THE
SEVENTH
SCROLL

WILBUR SMITH

THE
SEVENTH
SCROLL

St. Martin's Press
New York

"A Thomas Dunne Book"

Library of Congress Cataloging-in-Publication Data

Smith, Wilbur A.
The seventh scroll / Wilbur Smith.
p.   cm.
ISBN 0-312-11999-2
I. Title.
PR9405.9.S5S48   1995
823—dc20   95-768   CIP

First published in Great Britain by Macmillan London

First U.S. Edition: April 1995
10 9 8 7 6 5 4 3 2 1

Once more this book is for my wife Danielle.
Despite all the happy loving years we have spent
together I feel that we are only just beginning.
There is so much more to come.

THE
SEVENTH
SCROLL

The dusk crept in from the desert, and shaded the dunes with purple. Like a thick velvet cloak it muted all sounds, so that the evening was tranquil and hushed.

From where they stood on the crest of the dune they looked out over the oasis and the complex of small villages that surrounded it. The buildings were white with flat roofs and the date palms stood higher than any of them except the Islamic mosque and the Coptic Christian church. These bastions of faith opposed each other across the lake.

The waters of the lake were darkling. A flight of duck slanted down on quick wings to land with a small splash of white close in against the reed banks.

The man and the woman made a disparate couple. He was tall, though slightly bowed, his silvering hair catching the last of the sunlight. She was young, in her early thirties, slim, alert and vibrant. Her hair was thick and curling, restrained now by a thong at the nape of her neck.

'Time to go down now. Alia will be waiting.' He smiled down at her fondly. She was his second wife. When his first wife died he thought that she had taken the sunlight with her. He had not expected this last period of happiness in his life. Now he had her and his work. He was a man happy and contented.

Suddenly she broke away from him, and pulled the thong from her hair. She shook it out, dense and dark, and she laughed. It was a pretty sound. Then she plunged down the steep slip-face of the dune, her long skirts billowing around her flying legs. They were shapely and brown. She kept her balance until halfway down, when gravity overwhelmed her and she tumbled.

From the top he smiled down on her indulgently. Sometimes she was still a child. At others she was a grave and dignified woman. He was not certain which he preferred, but he loved her in both moods. She rolled to a halt at the bottom of the dune and sat up, still laughing, shaking the sand out of her hair.

'Your turn!' she called up at him. He followed her down sedately, moving with the slight stiffness of advancing age, keeping his balance until he reached the bottom. He lifted her to her feet. He did not kiss her, although the temptation to do so was strong. It was not the Arab way to show public affection, even to a beloved wife.

1

She straightened her clothing and retied her hair before they set off towards the village. They skirted the reed beds of the oasis, crossing the rickety bridges over the irrigation canals. As they passed, the peasants returning from the fields greeted him with deep respect.

'Salaam aleikum, Doktari! Peace be with you, doctor.' They honoured all men of learning, but him especially for his kindness to them and their families over the years. Many of them had worked for his father before him. It mattered little that most of them were Moslem, while he was a Christian.

When they reached the villa, Alia, the old housekeeper, greeted them with mumbles and scowls. 'You are late. You are always late. Why do you not keep regular hours, like decent folk? We have a position to maintain.'

'Old mother, you are always right,' he teased her gently. 'What would we do without you to care for us?' He sent her away, still scowling to cover her love and concern for him.

They ate the simple meal on the terrace together, dates and olives and unleavened bread and goat's milk cheese. It was dark when they finished, but the desert stars were bright as candles.

'Royan, my flower.' He reached across the table and touched her hand. 'It is time to begin work.' He stood up from the table and led the way to his study that opened out on to the terrace.

Royan Al Simma went directly to the tall steel safe against the far wall and tumbled the combination. The safe was out of place in this room, amongst the old books and scrolls, amongst the ancient statues and artefacts and grave goods that were the collection of his lifetime.

When the heavy steel door swung open, Royan stood back for a moment. She always felt this prickle of awe whenever she first looked upon this relic of the ages, even after an interval of only a few short hours.

'The seventh scroll,' she whispered, and steeled herself to touch it. It was nearly four thousand years old, written by a genius out of time with history, a man who had been dust for all these millennia, but whom she had come to know and respect as she did her own husband. His words were eternal, and they spoke to her clearly from beyond the grave, from the fields of paradise, from the presence of the great trinity, Osiris and Isis and Horus, in whom he had believed so devoutly. As devoutly as she believed in another more recent Trinity.

She carried the scroll to the long table at which Duraid, her husband, was already at work. He looked up as she laid it on the tabletop before him, and for a moment she saw the same mystical mood in his eyes that had affected her. He always wanted the scroll there on the table, even when there was no real call for it. He had the photographs and the microfilm to work with. It was as though he needed the unseen presence of the ancient author close to him as he studied the texts.

Then he threw off the mood and was the dispassionate scientist once more. 'Your eyes are better than mine, my flower,' he said. 'What do you make of this character?'

She leaned over his shoulder and studied the hieroglyph on the photograph of the scroll that he pointed out to her. She puzzled over the character for a moment before she took the magnifying glass from Duraid's hand and peered through it again.

'It looks as though Taita has thrown in another cryptogram of his own creation just to bedevil us.' She spoke of the ancient author as though he were a dear, but sometimes exasperating, friend who still lived and breathed, and played tricks upon them.

'We'll just have to puzzle it out, then,' Duraid declared with obvious relish. He loved the ancient game. It was his life's work.

The two of them laboured on into the cool of the night. This was when they did their best work. Sometimes they spoke Arabic and sometimes English; for them the two languages were as one. Less often they used French, which was their third common language. They had both received their education at universities in England and the United States, so far from this very Egypt of theirs. Royan loved the expression 'This very Egypt' that Taita used so often in the scrolls.

She felt a peculiar affinity in so many ways with this ancient Egyptian. After all, she was his direct descendant. She was a Coptic Christian, not of the Arab line that had so recently conquered Egypt, less than fourteen centuries ago. The Arabs were newcomers in this very Egypt of hers, while her own blood line ran back to the time of the pharaohs and the great pyramids.

At ten o'clock Royan made coffee for them, heating it on the charcoal stove that Alia had lit for them before she went off to her own family in the village. They drank the sweet, strong brew from thin cups that were half-filled with the heavy grounds. While they sipped, they talked as old friends.

For Royan that was their relationship, old friends. She had known Duraid ever since she had returned from England with her doctorate in archaeology and won her job with the Department of Antiquities, of which he was the director.

She had been his assistant when he had opened the tomb in the Valley of the Nobles, the tomb of Queen Lostris, the tomb that dated from about 1780 BC.

She had shared his disappointment when they had discovered that the tomb had been robbed in ancient times and all its treasures plundered. All that remained were the marvellous murals that covered the walls and the ceilings of the tomb.

3

It was Royan herself who had been working at the wall behind the plinth on which the sarcophagus had once stood, photographing the murals, when a section of the plaster had fallen away to reveal in their niche the ten alabaster jars. Each of the jars had contained a papyrus scroll. Every one of them had been written and placed there by Taita, the slave of the queen.

Since then their lives, Duraid's and her own, seemed to have revolved around those scraps of papyrus. Although there was some damage and deterioration, in the main they had survived nearly four thousand years remarkably intact.

What a fascinating story they contained, of a nation attacked by a superior enemy, armed with horse and chariot that were still alien to the Egyptians of that time. Crushed by the Hyksos hordes, the people of the Nile were forced to flee. Led by their queen, Lostris of the tomb, they followed the great river southwards almost to its source amongst the brutal mountains of the Ethiopian highlands. Here amongst those forbidding mountains, Lostris had entombed the mummified body of her husband, the Pharaoh Mamose, who had been slain in battle against the Hyksos.

Long afterwards Queen Lostris had led her people back northwards to this very Egypt. Armed now with their own horses and chariots, forged into hard warriors in the African wilderness, they had come storming back down the cataracts of the great river to challenge once more the Hyksos invader, and in the end to triumph over him and wrest the double crown of upper and lower Egypt from his grasp.

It was a story that appealed to every fibre of her being, and that had fascinated her as they had unravelled each hieroglyph that the old slave had penned on the papyrus.

It had taken them all these years, working at night here in the villa on the oasis after their daily routine work at the museum in Cairo was done, but at last the ten scrolls had been deciphered – all except the seventh scroll. This was the one that was the enigma, the one which the author had cloaked in layers of esoteric shorthand and allusions so obscure that they were unfathomable at this remove of time. Some of the symbols he used had never figured before in all the thousands of texts that they had studied in their combined working lives. It was obvious to them both that Taita had not intended that the scrolls should be read by any eyes other than those of his beloved queen. These were his last gift for her to take with her beyond the grave.

It had taken all their combined skills, all their imagination and ingenuity, but at last they were approaching the conclusion of the task. There were still many gaps in the translation and many areas where they were uncertain whether or not they had captured the true meaning, but

4

they had laid out the bones of the manuscript in such order that they were able to discern the outline of the creature it represented.

Now Duraid sipped his coffee and shook his head as he had done so often before. 'It frightens me,' he said. 'The responsibility. What to do with this knowledge we have gleaned. If it should fall into the wrong hands . . .' He sipped and sighed before he spoke again. 'Even if we take it to the right people, will they believe this material that is nearly four thousand years old?'

'Why must we bring in others?' Royan asked with an edge of exasperation in her voice. 'Why can we not do alone what has to be done?' At times like these the differences between them were most apparent. His was the caution of age, while hers was the impetuosity of youth.

'You do not understand,' he said. It always annoyed her when he said that, when he treated her as the Arabs treated their women in a totally masculine world. She had known the other world where women demanded and received the right to be treated as equals. She was a creature caught between those worlds, the Western world and the Arab world.

Royan's mother was an Englishwoman who had worked at the British Embassy in Cairo in the troubled times after World War II. She had met and married Royan's father, who had been a young Egyptian officer on the staff of Colonel Nasser. It was an unlikely union and had not persisted into Royan's adolescence.

Her mother had insisted upon returning to England, to her home town of York, for Royan's birth. She wanted her child to have British citizenship. After her parents had separated, Royan, again at her mother's insistence, had been sent back to England for her schooling, but all her holidays had been spent with her father in Cairo. Her father's career had prospered exceedingly, and in the end he had attained ministerial rank in the Mubarak government. Through her love for him she came to look upon herself as more Egyptian than English.

It was her father who had arranged her marriage to Duraid Al Simma. It was the last thing that he had done for her before his death. She had known he was dying at the time, and she had not found it in her heart to defy him. All her modern training made her want to resist the old-fashioned Coptic tradition of the arranged marriage, but her breeding and her family and her Church were against her. She had acquiesced.

Her marriage to Duraid had not proved as insufferable as she had dreaded it might be. It might even have been entirely comfortable and satisfying if she had never been introduced to romantic love. However, there had been her liaison with David while she was up at university.

5

He had swept her up in the hurly-burly, in the heady delirium, and, in the end, the heartache, when he had left her to marry a blonde English rose approved of by his parents.

She respected and liked Duraid, but sometimes in the night she still burned for the feel of a body as firm and young as her own on top of hers.

Duraid was still speaking and she had not been listening to him. She gave him her full attention once more. 'I have spoken to the minister again, but I do not think he believes in me. I think that Nahoot has convinced him that I am a little mad.' He smiled sadly. Nahoot Guddabi was his ambitious and well-connected deputy. 'At any rate the minister says that there are no government funds available, and that I will have to seek outside finance. So, I have been over the list of possible sponsors again, and have narrowed it down to four. There is the Getty Museum, of course, but I never like to work with a big impersonal institution. I prefer to have a single man to answer to. Decisions are always easier to reach.' None of this was new to her, but she listened dutifully.

'Then there is Herr von Schiller. He has the money and the interest in the subject, but I do not know him well enough to trust him entirely.' He paused, and Royan had listened to these musings so often before that she could anticipate him.

'What about the American? He is a famous collector,' she forestalled him.

'Peter Walsh is a difficult man to work with. His passion to accumulate makes him unscrupulous. He frightens me a little.'

'So who does that leave?' she asked.

He did not reply, for they both knew the answer to her question. Instead, he turned his attention back to the material that littered the work table.

'It looks so innocent, so mundane. An old papyrus scroll, a few photographs and notebooks, a computer printout. It is difficult to believe how dangerous these might be in the wrong hands.' He sighed again. 'You might almost say that they are deadly dangerous.'

Then he laughed. 'I am being fanciful. Perhaps it is the late hour. Shall we get back to work? We can worry about these other matters once we have worked out all the conundrums set for us by this old rogue, Taita, and completed the translation.'

He picked up the top photograph from the pile in front of him. It was an extract from the central section of the scroll. 'It is the worst luck that the damaged piece of papyrus falls where it does.' He picked up his reading glasses and placed them on his nose before he read aloud.

'"*There are many steps to ascend on the staircase to the abode of Hapi. With much hardship and endeavour we reached the second step and proceeded*

6

no further, for it was here that the prince received a divine revelation. In a dream his father, the dead god pharaoh, visited him and commanded him, 'I have travelled far and I am grown weary. It is here that I will rest for all eternity.'' Duraid removed his glasses and looked across at Royan, '"*The second step*". It is a very precise description for once. Taita is not being his usual devious self.'

'Let's go back to the satellite photographs,' Royan suggested, and drew the glossy sheet towards her. Duraid came around the table to stand behind her.

'To me it seems most logical that the natural feature that would obstruct them in the gorge would be something like a set of rapids or a waterfall. If it were the second waterfall, that would put them here—' Royan placed her finger on a spot on the satellite photograph where the narrow snake of the river threaded itself through the dark massifs of the mountains on either hand.

At that moment she was distracted and she lifted her head. 'Listen!' Her voice changed, sharpening with alarm.

'What is it?' Duraid looked up also.

'The dog,' she answered.

'That damn mongrel,' he agreed. 'It is always making the night hideous with its yapping. I have promised myself to get rid of him.'

At that moment the lights went out.

They froze with surprise in the darkness. The soft thudding of the decrepit diesel generator in its shed at the back of the palm grove had ceased. It was so much a part of the oasis night that they noticed it only when it was silent.

Their eyes adjusted to the faint starlight that came in through the terrace doors. Duraid crossed the room and took the oil lamp down from the shelf beside the door where it waited for just such a contingency. He lit it, and looked across at Royan with an expression of comical resignation.

'I will have to go down—'

'Duraid,' she interrupted him, 'the dog!'

He listened for a moment, and his expression changed to mild concern. The dog was silent out there in the night.

'I am sure it is nothing to be alarmed about.' He went to the door, and for no good reason she suddenly called after him.

'Duraid, be careful!' He shrugged dismissively and stepped out on to the terrace.

She thought for an instant that it was the shadow of the vine over the trellis moving in the night breeze off the desert, but the night was still. Then she realized that it was a human figure crossing the flagstones silently and swiftly, coming in behind Duraid as he skirted the fishpond in the centre of the paved terrace.

7

'Duraid!' She screamed a warning and he spun round, lifting the lamp high.

'Who are you?' he shouted. 'What do you want here?'

The intruder closed with him silently. The traditional full-length *dishdasha* robe swirled around his legs, and the white *ghutrah* headcloth covered his head. In the light of the lamp Duraid saw that he had drawn the corner of the headcloth over his face to mask his features.

The intruder's back was turned towards her so Royan did not see the knife in his right hand, but she could not mistake the upward stabbing motion that he aimed at Duraid's stomach. Duraid grunted with pain and doubled up at the blow, and his attacker drew the blade free and stabbed again, but this time Duraid dropped the lamp and seized the knife arm.

The flame of the fallen oil lamp was guttering and flaring. The two men struggled in the gloom, but Royan saw a dark stain spreading over her husband's white shirt front.

'Run!' he bellowed at her. 'Go! Fetch help! I cannot hold him!' The Duraid she knew was a gentle person, a soft man of books and learning. She could see that he was outmatched by his assailant.

'Go! Please! Save yourself, my flower!' She could hear by his tone that he was weakening, but he still clung desperately to his attacker's knife arm.

She had been paralysed with shock and indecision these few fatal seconds, but now she broke free of the spell and ran to the door. Spurred by her terror and her need to bring help to Duraid she crossed the terrace, swift as a cat, and he held the intruder from blocking her way.

She vaulted over the low stone wall into the grove, and almost into the arms of the second man. She screamed and twisted away from him as his outstretched fingers raked across her face, and almost broke free, but his fingers hooked in the thin cotton stuff of her blouse.

This time she saw the knife in his hand, a long silvery flash in the starlight, and it goaded her to fresh effort. The cotton tore in his grip and she was free, but not quickly enough to escape the blade. She felt the sting of it across her upper arm, and she kicked out at him with all the strength of panic and her hard young body behind it. She felt her foot slam into the softness of his lower body with a shock that jarred her knee and ankle, and her attacker cried out and fell to his knees.

Then she was away and running through the palm grove. At first she ran without purpose or direction. She ran simply to get as far from them as her flying legs would carry her. Then gradually she brought her panic under control. She glanced back, but saw nobody following her. As she reached the edge of the lake she slowed her run to conserve her strength, and she became aware of the warm trickle of her own blood down her arm and then dripping from her fingertips.

She stopped and rested her back against the rough bole of one of the palms while she tore a strip of cloth from her ripped blouse and hurriedly bound up her arm. She was shaking so much from shock and exertion that even her uninjured hand was fumbling and clumsy. She knotted the crude bandage with her teeth and left hand, and the bleeding slowed.

She was uncertain of which way to run, and then she saw the dim lamplight in the window of Alia's shack across the nearest irrigation canal. She pushed herself away from the palm trunk and started towards it. She had covered less than a hundred paces when a voice called from the grove behind her, speaking in Arabic, 'Yusuf, has the woman come your way?'

Immediately an electric torch flashed from the darkness ahead of her and another voice called back, 'No, I have not seen her.'

Another few seconds and Royan would have run full into him. She crouched down and looked around her desperately. There was another torch coming through the grove behind her, following the path she had taken. It must be the man she had kicked, but she could tell by the motion of the torchbeam that he had recovered and was moving swiftly and easily again.

She was blocked on two sides, so she turned back along the edge of the lake. The road lay that way. She might be able to meet a late vehicle travelling on it. She lost her footing on the rough ground and went down, bruising and scraping her knees, but she jumped up again and hurried on. The second time she stumbled, her out-thrust left hand landed on a round, smooth stone the size of an orange. When she went on she carried the stone with her; as a weapon it gave her a glimmer of comfort.

Her wounded arm was beginning to hurt, and she was driven by worry for Duraid. She knew he was badly wounded, for she had seen the direction and force of the knife thrust. She had to find help for him. Behind her the two men with torches were sweeping the grove and she could not keep her lead ahead of them. They were gaining on her – she could hear them calling to each other.

She reached the road at last, and with a small whimper of relief climbed out of the drainage ditch on to the pale gravel surface. Her legs were shaking under her so that they could hardly carry her weight, but she turned in the direction of the village.

She had not reached the first bend before she saw a set of headlights coming slowly towards her, flickering through the palm trees. She broke into a run down the centre of the road.

'Help me!' she screamed in Arabic. 'Please help me!'

The car came through the bend and before the headlights dazzled her she saw that it was a small, dark-coloured Fiat. She stood in the centre of the road waving her arms to halt the driver, lit by the headlights as though she were on a theatre stage.

The Fiat stopped in front of her, and she ran round to the driver's door and tugged at the handle. 'Please, you must help me—'

The door was opened from within, and then was thrown back with such force that she staggered off-balance. The driver leapt out into the roadway and caught her by the wrist of the injured arm. He dragged her to the Fiat and pulled open the back door.

'Yusuf! Bacheet!' he shouted into the dark grove. 'I have her.' And she heard the answering cries and saw the torches turn in their direction. The driver was forcing her head down and trying to push her into the back seat, but she realized then that she still had the stone in her good hand. She turned slightly and braced herself, and then swung her fist with the stone still clenched in it against the side of his head. It caught him squarely on the temple. Without another sound he dropped to the gravel surface and lay motionless.

Royan dropped the stone and pelted away down the road, but she found that she was running straight down the path of the headlights, and they lit her every movement. The two men in the grove shouted again and came up on to the gravel roadway behind her, almost shoulder to shoulder.

Glancing back, she saw them gaining on her swiftly, and she realized that her only chance was to get off the road and back into the darkness. She turned and plunged down the bank. Immediately she found herself waist-deep in the waters of the lake.

In the darkness and the confusion she had become disorientated. She had not realized that she had reached the point where the road skirted the embankment at the water's edge. She knew that she did not have time to climb back on to the road, and she knew also that there were thick clumps of papyrus and reeds ahead of her, that might give her shelter.

She waded out until the bottom sloped away steeply under her feet, and she found herself forced to swim. She broke into an awkward breast-stroke, hampered by her skirts and her injured arm. However, her slow and stealthy movements created almost no disturbance on the surface, and before the men on the road had reached the point where she had descended the bank, she reached a dense stand of reeds.

She eased her way into the thick of them and let herself sink. Before the water covered her nostrils she felt her toes touch the soft ooze of the lake bottom. She stood there quietly, with just the top of her head above the surface and her face turned away from the bank. She knew her dark hair would not reflect the light of a probing torch.

Though the water covered her ears, she could make out the excited voices of the men on the road. They had turned their torches down

10

towards the water and were shining them into the reeds, searching for her. For a moment one of the beams played full on her head, and she drew a deep breath ready to submerge, but the beam moved on and she realized that they had not picked her out.

The fact that she had not been seen even in the direct torchlight emboldened her to raise her head slightly until one ear was clear and she could make out their voices.

They were speaking Arabic, and she recognized the voice of the one named Bacheet. He appeared to be the leader, for he was giving the orders.

'Go in there, Yusuf, and bring the whore out.'

She heard Yusuf slipping and sliding down the bank and the splash as he hit the water.

'Further out,' Bacheet ordered him. 'In those reeds there, where I am shining the torch.'

'It is too deep. You know well I cannot swim. It will be over my head.'

'There! Right in front of you. In those reeds. I can see her head.' Bacheet encouraged him, and Royan dreaded that they had spotted her. She sank down as far as she could below the surface.

Yusuf splashed around heavily, moving towards where she cowered in the reeds, when suddenly there was a thunderous commotion that startled even Yusuf, so that he shouted aloud, 'Djinns! God protect me!' as the flock of roosting duck exploded from the water and launched into the dark sky on noisy wings.

Yusuf started back to the bank and not any of Bacheet's threats could persuade him to continue the hunt.

'The woman is not as important as the scroll,' he protested, as he climbed back on to the roadway. 'Without the scroll there will be no money. We always know where to find her later.'

Turning her head slightly, Royan saw the torches move back down the road towards the parked Fiat whose headlights still burned. She heard the doors of the car slam, and then the engine revved and pulled away towards the villa.

She was too shaken and terrified to make any attempt to leave her hiding-place. She feared that they had left one of their number on the road to wait for her to show herself. She stood on tiptoe with the water lapping her lips, shivering more with shock than with cold, determined to wait for the safety of the sunrise before she moved.

It was only much later when she saw the glow of the fire lighting the sky, and the flames flickering through the trunks of the palm trees, that she forgot her own safety and dragged herself back to the bank.

She knelt in the mud at the water's edge, shuddering and shaking and gasping, weak with loss of blood and shock and the reaction from

11

fear, and peered at the flames through the veil of her wet hair and the lake water that streamed into her eyes.

'The villa!' she whispered. 'Duraid! Oh please God, no! No!'

She pushed herself to her feet and began to stagger towards her burning home.

acheet switched off both the headlights and the engine of the Fiat before they reached the turning into the driveway of the villa and let the car coast down and stop below the terrace.

All three of them left the Fiat and climbed the stone steps to the flagged terrace. Duraid's body still lay where Bacheet had left it beside the fishpond. They passed him without a glance and went into the dark study.

Bacheet placed the cheap nylon tote bag he carried on the tabletop.

'We have wasted too much time already. We must work quickly now.'

'It is Yusuf's fault,' protested the driver of the Fiat. 'He let the woman escape.'

'You had a chance on the road,' Yusuf snarled at him, 'and you did no better.'

'Enough!' Bacheet told them both. 'If you want to get paid, then there had better be no more mistakes.'

With the torchbeam Bacheet picked out the scroll that still lay on the tabletop. 'That is the one.' He was certain, for he had been shown a photograph of it so that there would be no mistake. 'They want everything – the maps and photographs. Also the books and papers, everything on the table that they were using in their work. Leave nothing.'

Quickly they bundled everything into the tote bag and Bacheet zipped it closed.

'Now the *Doktari*. Bring him in here.'

The other two went out on to the terrace and stooped over the body. Each of them seized an ankle and dragged Duraid back across the terrace and into the study. The back of Duraid's head bounced loosely on the stone step at the threshold and his blood painted a long wet skid mark across the tiles that glistened in the torchlight.

'Get the lamp!' Bacheet ordered, and Yusuf went back to the terrace and fetched the oil lamp from where Duraid had dropped it. The flame was extinguished. Bacheet held the lamp to his ear and shook it.

'Full,' he said with satisfaction, and unscrewed the filler cap. 'All right,' he told the other two, 'take the bag out to the car.'

As they hurried out Bacheet sprinkled paraffin from the lamp over Duraid's shirt and trousers, and then he went to the shelves and splashed the remainder of the fuel over the books and manuscripts that crowded them.

He dropped the empty lamp and reached under the skirts of his *dishdasha* for a box of matches. He struck one of them and held it to the wet run of paraffin oil down the bookcase. It caught immediately, and flames spread upwards and curled and blackened the edges of the manuscripts. He turned away and went back to where Duraid lay. He struck another match and dropped it on to his blood- and paraffin-drenched shirt.

A mantle of blue flames danced over Duraid's chest. The flames changed colour as they burned into the cotton material and the flesh beneath it. They turned orange, and sooty smoke spiralled up from their flickering crests.

Bacheet ran to the door, across the terrace and down the steps. As he clambered into the rear seat of the Fiat, the driver gunned the engine and pulled away down the driveway.

The pain roused Duraid. It had to be that intense to bring him back from that far place on the very edge of life to which he had drifted.

He groaned. The first thing he was aware of as he regained consciousness was the smell of his own flesh burning, and then the agony struck him with full force. A violent tremor shook his whole body and he opened his eyes and looked down at himself.

His clothing was blackening and smouldering, and the pain was as nothing he had ever experienced in his entire life. He realized in a vague way that the room was on fire all around him. Smoke and waves of heat washed over him so that he could barely make out the shape of the doorway through them.

The pain was so terrible that he wanted it to end. He wanted to die then and not to have to endure it further. Then he remembered Royan. He tried to say her name through his scorched and blackened lips, but no sound came. Only the thought of her gave him the strength to move. He rolled over once, and the heat attacked his back that up until that moment had been shielded. He groaned aloud and rolled again, just a little nearer to the doorway.

Each movement was a mighty effort and evoked fresh paroxysms of agony, but when he rolled on to his back again he realized that a gale of fresh air was being sucked through the open doorway to feed the flames. A lungful of the sweet desert air revived him and gave him just

13

sufficient strength to lunge down the step on to the cool stones of the terrace.

His clothes and his body were still on fire. He beat feebly at his chest to try to extinguish the flames, but his hands were black burning claws.

Then he remembered the fishpond. The thought of plunging his tortured body into that cold water spurred him to one last effort, and he wriggled and wormed his way across the flags like a snake with a crushed spine.

The pungent smoke from his still cremating flesh choked him and he coughed weakly, but kept doggedly on. He left slabs of his own grilled skin on the stone coping as he rolled across it and flopped into the pond. There was a hiss of steam, and a pale cloud of it obscured his vision so that for a moment he thought he was blinded. The agony of cold water on his raw burned flesh was so intense that he slid back over the edge of consciousness.

When he came back to reality through the dark clouds he raised his dripping head and saw a figure staggering up the steps at the far end of the terrace, coming from the garden.

For a moment he thought it was a phantom of his agony, but when the light of the burning villa fell full upon her, he recognized Royan. Her wet hair hung in tangled disarray over her face, and her clothing was torn and running with lake water and stained with mud and green algae. Her right arm was wrapped in muddy rags and her blood oozed through, diluted pink by the dirty water.

She did not see him. She stopped in the centre of the terrace and stared in horror into the burning room. Was Duraid in there? She started forward, but the heat was like a solid wall and it stopped her dead. At that moment the roof collapsed, sending a roaring column of sparks and flames high into the night sky. She backed away from it, shielding her face with a raised arm.

Duraid tried to call to her, but no sound issued from his smoke-scorched throat. Royan turned away and started down the steps. He realized that she must be going to call for help. Duraid made a supreme effort and a crow-like croak came out between his black and blistered lips.

Royan spun round and stared at him, and then she screamed. His head was not human. His hair was gone, frizzled away, and his skin hung in tatters from his cheeks and chin. Patches of raw meat showed through the black crusted mask. She backed away from him as though he were some hideous monster.

'Royan,' he croaked, and his voice was just recognizable. He lifted one hand towards her in appeal, and she ran to the pond and seized the outstretched hand.

'In the name of the Virgin, what have they done to you?' she sobbed, but when she tried to pull him from the pond the skin of his hand came away in hers in a single piece, like some horrible surgical rubber glove, leaving the bleeding claw naked and raw.

Royan fell on her knees beside the coping and leaned over the pond to take him in her arms. She knew that she did not have the strength to lift him out without doing him further dreadful injury. All she could do was hold him and try to comfort him. She realized that he was dying – no man could survive such fearsome injury.

'They will come soon to help us,' she whispered to him in Arabic. 'Someone must see the flames. Be brave, my husband, help will come very soon.'

He was twitching and convulsing in her arms, tortured by his mortal injuries and racked by the effort to speak.

'The scroll?' His voice was barely intelligible. Royan looked up at the holocaust that enveloped their home, and she shook her head.

'It's gone,' she said. 'Burned or stolen.'

'Don't give it up,' he mumbled. 'All our work—'

'It's gone,' she repeated. 'No one will believe us without—'

'No!' His voice was faint but fierce. 'For me, my last—'

'Don't say that,' she pleaded. 'You will be all right.'

'Promise,' he demanded. 'Promise me!'

'We have no sponsor. I am alone. I cannot do it alone.'

'Harper!' he said. Royan leaned closer so that her ear touched his fire-ravaged lips. 'Harper,' he repeated. 'Strong – hard – clever man—' and she understood then. Harper, of course, was the fourth and last name on the list of sponsors that he had drawn up. Although he was the last on the list, somehow she had always known that Duraid's order of preference was inverted. Nicholas Quenton-Harper was his first choice. He had spoken so often of this man with respect and warmth, and sometimes even with awe.

'But what do I tell him? He does not know me. How will I convince him? The seventh scroll is gone.'

'Trust him,' he whispered. 'Good man. Trust him—' There was a terrible appeal in his 'Promise me!'

Then she remembered the notebook in their flat at Giza in the Cairo suburbs, and the Taita material on the hard drive on her PC. Not everything was gone. 'Yes,' she agreed, 'I promise you, my husband, I promise you.'

Though those mutilated features could show no human expression there was a faint echo of satisfaction in his voice as he whispered, 'My flower!' Then his head dropped forward, and he died in her arms.

The peasants from the village found Royan still kneeling beside the pond, holding him, whispering to him. By that time the flames were

15

abating, and the faint light of dawn was stronger than their fading glow.

All the senior staff from the museum and the Department of Antiquities were at the funeral service in the church of the oasis. Even Atalan Abou Sin, the Minister of Culture and Tourism and Duraid's superior, had come out from Cairo in his official black air-conditioned Mercedes.

He stood behind Royan and, though he was a Moslem, joined in the responses. Nahoot Guddabi stood beside his uncle. Nahoot's mother was the minister's youngest sister, which, as Duraid had sarcastically pointed out, fully made up for the nephew's lack of qualifications and experience in archaeology and for his ineptitude as an administrator.

The day was sweltering. Outside, the temperature stood at over thirty degrees, and even in the dim cloisters of the Coptic church it was oppressive. In the thick clouds of incense smoke and the drone of the black-clad priest intoning the ancient order of service Royan felt herself suffocating. The stitches in her right arm pulled and burned, and every time she looked at the long black coffin that stood in front of the ornate and gilded altar, the dreadful vision of Duraid's bald and scorched head rose before her eyes and she swayed in her seat and had to catch herself before she fell.

At last it was over and she could escape into the open air and the desert sunlight. Even then her duties were not at an end. As principal mourner, her place was directly behind the coffin as they walked in procession to the cemetery amongst the palm groves, where Duraid's relatives awaited him in the family mausoleum.

Before he returned to Cairo, Atalan Abou Sin came to shake her hand and offer her a few words of condolence. 'What a terrible business, Royan. I have personally spoken to the Minister of the Interior. They will catch the animals responsible for this outrage, believe me. Please take as long as you need before you return to the museum,' he told her.

'I will be in my office again on Monday,' she replied, and he drew a pocket diary from inside the jacket of his dark double-breasted suit. He consulted it and made a note, before he looked up at her again.

'Then come to see me at the Ministry in the afternoon. Four o'clock,' he told her. He went to the waiting Mercedes, while Nahoot Guddabi came forward to shake hands. Though his skin was sallow and there were coffee-coloured stains beneath his dark eyes, he was tall and elegant with thick wavy hair and very white teeth. His suit was impeccably tailored and he smelt faintly of an expensive cologne. His expression was grave and sad.

'He was a good man. I held Duraid in the highest esteem,' he told Royan, and she nodded without replying to this blatant untruth. There had been little affection between Duraid and his deputy. He had never allowed Nahoot to work on the Taita scrolls; in particular he had never given him access to the seventh scroll, and this had been a point of bitter antagonism between them.

'I hope you will be applying for the post of director, Royan,' he told her. 'You are well qualified for the job.'

'Thank you, Nahoot, you are very kind. I haven't had a chance to think about the future yet, but won't you be applying?'

'Of course,' he nodded. 'But that doesn't mean that no one else should. Perhaps you will take the job out from in front of my nose.' His smile was complacent. She was a woman in an Arab world, and he was the nephew of the minister. Nahoot knew just how heavily the odds favoured him. 'Friendly rivals?' he asked.

Royan smiled sadly. 'Friends, at least. I will need all of those I can find in the future.'

'You know you have many friends. Everyone in the department likes you, Royan.' That at least was true, she supposed. He went on smoothly, 'May I offer you a lift back to Cairo? I am certain my uncle will not object.'

'Thank you, Nahoot, but I have my own car here, and I must stay over at the oasis tonight to see to some of Duraid's affairs.' This was not true. Royan planned to travel back to the flat in Giza that evening but, for reasons that she was not very sure of herself, she did not want Nahoot to know of her plans.

'Then we shall see you at the museum on Monday.'

Royan left the oasis as soon as she was able to escape from the relations and family friends and peasants, so many of whom had worked for Duraid's family most of their lives. She felt numbed and isolated, so that all their condolences and pious exhortations were meaningless and without comfort.

Even at this late hour the tarmac road back through the desert was busy, with files of vehicles moving steadily in both directions, for tomorrow was Friday and the sabbath. She slipped her injured right arm out of the sling, and it did not hamper her driving too much. She was able to make reasonably good time. Nevertheless, it was after five in the afternoon when she made out the green line against the tawny desolation of the desert that marked the start of the narrow strip of irrigated and cultivated land along the Nile which was the great artery of Egypt.

As always the traffic became denser the nearer she came to the capital, and it was almost fully dark by the time she reached the apartment block in Giza that overlooked both the river and those great monuments of stone which stood so tall and massive against the evening sky, and which for her epitomized the heart and history of her land.

She left Duraid's old green Renault in the underground garage of the building and rode up in the elevator to the top floor.

She let herself into the flat and then froze in the doorway. The sitting room had been ransacked – even the rugs had been pulled up and the paintings ripped from the walls. In a daze she picked her way through the litter of broken furniture and smashed ornaments. She glanced into the bedroom as she went down the passage, and saw that it had not escaped. Her clothes and those of Duraid were strewn over the floor, and the doors of the cupboards stood ajar. One of these was smashed off its hinges. The bed was overturned, and the sheets and bolsters had been flung about.

She could smell the reek of broken cosmetic and perfume bottles from the bathroom, but she could not yet bring herself to go in there. She knew what she would find. Instead she continued down the passage to the large room that they had used as a study and workshop.

In the chaos the first thing that she noticed and mourned was the antique chess set that Duraid had given her as a wedding present. The board of jet and ivory squares was broken in half and the pieces had been thrown about the room with vindictive and unnecessary violence. She stooped and picked up the white queen. Her head had been snapped off.

Holding the queen in her good hand she moved like a sleepwalker to her desk below the window. Her PC was wrecked. They had shattered the screen and hacked the mainframe with what must have been an axe. She could tell at a glance that there was no information left on the hard drive; it was beyond repair.

She glanced down at the drawer in which she kept her floppy disks. That and all the other drawers had been pulled out and thrown on the floor. They were empty, of course; along with the disks, all her notebooks and photographs were missing. Her last connections with the seventh scroll were lost. After three years of work, gone was the proof that it had ever existed.

She slumped down on the floor, feeling beaten and exhausted. Her arm started to ache again, and she was alone and vulnerable as she had never been in her life before. She had never thought that she would miss Duraid so desperately. Her shoulders began to shake and she felt the tears welling up from deep within her. She tried to hold them back, but they scalded her eyelids and she let them flow. She sat amongst the wreckage of her life and wept until there was nothing more left within her, and then she curled up on the littered carpet and fell into the sleep of exhaustion and despair.

B y the Monday morning she had managed to restore some order into her life. The police had come to the flat and taken her statement, and she had tidied up most of the disarray. She had even glued the head back on her white queen. When she left the flat and climbed into the green Renault her arm was feeling easier, and, if not cheerful, she was at least a great deal more optimistic, and sure of what she had to do.

When she reached the museum she went first to Duraid's office and was annoyed to find that Nahoot was there before her. He was supervising two of the security guards as they cleared out all Duraid's personal effects.

'You might have had the consideration to let me do that,' she told him coldly, and he gave her his most winning smile.

'I am sorry, Royan. I thought I would help.' He was smoking one of his fat Turkish cigarettes. She loathed the heavy, musky odour.

She crossed to Duraid's desk, and opened the top right-hand drawer. 'My husband's day book was in here. It's gone now. Have you seen it?'

'No, there was nothing in that drawer.' Nahoot looked at the two guards for confirmation, and they shuffled their feet and shook their heads. It did not really matter, she thought. The book had not contained much of vital interest. Duraid had always relied on her to record and store all data of importance, and most of it had been on her PC.

'Thank you, Nahoot,' she dismissed him. 'I will do whatever remains to be done. I don't want to keep you from your work.'

'Any help you need, Royan, please let me know.' He bowed slightly as he left her.

It did not take her long to finish in Duraid's office. She had the guards take the boxes of his possessions down the corridor to her own office and pile them against the wall. She worked through the lunch-hour tidying up all her own affairs, and when she had finished there was still an hour until her appointment with Atalan Abou Sin.

If she was to make good her promise to Duraid, then she was going to be absent for some time. Wanting to take leave of all her favourite treasures, she went down into the public section of the huge building.

Monday was a busy day, and the exhibition halls of the museum were thronged with groups of tourists. They flocked behind their guides, sheep following the shepherd. They crowded around the most famous of the displays. They listened to the guides reciting their well-rehearsed spiels in all the tongues of Babel.

Those rooms on the second floor that contained the treasures of Tutankhamen were so crowded that she spent little time there. She managed to reach the display cabinet that contained the great golden death-mask of the child pharaoh. As always, the splendour and the romance of it quickened her breathing and made her heart beat faster. Yet as she stood before it, jostled by a pair of big-busted and sweaty middle-aged female tourists, she pondered, as she had so often before, that if an insignificant weakling king could have gone to his tomb with such a miraculous creation covering his mummified features, in what state must the great Ramessids have lain in their funeral temples. Ramesses II, the greatest of them all, had reigned sixty-seven years and had spent those decades accumulating his funerary treasure from all the vast territories that he had conquered.

Royan went next to pay her respects to the old king. After thirty centuries Ramesses II slept on with a rapt and serene expression on his gaunt features. His skin had a light, marble-like sheen to it. The sparse strands of his hair were blond and dyed with henna. His hands, dyed with the same stuff, were long and thin and elegant. However, he was clad only in a rag of linen. The grave robbers had even unwrapped his mummy to reach the amulets and scarabs beneath the linen bandages, so that his body was almost naked. When these remains had been discovered in 1881 in the cache of royal mummies in the cliff cave at Deir El Bahari, only a scrap of papyrus parchment attached to his breast had proclaimed his lineage.

There was a moral in that, she supposed, but as she stood before these pathetic remains she wondered again, as she and Duraid had done so often before, whether Taita the scribe had told the truth, whether somewhere in the far-off, savage mountains of Africa another great pharaoh slept on undisturbed with all his treasures intact about him. The very thought of it made her shiver with excitement, and goose pimples prickled her skin and raised the fine dark hair at the nape of her neck.

'I have given you my promise, my husband,' she whispered in Arabic. 'This will be for you and your memory, for it was you who led the way.'

She glanced at her wrist-watch as she went down the main staircase. She had fifteen minutes before she must leave for her appointment with the minister, and she knew exactly how she would spend that time. What she was going to visit was in one of the less-frequented side halls. The tour guides very seldom led their charges this way, except as a short-cut to see the statue of Amenhotep.

Royan stopped in front of the glass-fronted display case that reached from floor to ceiling of the narrow room. It was packed with small artefacts, tools and weapons, amulets and vessels and utensils, the latest of them dating from the twentieth dynasty of the New Kingdom, 1100 BC, whilst the oldest survived from the dim ages of the Old Kingdom almost five thousand years ago. The cataloguing of this accumulation was only rudimentary. Many of the items were not described.

At the furthest end, on the bottom shelf, was a display of jewellery and finger rings and seals. Beside each of the seals was a wax impression made from it.

Royan went down on her knees to examine one of these artefacts more closely. The tiny blue seal of lapis lazuli in the centre of the display was beautifully carved. Lapis was a rare and precious material for the ancients, as it had not occurred naturally in the Egyptian Empire. The wax imprint cut from it depicted a hawk with a broken wing, and the simple legend beneath it was clear for Royan to read: 'TAITA, THE SCRIBE OF THE GREAT QUEEN'.

She knew it was the same man, for he had used the maimed hawk as his autograph in the scrolls. She wondered who had found this trifle and where. Perhaps some peasant had plundered it from the lost tomb of the old slave and scribe, but she would never knew.

'Are you teasing me, Taita? Is it all some elaborate hoax? Are you laughing at me even now from your tomb, wherever it may be?' She leaned even closer, until her forehead touched the cool glass. 'Are you my friend, Taita, or are you my implacable adversary?' She stood up and dusted off the front of her skirt. 'We shall see. I will play the game with you, and we shall see who outwits whom,' she promised.

The minister kept her waiting only a few minutes before his male secretary ushered her into his presence. Atalan Abou Sin wore a dark, shiny silk suit and sat at his desk, although Royan knew that he preferred a more comfortable robe and a cushion on the rugs of the floor. He noticed her glance and smiled deprecatingly. 'I have a meeting with some Americans this afternoon.'

She liked him. He had always been kind to her, and she owed him her job at the museum. Most other men in his position would have refused Duraid's request for a female assistant, especially his own wife.

He asked after her health and she showed him her bandaged arm. 'The stitches will come out in ten days.'

They chatted for a while in a polite manner. Only Westerners would have the gaucherie to come directly to the main business to be discussed. However, to save him embarrassment Royan took the first opportunity he gave her to tell him, 'I feel that I need some time to myself. I need to recover from my loss and to decide what I am to do with the rest of my life, now that I am a widow. I would be grateful if you would consider my request for at least six months' unpaid leave of absence. I want to go to stay with my mother in England.'

Atalan showed real concern and urged her, 'Please do not leave us for too long. The work you have done has been invaluable. We need you to help carry on from where Duraid left off.' But he could not entirely conceal his relief. She knew that he had expected her to put before him her application for the directorship. He must have discussed it with his nephew. However, he was too kind a man to relish having to tell her that she would not be selected for the job. Things in Egypt were changing, women were emerging from their traditional roles, but not that much or that swiftly. They both knew that the directorship must go to Nahoot Guddabi.

Atalan walked with her to the door of his office and shook her hand in parting, and as she rode down in the lift she felt a sense of release and freedom.

She had left the Renault standing in the sun in the Ministry car park. When she opened the door the interior was hot enough to bake bread. She opened all the windows and fanned the driver's door to force out the heated air, but still the surface of the driver's seat burned the backs of her thighs when she slid in behind the wheel.

As soon as she drove through the gates she was engulfed in the swarm of Cairo traffic. She crawled along behind an overloaded bus that belched a steady blue cloud of diesel fumes over the Renault. The traffic problem was one that seemed to have no solution. There was so little parking available that vehicles lined the verge of the road three and four deep, choking the flow in the centre to a trickle.

As the bus in front of her braked and forced her to a halt, Royan smiled as she recalled the old joke that some drivers who had parked at the kerb had to abandon their cars there, for they were never able to extricate them from the tangle. Perhaps there was a little truth in this, for some of those vehicles she could see had not been moved for weeks. Their windscreens were completely obscured with dust and many of them had flat tyres.

She glanced in the rear-view mirror. There was a taxi stopped only inches from her back bumper, and behind that the traffic was backed up solidly. Only the motorcyclists had freedom of movement. As she watched in the mirror, one of these came weaving through the congestion with suicidal abandon. It was a battered red 200 cc Honda so covered with dust that the colour was hardly recognizable. There was a passenger perched on the pillion, and both he and the driver had covered the lower half of their faces with the corners of their white headcloths as protection against the exhaust fumes and dust.

Passing on the wrong side, the Honda skimmed through the narrow gap between the taxi and the cars parked at the kerb with nothing to spare on either side. The taxi-driver made an obscene gesture with thumb and forefinger, and called on Allah to witness that the driver was both mad and stupid.

The Honda slowed slightly as it drew level with Royan's Renault, and the pillion passenger leaned out and dropped something through the open window on to the passenger seat beside her. Immediately the driver accelerated so abruptly that for a moment the front wheel was lifted off the ground. He put the motorcycle over into a tight turn and sped away down the narrow alleyway that opened off the main thoroughfare, narrowly avoiding hitting an old woman in his path.

As the pillion passenger looked back at her the wind blew the fold of white cotton from his face, and with a shock she recognized the man she had last seen in the headlights of the Fiat on the road beside the oasis.

'Yusuf!' As the Honda disappeared she looked down at the object that he had dropped on to the seat beside her. It was egg-shaped and the segmented metallic surface was painted military green. She had seen the same thing so often on old TV war movies that she recognized it instantly as a fragmentation grenade, and at the same moment she realized that the priming handle had flown off and the weapon was set to explode within seconds.

Without thinking, she grabbed the door handle beside her and flung all her weight against the door. It burst open and she tumbled out in the road. Her foot slipped off the clutch and the Renault bounded forward and crashed into the back of the stationary bus.

As Royan sprawled in the road under the wheels of the following taxi, the grenade exploded. Through the open driver's door blew a sheet of flame and smoke and debris. The back window burst outwards and sprayed her with diamond chips of glass, and the detonation drove painfully into her eardrums.

A stunned silence followed the shock of the explosion, broken only by the tinkle of falling glass shards, and then immediately there was a hubbub of groans and screams. Royan sat up and clasped her injured arm to her chest. She had fallen heavily upon it and the stitches were agony.

The Renault was wrecked, but she saw that her leather sling bag had been blown out of the door and lay in the street close at hand. She pushed herself unsteadily to her feet and hobbled over to pick it up. All around her was confusion. A few of the passengers in the bus had been injured, and a piece of shrapnel or wreckage had wounded a little girl on the sidewalk. Her mother was screaming and mopping at the child's bloody face with her scarf. The girl struggled in her mother's grip, wailing pitifully.

Nobody was taking any notice of Royan, but she knew the police would arrive within minutes. They were geared up to respond swiftly to fundamentalist terror attacks. She knew that if they found her here she would be tied up in days of interrogation. She slung the bag over her shoulder and walked as swiftly as her bruised leg would allow her to the alleyway down which the Honda had disappeared.

At the end of the street was a public lavatory. She locked herself in one of the cubicles and leaned against the door with her eyes closed, trying to recover from the shock and to get her confused thoughts in order.

In the horror and desolation of Duraid's murder she had not until now considered her own safety. The realization of danger had been forced upon her in the most savage manner. She remembered the words of one of the assassins spoken in the darkness beside the oasis 'We always know where to find her later!'

The attempt on her life had failed only narrowly. She had to believe that there would be another.

'I can't go back to the flat,' she realized. 'The villa is gone, and anyway they would look for me there.'

Despite the unsavoury atmosphere she remained locked in the cubicle for over an hour while she thought out her next movements. At last she left the toilet and went to the row of stained and cracked washbasins. She splashed her face under the tap. Then in the mirror she combed her hair, touched up her make-up, and straightened and tidied her clothing as best she was able.

She walked a few blocks, doubling back on her tracks and watching behind her to make sure she was not being followed, before she hailed a taxi in the street.

She made the driver drop her in the street behind her bank, and walked the rest of the way. It was only minutes before closing time when she was shown into the cubicle office of one of the sub-accountants. She withdrew what money was in her account, which amounted to less than five thousand Egyptian pounds. It was not a great sum, but she had a little more in her Lloyds Bank account in York, and then she had her Mastercard.

'You should have given us notice to withdraw an article from safe deposit,' the bank official told her severely. She apologized meekly and played the helpless little-girl-lost so convincingly that he relented. He handed over to her the package that contained her British passport and her Lloyds banking papers.

Duraid had numerous relatives and friends who would have been pleased to have her to stay with them, but she wanted to remain out of sight, away from her usual haunts. She chose one of the two-star tourist hotels away from the river where she hoped she could remain anonymous amongst the multitudes of the tour groups. At this type of hotel there was a high turnover of guests, for most of them stayed only for a few nights before moving on up to Luxor and Aswan to view the monuments.

As soon as she was alone in her single room she phoned British Airways reservations. There was a flight to Heathrow the following morning at ten o'clock. She booked a one-way economy seat and gave them the number of her Mastercard.

It was after six o'clock by then, but the time difference between Egypt and the UK meant that it would still be office hours there. She looked up the number in her notebook. Leeds University was where she had completed her studies. Her call was answered on the third ring.

'Archaeology Department. Professor Dixon's office,' said a prim English school-marm voice.

'Is that you, Miss Higgins?'

'Yes, it is. To whom am I speaking?'

'It's Royan. Royan Al Simma, who used to be Royan Said.'

'Royan! We haven't heard from you for an absolute age. How are you?'

They chatted for a short while, but Royan was aware of the cost of the call. 'Is the Prof in?' she cut it short.

Professor Percival Dixon was over seventy and should have retired years ago. 'Royan, is it really you? My favourite student.' She smiled. Even at his age he was still the randy old goat. All the pretty ones were his favourite students.

'This is an international call, Prof. I just want to know if the offer is still open.'

'My goodness, I thought you said that you couldn't fit us in, what?'

'Change of circumstances. I'll tell you about it when I see you, if I see you.'

'Of course, we'd love to have you come and talk to us. When can you manage to get away?'

'I'll be in England tomorrow.'

'My goodness, that's a bit sudden. Don't know if we can arrange it that quickly.'

'I will be staying with my mother near York. Put me back to Miss Higgins and I will give her the telephone number.' He was one of the most brilliant men she knew, but she didn't trust him to write down a telephone number correctly. 'I'll call you in a few days' time.'

She hung up and lay back on the bed. She was exhausted and her arm was still hurting, but she tried to lay her plans to cover all eventualities.

Two months ago Prof Dixon had invited her to lecture on the discovery and excavation of the tomb of Queen Lostris, and the discovery of the scrolls. It was that book, of course, and more especially the footnote at the end of it, that had alerted him. Its publication had

25

caused a great deal of interest. They had received enquiries from Egyptologists, both amateur and professional, all around the world, some from as far afield as Tokyo and Nairobi, all of them questioning the authenticity of the novel and the factual basis behind it.

At the time she had opposed letting a writer of fiction have access to the transcriptions, especially as they had not been completed. She felt that the whole thing had reduced what should have been an important and serious academic subject to the level of popular entertainment, rather like what Spielberg had done to palaeontology with his park full of dinosaurs.

In the end her voice had been over-ruled. Even Duraid had sided against her. It had been the money, of course. The department was always short of funds to conduct its less spectacular work. When it came to some grandiose scheme like moving the entire Temple of Abu Simbel to a new site above the flood waters of the Aswan High Dam, then the nations of the world had poured in tens of millions of dollars. However, the day-to-day operational expenses of the department attracted no such support.

Their half share of the royalties from *River God*, for that was the book's title, had financed almost a year of research and exploration, but that was not enough to allay Royan's personal misgivings. The author had taken too many liberties with the facts contained in the scrolls, and had embroidered historical characters with personalities and foibles for which there was not the least evidence. In particular she felt he had portrayed Taita, the ancient scribe, as a braggart and a vainglorious poseur. She resented that.

In fairness she was forced to concede that the author's brief had been to make the facts as palatable and readable as possible to a wide lay public, and she reluctantly agreed that he had succeeded in doing so. However, all her scientific training revolted against such a popularization of something so unique and wonderful.

But she sighed and put these thoughts out of her head. The damage was done, and thinking about it only served to irritate her.

She turned her thoughts to more pressing problems. If she was to do the lecture that the Prof had invited her to deliver, then she would need her slides and these were still at her office in the museum. While she was still working out the best way to get hold of them without fetching them in person, exhaustion overtook her and she fell asleep, still fully clothed, on top of the bed.

In the end the solution to her problem was simplicity itself. She merely phoned the administration office and arranged for them to collect the box of slides from her office and send it out to the airport in a taxi with one of the secretaries.

When the secretary handed them over to her at the British Airways check-in desk, he told her, 'The police were at the museum when we opened this morning. They wanted to speak to you, Doctor.'

Obviously they had traced the registration of the wrecked Renault. She was pleased that she had her British passport. If she had tried to leave the country with her Egyptian papers she might have run into delays: the police would probably have placed a restriction order on all passport control points. As it was, she passed through the checkpoint with no difficulty and, once she was in the final departure lounge, she went to the news-stand and studied the array of newspapers.

All the local newspapers carried the story of the bombing of her car, and most of them had resurrected the story of Duraid's murder and linked the two events. One of them hinted at fundamentalist religious involvement. *El Arab* had a front-page photograph of herself and Duraid, which had been taken the previous month at a reception for a group of visiting French tour operators.

It gave her a pang to see the photograph of her husband looking so handsome and distinguished, with herself on his arm smiling up at him. She purchased copies of all the papers and took them on board the British Airways flight.

During the flight she passed the time by writing down in her notebook everything she could remember from what Duraid had told her of the man that she was going to find. She headed the page: 'Sir Nicholas Quenton-Harper (Bart).' Duraid had told her that Nicholas's great-grandfather had been awarded the title of baronet for his work as a career officer in the British colonial service. For three generations the family had maintained the strongest of ties with Africa, and especially with the British colonies and spheres of influence in North Africa: Egypt and the Sudan, Uganda and Kenya.

According to Duraid, Sir Nicholas himself had served in Africa and the Gulf States with the British army. He was a fluent Arabic and Swahili speaker and a noted amateur archaeologist and zoologist. Like his father, grandfather and great-grandfather before him, he had made numerous expeditions to North Africa to collect specimens and to explore the more remote regions. He had written a number of articles for various scientific journals and had even lectured at the Royal Geographical Society.

When his elder brother died childless, Sir Nicholas had inherited the title and the family estate at Quenton Park. He had resigned from the army to run the estate, but more especially to supervise the family museum that had been started in 1885 by his great-grandfather, the first baronet. It housed one of the largest collections of African fauna in private hands, and its ancient Egyptian and Middle Eastern collection of artefacts was equally famous.

However, from Duraid's accounts she concluded that there must be a wild, and even lawless, streak in Sir Nicholas's nature. It was obvious that he was not afraid to take some extraordinary risks to add to the collection at Quenton Park.

Duraid had first met him a number of years previously, when Sir Nicholas had recruited him to act as an intelligence officer for an illicit expedition to 'liberate' a number of Punic bronze castings from Gadaffi's Libya. Sir Nicholas had sold some of these to defray the expenses of the expedition, but had kept the best of them for his private collection.

More recently there had been another expedition, this time involving an illegal crossing of the Iraqi border to bring out a pair of stone bas-relief friezes from under Saddam Hussein's nose. Duraid had told her that Sir Nicholas had sold one of the pair for a huge amount of money; he had mentioned the sum of five million US dollars. Duraid said that he had used the money for the running of the museum, but that the second frieze, the finest of the pair, was still in Sir Nicholas's possession.

Both these expeditions had taken place years before Royan had met Duraid, and she wondered idly at Duraid's readiness to commit himself to the Englishman in this way. Sir Nicholas must have had unique powers of persuasion, for if they had been apprehended in the act there was no doubt that it would have meant summary execution for both of them.

As Duraid had explained to her, on each occasion it was only Nicholas's resourcefulness and his network of friends and admirers across the Middle East and North Africa, which he had been able to call on for help, that had seen them through.

'He is a bit of a devil,' Duraid had shaken his head with evident nostalgia at the memory, 'but the man to have with you when things are tough. Those days were all very exciting, but when I look back on it now I shudder at the risks we took.'

She had often pondered on the risks that a true in-the-blood collector was prepared to take to slake his passion. The risk seemed to be out of proportion to the reward, when it came to adding to his accumulations; and then she smiled at her own pious sentiments. The venture that she hoped to lead Sir Nicholas into was not exactly without risk, and she supposed that a circumlocution of lawyers might debate the legality of it endlessly.

Still smiling, she fell asleep, for the strain of these last few days had taken their toll. The air hostess woke her with an admonition to fasten her seat-belt for the landing at Heathrow.

Royan phoned her mother from the airport. 'Hello, Mummy. It's me.'

'Yes, I know that. Where are you, love?' Her mother sounded as unflappable as ever.

'At Heathrow. I am coming up to stay with you for a while. Is that all right?'

'Lumley's B and B,' her mother chuckled. 'I'll go and make your bed. What train will you be coming up on?'

'I had a look at the timetable. There is one from King's Cross that will get me into York at seven this evening.'

'I'll meet you at the station. What happened? Did you and Duraid have a tiff? Old enough to be your father. I said it wouldn't work.'

Royan was silent for a moment. This was hardly the time for explanations. 'I'll tell you all about it when I see you this evening.'

Georgina Lumley, her mother, was waiting on the platform in the gloom and cold of the November evening, bulky and solid in her old green Barbour coat with Magic, her cocker spaniel, sitting obediently at her feet. The two of them made an inseparable pair, even when they were not winning field trials cups. For Royan they painted a comforting and familiar picture of the English side of her lineage.

Georgina kissed Royan's cheek in a perfunctory manner. 'Never was one for all that sentimental fiddle-faddle,' she often said with satisfaction, and she took one of Royan's bags and led the way to the old mud-splattered Land Rover in the car park.

Magic sniffed Royan's hand and wagged his tail in recognition. Then in a dignified and condescending manner he allowed her to pat his head, but like his mistress he was no great sentimentalist either.

They drove in silence for a while and Georgina lit a cigarette. 'So what happened to Duraid, then?'

For a minute Royan could not reply, and then the floodgates within her burst and she let it all come pouring out. It was a twenty-minute drive north of York to the little village of Brandsbury, and Royan talked all the way. Her mother made only small sounds of encouragement and comfort, and when Royan wept as she related the details of Duraid's death and funeral, Georgina reached across and patted her daughter's hand.

It was all over by the time they reached her mother's cottage in the village. Royan had cried it out and was dry-eyed and rational again as they ate the dinner that her mother had prepared and left in the oven

29

for them. Royan could not remember when last she had tasted steak and kidney pie.

'So what are you going to do now?' Georgina asked as she poured what remained in the black bottle of Guinness into her own glass.

'To tell the truth, I don't know.' As she said it, Royan wondered ruefully why so many people used that particular phrase to introduce a lie. 'I have six months' leave from the museum, and Prof Dixon has arranged for me to give a lecture at the university. That is as far as it goes for the moment.'

'Well,' said Georgina as she stood up, 'there is a hot-water bottle in your bed and your room is there for as long as you wish to stay.' From her that was as good as a passionate declaration of maternal love.

Over the next few days Royan arranged her slides and notes for the lectures, and each afternoon she accompanied Georgina and Magic on their long walks over the surrounding countryside.

'Do you know Quenton Park?' she asked her mother during one of these rambles.

'Rather,' Georgina replied enthusiastically. 'Magic and I pick up there four or five times a season. First-class shoot. Some of the best pheasant and woodcock in Yorkshire. One drive there called the High Larches which is notorious. Birds so high they baffle the best shots in England.'

'Do you know the owner, Sir Nicholas Quenton-Harper?' Royan asked.

'Seen him at the shoots. Don't know him. Good shot, though,' Georgina replied. 'Knew his papa in the old days before I married your father.' She smiled in a suggestive way that startled Royan. 'Good dancer. We danced a few jigs together, not only on the dance floor.'

'Mummy, you are outrageous!' Royan laughed.

'Used to be,' Georgina agreed readily. 'Don't get many opportunities these days.'

'When are you and Magic going to Quenton Park again?'

'Two weeks' time.'

'May I come with you?'

'Of course – the keeper is always looking for beaters. Twenty quid and lunch with a bottle of beer for the day.' She stopped and looked at her daughter quizzically. 'What is all this about, then?'

'I hear there is a private museum on the estate. They have a world-renowned Egyptian collection. I wanted to get a look at it.'

'Not open to the public any more. Invitation only. Sir Nicholas is an odd chap, secretive and all that.'

'Couldn't you get an invitation for me?' Royan asked, but Georgina shook her head.

'Why don't you ask Prof Dixon? He is often one of the guns at Quenton Park. Great chum of Quenton-Harper.'

I t was ten days before Prof Dixon was ready for her. She borrowed her mother's Land Rover and drove to Leeds. The Prof folded her in a bear hug and then took her through to his office for tea.

It was nostalgic of her days as a student to be back in the cluttered room filled with books and papers and ancient artefacts. Royan told him about Duraid's murder, and Dixon was shocked and distressed, but she quickly changed the subject to the slides that she had prepared for the lecture. He was fascinated by everything she had to show him.

It was almost time for her to leave before she had an opportunity to broach the subject of the Quenton Park museum, but he responded immediately.

'I am amazed that you never visited it while you were a student here. It's a very impressive collection. The family has been at it for over a hundred years. As a matter of fact, I am shooting on the estate next Thursday. I'll have a word with Nicholas. However, the poor chap isn't up to much at the moment. Last year he suffered a terrible personal tragedy. Lost his wife and two little girls in a motor accident on the M1.' He shook his head. 'Awful business. Nicholas was driving. I think he blames himself.' He walked her out to the Land Rover.

'So we will see you on the twenty-third,' he told Royan as they parted. 'I expect that you will have an audience of at least a hundred, and I have even had a reporter from the *Yorkshire Post* on to me. They have heard about your lectures and they want to do an interview with you. Jolly good publicity for the department. You'll do it, of course. Could you come a couple of hours early to speak to them?'

'Actually I will probably see you before the twenty-third,' she told him. 'Mummy and her dog are picking up at Quenton Park on Thursday, and she has got me a job as a beater for the day.'

'I'll keep an eye open for you,' he promised, and waved to her as she pulled away in a cloud of exhaust smoke.

T he wind was searing cold out of the north. The clouds tumbled over each other, heavy and blue and grey, so close to earth that they brushed the crests of the hills as they hurried ahead of the gale.

31

Royan wore three layers of clothing under the old green Barbour jacket that Georgina had lent her, but still she shivered as they came up over the brow of the hills in the line of beaters. Her blood had thinned in the heat of the Nile valley. Two pairs of fisherman's socks were not enough to save her toes from turning numb.

For this drive, the last of the day, the head keeper had moved Georgina from her usual position behind the line of guns, where she and Magic were expected to pick up the crippled birds that came through to them, into the line of beaters.

Keeping the best for last, they were beating the High Larches. The keeper needed every man and woman he could get into the line to bring in the pheasant from the huge piece of ground on top of the hills and to push them off the brow, out over the valley where the guns waited at their pegs far below.

It seemed to Royan a supreme piece of illogical behaviour to rear and nurture the pheasants from chicks, and then, when they were mature, go to such lengths to make them as difficult to shoot as the keeper could devise. However, Georgina had explained to her that the higher and harder to hit the birds passed over the guns, the more pleased the sportsmen were, and the more they were willing to pay for the privilege of firing at them.

'You cannot believe what they will pay for a day's shooting,' Georgina had told her. 'Today will bring in almost £14,000 to the estate. They will shoot twenty days this season. Work that out and you will see that the shoot is a major part of the estate's income. Quite apart from the fun of working the dogs and beating, it gives a lot of us local people a very useful bit of extra money.'

At this stage of the day, Royan was not too certain just how much fun there was to be had from the job of beating. The walking was difficult in the thick brambles, and Royan had slipped more than once. There was mud on her knees and elbows. The ditch ahead of her was half-filled with water and there was a thin skin of ice across the surface. She approached it gingerly, using her walking-stick to balance herself. She was tired, for there had already been five drives, all as onerous as this one. She glanced across at her mother and marvelled at how she seemed to be enjoying this torture. Georgina strode along happily, controlling Magic with her whistle and hand signals.

She grinned at Royan now, 'Last lap, love. Nearly over.'

Royan was humiliated that her distress had been so obvious, and she used her stick to help her vault the muddy ditch. However, she miscalculated the width and fell short of the far bank. She landed knee-deep in the frozen water and it poured in over the top of her wellington boots.

Georgina laughed at her and offered her the end of her own stick to pull her out of the glutinous mud. Royan could not hold up the line by stopping to empty her flooded boots, so she went on, squelching loudly with each pace.

'Steady on the left!' the order from the head keeper was relayed over the walkie-talkie radio, and the line halted obediently.

The art and skill of the keeper was to flush the birds from the tangled undergrowth, not in one massed covey, but in a steady trickle that would pass over the waiting guns in singles and pairs, giving them the chance, after they had fired two barrels, to take their second gun from the loader and be ready for the next bird to appear in the sky high above them. The size of the keeper's tip and his reputation depended on the way he 'showed' the birds to the waiting guns.

During this respite Royan was able to regain her breath, and to look around her. Through a break in the grove of larches that gave the drive its name, she could see down into the valley.

There was an open meadow at the foot of the hills, the expanse of smooth green grass broken up by patches of dirty grey snow from the previous week's fall. Down this meadow the keeper had set a line of numbered pegs. At the beginning of the day's sport the guns had drawn lots to decide the peg number from which each of them would shoot.

Now each man stood at his allotted peg, with his loader holding his second gun ready behind him, ready to pass it over when the first gun was empty. They were all looking up expectantly to the high ground from which the pheasant would appear.

'Which is Sir Nicholas?' Royan called to her mother, and Georgina pointed to the far end of the line of guns.

'The tall one,' she said, and at that moment the keeper's voice on the radio ordered, 'Gently on the left. Start tapping again.' Obediently the beaters tapped their sticks. There was no shouting or hallooing in this delicate and strictly controlled operation.

'Forward slowly. Halt to the flush of birds.'

A step at a time the line moved ahead, and in the brambles and bracken in front of her Royan could hear the stealthy scuffle of a number of pheasants moving forward, reluctant to take to the air until they were forced to do so.

There was another ditch in their path, this one choked with an almost impenetrable thicket of brambles. Some of the larger dogs, like the Labradors, balked at entering such a thorny barrier. Georgina whistled sharply and Magic's ears went up. He was soaked and his coat was a matted mess of mud and burrs and thorns. His pink tongue lolled from the corner of his grinning mouth and the sodden stump of his tail was wagging merrily. At that moment he was the happiest dog in England. He was doing the work that he had been bred for.

'Come on, Magic,' Georgina ordered. 'Get in there. Get them out.'

Magic dived into the thickest and thorniest patch, and disappeared completely from view. There was a minute of snuffling and rooting around in the depths of the ditch, and then a fierce cackle and flurry of wings.

A pair of birds exploded out of the bushes. The hen led the way. She was a drab, nondescript creature the size of a domestic fowl, but the cock bird that followed her closely was magnificent. His head was capped with iridescent green and his cheeks and wattles were scarlet. His tail, barred in cinnamon and black, was almost as long again as his body and the rest of his plumage was a riot of gorgeous colour.

As he climbed he sparkled against the lowering grey sky like a priceless jewel thrown from an emperor's hand. Royan gasped with the beauty of the sight.

'Just look at them go!' Georgina's voice was thick with excitement. 'What a pair of crackerjacks. The best pair today. My bet is that not one of the guns will touch a feather on either of them.'

Up, and then on up, the two birds climbed, the hen drawing the cock after her, until suddenly the wind boiling over the hills like overheated milk caught them both and flung them away, out over the valley.

The line of beaters enjoyed the moment. They had worked hard for it. Their voices were tiny and faint on the wind as they urged the birds on. They loved to see a pheasant so high and fast that it could beat the guns.

'Forward!' they exulted. 'Over!' and this time the line came involuntarily to a halt as they followed the flight of the pair that were twisting away on the wind.

In the valley bottom the faces of the guns were turned upwards, pale specks against the green background. Their trepidation was almost palpable as they watched the pheasant reach their maximum speed, so that they could no longer beat their wings, but locked them into a back-swept profile as they began to drop down into the valley.

This was the most difficult shot that any gun would face. A high pair of pheasant with a half gale quartering from behind, dropping into the shot at their terminal rate of flight, set to pass over the line at the extreme effective range of a twelve-bore shotgun. For the men below it was a calculation of speed and lead in all three dimensions of space. The best of shots might hope to take one of them, but who would dare to think of both?

'A pound on it!' Georgina called. 'A pound that they both get through.' But none of the beaters who heard her accepted the wager.

The wind was pushing the birds gently sideways. They started off aimed at the centre of the line, but they were drifting towards the far

34

end. As the angle changed, Royan could see the men at the pegs below her brace themselves in turn as the birds appeared to be heading straight for them, and then relax as the wind moved them on. Their relief was evident as, one after the other, each of them was absolved from the challenge of having to make such an impossible shot with all eyes fastened upon him.

In the end only the tall figure at the extreme end of the line stood in their flight path.

'Your bird, sir,' one of the other guns called mockingly, and Royan found that instinctively she was holding her breath with anticipation.

Nicholas Quenton-Harper seemed unaware of the approach of the pair of pheasant. He stood completely relaxed, his tall frame slouching slightly, his shotgun tucked under his right arm with the muzzles pointing at the ground.

At the moment that the leading hen bird reached a point in the sky sixty degrees out ahead of him he moved for the first time. With casual grace he swung the shotgun up in a sweeping arc. At the instant that the butt touched his cheek and shoulder he fired, but the gun never stopped moving and went on to describe the rest of the arc.

The distance delayed the sound of the shot reaching Royan. She saw the barrels kick with the recoil, and a pale spurt of blue smoke from the muzzle. Then Nicholas lowered the gun as the hen suddenly threw back her head and closed her wings. There was no burst of feathers from her body, for she had been hit cleanly in the head and killed instantly. As she began the long plummet to earth Royan heard the thud of the shot.

By then the cock was high over Nicholas's head. This time as he mounted the gun in that casual sweeping gesture he arched his back to point upwards, his long frame bending from the waist like a drawn bow. Once again at the apex of the swing the weapon kicked in his grasp.

'He has missed!' Royan thought with a mixture of satisfaction and disappointment, as the cock sailed on seemingly unscathed. Part of her wanted the beautiful bird to escape, while part of her wanted the man to succeed. Gradually the profile of the high cock altered as the wings folded back and it rolled over in flight. Royan had no way of knowing that his heart had been struck through, until seconds later he died in mid-air and the locked wings lost their rigid set.

As the cock tumbled to earth, a spontaneous chorus of cheers ran down the line of beaters, faint but enthusiastic on the icy north wind. Even the other guns added their voices with cries of, 'Oh, good shot, sir!'

Royan did not join in the cheering, but for the moment her fatigue and cold were forgotten. She could only vaguely appreciate the skill that those two shots had called for, but she was impressed, even a little awed. Her very first glimpse of the man had fulfilled all the expectations that Duraid's stories about him had raised in her.

By the time the last drive ended it was almost dark. An old army truck came rumbling down the track through the forest along which the tired beaters and their dogs waited. As it slowed they scrambled up into the back. Georgina gave Royan a boost from behind before she and Magic followed her up. They settled thankfully on one of the long hard benches, and Georgina lit a cigarette as she joined in the chat and banter of the under-keepers and beaters around her.

Royan sat silently at the end of the bench, enjoying the sense of achievement at having come through such a strenuous day. She felt tired and relaxed, and strangely contented. For one whole day she had not thought either of the theft of the scroll or of Duraid's murder and the unknown and unseen enemy who threatened her with a violent death.

The truck ground down the hill and slowed as it reached the bottom, pulling in to the verge to let a green Range Rover pass. As the two vehicles drew level, Royan turned her head and looked down into the open driver's window of the expensive estate car, and into the eyes of Nicholas Quenton-Harper at the wheel.

This was the first time she had been close enough to him to see his features. She was surprised at how young he was. She had expected him to be a man of Duraid's age. She saw now that he was no older than forty, for there were only the first strands of silver in the wings of his thick, rumpled hair. His features were tanned and weatherbeaten, those of an outdoors man. His eyes were green and penetrating under dark, beetling brows. His mouth was wide and expressive, and he was smiling now at some witticism that the driver of the truck called to him in a thick Yorkshire accent, but there was a sense of sadness and tragedy in the eyes. Royan remembered what the Prof had told her of his recent bereavement, and she felt her heart go out to him. She was not alone in her loss and her mourning.

He looked directly into her eyes and she saw his expression change. She was an attractive woman, and she could tell when a man recognized that. She had made an impression on him, but she did not enjoy the fact. Her sorrow for Duraid was still too raw and painful. She looked away and the Range Rover drove on.

Her lecture at the university went off extremely well. Royan was a good speaker and she knew her subject intimately. She held them fascinated with her account of the opening of the tomb of Queen Lostris and of the subsequent discovery of the scrolls. Many of her audience had read the book, and during question time they pestered her to know how much of it was the truth. She had to tread very carefully here, so as not to deal too harshly with the author.

Afterwards Prof Dixon took Royan and Georgina to dinner. He was delighted with her success, and ordered the most expensive bottle of claret on the wine list to celebrate. He was only mildly disconcerted when she refused a glass of it.

'Oh, dear me, I forgot that you were a Moslem,' he apologised.

'A Copt,' she corrected him, 'and it's not on religious grounds. I just don't like the taste.'

'Don't worry,' Georgina counselled him, 'I don't have the same odd compulsion to masochism as my daughter. She must get it from her father's side. I'll give you a hand to finish the good stuff.'

Under the benign influence of the claret the Prof became expansive, and entertained them with the accounts of the archaeological digs he had been on over the decades. It was only over the coffee that he turned to Royan.

'Goodness me, I almost forgot to tell you. I have arranged for you to visit the museum at Quenton Park any afternoon this week. Just ring Mrs Street the day before, and she will be waiting to let you in. She is Nicholas's PA.'

Royan remembered the way to Quenton Park from when Georgina had driven them to the shoot, but now she was alone in the Land Rover. The massive main gates to the estate were made of ornate cast iron. A little further on, the road divided and a cluster of road signs pointed the way to the various destinations: 'Quenton Hall. Private', 'Estate Office' and 'Museum'.

The road to the museum curved through the deer park where herds of fallow deer grazed under the winter-bare oaks. Through the misty landscape she had glimpses of the big house. According to the guidebook that the Prof had given her, Sir Christopher Wren had designed the house in 1693, and the master landscapist, Capability Brown, had created the gardens sixty years later. The results were perfection.

The museum was set in a grove of copper beech trees half a mile beyond the house. It was a sprawling building that had obviously been added to more than once over the years. Mrs Street was waiting for her at the side door, and introduced herself as she let Royan in. She was middle-aged, grey-haired and self-assured. 'I was at your lecture on Monday evening. Fascinating! I have a guidebook for you, but you will find the exhibits well catalogued and described. I have spent almost twenty years at the job. There are no other visitors today. You will have the place to yourself. You must just wander around and please yourself. I shall not leave until five this evening, so you have all afternoon. If I can help you in any way my office is at the end of the passage. Please don't hesitate.'

From the first moment that Royan walked into the display of African mammals she was enthralled. The primate room housed a complete collection of every single species of ape and monkey from that continent: from the great silver-backed male gorilla to the delicate colobus in his long flowing mantle of black and white fur, they were all represented.

Although some of the exhibits were over a hundred years old, they were beautifully preserved and presented, set in painted dioramas of their natural habitat. It was obvious that the museum must employ a staff of skilled artists and taxidermists. She could guess what this must have cost. Wryly she decided that the five million dollars from the sale of the plundered frieze had been well spent.

She went through to the antelope room and stared around her in wonder at the magnificent beasts preserved here. She stopped before a diorama of a family group of the giant sable antelope of the now extinct Angolan variety, *Hippotragus niger variani*. While she admired the jet black and snowy-chested bull with his long, back-swept horns, she mourned his death at the hand of one of the Quenton-Harper family. Then she checked herself. Without the strange dedication and passion of the hunter-collector who had killed him, future generations might never have been able to look upon this regal presence.

She passed on into the next hall which was given over to displays of the African elephant, and paused in the centre of the room before a pair of ivory tusks so large that she could not believe they had ever been carried by a living animal. They seemed more like the marble columns of some Hellenic temple to Diana, the goddess of the chase. She stooped to read the printed catalogue card:

Tusks of the African Elephant, Loxodonta africana. *Shot in the Lado Enclave in 1899 by Sir Jonathan Quenton-Harper. Left tusk 289 lb. Right tusk 301 lb. Length of larger tusk 11' 4". Girth 32". The largest pair of tusks ever taken by a European hunter.*

They stood twice as high as she was tall, and they were half as thick again as her waist. As she passed on into the Egyptian room she marvelled at the size and strength of the creature that had carried them.

She came up short as her eyes fell upon the figure in the centre of the room. It was a fifteen-foot-high figure of Ramesses II, depicted as the god Osiris in polished red granite. The god-emperor strode out on muscular legs, wearing only sandals on his feet and a short kilt. In his left hand he carried the remains of a war-bow, with both the upper and lower limbs of the weapon broken off. This was the only damage that the statue had suffered in all those thousands of years. The rest of it was perfect – the plinth even bore the marks of the mason's chisel. In his right fist Pharaoh carried a seal embossed with his royal cartouche. Upon his majestic head he wore the tall double crown of the upper and lower kingdoms. His expression was calm and enigmatic.

Royan recognized the statue instantly, for its twin stood in the grand hall of the Cairo museum. She passed it every day on her way to her office.

She felt anger rising in her. This was one of the major treasures of her very Egypt. It had been plundered and stolen from one of her country's sacred sites. It did not belong here. It belonged on the banks of the great river Nile. She felt herself shaking with the strength of her emotion as she went forward to examine the statue more closely and to read the hieroglyphic inscription on the base.

The royal cartouche stood out in the centre of the arrogant warning: '*I am the divine Ramesses, master of ten thousand chariots. Fear me, O ye enemies of Egypt.*'

Royan had not read the translation aloud; it was a soft, deep voice close behind her that spoke, startling her. She had not heard anyone approaching. She spun round to find him standing close enough to touch.

His hands were thrust into the pockets of a shapeless blue cardigan. There was a hole in one elbow. He wore faded denim jeans over well-worn but monogrammed velvet carpet slippers – the type of genteel shabbiness that certain Englishmen often cultivate, for it would never do to seem too concerned with one's appearance.

'Sorry. Didn't mean to startle you.' He smiled a lazy smile of apology, and his teeth were very white but slightly crooked. Suddenly his expression changed as he recognized her.

'Oh, it's you.' She should have been flattered that he remembered her from so fleeting a contact, but there was that flash of something in his eyes again that offended her. Nevertheless, she could not refuse the hand he offered her. 'Nick Quenton-Harper,' he introduced himself. 'You must be Percival Dixon's old student. I think I saw you at the shoot last Thursday. Weren't you beating for us?'

His manner was friendly and forthright, so she felt her hackles subsiding as she responded, 'Yes. I am Royan Al Simma. I think you knew my husband, Duraid Al Simma.'

'Duraid! Of course, I know him. Grand old fellow. We spent a lot of time in the desert together. One of the very best. How is he?'

'He's dead.' She had not meant it to sound so bald and heartless, but then there was no other reply she could think of.

'I am so terribly sorry. I didn't know. When and how did it happen?'

'Very recently, three weeks ago. He was murdered.'

'Oh, my God.' She saw the sympathy in his eyes, and she remembered that he also had suffered. 'I telephoned him in Cairo not more than four months ago. He was his old charming self. Have they found the person who did it?'

She shook her head and looked around the hall to avoid having to face him and let him see that her eyes were wet. 'You have an extraordinary collection here.'

He accepted the change of subject at once. 'Thanks mostly to my grandfather. He was on the staff of Evelyn Baring – Over Bearing, as his numerous enemies called him. He was the British man in Cairo during—'

She cut him short. 'Yes, I have heard of Evelyn Baring, the first Earl of Cromer, British Consul-General of Egypt from 1883 to 1907. With his plenipotentiary powers he was the unchallenged dictator of my country for all that period. Numerous enemies, as you say.'

Nicholas's eyes narrowed slightly. 'Percival warned me you were one of his best students. He didn't, however, warn me of your strong nationalistic feelings. It is clear that you didn't need me to translate the Ramesses inscription for you.'

'My own father was on the staff of Gamal Abdel Nasser,' she murmured. Nasser was the man who had toppled the puppet King Farouk and finally broken the British power in Egypt. As president he had nationalized the Suez Canal in the face of British outrage.

'Ha!' he chuckled. 'Different sides of the track. But things have changed. I hope we don't have to be enemies?'

'Not at all,' she agreed. 'Duraid held you in the highest esteem.'

'As I did him.' He changed the subject again. 'We are very proud of our collection of royal *ushabti*. Examples from the tomb of every pharaoh from the old Kingdom onwards, right up to the last of the Ptolemys. Please let me show it to you.' She followed him to the huge display case that occupied one complete wall of the hall. It was lined with shelf after shelf of the doll-like figures which had been placed in the tombs to act as servants and slaves for the dead kings in the shadow world.

With his own key Nicholas opened the glazed doors of the case and reached up to bring down the most interesting of the exhibits. 'This is the *ushabti* of Maya who served under three pharaohs, Tutankhamen, Ay and Horemheb. It is from the tomb of Ay who died in 1343 BC.'

He handed the doll to her and she read aloud the three thousand-

40

year-old hieroglyphics as easily as though they had been the headlines of that morning's newspaper. 'I am Maya, Treasurer of the two Kingdoms. I will answer for the divine Pharaoh Ay. May he live for ever!' She spoke in Arabic to test him, and his reply in the same language was fluent and colloquial.

'It seems that Percival Dixon told me the truth. You must have been an exceptional student.'

Engrossed now in their common interest, speaking alternately Arabic and English, the initial sharp prickles of antagonism between them were dulled. They moved slowly round the hall, lingering before each display case to handle and examine minutely each object that it contained.

It was as though they were transported back over the millennia. Hours and days seemed of no consequence in the face of such antiquity, and so it startled both of them when Mrs Street returned to interrupt them, 'I am off now, Sir Nicholas. Can I leave it to you to lock up and set the alarm? The security guards are on duty already.'

'What time is it?' Nicholas answered his own question by glancing at the stainless steel Rolex Submariner on his wrist. 'Five-forty already, what on earth happened to the day?' He sighed theatrically. 'Off you go, Mrs Street. Sorry we kept you so long.'

'Don't forget to set the alarm,' she warned him, and then to Royan, 'He can be so absent-minded when he is off on one of his hobby-horses.' Her fondness towards her employer was obviously that of an indulgent aunt.

'You've given me enough orders for one day. Off you go,' Nicholas grinned, as he turned back to Royan. 'Can't let you go without showing you something that Duraid was in on with me. Can you stay for a few minutes longer?' She nodded and he reached out as if to take her arm, and then dropped his hand. In the Arab world it is insulting to touch a woman, even in such a casual manner. She was aware of the courtesy, and she warmed to his good manners and easy style a little more.

He led her out of the exhibition halls through a door marked 'Private. Staff Only', and down a long corridor to the room at the end.

'The inner sanctum.' He ushered her in. 'Excuse the mess. I must really get around to tidying up in here one of these years. My wife used to—' He broke off abruptly, and he glanced at the silver-framed photograph of a family group on his desk. Nicholas and a beautiful dark-haired woman sat on a picnic rug under the spreading branches of an oak. There were two little girls with them and the family resemblance to the mother was strong in both of them. The youngest child sat on Nicholas's lap while the elder girl stood behind them, holding the reins of her Shetland pony. Royan glanced sideways at him and saw the devastating sorrow in his eyes.

41

So as not to embarrass him she looked around the rest of the room, which was obviously his study and workshop. It was spacious and comfortable, a man's room, but it illustrated the contradictions of his character – the bookish scholar set against the man of action. Amongst the muddle of books and museum specimens lay fishing reels and a Hardy split cane salmon rod. On a row of wall hooks hung a Barbour jacket, a canvas shotgun slip and a leather cartridge bag embossed with the initials N.Q.-H.

She recognized some of the framed pictures on the walls. They were original nineteenth-century watercolours by the Scottish traveller David Roberts, and others by Vivant Denon who had accompanied Napoleon's *L'armée de l'Orient* to Egypt. They were fascinating views of the monuments drawn before the excavations and restorations of more modern times.

Nicholas went to the fireplace and threw a log on the fading coals. He kicked it until it flared up brightly and then beckoned her to stand in front of the floor-to-ceiling curtains that covered half of one wall. With a conjuror's flourish he pulled the tasselled cord that opened the curtains and exclaimed with satisfaction, 'What do you make of that, then?'

She studied the magnificent bas-relief frieze that was mounted on the wall. The detail was beautiful and the rendition magnificent, but she did not let her admiration show. Instead she gave her opinion in offhand tones.

'Sixth King of the Amorite dynasty, Hammurabi, about 1780 BC,' she said, pretending to study the finely chiselled features of the ancient monarch before she went on, 'Yes, probably from his palace site south-west of the ziggurat at Ashur. There should have been a pair of these friezes. They are worth in the region of five million US dollars each. My guess is that they were stolen from the saintly ruler of modern Mesopotamia, Saddam Hussein, by two unprincipled rogues. I hear that the other one of the pair is at present in the collection of a certain Mr Peter Walsh in Texas.'

He stared at her in astonishment, and then burst out laughing. 'Damn it! I swore Duraid to secrecy but he must have told you about our naughty little escapade.' It was the first time she had heard him laugh. It seemed to come naturally to his lips and she liked the sound of it, hearty and unaffected.

'You are right about the present owner of the second frieze,' he told her, still laughing. 'But the price was six million, not five.'

'Duraid also told me about your visit to the Tibesti Massif in Chad and southern Libya,' she remarked, and he shook his head in mock contrition.

'It seems I have no secrets from you.' He went to a tall *armoire*

42

against the opposite wall. It was a magnificent piece of marquetry furniture, probably seventeenth-century French. He opened the double doors and said, 'This is what Duraid and I brought back from Libya, without the consent of Colonel Muammar al Gadaffi.' He took down one of the exquisite little bronzes and handed it to her. It was the figure of a mother nursing her infant, and it had a green patina of age.

'Hannibal, son of Hamilcar Barca,' he said, 'about 203 BC. These were found by a band of Tuareg at one of his old camps on the Bagradas river in North Africa. Hannibal must have cached them there before his defeat by the Roman general Scipio. There were over two hundred bronzes in the hoard, and I still have fifty of the best of them.'

'You sold the rest of them?' she asked, as she admired the statuette. There was disapproval in her tone as she went on, 'How could you bear to part with something so beautiful?'

He sighed unhappily, 'Had to, I am afraid. Very sad, but the expedition to retrieve them cost me a fortune. Had to cover expenses by selling some of the booty.'

He went to his desk and brought out a bottle of Laphroaig malt whisky from the bottom drawer. He placed the bottle on the desk top and set two glasses beside it. 'Can I tempt you?' he asked, but she shook her head.

'Don't blame you. Even the Scots themselves admit that this brew should only be drunk in sub-zero weather on The Hill, in a forty-knot gale, after stalking and shooting a ten-point stag. May I offer you something a little more ladylike?'

'Do you have a Coke?' she suggested.

'Yes, but that is really bad for you, even worse than Laphroaig. It's all that sugar. Absolute poison.'

She took the glass he brought to her and returned his toast with it.

'To life!' she agreed, and then she went on, 'You are right. Duraid did tell me about these.' She replaced the Punic bronze in the *armoire*, then came to face him at the desk. 'It was also Duraid who sent me to see you. It was his dying instruction to me.'

'Aha! So none of this is coincidence then. It seems I am the unwitting pawn in some deep and nefarious plot.' He pointed to the chair facing his desk. 'Sit!' he ordered. 'Tell!'

He perched above her on the corner of the desk, with the whisky glass in his right hand and with one long, denim-clad leg swinging lazily as the tail of a resting leopard. Though he was smiling quizzically, he watched her face with a penetrating green gaze. She thought that it would be difficult to lie to this man.

She took a deep breath, 'Have you heard of an ancient Egyptian queen called Lostris, of the second intermediate period, co-existent with the first Hyksos invasions?'

43

He laughed a little derisively and stood up, 'Oh! Now we are talking about the book *River God*, are we?' He went to the bookcase and brought down a copy. Although well thumbed, it was still in its dust-jacket, and the cover illustration was a dreamy surrealistic view in pastel shades of green and rose purple of the pyramids seen over water. He dropped it on the desk in front of her.

'Have you read it?' she asked.

'Yes,' he nodded. 'I read most of Wilbur Smith's stuff. He amuses me. He has shot here at Quenton Park a couple of times.'

'You like lots of sex and violence in your reading, obviously?' She pulled a face. 'What did you think of this particular book?'

'I must admit that he had me fooled. Whilst I was reading it, I sort of wished that it might be based on fact. That was why I phoned Duraid.' Nicholas picked up the book again and flipped to the end of it. 'The author's note was convincing, but what I couldn't get out of my mind was the last sentence.' He read it aloud. '"*Somewhere in the Abyssinian mountains near the source of the Blue Nile, the mummy of Tenus still lies in the unviolated tomb of Pharaoh Mamose.*"'

Almost angrily Nicholas threw the book down on the desk. 'My God! You will never know how much I wanted it to be true. You will never know how much I wanted a shot at Pharaoh Mamose's tomb. I had to speak to Duraid. When he assured me it was all a load of bunkum, I felt cheated. I had built up my expectations so high that I was bitterly disappointed.'

'It's not bunkum,' she contradicted him, and then corrected herself quickly, 'well, at least not all of it.'

'I see. Duraid was lying to me, was he?'

'Not lying,' she defended him hotly. 'Just delaying the truth a little. He wasn't ready to tell you the whole story then. He didn't have the answers to all the questions that he knew you would ask. He was going to come to you when he was ready. Your name was at the top of the list of potential sponsors that he had drawn up.'

'Duraid did not have the answers, but I suppose you do?' He was smiling sceptically. 'I was caught once. I am not likely to fall for the same cock and bull a second time.'

'The scrolls exist. Nine of them are still in the vaults at the Cairo museum. I was the one who discovered them in the tomb of Queen Lostris.' Royan opened her leather sling bag and rummaged around in it until she brought out a thin sheaf of glossy 6 × 4 colour photographs. She selected one and passed it to him. 'That is a shot of the rear wall of the tomb. You can just make out the alabaster jars in the niche. That was taken before we removed them.'

'Nice picture, but it could have been taken anywhere.'

She ignored the remark and passed him another photograph. 'The ten scrolls in Duraid's workroom at the museum. You recognize the two men standing behind the bench?'

He nodded. 'Duraid and Wilbur Smith.' His sceptical expression had turned to one of doubt and bemusement. 'What the hell are you trying to tell me?'

'What the *hell* I am trying to tell you is that, apart from a wide poetic licence that the author took unto himself, all that he wrote in the book has at least some foundation in the truth. However, the scroll that most concerns us is the seventh, the one that was stolen by the men who murdered my husband.'

Nicholas stood up and went to the fireplace. He threw on another log and bashed it viciously with the poker, as if to give release to his emotions. He spoke without turning around, 'What was the significance of that particular scroll as opposed to the other nine?'

'It was the one that contained the account of Pharaoh Mamose's burial and, we believe, directions that might enable us to find the site of the tomb.'

'You believe, but you aren't certain?' He swung around to face her with the poker gripped like a weapon. In this mood he was frightening. His mouth was set in a tight hard line and his eyes glittered.

'Large parts of the seventh scroll are written in some sort of code, a series of cryptic verses. Duraid and I were in the process of deciphering these when—' she broke off and drew a long breath, 'when he was murdered.'

'You must have a copy of something so valuable?' He glared at her, so that she felt intimidated. She shook her head.

'All the microfilm, all our notes, all of it was stolen along with the original scroll. Then whoever killed Duraid went back to our flat in Cairo and destroyed my PC on to which I had transposed all our research.'

He threw the poker into the coal scuttle with a clatter, and came back to the desk. 'So you have no evidence at all? Nothing to prove that any of this is true?'

'Nothing,' she agreed, 'except what I have here.' With a long slim forefinger she tapped her forehead. 'I have a good memory.'

He frowned and ran his fingers through his thick curling hair. 'And so why did you come to me?'

'I have come to give you a shot at the tomb of Pharaoh Mamose,' she told him simply. 'Do you want it?'

Suddenly his mood changed. He grinned like a naughty schoolboy. 'At this moment I cannot think of anything I want more.'

'Then you and I will have to draw up some sort of working

45

agreement,' she told him, and she leaned forward in a businesslike manner. 'First, let me tell you what I want, and then you can do the same.'

It was hard bargaining, and it was one in the morning when Royan admitted her exhaustion. 'I can't think straight any more. Can we start again tomorrow morning?' They still had not reached an agreement.

'It's tomorrow morning already,' he told her. 'But you are right. Thoughtless of me. You can sleep here. After all, we do have twenty-seven bedrooms here.'

'No, thanks.' She stood up. 'I'll go on home.'

'The road will be icy,' he warned her. Then he saw her determined expression and held up his hands in capitulation. 'All right, I won't insist. What time tomorrow? I have a meeting with my lawyers at ten, but we should be finished by noon. Why don't you and I have a working lunch here? I was supposed to be shooting at Ganton in the afternoon, but I will cancel that. That way I will have the afternoon and evening clear for you.'

Nicholas's meeting with the lawyers took place the next morning in the library of Quenton Park. It was not an easy nor a pleasant session, but then he never expected it to be. This had been the year in which his world began to fall to pieces around his head. He gritted his teeth as he remembered how the year had opened with that fatal moment of fatigue and inattention at midnight on the icy motorway, and the blinding headlights of the truck bearing down on them.

He had not recovered from that before the next brutal blow had fallen. This was the financial report of the Lloyd's insurance syndicate on which Nicholas, like his father and grandfather before him, was a 'Name'. For half a century the family had enjoyed a regular and substantial income from their share of the syndicate profits. Of course, Nicholas had been aware that liability for his share of any losses that the syndicate suffered was unlimited. The enormity of that responsibility had weighed lightly; for there had never been serious losses to account for, not for fifty years, not until this year.

With the California earthquake and environmental pollution claims awarded against one of the multinational chemical companies, the syndicate's losses had amounted to over twenty-six million pounds sterling. Nicholas's share of that loss was two and a half million pounds – some of which had been settled, but the rest was due for payment in a little over eight months' time – together with whatever nasty surprises next year might hold.

Almost immediately after that the Quenton Park estate's crop of sugar beet, almost a thousand acres in total, had been hit by *rhizomania*, the mad root disease. They had lost the lot.

'We will need to find at least two and a half million,' said one of the lawyers. 'That should be no problem – the Hall is filled with valuable items, and what about the museum? What could we reasonably expect from the sale of some of the exhibits?'

Nicholas winced at the thought of selling the Ramesses statue, the bronzes, the Hammurabi frieze or any item of his cherished collection at the Hall or the museum. He acknowledged that their sale would cover his debts, but he doubted that he could live without them. Almost anything was preferable to parting with them.

'Hell, no,' Nicholas cut in, and the lawyer looked across at him coldly.

'Well, let's see what else we've got,' he continued remorselessly. 'There's the dairy herd.'

'That will bring in a hundred thousand, if we are lucky,' Nicholas grunted. 'Leaves only two point four million to find.'

'And your racing stud,' the accountant came into the conversation.

'I have only six horses in training. Another two hundred grand.' Nicholas smiled without humour, 'Brings us down to two point two. We are getting there slowly.'

'The yacht,' suggested the youngest lawyer.

'It's older than I am,' Nicholas shook his head, 'belonged to my father, for heaven's sake. You probably wouldn't be able to give it away. Sentimental is the only value it has. My shotguns would be worth more.'

Both lawyers bent their heads over their lists, 'Ah, yes! We have those. A pair of Purdey sidelock ejectors in good condition. Estimate forty thousand.'

'I also have some secondhand socks and underpants,' Nicholas admitted. 'Why don't you list those also?'

They ignored the jibe. 'Then there is the London house,' the elder lawyer went on unperturbed, inured to human suffering. 'Good address. Value one point five million.'

'Not in this financial climate,' Nicholas contradicted him. 'A million is more realistic.' The lawyer made a note in the margin of his document before going on, 'Of course we want to avoid, if at all possible, putting the entire estate up for sale.'

It was a hard and difficult meeting which ended with nothing definitely decided, and Nicholas feeling angry and frustrated.

He saw the lawyers off, and then went up to the family quarters to take a quick shower and change his shirt. As an afterthought, and for no good reason, he shaved and splashed aftershave on his cheeks.

He drove across the park and left the Range Rover in the museum car park. The snow had turned to sleet, and his bare head was sprinkled with cold droplets by the time he had crossed the car park.

Royan was waiting in Mrs Street's office. The two of them seemed to be getting along well together. He stopped outside the door to listen to her laughter. It made him feel a little better.

The cook had sent across a hot lunch from the main house. She seemed to believe that a substantial meal would keep this foul weather at bay. There was a tureen of thick, rich minestrone and a Lancashire hotpot, with a half bottle of red Burgundy for him and a jug of freshly squeezed orange juice for her. They ate in front of the fire, while the rain whipped against the windowpanes.

While they ate he asked her to give him the details of Duraid's murder. She left out nothing, including her own injuries, and drew back her sleeve to show him the dressing over the knife wound. He listened intently as she told him of the second attempt on her life in the streets of Cairo.

'Any suspicions?' he asked, when she had finished. 'Anybody you can think of who might be responsible?' But she shook her head.

'There was no warning of any kind,' she said.

They finished the meal in silence, each of them thinking their own thoughts. Over the coffee he suggested, 'All right, then. What about our agreement?'

They argued back and forth for nearly an hour.

'It's difficult to agree on your share of the booty, until I know just what your contribution is going to be,' Nicholas protested as he topped up their coffee cups. 'After all, I am going to be called on to finance and conduct the expedition—'

'You will just have to trust that my contribution will be worthwhile, otherwise there will simply be no booty, as you call it. Anyway you can be certain I am not going to tell you one thing more until we have an agreement, and have shaken hands on it.'

'A bit harsh?' he asked, and she gave him a wicked smile.

'If you don't like my terms, there are three other names on Duraid's list of possible sponsors,' she threatened.

'All right,' he cut in with a contrived look of martyrdom, 'I agree to your proposal. But how do we calculate equal shares?'

'I shall choose the first item of any archaeological artefacts we are able to retrieve, and you the next, and so on, turn about.'

'How about I choose first?' He raised an eyebrow at her.

'Let's spin for it,' she suggested, and he fished a pound coin from his pocket.

'Call!' He flipped the coin, and while it was in the air she called, 'Heads.'

'Damn!' he exclaimed, as he retrieved the coin and shoved it back into his pocket. 'So, you get first choice of the booty, if there ever is any.' He held out his hand across the lunch table. 'It will be yours to do exactly what you want to do with it. You can even donate it to the Cairo museum, if that is still your particular aberration. Deal?' he asked, and she took his hand.

'Deal!' she agreed, and then added, 'Partner.'

'Now let's get down to it. No more secrets between us. Tell me every detail that you have been holding back.'

'Bring that book,' she pointed to the copy of *River God*, and while he fetched it she pushed the dirty dishes aside. 'The first thing we should go over is the sections of the book that Duraid edited.' She turned to the last pages. 'Here. This is where Duraid's obfuscation begins.'

'Good word,' Nicholas smiled, 'but let's keep it simple. You have obfuscated me enough already.'

She did not even smile. 'You know the story to this point. Queen Lostris and her people are driven out of Egypt by the Hyksos and their superior chariots. They journey south up the Nile until they reach the confluence of the White and Blue Niles. In other words, present-day Khartoum. All this is reasonably faithful to the scrolls.'

'I recall. Go on.'

'In the holds of their river galleys they are carrying the mummified body of Queen Lostris's husband, Pharaoh Mamose the Eighth. Twelve years previously she has sworn to him as he lay dying of a Hyksos arrow through his lung that she would find a secure burial site for him, and that she would lay him in it with all his vast treasure. When they reach Khartoum she determines that the time has at last come for her to make good her promise to him. She sends out her son, the fourteen-year-old Prince Memnon, with a squadron of chariots to find the burial site. Memnon is accompanied by his mentor, the narrator of the history, the indefatigable Taita.'

'Okay, I remember this section. Memnon and Taita consult the black Shilluk slaves they have captured, and on their advice decide to follow the left-hand fork of the river, or what we know as the Blue Nile.'

Royan nodded and continued the story. 'They travelled eastwards and were confronted by formidable mountains, so high that they were described as a blue rampart. So far what you read in the book is a fairly faithful rendition of the scrolls, but at this point,' she tapped the open page, 'we come to Duraid's red herring. In his description of the foothills—'

Before she could continue, Nicholas interjected, 'I remember thinking when I originally read it that it didn't accurately describe the area where the Blue Nile emerges from the Ethiopian highlands. There are no foothills. There is only the sheer western escarpment of the massif. The river comes out of it like a snake out of its hole. Whoever wrote that description doesn't know the course of the Blue Nile.'

49

'Do you know the area?' Royan asked, and he laughed and nodded.

'When I was younger and even more stupid than I am now, I conceived the grandiose plan of boating the Abbay gorge from Lake Tana down to the dam at Roseires in the Sudan. The Abbay is the Ethiopian name for the Blue Nile.'

'Why did you want to do that?'

'Because it had never been done before. Major Cheesman, the British consul, had a shot at it in 1932, and nearly drowned himself. I thought I could make a film, and write a book about the voyage and earn myself a fortune from the royalties. I talked my father into financing the expedition. It was the kind of mad escapade that appealed to him. He even wanted to join the expedition. I studied the whole course of the Abbay river, not only on maps. I also bought myself an old Cessna 180 and flew down the gorge, five hundred miles from Lake Tana to the dam. As I said, I was twenty-one years old and crazy.'

'What happened?' She was fascinated. Duraid had never told her about this, but it was the type of adventure that she would have expected this man to launch into.

'I recruited eight of my friends from Sandhurst, and we devoted our Christmas holidays to the attempt. It was a fiasco. We lasted two days on those wild waters. The gorge is the most hellish corner of this earth that I know of. It's almost twice as deep and as rugged as the Grand Canyon of the Colorado river in Arizona. It smashed up our kayaks before we had covered twenty miles out of the five hundred. We had to abandon all our equipment and climb the walls of the gorge to reach civilization again.'

He looked serious for a moment, 'I lost two members of our party. Bobby Palmer was drowned, and Tim Marshall fell on the cliffs. We were not even able to recover their bodies. They are still down there somewhere. I had to tell their parents—' he broke off as he remembered the agony of it.

'Has anybody ever succeeded in navigating the Blue Nile gorge?' she asked, to distract him.

'Yes. I went back a few years later. This time not as leader, but as a very junior member of the official British Armed Forces Expedition. It took the army, the navy and the air force to beat that river.'

She stared at him with a feeling of awe. He had actually rafted the Abbay. It was as though she had been led to him by some strange fate. Duraid was right. There was probably no man in the world better qualified for the work in hand.

'So you know as much as anybody about the real nature of the gorge. I will try to give you a general indication of what Taita actually set down in the seventh scroll. Unfortunately this section of the scroll had suffered some damage and Duraid and I were obliged to extrapolate from parts of the text. You will have to tell me how this agrees with your own knowledge of the terrain.'

'Go ahead,' he invited her.

'Taita described the escarpment very much the way you did, as a sheer wall from which the river emerged. They were forced to leave their chariots, which were unable to cover the steep and rugged terrain of the canyon. They were forced to go forward on foot, leading the pack horses. Soon the gorge grew so steep and dangerous that they lost some of these animals, which fell from the wild goat tracks they were following and plunged into the river far below. This did not deter them and they pressed on at the orders of Prince Memnon.'

'I can see it exactly as he describes it. It's a fearsome bit of countryside.'

'Taita then describes coming to a series of obstacles, which he describes as "steps". Duraid and I could not decide with certainty what these were. But our best guess was that they were waterfalls.'

'No shortage of those in the Abbay gorge, either,' Nicholas nodded.

'This is the important part of his testimony. Taita tells us that after twenty days' travel up the gorge they came upon the "second step". It was here that the prince received a fortuitous message from his dead father, in the form of a dream, in which he chose this as the site of his own tomb. Taita tells us that they travelled no further. If we are able to determine what it was that stopped them, that would give us an accurate measurement of just how far into the gorge they penetrated.'

'Before we can go any further we will need maps and satellite photographs of the mountains, and I will have to go over my expedition notes and diary,' Nicholas decided. 'I try to keep my reference library up-to-date, and so we should have satellite photographs and the most recent maps on file here in the museum. If they are Mrs Street is the one to find them.'

He stood up and stretched, 'I will dig out my diaries this evening and read over them. My great-grandfather also hunted and collected in Ethiopia in the last century. I know he crossed the Blue Nile near Debra Markos in 1890-something. I'll get out his notes as well. They are preserved in our archives. The old boy may have written something there that could help us.'

He walked with her to the old green Land Rover in the car park, and as she started the engine he told her through the open window, 'I still think that you should stay over here at the Hall. It must be an hour-and-a-half's drive across to Brandsbury – each way that's three hours a day. We are going to have a lot of work to do before we can even think of leaving for Africa.'

'What would people think?' she asked, as she let out the clutch.

'I have never given a damn about people,' he called after her. 'What time will I see you tomorrow?'

51

'I have to stop off to see the doctor in York. He is going to take the stitches out of my arm. I won't be here before eleven,' she stuck her head out of the window to yell back at him.

The wind tossed her dark hair around her face. His fancy had always run towards dark-haired women. Rosalind had had that mysterious Eastern look. He felt guilty and disloyal making the comparison, but the memory of Royan was hard to shake off.

She was the first woman who had interested him since Rosalind had gone. The admixture of her blood drew him. She was exotic enough to pique his taste for the oriental, but English enough to speak his language and understand his sense of humour. She was educated and knowledgeable about those things that interested him, and he admired her spirit. Usually Eastern women were trained from birth to be self-effacing and compliant. This one was different.

Georgina had phoned her doctor in York to make an appointment to have the stitches removed from Royan's arm. They left after breakfast from the cottage in Brandsbury. Georgina was driving and Magic sat between them on the bench seat.

As they turned into the village street, Royan noticed a large MAN truck parked down near the post office, but she thought no more about it.

Once they were out in the countryside they found there were patches of heavy fog that in places reduced visibility to thirty yards, but Georgina made no concessions to the weather, and sent the Land Rover rattling and whining through it at the top of its speed, which Royan reflected thankfully was on the right side of sixty miles an hour.

She glanced over her shoulder to check the road behind them, and saw that the MAN truck was following them. Only the cab rose above the sea of low mist that surrounded it like the conning tower of a submarine. Even as she watched it, a bank of fog intervened and swallowed it up. She turned back to listen to her mother.

'This government is a troop of incompetent nincompoops.' Georgina squinted her eyes against the smoke from the cigarette that dangled from her lips. She drove single-handed, stroking Magic's flowing silken ear with her free hand, 'I don't mind ministers boffing themselves into a stupor, but when they start fiddling around with my pension I get really mad.' Her mother's pension from the foreign service was her sole source of income, and it wasn't much.

'You don't truly want a Labour government, now tell the truth, Mummy,' Royan teased her. Her mother had always been the arch Conservative.

Georgina wavered, and then avoided the choice, 'All I say is, bring back Maggie.'

Royan turned slightly in her seat and glanced through the dirty rear window again. The truck was still behind them, looming out of the fog and the trail of blue exhaust smoke that Georgina was laying behind her like the vapour trail of a jet aircraft. Up until now it had hung back, but suddenly it accelerated up behind them.

'I think he wants to pass you,' Royan told Georgina mildly.

The massive bonnet of the truck was only twenty feet from their rear bumper. The radiator was emblazoned with the chrome logo 'MAN' and stood taller than the cab of the Land Rover, so that she could not see the face of the driver from where she sat.

'Everybody wants to pass me,' lamented Georgina. 'Story of my life.' She held the centre of the narrow road doggedly.

Royan glanced back again, and saw that the truck was creeping still closer. It filled the rear window completely. The driver declutched and revved the gigantic engine menacingly.

'You'd better give over. I think he means business.'

'Let him wait,' Georgina grunted around her cigarette butt. 'Patience is a virtue. Anyway, can't let him through here. There is a narrow stone bridge ahead of us. Know this stretch of road like the way to my own bathroom.'

At that moment the truck-driver sounded his klaxon so close that it was deafening. Magic jumped up on the rear seat and barked in outrage.

'Stupid bastard,' Georgina swore bitterly. 'What does he think he is playing at? Write down his number plate. I am going to report him to the York police.'

'His plates are covered with mud. Can't make it out, but it looks like a continental registration. German, I think.'

As if the driver had heard her protest he slowed slightly and fell back until a gap of twenty yards opened between the two vehicles. Royan had swivelled right round in the seat to watch him.

'That's better,' Georgina said smugly. 'Ruddy Hun learning some manners.' She peered ahead through the fog, 'There is the bridge—'

For the first time Royan was able to see up into the driver's cab of the truck. The driver wore a balaclava helmet that covered all but his eyes and nose with dark blue wool. It gave him a sinister and evil aspect.

'Look out!' Royan screamed suddenly. 'He is coming straight at us!' The engine beat of the great truck rose to a bellow that engulfed them like the sound of a gale-driven sea. For a moment Royan saw nothing but glittering steel and then the front of the truck smashed into them from behind.

She was thrown half over the back of her seat by the impact. She dragged herself up and saw that the truck had picked them up like a fox with a bird in its jaws. It carried the Land Rover forward on the steel bull bars that protected the shining chromed radiator.

Georgina wrestled with the wheel, trying to maintain control, but the effort was futile. 'Can't hold her. The bridge! Try and get clear—'

Royan hit the quick-release buckle on her safety-belt and reached for the door handle. The stone walls of the bridge were racing towards them at a terrifying pace. The Land Rover was slewing across the road, completely out of control.

The door burst open in Royan's grip, but she could not push it all the way before the Land Rover was flung into the solid stonework columns that guarded the approaches to the bridge.

The two women screamed in unison as the vehicle crumpled, and the impact hurled them forward. The windscreen shattered as they bounced off the stone columns, and the body of the Land Rover flipped over as it went down the embankment and began to roll.

Royan was catapulted through the open door and flung clear. The slope of the bank broke her fall, but it knocked the wind out of her. She bounced and rolled down the incline and then dropped into the icy waters of the stream below the bridge.

Just before her head went under, she found herself looking up at the sky and the bridge above her. She caught one last glimpse of the truck before it roared away. It was towing two huge cargo trailers. The tall bodywork of the trailers stood higher than the guard rail of the bridge.

Both of the trailers were covered by a heavy green nylon tarpaulin roped down to the lugs on the body. She had only a subliminal glimpse of a large red trademark and company name painted on the side of the nearest trailer, but before she could register the name she was plunged below the surface of the stream and the cold and the force of her fall drove the air from her lungs.

She fought her way to the surface of the river, and found she had been washed some way downstream. Impeded by her sodden clothing, she floundered to the bank and used the branch of a tree to haul herself out.

She knelt in the mud, coughing up the water she had swallowed and trying to assess what injury she had suffered in the collision. Then her own plight was forgotten as she heard the terrible sounds of her mother's agony from the overturned wreck of the Land Rover.

In frantic haste she clawed herself to her feet and stumbled through the wet and frosted grass to where the Land Rover lay on its back at the foot of the embankment. The bodywork was crumpled and torn, and the bright silver aluminium metal shone through where the dark green paint had been stripped away. The engine had stalled, and the front wheels were still spinning aimlessly as she reached it.

'Mummy! Where are you?' she cried, and the terrible sounds never checked. She used the metal body of the vehicle to steady herself as she dragged herself towards the sound, dreading what she might find.

Georgina sat on the wet earth with her back against the side of the car. Her legs were thrust out straight ahead of her. The left one was twisted so that the toe of the booted foot was pointed down into the mud at an unnatural angle. The leg was obviously broken at the knee or very close to it.

This was not the cause of Georgina's distress. She held Magic in her lap, and was bowed over him in an attitude of abandoned grief; the sound of it bubbled up unchecked from deep inside her. The spaniel's chest had been crushed between metal and earth. His tongue lolled from the corner of his mouth in his last smile, but the blood dripped steadily from the pink tip and Georgina was using her scarf to wipe it away.

Royan sank down beside her mother and placed one arm around her shoulders. She had never before seen her mother weep. She hugged her hard and tried by main strength to quell the sound of her sorrow, but it went on and on.

She never knew how long they sat together like that. But at last the sight of her mother's maimed leg, and an awakening fear that the driver of the truck might return to finish the job, roused her. She crawled up the bank and tottered into the centre of the road to stop the next car that arrived on the scene.

N ot until Royan was two hours late for their meeting did Nicholas become sufficiently worried to phone the police in York. Fortunately he had noticed the licence plate of the Land Rover. It was an easy one for him to remember. The registration number was his mother's initials combined with an unlucky 13.

There was a delay while the woman constable checked her computer, and then she came back. 'I am sorry to have to tell you, sir, that Land Rover was involved in an accident this morning.'

'What happened to the driver?' Nicholas demanded brusquely.

'The driver and one passenger have been taken to the York Minster Hospital.'

'Are they all right?'

'I am sorry, sir. I don't have that information.'

It took Nicholas forty minutes to reach the hospital and almost as long again to trace Royan. She was in the women's surgical ward, sitting beside her mother's bed. Her mother had not yet come round from the anaesthetic.

She looked up when Nicholas stood over her. 'Are you all right? What the hell happened?'

'My mother – her leg is badly smashed up. The surgeon had to put a pin in her thigh – the femur.'

'How are you?'

'A few bruises and scrapes. Nothing serious.'

'How did it happen?'

'A truck – it pushed us off the road.'

'Not deliberate?' Nicholas felt something inside him quail as he remembered another truck on another road on another night.

'I think so. The driver wore a mask, a balaclava. He crashed into us from behind. It must have been deliberate.'

'Did you tell the police?'

She nodded. 'Apparently the truck was reported stolen early this morning, long before the accident, while the driver was stopped at one of those Little Chef cafés. He is German. Speaks no English.'

'That is the third time they have tried to kill you,' Nicholas told her grimly. 'So I am taking over now.'

He went out into the hospital waiting room and used the telephone there. The chief constable of the county was a personal friend, as was the hospital administrator.

By the time he returned, Georgina had come round from the anaesthetic. Although still woozy she was comfortable as they wheeled her off to the private ward that Nicholas had arranged. The orthopaedic surgeon arrived a few minutes later.

'Hello, Nick, what are you doing here?' he greeted Nicholas. Royan was surprised how many people knew him.

Then he turned his attention to Georgina. 'How are you feeling? We have got ourselves a nice little compound fracture. Looks like confetti in there. We've managed to put it all together again, but you're going to be with us for ten days at the very least.'

'Right you are, young lady,' Nicholas told Royan as they left Georgina sleeping. 'What more do you need to convince you? My housekeeper has made up a room for you at the Hall. I am not letting you wander around on your own any more. Otherwise, next time they try to cull you they may have a little more luck.'

She was still too shaken and upset to argue, and she climbed meekly into the front seat of the Range Rover and let him drive her first to have her stitches removed and then back to Quenton Park. As soon as they arrived, he sent her up to her bedroom.

'The cook will send dinner up to you. Make sure you take the sleeping pill that the doc gave you. Somebody will fetch your gear from Brandsbury if you give the key to your mother's cottage to Mrs Street. In the meantime my housekeeper has set out some nightclothes and a toothbrush in your room for you. I don't want to hear from you again before tomorrow morning.'

It was good to have him take control of her life. For the first time since that terrible night at the oasis she felt secure and safe. Still, she made one last gesture of independence and self-reliance; she flushed the Mogadon sleeping tablet down the toilet.

The nightdress that was laid on her pillow was full-length sheer silk with finest Cambrai lace at the cuffs and throat. She had never worn anything so luxurious and sensual against her skin before. She realized that it must have belonged to his wife, and the knowledge stirred mixed emotions in her. She climbed up into the four-poster bed, but even that lonely expanse of over-soft mattress and her unfamiliar surroundings did not keep her too long from sleep.

n the morning a young housemaid woke her with a copy of *The Times* and a pot of Earl Grey tea, then returned a few minutes later with her holdall.

'Sir Nicholas would like you to take breakfast with him in the dining room at eight-thirty.'

While she showered Royan inspected her naked body in the full-length mirror that covered one wall of the bathroom. Apart from the knife wound on her arm, which was still livid and only partially healed, there was a dark bruise on her thigh and another down her left flank and buttock, legacies of the car crash. Her shin was scraped raw, and gingerly she pulled a pair of slacks over the injury. She limped a little as she went down the main staircase to find the dining room.

'Please help yourself.' Nicholas looked up from his newspaper to greet her as she hesitated in the doorway. He waved at the display of breakfast dishes on the sideboard. As she spooned scrambled eggs on to her plate, she recognized the landscape on the wall in front of her as a Constable.

'Did you sleep well?' He didn't wait for an answer, but went on, 'I have heard from the police. They found the MAN truck abandoned in a lay-by near Harrogate. They are going over it now but they don't expect to find much. We seem to be dealing with someone who knows what he is doing.'

'I must phone the hospital,' she said.

'I have already done so. Your mother had an easy night. I left a message that you would visit her this evening.'

'This evening?' She looked around sharply. 'Why so late?'

'I intend to keep you busy until then. I want to get my money's worth out of you.'

He stood as she came to the table, and drew back her chair to seat her. She found the courtesy made her feel slightly uncomfortable, but she made no comment.

'The first attack on you and Duraid at your villa in the oasis – we can draw no conclusions from that, apart from the fact that the assassins knew exactly what they were after, and where to look for it.' She found the abrupt change of subject disconcerting. 'However, let's give some thought to the second attempt in Cairo. The hand grenade. Who knew you were going to the Ministry that afternoon, apart from the minister himself?'

She reflected as she chewed and swallowed a mouthful of egg. 'I am not sure. I think I told Duraid's secretary, maybe one of the other research assistants.'

He frowned and shook his head. 'So half the museum staff knew about your appointment?'

'That is about it, yes. Sorry.'

He pondered a moment, 'All right. Who knew you were leaving Cairo? Who knew you were staying at your mother's cottage?'

'One of the clerks from administration brought my slides out to the airport.'

'Did you tell him what flight you were leaving on?'

'No, definitely not.'

'Did you tell anybody at all?'

'No. That is—' she hesitated.

'Yes?'

'I told the minister himself during our interview, when I asked for leave of absence. Not him – surely not?' her expression reflected her horror at the thought.

Nicholas shrugged, 'Some funny things happen. Of course, the minister knew all about the work that you and Duraid were doing on the seventh scroll?'

'Not all the details, but – yes – in general terms he knew what we were up to.'

'All right. Next question, tea or coffee?' He poured coffee into her cup, and then went on, 'You said that Duraid had a list of possible sponsors for an expedition. Might give us some ideas as to a short-list of suspects?'

'The Getty Museum,' she said, and he smiled.

'Cross one from the list. They don't go around tossing grenades in the streets of Cairo. Who else was there on the list?'

'Gotthold Ernst von Schiller.'

'Hamburg. Heavy industry. Metal and alloy refineries. Base mineral production.' Nicholas nodded. 'Who was the third name on the list?'

'Peter Walsh,' she said. 'The Texan.'

'That's the one,' he nodded. 'Lives in Fort Worth. Fast-food franchising. Mail order retail.' There were very few collectors with the substance to compete with the major institutions when it came to making significant acquisitions of antiquities or to financing archaeological exploration. Nicholas knew them all, for it was a mutually antagonistic circle of no more than a couple of dozen men. He had competed with each of them at one time or another on the auction floors of Sotheby's and Christie's, not to mention other less salubrious venues where 'fresh' antiquities were sold. The adjective 'fresh' was used in the context of 'fresh out of the ground'.

'Those are two beady-eyed bandits. They would probably eat their own children if they felt peckish. What would they do if they thought you stood in their way to the tomb of Mamose? Do you know if either of them contacted Duraid after the book was published, the way I did?'

'I don't know. They may have.'

'I cannot imagine that either of those beauties would have missed such an easy trick. We must believe that they both know that Duraid had something going on. We will put their names on our list of suspects.' Then he inspected her plate. 'Enough? Another spoonful of egg? No? Very well, let's go down to the museum and see what Mrs Street has found for us to work on.'

When they walked into his study, she was impressed by the amount of organization that he had accomplished in such a short time. He must have been busy at it all last night, turning the room into a military-type headquarters. In the centre of the room stood a large easel and blackboard on which were pinned a set of overlapping satellite photographs. She went across to study them, and then glanced at the other material pinned on the board.

Along with a large-scale map covering the same area of south-western Ethiopia as the satellite photographs there were lists of names and addresses, lists of equipment and stores which he had obviously used on previous African expeditions, sheets of calculations of distance and what looked like a preliminary financial budget. At the top of the board was a schedule headed 'Ethiopia – General Information'. There were five closely typed foolscap sheets, so she did not read through the entire schedule, but she was impressed by his thoroughness in preparation.

Royan determined to study all this material at the earliest opportunity, but now she crossed to one of the two chairs he had set up at a table facing the board. He stood at the board and picked up a silver-topped swagger stick from the table, brandishing it like a schoolmaster's pointer.

'Class will come to order.' He rapped on the board. 'The first thing you have to do is convince me that we will be able to pick up the spoor of Taita again after it has had several thousand years to cool. Let us first consider the geographical features of the Abbay gorge.'

Nicholas described the course of the river on the satellite photograph with his pointer. 'Along this section the river has cut its way through the flood basalt plateaux. In places the cliffs of the sub-gorge are sheer, as high as four or five hundred feet on each side. Where there are intrusive strata of harder igneous schists the river has not been able to erode them. They form a series of gigantic steps in the course of the river. I think you are correct in your assumption that Taita's "steps" are actually waterfalls.'

He came to the table and picked out a photograph from amongst the bundles of papers that covered it. 'I took this in the gorge during the Armed Forces Expedition in 1976. It will give you an idea of what some of those falls are like.'

He passed her a black and white riverscape of towering cliffs on either hand and a cascade of water that seemed to fall from the heavens to dwarf the tiny figures of half-naked men and boats in the foreground.

'I had no idea it was like that!' She stared at it in awe.

'Doesn't do justice to the splendid desolation down there in the gorge,' he told her. 'From a photographer's point of view there is no place to stand from which you can get it all into perspective. But at least you can see how that waterfall would halt a party of Egyptians coming upriver on foot, or at least with pack horses. There is usually some sort of path alongside the cataracts made by elephant and other wild game over the ages. However, there is simply no way to bypass waterfalls such as this one, and to get around those cliffs.'

She nodded, and he went on, 'Even coming downstream we had to lower the boats and all our equipment down each set of waterfalls on ropes. It wasn't easy.'

'Let us agree that it was a waterfall that stopped them going further – the second waterfall from the westerly approaches,' she conceded.

Nicholas picked up the swagger stick and on the satellite photograph traced the course of the river up from the dark wedge shape of the Roseires dam in central Sudan. 'The escarpment rises on the Ethiopian side of the border, that is where the gorge proper begins. No roads or towns in there, and only two bridges far upstream. Nothing for five hundred miles except racing Nile waters and savage black basalt rock.' He paused to let that sink in.

'It is one of the last true wildernesses on earth, with an evil reputation as the haunt of wild animals and even wilder men. I have marked the main falls that show in the gut of the gorge here on the satellite photo.' With the pointer he picked them out, each circled neatly in red marker pen.

'Here is waterfall number two, about a hundred and twenty miles upstream from the Sudanese border. However, there are a number of factors we have to consider, not least the fact that the river may have altered its course during the last four thousand years since our friend, Taita, visited it.'

'Surely it could not have escaped from such a deep canyon, four thousand feet,' she protested. 'Even the Nile must be held captive by that?'

'Yes, but it would certainly have altered the existing bed. In the flood season the volume and force of the river exceeds my ability to describe it to you. The river rises twenty metres up the side walls and bores through at speeds of ten knots or more.'

'You navigated that?' she asked doubtfully.

'Not in the flood season. Nothing could survive that.'

They both stared at the photograph in silence for a minute, imagining the terrors of that mighty stretch of water in its full fury.

Then she reminded him, 'The second waterfall?'

'Here it is, where one of the tributary rivers enters the main flow of the Abbay. The tributary is the Dandera river and it rises at twelve thousand feet altitude, below the peak of Sancai Mountain in the Choke range, here about a hundred miles north of the gorge.'

'Do you remember the spot where it joins the Abbay from when you were there?'

'It was over twenty years ago, and even then we had been almost a month down there in the gorge, so it all seemed to merge into a single nightmare. The memory blurred with the monotonous surroundings of the cliffs and the dense jungle of the walls, and our senses were dulled by the heat and the insects and the roar of water and the repetitive, unremitting toil at the oars. But, strangely, I do remember the confluence of the Dandera and the Abbay for two reasons.'

'Yes?' She sat forward eagerly, but he shook his head.

'We lost a man there. The only casualty on the second expedition. Rope parted and he fell a hundred feet. Landed on his back across a spur of rock.'

'I am sorry. But what was the other reason you remember the spot.'

'There is a Coptic Christian monastery there, built into the rock face about four hundred feet above the surface of the river.'

'Down there in the depths of the gorge?' She sounded incredulous. 'Why would they build a monastery there?'

'Ethiopia is one of the oldest Christian countries on earth. It has over nine thousand churches and monasteries, a great many of them in similarly remote and almost inaccessible places in the mountains. This one at the Dandera river is the reputed burial site of St Frumentius, the saint who introduced Christianity to Ethiopia from the Byzantine Empire in Constantinople in the early third century. Legend has it that he was shipwrecked on the Red Sea shore and taken to Aksum, where he converted the Emperor Ezana.'

'Did you visit the monastery?'

'Hell, no!' he laughed. 'We were too busy just surviving, too eager to escape from the hell of the gorge to have any time for sightseeing. We descended the falls and kept on downriver. All I remember of the monastery are the excavations in the cliff face high above the pool of the river, and the distant figures of the troglodytic monks in their white robes lining the parapet of the caves to watch impassively as we passed. Some of us waved up to them, and felt quite rebuffed when they made no response.'

'How would we ever reach that spot again, without a full-scale river expedition?' she wondered aloud, staring disconsolately at the board.

'Discouraged already?' He grinned at her. 'Wait until you meet some of the mosquitoes that live down there. They pick you up and fly with you to their lairs before they eat you.'

'Be serious,' she entreated him. 'How would we ever get down there?'

'The monks are fed by the villagers who live up on the highlands above the gorge. Apparently, there is a goat track down the wall. They told us that it takes three days to get down that track into the gut of the gorge from the rim.'

'Could you find your way down?'

'No, but I have a few ideas on the subject. We will come to that later. Firstly, we must decide what we expect to find down there after four thousand years.' He looked at her expectantly. 'Your turn now. Convince me.' He handed her the silver-headed pointer, dropped into the chair beside her and folded his arms.

'First you have to go back to the book.' She exchanged the pointer for the copy of River God. 'You remember the character of Tanus from the story?'

'Of course. He was the commander of the Egyptian armies under Queen Lostris, with the title of Great Lion of Egypt. He led the exodus from Egypt, when they were driven out by the Hyksos.'

'He was also the Queen's secret lover and, if we are to believe Taita, the father of Prince Memnon, her eldest son,' she agreed.

'Tanus was killed during a punitive expedition against an Ethiopian chief named Arkoun in the high mountains, and his body was mummified and brought back to the Queen by Taita,' Nicholas expanded the story.

'Precisely.' She nodded. 'This leads me on to the other clue that Duraid and I winkled out.'

'From the seventh scroll?' He unfolded his arms and sat forward in his seat.

'No, not from the scrolls, but from the inscriptions in the tomb of Queen Lostris.' She reached into her bag and brought out another photograph. 'This is an enlargement of a section of the murals from the burial chamber, that part of the wall that later fell away and was lost when the alabaster jars were revealed. Duraid and I believe that the fact that Taita placed this inscription in the place of honour, over the hiding-place of the scrolls, was significant.' She passed the photograph to him, and he picked up a magnifying glass from the table to study it.

While he puzzled over the hieroglyphics Royan went on, 'You will recall from the book how Taita loved riddles and word games, how he boasts so often that he is the greatest of all bao players?'

Nicholas looked up from the magnifying glass, 'I remember that. I go along with the theory that bao was the forerunner of the game of chess. I have a dozen or so boards in the museum collection, some from Egypt and others from further south in Africa.'

'Yes, I would also subscribe to that theory. Both games have many of the same objects and rules, but bao is a more rudimentary form of the game. It is played with coloured stones of different rank, instead of chess men. Well, I believe that Taita was not able to resist the temptation to display his riddling skills and his cleverness to posterity. I believe that he was so conceited that he deliberately left clues to the location of the Pharaoh's tomb, both in the scrolls and amongst the murals that he tells us he painted with his own hands in the tomb of his beloved Queen.'

'You think that this is one of those clues?' Nicholas tapped the photograph with the glass.

'Read it,' she instructed him. 'It's in classical hieroglyphics – not too difficult compared to his cryptic codes.'

'"*The father of the prince who is not the father, the giver of the blue that killed him,*"' he translated haltingly, '"*guards eternally hand in hand with Hapi the stone testament of the pathway to the father of the prince who is not the father, the giver of blood and ashes.*"'

Nicholas shook his head, 'No, it doesn't make sense,' he protested, 'I must have made an error in the translation.'

'Don't despair. You are making your first acquaintance with Taita, the champion bao player and consummate riddler. Duraid and I puzzled over it for weeks,' she reassured him. 'To work it out, let's go back to the book. Tanus was not the father of Prince Memnon in name, but, as the Queen's lover, was his biological father. On his deathbed, he gave Memnon the blue sword that had inflicted his own mortal wound during the battle with the native Ethiopian chief. There is a full description of the battle in the book.'

'Yes, when I first read that section, I remember thinking that the blue sword was probably one of the very earliest iron weapons, and in an age of bronze would have been a marvel of the armourer's art. A gift fit for a prince,' Nicholas mused, and went on, 'So "*the father of the prince who is not the father*" is Tanus?' He sighed with resignation. 'For the moment I accept your interpretation.'

'Thank you for your trust and confidence in me,' she said sarcastically. 'But to proceed with Taita's riddle – Pharaoh Mamose was Memnon's father in name only, but not his blood father. Again the father who was not the father. Mamose passed down to the prince the double crown of Egypt, the red and white crowns of Upper and Lower Kingdoms – the blood and the ashes.'

'I am able to swallow that more easily. What about the rest of the inscription?' Nicholas was clearly intrigued.

'The expression "hand in hand" is ambiguous in ancient Egyptian. It could just as well mean very close to, or within sight of, something.'

'Go on. At last you have me sitting up and taking notice,' Nicholas encouraged her.

'Hapi is the hermaphroditic god or goddess of the Nile, depending on the gender he or she adopts at any particular moment. Throughout the scrolls Taita uses Hapi as an alternative name for the river.'

'So if we put the seventh scroll and the inscription from the Queen's tomb together, what then is your full interpretation?' he insisted.

'Simply this: Tanus is buried within sight of, or very close to, the river at the second waterfall. There is a stone monument or inscription on, or in, his tomb that points the way to the tomb of Pharaoh.'

He exhaled through his teeth. 'I am exhausted from all this jumping to conclusions. What other clues have you ferreted out for me?'

'That's it,' she said, and he looked at her with disbelief.

'That's it? Nothing else?' he demanded, and she shook her head.

'Just suppose that you are correct so far. Let us suppose that the river is recognizably the same in shape and configuration as it was nearly four thousand years ago. Let us further suppose that Taita was indeed pointing us towards the second waterfall at the Dandera river. Just what do we look for when we get there? If there is a rock inscription, will it still be intact or will it be eroded away by weather and the action of the river?'

'Howard Carter had an equally slender lead to the tomb of Tutankhamen,' she pointed out mildly. 'A single piece of papyrus, of dubious authenticity.'

'Howard Carter had only the area of the Valley of the Kings to search. It still took him ten years,' he replied. 'You have given me Ethiopia, a country twice the size of France. How long will that take us, do you think?'

She stood up abruptly, 'Excuse me, I think I should go and visit my mother in hospital. It's fairly obvious that I am wasting my time here.'

'It is not yet visiting hours,' he told her.

'She has a private room.' Royan made for the door.

'I will drive you to the hospital,' he offered.

'Don't bother. I will call a taxi,' she replied in a tone that crackled with ice.

'A taxi will take an hour to get here,' he warned, and she relented just enough to let him lead her to the Range Rover. They drove in silence for fifteen minutes, before he spoke.

'I am not very good at apologies. Not much practice, I am afraid, but I am sorry. I was abrupt. I didn't mean to be. Carried away by the excitement of the moment.'

She did not reply, and after a minute he added, 'You will have to talk to me, unless we are to correspond only by note. It will be a bit awkward down in the Abbay gorge.'

'I had the distinct impression that you were no longer interested in going down there.' She stared ahead through the windscreen.

'I am a brute,' he agreed, and she glanced sideways at him. It was her undoing. His grin was irresistible, and she laughed.

'I suppose I will just have to come to terms with that fact. You are a brute.'

'Still partners?' he asked.

'At the moment you are the only brute I have. I suppose that I am stuck with you.'

He dropped her off at the main hospital entrance. 'I will pick you up here at three o'clock,' he told her and drove on into the centre of York.

From his university days Nicholas had kept a small flat in one of the narrow alleys behind York Minster. The entire building was registered in the name of a Cayman Island company, and the unlisted telephone there did not route through an internal switchboard. No ownership could be traced to him personally. Before he had met Rosalind the flat had played an important part in his social life. But nowadays Nicholas only used it for confidential and clandestine business. Both the Libyan and the Iraqi expeditions had been planned and organized from here.

He hadn't used the flat for months, and it was cold and musty-smelling and uninviting. He put a match to the gas fire in the grate and filled the kettle. With a mug of steaming tea in front of him he placed a call to a bank in Jersey, followed immediately by another to a bank in the Cayman Islands.

'A wise rat has more than one exit from its burrow.' This was a family maxim, passed down through the generations. There should always be a little something tucked away for the day the heavens opened. He was going to need funds for the expedition, and the lawyers had most of those locked up already.

He gave the passwords and account numbers to each of the bank managers and instructed them to make certain transfers. It always amazed him how easily matters could be arranged, as long as you had money.

He checked his watch. It was still early morning in Florida, but Alison picked up the phone on the second ring. She was the blonde feminine dynamo who ran Global Safaris, a company that arranged hunting and fishing expeditions to remote areas around the world.

'Hello, Nick. We haven't heard from you in over a year. We thought you didn't love us any more.'

'I have been out of it for a while,' he admitted. How do you tell people that your wife and two little girls had died?

'Ethiopia?' She did not sound at all disconcerted by the request. 'When did you want to go?'

'How about next week?'

'You have to be joking. We only work with one hunter there, Nassous Roussos, and he is booked two years in advance.'

'Is there nobody else?' he insisted. 'I have to be in and out again before the big rains.'

'What trophies are you after?' she hedged. 'Mountain nyala? Mene-lik's bushbuck?'

'I am planning a collecting trip for the museum, down the Abbay river.' It was as much as he was prepared to tell her.

She hedged a little longer and then told him reluctantly, 'This is without our recommendation, do you understand. There is only one hunter who may take you on at such short notice, but I don't even know if he has a camp on the Blue Nile. He is a Russian, and we have had mixed reports about him. Some people say he is ex-KGB and was one of Mengistu's bunch of thugs.'

Mengistu was the 'Black Stalin' who had deposed and then murdered the old Emperor Haile Selassie, and in sixteen years of despotic Marxist rule had driven Ethiopia to its knees. When his sponsor, the Soviet Empire, had collapsed, Mengistu had been overthrown and fled the country.

'I am desperate enough to go to bed with the devil,' he told her. 'I promise I won't come back to you with any complaints.'

'Okay, then, no come-backs—' and she gave him a name and a telephone number in Addis Ababa.

'I love you, Alison darling,' Nicholas told her.

'I wish,' she said, and hung up on him.

He didn't expect that it would be easy to telephone Addis, and he wasn't disappointed in his expectations. But at last he got through. A woman with a sweet lisping Ethiopian accent answered and switched to fluent English when he asked for Boris Brusilov.

'He is out on safari at present,' she told him. 'I am Woizero Tessay, his wife.' In Ethiopia a wife did not take on her husband's name. Nicholas remembered enough of the language to know that the name meant Lady Sun, a pretty name.

'But if it is in connection with safari business I can help you,' said Lady Sun.

Nicholas picked Royan up outside the hospital entrance.

'How is your mother?'

'Her leg is doing well, but she is still distraught about Magic – about her dog.'

'You will have to get her a puppy. One of my keepers breeds first-class springers. I can arrange it.' He paused and then asked delicately, 'Will you be able to leave your mother? I mean, if we are going out to Africa?'

'I spoke to her about that. There is a woman from her church group who will stay with her until she is well enough to fend for herself again.'

Royan turned fully around in her seat to examine his face. 'You have been up to something since I last saw you,' she accused him. 'I can see it in your face.'

He made the Arabic sign against the evil eye, 'Allah save me from witches!'

'Come on!' He could make her laugh so readily, she was not sure if that was a good thing or not. 'Tell me what you have up your sleeve.'

'Wait until we get back to the museum.' He would not be moved, and she had to bridle her impatience.

As soon as they entered the building he led her through the Egyptian room to the hall of African mammals, and then stopped her in front of a diorama of mounted antelope. These were some of the smaller and medium-sized varieties – impala, Thompson's and Grant's gazelle, gerenuk and the like.

'Madoqua harperii.' He pointed to a tiny creature in one corner of the display. 'Harper's dik-dik, also known as the striped dik-dik.'

It was a nondescript little animal, not much bigger than a large hare. The brown pelt was striped in chocolate over the shoulders and back, and the nose was elongated into a prehensile proboscis.

'A bit tatty,' she gave her opinion carefully, unwilling to offend

67

him, for he seemed inordinately proud of this specimen. 'Is there anything special about it?'

'Special?' he asked with wonder in his voice. 'The woman asks if it is special.' He rolled his eyes heavenward and she had to laugh again at his histrionics. 'It is the only known specimen in existence. It is one of the rarest creatures on earth. So rare that it is probably extinct by now. So rare that many zoologists believe that it is apocryphal, that it never really existed. They think that my sainted great-grandfather, after whom it is named, actually invented it. One learned reference hinted that he may have taken the skin of the striped mongoose and stretched it over the form of a common dik-dik. Can you imagine a more heinous accusation?'

'I am truly appalled by such injustice,' she laughed.

'Darned right, you should be. Because we are going to Africa to hunt for another specimen of *Madoqua harperii*, to vindicate the honour of the family.'

'I don't understand.'

'Come with me and all will be explained.' He led her back to his study, and from the jumble on the tabletop picked out a notebook bound in red Morocco leather. The cover was faded and stained with water marks and tropical sunlight, while the corners and the spine were frayed and battered.

'Old Sir Jonathan's game book,' he explained, and opened it. Pressed between the pages were faded wild flowers and leaves that must have been there for almost a century. The text was illuminated by line drawings in faded yellow ink of men and animals and wild landscapes. Nicholas read the date at the top of one page.

2nd of February 1902. In camp on the Abbay river. All day following the spoor of two large bull elephants. Unable to come up with them. Heat very intense. My men played out. Abandoned the chase and returned to camp. On the return march spied a small antelope grazing on the river-bank, which I brought down with one shot from the little Rigby rifle. On close examination it proved to be a member of the genus Madoqa. *However, it was of a species that I had never seen before, larger than the common dik-dik and possessing a striped body. I believe that this specimen may be new to science.*

He looked up from the diary. 'Old great-grandpa Jonathan has given us the perfect excuse for going down into the Abbay gorge.' He closed the book, and went on, 'As you pointed out, to cater for our own expedition would require months of planning and organization, not to mention the expense. It would mean having to obtain approval and permission from the Ethiopian government. In Africa that can take months, if not years.'

'I don't imagine that the Ethiopian government would be too cooperative if they suspected our real intentions,' she agreed.

'On the other hand, there are a number of legitimate hunting safari companies operating throughout the country. They have all the necessary permits, governmental contacts, vehicles, camping equipment and logistic back-up necessary to travel and stay in even the remotest areas. The authorities are quite accustomed to foreign hunters arriving and leaving with these companies, whereas a couple of *ferengi* nosing around on their own would have the local military and everybody else down on them like a herd of angry buffalo.'

'So we are going to travel as a pair of dik-dik hunters?'

'I have already made the booking with a safari operator in Addis Ababa, the capital. My plan is to look upon the whole of our project in three distinct and separate stages. The first stage will be this reconnaissance. If we find the lead we are hoping for, then we will go back again with our own men and equipment. That will be stage two. Stage three, of course, will be getting the booty out of Ethiopia, and that I assure you from past experience will not be the easiest part of the operation.'

'How will you do that—' she began, but he held up his hands.

'Don't ask, because at this stage I don't have even the vaguest idea how we will do it. One stage at a time.'

'When do we leave?'

'Before I tell you when, let me ask you one more question. Your interpretation of the Taita riddle – did you explain that in the notes that were stolen from you at the oasis?'

'Yes, everything was either in those notes or on the microfilm. I am sorry.'

'So the uglies will have it all neatly laid out for them, just the way you laid it out for me.'

'I am afraid they will, yes.'

'Then to reply to your question as to when, the answer is *tout de suite*, and the tooter the sweeter! We must get into the Abbay gorge before the competition beats us to it. They have had your conclusions and suppositions for almost a month. For all we know they are on their way already.'

'When?' she repeated eagerly.

'I have booked two seats on the British Airways flight to Nairobi this Saturday – that is, in two days' time. We will connect there with an Air Kenya flight to Addis that will get us in on Monday at around midday. We will drive down to London this evening and stay over at my digs there. Are your yellow fever and hepatitis shots up to date?'

69

'Yes, but I have no equipment and hardly any clothing with me. I left Cairo in rather a hurry.'

'We will see to that in London. Trouble with Ethiopia is it's cold enough to emasculate a brass monkey in the highlands, and like a sauna bath down in the gorge.'

He crossed to the board and began to check off the items on his list. 'We will both start malarial prophylactics immediately. We are going into an area of chloroquine-resistant *P. falciparum* mosquitoes, so I will put you on Mefloquine—' He worked swiftly through the list.

'Of course all your travel documents are in order, or you wouldn't be here. We will both need visas for Ethiopia, but I have a contact who can arrange that in twenty-four hours.'

As soon as he completed the list he sent her up to her room to pack the few personal items she had brought with her from Cairo.

By the time they were ready to leave Quenton Hall it was dark outside, but still he stopped for an hour at the York Minster Hospital to allow her to say goodbye to her mother. He waited in the Red Lion pub across the road, and he smelt of Theakston's Old Peculier when she climbed back into the Range Rover beside him. It was a pleasant, yeasty aroma, and she felt so much at ease in his company that she lay back in the seat and fell asleep.

His London house was in Knightsbridge, but despite the fashionable address it was much less grand than Quenton Hall, and she felt more at home there, even if it was only for two days. During that time she saw little of Nicholas, for he was busy with all the last-minute arrangements, which included a number of visits to government offices in Whitehall. He returned with wads of letters of introduction to high officials and British Embassies and High Commissions throughout East Africa.

'Ask any Englishman,' she smiled to herself. 'There is no such thing as upper-class privilege any longer, nor is there an old-boy network that runs the country.'

While he was away, she went off with the shopping list he had given her. Even walking the streets of the safest capital city in the world she found herself looking back over her shoulder, and ducking in and out of ladies' rooms and tube stations to make certain that she was not being followed.

'You are acting like a terrified child without its daddy,' she scolded herself.

However, she felt a quite disproportionate sense of relief each evening when she heard his key in the street door of the empty house where she waited, and she had to control herself so as not to rush down the stairs to welcome him.

O n Saturday morning, when a taxi cab deposited them at the departures level of Heathrow Terminal Four, Nicholas surveyed their combined luggage with approval. She had only a single soft canvas bag, no larger than his, and her sling bag over her shoulder. His hunting rifle was cased in travel-worn leather, with his initials embossed on the lid. A hundred rounds of ammunition was packed in a separate brass-bound magazine and he carried a leather briefcase that looked like a Victorian antique.

'Travelling light is one of the great virtues. Lord save us from women with mountains of luggage,' he told her, refusing the services of a porter and throwing it all on to a trolley, which he pushed himself.

She had to step out to keep up with him as he strode through the crowded departures hall. Miraculously the throng opened before him. He tilted the brim of his panama hat over one eye and grinned at the girl at the check-in counter, so that she came over all girlish and flustered.

It was the same once they were aboard the aircraft. The two stewardesses giggled at everything he said, plied him with champagne and fussed over him outrageously, to the obvious irritation of the other passengers, including Royan herself. But she ignored him and them and settled back to enjoy the unaccustomed luxury of the reclining first-class seat and her own miniature video screen. She tried to concentrate on the screen images of Richard Gere, but found her attention wandering to other images of wild canyons and ancient stelae.

Only when Nicholas nudged her did she look around at him a little haughtily. He had set up a tiny travelling chessboard on the arm of the seat between them, and now he lifted an eyebrow at her and inclined his head in invitation.

When they landed at Jomo Kenyatta airport in Kenya they were still locked in combat. They were level at two games each, but she was a bishop and two pawns up in the final deciding game. She felt quite pleased with herself.

At the Norfolk Hotel in Nairobi he had booked a pair of garden bungalows, one for each of them. Within ten minutes of her flopping down on the bed, he called her from next door on the house phone.

'We are going to dinner with the British High Commissioner tonight. He is an old chum. Dress informal. Can you be ready at eight?'

One did not have to rough it too onerously when travelling around the world in this man's company, she thought.

t was a relatively short haul from Nairobi up to Addis Ababa, and the landscape below them unfolded in fascinating sequences that kept her glued to the cabin window of the Air Kenya flight. The hoary summit of Mount Kenya was for once free of cloud, and the snow-clad double peaks glistened in the high sunlight.

The bleak brown deserts of the Northern Frontier District were relieved only by the green hills that surrounded the oasis of Marsabit and, far out on the port side, the flashing waters of Lake Turkana, formerly Lake Rudolf. The desert finally gave way to the highlands of the great central plateau of the ancient land of Ethiopia.

'In Africa only the Egyptians go back further than this civilization,' Nicholas remarked as they watched it together. 'They were a cultured race when we peoples of northern climes were still dressing in untanned skins and living in caves. They were Christians when Europeans were still pagans, worshipping the old gods, Pan and Diana.'

'They were a civilized people when Taita passed this way nearly four thousand years ago,' she agreed. 'In his scrolls he writes of them as almost his cultural equals, which was rare for him. He disparaged all the other nations of the old world as his inferiors in every way.'

From the air Addis was like so many other African cities, a mixture of the old and the new, of traditional and exotic architectural styles, thatched roofs alongside galvanized iron and baked tiles. The rounded walls of the old *tukuls* built with mud and wattle contrasted with the rectangular shapes and geometrical planes of the brick-built multi-storeyed buildings, the blocks of flats and the villas of the affluent, the government buildings and the grandiose, flag-bedecked headquarters of the Organization of African Unity.

The distinguishing features of the surrounding countryside were the plantations of tall eucalyptus trees, the ubiquitous blue gums that provided firewood. It was the only fuel available to so many in this poor and war-torn land, which over the centuries had been ravaged by marauding armies and, more recently, by alien political doctrines.

After Nairobi the high-altitude air was cool and sweet when Royan and Nicholas left the aircraft and walked across the tarmac to the terminal building. As they entered, before they had even approached the row of waiting immigration officers someone called his name.

'Sir Nicholas!' They both turned to the tall young woman who glided towards them with all the grace of a dancer, her dark and delicate

72

features lit by a welcoming smile. She wore full-length traditional skirts which enhanced her movements.

'Welcome to my country of Ethiopia. I am Woizero Tessay.' She looked at Royan with interest, 'And you must be Woizero Royan.' She held out her hand to her and Nicholas saw that the two women liked each other immediately.

'If you will let me have your passports, I will see to the formalities while you relax in the VIP lounge. There is a man from your British Embassy waiting there to greet you, Sir Nicholas. I don't know how he knew that you were arriving.'

There was only one person waiting in the VIP lounge. He was dressed in a well-cut tropical suit and wore the orange, yellow and blue diagonally striped old Sandhurst tie. He stood up and came to greet Nicholas immediately, 'Nicky, how are you? It's good to see you again. Must be all of twelve years, isn't it?'

'Hello, Geoffrey. I had no idea they had stuck you out here.'

'Military attaché. His Excellency sent me down to meet you as soon as he heard that you and I had been at Sandhurst together.' Geoffrey looked at Royan with marked interest, and with a resigned air Nicholas introduced them.

'Geoffrey Tennant. Be careful of him. Biggest ram north of the equator. No girl safe within half a mile of him.'

'I say, steady on,' Geoffrey protested, looking pleased with the reference that Nicholas had given him. 'Please don't believe a word the man says, Dr Al Simma. Notorious prevaricator.'

Geoffrey drew Nicholas aside and quickly gave him a résumé of conditions in the country, particularly in the outlying areas. 'HE is a little worried. He doesn't like the idea of you swanning around out there on your own. Lots of nasty men down there in the Gojam. I told him that you knew how to look after yourself.'

In a remarkably short time Woizero Tessay was back. 'I have cleared all your luggage, including the firearm and ammunition. This is your temporary permit. You must keep it with you at all times whilst you are in Ethiopia. Here are your passports – the visas are stamped and in order. Our flight to Lake Tana leaves in an hour, so we have plenty of time to check in.'

'Any time you need a job, come and see me,' Nicholas commended her efficiency.

Geoffrey Tennant walked with them as far as the departures gate, where he shook hands, 'Anything I can do, it goes without saying. "*Serve to Lead*", Nicky.'

'"*Serve to lead*"?' Royan asked, as they walked out to the waiting aircraft.

'Sandhurst's motto,' he explained.

'How nice, Nicky,' she murmured.

'I have always considered Nicholas to be more dignified and appropriate,' he said.

'Yes, but Nicky is so sweet.'

n the high, thin air the Twin Otter aircraft that took them on the last, northern, leg pitched and yawed in the updraughts from the mountains below.

Although they were at fifteen thousand feet above sea level, the ground was close enough for them to make out the villages and the sparse areas of cultivation around them. Subjected for so many centuries to primitive agricultural methods and to the uncontrolled grazing of domestic herds, the land had a thin, impoverished look, and the bones of rock showed through the thin red fleshing of earth.

Abruptly ahead of them the plateau over which they were flying was rent through by a monstrous chasm. It was as though the earth had received a mighty sword-stroke that struck through to her very bowels.

'The Abbay river!' Tessay leaned forward in her seat to tap Royan's shoulder.

The rim of the gorge was clear-cut, and then the slope dropped away at an angle of over thirty degrees. The bare plains of the plateau gave way immediately to the heavily forested walls of the gorge. They could make out the candelabra shapes of giant euphorbia rising above the dense jungle. In places the walls had collapsed in scree slopes of loose rock, and in others they were up-thrust into bluffs and needles that erosion had sculpted with a monstrous artistry into the figures of towering humanoids and other fantastic creatures of stone.

Down and down it plunged, and they winged out over the void until they could look directly down, a mile and more, on to the glittering snake of the river in the depths. The funnel shape of the upper walls formed a secondary rim as they reached the sheer cliffs of the sub-gorge five hundred feet above the Nile water. Deep down there between its terrible cliffs the river gouged dark pools and long slithering runs through the red sandstone. In places the gorge was forty miles across, in others it narrowed to under ten, but through all its length the grandeur and the desolation were infinite and eternal. Man had made no impression upon it.

'You will soon be down there,' Tessay told them in a voice so awed that it was almost a whisper, and they were both silent. Words seemed superfluous in the face of such raw and savage nature.

Almost with relief they watched the northern wall rise to meet them, and the high mountains of the Choke range stood up against the tall blue African sky, higher than their fragile little craft was flying.

The aircraft banked into its descent and Tessay pointed over the starboard wingtip.

'Lake Tana,' she told them. It was a wide and lovely body of water, over fifty miles long, studded with islands on each of which stood a monastery or an ancient church. As they dropped in over the water on the final approach, they could make out the white-robed priests plying between the islands on their traditional little boats made from bundles of papyrus.

The Otter touched down on the dirt strip beside the lake and rolled out in a long trailing cloud of dust. It swung in and stopped engines beside the run-down terminal building of thatch and daub.

The sunlight was so bright that Nicholas pulled a pair of sunglasses from the breast pocket of his khaki jacket and placed them on his nose as he stood at the top of the boarding ladder. He took in the pock-marks of bullets and shrapnel on the dirty white walls of the terminal, and the burnt-out hull of a Russian T35 battle tank standing in the grass on the verge of the runway. The barrel of its turret gun pointed earthwards, and grass had grown up between the rusted tracks.

The other passengers pushed forward impatiently behind him, jostling him and jabbering with excitement as they saw friends and relatives waiting to greet them under the eucalyptus trees that shaded the building. There was only one vehicle parked out there, a sand-coloured Toyota Land Cruiser. The roundel on the driver's door had at its centre the painted head of a mountain nyala, with long corkscrew horns, and in a ribbon below it the title 'Wild Chase Safaris'. A white man lounged behind the wheel.

As Nicholas came down the ladder behind the two women, the driver slipped out of the truck and strode out on to the strip to meet them. He was dressed in a faded khaki bush suit, and he was tall and lean and walked with a spring to his step.

'Fortyish,' Nicholas judged his age from the grizzling in his short beard. 'One of the hard men,' Nicholas thought. His ginger hair was cropped short, his eyes were pale killer blue. There was a puckered white scar that ran across one cheek and up to twist and deform his nose.

Tessay introduced Royan to him first, and he made a short, choppy bow as he shook her hand. 'Enchanté,' he told her in an execrable French accent and then looked at Nicholas.

'This is my husband, Alto Boris,' Tessay introduced him. 'Boris, this is Alto Nicholas.'

'My English is bad,' Boris said. 'My French is better.'

'Not much to choose between them,' Nicholas thought, but he smiled easily and said, 'So we will speak French then. Bonjour, Monsieur

Brusilov. I am delighted to make your acquaintance.' He offered the Russian his hand.

Boris's grip was hard – too hard. He was making a contest out of the greeting, but Nicholas had expected it. He knew this type of old, and he had taken a deep grip so Boris could not crush his fingers. Nicholas held him without allowing any strain or effort to show on his lazy smile. Boris was the first to break the handshake, and there was just the trace of respect in those pale eyes.

'So you have come for a dik-dik?' he asked, just short of a sneer. 'Most of my clients come for big elephant, or at least for mountain nyala.'

'Bit rich for my nerves,' Nicholas grinned, 'all that big stuff. Dik-dik will suit me fine.'

'Have you ever been down in the gorge?' Boris demanded. His Russian accent overpowered the French words and made them difficult to follow.

'Sir Nicholas was one of the leaders of the 1976 river expedition,' Royan intervened sweetly, and Nicholas was amused by her unexpected intervention. She had picked up the antagonism between them very quickly, and come to his rescue.

Boris grunted, and turned to his wife. 'Have you got all the stores I ordered?' he demanded.

'Yes, Boris,' she answered meekly. 'They are all on board the aircraft.' She is afraid of him, Nicholas decided, probably with good reason.

'Let's get loaded up, then. We have a long journey ahead of us.'

The two men rode in the front seats of the Toyota, and the women sat behind them with many of the packages of stores packed in around them. Good African protocol, Nicholas smiled to himself: men first, women fend for themselves.

'You don't want to do the tourist run, do you?' Boris made it sound like a threat.

'The tourist run?'

'The outlet from the lake, and the power station,' he explained. 'The Portuguese bridge over the gorge and the point where the Blue Nile begins,' he added. But before they could accept he warned them, 'If you do, we won't get into camp until long after dark.'

'Thanks for the suggestion,' Nicholas told him politely, 'but I have seen it all before.'

'Good.' Boris made his approval evident. 'Let's get out of here.'

The road swung away into the west, below the high mountains. This was the Gojam, the land of the aloof mountaineers. It was well-populated country, and they passed many tall, thin men along the roadside as they strode along behind their herds of goats and sheep, with their long staffs held crossways over their shoulders. Both men and women wore *shammas*, woollen shawls, and baggy white jodhpur pants, with their feet in open sandals.

They were people with proud and handsome features, their hair dressed out into thick, bushy halos, and their eyes fierce as those of eagles. Some of the younger women in the villages they passed through were truly beautiful. Most of the men were heavily armed. They carried two-handed swords in chased silver scabbards, and AK-47 assault rifles.

'Makes them feel like big men,' Boris chuckled. 'Very brave, very macho.'

The huts in the villages were circular walled *tukuls*, surrounded by plantations of eucalyptus and spiky-headed sisal.

Bruised purple storm clouds boiled over the high peaks of the Choke and swept them with squalls of rain. Like silver coins, the huge drops rattled against the windscreen of the Land Cruiser and turned the road to a running river of mud under their wheels.

The condition of the road surface was appalling; in places it deteriorated into a rocky gully which even the four-wheel drive Toyota could not negotiate, and Boris was forced to make his own track across the rocky hillside. Often reduced to walking speed, they were nevertheless tossed about in their seats as the wheels bounced over the rough terrain.

'These damn blacks don't even think to repair the roads,' Boris grunted. 'They are happy to live like animals.' None of them replied, but Nicholas glanced up into the rear-view mirror at the faces of the two women. They were closed and neutral, hiding any hurt that either of them might have felt at the remark.

As they went on, the road, bad as it had been originally, became even worse. From here onwards the soft muddy surface had been torn up by the tyres and tracks of heavy traffic.

'Military traffic?' Nicholas raised his voice above the buffeting rain squalls, and Boris grunted.

'Some of it. There is a lot of *shufta* activity along the gorge – bandits and dissident warlords. However, most of this traffic is mineral-prospecting. One of the big mining companies has got concessions in Gojam and they are moving in to begin drilling.'

'We have passed no civilian vehicles,' Royan remarked, 'not even public buses.'

'We have just come through a terrible period in our long and troubled history,' Tessay explained to her. 'We are an agrarian-based economy. Once we were known as the bread basket of Africa, but when Mengistu seized power he drove us right over the edge of poverty. He

77

used starvation as a political weapon. We are still suffering terribly. Very few of our people can afford the luxury of a motor vehicle. Most of them are worried how they will be able to afford food for their children.'

'Tessay has an economics degree from Addis University,' Boris chuckled. 'She is very clever. She knows everything. You ask her, she will tell you. History, religion, economics – just ask her.' Tessay relapsed into silence at the rebuff.

In the middle of the afternoon the rain at last eased and a timid sun peered through the cloud banks. Boris stopped the Toyota in a deserted stretch of countryside. 'Pinkel pause,' he announced. 'Wee-wee stop. Pee-pee time.'

The two girls left the truck and wandered away amongst the rocks. When they returned to the vehicle they had changed their clothing. Both of them now wore the *shammas* and the jodhpur trousers of the country.

'Tessay has made me a gift of a traditional Tigrean costume,' said Royan, pirouetting for Nicholas's approval.

'Looks good, too,' he gave his opinion. 'You will be a lot more comfortable in pants.'

The sun was lowering as the road dropped into another rocky valley, down the length of which ran a river with steep, eroded banks. Above the river nestled a circular, white-walled church with a wooden Coptic cross set high on its reed-thatched roof. The village of *tukuls* huddled around the church.

'Debra Maryam,' Boris announced with satisfaction, 'the hill of the Virgin Mary, and the river is the Dandera. I sent my men on ahead in the big truck. They will have the camp ready and be waiting for us. We will sleep here tonight, and tomorrow we will follow the river downstream until we reach the rim of the gorge.'

Boris's camp staff had set up the tents in a eucalyptus grove just beyond the village.

'The second tent is yours,' Boris pointed it out.

'That will do fine for Royan,' Nicholas agreed. 'I will need a tent on my own.'

'Dik-dik and separate tents,' Boris looked at him with a flat, pale stare. 'A hell of a man. You impress me.'

He shouted for his men to erect Nicholas's tent alongside the other, the side walls almost touching.

'You may get up your courage during the night,' he leered at Nicholas. 'Don't want you to have too far to walk.'

The shower under which they bathed was a drum hung in the lower branches of one of the blue gum trees, with a roofless canvas screen set up around it. Royan used it first and came back looking cheerful and refreshed, and with a damp towel wrapped around her hair.

'Your turn, Nicky!' she called to Nicholas as she passed his tent. 'The water is beautifully hot.'

It was dark by the time Nicholas had showered and changed. He walked across to the dining tent where the rest of the party were already seated in camp chairs around the fire. The two women sat a little to one side, talking quietly, and Boris had his feet propped on the low table as he leaned back in his chair with a glass in one hand.

He indicated the vodka bottle on the table, as Nicholas stepped into the circle of firelight, 'Get yourself a drink. Ice in the bucket.'

'I prefer a beer,' Nicholas told him. 'Thirsty drive.' Boris shrugged and bellowed for his camp butler to bring a brown bottle from the portable gas refrigerator.

'Let me tell you something, a little secret.' He grinned at Nicholas as he poured himself another vodka. 'There is no such animal as a striped dik-dik these days, even if there ever was one. You are wasting your time and your money.'

'Fine,' Nicholas agreed mildly. 'It's my time and my money.'

'Just because some old fart shot one back in the Dark Ages, doesn't mean you are going to find another now. We could go up into the tea plantations for elephant. I saw three bulls there only ten days ago. All with tusks over a hundred pounds a side.'

As they argued, the level in Boris's vodka bottle fell like the Nile at the end of the inundation. When Tessay told them that the meal was ready, Boris carried the bottle with him; he stumbled on his way to the table. During the meal his only contribution to the conversation was to snarl at Tessay.

'The lamb is raw. Why don't you see to it that the cook does it properly? Damn monkeys, you have to watch everything they do.'

'Is your lamb under-cooked, Alto Nicholas?' Tessay asked without looking at her husband. 'I can have them cook it longer.'

'It's perfect,' he assured her. 'I like mine pink.'

By the end of dinner the vodka bottle at Boris's elbow was empty, and his face was flushed and swollen. He got up from the table without a word and disappeared into the darkness in the direction of his tent, swaying on his feet and occasionally catching his balance with a two-step jig.

'I apologize,' Tessay told them quietly. 'It is only in the evenings. In the day he is fine. It is a Russian tradition, the vodka.' She smiled brightly; only her eyes stayed sad.

'It is a lovely night, and too early yet for bed. Would you like to walk up to the church? It is very old and famous. I will have one of the servants bring a lantern, so that you may admire the murals.'

The servant walked ahead of them, lighting their way, and an ancient priest waited to welcome them on the portico of the circular building. He was thin and so very black that only his teeth flashed in the gloom. He carried a magnificent Coptic cross in massive native silver, set with carnelians and other semi-precious stones.

Both Royan and Tessay dropped on their knees in front of him to ask for his blessing. He slapped their cheeks lightly with the cross and genuflected over them, mumbling his benediction in Amharic. Then he ushered them into the interior.

The walls were covered with a magnificent display of paintings in brilliant primary colours. In the lantern light they blazed like gemstones. There was a strong Byzantine flavour to the style: the saints' eyes were huge and slanted, with great golden halos over their heads. Above the altar, with its tinsel and brass furnishing, the Virgin cradled her infant while the three wise men and a host of angels knelt in adoration. Nicholas slipped his Polaroid camera from the pocket of his jacket and adjusted the flash. He wandered around the church photographing these murals, while Tessay and Royan knelt before the altar side by side.

Once he had finished his photography Nicholas found a seat on the hand-hewn wooden pews and sat quietly watching their intent faces which the candlelight touched with golden highlights, and he was moved by the beauty of the moment.

'I wish I had that kind of faith,' he thought, as he had so often before. 'It must be a comfort in the hard times. I wish I were able to pray like that for Rosalind and the girls.' He could not stay longer, and he went out and sat on the church portico where he watched the night sky.

In these high altitudes, in the thin unpolluted air, the stars were such a dazzling blaze that it was difficult to pick out the individual constellations. After a while his sadness abated. It was good to be back in Africa.

When the two women emerged at last from the dark interior, Nicholas gave the old priest a one hundred birr note and a Polaroid photograph of himself which the old man clearly valued above the money. Then the three of them walked back down the hill together in companionable silence.

'Nicky!' Royan shook him awake. When he sat up and switched on his torch, he saw that she had thrown the woollen shawl over a pair of men's striped pyjamas before she had come into his tent.

'What is it?' he asked, but before she could answer he heard the sound of a hoarse and angry voice shouting invective in the night, and then the unmistakable thud of a clenched fist striking flesh and bone.

'He's beating her.' Royan's voice was tight with outrage. 'You have to make him stop.'

There was a cry of pain after the blow, and then sobs.

Nicholas hesitated. Only a fool interferes between a man and his wife, and his reward usually is to have them unite and turn savagely upon him.

'You must do something, Nicky, please.'

Reluctantly he swung his legs out of the cot and stood up. He slept in boxer shorts, and he did not bother to find his shoes. She followed him, also on bare feet, to the end of the grove where Boris's tent stood beyond the dining tent.

There was a lantern still burning within, and it threw magnified shadows on the canvas walls. He saw that Boris had his wife by the hair and was dragging her across the floor, roaring at her in Russian.

'Boris!' Nicholas had to shout his name three times to get his attention, and then they saw the shadow play on the canvas as he dropped Tessay and flung open the tent flap.

He was dressed only in a pair of underpants. His torso was lean and muscular, the chest flat and hard-looking, covered with coppery curls. On the floor behind him Tessay lay face down, sobbing into her cupped hands. She was naked, and the planes of her body were sleek as those of a panther.

'What the hell is going on here?' Nicholas demanded, his anger only just beginning to stir as he witnessed the gracious, gentle woman's distress and humiliation.

'I am giving this black whore a lesson in good manners,' Boris gloated, his face still swollen and flushed with drink and passion. 'It's none of your business, English, unless you want to pay some money and have a bit of pork for yourself.' He laughed, an ugly sound.

'Are you all right, Woizero Tessay?' Nicholas looked directly into Boris's face, sparing the woman the further humiliation of another man's eyes on her nudity.

Tessay sat up, lifted her knees against her chest, and hugged them with both arms to cover her body.

'It's all right, Alto Nicholas. Please go away before there is real trouble.' Blood was trickling from one nostril into her mouth, and dyeing her teeth pink.

'You heard my wife, English bastard. Go away! Mind your own business. Go away, before I give you a little lesson in good manners also.'

Boris staggered forward and thrust his open hand against Nicholas's chest. Nicholas moved as smoothly and as effortlessly as a matador avoiding the first wild charge of the bull. He swayed to one side, and used Boris's own momentum to send him on in the direction in which he was already committed. Completely off balance, the Russian reeled across the open ground in front of the tent until he collided with one of the camp chairs and went down in a sprawling heap.

'Royan, take Tessay to your tent!' he ordered softly. Royan ran into the tent and pulled a sheet from the nearest cot. She spread it over Tessay's shoulders and lifted her to her feet.

'Please, don't do this,' Tessay sobbed. 'You don't know him when he gets like this. He will hurt somebody.'

Royan dragged her, still protesting and weeping, out of the tent, but by now Boris was on his feet again. He bellowed with rage and picked up the camp chair that had tripped him. With a single jerk he tore off one of the legs and hefted it in his bunched fist.

'You want to play games, English? All right, we play!' He rushed at Nicholas, swinging the chair leg like a Ninja baton, so that it hissed with the force with which he aimed it at his head. As Nicholas ducked under it Boris reversed the swing, going for the side of his chest, under his upraised arm. It would have staved in his ribs if it had landed, but again Nicholas twisted away.

They circled each other warily, and then Boris charged again. If it had not been for the effect of the vodka on the Russian's reflexes Nicholas would never have taken a chance with an adversary of this calibre, but Boris was just loose enough in his control to allow him to duck in under the swinging chair leg. He straightened, with all his weight rolling into the punch, and his fist slogged into the pit of Boris's belly just under the sternum. The Russian's breath was driven out of him in a great gusty belch.

The chair leg flew from his grip, and he doubled over and collapsed. Clasping his middle, and heaving and wheezing for breath, Boris lay curled in the dust. Nicholas stooped over him and told him softly in English, 'This sort of behaviour simply isn't good enough, old chap. We don't bully girls. Please don't let it happen again.'

He straightened up and spoke to Royan, 'Get her to your tent and keep her there.' He combed his hair back from his face with his fingers. 'And now, if you have no serious objections, may we get a little sleep?'

It rained again during the early hours. The heavy drops drummed down on the canvas and the lightning lit the interior of the tents with an eerie brilliance. However, by the time that Nicholas went through to the dining tent for breakfast the next morning, the clouds had cleared and the sunshine was bright and cheering. The sweet mountain air smelt of wet earth and mushrooms.

Boris greeted Nicholas with hearty good fellowship. 'Good morning,

English. We had some fun last night. I still laugh to remember it. Very good jokes. One day soon we will have some more vodka, then we will make some more good jokes.' And he bellowed through to the kitchen tent, 'Hey! Lady Sun, bring your new boyfriend something to eat. He is hungry from all the sport last night.'

Tessay was quiet and withdrawn as she supervised the servants handing round breakfast. One eye was swollen almost closed, and her lip was cut. She did not look at Nicholas once during the meal.

'We will go on ahead,' Boris explained jovially as they drank coffee. 'My servants will break camp, and follow us in my big truck. With luck, we will be able to camp tonight on the rim above the gorge, and tomorrow we will begin the descent.'

As they were climbing into the truck, Tessay was able to speak to him softly for a moment, without danger of Boris overhearing her. 'Thank you, Alto Nicholas. But it was not wise. You don't know him. You must be careful now. He does not forget, nor does he forgive.'

From the village of Debra Maryam Boris took a branch road that ran alongside the Dandera river directly southwards. The road they had followed the previous day from Lake Tana was shown on the map as a major highway. It had been bad enough. But this track that they were now on was marked as a secondary road 'not passable in all weather'. To compound matters, it seemed that most of the heavy traffic that had torn up the main road had followed this same track. They came to a place where some huge vehicle had become bogged down in the rain-saturated earth, and the efforts to free it had left areas of ploughed land and an excavation like a bomb crater that resembled an old photograph of the battlefields of First World War Flanders.

Twice during the day the Toyota too became stuck in this foul ground. Each time this happened, the big truck that was following them came up and all the servants swarmed down from the cargo body to push and heave the Toyota through. Even Nicholas stripped to the waist to work with them in the mud to free it.

'If you had only listened to my advice,' Boris grumbled, 'we would not be here. There is no game where you want to go, and there are no roads worth the name either.'

In the early afternoon they stopped beside the river for an alfresco lunch. Nicholas went down to the pool beside the road to wash off the mud and filth of the morning's labours. He had been in the forefront of the efforts to keep the truck moving. Royan followed him down the slope and perched on a rock above the pool while he stripped off his shirt and knelt at the verge to splash himself with the cold mountain water. The river was muddy yellow and swollen from the rainstorms.

'I don't think Boris believes your story about the striped dik-dik,' she warned him. 'Tessay tells me that he is suspicious of what we are up

83

to.' She watched with interest as he sluiced his chest and upper arms. Where the sun had not touched it, his skin was very white and unblemished. His chest hair was thick and dark. She decided that his body was good to look at.

'He is the type that would go through our luggage if he gets a chance,' Nicholas agreed. 'You didn't bring anything with you that has any clues for him? No papers or notes?'

'Only the satellite photograph, and my notebooks are all in my own shorthand. He won't be able to make anything of them.'

'Be very careful of what you discuss with Tessay.'

'She is a dear. There is nothing underhand about her.' Heatedly Royan came to the defence of her new friend.

'She may be all right, but she's married to my chum Boris. Her first allegiance lies there. No matter what your feelings towards her, don't trust either of them.' He dried himself on his shirt, slipped it on and then buttoned it over his chest. 'Let's go and get something to eat.'

Back at the parked truck Boris was pulling the cork from a bottle of South African white wine. He poured a tumblerful for Nicholas. Chilled in the river, it was crisp and fruity. Tessay offered them cold roast chicken and *injera* bread, the flat, thin sheets of stone-ground unleavened bread of the country. The trials and labours of the morning's travels faded into insignificance as Royan lay beside Nicholas in the grass and they watched a bearded vulture sailing high against the blue. It saw them and drifted overhead curiously, twisting its head to look down at them. Its eyes were masked in black like those of a highwayman, and the distinctive wedge-shaped tail feathers flirted with the wind the way the fingers of a concert pianist would stroke the ivories of the keyboard.

When it was time to go on, Nicholas gave her his hand to lift her to her feet. It was one of their rare moments of physical contact, and she held on to his fingers for just a second or two longer than was strictly necessary.

There was no improvement in the surface of the track as they drew nearer to the rim of the gorge, and the hours passed in this bone-jarring, teeth-rattling progress. The track snaked over a rise and then dog-legged down the far slope. Halfway down Boris swore in Russian as they came round the hairpin bend of a high earthen bank to find a huge diesel truck slewed across the track, almost blocking it.

Even though they had been following the tracks of this convoy of vehicles since the previous day, this was the first of them that they had encountered, and it took Boris by surprise. He hit his brakes so suddenly that his passengers were almost catapulted from their seats, but on the steep incline in the mud the brakes did not bring them to a complete halt. Boris was forced to change down into his lowest gear and steer for the narrow gap between the bank and the truck.

From the back seat Royan looked out of the window beside her, up the high side of the diesel truck. There was a company name and logo emblazoned in scarlet on the green background.

A strong feeling of *déjà vu* overcame her as she stared at the image. She had seen this sign recently, but her memory cheated her: she could not recall the time or the place. She only knew that it was of vital importance that she should remember.

The side of the Toyota scraped against the metal of the truck, and then they were past it. Boris leaned out of his window and shook his fist at the driver of the larger vehicle.

He was a local man, probably recruited in Addis by the owner of the truck. Grinning at Boris's antics, he leaned out of his own cab to return the clenched fist salute, adding a nice little touch by jerking a raised forefinger upwards.

'Dung-eater!' Boris roared with outrage at being bested in the exchange, but he did not stop. 'No use even talking to them. What do they know? Black chimps!'

For the rest of the wearisome journey Royan remained silent and withdrawn, shaken and troubled by the conviction that she had seen the trademark of the winged red horse before, with, set above it in a pennant, the name of the company: 'PEGASUS EXPLORATION'.

As they approached the end of the day's journey at last they passed a signpost beside the track. The supporting legs of the sign were solidly set in concrete, and the artwork was of such high quality that it could only have been that of a professional signwriter.

Across the top of the board an arrow indicated a newly bulldozed road that headed off to the right, and the directions read:

PEGASUS EXPLORATION
BASE CAMP — ONE KILOMETRE
PRIVATE ROAD
NO ENTRY TO UNAUTHORIZED TRAFFIC

The scarlet horse reared in the centre of the board with its wings spread wide, on the point of flight.

Now she gasped aloud as the elusive memory came upon her with stunning clarity. She remembered where she had last seen the flying red horse. In an instant she was transported back into the icy waters of an English salmon river, flung from the rolling body of the Land Rover, the huge MAN truck roaring over the bridge above her, and, for a subliminal pulse of time, the prancing red horse upon its side.

'It's the same!' she almost shouted aloud, but controlled herself. The terror of the moment returned to her with full force, and she found herself breathing hard and her heart racing as though she had run a long way.

'It cannot be a coincidence,' she assured herself silently, 'and I am not mistaken. It is the same company. Pegasus Exploration.'

She was withdrawn and distracted for the last few miles of the journey, until the track they were following ended abruptly on the brink of the sheer cliffs of the escarpment. Here Boris pulled on to the grassy verge and stopped the engine.

'This is as far as we ride. We camp here tonight. My big truck is not far behind. They will make camp as soon as they arrive. Tomorrow we will go down into the gorge on foot.'

As they dismounted, Royan tugged at Nicholas's arm, 'I must speak to you,' she whispered urgently, and she followed him as he led her along the bank of the river.

He found a place for them to sit side by side, with their legs dangling over the drop. Beside them the swollen yellow river seemed to sense what lay ahead of it. The cold mountain waters speeded up, swirled amongst the rocks, and gathered themselves for that dizzying leap out into empty space. The cliff below them was a sheer wall of rock almost a thousand feet deep. It was so high that in the evening light the abyss far below was a dark, mysterious place, its bottom hidden from them by shadow and spray from the falls. As Royan looked down into it her sense of balance swirled with vertigo. She cringed back from the edge and found herself instinctively leaning against Nicholas's shoulder to steady herself. Only when they touched did she realize what she was doing, and she pulled away from him self-consciously.

The muddied waters of the Dandera river leaped from the brink, and were miraculously transformed into curtains of ethereal lacework as they fell. Like the skirts of a waltzing bride they shimmered and swirled, and rainbows of light played through them as though from an embroidery of seed pearls. Still falling, the columns of white spray twisted and changed into lovely but ephemeral shapes, until they struck the lower ledges of glistening black rock and exploded outwards into fresh clouds of white that at last screened the dark depths of the abyss with an opalescent veil.

It was with a conscious effort that Royan pulled her mind away from the awe-inspiring scene and back to the troubled present.

'Nicky, do you remember I told you about the truck that forced my mother and me over the bridge in the Land Rover?'

'Of course.' His expression was mystified as he studied her face. 'You are upset. What is it, Royan?'

'The truck had signwriting down the sides of the trailers that it was towing.'

86

'You told me, yes. Green and red. You told me that you didn't get a good enough look to read the sign.'

'It was the same as the truck we passed this afternoon. I saw the sign at the same angle as before and it came back to me. The red Pegasus, the flying horse.'

He studied her face for a while, 'Are you absolutely certain?'

'Absolutely!' She nodded vehemently.

Nicholas stared out over the magnificent panorama of the gorge spread below them. It was forty miles to the far wall of the canyon, but in the brilliant rain-washed air it seemed so close that he could reach across and touch it.

'A coincidence?' he wondered at last.

'Do you think so? A very strange and wonderful coincidence, then. Pegasus in both Yorkshire and Gojam? Do you accept that?'

'It doesn't make sense. The truck that hit you was stolen—'

'Was it?' she demanded. 'Are we sure of that?'

'If it wasn't, then let's hear your ideas.'

'If you were planning an assassination, would you rely on stealing a truck conveniently left at a Little Chef for you?'

He shook his head, 'Go on.'

'Suppose you arranged for your own truck to be placed there for you, and for your driver to report it stolen only after you had a good head start on the police.'

'It's possible,' he agreed without enthusiasm.

'Whoever murdered Duraid, and made two further attempts to kill me, obviously has considerable resources at his disposal. He is able to make arrangements in Egypt and England. On top of that, he has the seventh scroll in his possession. He has our notes and all our workings and translations which point him clearly to this spot on the Abbay river. Just suppose that he has control of a company like Pegasus – is there any reason why he can't be here in Ethiopia, just as we are, right at this moment?'

Nicholas was silent for a while. He picked up a stone from the ledge beside him and tossed it out over the cliff. They both watched it drop away, dwindling in size until it vanished in the veils of spray far below where they sat.

Abruptly Nicholas stood up and reached for her hand to pull her to her feet beside him. 'Come on,' he said.

'Where are we going?'

'Pegasus base camp. Let's go and have a chat to the site foreman.'

Boris protested angrily and hurried to intervene when Nicholas climbed into the Toyota and started the engine, 'Where the hell do you think you are going?'

'Sight-seeing.' Nicholas let in the clutch. 'Back in an hour.'

'Hey, English, my truck!' He ran to catch up with them, but Nicholas accelerated away.

'Charge me for the hire.' He grinned back at Boris in the rear-view mirror.

They reached the signposted turn-off and followed the side track over the ridge. The Pegasus camp lay on the far side. Nicholas braked to a halt on the crest of the rise and they studied it in silence.

An area of about ten acres had been cleared and levelled. It was surrounded by a barbed-wire security fence, with a single closed gate. Three of the massive diesel trucks in their green and red livery were parked in a rank inside the fence. There were also several smaller vehicles and a tall mobile drilling rig in the line. The rest of the yard was filled with prospecting equipment and stores. There were stacks of drilling rods and steel core boxes, wooden crates of spares, and several hundred forty-four-gallon drums of diesel and oil and drilling mud. The drums and the stores were stacked with a neatness and sense of good order that was startling in this wild and rocky landscape. Just inside the gate stood a small village of a dozen buildings made of corrugated sheet sections, of the Quonset type. They too were set out in a street of military precision.

'A big, well-organized outfit,' Nicholas commented. 'Let's go down and see who is in charge.'

There were two armed guards on the gate, dressed in the camouflage uniform of the Ethiopian army. They were clearly surprised by the arrival at the gate of the strange Land Cruiser, and when Nicholas sounded his horn one of them came forward suspiciously with his AK-47 rifle at the ready.

'I want to speak to the manager here,' Nicholas told him in Arabic, with enough haughty authority to make the sentry uncertain and uneasy.

The soldier grunted, went back and consulted his colleague, then lifted the handset of the two-way radio and spoke earnestly into the mouthpiece. There was a five-minute delay after he finished speaking, and then the door of the nearest Quonset building opened and a white man came out.

He was dressed in Khaki coveralls and a soft bush cap. His eyes, covered by mirrored sunglasses, were set in a deeply tanned, leathery face. His physique was short and chunky, and his sleeves were rolled up over hairy, work-thickened arms. After speaking a few words to the guards at the gate he came out to the Toyota.

'Yeah? What's going down here?' he demanded in a Texan drawl, speaking around the stub of an unlit cigar.

'The name is Quenton-Harper.' Nicholas dismounted from the truck to greet him, and held out his hand. 'Nicholas Quenton-Harper. How do you do?'

The American hesitated, and then took the hand as though he had been offered an electric eel to squeeze.

'Helm,' he said. 'Jake Helm, from Abilene, Texas. I am the foreman here.' His hand was that of an artisan, with calloused palms and lumpy scar tissue over the knuckles, and half moons of black grease under the fingernails.

'Terribly sorry to worry you. I am having some trouble with my truck. I wondered if you had a mechanic who could have a look at it for me.' Nicholas smiled winningly, but received no encouragement from the man.

'Not company policy.' He shook his head.

'I am prepared to pay for any—'

'Listen, buddy, I said no.' Jake removed the cigar from his mouth and examined it minutely.

'Your company – Pegasus. Can you tell me where your head office is situated? Who is your managing director?'

'I am a busy man. You are wasting my time.' Helm returned the cigar to his mouth and began to turn away.

'I will be hunting in this area over the next few weeks. I would not like to endanger any of your employees with a stray shot. Can you give me some idea of where you will be working?'

'I am running a prospecting outfit here, mister. I don't give out news flashes on my movements. Beat it!'

He turned and walked to the gate and gave brusque orders to the guards before marching back to his office building.

'Satellite disc on the roof,' Nicholas remarked. 'I wonder who our lad Jake is speaking to at this very moment.'

'Somebody in Texas?' Royan hazarded.

'Doesn't follow, necessarily,' Nicholas demurred. 'Pegasus is probably a multinational. Just because Jake is one, doesn't mean his boss is Texan also. Not a very instructive conversation, I am afraid.' He started the engine and U-turned the Toyota. 'But if someone at Pegasus is the ugly mixed up in this, he will recognize my name. We have given them notice of our arrival. Let's see what we have flushed out of the bushes.'

When they got back to the Dandera river falls, they found that Boris's truck had arrived, the tents had been erected, and the chef had brewed tea for them. Boris was less welcoming than his chef, and maintained a sullen silence while Nicholas tried to placate him for commandeering his truck. It was only after his first vodka of the evening that he mellowed sufficiently to speak again.

'The mules were supposed to be waiting for us here. Time means nothing to these people. We cannot start down into the gorge until they arrive.'

'Well, at least while we are waiting for them I will have a chance to sight in my rifle,' Nicholas remarked with resignation. 'In Africa it never pays to be in a hurry. Too wearing on the nerves.'

After a leisurely breakfast the next morning, when there was still no sign of the mules, Nicholas fetched his rifle case.

When Nicholas lifted the weapon out of its nest of green baize, Boris took it from him and examined it minutely.

'An old rifle?'

'Made in 1926,' Nicholas nodded. 'My grandfather had it made for himself.'

'They knew how to make them in those days. Not like the mass-produced crap they turn out today.' Boris pursed his lips critically. 'Short Mauser Oberndorf double square-bridge action, beautiful! But it has been rebarrelled, no?'

'The original barrel was shot out. I had it replaced with a Shilen match barrel. It will shoot the wings off a mosquito at a hundred paces.'

'Calibre 7 × 57, is it?' Boris asked.

'275 Rigby, as a matter of fact,' Nicholas corrected him, but Boris snorted.

'It is exactly the same cartridge – just your English bloodiness must call it something else.' He grinned. 'It will push a 150 grain bullet out there at 2800 feet per second. It is a good rifle, one of the best.'

'You will never know, my dear fellow, how much your approval means to me,' Nicholas murmured in English, and Boris chuckled as he handed the rifle back to him.

'English jokes! I love your English jokes.'

When Nicholas left camp carrying the little rifle in its slip case, Royan followed him down to the river and helped him fill two small canvas bags with white river sand. He laid them on top of a convenient rock and they formed a firm but malleable rest for the rifle as he settled it over them.

Using the open hillside as a safe back-stop, he stepped out two hundred yards and at that range set up a cardboard carton on which he had taped a Bisley-type target. He came back to where Royan waited and then settled down behind the rock on which the weapon lay.

Royan was unprepared for the report of the first shot from the dainty, almost feminine-looking rifle. She jumped involuntarily, and her ears sang.

'What a horrible, vicious thing!' she exclaimed. 'How can you bring yourself to kill lovely animals with a high-powered gun like that?' she demanded.

90

'Rifle,' he corrected her, as he noted the strike of the shot through his binoculars. 'Would it make you feel better if I used a low-powered rifle, or beat them to death with a stick?'

The shot had struck three inches right and two inches low. As he adjusted the telescopic sight he attempted to explain. 'An ethical hunter does everything in his power to kill as swiftly and as cleanly as is possible, and that means stalking in as close as he is able to do, using a weapon of adequate power and sighting it the best way he knows how.'

His next shot struck exactly on line but only an inch above the bullseye. He wanted it to shoot three inches high at that range. He worked on the sight again.

'Gun or rifle, but I don't understand why you would want to deliberately kill any of God's creatures,' she protested.

'That I can never explain to you.' He aimed deliberately and fired once. Even through the lower magnification of the sight lens he could see that the bullet had struck exactly three inches high.

'It is something to do with an atavistic urge that few men, no matter how cultured and civilized they deem themselves, can deny completely.' He fired a second time. 'Some of them work it out in the board room, others on the golf course or the tennis court, and some of us on a salmon river, in the ocean deeps or in the hunting field.'

He fired a third shot, merely to confirm the previous two, and then went on, 'As for God's creatures, he gave them to us. You are the believer. Quote me Acts 10, verses 12 and 13.'

'Sorry.' She shook her head. 'You tell me.'

'". . . *all manner of fourfooted beasts of the earth, and wild beasts, and creeping things, and fowls of the air,*" Nicholas obliged her. '"*And there came a voice to him, Rise, Peter; kill, and eat.*"'

'You should have been a lawyer,' she moaned in mock despair.

'Or a priest,' he suggested, and went forward to retrieve the target. He found that his last three shots had punched a tiny symmetrical rosette three inches above the bull, all three bullet holes just touching each other.

He patted the butt stock of the little rifle, 'That's my lovely darling, Lucrezia Borgia.' He had named the rifle for her beauty and for her murderous potential.

He slid the rifle back into its leather slip case and they walked back together. As they came in sight of the camp, Nicholas pulled up short.

'Visitors,' he said, and raised his binoculars. 'Aha! We have flushed something out of the undergrowth. That is a Pegasus truck parked there and, unless I am much mistaken, one of our visitors is the charming laddie from Abilene. Let's go down and find out what is going on.'

As they drew closer to camp, they realized that there were a dozen or more heavily armed, uniformed soldiers clustered around the red and green Pegasus truck, and that Jake Helm and an Ethiopian army officer were seated under the awning of the dining tent in serious and intent conversation with Boris.

As soon as Nicholas entered the tent, Boris introduced him to the bespectacled Ethiopian officer. 'This is Colonel Tuma Nogo, the military commander of the southern Gojam region.'

'How do you do?' Nicholas greeted him, but the colonel ignored the pleasantry.

'I want to see your passport, and your firearms licence,' he ordered arrogantly, while Jake Helm chewed complacently on the evil-smelling butt of an extinguished cigar.

'Yes, of course,' Nicholas agreed, and went to his own tent to fetch his briefcase. He opened it on the dining table, and smiled at the officer. 'I am sure you will also want to see my letter of introduction from the British Foreign Secretary in London, and this one from the British Ambassador in Addis Ababa. Here is another from the Ethiopian Ambassador to the Court of St James, and this *firman* is from your own Minister of Defence, General Siye Abraha.'

The colonel stared in consternation at this fruit salad of ornate official letterheads and scarlet beribboned seals. Behind the gold-rimmed glasses his eyes were bemused and confused.

'Sir!' He jumped to his feet and saluted. 'You are a friend of General Abraha? I did not know. Nobody informed me. I beg your pardon for this intrusion.'

He saluted again, and his embarrassment made him awkward and ungainly. 'I came to warn you only that the Pegasus Company is conducting drilling and blasting operations. There may be some danger. Please be alert. Also there are many bandits and outlaws, *shufta*, operating in this area.' Colonel Nogo was flustered and barely coherent. He stopped and drew a deep breath to steady himself. 'You see, I have been ordered to provide an escort for the employees of the Pegasus Company. If you yourself experience any trouble while you are here, or if you need assistance for any reason you have only to call on me, sir.'

'That is extremely civil of you, colonel.'

'I will detain you no longer, sir.' He saluted a third time and backed off towards the Pegasus truck, taking the Texan foreman along with him. Jake Helm had not uttered a word since their arrival, and now he left without a farewell.

Colonel Nogo gave Nicholas his fourth and final salute through the cab window as the truck pulled away.

'Deuce!' Nicholas told Royan, as he acknowledged the salute with a nonchalant wave. 'I think that point was definitely ours. Now at least we know that, for whatever reason, Mr Pegasus definitely does not want us in his hair. I think we can expect his next service fairly promptly.'

They walked back to where Boris sat in the dining tent and Nicholas told him, 'All we need now are your mules.'

'I have sent three of my men to the village to find them. They should have been here yesterday.'

The mules arrived early the next morning, six big sturdy animals, each accompanied by a driver dressed in the ubiquitous jodhpurs and shawl. By mid-morning they were loaded and ready to begin the descent into the gorge.

Boris paused at the head of the pathway, and looked out over that valley. For once even he seemed to be subdued and awed by the immensity of the drop and the rugged splendour of the gorge.

'You will be passing into another land in another age,' he warned them in an uncharacteristically philosophical mood. 'They say that this trail is two thousand years old, as old as Christ.' He spread his hands in a deprecating gesture. 'The old black priest in the church at Debra Maryam will tell you that the Virgin Mary passed this way when she fled from Israel after the crucifixion.' He shook his head. 'But then these people will believe anything.' And he stepped out on to the pathway.

It clung to the cliff, descending at such an angle that each pace was down a rock step so deep that it stretched the tendons and the sinews in their groins and knees, and jarred their spines. They were forced to use their hands to scramble the rougher and steeper sections, where it was almost as though they were descending a ladder.

It seemed impossible that the mules under their heavy packs could follow them down. The plucky beasts lunged down each of the rock steps, landing heavily on their forelegs, then gathered themselves for the next drop. The trail was so narrow that the bulky packs scraped against the rock wall on one hand, while on the other hand the drop sucked at them giddily.

When the path dog-legged and changed direction, the mules could not make the turn in one attempt. They were forced to back and fill, edging their way round the narrow trail, sweating with terror and their eyes rolling until the whites flashed. The drivers urged them on with wild cries and busy whips.

At places the pathway entered the body of the mountain, passing behind butts and needles of rock that time and erosion had prised away from the cliff face. These rocky gateways were so narrow that the mules had to be unloaded and the packs carried through by the drivers, and then the mules were reloaded on the far side.

'Look!' Royan cried in astonishment and pointed out into the void. A black vulture rose up out of the depths on widespread pinions and floated past them almost within arm's length, turning its gruesome naked head of pink lappeted skin to stare at them with inscrutable black eyes before sailing away.

'He is using the thermals of heated air from the valley for lift,' Nicholas explained to her. He pointed out along the cliff to an overhanging buttress on the same level as themselves. 'There is one of their nests.' It was a shaggy mound of sticks piled on an inaccessible ledge. The excrement of the birds that had inhabited it over the ages had painted the cliff face below with streaks of brilliant white, and even at this distance they could catch whiffs of rotting offal and decaying flesh.

All that day they clung to the precipitous track as they eased their way down that terrible wall. It was late afternoon, and they were only halfway down, when the trail turned back upon itself once more and they heard the rumble of the falls ahead. The sound grew louder and became a thunderous roar as they moved around the corner of another buttress and came in full sight of the falls.

The wind created by the torrent tugged at them and forced them to clutch for handholds. The spray blew around them and wetted their upturned faces, but the Ethiopian guide led them straight on until it seemed that they must be washed away into the valley still hundreds of feet below.

Then, miraculously, the waters parted and they stepped behind the great translucent curtain into a deep recess of moss-covered and gleaming wet rock, carved from the cliff by the force of water over the aeons. The only light in this gloomy place was filtered through the waterfall, green and mysterious like some undersea cavern.

'This is where we sleep tonight,' Boris announced, obviously enjoying their astonishment. He pointed to bundles of firewood piled at the rear of the cave, and the smoke-blackened wall above the stone hearth. 'The muleteers carrying food and supplies down to the priests in the monastery have used this place for centuries.'

As they moved deeper into the cavern, the sound of falling water became muted to a dull background rumble and the rock underfoot was dry. Once the servants had lit the fire, it became a warm and comfortable, not to say romantic, lodging.

With an old soldier's eye for the most comfortable spot, Nicholas laid out his sleeping bag in a corner at the back of the cave, and quite naturally Royan unrolled hers beside his. They were both tired out by the unusual exertion of climbing down the cliff wall, and after supper they stretched out in their sleeping bags in companionable silence and watched the firelight playing on the roof of the cave.

'Just think!' Royan whispered. 'Tomorrow we will be retracing the footsteps of old Taita himself.'

'To say nothing of the Virgin Mary,' Nicholas smiled.

'You are a horrid old cynic,' she sighed. 'And what is more, you probably snore.'

'You are about to find out the hard way,' he told her, but she was asleep before him. Her breathing was gentle and even, and he could just hear it above the sound of the water. It was a long time since he had had a lovely woman lying at his side. When he was sure she was deeply under, he reached across and touched her cheek gently.

'Pleasant dreams, little one,' he whispered tenderly. 'You have had a busy day.' That was the way he had often bid his younger daughter sleep.

The muleteers were stirring long before the dawn, and the whole party was on the pathway again as soon as the light was strong enough to reveal their footing. When the early sun struck the upper walls of the cliff face, they were still high enough above the valley floor to have an aerial view of the terrain. Nicholas drew Royan aside and they let the rest of the caravan go on down ahead of them.

He found a place to sit and unrolled the satellite photograph between them. Picking out the major peaks and features of the scene, they orientated themselves and began to make some order out of the cataclysmic landscape that rioted below them.

'We can't see the Abbay river from here,' Nicholas pointed out. 'It's still deep in the sub-gorge. We will probably only get our first glimpse of it from almost directly above.'

'If we have identified our present position accurately, then the river will make two ox-bow bends around that bluff over there.'

'Yes, and the confluence of the Dandera river with the Abbay is over there, below those cliffs.' He used his thumb knuckle as a rough scale measure. 'About fifteen miles from here.'

'It looks as though the Dandera has changed its course many times over the centuries. I can see at least two gullies that look like ancient river beds.' She pointed down: 'There, and there. They are all choked with jungle now.' She looked crestfallen, 'Oh, Nicholas, it is such a huge and confused area. How are we ever going to find the single entrance to a tomb hidden in all that?'

'Tomb? What tomb is this?' Boris demanded with interest. He had come back up the trail to find them. They had not heard his approach, and now he stood over them. 'What tomb are you talking about?'

'Why, the tomb of St Frumentius, of course,' Nicholas told him smoothly, showing no concern at having been overheard.

95

'Isn't the monastery dedicated to the saint?' Royan asked as smoothly, as she rolled up the photograph.

'*Da.*' He nodded, looking disappointed, as though he expected something of more interest. 'Yes, St Frumentius. But they will not let you visit the tomb. They will not let you into the inner part of the monastery. Only the priests are allowed in there.'

He removed his cap and scratched the short, stiff bristles that covered his scalp. They rasped like wire under his fingernails. 'This week is the ceremony of Timkat, the Blessing of the Tabot. There will be a great deal of excitement down there. You will find it very interesting, but you will not be able to enter the Holy of Holies, nor will you be able to see the actual tomb. I have never met any white man who has seen it.'

He squinted up at the sun. 'We must get on. It looks close, but it will take us two more days to reach the Abbay. It is bad ground down there. A long march, even for a famous dik-dik hunter.' He laughed delightedly at his own joke, and turned away down the path.

As they approached the bottom of the cliff, the gradient of the trail smoothed out and the steps became shallower and further apart. The going became easier and their progress swifter, but the air had changed in quality and taste. It was no longer cool, bracing mountain air but the languid, enervating air of the equator, with the smell and taste of the encroaching jungle.

'Hot!' said Royan, shrugging out of the woollen shawl.

'Ten degrees hotter, at least,' Nicholas agreed. He pulled his old army jersey over his head, leaving his hair in curly disarray. 'And we can expect it to get hotter before we reach the Abbay. We still have to descend another three thousand feet.'

Now the path followed the Dandera river for a while. Sometimes they were several hundred feet above it, and shortly afterwards they splashed waist-deep through a ford, hanging on to the panniers of the mules to keep themselves from being swept away on the flood.

Then the gorge of the Dandera river was too deep and steep to follow any longer, as sheer cliffs dropped into dark pools. So they left the river and followed the track that squirmed like a dying snake amongst eroded hills and tall red stone bluffs.

A mile or two further downstream they rejoined the river in a different mood as it rippled through dense forest. The dangling lianas swept the surface and tree moss brushed their heads as they passed, straggling and unkempt as the beard of the old priest at Debra Maryam. Vervet monkeys chattered at them from the treetops and ducked their heads in wide-eyed outrage at the human intrusion into these secret places. Once a large animal crashed away through the undergrowth, and Nicholas glanced across at Boris.

The Russian shook his head, laughing. 'No, English, not dik-dik. Only kudu.'

On the hillside above them the kudu paused to look back. He was a large bull with full twists to his wide corkscrew horns, a magnificent beast with a maned dewlap and pricked ears shaped like trumpets. He stared at them with huge, startled eyes. Boris whistled softly and his attitude changed abruptly.

'Those horns are over fifty inches. They would get a place right at the top of *Rowland Ward*.' He was referring to the register of big game which was the Bible of the trophy hunter. 'Don't you want to take him, English?' He ran to the nearest mule and pulled the Rigby rifle from its slip case, then ran back and offered it to Nicholas.

'Let him go.' Nicholas shook his head. 'Only dik-dik for me.'

With a flirt of his white powder-puff tail, the bull was gone over the ridge. Boris shook his head disgustedly and spat into the river.

'Why did he try to insist that you kill it?' Royan demanded as they went on.

'A photograph of a record pair of horns like that would look good on his advertising brochure. Suck in more clients.'

All day they followed the winding trail, and in the late afternoon they camped in a clearing above the river where it was evident that other caravans had camped many times before them. It seemed obvious that this road was divided into time-honoured stages: every traveller took three full days from the top of the falls to reach the monastery, and they all camped at the same sites.

'Sorry. No shower here,' Boris told his clients. 'If you want to wash, there is a safe pool around the first bend upstream.'

Royan looked appealingly at Nicholas, 'I am so hot and sweaty. Please won't you stand guard for me, where you can hear me call if I need you?'

So he lay on the mossy bank just below the bend, out of sight but close enough to hear her splash and squeal at the cold embrace of the water. Once when he turned his head he realized that the current must have drifted her downstream, for through the trees he caught a flash of a naked back, and the curve of a buttock, creamy and glistening wet with water. He looked away again guiltily, but he was startled by the intensity of his physical arousal brought on by that brief glimpse of lambent skin dappled with the late sunlight through the trees.

When she came downstream along the bank, singing softly, towelling her wet hair, she called to him, 'Your turn. Do you want me to stand guard for you?'

'I am a big boy now.' He shook his head, but as she passed him he noticed the saucy glint in her eye, and he wondered suddenly if she had been fully aware of just how far downstream she had swum, and how much he had seen. He was titillated by the thought.

He went upstream to the pool alone, and as he stripped he looked down at himself and felt guilty when he saw how she had moved him. Since Rosalind, no other woman had had this effect on him.

'A nice cold plunge won't do you any harm, my lad.' He threw his jeans over a bush, and dived into the pool.

As they sat at the campfire after the evening meal, Nicholas looked up suddenly and cocked his head.

'Am I hearing things?' he wondered.

'No,' Tessay laughed. 'That is singing you hear. The priests from the monastery are coming to welcome us.'

They saw the torches then, winding up the hillside in procession, flickering through the trees as they approached the camp. The muleteers and the servants crowded forward, singing and clapping rhythmically to greet the deputation from the monastery.

The deep male voices soared and then dropped away, almost to a whisper, then rose again in descant, haunting and beautiful, the sound of Africa in the night. It drove icy thrills down Nicholas's spine, so that he shivered involuntarily.

Then they saw the white robes of the priests, flitting like moths in the torchlight as they wound along the trail. The camp servants fell on their knees as the first of the holy men entered the perimeter of the camp. They were young acolytes, bare-headed and bare-footed. They were followed by the monks, wearing long robes and tall turbans. Their ranks wheeled aside and opened up, an honour guard for the phalanx of deacons and fully ordained priests in their gaudy embroidered robes and vestments.

Each of them carried a heavy Coptic cross, set on a tall staff and intricately chased and worked in native silver. They in turn opened into two ranks, still chanting, and allowed the canopied palanquin to be carried forward by four hefty young acolytes and placed in the centre of the camp. The crimson and yellow silk curtains shimmered in the light of the camp lanterns and the torches of the procession.

'We must go forward to welcome the abbot,' Boris told Nicholas in a stage whisper. 'His name is Jali Hora.' As they stepped up to the litter, the curtains were drawn dramatically aside and a tall figure stepped down to earth.

Both Tessay and Royan sank to their knees respectfully, and clasped their hands at the breast. However, Nicholas and Boris remained on their feet, and Nicholas inspected the abbot with interest.

Jali Hora was skeletally thin. Beneath the skirts of his robe his legs were like sticks of cured tobacco, tar-black and twisted, with desiccated sinew and stringy muscle. His robe was green and gold, worked with gold thread that glittered in the firelight. On his head he wore a tall hat with a flat top embroidered with a pattern of crosses and stars.

The abbot's face was dead sooty black, the skin wrinkled and riven with the deep etchings of age. There were few teeth behind his puckered lips, and even those were yellowed and askew. His beard was startling silver white, breaking like storm surf on the old bones of his jaw. One eye was opaque blue and blinded with tropical ophthalmia, but the other eye glistened like that of a hunting leopard.

He began to speak in a high, quavering voice. 'A blessing,' Boris warned Nicholas, and they both bowed their heads respectfully. The assembled priests came in with the chanted response each time the old man paused.

When at last he had finished giving his blessing Jali Hora made the sign of the cross in four directions, rotating slowly towards each point of the compass, while two altar boys swung their silver censers vigorously, deluging the night with pungent clouds of incense smoke.

After the blessing the two women came forward to kneel before the abbot. He stooped over them and struck them lightly on each cheek with his silver cross, chanting a falsetto blessing over them.

'They say the old man is over a hundred years old,' Boris whispered to Nicholas.

Two white-robed *debteras* brought forward a stool of African ebony, so beautifully carved that Nicholas eyed it acquisitively. He guessed that it was probably centuries old, and would have made a handsome addition to the museum collection. The two *debteras* took Jali Hora's elbows and gently seated him on the stool. Then the rest of the company sank to the earth in a congregation around him, their black faces lifted towards him attentively.

Tessay sat at his feet, and when her husband spoke she translated quietly for him into Amharic. 'It is a great pleasure and an honour for me to greet you again, Holy Father.'

The old man nodded, and Boris went on, 'I have brought an English nobleman of royal blood to visit the monastery of St Frumentius.'

'I say, steady on, old boy!' Nicholas protested, but all the congregation studied him with expectant interest.

'What do I do now?' he asked Boris out of the corner of his mouth.

'What do you think he came all this way for?' Boris grinned maliciously. 'He wants a gift. Money.'

'Maria Theresa dollars?' he enquired, referring to the centuries-old traditional currency of Ethiopia.

'Not necessarily. Times have changed. Jali Hora will be happy to take Yankee green-backs.'

'How much?'

'You are a nobleman of royal blood. You will be hunting in his valley. Five hundred dollars at least.'

Nicholas winced and went to fetch his bag from one of the mule panniers. When he came back he bowed to the abbot and placed the sheaf of currency in his outstretched, pink-palmed claw. The abbot smiled, exposing the yellow stumps of his teeth, and spoke briefly.

Tessay translated for him, 'He says, "Welcome to the monastery of St Frumentius and the season of Timkat." He wishes you good hunting on the banks of the Abbay river.'

Immediately the solemn mood of the devout company changed. They broke out in smiles and laughter, and the abbot looked expectantly at Boris.

'The holy abbot says it has been a thirsty journey,' Tessay translated.

'The old devil loves his brandy,' Boris explained, and shouted to the camp butler. With some ceremony a bottle of brandy was brought and placed on the camp table in front of the abbot, shoulder to shoulder with the bottle of vodka in front of Boris. They toasted each other, and the abbot tossed back a dram that made his good eye weep with tears, and his voice husky as he directed a question at Royan.

'He asks you, Woizero Royan, where do you come from, daughter, that you follow the true path of Christ the Saviour of man?'

'I am an Egyptian, of the old religion,' Royan replied. The abbot and all his priests nodded and beamed with approval.

'We are all brothers and sisters in Christ, the Egyptians and the Ethiopians,' the abbot told her. 'Even the word Coptic derives from the Greek for Egyptian. For over sixteen hundred years the Abuna, the bishop, of Ethiopia was always appointed by the Patriarch in Cairo. Only the Emperor Haile Selassie changed that in 1959, but we still follow the true road to Christ. You are welcome, my daughter.'

His *debtera* poured another dram of brandy and the old man swallowed it at a gulp. Even Boris looked impressed, 'Where does the skinny old black tortoise put it?' he wondered aloud. Tessay did not translate, but she lowered her eyes and the hurt she felt for the insult to the holy man showed on her madonna features.

Jali Hora turned to Nicholas. 'He wants to know what animals you have come to hunt here in his valley,' Tessay told him.

Nicholas steeled himself and then replied carefully. There was a long moment of disbelief, then the abbot cackled happily and the assembled priests shouted with incredulous mirth.

'A dik-dik! You have come to hunt a dik-dik! But there is no meat on an animal that size.'

Nicholas let them get over the first shock, and then produced a photograph of the mounted specimen of *Moquoda harperii* from the museum. He placed it on the table in front of Jali Hora.

'This is no ordinary dik-dik. It is a holy dik-dik,' he told them in portentous tones, nodding at Tessay for the translation. 'Let me recount the legend.' They were silenced by the prospect of a good story with religious overtones. Even the abbot arrested the glass on its way to his lips and replaced it on the table. His one eye swivelled from the photograph to Nicholas's face.

'When John the Baptist was dying of starvation in the desert,' Nicholas began, and a few of the priests crossed themselves at the mention of the saint's name, 'he had been thirty days and thirty nights without a morsel passing his lips—' Nicholas spun out the yarn for a while, dwelling on the extremities of hunger endured by the saint, details savoured by his audience who liked their holy men to suffer in the name of righteousness.

'In the end the Lord took mercy on his servant and placed a small antelope in a thicket of acacia, held fast by the thorns. He said unto the saint: "I have prepared a meal for you that you shall not die. Take of this meat and eat." Where John the Baptist touched the small creature, the marks of his thumb and fingers were imprinted upon its back for all time, and all generations to come.' They were silent and impressed.

Nicholas passed the photograph to the abbot. 'See the prints of the saint's fingers upon it.'

The old man studied the print avidly, holding it up to his single eye, and at last he exclaimed, 'It is true. The marks of the saint's fingers are clear to see.'

He passed it to his deacons. Encouraged by the abbot's endorsement, they exclaimed and wondered over the picture of the insignificant creature in its coat of striped fur.

'Have any of your men ever laid eyes upon one of these animals?' Nicholas demanded, and one after the other they shook their heads. The photograph completed the circle and was passed to the rank of squatting acolytes.

Suddenly one of them leaped to his feet prancing, brandishing the photograph and gibbering with excitement.

'I have seen this holy creature! With my very own eyes, I have seen it.' He was a young boy, barely adolescent.

There were cries of derision and disbelief from the others. One of them snatched the print from the boy's grasp and waved it out of his reach, taunting him with it.

'The child is soft in the head, and often possessed by demons and fits,' Jali Hora explained sorrowfully. 'Take no notice of him, poor Tamre!'

Tamre's eyes were wild as he ran down the rank of acolytes, trying desperately to recapture the photograph. But they passed it back and forth, keeping it just out of his reach, teasing him and jeering at his antics.

Nicholas rose to his feet to intervene. He found this taunting of a weak-minded lad offensive, but at that moment something tripped in the boy's mind, and he fell to the ground as though struck down by a club. His back arched and his limbs twitched and jerked uncontrollably, his eyes rolled back into his skull until only the whites showed, and white froth creamed on his lips that were drawn back in a grinning rictus.

Before Nicholas could go to him, four of his peers picked him up bodily and carried him away. Their laughter dwindled into the night. The others acted as though this was nothing out of the ordinary, and Jali Hora nodded to his *debtera* to refill his glass.

It was late when at last Jali Hora took his leave and was helped into the palanquin by his deacons. He took the remains of the brandy with him, clutching the half-empty bottle in one clawed hand and tossing out benedictions with the other.

'You made a good impression, Milord English,' Boris told him. 'He liked your story of John the Baptist, but he liked your money even more.'

When they set out the next morning, the path followed the river for a while. But within a mile the waters quickened their pace, and then raced through the narrow opening between high red cliffs and plunged over another waterfall.

Nicholas left the well-trodden trail and went down to the brink of the falls. He looked down two hundred feet into a deep cleft in the rock, only just wide enough to allow the angry river to squeeze through. He could have thrown a stone across the gap. There was no path nor foothold in that chasm, and he turned back and rejoined the rest of the caravan as it detoured away from the river and into another thickly wooded valley.

'This was probably once the course of the Dandera river, before it cut a fresh bed for itself through the chasm.' Royan pointed to the high ground on each side of the path, and then to the water-worn boulders that littered the trail.

'I think you are right,' Nicholas agreed. 'These cliffs seem to be an intrusion of limestone through the basalt and sandstone. The whole area has been severely faulted and cut up by erosion and the ever-changing river. You can be certain that those limestone cliffs are riddled with caves and springs.'

Now the trail descended rapidly towards the Blue Nile, falling away almost fifteen hundred feet in altitude in the last few miles. The sides of the valley were heavily covered with vegetation and at many places small springs of water oozed from the limestone and trickled down the old river bed.

The heat built up steadily as they went down, and soon even Royan's khaki shirt was stained with dark patches of sweat between her shoulder blades.

At one stage a freshet of clear water gushed from an area of dense bush high up the hillside and swelled the stream into a small river. Then they turned a corner of the valley and found that they and the stream had rejoined the main flow of the Dandera river. Looking back up the gorge, they could see where the river had emerged from the chasm through a narrow archway in the cliff. The rock surrounding the cleft was a peculiar pink in colour, smooth and polished, folded back upon itself, so that it resembled the mucous membrane on the inside of a pair of human lips.

The rock was of such an unusual colour and texture that they were both struck by it. They turned aside to study it while the mules went on downwards, the clatter of their receding hoofbeats and the voices of the men echoing and reverberating weirdly in this confined and unearthly place.

'It looks like some monstrous gargoyle, gushing water through its mouth,' Royan whispered, looking up at the cleft and at those strange rock formations. 'I can imagine how the ancient Egyptians, led by Taita and Prince Memnon, would have been moved if they had ever reached this place. What mystical connotations would they have attributed to such a natural phenomenon!'

Nicholas was silent, studying her face. Her eyes were dark with awe, and her expression solemn. In this setting she reminded him strongly of a portrait that he had in his collection at Quenton Park. It was a fragment of a fresco from the Valley of the Kings, depicting a Ramessidian princess.

'Why should that surprise you?' he asked himself. 'The very same blood runs in her veins.'

She turned to face him, 'Give me hope, Nicky. Tell me that I have not dreamed all this. Tell me that we are going to find what we are looking for, and that we are going to vindicate Duraid's death.'

Her face was up-turned to his, and it seemed to glow under the light dew of perspiration and the strength of her commitment. He was seized by an almost overwhelming urge to take her up in his arms and kiss those moistly parted lips, but instead he turned away and started down the trail.

He dared not look back at her until he had himself fully under control. After a while he heard her quick, light tread on the rock behind him. They went on down in silence, and he was so preoccupied that he was unprepared for the sudden stunning vista that opened abruptly before them.

They stood high on a ledge above the sub-gorge of the Nile. Below them was a mighty cauldron of red rock five hundred feet deep. The main flow of the legendary river plunged in a green torrent into the shadowy abyss. It was so deep that the sunlight did not reach down into it. Beside them the sparser waters of the Dandera river took the same leap, falling white as an egret's feather, twisting and blowing in the false wind of the gorge. In the depths the waters mingled, churning and roiling together in a welter of foam, turning upon themselves like a great wheel, weighty and viscous as oil, until at last they found the exit gorge and tore away down it with irresistible force and power.

'You sailed through that in a boat?' Royan asked, with awe in her voice.

'We were young and foolish, then,' Nicholas said with a sad little smile that was haunted by old memories.

They were silent for a long while. Then Royan said softly, 'One can see how this would have stopped Taita and his prince as they came upstream.' She looked about her, and then pointed down the gorge towards the west. 'They certainly could never have come up the sub-gorge itself. They must have followed the line of the top of the cliffs, right along here where we are standing.' Her voice took on an edge of excitement at the thought.

'Unless they came up the other side of the river,' Nicholas suggested to tease her, and her face fell.

'I hadn't thought of that. Of course it's possible. How would we ever cross over, if we find no evidence on this side?'

'Let's consider that only when it's forced upon us. We have enough to contend with as it is, without looking for more hardships.'

Again they were silent, both of them considering the magnitude and uncertainty of the task that they had taken on. Then Royan roused herself.

'Where is the monastery? I can see no sign of it.'

'It's in the cliff right under our feet.'

'Will we camp down there?'

'I doubt it. Let's catch up with Boris and find out what he intends to do.'

They followed the trail along the edge of the cauldron, and came up

104

with the mule caravan at a spot where the track forked. One branch turned away from the river into a wooded depression, while the other still hugged the rimrock.

Boris was waiting for them, and he indicated the track that led away from the river. 'There is a good campsite up there in the trees where I stayed last time I hunted down here.'

There were several tall wild fig trees throwing shade across this glade, and a spring of fresh water at the head. To minimize the loads, Boris had not carried tents down into the gorge. So as soon as the mules were unloaded he set his men to building three small thatched huts for their accommodation, and to digging a pit latrine well away from the spring.

While this work was going on, Nicholas beckoned to Royan and Tessay, and the three of them set off to explore the monastery. Where the trail forked, Tessay led them along the path that skirted the cliff top, and soon they came to a broad rock staircase that descended the cliff face.

There was a party of white-robed monks coming up the stone stairway, and Tessay stopped briefly to chat to them. As they went on she told Nicholas and Royan, 'Today is Katera, the eve of the festival of Timkat, which begins tomorrow. They are very excited. It is one of the major events of the religious year.'

'What does the festival celebrate?' Royan asked. 'It is not part of the Church calendar in Egypt.'

'It's the Ethiopian Epiphany, celebrating the baptism of Christ,' Tessay explained. 'During the ceremony the *tabot* will be taken down to the river to be rededicated and revitalized, and the acolytes will receive baptism, as did Jesus Christ at the hand of the Baptist.'

They followed the staircase down the sheer cliff face. The treads of the steps had been dished by the passage of bare feet over the centuries. Down they went, with the great cauldron of the Nile boiling and hissing and steaming with spray hundreds of feet below them.

Suddenly they came out on to a wide terrace that had been hewn by man's hand from the living rock. The red rock overhung it, forming a roof to the cloister with arches of stone left in place by the ancient builders to support it. The interior wall of the long covered terrace was riddled with the entrances to the catacombs beyond. Over the ages the cliff face had been mined and burrowed to form the halls and cells, the vestibules, churches and shrines of the monastic community which had inhabited them for well over a thousand years.

There were groups of monks seated along the length of the terrace. Some of them were listening to one of the deacons reading aloud from an illuminated copy of the scriptures.

'So many of them are illiterate,' Tessay sighed. 'The Bible must be read and explained to even the monks, for most of them are unable to read it for themselves.'

'This was what the Church of Constantine was like, the Church of Byzantium,' Nicholas pointed out quietly. 'It remains the Church of cross and book, of elaborate and sumptuous ritual in a predominantly illiterate world today.'

As they wandered slowly down the cloister they passed other seated groups who, under the direction of a precentor, were chanting and singing the Amharic psalms and hymns. From the interior of the cells and caves there came the hum of voices raised in prayer or supplication, and the air was thick with the smell of human occupation that had taken place over hundreds of years.

It was the smell of wood smoke and incense, of stale food and excrement, of sweat and piety, of suffering and of sickness. Amongst the groups of monks were the pilgrims who had made the journey, or been carried by their relatives, down into the gorge to make petition to the saint, or to seek from him a cure for their disease and suffering.

There were blind children weeping in their mothers' arms, and lepers with the flesh rotting and falling from their bones, and still others in the coma of sleeping sickness or some other terrible tropical affliction. Their whines and moans of agony blended with the chanting of the monks, and with the distant clamour of the Nile as it cascaded into the cauldron.

They came at last to the entrance to the cavern cathedral of St Frumentius. It was a circular opening like the mouth of a fish, but the surrounds of the portals were painted with a dense border of stars and crosses, and of saintly heads. The portraits were primitive, and rendered in ochre and soft earthy tones that were all the more appealing for their childlike simplicity. The eyes of the saints were huge and outlined in charcoal, their expressions tranquil and benign.

A deacon in a grubby green velvet robe guarded the entrance, but when Tessay spoke to him he smiled and nodded and gestured for them to enter. The lintel was low and Nicholas had to duck his head to pass under it, but on the far side he raised it again to look about him in amazement.

The roof of the cavern was so high that it was lost in the gloom. The rock walls were covered with murals, a celestial host of angels and archangels who flickered and wavered in the light of the candles and oil lamps. They were partially obscured by the long tapestry banners that hung down the walls, grimy with incense soot, their fringes frayed and tattered. On one of these St Michael rode a prancing white horse, on another the Virgin knelt at the foot of the cross, while above her the pale body of Christ bled from the wound of the Roman spear in his side.

This was the outer nave of the church. In the far wall the doorway to the middle chamber was guarded by a massive pair of wooden doors that stood open. The three of them crossed the stone floor, picking their way between the kneeling petitioners and pilgrims in their rags and tatters, in their misery and their religious ecstasy. In the feeble light of the lamps and the blue haze of incense smoke they seemed lost souls languishing eternally in the outer darkness of purgatory.

The visitors reached the set of three stone steps that led up to the inner doors, but their way was blocked at the threshold by two robed deacons in tall, flat-topped hats. One of these addressed Tessay sternly.

'They will not even let us enter the *qiddist*, the middle chamber,' Tessay told them regretfully. 'Beyond that lies the *maqdas*, the Holy of Holies.'

They peered past the guards, and in the gloom of the *qiddist* could just make out the door to the inner sanctum.

'Only the ordained priests are allowed to enter the *maqdas*, for it contains the *tabot* and the entrance to the tomb of the saint.'

Disappointed and frustrated, they made their way out of the cavern and back along the terrace.

They ate their dinner under a sky full of stars. The air was still stiflingly hot, and clouds of mosquitoes hovered just out of range of the repellents with which they had all smeared their exposed skin.

'And so, English, I have got you where you wanted to be. Now, how are you going to find this animal that you have come so far to hunt?' The vodka was making Boris belligerent again.

'At first light I want you to send out your trackers to work the country downstream from here,' Nicholas told him. 'Dik-dik are usually active in the early morning, and again late in the afternoon.'

'You are teaching your grandpapa to skin a cat,' said Boris, mangling the metaphor. He poured himself another vodka.

'Tell them to check for spoor.' Nicholas deliberately laboured his point. 'I imagine that the tracks of the striped variety will look very similar to those of the common dik-dik. If they find indications, then they must sit quietly along the edge of the thickest patches of bush and watch for any movement of the animals. Dik-dik are very territorial. They won't stray far from their own turf.'

'Da! Da! I will tell them. But what will you do? Will you spend the day in camp with the ladies, English?' He grinned slyly. 'If you are lucky, you may soon not need separate huts?' He guffawed at his own wit, and Tessay looked distressed and stood up with the excuse that she was going to the kitchen hut to supervise the chef.

Nicholas ignored the boorish pleasantry. 'Royan and I will work the riverine bush along the banks of the Dandera river. It looked very promising habitat for dik-dik. Warn your people to keep clear of the river. I don't want the game disturbed.'

They left camp the next morning in the glimmer of the dawn. Nicholas carried the Rigby rifle and a light day pack, and led Royan along the bank of the Dandera. They moved slowly, stopping every dozen paces to look and listen. The thickets were alive with the sounds and movements of the small mammals and birds.

'The Ethiopians do not have a hunting tradition, and I imagine the monks never disturb the wildlife here in the gorge.' He pointed to the tracks of a small antelope in the moist earth of the bank. 'Bushbuck,' he told her. 'Menelik's bushbuck. Unique to this part of the world. A much sought-after trophy.'

'Do you really expect to find your great-grandfather's dik-dik?' she asked. 'You seemed so determined when you discussed it with Boris.'

'Of course not,' he grinned. 'I think the old man made it up. It should rather have been named Harper's chimera. It probably was the skin of a striped mongoose that he used after all. We Harpers didn't get on in the world by always sticking to the literal truth.'

They paused to watch a Tacazze sunbird fluttering over a bunch of yellow blossoms on a creeper high above them in the canopy of the riverine forest. The tiny bird's plumage sparkled like a tiara of emeralds.

'Still, it gives us a wonderful excuse to fossick about in the bushes.' He glanced back to make certain that they were well clear of the camp, and then gestured for her to sit beside him on a fallen treetrunk. 'So, let's get it clear in our minds what we are looking for. You tell me.'

'We are looking for the remains of a funerary temple, or the ruins of the necropolis where the workers lived while they were excavating Pharaoh Mamose's tomb.'

'Any sort of masonry or stonework,' he agreed, 'especially some sort of column or monument.'

'Taita's stone testament,' she nodded. 'It should be engraved or chiselled with hieroglyphics. Probably badly weathered, fallen over, covered with vegetation – I don't know. Anything at all. We are fishing blind in dark waters.'

'Well, why are we still sitting here? Let's start fishing.'

In the middle of the morning Nicholas found the tracks of a dik-dik along the river bank. They took up a position against the bole of one of the big trees and sat quietly for a while in the shadows of the forest, until at last they were rewarded by a glimpse of one of the tiny creatures. It passed close to where they sat, wriggling its trunklike proboscis, stepping daintily on elfin hooves, nipping a leaf from a low-hanging

108

branch, and munching it busily. However, its coat was a uniform drab grey, unrelieved by stripes of any kind.

When it disappeared into the undergrowth, Nicholas stood up. 'No luck. Common variety,' he whispered. 'Let's get on.'

A little after noon they reached the spot where the river issued from between the pink flesh-coloured cliffs of the chasm. They explored these as far as they were able before their way was blocked by the cliffs. The rock fell straight into the flood, and there was no foothold at the water's edge that would allow them to penetrate further.

They retreated downstream, and crossed to the far bank over a primitive suspension bridge of lianas and hairy flax rope that Nicholas guessed had been built by the monks from the monastery. Once again they tried to push on into the chasm. Nicholas even attempted to wade around the first buttress of pink rock that barred the way, but the current was too strong and threatened to sweep him off his feet. He was forced to abandon the attempt.

'If we can't get through there, then it's highly unlikely that Taita and his workmen would have done so.'

They went back as far as the hanging bridge and found a shady place close to the water to eat the lunch that Tessay had packed for them. The heat in the middle of the day was stupefying. Royan wet her cotton neckerchief in the river and dabbed at her face as she lay beside him.

Nicholas lay on his back and studied every inch of the pink cliffs through his binoculars. He was looking for any cleft or opening in their smooth polished surfaces.

He spoke without lowering the binoculars. 'Reading *River God*, it looks as if Taita actually enlisted help to switch the bodies of Tanus, Great Lion of Egypt, and the Pharaoh himself.' He lowered the glasses and looked at Royan. 'I find that puzzling, for it would have been an outrageous thing to do in terms of his period and belief. Is that a fair translation of the scrolls? Did Taita truly switch the bodies?'

She laughed and rolled over to face him. 'Your old chum Wilbur has an overheated imagination. The only basis for that whole bit of story-telling is a single line in the scrolls. "*To me he was more a king than ever Pharaoh had been.*"' She rolled on to her back again. 'That is a good example of my objection to the book. He mixes fact and fantasy into an inextricable stew. As far as I know and believe, Tanus rests in his own tomb and the Pharaoh in his.'

'Pity!' Nicholas sighed and stuffed the book back in his pack. 'It was a romantic little touch that I enjoyed.' He glanced at his wrist-watch and stood up. 'Come on, I want to do a recce down the other spur of the valley. I spotted some interesting ground up there whilst we were on the approach march yesterday.'

It was late afternoon when they arrived back at the camp, and Tessay hurried out of her kitchen hut to greet them.

'I have been waiting for you to return. We have had an interesting invitation from Jali Hora, the abbot. He has invited us to a banquet in the monastery to celebrate Katera, the eve of Timkat. The servants have set up your shower, and the water is hot. There is just time for you to change before we go down to the monastery.'

T he abbot sent a party of young acolytes to escort them to the banqueting hall. These young men arrived in the short African twilight, carrying torches to light the way.

Royan recognized one of these as Tamre, the epileptic boy. When she singled him out for her warmest smile, he came forward shyly and offered her a bouquet of wild flowers that he had picked from beside the river. She was unprepared for this courtesy, and without thinking she thanked him in Arabic.

'Shukran.'

'Taffadali,' the boy replied immediately, using the correct gender of the response, and in an accent that told her instantly that he was fluent in her language.

'How do you speak Arabic so well?' she asked, intrigued.

The boy hung his head with embarrassment and mumbled, 'My mother is from Massawa, on the Red Sea. It is the language of my childhood.'

When they set off for the monastery, the boy monk followed Royan like a puppy.

Once more they descended the stairway down the cliff and came out on to the torchlit terrace. The narrow cloisters were packed with humanity, and as they made their way through the press, with the honour guard of acolytes clearing a way for them, black faces called Amharic greetings and black hands reached out to touch them.

They stooped through the low entrance to the outer nave of the cathedral. The chamber was lit with oil lamps and torches, so that the murals of saints and angels danced in the uncertain light. The stone floor was covered with a carpet of freshly cut reeds and rushes, their sweet herbal perfume leavening the heavy, smoky air. It seemed that the entire brotherhood of monks were seated cross-legged on this spongy carpet. They greeted the entrance of the little party of ferengi with cries of welcome and shouts of benediction. Beside each seated figure stood a flask of tej, the honey mead of the country. It was clear from the happy, sweaty faces that the flasks had already done good service.

The visitors were led forward to a spot that had been left clear for them directly in front of the wooden doors to the *qiddist*, the middle chamber. Their escort urged them to sit and make themselves comfortable in this space. As soon as they were settled, another party of acolytes came in from the terrace bearing flasks of *tej*, and knelt to place a separate pottery flask in front of each of them.

Tessay leaned across to whisper, 'Better you let me sample this *tej* before you try it. The strength and colour and taste vary in every place that it is served, and some of it is ferocious.' She raised her flask and drank directly from the elongated neck. When she lowered the flask she smiled, 'This is a good brew. If you are careful, you will be all right with it.'

The monks seated around them were urging them to drink, and Nicholas raised his flask. The monks clapped and laughed as he tasted the liquor. It was light and pleasant, with a strong bouquet of wild honey. 'Not bad!' he gave his opinion, but Tessay warned him, 'Later they will almost certainly offer you *katikala*. Be very careful of that! It is distilled from fermented grain and it will take your head off at the shoulders.'

The monks were concentrating their hospitality on Royan now. The fact that she was a Coptic Christian, a true believer, had impressed them. It was obvious also that her beauty had not gone entirely unremarked by this company of holy and celibate men.

Nicholas leaned close to her, and whispered, 'You will have to fake it for their benefit. Hold it up to your lips and pretend to swallow, or they will not leave you in peace.'

As she lifted the flask the monks hooted with delight and saluted her with their own upraised flasks. She lowered the flask again, and whispered to Nicholas.

'It's delicious. It tastes of honey.'

'You broke your vow of abstinence!' he chided her laughing. 'Did you?'

'Just a drop,' she admitted, 'and anyway I never made any vows.'

The acolytes knelt in turn in front of each guest, offering them a bowl of hot water in which to wash their right hands in preparation for the feast.

Suddenly there was the sound of music and drums, and a band of musicians filed through the open doors of the *qiddist*. They took up their positions along the side walls of the chamber, while the congregation craned expectantly to peer into its dim interior.

At last Jali Hora, the ancient abbot, appeared at the head of the steps. He wore a full-length robe of crimson satin, with a gold thread-embroidered stole around his shoulders. On his head was a massive

111

crown. Though it glittered like gold, Nicholas knew that it was gilt brass, and the multi-coloured stones with which it was set were just as certainly glass and paste.

Jali Hora raised his crook, which was surmounted by an ornate silver cross, and a weighty silence fell upon the company.

'Now he will say the grace,' Tessay told them, and bowed her head.

Jali Hora's grace was fervent and lengthy, his reedy falsetto punctuated by devout responses from the monks. When at last he came to the end, two splendidly robed *debteras* helped Jali Hora down the stairs and seated him on his carved *jimmera* stool at the head of the circle of senior deacons and priests.

The religious mood of the monks changed to one of festive bonhomie as a procession of acolytes entered from the terrace, each of them bearing upon his head a flat woven reed basket the size of a wagon wheel. They placed one of these in the centre of each circle of guests.

Then at a signal from Jali Hora, acting in unison they whipped the lid off each basket. A jovial cheer went up from the monks, for each basket contained a shallow brass bowl that was filled from rim to rim with round sheets of the flat grey unleavened *injera* bread.

Two acolytes staggered in from the terrace, barely able to carry between them a steaming brass pot filled with gallons of *wat*, a spicy stew of fat mutton. Over each of the bowls of *injera* bread they tipped the great pot and slopped gouts of the runny red-brown *wat*, the surface glistening with hot grease.

The assembly fell on the food voraciously. They tore off wads of *injera* and scooped up the mess of *wat* with it, and then stuffed the parcel into their open mouths, which remained open as they chewed. They washed it down with long swallows from the *tej* flasks, before wrapping themselves another parcel of running *wat*. Soon every one of them was greasy to the elbow and their chins were smeared thickly, as they chewed and drank and shouted with laughter.

The serving acolytes dumped thick cakes of another type of *injera* beside each guest. These were stiffer and less yeasty in taste, friable and crumbling, unlike the latex rubber consistency of the thin grey sheets of the first kind.

Nicholas and Royan tried to show their appreciation of the food without coating themselves with layers of it as the others were doing. Despite its appearance the *wat* was really rather tasty, and the dry yellow *injera* helped to cut the grease.

The communal brass bowls were emptied in remarkably short order. Only the churned up mess of bread and grease remained when the acolytes came tottering in under the weight of another set of pots, this time filled to overflowing with curried chicken *wat*. This was splashed into the bowls on top of the remains of the mutton, and again the monks had at it.

While they gobbled up the chicken, the *tej* flasks were replenished and the monks became more raucous.

'I don't think I can take much more of this,' Royan told Nicholas queasily.

'Close your eyes and think of England,' he advised her. 'You are the star of the evening. They aren't going to let you escape.'

As soon as the chicken was eaten, the servers were back with fresh pots, this time brimming with fiery beef *wat*. They dumped this on the remnants of both the mutton and the chicken.

The monk in the circle opposite Royan emptied his flask, and when an acolyte tried to refill it, he waved the lad away with a shout of, '*Katikala!*'

The cry was taken up by the other monks. '*Katikala! Katikala!*'

The acolytes hurried out and returned with dozens of bottles of the gin-clear liquor and brass bowls the size of tea cups.

'This is the stuff to be careful of,' Tessay told them. Surreptitiously both Nicholas and Royan were able to dribble the contents of their bowls into the mat of reeds on which they were sitting, but the monks guzzled theirs down greedily.

'Boris is getting his share,' Nicholas remarked to Royan. The Russian was red-faced and sweating, grinning like an idiot as he downed another bowlful.

Enlivened by the *katikala* the monks started playing a game. One of them would wrap a packet of beef *wat* with a sheet of *injera*, and then, as it dripped fat from his poised right hand, he would turn to the monk beside. The victim would open his mouth until his jaws were at full stretch, and the packet would be stuffed into it by his considerate neighbour. The morsel was, of course, as large as a human gape could possibly accommodate, and in order to engulf it the victim had to risk death by asphyxiation.

The rules of the game seemed to be that he was not allowed to use his hands to get it into his own mouth, neither should he dribble down the front of his robe, nor splutter gravy over those seated near to him. His contortions, together with his gulping and choking and gasping for air, were the source of uncontrollable hilarity. When at last he succeeded in getting it down, a brass bowl of *katikala* was held to his lips as a reward. He was expected to send the contents in the same direction as the parcel of *injera*.

Jali Hora, by now warmed with *tej* and *katikala*, lurched to his feet. In his right hand he held aloft a streaming parcel of *injera*. As he began an unsteady progress across the chamber, with his shiny crown awry, they did not at first realize his intentions. The entire company watched him with interest.

Then suddenly Royan stiffened and whispered with horror, 'No! Please, no. Save me, Nicky. Don't let this happen to me.'

'This is the price you pay for being the leading lady,' he told her. Jali Hora was making his rather erratic way towards where she sat. The gravy from the morsel he carried for her was trickling down his forearm and dripping from his elbow.

The band standing along the side wall struck up a lively air. As the abbot came to a halt in front of Royan, rocking on his suspension like an ancient carriage, they fiddled and fifed and the drummers broke out in a frenzy.

The abbot presented his gift, and with one last despairing glance at Nicholas Royan faced the inevitable. She closed her eyes and opened her mouth.

To roars of encouragement and the urgings of fife and drum, she struggled and chewed. Her face turned rosy and her eyes watered. At one point Nicholas thought she would have to admit defeat and spit it out on to the reed-covered floor. But slowly and courageously, a bit at a time, she forced it down and then fell back exhausted.

Her audience, clapping and hooting, loved every moment of it. The abbot sank stiffly to his knees in front of her and embraced her, almost losing his crown in the process. Then without relinquishing his embrace, he made himself a place beside her.

'It looks as though you have made another conquest,' Nicholas told her dryly. 'I think he will be on your lap at any moment, if you don't duck and run.'

Royan reacted swiftly. She reached across and grabbed a bottle of *katikala*, and a bowl which she filled to the brim.

'Drink it up, Pops!' she told him, and held the bowl to his lips. Jali Hora accepted the challenge, but he had to release her to drink from her hand.

Suddenly Royan started so violently that she spilled what was left in the bowl down the old man's robe. The blood drained from her face and she began to tremble as though in a high fever as she stared at Jali Hora's crown, which had slipped forward over his eyes.

'What is it?' Nicholas demanded quietly but urgently, and he reached across to steady her with a hand on her arm. Nobody else in the chamber had noticed her distress, but he was fully attuned to her moods by now.

Still staring ashen-faced at the crown, she dropped the bowl and reached down and grasped his wrist. He was startled by her strength. Her grip was painful, and he saw that she had driven her nails into his flesh so hard that she had broken the skin.

'Look at his crown! The jewel! The blue jewel!' she gasped.

He saw it then, amongst the gaudy shards of glass and pebbles of semi-precious garnets and rock crystal. The size of a silver dollar, it was a seal of blue ceramic, perfectly round, and baked to a hard, impervious finish. In the centre of the disc was an etching of an Egyptian war chariot, and above it the distinctive and unmistakable outline of the hawk with the broken wing. Around the circumference was a legend engraved in hieroglyphics. It took him only a few moments to read it to himself:

I COMMAND TEN THOUSAND CHARIOTS.
I AM TAITA, MASTER OF THE ROYAL HORSE.

Royan desperately wanted to escape from the oppressive atmosphere of the cavern. The parcel of *wat* that the abbot had forced upon her had mixed heavily with the few mouthfuls of *tej* she had swallowed, and this feeling in turn was aggravated by the smell of the dirty food bowls thick with congealing grease and the fumes of raw *katikala*. Already some of the monks were puking drunk, and the smell of vomit added to the cloying miasma of incense smoke within the chamber.

However, she was still the centre of the abbot's attention. He sat beside her stroking her bare arm and reciting garbled extracts from the Amharic scriptures; Tessay had long ago given up translating for her. Royan looked hopefully at Nicholas but he was withdrawn and silent, seeming oblivious of his surroundings. She knew that he was thinking about the ceramic seal in the abbot's crown, for his eyes kept returning thoughtfully to it.

She wanted to be alone with him to discuss this extraordinary discovery. Her excitement outweighed the distress of her overloaded stomach. She felt her cheeks flushed with it. Every time she looked up at the old man's crown her heart fluttered, and she had to make an effort to stop herself reaching up, seizing the shiny blue seal and ripping it from its setting to examine it more closely.

She knew how unwise it was to draw attention to the scrap of ceramic, but when she glanced across the circle she saw that Boris was far past noticing anything other than the bowl of *katikala* in his hand. In the end it was Boris who gave her the excuse for which she had been seeking. He tried to get to his feet, but his legs collapsed under him. He sagged forward quite gracefully, and his face dropped into the bowl of grease-sodden *injera* bread. He lay there snoring noisily, and Tessay appealed to Nicholas.

'Alto Nicholas, what am I to do?'

Nicholas considered the unlovely spectacle of the prostrate hunter. There were scraps of bread and beef stew sticking like confetti in his cropped ginger hair.

'I rather suspect Prince Charming has had enough for one night,' he murmured.

He stood up, stooped over Boris and gripped one wrist. With a sudden jerk he lifted him into a sitting position, and then heaved him upright and over his shoulder in a fireman's lift.

'Good night, all!' he told the assembled monks, very few of whom were in any condition to respond. Then he carried Boris away, draped over his shoulders with head and feet dangling. The two women had to hurry to keep up with Nicholas as he strode down the terrace and then up the stone stairway without a pause.

'I did not realize Alto Nicholas was so strong,' Tessay panted, for the stairs were steep and the pace was hard.

'I didn't either,' Royan admitted. She experienced a ridiculous proprietary pride in his feat, and smiled at herself in the darkness as they approached the camp.

'Don't be silly,' she admonished herself. 'He isn't yours to boast about.'

Nicholas threw his burden down on Boris's own bed in the thatched hut and stood back panting heavily, the sweat trickling down his cheeks.

'That's a pretty good recipe for a heart attack,' he gasped.

Boris groaned, rolled over and vomited copiously over his pillows and bedlinen.

'On that pleasant note I will bid you all goodnight and sweet dreams,' Nicholas told Tessay, stepping out of the hut into the warm African night.

He breathed in the smell of the forest and the river with relief, and then turned to Royan as she gripped his arm.

'Did you see—' she burst out excitedly, but he laid his fingers on her lips to silence her, and with a cautionary frown in the direction of Boris's hut led her away to her own hut.

'Did you see it?' she demanded, unable to contain herself longer. 'Could you read it?'

'"I command ten thousand chariots,"' he recited.

'"I am Taita, master of the royal horse,"' she completed it for him. 'He was here. Oh, Nicky! He was here. Taita was here. That's the proof we wanted. Now we know that we are not wasting our time.'

She flopped down on her camp bed and hugged herself ecstatically. 'Do you think the abbot will let us examine the seal?'

He shook his head, 'My guess is no. The crown is one of the monastery treasures. Even for you, his favourite lady, I don't think he would do it. Anyway, it would not be wise to show any great interest in it. Jali Hora obviously does not have any idea of its significance. Apart from that, we don't want to alert Boris.'

'I suppose you are right.' She moved over on the bed to make room for him. 'Sit down.'

He sat down beside her, and she asked, 'Where do you suppose the seal came from? Who found it? Where, and when?'

'Steady on, dear girl. That's four questions in one, and I don't have an answer to any of them.'

'Guess!' she invited him. 'Speculate! Throw some ideas around!'

'Very well,' he agreed. 'The seal was manufactured in Hong Kong. There is a little factory there that turns them out by the thousands. Jali Hora bought it from a souvenir store in Luxor when he was on holiday in Egypt last month.'

She punched his arm, hard. 'Be serious,' she ordered.

'Let's hear if you can do better,' he invited her, rubbing his arm.

'Okay, here I go. Taita dropped the seal here in the gorge while he was working on the construction of Pharaoh's tomb. Three thousand years later an old monk, one of the very first to live here at the monastery, picked it up. Of course, he could not read the hieroglyphics. He took it to the abbot, who declared it to be a relic of St Frumentius, and had it set in the crown.'

'And they all lived happily ever after,' Nicholas agreed. 'Not a bad shot.'

'Can you find any holes?' she demanded, and he shook his head. 'Then you agree that this proves that Taita really was here, and that it proves our theories are correct?'

'"Proves" is too strong a word. Let's just say that it points in that direction,' he demurred.

She wriggled around on the bed to face him squarely. 'Oh, Nicky, I am so excited. I swear I will not be able to sleep a wink tonight. I just can't wait for tomorrow, to get out there and start searching again.'

Her eyes were bright, and her cheeks flushed a warm rosy brown. Her lips were parted, and he could see the pink tip of her tongue between them. This time he could not stop himself. He leaned very slowly towards her, treating her gently, giving her every opportunity to pull away if she wished to avoid him. She did not move, but her shining expression turned slowly to one of apprehension. She stared into his eyes, as if seeking something, some reassurance. When their lips were an inch apart, Nicholas stopped, and it was she who made the last movement. She brought their mouths together.

At first it was soft, just a light mingling of their breath, and then it became harsher, more urgent. For a long, heart-stopping moment they devoured each other, and her mouth tasted soft and sweet as ripe fruit. Then suddenly she whimpered, and with a huge effort of will tore herself out of his arms. They stared at each other, both of them shaken and confused.

'No,' she whispered. 'Please, Nicky, not yet. I am not ready yet.'

He picked up her hand and turned it between his palms. Then lightly he kissed the tips of her fingers, savouring the smell and the taste of her skin.

'I'll see you in the morning.' He dropped her hand and stood up. 'Early. Be ready!' he said, and stooped out through the doorway of the hut.

As he was dressing the next morning he heard her moving around in her hut, and when he whistled softly at her door she stepped out to meet him, dressed and eager to start.

'Boris is not awake yet,' Tessay told them as she served their breakfast.

'Now that is a great surprise to me,' Nicholas said, without looking up from his plate. He and Royan were still slightly awkward in each other's presence, remembering the circumstances in which they had parted the previous evening. However, as Nicholas slung the rifle and the pack over his shoulder and they set off up the valley, their mood changed to one of anticipation.

They had been going for an hour when Nicholas glanced over his shoulder and then cautioned her with a frown. 'We are being followed.'

Taking her wrist, he drew her behind a slab of sandstone. He flattened himself against the rock and gestured at her to do the same. Then he poised himself, and suddenly leaped forward to seize the lanky figure in a dirty white *shamma* who was sneaking up the valley behind them. With a howl the creature fell to his knees, and began gibbering with terror.

Nicholas hauled him to his feet. 'Tamre! What are you doing following us? Who sent you?' he demanded in Arabic.

The boy rolled his eyes towards Royan. 'No, please, *effendi*, do not hurt me. I meant no harm.'

'Leave the child, Nicky. You will precipitate another fit,' Royan intervened. Tamre scurried behind her and clung to her hand for protection, peering out around her shoulder at Nicholas as though his life were in danger.

'Peace, Tamre,' Nicholas soothed him. 'I will not hurt you, unless you lie to me. If you do, then I will thrash you until there is no skin on your back. Who sent you to follow us?'

'I came alone. Nobody sent me,' blubbered the boy. 'I came to show you where I saw the holy animal with the fingermarks of the Baptist on his skin.'

Nicholas stared at him for a moment, before he began to laugh softly. 'I'll be damned if the boy doesn't really believe he saw great-grandfather's dik-dik.' Then he scowled ferociously. 'Remember what will happen to you, if you are lying.'

'It is true, *effendi*,' Tamre sobbed, and Royan came to his defence.

'Don't badger him. He is harmless. Leave the poor child.'

'All right, Tamre. I will give you a chance. Take us to where you saw the holy animal.'

Tamre would not relinquish his grip on Royan's hand. He clung to it as he danced beside her, leading her along, and within a hundred yards his terror had faded and he was smiling and giggling at her shyly.

For an hour he led them away from the Dandera river and up over the high ground above the valley, into an area of thick scrub and up-thrust ridges of weathered limestone. The thorny branches of the bush were densely intertwined, and grew so close to the ground that there seemed to be no way through them. However, Tamre led them on to a narrow twisting path, just wide enough for them to avoid the red-tipped hook thorns on each side of them. Then abruptly he stopped and pulled Royan to a halt beside him. He pointed down, almost at his own toes.

'The river!' he announced importantly. Nicholas came up beside them and whistled softly with surprise. Tamre had led them around in a wide circle to the west, and then brought them back to the Dandera river at a point where it still ran in the bed of the deep ravine.

Now they stood on the very edge of the chasm. He saw at once that, although the top of the rocky ravine was less than a hundred feet wide, the chasm opened out below the rim. From the surface of the water far below, the rock wall belled out in the shape of one of the pottery *tej* flasks. It narrowed again as it neared the top where they stood.

'I saw the holy thing over there.' Tamre pointed to the far side of the chasm where a small feeder spring meandered out of the thorny bush. Streamers of bright green moss, nourished by the spring, hung from the lip of the concave rock wall, and the water trickled down them and dripped from the tips into the river two hundred feet below.

'If you saw it there, why did you bring us to this side of the river?' Nicholas demanded.

Tamre looked as though he were on the point of tears. 'This side is easier. There is no path through the bush on the other side. The thorns would hurt Woizero Royan.'

'Don't be a bully,' Royan told him, and put her arm around the boy's shoulder.

Nicholas shrugged, 'It looks like the two of you are ganging up on me. Well, seeing that we are here, we might as well sit a while and see if great-grandpa's dik-dik puts in an appearance.'

He picked out a spot in the shade of one of the stunted trees that hung on the lip of the chasm, and with his hat swept the ground clear of fallen thorns until there was a place for them to sit. He placed his back against the trunk of the thorn tree and laid the Rigby rifle across his lap.

By this time it was past noon, and the heat was stifling. He passed the water bottle to Royan and, while she drank, glanced at Tamre and suggested to her in English, 'This might be a good time to find out what, if anything, the lad knows about the Taita ceramic in the crown. He is besotted with you. He will tell you anything you want to know. Question him.'

She began gently, chatting softly to the boy. Occasionally she stroked his head and petted him as though he were a puppy. She spoke to him of the previous night's banquet, the beauty of the underground church, and the antiquity of the murals and the tapestries, and then at last mentioned the abbot's crown.

'Yes. Yes. That is the stone of the saint,' he agreed readily. 'The blue stone of St Frumentius.'

'Where did it come from?' she asked. 'Do you know?'

The boy looked embarrassed, 'I do not know. It is very old, perhaps as old as Christ the Saviour. That is what the priests say.'

'You do not know where it was found?'

He shook his head, but then, eager to please her, he suggested, 'Perhaps it fell from heaven.'

'Perhaps.' Royan glanced at Nicholas, who rolled his eyes upwards and then pushed his hat forward to cover his face.

'Perhaps St Frumentius gave it to the first abbot when he died.' Tamre warmed to the subject. 'Or perhaps it was in his coffin with him when he was placed in his tomb.'

'All these things are possible, Tamre,' Royan agreed. 'Have you seen the tomb of St Frumentius?'

He looked around him guiltily. 'Only the ordained priests are allowed into the *maqdas*, the Holy of Holies,' he hung his head and whispered.

'You have seen it, Tamre,' she accused him gently, stroking his head. She was intrigued by the boy's guilt. 'You can tell me. I will not tell the priests.'

'Only once,' he admitted. 'The other boys. They sent me to touch the *tabot* stone. They would have beaten me if I had not. All the new acolytes are made to do this.' He began to babble with the horror of the memory of his initiation ordeal. 'I was alone. I was very afraid. It was after midnight when the priests were asleep. Dark. The *maqdas* is haunted by the ghost of the saint. They told me that if I was unworthy the saint would strike me down with lightning.'

Nicholas removed the hat from his face and straightened up slowly. 'My word, the child is telling the truth,' he said softly. 'He *has* been into

120

the Holy of Holies.' Then he looked across at Royan, 'Keep questioning him. He may just give us something useful. Ask him about the tomb of St Frumentius.'

'Did you see the tomb of the saint?' she asked, and the boy nodded vigorously. 'Did you go into the tomb?' This time he shook his head.

'No. There are bars across the entrance. Only the abbot is allowed into the tomb, on the birthday of the saint.'

'Did you look through the bars?'

'Yes, but it is very dark. I saw the coffin of the saint. It is wood and there is painting on it, the face of the saint.'

'Is he a black man?'

'No – a white man with a red beard. The painting is very old. The picture is faded, and the wood of the coffin is rotting and crumbling.'

'Is it lying on the floor of the tomb?'

Tamre screwed up his face in thought, then after careful consideration shook his head. 'No, it is on a shelf of stone in the wall.'

'Is there anything else you remember about the tomb of the saint?' Royan tried to prod his memory, but Tamre shook his head.

'It was very dark, and the opening in the bars is small,' he apologized.

'It does not matter. Is the tomb in the back wall of the *maqdas*?'

'Yes, it is behind the altar and the *tabot* stone.'

'What is the altar made of – stone?'

'No. It is wood, cedarwood. There are candles, and a big cross, and the many crowns of the abbot, and the chalice and staff.'

'Is it painted?'

'No, it is carved with pictures. But they are different from the pictures inside the tomb of the saint.'

'What is different? Tell me, Tamre.'

'I don't know. The faces are funny. They wear different clothes. There are horses.' He looked puzzled. 'They are different.'

Royan tried for a while to get a clearer description from him, but he became more and more confused and contradictory when she pushed him, so she changed tack.

'Tell me about the *tabot*,' she suggested, but Nicholas forestalled her.

'No, you tell me about the *tabot*,' he demanded of her. 'Is it similar to the Jewish Tabernacle?'

She turned to him, 'Yes, at least in the Egyptian Church it is. It is usually kept in a jewelled box and wrapped in an embroidered cloth of gold. The only difference is that the Jewish Tabernacle is carved with the ten commandments, but in our Church it is carved with the words of dedication of the particular church that houses it. It is the living heart of the Church.'

'What is the *tabot* stone?' Nicholas frowned with concentration.

'I don't know,' she admitted. 'Our Church does not have a *tabot* stone.'

'Ask him!'

'Tell me about the *tabot* stone, Tamre.'

'It is so high, and so square.' He indicated a height of a little above his own shoulder, and the width of his spread hands.

'And the *tabot* stands on top of this stone?' Royan guessed.

Tamre nodded.

'Why did they send you to touch the stone and not the *tabot* itself?' Nicholas demanded, but Royan shook her head to silence him.

'Let me do the talking. You are too harsh with him.' She turned back to the boy. 'Why the stone, rather than the Ark of the *tabot* that stands on top of it?'

Tamre shrugged helplessly. 'I don't know. They just did.'

'What does the stone look like? Are there paintings on it also?'

'I don't know.' He looked distraught at not being able to satisfy her. He wanted desperately to please her. 'I don't know. The stone is wrapped with cloth.'

Nicholas and Royan exchanged startled glances, and then Royan turned back to the boy.

'Covered?' Royan leaned closer to him. 'The stone is covered?'

'They say that it is only uncovered by the abbot on the birthday of St Frumentius.'

Again Nicholas and Royan stared at each other, and then he smiled thoughtfully. 'I would rather like to have a look at the tomb of the saint, and the *tabot* stone – in its uncovered state.'

'You'd have to wait for the saint's birthday,' she said, 'and have yourself ordained. Only the priests—' she broke off and stared at him again. 'You aren't thinking of – no, you wouldn't, would you?'

'Who, me?' he grinned. 'Perish the thought.'

'If they caught you in the *maqdas*, they would tear you to little pieces.'

'The answer, then, would be not to let them catch me.'

'If you go, I am going with you. How are we going to manage it?'

'Throttle back, dear girl. The thought only occurred to me ten seconds ago. Even on my good days, I need at least ten minutes to come up with a brilliant plan of action.'

They both stared out across the chasm in silence, until Royan whispered softly, 'The covered stone. Taita's stone testament?'

'Don't say it aloud,' he pleaded, and made the sign against the evil eye. 'Don't even think it aloud. The Devil is listening.'

They were silent again, both of them thinking furiously. Then

122

Royan started, 'Nicky, what if—' she broke off. 'No, that won't work.' She relapsed into frowning silence again.

Tamre broke the quiet with a sudden squeak of excitement, 'There it is. Look!'

They were both startled by the interruption. 'What is it?' Royan turned to him.

Tamre seized her arm and shook it. He was trembling with emotion. 'There it is. I told you.' With his other hand he was pointing out across the river, 'There at the edge of the thorn bushes. Can't you see it?'

'What is it? What can you see?'

'The animal of John the Baptist. The holy marked creature.'

Following the direction of his outflung arm, she picked out a soft, brownish blur of movement at the edge of the thicket on the far bank. 'I don't know. It is too far—'

Nicholas scrabbled in his pack and brought out his binoculars. He lifted and focused them, and then he began to chuckle.

'Hallelujah! Great-grandpa's reputation is safe at last.' He passed the binoculars to Royan. She focused them and found the little creature in the field. It was three hundred yards away, but through the ten-power lens she could make it out in detail.

It was almost half as large again as the common dik-dik that they had seen the previous day, and instead of drab grey its coat was a rich red brown. Its most striking feature, however, was the distinct dark bars of chocolate colour across its shoulders and back – five evenly spaced markings that did indeed look like the imprint of fingers and thumb.

'*Madoqua harperii*, no less,' Nicholas whispered to her. 'Sorry, great-grandfather, for doubting you.'

The dik-dik stood half in shadow, wriggling its nose as it snuffled the air. Its head was held high, suspicious and alert. The soft breeze was quartering between them and the animal, but every so often a wayward eddy gave it the faint whiff of humanity that had alarmed it.

Royan heard the snick of the rifle action as Nicholas worked the bolt and chambered a round. Hurriedly she lowered the glasses, and glanced at him. 'You aren't going to shoot it?' she demanded.

'No, not at that range. Over three hundred yards, and a small target. I'll wait for it to get closer.'

'How can you bring yourself to do it?'

'How can I not? That's what I came here to do, amongst other things.'

'But it's so beautiful.'

'I take it, then, that it would be perfectly all right to whack it if it were ugly?'

She said nothing, but raised the binoculars again. The eddy of the wind must have changed, for the dik-dik lowered its head to nibble at a tuft of coarse brown grass. Then lifted its head again and came on down the clearing in the thorn scrub, stepping daintily, pausing every few paces to feed again.

'Go back!' She tried to will it into safety, but it kept on coming, meandering towards the edge of the chasm.

Nicholas rolled on to his stomach and settled himself behind the root of the tree. He screwed up his hat into a soft pad on which to rest the rifle.

'Two hundred yards,' he muttered to himself. 'That's a fair shot. No further.' Resting the cushioned rifle on the twisted root, he aimed through the telescopic sight. Then he lifted his head, waiting to let it come within certain range.

Abruptly the dik-dik lifted its head again and came to a halt, quivering with tension.

'Something he doesn't like. Dammit all, wind must have changed again,' Nicholas growled. At that moment the little antelope bolted. It streaked across the clearing, back the way it had come, and disappeared into the thorn scrub.

'Go, dik-dik, go!' said Royan smugly, and Nicholas sat up and grunted with disgust.

'I can't make out what frightened him.' Then his expression changed and he cocked his head. There was an alien sound on the air, growing each second – a harsh, rising clatter and a shrill, whining whistle.

'Chopper! What the hell!' Nicholas recognized the sound immediately. He took the binoculars from Royan's hand and turned them to the sky, sweeping the cloudless blue emptiness above the crenellated tops of the escarpment.

'There it is,' he said grimly, adding, 'Bell Jet Ranger,' as he recognized the profile. 'Coming this way, by the looks of it. No point in drawing attention to ourselves. Let's get under cover.'

He shepherded Royan and the boy under the spread branches of the thorn tree. 'Sit tight,' he told her. 'No chance they will spot us under here.'

He watched the approaching helicopter through the binoculars. 'Probably Ethiopian air force,' he said softly. 'Anti-*shufta* patrol, most likely. Both Boris and Colonel Nogo warned us that there are a lot of rebels and bandits operating down here in the gorge—' he broke off abruptly. 'No. Hold on. That's not military. Green and red fuselage, and the red horse emblem. None other than your old friends from Pegasus Exploration.'

The sound of the rotors crescendoed, and now with her naked eye the camp. However, when they neared the grove he slipped away in the direction of the monastery.

That evening, while it was still light, Nicholas took Royan back to the monastery.

'I believe that the criminal fraternity refer to a reconnaissance of this nature as "casing the joint",' he remarked, as they stooped through the entrance of the rock cathedral and joined the throng of worshippers in the outer chamber.

'From what Tamre says, it sounds as though the novices wait until they know that the priests on duty are ones that will nod off during their watch,' Royan told him softly, as they paused to gaze through the doors into the middle chamber.

'We don't have that sort of insider knowledge,' Nicholas pointed out.

There were priests passing backwards and forwards through the doors as they watched.

'There doesn't seem to be any sort of procedure,' Nicholas noted. 'No password or ritual to allow them through.'

'On the other hand, they greeted the guards at the door by name. It's a small community. They must all know each other intimately.'

'There doesn't seem any chance at all that I could dress up like a monk and brazen my way through,' Nicholas agreed. 'I wonder what they do to intruders in the sacred areas?'

'Throw them off the terrace to the crocodiles in the cauldron of the Nile?' she suggested maliciously. 'Anyway, you are not going in there without me.'

This was not the time to argue, he decided, and instead he tried to see as much as possible through the open doors of the *qiddist*. The middle chamber seemed much smaller than the outer chamber in which they stood. He could just make out the shadowy murals that covered the portions of the inner walls that he could see. In the facing wall was another doorway. From Tamre's description, he realized that this must be the entrance to the *maqdas*. The opening was barred by a heavy grille gate of dark wooden beams, the joints of the cross-pieces reinforced with gussets of hand-hammered native iron.

On each side of the doorway, from rock ceiling to floor, hung long embroidered tapestries depicting scenes from the life of St Frumentius. In one he was preaching to a kneeling congregation, with the Bible in one hand and his right hand raised in benediction. In the other tapestry he was baptizing an emperor. The king wore a high golden crown like that of Jali Hora, and the saint's head was surrounded by a halo. The saint's face was white, while the emperor's was black.

'Politically correct?' Nicholas asked himself, with a smile.

'What is amusing you?' Royan asked. 'Have you thought of a way of getting in there?'

'No, I was thinking of dinner. Let's go!'

At dinner Boris showed no ill effects from the previous night's debauch. During the day he had taken out his shotgun and shot a bunch of green pigeons. Tessay had marinated these and barbecued them over the coals.

'Tell me, English, how was the hunting today? Did you get attacked by the deadly striped dik-dik? Hey? Hey?' He bellowed with laughter.

'Did your trackers have any success?' Nicholas asked mildly.

'Da! Da! They found kudu and bushbuck and buffalo. They even found dik-dik, but no stripes. Sorry, no stripes.'

Royan leaned forward and opened her mouth to intervene, but Nicholas cautioned her with a shake of the head. She shut her mouth again and looked down at her plate, slicing a morsel from the breast of a pigeon.

'We don't really need company tomorrow,' Nicholas explained mildly in Arabic. 'If he knew, he would insist on coming with us.'

'Did your Mummy never teach you no manners, English? It's rude to talk in a language that others can't understand. Have a vodka.'

'You have my share,' Nicholas invited him. 'I know when I am outclassed.'

During the rest of the meal Tessay replied only in low monosyllables when Royan tried to draw her into the conversation. She looked tragic and defeated. She never looked at her husband, even when he was at his loudest and most overbearing. When the meal ended, they left her sitting with Boris at the fire. Boris had a fresh bottle of vodka on the table beside him.

'The way he is pumping the liquor, it looks as if I might be called out on another midnight rescue mission,' Nicholas remarked as they made their way to their own huts.

'Tessay has been in camp all day with him. There has been more trouble between them. She told me that as soon as they get back to Addis Ababa she is going to leave him. She can't take any more of this.'

'The only thing I find surprising is that she ever got mixed up with an animal like Boris in the first place. She is a lovely woman. She could pick and choose.'

'Some women are drawn to animals,' Royan shrugged. 'I suppose it must be the thrill of danger. Anyway, Tessay has asked me if she can come with us tomorrow. She cannot stand another day in camp with

128

Boris on her own. I think she is really afraid of him now. She says that she has never seen him drink like this before.'

'Tell her to come along,' Nicholas said resignedly. 'The more of us the merrier. Perhaps we will be able to frighten the dik-dik to death by sheer weight of numbers. Save me wasting ammunition.'

It was still dark when the three of them left camp the next morning. There was no sign of Boris and, when Nicholas asked about him, Tessay said simply, 'After you went to bed last night he finished the bottle. He won't be out of his hut before noon. He won't miss me.'

Carrying the Rigby, Nicholas led them up into the weathered limestone hills, retracing the path along which Tamre had taken them the previous day. As they walked, Nicholas heard the two women talking behind him. Royan was explaining to Tessay how they had sighted the striped dik-dik, and what they planned.

The sun was well up by the time they again reached the spot under the thorn tree on the lip of the chasm, and settled down to wait in ambush.

'How will you retrieve the carcass, if you do manage to shoot the poor little creature?' Royan asked.

'I made certain of that before we left camp,' he explained. 'I spoke to the head tracker. If he hears a shot he will bring up the ropes and help me get across to the other side.'

'I wouldn't like to make the journey across there.' Tessay eyed the drop below them.

'They teach you some useful things in the army, along with all the rubbish,' Nicholas replied. He made himself comfortable against the thorn tree, the rifle ready in his lap.

The women lay close by him, talking together softly. It was unlikely that the sound of their low voices would carry across the ravine, Nicholas decided, so he did not try to hush them.

He expected that if it came at all, the dik-dik would show itself early. But he was wrong. By noon there was still no sign of it. The valley sweltered in the midday sun. The distant wall of the escarpment, veiled in the blue heat haze, looked like jagged blue glass, and the mirage danced across the rocky ridges and shimmered like the waters of a silver lake above the tops of the thorn thickets.

The women had long ago given up talking, and they lay somnolent in the heat. The whole world was silent and heat-struck. Only a bush dove broke the silence with its mournful lament, 'My wife is dead, my children are dead, Oh, me! Oh, my! Oh, me!' Nicholas found his own eyelids becoming leaden. His head nodded involuntarily, and he jerked it up only to have it flop forward again. On the very edge of sleep he heard a sound, close by in the thorn scrub behind him.

It was a tiny sound, but one that he knew so well. A sound that whiplashed across his nerve endings and jerked him back to full consciousness, with his pulse racing and the coppery taste of fear in the back of his throat. It was the metallic sound of the safety-catch on an AK-47 assault rifle being slipped forward into the 'Fire' position.

In one fluid movement he lifted the rifle out of his lap and rolled twice, twisting his body to cover the two women who lay beside him. At the same time he brought the Rigby into his shoulder, aimed into the scrub behind him from where the sound had come.

'Down!' he hissed at his companions. 'Keep your heads down!'

His finger was on the trigger and, even though it was a puny weapon with which to take on a Kalashnikov, he was ready to return fire. He picked up his target immediately, and swung on to it.

There was a man crouched twenty paces away, the assault rifle he carried aimed into Nicholas's face. He was black, dressed in worn and tattered camouflage fatigues and a soft cap of the same material. His webbing held a bushknife and grenades, water bottle and all the other accoutrements of a guerrilla fighter.

'Shufta!' thought Nicholas. 'A real pro. Don't take chances with this one.' Yet at the same time he realized that if the intention had been to kill him, then he would be dead already.

He aimed the Rigby an inch over the muzzle of the assault rifle, into the bloodshot right eye of the shufta behind it. The man acknowledged the stand-off with a narrowing of his eyes, and then gave an order in Arabic.

'Salim, cover the women. Shoot them if he moves.'

Nicholas heard movement on his flank and glanced in that direction, still keeping the shufta in his peripheral vision.

Another guerrilla stepped out of the scrub. He was similarly dressed, but he carried a Soviet RPD light machine gun on his hip. The barrel was sawn off short to make the weapon more handy for bush fighting, and there was a loop of ammunition belt draped around his neck. He came forward carefully, the RPD aimed point-blank at the two women. Nicholas knew that, with a touch on the trigger, he could chop them both to mincemeat.

There were other stealthy rustling sounds in the bush all around them. These two were not the only ones, Nicholas realized. This was a large war party. He might be able to get off one shot with the Rigby, but by then Royan and Tessay would be dead. And he would not be far behind them.

Very slowly and deliberately he lowered the muzzle of the rifle until it was pointing at the ground. Then he laid the weapon down and raised his hands.

'Get your hands up,' he told the women. 'Do exactly what they tell you.'

The guerrilla leader acknowledged his surrender by coming to his full height and speaking rapidly to his men, still in Arabic.

'Get the rifle and his pack.'

'We are British subjects,' Nicholas told him loudly, and the guerrilla looked surprised by his use of Arabic. 'We are simple tourists. We are not military. We are not government people.'

'Be quiet. Shut your face!' he ordered, as the rest of the guerrilla patrol emerged from cover. Nicholas counted five of them all told, though he knew there were probably others who had not come forward. They were very professional as they rounded up their prisoners. They never blocked each other's field of fire, nor offered an opportunity of escape. Quickly they searched them for weapons, then closed in around them and hustled them on to the path.

'Where are you taking us?' Nicholas demanded.

'No questions!' The butt of an AK-47 smashed between his shoulder blades and almost knocked him off his feet.

'Steady on, chaps,' he murmured mildly in English. 'That wasn't really called for.'

They were forced to keep marching through the heat of the afternoon. Nicholas kept a check on the position of the sun and the distant glimpses of the escarpment wall. He realized that they were heading westwards, following the course of the Nile towards the Sudanese border. It was late afternoon, and Nicholas estimated that they had covered some ten miles, before they came upon a side shoot of the main valley. The slopes were heavily wooded, and the three prisoners were herded into a patch of this forest.

They were actually within the perimeter of the guerrilla camp before they were aware of its existence. Cunningly camouflaged, it consisted merely of a few crude lean-to shelters and a ring of weapons emplacements. The sentries were well placed, and all the light machine guns in the foxholes were manned.

They were led to one of the shelters in the centre of the camp, where three men were squatting around a map spread on a low camp table. These were obviously officers, and there was no mistaking which of the three was the commander. The leader of the patrol which had captured them went to this man, saluted him deferentially and then spoke to him urgently, pointing at his captives.

The guerrilla commander straightened up from the table, and came out into the sunlight. He was of medium height, but was imbued with such an air of authority that he seemed taller. His shoulders were broad and his body square and chunky, with the beginning of a dignified spread

131

around the waist. He wore a short curly beard which contained a few strands of grey, and his features were refined and handsome. His skin tones were amber and copper. His dark eyes were intelligent, his gaze quick and restless.

'My men tell me that you speak Arabic,' he said to Nicholas.

'Better than you do, Mek Nimmur,' Nicholas told him. 'So now you are the leader of a bunch of bandits and kidnappers? I always told you that you would never get to heaven, you old reprobate.'

Mek Nimmur stared at him in astonishment, and then began to smile. 'Nicholas! I did not recognize you. You are older. Look at the grey on your head!'

He opened his arms wide and folded Nicholas into a bear hug.

'Nicholas! Nicholas!' He kissed him once on each cheek. Then he held him at arm's length and looked at the two women, who were standing amazed.

'He saved my life,' he explained to them.

'You make me blush, Mek.'

Mek kissed him again, 'He saved my life twice.'

'Once,' Nicholas contradicted him. 'The second time was a mistake. I should have let them shoot you.'

Mek laughed delightedly. 'How long ago was it, Nicholas?'

'It doesn't bear thinking about.'

'Fifteen years ago at least,' Mek said. 'Are you still in the British army? What is your rank? You must be a general by now!'

'Reserves only,' Nicholas shook his head. 'I have been back in civvy street a long time now.'

Still hugging Nicholas, Mek Nimmur looked at the women with interest. 'Nicholas taught me most of what I know about soldiering,' he told them. His eyes flicked from Royan to Tessay, and then stayed on the Ethiopian girl's dark and lovely face.

'I know you,' he said. 'I saw you in Addis, years ago. You were a young girl then. Your father was Alto Zemen, a great and good man. He was murdered by the tyrant Mengistu.'

'I know you also, Alto Mek. My father held you in high esteem. There are many of us who believe that you should be the president of this Ethiopia of ours, in place of that other one.' She dropped him a graceful little curtsey, hanging her head in a shy but appealing gesture of respect.

'I am flattered by your opinion of me.' He took her hand and lifted her to her full height. Then he turned back to Nicholas, 'I am sorry for the rough welcome. Some of my men are over-enthusiastic. I knew that there were *ferengi* asking questions at the monastery. But enough, you are with friends here. I bid you welcome.'

Mek Nimmur led them to his shelter, where one of his men brought a soot-blackened kettle from the fire and poured viscous black coffee into mugs for them.

He and Nicholas plunged into reminiscences of the days prior to the Falklands war when they had fought side by side, Nicholas as a covert military adviser, and Mek as a young freedom fighter opposing the tyranny of Mengistu.

'But the war is over now, Mek,' Nicholas remonstrated at last. 'The battle is won. Why are you still out in the bush with your men? Why aren't you getting rich and fat in Addis, like all the others?'

'In the interim government in Addis there are enemies of mine, men like Mengistu. When we have got rid of them, then I will come out of the bush.'

He and Nicholas embarked into a spirited discussion of African politics, so deep and complicated that Royan knew very few of the personalities whom they were discussing. Nor could she follow the nuances and the subtlety of religious and tribal prejudices and intolerance that had persisted for a thousand years. She was, however, impressed by Nicholas's knowledge and understanding of the situation, and the way in which a man like Mek Nimmur asked his opinion and listened to his advice.

In the end Nicholas asked him, 'So now you have carried the war beyond the borders of Ethiopia itself? You are operating in Sudan, as well?'

'The war in the Sudan has been raging for twenty years,' Mek confirmed. 'The Christians in the south fighting against the persecution of the Moslem north—'

'I am well aware of that, Mek. But that is not Ethiopia. It's not your war.'

'They are Christians, and they suffer injustice. I am a soldier and a Christian. Of course it is my war.' Tessay had been listening avidly to every word that Mek spoke, and now she nodded her head in agreement, her eyes dark and solemn with hero worship.

'Alto Mek is a crusader for Christ and the rights of the common man,' Tessay told Nicholas in awed tones.

'And he dearly loves a good fight,' Nicholas laughed, punching his shoulder affectionately. It was a familiar gesture which could easily have given offence, but Mek accepted it readily and laughed back at him.

'What are you doing here yourself, Nicholas, if you are no longer a soldier? There was a time when you also loved a good fight.'

'I am completely reformed. No more fighting. I have come to the Abbay gorge to hunt dik-dik.'

'Dik-dik?' Mek Nimmur stared at him with disbelief, and then he roared with laughter. 'I don't believe it. Not you. Not dik-dik. You are up to something.'

'It is the truth.'

'You are lying, Nicholas. You never could lie to me. I know you too well. You are up to something. You will tell me about it when you need my help.'

'And you will still give me your help?'

'Of course. You saved my life twice.'

'Once,' said Nicholas.

'Even once is enough,' said Mek Nimmur.

W hile they talked, the sun slanted down the sky.

'You are my guests for tonight,' Mek Nimmur told them formally. 'In the morning I will escort you back to your camp at the monastery of St Frumentius. That is also my destination. My men and I are going to the monastery to celebrate the festival of Timkat. The abbot, Jali Hora, is a friend and an ally.'

'And the monastery is probably your deep cover base. You use it and the monks for resupply and intelligence. Am I right?'

'You know me too well, Nicholas.' Mek Nimmur shook his head ruefully. 'You taught me much of what I know, so why should you not be able to guess my strategy? The monastery makes a perfect base of operations. It's close enough to the border—' he broke off, smiling. 'But there is no need to explain it to you, of all people.'

Mek had his men build a night shelter for Nicholas and Royan, and cut a mattress of grass to cushion their sleep. They lay close together under the flimsy roof. The night was sultry, and they did not miss their blankets. Nicholas had a tube of insect repellent in his pack to keep the mosquitoes at bay.

After they had settled down on the grass mattress, their heads were close enough together to allow them to converse in quiet tones. When he turned his head Nicholas could see the dark silhouettes of Mek Nimmur and Tessay still sitting close together by the fire.

'Ethiopian girls are different from the Arabs, and from most other African women.' Royan too was watching the other couple. 'No Arab girl would dare be alone with a man like that. Especially if she were a married woman.'

'Any way you cut it, they make a damned fine pair,' he gave his opinion. 'Good luck to them. Tessay hasn't had much of that lately – she is overdue.'

He turned his head and looked into her face, 'What about you, Royan, what are you? Are you a decorous, submissive Arab, or an independent, assertive Western girl?'

'It's both a little early and much too late for intimate questions of that nature,' she told him, and turned over, presenting him with her back.

'Ah, we are standing on ceremony this evening! Goodnight, Woizero Royan.'

'Goodnight, Alto Nicholas,' she replied, keeping her face turned away from him so that he could not see her smile.

The guerrilla column moved out before dawn the next morning. They marched in full battle order, with scouts moving ahead and flankers covering each side of the path.

'The army come down here into the gorge very seldom, but we are always ready for them when they do come,' Mek Nimmur explained. 'We try to give them a hearty welcome.'

Tessay was watching Mek Nimmur as he spoke; indeed, she had seldom taken her eyes off him that morning. Now she murmured to Royan, 'He is a truly great man, a man who could unite our land, perhaps for the first time in a thousand years. I feel humble in his presence, and yet I also feel like a young girl again, filled with joy and hope.'

The march back to the monastery took the entire morning. When they came in sight of the Dandera river, Mek Nimmur drew his men back off the path into thick bush, while sending only one scout forward. After an hour's wait, a party of acolytes came up from the monastery, each carrying a large bundle balanced upon his head.

They greeted Mek with deep reverence, and handed over their bundles to his men before returning down the pathway into the gorge of the Abbay.

The bundles contained priestly *shammas*, headcloths and sandals. Mek's men changed out of their camouflage fatigues into these garments, all of which were well worn and unwashed for the sake of authenticity. They wore only their sidearms under the robes. All their other weapons and equipment they cached in one of the caves in the limestone cliffs, and left a detachment to guard them.

Now as a party of monks they covered the last few miles to the monastery, to be welcomed joyously by the community there. Here Nicholas and the women left Mek, and climbed the steep path up into the grove of wild fig trees. Boris was waiting for them, pacing about the camp, angry and frustrated.

'Where the hell have you been, woman?' he snarled at Tessay. 'Been whoring around all night, have you?'

'We lost our way yesterday evening.' Nicholas fed him the cover story that they had agreed with Mek Nimmur, to maintain his security. Boris was hardly the man to trust. 'And we were picked up by a party of monks from the monastery this morning. They brought us back.'

'You are the big hunter and tracker, are you?' Boris sneered at him. 'You didn't need me to guide you, hey? You got yourself lost, did you, English? I see now why you want only to shoot dik-dik.' He guffawed without humour, and looked at Tessay with those pale dead eyes. 'I will talk to you later, woman. Go and see to the food.'

Despite the heat, both Nicholas and Royan were hungry. In short order, Tessay was able to serve a tasty cold lunch under the shady branches of the fig trees. Nicholas refused the wine that Boris offered him.

'I want to go out hunting again this afternoon. I have lost almost a whole day.'

'You want me to hold your hand this time, English? Make sure you don't lose yourself again?'

'Thanks, old chap, but I think I can manage without you.'

While they ate Nicholas nudged Royan and told her, 'Your admirer has arrived.'

He jerked his head at the lanky, ungainly figure of Tamre, who had sneaked up quietly and was now sitting near the kitchen hut. As soon as Royan looked at him his face split into a doting idiotic grin, and he bobbed his head and squirmed with ecstatic shyness.

'I will not come with you this afternoon,' Royan told Nicholas quietly, when Boris was not listening. 'I think there is going to be trouble between him and Tessay. I want to stay here with her. Take Tamre with you.'

'My word, what an attractive alternative. All my life I have waited for this moment.' But when he had picked up his rifle and pack, he beckoned the boy to follow him. Tamre looked around eagerly for Royan, but she was in her hut. At last, dragging his feet, he followed Nicholas up the valley.

'Take me to the other side of the river,' he told the boy. 'Show me how to reach the side where the holy creature lives.' Tamre perked up at the prospect, and broke into a shambling trot as he led Nicholas over the suspension bridge below the pink cliffs.

For an hour they followed the path, but gradually it petered out until it ended in bad and broken ground amongst the erosion-carved hills. Undeterred, Tamre plunged into the thorny scrub, and for another two hours they scrambled over rocky ridges and through thorn-choked valleys.

'I can see why you didn't want to bring Royan this way round,' Nicholas grunted. His bare arms were scored by thorn, and the legs of his trousers were ripped in half a dozen places. However, he was memorizing the route and knew that he could find his way back again without difficulty.

At last they topped another ridge and Tamre stopped and pointed down over the far side. Below them Nicholas could make out the cleft of the chasm, and the small open glade from which the dik-dik spring issued. He could even recognize the thorn tree on the far bank of the Dandera river under which they had been sitting when Mek's men had surprised them.

He rested a few minutes and swallowed a few mouthfuls from the water bottle before passing it to Tamre. 'He's a monk, for goodness' sake,' he consoled himself. 'The little devil is not going to have AIDS, now, is he?' But he wiped the mouth of the bottle carefully when Tamre handed it back to him.

Before starting down the slope he checked the Rigby rifle again, blowing dust off the lens of the scope. Then he sighted through it at a dik-dik-sized rock at the foot of the slope, whilst he twisted the ring on the telescope down to its lowest magnification. He was now ready for a quick shot at close range in thick bush. Satisfied at last, he chambered a round, set the safety-catch and stood up.

'Keep behind me,' he told the boy. 'And do what I do.'

He drifted down the slope, pausing after every few slow steps to check the thorn scrub ahead and on both sides. When he reached the spring head, the earth was damp and soft. A number of animals and birds had been drinking here. He recognized the spoor of both kudu and bushbuck, but amongst these were the tiny, heart-shaped prints of his quarry.

He moved on quietly and at the edge of the scrub he found a midden, a boundary post which the dik-dik had used to mark out its chosen territory. The pile of buckshot-sized pellets of dung would be added to each time the little antelope returned to defecate at this spot.

By now Nicholas was totally absorbed in the hunt. His earlier failures had merely served to pique his fascination. He brought as much concentration to bear as if it had been a man-eating lion he was following. He crept forward a pace at a time, checking the ground before he let his foot fall on a dry twig or patch of rustling leaves, his eyes moving more swiftly than his feet, picking out any movement or touch of colour in the thorny palisade.

It was a flicker of an ear that gave the creature away. It was standing half in shadow, its ruddy coat blending into the backdrop of dried branches, still as if carved from mahogany. Only that small movement betrayed it. It was so close that Nicholas could see the reflection of light from one eye bright as polished onyx, and then the elongated nose wriggled with agitation. It was aware of danger, but uncertain from what quarter it was to come.

Achingly slowly, Nicholas lifted the Rigby to his shoulder. Through the lens he could make out every hair in the tuft between the pricked ears and the little black needle horns. He moved the cross hairs down on to the junction between neck and head. He wanted to restrict the damage to the pelt, so as to make the mounting and taxidermy easier.

'It is the holy creature. Praise God and St John the Baptist!' cried Tamre in a loud voice at his elbow, and he fell to his knees with his hands clasped in front of his eyes.

The dik-dik dissolved like a puff of brown smoke out of the field of the lens, and there was only a soft rustle in the scrub as it fled. Nicholas lowered the rifle slowly and looked down at the boy. He was still on his knees, gabbling out praises and prayers.

'Nice work. I think Woizero Royan must have you in her pay,' he said in English. He reached down, hauled the boy to his feet and switched into Arabic. 'You will stay here. You will not move. You will not speak. You will even breathe very, very quietly, until I come back to fetch you. If you utter even one little prayer before I return, I will personally start you on your journey to meet St Peter at the gates of heaven. Do you understand me?'

He went forward alone, but the little antelope was thoroughly alarmed by now. Nicholas saw it twice more, but he only had fleeting glimpses of ruddy brown movement almost entirely screened by bush. He stood directing bitter imprecations towards the boy monk and listening to the tick of small hooves on dry earth as it raced away, deeper into the thickets. In the end he was forced to give up the hunt for that day.

It was after dark when he and Tamre got back to camp. As soon as Nicholas stepped into the circle of firelight, Royan came to meet him.

'What happened?' she asked. 'Did you see the dik-dik again?'

'Don't ask me. Ask your accomplice. He scared it off. It is probably still running.'

'Tamre, you are a fine young man, and I am very proud of you,' she told him. The boy wriggled like a puppy, giggling and hugging himself with the joy of her approval as he scurried away down the path to the monastery.

Royan was so pleased with the outcome of the hunt that she poured Nicholas a whisky with her own hand and brought it to him as he sagged wearily by the fire.

He tasted it and shuddered, 'Never let a teetotaller pour for you. With a heavy hand like that you should take up tossing the caber or blacksmithing.' Despite the complaint, he took another tentative sip.

She sat close to him, fidgeting with excitement, but it was a while before he became aware of her agitation.

'What is it? Something is eating you alive.'

She threw a cautionary glance in the direction of where Boris sat on the opposite side of the fire, and then dropped her voice, leaned close to him and spoke in Arabic.

'Tessay and I went down to the monastery this afternoon to see Mek Nimmur. Tessay asked me to go with her, just in case Boris – well, you know what I mean.'

'I have a vague idea. You were playing chaperone.' Nicholas took another sip of the whisky and gasped. He exhaled sharply and his voice was husky. 'Go on,' he invited her.

'At one stage, before I left them alone together, we were discussing the festival of Timkat. On the fifth day the abbot takes the *tabot* down to the Abbay. Mek tells us there is a path down the cliff to the water's edge.'

'Yes, we know that.'

'This is the interesting part – this you didn't know. Everybody joins the procession down to the river. Everybody. The abbot, all the priests, the acolytes, every true believer, even Mek and all his men, they all go down to the river and stay there overnight. For one whole day and night the monastery is deserted. Empty. Nobody there at all.'

He stared at her over the rim of his glass, and then slowly he began to smile, 'Now that is very interesting indeed,' he admitted.

'Don't forget, I am coming with you,' she told him severely. 'Don't you dare to even think of leaving me behind.'

Nicholas went to her hut again that evening after dinner. This was the only place in camp where they could be sure of privacy, and where they were safe from eavesdropping. However, this time he did not make the mistake of sitting on her bed. While she perched on the end of it, he took the stool opposite her.

'Before we start planning this thing, let me ask you one question. Have you considered the possible consequences?'

'You mean, what happens if the monks catch us at it?' Royan asked.

'At the very least we can expect them to run us out of the valley. The abbot has a tremendous amount of power. At the worst we can be physically attacked,' Nicholas told her. 'This is one of the most sacred sites in their religion, and don't underestimate that fact. There is a great deal of danger involved. It could go as far as a knife between the ribs, or something nasty in our food.'

'We would also alienate Tessay. She is a deeply religious woman,' Royan added.

'Even more importantly, we would probably outrage Mek Nimmur as well.' Nicholas looked distressed at the thought. 'I don't know what he would do, but I don't think our friendship would stand the test.'

They were both quiet for a while, considering the cost that they might have to pay. Nicholas broke the silence.

'Then again, have you considered your own position? After all, it is your own Church that we will be desecrating. You are a committed Christian. Can you justify this to yourself?'

'I have thought about it,' she admitted. 'And I am not altogether happy about it, but it isn't really my Church. It's a different branch of the Coptic Church.'

'Splitting hairs, aren't we?'

'The Egyptian Church does not deny anyone access to even the most sacred precincts of its church building. I do not feel myself bound by the abbot's prohibition. I feel that as a believing Christian I have the right to enter any part of the cathedral that I wish.'

He whistled softly, 'And you are the one who once said that I should have been a lawyer.'

'Please don't, Nicky. It's not something you should joke about. All I know is that, no matter what, I have to go in there. Even if I give offence to Tessay and Mek and all the priesthood, I have to do it.'

'You could let me do it for you,' he suggested. 'After all, I am an old heathen. It would not spoil my chances of salvation. I don't have any.'

'No.' She shook her head firmly. 'If there is an inscription or something of that nature, I need to see it. You read hieroglyphics quite well, but not as well as I do, and you don't know the hieratic script. I am the expert – you are just a gifted amateur. You need me. I am going in there with you.'

'All right. That is settled, then,' he said with finality. 'Let's start planning. We had better draw up a list of equipment that we may need. Flashlight, knife, Polaroid camera, spare film—'

'Art paper and soft pencils to lift an impression of any inscriptions,' she added to the list.

'Hell!' He snapped his fingers with chagrin. 'I didn't think to bring any.'

'See what I mean? Amateur. I did.'

They talked on until late, and at last Nicholas glanced at his wristwatch and stood up.

'Long after midnight. I am scheduled to turn into a pumpkin at any moment. Goodnight.'

'There are still two days of the festival before the *tabot* is taken down to the river. Nothing we can do until then. What are your plans?'

'Tomorrow I am going back after that damned little Bambi. It has made a fool of me twice already.'

140

'I am coming with you,' she said firmly, and that simple declaration gave him a disproportionate amount of pleasure.

'Just as long as you leave Tamre at home,' he warned her as he stooped out through the door.

The tiny antelope stepped out from the deep shadow of the thorn thicket, and the early morning sunlight gleamed on the silky pelt. It kept walking steadily across the narrow clearing.

Nicholas's breathing quickened with excitement as he followed it with the telescopic sight. It was ridiculous that he should feel so wrought up with the hunting of such a humble little animal, but his previous failures had sharpened his anticipation. Added to that was the peculiar passion that drives the true collector. Since he had lost Rosalind and the girls, he had thrown all his energy into the building up of the collection at Quenton Park. Now, suddenly, procuring this specimen for it had become a matter of supreme importance to him.

His forefinger rested lightly on the side of the trigger guard. He would not fire until the dik-dik came to a standstill. Even that walking pace would make the shot uncertain. He had to place his bullet precisely, to kill swiftly but at the same time to inflict the least possible damage to the skin.

To this end he had loaded the Rigby with full metal jacket bullets – ones that would not expand on impact and open a wide wound channel, nor rip out a gaping hole in the coat as they exited. These solid bullets would punch a tiny hole the size of a pencil that the taxidermist at the museum would be able to repair invisibly.

He felt his nerves screwing up as he realized that the dik-dik was not going to stop in the open. It made steadily for the thick scrub on the far side of the clearing. This might be his last chance. He fought the temptation to take the shot at the moving target, and it required an effort of will to lift his finger off the trigger again.

The antelope reached the wall of thorn scrub and, the moment before it disappeared, stopped abruptly and thrust its tiny head into the depths of one of the low bushes. Standing broadside to Nicholas, it began to nibble at the pale green tufts of new leaves. The head was screened, so he had to abandon his intention of going for that shot. However, the shoulder was exposed. He could make out the clear outline of the blade beneath the glossy red-brown skin. The dik-dik was angled slightly away from him, in the perfect position for the heart shot, tucked in low behind the shoulder.

Unhurriedly he settled the reticule of the scope on the precise spot, and squeezed the trigger.

The shot whip-cracked in the heavy heated air and the tiny antelope bounded high, coming down to touch the earth already at a full run. Like a rapier rather than a cutlass, the solid bullet had not struck with sufficient shock to knock the dik-dik over. Head down, the dik-dik dashed away in the typical frantic reaction to a bullet through the heart. It was dead already, running only on the last dregs of oxygen in its bloodstream.

'Oh, no! Not that way,' Nicholas cried as he jumped to his feet. The tiny creature was racing straight towards the lip of the cliff. Blindly it leaped out into empty space and flipped into a somersault as it fell, dropping from their sight, down almost two hundred feet into the chasm of the Dandera river.

'That was a filthy bit of luck.' Nicholas jumped over the bush that had hidden them and ran to the rim of the chasm. Royan followed him and the two of them stood peering down into the giddy void.

'There it is!' She pointed, and he nodded. 'Yes, I can see it.'

The carcass lay directly below them, caught on an islet of rock in the middle of the stream.

'What are you going to do?' she asked.

'I'll have to go down and get it.' He straightened up and stepped back from the brink. 'Fortunately it's still early. We have plenty of time to get the job done before dark. I'll have to go back to camp to fetch the rope and to get some help.'

t was afternoon before they returned, accompanied by Boris, both his trackers and two of the skinners. They brought with them four coils of nylon rope.

Nicholas leaned out over the cliff and grunted with relief. 'Well, the carcass is still down there. I had visions of it being washed away.' He supervised the trackers as they uncoiled the rope and laid it out down the length of the clearing.

'We will need two coils of it to get down to the bottom,' he estimated and joined them, painstakingly tying and checking the knot himself. Then he plumbed the drop, lowering the end of the rope down the cliff until it touched the surface of the water, and then hauling it back and measuring it between the spread of his arms.

'Thirty fathoms. One hundred and eighty feet. I won't be able to climb back that high,' he told Boris. 'You and your gang will have to haul me back up.'

He anchored the rope end with a bowline to the bole of one of the

142

wiry thorn trees. Then he again tested it meticulously, getting all four of the trackers and skinners to heave on it with their combined weight.

'That should do it,' he gave his opinion as he stripped to his shirt and khaki shorts and pulled off his chukka boots. On the lip of the cliff he leaned out backwards with the rope draped over his shoulder and the tail brought back between his legs in the classic abseil style.

'Coming in on a wing and a prayer!' he said, and jumped out backwards into the chasm. He controlled his fall by allowing the rope to pay out over his shoulder, braking with the turn over his thigh, swinging like a pendulum and kicking himself off the rock wall with both feet. He went down swiftly until his feet dangled into the rush of water, and the current pushed him into a spin on the end of the rope. He was a few yards short of the spur of rock on which the dead dik-dik lay, and he was forced to let himself drop into the river. With the end of the rope held between his teeth he swam the last short distance with a furious overarm crawl, just beating the current's attempt to sweep him away downstream.

He dragged himself up on to the island and took a few moments to catch his breath, before he could admire the beautiful little creature he had killed. He felt the familiar melancholy and guilt as he stroked the glossy hide and examined the perfect head with the extraordinary proboscis. However, there was no time now for regrets, nor for the searching of his hunter's conscience.

He trussed up the dik-dik, tying all four of its legs together securely, then he stepped back and looked up. He could see Boris's face peering down at him.

'Haul it up!' he shouted, and gave three yanks on the rope as the agreed signal. The trackers were hidden from his view, but the slack in the rope was taken up and then the dik-dik lifted clear of the island and rose jerkily up the wall of the chasm. Nicholas watched it anxiously. There was a moment when the rope seemed to snag when the carcass was two-thirds of the way to the top, but then it freed itself and snaked on up the cliff.

Eventually the dik-dik disappeared from his sight, and there was a long delay until the rope end dropped back over the lip. Boris had been sensible enough to weight it with a round stone the size of a man's head, and he was hanging over the top of the cliff, watching its progress and signalling to his men to control the descent.

When the end of the weighted line touched the surface of the water it was just out of Nicholas's reach. From the top of the cliff Boris began to swing the line until the end of it pendulumed close enough for Nicholas to grab it. With a bowline knot Nicholas tied a loop in the end of the line and slipped it under his armpits. Then he looked up at Boris.

'Heave away!' he yelled, and tugged the dangling rope three times. The slack tightened and then he was lifted off his feet. He began to ascend in a series of spiralling jerks and heaves. As he rose, the belled wall of the chasm arched in to meet him, until he could fend off from the rock with his bare feet and stop himself spiralling at the end of the rope. He was fifty feet from the top of the cliff when suddenly he stopped abruptly, dangling helplessly against the rock face.

'What's going on?' he shouted up at Boris.

'Bloody rope has jammed,' Boris yelled back. 'Can you see where it is stuck?'

Nicholas peered up and realized that the rope had rolled into a vertical crack in the face, probably the same one that had almost stopped the dik-dik reaching the top. However, his own weight was almost five times that of the little antelope, and had forced the rope much more deeply into the crack.

He was suspended high in the air, with a drop of almost a hundred feet under him.

'Try and swing yourself loose!' Boris shouted down at him. Obediently, Nicholas kicked himself back and twisted on the rope to try and roll it clear. He worked until the sweat streamed down into his eyes and the rope had rubbed him raw under the arms.

'No use,' he shouted back at Boris. 'Try to haul it out with brute force!'

There was a pause, and then he saw the rope above the crack tighten like a bar of iron as five strong men hauled on the top end with all their strength. He could hear the trackers chanting their working chorus as they threw all their combined weight on the line.

His end of the line did not budge. It was a solid jam, and he knew then that they were not going to clear it. He looked down. The surface of the water seemed much further than a hundred feet below.

'The terminal velocity of the human body is one hundred and fifty miles an hour,' he reminded himself. At that speed the water would be like concrete. 'I won't be going that fast when I hit, will I?' he tried to reassure himself.

He looked up again. The men on the top of the cliff were still hauling with all their weight and strength. At that moment one of the strands of the nylon rope sheared against the cutting edge of the rock crack, and began to uncurl like a long green worm.

'Stop pulling!' Nicholas screamed. 'Vast heaving!' But Boris was no longer in sight. He was helping his trackers, adding his weight to the pull.

The second strand of the rope parted and unravelled. There was only a single strand holding him now.

It was going to go at any moment, he realized. 'Boris, you ham-fisted

144

bastard, stop pulling!' But his voice never reached the Russian, and with a pop like a champagne cork the third and final strand of the rope parted.

He plunged downwards, with the loose end of the severed rope fluttering above his head. Flinging both arms straight upwards over his head to stabilize his flight, he straightened his legs, arrowing his body to hit feet first.

He thought about the island under him. Would he miss its red rock fangs or would he smash into it and shatter every bone in his lower body? He dared not look down to judge it in case he destabilized his fall and tumbled in mid-air. If he hit the water flat it would crush his ribs or snap his spine.

His guts seemed to be forced into his throat by the speed of his fall, and he drew one last breath as he hit the surface feet first. The force of it was stunning. It was transmitted up his spine into the back of his skull, so that his teeth cracked against each other and bright lights starred his vision. The river swallowed him under. He went down deep, but he was still moving so fast when he hit the rocky bottom that his legs were jarred to the hips. He felt his knees buckle under the strain, and he thought that both his legs had been broken.

The impact drove the air out of his lungs, and it was only when he kicked off the bottom, desperate for air, that he realized with a rush of relief that both his legs were still intact. He broke out through the surface, wheezing and coughing, and realized that he must have missed the island by only the length of his body. However, by now the current had carried him well clear of it.

He trod water on the racing stream, shook the water from his eyes and looked around him swiftly. The walls of the chasm were streaming past him, and he estimated his speed at around ten knots – fast enough to break bone if he hit a rock. As he thought it, another small island flashed past him almost close enough to touch. He rolled on to his back and thrust both feet out ahead of him, ready to fend off should he be thrown on to another outcrop.

'You are in for the whole ride,' he told himself grimly. 'There is only one way out, and that is to ride it to the bottom.'

He was trying to calculate how far he was above the point where the river debouched from the chasm through the pink stone archway, how far he still had to swim.

'Three or four miles, at the least, and the river falls almost a thousand feet. There are bound to be rapids and probably waterfalls ahead,' he decided. 'From here it does not look good. I'd say the betting is three to one against getting through without leaving some skin and meat on the rocks behind you.'

He looked up. The walls canted in from each side, so that at places they almost met directly over his head. There was only a narrow strip of blue sky showing, and the depths were gloomy and dank. Over the ages the river had scoured the rock as it cut its way through.

'Damned lucky this is the dry season. What is it like down in here in the rainy season?' he wondered. He looked up at the high-water mark etched on the rock fifteen or twenty feet above his head.

Shuddering at the image he looked down again, concentrating on the river ahead. He had his breath back by now, and he checked his body for any damage. With relief he decided that, apart from some bruising and what felt like a sprained knee, he was unhurt. All his limbs were responding, and when he swam a few strokes to one side to avoid another spur of rock, even the sore knee worked well enough to get him out of trouble.

Gradually he became aware of a new sound in the canyon. It was a dull roar, growing stronger as he sped onwards. The walls of the chasm converged upon each other, the gut of rock narrowed and the flood seemed to accelerate as it was squeezed in and confined. The sound of water built up rapidly into a thunder that reverberated in the canyon.

Nicholas rolled over and swam with all his strength across the current until he reached the nearest rock wall. He tried to find a handhold, a place where he could anchor himself, but the rock was polished smooth by the river. It slipped past under his desperately grasping hands, and the river bellowed in his head. He saw the surface around him flatten out and smooth like solid glass. Like a horse laying back its ears as it gathers itself for a jump, the river had sensed what lay ahead.

Nicholas pushed himself away from the rock wall to try and give himself room in which to manoeuvre, and pointed his feet once more downriver. Abruptly the air opened under him and he was launched out into space. All around him white spuming water filled the air, and he was swirled off balance and tossed like a leaf in the torrent. The drop seemed to last for ever, and his stomach swooped against his ribs. Then once more he struck with all his weight and was driven far below the surface.

He fought his way up and abruptly burst out through the surface with his breathing whistling up his throat. Through streaming eyes he saw that he was caught up in the bowl of swirling water below the falls. The waters revolved and eddied, turning in a stately minuet upon themselves.

As he turned, he saw first the high sheet of white water of the falls down which he had tumbled, and then, still turning, the narrow exit from the basin through which the river resumed its mad career downstream. But for the moment he was safe and quiet here in the back-eddy below the falls. The current pushed him against the side of the basin, close in beneath the chute of the falls. He reached out and found a handhold on a clump of mossy fern growing out of a crack in the wall.

Here, at last, he had a chance to rest and consider his position. It did not take him long, however, to realize that his only way out of the chasm was to follow the course of the river and to take his chances with whatever lay downstream. He could expect rapids, if not another set of falls like this one that thundered away close beside him.

If only there were some way up the wall! He looked up, but his spirits quailed as he considered the overhang that formed a cathedral roof high above him.

While he still stared upwards, something caught his eye. Something too regular and regimented to be natural. There was a double row of dark marks running vertically up the wall of rock, beginning at the surface of the water and climbing up the wall to the rim almost two hundred feet overhead. He relinquished his hold on the clump of fern and dog-paddled slowly down to where these marks reached the water.

As he reached them he realized that they were niches, cut about four inches square into the wall. The two rows were twice the spread of his arms apart, and the niche in one row lined up in the horizontal plane exactly with its neighbour in the second row.

Thrusting his hand into the nearest opening, he found that it was deep enough to accommodate his arm to the elbow. This opening, being below the flood level of the waters, was smoothed and worn, but when he looked to those higher up the wall, above the water mark, he saw that they had retained their shape much more clearly. The edges were sharp and square.

'My word, how old are they to have been worn like that?' he marvelled. 'And how the hell did anybody get down here to cut them?'

He hung on to the niche nearest him and studied the pattern in the cliff face. 'Why would anybody go to all that amount of trouble?' He could think of no reason nor purpose. 'Who did this work? What would they want down here?' It was an intriguing mystery.

Then suddenly something else caught his eye. It was a circular indentation in the rock, precisely between the two rows of niches and above the high-water mark. From so far below it looked to be perfectly round – another shape that was not natural.

He paddled further around, trying to reach a position from which he would have a clearer view of it. It seemed to be some sort of rock engraving, a plaque that reminded him strongly of those marks in the black boulders that flank the Nile below the first cataract at Aswan, placed there in antiquity to measure the flood levels of the river waters. But the light was too poor and the angle too acute for him to be certain that it was man-made, let alone to recognize or read any script or lettering that might have been incorporated in the design.

Hoping to devise some way of climbing closer, he tried to use the stone niches as aids. With a great deal of effort, using them as foot- and hand-holds, he managed to lift himself out of the water. But the distances between holds were too great and he fell back with a splash, swallowing more water.

'Take it easy, my lad – you still have to swim out of here. No profit in exhausting yourself. You will just have to come back another day to get a closer look at whatever it is up there.'

Only then did he realize how close he was to total exhaustion. This water coming down from the Choke mountains was still cold with the memories of the high snows. He was shivering until his teeth chattered.

'Not far from hypothermia. Have to get out of here now, while you still have the strength.'

Reluctantly he pushed himself away from the wall of rock and paddled towards the narrow opening through which the Dandera river resumed the headlong rush to join her mother Nile. He felt the current pick him up and bear him forward, and he stopped swimming and let it take him.

'The Devil's roller-coaster!' he told himself. 'Down and down she goes, and where she stops nobody knows.'

The first set of rapids battered him. They seemed endless, but at last he was spewed out into the run of slower water below them. He floated on his back, taking full advantage of this respite, and looked upwards. There was very little light showing above him, for the rock almost met overhead. The air was dank and dark and stank of bats. However, there was little time to examine his surroundings, for once again the river began to roar ahead of him. He braced himself mentally for the assault of turbulent waters, and went cascading down the next steep slide.

After a while he lost track of how far he had been carried, and how many cataracts he had survived. It was a constant battle against the cold and the pain of sodden lungs and strained muscle and overtaxed sinew. The river mauled him.

Suddenly the light changed. After the gloom at the bottom of the high cliffs it was as though a searchlight had been shone directly into his eyes, and he felt the force and ferocity of the river abating. He squinted up into bright sunlight, and then looked back and saw that he had passed out below the archway of pink rock into that familiar part of the river which he had explored with Royan. Coming up ahead of him was the rope suspension bridge, and he had just sufficient strength remaining to paddle feebly towards the small beach of white sand below it.

One of the hairy tattered ropes dangled to the surface of the water, and he managed to catch hold of it as he drifted past and swing himself in towards the beach. He tried to crawl fully ashore, but he collapsed with his face in the sand and vomited out the water he had swallowed. It felt so good just to be able to lie without effort and rest. His lower body still hung into the river, but he had neither the strength nor the inclination to drag himself fully ashore.

'I am alive,' he marvelled, and fell into a state halfway between sleep and unconsciousness.

He never knew how long he had been lying like that, but when he felt a hand shaking his shoulder, and a voice calling softly to him, he was annoyed that his rest had been disturbed.

'*Effendi*, wake up! They seek you. The beautiful Woizero seeks you.'

With a huge effort Nicholas roused himself and sat up slowly. Tamre knelt over him, grinning and waggling his head.

'Please, *effendi*, come with me. The Woizero is searching the river bank on the far side. She is weeping and calling your name,' Tamre told him. He was the only person Nicholas had ever met who contrived to look worried and to grin at the same time. Nicholas looked beyond him and saw that it must be late afternoon, for the sun sat fat and red on the lip of the escarpment.

While still sitting in the sand Nicholas checked his body, making an inventory of his injuries. He ached in every muscle, and his legs and arms were scraped and bruised, but he could detect no broken bones. And although there was a tender lump on the side of his head where he had glanced off a rock, his mind was clear.

'Help me up!' he ordered Tamre. The boy put his shoulder under Nicholas's armpit, where the rope had burnt him, and hoisted him to his feet. The two of them struggled up to the bank and on to the path, and then hobbled slowly across the swinging bridge.

He had hardly reached the other bank when there was a joyous shout from close at hand.

'Nicky! Oh, dear God! You are safe.' Royan ran down the path and threw her arms around him. 'I have been frantic. I thought that—' she broke off, and held him at arm's length to look at him. 'Are you all right? I was expecting to find your broken body—'

'You know me,' he grinned at her and tried not to limp. 'Ten feet tall and bullet-proof. You don't get rid of me that easily. I only did it just to get a hug from you.'

She released him hurriedly. 'Don't read anything into that. I am kind to all beaten puppies, and other dumb animals.' But her smile belied the words. 'Nevertheless, it's good to have you back in one piece, Nicky.'

'Where is Boris?' he asked.

'He and the trackers are searching the banks lower down the river. I think he is looking forward to finding your corpse.'

'What has he done with my dik-dik?'

'There is certainly nothing too much the matter with you if you can worry about that. The skinners have taken it down to the camp.'

'Damn it to hell! I must supervise the skinning and preparation of the trophy myself. They will ruin it!' He put his arm around Tamre's shoulder. 'Come on, my lad! Let's see if I can break into a trot.'

Nicholas knew that in this heat the carcass of the little antelope would decompose swiftly, and the hair would slough from the hide if it were not treated immediately. It was imperative to skin it out immediately. Already it had been left too long, and the preparation of a hide for a full body mount was a skilled and painstaking procedure.

It was already dark as they limped into the camp. Nicholas shouted for the skinners in Arabic.

'Ya, Kif! Ya, Salin!' and when they came running from their living huts he asked anxiously, 'Have you begun?'

'Not yet, *effendi*. We were having our dinner first.'

'For once gluttony is a virtue. Do not touch the creature until I come. While you are waiting for me, fetch one of the gas lights!' He limped to his own hut as fast as his aches would allow. There he stripped and anointed all his visible scrapes and abrasions with mercurochrome, flung on fresh dry clothes, rummaged in his bag until he found the canvas roll which contained his knives, and hurried down to the skinning hut.

By the brilliant white glare of the butane gas lantern he had only just completed the initial skin incisions down the inside of the dik-dik's legs and belly when Boris pushed open the door of the hut.

'Did you have a good swim, English?'

'Bracing, thank you.' Nicholas smiled. 'I don't expect you want to eat your words about my striped dik-dik, do you?' he asked mildly. 'No such bloody animal, I think you said.'

'It is like a rat. A true hunter would not bother himself with such rubbish,' Boris replied haughtily. 'Now that you have your rat, perhaps we can go back to Addis, English?'

'I paid you for three weeks. It is my safari. We go when I say so,' Nicholas told him. Boris grunted and backed out of the hut.

Nicholas worked swiftly. His knives were of a special design to facilitate the fine work, and he stropped them at regular intervals on a ceramic sharpening rod until he could shave the hairs from his forearm with just the lightest touch.

The legs had to be skinned out with the tiny hooves still attached. Before he had completed this part of the work, another figure stooped into the hut. He was dressed in a priest's *shamma* and headcloth, and until he spoke Nicholas did not recognize Mek Nimmur.

'I hear that you have been looking for trouble again, Nicholas. I came to make sure that you were still alive. There was a rumour at the monastery that you had drowned yourself, though I knew it was not possible. You will not die so easily.'

'I hope you are right, Mek,' Nicholas laughed at him.

Mek squatted opposite him. 'Give me one of your knives and I will finish the hooves. It will go quicker if I help you.'

Without comment Nicholas passed him one of the knives. He knew that Mek could skin out the hooves, for years before he had taught him the art. With two of them working on the pelt, it would go that much faster. The sooner the skin was off, the less chance there would be of deterioration.

He turned his attention to the head. This was the most delicate part of the process. The skin had to be peeled off like a glove, and the eyelids and lips and nostrils must be worked from the inside. The ears were perhaps the most difficult to lift away from the gristle in one piece. They worked in companionable silence for a while, which Mek broke at last.

'How well do you know your Russian, Boris Brusilov?' he asked.

'I met him for the first time when I stepped off the plane. He was recommended by a friend.'

'Not a very good friend.' Mek looked up at him and his expression was grim. 'I came to warn you about him, Nicholas.'

'I am listening,' said Nicholas quietly.

'In '85 I was captured by Mengistu's thugs. They kept me in the Karl Marx prison camp near Addis. Brusilov was one of the interrogators there. He was KGB in those days. His favourite trick was to stick the pressure hose from a compressor up the anus of the man or woman he was questioning and turn on the tap. They blew up like a balloon, until the gut burst.' He stopped speaking while he moved around to work on the other hoof of the antelope. 'I escaped before he got around to questioning me. He retired when Mengistu fled, and went hunting. I don't know how he persuaded Woizero Tessay to marry him, but knowing what I do of the man, I expect she did not have much choice in the matter.'

'Of course, I had my suspicions about him,' Nicholas admitted.

They were quiet after that until Mek whispered, 'I came to tell you that I may have to kill him.'

Neither of them spoke again until Mek had finished working on all

151

four hooves. Then he stood up. 'These days, life is uncertain, Nicholas. If I have to leave here in a hurry, and I do not have a chance to say goodbye to you, then there is somebody in Addis who will pass a message to me if you ever need me. His name is Colonel Maryam Kidane in the Ministry of Defence. He is a friend. My code name is the Swallow. He will know who you are talking about.'

They embraced briefly. 'Go with God!' said Mek, and left the hut quietly. The night swallowed his robed figure and Nicholas stood for a long time at the door, until at last he turned back to finish the work.

It was late by the time he had rubbed every inch of the skin with a mixture of rock salt and Kabra dip to cure it and protect it from the ravages of the bacon beetle and other insects and bacteria. At last he laid it out on the floor of the hut with the wet side uppermost and packed more rock salt on the raw areas.

The walls of the hut were reinforced with mesh netting to keep out hyenas. One of these foul creatures could gobble down the pelt in a few seconds. He made certain the door was wired shut before he carried the lantern up to the dining hut. The others had all eaten and gone to bed hours earlier, but Tessay had left his dinner in the charge of the Ethiopian chef. He had not realized how hungry he was until he smelt it.

The next morning Nicholas was so stiff that he hobbled down to the skinning hut like an old man. First he checked the pelt and poured fresh salt over it, then he ordered Kif and Salin to bury the skull of the dik-dik in an ant heap to allow the insects to remove the surplus flesh and scour the brain pan. He preferred this method to boiling the skull.

Satisfied that the trophy was in good condition, he went on down to the dining hut, where Boris greeted him jovially.

'And so, English. We leave for Addis now, da? Nothing more to do here.'

'We will stay to photograph the ceremony of Timkat at the monastery,' Nicholas told him. 'And after that I may want to hunt a Menelik's bushbuck. Who knows? I've told you before. We go when I say so.'

Boris looked disgruntled. 'You are crazy, English. Why do you want to stay in this heat to watch these people and their mumbo-jumbo?'

'Today I will go fishing, and tomorrow we will watch Timkat.'

'You do not have a fishing rod,' Boris protested, but Nicholas opened the small canvas roll no larger than a woman's handbag and showed him the four-piece Hardy Smuggler rod nestling in it.

He looked across the table at Royan, 'Are you coming along to ghillie for me?' he asked.

They went upstream to the suspension bridge where Nicholas set up the rod and tied a fly on to his leader.

'Royal Coachman.' He held it up for her appraisal. 'Fish love them anywhere in the world, from Patagonia to Alaska. We shall soon find out if they are as popular here in Ethiopia, as well.'

She watched from the top of the bank as he shot out line, rolling it upon itself in flight, sailing the weightless fly out to midstream, and then laying it gently on the surface of the water so that it floated lightly on the ripples. On his second cast there was a swirl under the fly. The rod tip arced over sharply, the reel whined and Nicholas let out a whoop.

'Gotcha, my beauty!'

She watched him indulgently from the top of the bank. In his excitement and enthusiasm he was like a small boy. She smiled when she noticed how his injuries had miraculously healed themselves, and how he no longer limped as he ran back and forth along the water's edge, playing the fish. Ten minutes later he slid it, gleaming like a bar of freshly minted gold as long as his arm, flopping and flapping up on to the beach.

'Yellow fish,' he told her triumphantly. 'Scrumptious. Breakfast for tomorrow morning.'

He came up the bank and dropped down in the grass beside her. 'The fishing was really just an excuse to get away from Boris. I brought you here to tell you about what I found up there yesterday.' He pointed up through the archway of pink stone above the bridge. She came up on her elbow and watched him with her full attention.

'Of course, I have no way of telling if it has anything to do with our search, but somebody has been working in there.' He described the niches that he had found carved into the canyon wall. 'They reach from the lip right down to the water's edge. Those below the high-water mark have been severely eroded by the floods. I could not reach those higher up, but from what I could see they have been protected from wind and rain by the dished shape of the cliff; it has formed a veranda roof over them. They appear to be in pristine condition, very much in contrast to those lower down.'

'What do we deduce from that?' she asked.

'That they are very old,' he answered. 'Certainly the basalt is pretty hard. It has taken a long, long time for water to wear it down the way it has.'

'What do you think was the purpose of those holes?'

'I am not sure,' he admitted.

'Could it be that they were the anchor points for some sort of scaffolding?' she asked, and he looked impressed.

'Good thinking. They could be,' he agreed.

'What other ideas occur to you?'

'Ritual designs,' he suggested. 'A religious motif.' He smiled as he saw her expression of doubt. 'Not very convincing, I agree.'

'All right, let's consider the idea of scaffolding. Why would anybody want to erect scaffolding in a place like that?' She lay back in the grass and picked a straw which she nibbled reflectively.

He shrugged. 'To anchor a ladder or a gantry, to gain access to the bottom of the chasm?'

'What other reason?'

'I can't think of any other.'

After a while she shook her head. 'Nor can I.' She spat out the piece of grass. 'If that is the motive, then they were fairly committed to the project. From your description it must have been a substantial structure, designed to support the weight of a lot of men or heavy material.'

'In North America the Red Indians built fishing platforms over waterfalls like that from which they netted the salmon.'

'Have there ever been great runs of fish through these waters?' she asked, and he shrugged again.

'Nobody can answer that. Perhaps long ago – who knows.'

'Was that all you saw down there?'

'High up the wall, aligned with mathematical precision between the two lines of stone niches, there was something that looked like a bas-relief carving.'

She sat up with a jerk and stared at him avidly. 'Could you see it clearly? Was it script, or was it a design? What was the style of the carving?'

'No such luck. It was too high, and the light is very poor down there. I am not even certain that it wasn't a natural flaw in the rock.'

Her disappointment was palpable, but after a pause she asked, 'Was there anything else?'

'Yes,' he grinned. 'Lots and lots of water moving very very fast.'

'What are we going to do about this putative bas-relief of yours?' she asked.

'I don't like the idea in the least, but I will have to go back in there and have another look.'

'When?'

'Timkat tomorrow. Our one chance to get into the *maqdas* of the cathedral. After that we will make a plan to explore the gorge.'

'We are running out of time, Nicky, just when things are getting really interesting.'

'You can say that again!' he murmured. She felt his breath on her lips, for their faces were as close together as those of conspirators or of lovers, and she realized the double meaning of her own words. She jumped to her feet and slapped the dust and loose straw from her jodhpurs.

'You only have one fish to feed the multitude. Either you have a very high opinion of yourself, or you had better get fishing.'

Two *debteras* who had been detailed by the bishop to escort them tried to force a way for them through the crowds. However, they had not reached the foot of the staircase before the escort itself was swallowed up and lost. Nicholas and Royan became separated from the other couple.

'Keep close,' Nicholas told Royan, and maintained a firm grip on her upper arm as he used his shoulder to open a path for them. He drew her along with him. Naturally, he had deliberately contrived to lose Boris and Tessay in the crush, and it had worked out nicely the way he had planned it.

At last they reached a position where Nicholas could set his back firmly against one of the stone columns of the terrace, to prevent the crowd jostling him. He also had a good view of the entrance to the cavern cathedral. Royan was not tall enough to see over the heads of the men in front of her, so Nicholas lifted her up on to the balustrade of the staircase and anchored her firmly against the column. She clung to his shoulder for support, for the drop into the Nile opened behind her.

The worshippers kept up a low monotonous chant, while a dozen separate bands of musicians tapped their drums and rattled their sistrums. Each band surrounded its own patron, a chieftain in splendid robes, sheltering under a huge gaudy umbrella.

There was an air of excitement and expectation almost as fierce as the heat and the stink. It built up steadily and, as the singing increased in pitch and volume, the crowd began to sway and undulate like a single organism, some grotesque amoeba, pulsing with life.

Suddenly from within the precincts of the cathedral there came the chiming of brass bells, and immediately a hundred horns and trumpets answered. From the head of the stairway there was a fusillade of gunfire as the bodyguards of the chieftains fired their weapons in the air.

Some of them were armed with automatic rifles, and the clatter of AK-47 fire blended with the thunder of ancient black powder muzzle-loaders. Clouds of blue gunsmoke blew over the congregation, and bullets ricocheted from the cliff and sang away over the gorge. Women shrieked and ululated, an eerie, blood-chilling sound. The men's faces were alight with the fires of religious fervour. They fell to their knees and lifted their hands high in adoration, chanting and crying out to God for blessing. The women held their infants aloft, and tears of religious frenzy streaked their dark cheeks.

From the gateway of the underground church emerged a procession of priests and monks. First came the *debteras* in long white robes, and then the acolytes who were to be baptized at the riverside. Royan recognized Tamre, his long gangling frame standing a head above the boys around him. She waved over the crowd and he saw her and grinned shyly before he followed the *debteras* on to the pathway to the river.

By this time night was falling. The depths of the cauldron were obscured by shadows, and hanging over it the sky was a purple canopy pricked by the first bright stars. At the head of the pathway burned a brass brazier. As each of the priests passed it he thrust his unlit torch into the flames and, as soon as it flared, he held it aloft.

Like a stream of molten lava the torchlit procession began to uncoil down the cliff face, the priests chanting dolefully and the drums booming and echoing from the cliffs across the river.

Following the baptism candidates through the stone gateway came the ordained priests in their tawdry robes, bearing the processional crosses of silver and glittering brass, and the banners of embroidered silk, with their depictions of the saints in the agony of martyrdom and the ecstasy of adoration. They clanged their bells and blew their fifes, and sweated and chanted until their eyes rolled white in dark faces.

Behind them, borne by two priests in the most sumptuous robes and tall, jewel-encrusted head-dresses, came the *tabot*. The Ark of the Tabernacle was covered with a crimson cloth that hung to the ground, for it was too holy to be desecrated by the gaze of the profane.

The worshippers threw themselves down upon the ground in fresh paroxysms of adoration. Even the chiefs prostrated themselves upon the soiled pavement of the terrace, and some of them wept with the fervour of their belief.

Last in the procession came Jali Hora, wearing not the crown with the blue stone, but another even more splendid creation, the Epiphany crown, a mass of gleaming metal and flashing *faux* jewels which seemed too heavy for his ancient scrawny neck to support. Two *debteras* held his elbows and guided his uncertain footsteps on to the stairway that led down to the Nile.

As the procession descended, so those worshippers nearest to the head of the stairs rose to their feet, lit their torches at the brazier and followed the abbot down. There was a general movement along the terrace to join the flow, and as it began to empty, Nicholas lifted Royan down from her perch on the balustrade.

'We must get into the church while there are still enough people around to cover us,' he whispered. Leading her by the hand, with his other hand hanging on to the strap of his camera bag, he joined the movement down the terrace. He allowed them to be carried forward, but all the time he was edging across the stream of humanity towards the entrance to the church. He saw Boris and Tessay in the crush ahead of him, but they had not seen him, and he crouched lower so as to screen himself from them.

As he and Royan reached the gateway to the outer chamber of the church, he eased them out of the throng of humanity and drew her gently through the low entrance into the dim, deserted interior. With a quick glance he made certain that they were alone, and that the guards were no longer at their stations beside the inner gates. Then he moved quickly along the side wall, to where one of the soot-grimed tapestries hung from the ceiling to the stone floor. He lifted the folds of heavy woven wool and drew Royan behind them, letting them fall back into place, concealing them both.

They were only just in time, for hardly had they flattened their backs against the wall and let the tapestry settle when they heard footsteps approaching from the *qiddist*. Nicholas peeked around the corner of the tapestry and saw four white-robed priests cross the outer chamber and swing the main doors closed as they left the church. There was a weighty thud from outside as they dropped the locking beam into place, and then a profound silence pervaded the cavern.

'I didn't reckon on that,' Nicholas whispered. 'They have locked us in for the night.'

'At least it means that we won't be disturbed,' Royan replied briskly. 'We can get to work right away.'

Stealthily they emerged from their hiding-place, and moved across the outer chamber to the doorway of the *qiddist*. Here Nicholas paused and cautioned her with a hand on her arm. 'From here on we are in forbidden territory. Better let me go ahead and scout the lie of the land.'

She shook her head firmly. 'You are not leaving me here. I am coming with you all the way.' He knew better than to argue.

'Come on, then.' He led her up the steps and into the middle chamber.

It was smaller and lower than the room they had left. The wall hangings were richer and in a better state of repair. The floor was bare, except for a pyramid-shaped framework of hand-hewn native timber upon which stood rows of brass lamps, each with the wick floating in a puddle of melted oil. The meagre light they provided was all that there was, and it left the ceiling and the recesses of the chamber in shadow.

As they crossed the floor towards the gates that closed off the *maqdas*, Nicholas took two electric torches from his camera bag and handed one to her. 'New batteries,' he told her, 'but don't waste them. We may be here all night.'

They stopped in front of the doors to the Holy of Holies. Quickly

Nicholas examined them. There were engravings of St Frumentius on each panel, his head enclosed in a nimbus of celestial radiance and his right hand lifted in the act of benediction.

'Primitive lock,' he murmured, 'must be hundreds of years old. You could throw your hat through the gap between the hasp and the tongue.' He slipped his hand into the bag and brought out a Leatherman tool.

'Clever little job, this is. With it you do anything from digging the stones out of a horse's hoof, to opening the lock on a chastity belt.'

He knelt in front of the massive iron lock and unfolded one of the multiple blades of the tool. She watched anxiously as he worked, and then gave a little start as with a satisfying clunk the tongue of the lock slid back.

'Mis-spent youth?' she asked. 'Burglary amongst your many talents?'

'You don't really want to know.' He stood up and put his shoulder to one leaf of the door. It gave with a groan of unlubricated hinges, and he pushed it open only just wide enough for them to squeeze through, then immediately shut it behind them.

They stood side by side on the threshold of the *maqdas* and gazed about them in silent awe.

The Holy of Holies was a small chamber, much smaller than either of them had expected. Nicholas could have crossed it in a dozen strides. The vaulted roof was so low that by standing on tiptoe he could have touched it with his outstretched fingertips.

From the floor upwards the walls were lined with shelves upon which stood the gifts and offerings of the faithful, icons of the Trinity and the Virgin rendered in Byzantine style, framed in ornate silver. There were ranks of statuettes of saints and emperors, medallions and wreaths made of polished metal, pots and bowls and jewelled boxes, candelabra with many branches, on each of which the votive candles burned providing an uncertain wavering light. It was an extraordinary collection of junk and treasures, of objects of virtue and garish bric-à-brac, offered as articles of faith by the emperors and chieftains of Ethiopia over the centuries.

In the centre of the floor stood the altar of cedarwood, the panels carved with visionary scenes of revelation and creation, of the temptation and the fall from Eden, and of the Last Judgement. The altar cloth was crocheted raw silk, and the cross and the chalice were in massive worked silver. The abbot's crown gleamed in the candlelight, with the blue ceramic seal of Taita in the centre of its brow.

Royan crossed the floor and knelt in front of the altar. She bowed her head in prayer. Nicholas waited respectfully at the threshold until she rose to her feet again, and then he went to join her.

'The *tabot* stone!' He pointed beyond the altar, and they went forward side by side. At the back of the *maqdas* stood an object covered with a heavy damask cloth encrusted with embroidered thread of silver and gold. From the outline beneath the covering they could see that it was of elegant and pleasing proportions, as tall as a man, but slender with a pedestal topping.

They both circled it, studying the cloaked shape avidly, but reluctant to touch it or to uncover it, fearful that their expectations might prove unwarranted, and that their hopes would be dashed like the turbulent river waters plunging into the cauldron of the Nile. Nicholas broke the tension that gripped them by turning away from the *tabot* stone to the barred gate in the back wall of the sanctuary.

'The tomb of St Frumentius!' he said, and went to the grille. She came to his side, and together they peered through the square openings in the woodwork that was black with age. The interior was in darkness. Nicholas prodded his torch through one of the openings and pressed the switch.

The tomb lit up in a rainbow of colour so bright in the beam of the torch that their eyes took a few moments to adjust and then Royan gasped aloud.

'Oh, sweet heaven!' She began to tremble as if in high fever, and her face went creamy pale as all the blood drained from it.

The coffin was set into a stone shelf in the rear wall of the cell-like tomb. On the exterior was painted the likeness of the man within. Although it was badly faded and most of the paint had flaked away, the pale face and reddish beard of the dead man were still discernible.

This was not the only reason for Royan's amazement. She was staring at the walls above and on either side of the shelf on which the coffin lay. They were a riot of colour, every inch of them covered with the most intricate and elaborate paintings that had miraculously weathered the passage of the millennia.

Nicholas played his torchbeam over them in awestruck silence, and Royan clung to his arm as if to save herself from falling. She dug her sharp nails into his flesh, but he was heedless of the pain.

There were scenes of great battles, fighting galleys locked in terrible combat upon the blue eternal waters of the river. There were scenes of the hunt, the pursuit of the river horse and of great elephants with long tusks of gleaming ivory. There were battle scenes of regiments plumed and armoured, raging in their fury and blood lust. Squadrons of chariots wheeled and charged each other across these narrow walls, half obscured by the dust of their own mad career.

The foreground of each mural was dominated by the same tall heroic figure. In one scene he drew the bow to full stretch, in another he swung high the blade of bronze. His enemies quailed before him, he trod them underfoot or gathered together their severed heads like a bouquet of flowers.

Nicholas played the beam over all this splendid array of art, and brought it to a stop upon the central panel that covered the entire main wall above the shelf on which the rotting coffin lay. Here the same godlike figure rode the footplate of his chariot. In one hand he held the bow and in the other a bundle of javelins. His head was bare of any helmet, and his hair flowed out behind him in the wind of his passage, a thick golden braid like the tail of a lion. His features were noble and proud, his gaze direct and indomitable.

Below him was a legend in classical Egyptian hieroglyphics. In a sepulchral whisper Royan translated them aloud:

> Great Lion of Egypt.
> Best of One Hundred Thousand
> Holder of the Gold of Valour
> Pharaoh's Sole Companion
> Warrior of all the Gods
> May you live for ever!

Her hand shook upon his arm, and her voice choked and died away, stifled with emotion. She gave a little sob, and then shook herself as she brought herself back under control.

'I know this artist,' she said softly. 'I have spent five years studying his work. I would know it anywhere.' She drew a breath. 'I know with utter certainty that nearly four thousand years ago Taita the slave decorated these walls and designed this tomb.'

She pointed to the name of the dead man carved into the stone above the shelf on which his coffin lay.

'This is not the tomb of a Christian saint. Centuries ago some old priest must have stumbled upon it and, in his ignorance, usurped it for his own religion.' She drew another shaky breath. 'Look there! That is the seal of Tanus, Lord Harreb, the commander of all the armies of Egypt, lover of Queen Lostris and the natural father of Prince Memnon, who became the Pharaoh Tamose.'

They were both silent then, lost in the wonder of their discovery. Nicholas broke the silence at last.

'It's all true, then. The secrets of the seventh scroll are all here for us, if we can find the key to them.'

'Yes,' she said softly. 'The key. Taita's stone testament.' She turned back towards the *tabot* stone and approached it slowly, almost fearfully.

'I can't bring myself to look, Nicky. I am terrified that it's not what we hope it is. You do it!'

He went directly to the column, and with a magician's flourish jerked away the damask cloth that covered it. They stared at the pillar of pink mottled granite that he had revealed. It was about six feet high and a foot square at the base, tapering up to half that width at the flat pedestal of the summit. The granite had been polished, and then engraved.

Royan stepped forward and touched the cold stone, running her fingers lingeringly over the hieroglyphic script in the way a blind man reads Braille.

'Taita's letter to us,' she whispered, picking out the symbol of the hawk with a broken wing from the mass of close-chiselled script, tracing the outline with a long, slim forefinger that trembled softly. 'Written almost four thousand years ago, waiting all these ages for us to read and understand it. See how he has signed it.' Slowly she circled the granite pillar, studying each of the four sides in turn, smiling and nodding, frowning and shaking her head, then smiling again as if it were a love letter.

'Read it to me,' Nicholas invited. 'It's too complicated for me – I understand the characters, but I cannot follow the sense or the meaning. Explain it to me.'

'It's pure Taita.' She laughed, her awe and wonder at last giving way to excitement. 'He is being his usual obscure and capricious self.' It was as though she were talking of a beloved but infuriating old friend. 'It's all in verse and is probably some esoteric code of his own.' She picked out a line of hieroglyphics, and followed them with her finger as she read aloud, '"*The vulture rises on mighty pinions to greet the sun. The jackal howls and turns upon his tail. The river flows towards the earth. Beware, you violators of the sacred places, lest the wrath of all the gods descend upon you!*"'

'It's nonsense jargon. It does not make sense,' he protested.

'Oh, yes, it makes sense all right. Taita always makes sense, once you follow the way his oblique mind is working.' She turned to face him squarely. 'Don't look so glum, Nicky. You can't expect to read Taita like an editorial in *The Times*. He has set us a riddle that may take weeks and months of work to unravel.'

'Well, one thing is certain. We can't stay here in the *maqdas* for weeks and months while we puzzle it out. Let's get to work.'

'Photographs first.' She became brisk and businesslike. 'Then we can lift impressions from the stone.'

He set down the camera bag and knelt over it to open the flap. 'I will shoot two rolls of colour first, and then use the Polaroid. That will give us something to work on until we can have the colour developed.'

She stood out of his way as he circled the pillar on his knees, keeping the angle correct so as not to distort the perspective. He took a series of shots of each of the four sides, using different shutter speeds and exposures.

'Don't use up all your film,' she warned him. 'We need some shots of the walls of the tomb itself.'

Obediently he went to the grille gates and studied the locking system. 'This is a bit more complicated than the outer gate. If I try to get in here, I might do some damage. I don't think it will be worth the risk of being discovered.'

'All right,' she agreed. 'Work through the openings in the grille.'

He filmed as best he was able, extending the camera through the openings at the full stretch of his arms, and estimating his focus.

'That's the lot,' he told her at last. 'Now for the Polaroids.' He changed cameras and repeated the entire process, but this time Royan held a small tape measure against the pillar to give the scale.

As he exposed each plate he handed it to her to check the development. Once or twice when the flash setting on the camera had either overexposed or rendered the subject too dull, or for some other reason she was not satisfied, she asked him to repeat the shot.

After almost two hours' work they had a complete set of Polaroids, and Nicholas packed his cameras away and brought out the roll of art paper. Working together, they stretched it over one face of the pillar and secured it in place with masking tape. Then he started at the top and she at the bottom. Each with a black art crayon, they rubbed the precise shape and form of the engravings on to the sheet of blank paper.

'I have learned how important this is when dealing with Taita. If you are not able to work with the original, then you must have an exact copy. Sometimes the most minute detail of the engraving may change the entire sense and meaning of the script. He layers everything with hidden depths. You have read in *River God* how he considers himself to be the riddler and punster *par excellence* and the greatest exponent of the game of bao that ever lived. Well, that much of the book is accurate. Wherever he is now, he knows the game is on and he is revelling in every move we make. I can just imagine him giggling and rubbing his hands together with glee.'

'Bit fanciful, dear girl.' He settled back to work. 'But I know what you mean.'

The task of transferring the outline of the designs on to the blank sheets of art paper was painstaking and monotonous, and the hours passed as they laboured on hands and knees or crouched over the granite pillar. At last Nicholas stepped back and massaged his aching back.

'That does it, then. All finished.'

She stood up beside him. 'What time is it?' she asked, and he checked his wrist-watch.

'Four in the morning. We had better tidy up in here. Make certain we leave no sign of our visit.'

'One last thing,' Royan said, tearing a corner off one of the sheets of art paper. With it she went to the altar where the abbot's crown lay. Quickly she taped the scrap of paper over the blue ceramic seal in the

162

centre of the crown, and filled it with a rubbing of the design of the hawk with a broken wing.

'Just for luck,' she explained to him, as she came back to help him fold the long sheets of paper and pack them back in the bag. Then they gathered up the shreds of discarded masking tape and the empty film wrappers that he had strewn on the stone slabs.

Before they covered the granite stele with the damask cloth, Royan caressed the stone panels of script as if to take leave of them for ever. Then she nodded at Nicholas.

He spread the cloth over the pillar and they adjusted the folds to hang as they had found them. From the threshold of the brass-bound door they surveyed the *maqdas* for the last time, then he opened the door a crack.

'Let's go!' She squeezed through and he followed her out into the *qiddist* of the church. It took him only a few minutes to slide the tongue of the lock back into place.

'How will we get out through the main doors?' she asked.

'I don't think that will be necessary. The priests obviously have another entrance from their quarters directly into the *qiddist*. You very seldom see them using the main gates.' He stood in the centre of the floor, and looked around carefully. 'It must be on this side if it leads directly into the monks' living quarters—' he broke off with a grunt of satisfaction. 'Aha! You can see where all their feet have actually worn a pathway over the centuries.' He pointed out a smooth area of dished and worn stone near the side wall. 'And look at the marks of grubby fingers on the tapestry over there.' He crossed quickly to the hanging and drew a fold aside. 'I thought as much.' There was a narrow doorway concealed behind the hanging. 'Follow me.'

They found themselves in a dark passageway through the living rock. Nicholas flashed his torch down its length, but he masked the bulb with his hand to show only as much light as they needed. 'This way.'

The passage turned at right-angles and ahead they could make out a dull illumination. Nicholas switched off the torch and led her on.

Now there was the smell of stale food and humanity, and they passed the doorless entrance to a monk's rock cell. Nicholas flashed his torch into it. It was deserted and bare. A wooden cross hung on the wall with a truckle bed below it. There were no other furnishings. They went on past a dozen others which were almost identical.

At the next turning of the passage Nicholas paused. He felt a tiny draught on his cheek, and the taste of fresh air on his tongue. 'This way,' he whispered.

They hurried on, until suddenly Royan grabbed his shoulder from behind and forced him to stop.

'What—' he began, but she squeezed his shoulder to silence him. He heard it then, the sound of a human voice, echoing eerily through the labyrinth of passageways.

Then came a weird haunting cry, that of a soul in agony, wailing and sobbing. They crept forward, trying to make their escape before they were discovered, but the sounds grew stronger as they went on.

'Dead ahead,' Nicholas warned her in a whisper. 'We are going to have to sneak past.'

Now they saw soft yellow lamplight spilling from the doorway of one of the cells into the passage. There came another heart-rending female cry that echoed down the passage and froze them in their tracks.

'That's a woman's voice. What is happening?' Royan breathed, but he shook his head for silence and led her on.

They had to pass the open door of the lit cell. Nicholas edged towards it with his back flattened to the opposite wall. She followed him, keeping close and clinging to his arm for comfort.

As they looked into the cell the woman cried out again, but this time her voice blended with that of a man. It was a duet without words, but racked with all the feral agony of a passion too fierce to be borne in silence.

In their full view a couple lay naked upon the truckle bed. The woman lay spread-eagled, holding the man's hips between her uplifted knees. Her arms wound hard around his back, upon which each separate muscle stood out proudly and gleamed with sweat. He thrust down into her savagely, his buttocks bunching and pounding with the force of a great black battering ram.

She rolled her head from side to side as another incoherent cry was torn from her straining throat. It seemed too much for the man above her to bear, and he reared back like a flaring cobra, his pelvis still locked to hers, but his back arched like a war bow. Spasm after spasm gripped him. The sinews in the back of his legs were stretched to snapping point, and the muscles in his back fluttered and jumped like separate living creatures.

The woman opened her eyes and looked directly at them as they stood transfixed in the doorway, but she was blinded with the strength of her passion. Her eyes were sightless, as she cried aloud to the man above her.

Nicholas drew Royan away, and they slipped down the passageway and out on to the deserted terrace. They stopped at the foot of the staircase, and breathed the sweet cool night air that was perfumed by the waters of the Nile.

'Tessay has gone to him,' Royan whispered softly.

'For tonight at least,' Nicholas agreed.

'No,' Royan denied. 'You saw her face, Nicky. She belongs to Mek Nimmur now.'

The dawn was flushing the serrated crests of the escarpment to the colours of port wine and roses when they reached camp and separated at the door to Royan's hut.

'I am bushed,' she told Nicholas. 'The excitement has been too much for me. You won't see me again before noon.'

'Good thinking! Sleep as long as you wish. I want you scintillating and perceptive when we start going over the material which we gathered last night.'

It was long before noon, however, when Nicholas was woken from a deep sleep by the harsh and intrusive bellows of Boris as he stormed into the hut.

'English, wake up! I must talk to you. Wake up, man, wake up.'

Nicholas rolled over and thrust one arm out from under the mosquito net as he groped for his wrist-watch. 'Damn you, Brusilov! What the hell do you want?'

'My wife! Have you seen my wife?'

'Now what has your wife got to do with me?'

'She has gone! I have not seen her since last night.'

'The way you treat her, that comes as no stunning surprise. Now go away and leave me to sleep.'

'The whore has run off with that black bastard, Mek Nimmur. I know all about them. Don't try and protect her, English. I know everything that goes on around here. You are trying to cover for her – admit it!'

'Get out of here, Boris. Don't try and involve me in your sordid private life.'

'I saw you and that *shufta* bastard talking in the skinning hut the other night. Don't try to deny it, English. You are in this thing with them.'

Nicholas flung back the mosquito net and jumped out of his bed. 'Kindly moderate your language when you talk to me, you great oaf.'

Boris backed off towards the door. 'I know that she has run away with him. I searched for them all last night at the river. They have gone, and most of his men with them.'

'Good for Tessay. She is showing some taste in men for a change.'

'You think I will let the whore get away with this? You are wrong, very wrong. I am going to follow them and kill them both. I know which way they are headed. You think I am a fool. I know all about Mek Nimmur. I was head of intelligence—' He broke off as he realized

165

what he had said. 'I will shoot him in the belly and let that whore Tessay watch him die.'

'If you are going after Mek Nimmur, then my bet is that you won't be coming back.'

'You don't know me, English. You beat me up one night when I had a bottle of vodka in my belly, so you think I am easy, *da?* Well, Mek Nimmur will see now how easy I am.'

Boris flung out of the hut. Nicholas pulled on a shirt over his shorts and followed him.

Back in his own hut, Boris had flung a few essential items into a light pack. Now he was stuffing cartridges into the magazine of his 30/06 hunting rifle.

'Let them go, Boris,' Nicholas advised him in a more reasonable tone of voice. 'Mek is a tough lad – they don't come tougher – and he has a war party of fifty men with him. You are old enough to know that you can never hold on to a woman by force. Let her go!'

'I do not want to hold on to her. I want to kill her. The safari is over, English.' He flung a pair of keys on a leather tag on the floor at Nicholas's feet. 'There are the keys of the Land Cruiser. You can make your own way back to Addis from here. I will leave four of my best men to look after you, and hold your hand. Leave the big truck for me to use. When you get to Addis, leave the keys of the Land Cruiser with my tracker, Aly. I will know where to find him later. I will send you the money I owe you for cancellation. Don't worry – I am a man of principles.'

'How could I ever doubt it?' Nicholas smiled. 'Goodbye, old chum. I wish you luck. You'll need plenty of that if you are going up against Mek Nimmur.'

Boris was several hours behind his quarry, and as soon as he had left the camp he broke into a jog trot that carried him down the pathway to join the main track to the west, towards the Sudanese border. He ran like a scout, with an easy swinging gait that ate up the ground.

'Looks as though he is still in good shape, even with the vodka.' Despite himself Nicholas was impressed as he watched him go. 'But I wonder how long he will be able to keep up that pace?'

He turned back to his own quarters to get a little more sleep, but as he passed her hut Royan popped her head out. 'What was all the shouting about? I thought that you and Boris were having another little difference of opinion.'

'Tessay has done a bunk. Boris has guessed that she has gone off with Mek, and he is chasing after them.'

'Oh, Nicky! Can't we warn them?'

'No chance of that, but unless Mek has gone soft he will be

expecting Boris to come after him. In fact, now that I come to think of it, he is probably hoping for just that chance to even the score. No, Mek doesn't need any more help from us. Go back to sleep!'

'I can't possibly sleep now. I am so worked up. I have been looking at the Polaroids that we took last night. Taita has given us an overflowing cup. Come and have a look at this.'

'Just one hour's sleep more?' He made a mock plea.

'Immediately, if not sooner.' She laughed at him.

In her hut she had the Polaroids and the rubbings spread out on the camp table, and she beckoned him to take the seat beside her.

'While you were snoring your head off, I made some progress.' She laid four Polaroids side by side, and placed her large magnifying glass over them. It was a professional land surveyor's model on folding legs, and under it every detail of the photographs was revealed. 'Taita has headed each of the sides of the stele with the name of one of the seasons of the year – spring, summer, autumn and winter. What do you think he was getting at?'

'Page numbers?'

'Exactly my own thought,' she agreed. 'The Egyptians considered spring as the beginning of all new life. He is telling us in which order to read the panels. This one is spring.' She selected one of the photographs.

'It starts with four standard quotations from the *Book of the Dead*.' She quoted the first few lines of the opening section: '"*I am the first breeze blowing softly over the dark ocean of eternity. I am the first sunrise. The first glimmer of light. A white feather blowing in the dawn wind. I am Ra. I am the beginning of all things. I will live for ever. I shall never perish.*"' Still holding the glass poised, she looked up at him. 'As far as I can see, they do not differ substantially from the original. My instinct is to set these aside for the time being. We can always come back to them later.'

'Let's go with your instinct,' he suggested. 'Read the next section.'

She held the glass to the Polaroid. 'I am not going to look at you while I read this. Taita can be as earthy as Rabelais when he is in the mood. Anyway, here goes. "*The daughter of the goddess pines for her dam. She roars like a lioness as she hurries to meet her. She leaps from the mountain, and her fangs are white. She is the harlot of all the world. Her vagina pisseth out great torrents. Her vagina has swallowed an army of men. Her sex eateth up the masons and the workers of stone. Her vagina is an octopus that has swallowed up a king.*"'

'Whoa there!' Nicholas chuckled. 'Pretty fruity stuff, don't you think?' He leaned forward to study her face, for it was still turned away from him. 'Och, lassie, you have roses in your bonny cheeks. Not a blush, surely not?'

167

'Your Scots accent is not in the least convincing,' she told him coldly, still not looking at him. 'When you have finished being clever at my expense, what do you think of what I have just read?'

'Apart from the obvious, I haven't any idea.'

'I want to show you something.' She stood up and packed the photographs and the rolls of art paper back into the haversack. 'You'll need to get your boots on. I am taking you on a little walk.'

An hour later they stood in the centre of the suspension bridge, swaying gently high above the swift waters of the Dandera river.

'Hapi is the goddess of the Nile. Is this river not then her daughter, pining to meet her, leaping from the mountain top, roaring like a lioness, her fangs white with spume?' she asked him.

They stared in silence at the archway of pink stone through which the river poured, and suddenly Nicholas grinned lasciviously. 'I think that I know what you are going to say next. That's what I first thought of when I looked at that cleft. You said it was like a gargoyle's mouth, but I had another image.'

'All I can say is that you must have some extraordinary lady friends,' she said, and then covered her mouth. 'Ooops! I didn't mean to say that. I am being as disgusting as either you or Taita.'

'The workmen swallowed up in there!' His voice became more excited. 'The masons and the workers in stone!'

'Pharaoh Mamose was a god. The river has swallowed up a god with her – with her stone archway.' She was equally excited. 'I must admit that I would not have made the association if you hadn't explored the interior of the cavern, and found those niches in the wall.' She shook his arm. 'Nicky, we have to get in there again. We have to get a clearer look at that bas-relief you found on the cavern wall.'

'It will take some preparation,' he said dubiously. 'I will have to splice the ropes and make some sort of pulley system, and I will have to drill Aly and the other men to avoid a repetition of my last little fiasco. We won't be ready to make the attempt until tomorrow morning at the very earliest.'

'You get on with it. I will have plenty to keep me occupied with the translation of the stele.' Then she stopped and looked up at the sky. 'Listen!' she whispered.

He cocked his head and above the sound of the river, heard the whining flutter of rotors in the air.

'Dammit!' he snapped. 'I thought we had lost the Pegasus presence. Come on!' He grabbed her arm and hustled her off the bridge. When they reached the land he jumped down on to the beach, and she followed him. The two of them crept under the hanging eaves of the bridge.

168

They sat quietly on the white sandy beach and listened to the Jet Ranger helicopter approaching swiftly, and then circling back over the hills beyond the pink cliffs. This time the pilot had not spotted them, for he turned away and began to patrol up and down the line of the chasm. Suddenly the engine-beat changed dramatically as the pitch altered and the pilot pulled up the collective.

'Sounds as if he is going in for a landing up there in the hills,' Nicholas said as he crawled out from under the bridge. 'I would feel a lot easier without them snooping around.'

'I don't think we have too much to worry about,' Royan disagreed. 'Even if they are connected with Duraid's killers, we are still way out ahead of them. Obviously they have not tumbled to the importance of the monastery, and the stele.'

'I hope you are right. Let's get back to camp. We must not let them see us in the vicinity of the chasm again. It will be too much of a coincidence for them to find us hanging around here every time they come this way.'

While Royan went to her hut and pored over her photographs and etchings, Nicholas worked with the trackers and skinners. He spliced the unravelled end of the nylon rope to the second hank, to make a single length five hundred feet long. Then he cannibalized the canvas fly of the cooking hut, cutting it up and whipping the raw edges to make a sling seat. He fashioned the ends of the rope into a harness which he spliced into the four corners of the canvas seat.

He had no block and tackle, so he put together a crude gantry of poles which could be extended out over the cliff edge to keep the rope clear of the rock. The rope would run through the groove that he drilled in the end of the central beam with a red-hot iron. He lubricated it with cooking lard.

It was the middle of the afternoon by the time he had completed his preparations. Then, leaving Royan in camp, he led his men, burdened with the coils of rope and the pole sections of the gantry, back up the pathway to the spot where he had abseiled down into the ravine to retrieve the carcass of the dik-dik. From there they worked their way downstream, following the rim of the cliff. It was heavy going for thorn scrub grew right up to the edge, and in many places they were forced to use their machetes to hack their way through.

The sound of the waterfall guided him. As they moved downriver it grew louder, until the rock seemed to quiver under his feet with the roar of falling waters. Finally, by leaning out over the edge and peering downwards, Nicholas could make out the flash of spray in the depths below.

'This is the spot.' He grunted with satisfaction, and explained to Aly in Arabic what he wanted done.

In order to determine the exact position in which to set up the gantry, Nicholas climbed into the canvas sling seat and had them lower him twenty feet down the cliff face, just as far as the beginning of the overhang. Up to that point he was able to keep the nylon rope from abrading on the rock, but he was also able to see around the bulge of the face.

Hanging backwards over the falls and the rocky bowl of the river one hundred and fifty feet below him, he was able at last to see the double row of niches in the rock face. However, the bas-relief engraving was still hidden from view by the tumblehome of the cliff. He gave Aly the signal and they hauled him up.

'We must set up the gantry a little further down,' he told him, and directed them as they hacked away the dense shrubbery that choked the rim. Then suddenly he exclaimed, 'I'll be damned!' He went down on one knee to examine the rim rock that the thorns had concealed. 'There are more excavations here.'

Exposed to the elements, unlike those works further down that had been protected by the overhang, these were badly eroded. There were just vague traces remaining in the rim rock, but he was certain that these indentations were the upper anchor points for the ancient scaffolding. They set up their own gantry on the same levelled area, and extended the long pole out over the drop. Then they rigged and secured it with a crude cantilever system of ropes and lighter poles.

When they were finished, Nicholas crawled out to the end to test the structure and to run the end of the rope through the slot he had prepared for it. The whole structure seemed solid and firm. Nevertheless, it was with relief that he crawled back to solid ground.

He stood up and looked over the tops of the thorn scrub to where the lowering sun was fuming red and angry on the horizon.

'Enough for one day,' he decided. 'The rest can wait for tomorrow.'

The next morning Nicholas and Royan were both up and drinking coffee at the campfire while it was still dark. Aly and his men were squatting at their own fire near by, talking quietly and coughing over the first cigarettes of the day. The project seemed to have caught their imagination. They had no inkling of the reason for this second descent into the chasm, but the enthusiasm of the two *ferengi* was infectious.

As soon as it was light enough to see the path, Nicholas led them back up into the hills. The men chatted cheerfully amongst themselves in Amharic as they hurried through the thorn scrub, and they came out on the rim rock just as the sun broke out over the eastern escarpment of the valley. Nicholas had drilled the men the previous day, and he and Royan had sat half the night going over the plans, so each of them knew their part and they lost little time in setting themselves up for the descent.

Nicholas had stripped to shorts and tennis shoes, but this time he had brought along an old Barbarians rugby jersey for warmth. While he pulled this over his head he pointed out to Royan the platform that had been dug out from the solid rock.

She examined it carefully. 'It's very hard to be sure, but I think you are right. This probably is man-made.'

'When you get further down you will have no doubts. There is very little weathering of the face under the overhang, and the niches are almost perfectly preserved – until they reach the high-water mark, that is,' he told her, as he took his seat in the sling and swung out over the cliff. Dangling from the end of the gantry he gave Aly the sign, and the men lowered him down into the gorge. The rope ran smoothly through the lubricated slot.

He saw at once that he had judged it correctly, and that he was descending in line with the double row of niches. He came level with the enigmatic circle on the cliff face, but it was fifty feet from him, and a growth of gaudy-coloured lichens had streaked and discoloured the rock, partially obscuring the details, so that he still could not be certain that it was not a natural flaw. He passed it and went on down as Aly and his team paid out the rope from above.

When he reached the surface of the water he slipped out of the sling and dropped in. The water was very cold. He trod water, gasping, until his body became acclimatized. Then he gave Aly three tugs on the signal rope. While the canvas seat was hauled up he swam to the side of the pool and held on to one of the carved stone niches for support. He had forgotten how gloomy and cold and lonely it was here in the bottom of the chasm.

After a long delay he craned his head backwards and watched Royan come into sight around the bulge of the overhang, dangling in the sling seat and revolving slowly at the end of the nylon rope. She looked down and waved at him cheerfully.

'Full marks to that girl,' he grinned. 'Not much puts the wind up her.' He wanted to shout encouragement, but he knew it was futile because the thunder of the falls smothered all other sound. So he contented himself with returning her wave.

Halfway down he saw her tugging frantically on the signal rope. Aly had been warned to expect this, and her descent was halted immediately. Then she leaned back in the sling, hanging on with only her left hand, as she groped for Nicholas's binoculars which hung from their strap on to her chest. She was twisted at an awkward angle as she held the glasses to her eyes and tried to manipulate the focus wheel with one hand. He saw that she was obviously having difficulty picking up the round mark on the wall and keeping it in the field of the lens, for the sling was swinging from side to side and at the same time revolving slowly.

She struggled at the end of the rope for what seemed to Nicholas a very long time, but probably was no more than a few minutes. Then abruptly she dropped the binoculars on to her chest, threw back her head and let out a scream that, despite the roar of falling water, carried clearly to Nicholas a hundred feet beneath her. She was kicking her legs joyfully and waving her free hand at him, wild with excitement, as Aly began paying out the rope once more. Still screaming incoherently, she was looking down at him with a face that seemed to light up the cathedral gloom of the gorge.

'I can't hear you,' he yelled back, but the falls defeated both their efforts to communicate.

Royan was wriggling about in her seat, shouting and gesticulating wildly, and now she let go the harness with her other hand and leaned further out to keep him in sight as the sling revolved. She was still twenty feet above the water when she almost lost her balance entirely, and very nearly toppled backwards out of the sling.

'Careful there,' he yelled up at her. 'Those glasses are Zeiss. Two thousand quid at the Zurich duty-free!'

This time his voice must have carried, for she stuck her tongue out at him in a schoolgirlish gesture. But her movements became more circumspect. When her feet were almost touching the water she signalled on the rope to stop her descent and hung there, fifty feet across the pool from him.

'What did you find?' he shouted across.

'You were right, you wonderful man!'

'Is it man-made? Is it an inscription? Could you read it?'

'Yes, yes and yes to all three of your questions!' She grinned triumphantly as she teased him.

'Don't be infuriating. Tell me.'

'Taita's ego got the better of him once again. He couldn't resist signing his work.' She laughed. 'He has left us his autograph – the hawk with a broken wing!'

'Marvellous! Plain bloody marvellous!' he exalted.

'Proof that Taita was here, Nicky. To carve that cartouche, he must have been standing on a scaffolding. Our first guess was right. That niche you are holding on to is part of his ladder to the bottom of the gorge.'

'Yes, but why, Royan?' he yelled back at her. 'Why was Taita down here? There is no evidence of any excavation or building work.'

They both looked around the gloomy cavern. Apart from the tiny rows of niches, the walls were unbroken, smooth and inscrutable until they plunged into the dark water.

'Under the falls?' she shouted across. 'Is there a cutback in the rock? Can you get across there?'

He pushed off from the cliff, and swam towards the thundering chute of water. Halfway across, the current caught him and he had to swim with all his strength to make any headway against it. Thrashing the water with flailing arms and kicking out strongly, he managed to reach a spur of polished, algae-slick rock at the nearest end of the falls.

The water crashed over his head, but he edged his way along under the rock step into the heart of the cascade. Halfway across, the water overwhelmed him. It tore him off his precarious perch, hurled him back into the basin below and swirled him end over end. He surfaced in the middle of the pool, and once again had to swim with all his strength to break free of the grip of the current and to reach the slack water below the wall again. He clung to his handhold in the stone niche, and panted like a bellows.

'Nothing?' she called.

He shook his head, unable to answer until he had finally regained his breath. Finally he managed: 'Nothing. It's a solid rock wall behind the falls.' He gasped another breath, and then invited sarcastically, 'Next bright idea, madam?'

She was silent and he was glad of the respite. Then she called again, 'Nicky, how far do those niches go down?'

'You can see,' he told her, 'right to the one I am holding on to.'

'What about below the surface?'

'Don't be silly, woman.' He was getting cold and irritable. 'How the hell could there be cuttings below the surface?'

'Try!' she yelled almost as irritably. He shook his head pityingly, and drew a deep breath. Still clinging to his handhold, he extended his limbs and body to their full stretch. Then his head went under the dark surface as he groped down as far as he could reach with his toes.

Suddenly he shot back, snorting for air with a startled look on his face. 'By Jove!' he shouted. 'You are right! There is another niche down there!'

'I hate to say I told you so.' Even at that range he could see the smug expression on her face.

'What are you? Some kind of witch?' Then he broke off and rolled his eyes heavenward in despair. 'I know what you are going to ask me to do next.'

'How far do the niches go down?' she called in honeyed tones. 'Will you dive down for me, dear Nicky?'

'That's it,' he said. 'I knew it. I am going to speak to my shop steward. This is slave labour. From now onwards I am on strike.'

'Please, Nicky!'

He hung in the water, pumping air in and out of his lungs, hyperventilating, flushing his bloodstream with oxygen to increase his underwater endurance to its limits. In the end he expelled the contents of his lungs completely, squeezing out the last breath until his chest ached with the effort, and then he sucked in again, filling his lungs to their capacity with fresh air. Finally, with his chest fully expanded, he duckdived, standing on his head with his legs high out of the water and letting their weight drive him under.

Sliding head-first down the submerged wall, he reached down, groping for the next niche below the surface. He found it, and used it to accelerate his dive, pulling himself on downwards.

He found the second niche below that, and pulled himself on downwards. The niches were about six feet apart – a nautical fathom. Using them as a measure, he was able to calculate his progress accurately.

Swimming on downwards, he found another niche, then another. Four rows of niches, twenty-four feet below the surface. His ears were popping and squeaking as the pressure squeezed the air out of his Eustachian tubes.

He kept on downwards and found the fifth row of niches. Now the air in his lungs was compressing to almost half its surface volume, and as his buoyancy decreased so his descent became easier and more rapid.

His eyes were wide open, but the waters below him were dark and turbid. He could make out only the surface of the wall directly in front of his face. He saw the sixth niche appear ahead of him and he grasped it, then hesitated.

'Thirty-six feet of depth already, and no sign yet of bottom,' he thought. There had been a time, when he was spearfishing competitively with the army team, that he could free-dive to sixty feet and stay at that depth for a full minute. But he had been younger then and in peak physical condition.

'Just one more niche,' he promised himself, 'and then back up to the surface.' His chest was beginning to throb and burn with the need to breathe, but he pulled hard on his handhold and shot down. He saw the vague shape of the seventh niche appear out of the murk below him.

'They go right to the bottom,' he realized with amazement. 'How on earth did Taita do it? They had no diving equipment.' He grasped the

174

niche and hovered there for a moment, undecided if he should risk going further. He knew he was almost at his physical limit. Already he was hunting for air, his chest beginning to convulse involuntarily.

'What about one more for the hell of it!' He was beginning to feel light-headed, and a strange glow of euphoria came over him. He recognized the danger signs, and looked down at his own body. Through the murk he saw that his skin was wrinkled and folded by the pressure of water. There were over two atmospheres' weight bearing down upon him, crushing in his chest. His brain was becoming starved of oxygen, and he felt reckless and invulnerable.

'Once more into the breach, dear friends,' he thought drunkenly, and went on down.

'Number eight, and the doctor's at the gate.' He felt the eighth niche under his fingers. He was thinking in gibberish now: 'Number eight, and I'll have her on a plate.'

He turned to go up again, and his feet touched bottom. 'Fifty feet deep,' he realized even through his fuddled state. 'I have left it too late. Got to get back. Got to breathe.'

He was bracing himself to push off from the bottom when something grabbed his legs and dragged him hard against the rock wall.

'Octopus!' he thought, remembering the line from Taita's stele, 'Her vagina is an octopus that has swallowed up a king.'

He tried to kick out, but his legs were bound as if by the arms of a sea monster; some cold, insidious embrace held him captive. 'Taita's octopus. My oath! He meant it literally. It's got me.'

He was pinned against the wall, crushed, helpless. Terror seized him, and the rush of it through his blood flushed away the hallucinations of his oxygen-impoverished brain. He realized what had happened to him.

'No octopus. This is water pressure.' He had experienced the same phenomenon once before. On an army training exercise, while diving near the inlet to the turbines of the generators in Loch Arran, his buddy diver who was roped to him had drifted into their terrible suction. His companion had been sucked against the grille of the intake and his body had been crushed so that the splinters of his ribs had been driven through the flesh of his chest and had come out through the black neoprene rubber of his suit like daggers.

Nicholas had narrowly escaped the same fate. The fact that he was a few feet to one side of his buddy had meant that he escaped the full brunt of the rush of water into the turbine intake. Nevertheless, one of his legs was broken, and it had taken the strength of two other army divers to prise him out of the grip of the current.

This time he was at the limit of his air, and there was no other diver to assist him. He was being sucked into a narrow opening in the rock, the mouth of an underwater tunnel, a subaqueous shaft that bored into the rock wall.

His upper body was free of the baleful influence of the rushing flood, but his legs were being drawn inexorably into it. He was aware that the surrounds of the opening were sharply demarcated, as straight and as square as a lintel hewn by a mason. He was being dragged over and around this lintel. Spreading out his arms, he resisted with all his strength, but his hooked fingers slid over the polished, slimy surface of the rock.

'This is the big one,' he thought. 'This is the one punch that you can't duck.' He hooked his fingers, and felt his nails tear and break as they rasped against the rock. Then suddenly they locked into the last niche in the wall above the sink-hole which was sucking him under.

Now at least he had an anchor point. With both hands he clung to the niche, and fought the pull of the water. He fought it with all his remaining strength and all his heart, but he was near the end of his store of both. He strained until he felt the muscles in both arms popping, until the sinews in his neck stood out in steely cords and he felt something in his head must burst. But he had halted the insidious slide of his body into the sink-hole.

'One more,' he thought. 'Just one more try.' And he knew that was all he had left within him. His air was all used up, and so were his courage and his resolve. His mind swirled, and dark shapes clouded his vision.

From somewhere deep inside himself he drew out the last reserves, and pulled until the darkness in his head exploded in sheets of bright colours, shooting stars and Catherine wheels that dazzled him. But he kept on pulling. He felt his legs coming out of it, the grip of the waters weakening, and he pulled once more with strength that he had never realized he possessed.

Then suddenly he was free and shooting towards the surface, but it was too late. The darkness filled his head and in his ears was a sound like the roaring of the waterfall in the abyss. He was drowning. He was all used up. He had no knowledge of where he was, how much further he had to go to the surface, but he knew only that he was not going to make it. He was finished.

When he came out through the surface, he did not know that he had done so, and he did not have enough strength left to lift his face out of the water and to breathe. He wallowed there like a waterlogged carcass, face down and dying. Then he felt Royan's fingers lock into the hair in the back of his head, and the cold air on his face as she lifted it clear.

'Nicky!' she screamed at him. 'Breathe, Nicky, breathe!'

He opened his mouth and let out a spray of water and saliva and stale air, and then gagged and gasped.

'You're still alive! Oh, thank God. You were down for so long. I thought you had drowned.'

As he coughed and fought for air and his senses returned, he realized in a vague way that she must have dropped out of the sling seat and come to his aid.

'You were under for so long. I could not believe it.' She held his head up, clinging with her free hand to the niche in the wall. 'You are going to be all right now. I have got you. Just take it easy for a while. It's going to be all right.'

It was amazing how much her voice encouraged him. The air tasted good and sweet and he felt his strength slowly returning.

'We have to get you up,' she told him. 'A few minutes more to get yourself together, and then I will help you into the sling.'

She swam with him across to the dangling sling and signalled to the men at the top of the cliff to lower it into the water. Then she held the folds of canvas open so that he could slip his legs into them.

'Are you all right, Nicky?' she demanded anxiously. 'Hang on until you get to the top.' She placed his hands on the side ropes of the harness. 'Hold tight!'

'Can't leave you down here,' he blurted groggily.

'I'll be fine,' she assured him. 'Just have Aly send the seat down again for me.'

When he was halfway up he looked down and saw her head bobbing in the dark waters. She looked very small and lonely, and her face pale and pathetic.

'Guts!' His voice was so weak and hoarse that he did not recognize it. 'You've got real guts.' But already he was too high for the words to carry down to her.

Once they had got Royan safely up out of the ravine, Nicholas ordered Aly to dismantle the gantry and hide the sections in the thorn scrub. From the helicopter it would be highly visible and he did not wish to stir Jake Helm's curiosity.

He was in no shape to give the men a hand, but lay in the shade of one of the thorn trees with Royan tending to him. He was dismayed to find how much his near-drowning had taken out of him. He had a blinding headache, caused by oxygen starvation. His chest was very painful and stabbed him every time he breathed: in his struggles he must have torn or sprained something.

177

He was impressed with Royan's forbearance. She made no attempt to question him about his discoveries in the bottom of the gorge, and seemed genuinely more concerned with his wellbeing than with the progress of their exploration.

When she helped him to his feet and they started back towards camp, he moved like an old man, lame and stiff. Every muscle and sinew in his body ached. He knew that the lactic acid and nitrogen that had built up in his tissues would take some time to be reabsorbed and dispersed.

Once they reached camp Royan led him to his hut and fussed over him as she settled him under the mosquito net. By this time he was feeling a lot better, but he neglected to inform her of this fact. It was pleasant to have a woman caring for him again. She brought him a couple of aspirin tablets and a steaming mug of tea, stiff with sugar. He was putting it on a little when he asked weakly for a second mugful.

Sitting beside his bed, she solicitously watched him drink it. 'Better?' she asked, when he had finished.

'The odds are two to one that I will survive,' he told her, and she smiled.

'I can see that you are better. Your cheek is showing again. You gave me an awful scare, you know.'

'Anything to get your attention.'

'Now that we have decided that you will live, tell me what happened. What sort of trouble did you run into down there in the pool?'

'What you really want to know is what I found down there. Am I correct?'

'That too,' she admitted.

Then he told her everything that he had discovered and how he had been caught in the inflow of the underwater sink-hole. She listened without interruption, and even when he had finished speaking she said nothing for a while, but frowned with concentrated thought.

At last she looked up at him. 'You mean that Taita was able to take those stone niches right down to the very bottom of the pool, fifty feet below the surface?' and when he nodded, she was silent again. Then she said, 'How on earth did he accomplish that? What are your thoughts on the subject?'

'Four thousand years ago the water level may have been lower. There may have been a drought year when the river dried up, and enabled him to get in there. How am I doing?'

'Not a bad try,' she admitted, 'but then why go to all the trouble of building a scaffold? Why not just use the dry river bed as an access? Then again, surely the attraction of the spot for Taita was the river. If it was dry, then it would be just like a thousand other places in this gorge.

178

No, I have a feeling that the fact that it was so inaccessible was the main, if not the only, reason he chose to work there.'

'I suspect that you are correct,' he agreed.

'So if the river was running, even at its lowest level as it is now, how on earth did he manage to carve those niches below the surface? And what would be the point in having scaffolding under water?'

'Beats me. I have no idea,' he admitted.

'All right, let's leave that for the moment. Now let's go over your description of the sink-hole that almost sucked you in. Did you form any estimate of the size of the opening?'

He shook his head. 'It is almost totally dark down there. I could not see more than two or three feet in front of me.'

'Was the entrance directly between the two rows of niches?'

'No, not directly,' he said thoughtfully. 'It was slightly to one side. I hit the bottom of the pool with my feet, and was just about to push off when it grabbed me.'

'So it must be at the very bottom of the pool, and slightly downstream from the scaffolding. You say that the entrance seemed to have a square coping?'

'I am not absolutely sure of that – remember that I could see very little. But that was the impression I received.'

'It may have been another man-made structure, then – perhaps some type of adit shaft driven into the side of the pool?'

'It's possible,' he agreed reluctantly. 'But on the other hand it could just as easily be a natural fault in the strata that the river is draining into.'

She stood up to leave, and he demanded, 'Where are you going?'

'I won't be long. I am going to my hut to fetch my notes, and the material from the stele. Back in a moment.'

When she returned she sat on the floor beside his bed, with her legs drawn up under her in that double-jointed feminine fashion. As she spread her papers around her, he pulled up the edge of the mosquito net and looked down at what she was doing.

'Yesterday, while you were busy building the gantry, I was able to decipher most of the rest of the "spring" face of the stele.' She moved her notebook so that he was able to overlook the pages she had opened. 'These are my preliminary notes. You will see where I have inserted a number of question marks – here and here, for instance. That is where I am uncertain of the translation, or where Taita has used a new and strange symbol. I will have to give more time and consideration to those later.'

'I follow you,' he said, and she went on.

'These sections that I have highlighted with green are quotations from the standard version of the *Book of the Dead*. Take this one here:

"*The universe is drawn in circles, the disc of the sun god, Ra. The life of man is a circle that begins in the womb and ends in the tomb. The circle of the chariot wheel foreshadows the death of the serpent that it crushes beneath its rim.*"'

'Yes, I recognize the quotation,' he said.

'On the other hand, these parts of the text that I have highlighted in yellow are original Taita writings, or at least are not quotations from the *Book of the Dead* or any other source that I am aware of. This paragraph here in particular is the one that I wanted to bring to your attention.'

She traced a section with her forefinger as she read it aloud, '"*The daughter of the goddess has conceived. She has been impregnated by the one who is without seed. She has begotten her own twin sister. The foetus lies for ever coiled in her own womb. Her twin shall never be born. She will never see the light of Ra. She will live for ever in the darkness. In the womb of the sister her bridegroom claims her in eternal marriage. The unborn twin becomes the bride of the god, who was a man. Their destinies are intertwined. They shall live for ever. They shall not perish.*"'

She looked up from the notebook. 'When I first read it, I was satisfied that the daughter of the goddess was the Dandera river, as we had already agreed. I was also pretty sure that the god that was once a man must be Pharaoh. Mamose was only deified on his ascension to the throne of Egypt. Before that he was a man.'

Nicholas nodded. 'The seedless one is obviously Taita himself. He makes repeated references to the fact that he was a eunuch. But now,' he suggested, 'if you have some new ideas about the mysterious twin sister, let's hear them.'

'The twin of the river would most likely be a branch, or a fork of the stream, wouldn't it?'

'Ah, I see what you are driving at. You are suggesting that the sink-hole is the twin. Down there in the gorge it will never see the light of Ra. Taita, the seedless one, claims paternity, so he is telling us that he is the architect.'

'Exactly, and he has married the twin of the river to Pharaoh Mamose for all eternity. Putting that all together, I have come to the conclusion that we will never find the location of Pharaoh Mamose's tomb until we explore thoroughly that sink-hole that nearly drowned you.'

'How do you suggest we do that?' he asked, and she shrugged.

'I am not the engineer, Nicky. I leave that to you to arrange. All I know is that Taita devised some way of doing it – not only of getting there but of working down there. If our interpretation of the stele is correct, then he carried out extensive mining operations at the bottom of the pool. If he could do it, then there is no reason why you can't do it also.'

'Ah!' he demurred. 'Taita was a genius. He says so repeatedly. I am just an old plodder.'

'I have got all my bets on you, Nicky. You won't let me down, will you?'

There was no call for intensive bushcraft to follow this spoor. His quarry had taken very few anti-tracking precautions. Quite openly they were following the main trail down the Abbay gorge, heading directly westwards towards the Sudanese border. Mek Nimmur was on his way back to his own stronghold.

Boris estimated that he had between fifteen and twenty men with him. It was difficult to be certain, for the tracks on the pathway overlapped each other, and of course he would have scouts on the point ahead of him and sweeping his flanks. There would also be a rearguard dragging the trail behind him.

They were making good time, but such a large party would not be able to outpace a single pursuer. He was sure he was gaining on them. He reckoned that he had started four hours behind them, but judging by recent signs he was now less than two hours adrift.

Without breaking his trot, he stooped to pick something up from the path. As he ran on he examined it. It was a twig, the soft tip shoot of a kusagga-sagga plant that grew beside the track. One of the men ahead of him had brushed against it as he passed, and snapped it off the main branch. It gave Boris a fairly accurate gauge of how far he was behind. Even in the heat of the gorge, the tender shoot had barely begun to wilt. He was even closer than he had estimated.

He slowed down a little as he considered his next move. He knew this part of the valley fairly well. The previous year he had hunted over much of this terrain with an American client, who had been looking for a trophy Walia ibex. They had spent almost a month combing these same gullies and wooded ravines before they had brought down a huge old ram, black with age and carrying a pair of curled, back-sweeping horns that ranked as the tenth largest ever in the *Rowland Ward* record book.

He knew that two or three miles ahead the Nile began another oxbow loop out to the south, and that it then doubled back upon itself. The main trail followed the river, because a series of sheer and formidable cliffs guarded the high ground in the centre of the loop of the river. It was, however, possible to cut the corner. Boris had done it before, while following the wounded ibex.

The American hunter had not killed cleanly – his bullet had struck the ram too far back, missing the heart-lung cavity and piercing the gut. The stricken wild goat had taken to the high ground, following one of its secret paths up amongst the crags. Boris and the American had followed it up and over the mountain. Boris remembered how dangerous and treacherous the path had been, but when it descended the far side of the mountain it had cut off nearly ten miles.

If he could find the beginning of the goat path again, there was every chance that he would be able to get ahead of Mek Nimmur and be lying in wait for him on the far side. That would give him an enormous advantage. The guerrilla leader would be expecting pursuit, not ambush. He would be covering his back trail, and it was highly unlikely that Boris would be able to slip past the rearguard without alerting his intended victims. On the other hand, once he was ahead of them he would be in control. Then he could choose his own killing ground.

As the trail and the main flow of the Nile started to turn away towards the south, he kept watching the high ground above it, seeking a familiar landmark. He had not gone another half-mile before he found it. Here there was a break in the line of dark cliffs, a heavily forested re-entrant, that cut into the wall of basalt.

He stopped and mopped the sweat from his face and neck. 'Too much vodka,' he grunted, 'you are getting soft.' His shirt was as sodden as though he had plunged in the river.

He changed the sling of the rifle to his other shoulder, lifted his binoculars and swept the sides of the wooded gully. They appeared sheer and unscalable, but then he picked out the stunted shape of a small tree that grew out of a narrow crack in the face. It looked like a Japanese bonsai, with a twisted, malformed trunk and tortured branches.

The Walia ibex had been standing on the ledge just above that tree when the American had fired. In his mind's eye Boris could still see the way in which the wild goat had hunched its back as the bullet struck, and then spun around and raced away up the cliff. He panned the glasses upwards gently, and could just make out the inclination of the narrow ledge as it angled up the face.

'Da, da. This is the spot.' He was thinking in his mother tongue again. It was a relief after these last days of having to struggle in French and English.

Before he began the climb, he left the trail and scrambled down the boulder-strewn slope to the river. He knelt at the edge of the Nile and splashed double handfuls over himself, soaking his cropped head and sluicing the sweat from his face and neck. He drained and refilled his water bottle, then drank until his belly was painfully full. Then he rinsed out the bottle and refilled it. There was no water on

182

the mountain. Finally he dipped his bush hat in the river and placed it back on his head, sodden and streaming water down his neck and face.

He climbed back to the main trail and followed it for another hundred paces, moving slowly and studying the ground. At one place there was a rock boulder almost blocking the path. The men ahead of him had been forced to step over this obstruction, on to a patch of talcum-fine dust beyond it. They had left perfect impressions of their footprints for him to read.

Most of the men were wearing Israeli-style para boots with a zigzag-patterned sole, and those coming up from behind had overtrodden the spoor of the leaders. He had to go down on one knee to examine the signs minutely before he could pick out the imprint of a much smaller and more delicately formed foot, a lighter, unmistakably feminine tread. It was partially obliterated by other larger masculine footprints, but the outline of the toe was clear, and the pattern was that of a smooth rubber-soled Bata tennis shoe. He would have recognized it from ten thousand others.

He was relieved to find that Tessay was still with the group, and that she and her lover had not left and taken another path. Mek Nimmur was a sly one, and cunning. He had escaped from Boris's clutches once before. But not this time! The Russian shook his head vehemently: not this time.

He gave his full attention to the female footprint once again. It gave him a pang to look at it. His anger returned in full force. He did not consider his feelings for the woman. Love and desire did not enter into the equation. She was his chattel, and she had been stolen from him. It was only the insult that had significance for him. She had rejected and humiliated him, and for that she was going to die.

He felt the old thrill run through his blood at the thought of the kill. Killing had always been his trade and his vocation, but no matter how often he exercised his craft the thrill was never blunted, the pleasure never satiated. Perhaps it was the only true pleasure left to him, pure and unjaded – not even the vodka could weaken and dilute it as it had the physical act of copulation. He would enjoy killing her even more than he had once enjoyed coupling with her.

These past few years he had hunted only the lower animals, but he had never forgotten what it was like to hunt down and to kill a human being, more especially a woman. He wanted Mek Nimmur, but he wanted the woman more.

In the days of President Mengistu, when he had been the head of counter-intelligence, his men had known his tastes and had picked the pretty ones for him. He had only one regret now, and that was that this time he would have to do it swiftly. There could be no question of drawing it out and savouring the pleasure. Not like some of the other experiences, which had lasted for hours, sometimes for days.

'Bitch,' he mouthed, and kicked at the dust, stamping on the faint outline of her footprint, obliterating it just as he would do to her. 'Black fornicating bitch.'

He ran now with fresh strength and determination as he left the trail and climbed up towards the deformed tree and the beginning of the goat track up the cliff.

Exactly where he expected it, he found the start of the track and followed it upwards. The higher he climbed, the steeper it became. Often he had to use both hands to haul himself up a gradient, or to work his way along a narrow traverse.

The first time he had climbed this mountain he had been following the blood spoor of the wounded ibex, but now he did not have those splattered droplets to guide him, and twice he missed the path and found himself in a dead end on the cliff face. He was forced to edge back from the drop and retrace his footsteps until he found the correct turning. Each time he did so he was aware that he was losing time, and that Mek Nimmur might pass before he was able to intercept him.

Once he startled a small troop of wild goats which were lying on a ledge halfway up the cliff. They went bounding away up the rock face, more like birds than animals bound by the laws of gravity. They were led by a huge male with a streaming beard and long spiral horns, which in its flight showed Boris a direct route to the top of the cliff.

He tore the skin off his fingertips dragging himself up the last steep pitch, but finally he reached the top and wormed his way over the skyline, never lifting his head. A human form silhouetted against the clear, eggshell-blue sky would be visible from miles around. He moved along behind the crest until he found a small clump of sanseveria to give him cover, and used the erect, spiny leaves to break up the outline of his head as he surveyed the valley a thousand feet below through the binoculars.

From this height the Nile was a broad, glittering serpent uncoiling into the first bend of the oxbow, its surface ruffled by rapids and rocky reefs. The high ground on either bank formed standing waves of upthrust basalt, turbulent and chopped into confusion like a storm sea in a tropical typhoon. The whole danced and shimmered in the heat and the sun beat down with the blows of an executioner's axe, pounding this universe of red rock into heat-exhausted submission.

Though the air danced and trembled with the mirage in the lenses of his binoculars, Boris traced out the rough trail beside the river, and followed it down the valley to the point where it was hidden by the bend. It was deserted, with no sign of human presence, and he knew that his quarry had moved on out of sight. He had no way of telling how far down the trail they had travelled – he knew only that he must hurry on if he were to cut them off on the far side of the mountain.

For the first time since he had left the river, he drank sparingly from the water bottle. He realized how the heat and the exertion of the climb had dehydrated him. In these conditions a man without water might be dead in hours. It was not in the least surprising that there was so little permanent human habitation down here in the gorge.

When he backed off the skyline he felt rejuvenated, and set out to cross the saddle of the mountain. It was less than a mile across, and without warning he came out on the top of the cliffs on the far side. One more unwary pace and he would have stepped off into space and plunged down a thousand feet. Once again he moved along the crest until he found a concealed vantage point from which to spy the terrain below.

The river was the same – a wide and confused expanse of white-ruffled rapids, running back towards him as it turned through the leg of the oxbow. The trail followed the near bank, except where it was forced to detour inland by the rugged bluffs and stone needles which rose out of the Nile waters.

In the great desolation of the gorge he could pick out no movement other than the run of wild waters and the ceaseless dance of the heat mirage. He knew it was not possible that Mek Nimmur had moved fast enough to have passed completely ahead of him; therefore he must still be coming around the bend of the oxbow.

Boris drank again, and rested for almost half an hour. At the end of that time he felt strong and fully recovered. He debated with himself whether to descend immediately and stake out an ambush on the trail, but in the end decided to keep to the high ground until he had his quarry in sight.

He checked his rifle carefully, making sure that the telescopic sight had not been bumped out of alignment during the climb, and then emptied the magazine and examined the five cartridges. The brass case of one of them was dented and discoloured, so he discarded it and reloaded with another from his belt. He chambered a round and set the safety-catch.

He set the weapon aside while he changed his sweat-dampened socks with a fresh dry pair from his pack and retied his bootlaces with care. Only a novice would risk blistered feet in these conditions, for within hours they would be infected and festering.

He drank once more, and then stood up and slung the 30/06 on his shoulder. Ready now for anything that the goddess of the chase could send his way, he moved off along the crest to intercept the war party.

From every vantage point along the rim he glassed the valley below, each time without spying his quarry, and the afternoon passed swiftly. He was just beginning to worry that Mek Nimmur had somehow managed to slip past him unseen, that he had crossed the river at some secret ford or taken another path through a hidden valley, when there came a plaintive and querulous cry on the heat-hushed air. He looked up. A pair of kites were circling over one particular clump of thorn scrub on the river bank.

The yellow-billed kite is one of the most ubiquitous scavengers in Africa. It exists in close symbiotic association with man, feeding off his rubbish, picking up his leavings, soaring and circling over his villages or his temporary campsites, watching for his scraps or waiting patiently for him to squat in the bushes and then dropping down immediately he has finished his private business, acting as a universal sewage disposal agent.

Boris studied this pair of birds through his binoculars as they sailed idly in the heated air, always circling directly over that same patch of riverine bush. They had a distinctive manner of steering with their long bifurcated tails, twisting them from side to side as they flirted with the breeze. Their bright yellow beaks showed clearly as they turned their heads to look down at something in the scrub.

He smiled coldly to himself. 'Da! Nimmur has gone into camp early. Perhaps the heat and the pace are too fierce for his new woman, or perhaps he has stopped to play with her a little.'

He moved on along the rim until he could look down directly into the patch of bush. He studied it through the binoculars, but without picking out any signs of human presence. After almost two hours he was becoming uncertain of his original assumption. The only thing that retained his attention was the pair of kites, which had settled in a treetop overlooking the patch of scrub. He had to trust that they were watching the men hidden in the scrub.

He glanced at the sun anxiously. It was sliding down towards the horizon at last and losing its furious heat. Then he looked down into the valley again.

Directly below the patch of bush was an indentation in the river bank that formed a backwater, almost a small lagoon. When the river was in flood it would be inundated, but now there was a small strip of gravel bank exposed. On this bank stood a number of boulders that had tumbled down from the cliff above. Some of them were lying on the beach, while others had rolled into the river and were half-submerged. The largest was the size of a cottage, a great round mass of dark rock.

As he watched, a man emerged unexpectedly from the scrub. Boris's pulse quickened as he watched him scramble down on to one of the smaller boulders and jump from there on to the gravel bank. He knelt at

186

the water's edge and filled a canvas bucket with water, then climbed back and disappeared into the bush again.

'Ah! The heat is too much even for them. They must drink, and that gives them away. If it had not been for the birds I would never have known that they were there.' He clucked softly with reluctant admiration. 'Nimmur is a careful man. No wonder he has survived so long. He keeps tight control. But even he must have water.'

Boris kept watching through the glasses as he tried to guess what Mek Nimmur would do next. 'He has lost much time here by sheltering from the heat. He will march again as soon as it is cooler. He will make a night march,' he decided, as he looked at the sun again. 'Three hours until dark. I must make my move before then. Once it is dark it will be difficult to pick my targets.'

Before he stood up he wriggled back from the skyline. He retraced his steps back along the mountainside until a bluff shielded him from the eyes of Mek Nimmur's sentries. Then he started down. There was no goat track here and he had to make his own going, but after a few false starts he discovered an inclined rock shelf that afforded him a fairly easy path down the face. When he reached the bottom of the gorge, he took careful stock of the lie and run of the stratum so as to be able to find it again in an emergency. It was a good escape route, and he knew that he might soon be under pursuit and duress.

It had taken him over an hour to negotiate the descent, and he knew that he was running out of time. He reached the trail at the water's edge, and started back along it towards Mek Nimmur's camp. He was in a hurry now, but even then he was careful to take anti-tracking precautions. He walked on the edge of the trail, stepping only on the stony ground, careful to leave no sign of his passing. But despite his caution, he nearly walked right into them.

He had not covered the first two hundred metres when in the back of his mind he registered the low, mournful whistle of a pale-winged starling, and almost ignored it until alarm bells sounded in his mind. The timing was all wrong. The starling only gave that particular call at dawn when it left its nesting site high up in the cliffs. This was late afternoon down in the heated depths of the gorge. He guessed that it was a signal from one of the scouts coming up the trail towards him. Mek Nimmur's party was on the move.

Boris reacted instantly. He slipped off the trail, and ran back the way he had come until he reached the beginning of the pathway along which he had descended the cliff. He climbed just high enough to be able to overlook the trail. However, he realized that he had lost much of the advantage that he had built up by cutting across the mountain. This was not the ideal ambush position, and his escape route was exposed to enemy fire from below – he would be lucky to make it to the top. But the idea of abandoning his vengeance never occurred to him. As soon as his targets were in his sights, he would shoot from this stance.

However, he acknowledged to himself that Mek Nimmur had taken him by surprise. Boris had not anticipated that he would move before the sun had set. He had expected to be able to take up a position above the camp in the thorn patch and to be able to get off two careful, well-aimed shots before he was forced to run.

It was also part of his calculations that, once he had dropped Mek Nimmur, his men would not be eager to follow up with too much despatch. Boris planned to make a running retreat, stopping at every defensible strong point to fire a few shots, knock down one or two of them, and keep the pursuit circumspect and cautious until they eventually lost their taste for the game and let him go.

However, all that had now changed. He would have to take the first opportunity that presented itself – almost certainly a moving target – and as soon as he had fired he would be exposed on the path up the cliff face. His one advantage here was that his hunting rifle was a superbly accurate piece, whereas Mek Nimmur's men were all armed with AK-47 assault rifles, rapid-firing but notoriously wild at longer range, and more especially in the hands of these *shufta*. With proper training, the fighting tribesmen of Africa made some of the finest troops in the world. They possessed all the necessary skills, with one exception – they were notoriously poor marksmen.

He lay flat on the ledge, and the rock under him was so hot from the direct sunlight that it burned painfully even through his clothing. He pulled the pack from his back and set it up in front of him, settling the forestock of the rifle over it to give himself a dead rest. He peered through the telescope, wriggling into a comfortable position, sighting on a small rock beside the main trail and then swinging the barrel from side to side to make certain that he had a clear arc of fire.

Satisfied that this was the best stance he could find in the short time left to him, he set the rifle aside and picked up a handful of dirt. He rubbed this gently into his face, and the sweat turned it to mud that coated his pale skin and dulled the shine that an alert scout might pick out at long range. His last concern was to check the angle of the sun, and to satisfy himself that it was not reflecting off the lens of his scope or off any of the metal parts of the rifle. He reached over and pulled at the branch of the shrub beside him so that it cast its shadow over the weapon.

At last he settled down behind the rifle and cuddled the butt into his shoulder, regulating his breathing to a deep slow rhythm, dropping his pulse rate and steadying his hands. He did not have long to wait. He heard the bird-call again, but this time much nearer at hand. It was answered immediately from the far side of the trail, down closer to the river bank.

'The flankers will be having difficulty maintaining station over this terrain.' He grinned without humour, a death's-head grimace. 'They will be bunching and straggling.' As he thought it, a man came into view around the bend of the trail, about five hundred metres dead ahead.

Boris picked him up in the magnified field of the lens. He was a typical African guerrilla, a *shufta* dressed in a tattered and faded motley of camouflage and civilian clothing, festooned with pack and water bottle, ammunition and grenades, carrying his AK at high port. He halted the moment he came through the turn, and crouched into cover behind a boulder at the side of the trail.

For a long minute he surveyed the lie of the land ahead of him, his head turning slowly from side to side. At one point he seemed to be staring directly at Boris, who held his breath and lay as still as the rock beside him. But finally the *shufta* straightened up and gave a hand signal to those out of sight behind him. Then he came on down the trail at a trot. When he had covered fifty metres the rest of the party began to appear, keeping their intervals as precisely as beads on a string. It would not be possible to enfilade this line even with an RPD from a prepared position.

'Good!' Boris approved. 'These are crack troops. Mek must have hand-picked them.' He watched them through the lens, examining the features of each man as he came into view, searching for Mek Nimmur. There were seven of them spread out down the trail now, but still no sign of their leader. The man on the point drew level with Boris's position and then went on past him. A pair of flankers passed directly beneath where he lay, rustling softly by in the scrub not more than a dozen paces from him. He lay like a stone and let them go. The rest of them passed his position, well spaced and moving swiftly. For some minutes after the last of them had gone, the gorge seemed deserted and devoid of all human presence. Then there was another stealthy movement out there.

'The rearguard,' Boris grunted softly. 'Mek is keeping the woman at the rear. His new plaything. He is taking great care of her.'

He slipped the safety-catch on the rifle gently, making certain that no alien metallic sound fell on the heated and hushed air.

'Now let them come,' he breathed. 'I will take Mek first. Nothing fancy, no head shots. Squarely in the centre of the chest. The woman will freeze when he goes down. She does not have the reflexes of a warrior. She will give me a second unhurried shot. At this range there will be no question of a miss. Right between those pretty little black tits of hers.' He became sexually charged by the image of blood and violent death set opposite Tessay's loveliness and grace. 'I might even have a chance to get one of the others. But I can't bank on that. These men are good. More likely that they will dive into cover before I have even had time to kill the woman.'

He watched the faces of the rearguard as, one at a time, carefully spaced, they came into view. Each time he felt his heart trip with disappointment. In the end there were three of them on the path, moving past him at a steady, businesslike jog-trot. But no sign of Mek and the woman. The rearguard disappeared down the path, and the small sounds of their progress dwindled into silence. Boris lay alone on the ledge, his heart thumping and the sour taste of disappointment in the back of his throat.

'Where are they?' he thought bitterly. 'Where the hell is Mek?' And the obvious answer to his own question occurred to him immediately. They had taken a different trail. Mek had used this patrol as a decoy to lure him away.

He lay quietly for a measured five minutes by his wrist-watch, just in case there might be more men coming up the trail. His mind was racing. His last definite placing of Tessay had been the glimpse of her footprint on the trail at the far bend of the oxbow.

That was several hours ago, and if she and Mek had given him the slip they could be anywhere by now. Mek might have won himself a start of a full day or more – it might take Boris that long to work the spoor through. Feeling waves of anger overwhelm him, he had to close his eyes and fight it off in order to keep his sense of reason from being swamped. He had to think clearly now, not go rushing at the problem like a wounded buffalo. He knew that this was one of his weaknesses: he had to keep tight control of himself.

When he opened his eyes again, his anger had become cold and functional. He knew precisely what he had to do and the order in which he must do it. The very first task was to sweep and check the back trail. He had to establish the point at which Mek had left the main detachment of *shufta*.

He slipped down off the ledge and through the scrub to the open trail. Still anti-tracking, but moving swiftly, he made his way upstream, back towards the patch of thorn scrub where the party of *shufta* had lain up in the heat of the day. The first thing he noticed was that the pair of kites had gone. But he did not take this as proof that the bush was deserted, and began to circle it carefully. First he worked the incoming trail on the far side of the patch of bush. Although several hours old now, it was still clear enough to read.

Suddenly he stopped in the centre of the trail and felt the hair rise on his forearms and down the back of his neck as he stared at the sign in the dust of the path. He realized that he had walked into Mek's trap. There lay the distinctive imprint of a Bata tennis shoe.

Mek and the woman had gone into the patch of scrub and had not come out again. They were still in there, and Boris was seized by the strong premonition that Mek was watching him even at that moment, over the open sights of his AK. While he was out in the open like this, stooped over the spoor, Boris was completely vulnerable.

Hurling himself sideways off the path, he landed like a cat in the wire grass beside it, with the rifle at the ready. It took many minutes for his heartbeats to return to normal, and then he rose again into a stealthy crouch and began circling the patch of scrub very cautiously. His nerves were as taut as guitar strings, and his pale eyes darted from side to side. His finger lay upon the trigger of the 30/06 and he kept the muzzle weaving slowly, like the head of a cobra ready to strike in any direction.

He moved down towards the bank of the river, where the noise of the rapids would mask any sound he might make. But when he had almost reached the shelter of the house-sized boulder that he had noticed from the mountain crest he froze again. He had heard a sound that carried over the sound of Nile waters – a sound so incongruous in this place and at this time that for a moment he doubted his own hearing. It was the sound of a woman's laughter, sweet and clear as the tinkle of a crystal chandelier swinging in the breeze.

The sound came from below him, from the river bank beyond the tumbled boulder. He crept towards the boulder, determined to use it for cover and as a vantage point from which he could cover the bank beyond it. But before he reached it he heard the splash of some heavy object striking the surface of the river, and an excited female squeal, both playful and provocative.

Reaching the side of the boulder, and keeping close in under its protective bulk, he stole towards the corner, from which he could overlook the gravel bank beyond. Then, peeping cautiously around the angle of the boulder, he stared in amazement. He could barely believe what he was seeing. He could not credit this kind of stupidity from a man like Mek Nimmur. This was the hard man, the seasoned warrior and survivor of twenty years of bloody bush war acting like a love-sick teenage booby.

Mek Nimmur had sent his men away so that he could be alone to frolic with his new paramour. Boris took time to make absolutely certain that this was not some elaborate trap that had been set for him. It seemed too fortuitous, too heaven-sent to be really true. He searched every inch of the bank in both directions for hidden gunmen before he smiled his cold little smile.

'Of course they are alone. Mek would never let one of his men see Tessay naked like this.' His smile grew broader as he recognized the full extent of his luck. 'He must have gone crazy. Did he not realize that I would follow him? Did he think he was far enough ahead to be able to indulge himself like this? Is there anything in this world as stupid and as short-sighted as a standing prick?' Boris was gloating delightedly now.

The couple had stripped off their clothes and left them in a pile on the beach of grey basalt gravel in the shade of the tall boulder. They were splashing together in the slack water of the river at the edge of the main current. Both of them were stark mother-naked. Mek Nimmur was broad-shouldered, with a heavily muscled back and hard, tight buttocks. Beside him Tessay was slim as a river reed, her waist tiny and her hips narrow. Her skin was the colour of wild honey. They were completely absorbed in each other, without eyes or ears for anything else in this world.

'He must have left men guarding his back trail.' Boris gave Mek the benefit of some sense. 'He never expected me to be ahead of him on the trail. He thinks they are completely secure. Look at the fool,' he gloated, as Mek chased the girl and she let herself be caught. They fell into the shallow water locked in each other's embrace, mouths seeking each other as they surfaced again, laughing as the water streamed down their darkly beautiful faces, the epitome of handsome masculinity and lovely womanhood, the image of an African Adam and Eve captured for a moment in their own little carefree paradise.

Boris tore his eyes from them, and looked to where their clothing had been abandoned on the gravel bar. Mek's AK rifle lay carelessly on top of his camouflage jacket, within a few paces of where Boris stood. He crossed the open gravel bar with a few quick strides, picked up the AK, unclipped the curved magazine and dropped it into his pocket, ejected the round from the chamber and let it fly away into the gravel, replaced the unloaded rifle on the jacket, and rapidly returned to the lee of the boulder. Both Mek and Tessay remained utterly oblivious to what had happened.

Boris stood there quietly in the shadow of the rock, watching them at play in the river. They were almost childlike in their love and their complete preoccupation with each other.

Tessay at last broke from Mek's embrace and left the water. She came up the gravel bar, running long-legged and coltish, her wet silken breasts swinging and jostling each other at each stride as she looked back at him over her shoulder in open invitation. Mek followed her out, the water glistening in the dense curls of his barrel chest, his genitals weighty and puissant.

He caught her before she could reach her clothing and she struggled playfully for a while in his arms, until his mouth clamped down over

192

hers. Then she gave herself up to him completely. While he kissed her his hands ran down her back and over her wet glistening buttocks. Pressing herself against him she moved her feet apart and spread her thighs, inviting him to explore the secrets of her body. She groaned with desire as his hand cupped her sex gently.

Boris felt his anger mingle with the perverse voyeuristic thrill of watching his own wife being taken by another man. A devil's brew of emotions bubbled up inside him. He felt his loins engorging and stiffening almost painfully with excitement, but at the same time his rage shook him like the branch of a tree in a gale of wind.

The lovers sank down on to their knees. Still locked together, Tessay fell backwards and pulled him over on top of herself.

Boris called out loudly, 'By God, Mek Nimmur, you will never know how ridiculous you look with your bare backside in the air like that.'

Mek reacted as swiftly as a leopard surprised on his kill. With a blur of movement he flipped over and reached for the AK-47. Although Boris was ready for him, covering him with the 30/06, aiming at the back of his neck when he shouted to him, Mek was so quick that he had swept up the AK from where it lay and had it pointed at Boris's belly before he could move. Mek pressed the trigger in the same instant as the muzzle came to bear.

The firing pin fell on the empty chamber with a futile click, and the two men stared at each other across the gravel beach, both with their weapons levelled. Tessay was curled naked where Mek had left her, her dark eyes liquid with pain and horror as she watched her husband and realized that Mek was about to die.

Boris chuckled softly, throatily. 'Where do you want it, Mek? How about I shoot the head off that filthy black tool of yours, while it is still standing up in the air like that?'

Mek Nimmur's eyes darted away from his adversary's face, back towards the mountain, and Boris realized that his guess had been correct. Mek had some of his men up there, but they were keeping out of view of the beach while their commander indulged himself.

'Don't worry about them. You will both be dead long before your chimps can get down here to save you.' Boris chuckled again. 'I am enjoying this. You and I had an appointment once before, but you broke it. Never mind – this is going to be even more fun.' He knew that it was not wise to delay with a man like this. Mek had made one mistake, and it was highly unlikely that he would make another. He should blow his head off now, and that would give him a few minutes more to deal with Tessay. But the temptation to gloat over him was too strong.

'I have good news for you, Mek. You will live a few seconds longer. I am going to kill the whore first, and I am going to let you watch. I hope you enjoy it as much as I am going to.' He sidled away from the

193

shelter of the boulder, edging towards where Tessay lay curled on the gravel beach. She was turned half away from him, trying to cover her breasts and her pubic area with hands too small and delicate for the job. Even as he approached the woman, Boris was watching Mek with his full attention. Mek was the danger, and he never took his eyes off him. It was a mistake. He had underestimated the woman.

While pretending to turn away from him modestly, Tessay had reached down between her thighs and found a round, water-worn stone that fitted neatly into her small fist. Suddenly she uncoiled her lithe body and used all the strength of it to hurl the stone at his head. Boris caught the movement from the corner of his eye and flung up his arm to shield his head.

The stone, flying with surprising force at close range, never struck its target. Instead it caught the point of Boris's upraised elbow. His sleeves were rolled up high around his biceps, and there was no padding to cushion the impact of the stone; his arm was bent and flexed, the thin covering of skin drawn tightly over the bone of the joint. The head of the ulna cracked like glass, and Boris howled at the excruciating agony. His hand opened involuntarily, and his forefinger jerked away from the trigger without the strength to fire the shot he was aiming at Mek's belly.

Mek rolled to his feet, and before Boris could change the rifle to his other hand he disappeared behind the angle of the giant boulder.

With his left hand Boris swung the butt of the rifle at Tessay's head, knocking her backwards into the sand. Then he thrust the muzzle into her throat, pinning her there while he shouted angrily. 'I am going to kill her, you black bastard! If you want your whore, you'd better come fetch her!' The pain of the shattered elbow rendered his voice hoarse and brutish.

From somewhere behind the boulder Mek Nimmur's voice rang out strongly and clearly, calling a single word in Amharic that echoed along the cliffs. Then he spoke in English, 'My men will be here in a moment. Leave the woman and I will spare you. Harm her and I will make you plead for death.'

Boris stooped over Tessay and dragged her to her feet with his good arm locked around her throat. He held the rifle in the same hand, pointing it over her shoulder. The hand of his injured arm had recovered sufficiently from the first shock to be able to hold the pistol grip and to manipulate the trigger.

'She will be dead long before your men get here,' he shouted back as he started to drag her away from the boulder. 'Come and get her yourself, Mek. She is here if you want her.'

He tightened his lock around her throat, choking her until she struggled and gasped, tearing at his arm with her nails and leaving long red welts across the tanned skin.

'Listen to her! I am crushing this pretty neck. Listen to her choking.' He tightened his grip, forcing the sounds of distress out of her.

Boris was watching the corner of the boulder where Mek had disappeared. At the same time he was backing away from it, giving himself space in which to work. His mind was racing, for he knew that he could not escape. His right arm was barely usable, and there were too many of Mek's *shufta* companions. He had the woman, but he wanted the man as well. That was the best trade that he could hope for – both of them, he had to have both of them.

He heard a shout, a strange voice from higher up the slope. Mek's men were on their way. He was desperate now. Mek was not going to be drawn; he had not heard him speak or move for almost two minutes. He had lost him – by this time he could be anywhere.

'Too late,' Boris realized. 'I am not going to get him. Only the woman. But I must do it now.' He forced her to her knees and stooped over her, shifting the lock of his arm around her throat.

'Goodbye, Tessay,' he grated in her ear. He tightened his arm muscles and felt the vertebrae in her neck arched to breaking point. It needed only an ounce more pressure.

'It's all over for you,' he whispered, and began the final pressure. He knew from long experience the sound that the vertebrae would make as they gave, and he tensed himself for it, poised for that crackle like the breaking of a green branch, and the slack weight of her corpse in his grip.

Then something crashed into his back with a force that seemed to drive in his backbone and crush his ribs. Both the strength and the direction were entirely unexpected. It did not seem possible that Mek Nimmur could have moved so far and so swiftly. He must have left the shelter of the boulder and circled out through the scrub. Now he had come at Boris from behind.

His attack was so savage that the arm that Boris had wound around Tessay's neck opened. She drew in a wheezing, strangled breath and twisted out of his grip. Boris tried to turn and swing the rifle around, but Mek was on him again, seizing the rifle and trying to wrest it from Boris's hands.

The Russian's finger was still on the trigger, and a shot went off while the muzzle was level with Mek's face. The detonation stunned him for an instant, and he released the rifle and staggered backwards with his ears ringing.

Boris backed away from him, struggling with the weapon, trying to open the bolt and crank another cartridge into the chamber, but his crippled right arm made his movements clumsy and awkward. Mek gathered himself and charged head down across the gravel beach. He drove into Boris with all his weight, and the rifle flew out of the Russian's hands. Locked chest to chest the two of them spun around in a macabre waltz, trying to throw each other, wrestling for the advantage, until they tripped and went over backwards into the river.

They came to the surface still grappling and rolling over each other, first one on top and then the other, a fearful parody of the lovemaking which Boris had watched a few minutes earlier. Punching and straining and tripping each other, they struggled in the shallows. But every time they fell back into the water the slope of the bank beneath their feet forced them further out, until, when they were waist-deep, the main current of the Nile suddenly picked them up and swept them away downstream. They were still locked together, their heads bobbing in the tumble of waters, their arms thrashing the water white around them, bellowing at each other in primeval rage.

Tessay heard the men that Mek had called coming down through the scrub at the run. She snatched up her *shamma* and pulled it over her head as she ran to meet them. As the first of them burst on to the gravel bar with his AK cocked, she shouted to him in Amharic.

'There! Mek is in the water. He is fighting the Russian. Help him!' She ran with them along the bank. As they drew level with the two men in midstream one of the men stopped and levelled his AK, but Tessay rushed at him and struck up the barrel.

'You fool!' she shouted angrily. 'You will hit Mek.'

Jumping to the top of one of the riverside boulders, she shaded her eyes against the dazzling reflection of the low sun off the water. With a sick feeling in the pit of her stomach she saw that Boris had managed to get behind Mek and had a half nelson hold around his throat. He was forcing Mek's head under the surface. Mek was struggling like a hooked salmon in his grip as they were swept into a long chute of white water.

Tessay jumped down from the rock and ran on down the bank to the next point, from which she could only watch helplessly.

Boris was still holding Mek's head under water as they were borne together into the head of the chute. Fangs of black rock flashed by them on each side as they gathered speed. Mek was a powerful man and Boris had to exert every last ounce of his own strength to hold him, and he knew he could not do so much longer. Suddenly Mek reared back, and for a moment his head came out. He sucked a quick breath of air before Boris could force him under again, but that breath seemed to have renewed his strength.

Desperately Boris looked ahead to the tail of the chute as they sped towards it. There were more rocks there. Boris picked out one great black slab over which the waters poured in a standing wave three feet high. He steered for it, kicking and hauling Mek's body around with the last of his strength.

They flew down the slope of racing water with the rock slab waiting for them at the end like a lurking sea-monster. Boris continued to wrestle with Mek, until he had turned him into a position ahead of him. He planned to steer him into a head-on collision with the rock and use Mek's body to cushion his own impact.

At the very last moment before they struck Mek dragged his head out from the surface, and as he grabbed a precious lungful of air he saw the rock and realized the danger. With a single violent effort he ducked forward below the surface again and rolled over head-first. It was so powerful and unexpected that Boris was unable to resist. Instinctively he maintained his lock around Mek's neck and was carried forward over his back until their positions were reversed. Now Mek had managed to interpose Boris between himself and the rock, so that when they slammed into it it was the Russian who bore the full brunt of the impact.

Boris's right shoulder crunched like a walnut in the jaws of a steel cracker. Although his head was still under water he screamed at the brutal agony of it, and his lungs filled with water. He relinquished his grip and was flung clear of Mek. When he came to the surface he was floundering like a drowned insect, his right arm shattered in two places, his good arm flailing weakly, and his sodden lungs wheezing and pumping.

Mek exploded through the surface only a few yards behind him. Looking around quickly as he strained for air, he spotted Boris's bobbing head almost immediately and with a few powerful overarm strokes came up behind him.

Boris was so far gone that he was not aware of Mek's intentions until he seized his shirt collar from behind and twisted it like a strangler's garotte. With his other hand, below the surface, Mek secured a grip on the back of Boris's wide leather belt and used it like the helm of a rudder to steer him towards the next reef of rocks that was boiling the water ahead of them.

Through his waterlogged lungs Boris was trying to shout invective at him. 'Bastard! Black swine! Filthy—' But his voice was barely audible above the rush of the waters and the growl of the rocky spur that lay across their path. Mek rode him head-first into the rock and he felt the impact transferred through Boris's skull to jolt the straining muscles of his forearms. Instantly Boris went slack in his grip, his head lolled and his limbs became as limp and soft as strands of kelp washing in the surf.

As they tumbled into the next run of open water, Mek used his grip on the back of Boris's collar to lift the Russian's face above the surface. For a moment even he was struck with horror at the injury that he had inflicted. Boris's forehead was staved in. The skin was unbroken, but there was a deep indentation in his skull into which Mek could have thrust his thumb. And Boris's eyes bulged, pushed out of their sockets like those of a battered doll.

Mek swung the inert carcass around in the water, and stared at the broken head from a distance of only a few inches. He reached up and touched the depressed area of the skull with his fingertips, and felt the shards of splintered bone grate and give beneath the skin.

Once again he thrust the shattered head below the surface and held it there, while he crabbed sideways across the current towards the bank. There was no resistance from Boris, but Mek kept his head submerged for the rest of that long tortuous swim across the Nile.

'How do you kill a monster?' he thought grimly. 'I should bury him at a crossroads with a stake through his heart.' But instead he drowned him fifty times over, and at the next bend of the river they were washed into the bank.

Mek's men were waiting for him there. They supported him when his legs sagged under him, and they helped him up the bank. When they started to drag Boris's corpse out of the river, Mek stopped them abruptly.

'Leave him for the crocodiles. After what he has done to our country and our people, he deserves nothing better.' But even in his anger and his hatred he did not want Tessay to have to look at that mutilated head. She had been unable to keep pace with the men, but she was coming along the bank towards him now.

One of his men pushed Boris's corpse back into the current, and as it floated away he unslung his AK rifle from his shoulder and let off a burst of automatic fire. The bullets chopped up the surface around Boris's head, and socked heavily into his back. They tore holes in his wet shirt and kicked out lumps of raw flesh. The other men on the bank shouted with laughter and joined in the fusillade, emptying their magazines into the lifeless body. Mek did not attempt to prevent them. Some of their close relatives had died most horribly under the Russian's care. The corpse rolled over in a pink cloud of its own blood, and for a moment Boris's pale bulging eyes stared at the sky. Then he sank away beneath the surface.

Mek stood up slowly and went to meet Tessay. He took her in his arms, and as he held her to his chest he whispered to her softly.

'It's all right. He won't ever hurt you again. It's all over. You are my woman now – for ever!'

ince Boris and Tessay had left the camp there was no longer any reason to maintain security, and Nicholas and Royan were no longer obliged to skulk in Royan's hut when they discussed their search for the tomb.

Nicholas transferred their headquarters into the dining hut, and had the camp staff build another large table on which they could spread the satellite photographs and all the other maps and material that they had accumulated. The chef sent a steady supply of coffee from the kitchen, while they pored over the papers and discussed their discoveries in Taita's pool and every theory that either of them dreamed up, no matter how far-fetched.

'We will never be certain if that shaft was made by Taita, or whether it was a natural sink-hole, until we can get back in there with the right equipment.'

'What type of equipment are you talking about?' she wanted to know.

'Scuba, not oxygen rebreathers. Although the navy rebreathing outfits are much lighter and more compact, you cannot use them below a depth of thirty-three feet, the equivalent of one atmosphere of water. After that pure oxygen becomes lethal. Have you ever used an aqualung?'

She nodded. 'When Duraid and I were on honeymoon at a resort on the Red Sea. I had a few lessons and made three or four open-water dives, but let me hasten to add that I am no expert.'

'I promise not to send you down there,' he smiled, 'but I think we can safely say that we have found enough evidence both in Tanus's tomb and Taita's pool to make it imperative that we mount the second phase of this operation.'

She nodded agreement. 'We will have to return with a much more extensive range of equipment, and some expert help. But you are not going to be able to pose as a tourist sportsman next time around. What possible excuse are we going to find for returning that will not set off all the alarm bells in the minds of Ethiopian bureaucracy?'

'You are speaking to the man who has paid unofficial and uninvited visits to both those charming lads Gadaffi and Saddam. Ethiopia should be a Sunday-school picnic in comparison.'

'When do the big rains start up in the mountains?' she asked suddenly.

'Yes!' His expression became serious. 'That is the jackpot question. You only have to look at the high-water mark on the walls of Taita's pool to have some idea what it must be like in there when the river is in full flood.' He flipped over the pages of his pocket diary. 'Luckily, we still have a bit of time – not a great deal, but enough. We will need to move pretty smartly. We have to get back home before I can start work on planning phase two.'

'We should pack up right away, then.'

'Yes, we should. But it seems a damned shame not to take full advantage of every moment we are here, having come all this way. I think we can spare just a few more days to sound out some ideas that I have about Taita's pool and the sink-hole, to try to arrive at some sort of informed guess about what we will need when we return.'

'You are the boss.'

'My word, how pleasant to hear a lady say that.'

She smiled sweetly. 'Enjoy the moment,' she counselled him, 'it may never happen again.' And then she became serious again. 'What are these ideas that you have?'

'What goes up must come down, what goes in must come out,' he said mysteriously. 'The water going into the sink-hole under such pressure must be going somewhere. Unless it joins a subterranean water system and makes its way into the Nile that way, then it should come to the surface where we can find it.'

'Go on,' she invited.

'One thing is certain. Nobody is going to get into the sink-hole from the pool. The pressure is lethal. But if we can find the outlet, we may be able to explore it from the other end.'

'That's a fascinating possibility.' She looked impressed, and turned to the satellite photograph. Nicholas had identified the monastery and ringed it on the photograph. He had marked in the approximate course of the river through the chasm, although the gorge itself was too narrow and covered with bush to show up on the small-scale picture, even under the high-powered magnifying lens.

'Here is the point where the river enters the chasm.' She pointed it out to him. 'And here is the side valley down which the trail detours. Okay?'

'Okay,' he nodded. 'What are you driving at?'

'On our approach march, we remarked that this valley might at one time have been the original course of the Dandera river, and that it seemed to have cut a new bed for itself through the chasm.'

'That's right,' Nicholas agreed. 'I am still listening.'

'The fall of the land towards the Nile is very steep at this point, isn't it? Well, do you recall we crossed another smaller, but still pretty substantial, stream on our way down the dry valley? That stream seemed to emerge from somewhere on the eastern side of the valley.'

'All right, I am with you now. You are suggesting that this may be the overflow from the sink-hole. Clever little devil, aren't you?'

'Just capitalizing on your genius.' She cast down her eyes modestly, and looked up at him from under her lashes. She was clowning, but her lashes were long and dense and curling, and her eyes were the colour of burnt honey with tiny golden highlights in their depths. At this close range he found them disturbing.

He stood up and suggested, 'Why don't we go and take a look?'

Nicholas went to fetch his camera bag and the light day-pack from his hut, and when he returned he found Royan ready to go. But she was not alone.

'I see that you are bringing your chaperon with you,' he remarked with resignation.

'Unless you are tough enough to send him away.' Royan smiled encouragement at Tamre who stood at her side, grinning and bobbing and hugging his shoulders in the ecstasy of being in the presence of his idol.

'Oh, very well.' Nicholas gave in without a struggle. 'Let the little devil come along.'

Tamre lolloped away up the path ahead of them, his grubby *shamma* flapping around his long skinny legs, chanting the repetitive chorus of an Amharic psalm, and every few minutes looking back to make certain that Royan was still following him. It was a hard pull up the valley, and the noonday heat was debilitating. Although Tamre seemed totally unaffected, the other two were both sweating in dark patches through their shirts by the time they reached the point where the stream debouched into the valley. Gratefully, they sought the shade of a patch of acacia trees, and while they rested Nicholas glassed the side of the valley through his binoculars.

'How are they after the dunking I gave them?' she asked.

'Waterproof,' he grunted, 'full marks to Herr Zeiss.'

'What do you see up there?'

'Not much. The bush is too thick. We will have to foot-slog up the side. Sorry.'

They left the shade and made their way up the side of the valley in the direct burning sunlight. The stream tumbled down a series of cascades, each with a pool at its foot. The bush crowded the banks, lush and green where the roots had been able to reach the water. Clouds of black and yellow butterflies danced over the pools, and a black and white wagtail patrolled the moss-green rocks along the edge, its long tail gyrating back and forth like the needle of a metronome.

Halfway up the slope they paused beside one of the pools to rest, and Nicholas used his hat like a fly-swatter to stun a brown and yellow grasshopper. He tossed the insect on to the surface of the pool, and as it kicked weakly and floated towards the exit a long dark shadow rose from the bottom. There was a swirl and a mirrorlike flash of a scaly silver belly, and the grasshopper disappeared.

'Ten-pounder,' Nicholas lamented. 'Why didn't I bring my rod?'

Tamre was crouched near Nicholas on the pool bank, and suddenly he lifted his hand and held it out. Almost at once one of the circling butterflies settled upon his finger. It perched there with its velvety black and yellow wings fanning gently. They stared at him in astonishment, for it was as though the insect had come to his bidding. Tamre giggled and offered the butterfly to Royan. When she held out her hand, he gently transferred the gorgeous insect to her palm.

'Thank you, Tamre. That is a wonderful gift. Now my gift to you is to set it free again.' She pursed her lips and blew it softly into flight. They watched the butterfly climb high above the pool, and Tamre clapped his hands and laughed with delight.

'Strange,' Nicholas murmured. 'He seems to have a special empathy with all the creatures of the wilderness. I think that Jali Hora, the abbot, does not try to control him, but lets him do very much as his simple fancy dictates. Special treatment for a fey soul, one that hears a different tune and dances to it. I must admit that, despite myself, I am becoming quite fond of the lad.'

It was only another fifty feet higher that they came to the source. There was a low cliff of red sandstone, from a grotto at whose foot the stream gushed. The entrance was screened by a heavy growth of ferns, and Nicholas went down on his knees to pull them aside and peer into the low opening.

'What can you see?' Royan demanded behind him.

'Not much. It's dark in there, but it seems to go in for quite some way.'

'You are too big to get in there. You had better let me go in.'

'Good place for water cobra,' he remarked. 'Lots of frogs for them to eat. Are you sure you want to go?'

'I never said that I wanted to.' She sat on the bank while she unlaced her shoes, then lowered herself into the stream. It came halfway up her thighs, and she waded forward against the flow with difficulty.

She was forced to bend almost double to creep under the overhanging roof of the grotto. As she moved deeper in, her voice came back to him.

'The roof gets lower.'

'Be careful, dear girl. Don't take any chances.'

'I do wish you wouldn't call me "dear girl".' Her voice resonated strangely from the cave entrance.

'Well, you are both those things, a girl and dear. How about if I call you "young lady"?'

'Not that either. My name is Royan.' There was silence for a while, then she called again. 'This is as far as I can go. It all narrows down into a shaft of some sort.'

'A shaft?' he demanded.

'Well, at least a roughly rectangular opening.'

'Do you think it is the work of humans?'

'Impossible to tell. The water is coming out of it like the spout of a bath tap. A solid jet.'

'No evidence of any excavation? No marks of tools on the rock?'

'Nothing. It's slick and water-worn, covered with moss and algae.'

'Could a man get into the opening, I mean if it were not for the water pressure?'

'If he was a pygmy or a dwarf.'

'Or a child?' he suggested.

'Or a child,' she agreed. 'But who would send a child in there?'

'The ancients often used child-slaves. Taita might have done the same.'

'Don't suggest it. You are destroying my high opinion of Taita,' she told him as she backed out of the entrance of the grotto. There were pieces of fern and moss in her hair, and she was soaked from the waist downwards. He gave her a hand and boosted her back on to the bank. The curve of her bottom was clearly visible through her wet trousers. He forced himself not to dwell upon the view.

'So we have to conclude that the shaft is a natural flaw in the limestone, and not a man-made tunnel?'

'I didn't say that. No. I said that I couldn't be sure. You might be correct. Children might have been used to dig it. After all, they were used in the coalmines during the industrial revolution.'

'But there is no way that we would be able to explore the tunnel from this end?'

'Impossible.' She was vehement. 'The water is pouring out under enormous pressure. I tried to push my arm up the shaft, but I did not have the strength.'

'Pity! I was hoping for some more irrefutable evidence, or at least another lead.' He sat down beside her on the bank, and ferreted in his pack. She looked at him quizzically when he brought out a small black anodized instrument and opened the lid.

'Aneroid barometer,' he explained. 'Every good navigator should have one.' He studied it for a moment and then made a note of the reading.

'Explain,' she invited.

'I want to know if this spring is below the level of the entrance to the sink-hole in Taita's pool. If it is not, then we can cross it off our list of possibilities.'

He stood up. 'If you are ready, we can move on.'

'Where to?'

'Why, Taita's pool, of course. We need a reading up there to establish the difference in altitude between the two points.'

O nce Tamre knew where they were headed he showed them a short-cut, so it took them just under two hours from the fountain head to the top of the cliff face above Taita's pool.

While they rested, Royan remarked, 'Tamre seems to spend most of his days wandering around in the bush. He knows every path and game trail. He is an excellent guide.'

'Better than Boris, at least,' Nicholas agreed, as he fished out his barometer and took another reading.

'You look particularly pleased with yourself.' Royan watched his face as he studied the instrument.

'Every reason to be,' he told her. 'Allowing one hundred and eighty feet for the height of the cliff below us, and another fifty feet for the depth of the pool, the entrance to the sink-hole is still over a hundred feet higher than your outlet through the fern grotto on the other side of the ridge.'

'Which means?'

'Which means that there is a distinct possibility that the streams are one and the same. The inflow is here in Taita's pool and the outflow is from your grotto.'

'How on earth did Taita do it?' she puzzled. 'How did he get to the bottom of the pool? You are the engineering marvel. Tell me how you would do it.'

He shrugged, but she persisted. 'I mean, there must be some established way of doing things like that, of working under water. How do they build the piers of a bridge, or the foundations of a dam, or – or – or how did Taita himself build the shaft below the level of the Nile to measure the flow of the river? You remember the description that he gives of his hydrograph in *River God?*'

'The accepted technique is to build a coffer dam,' Nicholas said casually, and then broke off and stared at her. 'My oath, you really are a corker. A dam! What if that old ruffian, Taita, dammed the whole flipping river!'

'Would that have been possible?'

'I am beginning to believe that with Taita anything is possible. He certainly had unlimited manpower at his disposal, and if he could build the hydrograph on the Nile at Aswan, then he understood very clearly the principles of hydrodynamics. After all, the old Egyptians' lives were completely bound up with the seasonal inundations of the river and the management of the floods. From what we have gathered about the old man, it certainly seems possible.'

'How could we prove it?'

'By finding the remains of his dam. It had to be a hell of a work to hold the Dandera river. There is a good chance that some evidence of it remains.'

'Where would he have built the dam?' she asked excitedly. 'Or let me put it another way, where would you site the dam if you had to do it?'

'There is one natural place for it,' he answered promptly. 'The spot where the trail leaves the river and detours down the valley, and the river falls into the chasm.' They both turned their heads in unison and looked upstream.

'What are we waiting for?' she asked, and sprang to her feet. 'Let's go look-see!'

Their excitement was infectious, and Tamre giggled and danced ahead of them along the trail through the thorns and then up the valley to the point where it rejoined the river. The sun had lost the worst of its heat by the time they stood once again above the falls where the Dandera river plunged into the mouth of the chasm, and began its last lap in the race to join the Nile.

'If Taita had thrown a dam across here – ' Nicholas made a sweep of his arms across the mouth of the gorge, ' – he could have diverted the river down the side valley here.'

'It looks possible,' she laughed. Tamre giggled in sympathy, not understanding a word of what they were saying, but enjoying himself immensely.

'I would need a dumpy level to take some shots of the actual fall of the land. It can be very deceptive, but with the naked eye it does look possible, as you say.' He shaded his eyes and looked up the bluffs on each side of the waterfall. They formed two craggy portals of limestone, between which the river roared as it plunged over the lip.

'I would like to climb up there to get a clearer picture of the layout of the terrain. Are you game?'

'Try and stop me,' she challenged him, and led the climb. It was a heavy scramble, and in some places the limestone was rotten and crumbling dangerously. However, when they came out on the summit of the eastern portal they were rewarded with a splendid overall view of the ground below.

Directly to the north, the escarpment rose like a sheer wall with its battlements crenellated and serrated. Above and beyond it there was a dream of further mountains, the high peaks of the Choke, blue as a heron's plumage against the clearer distant blue of the African sky.

All around them were the badlands of the gorge, a vast confusion of ridges and spines and reefs of rock of fifty different hues, some ash-grey and white, others black as the hide of a bull buffalo, or red as his heart blood. The riverine bush was green, the poisonous vivid green of the mamba in the treetop, while further from the water the scrub was grey and sear, and along the spines of the broken kopjes stood the stark outlines of ancient drought-struck trees, their tortured limbs twisted and black against the sky.

'The picture of devastation,' Royan whispered as she looked around her, 'untamed and untamable. No wonder Taita chose this place. It repels all intruders.'

They were both silent for a while, awed by the wild grandeur of the scene, but as soon as they had recovered from the exertion of the climb their enthusiasm resurfaced.

'Now you can get a good picture of it.' Nicholas pointed down into the valley below them. 'There is a clear divide at the fork of the valley. You can see the natural fall of the ground. There, from that side of the gorge to that point below us, is the narrowest part. It is a neck where the river squeezes through – the natural site for a dam.' He swivelled and pointed down to the left of where they sat. 'It would not take much to spill the river into the valley. Once he had finished whatever he was up to in the chasm, it would taken even less to break down the wall of the dam and let the river resume its natural course again.'

Tamre watched their faces eagerly, turning his head to each speaker in turn, uncomprehending, but aping Royan's expression like a mirror. If she nodded he nodded, when she frowned he did the same, and when she smiled he giggled happily.

'It's a big river.' Royan shook her head, while Tamre wagged his from side to side in sympathy and looked wise. 'What method would he have used? An earthen dam? Surely not?'

'The Egyptians used earthen canals and dams for a great many of their irrigation works,' Nicholas mused. 'On the other hand, when they had rock available to work with they used it extensively. They were expert masons. You have stood in the quarries at Aswan.'

'Not much topsoil here in the gorge,' she pointed out. 'But on the other hand, there is plenty of rock. It's like a geological museum. Every type of rock that you could wish for.'

'I agree,' he said. 'Rather than an earthen wall, Taita would most probably have used a masonry and rock fill. That is the type of dam the ancients built in Egypt, long before his time. If that is the case, there is a chance that traces of it have survived.'

'Okay. Let's work on that hypothesis. Taita built a dam of rock slabs, and then he breached it again. Where would we find the remains of it?'

'We would have to start searching on the actual site,' he answered.

'There at the neck of the gorge. Then we would have to search downstream from there.'

They scrambled down the slope again, with Tamre picking out the easiest route for Royan, stopping to beckon her whenever she faltered or paused for breath. They came out in the neck of the valley and stood on the rocky bank of the river, looking about them.

'How high would the wall have been?' Royan asked.

'Not too high. Again, I can't give you a precise answer until I have shot the levels.' He climbed a little way up the side of the wall. There he squatted and turned his head back and forth, looking first down the length of the valley and then towards the lip of the waterfall that dropped into the mouth of the chasm.

Three times he changed his position, on each occasion moving a few paces higher up the slope. The cliff became steeper the higher he climbed. In the end he was clinging precariously to the side of it, but he seemed satisfied. Then he called down to her.

'I would say this is about it, where I am now. This would be the height of the dam wall. It looks about fifteen feet high to me.'

Royan was still standing on the bank, and now she turned and stared across at the far bank of the river, estimating the distance to the limestone cliff rising above it.

'Roughly a hundred feet across,' she shouted up to him.

'About that,' he agreed. 'A lot of work, but not impossible.'

'Taita was never one to be daunted by size or difficulty.' She cupped her hands around her mouth to shout up to him. 'While you are up there, can you see any sign of works? Taita would have had to pin the dam wall into the cliff.'

He scrambled along the cliff, keeping to the same level, until he was almost directly above the falls and could go no further. Then he slid down to where Royan and Tamre waited.

'Nothing?' she anticipated, and he shook his head.

'No, but you can't really expect that there would be anything left after nearly four thousand years. These cliffs have been exposed to wind and weather for all that time. I think our best bet will be to look for any surviving blocks from the dam wall that might have been carried away when Taita breached it to flood the chasm again.'

They started down the valley, where Royan came upon a chunk of stone that seemed to be of a different type from the surrounding country rock. It was the size of an old-fashioned cabin trunk. Although it was half-covered by undergrowth, the uppermost end – the one that was exposed – had a definite right-angled corner to it. She called Nicholas across to her.

'Look at that.' Royan patted it proudly. 'What do you think of that?'

He climbed down beside her and ran his hands over the exposed surface of the slab. 'Possible,' he repeated. 'But to be certain we would have to find the chisel marks where the old masons started the fracture. As you know, they chiselled a hole into the stone, and then wedged it open until it split.'

Both of them went over the exposed surface carefully, and although Royan found an indentation that she declared was a weathered chisel mark, Nicholas gave her only four out of ten on the scale of probability.

'We are running out of time,' he said, enticing her away from her find, 'and we still have a lot of ground to cover.'

They searched the valley floor for half a kilometre further, and then Nicholas called it off. 'Even in the heaviest flood it is unlikely that any blocks would have been carried down this far. Let's go back and see if anything was washed over the falls into the mouth of the chasm.'

They returned to the bank of the Dandera and worked their way down as far as the falls. Nicholas peered over.

'It's not as deep here as it is further down,' he estimated. 'I would guess that it is less than a hundred feet.'

'Do you think you could get down there?' she asked dubiously. Spray blew back out of the depths into their faces, and they had to shout at each other to make themselves heard over the thunder of the waters.

'Not without a rope, and some muscle men to haul me back out of there.' He perched himself on the brink and focused the binoculars down into the bowl. There was a jumble of loose rock down there – small, rounded boulders, and one or two very much larger. Some of them were angular, and some with a little imagination could be called rectangular. However, their surfaces had been smoothed by the rushing waters, and were gleaming wet. All of them seemed partially submerged or obscured by spray.

'I don't think we can decide anything from up here, and to tell the truth I don't fancy going down there – not this evening anyway.'

Royan sat down beside him and hugged her knees to her chest. She was dispirited. 'So there is nothing we can be certain about. Did Taita dam the river, or didn't he?'

Quite naturally he placed his arm around her shoulders to console her, and after a moment she relaxed and leaned against him. They stared down into the chasm in silence. At last she drew back from him gently, and stood up.

'I suppose we should start back to camp. How long will it take us?'

'At least three hours.' He stood up beside her. 'You are right. It will be dark before we get back, and there is no moon tonight.'

'Funny how tired you feel after a disappointment,' she said, and stretched. 'I could lie down and sleep right here on one of Taita's stone blocks.' She broke off and stared at him. 'Nicky, where did he get them?'

'Where did he get what?' He looked puzzled.

'Don't you see! We are going at it from the wrong end. We have been trying to find out what happened to the blocks. This morning you mentioned the quarries at Aswan. Shouldn't we consider where Taita found the blocks for his dam, rather than what happened to them afterwards?'

'The quarry!' Nicholas exclaimed. 'My word, you are right. The beginning, not the end. We should be looking for the quarry, not the remnants of the dam wall.'

'Where do we start?'

'I hoped you were going to tell me.' He laughed out loud, and immediately Tamre bubbled with sympathetic laughter. They both looked at the boy.

'I think we should start with Tamre, our faithful guide,' she said, and took his hand. 'Listen to me, Tamre. Listen very carefully!' Obediently he cocked his head and stared at her face, summoning all his errant concentration.

'We are looking for a place where the square stones come from.' He looked mystified, so she tried again. 'Long ago there were men who cut the rock from the mountains. Somewhere near here, they left a big hole. Perhaps there are still square blocks of stone lying in the hole?'

Suddenly the boy's face cleared and split into a beatific smile. 'The Jesus stone!' he cried happily.

He sprang to his feet without relinquishing his grip on her hand. 'I show you my Jesus stone.' He dragged her after him as he bounded away down the valley.

'Wait, Tamre!' she pleaded. 'Not so fast.' But in vain. Tamre kept up the pace and burst into an Amharic hymn as he ran. Nicholas followed at a more sedate pace, and caught up with them a quarter of a mile down the valley.

There he found Tamre on his knees, pressing his forehead against the rock wall of the valley, his eyes shut tightly as he prayed. He had dragged Royan down beside him.

'What on earth are you doing?' Nicholas demanded, as he came up.

'We are praying,' she told him primly. 'Tamre's instructions. We have to pray before we can go to the Jesus stone.'

She turned away from Nicholas, closed her eyes and clasped her hands in front of her eyes, then began to pray softly.

Nicholas found a seat on a boulder a little way from them. 'I don't suppose it can do any harm,' he consoled himself, as he settled down to wait.

Abruptly Tamre sprang to his feet and performed a giddy little dance, flapping his arms and whirling around until he raised the dust.

Then he stopped and chanted. 'It is done. We can go in to the Jesus stone.'

Once again he seized Royan's hand and led her to the rock wall. In front of Nicholas's eyes the two of them seemed to vanish, and he stood up in mild alarm.

'Royan!' he called. 'Where are you? What's going on?'

'This way, Nicky. Come this way!'

He went to the wall and exclaimed with astonishment, 'My oath! We would never have found this in a year of searching.'

The cliff face was folded back upon itself, forming a concealed entrance. He walked through the opening, gazing up the vertical sides, and within thirty paces came out into an open amphitheatre that was at least a hundred yards across and open to the sky. The walls were of solid rock, and he could see at a glance that it was the same micaceous schist as the block which Royan had found lying on the floor of the valley.

It was apparent that the bowl had been quarried out of the living rock, leaving tiers rising up to the top of the walls. The recesses from which the blocks had been hacked were still plain to see and had left deep steps with right-angled profiles. Some scrub and undergrowth had found a precarious foothold in the cracks, but the open quarry was not choked with this growth and Nicholas could see that a stockpile of finished granite blocks remained scattered about the bottom of the excavation. He was so awed by the discovery that he could find no words to express himself. He stood just inside the entrance, his head slowly turning from side to side as he tried to take it all in.

Tamre had led Royan to the centre of the quarry where one large slab lay on its own. It was obvious that the ancients had been on the point of removing it and transporting it up the valley, for it was finished and dressed into a perfect rectangle.

'The Jesus stone!' Tamre chanted, kneeling before the slab and pulling Royan down beside him. 'Jesus led me here. The first time I came here I saw him standing on the stone. He had a long white beard and eyes that were kind and sad.' He crossed himself and began to recite one of the psalms, swaying and bobbing to the rhythm.

As Nicholas moved up quietly behind them he saw the evidence that Tamre had visited this sacred place of his regularly. The Jesus stone was his own private altar, and his pathetic little offerings were lying where he had laid them. There were old *tej* flasks and baked clay pots, most of them cracked and broken. In them stood bunches of wild flowers that had long ago wilted and dried out. There were other treasures that he had gathered and placed upon his altar – tortoise shells and porcupine quills, a cross that had been hand-carved from wood and decorated with scraps of coloured cloth, necklaces of lucky beans, and models of animals and birds moulded from blue river clay.

Nicholas stood and watched the two of them kneeling and praying together in front of the primitive altar. He felt deeply moved by this evidence of the boy's faith, and by his childlike trust in bringing them to this place.

At last Royan stood up and came to join him. Together she and Nicholas began to make a slow circuit of the quarry floor. They spoke little, and then only in whispers as though they were in a cathedral or some holy place. She touched his arm and pointed. A number of the square blocks still lay in their original positions in the quarry walls. They had not been completely freed from the mother rock, like a foetus attached by an umbilical cord which had never been severed by the ancient masons.

It was a perfect illustration of the quarrying methods used by the ancients. Work could be seen in progress in all the various stages, from the marking out of the blocks by the master craftsman, the drilling of the tap holes, the wedging of the cleavage lines, right up to the finished product lifted out of the wall and ready for transport to the dam site.

The sun had set and it was almost dark by the time they came round to the entrance of the quarry again. They sat together on one of the finished blocks, with Tamre sitting at their feet like a puppy, looking up at Royan's face.

'If he had a tail he would wag it,' Nicholas smiled.

'We can never betray his trust, and desecrate this place in any way. He has made it his own temple. I don't think he has ever brought another living soul here. Will you promise me that we will always respect it, no matter what?'

'That is the very least I can do,' he agreed. Then, turning to Tamre, he said, 'You have done a very good thing by bringing us here to your Jesus stone. I am very pleased with you. The lady is very pleased with you.'

'We should start back to camp now,' Royan suggested, looking up at the patch of sky above them. Already it was purple and indigo, shot through with the last rays of the sunset.

'I don't think that would be very wise,' he disagreed. 'Because it is a moonless night one of us could very easily break a leg in the dark. That is something not to be recommended out here. It might take a week to get back to any adequate medical attention.'

'You plan to sleep here?' she asked, with surprise.

'Why not? I can whip up a fire in no time and I also have a pack of survival rations for dinner – I have done this kind of thing before, you know! And you have your chaperon with you, so your honour is safe. So why not?'

'Why not, indeed?' she laughed. 'We will be able to make a more detailed inspection of the quarry tomorrow early.'

He stood up to start gathering firewood, but then stopped and looked up at the sky. She heard it too, that now familiar fluttering whistle in the air.

'The Pegasus helicopter once again,' he said unnecessarily. 'I wonder what the hell they are up to at this time of day?'

They both stared up into the gathering darkness and watched the navigational lights of the aircraft pass a thousand feet overhead, flashing red and green and white as it headed southwards in the direction of the monastery.

Nicholas built a small fire in the corner of the quarry nearest the entrance, and as they sat around it he divided the pack of dry survival rations into three parts. They nibbled them, and washed down the sweet and sticky concentrated tablets with water from his bottle.

The fire threw ghostly reflections up the side of the quarry wall, and enhanced the moving shadows. When a nightjar uttered its warbling cry from a niche high up the wall, it was so eerie and evocative that Royan shivered and moved a little closer to Nicholas.

'I wonder if somewhere on the other side Taita is aware of our progress,' she said. 'I get the feeling that we have him a little worried by now. We have untangled the first part of the conundrum that he set for us, and I'll bet he never expected anybody to do that well.'

'The next step will be to get to the bottom of his pool. That will be really one up on the old devil. What do you hope we might find down there?'

'I hesitate to put it into words,' she replied. 'I might talk it away, and put a jinx on us.'

'I am not superstitious. Well, not much anyway. Shall I say it for you?' he offered, and she laughed and nodded. He went on, 'We hope to find the entrance to the tomb of Pharaoh Mamose. No more hints and riddles and red herrings. The veritable tomb.'

She crossed her fingers. 'From your lips to God's ear!' Then she grew serious. 'What do you think of our chances? I mean of finding the tomb intact?'

He shrugged. 'I will answer that once we get to the bottom of the pool.'

'How are we going to do that? You have ruled out the use of an aqualung.'

'I don't know,' he confessed. 'At this stage I just don't know. Perhaps we might be able to get in there with full-helmeted diving suits.'

212

She was silent as she considered the seeming impossibility of the task ahead.

'Cheer up!' He put his arm around her shoulders, and she made no move to pull away from him. 'There is one consolation. If Taita has made it so tough for us, he has also made it tough for anyone else to have got in there ahead of us. I think that if the tomb is really down there, no other grave robbers have beaten us to it.'

'If the entrance to the tomb is at the bottom of the pool, then his descriptions in the scrolls are deliberately misleading. The information that has come down to us has been garbled by Taita, then by Duraid, and finally by Wilbur Smith. We are faced with the task of finding our way through this labyrinth of deliberate misinformation.'

They were silent again for a while and then Royan smiled in the firelight, her face lighting up with anticipation.

'Oh, Nicky! It is such an exciting challenge.' Then her voice descended an octave. 'But is there a way? Is it possible to get in there?'

'We will find out.'

'When?'

'In due course. I haven't thought it out fully as yet. All I am certain of is that it is going to take a prodigious amount of planning and hard work.'

'You are still committed, then?' She wanted his assurance. She knew that she could never do it alone. 'You aren't daunted by the project?'

Nicholas chuckled. 'I will admit that I never expected Taita to lead us on such a merry chase. I imagined simply breaking open a stone gateway and finding it all waiting for us there, like Howard Carter walking into the tomb of Tutankhamen. However, to answer your question, yes, I am daunted by what it's going to involve – but hell, nothing could stop me now! I have the smell of glory in my nostrils and the gleam of gold in my eye.'

While they talked, Tamre curled up in the dust on the other side of the fire, and pulled his *shamma* over his head. His rest must have been interrupted by dreams and fantasies, for he burbled and squeaked and giggled in his sleep.

'I wonder what goes on in that poor demented head, and what visions he sees,' Royan whispered. 'He says he saw Jesus here in the quarry, and I am sure that he really believes that he did.'

Their voices became softer and drowsier as the fire burned down, and Royan murmured, just before she fell asleep on Nicholas's shoulder, 'If the tomb of Pharaoh Mamose is below the level of the river, then surely the contents will be water-damaged?'

'I can't believe that Taita would have built his dam and spent fifteen years working on the tomb, as he says that he did in the scrolls, only to

213

flood it deliberately and despoil the mummy of his king and ruin his treasure,' Nicholas murmured, with her hair tickling his cheek. 'No, that would have precluded Pharaoh's resurrection in the other world, and brought all his work to nothing. I think Taita has taken all that into his calculations.'

She snuggled closer, and sighed with satisfaction.

A little while later he said softly, 'Goodnight, Royan,' but she did not reply and her breathing was deep and even. He smiled to himself, and gently kissed the top of her head.

Nicholas was not certain what had woken him. He took a few moments to place himself, and then he realized that he was still in the quarry. There was no moon but the stars hung down close to the earth, as big and fat as bunches of ripe grapes. By their light he saw that Royan had slipped down and was lying flat on the ground beside him.

He stood up carefully, so as not to disturb her, and moved well away from the dead fire to empty his bladder. The night was deathly quiet. No night bird called, nor was there the sound of any of the other nocturnal creatures. The rocks around him still radiated the heat of the previous day's sunlight.

Suddenly the sound that had woken him was repeated. It was a faint and distant susurration that echoed along the cliffs, so that he could form no judgement as to the direction from which it came. But he was in no doubt what the sound was. He had heard it so often before. It was the sound of faraway automatic gunfire, almost certainly an AK-47 assault rifle firing, not long ragged bursts, but short taps of three rounds, an art that took expertise and practice. He was sure that the person doing the shooting was a trained professional.

He tilted his wrist so that the luminescent dial of his watch caught the starlight, and he saw that it was a few minutes after three o'clock in the morning.

He stood listening for a long time, but the firing was not repeated. At last he returned to where Royan lay and settled down beside her again. However, he slept only shallowly and intermittently, and kept starting awake listening for more gunfire in the night.

Royan began to stir at the first lemon and orange flush of dawn in the eastern sky, and while they ate the remains of the survival rations for their breakfast he told her about the noise that had woken him during the night.

'Do you think it could have been Boris?' she asked. 'He may have caught up with Mek and Tessay.'

'I doubt that very much. Boris has already been gone several days. He should be well out of earshot by now, even beyond the sound range of the heaviest weapons.'

'Who do you suppose it was, then?'

'I have no idea. But I don't like it. We should start back to camp as soon as we have had another look around the quarry. After that there is nothing further that we can do at this stage. We should make tracks for home and mother.'

As soon as the light was strong enough, Nicholas shot a spool of film to make a record of the quarry. For comparison of scale, Royan posed beside the wall in which the embryonic blocks still lay. As she warmed to her role as a model she started to clown for him. She climbed on to the biggest of the slabs and hammed it up for the camera, pouting with one hand behind her head in the style of Marilyn Monroe.

When, finally, they went off down the valley towards the monastery they were both exultant and garrulous after their success. Their discussion was animated as they bounced ideas back and forth, and laid their plans for the further exploitation of these wonderful discoveries. By the time they reached the pink cliffs at the lower end of the chasm it was late morning. There they met a small party of monks from the monastery coming up the trail.

Even from a distance it was obvious that something dreadful had happened during their absence: the sorrowful ululations of the monks sent chills down Royan's spine. It was the universal African sound of mourning, the harbinger of death and disaster. As they approached they saw that the monks were picking up handfuls of dust from the track and pouring it over their heads as they wailed and lamented.

'What is it, Tamre?' Royan asked the boy. 'Go and find out for us!' Tamre ran ahead to meet his brother monks. They stopped in the middle of the path and fell into a high-pitched discussion, weeping and gesticulating. Then Tamre ran back to them.

'Your people at the camp. Something terrible has happened. Bad men came in the might. Many of the servants are dead,' he screamed.

Nicholas grabbed Royan's hand. 'Come on!' he snapped, 'let's find out what is going on here.'

They ran the last mile to the camp, and arrived to find another circle of monks gathered around something in front of the kitchen hut. Nicholas pushed them aside and elbowed his way to the front. There he stopped and stared with a sinking feeling in his gut, and the sweat on his face turned cold with horror. Under a buzzing blue pall of flies lay the blood-splattered corpse of the

215

cook and three other camp servants. Their hands had been bound behind their backs, and then they had been forced to kneel before being shot in the back of the head at close range.

'Don't look!' Nicholas warned Royan as she came up. 'It's not very pretty.'

But she ignored his advice and came to stand beside him. 'Oh, sweet heavens. They have been slaughtered like cattle in an abattoir.' She gagged.

'This explains the sound of gunfire that I heard last night,' he answered grimly. He went forward to identify the dead men. 'Aly and Kif are not here. Where are they?' He raised his voice and called in Arabic, turning to face the crowd. 'Aly, where are you?'

The tracker pushed his way forward. 'I am here, *effendi*.' His voice was shaky and his face was haggard. There was blood on the front of his shirt.

'How did this happen?' Nicholas seized his arm and steadied him.

'Men came in the night with the guns. *Shufta*. They shot into the huts where we were sleeping. They gave us no warning. They just started shooting.'

'How many of them? Who were they?' Nicholas demanded.

'I do not know how many of them there were. It was dark. I was asleep. I ran away when the shooting began. They were *shufta*, bandits, killers. They were hyenas and jackals – there was no reason for what they have done. These men were my brothers, my friends.' He began to sob, and the tears streamed down his face.

Royan turned away, sickened and horrified. She went to her hut and stopped in the doorway. It had been ransacked. Her bags had been turned out on to the floor. Her bedding had been stripped, and the mattress thrown into the corner. As though she were a sleep-walker in a nightmare, she crossed the floor and picked up the canvas folder in which she kept her papers. She turned it upside down and shook it. It was empty. The satellite photographs and the maps, all her rubbings of the stele, the Polaroids that Nicholas had taken in Tanus's tomb – everything was gone.

Royan picked up the bed and set it the right way up. She sat down on it, and tried to gather her thoughts. She felt confused and shaken. The image of those bloody, bullet-ripped corpses laid out in front of the kitchen haunted her, and she found it difficult to concentrate and to think clearly.

Nicholas burst into her hut and looked around quickly. 'They did the same thing to me. Ransacked the place. My rifle has gone, and all my papers. But at least I had the passports and travellers' cheques in my day-pack—' He broke off as he saw the empty canvas folder lying at her feet. 'Have they taken the—'

'Yes!' she forestalled his question. 'They have cleaned out all our research material, even the Polaroids. Thank God you had the undeveloped rolls of film with you. It's the same as happened to Duraid and me all over again. We aren't safe from them, even here, even out in the remotest part of the bush.' There was the edge of hysteria in her voice. She jumped up from the bed and ran to him.

'Oh, Nicky, what would have happened if we had been in camp last night?' She threw her arms around him, and clung to him. 'We would be lying out there in the sun now, all bloody and covered with flies.'

'Steady on, my dear. Let's not jump to any conclusions. This could just be a chance raid by bandits.'

'Then why did they steal our papers? What value would ordinary *shufta* place on rubbings and Polaroids? Where was the Pegasus helicopter heading just before the raid? They were after us, Nicky. I feel it so strongly. They wanted to kill us just as they did Duraid. They could return at any time, and now we are unarmed and helpless.'

'All right, I agree with you that we are pretty vulnerable here. It would be wise to get out as soon as possible. There isn't any point in staying on here anyway. There's nothing more we can do at this stage.' He hugged her and shook her gently. 'Brace up! We will salvage what we can from this mess, and then get moving back to the vehicles right away.'

'What about the dead men?' She stood back, and with an effort forced back her tears and brought herself under control. 'How many of our people survived?'

'Aly, Salin and Kif escaped. They dived out of their huts and ran off into the darkness as soon as the shooting started. I have told them to get ready to leave right away. I have spoken to one of the senior priests. They will take care of the burial of the dead, and will report to the authorities as soon as they are able. But they agree that the attack was aimed at us, and that we are still in danger, and that we should get away as soon as possible.'

Within the hour they were ready to start. Nicholas had decided to leave all the camping equipment and Boris's personal gear in the charge of Jali Hora. The mules were lightly loaded, and he planned to make a forced march out of the gorge.

The abbot had given them an escort of monks to accompany them to the top of the escarpment. 'Only a truly Godless man would attack you while you are under the protection of the cross,' he explained.

Nicholas found the dried hide and head of the striped dik-dik still in the skinning shed. He rolled it into a bundle and strapped it on to the load atop one of the mules, and then gave the order for the attenuated caravan to move out.

Tamre had insinuated himself into the group of monks who were

217

escorting the party. He kept close behind Royan as they set off up the trail, with the lamentations and farewells of the monastic community following them for the first mile.

It was hot in this brutal midday. There was no movement of air to bring relief, and the stone walls of the valley sucked up the heat of that awful sun and spewed it back over them as they toiled up the steep gradients. It dried their sweat even as it oozed through their pores, leaving patterns of white salt crystals on their skins and clothing. The muleteers, spurred on by fear, set a killing pace, trotting behind their beasts and prodding their testicles with a sharpened stick to keep them moving at their best pace.

By mid-afternoon they had retraced the morning's travel and once more reached the putative site of Taita's dam wall. Nicholas and Royan took a few minutes' breather to dip their heads in the river and sluice the salt and sweat from their faces and necks. Then they stood together above the falls and took a brief farewell of the chasm in which lay all their hopes and dreams.

'How long until we return?' she asked.

'We cannot afford to leave it too long,' he told her. 'Big rains are due soon, and the hyenas have got the scent and are crowding in. From now on every day will be precious, and every hour we lose may be crucial.'

She stared down into the chasm and said softly, 'You haven't won yet, Taita. The game is still afoot.'

They turned away together and followed the mules up the trail towards the escarpment wall. That evening they did not stop at the traditional campsite beside the river, but pressed on several miles further until darkness forced a halt. There was no attempt to build a comfortable camp. They dined on cakes of *injera* bread dipped in the *wat* pot that the monks had carried with them. Then Nicholas and Royan spread their bedrolls side by side on the stony earth and, using the mule packs as pillows, fell into exhausted, dreamless sleep.

The next morning, while the mules were being loaded in the pre-dawn darkness, they drank a bowl of strong bitter black Ethiopian coffee. Then they started out along the trail again.

As the rising sun lit the sheer walls of the escarpment ahead of them they seemed close enough to touch, and Nicholas remarked to Royan, as she swung along long-legged beside him, 'At this pace we should reach the foot of the escarpment this afternoon, and there is a good chance that we might sleep tonight in the cavern behind the waterfall.'

'That means we could cut a couple of days off the journey and reach the trucks some time tomorrow.'

'Possibly,' he said. 'I'll be glad to get out of here.'

'It feels like a trap,' Royan agreed, looking at the rocky, broken ground that rose on either hand, hemming them into the narrow bottom of the Dandera river. 'I have been doing a bit of thinking, Nicky.'

'Let's hear your conclusions.'

'No conclusions, only some disturbing thoughts. Suppose somebody at Pegasus who can understand them is now in possession of our rubbings and Polaroids. What will their reaction be if they know how much progress we have made in the search?'

'Not very happy thoughts,' he agreed. 'But on the other hand there is not much we can do about any of that until we get back to civilization, except keep our eyes wide open and our wits about us. Hell, I haven't even got the little Rigby rifle. We are a flock of sitting ducks.'

Aly, the muleteers and the monks seemed to be of the same opinion, for they never slackened the pace. It was midday before they called the first brief halt to brew coffee and to water the mules. While the men lit fires, Nicholas took his binoculars from the mule pack and began to climb the rock slope. He had not covered much ground before he glanced back and saw Royan climbing after him. He waited for her to catch up.

'You should have taken the chance to rest,' he told her severely. 'Heat exhaustion is a real danger.'

'I don't trust you going off on your own. I want to know what you are up to.'

'Just a little recce. We should have scouts out ahead, not just go charging blindly along the trail like this. If I remember correctly from the inward march, some of the worst ground lies just ahead of us. Lord knows what we may run into.'

They went on upwards, but it was not possible to reach the crest for a sheet of unscalable vertical cliff barred their way. Nicholas chose the best vantage point below this barrier, and glassed both slopes of the valley ahead of them. The terrain was as he had remembered it. They were approaching the foot of the escarpment wall and the ground was becoming more rugged and severe, like the swell of the open ocean sensing the land and rising up in alarm before breaking in confusion upon the shore. The trail followed the river closely. The cliffs hung over the narrow aisle of ground that made up the bank, sculpted by wind and weather into strange, menacing shapes, like the battlements of a wicked witch's castle in an old Disney cartoon. At one point a buttress of red

219

sandstone overhung the trail, forcing the river to detour around it, and the trail was reduced so much that it would be difficult for a laden mule to negotiate without being pushed off the bank into the river.

Nicholas studied the bottom of the valley carefully through the lens. He could pick out nothing that seemed suspicious or untoward, so he raised his head and swept the cliffs and their tops.

At that moment Aly's voice came up from the valley below, echoing along the slope as he shouted, 'Hurry, *effendi!* The mules are ready to go on!'

Nicholas waved down to him, but then lifted the binoculars for one more sweep of the ground ahead. A wink of bright light caught his eye – a brief ephemeral stab of brilliance like the signal of a heliograph. He switched his whole attention to the spot on the cliff from which it had emanated.

'What is it? What have you seen?' Royan demanded.

'I am not sure. Probably nothing,' he replied, without lowering the binoculars. It may have been a reflection from a polished metal surface, or from the lens of another pair of binoculars, or from the barrel of a sniper's rifle, he thought. On the other hand, a chip of mica or a pebble of rock crystal could reflect sunlight the same way, and even some of the aloes and other succulent plants have shiny leaves. He watched the spot carefully for a few more minutes, and then Aly's voice floated up to them again.

'Hurry, *effendi*. The mule-drivers will not wait!'

He stood up. 'All right. Nothing. Let's go.' He took Royan's arm to help her over the rough footing, and they started down. At that moment he heard the rattle of stones from further up the slope, and he stopped her and held her arm to keep her quiet. They waited, watching the skyline.

Abruptly a pair of long curling horns appeared over the crest, and under them the head of an old kudu bull, his trumpet-shaped ears pricked forward and the fringe of his dewlap blowing in the hot, light breeze. He stopped on the edge of the cliff just above where they crouched, but he had not seen them. The kudu turned his head and stared back in the direction from which he had come. The sunlight glinted in his nearest eye, and the set of his head and the alert, tense stance made it clear that something had disturbed him.

For a long moment he stood poised like that, and then, still without being aware of the presence of Nicholas and Royan, he snorted and abruptly leaped away in full flight. He vanished from their sight behind the ridge and the sound of his run dwindled into silence.

'Something scared the living daylights out of him.'

'What?' enquired Royan.

'Could have been anything – a leopard, perhaps,' he replied, and he hesitated as he looked down the slope. The caravan of mules and monks had set off already and was following the trail up along the river bank.

'What should we do?' Royan asked.

'We should reconnoitre the ground ahead – that is if we had the time, which we haven't.' The caravan was pulling away swiftly. Unless they went down immediately they would be left behind alone, unarmed. He had nothing concrete to act upon, and yet he had to make an immediate decision.

'Come on!' He took her hand again, and they slid and scrambled down the slope. Once they reached the trail they had to break into a run to catch up with the tail of the caravan.

Now that they were again part of the column, Nicholas could turn his attention to searching the skyline above them more thoroughly. The cliffs loomed over them, blocking out half the sky. The river on their left hand washed out any other sounds with its noisy, burbling current.

Nicholas was not really alarmed. He prided himself on being able to sense trouble in advance, a sixth sense that had saved his life more than once before. He thought of it as his early-warning system, but now it was sending no messages. There were any number of possible explanations for the reflection he had picked up from the crest of the cliff, and for the behaviour of the bull kudu.

However, he was still a little on edge, and he was giving the high ground above them all his attention. He saw a speck flick over the top of the cliff, twisting and falling – a dead leaf on the warm, wayward breeze. It was too small and insignificant to be of any danger, but nevertheless he followed the movement with his eye, his interest idle.

The brown leaf spiralled and looped, and finally touched lightly against his cheek. He lifted his hand as a reflex, and caught it. He rubbed the brown scrap between his fingers, expecting it to crackle and crumble. Instead it was soft and supple, with a fine, almost greasy texture.

He opened his hand and studied it more closely. It was no leaf, he saw at once, but a torn scrap of greased paper, brown and translucent. Suddenly all his early-warning bells jangled. It was not just the incongruity of manufactured paper suddenly materializing in this remote setting. He recognized the quality and texture of that particular type of paper. He lifted it to his nose and sniffed it. The sharp, nitrous odour prickled the back of his throat.

'Gelly!' he exclaimed aloud. He knew the smell instantly.

Blasting gelignite was seldom employed for military purposes in this age of Semtex and plastic explosives, but was still widely used in the mining industry and in mineral exploration. Usually the sticks of nitrogelatine in a wood pulp and sodium nitrate base was wrapped in that distinctive brown greased paper. Before the detonator was placed in the head of the stick, it was common practice to tear off the corner of the paper wrapper to expose the treacle-brown explosive beneath. He had used it often enough in the old days never to forget the odour of it.

His mind was racing now. If somebody was expecting them and had mined the cliff with gelignite, then the reflection he had picked up could have been from the coils of copper wiring strung between the explosive in the rock, or it could have been from some other item of equipment. If that was so, then the operator might even at this moment be lying concealed up there, ready to press the plunger on the circuit box. The kudu bull might have been fleeing from the concealed human presence.

'Aly!' he bellowed down to the head of the caravan, 'Stop them! Turn them back!'

He started to run forward towards the head of the caravan, but in his heart he knew it was already too late. If there was somebody up there on the cliff, he was watching every move that Nicholas made. Nicholas could never hope to reach the head of the column and turn the mules around on the narrow trail, and get them back to safety before . . . He came up short and looked back at Royan. Her safety was his main concern. He turned and ran back to grab her arm.

'Come on! We have to get off the track.'

'What is it, Nicky? What are you doing?' She was resisting him, pulling back against his grip on her arm.

'I'll explain later,' he snapped at her brusquely. 'Just trust me now.' He dragged her a couple of paces before she gave in and began to run with him, back in the direction from which they had come.

They had not covered fifty yards before the cliff face blew. A vast disruption of air swept over them with a force that made them stagger. It clapped painfully in their skulls and threatened to implode the delicate membranes of their eardrums. Then the main force of the blast swept over them, not a single blast but a long, rolling detonation like thunder breaking directly overhead. It stunned and battered them so that they reeled into each other and lost the direction of their flight.

Nicholas seized her in a steadying embrace, and looked back. He saw a series of explosions leap from the crest of the cliff. Tall, dancing fountains of dirt and dust and rubble, pirouetting one after the other in strict choreography, like a chorus-line of hellish ballerinas.

Even in the terror of the moment he could appreciate the expertise with which the gelignite had been laid. This was a master bomber at work. The leaping columns of rubble subsided upon themselves, leaving the fine, tawny mist of dust drifting and spiralling against the clear blue of the sky, and for a moment longer it seemed that the destruction was complete. Then the silhouette of the cliff began to alter.

Slowly at first the wall of rock started to lean outwards. He saw great

222

cracks appear in the face, opening like leering mouths. Sheets of rock collapsed and in slow motion slithered down upon themselves like the silken skirts of a curtseying giantess. The rock groaned and crackled and rumbled as the entire cliff began to fall into the river far below.

Nicholas was mesmerized by the awful sight, and his brain seemed to have been numbed by the explosion. It took a huge effort to force himself to think and to act. He saw that the centre of the explosion had occurred further down the trail, near the head of the mule caravan. Tamre was up there, beside Aly. He and Royan were at the tail of the caravan. The bomber up on the cliff had obviously been waiting for them to come directly into the epicentre of his explosive trap, but had been forced to trigger it when he saw them running back down the trail and realized that they had been alerted and were about to escape.

Yet they were not clear – they were about to catch the peripheral force of the landslide that was developing above them. Still holding Royan, Nicholas stared up the falling cliff face and made a desperate calculation.

He watched in petrified fascination as the vast tide of falling rock swept over the trail ahead of him, picking up men and mules and carrying them with it over the edge and down into the river bed. It swallowed them, lapping them up like the tongue of some fearsome monster and chewing them to pulp with razor fangs of red rock. Even above the rumbling roar of the rock tide he heard the terrified screams of men and animals as they were ploughed under.

The wave of destruction spread towards where he and Royan stood upon the trail. If they had been directly under the explosion they would have stood as little chance as those others, but as it ran down the cliff its destructive momentum was dissipating. On the other hand, Nicholas realized that there was no hope that they would be able to outrun it, and what was about to fall upon them would still be devastating.

There was no time to explain to Royan what they had to do – he had only seconds left in which to act. Sweeping her up in his arms, he leaped over the bank towards the river. He lost his footing almost immediately and they went down together, rolling end over end, but thirty feet down there was a spur of rock the size of a house. As they came up against the upper side of it, it broke their fall.

They were half-stunned, but Nicholas dragged Royan to her feet and guided her into the lee of the rock wall. There was a cut-back here, and they crept into it and crouched flat. Pressing themselves hard against the wall, they both held their breath as the first chunk of cliff came bounding and bouncing down towards them like a gigantic rubber ball, picking up speed with gravity, until it smashed into their shelter with a force that made the solid rock against which they were cringing vibrate and resound like a cathedral bell, and the hurtling missile leaped high

223

over their heads, spinning massively in flight before it dropped into the river. It raised a tidal wave from the surface that broke like storm surf on both banks.

This was merely the forerunner of the maelstrom that now poured over them. It seemed that half the mountain was falling upon them. As each slab crashed into their shelter daggers and splinters burst from its leading edges, filling the air they breathed with fine white dust and the sulphurous stink of sparking flint. This immense cascade flew over their heads or piled up in front of their shelter, and loose chips and pebbles rained down upon them.

Nicholas crawled over the top of Royan, and covered her with his body. A stone struck the side of his head a glancing blow that made his ears ring, but he gritted his teeth and fought the impulse to lift his head and look up. He felt something warm and ticklish snaking through the short hairs behind his right ear. It crept down his cheek like a living thing, and it was only when it reached the corner of his mouth and he tasted the metallic salt that he realized it was a trickle of blood.

The fine talcum dust powdered them and irritated their throats, so that they coughed and choked in the uproar. The dust seeped into their eyes, and they were forced to clench their lids and keep them tightly shut.

One mass of rock the size of a wagon sprang high in the air and then fell back close beside where they lay. The impact made the earth jump so violently that Royan, with Nicholas's weight on top of her, was struck in the belly and diaphragm with a force that drove the wind from her lungs, and she thought that her ribs had been crushed.

Then gradually the downpouring of earth and rock began to subside. The breath-stopping impact of great boulders into their shelter became less frequent. The fine dust they were breathing began to settle. The rumbling and roaring let up gradually, until the only sound was the slip and slide of settling earth and rock and the burble of the river below them.

Warily, Nicholas at last lifted his head and tried to blink the dust off his eyelashes. Royan stirred under him, and he crawled back to let her sit up. They stared at each other. Their faces were caked into kabuki masks with the antimony-white dust, and their hair was powdered like the wigs of eighteenth-century French aristocrats.

'You are bleeding,' Royan whispered, her voice husky with dust and terror.

Nicholas lifted his hand to his face and it came away covered with a paste of dust and blood. 'It's just a nick,' he said. 'How are you?'

'I think I may have twisted my knee. I felt something give when we fell. I don't think it's serious. There is very little pain.'

224

'Then we have both been ridiculously lucky,' he told her. 'Nobody deserved to survive that.'

She made an effort to stand, but he restrained her with a hand on her shoulder. 'Wait! The entire slope above us is broken and unstable. Give it time. There will be loose rocks coming down for a while yet.' He untied the Paisley bandana from around his throat and handed it to her. 'Besides which, we don't want—' But he changed his mind and did not finish his sentence.

While she wiped her face she asked shakily, 'You were going to say, besides which—?'

'Besides which, we don't want to give those bastards up there any idea that we have survived their little party. Otherwise we will have them down here finishing the job, cutting throats. Much better they believe that we snuffed it, as intended.'

She stared at him. 'Do you think they are still up there, watching us?'

'Count on it,' he answered grimly. 'They must be pretty chuffed with the fact that they have at last succeeded in getting rid of you. We don't want to pop our heads up right now and spoil it for them.'

'How did you know what was going to happen?' she asked. 'If you hadn't grabbed me—' Her voice petered out.

In a few words he explained about the scrap of gelignite wrapping. 'Simplest thing in the world to pick one of the narrowest sections of the trail and mine the cliff—' He broke off as, faintly but unmistakably, there came the sound of an aircraft engine and the flutter of rotors in fully fine pitch for take-off.

'Quickly,' he snapped at her. 'Get in as close as you can to the overhang.' He pushed her back against the sheltering boulder. 'Lie flat!' When she obeyed without question, he lay beside her and piled loose rubble over them both.

'Lie still. Don't move, whatever you do.'

They lay and listened to the sound of the helicopter approaching, and circling overhead. It moved up and down the valley, flying a few feet above the surface of the river. At one point it was directly above the ledge on which they lay, and they were buffeted by the down-draught of the rotors.

'Looking for survivors,' said Nicholas grimly. 'Don't move. They haven't spotted us yet.'

'If they were watching us before the blast, they should have been able to come directly to where we are,' she whispered. 'They seem confused.'

'They must have lost us in the dust of the avalanche and the break-up of the cliff face. They aren't sure where we are lying.' The sound of the helicopter moved off slowly along the river, and Nicholas told her, 'I am going to risk a peep, to make sure it's the Pegasus job – not that there can be many other choppers in this area. Keep your head down!'

He lifted his head slowly and cautiously, and one glance was sufficient to confirm all his speculations. Half a mile upstream, the Pegasus Jet Ranger hovered over the river. It was moving slowly away from him, so that from this angle Nicholas was unable to see through the windscreen into the cockpit. But at that moment the engine beat changed as the pilot changed pitch and pulled on the collective.

As the aircraft rose vertically and turned northwards, Nicholas caught a glimpse of the passengers. Jake Helm sat in the front seat beside the pilot, and Colonel Nogo was in the seat behind him. They were both staring down into the river valley, but in seconds the helicopter lifted them away and the machine disappeared beyond the ridge, flying in the direction of the escarpment, and the sound of its engines dwindled into silence. Nicholas crawled out from beneath the boulder and pulled Royan to her feet.

'No more doubts. We know who we are dealing with now. That was Helm and Nogo in the chopper. Helm almost certainly laid the gelly, and Nogo probably led the men who hit our camp last night. Each of them doing the job he does best,' Nicholas told her. 'So that confirms it. Whoever owns Pegasus is the ugly behind all this. Helm and Nogo are merely the stooges.'

'But Nogo is an officer in the Ethiopian army,' she protested.

'Welcome to Africa.' He did not smile as he said it. 'Here everything is for sale at a price, including government officials and army officers.' Now he scowled so that the caked dust on his face was dislodged and filtered down in a fine powdering. 'Now, however, our main concern is to get out of the gorge and back to civilization.'

He looked up the slope. The trail above them had been obliterated beneath the rock fall. 'We can't get back that way,' he told her, and took her hand. But when he lifted her to her feet she gasped and quickly shifted her weight to her right leg.

'My knee!' Then she smiled bravely. 'It will be all right.'

However, she was limping heavily as they scrambled down to the river, terrified that their movements would set off another rock slide. They ended up waist-deep in the water under the bank.

Royan stood behind Nicholas and washed the blood and dust from the wound in his scalp. 'Not too bad,' she told him. 'Doesn't need a stitch.'

'I have a tube of Betadyne in my pack,' he said. He fished it out, and she smeared the wound with the yellow-brown ointment before binding it up with the Paisley bandana.

'That will do.' She patted his shoulder.

'Thank the Lord for my bum-bag,' Nicholas remarked as he zipped it closed. 'At least we have a few essentials with us. Now our next job is to look for any other survivors.'

'Tamre!' she exclaimed.

They floundered along the bank. The river was clogged with loose rock and earth that had fallen from the cliff. In the deeper places they were forced in up to their armpits, and Nicholas carried his pack at arm's length above his head. The loose rock was treacherous, and gave way under them when they tried to scramble out of the water to search for the other members of the caravan.

They found the bodies of two of the monks, both of them crushed and half-buried. They did not even attempt to dig them free. One of the mules lay with one leg in the air and the rest of its body completely covered with broken rock. The pack that it had carried had burst open and the contents were scattered about. The rolled skin and trophies of the dik-dik had been churned into the muck. Nicholas rescued them and strapped them on to his bum-bag.

'More to carry,' Royan warned him.

'Only a pound or two, but worth it,' he replied.

They made their way towards the point below the trail where they had last seen Tamre and Aly. But though they searched for almost an hour they found no sign of either of them. The slope above them was devastated: raw ravaged earth, great rocks shattered, bushes and trees uprooted and smashed to kindling.

Royan climbed as high as her injured leg enabled her, then cupped her hands around her mouth and shouted, 'Tamre! Tamre! Tamre!' The echoes took her cry and flung it from wall to valley wall.

'I think he is done for. The poor little devil has been buried,' Nicholas called up to her. 'We have been at it an hour now. We cannot afford more time, if we are to get out ourselves. We will have to leave him.'

She ignored him and worked her way along the rock-slide, loose scree rolling under her feet, and he could see that the knee was giving her pain.

'Tamre! Answer me,' she called in Arabic. 'Tamre! Where are you?'

'Royan! That's enough. You are going to damage that knee even more. You are putting both of us at risk now. Give it up!'

At that moment they both heard a soft groan from higher up the slope. Royan scrambled up towards the sound, slipping and sliding back almost as far as she climbed, but at last she gave a cry of horror. Nicholas dumped his pack and went up after her. When he reached her side, he too dropped to his knees.

Tamre was pinned down in the rubble. His face was barely recognizable. It was torn and lacerated, with half the skin ripped off. Royan had lifted his head into her lap, and was using her sleeve to wipe the filth out of his nostrils to allow him to breathe more freely. Blood was oozing from the corner of his mouth, and when he groaned again it welled up in a fresh flood. Royan dabbed at it, smearing it across his chin.

His lower body was buried, and Nicholas tried to clear the broken rock; but almost immediately he realized the futility of it. A lump of raw rock the size of a billiard table lay across him. It weighed many tons, and must certainly have crushed his spine and pelvis. No single man would be able to move that massive weight unaided. Even if it were possible, the grinding action of any movement would inevitably aggravate the terrible injuries that Tamre had already sustained.

'Do something, Nicky,' Royan whispered. 'We have to do something for him.'

Nicholas looked at her and shook his head. Royan's eyes flooded with tears, and they broke over her lower lids and scattered like raindrops into Tamre's upturned face, diluting the blood to the pink of rosé wine.

'We can't just sit here and let him die,' she protested, and at the sound of her voice Tamre opened his eyes and looked into her face.

He smiled through the blood, and that smile lit his dusty, broken face. 'Ummee!' he whispered. 'You are my mother. You are so kind. I love you, my mother.'

The words were bitten off and a spasm stiffened his body. His face contorted with agony and he gave a soft, strangled cry, and then slumped. The rigidity went out of his shoulders and his head rolled to one side.

Royan sat for long time holding his head and weeping softly, but bitterly, until Nicholas touched her hand and said gently, 'He is dead, Royan.'

She nodded. 'I know. He held on just long enough to say goodbye to me.'

He let her mourn a little longer, and then he told her softly, 'We must go, my dear.'

'You are right. But it is so hard to leave him here. He never had anybody. He was so alone. He called me mother. I think he truly loved me.'

'I know he did,' Nicholas assured her, lifting the boy's dead head from her lap and helping her to her feet. 'Go down and wait for me. I will cover him the best I can.'

Nicholas crossed Tamre's hands upon his chest, and folded his fingers around the silver crucifix that hung around his neck. Then he piled loose rock carefully over him, covering his head so that the crows and vultures could not reach him.

He slid down to where she waited in the water, and slung his pack over one shoulder.

'We must go on,' he told Royan.

She wiped away the tears with the back of her hand and nodded. 'I am ready now.'

They waded upstream, pushing hard against the current. The rock-slide had blocked half the river bed and the waters squeezed through the gap that was left. When at last they reached the point on the bank above the avalanche, they climbed out of the river and picked their way up the steep bank until at last they could crawl out on to the intact section of the pathway.

They took a moment to recover and looked back. The river below the rock-slide was running red-brown with mud. Even if the monks at the monastery downstream had not heard the explosions, they would be alarmed by that flood of discoloured water and would come to investigate. They would find the bodies and take them down for decent burial. That thought comforted Royan a little as they struck out along the trail, with two days' hard travel still ahead of them.

Royan was limping heavily now, but each time Nicholas tried to help her she brushed his hand away. 'I am all right. It's just a bit stiff.' She would not allow him to inspect the knee, but kept on stubbornly along the trail ahead of him.

They marched mostly in silence for the rest of that day. Nicholas respected her grief and was grateful for her reticence. This ability to be quiet and yet not give out a sense of alienation and withdrawal to those around her was one of the qualities he admired in her. They spoke briefly late that afternoon while they paused to rest beside the path.

'The only consolation is that now Pegasus will believe that we are safely buried under the rock-slide and they won't bother to come looking for us again. We can push on without wasting time scouting the trail ahead,' Nicholas told her.

They camped that night below the escarpment, just before the path began the climb up the vertical wall. Nicholas led her well off the path, into a heavily wooded gully, and built a small screened fire that could not be seen from the trail.

Here at last she relented and allowed him to examine her knee. It was bruised and swollen, and hot to the touch. 'You shouldn't be walking on this,' he told her.

'Do I have any option?' she asked, and he had no reply. He wetted his bandana from the water bottle and bound up her leg as tightly as he dared without cutting off the circulation. Then he found a phial of Brufen in his bum-bag and made her take two of these anti-inflammatories.

'It feels better already,' she told him.

They shared the last bar of survival rations from his pack, sitting hunched up over the fire and talking quietly, still subdued and shaken by their experiences.

'What will happen when we reach the top?' Royan asked. 'Will the trucks still be parked where we left them? Will the men that Boris left to guard them still be there? What will happen if we run into the men from Pegasus again?'

'I can't give you any answers. We will just have to face each problem as it comes up.'

'One thing I am looking forward to when we reach Addis Ababa – reporting the massacre of Tamre and the others to the Ethiopian police. I want Helm and his gang to pay for what they have done.'

He was quiet for a while before he replied. 'I don't know if that is the wisest thing to do,' he ventured at last.

'What do you mean? We were witnesses to murder. We cannot let them get away with it.'

'Just remember that we want to return to Ethiopia. If we make a huge fuss now, we will have the entire valley swarming with troops and police. It may put an end to our further attempts to solve Taita's riddle, and to trace the tomb of Mamose.'

'I hadn't thought of that,' she said thoughtfully. 'But still, it was murder, and Tamre—'

'I know, I know,' he soothed her. 'But there are more certain ways of wreaking vengeance on Pegasus than trying to turn them over to Ethiopian justice. Consider for the moment the fact that Nogo is working with Helm. We saw him in the helicopter. If Pegasus have an army colonel in their pay, who else is working for them? The police? The head of the army? Members of the cabinet? We just don't know at this stage.'

'I hadn't thought about that either,' she admitted.

'Let's begin to think African from here on, and take a leaf out of Taita's scrolls. Like him we must be devious and cunning. We don't go rushing in shouting accusations. If we could just sneak out of the country, leaving everybody to believe that we are buried under the avalanche, that might be ideal. It would make our return to the gorge that much easier. Unfortunately I don't think we will be able to get away with that. But from now on, we should be as cagey and careful as circumstances permit.'

She stared into the dancing flames for a long while, then sighed and asked, 'You said there is a better vengeance to be had on Pegasus. What did you have in mind?'

'Why, simply whisking Mamose's treasure out from under their noses.'

She laughed for the first time that long cruel day. 'You are right, of course. Whoever owns Pegasus wants it desperately enough to kill for it.

We must hope that depriving him of it will hurt him almost as badly as he has hurt us.'

Both of them were so tired that it was already half-light when they woke the next morning. As soon as Royan tried to stand she groaned and sank back. He went to her immediately, and she made no protest when he placed her bare leg across his lap.

He unwrapped the bandana, and frowned as he saw the knee. It was nearly twice its normal girth, and the bruising was plum and ripe grape. He wet the bandana again, and rewrapped the knee. He made her take the last two Brufen from the phial, and then helped her to her feet.

'How does it feel?' he asked anxiously, and she hobbled a few paces and smiled at him bravely.

'It will be all right as soon as I walk the stiffness out of it, I'm sure.'

He looked up the escarpment. So close in under the wall, the height was foreshortened, but he recalled every tortuous step of the way. It had taken them a full day to come down.

'Of course it will.' He smiled encouragement at her, and took her arm. 'Lean on me. It'll be a stroll in the park.'

They toiled upwards all that morning. The trail seemed to rise more steeply with every pace they took. She never complained, but she was ashen pale and sweating with the pain. By midday they had not yet reached the waterfall, and Nicholas made her stop to rest. They had nothing to eat, but she drank thirstily from the water bottle. He did not try to ration her, but limited himself to a single mouthful.

When she tried to rise, and go on, she gasped and staggered so violently that she might have fallen if he had not steadied her.

'Damn! Damn! Damn!' she swore bitterly. 'It's stiffened up on me.'

'Never mind,' he said cheerfully, and stripped his bum-bag of all but the most crucial items of equipment. He kept the dik-dik skin, however, rolling it into a tight ball and stuffing it into the bag. Then he rebuckled it around his waist, and grinned at her cheerfully. 'Skinny little thing like you. Hop on my back.'

'You can't carry me up there.' She looked up the trail, steep as a ladderway, and was aghast.

'It's the only train leaving from this station,' he told her, and offered her his back. She crawled up on to it.

'Don't you think you should dump the dik-dik skin?' she asked.

'Perish the thought!' he said, and started up.

It was slow and heavy-going. After a while he had nothing left over for talking, and he trudged upwards in dogged silence. Sweat drenched his shirt, but she found neither the wet warmth of it that permeated her

231

blouse on to her own skin, nor the strong masculine odour of it offensive. Instead, it was comforting and reassuring.

Every half-hour he stopped and lowered her to the ground, and lay quietly with his eyes closed until his breathing became regular and even again. Then he opened his eyes and grinned at her.

'Hi ho, Silver!' He pushed himself to his feet, and bowed his back for her to scramble aboard.

As the day wore on, his jokes became more forced and feeble. By late afternoon the pace was down to an exhausted plod, and at the more difficult places he had to pause and gather himself before stepping up. She tried to help him by climbing down from his back, and supporting herself on his shoulder as they struggled over the more arduous pitches, but even with this respite she knew that he was burning up the very last of his strength.

Neither of them could truly credit their achievement when they reeled around another corner of the track and saw before them the waterfall, spilling down like a white lacy curtain across the trail. Nicholas staggered into the cavern behind the sheet of falling water and lowered her to the floor. Then he collapsed and lay like a dead man.

It was dark when he had at last recovered sufficiently to open his eyes and sit up. While he was resting Royan had gathered some wood from the monks' stockpile and managed to get a small fire going.

'Good girl,' he told her. 'If ever you want a job as a housekeeper—'

'Don't tempt me.' She hobbled over to him, and examined the cut in his scalp. 'Nice healthy scab,' she told him, and then suddenly and impulsively she hugged his head to her bosom and stroked his dusty, sweat-stiff hair off his forehead.

'Oh, Nicky! How can I ever repay you for what you did for me today?'

A flippant reply rose to his lips, but even in his weakened state he had the good sense to bite it back. He was in no state to attempt any further intimacy. So he lay in her embrace, enjoying the feel of her body against his, but not taking the risk of scaring her off with a move of his own.

At last she released him gently, and sat back. 'I very much regret, sir, that the housekeeper cannot offer you smoked salmon and champagne for your dinner. How about a mug of mountain water, pure and nourishing?'

'I think we can do better than that.' He took the dry-cell torch from his bum-bag, and by its beam selected a round, fist-sized stone from the floor of the cavern. With this in his right hand he turned the light upwards, and played it over the cavern roof. Immediately there was a rustling of wings and the alarmed cooing of the rock pigeons that were roosting on the ledges. Nicholas manoeuvred into position below them, dazzling them with the torchbeam.

With his first throw he brought down a brace of them, fluttering and squawking to the cavern floor, while the rest of the flock exploded out into the night in a great clattering uproar of frantic wings. Nicholas pounced on the downed birds and with a practised flick of the wrist wrung their necks.

'How do you fancy a juicy slice of roast pigeon?' he asked her.

She lay propped on one elbow, and he sat cross-legged facing her, each of them plucking the vinous-maroon and grey feathers from one of the pigeon carcasses. Even when it came to drawing the bird, she was not squeamish, as many other women might have been faced with the same task. This, together with her stoical performance during the day's struggle up the mountain, enhanced his opinion of her. She had repeatedly proved to him how game and plucky she was. His feelings towards her were strengthening and maturing every day.

Concentrating on removing the fine bristles from the puckered breast skin of the bird, she said, 'It is beyond all doubt now that the material stolen in the raid on our camp is in Pegasus hands.'

'I was thinking the same thing,' Nicholas nodded, 'and we know from the antennae at their base camp above the falls that they have satellite communications. We can place a pretty certain bet that Jake Helm has already telefaxed it through to the big man, whoever he may be.'

'So he has all the details of the stele in Tanus's tomb. We know that he already has the seventh scroll in his possession. If he isn't an expert Egyptologist himself, he must have somebody in his pay who is. Wouldn't you agree with that?'

'I would guess that he can read hieroglyphics himself. I would think that he must be an avid collector. I know the type. It is an obsession with them.'

'I know the type as well.' She smiled at him. 'There is one sitting not a thousand miles away from me at this very moment.'

'Touché!' he laughed, and held up his hands in surrender. 'But I have only been lightly bitten by the bug, compared to others I could name. Those other two on Duraid's list, for instance.'

'Peter Walsh and Gotthold von Schiller,' she reeled off the names.

'Those two are homicidal collectors,' he confirmed. 'I am sure neither of them would hesitate to kill for the chance of having Pharaoh Mamose's treasure to themselves.'

'But from what I know about them, both of them are billionaires, at least in dollar terms.'

'Money has nothing to do with it, don't you see. If they laid hands upon it, they would never ever dream of selling a single artefact from the hoard. They would lock it all away in some deep vault, and not let another living soul lay eyes upon it. They would gloat on it in private – it's a bizarre, masturbatory passion.'

'What an odd word to describe it,' she protested.

'But accurate, I assure you. It's a sexual thing, a compulsion, like that of a serial killer.'

'I love all things Egyptian, but I don't think I can even imagine a craving that intense.'

'You must remember that these are not ordinary men whom we are considering. Their wealth allows them to pander to any appetite. All the normal, natural human appetites soon become jaded and satiated. They can have anything they want. Any man or any woman. Any thing, any perversion, whether legal or not. In the end they have to find something that no one else can ever have. It's the only thing that can still give them the old thrill.'

'So in whoever is behind Pegasus we are dealing with a madman?' she asked softly.

'Much more than that,' he corrected her. 'We are dealing with an enormously wealthy and powerful maniac, who in his disease will stop at nothing.'

They picked the cold carcasses of the roasted pigeons for their breakfast. Then, while the other one tactfully went to the back of the cavern and averted his or her gaze, they took turns to strip naked and bathe under the waterfall.

After the heat of the gorge the water was icy cold. It battered them with the force of a fire hose. Royan hopped on her good leg, gasping and whimpering under the torrent, and emerged covered in goose-pimples and shuddering blue with cold. However, it refreshed her, and even in her filthy, sweat-stinking clothes it gave her heart to start out on the last bitter climb to the summit.

Before leaving the cavern they examined each other's injuries again. Nicholas's scalp wound was healing cleanly, but Royan's knee was no better than the previous day. The bruises were starting to turn a virulent puce, the colour of decomposing liver, and the swelling was unabated. There was very little he could do for it, other than strapping it again with the bandana.

At last Nicholas admitted defeat, and abandoned his bum-bag and the roll of dik-dik skin. He knew that he was reaching the limit of his physical reserves, and he realized that, light as these items were, every extra pound that he carried today might mean the difference between reaching the summit or breaking down on the trail. He retained only the three rolls of undeveloped film, each in its plastic capsule. These were their only record of the hieroglyphics on the stele in Tanus's tomb. He dared not risk losing them, so he buttoned them into the breast pocket of his khaki shirt. He tucked both the bag and the skin into a crack in the wall at the back of the cavern, determined to retrieve them at some later date.

And so they started out on the last but most onerous leg of the trail. To begin with Royan was on her own two feet, but leaning heavily on his shoulder. However, before the first hour was over her knee could no longer take the strain, and she subsided on to a rock on the edge of the pathway.

'I am being an awful nuisance, aren't I?'

'Come on board, lady. Always room for a small one.'

With Royan perched on Nicholas's back, her injured leg sticking out stiffly in front of her, they toiled upwards, but their progress was even slower than it had been the day before. Nicholas was forced to pause and rest at shorter and shorter intervals. On the easier pitches she dismounted and hopped along on one leg beside him, steadying herself with one hand on his shoulder. Then she would collapse, and he had to lift her to her feet and pull her up on to his back once again.

The journey descended into nightmare, and both of them lost all sense of the passage of time. Hours blended with hours into a single unremitting agony. At one stage they lay beside each other on the path, sick and nauseated with thirst and exhaustion and pain. They had emptied the water bottle an hour ago, and there was no more on this section of the path – nothing to drink until they reached the summit and were reunited with the Dandera river.

'Go on and leave me here,' she whispered hoarsely.

He sat up immediately and stared at her aghast. 'Don't be silly. I need you for ballast.'

'It can't be much further to the top,' she insisted. 'You can come back with some of Boris's men to help carry me.'

'If they are still there, and if Pegasus doesn't find you first.' He stood up a little unsteadily. 'Forget it. You are coming along on this ride, all the way.' And he hoisted her to her feet.

He made her count aloud every step he took, and at every hundredth he paused and rested. Then he started the next hundred, with her counting softly in his ear, clinging with both arms around his neck. The whole universe seemed to shrink in upon them to the ground directly at his feet. They no longer saw the rock cliff on one side nor the deep void of space on the other. When he lurched or jolted her and the pain shot through her knee, she closed her eyes and tried not to let her voice betray it to him as she kept counting.

When he rested, he had to lean against the cliff face, not trusting his legs to get him up again if he lay down. He dared not lower her to the ground. The effort of lifting her again would be too much. He no longer had the strength for it.

'It's almost dark,' she whispered in his ear. 'You must stop here for the night. It's enough for one day. You are killing yourself, Nicky.'

'Another hundred,' he mumbled.

'No, Nicky. Put me down!'

For answer he pushed off from the rock wall with his shoulder and staggered on upwards.

'Count!' he ordered.

'Fifty-one, fifty-two,' she obeyed. Suddenly the gradient altered so sharply under his feet that he almost fell. The path had levelled out, and like a drunkard he reached up for a step that wasn't there.

He staggered and then caught his balance. He stood teetering on the brink of the precipice and peered into the dusk ahead of him, at first unable to credit what he was seeing. There were lights in the gloom, and he thought that he had begun to hallucinate. Then he heard men's voices, and he shook his head to clear it and bring himself back to reality.

'Oh, dear God. You have made it. We are at the top, Nicky. There are the vehicles. You did it, Nicky. You did it!'

He tried to speak, but his throat had closed up and no words came. He reeled forward towards the lights, and Royan cried out weakly on his back.

'Help us here. Please help us.' First in English and then in Arabic. 'Please help us.'

There were startled cries and the sounds of running men. Nicholas sank down slowly into the fine highland grass and let Royan slide off his back. Dark figures gathered around them, chattering in Amharic, and friendly hands seized them and half-carried, half-dragged them towards the lights. Then a torch was shone into Nicholas's face and a very English voice said, 'Hello, Nicky. Nice surprise. I came down from Addis to look for your corpse. Heard you were dead. Bit premature, what?'

'Hello, Geoffrey. Good of you to take the trouble.'

'I dare say you could use a cup of tea. You look a bit done in,' said Geoffrey Tennant. 'Never realized that your beard had ginger and grey bits in it. Designer stubble. Fashionable. Suits you actually.'

Nicholas realized what a picture he must present, ragged and unshaven, filthy and haggard with exhaustion.

'You remember Dr Al Simma? She has a bit of a dicky knee. Wonder if you would mind taking care of her?'

Then his legs gave way under him, and Geoffrey Tennant caught him before he fell.

'Steady on, old boy.' He led him to a canvas-backed camp chair, and seated him solicitously. Another chair was brought for Royan.

'*Letta chai hapa!*' Geoffrey gave the universal call of an Englishman in Africa, and minutes later thrust mugs of steaming over-sweetened tea into their hands.

Nicholas saluted Royan with his mug. 'Here's to us. There's none like us!'

They both drank deeply, scalding their tongues, but the caffeine and sugar hit their bloodstreams like a charge of electricity.

'Now I know I am going to live,' Nicholas sighed.

'Don't want to be pushy, Nicky, but do you mind telling me what the hell is going on here?' Geoffrey asked.

'Why don't you tell me?' Nicholas countered. He needed time to evaluate the situation. What did Geoffrey know and who had told him? Geoffrey obliged immediately.

'First thing we heard was that white hunter chappie of yours, Brusilov, had been fished out of the river near the Sudanese border, absolutely riddled with bullet holes. The crocs and catfish had snacked on his face, so the border police identified him by the documents in his money belt.'

Nicholas glanced across at Royan and cautioned her with a frown.

'Last time we saw him, he went off on a scouting expedition on his own,' Nicholas explained. 'He probably ran into the same bunch of *shufta* who raided our camp four nights ago.'

'Yes, we heard about that too. Colonel Nogo here radioed in a report to Addis.'

Neither of them had recognized Nogo in the crowd of men. It was only when he stepped forward into the light of the camp lanterns that Royan stiffened, and such an expression of loathing flashed across her face that Nicholas reached across surreptitiously and took her hand to restrain her from any indiscretion. After a moment she relaxed and composed her features.

'I am very relieved to see you, Sir Quenton-Harper. You have given us all a very worrying few days,' said Nogo.

'I do apologize,' said Nicholas smoothly.

'Please, sir, I meant no offence. It is just that we had a report from the Pegasus Exploration Company that you and Dr Al Simma had been caught up in a blasting accident. I was present when Mr Helm of the exploration company warned you that they were conducting blasting in the gorge.'

'But you—' Royan flared bitterly, and Nicholas squeezed her hand hard to stop her going on.

'It was probably our own carelessness, as you suggest. Nevertheless, Dr Al Simma has been injured and we are both badly shaken up by the accident. More important than that, however, is the fact that a number of other people, camp staff and monks from the monastery, have been killed in the *shufta* raid and in the blasting accident. As soon as we get back to Addis I will make a full statement to the authorities.'

'I do hope that you don't think any blame attaches—' Nogo started, but Nicholas cut him short.

'Of course not. Not your fault at all. You warned us about the danger of *shufta* in the gorge. You were not present, so what could you have done to prevent any of this? I would say that you have done your duty in the most exemplary fashion.'

Nogo looked relieved. 'You are most gracious to say so, Sir Quenton-Harper.'

Nicholas studied him for a moment longer. He seemed the most amiable of young men behind the metal-rimmed spectacles, so concerned and eager to please. For a moment Nicholas almost believed that he had been mistaken, and that it had been somebody else that he had seen in the Jet Ranger, hovering over the avalanche site like a vulture, searching for their dead bodies.

Nicholas forced himself to smile in his most friendly manner. 'I would be most grateful if you could do me a favour, Colonel.'

'Of course,' Nogo agreed readily. 'Anything at all.'

'I left a bag and one of my hunting trophies in the cavern under the Dandera waterfall. The bag contains our passports and travellers' cheques. Very grateful if you could send one of your men down to bring it up for me.'

While giving Nogo directions on how to find his possessions, he derived a perverse enjoyment from sending his would-be assassin on such a trivial errand. Then he turned back to his friend so that Nogo would not pick up the vindictive glint in his eyes. 'How did you get here, Geoffrey?'

'Light plane to Debra Maryam. There is an emergency landing field there. Colonel Nogo met us, and brought us the rest of the way by army jeep,' Geoffrey explained. 'The pilot and the aircraft are waiting for us at Debra Maryam.'

Geoffrey broke off and spoke to the camp staff in execrable Amharic, before turning back to Nicholas. 'I have just arranged a hot bath for you and Dr Al Simma. After that, a meal and a good night's sleep should work wonders. Tomorrow we can fly back to Addis. No reason why we shouldn't be there by tomorrow evening at the latest.'

He patted Royan's shoulder, disguising his carnal interest in her behind a benign avuncular smile. 'I must say I am rather pleased not to have to go traipsing down into the Abbay gorge looking for the pair of you. I hear that it's a pretty beastly part of the world.'

'Do you mind, Dr Al Simma, if I sit in front? Terribly rude of me, but I am inclined to suffer from mal de air. Ha ha!' Geoffrey explained to Royan as they waited for three small boys to chase the goats off the emergency airfield at Debra Maryam. In the meantime Nicholas was stuffing the roll of dik-dik skin under the rear passenger seat. One of Nogo's sergeants had made a night descent of the escarpment, and had delivered both his bag and the skin while they were breakfasting that morning.

Nogo gave them a smart salute as they taxied out in a cloud of dust. Nicholas waved and smiled at him through the side window, murmuring, 'Screw you, Nogo, screw you very much indeed.'

When at last the pilot lifted the little Cessna 260 off the rough grass strip, the horizon over the Abbay gorge resembled a field of cosmic mushrooms, vast thunderheads reaching up into the stratosphere. The air beneath them was turbulent as a storm sea and they were thrown about mercilessly in the rear seats. Up in front Geoffrey seemed to be faring no better. He was very quiet and took no interest in their conversation.

There had been no opportunity for them to talk privately the previous evening, what with either Geoffrey or Nogo hovering within earshot at all times. Now with their heads close together, the engine beat covering their voices and Geoffrey occupied with his own queasy thoughts, they were able to concoct their story.

Geoffrey had made it clear that the British Ambassador in Addis was less than delighted with the inconvenience they had caused him. Apparently there had been a string of faxes from Whitehall since they had been reported missing. Added to that, the Ethiopian Commissioner of Police was anxious to question them. They had to make sure that they did not implicate Mek Nimmur in the killing of Boris Brusilov, and at the same time they must not alert or alarm Pegasus in any way. They realized that the reaction from that quarter would be swift and probably lethal if they gave the least suspicion that they knew who the other players were in Taita's game.

Most of all they must avoid antagonizing the Ethiopian authorities, or give them any cause to cancel their visas and declare them to be undesirable immigrants. They agreed to feign ignorance and play the role of innocents caught up in affairs which they had not precipitated and which they did not understand.

By the time that they landed at Addis Ababa they had prepared their story and rehearsed it thoroughly. As soon as the Cessna pulled on to the hardstand in front of the airport buildings and the pilot cut the engine, Geoffrey came back to life again, only a little green around the gills, and handed Royan down the aircraft steps with a flourish.

'Of course, you will stay at the residence,' he told them. 'The hotels in town are too dreadful to contemplate, and HE has a half-decent chef and a passable wine cellar. I will rustle up some togs for both of you. My missus is about the same size as you, Dr Al Simma, and Nicky will fit into my gear at a pinch. Thank God, I have a spare dinner jacket. HE is a bit of a stickler for form.'

T he British Ambassador's residence had been built during the reign of the old Emperor, Haile Selassie, before Mussolini's invasion in the 1930s. Set on the outskirts of the town, it was an example of the better colonial architecture, with a thatched roof and wide verandas. The lawns, tended by a host of gardeners, were wide and green, contrasting with the brilliant crimson of the poinsettia. The mansion had survived both the revolution and the war of liberation that followed.

At the front entrance Geoffrey handed them over to an Ethiopian butler in a long, spotlessly white *shamma*, who showed them to adjoining bedrooms on the second floor. Nicholas heard the bathwater running in Royan's suite next door as he lay in his own brimming bath, sipping a whisky and soda and twiddling the taps with his big toe. Then there was the murmur of the doctor's voice from next door as he attended to Royan's knee.

Geoffrey's dinner jacket was loose round his waist and too short in the arms and legs, and his shoes pinched, added to which Nicholas was in need of a haircut, he realized, as he surveyed himself in the mirror.

'No help for it, now,' he decided with resignation, and went to knock on Royan's door.

'I say!' he exclaimed as she opened it. Sylvia Tennant had loaned her a lime-green cocktail dress that set off Royan's olive skin marvellously well. Royan had washed her hair and left it loose on her shoulders. He felt his pulse accelerate like a teenager on his first date, and laughed at himself.

'You look absolutely scrumptious,' he told her, and meant it.

'Thank you, sir,' she laughed back at him, 'and you look very dashing yourself. May I take your arm?'

'I was hoping to carry you. Addictive activity.'

'Those days are over,' she told him, and brandished the carved ebony walking-stick with which the butler had provided her. She used it on her bad side. As they started down the long corridor, she asked in a whisper, 'What is the name of our host?'

'Her Britannic Majesty's Ambassador, Sir Oliver Bradford KCMG.'

'Which stands for Knight Commander of St Michael and St George, right?' she asked.

'No,' he corrected her, 'it stands for Kindly Call Me God.'

'You are impossible!' She giggled, and then became serious. 'Did you manage to send the fax to Mrs Street?'

'It went through at the first attempt and she acknowledged. Sends you her salaams, and promises to have some information about Pegasus double pronto.'

It was a mild evening and Sir Oliver was waiting to greet them on the veranda. Geoffrey hurried forward to make the introductions. The Ambassador had a bush of white hair and a red face. Geoffrey had warned them about him and his view on troublesome tourists, but his hostile frown started to fade as soon as he laid eyes on Royan.

There were a dozen other guests for dinner apart from Geoffrey and Sylvia Tennant, and Sir Oliver took Royan's arm and led her around the group introducing her. Nicholas trailed along behind them, resigned by now to the fact that Royan had that effect on most men.

'May I present General Obeid, the Commissioner of Police,' Sir Oliver said. The head of the Ethiopian police force was tall and very dark-complexioned, suave and elegant in his blue mess uniform. He bowed over Royan's hand.

'I believe that we have an appointment to meet tomorrow morning. I look forward to that with the keenest pleasure.'

Royan glanced at Sir Oliver uncertainly. She had been told nothing of this.

'General Obeid wants to know from you and Sir Nicholas a little more about this business in the Abbay gorge,' Sir Oliver explained. 'I took the liberty of having my secretary make the appointment.'

'Just a routine interview, I assure you both, Dr Al Simma and Sir Nicholas. I will take up very little of your time, I promise you that.'

'Of course we will do everything that we can to assist you,' Nicholas told him politely. 'What time are we coming to see you?'

'I believe we are meeting at eleven in the morning, if that suits you.'

'A most civilized hour,' Nicholas agreed.

'My driver will pick you up at ten-thirty, and take you down to police headquarters,' Sir Oliver promised.

At the dinner table Royan was seated between Sir Oliver and General Obeid. She was pretty and charming, and both men were attentive. Nicholas realized that he would have to become accustomed to sharing her company with other men; he had had her to himself for much too long.

For his own part, Nicholas found Lady Bradford at the other end of the table rather heavy-going. She was a second wife, thirty years younger than her husband, with a pronounced London accent and an even more pronounced common streak, with a mane of dyed blonde hair and an improbable bust which overflowed her sequined *décolletage*. An old man's folly, Nicholas concluded. It appeared that she had made herself an expert on the genealogy of the English aristocracy – in other words she was an arrant snob. She questioned him closely on his antecedents, insisting on going back several generations.

In the end she called to her husband down the table, 'Sir Nicholas owns Quenton Park. Did you know that, dear?' And then she turned back to Nicholas. 'My husband is a very keen shot.'

Sir Oliver looked suitably impressed by his wife's intelligence. 'Quenton Park, hey? I read an article in the *Shooting Times* the other day. You have a drive there called the "High Beeches". Is that right?'

'The "High Larches",' Nicholas corrected him.

'Some of the best birds in Britain. That's what they said,' Sir Oliver enthused, looking eager and expectant.

'I don't know about that,' Nicholas protested modestly. 'But we are rather proud of them. You must come and have a shot at them next time you are home – as my guest, of course.'

From that moment Sir Oliver's attitude towards Nicholas altered dramatically. He became affable and solicitous, even going so far as to send the butler to fetch a bottle of the 1954 Lafite.

'You have made a good impression,' Geoffrey murmured wryly. 'HE doesn't waste the 1954 on anybody but the chosen few.'

It was after midnight when Nicholas was at last able to escape from his hostess and rescue Royan from Sir Oliver and General Obeid. He led her away, supporting her as she limped along fetchingly at his side, avoiding Geoffrey Tennant's knowing and speculative gaze until they had negotiated the first landing of the staircase.

'Well, you were definitely the star of the evening,' he told her.

'You had Lady Bradford purring like a cat,' she counter-attacked, and he was delighted to hear the faint tone of possessive jealousy in her voice. He had not been the only one.

At her door she solved any problems by offering him her cheek, and he kissed it chastely.

'Those bosoms!' she murmured. 'Don't have nightmares about them.' And she closed the door behind her.

He felt quite jaunty as he went to his own room, but as he opened the door he saw the envelope lying at the threshold. During dinner, one of the servants must have pushed it under the door. Quickly he tore open the flap of the envelope and unfolded the pages that it contained. His expression changed as he scanned through them, and he left the bedroom and went back to tap on Royan's door.

After a moment she opened it a crack, and peeped out at him. He saw the confusion in her eyes, and he hurried to allay her suspicions.

'Reply to my fax.' He showed her the sheaf of papers. 'Are you decent?'

'One moment.' She closed the door, and opened it again only seconds later. 'Come in,' she said.

She indicated the decanter on the cabinet. 'Would you like a nightcap?'

'I think I need one. We know who runs Pegasus now.'

'Tell me!' she ordered, but he took his time pouring a Scotch, and then smiled at her over his shoulder. 'How about a soda water for you?'

'Damn you, Nicholas Quenton-Harper.' She stamped her stockinged foot. 'Don't you dare torment me. Who is it?'

'When I first met you, you were a dutiful little Arab girl. One who realized the superiority of the male species. Listen to you now. I think I have spoiled you.'

'I think I should warn you that you are flirting with disaster.' She tried to suppress her smile. 'Tell me, please, Nicky.'

'Sit down,' he ordered, and took the armchair facing her. He unfolded the fax and then looked up at her. 'Mrs Street has worked fast. In my fax, I suggested that she rang my stockbroker in the city. We are three hours ahead of Greenwich Mean Time, so it seems that she must have caught him before he left his office. Anyway, she has all the information I asked for.'

'Stop it, Nicky, or I will tear my bodice and scream and cause a scandal. Tell me!'

He rustled the pages, and then read. 'Pegasus Exploration is registered on the Sydney Stock Exchange in Australia with a share capital of twenty million—'

'Don't go through all the details,' she pleaded. 'Just name the man.'

'Sixty-five per cent of the shares in Pegasus are owned by Valhalla Mining Company,' he continued imperturbably, 'and the remaining thirty-five per cent are owned by Anaconda Metals of Austria.'

She had given up pleading with him and sat forward in her chair, watching him with a fixed gaze.

'Both Valhalla and Anaconda are fully-owned subsidiaries of HMI, Hamburg Manufacturing Industries. All the shares in HMI are owned by the von Schiller family trust, the sole trustees of which are Gotthold Ernst von Schiller and his wife, Ingemar.'

'Von Schiller,' she repeated softly, still staring at him. 'Duraid had him on his list of possible sponsors. He must have read the Wilbur Smith book – I know it has been translated into German. He probably contacted Duraid just the way that you did. But he was not put off as easily as you were by Duraid's denials.'

'That's the way I read it also,' Nicholas nodded. 'It would have been easy to sniff around the Cairo museum, and find that Duraid and you were working on something big. The rest of it we know only too well.'

'But how did he move Pegasus into Ethiopia so quickly?' she demanded.

'That must have been a stroke of luck on von Schiller's side – the luck of the devil. Geoffrey tells me that Pegasus obtained a concession to prospect for copper from President Mengistu five years ago, just before he was ousted. Von Schiller was already in place, even before he heard about the scrolls. All it involved was moving the base camp down from the north where they were working and relocating it on the escarpment of the Abbay gorge, to be ready to take advantage of any fresh developments. We will probably find that Jake Helm is one of his heavies, his dirty tricks specialist that he sends to any of his trouble spots around the world. It's apparent that he has Nogo in his pocket. We waltzed right into their arms.'

Royan looked thoughtful. 'It all makes sense. As soon as Helm reported our arrival to his master, von Schiller must have ordered him to set up the *shufta* raid on our camp. Oh, sweet heaven, I hate him. I have never laid eyes on him, but I hate him more than I thought I was capable of hating anything or anybody.'

'Well, at least we know now who we are dealing with.'

'Not altogether,' she demurred. 'Von Schiller must have had a man in Cairo. Somebody on the inside there.'

'What is the name of your minister?' Nicholas wanted to know.

'No,' she denied it instantly. 'Not Atalan Abou Sin. I have known him all my life. He is a tower of integrity.'

'It's amazing what effect a bribe of a hundred thousand dollars or so can have on the foundations of even the best-constructed tower,' Nicholas observed quietly, and she looked stricken.

They were the only two at breakfast. Sir Oliver had left for his office an hour earlier, and Lady Bradford had not yet risen to greet the clear, cool highland morning.

'I hardly slept last night, thinking about Atalan. Oh, Nicky, I can't bear even the suspicion that he might be involved in Duraid's murder.'

'Sorry if I gave you a rough night, but we have to consider all the angles,' he tried to soothe her, and then changed the subject. 'We have wasted enough time here. Pegasus have got a clear run of the field at the moment. I want to get back home, and start putting together our own expeditionary force for the return.'

'Would you like me to get on to the airline and make our reservations?' She stood up immediately. 'I will go off and find a phone.'

'Finish your breakfast first.'

'I have had all I want.' She made for the door, and he called after her.

'No wonder you are so skinny. They tell me anorexia nervosa is a rotten way to go.' And he helped himself to another slice of toast and marmalade.

She was back within fifteen minutes. 'Tomorrow afternoon at three-thirty. Kenya Airways to Nairobi, connecting the same evening with British Airways to Heathrow.'

'Well done.' He wiped his mouth on his napkin, and stood up. 'Our car is waiting to take us down to police headquarters to speak to your new admirer, General Obeid. Let's go.'

There was a police officer waiting to meet them and usher them into the headquarters building, through the private entrance. He introduced himself as Inspector Galla and treated them with the greatest deference as he led them through to the Commissioner's suite.

General Obeid rose to his feet as soon as they entered his office, and came around his desk to greet them. He was charming and affable, fussing over Royan as he led them through to his private sitting room. Once they were seated, Inspector Galla poured the inevitable tiny bowls of bitter black coffee.

After a polite interval of small talk the general came directly to the business in hand. 'As I promised, I won't detain you longer than is absolutely necessary. Inspector Galla here will be recording your statements. Firstly I would like to deal with the disappearance and death of Major Brusilov. I presume you are aware that he was formerly an officer in the Russian KGB?'

The interview lasted much longer than they had expected. General Obeid was thorough, but unfailingly polite. Finally he had their statements typed out by a police stenographer, and after they had read and signed them, the general walked with them as far as the entrance where their car was waiting. Nicholas recognized this as a mark of special favour.

'If there is anything I can do for you, anything that you need, please do not hesitate to call upon me. It has been a great pleasure meeting you, Dr Al Simma. You must come back to Ethiopia and visit us again soon.'

'Despite our little misadventure, I have thoroughly enjoyed your beautiful country,' she told him sweetly. 'You may see us again sooner than you expect.'

'What a charming man,' she remarked, as they settled into the back seat of Sir Oliver's Rolls. 'I really like him.'

'It would seem to be mutual,' said Nicholas.

oyan's words were prophetic. There were identical envelopes addressed to each of them lying at their places on the dining-room table the next morning when they came down to breakfast.

Nicholas opened his as he ordered coffee from the waiter in his ankle-length *shamma*, and his expression changed as he read the note.

'Hello!' he exclaimed. 'We made an even bigger impression on the boys in blue than we realized. General Obeid wants to see me again.' He read aloud from the note, '"You are ordered to present yourself at police headquarters at or before noon."' Nicholas whistled softly. 'Strong language. No please or thank you.'

'Mine is identical.' Royan glanced at the note on an official police letterhead. 'What on earth do you suppose it means?'

'We will find out soon enough,' Nicholas promised her. 'But it sounds a little ominous. Methinks the love affair is over.'

This morning, when they arrived at police headquarters, there was no reception committee to welcome them. The guard at the private entrance sent them around to the general charge office, where they were involved in a long, confused discussion with the desk officer, who had only a rudimentary knowledge of English. From previous experience in Africa Nicholas knew better than to lose his temper, or even to let his irritation show. Finally the desk officer held a long whispered telephone conversation with some unknown person, at the end of which he waved them airily towards a hard wooden bench against the far wall.

'You wait. Man come soon.'

For the next forty minutes they shared their seat with a colourful selection of other supplicants, applicants, complainants and petty criminals. One or two of them were bleeding copiously from assault by persons unknown, and yet others were in manacles.

'It seems our star is on the wane,' Nicholas remarked as he held a handkerchief to his nose. It was obvious that some of his neighbours had not had a close acquaintance with soap and water for some time. 'No more VIP treatment.'

At the end of forty minutes Inspector Galla, he who had treated them so deferentially the day before, looked over the partition and beckoned to them in a high-handed fashion.

He ignored Nicholas's outstretched right hand and led them through to one of the back rooms. There he did not offer them a seat but addressed Nicholas coldly. 'You are responsible for the loss of a firearm that was in your possession.'

'That is correct. As I explained to you in my statement yesterday—'

Inspector Galla cut him off. 'The loss of a firearm due to negligence is a very serious offence,' he said severely.

'There was no negligence on my part,' Nicholas denied.

'You left the firearm unguarded. You made no attempt to lock it in a steel safe. That is negligence.'

'With respect, Inspector, there is a notable dearth of steel safes in the Abbay gorge.'

'Negligence,' Galla repeated. 'Criminal negligence. How are we to know that the weapon has not fallen into the hands of elements opposed to the government?'

'You mean some unknown person may overthrow the government with a 275 Rigby?' Nicholas smiled.

Inspector Galla ignored the sally, and produced two documents from the drawer of his desk. 'It is my duty to serve these deportation orders on both you and Dr Al Simma. You have twenty-four hours to leave Ethiopia, and thereafter you will be considered to be prohibited immigrants, both of you.'

'Dr Al Simma has not lost any weapons,' Nicholas pointed out mildly. 'In fact as far as I am aware, she has never been even mildly negligent in her entire life.' And again his comment was ignored.

'Please sign here to acknowledge that you have received and understood the orders.'

'I would like to speak to General Obeid, the Commissioner of Police,' said Nicholas.

'General Obeid left this morning for an inspection tour of the northern frontier districts. He will not return to Addis Ababa for some weeks.'

'By which time we will be safely back in England?'

'Exactly.' Inspector Galla smiled for the first time, a thin, wintry smirk. 'Please sign here, and here.'

'What happened?' Royan demanded, as the driver opened the door of the Rolls for her and she settled into the seat beside Nicholas. 'It was all so sudden and unexpected. One moment everybody loved us, and the next we are being booted down the stairs.'

'Do you want my guess?' Nicholas asked, and then went on without waiting for her reply. 'Nogo is not the only one in Pegasus's back pocket. Overnight Obeid has been in contact with von Schiller, and received his orders.'

'Do you realize what this means, Nicky? It means that we will not be able to return to Ethiopia. That puts the tomb of Mamose beyond our grasp.' She stared at him with large dark eyes full of dismay.

'When Duraid and I visited Iraq and Libya, neither of us had letters of invitation from either Saddam or Gadaffi, as I recall.'

'You look delighted at the prospect of breaking the law,' she accused. 'You are smirking all over your face.'

'After all, it is only Ethiopian law,' he pointed out virtuously. 'Not to be taken too seriously.'

'And it will be an Ethiopian prison they toss you into. That you can take seriously.'

'You too,' he grinned, 'if they catch us.'

'You can be certain that HE has already registered a formal complaint with the President's office,' Geoffrey told them as he drove them to the airport the next day. 'He is most upset at the whole business, I can tell you. Deportation orders and all that rot. Never heard the likes.'

'Don't fuss yourself, old boy,' Nicholas told him. 'As it is, neither of us intends coming back here again. No harm done.'

'It's the principle of the thing. Prominent British subject being treated like a common criminal. No respect shown.' He sighed. 'Sometimes I wish I had been born a hundred years ago. We wouldn't have to put up with this sort of nonsense. Just send a gunboat.'

'Quite so, Geoffrey, but please don't let it upset you.'

Geoffrey hovered around them like a cat with kittens while they checked in at the Kenya Airways counter. They had only their hand luggage, two small cheap nylon holdalls that they had bought that morning at a street market. Nicholas had rolled his dik-dik skin into a ball and wrapped it in an embroidered *shamma* that he had purchased in the same market.

Geoffrey waited with them until their flight was called and waved to them after they passed through the barrier, aiming this affectionate display more at Royan than Nicholas.

They had been allocated seats behind the wing, and Royan was beside the window. The Kenya Airways plane started its engines and began to taxi slowly past the airport buildings. Nicholas was arguing with a stewardess who wanted him to stow his precious dik-dik skin in its purple nylon bag in the overhead locker, while Royan peered out of the porthole beside her for her last glimpse of Addis during take-off.

Suddenly Royan stiffened in her seat, and while still gazing out of the window reached across and seized Nicholas's arm.

'Look!' she hissed with such venom in her tone that he leaned across her to see what had excited her.

'Pegasus!' she exclaimed, and pointed to the Falcon executive jet that had just taxied in and parked at the far end of the airport buildings. The small, sleek aircraft was painted green and on its tall tail fin the scarlet horse reared on its hind legs in that stylized pose. While they watched through the window, the door in the fuselage of the green Falcon was lowered, and a small reception committee waiting on the

248

tarmac pressed forward expectantly to greet the passengers as they appeared in the doorway of the jet.

The first of these was a small man, neatly dressed in a cream tropical suit and a white panama straw hat. Despite his size he exuded an air of confidence and command, that special aura of power. His face was pale, as though he had come from a northern winter, and it looked incongruous in this setting. His jaw was firm and stubborn, his nose prominent and his gaze beneath dark beetling eyebrows penetrating.

Nicholas recognized him immediately. He had seen him often enough on the auction floors at Sotheby's and Christie's. This man was not the type of person whom anyone would forget in a hurry.

'Von Schiller!' he exclaimed, as the German surveyed with an imperial gaze the men who waited on the tarmac below him.

'He looks like a bantam rooster,' Royan murmured, 'or a standing cobra.'

Von Schiller raised his panama hat and ran down the steps of the Falcon with a light, athletic tread, and Nicholas said quietly, 'You wouldn't think that he is almost seventy.'

'He moves like a man of forty,' Royan agreed. 'He must dye his hair and eyebrows – see how dark they are.'

'My oath!' Nicholas was startled. 'Look who is here to greet him.'

There was the glint of sunlight on decorations and regimental insignia. A tall figure in blue uniform detached itself from the welcoming group and touched the shiny patent-leather brim of his cap in a respectful salute, before taking von Schiller's hand and shaking it cordially.

'Your erstwhile admirer, General Obeid. No wonder he could not meet us yesterday. He was much too busy.'

'Look, Nicky,' Royan gasped. She was no longer watching the pair at the foot of the steps, who were still clasping hands as they chatted with animation. Her whole attention was focused on the top of the steps of the Falcon jet, where another, younger, man had appeared. He was bare-headed, and Nicholas had the impression of sallow skin and dense, dark, wavy hair.

'Never seen him in my life before. Who is he?' Nicholas asked her.

'Nahoot Guddabi. Duraid's assistant from the museum. The man who now has his job.'

As Nahoot started down the steps of the Falcon their own aircraft trundled on down the tarmac, then swung out on to the main taxi-way and blocked any further view of the gathering beside the Pegasus jet. Both of them fell back in their seats and stared at each other for a long moment. Nicholas recovered his voice first.

'A witches' sabbath. A convocation of the ugly ones. We were lucky to witness it. There are no more secrets now. We know very clearly who the opposition is.'

'Von Schiller is the puppet-master,' she agreed, breathless with anger and horror. 'But Nahoot Guddabi is his hunting dog. Nahoot must be the one who hired the killers in Cairo and turned them loose on us. Oh God, Nicky, you should have heard him at the funeral, going on about how much he admired and respected Duraid. The filthy, murderous hypocrite!'

They were both silent until the aircraft had taken off and climbed to cruise altitude, then Royan said quietly, 'Of course, you were right about Obeid. He is deep in von Schiller's pocket also.'

'He may simply have been acting as the representative of the Ethiopian government, paying respect to a major foreign concession-holder, somebody who they hope is going to discover fabulous copper deposits in their poverty-stricken country and make them all rich.'

She shook her head firmly. 'If it was as simple as that, it would be one of the cabinet ministers meeting him, not the chief of police. No, Obeid has the stink of treachery on him, just the same as Nahoot.'

Seeing her husband's killers in the flesh had reopened the half-healed wounds of Royan's grief and mourning. These bitter emotions were a flame that was burning her up, like the bushfire in the trunk of a hollow forest tree, consuming her from within. Nicholas knew that he could not quench that flame, that he could only hope to distract her for a while. He talked to her quietly, turning her dark thoughts away from death and vengeance to the challenge of Taita's game and the riddle of the lost tomb.

By the time that they had changed planes at Nairobi and landed at Heathrow the following morning, the two of them had sketched out a plan of action for their return to the Nile gorge and the exploration of Taita's pool in the chasm. But although now Royan appeared on the surface to be her usual calm and cheerful self once again, Nicholas knew that the pain of her loss was still there beneath the surface.

They landed at Heathrow so early that they walked through the immigration gates without running into a queue, and since they had no bags in the hold they did not have to play the customary game of roulette at the luggage carousel – will they arrive or won't they?

Carrying the dik-dik skin in the nylon bag under his arm, and with Royan limping on her cane on his other arm, Nicholas sauntered through the green channel of HM Customs, as innocent as a cherub from the roof of the Sistine Chapel.

'You are so brazen,' she whispered to him once they were through and clear. 'If you can lie so convincingly to Customs, how can I ever trust you again?'

Their luck held. There was no queue at the taxi rank, and in a little over an hour after touch-down the taxi deposited them on the pavement outside Nicholas's town house in Knightsbridge. It was only eight-thirty on a Monday morning.

While Royan showered, Nicholas went down to the corner shop under an umbrella to fetch some groceries. Then they shared the task of cooking breakfast, Royan taking care of the toast while Nicholas whipped up his speciality, a herb omelette.

'Surely your going to need expert help when we go back to the Abbay gorge?' Royan observed, as she let the butter melt into the hot toast.

'I already have the right man in mind. I have worked with him before,' he told her. 'Ex-Royal Engineers. Expert in diving and under-water construction. Retired and living in a little cottage in Devon. I suspect he is a little short of the ready, and bored out of his considerable mind. I expect him to jump at any opportunity to alleviate either condition.'

As soon as they had finished breakfast, Nicholas told her, 'I will do the dishes. You take the films of the stele to be developed. There is a one-hour service at the branch of Boots opposite Harrods.'

'That's what I call a fair distribution of labour,' she remarked with a long-suffering air. 'You have a dishwasher, and it's raining again outside.'

'All right,' he laughed. 'To sweeten the pill, I'll lend you my raincoat. While you are waiting for the films to be developed you can go shopping to replace the togs you lost in the rock-fall. I have some crucial phone calls to make.'

As soon as she had left, Nicholas settled at his desk with a notepad at one hand and the telephone at the other. His first call was to Quenton Park, where Mrs Street tried not to show how delighted she was to have him home.

'Your desk is about two feet deep with mail awaiting your return. It's mostly bills.'

'Cheerful, aren't we?'

'The lawyers have been pestering me, and Mr Markham from Lloyd's has been ringing every day.'

'Don't tell any of them that I am back, there's a good girl.' Nicholas knew exactly what they wanted from him – the same thing that persistent callers always wanted: money. In this case it was not simply five hundred guineas for an overdue tailor's bill, but two and a half million pounds. 'It's probably better if I stay in York, rather than at Quenton,' he told Mrs Street. 'They won't be able to find me at the flat.'

He pushed his debts to the back of his mind, and concentrated on the task at hand. 'Have you got your pencil and notepad ready? All right, here's what I want you to do.'

It took him ten minutes to finish his dictation, and then Mrs Street read it back to him. 'Okay. Get on with it, will you. We'll be back this evening. Dr Al Simma will be staying indefinitely. Ask the housekeeper to prepare the second bedroom for her at the flat.'

Next he rang the number in Devon, and while the phone rang he imagined the converted coastguard's cottage on top of the cliffs overlooking a grey, storm-whipped winter sea. Daniel Webb was probably in his workshop in the back garden, either tinkering with his 1935 Jaguar, the great love of his life, or tying salmon flies. Fishing was his other passion, the one that had originally brought them together.

'Hello?' Daniel's voice was guarded and suspicious. Nicholas could imagine him, his bald head freckled like a plover's egg, gripping the telephone with a hairy, work-scarred fist.

'Sapper, I have a job for you. Are you a starter?'

'Where are we headed, Major?' Although it had been three years, he recognized Nicholas's voice instantly.

'Sunny climes and dancing girls. Same pay as the last time.'

'I'm a starter. Where do we meet?'

'At the flat. You remember it from last time. Tomorrow. Bring your slide rule.' Nicholas knew that Danny put no store by these new-fangled pocket computers.

'The Jag is still in good nick. I'll leave early and be there for lunch tomorrow.'

Nicholas hung up, and then made two more calls: one to his Jersey bank, and the other to the Cayman Islands. The funds in both his emergency accounts were running low. His budget for the expedition that he had worked out with Royan on the flight was two hundred and thirty thousand. Like all budgets, he knew that it was optimistic.

'Always add fifty per cent,' he warned himself. 'Which means that the cupboard will be bare by the time we are finished. Let's hope and pray that you are not pulling our legs, Taita.'

He gave the passwords to the respective bank accountants and instructed them to make transfers into his holding accounts, ready to draw on immediately.

There were two more calls he had to make before they left for York. The fate of all their plans hung on them, and the contacts that he had for both of them were at the best tenuous, and at the worst chimerical.

The first number was engaged. He rang it five times more, and on each occasion got the irritating high-pitched busy tone in his ear. He tried one last time and was answered by a reassuring west country accent.

'Good afternoon. British Embassy. How may I help you?' Nicholas glanced at his wrist-watch. There was a three-hour time difference. Of course, it would be afternoon in Addis.

'This is Sir Nicholas Quenton-Harper calling from the UK. Is Mr Geoffrey Tennant, your military attaché, available, please?'

Geoffrey came on the line almost immediately. 'My dear boy. So you made it all the way home. Lucky you.'

'Just thought I would set your mind at rest. Knew you would be losing sleep.'

'How is the charming Dr Al Simma?'

'She sends her love.'

'I wish I could believe you.' Geoffrey sighed dramatically.

'Big favour, Geoff. Do you know a Colonel Maryam Kidane at the Ministry of Defence?'

'First-rate chap,' Geoffrey affirmed immediately. 'Know him well. Played tennis with him last Saturday, actually. Demon back-hand.'

'Please ask him to contact me urgently.' He gave Geoffrey the telephone number of the flat in York. 'Tell him it's in connection with a rare breed of Ethiopian swallow for the museum collection.'

'Up to your shenanigans again, Nicky. Not enough that you get slung out of Ethiopia on your ear. Now you are trading in rare birds. Probably CITES Schedule One. Endangered species.'

'Will you do it for me, Geoff?'

'Of course. Serve to Lead, old boy. Always the sucker.'

'I owe you one.'

'More than one. Half a dozen, more like it.'

He had less success with his next call. International Enquiries gave him a number in Malta. On his first attempt he received an encouraging ringing tone.

'Pick it up, Jannie,' he pleaded in a whisper, but on the sixth ring an answering machine cut in.

'You have reached the head office of Africair Services. There is nobody available to take your call at the moment. Please leave your name and number and a short message after the tone. We will get back to you as soon as possible. Thank you.' Jannie Badenhorst's rich South African accent was unmistakable.

'Jannie. This is Nicholas Quenton-Harper. Is that broken-down old Herc of yours still airworthy? This job should be a lark. What's more, the money is good. Call me at the flat in the UK. No hurry. Yesterday, or the day before, will do just fine.'

Royan rang the doorbell a minute after he finished the last call, and he ran down the stairs.

'Your timing is impeccable,' he told her as she came in with the end of her nose pink with cold, shaking the raindrops off the coat he had lent her. 'Did you get the films developed?'

She pulled the yellow packet out of the coat pocket and brandished it triumphantly.

'You are a master photographer,' she told him. 'They have turned out perfectly. I can read every character on the stele with the naked eye. We are back in Taita's game again.'

They spread the glossy photographs across his desktop and gloated over them.

'You have had duplicates made? A set for each of us. Excellent,' Nicholas approved. 'The negatives will go into the safe deposit box at my bank. We won't take a chance on losing them the second time around.'

Using his large magnifying glass, Royan studied each of the prints in turn, and she picked out the clearest shot of each of the four sides of the stele.

'These will be our working copies. I don't think we are really going to miss the rubbings that we lifted from the stone. These should suffice.' She read aloud a snippet from one of the blocks of hieroglyphics. '"*The cobra uncoils and lifts his jewelled hood. The stars of morning shine within his eyes. Three times his black and slippery tongue kisses the air.*"' She was flushed with excitement. 'I wonder what Taita is telling us with that verse. Oh, Nicky, it's so exciting to be unravelling the mysteries again!'

'Leave it alone now,' he ordered sternly. 'I know you. Once you start, we'll be here all night. Let's get the Range Rover packed up. It's a long, hard haul up to York, and there is an AA warning of black ice on the motorway. A bit of a change from the weather in the Abbay gorge.'

She straightened up and shuffled the prints into a neat pile. 'You are right. Sometimes I do tend to get carried away.' She stood up. 'Before we go, may I make a phone call home?'

'By home, I take it that you mean Cairo?'

'Sorry. Yes, to Cairo. Duraid's family—'

'Please! No need to explain. There is the phone. Help yourself. I'll be waiting downstairs in the kitchen when you are finished. We both need a cup of tea before we get going.'

She came down into the kitchen half an hour later looking guilty, and told him directly, 'I am afraid that I am going to be a nuisance again. I have a confession to make.'

'Spit it out,' he invited.

'I have to go back home – to Cairo,' she said, and he looked at her startled. 'Just for a few days,' she qualified hurriedly. 'I was speaking to Duraid's brother. There are some of Duraid's affairs that I have to see to.'

'I don't like you going back there on your own,' he shook his head, 'after your last experiences.'

'If our theory is correct, and Nahoot Guddabi was the danger, then he is in Ethiopia now. I should be quite safe.'

'Still, I don't like it. You are the key to Taita's game.'

'Thank you kindly, sir,' she said with mock outrage. 'Is that the only reason you don't want me bumped off?'

'If forced into a corner, I may admit that I have also grown rather partial to having you around.'

'I'll be back before you know I've even gone. Besides which, you will have plenty to keep you busy while I am away.'

'I don't suppose that I can stop you,' he grumbled. 'When do you plan to leave?'

'There's a flight at eight this evening.'

'A bit sudden. I mean, we have only just arrived.' He made one last feeble protest, then capitulated. 'I will run you out to the airport.'

'No, Nicky. Heathrow is out of your way. I can catch the train.'

'I insist.'

On a Monday evening the traffic was reasonably light and, once they had cleared the main built-up area, they made good time. The journey was further lightened by their animated discussion as he related the contents of the phone calls he had made in her absence.

'Through Maryam Kidane, I hope to be in contact with Mek Nimmur again pretty soon. Mek is the kingpin of the whole plan. Without him we can't even make the first move on Taita's bao board.'

He dropped her off at the departures entrance at Heathrow. 'Phone me tomorrow morning from Cairo to let me know you are all right, and when you are coming back. I'll be at the flat.'

'Reversed charges,' she warned him as she offered him her cheek to kiss. Then she slid across the seat and slammed the door behind her.

He watched her waiflike figure in the rear-view mirror as he pulled away, and he was filled with melancholy and a sense of loss. Then quite suddenly he was aware of a new sensation of disquiet. His early-warning bells were jangling. Something unpleasant was afoot. Something nasty was about to happen when she reached Egypt. Another dangerous beast had escaped from its cage and was prowling the darkness waiting its opportunity to pounce, but it was still too early for him to discern its colour or shape.

'Please don't let anything happen to her,' he spoke aloud, but he did not know to whom his plea was addressed. He thought of turning back and making her stay with him, but he had no rights in the matter, and he knew she would not obey him. Short of physical force, there was no way he could impose his will upon her. He had to let her go.

'But I don't like it one little bit,' he reaffirmed.

His private secretary, and the other men who worked for him, knew exactly what he expected of them. Everything was as he required it. Gotthold von Schiller looked around the interior of the Quonset hut with approval. Helm had done well in the time that he had been given to prepare the base for his boss's arrival.

His own private quarters occupied half the long portable building. They were spartan, but sterilely clean and neat. His clothes hung in the cupboard and his cosmetics and medicines were set out in the bathroom cabinet. His private kitchen was fully equipped and stocked with provisions. His own Chinese chef had flown out in the Falcon with him, bringing everything with him that he needed to provide the meals that his master demanded.

Von Schiller was a vegetarian, a non-smoker and a teetotaller. Twenty years ago he had been a famous trencherman who loved the hearty food of the Black Forest, the wines of the Rhine valley and the rich dark tobaccos of Cuba. In those days he had been obese, with rolls of chin sagging over his collar. Now, despite his age, he was as lean and fit and vital as a racing greyhound.

In the autumn of his life, the pleasures were of the mind and the emotions, more than of the physical senses. He placed a higher value on inanimate objects than on living creatures, either human or animal. A piece of stone carved by masons who had been dead for thousands of years could excite him more than the soft warm body of the most lovely young woman. He loved order and control. Power over men and events sustained him more than did the taste of food. Power and the possession of beautiful and unique objects were his passions, now that his body was running down and his animal appetites were losing their zest.

Every item of all that vast and priceless collection of ancient treasures that he had already assembled had been discovered by other men. This was his chance, his very last chance to make his own discovery, to break the seals on the door of a Pharaoh's tomb and be the first man in four thousand years to gaze upon the contents. Perhaps that was his real hope for immortality, and there was no price in gold and human life he was not fully prepared to pay for it. Already men had died in this passion of his, and he cared not that there would be other sacrifices. No price was too high.

He checked his image in the full-length mirror that hung on the wall opposite his bed. He smoothed the thick, coarse, dark hair. Of course it was dyed, but that was one of his few remaining conceits. Then he crossed the uncarpeted wooden floor of his own quarters, and opened the door into the long conference room which would be his headquarters over the days to come.

The persons seated there rose to their feet immediately, their attitudes servile and their expressions obsequious. Von Schiller strode to the head of the long table and stepped up on to the block of wood covered with carpeting that his private secretary had placed there for him. This block went everywhere with him. It was nine inches high. From this elevation von Schiller looked down upon the men and one woman who waited for him. He looked them over unhurriedly, letting them stand a while. From the vantage point of his block, he was taller than any of them.

First he looked at Helm. The Texan had worked for him for over a decade. Completely reliable, he was strong both physically and mentally and would follow orders without question or qualms. Von Schiller had come to rely on him. He could send him anywhere in the world, from Zaïre to Queensland, from the Arctic Circle to the steaming equatorial forests, and Helm would get the job done with the minimum of fuss and with very few unpleasant consequences. He was ruthless but discreet, and like a good hunting dog he knew his master.

From Helm he looked at the woman. Utte Kemper was his private secretary. She ordered and directed the details of his life, from his food to his block, from his medicine to his social calendar, No man or woman was ever received into his presence without her prior arrangement. She was also his communications expert. The mass of electronic equipment that occupied one wall of the hut was her preserve. Utte was able to find her way through the ether with the infallible instinct of a homing pigeon. From the archaic art of the keyboard and Morse code to burst transmissions and random switching he had never known another person, male or female, who could match her wizardry. She was at that perfect age for a woman, forty, slim and blonde, with slanting green eyes over high cheekbones, resembling the young Dietrich.

Von Schiller's own wife, Ingemar, had been an invalid for the last twenty years, and Utte Kemper had stepped into the void she had left in his life. Yet she was more than either secretary or wife to him.

When he had first met Utte, she had been holding a very senior position in the technical section of the German national telecommunications network, and moonlighting as a pornographic actress – not for the money but for love of the job. Copies of the videos she had made at that time were amongst von Schiller's most precious possessions, after his collection of Egyptian antiquities. Like Helm, she had no qualms. There was nothing she would not do to him, or allow him to do to her, to fulfil his most bizarre fantasies. When he watched her videos and she did some of these things to him, she was the only woman who could still bring him to orgasm. Yet even this happened less frequently with every month that passed, and each time the spasms of sexual release she could evoke from his aging body were less intense.

Utte had her recording equipment set up before her on the table. It was part of her multifarious duties to keep accurate and complete records of every meeting and conversation. Then von Schiller looked past these two trusted employees to the two other men standing at the table.

Colonel Nogo he had met for the first time that morning, as he stepped down from the Jet Ranger helicopter that had flown them down from Addis Ababa to the base camp here on the summit of the escarpment of the Nile gorge. He knew very little about him, except that Helm had selected him, and was so far satisfied with his performance. Von Schiller himself was not equally impressed. There had already been some bungling. Nogo had allowed Quenton-Harper and the Egyptian woman to slip through his clutches. After a lifetime of operating in Africa, von Schiller placed little trust or store in blacks and preferred to work with Europeans. However, he realized that for the time being Nogo's services were indispensable. He was, after all, the military commander of the southern Gojam. No doubt once he had served his purpose he could be taken care of. Helm would see to that. He would not have to bother himself with the details.

Von Schiller looked now at the last man at the table. Here was another who was indispensable for the time being. Nahoot Guddabi was the one who had brought the existence of the seventh scroll to his attention. Apparently some English author had written a fictionalized version of the scrolls, but von Schiller never read fiction of any sort, either in German or in any of the four foreign languages in which he was fluent. Without Nahoot bringing the existence of the Taita scrolls to his notice, he might have overlooked this opportunity of his lifetime.

The Egyptian had come to him as soon as the original translation of the scrolls had been completed by Duraid Al Simma, and the existence of an unrecorded Pharaoh and his tomb had been mooted. Since then they had been in constant contact, and when the time came that Al Simma and his wife had started to make too much headway with their investigations, von Schiller had employed Nahoot to get rid of them and to bring the seventh scroll to him.

The scroll was now the shining star of his collection, safely housed with his other ancient treasures in the steel and concrete vaults below the Schloss in the mountains that was his private retreat, his Eagle's Nest.

Despite this, the choice of Nahoot to undertake the more sensitive work of ridding him of Al Simma and his wife had proved to be a mistake. He should have sent a professional to take care of them, but Nahoot had argued that he was capable of seeing it through, and he had been well paid for the work that he had mismanaged so ineptly. He too would be disposable in time, but right now von Schiller still needed him.

There was no question that Nahoot's understanding of Egyptology and hieroglyphics was far in advance of von Schiller's own. After all, Nahoot had spent most of his life studying them, while von Schiller was an amateur and only a comparatively recent enthusiast. Nahoot was able to read the scrolls and this new material that they had acquired as though they were letters from a friend, whereas von Schiller was obliged to puzzle over each symbol and resort frequently to his reference books. Even then, he was not capable of picking up the finer nuances of meaning in the text. Without Nahoot's assistance he could not hope to solve the riddles which confronted him in the search for Mamose's tomb.

This was the team who were now assembled beneath him, waiting for him to start the proceedings. 'Sit down, please, Fräulein Kemper,' he said at last. 'You too, gentlemen. Let us get started.'

Von Schiller remained standing on his block at the head of the table. He enjoyed the feeling of superior height. His short stature had been a source of humiliation ever since his school-days when he had been nicknamed 'Pippa' by his peers.

'Fräulein Kemper will be recording everything which is said here this afternoon. She will also issue each of you with a folder of documents which she will collect from you again at the end of this meeting. I want to make it very clear that none of this material will ever leave this room. It is of the most confidential nature, and belongs to me alone. I will take a most stringent view of any breach of this instruction.'

As Utte handed out the folders, von Schiller looked at each recipient in turn. His expression made it clear what the penalty would be for any contravention of his instructions.

Then von Schiller opened the dossier that lay on the tabletop in front of him. He stood over it, leaning forward on his bunched fists.

'In your folders you will find copies of the Polaroid photographs that were recovered from Quenton-Harper's camp. Please look at these now.'

Each of them opened their own folder.

'Since our arrival Dr Nahoot has had an opportunity to study these, and he is of the opinion that they are genuine, and that the stele in the photographs is an authentic artefect of ancient Egyptian origin, almost certainly dating from the Second Intermediate Period, circa 1790 BC. Is there anything you wish to add to that, Doctor?'

'Thank you, Herr von Schiller.' Nahoot smiled oleaginously, but his dark eyes were nervous. There was something cold and dispassionate about the old German that terrified him. He had displayed no emotion whatsoever as he ordered Nahoot to arrange the death of Duraid Al Simma and his wife. Nahoot knew that he would be equally unmoved if he were to order Nahoot's own murder. He realized that he was riding the tiger's back. 'I would just like to qualify that statement. I said that the stele pictured in these prints *appeared* to be genuine. Of course, I would not be able to give you a definite opinion until I was able to examine the actual stone at first hand.'

'I note your qualification,' von Schiller nodded, 'and we are assembled here to find the means to obtain the stele for your examination and verdict.' He picked up the glossy print that Utte had made from the original that morning in the laboratory darkroom in the adjoining hut. Photography was not the least of her many talents and skills, and she had done a very competent job. The copies of the Polaroids that Helm had transmitted to him in Hamburg had been blurred and distorted, but still they had been sufficient to bring him rushing across the continents in all this haste. Now he held these clear likenesses in full colour, and his excitement threatened to suffocate him.

While they were all silent, he caressed the print as lovingly as if it had been the actual object that it portrayed. If this were genuine, as he knew instinctively that it was, then it alone would be well worth the considerable cost in time and money and human life that he had already paid. It was a marvellous treasure, to match even the original seventh scroll which was already in his collection. The condition and state of preservation of the stele after four thousand years seemed to be extraordinary. He lusted for it as he had for few things in his long life. It required an effort to set aside this pervasive longing, and to apply his mind to the task ahead of him.

'If, however, the stele is genuine, Doctor, can you tell us, or rather, can you suggest to us where it may be situated, and where we should direct our search?'

'I believe that we should not consider the stele in isolation, Herr von Schiller. We should look at the other Polaroids that Colonel Nogo was able to recover for us, and which Fräulein Kemper has so ingeniously copied.' Nahoot set aside the one print, and selected another from the pile in the folder in front of him. 'This one, for example.'

The others riffled through their own folders and selected the same print as he was displaying.

'If you study the background of this copy, you will see that in the shadows behind the stele there appears to be the wall of some type of cave or cavern.' He looked up at von Schiller, who nodded encouragement. 'There also appears to be some type of barred doorway.' Nahoot set the print aside and selected another. 'Now, see here. This is a photograph taken of another subject. It is, I believe, of a mural decoration painted upon either a plastered wall or the bare rock of a cave, possibly an excavated tomb. It seems to have been taken through the grille of the gate which I pointed out to you in the first photograph of the stele. This mural is almost certainly Egyptian in style and influence. In fact it very strongly reminds me of those murals that decorated the tomb of Queen Lostris in Upper Egypt in which the original Taita scrolls were uncovered.'

'Yes. Yes. Go on!' von Schiller encouraged him.

'Very well, then. Using the barred gate as the connecting factor, there is every reason to believe that both stele and murals are located in the same cave or tomb.'

'If that is so, what indications do we have as to where Quenton-Harper photographed these Polaroids?' Von Schiller was still frowning angrily as he looked at each of them in turn. They all tried to avoid his blue, penetrating scrutiny.

'Colonel Nogo,' von Schiller singled him out, 'this is your country. You know the terrain intimately. Let's hear your thoughts on the subject.'

Colonel Nogo shook his head. 'This man, this Egyptian—' he used the epithet disparagingly, 'is mistaken. This is not an Egyptian tomb in the photographs.'

'Why do you say that?' Nahoot challenged him angrily. 'What do you know about Egyptology? I have spent twenty-five years—'

'Wait,' von Schiller silenced him peremptorily. 'Let him finish.' He looked at Nogo. 'Go on, colonel.'

'I agree that I don't know anything about Egyptian tombs, but these photographs were taken in a Christian church.'

'What makes you so sure?' Nahoot demanded bitterly, his authority challenged.

'Let me explain to you that I was ordained as a priest fifteen years ago. Later, I became disillusioned with Christianity and all other religions, and left the Church to become a soldier. I tell you this so that you may believe that I know what I am talking about.' He smiled with supercilious malice at Nahoot, before going on. 'Look at this first print again, and you will be able to make out on the wall in the background, near the corner of the grille gate, the outline of a human hand and the stylized picture of a fish. Those are symbols of the Coptic Church. You can see them reproduced in any church or cathedral in the land.'

Each of them peered at their own copy of the same print, but none of them ventured an opinion until von Schiller had given his.

'You are right,' von Schiller said softly. 'There is, as you say, the hand and the fish.'

'But I assure you the hieroglyphics on the stele and the murals and the wooden coffin are all Egyptian,' Nahoot defended himself stoutly. 'I would stake my life on it.'

Nogo shook his head, and began to argue. 'I know what I am saying—'

Von Schiller held up his hand to silence them both while he considered the problem. At last he came to some decision.

'Colonel Nogo, show me on the satellite photograph the site of Quenton-Harper's camp where you obtained these Polaroids.'

Nogo stood up, and came around the table to stand beside von Schiller. He leaned over the satellite photograph and prodded his forefinger at the spot near where the Dandera river joined the Nile. The photograph had once been in the possession of Quenton-Harper, and had been captured in the raid on his camp. There were numerous markings in coloured marker pen on the copy, which Nogo presumed had been placed there by the Englishman.

'It was here, sir. You can see that Quenton-Harper has marked the spot with a green circle.'

'Now show me where the nearest Coptic church is situated.'

'Why, Herr von Schiller, it's right here. Again Quenton-Harper has marked it with red ink. It is situated only a mile from the campsite. The monastery of St Frumentius.'

'There is your answer, then.' Von Schiller was still frowning. 'Coptic and Egyptian symbols together. The monastery.'

They stared at him, none of them daring to question his conclusion.

'I want that monastery searched,' he said softly. 'I want every room and every inch of every wall examined.' He turned back to Nogo. 'Can you get your men in there?'

'Of course, Herr von Schiller. I already have one of my reliable men in the monastery – one of the monks is in my pay. Added to that, there is still martial law in force here in Gojam. I am the military commander. I am fully empowered to search for rebels and dissidents and bandits wherever I suspect they may be sheltering.'

'Will your men enter a church to perform their duty?' Helm wanted to know. 'Do you personally have any religious scruples? It may be necessary to – how can I put it – desecrate hallowed premises.'

'I have already explained to you that I have renounced religion for other more worldly beliefs. I would take pleasure in destroying such superstitious and dangerous symbols as will certainly be found in the monastery of St Frumentius. As for my men, I will select only Moslems or Animists who are hostile to the cross, and all it stands for. I will lead them personally. I assure you that there will be no difficulty in that respect.'

'How will you explain this to your superiors in Addis Ababa? I do not want to be associated in any way with your actions at the monastery,' von Schiller said.

'I have been ordered by the high command in Addis to take all possible steps against the dissident rebels that are operating in the Abbay gorge. I will be completely able to justify any search of the monastery.'

'I want that stele. I want it at any cost. Do you understand me, colonel?'

'I understand you perfectly, Herr von Schiller.'

'As you already know, I am a generous man to those who serve me well. Bring it to me in good condition and you will be well rewarded. You may call on Mr Helm for any assistance that he can give you, including the use of Pegasus equipment and personnel.'

'If we are able to use your helicopter, it will save a great deal of time. I can take my men down there tomorrow, and if the stone is in the monastery I will be able to deliver it to you by tomorrow evening.'

'Excellent. You will take Dr Guddabi with you. He must search the area for other valuables and translate any inscriptions or engravings that you find in the monastery. Please provide him with military uniform. He must appear to be one of your troopers. I do not want to become involved in recriminations at a later date.'

'We will leave as soon as it is light enough to take off tomorrow morning. I will commence the arrangements immediately.' Tuma Nogo saluted von Schiller and strode eagerly from the hut.

Although Colonel Nogo had never entered either the *qiddist* or the *maqdas*, he had often visited the monastery of St Frumentius. He was therefore fully aware of the magnitude of the task ahead of him, and the likely reaction of the monks and the congregation to his forced entry to their premises. In addition, he was familiar with numerous similar rock cathedrals in other parts of the country. In fact he had been ordained in the famous cathedral of Lalibelela, so he knew just how labyrinthine one of these subterranean warrens could be.

He estimated that he would need at least twenty men to secure and search the monastery, and to fend off the outraged retaliation of the abbot and his monks. He selected his best men personally. None of them was squeamish.

Two hours before dawn he paraded them within the security of the Pegasus compound, under the glare of the floodlights, and briefed them carefully. At the end of the briefing he made each man step from the ranks in turn and recite his orders to ensure there was no misunderstanding. Then he inspected their arms and equipment meticulously.

Tuma Nogo was painfully conscious of his own culpability in allowing the Englishman and the Egyptian woman to escape, and he could sense the danger in Herr von Schiller's attitude towards him. He had few illusions about the consequences if he were to fail again. In the short time since he had made the acquaintance of Gotthold von Schiller, Nogo had come to fear him as he had never feared God or the Devil in

263

the days of his priesthood. He realized that this raid was an opportunity to reinstate himself with the formidable little German.

The Jet Ranger was standing by, the pilot at the controls, the engines running and the rotors turning lazily, but it could not carry such a large number of fully equipped men. It would need four round trips to ferry them all down to the assembly point in the gorge. Nogo flew with the first flight, and took Nahoot Guddabi with him. The helicopter dropped them three miles from the monastery, in a clearing on the banks of the Dandera river, the same drop area as they had used for the raid on Quenton-Harper's camp.

The drop area was just far enough from the monastery for the engine noise of the Jet Ranger not to alarm the monks. Even if they did hear it, Nogo was banking on the probability that they were by this time thoroughly conditioned to the frequent sorties of the machine, and would not associate it with any threat to themselves.

The men waited in the darkness, warned to silence and not even allowed by Nogo to smoke, while the Jet Ranger ferried in the remaining troopers. When the last flight came in Nogo ordered his detachment to fall in, and led them in single file down the path beside the river. They were all trained bush fighters in top physical condition, and they moved swiftly and purposefully through the night. Only Nahoot was a soft urbanite, and within half a mile he was wheezing and whining for a chance to rest. Nogo smiled vindictively to himself as he listened to Nahoot's pathetic whispered pleas for mercy as he was prodded along by the men behind him.

Nogo had timed his arrival at the monastery to coincide with the hour of matins and lauds, the break of day. He led his contingent down the cliff staircase at a trot. Their weapons were at high port, all the equipment was carefully muted so as not to clatter or creak, and their rubber-soled paratrooper boots made little noise on the stone paving as they hurried along the deserted cloisters to the entrance of the underground cathedral.

From the interior echoed the monotonous chanting and drumming of the ceremony, punctuated at intervals by the higher treble descant of the abbot leading the service. Colonel Nogo paused outside the doors, and his men drew up in double ranks behind him. There was no need for orders, for his briefing had covered every aspect of the raid. He looked the men over for a moment, then nodded at his lieutenant.

The outer chamber of the church was empty, as the monks were gathered in the middle chamber, the *qiddist*. Nogo crossed the outer nave swiftly, with his detachment moving up close behind him. Then he ran up the steps to the wooden doors of the *qiddist*, which stood open. As he entered, his men fanned out in two files behind him and swiftly took up their positions along the side walls of the *qiddist*, their assault rifles cocked and locked, and with bayonets fixed, covering the kneeling congregation.

It was done so silently and swiftly that it was some minutes before the monks gradually became aware of this alien presence in their holy place. The chanting and drumming died away, and the dark faces turned apprehensively towards the ranks of armed men. Only Jali Hora, the ancient abbot, was unaware of anything untoward happening. Completely absorbed in his devotions, he continued kneeling before the doors of the *maqdas*, the Holy of Holies, his quavering voice the lonely cry of a lost soul.

In the silence Colonel Nogo marched down the centre of the nave, kicking the kneeling monks out of his way. When he came up behind Jali Hora he seized him by his skinny black shoulder and threw him roughly to the ground. The tinsel crown flew from his silvered pate and rolled across the slabs with a brassy clatter.

Nogo left him sprawling and turned to face the rows of monks in their white *shammas*, addressing them imperiously in Amharic.

'I am here to search this church and the other buildings of this monastery, on suspicion that there are dissident rebels and other bandits harboured here.' He paused and surveyed the cowering holy men haughtily and threateningly. 'I must warn you that any attempt to prevent my men performing their duties will be regarded as an act of banditry and provocation. It will be met with force.'

Jali Hora crawled to his knees and then, using one of the embroidered hangings for support, slowly hoisted himself to his feet. Still clinging to the tapestry of the Virgin and child, he gathered himself with an effort.

'These are hallowed precincts,' he cried, in a surprisingly clear and strong voice. 'We are dedicated to the service and worship of almighty God, the Father, the Son and the Holy Ghost.'

'Silence!' Nogo bellowed at him. He unbuckled the flap of the webbing holster on his hip and placed his hand threateningly on the grip of the Tokarev pistol it contained.

Jali Hora ignored the threat. 'We are holy men in a place of God. There are no *shufta* here. There are no law-breakers amongst us. In the name of God the most high, I call upon you to be gone, to leave us to our prayers and our worship, and not to desecrate—'

Nogo drew the pistol and in the same movement swung the black steel barrel into the abbot's face with a vicious back-handed blow. Jali Hora's mouth burst open like the rind of a ripe pomegranate; the red juice burst from his crushed lips and flooded down the front of his tattered velvet vestments. A low moan of horror went up from the ranks of squatting monks.

Still clinging to the tapestry, Jali Hora kept his feet, but he was swaying and teetering wildly. He opened his shattered mouth to speak again, but the only sound that came from it was a high-pitched cawing, like that of a dying crow, and the blood splattered in bright droplets from his lips.

Nogo laughed and kicked his legs from under him. Jali Hora collapsed like a heap of dirty laundry and lay on the paving, groaning in his own blood and spittle.

'Where is your God now, you old baboon? Bleat to him as loud as you will, and he will never answer you,' Nogo chuckled.

With the pistol he gestured to his lieutenant across the church. He left six of his men guarding the monks, four at the doorway and one at each side wall. The others bunched up and followed him to the entrance to the *maqdas*.

The doors were locked. Nogo rattled the ancient padlock impatiently. 'Open this immediately, you old crow!' he shouted at Jali Hora who still lay in a bundle, moaning and sobbing.

'He is too far gone in senility,' the lieutenant shook his head. 'His mind has gone, colonel. He does not understand the command.'

'Break it open, then,' Nogo ordered. 'No, don't waste any more time. Shoot the lock away. The wood is rotten.'

Obediently the lieutenant stepped up to the door, and gestured his men to stand well clear. He aimed his AK-47 into the wood of the door lintel and fired a long, continuous burst.

Dust and chips of wood and stone flew in a cloud, and fresh yellow splinters splattered the paving. The noise of gunfire and the whine of ricochets was deafening in the echoing hall of the *qiddist*, and the monks wailed and howled and covered their ears and their eyes where they knelt. The lieutenant stepped back from the shattered door. The black wrought-iron hasp and staple hung at an angle, the supporting woodwork almost shot through.

'Break it down now!' Nogo ordered, and five of his men ran forward and put their shoulders to the sagging door. At their combined thrust there was a crackling, rending sound, and now the monks were screaming. Some of them had covered their heads with the skirts of their *shammas* so as not to have to witness this sacrilege; others were tearing at their faces with their fingernails, leaving long bloody gouges down their own cheeks.

'Again!' roared Nogo, and his men rushed the door once more, using their shoulders in unison. The lock was ripped away from its fastenings, and they pushed the massive door fully open and peered into the dim recesses of the *maqdas* beyond. The chamber was lit only by a few smoky oil lamps.

Now suddenly even these non-Christians were reluctant to cross

266

that threshold into the holy place. They all hung back, even Tuma Nogo, despite his defiant protestations of non-belief.

'Nahoot!' He looked back over his shoulder at the bedraggled and still sweating Egyptian. 'This is your job now. Herr von Schiller has ordered you to find the things we want. Come here.'

As Nahoot came forward, Nogo seized his arm and thrust him through the doorway. 'Get in there, oh follower of the Prophet. The Trinity of Christian gods cannot harm you.'

He stepped into the *maqdas* immediately after Nahoot and shone his torch around the low chamber. The beam of light danced over the shelves of votive offerings, sparkling on the glass and precious stones, on the brass and gold and silver. It stopped on the high cedarwood altar, lighting the Epiphany crown and the chalices, reflected from the communion plate and the tall silver Coptic cross.

'Beyond the altar,' Nahoot cried out with excitement. 'The barred gateway! This is the place where the Polaroids were taken.'

He broke away from the group in the doorway and ran wildly across the chamber. Gripping the bars of the gate in his clenched fists, he peered between them like a prisoner sentenced to life imprisonment.

'This is the tomb. Bring the light!' His voice was a high-pitched and frantic scream.

Nogo ran to join him, brushing past the damask-covered *tabot* stone. He shone the torch through the bars of the gate.

'By the sweet compassion of God, and the eternal breath of his Prophet,' Nahoot's voice sank from a scream to a whisper, 'these are the murals of the ancient scribe. This is the work of the slave Taita.' As Royan had done, he recognized the style and the execution immediately. Taita's brush was so distinctive, and his talent had outlasted the ages.

'Open this gate!' Nahoot's tone rose again, becoming strident and impatient.

'Here, you men!' Nogo responded, and they crowded around the ancient structure, trying at first to rip it from the cavern wall by main strength. Almost at once it became apparent that this was a futile effort, and Nogo stopped them.

'Search the monks' quarters!' he ordered his lieutenant. 'Find me tools to do the job.'

The junior officer hurried from the chamber, taking most of the troopers with him. Nogo turned from the gate and studied the rest of the interior of the *maqdas*.

'The stele!' he rasped. 'Herr von Schiller wants the stone above everything else.' He played the torchbeam around the chamber. 'From what angle was the Polaroid taken—'

He broke off abruptly, and held the light on the damask-covered *tabot* stone, on which the velvet-cloaked tabernacle stood.

267

'Yes,' cried Nahoot at his shoulder. 'That is it.'

Tuma Nogo crossed to the pillar with half a dozen strides and seized the gold-tasselled border of the tabernacle cloth. He pulled it away. The tabernacle was a simple chest carved from olive wood, glowing with the patina that priestly hands had imparted to the wood over the centuries.

'Primitive superstitions,' Nogo muttered contemptuously and, picking it up in both hands, hurled it against the cavern wall. The wood splintered and the lid of the chest burst open. A stack of inscribed clay tablets spilled out on to the cavern paving slabs, but neither Nogo nor Nahoot took any notice of these sacred items.

'Uncover it,' Nahoot encouraged him. 'Uncover the stone.'

Nogo tugged at the corner of the damask cloth, but it caught on the angle of the pillar beneath it. Impatiently he heaved at it with all his strength, and the old and rotten material tore with a soft ripping sound.

Taita's stone testament, the carved stele, was revealed. Even Nogo was impressed by the discovery. He backed away from it with the torn covering cloth in his hand.

'It is the stone in the photograph,' he whispered. 'This is what Herr von Schiller ordered us to find. We are rich men.'

His words of avarice broke the spell. Nahoot ran forward, and threw himself on his knees in front of the stele. He clasped it with both arms, like a lover too long deprived. He sobbed softly, and with amazement Nogo saw tears streaming unashamedly down his cheeks. Nogo himself had considered only the value of the reward that it would bring. He had never thought that any man could long so deeply for an inanimate object, especially something so mundane as this pillar of ordinary stone.

They were still posed like this, Nahoot kneeling at the stele like a worshipper and Nogo standing silently behind him, when the lieutenant ran back into the cavern. Somewhere he had found a rusty mattock with a raw timber handle.

His arrival roused both men from their trance, and Nogo ordered him, 'Break open the gate!'

Although the gate was antique and the wood brittle, it took the efforts of several men working in relays to rip the stanchions out of their foundations in the rock of the cavern wall.

At last, however, the heavy gate sagged forward. As the workers jumped aside it fell with a shattering crash to the slabs, raising a mist of red dust that dimmed the light of the lamps and the electric torch.

Nahoot was the first one into the tomb. He ran through the veil of swirling dust and once again threw himself to his knees beside the ancient crumbling wooden coffin.

'Bring the light,' he shouted impatiently. Nogo stepped up behind him and shone the torchlight on the coffin.

The portraits of the man were three dimensional, not only on the sides, but on the lid too. Clearly the artist was the same as the one who had executed the murals. The upper portrait was in excellent condition. It depicted a man in the prime of life with a strong, proud face, that of a farmer or a soldier with a calm and unruffled gaze. He was a handsome man, with thick blond tresses, skilfully painted as if by someone who had known him well and loved him. The artist seemed to have captured his character, and then eulogized his salient virtues.

Nahoot looked up from the portrait to the inscription on the wall of the tomb above it. He read it aloud, and then, with tears still backing up behind his eyelids, he looked down again at the coffin and read the cartouche that was painted below the portrait of the blond general.

'Tanus, Lord Harrab.' His voice choked up with emotion, and he swallowed noisily and cleared his throat. 'This follows exactly the description in the seventh scroll. We have the stele and the coffin. They are great and priceless treasures. Herr von Schiller will be delighted.'

'I wish I could believe what you say,' Nogo told him dubiously. 'Herr von Schiller is a dangerous man.'

'You have done well so far,' Nahoot assured him. 'It remains only for you to move the stele and the coffin out of this monastery to where the helicopter can fly them to the Pegasus camp. If you can do that, you will be a very rich man. Richer than you ever believed was possible.'

This spur was enough for Nogo. He stood over his men as they laboured around the base of the stele, digging in clouds of dust, levering the paving slabs out of their mooring. Finally they freed the foundation of the stele and between them lifted the stone out of the position in which it had stood for nearly four thousand years.

Only once it was free did they realize the weight of the stone. Although slender, it was a solid half-ton weight. Nahoot went back into the *qiddist* and, ignoring the rows of squatting monks, pulled down a dozen of the thick woollen tapestries from the walls and had the troopers carry them back into the *maqdas*.

He wrapped both the stele and the coffin in the heavy folds of coarse-spun wool. It was tough as canvas, and afforded the men who were to carry it a secure handhold. Ten of the burly troopers were able to lift and carry the stele, while three men were able to handle the wooden coffin and its desiccated contents. This left seven armed men free to provide an escort. Then the heavily burdened procession moved out through the ruined doorway of the Holy of Holies into the crowded central *qiddist*.

As soon as the assembled monks realized what they were carrying away with them, a shocked babble of voices, of lamentations and exhortations, rose from the squatting ranks of holy men.

'Quiet!' Nogo roared. 'Silence! Keep these fools quiet.'

The guards waded forward into the mass of humanity, clearing a passage for the treasures they were plundering, laying about them with boot and rifle butt, shouting at the monks to give way and to let the staggering porters through. The hubbub rose louder, the monks encouraging each other with their howls of protest, whipping themselves into a frenzy of religious outrage. Some of them leaped to their feet, defying the commands bellowed at them to remain seated. They crowded closer and closer to the armed troopers, clutching at their uniforms, chanting and whirling about them in a challenging display of mounting hostility.

In the midst of this uproar, suddenly the spectral figure of Jali Hora reappeared. His beard and robes were stained with blood, his eyes were crazy, bloodshot and staring. From his battered lips and ruined mouth issued a long, sustained shriek. The ranks of dancing monks opened to let him through, and he rushed like an animated scarecrow with his skirts flapping around his thin legs straight at Colonel Nogo.

'Get back, you old maniac!' Nogo warned him, and lifted the muzzle of his assault rifle to fend him away.

Jali Hora was far past any earthly restraint. He did not even check, but ran straight on to the point of the bayonet that Nogo was aiming at his belly.

The needle-pointed steel stabbed through his gaudy robes and ran into the flesh beneath them as easily as a gaff into the body of a struggling fish. The point of the bayonet emerged from the middle of his back, pricking through the velvet cloak, all pinkly smeared with the old man's blood. Spitted upon the steel, Jali Hora wriggled and contorted, a dreadful squeal bursting from his bloody lips.

Nogo tried to pull the bayonet free, but the wet clinging suction of the abbot's guts held the steel fast, and when Nogo jerked harder, Jali Hora was tossed about like a puppet, his arms flapping and his legs kicking and dancing comically.

There was only one way to free the blade of a bayonet that was trapped like this. Nogo slipped the rate-of-fire selector on the AK-47 to 'Single Shot'. He fired once.

The detonation of the shot was muffled by Jali Hora's body, but was yet so thunderous that for a moment it stilled the outcry of the monks. The high-velocity bullet tore down the entry track of the blade. It was moving at three times the speed of sound, creating a wave of hydrostatic shock behind it that turned the old man's bowels to jelly and liquidized his flesh. The suction that had held the bayonet was broken, and the blast of shot hurled Jali Hora's carcass off the point of the blade, flinging it into the arms of the monks who were crowding close behind him.

For a moment longer the strained, unnatural silence persisted, and then it was shattered by a higher, more angry chorus of horror from the monks. It was as though they were compelled by a single mind, a single instinct. Like a flock of white birds they flew at the band of armed men in their midst and descended upon them, intent on retribution for murder. They counted no cost to themselves, but with their bare hands they tore at them, hooked fingers clawing for their eyes, seizing the barrels of the levelled rifles. Some of them even grasped the blades of the bayonets with their naked hands, and the razor steel sliced through flesh and tendons.

For a short while it seemed that the soldiers would be overwhelmed and smothered by the sheer weight of numbers, but then those troopers carrying the stele and the coffin dropped their loads and unslung their weapons.

The monks crowded them too closely for them to swing the rifles, and they were forced to hack and stab with the bayonets to clear a space around them in which to do their work. They did not need much room, for the AK-47 has a short barrel and compact action. Their first burst of fully automatic fire, aimed into the monks at belly height and point-blank range, scythed a windrow through them. Every bullet told, and the full metal jacket ball whipped through one man's torso with almost no check, going on to kill the man behind him.

By now all the troopers were firing from the hip, traversing back and forth, spraying the packed ranks of monks like gardeners hosing a bed of white pansies. As one magazine of twenty-eight rounds emptied they snapped it off and replaced it with another, fully loaded.

Nahoot cowered behind the fallen pillar, using it as a shield. The roar of gunfire deafened and confused him. He stared around him and could not credit the carnage he was witnessing. At such close range the 7.62 round is a terrible missile, which can blow off an arm or a leg as efficiently as an axe-stroke, but more messily. Taken in the belly, it can gut a man like a fish.

Nahoot saw one of the monks hit in the forehead. His skull erupted in a cloud of blood and brain tissue, and the gunman who had shot him laughed as he fired. They were all caught up in the madness of the moment. Like a pack of wild dogs that had run down their prey, they kept on firing and reloading and firing again.

The monks in the front rows turned to flee and ran into those behind. They struggled together, howling with agony and terror, until the storm of bullets swept over them, killing and maiming, and they fell upon the heaps of dead and dying. The floor of the chamber was carpeted with the dead and the wounded. Trying to escape the hail of bullets the monks blocked the doorway, plugging it tight with their struggling white-clad bodies, and now the troopers standing clear in the centre of the *qiddist* turned their guns upon this trapped mass of humanity. The bullets socked into them and they heaved and tossed like the trees of

271

the forest in a gale of wind. Now there was very little screaming; the guns were the only voices that still clamoured.

It was some minutes before the guns stuttered into silence, and then the only sound was the groans and the weeping of the wounded. The chamber was filled with a blue mist of gunsmoke and the stink of burned powder. Even the laughter of the soldiers was silenced as they stared around them, and realized the enormity of the slaughter. The entire floor was carpeted with bodies, their *shammas* splashed and speckled with gouts of scarlet, and the stone paving beneath them was awash with sheets of fresh blood in which the empty brass cartridge cases sparkled like jewels.

'Cease firing!' Nogo gave the belated order. 'Shoulder arms! Pick up the load! Forward march!'

His voice roused them, and they slung their weapons and stooped to lift their heavy, tapestry-wrapped burdens. Then they staggered forward, their boots squelching in the blood, tripping over the corpses, stepping on bodies that either convulsed or lay inert. Gagging in the stench of gunsmoke and blood, of bowels and guts ripped wide open by the bullets, they crossed the chamber.

When they reached the doorway and staggered down the steps into the deserted outer chamber of the church, Nahoot saw the relief on the faces of even these battle-hardened veterans as they escaped from the reeking charnel-house. For Nahoot it was too much. Never in his worst nightmares had he seen sights such as these.

He tottered to the side wall of the chamber and clung to one of the woollen hangings for support; then, heaving and retching, he brought up a mouthful of bitter bile. When he looked around him again, he was alone except for a wounded monk who was dragging himself across the flags towards him, his spine shot through and his paralysed legs slithering behind him, leaving a slimy snail's trail of blood across the stone floor.

Nahoot screamed and backed away from the wounded monk, then whirled and fled from the church, along the cloisters above the gorge of the Nile, following the group of soldiers as they carried their burdens up the stone staircase. He was so wild with horror that he did not even hear the approach of the helicopter until it was hovering directly overhead on the glistening silver disc of its spinning rotor.

Gotthold von Schiller stood outside the front door of the Quonset hut, with Utte Kemper waiting a pace behind him. The pilot had radioed ahead while the Jet Ranger was in flight, so all was in readiness to receive the precious cargo it was carrying. The helicopter raised a cloud of pale dust from the landing circle as it sank down to the earth. The long tapestry-covered load it carried had not been able to fit into the cabin, and was strapped across the landing skids of the aircraft. The instant that the skids kissed the ground and the pilot cut back the throttle, Jake Helm led out a team of a dozen men to loosen the nylon retaining straps and lift the heavy bundle down. Between them the gang of overall-clad workers carried the stele to the hut and eased it through the door. Helm hovered close at hand, issuing terse orders.

A space had been cleared in the centre of the conference room, the long table pushed back against the wall. With extreme care the stele was laid there, and minutes later the coffin of Tanus, the Great Lion of Egypt, was laid beside it.

Brusquely Helm dismissed the gang and closed and bolted the door behind them as they left. Only the four of them remained in the room. Nahoot and Helm crouched beside the stele, ready to unwrap the woollen tapestry. Von Schiller stood at the head of it, with Utte at his side.

'Shall we begin?' Helm asked softly, watching von Schiller's face the way a faithful dog watches its master.

'Carefully,' von Schiller warned him in strangled tones. 'Do not damage anything.' He was sweating in a sheen across his forehead, and his face was very pale. Utte edged protectively closer to him, but he did not glance in her direction. He was staring fixedly at the treasure that lay at his feet.

Helm opened his clasp-knife and cut away the tasselled cords that secured the covering. As he watched, von Schiller's breathing became louder. It rasped in his throat like a man in the terminal stages of emphysema.

'Yes,' he whispered hoarsely, 'that's the way to do it.' Utte Kemper watched his face. He was always like this when he made another significant addition to his collection of antiquities. He seemed on the verge of a seizure, of a massive heart attack, but she knew he had the heart of an ox.

Helm came to the top end of the pillar and carefully opened a small slit in the cloth. He eased the point of the blade into this opening, and then ran it slowly down towards the base, like a zip fastener. The blade was razor-sharp and the cloth fell away to reveal the inscribed stone beneath it.

The sweat burst out like a heavy dew on von Schiller's skin. It dripped from his chin on to the front of his khaki bush jacket. He made a small moaning sound as he saw the carved hieroglyphics. Utte watched him, her own excitement mounting. She knew what to expect of him, when he was caught up in this paroxysm of emotion.

'See here, Herr von Schiller.' Nahoot knelt beside the obelisk and traced the outline of a broken-winged hawk with his finger. 'This is the signature of the slave, Taita.'

'Is it genuine?' Von Schiller's voice was that of a very sick man, wheezing and gusty.

'It is genuine. I will guarantee it with my life.'

'It may come to that,' von Schiller warned him. His eyes were glittering with the hard brilliance of pale sapphires.

'This column was carved nearly four thousand years ago,' Nahoot repeated stoutly. 'This is the veritable seal of the scribe.' He translated glibly and easily from the blocks of figures, his face shining with an almost religious rapture: '"*Anubis, the jackal-headed, the god of the cemeteries, holds in his paws the blood and the viscera, the bones and the lungs and the heart that are my separate parts. He moves them like the stones of the bao board, my limbs serve him as counters, my head is the great bull of the long board*"—'

'Enough!' von Schiller commanded. 'There will be time for more later. Go now. Leave me alone. Do not return until I send for you.'

Nahoot looked startled and scrambled to his feet uncertainly. He had not expected to be dismissed so abruptly in the moment of his triumph. Helm beckoned him, and the two of them went quickly to the door of the hut.

'Helm,' von Schiller called thickly after him, 'make certain that nobody disturbs me.'

'Of course, Herr von Schiller.' He glanced enquiringly at Utte Kemper.

'No,' said von Schiller. 'She stays.'

The two men left the room, and Helm shut the door carefully behind them. Utte crossed the room and turned the key. Then she faced von Schiller with her hands behind her and her back pressed to the door.

Her breasts were thrust forward, firm and pointed. The nipples showed clearly through the thin cotton blouse, hard as marbles.

'The costume?' she asked. 'Do you want the costume?' Her own voice was tight and strained. She enjoyed this game almost as much as he did.

'Yes, the costume,' he whispered.

She crossed the room and disappeared through the door into his private quarters. As soon as she was gone von Schiller began to undress. When he stood mother-naked in the centre of the room, he threw his clothing in a heap into one corner and turned to face the door through which she would return.

Suddenly she stood in the doorway, and he gasped at the transformation. She wore the wig of tight Egyptian braids and over it the *uraeus*, the golden circlet with the hooded cobra standing erect above her forehead. The crown was genuine, as old as the ages – von Schiller had paid five million Deutschmarks for it.

'I am the reincarnation of the ancient Egyptian Queen Lostris,' she purred. 'My soul is immortal. My flesh is incorruptible.' She wore golden sandals from the tomb of a princess, and bracelets and finger rings and earrings from the same tomb. All were authentic royal relics.

'Yes.' His voice was choking, his face as pale as death.

'Nothing can destroy me. I will live for ever,' she said. Her skirt was diaphanous yellow silk, belted with gold and precious stones.

'For ever,' he repeated.

She was naked above the waist. Her breasts were big and white as milk. She cupped them in her own hands.

'These have been young and smooth for four thousand years,' she purred. 'I offer them to you.'

She stepped out of the open golden sandals and her feet were slim and neat. She parted the frontal split in the yellow skirts and held it so that her lower body was exposed. All her movements were slow and calculated. She was a clever actress.

'This is the promise of eternal life.' She placed her right hand on her dense honey-coloured pubic bush. 'I offer it to you.'

He groaned softly and blinked the streaming sweat out of his eyes, watching her avidly.

She undulated her hips, slowly and lewdly as an uncoiling cobra. She moved her feet apart and opened her thighs. With her fingers she spread the lips of her vulva.

'This is the gateway to eternity. I open it for you.'

Von Schiller groaned aloud. No matter how often repeated, the ritual never failed. Like a man in a trance he moved towards her. His body was thin, dried out like a thousand-year-old mummy. His chest hair was a silver fuzz, the skin of his sunken belly was folded and wrinkled, but his pubic hair was dark and thick as the hair on his head. His penis was huge, out of all proportion to the skinny old frame from which it dangled. As she moved slowly to meet him it filled out and hung at a different angle, and of its own accord the wizened foreskin peeled back to reveal the massive purple head beneath it.

'On the stele,' he grunted. 'Quickly! On the stone.'

She turned her back to him and knelt upon the stone, watching him over her shoulder as he came up behind her. Her buttocks were round and white as a pair of ostrich eggs.

elm and his men worked late that night in the Pegasus workshop, making the wooden crates to house both the stele and the coffin securely. At dawn the next day they were loaded on to one of the heavy trucks, cushioned with thick rubber matting and strapped down on to specially fitted cradles.

At his own suggestion Nahoot rode in the back of the truck, which would take just over thirty hours to cover the long and arduous journey to Addis Ababa. The Pegasus Falcon was standing on the airport tarmac when the dusty truck trundled out through the security gates and parked beside it.

Von Schiller and Utte Kemper had made the journey in the company helicopter. General Obeid was with them. He had come to wish them *au revoir* and Godspeed.

While the wooden crates were loaded into the jet, Obeid spoke to the waiting Customs officer. He stamped the documents clearing the two cases of 'Geological Samples' for export, and then discreetly retired.

'Loaded and ready to start engines, Herr von Schiller,' said the uniformed Pegasus chief pilot, saluting.

Von Schiller shook hands with Obeid and clambered up the boarding ladder. Utte and Nahoot Guddabi followed him. The rings under Nahoot's eyes were even darker and deeper than usual. The journey had come close to exhausting him entirely, but he would not let the wooden cases out of his sight.

The Falcon climbed up into a bright clear sky over the mountains and headed northwards. A few moments after the pilot extinguished the Seat Belt panel, Utte Kemper thrust her lovely blonde head through the cockpit door and asked the chief pilot, 'Herr von Schiller would like to know our ETA.'

'I expect to touch down at Frankfurt at 2100 hours. Please inform Herr von Schiller that I have already radioed head office to give instructions for transport to be awaiting our arrival at the airport.'

The Falcon landed a few minutes ahead of schedule and taxied to the private hangar. The senior Customs and Immigration officials who were waiting for them were old acquaintances who were always on hand when the Falcon carried a special cargo. After they had completed the formalities they drank a schnapps with Gotthold von Schiller at the Falcon's tiny fitted bar, and discreetly pocketed the envelopes that lay on the bar counter beside each crystal glass.

The drive up into the mountains took most of the rest of the night. Von Schiller's chauffeur followed the covered Pegasus truck along the icy winding mountain road, never letting it and its cargo out of sight. At five in the morning they drove through the stone gate of the Schloss, where the snow lay half a metre deep in the deer park. The castle itself, with its dark stone battlements and arrow-slit windows, looked like something from Bram Stoker's novel. However, even at this hour the butler and all his staff were on hand to welcome the master.

Herr Reeper, the custodian of von Schiller's collection, and his most trusted assistants were also waiting, ready to move the two wooden cases down into the vault. Reverently they loaded them on to the forklift and rode down with them in the specially installed elevator.

While they unpacked the crates, von Schiller returned to his suite in the north tower. He bathed and ate a light breakfast, prepared by the Chinese chef. When he had eaten, he went to his wife's bedroom. She was even frailer than she had been when last he had seen her. Her hair was now completely white, her face pinched and waxy. He sent the nurse away, and kissed his wife's forehead tenderly. The cancer was eating her away slowly, but she was the mother of his two sons, and in his own peculiar way he still loved her.

He spent an hour with her, and then went to his own bedroom and slept for four hours. At his age he never needed more sleep than that, no matter how tired he might be. He worked until mid-afternoon with Utte and two other secretaries, and then the custodian called on the house intercom to tell him that they were ready for him in the vault.

Von Schiller and Utte rode down together in the elevator, and when the door slid open both Herr Reeper and Nahoot were waiting for them. One look at their faces told von Schiller that they were beside themselves with excitement, bubbling over with news for him.

'Are the X-rays completed?' von Schiller demanded as they hurried after him down the subterranean passageway to the vault.

'The technicians have completed their work,' Reeper told him. 'They have done a fine job. The plates are wonderful. *Ja, wunderbar!*'

Von Schiller had endowed the clinic, so any request of his was treated as a royal command. The director had sent down his most modern portable X-ray equipment and two technicians to photograph the mummy of Lord Harrab, and a senior radiologist to interpret the plates.

Reeper inserted his plastic pass card into the lock of the steel vault door, and with a soft pneumatic hiss it slid open. They all stood aside for von Schiller to enter first. He paused in the doorway, and looked around the great vault. The pleasure never palled. On the contrary, it seemed to grow more intense every time he entered this place.

The walls were enclosed in two metres of steel and concrete, and were guarded by every electronic device that genius could devise. But this was not apparent when he viewed the softly lit and elegantly appointed main display room. It had been planned and decorated by one of Europe's foremost interior designers. The theme colour was blue.

Each item of the collection was housed in its own case, and each of these was cunningly arranged to show it to its best advantage.

Everywhere was the soft glimmer of gold and precious gems nestling on midnight-blue velvet cushions. Artfully concealed spotlights illuminated the lustre of lovingly polished alabaster and stone, the glow of ivory and obsidian. There were marvellous statues. The pantheon of the old gods were here assembled: Thoth and Anubis, Hapi and Seth, and the glorious trinity of Osiris and Isis and Horus, the son. They gazed out with those inscrutable eyes which had looked upon the procession of the ages.

On its temporary plinth in the centre of the room, in pride of place, stood the latest addition to this extraordinary hoard, the tall, graceful stone testament of Taita. Von Schiller stopped beside it to caress the polished stone before he passed on into the second room.

Here the coffin of Tanus, Lord Harrab, lay across a pair of trestles. A white-coated radiologist hovered over her back-lit display board on which the X-ray plates were clipped. Von Schiller went directly to the display and peered at the shadowy pictures upon it. Within the outline of the wooden coffin, the reclining human shape with hands crossed over its chest was very clear. It reminded him of a carved effigy atop the sarcophagus of an old knight in the precincts of a medieval cathedral.

'What can you tell me about this body?' he asked the radiologist without looking at her.

'Male,' she said crisply. 'Late middle age. Over fifty and under sixty-five at death. Short stature.' All the listeners winced and glanced at von Schiller. He seemed not to have noticed this solecism. 'Five teeth missing. One front upper, one eye tooth and three molars. Wisdom teeth impacted. Extensive caries in most surviving teeth. Evidence of chronic bilharzia infection. Possible poliomyelitis in infancy, withering in left leg.' She recited her findings for five minutes, and then ended, 'Probable cause of death was a puncture wound in upper right thorax. Lance or arrow. Extrapolating from the entry angle, the head of the lance or arrow would have transfixed the right lung.'

'Anything else?' von Schiller asked when she fell silent. The radiologist hesitated, and then went on.

'Herr von Schiller, you will recall that I have examined several mummies for you. In this instance, the incisions through which the viscera were removed appear to have been made with more skill and finesse than those of the other cadavers. The operator seems to have been a trained physician.'

'Thank you.' Von Schiller turned from her to Nahoot. 'Do you have any comments, at this stage?'

'Only that these descriptions do not fit those given in the seventh scroll for Tanus, Lord Harrab, at the time of his death.'

'In what way?'

'Tanus was a tall man. Much younger. See the portraits on the coffin lid.'

'Go on,' von Schiller invited.

Nahoot stepped up to the display of X-ray plates and pointed out several solid dark objects, all of them with clean outlines, that adorned the body.

'Jewellery,' he said. 'Amulets. Bracelets. Pectorals. Several necklaces. Rings and earrings. But, most significant,' Nahoot touched the dark circle around the dead brow, 'the *uraeus* crown. The outline of the sacred serpent is quite unmistakable, beneath the bandages.'

'What does that indicate?' Von Schiller was puzzled.

'This was not the body of a commoner, or even of a noble. The extent of ornamentation is too extensive. But most significant, the *uraeus* crown. The sacred cobra. That was only worn by royalty. I believe that what we have here is a royal mummy.'

'Impossible,' snapped von Schiller. 'Look at the inscription on the coffin. Those that were painted on the walls of the tomb. Clearly this is the mummy of an Egyptian general.'

'With respect, Herr von Schiller. There is a possible explanation. In the book written by the Englishman, *River God*, there is an interesting suggestion that the slave Taita swopped the two mummies, that of Pharaoh Mamose and his good friend, Tanus.'

'For what earthly reason would he do that?' Von Schiller looked incredulous.

'Not for any earthly reason, but for a spiritual and supernatural reason. Taita wished his friend to have the use and ownership of all Pharaoh's treasure in the after-world. It was his last gift to a friend.'

'Do you believe that?'

'I do not disbelieve it. There is one other fact that tends to support this theory. It is quite obvious from the X-rays that the coffin is too large for the body within. To me, it seems obvious that it was designed to accommodate a larger man. Yes, Herr von Schiller, I do believe that there is an excellent chance that this is a royal mummy.'

Von Schiller had gone ashen pale as he listened. Sweat beaded upon his forehead, and his voice was hoarse and chesty as he asked,

'A royal mummy?'

'It may very well be so.'

Slowly von Schiller moved closer to the sealed coffin on its trestle, until he was staring down at the portrait of the dead man upon its lid.

'The golden *uraeus* of Mamose. The personal jewellery of a pharaoh.' His hand was shaking as he laid it on the coffin lid. 'If that is so, then this find exceeds our most extravagant hopes.'

Von Schiller drew a deep steadying breath. 'Open the coffin. Unwrap the mummy of the Pharaoh Mamose.'

t was painstaking work. Nahoot had performed the same task many times before, yet never on the earthly remains of such an illustrious personage as an Egyptian pharaoh.

Nahoot first had to establish where the joint of the lid lay beneath the paint. Once he had done this, he could whittle away at the ancient varnish and glues that secured the lid in place. Great care had to be taken to inflict as little damage as possible: the fragile coffin in itself was a priceless treasure. This work took the greater part of two days.

When the lid was free and ready to be lifted, Nahoot sent a message to von Schiller, who was in an executive meeting with his sons and the other directors of his company in the library upstairs. Von Schiller had refused to go into the city for this meeting: he could not bear to be separated from his latest treasure. Immediately he heard from Nahoot he adjourned the meeting until the following Monday, and dismissed his directors and his offspring unceremoniously. Then, without waiting to see them into their waiting limousines, he hurried down to the vaults.

Nahoot and Reeper had rigged a light scaffold over the coffin, from which hung two sets of block and tackle. As soon as von Schiller entered the vault, Reeper sent away his assistants. Only the three of them would be present to witness the opening of the coffin.

Reeper brought him the carpet-covered block for him to stand on and positioned it at the head of the coffin, so that von Schiller would be able to see inside as they worked. From this eminence the old man nodded to them to proceed. The ratchets of the two blocks clicked, one pawl at a time, as both Reeper and Nahoot gently put pressure on the tackle. There was a faint crackling and tearing sound, at which von Schiller winced.

'It is only the last shreds of glue holding the lid,' Nahoot reassured him.

'Go on!' von Schiller ordered, and they lifted the lid another six inches until it hung suspended over the body of the coffin. The scaffolding was on nylon castors which rolled smoothly over the tiled floor. They wheeled away the entire structure, with the coffin lid still suspended from it.

Von Schiller peered into the open coffin. His expression changed to one of astonishment. He had expected to see the neatly swathed human form lying serenely in the traditional funereal pose. Instead, the interior of the coffin was stuffed untidily with loose linen bandages that entirely hid the body from view.

'What on earth—' von Schiller exclaimed with astonishment. He reached out to take a handful of the old discoloured wrappings, but Nahoot stopped him.

'No! Don't touch it,' he cried out excitedly, and then was immediately apologetic. 'Forgive me, Herr von Schiller, but this is fascinating. It strongly supports the theory of an exchange of bodies. I think we should study it, before we proceed with the unwrapping. With your permission of course, Herr von Schiller.'

Von Schiller hesitated. He was anxious to discover what lay beneath this rat's nest of old rags, but he realized the virtue of caution and prudence now. A hasty move might do irreparable damage. He straightened up and stepped down from his block.

'Very well,' he grunted. He pulled a handkerchief from the breast pocket of his dark blue double-breasted suit jacket, and mopped the heavy sweat from his face. His voice was shaky as he asked, 'Is it possible? Could this be Mamose himself?'

Stuffing the handkerchief back into his trouser pocket, he discovered with mild surprise that he had a painful erection. With his hand in his pocket he rearranged it to lie flat against his stomach. 'Remove the loose wrappings.'

'With your permission, Herr von Schiller, we should take the photographs first,' Reeper suggested tactfully.

'Of course,' von Schiller agreed at once. 'We are scientists, archaeologists, not common looters. Take the photographs.'

They worked slowly, and von Schiller found the delay tantalizing. There was no sense of the passage of time down here in the vault, but at one stage von Schiller, now in his shirtsleeves, glanced at his gold wristwatch and was surprised to see that it was past nine o'clock at night. He unknotted his necktie, threw it on the bench where his jacket already lay, and reapplied himself to the task.

Gradually the shape of a human body emerged from under the compacted mass of ancient bindings, but it was after midnight when at last Nahoot teased away the last untidy clump of old cloth from the mummy's torso. They blinked at the glimpse of gold just visible through the neat layers of bandages laid upon the corpse by the meticulous and skilful hands of the embalmers.

'Originally, of course, there would have been several massive outer coffins. These are missing, as are the masks. Those must still be in Pharaoh's original sarcophagus, covering the body of Tanus in the royal tomb that still awaits discovery. What we have left here is only the inner dressing of the royal mummy.'

With long forceps he peeled away the top layer of bandage as von Schiller, perched on his block, grunted and shuffled his feet.

'The pectoral medallion of the royal house of Mamose,' Nahoot whispered reverently. The great jewel blazed under the arc light. Resplendent in blue lapis lazuli and red carnelian and gold, it covered the entire chest of the mummy. The central motif was of a vulture in flight, soaring on wide pinions, and in its talons it clutched the golden cartouche of the king. The craftsmanship was marvellous, the design splendid.

'There is no doubt now,' von Schiller whispered. 'The cartouche proves the identity of the body.'

Next they unwrapped the king's hands, clasped over the great medallion. The fingers were long and sensitive, each of them loaded with circle after circle of magnificent rings. Clasped in his dead hands were the flail and sceptre of majesty, and Nahoot exulted when they saw them.

'The symbols of kingship. Proof on proof that this is Mamose the Eighth, ruler of the Upper and Lower Kingdoms of ancient Egypt.'

He moved up to the king's still veiled head, but von Schiller stopped him. 'Leave that until last!' he ordered. 'I am not yet ready to look upon the face of Pharaoh.'

So Nahoot and Reeper transferred their attention to the king's lower body. As they lifted away each layer of linen, so were revealed scores of amulets that the embalmers had placed beneath the bandages as charms to protect the dead man. They were of gold and carved jewels and ceramic in glowing colours and marvellous shapes – all the birds of the air and the creatures of the land and the fish of the Nile waters. They photographed each amulet *in situ* before working it free and placing it into a numbered slot in the trays that had been set out upon the workbench.

Pharaoh's feet were as small and delicate as his hands, and each toe was laden with precious rings. Only his head was still covered, and both men looked enquiringly at von Schiller. 'It is very late, Herr von Schiller,' Reeper said, 'if you wish to rest—'

'Continue!' he ordered brusquely. So they moved up on each side of the mummy's head, while von Schiller remained on his stand between them.

Gradually the king's face was exposed to the light, for the first time in nearly four thousand years. His hair was thin and wispy, still red with the henna dye he had used in his lifetime. His skin had been cured with aromatic resins until it was hard as polished amber. His nose was thin and beaked. His lips were drawn back in a soft, almost dreamy smile which exposed the gap in his front teeth.

The resin coated his eyelashes, so that they seemed wet with tears and the lids only half-shut. Life seemed to gleam there still, and only when von Schiller leaned closer did he realize that the light in those ancient sockets was the reflection from the white porcelain discs that the undertakers had placed in the empty sockets during the embalming.

On his brow the Pharaoh wore the sacred *uraeus* crown. Every detail of the cobra head was still perfect. There was no wearing or abrading of the soft metal. The serpent's fangs were sharp and recurved, and the long forked tongue curled between them. The eyes were of shining blue glass. On the band of gold beneath the hooded asp was engraved the royal cartouche of Mamose.

'I want that crown.' Von Schiller's voice was choking with passion. 'Remove it, so that I can hold it in my own hands.'

'We may not be able to lift it without damaging the head of the royal mummy,' Nahoot protested.

'Do not argue with me. Do as I tell you.'

'Immediately, Herr von Schiller,' Nahoot capitulated. 'But it will take time to free it. If Herr von Schiller wishes to rest now, we will inform you when we have loosened the crown and have it ready for you.'

The circle of gold had adhered to the resin-soaked skin of the king's forehead. In order to remove it Nahoot and Reeper first had to lift the complete body out of the coffin and lay it on the stainless steel mortuary stretcher which already waited to receive it. Then the resin had to be softened and removed with specially prepared solvents. The whole process took as long as Nahoot had predicted, but finally it was completed.

They laid the golden *uraeus* upon a blue velvet cushion, as if for a coronation ceremony. They dimmed all the other lights in the main chamber of the vault, and arranged a single spot to fall upon the crown. Then they both went upstairs to inform von Schiller.

He would not let the two archaeologists accompany him when he returned to the vaults to view the crown. Only Utte Kemper was with him when he keyed the lock to the armoured door of the vault, and the heavy door slid open.

The first thing that caught von Schiller's eye as he entered the vault was the glittering crown in its velvet nest.

Immediately he began to wheeze for air like an asthmatic, and he seized her hand and squeezed until her knuckles crackled with the pressure and she whimpered with pain. But the pain excited her. Von Schiller undressed her, placed the golden crown upon her head and laid her naked in the open coffin.

'I am the promise of life,' she whispered from the ancient coffin. 'Mine is the shining face of immortality.'

He did not touch her. Naked, he stood over the coffin with his inflamed and swollen rod thrusting from the base of his belly like a creature with separate life.

She ran her hands slowly down her own body, and as they reached her mons Veneris, she intoned gravely, 'May you live for ever!'

The wondrous efficacy of the crown of Mamose was proven beyond any doubt. Nothing before had produced this effect upon Gotthold von Schiller. For at her words, the purple head of his penis erupted of its own accord and glistening silver strings of his semen dribbled down and splattered upon her soft white belly.

In the open coffin Utte Kemper arched her back, and writhed in her own consuming orgasm.

It seemed to Royan that she had been away from Egypt for years instead of weeks. She realized just how much she had missed the crowded and bustling streets of the city, the wondrous smells of spices and food and perfume in the bazaars, and the wailing voice of the muezzin calling the faithful to prayer from the turrets of the mosques.

That very first morning she left her flat in Giza while it was still dark, and since her injured knee was still swollen and painful she used her stick as she limped along the banks of the Nile. She watched the dawn cobble the river waters with a pathway of gold and copper and set the triangular sails of the feluccas ablaze.

This was a different Nile from the one she had encountered in Ethiopia. This was not the Abbay, but the true Nile. It was broader and slower, and the muddy stink of it was familiar and well beloved. This was her river and her land. She found that her resolve to do what she had come home to do was reinforced. Her doubts were set at rest, her conscience soothed. As she turned away from it she felt strong and sure of herself and the course that she must take.

She visited Duraid's family. She had to make amends to them for her sudden departure and her long, unexplained absence. At first her brother-in-law was cool and stiff towards her; but after his wife had wept and embraced Royan and the children had clambered all over her – she was always their favourite *ammah* – he warmed to her and relented sufficiently to offer to drive her out to the oasis. When she explained that she wanted to be alone when she visited the cemetery, he unbent so far as to lend her his beloved Citroën.

As she stood beside Duraid's grave the smell of the desert filled her nostrils and the hot breeze fidgeted with her hair. Duraid had loved the desert. She was glad for him that from now onwards he would always be close to it. The headstone was simple and traditional: just his name and dates under the outline of the cross. She knelt beside it and tidied the grave, renewing the wilted and dried bouquets of flowers with those that she had brought with her from Cairo.

Then she sat quietly beside him for a long while. She made no rehearsed speeches, but simply ran over in her mind so many of the good quiet times they had passed together. She remembered his kindness and his understanding, and the security and warmth of his love for her. She regretted that she had never been able to return it in the same measure, but she knew that he had accepted and understood that.

She hoped that he also understood why she had come back now. This was a leave-taking. She had come to say goodbye. She had mourned him and, although she would always remember him and he would always be a part of her, it was time for her to move on. It was time for him to let her go. When at last she left the cemetery, she walked away without looking back.

She took the long road around the south side of the lake to avoid having to pass the burnt-out villa; she did not wish to be reminded of that night of horror on which Duraid had died there. It was therefore after dark when she returned to the city, and the family were relieved to see her. Her brother-in-law walked three times around the Citroën, checking for damage to the paintwork, before ushering her into the house where his wife had set a feast for them.

Atalan Abou Sin, the minister whom Royan had come specifically to see, was out of Cairo on an official visit to Paris. She had three days to wait for his return, and because she knew that Nahoot Guddabi was no longer in Cairo, she felt safe and able to spend much of that time at the museum. She had many friends there, and they were delighted to see her and to bring her up to date with all that had happened during the time that she had been away.

The rest of the time she spent in the museum reading room, going over the microfilm of the Taita scrolls, searching for any clues that she might have missed in her previous readings. There was a section of the second scroll which she read carefully and from which she made extensive notes. Now that the prospect of finding the tomb of Pharaoh Mamose intact had become real and credible, her interest in what that tomb might contain had been stimulated.

The section of the scroll upon which she concentrated was a description that the scribe, Taita, had given of a royal visit by the Pharaoh to the workshops of the necropolis, where his funerary treasure was being manufactured and assembled within the walls of the great temple that he had built for his own embalming. According to Taita they had visited the separate workshops, first the armoury with its collection of accoutrements of the battlefield and the chase, and then the furniture workshop, home of exquisite workmanship. In the studio of the sculptors, Taita described the work on the statues of the gods and the life-sized images of the king in every different activity of his life that would line the long causeway from the necropolis to the tomb in the Valley of the Kings. In this workshop the masons were also hard at work on the massive granite sarcophagus which would house the king's mummy over the ages. However, according to Taita's later account history had cheated Pharaoh Mamose of this part of his treasure, and all these heavy and unwieldy items of stone had been abandoned and left behind in the Valley of the Kings when the Egyptians fled south along the Nile to the land they called Cush, to escape the Hyksos invasion that overwhelmed their homeland.

As Royan turned with more attention to the scribe's description of the studio of the goldsmiths, the phrase which he used to describe the golden death-mask of the Pharaoh struck her forcibly. *'This was the peak and the zenith. All the unborn ages might one day marvel at its splendour.'* Royan looked up dreamily from the microfilm and wondered if those words of the ancient scribe were not prophetic. Was she destined to be one of those who would marvel at the splendour of the golden death-mask? Might she be the first to do so in almost four thousand years? Might she touch this wonder, take it up in her hands and at last do with it as her conscience dictated?

Reading Taita's account left Royan with a sense of ancient suffering, and a feeling of compassion for the people of those times. They were, after all – no matter how far removed in time – her own people. As a Coptic Egyptian, she was one of their direct descendants. Perhaps this empathy was the main reason why, even as a child, she had originally determined to make her life's work a study of these people and the old ways.

However, she had much else to think of during those days of waiting for the return of Atalan Abou Sin. Not least of these were her feelings for Nicholas Quenton-Harper. Since she had visited the little cemetery at the oasis and made her peace with Duraid's memory, her thoughts of Nicholas had taken on a new poignancy. There was so much she was still uncertain of, and there were so many difficult choices to make. It was not possible to fulfil all her plans and desires without sacrificing others almost equally demanding.

When at last the hour of her appointment to see Atalan came around, she had difficulty bringing herself to go to him. Like somebody in a trance she limped through the bazaars, using her stick to protect her injured knee, hardly hearing the merchants calling their wares to her.

From her skin tone and European clothing they presumed she must be a tourist.

She hesitated so long over taking this irrevocable step that she was almost an hour late for the appointment. Fortunately this was Egypt, and Atalan was an Arab to whom time did not have the same significance as it did to the Western part of Royan's make-up.

He was his usual urbane and charming self. Today, in the privacy of his own office, he was comfortably dressed in a white *dishdasha* and a headcloth. He shook hands with her warmly. If this had been London he might have kissed her cheek, but not here in the East where a man never kissed any woman but his wife and then only in the privacy of their home.

He led her through to his private sitting room, where his male secretary served them small cups of tar-thick coffee and lingered to preserve the propriety of this meeting. After an exchange of compliments and the obligatory interval of polite small-talk, Royan could come obliquely to the main reason for her visit.

'I have spent much of the last few days at the museum, working in the reading room. I managed to see many of my old colleagues there, and I was surprised to hear that Nahoot had withdrawn his application for the post of director.'

Atalan sighed, 'My nephew is a headstrong boy at times. The job was his, but at the very last moment he came to tell me that he had been offered another in Germany. I tried to dissuade him. I told him that he would not enjoy the northern climate after being brought up in the Nile valley. I told him that there are many things in life such as country and family that no amount of money can recompense. But—' Atalan spread his hands in an eloquent gesture.

'So who have you chosen to fill the post of director?' she asked with an innocence that did not deceive him.

'We have not yet made any permanent appointment. Nobody automatically comes to mind, now that Nahoot has withdrawn. Perhaps we will be forced to advertise internationally. I for one would be very sad to see it go to a foreigner, no matter how well qualified.'

'Your excellency, may I speak to you in private?' Royan asked, and glanced significantly at the male secretary hovering at the doorway. Atalan hesitated only a moment.

'Of course.' He gestured to the secretary to leave the room, and when he had withdrawn and closed the door behind him Atalan leaned towards her and dropped his voice slightly. 'What is it that you wish to discuss, my dear lady?'

It was an hour later that Royan left him. He walked with her as far as the lift outside his suite of offices.

287

As he shook hands his voice was low and mellifluous, 'We will meet again soon, inshallah.'

When the Egyptair flight landed at Heathrow and Royan left the airport arrivals hall for a place in the queue at the taxi rank outside, it seemed that the temperature difference from Cairo was at least fifteen degrees. Her train arrived at York in the damp misty cold of late afternoon. From the railway station she phoned the number that Nicholas had given her.

'You silly girl,' he scolded her. 'Why didn't you let me know you were on your way? I would have met you at the airport.'

She was surprised at how pleased she was to see him, and at how much she had missed him, as she watched him step out of the Range Rover and come striding towards her on those long legs. He was bare-headed and obviously had not subjected himself to a haircut since she had last seen him. His dark hair was rumpled and wind-tossed and the silver wings fluffed over his ears.

'How's the knee?' he greeted her. 'Do you still need to be carried?'

'Almost better now. Nearly time to throw away the stick.' She felt a sudden urge to throw her arms around his neck, but at the last moment she prevented herself from making a display and merely offered him a cold, rosy brown cheek to kiss. He smelt good – of leather and some spicy aftershave, and of clean virile manhood.

In the driver's seat he delayed starting the engine for a moment, and studied her face in the street light that streamed in through the side window.

'You look mighty pleased with yourself, madam. Cat been at the cream?'

'Just pleased to see old friends,' she smiled, 'but I must admit Cairo is always a tonic.'

'No supper laid on. Thought we would stop at a pub. Do you fancy steak and kidney pud?'

'I want to see my mother. I feel so guilty. I don't even know how her leg is mending.'

'Popped in to see her day before yesterday. She's doing fine. Loving the new puppy. Named it Taita, would you believe?'

'You are really a very kind person – I mean, taking the trouble to visit her.'

'I like her. One of the good old ones. They don't build them like that any more. I suggest we have a bite to eat, and then I will pick up a bottle of Laphroaig and we will go and see her.'

It was after midnight when they left Georgina's cottage. She had dispensed rough frontier justice to the malt whisky that Nicholas had brought and now she waved them off, standing in the kitchen doorway, clutching her new puppy to her ample bosom and teetering slightly on her plaster-cast leg.

'You are a bad influence on my mother,' Royan told him.

'Who's a bad influence on whom?' he protested. 'Some of those jokes of hers turned the Stilton a richer shade of blue.'

'You should have let me stay with her.'

'She has Taita to keep her company now. Besides, I need you close at hand. Plenty of work to do. I can't wait to show you what I have been up to since you went swanning off to Egypt.'

The Quenton Park housekeeper had prepared her a bedroom in the flat in the lanes behind York Minster.

As Nicholas carried her bags up the stairs rip-saw snoring came from behind the door of the bedroom on the second landing, and she looked at Nicholas enquiringly.

'Sapper Webb,' he told her. 'Latest addition to the team. Our own engineer. You will meet him tomorrow, and I think you will like him. He is a fisherman.'

'What's that got to do with me liking him?'

'All the best people are fishermen.'

'Present company excluded,' she laughed. 'Are you staying at Quenton Park?'

'Giving the house a wide berth, for the time being.' He shook his head. 'Don't want it bruited about that I am back in England. There are some fellows from Lloyd's that I would rather not speak to at the moment. I will be in the small bedroom on the top floor. Call if you need me.'

When she was alone she looked around the tiny chintzy room with its own doll's house bathroom, and the double bed that took up most of the floor area. She remembered his remark about calling if she needed him, and she looked up at the ceiling just as she heard him drop one of his shoes on the floor.

'Don't tempt me,' she whispered. The smell of him lingered in her nostrils, and she remembered the feel of his lean hard body, moist with sweat, pressed against hers as he had carried her up out of the Abbay gorge. Hunger and need were two words she had not thought of for many years. They were starting to loom too large in her existence.

'Enough of that, my girl,' she chided herself, and went to run a bath.

icholas pounded on her door the next morning on his way downstairs.

'Come along, Royan. Life is real. Life is urgent.'

It was still pitch dark outside, and she groaned softly and asked, 'What time is it?' But he was gone, and faintly she could hear him whistling 'The Big Rock Candy Mountain' somewhere downstairs.

She checked her watch and groaned again. 'Whistling at six-thirty, after what he and Mummy did to the Laphroaig last night. I don't believe it. The man is truly a monster.'

Twenty minutes later she found him in a dark blue fisherman's sweater and jeans and a butcher's apron, working in the kitchen.

'Slice toast for three, there's a love.' He gestured towards the brown loaf that lay beside the electric toaster. 'Omelettes coming up in five minutes.'

She looked at the other man in the room. He was middle-aged, with wide shoulders and sleeves rolled up high around muscular biceps, and he was as bald as a cannonball.

'Hello,' she said, 'I am Royan Al Simma.'

'Sorry.' Nicholas waved the egg-whisk. 'This is Danny – Daniel Webb, known as Sapper to his friends.'

Danny stood up with a cup of coffee in his big competent-looking fist. 'Pleased to meet you, Miss Al Simma. May I pour you a cup of coffee?' The top of his head was freckled, and she noticed how blue his eyes were.

'Dr Al Simma,' Nicholas corrected him.

'But please call me Royan,' she cut in quickly, 'and yes, I'd love a cup.'

There was no mention of Ethiopia or Taita's game during breakfast, and Royan ate her omelette and listened respectfully to a passionate dissertation on how to catch sail fish on a fly rod from Sapper, while Nicholas heckled him mercilessly, calling into question almost every statement he made. Very obviously they had a good relationship, and she supposed she would become accustomed to all the angling jargon.

As soon as breakfast was over, Nicholas stood up with the coffee pot in one hand. 'Bring your mugs, and follow me.'

He led Royan to the front sitting room. 'I have a surprise for you. My people up at the museum worked round the clock to get it ready for you.'

He threw open the door of the sitting room, with an imitation of a trumpet flourish, 'Tarantara!'

On the centre table stood a fully mounted model of the striped dik-dik, crowned with the pricked horns and clad in the skin that Nicholas had smuggled back from Africa. It was so realistic that for a moment she expected it to leap off the table and dash away as she walked towards it.

'Oh, Nicky. It's beautifully done!' She circled it appraisingly. 'The artist has captured it exactly.'

The model brought back to her vividly the heat and smell of the bush in the gorge, and she felt a twinge of nostalgia and sadness for the delicate, beautiful creature. Its glass eyes were deceptively lifelike and bright, and the end of its proboscis looked wet and gleaming as though it was about to wiggle it and sniff the air.

'I think it's splendid. Glad you agree with me.' He stroked the soft, smooth hide. She felt this was not the moment to spoil his boyish pleasure. 'As soon as we have sorted out Taita's puzzle, I intend writing a paper on it for the Natural History Museum, the same lads that called Great-grandpapa a liar. Restore the family honour.' He laughed and spread a dust-sheet over the model. Carefully he lifted it down from the table and placed it safely in a corner of the room where it was out of harm's way.

'That was the first surprise I had saved up for you. But now for the big one.' He pointed to a sofa against one wall. 'Take a seat. I don't want you to be bowled over by this.'

She smiled at his nonsense, but went obediently to the furthest end of the sofa and curled her legs under her as she settled there. Sapper Webb came to sit awkwardly at the other end, obviously uncomfortable at being so close to her.

'Let's talk about how we are going to get into the chasm on the Dandera river,' Nicholas suggested. 'Sapper and I have talked about nothing else the whole time that you have been away.'

'That and catching fish, I'll warrant.' She grinned at him, and he looked guilty.

'Well, both subjects involve water. That is my justification.' His expression became serious. 'You recall that we discussed the idea of exploring the depths of Taita's pool with scuba gear, and I explained the difficulties.'

'I remember,' she agreed. 'You said the pressure into the underwater opening was too great, and that we would have to find another method of getting in there.'

'Correct.' Nicholas smiled mysteriously. 'Well, Sapper here has already earned the exorbitant fee that I have promised him – promised, I emphasize, not yet paid. He has come up with the alternative method.'

Now she too became serious and unfolded her legs. She placed both feet on the floor and leaned forward attentively, with her elbows on her knees and her chin cupped in her hands.

'It must have been all those brains of his that pushed out his hair. I mean, it's very neat thinking. Although it was staring us both in the face, neither you nor I thought of it.'

'Stop it, Nicky,' she told him ominously, 'you are doing it again.'

'I am going to give you a clue.' He ignored the warning and went on teasing her blithely. 'Sometimes the old ways are the best. That's the clue.'

'If you are so clever, how come you aren't famous?' she began, and then broke off as the solution occurred to her. 'The old ways? You mean, the same way as Taita did it? The same way he reached the bottom of the pool without the benefit of diving equipment?'

'By George! I think she's got it!' Nicholas put on a convincing Rex Harrison imitation.

'A dam.' Royan clapped her hands. 'You propose to redam the river at the same place where Taita built his dam four thousand years ago.'

'She's got it!' Nicholas laughed. 'No flies on our girl! Show her your drawings, Sapper.'

Sapper Webb made no attempt to disguise his self-satisfaction as he went to the board that stood against the facing wall. Royan had noticed it, but had paid no attention to it, until now he pulled away the cover and proudly displayed the illustrations that were pegged to it.

She recognized immediately the enlargements of the photographs that Nicholas had taken at the putative site of Taita's dam on the Dandera river, and others that he had taken in the ancient quarry that Tamre had shown them. These had been liberally adorned with calculations and lines in thick black marker pen.

'The major has provided me with estimates of the dimensions of the river bed at this point, and he has also calculated the height that we will have to raise the wall to induce a flow down the former course. I have, of course, allowed for errors in these calculations. Even if these errors are in the region of thirty per cent, I believe that the project is still feasible with the very limited equipment we will have available to us.'

'If the ancient Egyptians could do it, it will be a breeze for you, Sapper.'

'Kind of you to say so, major, but "breeze" is not the word I would have chosen.'

He turned to the drawings pegged beside the photographs on the board, and Royan saw that they were plans and elevations of the project based upon the photographs and Nicholas's estimates.

'There are a number of different methods of dam construction, but these days most of them presuppose the availability of reinforced concrete and heavy earth-moving equipment. I understand that we will not have the benefit of these modern aids.'

'Remember Taita,' Nicholas exhorted him. 'He did it without bulldozers.'

'On the other hand, the Egyptians probably had unlimited numbers of slaves at their disposal.'

'Slaves I can promise you. Or the modern equivalent thereof. Unlimited numbers? Well, perhaps not.'

'The more labour you can provide, the sooner I can divert the flow of the river for you. We are agreed that this has to be done before the onset of the rainy season.'

'We have two months at the most.' Nicholas dropped his flippant attitude. 'As regards the provision of labour, I will be relying on enlisting the aid of the monastic community at St Frumentius. I am still working out a sound theological reason that might convince them to take part in the building of the dam. I don't think they will fall for the idea that we have discovered the site of the Holy Sepulchre in Ethiopia and not in Jerusalem.'

'You find me the labour, and I will build your dam,' Sapper grunted. 'As you said earlier, the old ways are the best. It is almost certain that the ancients would have used a system of gabions and coffer dams to lay the foundations of the original dam.'

'Sorry,' Royan interrupted. 'Gabions? I don't have an engineering degree.'

'I am the one who must apologize.' Sapper made a clumsy attempt at chivalry. 'Let me show you my drawings.' He turned to the board. 'What this fellow Taita probably did was to weave huge bamboo baskets, which he placed in the river and filled with rock and stone. These are what we call gabions.' He indicated the plans on the board. 'After that he would have used rough-cut timber to build circular walls between the gabions – the coffer dams. These he would also have filled with stone and earth.'

'I get the general idea,' Royan said, sounding dubious, 'but then it is not really necessary for me to understand all the details.'

'Right you are!' Sapper agreed heartily. 'Although the major assures me that there is all the timber we will need on the site, I plan to use wire mesh for the construction of the gabions and human labour for the filling of the mesh nets with stone and aggregate.'

'Wire mesh?' Royan demanded. 'Where do you hope to find that in the Abbay valley?'

Sapper began to reply, but Nicholas forestalled him. 'I will come to that in a moment. Let Sapper finish his lecture. Don't spoil his fun. Tell Royan about the stone from the quarry. She will enjoy that.'

'Although I have designed the dam as a temporary structure, we have to make certain that it is capable of holding back the river long enough to enable the members of our team to enter the underwater tunnel in the downstream pool safely—'

'We call it Taita's pool,' Nicholas told him, and Sapper nodded.

'We have to make sure that the dam does not burst while people are in there. You can imagine the consequences, should that happen.'

He was silent for a moment while he let them dwell upon the possibility. Royan shuddered slightly and hugged her own arms.

'Not very pleasant,' Nicholas agreed. 'So you plan to use the blocks?' he prompted Sapper.

'That's right. I have studied the photographs taken in the quarry. I have picked out over a hundred and fifty granite blocks lying there completed or almost completed, and I calculate that if we use these in combination with the steel mesh gabions and the timber coffer walls, this would give us a firm foundation for the main dam wall.'

'Those blocks must weigh many tons each,' Royan pointed out. 'How will you move them?' Then, as Sapper opened his mouth to explain, she changed her mind. 'No! don't tell me. If you say it's possible, I will take your word for it.'

'It's possible,' Sapper assured her.

'Taita did it,' Nicholas said. 'We will be doing it all his way. That should please you. After all, he is a relative of yours.'

'You know, you are right. In a strange sort of way, it does give me pleasure.' She smiled at him. 'I think it's a good omen. When does all this happen?'

'It's happening already,' Nicholas told her. 'Sapper and I have already ordered all the stores and equipment that we will be taking with us. Even the mesh for the gabions has been precut to size by a small engineering firm near here. Thanks to the recession, they had machines standing idle.'

'I have been down there at their workshop every day, supervising the cutting and packing,' Sapper butted in. 'Half the shipment is already on its way. The rest of it will follow before the weekend.'

'Sapper is leaving this afternoon to take charge and get it all loaded. You and I have some last-minute arrangements to see to, and then we will follow him at the end of the week. You must remember I was not expecting you back from Cairo so soon,' Nicholas said. 'If I had known, I could have arranged for us all to fly down to Valletta together.'

'Valletta?' Royan looked mystified. 'As in Malta? I thought we were going to Ethiopia.'

'Malta is where Jannie Badenhorst has his base.'

'Jannie who?'

'Badenhorst. Africair.'

'Now you have really lost me.'

'Africair is an air transport company that owns one old ex-RAF Hercules, flown by Jannie and his son Fred. They use Malta as their base. It's a stable and pragmatic little country – no African politics, no corruption – and yet it is the door to most of the destinations in the Middle East and in the northern half of Africa where Jannie and Fred do most of their work. His main employment is smuggling booze into the Islamic countries, where of course it is prohibited. He's the Al Capone of the Mediterranean. Bootlegging is big business in that part of the world, but he does take on other work. Duraid and I flew into Libya from there with Jannie on our little jaunt to the Tibesti Massif. Jannie will be taking us down to the Abbay.'

'Nicky, I don't want to be a killjoy, but you and I are now undesirable immigrants to Ethiopia. Had you overlooked that little fact? How do you propose to get back in there?'

'Through the back door,' Nicholas grinned, 'and my old pal Mek Nimmur is the gatekeeper.'

'You have been in contact with Mek?'

'With Tessay. It seems that she is now his go-between. I imagine it's very convenient for Mek to have her on board. She has all the right connections, and she can slip in and out of Khartoum or Addis or places where it might be awkward or even dangerous for him to be seen.'

'Well, well!' Royan looked impressed. 'You have been busy.'

'Not all of us can afford a holiday in Cairo whenever the fancy takes us,' he told her tartly.

'One more little question.' She ignored the jibe, although she realized that despite his easy smile her absence must have irked him. 'Does Mek know about Taita's game?'

'Not in detail.' Nicholas shook his head. 'But he has some suspicions, and anyway I know I can rely on him.' He hesitated, and then went on. 'Tessay was very cagey when I spoke to her on the phone, but it seems that there has been some sort of attack on St Frumentius monastery. Jali Hora and thirty or forty of his monks were massacred, and most of the sacred relics from the church were stolen.'

'Oh, dear God, no!' Royan looked stricken. 'Who would do a thing like that?'

'The same people who murdered Duraid, and made three attempts to wipe you out.'

'Pegasus.'

'Von Schiller,' he agreed.

'Then we are directly responsible,' Royan whispered. 'We led them to the monastery. The Polaroids they captured from us when they raided our camp would have shown them the stele and the tomb of Tanus. Von Schiller wouldn't have to be a clairvoyant to guess where we had taken them. Now there is more blood on our hands.'

'Hell, Royan, how can you take responsibility for von Schiller's madness? I am not going to let you punish yourself for that.' Nicholas's tone was sharp and angry.

'We started this whole thing.'

'I don't agree with that, but I admit that von Schiller is the one who must have cleaned out the *maqdas* of St Frumentius and that the stele and the coffin are now almost certainly part of his collection.'

'Oh, Nicky, I feel so guilty. I never realized what a danger we were to those simple devout Christians.'

'Do you want to call off the whole thing?' he asked cruelly.

She thought about it seriously for a while, then shook her head.

'No. Perhaps when we go back we will be able to compensate the monks for their losses with what we find in the bottom of Taita's pool.'

'I hope so,' he agreed fervently. 'I do hope so.'

he giant Hercules C-Mk1 four-engined turbo-prop aircraft was painted a dusty nondescript brown, and the identification lettering on the fuselage was faded and indistinct. There was no Africair legend displayed anywhere on the machine, and it had a tired and scruffy appearance that spoke eloquently of the fact that it was almost forty years old and had flown well over half a million hours even before it had fallen into Jannie Badenhorst's hands.

'Does that thing still fly?' Royan asked, as she looked at it standing forlornly in a back corner of the Valletta airfield. Its drooping belly gave it the air of a sad old street-walker who had been put out of business by an unexpected and unlooked-for pregnancy.

'Jannie keeps it looking that way deliberately,' Nicholas assured her. 'The places that he flies to, it's best not to draw envious eyes.'

'He certainly succeeds.'

'But both Jannie and Fred are first-rate aero-engineers. Between them they keep Big Dolly perfect under her engine cowlings.'

'Big Dolly?'

'Dolly Parton. Jannie is an avid fan.' The taxi dropped them and their meagre luggage outside the side door of the hangar, and Nicholas paid the driver while Royan thrust her hands into the pockets of her anorak and shivered in the cold wind off the Mediterranean.

'There's Jannie now.' Nicholas pointed to the bulky figure in greasy brown overalls coming down the loading ramp of the Hercules. He saw them and jumped down off the ramp.

'Hello, man! I was beginning to give up on you,' he said as he came shambling across the tarmac. He looked like a rugby player, as he had been in his youth, and the slight limp was from an old playing-field injury.

'We were late leaving Heathrow. Strike by French air traffic control.

The joys of international travel,' Nicholas told him, and then introduced Royan.

'Come and meet my new secretary,' Jannie invited. 'She may even give you a cup of coffee.'

He led them through a wicket in the main hangar door and into the cavernous interior. There was a small office cubicle beside the entrance with a sign over the door saying 'Africair' and the company logo of a winged battleaxe. Mara, Jannie's new secretary, was a Maltese lady only a few years younger than himself. What she lacked in youth and beauty she fully made up for across the chest.

'Jannie likes them mature and with plenty of top hamper,' Nicholas murmured to Royan from the side of his mouth.

Mara gave them coffee, while Jannie went over his flight plan with Nicholas.

'It's a little complicated,' he apologized. 'As you can imagine, we will have to do a bit of ducking and diving. Muammar Gadaffi is not wallowing in affection for me at the moment, so I'd rather not overfly any of his territory. We will be going in through Egypt, but without landing there.' He pointed out their flight path on the maps spread over his desk.

'Bit of a problem over the Sudan. They are having a little civil war there.' He winked at Nicholas. 'However, the northern government are not equipped with the most up-to-date radar in the world. Lot of old Russian reject stuff. It's an enormous bit of country, and Fred and I have worked out their blank spots. We will be keeping well clear of their main military installations.'

'What's our flying time?' Nicholas wanted to know.

Jannie pulled a face. 'Big Dolly is no sprinter, and as I have just told you we will not be taking any short-cuts.'

'How long?' Nicholas insisted.

'Fred and I have rigged up bunks and a kitchen, so that during the flight you will have all the comforts of home.' He lifted his cap and scratched his head before he admitted, 'Fifteen hours.'

'Has Big Dolly got that sort of endurance?' Nicholas wanted to know.

'Extra tanks. Seventy-one thousand kilos of fuel. Even with the load you have given us, we can get there and back without refuelling.' He was interrupted by the huge hangar doors rolling open, and a heavy truck being driven through. 'That will be Fred and Sapper now.' Jannie swigged the last of his coffee and hugged Mara. She giggled, and her bosom quivered like a snowfield on the point of an avalanche.

The truck parked at the far end of the hangar, where an array of equipment and stores was already neatly stacked, ready for loading.

When Fred climbed down from the cab, Jannie introduced him to Royan. He was a younger version of the father, already beginning to spread around the waist, and with an open bucolic face, more like a Karroo sheep farmer than a commercial pilot.

'That's the last truckload.' Sapper came around the front of the truck and shook Nicholas's hand. 'All set to begin loading.'

'I want to take off before four o'clock tomorrow morning. That will get us into our rendezvous at the optimum time tomorrow evening,' Jannie cut in. 'We have a bit of work to do, if we are going to get some sleep before we leave.' He gestured to the pallets waiting to be loaded. 'I wanted to get some of the local lads to give a hand with the loading, but Sapper wouldn't hear of it.'

'Quite right,' Nicholas agreed. 'The fewer who are in on this, the merrier. Let's get cracking.'

The cargo had been prepacked on the steel pallets, secured with heavy nylon strapping and covered with cargo netting. There were thirty-six loaded pallets, and the canvas packs containing the parachutes formed an integral part of each load. This huge cargo would require two separate flights to ferry it all across to Africa.

Royan called out the contents of each pallet from the typed manifest, while Nicholas checked it against the actual load. Nicholas and Sapper had worked out the loads carefully to ensure that the items that would be required first were on the initial flight. Only when he was certain that each pallet was complete in every detail did he signal to Fred, who was operating the forklift. Fred ran the arms into the slots of the pallet and lifted it, then he drove it out of the hangar and up the ramp of the Hercules.

In the hold of the enormous aircraft, Jannie and Sapper helped Fred to position each pallet precisely on the rollers and then strap it down securely. The last part of the cargo to go aboard was the small front-end-loading tractor. Sapper had found this in a secondhand yard in York, and after testing it exhaustively declared it to be a 'steal'. Now he drove this up the ramp under its own power, and lovingly strapped it down to the rollers.

The tractor made up almost a third of the total weight of the entire shipment, but it was the one item that Sapper considered essential if they were to complete the earthworks for the dam in the time that Nicholas had stipulated. He had calculated that it would require a cluster of five cargo parachutes to get the heavy tractor back to earth without damage. Fuel for it would of course present a problem, and the bulk of the second cargo would be made up of dieseline in special nylon tanks that could withstand the impact of an airdrop.

It was after midnight before the aircraft was loaded with the first shipment. The remaining pallets were still stacked against the hangar wall awaiting Big Dolly's return for the second flight. Now they could turn their full attention to the farewell banquet of island specialities that Mara had laid out for them in the tiny Africair office.

'Yes,' Jannie assured them, 'she's also a good cook,' and gave Mara a loving squeeze as she rested her bosom on his shoulder, leaning over him to refill his plate with calamari.

'Happy landings!' Nicholas gave them the toast in red Chianti.

'Eight hours between the throttle and the bottle,' Jannie apologized, as he drank the toast in Coca-Cola.

They lay down in their clothes to get a few hours' sleep on the bunks bolted to the bulkhead behind the flight deck, but it seemed to Royan that she was woken only a few minutes later by the quiet voices of the two pilots completing their pre-take-off checks, and the whine of the starters on the huge turbo-prop engines. As Jannie spoke on the radio to the control tower, and Fred taxied out to the holding point, the three passengers climbed out of their bunks and strapped themselves into the folding seats down the side of the main cabin. Big Dolly climbed into the night sky and the lights of the island dwindled and were swiftly lost behind them. Then there was only the dark sea below and the bright pricking of the stars above. Royan turned her head to smile at Nicholas in the dim overhead lights of the cabin.

'Well, Taita, we are back on court for the final set.' Her voice was tight with excitement.

'The one good thing about being forced to sneak about like this is that Pegasus may take a while to find out that we are back in the Abbay gorge.' Nicholas looked complacent.

'Let's hope that you are right.' Royan held up her right hand and crossed her fingers. 'We will have enough to worry about with what Taita has in store for us, without Pegasus muscling in on us again just yet.'

'They are on their way back to Ethiopia,' said von Schiller with utter certainty.

'How can we be certain of that, Herr von Schiller?' Nahoot asked.

Von Schiller glared at him. The Egyptian irritated him intensely, and he was beginning to regret having employed him. Nahoot had made very little headway in deciphering the meaning of the engravings on the stele that they had taken from the monastery.

The actual translation had offered no insurmountable problems. Von Schiller was convinced that he could have done this work himself, without Nahoot's assistance, given time and the use of his extensive library of reference works. It comprised, for the most part, nonsensical rhymes and extraneous couplets out of place and context. One face of the stele was almost completely covered by columns of letters and figures that bore no relation whatsoever to the text on the other three faces of the column.

But although Nahoot would not admit it, it was clear that the underlying meaning behind most of this had eluded him. Von Schiller's patience was almost exhausted. He was tired of listening to Nahoot's excuses, and to promises that were never fulfilled. Everything about him, from his oily ingratiating tone of voice to his sad eyes in their deep lined sockets, had begun to annoy him. But especially he had come to detest his exasperating habit of questioning the statements that he, Gotthold von Schiller, made.

'General Obeid was able to inform me of their exact flight arrangements when they left Addis Ababa. It was very simple to have my security men at the airport when they arrived in England. Neither Harper nor the woman are the kind of people that are easily overlooked, even in a crowd. My men followed the woman to Cairo—'

'Excuse me, Herr von Schiller, but why did you not have her taken care of if you were aware of her movements?'

'*Dummkopf!*' von Schiller snapped at him. 'Because it now seems that she is much more likely to lead me to the tomb than you are.'

'But, sir, I have done—' Nahoot protested.

'You have done nothing but make up excuses for your own failure. Thanks to you, the stele is still an enigma,' von Schiller interrupted him contemptuously.

'It is very difficult—'

'Of course it is difficult. That's why I am paying you a great deal of money. If it were easy I would have done it myself. If it is indeed the instruction to find the tomb of Mamose, then the scribe Taita meant it to be difficult.'

'If I am allowed a little more time, I think I am very near to establishing the key—'

'You have no more time. Did you not hear what I have just told you? Harper is on his way back to the Abbay gorge. They flew from Malta last night in a chartered aircraft that was heavily loaded with cargo. My men were not able to establish the nature of that cargo, except that it included some earth-moving equipment, a front-end-loading tractor. To me, this can mean only one thing. They have located the tomb, and they are returning to begin excavating it.'

'You will be able to get rid of them as soon as they reach the monastery.' Nahoot relished the thought. 'Colonel Nogo will—'

'Why do I have to keep repeating myself?' Von Schiller's voice turned shrill and he slapped his hand down on the tabletop. 'They are now our best chance of finding the tomb of Mamose. The very last thing that I want to happen is that any harm should come to them.' He glared at Nahoot. 'I am sending you back to Ethiopia immediately. Perhaps you will be of some use to me there. You are certainly no use here.'

Nahoot looked disgruntled, but he had better sense than to argue again. He sat sullenly as von Schiller went on, 'You will go to the base camp and place yourself under the command of Helm. You will take your orders from him. Treat them as if they come directly from me. Do you understand?'

'Yes, Herr von Schiller,' Nahoot muttered sulkily.

'Do not interfere in any way with Harper and the woman. They must not even know that you are at the base camp. The Pegasus geological team will carry on its normal duties.' He paused and smiled bleakly, then went on, 'It is most fortunate that Helm has actually discovered very promising evidence of large deposits of galena, which as you may know is the ore from which lead is obtained. He will continue the exploratory work on these deposits, and if they bear out their promise they will make the entire operation highly profitable.'

'What exactly will be my duties?' Nahoot wanted to know.

'You will be playing the waiting game. I want you there ready to take advantage of any progress that Harper makes. However, you are to give him plenty of elbow room. You will not alert him by any overflights with the helicopter, or by approaching his camp. No more midnight raids. Every move that you make must be cleared with me before, I repeat before, you take any action.'

'If I am to operate under these restrictions, how will I know if Harper and the woman have made any progress?'

'Colonel Nogo already has a reliable man, a spy, in the monastery. He will inform us of every move that Harper makes.'

'But what about me? What will be my work?'

'You will evaluate the intelligence that Nogo collects. You are familiar with archaeological methods. You will be able to judge what Harper is trying to achieve, and you will be able to tell what success he is enjoying.'

'I see,' Nahoot muttered.

'If it were possible I would have gone back to the Abbay gorge myself. However, this is not possible. It may take time, months perhaps, before Harper makes any important progress. You know as well as anybody that these things take time.'

'Howard Carter worked for ten years at Thebes before he found the tomb of Tutankhamen,' Nahoot pointed out maliciously.

'I hope that it will not take that long,' said von Schiller coldly. 'If it does, it is very unlikely that you will still be involved with the search. As for myself, I have a series of very important negotiations coming up here in Germany, as well as the annual general meeting of the company. These I cannot miss.'

'You will not be coming back to Ethiopia at all, then?' Nahoot perked up at the prospect of escaping from von Schiller's malignant influence.

'I will come as soon as there is something for me there. I will be relying on you to decide when my presence is needed.'

'What about the stele? I should—'

'You will continue to work on the translation.' Von Schiller forestalled his objections. 'You will take a full set of photographs with you to Ethiopia, and you will continue your work while you are there. I shall expect you to report to me by satellite, at least once a week, on your progress.'

'When do you want me to leave?'

'Immediately. Today if that is possible. Speak to Fräulein Kemper. She will make your travel arrangements.'

For the first time during the interview Nahoot looked happy.

ig Dolly droned on steadily south-eastwards, and there was very little to relieve the boredom of the flight. The dawn was just breaking when they crossed the African coast at a remote and lonely desert beach that Jannie had chosen for just this reason. Once they were over the land there was as little of interest to see as there had been over the sea. The desert stretched away, bleak and brown and featureless in every direction.

At irregular intervals they heard Jannie in the cockpit speaking to air traffic control, but as they were able to hear only half the conversation they had no idea as to the identity or the nationality of the station. Occasionally Jannie dropped the heavily accented English he was affecting and broke into Arabic. Royan was surprised by Jannie's fluency in the language, but then as an Afrikaner the guttural sounds came naturally to him. He was even able to mimic the different accents and dialecs of Libyan and Egyptian convincingly as he lied his way across the desert.

For the first few hours Sapper pored over his dam drawings; then, unable to proceed further until he had the exact measurements of the site, he curled up on his bunk with a paperback novel. The unfortunate author was unable to hold his attention for long. The open book sagged down over his face, and the pages fluttered every time he emitted a long grinding snore.

Nicholas and Royan huddled on her bunk with the chessboard between them, until hunger overtook them and they moved to the makeshift galley. Here Royan took the subservient role of bread-slicer and coffee-maker, while Nicholas demonstrated his artistry in creating a range of Dagwood sandwiches. They shared the food with Jannie and Fred, perched up behind the pilots' seats in the cockpit.

'Are we still over Egyptian territory?' Royan asked.

With his mouth full, Jannie pointed out over the port wingtip of Big Dolly. 'Fifty nautical miles out there is Wadi Halfa. My father was killed there in 1943. He was with the Sixth South African Division. They called it Wadi Hellfire.' He took another monstrous bite of sandwich. 'I never knew the old man. Fred and I landed there once. Tried to find his grave.' He shrugged eloquently. 'It's a hell of a big piece of country. Lots of graves. Very few of them marked.'

Nobody spoke for a while. They chewed their sandwiches, thinking their own thoughts. Nicholas's father had also fought in the desert against Rommel. He had been more fortunate than Jannie's father.

Nicholas glanced across at Royan. She was staring out of the window at her homeland, and there was something so passionate and fraught in her gaze that Nicholas was startled. The temptation to think of her as an English girl, like her mother, was at most times irresistible. It was only in odd moments such as these that he became intensely aware of the other facets of her being.

She seemed unaware of his scrutiny. Her preoccupation was total. He wondered what she was thinking – what dark and mysterious thoughts were smouldering there. He remembered how she had seized the very first opportunity on their return from Ethiopia to hurry back to Cairo, and once again a feeling of disquiet came over him. He wondered if other emotional ties of which he was unaware might not transcend those loyalties which he had taken for granted. He realized with something of a shock that they had been together for only a few short weeks, and despite the strong attraction that she exerted over him he knew very little about her.

At that moment she started and looked round at him quickly. Crowded as they were at the portside window, they stared into each other's eyes from a distance of only a foot or so. It was only for a few seconds but what he saw in her eyes, the dark shadows of guilt or some other emotion, did nothing to allay his misgivings.

She turned back to Jannie, leaning over his shoulder to ask, 'When will we cross the Nile?'

'On the other side of the border. The Sudanese government concentrate all their attentions on the rebels in the far south. There are some stretches of the river here in the north that are completely deserted. Pretty soon now we will be going down right on the deck, to get under the radar pings from the Sudanese stations around Khartoum. We will slip through one of the gaps.'

Jannie lifted the aeronautical map on its clipboard from his lap, and held it so she could see it. With one thick, stubby finger he showed Royan their intended route. It was drawn in with blue wax pencil, 'Big Dolly has taken this route so often that she could fly it without my hands on the stick, couldn't you, old girl?' He patted the instrument panel affectionately.

Two hours later, when Nicholas and Royan were back at the chess board in the main cabin, Jannie called them on the PA, 'Okay, folks. No need to panic. We are going to lose some altitude now. Come up front and watch the show.'

Strapped into fold-down seats in the back of the flight deck, they were treated to a superb exhibition of low flying by Fred. The descent was so rapid that Royan felt they were about to fall out of the sky, and that she had left her stomach back there somewhere at thirty thousand feet. Fred levelled Big Dolly out only feet above the desert floor, so low that it was like riding in a high-speed bus rather than flying. Fred lifted her delicately over each undulation of the tawny, sun-scorched terrain, skimming the black rock ridges and standing on a wingtip to swerve around the occasional wind-blasted hill.

'Nile crossing in seven and a half minutes.' Jannie punched the stopwatch fixed to the control wheel in front of him. 'And unless my navigation has gone all to hell there should be an island shaped like a shark directly under us as we cross.'

As the needle of the stopwatch came up to the mark, the broad, glittering expanse of the river flashed beneath them. Royan caught a brief glimpse of a green island with a few thatched huts on the tip, and a dozen dugout canoes lying on the narrow beach.

'Well, the old man hasn't lost his touch yet,' Fred remarked. 'Still good for a few thousand miles before we trade him in.'

'Not so much of the old man stuff, you little squirt. I have some tricks up my sleeve that I haven't even used yet.'

'Ask Mara.' Fred grinned affectionately at his father as he banked on to a new southwesterly heading, and with his wingtip so close to the ground that he scattered a herd of camels feeding in the sparse thorn scrub. They lumbered away across the plain, each trailing a wisp of white dust like a wedding train.

'Another three hours' flying time to the rendezvous.' Jannie looked up from the map. 'Spot on! We should land forty minutes before sunset. Couldn't be better.'

'I'd better go and change into my hiking gear, then.' Royan went back into the main cabin, pulled her bag from under the bunk and disappeared into the lavatory. When she emerged twenty minutes later she wore khaki culottes and a cotton top.

'These boots were made for walking.' She stamped them on the deck.

'That's fine.' Nicholas watched her from the bunk. 'But how about that knee?'

'It will get me there,' she said, defensively.

'You mean I am to be deprived of the pleasure of back-packing you again?'

The Ethiopian mountains came up so subtly on the eastern horizon that Royan was not aware of them until Nicholas pointed out to her the faint blue outline against the brighter blue of the African sky.

'Almost there.' He glanced at his wrist-watch. 'Let's go up to the flight deck.'

Looking forward through the windshield there was no landmark ahead of them – just the vast brown savannah, speckled with the black dots of acacia trees.

'Ten minutes to go,' Jannie intoned. 'Anyone see anything?' There was no reply, and they all stared ahead.

'Five minutes.'

'Over there!' Nicholas pointed over his shoulder. 'That's the course of the Blue Nile.' A denser grove of thorn trees formed a dark line far ahead. 'And there is the smokestack of the derelict sugar-mill on the river bank. Mek Nimmur says that the airstrip is about three miles from the mill.'

'Well, if it is, it's not shown on the chart,' Jannie grumbled. 'One minute before we are on the coordinates.' The minute ticked off slowly on the stopwatch.

'Still nothing—' Fred broke off as a red flare shot up from the earth directly ahead and flashed past Big Dolly's nose. Everyone in the cockpit smiled and relaxed with relief.

'Right on the nose.' Nicholas patted Jannie's shoulder in congratulations. 'Couldn't have done better myself.'

Fred climbed a few hundred feet and came round in a one-eighty turn. Now there were two signal fires burning out there on the plain – one with black smoke, the other sending a column of white straight up into the still evening sky. It was only when they were a kilometre out that they were able to make out the faint outline of the overgrown and long-disused landing strip. Roseires airstrip had been built twenty years before by a company that tried to grow sugar cane under irrigation from the Blue Nile. But Africa had won again and the company had passed into oblivion, leaving this feeble scrape mark on the plain as its epitaph. Mek Nimmur had chosen this remote and deserted place for the rendezvous.

'No sign of a reception committee,' Jannie grunted. 'What do you want me to do?'

'Continue your approach,' Nicholas told him. 'There should be another flare – ah, there it is!' The ball of fire shot up from a clump of thorn trees at the far end of the runway, and for the first time they were able to make out human figures in the bleak landscape. They had stayed hidden until the very last moment.

'That's Mek, all right! Go ahead and land.'

As Big Dolly finished her roll-out and the end of the rough and pitted runway came up ahead, a figure in camouflage fatigues popped up ahead of them. With a pair of paddles it signalled them to taxi into the space between two of the tallest thorn trees.

Jannie cut the engines and grinned at them over his shoulder. 'Well, boys and girls, looks like we pulled off another lucky one!'

Even from the height of Big Dolly's cockpit there was no mistaking the commanding figure of Mek Nimmur as he emerged from the cover of the clump of acacia trees. Only now did they realize that the trees had been shrouded with camouflage netting; this was why they had not been able to spot any sign of human presence from the air. As soon as the loading ramp was lowered, Mek Nimmur came striding up it.

'Nicholas!' They embraced and, after Mek had kissed him noisily on each cheek, he held Nicholas at arm's length and studied his face, delighted to see him again. 'So I was right! You are up to your old tricks. Not simply a dik-dik shoot, was it?'

'How can I lie to an old friend?' Nicholas shrugged.

'It always came easy to you,' Mek laughed, 'but I am glad we are going to have some fun together. Life has been very boring recently.'

'I bet!' Nicholas punched his shoulder affectionately.

A slim, graceful figure followed Mek up the ramp. In the olive-green fatigues Nicholas hardly recognized Tessay until she spoke. She wore canvas para boots and a cloth cap that made her look like a boy.

'Nicholas! Royan! Welcome back!' Tessay cried. The two women embraced as enthusiastically as the men had done.

'Come on, you Ous!' Jannie protested. 'This isn't Woodstock. I have to get back to Malta tonight. I want to take off before dark.'

Swiftly Mek took charge of the offloading. His men swarmed aboard and manhandled the pallets forward on the rollers, while Sapper started up his beloved front-end loader and used it to run the cargo down the ramp and stack it in the acacia grove under the camouflage netting. With so many hands to help it went swiftly, and Big Dolly's hold was emptied just as the sun settled wearily on to the horizon, and the short African twilight bled all colour from the landscape.

Jannie and Nicholas had one last hurried discussion in the cockpit while Fred completed his flight checks. They went over the plans and radio procedures one last time.

'Four days from today,' Jannie agreed, as they shook hands briefly.

'Let the man go, Nicholas,' Mek bellowed from below. 'We must get across the border before dawn.'

They watched Big Dolly taxi down to the end of the strip and swing around. The engine beat crescendoed as she came tearing back in a long rolling shroud of dust and lifted off over their heads. Jannie waggled his wings in farewell and, without navigation lights showing, the great aircraft blended like a black bat into the darkening sky and disappeared almost immediately.

'Come here.' Nicholas led Royan to a seat under the acacia. 'I don't want that knee to play up again.' He pushed her culottes halfway up her thigh and strapped the knee with an elastic bandage, trying not to make his pleasure in this task too apparent. He was pleased to see that the bruising had almost faded and there was no longer any swelling.

He palpated it gently. Her skin was velvety and the flesh beneath it firm and warm to the touch. He looked up, and from the expression on her face realized that she was enjoying this intimacy as much as he was. As he caught her eye she flushed slightly, and quickly smoothed down her culottes.

She jumped up and said, 'Tessay and I have a lot of catching up to do,' and hurried across to join her.

'I am leaving a full combat platoon to guard your stores here,' Mek explained to Nicholas as Tessay led Royan away. 'We will travel in a very small party as far as the border. I don't expect any trouble. There is very little enemy activity in this sector at the moment. Lots of fighting in the south, but we are quiet here. That is why I chose this rendezvous.'

'How far to the Ethiopian border?' Nicholas wanted to know.

'Five hours' march,' Mek told him. 'We will slip through one of our pipelines after the moon has set. The rest of my men are waiting in the entrance to the Abbay gorge. We should rendezvous with them before dawn tomorrow.'

'And from there to the monastery?'

'Another two days' march,' Mek replied. 'We will be there just in time to receive the drop from your fat friend in the fat plane.'

He turned away and gave his last orders to the platoon commander who would remain at Roseires to guard the stores. Then he assembled the party of six men who would form their escort across the border. Mek divided up the loads between them. The most important single item was the radio, a modern military lightweight model which Nicholas carried himself.

'Those bags of yours are too difficult to carry. You will have to repack them,' Mek told Nicholas and Royan. So they emptied their bags and stuffed the contents into the two canvas haversacks that Mek had ready for them. Two of his men slung the haversacks over their shoulders and disappeared into the darkness.

'He is not taking that!' Mek stared aghast at the bulky legs of the theodolite that Sapper had retrieved from one of the pallets. Sapper spoke no Arabic, so Nicholas had to translate.

'Sapper says that it is a delicate instrument. He cannot allow it to be dropped from the aircraft. He says that if it is damaged he will not be able to do the work he was hired for.'

'Who is going to carry it?' Mek demanded. 'My men will mutiny if I try to make them do it.'

'Tell the cantankerous bugger that I will carry it myself.' Sapper drew himself up with dignity. 'I wouldn't let one of his great clumsy oafs lay a finger on it.' He picked up the bundle, placed it over his shoulder and stalked away with a stiff back.

Mek let the advance guard have a five-minute start, and then he nodded. 'We can go now.'

Thirty minutes after Big Dolly had taken off, they left the airfield and set out across the dark and silent plain, headed into the east. Mek set a hard pace. He and Nicholas seemed to have the eyes of a pair of cats, Royan thought, as she followed close behind them. They could see in the darkness, and only a whispered warning from one of them prevented her falling into a hole or tripping over a pile of rocks in the darkness. When she did stumble, Nicholas seemed always to be there, reaching back to steady her with a strong, firm grip.

They marched in complete and disciplined silence. It was only every hour, when they rested for five minutes, that Nicholas and Mek sat close together, and from the few quiet words she picked up Royan realized that Nicholas was explaining to him the full reasons for their return to the Abbay gorge. She heard Nicholas repeat the names 'Mamose' and 'Taita' often, and Mek's deep voice questioning him at length. Then they would be up again and moving forward in the night.

After a while she lost all sense of the distance they had travelled. Only the hourly rest periods orientated her to the passage of time. Fatigue crept over her slowly, until it required an effort to lift her foot for each pace. Despite her boast, her knee was beginning to ache. Now and then she felt Nicholas touch her arm, guiding her over the rough places. At other times they would stop abruptly at some whispered warning from up front. Then they would stand quietly waiting in the darkness, nerves tensed, until at another whisper they would move on again at the same pressing pace. Once she smelt the cool muddy effluvium of the river on the dry warm night air, and she knew that they must be very close to the Nile. Without a word being spoken she sensed the nervous tension in the men ahead of her, and was aware of the alertness in the way they carried themselves and their weapons.

'Crossing the border now,' Nicholas breathed close to her face, and the tension was infectious. She forgot her tiredness, and heard her pulse beating in her own ears.

This time they did not stop for the usual rest break, but continued for another hour until slowly she felt the mood of the men changing. Someone laughed softly, and there was a lightness in their pace as they swung on towards the luminescence in the eastern sky. Abruptly the moon thrust its crescent horns above the dark silhouette of far-off mountain ranges.

'All clear. We are through,' Nicholas told her in his normal voice. 'Welcome back to Ethiopia. How are you feeling?'

'I'm okay.'

'I am tired too.' He grinned at her in the moonlight. 'Pretty soon we will camp and rest. Not much further.'

He was lying, of course: the march went on and on until she wanted to weep. And then suddenly she heard the sound of the river again, the soft rushing flow of the Nile in the dawn. Up ahead she heard Mek talking to the men who were waiting for them, and then Nicholas guided her off the path and made her sit while he knelt in front of her and unlaced her boots.

'You did well. I am proud of you,' he told her, as he stripped off her socks and examined her feet for blisters. Then he unbandaged the knee. It was slightly swollen, and he massaged it with a skilled and tender touch.

She sighed softly, 'Don't stop. That feels good.'

'I'll give you a Brufen for the inflammation.' He dug the pills out of his pack and then spread his padded jacket for her to lie on. 'Sorry, the sleeping bags are with our other gear. Have to rough it until Jannie makes his air drop.'

He passed her the water bottle, and while she swallowed the pill he pulled the tab on a pack of emergency rations. 'Not exactly gourmet fare.' He sniffed the contents. 'In the army we call them rat packs.' She fell asleep with her mouth still half-filled with tasteless meat loaf and plastic cheese.

When Nicholas woke her with a mug of hot sweet tea, she saw it was already late afternoon. He sat beside her and sipped at his own mug, noisily blowing away the steam between each mouthful.

'You will be pleased to know that Mek is now fully in the picture. He has agreed to help us.'

'What have you told him?'

'Just enough to keep him interested.' Nicholas grinned. 'The theory of progressive disclosure. Never tell everything all at once, feed it to them a little at a time. He knows what we are looking for, and that we are going to dam a river.'

'What about men to work on the dam?'

'The monks at St Frumentius will do whatever he tells them. He is a great hero.'

'What have you promised him in return?'

'We haven't got round to that yet. I told him that we have no idea what we are going to find, and he laughed and said he would trust me.'

'Silly boy, isn't he?'

'Not exactly how I would describe Mek Nimmur,' he murmured. 'I think when the time is ripe he will let us know what the price of his cooperation is.' He looked up at that moment. 'We were just talking about you, Mek.'

Mek strode up to them, and then squatted on his haunches beside Nicholas.

'What were you saying about me?'

'Royan says you are a hard bastard, pushing her on a forced march all night.'

'Nicholas is spoiling you. I have been watching him fussing over you,' he chuckled. 'What I say is, treat them rough. Women love it.' Then he grew serious. 'I am sorry, Royan. The border is always a bad place. You will find me less of a monster now we are on home ground.'

'We are very grateful for all you are doing.'

He inclined his head gravely, 'Nicholas is an old friend, and I hope that you are a new friend.'

'I have been terribly distressed. Tessay told me last night that there had been trouble at the monastery.'

Mek scowled and tugged at his short beard, pulling a tuft of hair from his own chin with the force of his anger. 'Nogo and his killers. This is just a sample of what we are fighting against. We have been rescued from the tyranny of Mengistu, only to be plunged into fresh horror.'

'What happened, Mek?'

Speaking tersely but vividly, he described the massacre and the plunder of the monastery's treasures. 'There was no doubt it was Nogo. Every one of the monks that escaped knows him well.'

His anger was too fierce for him to contain, and he stood up abruptly. 'The monastery means much to all the people of the Gojam. I was christened there, by Jali Hora himself. The murder of the abbot and the desecration of the church is a terrible outrage.' He jammed his cap down on his head. 'And now we must get on. The road ahead is steep and difficult.'

N ow that they were clear of the border, it was safe to move in daylight. The second day's march carried them into the depths of the gorge. There were no foothills: it was like entering through the keep of a vast castle. The walls of the great central massif rose up almost four thousand feet on either hand, and the river snaked along in the depths, its entire length churned by rapids and breaking white water. At noon Mek broke the march to rest in a grove of trees beside the river. There was a beach below them, sheltered by massive boulders which must have rolled down from the cliffs that hung like a rampart above them.

The five of them sat a little apart from each other. Sapper was still smarting from his altercation over the theodolite with Mek, and keeping himself aloof. He placed the heavy instrument in a conspicuous position and sat ostentatiously close to it. Mek and Tessay seemed strangely quiet and withdrawn, until suddenly Tessay reached out and grasped Mek's hand.

'I want to tell them,' she blurted out impulsively.

Mek looked away at the river for a moment before he nodded. 'Why not?' he shrugged at last.

'I want them to know,' Tessay insisted. 'They knew Boris. They will understand.'

'Do you want me to tell them?' Mek asked softly, and he was still holding her hand.

'Yes,' she nodded, 'it is best that it comes from you.'

Mek was silent for a while, gathering his words, and then he started in that low rumbling voice, not looking at them, but watching Tessay's face. 'The very first moment I looked upon this woman, I knew that she was the one that God had sent my way.'

Tessay moved closer to him.

'Tessay and I said our vows together on the night of Timkat and asked for God's forgiveness, and then I took her away as my woman.'

She laid her head upon his great muscular shoulder.

'The Russian followed us. He found us here, on this very spot. He tried to kill us both.'

Tessay looked down at the beach upon which she and Mek had so nearly died, and she shuddered at the memory.

'We fought,' he said simply, 'and when he was dead, I sent his body floating away down the river.'

'We knew he was dead,' Royan told them. 'We heard from the people at the embassy that the police found his body downstream, near the border. We didn't know how it had happened.'

They were all quiet for a while, and then Nicholas broke the silence, 'I wish I had been there to watch. It must have been one hell of a fight.' He shook his head in awe.

'The Russian was good. I am glad I don't have to fight him again,' Mek admitted, and stood up. 'We can reach the monastery before dark, if we start now.'

Mai Metemma, the newly elected abbot of St Frumentius, met them on the terrace of the monastery overlooking the river. He was only a little younger than Jali Hora had been, tall and with a dignified silver head, and today he was wearing the blue crown in honour of such a distinguished guest as Mek Nimmur.

After the visitors had bathed and rested for an hour in the cells that had been set aside for them, the monks came to lead them to the welcome feast that had been prepared. When the *tej* flasks had been refilled for the third time, and the mood of the abbot and of his monks had mellowed, Mek began to whisper into the old man's ear.

'You recall the history of St Frumentius – how God cast him up on our shore from the storm-tossed sea, so that he might bring the true faith to us?'

The abbot's eyes filled with tears. 'His holy body was entombed here, in our *maqdas*. The barbarians came and stole the relic away from us. We are children without a father. The reason for the building of this church and monastery has been taken away,' he lamented. 'No longer will the pilgrims come from every corner of Ethiopia to pray at his shrine. We will be forgotten by the Church. We are undone. Our monastery will perish and our monks will be blown away like dead leaves on the wind.'

'When St Frumentius came to Ethiopia he was not alone. Another Christian came with him from the High Church in Byzantium,' Mek reminded him in a soft, soothing rumble.

'St Antonia.' The abbot reached for his *tej* flask to allay the intensity of his sorrow.

'St Antonia,' Mek agreed. 'He died before St Frumentius, but he was no less holy than his brother.'

'St Antonia was also a great and holy man, deserving of our love and veneration.' The abbot took a long swallow from the flask.

'The ways of God are mysterious, are they not?' Mek shook his head at the wonder of the workings of the universe.

'His ways are deep and not for us to question or understand.'

'And yet he is compassionate, and he rewards the devout.'

'He is all-compassionate.' The abbot's tears overflowed and ran down his cheeks.

'You and your monastery have suffered a grievous loss. The sacred relic of St Frumentius has been taken from you – alas, never to be recovered. But what if God were to send you another? What if he were to send you the sacred body of St Antonia?'

The abbot looked up through his tears, his expression suddenly calculating. 'That would be a miracle indeed.'

Mek Nimmur placed his arm around the old man's shoulders and whispered quietly in his ear, and Mai Metemma stopped weeping and listened intently.

'I have obtained your workers for you,' Mek told Nicholas as they began the march up the valley the next morning. 'Mai Metemma has promised to give us a hundred men within two days and another five hundred to follow them within the next week. He is handing out indulgences to all those who volunteer to work on the dam. They will be spared the fires of purgatory if they take part in such a glorious project as the recovery of the holy relic of St Antonia.'

Both the women stopped in their tracks and stared at him.

'What did you promise the poor old man?' Tessay demanded.

'A body to replace the one that Nogo plundered from the church. If we do discover the tomb, then the monastery's share will be the mummy of Mamose.'

'That's a mean thing to do,' Royan exploded. 'You will cheat him into helping us.'

'It is not a cheat.' Mek's dark eyes flashed at the accusation. 'The relic that they lost was not the veritable body of St Frumentius, and yet for hundreds of years it served the purpose of uniting the community of monks and drawing Christians from all over this land. Now that it is gone, the very existence of the monastery is threatened. They have lost their reason for continuing.'

'So you are tempting them with a false promise!' Royan was still angry.

'The body of Mamose is every bit as authentic as the one they lost. What does it matter if it is the body of an ancient Egyptian rather than that of an ancient Christian, just as long as it serves as a focus for the faith and if it is the means by which the monastery might survive for another five hundred years?'

'I think Mek is making sense.' Nicholas gave his opinion.

'Since when have you been an expert in Christianity? You are an atheist,' Royan flashed at him, and he held up his hands as if to ward off a blow.

'You are right. What do I know about it anyway? You argue it out

313

with Mek. I am going to discuss the theory of dam-building with Sapper Webb.' He sauntered up to the head of the file of men and fell in beside his engineer.

From time to time he heard heated voices raised behind him, and he grinned. He knew Mek, but he was also beginning to understand the lady. It would be fascinating to see who would win this argument.

They reached the head of the chasm in the middle of the afternoon, and while Mek searched out a campsite Nicholas took Sapper immediately to the narrow neck of the river just above where it plunged over the waterfall. While Sapper set up the theodolite, Nicholas took the graduated levelling staff. Sapper ordered him up and down the face of the cliff with peremptory hand signals, all the while peering into the lens of the theodolite, while Nicholas teetered on insecure footing and tried to keep the staff upright for Sapper to take his sightings.

'Okay!' Sapper bellowed, after taking his twentieth shot. 'Now I want you on the other side of the river.'

'Fine!' Nicholas bellowed back. 'Do you want me to fly or swim?'

Nicholas hiked three miles upstream to the ford where the trail crossed the Dandera river, and then fought his way back through the tangled riverine undergrowth to the point on the bank opposite which Sapper lay in the shade smoking a soothing cigarette.

'Don't rupture yourself, will you?' Nicholas yelled across the water at him.

It was almost dark before Sapper had made all the shots he wanted, and Nicholas was still faced with the long return trip over the ford. He covered the last mile in almost total darkness, guided only by the flicker of the campfires. Wearily he stumbled into the camp and flung down the levelling staff.

'You had better tell me that it was worth it,' he growled at Sapper, who did not look up from his slide rule. He was working over his revised drawings by the glaring light of a small butane lantern.

'You weren't too far out in your estimates,' he congratulated Nicholas. 'The river is forty-one yards wide at the critical point above the falls, where I want to site the structure.'

'All I want to know is if you will be able to throw a dam across it.'

Sapper grinned and laid his finger down the side of his nose, 'You get me my ruddy front-ender, and I'll dam the bleeding Nile itself.'

After they had eaten their dinner – another of the rat packs – Royan glanced across the fire at Nicholas. When she caught his eye she inclined her head in invitation. Then she stood up and casually drifted out of camp, looking back once to make sure he was following her. Nicholas lighted the path with his torch as they picked their way back to the dam site and found a boulder overlooking the water on which to sit.

He switched off the torch and they were silent for a while as their eyes adjusted to the starlight, and then Royan whispered, 'There were times that I thought we would never return here – that it was all a dream, and that Taita's pool never existed.'

'For us perhaps it never will, without the help of the monks from the monastery.' There was a note of enquiry in his voice.

'You and Mek Nimmur win,' she chuckled softly. 'Of course we have to accept their help. Mek's arguments were very convincing.'

'So you agree that their reward should be the mummy of Mamose?'

'I agree that they may take whatever mummy we discover, if we discover one at all,' she qualified. 'For all we know, the true mummy of Mamose may be the one that Nogo stole.'

Quite naturally he slipped his arm around her shoulders, and after a moment she relaxed against him.

'Oh, Nicky, I am afraid and excited. Afraid that all our hopes are vain, and excited that we might have found the key to Taita's game.' She turned her face to his, and he felt her breath on his lips.

He kissed her, tenderly. Then he drew back with the warmth of her lingering on his lips and studied her face in the starlight. She made no movement to pull away from him. Instead she swayed towards him, and kissed him back. At first it was a staid sisterly kiss, with her mouth tightly closed. He brought his right hand up behind her head and weaved his fingers into her hair, holding her face to his. He opened his mouth over hers, and she made a little sound of dissent through her closed lips.

Slowly, voluptuously, he worked her lips apart, and her protests died away as he probed her mouth deeply with his tongue. She was making a contented little mewling sound now, like a kitten nursing on the teat, and her arms went around him. She kneaded his back with strong supple fingers, her mouth wide open to his kiss, her tongue sinuous and slippery as it twined around his.

He slid his other hand up between their bodies and unhooked the buttons of her shirt down as low as her belt. She leaned back slightly in his embrace to make it easier for him. With a delicious shock he discovered that her breasts were naked under the thin cotton shirt. He cupped one of them in his hand: it was small and firm, only just filling his hand. When he pinched the nipple gently, it stiffened between his fingers like a tiny ripe strawberry.

He broke off the kiss and bowed his head to her bosom. She moaned softly, and with one hand guided him down. When he sucked her nipple into his mouth she gasped and hooked the nails of her other hand into his back, like a cat responding to a caress. Her whole body undulated in his embrace, and after a while she pulled his mouth away. He thought for a moment that she was rejecting him, but then she moved his head across and placed her other nipple in his mouth. Once again she gasped as he sucked it in.

Her movements became more abandoned, keeping pace with his own arousal. He could restrain himself no longer and he reached up under her khaki culottes and laid his hand on the plump mound of her sex. Then with one swift lithe movement she broke away and sprang to her feet. She stood back from him, smoothing down her culottes and buttoning her shirt with fingers that trembled.

'I am so sorry, Nicky. I want to, oh God, you will never know how much I want to. But—' she shook her head and she was panting wildly, 'not yet. Please, Nicky, forgive me. I am caught between two worlds. One half of me wants this so very much, but the other half will not allow me—'

He stood up and kissed her chastely. 'There is no hurry. Good things are worth waiting for,' he told her with his mouth just touching hers. 'Come! I will take you home now.'

While it was still dark the next morning, the first levy of priests that Mai Metemma had promised came filing up the valley. Their chanting awoke the camp, and everyone came sleepily out of their thatched lean-to shelters to welcome the long column of holy men.

'Sweet heavens,' Nicholas yawned, 'it looks as though we have started another crusade. They must have left the monastery in the middle of the night to get here at this hour.' He went to find Tessay, and when he did he told her, 'You are hereby appointed official translator. Sapper speaks not a word of either Arabic or Amharic. Stick close to him.'

As soon as it was fully light, Mek and Nicholas left camp to reconnoitre a drop site. By noon they had agreed that there was only one possibility: they would have to use the valley itself. Compared to the rocky ridges that surrounded them, the floor of the valley was level and fairly free of obstructions. It was imperative that the drop should take place as close to the dam site as possible, for every mile that the stores must be manhandled would add immeasurably to the time and effort needed for the work.

'Time is the major factor,' Nicholas told Mek as they stood in the chosen drop zone the following morning. 'Every day counts from now until the rains break.'

Mek looked up at the sky. 'Pray God for late rains.'

They marked out their drop site a mile down from the river, along the stretch where the valley was widest and there was a clear approach through a gap in the hills. Jannie would need to fly straight and level for five miles under full flap and with the loading ramp down.

'Cutting it fine,' Mek remarked, as they surveyed the rugged slopes and frowning peaks that surrounded them. 'Can your fat friend fly?'

'Fly? He is half-bird,' Nicholas told him.

They moved down the valley to check the placement of the flares and the markers. The markers consisted of crosses of quartz stones laid out down the centre of the valley floor, and they would be highly visible from the air. Sapper was up at the head of the valley. They could see him there on the skyline as he moved around, setting out his smoke flares to mark the approach to the drop zone.

When Nicholas turned around and looked in the opposite direction, he could see the two women sitting on a rock together at the far end of the valley. Sapper had already helped them to set up their flares. These would mark the far limit of the zone, and give Jannie a mark for his climb out of the valley.

Nicholas then turned his attention back to Mek's men as they finished laying out the stark white quartz markers. Once these were all in place, Mek ordered the area to be cleared. Then, lugging the radio, they climbed up to join Sapper on the high ground at the head of the valley. Mek helped Nicholas string out the aerial. Then Nicholas switched on and adjusted the gain carefully before he thumbed the microphone.

'Big Dolly. Come in, Big Dolly!' Nicholas invited, but the static hummed and whined.

'They must be running late.' Nicholas tried not to let his disquiet show. 'Jannie will be coming straight in from Malta on this run. After the first drop he will go back to your base at Roseires and pick up the second load. With luck, both loads should all be dropped before noon tomorrow.'

'If the fat man comes at all,' Mek remarked.

'Jannie is a pro,' Nicholas grunted. 'He will come.' He held the microphone to his lips, 'Big Dolly. Do you read? Over.'

Every ten minutes he called out into the empty echoing silence.

Each time his call went unanswered he had visions of Sudanese MiG interceptors racing in with their missiles cocked and locked, and the old Hercules plunging earthwards in flames.

'Come in, Big Dolly!' he pleaded, and at last a thin, scratchy voice floated into his headset. 'Pharaoh. This is Big Dolly. ETA forty-five minutes. Standing by.' Jannie's transmission was terse. He was too much of an old hand at the smuggling game to give a hostile listener time to fix his position.

'Big Dolly. Understand four five. Pharaoh standing by.' Nicholas grinned at Mek. 'Looks like we are in business after all.'

Mek heard it first. His ear was battle-tuned. In this land, if you wanted to go on living it paid to pick up any aircraft long before it arrived. Nicholas was out of training, so it was almost five minutes later that he picked up the distinctive drone of the multi-props echoing weirdly off the cliffs of the gorge. It was impossible to be certain of the direction, but they shaded their eyes and stared into the west.

'There she is.' Nicholas redeemed himself as he spotted the tiny dark speck, so low as almost to blend into the background of the escarpment wall. He nodded at Sapper.

Sapper ran out to his flares and fussed over them briefly. When he backed away they bloomed into clouds of dense marigold-yellow smoke that drifted out sluggishly on the light breeze. The smoke would give Jannie the strength and direction of the wind, as well as his orientation for the drop zone.

Nicholas lifted his binoculars and gazed towards the other end of the narrow valley. He saw that Royan and Tessay were busy with their flares. Suddenly crimson smoke billowed from them, and the women ran back to their original position and stood staring up at the sky.

Nicholas called softly into the microphone. 'Big Dolly. Smoke is up. Do you have it visual?'

'Affirmative. You are visual. For what you are about to receive may you be truly thankful.' Jannie's South African accent was unmistakable as he uttered the cheerful blasphemy.

They watched the aircraft grow in size until its wings seemed to fill half the sky, and then its profile altered as the great wing flaps dropped and the ramp below its belly drooped open. Big Dolly slowed her flight so dramatically that she seemed to hang suspended on an invisible thread from the high African sun. Slowly she came around, banking steeply as Jannie lined her up on the smoke flares, dropping lower and still lower, headed directly at where they stood.

With a savage roar that made all three of them duck, she passed so low over their heads that it seemed she would wipe them off the crest. Nicholas had a glimpse of Jannie peering down at him from the cockpit, a fat smile on his face and one hand raised in a laconic wave, and then he was past.

Nicholas straightened up and watched Big Dolly sweep majestically down the centre of the valley. The first pallet dropped out of her and plunged earthwards, until at the last moment its parachutes burst open like a bride's bouquet. The fall of the heavy container was arrested abruptly. It dangled and swung, and seconds later struck the floor of the valley in a cloud of yellow dust and with a crash they could hear up on the ridge. Then two more loads dropped from her, and they too hung for a moment on their chutes before they slammed in.

Big Dolly's engines howled under full throttle and her nose lifted as she bored for height while she passed over the crimson smoke clouds, and then climbed out of the deadly trap of the valley. She came round in another wide turn and lined up for the second run. Once again the pallets dropped out of her as she roared over the quartz markers and then climbed out over the end wall of the valley, skimming the rocky spikes that would have clawed her down.

Six times Jannie repeated the dangerous manoeuvre, and each time he dropped three of the heavy rectangular loads. They lay strewn down the length of the valley, shrouded by the tumbled white silk of their own parachutes.

As Jannie climbed away from the last pass, his voice echoed in Nicholas's earphones. 'Don't go away, Pharaoh! I will be back.' Then Big Dolly lifted her belly ramp like an old lady hoisting her knickers and headed away westwards.

Nicholas and Mek ran down into the valley, where the monks were already jabbering and laughing around the pallets. Quickly the two of them took control, sorting the men into gangs and directing them as they broke down the loads and carried them away.

Nicholas and Sapper had planned that the pallets should be dropped in the order that their contents would be needed. The first pallet contained canned and dried food, all their personal effects and camping equipment, along with those other little creature comforts that Nicholas had allowed, including mosquito nets and a case of malt whisky. He was relieved to see that there was no leakage from the precious case: not one of the bottles had been broken in the drop.

Sapper took charge of the building material and heavy equipment. With Tessay relaying his orders, it was dragged and manhandled away to the ancient quarry where it would be packed and stored until needed on site. Darkness fell with more than half the pallets still not unpacked, lying where they had fallen. Mek placed an armed guard over them, and they all traipsed wearily back up the valley to the camp.

That night, with a dram of whisky and a decent meal warming his

319

belly, a mosquito net over his head and a thick foam mattress under him, Nicholas drifted off to sleep with a smile on his face. They were off to a good start.

The chanting of the monks at their matins woke him, 'We won't need an alarm clock here,' he groaned, and staggered down to the river to wash and shave.

As the sun gilded the battlements of the escarpment, he and Mek were already at their post on the heights, searching the western sky. The plan had been for Jannie to spend the night at Roseires, while Mek's men assisted him with the loading of the cargo they had stored there on their first flight out from Malta. This was one of the vulnerable stages of the operation. Although Mek had assured them that there was little military presence in the area at the moment, it needed only a stray Sudanese government patrol to stumble on Big Dolly while she was on the ground to plunge them all into disaster. So it was with a leap of the heart that they heard the familiar drone of the turbo-props reverberating off the cliffs.

Big Dolly lined up again for her first pass down the valley, and as she flew over the quartz crosses the huge yellow front-end loader tumbled out of her hold. Instinctively Nicholas held his breath as he watched it come hurtling down and then jerk up short on the parachute shrouds. It swayed wildly all over the sky, yoyoing on the nylon ropes, and the monks howled with amazement and excitement as they watched it drop in. It struck in a cloud of dust.

Sapper was standing next to Nicholas, groaning and covering his eyes so that he did not have to watch the cloud of dust rising into the air. 'Shit!' he said in a hollow voice.

'Is that a command, or merely a request?' Nicholas asked, but he wasn't really amused.

As the last pallet dropped, and the aircraft climbed away under full power, Nicholas called Jannie on the radio.

'Many thanks, Big Dolly. Safe flight home.'

'Inshallah! If God wills!' Jannie called back.

'I will call you when I need a lift back.'

'I'll be waiting.' Big Dolly trundled away. 'Break a leg!'

'Well now.' Nicholas slapped Sapper's back. 'Let's go down and see if you still have a front ender.'

The battered yellow machine lay on its side with oil pouring out of her, like blood from a heart-shot dinosaur.

'You can push off. Just leave me a dozen of these black guys to help me,' Sapper told them as sorrowfully as if he was standing at the graveside of his beloved.

Sapper did not return to camp for dinner, so Tessay sent a bowl of *wat* and some *injera* bread down to him to eat while he worked. Nicholas considered going down to offer his help with repairing the damaged tractor, but thought better of it. From bitter experience he knew that at certain times Sapper wanted to be left alone, and that this was one of those times.

In the small dark hours of the morning the camp was lit up by the blaze of headlights and the hills reverberated to the roar of a diesel engine. With even his bald head covered with grease and dust, hollow-eyed but triumphant, Sapper drove the yellow tractor into the camp and shouted at them from the high driver's seat.

'Okay, knaves and nymphs! Drop your cocks and grab your socks. Let's go build a dam.'

It took them another two full days to gather in all the pallets that lay strewn down the valley and to carry the stores into the ancient quarry. There they stacked them carefully in accordance with the manifest that Nicholas and Sapper had drawn up in England. It was essential that they knew where every item was stored, and that they had immediate access to it when needed. In the meantime Sapper was at work on the dam site, laying out his foundations, driving numbered wooden pegs into the banks of the river, and taking his final measurements with the long steel surveyor's tape.

During this preliminary work Nicholas was watching the performance of the monks, and getting to know them individually. He was able to pick out the natural leaders and the most intelligent and willing men amongst them. He was also able to identify those who spoke Arabic or a little English. The most promising of these was a monk named Hansith Sherif, whom Nicholas made his personal assistant and interpreter.

Once they were settled into the camp, and had worked out a relationship with the monks, Mek Nimmur took Nicholas aside out of earshot of the two women.

'From now on, my work will be the security of the site. We will have to be ready to prevent another raid like the one on your camp, and the slaughter at St Frumentius. Nogo and his thugs are still out there. It won't take long for him to hear that you are back in the gorge. When he comes, I will be waiting for him.'

'You are better with an AK-47 than with a pickaxe,' Nicholas agreed. 'Just leave Tessay here with me. I need her.'

'So do I.' Mek smiled and shook his head ruefully. 'I am only just learning how much. Look after her for me. I will be back every night to check on her.'

Mek took his men into the bush and deployed them in defensive positions along the trail and around the camp. When Nicholas looked up from his own work he could often make out the figure of one of Mek's sentries on the high ground above the camp. It was reassuring to know that they were there.

However, as he had promised, Mek was back in camp most evenings, and often in the night Nicholas heard, coming from the shelter he shared with Tessay, his deep rumbling laughter blending with her sweet silvery tones. Then Nicholas lay awake and thought about Royan in the hut so close, but yet so far away from where he lay.

On the fifth day the second draft of three hundred labourers that Mai Metemma had conscripted for them arrived, and Nicholas was astonished. Things seldom worked that way in Africa. Nothing ever happened ahead of the promised time. He wondered what exactly Mek had told the abbot, but then decided that he didn't really want to know, for now the main construction work could begin.

These men were not monks, for St Frumentius had already given its all to the sacred labour, but villagers who lived up on the highlands of the escarpment. Mai Metemma had coerced them with promises of religious indulgences and threats of hellfire.

Nicholas and Sapper divided this workforce into gangs of thirty men each, and set one of the picked monks as foreman over each gang. They were careful to grade the men by their physical appearance, so that the big strapping specimens were all grouped together as the project stormtroopers, while the smaller, more wiry men could be reserved for the tasks in which brute strength was not a necessity.

Nicholas dreamed up a name for each gang – the Buffaloes, the Lions, the Axes and so on. It taxed his powers of invention, but he wanted to inspire in them a sense of pride and, to his own particular advantage, to encourage the gangs to compete with one another. He paraded them in the quarry, each group headed by its newly appointed ecclesiastical foreman. Using one of the ancient stone blocks as a platform, and with Tessay interpreting for him, he harangued them heartily and then told them that they would be paid in silver Maria Thereon dollars. He set their wages at three times the going rate.

Up to this stage the men had listened to him with a sullen air of resignation, but now a remarkable transformation came over them. None of them had expected to be paid for the work, and most of them were wondering how soon they could desert and go home. Now Nicholas was promising them not only money, but silver dollars. In Ethiopia for the past two hundred years the Maria Theresa dollar had been regarded as the only true coinage. For this reason they were still minted with the original date of 1780 and the portrait of the old Empress, with her double chin and her *décolletage* exposing half her great bust. One of these coins was more prized than a sackful of the worthless paper birr issued by the regime in Addis. To pay his labour bills, Nicholas had included a chest of these silver coins in the first pallet load that Jannie had dropped.

Celestial grins bloomed as they listened, and white teeth sparkled in their ebony faces. Someone began to sing, and they all stamped and danced and cheered Nicholas as they trooped off to queue for their tools. With mattocks and shovels at the slope they filed off up the valley to the dam site, still singing and prancing.

'St Nicholas,' Tessay laughed. 'Father Christmas. They will never forget you now.'

'They may even enshrine you and build a monastery over you,' Royan suggested sweetly.

'What they don't know is that they are going to earn every single dollar, the hard way.'

From then onwards the work began as soon as it was light enough to see, and stopped only when it was too dark to continue. The men came back to their temporary compound each night by the light of grass torches, too weary to sing. However, Nicholas had contracted with the headmen from the highland villages to supply a slaughter beast every day. Each morning the women came down the trail driving the animal before them, and with huge pots of *tej* balanced on their heads.

Over the days that followed, there were no deserters from Nicholas's little army of workers.

Mounted on the high seat of the front-ender, Sapper lifted the first filled mesh gabion in the hydraulic arms. The mesh-bound parcel of boulders weighed several tons, and all work on the site came to a halt as the men crowded the banks of the Dandera river to watch. A hum of astonishment went up as Sapper eased the yellow tractor down the steep bank and, with the gabion held high, drove the vehicle into the water. The current, affronted by this invasion, swirled angrily around the high rear wheels, but Sapper pushed in deeper.

The crowds lining the bank began to chant and clap encouragement as the water reached as high as the belly of the machine, and clouds of steam hissed from the hot steel of the sump. Sapper locked the brakes, and then lowered the heavy gabion into the flood before reversing back up the bank. The men cheered him wildly, even though the first gabion was instantly submerged and only a whirlpool on the river's surface marked its position. Another filled gabion lay ready. The front-ender waddled up to it, lowered its steel arms and picked it up as tenderly as a mother gathering up her infant.

Nicholas shouted at the foremen to get their gangs back to work. The long lines of men came up the valley, naked except for their brief white loincloths. Sweating heavily in the heat of the gorge, their skin glistened like anthracite freshly cut from the coal face. Each of them carried on his head a basket of stone aggregate, which he dumped into the mouth of the waiting gabion. Then he returned with his empty basket down the hill to the quarry. As each gabion was filled, another team fitted the mesh lid and laced it closed with heavy eight-gauge wire.

'Twenty dollars bonus to the team with the most baskets filled today!' Nicholas bellowed. They shouted with glee and redoubled their efforts, but they were unable to keep up with Sapper on the front-ender. He laid his stone piers artfully, working out from the shallow water alongside the bank so that each gabion lay against its neighbour, keying into the wall to give mutual support.

At first there was little evident progress, but as a solid reef was built up beneath the surface the river began to react savagely. The voice of the water changed from a low rustle to a dull roar as it tore at Sapper's wall.

Soon the top of the wall of gabions thrust its head above the surface, and the river was constricted to half its former width. Now its mood was truculent. It poured through the gap in a solid green torrent, and crept almost imperceptibly up the banks as it was forced to back up behind the barrier. The river worried the foundations of the dam, clawing at it to find its weak spots, and the progress of the work slowed down as the waters rose higher.

Up in the riverine forests along the banks the axemen were at work, and Nicholas winced each time one of the great trees toppled, groaning and shrieking like a living creature. He liked to think of himself as a conservationist, and some of these trees had taken centuries to reach this girth.

'Do you want your bleeding dam, or your pretty trees?' Sapper demanded ferociously, when Nicholas lamented in his hearing. Nicholas turned away without replying.

They were all becoming tired with the unremitting labour. Their nerves were stretching towards snapping point, and tempers were mercurial. Already there had been a number of murderous fights amongst the workmen, and each time Nicholas had been forced to duck in under the swinging steel mattocks to break it up and separate the combatants.

lowly they squeezed the river in its bed as the pier crept out from the bank, and the time came when they had to transfer their efforts to the far bank. It required the combined efforts of their entire labour force to build a new road along the bank as far as the ford. There they manhandled the front-ender into the water, and, with a hundred men hauling on the tow ropes and her tall lugged rear wheels spinning and churning the surface to a froth, they dragged her across.

Then they had to build another road back along the far bank to reach the dam site. They cut out the treetrunks that obstructed them and levered the boulders out of the way to get the tractor through. Once they had her back at the dam site they could begin the same process of laying out gabions from the far bank.

Gradually, a few metres each day, the two walls crept closer to each other, and as the gap between them narrowed the water rose higher and became more raucous, making the work more difficult.

In the meanwhile, two hundred metres upstream of the dam site, the Falcons and the Scorpions were at work. These two teams were building the raft of treetrunks that they had hacked from the forest. The timbers were lashed together to form a grating. Over this was laid heavy PVC sheeting to make it waterproof; then a second grating of treetrunks went over this to form a gigantic sandwich. It was all lashed together with heavy baling wire. Finally, one end of the grating was ballasted with boulders.

Sapper arranged the ballast of boulders to make the raft one-side heavy, so that it would float almost vertically in the water, with one end of it scraping the bottom of the river and the other sticking up above the surface. The dimensions of the completed raft were carefully related to the gap between the two buttresses of the dam. And while the work on the raft and the wall continued Sapper built up a stockpile of filled gabions, which he stacked on both banks below the dam.

Three other full work teams, the Elephants, the Buffaloes and the Rhinos, comprising the biggest and strongest men in the force, laboured at the head of the valley. They were digging out a deep canal into which the river could be diverted.

'Your hot-shot engineer, Taita, never thought of that little refinement,' Sapper gloated to Royan as they stood on the lip of the trench. 'What it means is that we only have to raise the level of the river another six feet before it will start flowing down the canal and into the valley. Without it we would have had to lift the water almost twenty feet to divert it.'

'Perhaps the river levels were different four thousand years ago.' Royan felt a strange loyalty to the long-dead Egyptian, and she defended him. 'Or perhaps he dug a canal but all traces of it have been obliterated.'

'Not bleeding likely,' Sapper grunted. 'The little perisher just plain didn't think of it.' His expression was smug and self-satisfied. 'One up on Mr Taita, I think.'

Royan smiled to herself. It was strange how even the practical and down-to-earth Sapper felt that this was a direct personal challenge from down the ages. He too had been caught up in Taita's game.

By dint of neither threat nor heavenly reward could the monks be inveigled into working on Sundays. Each Saturday evening they knocked off an hour earlier and trooped away down the valley on the trail to the monastery, so as to be in time for Holy Communion the next day. Although Nicholas grumbled and scowled at their desertion, secretly he was as relieved as any of them for the chance to rest. They were all exhausted, and for once there would be no chanting of matins to wake them at four o'clock the next morning.

So on Saturday night they all swore to each other that they would sleep late the next morning, but from force of habit Nicholas found himself awake and fully alert at that same iniquitous hour. He could not stay in his camp bed, and when he came back from his ablutions at the riverside he found that Royan was also awake and dressed.

'Coffee?' She lifted the pot off the fire and poured a mugful for him.

'I slept terribly badly last night,' she admitted. 'I had the most ridiculous dreams. I found myself in Mamose's tomb, lost in a labyrinth of passages. I was searching for the burial chamber, opening doors, but there were always people in the rooms that I looked into. Duraid was working in one room and he looked up and said, "Remember the protocol of the four bulls. Start at the beginning." He was so real and alive. I wanted to go to him but the door closed in my face, and I knew I would never see him again.' Tears filled her eyes and glistened in the light of the campfire.

Nicholas sought to distract her from the painful memory. 'Who were in the other rooms?' he asked.

'In the next room was Nahoot Guddabi. He laughed spitefully and said, "The jackal chases the sun," and his head changed into the head of Anubis, the jackal god of the cemetery, and he yelped and barked. I was so frightened that I ran.'

She sipped her coffee. 'It was all meaningless and silly, but von Schiller was in the next room, and he rose in the air and flapped his wings and said, "The vulture rises, and the stone falls." I hated him so much I wanted to strike him, but then he was gone.'

'And then you woke up?' Nicholas suggested.

'No. There was one other room.'

'Who was in it?'

She dropped her eyes, and her voice was small, 'You were,' she said.

'Me? What did I say?' He smiled.

'You didn't say anything,' she whispered, and blushed so suddenly and fiercely that he was instantly intrigued.

'What did I do then?' He was still smiling.

'Nothing. I mean, I can't tell you.' The dream returned to her, vivid and real as life, every detail of his naked body, even the smell and the feel of him. She forced herself to stop thinking about it. She felt vulnerable as she had been in the dream.

'Tell me about it,' he insisted.

'No!' She stood up quickly, confused and still blushing, trying to thrust the images from her.

Last night had been the first time in her life that she had ever dreamed of a man in that way, the first time she had ever experienced a full orgasm in her sleep. This morning, when she awoke, she found that she had soaked right through her pyjamas bottoms.

'We have a full day ahead of us with no work to do,' she blurted – the first thought that came into her mind.

'On the contrary.' He stood up with her. 'We still have to make the arrangements for getting out of here. When the time comes, we will probably be in something of a hurry.'

'Mind if I tag along?' she asked.

Two teams, the Buffaloes and the Elephants, with only their foremen missing, were waiting for them at the quarry. They comprised sixty of the strongest men in the labour force. Nicholas unpacked the inflatable Avon rafts from one of the pallets. Each raft was deflated and folded into a neat pack, with the paddles strapped along the sides. These craft had been specifically designed for river-running in turbulent water, and each was capable of carrying sixteen crew and a ton of cargo.

Nicholas directed them to strap the heavy packs on to the carrying poles that they had cut for that purpose. Five men on each end of the long poles, with the bundle of the boat slung in the centre, made light of the load. They set off at a cracking pace down the trail, and as soon as one team tired the next was ready to take over. They made the exchange without even stopping, the new porters slipping their shoulders under the pole on the run while the exhausted team dropped out.

Nicholas carried the radio in its shockproof and waterproof fibreglass case. He would not trust such a precious instrument to one of the porters. He and Royan trotted along behind the caravan, joining in the chorus of the work chant that the porters sang as they carried their loads down to the monastery.

Mai Metemma was waiting on the terrace outside the church of St Frumentius to welcome them. He led them down the staircase hewn out of the rock of the cliff, two hundred feet to the very water's edge. There was a narrow rocky ledge against which the Nile waters dashed, and the spray from the high waterfalls drifted over them like a perpetual drizzle of rain. After the heat and the bright sunlight above, it was cold and gloomy and dank down here in the depths of the gorge. The black cliffs ran with water, and the ledge on which they stood was wet and slippery underfoot.

Royan shivered as she watched the river racing by, forming a great spinning vortex as it swirled around the deep rock bowl and then raced out through the narrow throat of the gorge on its long hectic journey towards Egypt and the north.

'If only I had known that this was the road you were planning on taking home—' she eyed the river dubiously.

'If you would prefer to walk, it's okay by me,' Nicholas told her. 'With luck we will be carrying some extra baggage. The river is the logical escape route.'

'I suppose it makes sense, but still it's not terribly inviting.' She broke off a piece of driftwood from a stranded tangle that lay trapped upon the ledge and tossed it into the river. It was whipped away, and raced over the standing wave where some submerged obstacle forced the surface to bulge up.

'What speed is that current?' she asked in a subdued voice as the splinter of driftwood was sucked below the surface.

'Oh, not much more than eight or nine knots,' he told her offhandedly, 'but that's nothing. The river is still very low. Just wait until it starts raining up in the mountains, then you will really see some water passing through here. It will be great fun. Lots of people would pay good money for the chance to run a river like this. You are going to love it.'

'Thanks,' she said drily. 'I can't wait.'

Fifty feet above the ledge, out of reach of the Nile's highest water level, was a small cavern – the Epiphany shrine. Long ago the monks had cut this passage deeply into the rock face, and it ended in a spacious, candle-lit chamber that housed a life-sized statue of the Virgin, dressed in faded velvet robes, with the infant in her arms. Mai Metemma gave them his sanction to store the rafts in the shrine, and they stacked them against a side wall. When the porters had left, Nicholas showed Royan how to operate the quick-release handles on the packs, and the CO$_2$ cylinders which would inflate the rafts within minutes. He wrapped the radio case and his small emergency pack in a sheet of plastic and stowed them in one of the boat packs, where he could lay his hands on them again in a hurry.

'You do intend coming along on this joy ride?' she asked anxiously. 'You aren't planning on sending me down on my ownsome?'

'It is best that you know how it all works,' he told her. 'If things start to get a little hairy when the time comes to leave here, I may need your help in launching the rafts.'

When they climbed back up the staircase into the warmth and the sunlight, Royan's uncertain mood had changed. 'It's not yet noon, and we have the rest of the day to ourselves. Let's go back to Taita's pool again,' she suggested, and he shrugged indulgently.

The Buffaloes and the Elephants accompanied them as far as the branch in the trail. Here the teams headed back towards the dam, and shouted and hallooed their farewells after Nicholas and Royan.

Even in the short time since their last visit, the path through the undergrowth had become overgrown. Nicholas was forced to use his machete to hack a way through, and they ducked under the trailing thorn branches. It was mid-afternoon when they eventually crossed the high ridge and stood once again on the cliff directly above Taita's pool.

'It looks as though we were the last ones here.' Nicholas's tone was relieved. 'No signs of any other visitors since us.'

'Were you expecting any?'

'You never know. Von Schiller is a formidable character, and he has some charming lads working for him. Helm is one that worries me, and I had a nasty feeling that he might have been snooping around here. I am going to take a closer look.'

He worked quickly around the entire area, casting widely for any sign of intruders. Then came back to where she sat on the lip of the abyss and dropped down beside her.

'Nothing,' he admitted. 'We have still got the running to ourselves.'

'Once Sapper stops the river upstream, this is going to be our main area of operations, isn't it?' she asked.

'Yes, but even before Sapper closes the dam I want to open a fly camp here, and move all the gear and equipment we will need from the quarry to have it handy when we start the exploration of the pool.'

'How are we going to get down into the pool? Down the river bed, once it is dry?'

'I suppose we could use the dry river bed as a road, and come down it from below the dam or up from the monastery end, through the pink cliffs.'

'But that is not the way you are planning to get in, is it?' she guessed.

'Even with no water in it, the river bed will be a long way round. It's a three- or four-mile haul from either end of the abyss, added to which it will be a pretty rough road to travel.' He grinned ruefully. 'You are speaking to an expert on the subject. I went down it the hard way, and I wouldn't want to do it again. There are at least five chutes and rock jams that I can remember being thrown over.'

'What is your better idea, then?' she asked.

'It's not my idea,' he contradicted her. 'It's Taita's idea really.'

She peered over the edge. 'You mean to build a scaffold down the cliff, just the way he did it?'

'What's good enough for Taita is good enough for me,' he acknowledged. 'The old boy probably had a good look at the alternative of using the river bed as an access road, and abandoned the idea.'

'When will you start work on the scaffold, then?'

'One of our teams is already cutting bamboo poles higher up the gorge. Tomorrow we will begin carrying them up here, and stacking them. We can't waste a day. Once the dam is closed, we have to get into the dry pool as soon as possible.'

As if to add weight to his words there came a far-off mutter of thunder, and they both craned their heads to peer up with trepidation at the escarpment. Probably a hundred miles to the north, faintly washed as a sepia print superimposed upon the razor-edged blue silhouette of the escarpment wall, rose high tumbled towers of cumulo-nimbus clouds. Neither of them spoke about it, but both were aware of how ominously the storm clouds were settling on the distant mountains.

Nicholas glanced at his wrist-watch and stood up. 'Time to start back if we are to get into camp before dark.'

He gave her his hand and lifted her to her feet. She dusted off her clothes and then stepped right to the very lip of the canyon.

'Wake up, Taita. We are hot on your tracks,' she called down into the shadows.

'Don't challenge him.' Nicholas took her arm and drew her back. 'The old ruffian has given us enough trouble already.'

The axemen had left the stumps of several great trees standing on the banks of the Dandera upstream from the dam. Sapper used these as anchor points for the heavy cables that he strung across the river. Through the cables he had rigged a cunning series of pulley blocks. The main cable was run back and connected to the tow hitch on the front-ender. Two other cables were laid out, one to each bank, where the Buffaloes and the Elephants stood ready to handle them. One team was under the direction of Nicholas, and the other under Mek Nimmur. For this crucial part of the construction, Mek had come down from the hills to lend a hand.

The grating of massive treetrunks lay on the river verge, already half in the water. Heavily weighted with boulders, it was an unwieldy structure that would require all their combined efforts to manoeuvre into position. Sapper slitted his eyes as he studied the layout, and then looked downstream to the partially completed dam. The two walls of gabions stretched out from either bank, but the gap in the middle of the river was twenty feet across and the whole volume of the river roared through it.

'The one thing we don't want is to let the bleeding plug run away from us and slam into the ruddy wall,' he warned Nicholas and Mek. 'Otherwise we are going to lose a big chunk of what we have done so far. I want to cuddle her in there, nice and softly, and let her sit snug in the gap. Any questions? This is your last chance to ask. You all know the signals.'

Sapper took one last drag on his cigarette, and flicked the stub into the river. Then, looking lugubrious, he said, 'Okay, gents. The last one in the water is a sissy.'

Compared to their men, Nicholas and Mek were overdressed in their khaki shorts. The others were all stark naked. When the order was given they trooped waist-deep into the river and took up their stations along the cables.

Before he followed them into the river, Nicholas took one last look round. At breakfast that morning Royan had innocently asked to borrow his binoculars. Now he knew why. She and Tessay were perched up on top of the slope high above the gorge. Even as Nicholas watched, he saw Royan pass the binoculars to Tessay. They were not missing a moment of this fateful operation.

Nicholas looked back from the ridge to the rows of big naked men, pulled a face and muttered, 'My oath, there are some prize specimens around here. I just hope that Royan isn't making comparisons.'

Sapper climbed up on to the yellow tractor, and with a roar and a cloud of diesel smoke the engine burst into life. He raised one hand above his head with the fist clenched, and Nicholas relayed the order to his team: 'Take the strain.'

The foremen repeated it in Amharic, and the men leaned back against the cables. Sapper threw the tractor into extra low, and eased her forward. The belly straightened in the lines, the sheave wheels squealed, and the timber grating slid ponderously down the bank into the river. The weighted end of the grating sank immediately and bumped along the bottom, while the lighter end floated high. Slowly they hauled it out into midstream, until it was hanging vertically in the water.

The current seized it and began to bear it away, straight at the wall of gabions. It picked up speed alarmingly. The tractor bellowed and blew out clouds of black smoke as Sapper threw her into reverse and backed up on the cables. The teams of naked black men heaved and chanted – some of them had already been dragged in neck-deep as they hauled on the lines.

The grating steadied across the current, and they let it fall away at a more sedate pace, down towards the open gap in the wall. As it began to slew towards one bank, Sapper lifted his right arm and windmilled it. Obediently, Mek's team on the far bank paid out rope and Nicholas's team on the near bank picked it up. Once again the grating was lined up on the gap.

'Rock and roll. Close the hole,' bellowed Sapper, and now the full current was too powerful to resist. It dragged both teams into the river until some of them were in over their heads, losing their hold on the lines and floundering and swimming. However, those men who still had their footing managed to slow the rush of the grating just enough to prevent it smashing out of control into the dam. It settled firmly across the gap, like a mammoth plug in the outlet of a giant's bathtub, and instantly the current was cut off.

While the men in the water struggled ashore, their bodies wet and gleaming in the sunlight, Sapper threw off the cables from his tow hitch and roared along the bank with the front-ender in its highest gear. As it passed him, Nicholas grabbed a handhold and swung himself up on to the footplate behind Sapper's seat.

'Got to shore up now, before the grating bursts,' Sapper yelled.

From his vantage point, clinging to the rear of the tall machine, Nicholas had a moment to assess the position. The dam was holding, but only just. Numerous jets of water spurted through every gap between the grating and the gabions. The pressure of water against the sheets of PVC in the grating was enormous. It was taking the full thrust of the river, flexing and bowing before it like a castle portcullis attacked with a battering ram.

Sapper picked up one of the gabions that were standing ready on the bank and drove down into the river bed below the dam. The flow of the water had shrivelled to a mere knee-deep trickle. Jets of water squirted through every chink in the wall, and the gabions were not impermeable; water was finding its way through the tightly packed stones.

As the front-ender churned and lurched over the rough bed at the back of the wall, Nicholas and Sapper were drenched by the jets spurting over them. It was like working under a cold shower. Sapper drove in close behind the straining grating and placed the heavy gabion against it. He threw the tractor into reverse and climbed up the bank to pick up another gabion. Slowly he built up a retaining wall behind the grating, placing the gabions in sloping ranks, until this revetment was as strong as the side piers.

Nicholas jumped down from the tractor and left Sapper to it while he ran back upstream to the canal that the teams had dug at the head of the valley. Most of the workers had gathered along the banks of this cutting already, and Nicholas saw both Royan and Tessay in the front row of the excited crowd.

Nicholas pushed his way through to Royan's side, and she grabbed his hand. 'It's working, Nicky. The dam wall is holding.'

Even as they watched they could see the level of the trapped waters rising up the wall of grating and gabions. While the men chattered and laughed and urged it on, the river lapped at the entrance of the canal.

Fifty men seized their tools and jumped down into the bottom of the canal. Dust flew in clouds as they shovelled the broken earth aside to lead the first trickle of water into the mouth of the canal. The men on the banks above them whooped and chanted to encourage them, and a thin snake of river water found its way into the mouth of the canal. The men with the mattocks and shovels ran ahead of it, enticing it on down the cutting. Every time it met any obstruction and faltered, they fell upon the blockage and tore it away.

At last the thin trickle of water felt the gradient fall away as the valley opened before it. The trickle increased to a freshet, and then to a torrent. With its new strength it gouged out the canal and burst through with the full flow of the river behind it.

The men in the bottom of the cutting yelled with fright at the suddenness and ferocity of it, and scrambled up the sides of the canal. But some of them were not quick enough and were swept away, struggling and screaming for help. The men on the banks ran alongside them, throwing ropes and dragging them sodden and muddy from the flood.

Now the river roared through the canal and tore on down the valley, rediscovering the ancient course that it had not followed for thousands of years. For almost an hour they stood upon the bank watching it, for it exercised over them the particular spell that turbulent waters always have over men. They were forced to retreat step by step as the river cut the banks out from under their feet.

At last Nicholas roused himself, and went back to where Sapper was still shoring up the dam wall. By now he had erected a sloping revetment on the downstream side of the dam wall, with four rows of gabions on the bottom course gradually narrowing as it reached the top of the retaining wall. For the time being the dam was secure, the vulnerable grating had been shored up with the heavy, stone-filled mesh baskets, and the overflow through the canal into the valley had relieved much of the pressure upon it.

'Do you think it will hold?' Royan eyed the structure with suspicion.

'Until the rains come, we hope.' Nicholas drew her away. 'We don't want to waste any more time here. Time to go on downstream to begin work at Taita's pool.'

They followed the banks of the new river that they had created, down the length of the long valley. At places they were forced to detour higher up the slope because the overflow from the dam had cut away and submerged the old trail. Eventually they reached the confluence of the stream that had as its source the butterfly fountain that they had explored with Tamre. They paused on the bank, and Nicholas and Royan looked at each other wordlessly. The stream had dried up.

Turning aside, they followed the empty stream bed up the hills and at last scrambled out on to the ledge from which the butterfly fountain had poured. The cave was still surrounded by lush green ferns, but it was like the eye socket in a skull, dark and empty.

'The spring has dried up!' Royan whispered. 'The dam has shrivelled it. That's the proof that the fountain was fed from Taita's pool. Now we have diverted the river we have killed the fountain.' Her eyes were bright and sparkling with excitement. 'Come on. Let's waste no more time here. Let's get on up to Taita's pool.'

Nicholas was the first one down into Taita's pool. This time he had a bosun's chair to sit in and a properly rigged block and tackle to lower him over the cliff. As he swung down around the overhang of the cliff, the chair swung awkwardly against the rock and the thumb of his right hand was trapped between the wooden seat of the chair and the wall. He exclaimed with the pain and, when he wrenched it free, he found that the skin had been torn from the knuckle and that blood was oozing up and dripping down his legs. It was painful but not serious, and he sucked the wound clean. It was still weeping drops of blood, but he had no time to attend to the injury now.

He was around the overhang, and the abyss opened under him, sombre and repellent. His eye was drawn irresistibly to the engraving on the wall, etched between the vertical rows of niches. Now that he knew what to look for, he could make out the outline of the maimed hawk. It cheered and encouraged him. Since their flight from the gorge over a month previously he had often been haunted by the feeling that they had imagined it all, that the cartouche of Taita was a hallucination, and that when they returned they would find the cliff wall smooth and unblemished. But there it was, the signpost and the promise.

He peered down past his own feet to the bottom of the gorge, and saw at once that the waterfall above the pool had been reduced to a trickle. The water still coming down the smooth black chute of polished rock was that which was filtering through the gaps and chinks in the dam wall upstream and the last drainage from the sandbanks and the pools higher up the gorge.

The level of the great pool under him had fallen drastically. He could make out the high-water level by the wet markings on the rock cliff. Fifty feet of the wall that had previously been submerged was now exposed. Another eight pairs of chiselled niches were visible in the face. Where once he had been forced to swim down to them, they were now high and dry.

However, the pool was not completely drained. It was dished below the level of the downstream outlet, so that it was unable to empty itself by gravitational flow. There was still a puddle of black water trapped in the centre, with a narrow ledge surrounding it. Nicholas landed on this ledge and stepped out of the bosun's chair. It was strange to stand on firm rock down here where last he had struggled for his life and very nearly been sucked under and drowned.

He looked up to where beams of sunlight penetrated the upper levels of the chasm. It was like being in the bottom of a mineshaft, and he shuddered at the feel of the clammy air on his bare arms and the eerie sensation in the pit of his stomach. He tugged on the line to send the rope chair back to the surface, and then edged his way along the slippery rock ledge towards the cliff face where the rows of dark niches stood out clearly against the lighter stone.

Now he could make out the shape of the opening in the wall that had so nearly sucked him down into its dark and slimy throat. It was almost completely submerged in a deeper corner where the pool flowed back against the cliff. All that was visible above the surface was the top arch of an irregular entrance at the foot of the descending rows of niches. The rest of it was still submerged.

The ledge narrowed as he worked his way along the foot of the cliff until he had his back to the rock and was moving sideways with his toes in the water. Eventually he could go no further without actually stepping down into the water. He had no way of judging the depth of the waters, which were turbid and uninviting.

Still trying to keep his feet dry, he squatted down on the narrow ledge and leaned out so far that his balance was threatened. He steadied himself with one hand against the wall, and with the other reached out towards the partially submerged opening.

The lip of the hole was smooth, as he had remembered it, and once again it seemed to him that it was too square and straight to be anything other than man-made. As he rolled up his sleeve he noticed that his injured thumb was still bleeding, but he ignored it and thrust his arm down below the surface of the pool. He groped downwards, trying to trace the sill of the opening. He felt what seemed to be blocks of roughly dressed masonry, and reached down further until the water reached halfway up his biceps.

Suddenly some living creature, swift and weighty, swirled in the dark waters right in front of his face, and as an immediate reflex he jerked his arm out of the water. The thing followed his arm up to the surface, slashing at his bare flesh with long, needle-sharp fangs, and he had a glimpse of a head as evil and villainous as that of a barracuda. He realized instinctively that it must have been attracted by the smell of the blood from his injured thumb.

He leaped to his feet and teetered on the narrow ledge, clutching his arm. Only one of the creature's frontal fangs had touched him, but it had opened the skin like a razor cut, a long shallow wound across the back of his right hand from which fresh blood dribbled and splattered into the pool at his feet.

Instantly the black waters seemed to come alive, roiling and seething with frenzied writhing aquatic shapes. Nicholas, his back flattened against the rock wall, stared down at them with loathing and horror. He could vaguely make out the shape of them, sinuous and ribbonlike, some of them as thick as his calf, black and gleaming.

One of them thrust its head out on to the ledge and snapped its jaws. Its eyes were huge and glistening and its snout was elongated, the long jaws lined with fangs that overlapped its thin lips. The body behind the head was six feet long, and lashed like a whip as it drove itself high up on to the ledge, reaching out for Nicholas's bare legs. He shouted with revulsion and leaped back, stumbling and splashing on to safer footing. Clutching his bleeding hand, he stared back. The evil head had disappeared, but the surface of the pool was still agitated by the lithe ophidian shapes.

'Eels!' he realized. 'Giant tropical eels.'

Of course the blood had excited them. The fall in the water-level had trapped them in the pool, congregated them in such numbers that they had probably already devoured the fish that they depended upon for food. Now they were ravenous. Probably all the pools of water that remained in the abyss were infested with these fearsome creatures. He was thankful that during his last swim in this pool he had not bled into the water.

He unwound the cotton kerchief from his neck and wrapped it round his wounded hand. The eels were a deadly threat to any attempt to explore the opening in the cliff. But already he was considering ways of ridding the pool of them and of gaining access to the underwater opening.

Slowly the frenzy in the pool quietened and its surface grew still again. Nicholas looked up to see the bosun's chair descending, with Royan's slim, shapely legs dangling below the wooden seat.

'What have you found?' she called down to him excitedly. 'Is there a tunnel—' then she broke off suddenly as she saw the blood on his clothing, and the bandage swathing his hand.

'Oh dear God,' she exclaimed. 'What have you done? You are hurt. How badly?' Her feet touched the ledge beside him and she slid from the chair and took his injured hand gently. 'What have you done to yourself?'

'It's not as bad as it looks,' he assured her. 'Lots of blood but not deep.'

'How did you do it?' she insisted.

For an answer he tore a corner off the bloodstained kerchief. 'Watch!' he instructed her, wadding it into a ball and tossing it out into the pool.

Royan screamed with horror as the waters boiled with the long fleeting shapes. One of them wriggled half its monstrous length out on to the ledge, before flopping back. It left a shining trail of silver slime across the black stones.

'Taita has left his guard dogs to see us off,' Nicholas remarked. 'We are going to have to take care of those beauties before we can explore the entrance below the surface.'

The bamboo scaffolding that Sapper and Nicholas had built down the cliff was anchored in the niches that had been cut into the rock nearly four thousand years before. Taita had probably lashed his framework together with bark rope, but Sapper had used heavy-gauge galvanized wire, and the structure was strong enough to bear the weight of many men. The Buffaloes formed a living chain and passed all the material and equipment down the scaffolding from hand to hand.

The very first piece of equipment to reach the floor of the cavern was the portable Honda EM500 generator. Sapper connected it up to the lights that he had rigged along the foot of the cliff. The small petrol engine ran smoothly and quietly, but the amount of power it put out was impressive. The floodlights chased the shadows from the furthest corners of the cavern, and lit the deep rock bowl like a stage.

Immediately the mood changed. Everybody became more cheerful and confident. There was laughter and excited chatter from the chain of men on the scaffolding as Royan climbed down to join Sapper and Nicholas at the side of the pool.

337

'Now that we know that they are working, switch off those lights,' Nicholas ordered.

'It's so dark and gloomy without them,' Royan protested.

'Saving fuel,' Nicholas explained. 'No filling station on the corner. We only have two hundred litres in reserve, and although the little Honda is pretty economical we have to be careful. We don't know how long we are going to need it in the tunnel.'

Royan shrugged with resignation, and when Sapper cut the generator the cavern was plunged once more into gloom and shadow. She looked at the dark pool and pulled a face.

'What are you going to do about those horrid pets of yours?' she demanded, glancing at Nicholas's bandaged right hand.

'Sapper and I have worked out a plan. We thought of trying to empty the pool completely, using a bucket chain. But the amount of water still coming down the river bed makes that a poor choice.'

'We would be lucky to hold our own against that flow, even working around the clock with buckets,' Sapper grunted. 'If only the major had thought to bring along a high-speed water pump—'

'Even I can't think of everything, Sapper. What we are going to do is to build a small coffer dam around the underwater opening, and bale that out with buckets.'

Royan stood back and watched the preparations. Half a dozen of the empty mesh gabions were carried down the scaffolding and placed at the edge of the pool. Here they were partially filled with boulders that the men gathered up from the river bed. However, the gabions were not filled so full that they became too heavy to handle. There was no front-ender down here to move them around, and they would be forced to rely on old-fashioned manpower. There was just sufficient of the yellow PVC sheeting left over to wrap around each gabion and render it waterproof.

'What about your eels?' Royan was fascinated by these loathsome creatures, and she hung well back from the edge of the pool. 'You can't send any of your men in there!'

'Watch and learn.' Nicholas grinned at her. 'I have a little treat in store for your favourite fish.'

Once all the preparations for the construction of the coffer were complete, Nicholas cleared the cavern, sending Royan and Sapper and all of the men up the scaffolding. He alone remained at the edge of the pool, with the bag of fragmentation grenades that he had begged from Mek Nimmur slung over his shoulder.

With a grenade in each hand, he hesitated. 'Seven-second delay,' he reminded himself. 'Quenton-Harper dry flies. More effective than the Royal Coachman!'

He pulled the pins from each of the grenades and then lobbed them

338

out into the middle of the pool. Quickly he turned away and hurried to the furthest corner of the cavern. He knelt with his face to the rock wall and covered his ears with both hands.

Squeezing his eyes shut, he braced himself. The rock floor jumped under him and the double shock waves from the explosions swept over him in quick succession, with a savage power that drove in his chest and stopped his breath. In the confines of the chasm the detonations were thunderous, but his ears were protected and the deep water of the pool absorbed much of the blast. A twin fountain of water shot high into the air and splashed against the cliff above his head. It poured down in a sheet over him, soaking his clothing.

As the echoes died away, he stood up. His hearing had not been adversely affected, and he had suffered no injury other than the shower of cold water. Back at the edge of the pool the water shimmered with movement. Scores of the great eels flopped and writhed on the surface, flashing their white bellies as they twisted. Many of them were dead, their bellies burst open, floating inert, while others were merely stunned by the blast. Knowing how tenaciously they clung to life he suspected that they would soon recover, but for the time being they were no longer a danger.

He bellowed up toward the top of the cliff. 'All clear, Sapper. Send them down.'

The men came swarming down the scaffolding, amazed by the carnage that the grenades had wreaked in the pool. They lined the bank and began to fish out the bodies of the dead eels.

'You eat them?' Nicholas demanded of one of the monks.

'Very good!' The monk rubbed his belly in anticipation.

'Enough of that, you greedy perishers.' Sapper drove them back to work. 'Let's get those gabions in place before they wake up and start eating you.'

With a bamboo pole Nicholas sounded the depth of the water that covered the entrance to the shaft, and found that it was well over the height of a man's head. They were forced to roll the gabions down into it, and complete the filling once they were in position. It was difficult and taxing work, and took almost two days to complete, but at last they had built a half-moon-shaped weir around the underwater entrance, walling it off from the main body of water in the pool.

Using leather buckets and clay *tej* pots the Buffaloes began to bale out the coffer and scoop the water over the wall into the main pool. Nicholas and Royan watched with silent trepidation as the level in the coffer fell and the opening in the cliff was gradually revealed.

Very soon they were able to see that it was almost rectangular, about three metres wide by two metres high. The sides and the roof had been eroded by the rush of water through the opening, but as the level fell lower they could see the remains of shaped stone blocks that had probably once sealed the opening. Four courses of them still stood where the ancient masons had placed them across the threshold of the opening, but the others had been torn out by thousands of years of flood seasons and thrown into the tunnel behind, partially blocking it.

Eagerly Nicholas climbed down into the coffer. It was not yet empty, but he could not control his impatience. The water was knee-deep as he crawled forward into the opening, and with his bare hands tried to shift some of the rock debris that choked it.

'It's definitely some sort of shaft,' he shouted back, and Royan could not restrain herself either. She came slithering and sloshing down into the coffer, and pushed into the opening beside him.

'There's an obstruction,' she cried in disappointment. 'Did Taita do that deliberately?'

'Might have,' Nicholas gave his opinion. 'Hard to tell. A lot of this rubble and flotsam has been sucked in from the main flow of the river, but he might have filled the tunnel behind him as he pulled out.'

'It's going to take a tremendous amount of work just to clear it enough to find out where this passage leads to.' Royan's voice had lost its ring of excitement.

'I am afraid it is,' Nicholas agreed. 'We are going to have to clear every bit of this rubbish by hand, and there won't be time for the niceties of formal archaeological excavation. We are just going to rip it out.' He clambered back out of the coffer, and reached back to hand her up the bank. 'Well, at least we have the floodlights,' he added. 'We can keep the men working in shifts, night and day, until we get through.'

'They have dammed the Dandera river,' said Nahoot Guddabi, and Gotthold von Schiller stared at him in astonishment.

'Dammed the river? Are you certain?' he demanded.

'Yes, Herr von Schiller. We have a report from our spy in Harper's camp. He has over three hundred men working in the gorge. That is not all. He has air-dropped huge amounts of equipment and supplies. It is like a military operation. Our spy tells us that he even has an earth-moving machine, some sort of tractor, which he has brought in.'

Von Schiller looked across the table at Jake Helm for confirmation, and Helm nodded. 'Yes, Herr von Schiller. That is true. Harper must have spent a large amount of money. The air charter alone could have cost him fifty grand.'

Von Schiller felt the first stirrings of real passion since the urgent satellite message had summoned him from Frankfurt. He had flown directly to Addis Ababa, where the Jet Ranger had been waiting to carry him to the Pegasus base camp on the escarpment above the Abbay gorge.

If this was true, and he did not doubt Helm's word, then Harper was on to something of enormous importance. He looked out of the window of the Quonset hut to where the Dandera flowed down the valley below the base camp. It was a large river. To dam that volume of water would be an expensive and difficult project in this remote and primitive situation – not a project to be taken on lightly without the prospect of substantial reward.

He felt a reluctant admiration for the Englishman's achievement. 'Show me where he has placed his dam!' he ordered, and Helm came around the table to stand beside him. Von Schiller was standing on his block, and their eyes were on the same level.

Helm bent over the satellite photograph and carefully marked in the site of the dam. They both studied it for a minute, and then von Schiller asked, 'What do you make of it, Helm?'

Helm shook his head, hunching it down on his bull-like shoulders. 'I can only guess.'

'Guess then,' said von Schiller, but still Helm hesitated.

'Go on!'

'Either he wants to move the water to another area downstream, to use it for washing out a deposit, gold nuggets or artefacts made of precious metals, perhaps even to use it for hosing the overburden off the site of the tomb—'

'Highly unlikely!' von Schiller interjected. 'That would be an inefficient and expensive manner of excavation.'

'I agree that it is far-fetched.' Nahoot obsequiously followed von Schiller's lead, but no one even looked at him.

'What is your other supposition?' Von Schiller glared at Helm.

'The only other reason for damming the river, that I can think of, would be to reach something that has been covered by the water. Something lying in the bed of the river.'

'That is more logical,' von Schiller mused, and turned his attention back to the photograph. 'What is there below this dam site?'

'The river enters a deep and narrow ravine here.' Helm pointed at the spot. 'Just below his dam. The ravine stretches about eight miles, down to this point, just above the monastery. I have flown over it in the helicopter, and it seems to be impassable, and yet—' he broke off.

'Yes, go on! And yet – what?'

'On one flight over the area, we found Harper and the woman on the high ground above the ravine. They were at this spot here.' He touched the photograph, and von Schiller leaned forward to peer at it.

'What were they doing there?' he demanded, without looking up.

341

'Nothing. They were merely sitting on the top of the cliff above the ravine.'

'But they were aware of your presence?'

'Of course. We were in the helicopter. They heard our approach. They were watching us, and Harper even waved.'

'And so they would have ceased whatever activity they were engaged in when they became aware of your approach?'

Von Schiller was silent for so long that they began to fidget uncomfortably and exchange glances. When he spoke it was so unexpected that Nahoot started.

'Harper obviously has reason to believe that the tomb lies in the gorge below the dam. When and how do you make contact with your spy that you have in Harper's camp?'

'Harper is receiving some of his supplies from the villages here on the escarpment. The women are driving down slaughter cattle to feed his men, and carrying down pots of *tej*. Our man sends back his reports with the women when they return.'

'Very well. Very well!' Von Schiller waved him to silence. 'I don't need to know his life history. All I want to know is if Harper is working in the ravine below his dam. How soon can you find this out?'

'By the day after tomorrow at the latest,' Helm promised him.

Von Schiller turned to Colonel Nogo at the far end of the conference table. So far he had not spoken, but had watched and listened quietly to the others.

'How many men have you deployed in this area?' von Schiller asked.

'Three full companies, over three hundred men. All well trained. Many are battle-hardened veterans.'

'Where are they? Show me on the map.'

The colonel came to stand beside him. 'One company here, another billeted at the village of Debra Maryam, and the third company at the foot of the escarpment, ready to move forward and attack Harper's camp.'

'I think you should attack them now. Wipe them out, before they can uncover the tomb—' Nahoot came in again.

'Shut your mouth,' von Schiller snapped without looking up at Nahoot. 'I will ask for your opinion when I need it.'

He considered the map for a while longer, then asked Nogo, 'How many men has this guerrilla commander, what is his name, the one who has allied himself to Harper?'

'Mek Nimmur is not a guerrilla. He is a bandit, and notorious *shufta* terrorist,' Nogo corrected him hotly.

'One man's freedom fighter is the next man's terrorist,' von Schiller remarked drily. 'How many men has he under his command?'

'Not many. Fewer than a hundred, perhaps no more than fifty. He has them all guarding Harper's camp, and the dam.'

Von Schiller nodded to himself, plucking at the lobe of his ear. 'How did Harper and his gang return to Ethiopia?' he mused. 'I know he flew from Malta, but it is not possible that the aircraft could have landed down there in the gorge.'

He hopped down off his block and strutted to the window of the hut through which he had a panoramic view spread below him. He stared down into the depths of the gorge, a vista of cliffs and broken hilltops and wild tablelands, smoked blue with distance.

'How did they get in without being discovered by the authorities? Did he parachute in, the same way as he dropped his supplies?'

'No,' said Nogo. 'My informer tells us that he marched in with Mek Nimmur, some days before the supplies were dropped to him.'

'So from where did he march?' von Schiller pondered. 'Where is the nearest airfield where a heavy aircraft could land?'

'If he came in with Mek Nimmur, then they almost certainly came in from the Sudan. That is where Nimmur operates from. There are many old abandoned airfields near the border. The war,' Nogo shrugged expressively, 'the armies are always on the move, that war has been going on for twenty years.'

'From the Sudan?' Von Schiller picked out the border on the map. 'So they must have trekked in along the river.'

'Almost certainly,' Nogo agreed.

'Then just as certainly Harper plans to escape the same way. I want you to move the company of men that you have at Debra Maryam and deploy them here and here. On both banks of the river, below the monastery. They must be in a position to prevent Harper reaching the Sudanese border, if he should try to make a run for it.'

'Yes. Good! I understand. That is good tactics,' Nogo nodded gloatingly, his eyes bright behind the lenses of his spectacles.

'Then I want your remaining men moved down to the foot of the escarpment. Tell them to avoid contact with Mek Nimmur's men, but to be in a position to move forward very quickly and seize the dam area, and to block off the ravine below the dam as soon as I give you the word.'

'When will that be?' Nogo asked.

'We will continue to watch him carefully. If he makes a discovery, he will start moving the artefacts out. Many of them will be too large to conceal. Your informer will know about it. That is when we will move in on him.'

'You should move in now, Herr von Schiller,' Nahoot advised him, 'before he gets a chance to open the tomb.'

'Don't be an idiot,' von Schiller snarled at him. 'If we strike too soon, we might never discover what he obviously has learned about the whereabouts of the tomb.'

'We could force him—'

'If I have learned anything in my life, it is that you cannot force a man like Harper. There is a certain type of Englishman – I remember during the last war with them—' He broke off and frowned. 'No. They are very difficult people. We must not rush it now. When Harper makes a discovery in the ravine, that will be the time to pounce.' The frown faded and he smiled a small, cold smile. 'The waiting game. In the meantime, we play the waiting game.'

The debris that filled the shaft was not so tightly packed that it completely blocked the flow of water through it. If it had done so, Nicholas would never have been sucked in by the current, as he had been on his first dive into the pool. There were still gaps in the blockage where the larger boulders had lodged or where a treetrunk had been sucked in and jammed sideways across the width of the tunnel. Through these sections the water had found the weak spots and kept them open.

Nevertheless, the debris had taken centuries to wedge itself in, and it required back-breaking effort to prise it apart. The clearing operation was further hampered by the lack of working space in the shaft. Only three or four of the big men from the Buffaloes were able to work in the shaft at any one time. The rest of the team were employed in passing back the rubble as it was levered out.

Nicholas changed the shifts every hour. They had more labour than they needed, and changing them often meant that the men at the face were always rested and strong, and eager to earn the bonus of silver dollars that Nicholas promised them for their progress along the shaft. At each change of shift, Nicholas disappeared into the mouth of the tunnel with Sapper's steel tape and measured the advance.

'One hundred and twenty feet! Well done, the Buffaloes,' he told Hansith Sherif, the foreman monk, and then watched the water trickling past his feet. The floor of the tunnel was still sloping downwards at a constant angle. He looked back along it towards the pool, and now in the floodlights the rectangular shape of the walls was very clear to see. It was obvious that the tunnel had been designed and surveyed by an engineer.

He transferred his attention back to the floor of the tunnel and watched the run of water, trying to judge how deep they were below the original river level.

'Eighty or ninety feet,' he estimated. 'No wonder the pressure in the mouth of the tunnel almost crushed me—' he broke off as an unusually shaped fragment in the muck at his feet caught his eye. He stooped and picked it up. Then took it to one of the floodlamps and by its light examined it closely. As he rubbed it clean between finger and thumb, he began to grin.

Sloshing back along the tunnel, he yelled, 'Royan!' Triumphantly brandishing the fragment, he demanded, 'What do you make of that, then?'

She was sitting on the wall of the coffer, and reached down and snatched the object out of his grasp.

'Oh, sweet Mary! Where did you find this, Nicky?'

'Lying in the mud. Right there in the adit, where it's been for the last four thousand years. Where one of Taita's workmen dropped and broke it, probably while he was sneaking a sup of wine behind the slave driver's back.'

Eagerly Royan held the broken shard of pottery up to the lamplight. 'You are right, Nicky,' she exclaimed. 'It's part of a wine vessel. Look at the flared neck and belled lip. But if there was any doubt, which there isn't, the black firing around the rim dates it perfectly in our period. No older than 2000 BC.'

Still clutching the fragment of broken pottery, she jumped down into the mud and slush of the coffer and flung both arms around his neck.

'Further proof, Nicky. We are on Taita's tracks. Can't you get them to clear any faster? We are breathing down the back of the old rogue's neck.'

Halfway through the next shift an excited yelling echoed out of the mouth of the tunnel, and Nicholas hurried back down to the face.

'What is it, Hansith?' he demanded in Arabic of the foreman monk. 'What are you shouting about?'

'We have broken through, *effendi*.' Hansith Sherif grinned at him, his teeth gleaming in his black and mud-smeared face. Nicholas eagerly pushed his way through the workmen. They had levered a huge round boulder out of the pack, and beyond it lay an opening. He shone his electric torch through this window in the wall, but could make out very little except empty black space.

Stepping back, he slapped the monk on the back. 'Well done, Hansith. A dollar bonus for every man in the team. But keep them working! Clear away all this rubbish.' But it was not as easily done as he had ordered. The shifts changed twice more before the shaft was cleared completely of the last of the extraneous rubble and broken rock. Only then could Nicholas and Royan stand in the threshold of the cavern beyond the tunnel.

345

'What has happened here? What has caused this?' Royan's voice was puzzled as Nicholas played his torch out into the void.

'I think this is a cave-in area. There was probably a fault in the rock strata running through here and here.' He picked out the cracks in the roof of the cavern.

'You think the flow of the water through the shaft has scoured it out?' she asked.

'I would say so, yes.' Nicholas turned the beam of light downwards. 'The floor has fallen out of the shaft also.'

The rock had subsided in front of them, leaving a deep hole. Ten feet below where they stood the hole was filled with water, forming a large circular pool with vertical rock sides. Overhead the roof had fallen in and was now a high dome of irregular rock, and the far side of the pool was shrouded in shadows a hundred feet or more in front of them.

There was no apparent way around this obstacle without entering the water. Nicholas shouted to Hansith to bring one of the long bamboo poles that they had used for the scaffolding. The pole was thirty feet long and they had to manoeuvre its length down the tunnel. Nicholas sounded the pool with the bamboo, probing it down into the turbid water as deeply as he could reach.

'No bottom.' He shook his head. 'Do you know what I think?' He retrieved the pole and passed it back to Hansith.

'Tell me,' Royan invited.

'I think that this is the natural fault that leads the water away to the other side of the hills, and comes to the surface again at the butterfly fountain. The river has carved its own path.'

'Why hasn't it drained, then?' Royan looked down dubiously in the pool below them.

'A U-bend in the shaft, probably. Water still trapped in the top of the shaft like the bowl of a lavatory.'

He probed the waters of the pool with the beam of his torch, and Royan exclaimed with horror and disgust as one of the giant eels came racing to the surface, attracted by the light.

'The filthy creatures!' She stepped back involuntarily. 'The whole river must be infested with them.'

The long dark shape circled the pool swiftly and then disappeared back into the depths as suddenly as it had appeared.

'If you are right, and a section of Taita's adit has collapsed, then the continuation of his tunnel should be on the far side of this.' She pointed across the pool, and Nicholas lifted the beam of the torch and shone it in the direction she indicated.

'Look, Nicky!' she cried. 'There it is.'

The dark rectangular opening yawned at them from across the pool.

'How do we get across there?' Royan asked, disconsolate.

'The answer to that is, not very easily. Dammit to hell!' Nicholas swore heartily. 'This is going to cost us another couple of days that we can ill afford. We are going to have to build some sort of bridge across it.'

'What kind of bridge?'

'Get Sapper down here. This is his department.'

Sapper stood at the brink of the sink-hole and glared across at the far bank.

'Pontoons,' he grunted. 'How many of those inflatable rafts have you got squirrelled away?'

'Forget it, Sapper!' Nicholas shook his head. 'You are not getting those dirty great paws of yours on my rafts.'

'Suit yourself.' Sapper spread his hands in resignation. 'It would be the easiest and quickest way of doing it. Anchor a raft in the middle and build a catwalk over the top of it. I need something that floats high—'

'Baobab.' Nicholas snapped his fingers. 'That should do the trick very nicely. When it's dried out, baobab wood is as light as balsa. Floats just as well as one of my inflatable rafts.'

'Plenty of baobabs growing along the hills,' Sapper agreed. 'Every second tree in this valley seems to be a ruddy baobab.'

Three hundred yards from the top of the cliff grew a massive specimen of *Adansonia digitata*. Its smooth bark resembled the skin of one of the great reptiles from the age of the dinosaurs. Its girth was tremendous – twenty men with outstretched arms could not have encircled it. The upper branches were bare and twisted, and it looked as though it had been dead for a hundred years. Only the heavy velvet-covered pods proved that it still lived; they hung thickly from the high branches, bursting open to spill the black seeds which were coated thickly with white cream of tartar.

'The Zulus say that the Nkulu Kulu, the Great Spirit, planted the baobab upside down with its roots in the air to punish it,' Nicholas told Royan as they looked up at the enormous spread of its branches.

'Why would he want to do that?' she wanted to know. 'What did the poor old baobab do that was so bad?'

'It boasted that it was the tallest and thickest tree of the forest, and so the Nkulu Kulu decided to teach it a little lesson in humility.'

One of the gigantic branches had snapped off under its own weight, and lay on the rocky ground beneath the trunk. The wood was white and fibrous, light as cork. Under Nicholas's direction the axemen cut it into manageable lengths. Once they had been carried down the adit shaft to the sink-hole, Sapper stapled the logs together and floated them across the pool to form a causeway. He anchored this to the rock face at either end, and then over it he laid a catwalk of bamboo poles. The bridge of baobab logs floated high, and although it bobbed and swayed, it could easily support the weight of a dozen men at a time.

Nicholas was the first one across the sink-hole. He placed a roughly made ladder against the high vertical bank, and scrambled up into the mouth of the adit on the far side of the pool. Royan was close behind him.

The two of them stood in the entrance to this continuation of the shaft, and as soon as Nicholas shone his torch into it they realized that the nature of the construction had changed. This section had not been so heavily scoured out and eroded by the rush of river water through it. The main flow must have drained away through the sink-hole. The dimensions were the same, three metres wide by two high, but the rectangular shape was more precise and although the walls and roof were rough, like those of a mine, the marks of the tools that had shaped it were now clearly visible. The footing of the tunnel was roughly paved with slabs of crudely dressed stone.

This whole length of the tunnel had also been submerged, for it lay below the natural level of the river before it had been dammed. The paving under their feet was wet and covered with a slime that had not yet had time to dry out since it had been exposed by the receding waters. The roof and walls of the tunnel ran with moisture, and the air was dank and cold and smelled of mud and rot.

They waited for Sapper to string the cables for the lights across the causeway. He set up the lamps and switched them on. At once they were aware that ahead of them the shaft had begun to rise at an angle of about twenty degrees.

'You can see what the old devil Taita was up to here. He has taken us down well below water level to flood the tunnel to a length and depth that nobody would be able to swim along. Now he is angling up again,' Nicholas pointed out to Royan. They started forward, moving slowly up the ascending shaft, and Nicholas counted aloud each pace he took.

'One hundred and eight, one hundred and nine, one hundred and ten—' suddenly they came to the recent low river level. It was clearly marked as a dry line on the walls of the tunnel. The paving under their feet was also dry and free of the slippery coating of slime. Fifty paces further on they passed the high flood level of the river, which was just as clearly etched on the rock floor and the walls. Beyond that the tunnel had never been immersed, and the walls were in the same condition as the Egyptian slave workmen had left them four thousand years earlier. The marks of the bronze chisels were as pristine as if they had been inflicted just days before.

Only ten feet beyond the highest point that the river waters had ever reached, they came out upon a stone landing. Here the floor levelled out, and then the tunnel turned sharply back upon itself.

'Let's spare a minute just to think about this as a feat of engineering.' Nicholas took Royan's arm and pointed back down the tunnel. 'Taita has placed this landing on which we are standing precisely above the high-water mark of the river. How did he work it out so exactly? He had no dumpy level, and only the crudest measuring equipment. And yet he calculated it as accurately as this. It's a hell of a piece of work.'

'Well, he tells us repeatedly in the scrolls that he is a genius. I suppose we will have to believe him now.' She pulled against his grip. 'Let's go on. I must see what lies around this corner,' she urged.

Side by side they turned through the one hundred and eighty degree corner and Nicholas held the hand lamp high, with the electrical cable trailing back down the shaft behind him. As he lit the way ahead, Royan exclaimed aloud and seized Nicholas's free hand. Both of them froze with astonishment.

Taita had designed the turning of the ascending ramp for dramatic effect. The lower section of the shaft through which they had passed was crudely constructed, the walls irregular and undressed, the roof lumpy and cracked. Taita had calculated his levels so finely that he had known that the lower levels of the shaft would be submerged and damaged by the water. He had wasted no effort on beautifying them.

Now before them rose a wide stairway. The angle of its ascent was such that, from where they stood on the landing, the top of it was hidden from their view. Each step stretched the full width of the tunnel, and rose a hand's breadth. The treads were cut from slabs of mottled gneiss, polished and fitted to each other so precisely that the joints between them were barely visible. The roof of the tunnel was three times as high as it had been in the lower reaches of the tunnel, perfectly domed and proportioned. The walls and the curved roof were of beautifully dressed blue granite blocks, keyed into each other with marvellous precision and symmetry. The whole was a masterpiece of the mason's art, majestic and portentous. There was both a promise and a menace in this vestibule to the unknown. Its simplicity and lack of ornamentation made it even more impressive.

Royan tugged softly at Nicholas's hand and together they stepped on to the first tread of the stairway. It was carpeted with a fine layer of dust, soft and white as talcum powder. The dust rose in soft eddies and wisps around their knees and then subsided as they passed on upwards. It muted the harsh glare of the electric lamp that Nicholas carried high in his right hand.

Gradually, as they went on upwards, the top of the staircase came into view ahead of them. Royan dug her fingernails into the palm of Nicholas's hand as she saw what lay ahead. The staircase ended on another level landing, across which a rectangular doorway faced them. They stepped up on to the landing and stood before the doorway. Neither of them had words to express this supreme moment: they stood in silence for what seemed like an eternity, holding each other's hand with a fierce and possessive grip.

Finally Nicholas tore his eyes off the gateway, and looked down at Royan. He saw his own feelings mirrored in her face, her eyes shone as though lit from within by an incandescent passion. There was no other person alive with whom he would wish to share this moment. He wanted it to last for ever.

She turned her head and looked at him. They stared deeply and solemnly into each other's eyes. Both of them were aware that this was a high tide in their lives, one that could never be repeated. She tightened her grip on his hand, and looked back to the doorway facing them. It had been plastered over with white river clay, a surface that had mellowed to the shade of ivory. There was no crack or blemish in its smooth expanse, like the flawless skin of a beautiful virgin.

Their eyes fastened avidly on the two embossed seals in the centre of the expanse of white clay. The upper one was in the shape of the royal cartouche, the rectangular knot surmounted by the scarab, the horned beetle that signified the great circle of eternity.

Royan's lips formed the words as she read them from the hieroglyphics, but she uttered no sound. '"The Almighty. The Divine. Ruler of the Upper and Lower Kingdoms of Egypt. Familiar of the god, Horus. Beloved of Osiris and of Isis. Mamose, may he live for ever!"'

Below this magnificent royal seal was a smaller, simpler design in the shape of a hawk, with one broken wing drooping across its barred breast, and the legend: 'I, Taita the slave, have obeyed your command, divine Pharaoh.' Underneath the maimed hawk was a single column of hieroglyphics that spelled out the stern warning: 'Stranger! The gods are watching. Disturb the king's eternal rest at your peril!'

Breaking the seals on the doorway was a momentous act, and despite the fact that the time before the onset of the rains was fast running out, neither of them was prepared to undertake it lightly. They had to make every effort to keep permanent records of everything they discovered, and to inflict as little damage as possible while gaining access.

They spent one of their precious remaining days preparing for the break-in to the tomb. Naturally, Nicholas's first concern was the security of the tomb area. He asked Mek Nimmur to place an armed guard on the causeway over the sink-hole in the approach tunnel, and access beyond this point was restricted. Only Nicholas, Royan, Sapper, Mek, Tessay and four of the monks whom Nicholas had selected were allowed across the bridge.

Hansith Sherif had proved himself repeatedly during the clearing of the lower tunnel. Physically strong, willing and intelligent, he had become Nicholas's principal assistant. It was Hansith who carried the tripod and spare camera equipment while Nicholas photographed the approach tunnel and the sealed doorway. He shot three rolls of high-speed film to make certain that they had a complete record of the unbroken seals and the doorway surrounds. Only when the filming was completed would Nicholas allow Hansith and the other three monks to bring up the tools needed for the break-in.

Sapper moved the Honda generator up as far as the sink-hole, to reduce the voltage drop over the distance that the current had to travel down the cable. Then he set up the floodlights on the upper landing of the staircase and focused them on the white expanse of the plastered doorway.

When they assembled at the threshold they were all in a sober mood. Despite the fact that the tomb was thousands of years old, it was still an act of desecration that they were about to perpetrate. Royan had translated the hieroglyphic warning on the sealed doorway to Sapper, Mek and Tessay, and none of them was prepared to take it lightly.

Nicholas marked out the square opening he intended cutting through the plaster covering. This was large enough to afford access, but it also enclosed the royal cartouche and Tatia's maimed hawk seal. He intended lifting these out in one piece, and preserving them intact. In his imagination, he could already see them displayed in a prominent position in the museum at Quenton Park.

Nicholas began on the right-hand upper corner of the opening. First he used a long, needle-sharp awl as a probe. He pressed and twisted the needle point through the dried clay in an attempt to determine exactly what lay beneath the surface. Very soon he found out that the plaster had been laid over laths of finely interwoven reeds.

'That makes it a lot easier,' he told Royan. 'The reed mat will help to hold the plaster together and prevent it cracking and breaking up.'

He kept working the point of the awl deeper, until suddenly the resistance gave way and the blade ran in its full length.

'Six inches,' he said, measuring the thickness of the door off the blade. 'Taita never skimps, does he? It's a heavy bit of work.'

Still using the awl, Nicholas drilled all four corners of the square opening he intended cutting. Then he stepped back and gestured for Hansith to bring up the heavy four-inch gimlet to enlarge them. This was the type of drill that fishermen use for cutting through lake ice in winter.

As soon as the gimlet broke through, Nicholas impatiently pulled Hansith aside and peered into the hole. Beyond the opening all was completely dark, but he caught a whiff of the faint breath of ancient air that washed through the opening. The odour was dry and dead and austere, the smell of the ages long past.

'What do you see?' Royan demanded at his elbow.

'The light! Give me the light!' he ordered, and when Sapper handed it to him, he held it to the opening.

'Tell me!' Royan was dancing beside him with impatience. 'What do you see now?'

'Colours!' he whispered. 'The most marvellous, indescribable colours.' He stepped back and, lifting her around the waist, held her so that she could look into the aperture.

'Beautiful!' she cried. 'It's so beautiful.'

Sapper rigged up the heavy-duty electric blower fan which would circulate the air in the shaft, while Nicholas prepared the chain-saw. When he was ready, Nicholas handed Royan a pair of goggles and a dust mask and helped her to adjust them. Then he made her fit a pair of wax ear plugs.

Before he started the chain-saw, he sent the rest of them back down the tunnel as far as the causeway over the sink-hole. In the confined space the exhaust fumes from the chain-saw and the dust, together with the noise of the petrol engine, would be overpowering, but apart from that he wanted only Royan with him at the moment of the break-in.

When they were alone, Nicholas switched the blower fan to its highest speed, then donned his own mask and goggles and plugged his ears. He pulled the starter cord of the chain-saw motor and it burst into life in a cloud of blue exhaust smoke.

Nicholas braced himself and pressed the spinning chain blade into the gimlet hole in the plastered doorway. It cut through the thick white plaster and the laths beneath it like a knife through the icing on a wedding cake. Carefully he ran the cutting edge down the line he had marked out.

A cloud of flying white plaster dust filled the air. Within seconds they could see only a few feet in front of their eyes. Doggedly Nicholas kept the cut going, down the right-hand side, across the bottom, then up the left side. Finally he made the last cut across the top, and when the square trapdoor began to sag forward under its own weight he killed the engine of the chain-saw and set it aside.

Royan jumped forwards to help him, and together in the eddies of dust and smoke they steadied the square of plaster and prevented it from

352

crashing to the paving and shattering into a thousand pieces. Gently they lifted it out of the opening and, with the seals still intact, laid it against the side wall of the landing.

The open hatchway they had cut through the plaster was a dark square. Nicholas adjusted the floodlight to shine through it, but the dust was still too dense for them to be able to see much of the interior. Nicholas climbed through the hatch into the space beyond. All was obscured by a dense fog of dust that not even the lamps could penetrate.

He did not attempt to explore further, but immediately turned back to help Royan through the opening after him. He recognized her right to share every moment of this discovery. Beyond the wall they stood quietly together, waiting for the blower fan to clear the air. Slowly the dust fog began to dissipate, and the first thing they became aware of was the floor beneath their feet.

No longer made of stone slabs, it was covered with tiles of yellow agate that had been polished to a gloss and fitted together so cunningly that no joints were visible. It was like a single sheet of lovely opaque glass, dulled only by the film of fine talcum dust that had settled upon it. Where their feet had disturbed the layer of dust the agate sparkled through it, catching the light of the floodlamp.

Then the fog of dust that surrounded them thinned, and gradually a miraculous blaze of colours and shapes began to appear through the murk. Royan lifted the dust mask from her face and let it drop to the agate floor. Nicholas followed her example, and took a breath of the stagnant air. No draught had disturbed it for thousands of years and it had the odour of great antiquity, the musty smell of the linen bandages of an embalmed corpse.

Now the miasma of dust faded away and before them opened a long straight passageway, the end of which was hidden in shadow and darkness. Nicholas turned back to the opening in the sealed door behind them, and reached through it to bring in the floodlight on its stand. Quickly he arranged it to illuminate the full length of the passageway ahead of them.

As they started forward, the images of the old gods hovered around them. They glowered at the intruders from the walls and hung over them, watching them with huge and hostile eyes from the ceiling high overhead. Nicholas and Royan passed on slowly. Their footfalls on the agate tiles were muted by the thin carpet of dust, and the dust that still hung in the air reflected the light and cast over them a luminous net that had an ethereal, dreamlike quality.

Inscriptions covered every inch of space upon the walls and the high roof. There were long quotations from all the mystical writings, from the *Book of Breathings*, the *Book of the Pylons* and the *Book of Wisdom*. Other blocks of hieroglyphics recited the history of Pharaoh Mamose's

353

existence on this earth, and extolled those virtues that made the gods love him.

Further along they came to the first of eight shrines set into the walls of the long funeral gallery. This one was the shrine of Osiris. It was a circular chamber, the curved wall decorated with texts in praise of the god, and in its niche a small statue of Osiris in his tall feathered head-dress, with eyes of onyx and rock crystal which stared at them so implacably that Royan shivered. Nicholas reached out and touched the foot of the god.

He said one word, 'Gold!'

Then he looked up at the towering mural that covered the wall and half the domed ceiling above and around the shrine. It was another gigantic figure of the father Osiris, god of the Underworld, with his green face and false beard, his arms crossed upon his chest, holding the flail and the crook, wearing his tall feathered head-dress and with the erect cobra on his brow. They gazed up at him with a sense of awe. As the lamplight wavered in the shifting dust cloud the god seemed to become imbued with life, and to move and sway before their eyes.

They did not linger at the first shrine, for beyond it the gallery ran on, straight as the flight of an arrow to its target. They followed it. The next shrine set into the wall was dedicated to the goddess. The golden figure of Isis sat in her niche, upon the throne that was her symbol. The infant Horus suckled at her breast. Her eyes were ivory and blue lapis lazuli.

Her murals covered the walls around her niche. There she was, the mother with great kohl-lined eyes as black as night, wearing the sun disc and the horns of the sacred cow upon her head. All around her, hieroglyphic symbols covered the wall, so bright that they glowed like a cloud of fireflies; for she possessed a hundred diverse names. Amongst these were Ast and Net and Bast. She was also Ptah and Seker and Mersekert and Rennut. Each of these names was a word of power, for her sanctity and her benevolent aura had lived on where most of the old gods had withered away for lack of worshippers to repeat and keep alive these mystic names.

In ancient Byzantium and later in Christian Egypt they had bestowed the old goddess's virtues and attributes upon the Virgin Mary. The image of her suckling the infant Horus had been perpetuated in the icons of the Madonna and child. Thus Royan responded to the goddess in all her entities, the mingled blood of Royan's forefathers in her veins acknowledging both Isis and Mary, heresy and truth mingling inextricably in her heart, so that she felt at once both guilt and religious elation.

In the next shrine was a golden figure of Horus, the falcon-headed, the last of the holy trinity. In his right hand he held the war-bow and in his left the *ankh*, for life and death were his to dispense. His eyes were red carnelians.

Portraits of his other entities surrounded the statue: Horus the infant, suckling at the breast of Isis, Horus as the divine youth Harpocrates, proud and lithe and beautiful, one finger touching his chin in the ritual gesture, striding out on sandalled feet under his short, stiff kilt. Then Horus the falcon-headed, sometimes with the body of a lion and then with the body of a young warrior, wearing the great crown of the south and the north united. Beneath him was the inscription: '*Great God and Lord of Heaven, of manifest power, Mighty one amongst all the gods, whose strength has vanquished the foes of his divine father, Osiris.*'

In the fourth shrine stood Seth, the arch-fiend, the god of violence and discord. His body was gold, but his head was the head of a black hyena.

In the fifth shrine stood the god of the dead and of the cemeteries, Anubis the jackal-headed. It was he who officiated at the embalming, and whose duty it was to examine the tongue of the great balance when the heart of the deceased was weighed. If the beam of the scales were exactly horizontal, then the dead man was declared worthy, but if the balance tipped against him Anubis threw the heart to the crocodile monster and it was devoured.

The sixth shrine was dedicated to the god of writing, Thoth. He had the head of a sacred ibis and his stylus was in his hand. In the seventh shrine the sacred cow Hathor stood squarely on all four hooves, her piebald body spotted black and white, her face benignly human but with huge, trumpet-shaped ears. The eighth shrine was the largest and most splendid of all, for it belonged to Amon-Ra, father of all creation. He was the sun, an enormous golden disc from which the slanting golden rays emanated.

Nicholas paused here and looked back down the long gallery. Those eight sacred statues comprised a treasure that matched anything that Howard Carter and Lord Carnarvon had discovered in the tomb of Tutankhamen. He felt in his heart that it was crass even to consider their monetary value. However, the simple truth was that even one of these extraordinary works of art would be sufficient to pay off all his debts many times over. But he thrust the thought aside and turned once more to face the commodious chamber at the far end of the gallery.

'The burial chamber,' Royan murmured with awe. 'The tomb.'

As they walked towards it the shadows retreated before them, like the ghost of the long-dead pharaoh scurrying back to its final resting place. Now they could see into the tomb. Its walls were aflame with still more magnificent murals. Though they had gazed upon so many of these already, their eyes and their senses were not yet jaded or wearied by such profusion.

A single elongated figure rose up the far wall, and then stooped across the ceiling. It was the supple, sinuous body of the goddess Nut, giving birth to the sun. The golden rays poured forth from her open womb, suffusing the sarcophagus of the pharaoh and endowing the dead king with new life.

The royal sarcophagus stood in the centre of the chamber, a massive coffin hewn from a solid granite block. How many slaves must have laboured to bring this mass of stone along the subterranean passages, Nicholas wondered. He could imagine their sweating bodies gleaming in the lamplight, and hear the grating squeal of the wooden rollers under the immense weight of the coffin.

Then Nicholas looked down into the coffin, and felt the plunge of his spirits as he realized that the sarcophagus was empty. The massive granite lid had been lifted from its seat, and flung aside with such violence that it had cracked across its width and now lay in two pieces on the floor beside the coffin.

They moved forward slowly, the bitter taste of disappointment mingling with the dust upon their tongues, until they could look down into the open sarcophagus. It contained only the shattered fragments of the four canopic jars. These vessels had been carved from alabaster to contain the entrails, liver and other internal organs of the king. The broken lids were decorated with the heads of gods and fabulous creatures from beyond the grave.

'Empty!' whispered Royan. 'The body of the king has gone.'

O ver the following days, while they photographed the murals and packed the statues of the eight gods and goddesses from the funeral gallery, Royan and Nicholas discussed and argued the disappearance of the royal mummy from its sarcophagus.

'The seals on the gate of the tomb were intact,' Royan pointed out repeatedly.

'There is probably an explanation for that,' Nicholas told her. 'Taita himself might have removed the treasure and the body. Many times in the writing of the seventh scroll he laments the waste of such treasure. He points out that it could have been much better spent in protecting and nurturing the nation and its people.'

'No, it does not make sense,' Royan argued, 'to go to such lengths as to dam the river and tunnel under the pool, to build this elaborate tomb, and then to remove and destroy the king's mummy. Taita was always a logical person. In his own way he revered the gods of Egypt. It shows in all his writings. He would never have flouted the religious traditions in which he believed so strongly. Something about this tomb does not ring true for me – the mysterious and almost offhanded disappearance of the body, even the paintings and the inscriptions upon the walls.'

'I agree with you about the missing corpse, but what do you find illogical about the decorations?' Nicholas wanted to know.

'Well, the paintings first.' She indicated the image of Isis with a wave of her hand. 'They are lovely, and they are the work of a competent classical artist, but they are hackneyed and stylized in form and choice of colour. The figures are stiff and wooden – they do not move and dance. They lack that spark of genius that we were shown in the tomb of Queen Lostris where the original scrolls in their alabaster jars were hidden.'

Nicholas considered the murals thoughtfully. 'I see what you mean. Even the murals in the tomb of Tanus at the monastery are in a different class from these.'

'Exactly!' she said forcefully. 'Those were the paintings of Taita himself. These are not. They were done by one of his hacks.'

'What else is there about the inscriptions that you don't like?'

'Have you ever heard of another tomb that did not have the text of the *Book of the Dead* inscribed upon its walls, or that did not depict the dead person's journey through the seven pylons to reach the paradise beyond?'

Nicholas looked startled; he had never considered that fact. Without replying he left her and went back down the long gallery, ostensibly to supervise the packing of the sacred statues, but in reality to give himself more time to consider what she had said.

Before leaving England Nicholas had seen to it that all of the more vulnerable and breakable equipment that they had air-freighted into the gorge had been packed in sturdy metal ammunition crates. All these crates had waterproof rubber seals and strong lever fastenings. The original contents had been padded and protected with polystyrene packing. When they left Ethiopia the equipment would be abandoned, but the crates, together with the packing material, had been carefully preserved for transporting the treasures that they might find in the tomb.

While six of the sacred statues fitted neatly into the crates, the images of Hathor the cow and satanic Seth were too large. However, Nicholas discovered that these had been carved in separate parts. The heads were detachable, and the hoofed legs of Hathor were held into the body by wooden pins that were rotted to dust. Broken down into their separate parts, even these two larger statues could also be packed into the metal cases.

Nicholas watched Hansith packing Seth's ferocious head of ebony and black resin into one of the crates. Then after a while he went back to where Royan was working on the inscriptions on the wall above the empty sarcophagus.

'Very well. I agree. You are right about the lack of inscriptions from the *Book of the Dead*. It does seem strange. But what can we do about it, other than accepting it as a mystery which we can never unravel?'

'Nicky, there is something more here. This is not everything. I feel it in every fibre of my being. We are missing something.'

'Who am I, a mere male, to question the veracity of a woman's instincts.'

'Stop being superior,' she snapped. 'How long do I have to work over the inscriptions from the stele?'

'A week or two at the most. I have to set up an RV with Jannie. We have to be there at Roseires airstrip when he comes in to pick us up. That's one date we dare not break.'

'Good Lord. I thought you would have arranged that long ago. How will you contact Jannie from here?'

'Quite simple really.' Nicholas smiled. 'There is a public telephone at the post office in Debra Maryam. Tessay can move freely anywhere in the Gojam. She will go up the escarpment with an escort of monks and telephone Geoffrey Tennant at the British Embassy in Addis. I have already arranged it with Geoffrey. He will relay a message on to Jannie.'

'Will Tessay do it for you?'

He nodded. 'She has agreed to go up to Debra Maryam tomorrow. Jannie must have as much notice as possible to get himself prepared for the flight out from Malta. It's going to need some fine timing for all of us to arrive at the airstrip simultaneously. It will be asking for trouble for one party to sit around waiting at Roseires for the others to arrive.'

'Dawn on the first of April,' Nicholas gave Tessay the message. 'Tell Jannie we will be there on April Fools' Day! A nice easy one to remember.'

They watched Tessay set off along the trail with her escort of monks and Royan asked Mek Nimmur quietly, 'Don't you worry about her going off like this on her own?'

'She is a very competent person, and she is well known and liked throughout the Gojam. She is as safe as any person can be in a dangerous land.' Mek watched Tessay's slim figure in *shamma* and jodhpur pants becoming smaller with distance. 'I wish I could go with her, but—' Mek shrugged.

Suddenly Royan exclaimed, 'There is something that I forgot to ask her.' She left Nicholas and Mek standing, and ran down the trail calling

358

after the other woman. Her voice floated back to where Nicholas stood watching her.

'Tessay! Wait! Come back!'

Tessay turned and waited for Royan to catch up with her. While the two women stood talking together, Nicholas lost interest and turned to study the distant silhouette of the escarpment. With a sinking feeling in the pit of his stomach he saw that the thunderheads on the mountain tops were denser and more ominous than they had been only days before. The rains were building up swiftly now. He wondered if they really had as long as they hoped before the dam was threatened and they were driven out of the gorge by the rising waters.

He looked back down the path just in time to see Royan pass something to Tessay, who nodded and pushed it into the pocket of her jodhpurs. Then at last the two women embraced warmly, and Tessay turned away. Royan stood in the middle of the trail, watching until a bend in the valley hid Tessay from her. Then she walked slowly back to where Nicholas waited.

'What was all that about?' he wanted to know, and she smiled mysteriously.

'Girls' secrets. There are some things that it's best you brutish males don't know about.' But when Nicholas raised an eyebrow at her, she relented and told him, 'Tessay will ask Geoffrey Tennant to send a message to Mummy, just to let her know that I am all right. I don't want her to worry about me.'

As they climbed back down the scaffolding to where the fly camp had been set up on the rock ledge beside Taita's pool, Nicholas thought how fortuitous it was that Royan had her mother's phone number already written down to hand to Tessay, and he wondered at this sudden urge of Royan's to report her whereabouts to her mother. 'I wonder what she is really up to?' he mused. 'I will try and wheedle it out of Tessay when she returns.'

Royan would have preferred to camp in the tomb itself, so as to be in the midst of the inscriptions on which she was working, but Nicholas had insisted that they sleep in the open air, and the ledge was as close as they could get to their workplace. 'The musty air in the tomb is very probably unhealthy,' he told her. 'Cave disease is a real danger in these old enclosed places. They say that is what killed some of Howard Carter's people working in the tomb of Tutankhamen.'

'The fungus spores that cause cave disease breed in bat dung,' she pointed out. 'There are no bats in Mamose's tomb. Taita sealed it up too tightly.'

'Humour me,' he begged. 'You cannot work in there for days on end. I want you at least to get out of the tomb for a few hours each day.'

She shrugged. 'Only as a special favour to you,' she agreed, but as they reached the foot of the scaffolding she gave her new sleeping quarters only a perfunctory glance and then headed for the coffer dam and the entrance to the approach tunnel.

They had converted the landing at the top of the staircase, outside the plaster-sealed entrance to the tomb, into their workshop. Royan spread her drawings and photographs and reference books on the rough table of hand-hewn planks that Hansith made for her. Sapper had placed one of the floodlamps above this crude desk so that she had good light to work by. Against one wall of the landing they had stacked the ammunition crates which contained the eight sacred statues. Nicholas had insisted on storing all their discoveries where he could safeguard them adequately. Mek's armed men still kept a twenty-four-hour guard on the causeway over the sink-hole.

While Nicholas completed his photographic record of the walls of the long gallery and the empty burial chamber, Royan sat at her table and pored over her papers for hours at a time, scribbling notes and calculations from them into her notebooks. Now and then she would jump up from her desk and dart through the hatch in the white plaster doorway into the long gallery to study a detail on the decorated walls.

Whenever this happened, Nicholas straightened up from his camera tripod and watched her with a fond and indulgent expression. So intent was she that she seemed completely oblivious of him and everybody else about her. Nicholas had never seen her in this mood, and the depth of her powers of concentration impressed him.

When she had worked for fifteen hours without a break he went out on to the landing to rescue her and to lead her, protesting, back down the tunnel to the pool where there was a hot meal waiting for them. After she had eaten he led her to her hut and insisted that she lie down on her inflatable mattress.

'You are going to sleep now, Royan,' he ordered.

He woke to hear her creeping stealthily out of the hut next door to his, back along the ledge to the entrance to the tomb. He checked his watch and grunted with disbelief when he realized that they had slept for only three and a half hours. He shaved quickly and bolted back a slab of toasted *injera* bread and a cup of tea before following her into the tomb.

He found her standing in the long gallery before the empty niche in the shrine where the statuette of Osiris had stood. She was so preoccupied that she did not hear him come up behind her, and she started violently when he touched her arm.

'You startled me,' she scolded him.

'What are you staring at?' he asked. 'What have you discovered?'

'Nothing,' she denied swiftly, and then after a moment, 'I don't know. It's just an idea.'

'Come on! What are you up to?'

'It's easier for me to show you.' She led him back to her table on the stone landing, and rearranged her notebooks carefully before she spoke again.

'What I have been doing these last few days is going through the material on the stele of Tanus's tomb, picking out all the quotations that I recognize from the classical books of mystery, the *Book of Breathings*, the *Book of the Pylons* and the *Book of Thoth*, and setting those on one side.' She showed him fifteen pages in her neat small script. 'All this is ancient material, none of it original compositions by Taita. I have discarded it for the time being.'

She set the first notebook aside and picked up the next. 'All this is from the fourth face of the stele. It's nothing that I recognize, but seems to be only long lists of numbers and figures. Some sort of code, perhaps? I am not sure, but I do have some ideas on it that I will come to later.

'Now this here,' she showed him the next book, 'this is all fresh material that I don't remember reading in any of the ancient classics. Much of it, if not all of it, must be original Taita writings. If he has left any more clues for us, I believe they will be here, in these sections.'

He grinned, 'Like that marvellous quotation describing the pink and private parts of the goddess. Is that what you are referring to?'

'Trust you not to forget that.' She flushed lightly and refused to look up from her notebook. 'Look at this quotation from the head of the third face of the stele, the side Taita has headed "*autumn*". It's the very first one that caught my attention.'

Nicholas leaned forward and read the hieroglyphics aloud: '"*The great god Osiris makes the opening coup with deference to the protocol of the four bulls. At the first pylon he bears full testimony to the immutable law of the board.*"' He looked up at her. 'Yes, I remember that quotation. Taita is referring to bao, the game that the old devil loved so passionately.'

'That's right.' Royan looked slightly embarrassed. 'But do you also remember that I told you about a dream that I had in which I saw Duraid again in one of the chambers of the tomb?'

'I remember.' He chuckled at her discomfort. 'He said something to you about the protocol of the four bulls. Now we are going into the realm of divination by dreams, are we?'

She looked annoyed by his levity. 'All I am suggesting is that my subconscious had been digesting the quotation and come up with an answer, which it put into the mouth of Duraid in the dream. Can't you be serious just for one moment?'

'Sorry.' He was contrite. 'Remind me what you heard Duraid say.'

'In the dream he told me, "*Remember the protocol of the four bulls – Start at the beginning.*"'

361

'I am no expert on the game of bao. What did he mean?'

'The rules and subtleties of the game have been lost in the mists of antiquity. But as you know, we have found examples of the bao board amongst the grave goods in the tombs of the eleventh to the seventeenth dynasties, and we can only guess that it was an early form of chess.' She began to sketch for him on one of the blank pages at the back of her notebook.

'The wooden board was laid out like a chessboard, eight rows of cups wide and eight rows deep. Like this.' She drew it in with quick, deft strokes of her ballpoint pen. 'The pieces were coloured stones that moved in a prescribed fashion. I won't go into all the details, but the protocol of the four bulls was an opening gambit in the game favoured by grand masters of Taita's calibre. It consisted of making sacrifices to mass the highest-ranking stones in the first cup from where they could dominate the important central files of the board.'

'I am not sure where we are going, but lead on. I am listening.' Nicholas tried not to look too mystified.

'The first cup of the board.' She indicated it on her sketch, as though instructing a backward child. 'The beginning. Duraid said, "Start at the beginning." Taita said, "The great god Osiris makes the opening coup."'

'I still don't follow you.' Nicholas shook his head.

'Come with me.' Carrying the notebooks, she led him through the hatch in the white plaster doorway and stood beside him at the shrine of Osiris. 'The opening coup. The beginning.'

She turned and faced down the gallery. 'This is the first shrine. How many shrines are there altogether?'

'Three for the trinity, then Seth, Thoth, Anubis, Hathor and Ra,' he listed. 'Eight altogether.'

'Glory be!' She laughed. 'The lad can count! How many cups in the files of the bao board?'

'Eight across, and eight down—' he broke off and stared at her. 'You think—?'

She did not answer, but opened the notebook. 'All of these numbers and extraneous symbols – they spell no coherent words. They do not relate to each other in any way, except that no number in the list is greater than eight.'

'I thought I had caught up with you, but I just lost you again.'

'If somebody were to read the notations of a game of chess four thousand years from now, what would he make of it?' she asked. 'Wouldn't it just be lists of numbers and extraneous symbols to him? You really are being extremely dense, aren't you? This is like pulling teeth.'

'Oh, Lordy, Lordy!' His face cleared. 'You clever lady! Taita is playing the game of bao with us.'

'And this is the first pylon, where it starts.' She gestured to the shrine. 'This is where the great god Osiris makes the opening coup. This is where we must start at the beginning of the sacred bao board. This is where we counter his opening move.'

They both looked around the shrine for a while, studying the curved walls and the high domed roof, and then Nicholas broke the silence. 'At the risk of being called extremely dense and having my teeth pulled, may I ask a question? How the hell do we play a game when we don't even know the rules?'

Colonel Nogo exuded confidence and self-importance as he swaggered into the conference room to answer von Schiller's summons. Nahoot Guddabi bustled along behind him, determined not to be excluded from any of the proceedings. He too tried to look confident and important, but in truth he felt his position was very insecure and that he needed to justify himself to his master.

Von Schiller was dictating correspondence to Utte Kemper, but as soon as they entered the room he stood up quickly and stepped on to the carpeted block.

'You promised that you would have a report for me yesterday,' he snapped at Nogo, ignoring Nahoot. 'Have you not heard anything from this informer of yours in the gorge?'

'I apologize for keeping you waiting like this, Herr von Schiller.' Nogo was immediately deflated by this sharp attack, and he became restless and uneasy. The German frightened him. 'The women were a day late returning from Harper's camp. They are very unreliable, these country people. Time means very little to them.'

'Yes, yes.' Von Schiller was impatient. 'I know the failings of your black brethren, and I might add you are not completely innocent of these yourself, Nogo. But tell me what news you have for me.'

'Harper finished work on the dam seven days ago, and immediately he moved his camp downstream, to a new place on the hills above the ravine. He then built some sort of bamboo ladder down into the ravine. My informer tells me that they are clearing a hole at the bottom of the empty pool—'

'A hole? What kind of hole?' Von Schiller turned pale as he listened, and began sweating in a light sheen across his forehead.

'Are you all right, Herr von Schiller?' Nogo was alarmed. The German looked very ill, as if he were about to collapse.

'I am perfectly well,' von Schiller shouted at him. 'What hole was this? Describe it to me.'

'The woman bringing the message is a stupid peasant.' Nogo was uncomfortable, squirming under von Schiller's grilling. 'She says only that when the river water fell, there was a hole in the bottom that was filled with rock and rubbish and that they have cleared this out.'

'A tunnel!' Nahoot could contain himself no longer. 'It must be the entrance tunnel to the tomb.'

'Be quiet!' Von Schiller turned on him furiously. 'You have no facts to back up that supposition. Let Nogo finish.' He turned back to the colonel. 'Go on. Give me the rest of it.'

'The woman says that there is a cave at the end of the hole. Like a rock shrine, with pictures on the walls—'

'Pictures? What pictures?'

'The woman said they were pictures of the saints.' Nogo made a deprecating gesture. 'She is a very uneducated woman. Stupid—'

'Christian saints?' von Schiller demanded.

Nahoot interjected, 'That is not possible, Herr von Schiller. I tell you that Harper has discovered the tomb of Mamose. You must act swiftly now.'

'I will not warn you again, you miserable little man,' von Schiller snarled at him. 'Keep quiet.'

He turned back to Nogo. 'Was there anything else in the cavern? Tell me everything the woman said.'

'Pictures and statues of the saints.' Nogo spread his hands. 'I am sorry, Herr von Schiller, that's what she said. I know this is all nonsense, but that is what the woman told me.'

'I will judge what is and what is not nonsense,' von Schiller told him. 'What did she say happened to these statues of the saints?'

'Harper has packed them in boxes.'

'Has he removed them from the shrine?'

'I do not know, Herr von Schiller. The woman did not say.'

Von Schiller stepped down from his block. He began to pace up and down the length of the hut, muttering to himself distractedly.

'Herr von Schiller—' Nahoot began, but the German waved him to silence. At last he stopped in front of Nogo and stared up at him.

'Did they find a mummy, a body, in the shrine?' he demanded.

'I do not know, Herr von Schiller. The woman did not say.'

'Where is she?' Von Schiller was so agitated that he clutched the front of Nogo's uniform jacket and stood on tiptoe to thrust his face up close to his. 'Where is this woman? Have you let her go?' Tiny droplets of spittle flew into Nogo's face and he blinked and tried to duck, but von Schiller had him in a death grip.

'No, sir. She is still here. I did not want to bring her to you—'

'You fool. All you are telling me is secondhand. Bring her in here immediately. I want to question her face to face.' He shoved Nogo away from him. 'Go and fetch her.'

Nogo returned minutes later dragging the woman into the room by one arm. She was young, and despite the blue tattoos across her cheeks and chin she was pretty. She wore the long black robes and head-covering of a married woman, and carried an infant on her hip.

As soon as Nogo released her arm she sank to the floor and whimpered with terror. The child she carried whined in sympathy. Its nostrils were plugged with white crusts of dried snot. The woman opened the top of her robe with a shaking hand, fished out one of her milk-swollen breasts and thrust the nipple into the child's mouth. Infant and mother stared at von Schiller with terrified eyes.

'Ask her if there was a coffin or body of the saint in the shrine,' von Schiller ordered, eyeing the woman with distaste.

Nogo questioned her for a minute and then shook his head. 'She does not know anything about a body. She is very stupid. She does not understand very well.'

'Ask her about the statues of the saints. What has Harper done with them? Where are they now? Has he removed them from the shrine?'

After another long exchange with the woman, Nogo shook his head. 'No. She says that the statues are still in the shrine. The white man has packed them into boxes and the soldiers are guarding them.'

'Soldiers? What soldiers?'

'Soldiers of Mek Nimmur, the *shufta* commander that I told you about. He is still with Harper.'

'How many boxes are there?' In his impatience von Schiller went up to where the woman sat and prodded her with the toe of his boot. 'How many statues are there?'

The woman wailed with terror and shrank away from him. Von Schiller recoiled from her at the same time, with an expression of disgust.

'Gott im Himmel!' He pulled a handkerchief from his pocket and patted his mouth and nose with it. 'She stinks like an animal. Ask her how many boxes.'

'Not many,' Nogo translated, 'perhaps five, not more than ten. She is not sure.'

'What size? How big are they?'

When Nogo put the question to her, the woman indicated the length of her arm. Von Schiller's disappointment registered clearly in his face.

'So few pieces, and so insignificant.' He turned away from the woman and went to stare out of the south-facing window of the hut, down over the escarpment rim into the wilderness of the gorge. 'If what this creature says is true, then Harper has not yet discovered the treasure of Mamose. There should be more, much more.'

Nogo was talking rapidly to the woman again, and now he turned back to von Schiller. 'She says that one of Harper's party has left the camp in the gorge, and gone to Debra Maryam.'

Von Schiller spun away from the window and stared at him. 'One of his party? Who? Which one?'

'She is an Ethiopian woman. The concubine of Mek Nimmur. A woman she calls Woizero Tessay. I know of her. She was married to the Russian hunter, before she became Mek Nimmur's whore.'

Von Schiller rushed across the room and seized the woman by the front of her robe. He hauled her to her feet with such violence that the infant was jerked from her grip and fell howling to the floor.

'Ask her where the woman is now,' he instructed Nogo.

The mother pulled free from his grip and grovelled on the floor, trying to pick up and console her screaming infant. Nogo grabbed her and slapped her face resoundingly to get her attention. She clasped her baby to her breast and gabbled out a reply.

'She does not know,' Nogo admitted. 'She thinks she is still at Debra Maryam.'

'Get that filthy bitch out of here!' Von Schiller jerked his head at the woman and her child. Nogo dragged them from the hut.

'What else do you know of this woman of Mek Nimmur's?' he asked in milder tones when Nogo returned.

'She is from one of the noble families in Addis Ababa, a blood relative of Ras Tafari Makonnen, the old Emperor Haile Selassie.'

'If she is Mek Nimmur's woman, and has come directly from Harper's camp, then she will be able to answer the questions that this other creature could not.'

'That is true, Herr von Schiller. But she may not wish to tell us.'

'I want her,' von Schiller said. 'Bring her here. Helm will speak to her. I am sure he will be able to make her see reason.'

'She is an important person. Her family has much influence.' Nogo thought about it for a moment. 'But on the other hand, she has been consorting with a notorious bandit. That is all the reason I need for bringing her in. I will send a detachment of my men, under one of my most trusted officers, to arrest her immediately.' He hesitated. 'If the woman is questioned severely, it would be as well that she were not allowed to return to her friends in Addis. They could make trouble for all of us. Even for you, Herr von Schiller.'

'What do you propose?' von Schiller wanted to know.

'When she has answered your questions, there will have to be a little accident,' Nogo suggested.

'Do what is necessary,' von Schiller ordered. 'I will leave the details to you, but make sure that if it is necessary to dispose of the woman it is done properly. I have had enough bungling.' As he spoke these words he looked across at Nahoot Guddabi, who lowered his gaze and flushed angrily.

They had spent almost two full days at the shrine of Osiris in the long gallery. No ancient worshipper had ever studied the texts upon those walls more avidly than Nicholas and Royan, or examined the flamboyant murals of the great god with more minute attention.

They took it in turn to recite aloud the extracts from the stele of Tanus that Royan had picked out and recorded in her notebooks, repeating them until they knew each quotation by heart. While one read aloud, the other concentrated his or her full attention upon the walls, trying to discover some connecting link.

'"My love is a flask of cold water in the desert. My love is a banner unfurling in the breeze. My love is the first shout of the newborn infant,"' Nicholas read.

Royan looked up at him from where she squatted attentively before the shrine, and smiled. 'At times Taita was really rather cute, wasn't he?' she said. 'Such a romantic.'

'Concentrate, for heaven's sake. This isn't a poetry appreciation class. We are doing serious business here.'

'Barbarian!' she muttered under her breath, but turned back to the wall of inscriptions.

'Try this one again,' Nicholas ordered, and read out, '"We lie in the vale of a thousand joinings, of infant to mother, of man to woman, of friend to friend, of teacher to pupil, of sex to sex."'

'That's the third time you have picked out that particular quotation this morning. What is there about it that appeals to you so strongly?' She did not look up at him, but the back of her neck turned a ruddier shade of brown.

'Sorry! Thought you might find that one as romantic as the other,' he mumbled. 'Let's try this one then. "I have suffered and loved. I have withstood the wind and the storm. The arrow pierced my flesh but did not harm me. I have eschewed the false path that lies straight before me. I have taken the hidden stairway to the seat of the gods."'

Royan rocked back on her heels and glanced down the long gallery. 'Something there perhaps. "The false path that lies straight before me. The hidden stairway"?'

'We are straining a bit now. Snapping at gnats like a hungry trout.'

She stood up and pushed the tendrils of sweaty hair off her forehead. 'Oh, Nicky. It's so discouraging. We don't even know where to begin.'

'Courage, lassie.' He feigned the cheerfulness he did not feel. 'We begin at the beginning like your friend Taita said we must. Let me try you with this one again.' He placed his hand over his heart like a Victorian actor and emoted, '"*The vulture rises on mighty pinions to greet the sun*"—'

She laughed softly at his clowning, and then her eyes wandered from his face and passed over his shoulder. Suddenly she started.

'The vulture!' she blurted, and pointed at the wall behind him.

He spun around and stared in the direction she was indicating.

There was the vulture, a magnificent image of the bird, the fierce eyes glaring and the yellow beak hooked and pointed. Its wings were spread wide, with each feather outlined in jewel-like colours. It stood as tall as Nicholas, but its wing-spread covered half the wall. They stared at it together, and then Royan lifted her eyes to the ceiling high above where they stood. She touched his arm and motioned him to do the same.

'The sun!' she whispered. The golden sun disc of Ra was painted in the highest portion of the roof. Its warmth seemed to illuminate the shadows. Its rays spread out in every direction, but one of these beams followed the curve of the wall and descended to envelop the vulture image in its spreading luminosity.

'"*The vulture rises to greet the sun*",' she repeated. 'Does Taita mean it literally?'

He moved closer to the mural and examined it minutely, running his hands over the wings and down its belly to the cruel curved talons. Beneath the paint the plastered wall was smooth. There was no projection or any irregularity.

'The head, Nicky. Look at the head of the bird!' She jumped up and tried to reach it, but her fingers fell short and she turned to him with a desperate edge to her voice. 'You do it – you are much taller than I am.'

Only then did he see the slight shadow down one side of the bird's head where the floodlamp caught it, and as he touched it he realized that the head was in relief, standing slightly above the level of the surrounding wall. He ran his fingers over the raised head and found that the beak was part of the relief.

'Can you feel any joint in the plaster?' Royan demanded.

He shook his head. 'No. It's smooth. It all seems to be part of the main wall.'

'"*The vulture rises to greet the sun*",' she insisted. 'Can't you detect any movement? Try pushing the head upwards towards the sun painting.'

He placed the heel of his hand under the bulge of the head and pushed upwards. 'Nothing!' he grunted.

'It's been there for almost four thousand years.' She was hopping from one foot to the other with frustration. 'Dammit, Nicky, if there is a moving part, it will be stiff. Harder! Push harder!'

He shifted his feet to get well under it and placed both hands under the projection of the head. Slowly he brought all his strength to bear. The cords in his neck stood out and blood flooded his face, turning it a deep, angry red.

'Harder!' she implored him, but at last he dropped his arms to his sides and stood back.

'No.' His voice was hoarse and strained with the effort. 'It's solid. Won't budge.'

'Lift me up. Let me look.'

'With the greatest of pleasure. Any excuse to lay lascivious hands on you.' He stepped behind her and placed both arms around her waist, then lifted her until she was able to touch the bird's head.

Quickly she explored it with her fingertips, and then she let out a small cry of triumph.

'Nicky! You have started something. The paint is cracked all around the outline of the head. I can feel it. Lift me higher!'

He grunted with the effort but raised her another foot off the floor.

'Yes, definitely!' she exclaimed. 'Something has moved. There is a hairline crack in the wall above the head, as well. You have a look!'

He fetched one of the empty ammunition crates from the landing outside the entrance and placed it below the vulture image. When he stepped up on to it he was on a level with the vulture's eye.

His expression changed. Quickly he groped in his pocket and brought out his clasp knife. He opened the blade and probed carefully around the outline of the head. Tiny specks of dried paint and plaster filtered down as he worked.

'It does look as though the head is a separate detached piece,' he admitted.

'Look on top of it, higher up the wall. There along the edge of the sunbeam. Can't you see a vertical crack in the plaster?'

'You are right, you know,' he admitted. 'But if I try to open that crack I am going to damage the mural. Do you want me to do that?'

She hesitated only a moment. 'This tomb is going to be reflooded when the river rises, so we are going to lose it again anyway. It's worth the risk. Do it, Nicky!'

He pressed the point of the knife-blade into the fine crack and twisted it gently. A slab of painted plaster the size of his spread hand fell out of the wall and splattered into the dust on the agate tiles of the floor.

369

He peered into the cavity that it had left in the wall.

'It looks like some kind of slot or groove in the wall,' he said. 'I am going to clear its full length.' Carefully he worked at the cavity he had opened, and more loose plaster rained down.

Royan sneezed in the dust, but would not retreat. Particles of debris lodged in her hair like confetti.

'Yes,' he said at last. 'There is a vertical groove running up here.'

'Chip the plaster away from the crack around the vulture's head,' she ordered, and he wiped the blade against his trouser leg and attacked the wall again.

'It's free,' he said at last. 'It looks as though the head will travel up the groove. Anyway, I am going to try it. Stand back and give me room to work.'

He placed the heels of both hands under the head of the vulture, and heaved upwards against it. Royan bunched her hands into fists and screwed up her face in sympathy with his effort.

There was a soft grating sound, and the head began to move jerkily up the exposed groove in the wall. It reached the top of the slot and Nicholas jumped down from the crate. They both stared expectantly at the disembodied head, now disfigured by the chipped and damaged plaster.

After a long, breathless wait, Royan whispered dejectedly, 'Nothing! It hasn't changed anything.'

'The rest of the quotation from the stele,' he reminded her. 'There was more to it than just the vulture and the sun.'

'You are right.' She looked around the rest of the wall eagerly. '"*The jackal howls and turns upon his tail.*"'

She pointed with a trembling finger at the small, almost insignificant figure of Anubis, the jackal-headed god of the graveyards, on the wall opposite the vulture that they had mutilated. Standing at the foot of the huge, towering painting of Osiris, he was only a little larger in size than the ringed and bejewelled big toe of the husband of Isis and father of Horus.

Royan ran to the wall, and the moment she touched Anubis she felt that his image too was raised. She flung all her strength against the tiny figure, trying to twist it first one way and then the other.

'"*The jackal turns upon his tail*",' she panted as she wrestled with him. 'He must turn!'

'Here, let me do that.' Gently Nicholas pulled her away, and knelt before the black-headed god image. Once again he used the blade of his clasp knife to chip away the plaster and the thick layer of paint from around the outline.

'It seems to be carved in some sort of hard wood and then it's been plastered over,' he told her, as he tested the construction of the figure with the point of the blade.

When at last he had chipped it clear he tried to twist it in a clockwise direction, and grunted with the effort.

'No!' He gave up at last.

'They had no clock dials in ancient Egypt,' she reminded him agitatedly. 'The other way. Turn it the other way.'

When he tried to turn it counter-clockwise, there was another rasping, gritty sound from behind the wall panel. The tiny figure revolved slowly in his hands, until the black head pointed down towards the yellow tiles.

They both stood well back from the wall, looking expectantly at it, but after another long wait even Nicholas was disheartened.

'I don't know what to expect, but whatever it is, it isn't happening,' he grunted with disgust.

'There is still the last part of the quotation,' Royan whispered. '"*The river flows towards the earth. Beware, you violators of the sacred places, lest the wrath of all the gods descend upon you!*"'

'The river?' Nicholas asked. 'As Sapper might say, I don't see no perishing river.'

Royan did not even smile at the cockney accent. Instead she searched the profusion of writing and images that covered all the walls around them. Then she saw it.

'Hapi!' Her voice was shrill with excitement. 'The god of the Nile! The river!'

High up the wall, on a level with the head of the great god Osiris, the god of the river looked down upon them. Hapi was a hermaphrodite, with the breasts of a woman and the genitals of a man protruding from under the pendulous belly. The mouth in his hippo-potamus head gaped wide to display the great curved tusks that lined his cavernous jaws.

Standing on a pile of ammunition boxes, Nicholas was able to reach the Hapi image at the full stretch of his arms. As he touched it he exulted, 'This one is raised also.'

'"*The river flows towards the earth*,"' she called up to him. 'It must move downwards. Try it, Nicky.'

'Give me a chance to clear the edges.' He used the point of the blade to chip the outline of the god free, and then he probed the plaster beneath it and found another vertical slot running towards the floor.

'Ready to give it a go now.' He folded the knife and tucked it back into his pocket. 'Hold your breath and say a little prayer for me,' he instructed.

He settled both hands on the image of the god and began to pull steadily downwards. Gradually he brought more pressure to bear upon it, until he was hanging all his weight on it. Nothing moved.

'It's not working,' he grunted.

'Wait!' she ordered. 'I am coming up.'

She scrambled up on to the boxes behind him and placed both arms around his neck. 'Hang on tight,' she ordered.

'Every little bit helps, I suppose,' he agreed, as she lifted her feet and hung her full weight on his shoulders.

'It's moving!' he shouted. Suddenly the image of Hapi gave way under his hands, and with a sharp grating sound travelled down to the bottom end of the groove in the wall.

Nicholas lost his grip on the smoothly rounded shape as it came up hard against the end of its slot. The stack of boxes under them toppled, and both he and Royan dropped back to the floor of the gallery. She was still hanging around his neck, and he lost his balance as she pulled him over backwards. The two of them sprawled on the agate floor in an untidy tangle of arms and legs. Nicholas scrambled to his feet and pulled her up beside him.

'What has happened?' she gasped, looking up wildly at the damaged Hapi figure and then around the walls of the gallery.

'Nothing,' he said. 'Nothing has moved.'

'Perhaps there is another—' she began, but broke off at a sound from the roof above them. They both stared upwards, startled and filled with sudden trepidation. There was a ponderous movement from above the high plastered ceiling.

'What is that?' Royan whispered. 'There is something up there. It sounds like a living thing.'

A giant was moving, coming awake after slumbering for thousands of years, stretching and turning as he awoke.

'Is it—?' She could not finish the question. She had an image in her mind of the great god himself stirring in a hidden chamber in the rock, opening those baleful, slanted eyes, rising on one elbow to discover who had disturbed him from his eternal sleep.

Then there was another sound, a creaking and rumbling as though the arm of a mighty balance was swinging slowly across, as its equilibrium altered. Softly at first, then louder, the movement gathered momentum, like the beginning of a mountain avalanche. Then there was a report like the shot of a cannon.

A crack appeared in the high ceiling, running the length of the gallery. Dust smoked from the jagged opening, and then, slowly as a nightmare, the roof began to sag down over where they stood. Both of them were paralysed with superstitious horror, unable to tear their gaze from the slow, inexorable collapse of the ceiling upon them. Then a chunk of plaster struck Nicholas's upturned face, slamming into his cheek, tearing the skin and sending him staggering backwards against the wall. The shock and pain aroused him at last.

'The warning!' he blurted. 'Taita's warning. The wrath of the gods.' He sprang to her side and grabbed her hand, 'Run!' He pulled her after him. 'Taita has booby-trapped the roof!'

They raced back along the gallery towards the opening in the sealed entrance. Lumps of stone and plaster began to rain down and dust filled the passageway, half-blinding them. The dull rumble overhead became a rising roar as progressively the roof collapsed. They did not dare to look back as the thunder of falling masonry swept towards them, threatening to overtake and overwhelm them before they were able to reach the entrance.

A jagged piece of rock as large as her head struck Royan a glancing blow on her shoulder, and her legs sagged under her. She would have gone down if he had not flung one arm around her and held her upright, dragging her along the gallery. The dust obscured the passage ahead of them, so that the square opening that offered their only chance of escape receded in the choking fog.

'Keep going!' he yelled at her. 'Almost there.' As he spoke, a thick sheet of plaster came crashing down and smashed into the tripod stand of the floodlamp. Instantly the gallery was plunged into utter darkness.

Completely unsighted, Nicholas's first instinct was to come up short and try to orientate himself. But all around him the rubble of the roof was falling heavier and faster. He knew that at any second the entire roof would come down on top of them, burying and crushing them. Running on without a check, he dragged Royan along behind him in the darkness. He reached the end wall at full tilt, and the impact knocked the breath out of him. Now, through the swirling dust cloud, he was just able to make out the rectangular opening in the plaster wall in front of him, back-lit by the lamps on the landing at the head of the staircase outside.

As he reeled backwards he seized Royan around the waist and lifted her bodily off her feet. He hurled her through the opening and heard her cry out as she fell heavily on the far side. Another piece of rubble struck him on the back of his head and knocked him to his knees. He felt himself teetering on the very brink of consciousness, but crawled forward, groping frantically until he touched the jagged edge of the opening. With this handhold he was able to drag himself over the sill, just as the full weight of the roof came thundering down along the entire gallery.

Here on the upper landing of the staircase Royan was crouching on her knees. She crawled towards him, guided once more by the lamplight.

'Are you all right?' she panted. A trickle of blood snaked down her cheek from a wound in her scalp line. It cut a dark glistening runnel through the caked white dust that powdered her face.

He did not answer, but dragged himself to his feet and pulled Royan up beside him. 'Can't stay here,' he croaked, just as a thick white breath of dust blew through the mouth of the opening and swept over them, choking them and dimming the floodlamps to a faint glimmer.

'Not safe.' He pulled her away from the opening. 'The whole thing might cave in.' His voice was rough, his throat closing with the dust.

He dragged her to the head of the steps and they staggered down together, stumbling against each other, their feet sliding under them as they came on to the algae-slippery footing. Through the dust mist ahead of them loomed the broad square figure of Sapper.

'What the ruddy hell is going on?' he bellowed with relief as he saw them.

'Give me a hand here,' Nicholas yelled back at him. Sapper lifted Royan in his arms and together they ran back down the tunnel, only stopping to draw breath when they reached the causeway over the sink-hole.

The post office in the village of Debra Maryam was a small building in the dusty street behind the church. Its walls were of unplastered unburnt and unpainted brick, and its galvanized iron roof glared like a mirror in the high mountain sunlight. The public telephone should have been in its booth outside the front door. However, the instrument had long since vanished – stolen, vandalized or, more likely, removed by the military to prevent it being used by political dissidents and rebels.

Tessay had expected this, and hardly glanced into the booth before she strode into the small room which was the main post office. It was filled with a motley crowd of peasants and villagers, queuing to conduct their leisurely business with the elderly postmaster, the only person behind the barred counter. Some of the customers had spread their cloaks on the floor and settled in for a long wait, chatting and smoking while their children romped and crawled around them.

Most of the patient crowd recognized Tessay as soon as she entered the room. Even those who had waited most of the morning in the lines at the counter greeted her respectfully and stood aside to allow her to go to the head of the queue. Despite two decades of African socialism, the feudal instincts of the rural population were still strong. Tessay was a noblewoman and she was entitled to this preference.

'Thank you, my friends.' She smiled at them and shook her head. 'You are kind, but I will wait my turn.'

They were embarrassed by her refusal, and when the old postmaster

374

leaned over his counter top and added his insistence to the others, one of the older women seized Tessay's arm and forcefully propelled her forward.

'Jesus and all the saints bless you, Woizero Tessay.' The postmaster clapped his hands in respectful greeting. 'Welcome back to Debra Maryam. What is it that your ladyship desires?'

The entire clientele of the post office crowded around Tessay so as not to miss a detail of her transaction.

'I want to make a telephone call to Addis,' she told the postmaster and there was a hum of comment and discussion. This was unusual and important business indeed.

'I will take you to the telephone exchange,' the postmaster told her importantly, and donned his official blue cap for the occasion. He came around the counter shouting and hectoring the other customers, pushing them aside to make way for Lady Sun. Then he ushered her through to the back room of the building, where the telephone exchange occupied a cubicle the size of a small lavatory.

Tessay, the postmaster and as many of the other customers who could find standing room pushed their way into the tiny room. The exchange operator was almost overcome by the honour being accorded him by the beautiful Tessay, and he shouted into his headset like a sergeant major commanding a flag party.

'Soon now!' he beamed at Tessay. 'Only small delay. Then you speak to British Embassy in Addis.'

Tessay, who knew well what a small delay constituted, retired to the front veranda of the post office and sent for food and flasks to be brought from the village *tej* shop. She treated her escort of monks, together with half the population of Debra Maryam, to a happy picnic while she waited for her call to be patched through half a dozen antiquated village exchanges to the capital. Thanks to the *tej*, spirits were high amongst her entourage when finally, an hour later, the postmaster rushed out to tell her proudly that they had succeeded and that her party was awaiting her on the line in the back room.

Tessay, the monks and fifty villagers followed the postmaster back into the exchange and crowded, jabbering, into the cubicle. The overflow backed up into the main post hall.

'Geoffrey Tennant speaking.' The upper-class English accent was tinny with distance and static.

'Mr Tennant, this is Woizero Tessay.'

'I was expecting your call.' Geoffrey's voice lightened as he realized that he was talking to a pretty girl. 'How are you, my dear?'

Tessay passed Nicholas's message to him.

'Tell Nicky it's as good as done,' Geoffrey acknowledged, and hung up.

'Now,' Tessay addressed the postmaster, 'I want to place another call to Addis – to the Egyptian Embassy.'

There was a buzz of delight from her audience when they realized that the entertainment was not yet over for the day. Everybody repaired to the veranda for more *tej* and conversation.

The second call took even longer to connect, and it was after five o'clock when Tessay was at last put in contact with the Egyptian cultural attaché. Had she not once met him at one of those ubiquitous cocktail parties on the diplomatic circuit in Addis, and made a profound impression on him then, he would probably not have accepted her call now.

'You are very lucky to have reached me so late,' he told her. 'We usually close at four-thirty, but there is a meeting of the Organization of African Unity on at the moment and I am working late. Anyway, how may I help you, Woizero Tessay?'

As soon as she told him the name and rank of the person in Cairo to whom Royan's message was addressed, his superior and condescending attitude altered dramatically and he became effusive and eager to please. He wrote down everything she said in detail, asking her to repeat and spell the names of people and places. Finally he read his notes back to her for confirmation.

At the end of the long conversation, he dropped his voice to an intimate level and told her. 'I was greatly saddened to hear of your recent bereavement, Lady Sun. Colonel Brusilov was a man I held in high regard. Perhaps when you return to Addis you would do me the honour of dining with me one evening.'

'How kind and thoughtful of you.' Tessay's tones were honeyed. 'I would so much enjoy meeting your charming wife again.' She hung up while he was still making confused noises of assent and denial.

By this time the sun was already setting behind the sky castles of cumulo-nimbus, and there was the smell of rain in the air. It was too late to start the journey back down the escarpment that evening, so Tessay was relieved when the headman of Debra Maryam village sent one of his teenage daughters to invite her to spend the night as a guest in his home.

The headman's house was the finest in the village, not one of the circular *tukuls*, but a square brick building with an iron roof. His wife and daughters had prepared a banquet in Tessay's honour, and all the village notables, including the priests from the church, had been invited. It was therefore after midnight before Tessay was able to escape to the principal bedroom, which the headman and his wife had vacated for her.

Just before Tessay fell asleep she heard the heavy raindrops rattling on the corrugated iron roof over her head. It was a comforting sound, but she thought briefly of the dam further downstream in the gorge, and hoped that this shower was merely the harbinger and not the true onset of the big rains.

When she started awake much later the rain had passed. Beyond her uncurtained window the night was moonless and silent, except for the howling of a pariah-dog down in the village. She wondered what had woken her, and was filled suddenly with a premonition of impending disaster, a legacy from the Mengistu days, when any sound in the night might warn of the arrival of the security police. So strong was this feeling that she could not get to sleep again. Creeping quietly out of her bed, she began dressing in the dark. She had decided to call her monks and start back along the trail in the darkness. Only when she was at Mek Nimmur's side once again would she feel secure.

She had just pulled on her jodhpurs and was searching beneath the bed for her sandals when she heard the sound of a truck engine in the distance. She went to the window and listened. The air had been cooled by the rain and she felt the chill on her naked arms and chest.

The truck sounded as though it was approaching the village from the south, up the track that followed the river bank. It was coming fast, and her sense of unease sharpened. The villagers had spoken to the monks, and it was now common knowledge that she was Mek Nimmur's woman. Mek was a wanted man. Suddenly she felt very vulnerable and alone.

Quickly she pulled the woollen *shamma* over her head and thrust her feet into her sandals. As she crept from the room she heard the headman snoring in the front room where he and his wife had moved to make room for her. She turned down the short passage to the kitchen. The fire in the hearth had burned down, but she could make out the shapes of the sleeping monks on the mud floor. They lay with their *shammas* pulled over their heads, completely covered, like a row of bodies on mortuary tables. She knelt beside the nearest of them and shook him, but obviously he had enjoyed the *tej* at dinner because he was difficult to rouse.

The sound of the approaching truck was much louder and closer by now, and she felt her uneasiness take on a tinge of panic. Realizing that in an emergency the monks would probably be of little real help to her, she stood up and groped her way quickly towards the back door.

The truck was right outside the front of the house now. The headlights flashed across the front windows and were briefly reflected down the passageway. Abruptly the engine roar sank to a burble as the driver decelerated, and she heard the squeal of brakes and the crunch of tyres in the gravel outside. Then there was shouting and the trampling of many feet as men jumped down from the back of the stationary truck.

Tessay froze halfway across the small kitchen, her head cocked to listen. Suddenly there was a loud banging on the flimsy front door, and chillingly familiar shouts of, 'Open up here! Central Intelligence! Open the door! Nobody leave the house!'

Tessay ran for the back door, but in the darkness she tripped over a low table covered with dirty dishes from the previous evening's meal. She fell heavily and the bowls and *tej* flasks crashed to the floor and shattered. Instantly the men at the front door put their shoulders to it, tearing it off its hinges. They burst into the house, shouting and breaking furniture, torches flashing as they searched the front rooms. There was a confused babble of alarm as the headman and his family struggled awake, and then the sound of heavy blows with club and rifle butt, followed by shrieks of pain and terror.

Tessay reached the back door and struggled to open it. The sound of strange men rampaging through the house made her fingers clumsy. She struggled with the lock. All the while she could hear other men outside running through the yard to surround the house completely. At last she got the door open. It was dark and the area was unfamiliar so she did not know in which direction to run, but she heard the river close by in the night.

'If I can only reach the bank,' she thought, and started across the yard.

As she did so the beam of an electric torch blinded her, and a coarse voice bellowed, 'There she is!'

Any doubt that she was the prey was instantly dispelled, and she fled like a startled hare in the beam of the light. They bayed behind her like a pack of hounds. She reached the bank of the river and spun off to the right, downstream. A pistol cracked out behind her and she ducked as a shot fluted past her head.

'Don't shoot, you baboons!' a voice roared in commanding tones. 'We want her for questioning.'

In the torchbeam her white *shamma* flashed like the wings of a moth flitting around the candle flame.

'Stop her!' shouted the officer behind her. 'Don't let her get away.'

But she was fleet as a gazelle, and her lightly sandalled feet flew across the rough terrain while the heavily equipped soldiers blundered along behind her. Her spirits soared as she realized that she was pulling away from them.

The sound of the pursuit dwindled behind her and she had reached the limit of the effective range of the torchbeam when she ran into a fence of rusty barbed wire. Three wire strands whipped across her lower body, at the level of her knees, her hips and her diaphragm. The top strand drove the breath from her lungs, and the barbs tore through the wool of her clothing and into her flesh. They snagged her like a fish in the mesh of a net, and she hung there struggling helplessly. Rough hands seized her and dragged her off the wire, and she sobbed with despair and with the pain of the sharp wire spurs tearing her skin. One of the soldiers grabbed her wrist and twisted it up between her shoulder-blades, laughing with sadistic relish when she cried out at the pain.

The officer came up panting over the rough ground. He was overweight, and even in the cold night air he was sweating heavily. It greased his fat cheeks and glistened in the light of the torch.

'Do not hurt her, you oaf,' he gasped. 'She is not a criminal. She is a high-bred lady. Bring her to the truck, but treat her with respect.'

With a man on each arm they marched her to the truck, holding her so that her feet barely touched the rough ground, and then shoved her up into the cab on to the seat beside the uniformed driver. The plump officer climbed in heavily after her, and she found herself wedged in firmly between the two men. The soldiers scrambled up into the rear of the truck, and the driver revved the engine and let out the clutch.

Tessay was sobbing softly, and the officer glanced sideways at her. She saw in the reflection of the headlights that his expression was gentle and sympathetic, completely at odds with his actions.

'Where are you taking me?' she asked softly, stifling her sobs. 'What have I done wrong?'

'I have been ordered to take you to Colonel Nogo, the district commander, for questioning in connection with *shufta* activities in the Gojam,' he told her, as they jolted and bounced down the rough track.

They were both silent for a while, and then the officer said quietly in English, 'The driver speaks only Amharic. I wanted to tell you that I knew your father, Alto Zemen. He was a good man. I am sorry for what is happening here tonight, but I am only a lieutenant. I have to follow my orders.'

'I understand that it is not your choice, or your blame.'

'My name is Hammed. If I can, I will help you. For Alto Zemen's sake.'

'Thank you, Lieutenant Hammed. I need friends now.'

While they waited for the dust of the cave-in to settle, and for any loose hanging rock to fall or stabilize, Nicholas dressed the minor injuries that Royan had sustained. The cut over her temple was not deep, barely more than a scratch. Nicholas saw that it did not require a stitch. He disinfected it and covered it with a Band Aid. However, her shoulder, which the falling rock had struck, was badly bruised. He massaged it with arnica cream.

His own bruises he treated less ceremoniously. Within an hour of the cave-in he was ready to go back up the tunnel. He ordered Royan and Sapper to remain on the causeway over the sink-hole while he returned to the landing at the top of the stairs alone. He carried a bamboo pole and a hand lamp connected to the Honda generator.

Nicholas proceeded with the utmost caution, probing the roof of the tunnel for weakness as he went. When he reached the landing he saw at once that the rock fall had smashed down what remained of the white plaster door that had originally sealed the entrance to the tomb. The ammunition crates, eight of which contained the statues from the shrines, had been knocked about and scattered, and some of them were partially buried under the fallen rubble. He retrieved them and opened each of the packed crates in turn to check the contents. With immense relief he discovered that the stout metal containers had withstood the rough treatment and there was no damage to the precious statues they held. One at a time he carried them back down the tunnel as far as the causeway and handed them into Sapper's care.

When he returned to the landing outside the tomb, Royan insisted on accompanying him. Even his lurid descriptions of the danger of a further rock-fall could not dissuade her. Her dismay when she stood outside the shattered gallery was overwhelming.

'It's totally destroyed,' she whispered. 'All those marvellous works of art. I cannot believe that Taita wanted this to happen.'

'No,' Nicholas agreed ruefully. 'His plan was to give us a big send-off along the road past the seven pylons to the happy hunting grounds. And he damned nigh succeeded.'

'It's going to take a lot of hard work to clear up this mess,' she said.

'What on earth are you talking about?' He turned on her in genuine alarm. 'We have saved the statues, and that's all we can hope for. Now I think it's time to cut our losses and get out of here.'

'Get out of here? Are you crazy?' She rounded on him furiously. 'Are you out of your mind?'

'At least the statues will pay our costs,' he explained, 'and there might even be something left over to divvy up between us, in accordance with our agreement.'

'You aren't dreaming of giving up now, when we are so close?' Her voice rose sharply with agitation.

'The gallery is destroyed—' he began in more reasonable tones, but she stamped her foot with agitation and shouted him down.

'The tomb is still there. Dammit, Nicky, Taita would not have gone to those lengths if it were not. We are getting too close now – that is why he fired that warning shot across our bows. Don't you see? We have him really worried now. We can't give up with the prize almost in sight.'

'Royan, be reasonable.'

'No! No! You be reasonable.' She refused to listen. 'You have to start clearing the gallery right away. I know the entrance is open now. All we have to do is clear this mess, and I am certain that we will find the true entrance to the tomb behind the rubble that Taita deliberately dropped on us.'

'I think that bang on your head has loosened a couple of nuts and bolts.' He threw up his hands in resignation. 'But what's the use arguing with a crazy woman? We will clear just enough of the scree to prove to you that there is nothing more to discover in there.'

'The dust is going to be our big problem.' Sapper eyed the blocked gallery entrance when they told him what they intended. 'As soon as we touch that rubble there is going to be clouds of it – more than our little blower fan can handle.'

'Right,' Nicholas agreed briskly. 'We will have to wet it all down. Two lines of men back down the tunnel to the sink-hole. One chain passing up water buckets, and the other chain passing back the rubble from the cave-in.'

'It's going to take a lot of work.' Sapper sucked his bottom lip lugubriously.

'You signed on to be tough,' Nicholas reminded him. 'No time to start whinging now.'

The monks, still convinced that they were engaged on the Lord's work, accepted this new task cheerfully. They sang as they passed the chunks of broken plaster and rock in one direction and the clay pots of water from the sink-hole in the other. Nicholas worked at the rock-fall with the gang of Buffaloes, led by Hansith. It was hard, messy and dangerous work, for each piece of rubble had to be doused with water before it could be levered out of the pack and passed down the chain. The staircase was soon running with muddy water and the steps were treacherous underfoot. The fallen rock was loose and unstable, and there was always the danger of a secondary collapse.

So many men working in the confined spaces of the gallery and tunnel taxed the ability of the little blower fan to recirculate the air, and it was hot and oppressive. The men stripped to loincloths and their bodies glistened with sweat. The rubble passed back down the tunnel was dumped into the sink-hole. Even that large volume of material made no difference to the level of the black waters. It was simply swallowed up into the depths without trace.

Nicholas found the crowded workings so humid and claustrophobic that at the change of the first shift he had to escape into the open air, if only for a few minutes. Even the dark and forbidding chasm of Taita's pool was a relief after the close confines of the underground workings. Mek Nimmur was waiting for him when he climbed out over the wall of the coffer dam on to the ledge beside the pool.

'Nicholas!' Mek's handsome dark face was grave. 'Has Tessay returned from Debra Maryam yet? She should have been back yesterday.'

'I have not seen her, Mek. I thought she was with you.'

381

Mek shook his head. 'I wanted to make certain that she had not returned without my men seeing her, before I send a patrol up the trail to search for her.'

'I am sorry, Mek. I did not anticipate any danger in sending her up the escarpment.' Nicholas felt a stab of guilt.

'If I had thought there was any danger, I would not have allowed her to go,' Mek agreed. 'I have sent men to search for her.'

But Tessay's absence was another worry for Nicholas. It lurked at the edge of his mind during the days that followed, as the clearing of the long funeral gallery proceeded too slowly for his satisfaction.

Royan spent as much time at the face as Nicholas did, and both of them were as filthy with mud and dirt as the Buffaloes who were labouring there beside them. She mourned over each fragment of the shattered murals. Before they were carried away to be thrown into the sink-hole, she tried to retrieve those on which significant portions of the paintings were still intact. There was one jagged piece of plaster on which the lovely head of Isis was still in one piece, and another on which the entire figure of Thoth, the god of writing, was preserved. However, most of the paintings were destroyed beyond any hope of ever restoring them, and sadly they were consigned to the pit.

There was no sense of time in the long gallery, and they could not tell night from day. It was always a surprise to leave the precincts of the tomb and find that the stars were shining in the narrow strip of sky that showed above Taita's pool, or to find the bright African sun burning hotly down out of the cloudless blue. They ate and slept only when their bodies demanded it, not according to the passage of the hours.

Re-entering the tomb after a few hours' sleep in their shelters beside the pool, they were crossing the causeway over the sink-hole when a wild cry reverberated down the shaft ahead of them. Immediately there was a hullabaloo of query and answer, and excited shouts from the men working in the upper levels of the tunnel.

'Hansith has found something,' Royan cried. 'Dammit, Nicky, I knew we should have stayed—' She began to run, and he hurried after her.

They came out on the landing in front of the gallery to find it crowded with chattering, gesticulating, half-naked workmen. Nicholas forced his way through them with Royan on his heels. They realized that Hansith had cleared the gallery as far as where the shrine of Osiris had once stood. The roof above them was jagged and broken, and lying amongst the rubbish on the ruined agate tiles of the floor Nicholas made out the remains of the mechanism which Taita had placed in the roof, and which they had brought crashing down when they had activated the device. The main part of this was an enormous stone wheel, resembling a mill wheel and weighing many tons. Nicholas stopped to give it a cursory examination.

'When you read *River God*, you realize that Taita had an obsession with the wheel,' he told Royan. 'Chariot wheels, water wheels, and now this must have been the balance wheel of his booby-trap. When we moved the levers, we toppled the wedges that held this monstrosity in place. Once it started rolling, it tumbled all the drop-stones that he had stacked above the ceiling of the gallery.' He glanced up at the shattered roof.

'Not now, Nicky!' Royan was hopping with impatience. 'Time for your lectures later. Taita's death-trap is not what has excited Hansith. He has found something else. Come on!'

They pushed their way through the pack of workmen until they reached Hansith's tall figure.

'What is it?' Nicholas shouted over the heads of the others. 'What have you found, Hansith?'

'Here, *effendi*,' Hansith shouted back. 'Come quickly.'

They pushed their way to the face, and stopped beside the monk at the end of the blocked gallery.

'There!' Hansith pointed proudly.

Nicholas went down on one knee in the shattered remains of the shrine. Small pieces of the painted plaster still adhered to the fractured rock wall. Hansith pulled a slab out of the collapsed face, and pointed into the space it had left. Nicholas peered into it and felt his pulse begin to race. There was an opening in the side of the gallery. Even at first glance he realized that it was the mouth of another tunnel leading off at right-angles from the long gallery. It had been concealed behind the plaster-covered image of the great god.

As he stared into it with awe, he felt Royan's hand on his arm and her warm breath on his cheek. 'This is it, Nicky. The entrance to the true tomb of Mamose. This gallery was a bluff. Taita's red herring. This is the veritable tomb.'

'Hansith!' Nicholas called to him in a voice that was hoarse with emotion. 'Get your men to clear this doorway.'

As the workmen moved the rocks Nicholas and Royan hovered close behind them, so that they were able to watch the shape of the doorway as it was fully revealed. It proved to be a dark rectangle, of the same dimensions as the tunnel leading up from the sink-hole, three metres wide by two high. The lintel and the door jambs were of beautifully cut and dressed stone, and when Nicholas shone his lamp into the opening he saw a flight of stone steps rising before him.

They moved the cables and the lights into the gallery and arranged them at the entrance to this new doorway, but when Nicholas set foot on the first step he found Royan at his side.

'I am coming with you,' she told him firmly.

'It's probably booby-trapped,' he warned her. 'Taita is lying in wait for you around the first bend.'

'Don't try that. It just won't work, mister! I am coming.'

They went slowly up the steep steps, pausing on each one to survey the walls and the way ahead. Twenty steps from the bottom they reached another landing. A pair of doorways led off it, one on either side. However, the staircase continued climbing directly ahead of them.

'Which way?' Nicholas asked.

'Keep going up,' Royan urged him. 'We can explore these side passages later.'

Cautiously, they continued climbing. After twenty more steps they came out on an identical landing, with a doorway on each side and the stairway in front of them.

'Keep going up,' Royan ordered, without waiting for him to ask.

Twenty more steps and there was another landing, with the familiar openings on either side and the stairway straight ahead.

'This isn't making sense,' Nicholas protested, but she prodded him in the back.

'We should keep going on upwards,' she told him, and he did not protest further. They passed another landing and then yet another, each of them the exact image of those that they had passed lower down.

'At last!' Nicholas exclaimed when they came out at the top of the staircase, with the expected doorway on each side but now a blank wall in front of them. 'This is as far as it goes.'

'How many landings are there?' she asked. 'How many altogether?'

'Eight,' he answered.

'Eight,' she agreed. 'Isn't that a familiar number by now?'

He turned to stare down at her in the lamplight. 'You mean—'

'I mean the eight shrines in the long gallery, these eight landings, and the eight cups of the bao board.'

They stood silent and undecided on the top landing and looked about them.

'Okay,' he said at last, 'if you are so damned clever, tell me which way to go now.'

'Eeny-meeny-miny-moe,' she recited. 'Let's try the right-hand doorway.'

They followed the right-hand passage only a short distance before they were confronted by a T-junction – a blank wall with identical twin passageways on each side.

'Take the right one again,' she counselled, and they followed it. But when they came to the next T-junction Nicholas stopped and faced her.

'You know what is happening here, don't you?' he demanded. 'This is another one of Taita's tricks. He has led us into a maze. If it were not for the cable, we would be lost already.'

With a bemused expression she looked back the way they had come, and then down the unexplored passages to their right and left.

'When he built this, Taita could not have anticipated the age of electricity. He expected any grave robber to be equipped the same way he was. Imagine being caught in here without the electric cable to follow back the way we have come,' Nicholas said softly. 'Imagine having only an oil lamp for light. Imagine what would happen to you when the oil burnt out and you were lost in here in the utter darkness.'

Royan shivered and gripped his arm. 'It's scaring!' she whispered.

'Taita is beginning to play rough,' Nicholas said softly. 'I was developing rather a soft spot for the old boy. But now I am beginning to change my mind.'

She shuddered again. 'Let's go back,' she whispered, 'We should never have rushed in here like this. We must go back and work it out carefully. We are unprepared. I have the feeling that we are in danger – I mean real danger, the same as we were in the long gallery.'

As they started back through the twists and turns, picking up the electric cable as they retreated down the stone passageways, the temptation to break into a run became stronger with each step. Royan hung tightly to Nicholas's arm. It seemed to both of them that some intelligent and malignant presence lurked behind them in the darkness, following them, watching them and biding its time.

The army truck carrying Tessay drove back through the village of Debra Maryam, and then turned off on to the track that followed the Dandera river downstream towards the escarpment of the Abbay gorge.

'This is not the way to army headquarters,' Tessay told Lieutenant Hammed, and he shifted awkwardly on the seat beside her.

'Colonel Nogo is not at his headquarters. I have orders to take you to another location.'

'There is only one other place in this direction,' she said. 'The base camp of the foreign prospecting company, Pegasus.'

'Colonel Nogo is using that as a forward base in his campaign against the *shufta* in the valley,' he explained. 'I have orders to take you to him there.'

Neither of them spoke again during the long, bumpy ride over the rough track. It was almost noon when at last they reached the edge of the escarpment and turned off on to the fork that brought them at last to the Pegasus camp. The camouflage-clad guards at the gate saluted when they recognized Hammed. The truck drove through the gates, and parked in front of one of the long Quonset huts within the compound.

'Please wait here.' Hammed got down and went into the hut, but was gone for only a few minutes.

'Please come with me, Lady Sun.' He looked awkward and embarrassed, and could not meet her eyes as he helped her down from the cab. He led her to the door of the hut, and stood aside to let her enter first.

She looked around the sparsely furnished room, and realized that it must be the company's administration centre. A conference table ran almost the full length of the room, and there were filing cabinets and two desks set against the side walls. A map of the area and a few technical charts were the only decorations on the bare walls. Two men sat at the table, and she recognized both of them immediately.

Colonel Nogo looked up at her, and his eyes were cold behind his metal-framed spectacles. As always, his long, thin body was immaculately uniformed; but his head was bare. His maroon beret lay on the table in front of him. Jake Helm leaned back in his chair with his arms folded. At first glance, his short-cropped hair made him look like a boy. Only when she looked closer did she see how his skin was weathered, and notice the crows' feet at the corners of his eyes. He wore an open-necked shirt and blue jeans that were bleached almost white. His belt buckle was of ornate Indian silver, the shape of a wild mustang's head. The sleeves of his cotton shirt were rolled high around his lumpy biceps. He chewed upon the dead butt of a cheap Dutch cheroot, and the smell of the strong tobacco was rank and offensive.

'Very well, lieutenant,' Nogo dismissed Hammed in Amharic. 'Wait outside. I will call you when I need you.'

Once Hammed had left the room, Tessay demanded, 'Why have I been arrested, Colonel Nogo?'

Neither man acknowledged the question. They both regarded her expressionlessly.

'I demand to know the reason for this high-handed treatment,' she persisted.

'You have been consorting with a band of notorious terrorists,' said Nogo softly. 'Your actions have made you one of them, a *shufta*.'

'That is not true.'

'You have trespassed in a mineral concession in the Abbay valley,' said Helm. 'And you and your accomplices have begun mining operations in the area which belongs to this company.'

'There are no mining operations,' she protested.

'We have other information. We have evidence that you have built a dam across the Dandera river—'

'That is nothing to do with me.'

386

'So you do not deny that there is a dam?'

'It is nothing to do with me,' she repeated. 'I am not a member of any terrorist group, and I have not taken part in any mining operations.'

They were both silent again. Nogo made an entry in the notebook in front of him. Helm stood up and sauntered across to the window behind her right shoulder. The silence drew out until she could bear it no longer. Even though she knew it was part of the campaign of nerves they were waging against her, she had to break it.

'I have travelled most of the night in an army truck,' she said. 'I am tired, and I need to go to a lavatory.'

'If what you need to do is urgent you can do it where you are standing. Neither Mr Helm nor I will be offended.' Nogo tittered in a surprisingly girlish manner, but did not look up from his book.

She looked over her shoulder at the door, but Helm crossed to it and turned the key in the lock, slipping the key into his pocket. She knew she must show no weakness in front of these two, and, though she was tired and afraid and her bladder ached, she feigned an air of confidence and assurance and crossed to the nearest chair. She pulled it from the table and sat down in it easily.

Nogo looked up at her and frowned. He had not expected her to react this way.

'You know the *shufta* bandit Mek Nimmur,' he accused abruptly.

'No,' she said coldly. 'I know the patriot and democratic leader Mek Nimmur. He is no *shufta*.'

'You are his concubine, his whore. Of course, you will say this.'

She looked away from him with disdain, and his voice rose shrilly. 'Where is Mek Nimmur? How many men does he have with him?' Her composure was beginning to rattle him.

She ignored the question, and Nogo scowled at her furiously. 'If you do not cooperate with us, I will have to use stronger methods to make you answer my questions,' he warned.

She turned in her chair and stared out of the window. In the long silence that followed, Jake Helm crossed the room and went to the door behind Nogo that led through to the rooms at the rear of the hut. He disappeared through it, and closed it behind him. The walls of the hut were thin, and Tessay made out the murmur of voices from the room beyond. The cadence and inflection were neither English nor Amharic. They were using a foreign language in there. She guessed that Helm was receiving instructions from a superior, who did not want her to be able to recognize him at some later date.

After a few minutes Helm re-emerged and closed the door behind him without locking it. He nodded to Nogo, who at once stood up. They both came across to stand in front of Tessay.

'I think that it will be better for all of us if we finish this business as quickly as possible,' said Helm softly. 'Then you can go to the bathroom, and I can go to my breakfast.'

She raised her chin and stared at him defiantly, but did not answer him.

'Colonel Nogo has tried to be reasonable. He is bound by certain niceties of his official position. Fortunately I do not have the same restraints. I am going to ask you the same questions that he did, but this time you will answer them.'

He took the dead cheroot from his mouth and examined the tip. Then he threw the butt into a corner of the room and took a flat tin from his hip pocket. From it he selected a fresh cheroot, long and black, and lit it carefully, holding the match to it until it was drawing evenly. Then, amid a cloud of pungent tobacco smoke, he waved the match to extinction and asked,

'Where is Mek Nimmur?'

She shrugged and looked away, out of the side window of the hut.

Abruptly, without signalling the blow in any way, he hit her open-handed across her face. It was a savage blow, delivered with a force that snapped her head around. Then, before she could recover, he swung back again and slammed his knuckles across her jawline. Her head was thrown back violently in the opposite direction and she was knocked flying from her chair.

Nogo stooped over her and seized her arms, twisting them up behind her back. He lifted her back into the seat and stood behind her. He held her in such a surprisingly powerful grip that she could feel the skin of her upper arms bruising beneath his fingers.

'I have no more time to waste,' Helm said quietly, taking the burning cheroot from his lips to inspect the glowing tip. 'Let us start again. Where is Mek Nimmur?'

Tessay's left eardrum felt as if it had burst with the ferocity of those blows. Her hearing buzzed and sang. Her teeth had been driven halfway through the flesh of her cheek, and her mouth filled slowly with her own blood.

'Where is Mek Nimmur?' Helm repeated, leaning his face closer to hers. 'What are your friends doing with the dam in the Dandera river?'

She gathered the blood and saliva in her mouth, and suddenly and explosively spat it into his face

He recoiled violently and wiped the bloody mess from his eyes with the palm of his hand.

'Hold her!' he said to Nogo, and seized the front of her blouse. With one heave he ripped it open down to her waist, and Nogo giggled and leaned forward over her shoulder to look at her breasts. He giggled again as Helm took one of them in his hand and squeezed out the nipple between his finger and thumb. It was the dark purple colour of a ripe mulberry.

He held her like that, pinching her flesh with his nails until the skin tore and a droplet of blood welled up and trickled over his thumb. Then with his other hand he took the burning cheroot from his lips and blew on the top until it glowed hotly.

'Where is Mek Nimmur?' he asked, and lowered the cheroot towards her breast. 'What are they doing in the Dandera river?'

She stared down in horror as he brought the burning cheroot closer, and tried to wriggle away from him. But Nogo held her firmly from behind. She screamed once, on an agonized drawn-out note, as the glowing coal touched the tip of her nipple and the delicate skin began to blister.

'Winter,' said Royan, spreading the enlargement of the fourth face of the stele from Tanus's tomb under the bright glare of the floodlamp. 'This is the side that contains Taita's notations, which I am postulating are those of the bao board. I don't understand all of them, but by a process of elimination I have determined that the first symbol denotes one of the four sides, or as he terms them the castles of the board.'

She showed him the pages of her notebook on which she had made her calculations.

'See here, the seated baboon is the north castle, the bee is the south, the bird is the west and the scorpion the east.' She pointed out to him the same symbols on the photograph of the stele. 'Then the second and third figures are numbers – I believe that they designate the file and the cup. With these we can follow the moves of his imaginary red stones. The reds are the highest-ranking colours on the board.'

'What about the verses between each set of notations?' Nicholas asked. 'Such as this one here, about the north wind and the storm?'

'I am not sure about those. Probably merely smokescreens, if I know Taita. He is never one to make life too easy for us. Perhaps they do have significance, but we can only hope to unravel them as we work through the moves of our stones.'

Nicholas studied her figures a while, then grinned ruefully. 'Just think how remote was the possibility that anybody would ever be able to decipher the clues he left behind. The first requirement is that the searcher must have access to both chronicles, the seventh scroll and the stele of Tanus, before he had any chance of understanding the key to the tomb.'

She laughed – a throaty, well-satisfied sound. 'Yes, he must have believed that he was perfectly safe. Well, we will see now, Master Taita. We will see just how clever you really were.' Then, sober and business-like once more, she looked up the stone staircase that led to Taita's maze.

'Now we have to see if my figures and theories fit into the hard stones and walls of Taita's architecture. But where do we start?'

'At the beginning,' Nicholas suggested, 'the god plays the first coup. That's what Taita told us. If we start here in the shrine of Osiris, at the foot of the staircase, then perhaps that will give us the alignment of his imaginary bao board.'

'I had the same idea,' she agreed immediately. 'Let's postulate that this is the north castle of Taita's board. Then we work the protocol of the four bulls from here.'

It was slow and painstaking work, trying to work their way into the mind of the ancient scribe by probing the labyrinth of passages and tunnels that he had built four thousand years previously. This time they moved into the maze with more circumspection. Nicholas had filled his pockets with lumps of dried white river clay, and he used these like a schoolmaster's stick of chalk to write on the stone walls at each branch and fork of the tunnels, setting out the notations from the winter face of the stele and marking a signpost to enable them not only to find their way through the maze but to relate it to the model that Royan was drawing up in her notebook.

They found that their first assumption that the shrine of Osiris was the north castle of the board seemed to be correct, and they happily believed that with this as the key it would be a simple matter to follow the moves of play to their conclusion. But these hopes were soon dashed as they realized that Taita was not thinking in the simple two dimensions of the conventional board. He had added the third dimension to the equation.

The stairway leading up from the shrine of Osiris was not the only link between the eight landings. Each of the passages leading off from it was subtly angled either upwards or downwards. As they followed the twists and turns of one of these tunnels they did not detect the fact that they were changing levels. Then suddenly they re-emerged on to the central staircase, but on a landing higher than the one they had entered from.

They stood there and stared at each other in horrified disbelief.

Royan spoke first. 'I didn't even have the feeling that we were ascending,' she whispered. 'The whole thing is infinitely more complex than I first assumed.'

'It must be constructed like one of those nuclear models of some complicated carbon atom,' Nicholas agreed with awe. 'It interlinks on all eight planes. Quite frankly, it's terrifying.'

'Now I have some inkling what those extraneous symbols signify,' Royan muttered. 'They set out the levels. We are going to have to rethink the entire concept.'

'Three-dimensional bao, played to enigmatic rules. What chance have we got against him?' Nicholas shook his head ruefully. 'What we really need is a computer. Taita wasn't puffing his own virtues without good reason. The old hooligan really was a mathematical genius.' He shone the lamp back down the tunnel from which they had come. 'Even when you know it's there you cannot actually see the fall in the floor level. He designed and built it without even a slide rule or a spirit level in his back pocket. This maze is an extraordinary piece of engineering.'

'You can form your fan club later,' she suggested. 'But right now let's start grinding those numbers again.'

'I am going to move the lights and the desks up here, on to this central landing of the staircase.' Nicholas agreed, 'I think we should work from the centre of the board. It may help us to visualize it. Right now he has got me thoroughly confused.'

The only sound in the room was the soft sobbing of the woman who lay curled on the floor in a puddle of her own blood and urine.

Tuma Nogo sat at the long conference table and lit a cigarette. His hands trembled slightly, and he looked sickened. He was a soldier, and he had lived through the Mengistu terror. He was a hard man and accustomed to violence and cruelty, but he was shaken with what he had just witnessed. He knew now why von Schiller placed such reliance on Helm. The man was barely human.

Across the room Jake Helm was washing his hands in the small basin. He dried them fastidiously and then dabbed at the stains on his clothing with the towel as he came back and stood over Tessay.

'I don't think there is anything else she can tell us,' he said calmly. 'I don't think she held anything back.'

Nogo glanced down at the woman, and saw the livid burns that spotted her chest and her cheeks like the running ulcerations of some dreadful smallpox. Her eyes were closed, and her lashes were frizzled away. She had held out well. It was only when Helm had touched her eyelids with the burning cheroot that she had at last capitulated, and gabbled out the answers to his questions.

Nogo felt queasy, but he was relieved that it had not been necessary to hold her lids open, as Helm had ordered, and to watch as he quenched the flame of the cheroot against her weeping eyeballs.

'Watch her,' Helm ordered, as he rolled down his sleeves. 'She is a tough one. Don't take any chances with her.'

Helm walked past him, and went to the door in the far end of the hut. He left the door open, and Nogo could hear their voices, but they were speaking in German so he could not understand what they were saying. He understood now why von Schiller had chosen not to be present during the questioning. He obviously knew how Helm worked.

Helm came back into the room, and nodded at Nogo. 'Very well. We are finished with her. You know what to do.'

Nogo stood up nervously and placed his hand on the webbing holster at his side.

'Here?' he asked. 'Now?'

'Don't be a bloody fool,' Helm snapped. 'Take her away. Far away. Then get somebody in here to clean up this mess.' Helm turned on his heel and went back into the rear room.

Nogo roused himself and then went to the door of the hut. He walked wide of where Tessay lay, so as not to soil his canvas paratrooper boots.

'Lieutenant Hammed!' he called through the door.

Hammed and Nogo lifted Tessay to her feet. Neither of them spoke and they were subdued, almost chastened, as they helped her into her torn and bloodied clothing. Hammed averted his eyes from her naked body and the burns and other injuries that marred her glossy amber skin. He draped the *shamma* over her shoulders, and led her towards the door. When she stumbled he caught her before she fell and supported her with a hand under her elbow. He led her down the steps to the truck, and she moved slowly, like a very old woman. She sat in the passenger seat with her burned and swollen face in her cupped hands.

Nogo summoned Hammed with a jerk of his head, and led him aside. He spoke quietly to him, and Hammed's expression became stricken as he listened to his orders. At one point he started to protest, but Nogo snarled at him savagely and he chewed his lower lip in silence.

'Remember!' Nogo repeated. 'Well away from any of the villages. Make certain that there are no witnesses. Report back to me immediately.'

Hammed straightened his shoulders and saluted before he marched back to the truck and climbed up into the seat beside Tessay. He gave the driver a curt order and they drove out of the camp, following the track back towards Debra Maryam.

Tessay was so confused and in such pain that she had lost all sense of time. Only half-conscious, she lurched about in the seat when the truck hit a particularly rough stretch of the track, and her head rolled loosely on her shoulders. Her face was so swollen that it required an effort to force her eyelids apart, and when she did she thought that her vision was failing and that she was going blind. Then she realized that the sun had set and darkness had fallen. She must have spent the whole day in the hut with Helm.

She felt a mild lift of relief that the burns on her eyelids had not done more damage. At least she was still able to see. She peered out through the windscreen, and found that in the headlights the road was unfamiliar.

'Where are you taking me?' she mumbled. 'This is not the way back to the village.'

Lieutenant Hammed sat slumped beside her in the seat and would not answer. She relapsed into a daze of pain and exhaustion.

She was jerked awake when the truck braked abruptly and the driver switched off the ignition. Rude hands dragged her out of the cab and into the glare of the headlights. Her hands were jerked behind her back and her wrists were bound together with a raw-hide thong.

'You are hurting me,' she whimpered. 'You are cutting my wrists.' She had used up the last of her strength and courage. She felt beaten and pathetic, with no fight left in her.

One of the soldiers yanked on her bound wrists and shoved her off the road. Two others followed, each carrying trenching tools. There was enough of a moon for her to see a grove of eucalyptus trees about a hundred metres from the side of the road, and they led her there. They pushed her down at the base of one of the trees and the man who had tied her wrists stood over her, holding his rifle casually aimed down at her and smoking a cigarette with his free hand. The others stacked their rifles and began digging. They seemed to take no interest in her at all, but were discussing the All Africa Soccer Championships that were being held in Lusaka, and the Ethiopian team's chances of reaching the finals.

It was only after a while that it began to sink into Tessay's befuddled mind that they were digging a grave for her. The saliva in her injured mouth dried up and she looked around desperately for Lieutenant Hammed. But he had stayed with the truck.

'Please,' she whispered to her guard, but before she could say more he kicked her painfully in the belly.

'Keep quiet!' he used the derogatory term of address only applied to an animal or a person of the lowest order, and as she lay doubled up on the ground she realized the futility of appealing to them. A feeling of weakness and resignation overwhelmed her and she found herself weeping softly and hopelessly in the darkness.

When she looked up again through her swollen lids, there was sufficient moonlight for her to see that the grave was now so deep that the two men still digging in it were out of her line of sight. Spadefuls of dirt flew over the lip of the hole and splattered on to the growing pile. Her guard left her side for a moment and sauntered over to the edge of the hole. He looked down in it and then grunted.

'Good. That is deep enough. Call the lieutenant.'

The two soldiers scrambled up out of the grave, then gathered up their tools and weapons and traipsed off into the darkness of the grove. Chatting amicably amongst themselves they headed back towards where the truck was parked, leaving Tessay and her guard.

She lay there shivering with the cold and with terror, while her guard squatted at the lip of her grave and puffed on his cigarette. She thought that if she could get to her feet she could kick him into the hole and make a run for it, back through the trees. But when she tried to sit up her movements were stiff and slow, and she had no feeling in her hands or feet. She tried to force herself to move, but at that moment she heard Lieutenant Hammed coming from the truck and she slumped back in despair.

Hammed was carrying an electric torch. He flashed it down into the grave.

'Good,' he said loudly. 'That is deep enough.'

He switched off the torch and said to the man guarding her, 'No witnesses. Go back and wait at the truck. When you hear the shots, come back with the others to help me fill the hole.'

The guard slung his rifle over his shoulder and disappeared amongst the trees. Hammed waited until the man was well out of earshot, then he came to Tessay and hoisted her to her feet. He pushed her to the edge of the grave, and then she felt him fumbling with her clothing. She tried to lash out at him, but her arms were still bound behind her.

'I want your *shamma*.' He pulled the white woollen cloak off over her shoulders, and then went with it to the edge of the grave. He jumped down into the hole and she heard him scuffling about in the bottom.

His voice came back to her, speaking softly. 'They must see something here. A body—'

He climbed back beside her, puffing with the exertion, and stepped behind her. She felt the touch of cold metal on the inside of her wrists, and then he was sawing at the leather thong. She felt her bonds fall away, and she gasped at the pain as the blood poured back into her numb hands.

'What are you doing?' she whispered in confusion. She looked down into the grave and saw the pale *shamma* arranged to look like a human body. 'Are you going—'

'Please don't talk,' he instructed her softly, as he took her by the shoulder and led her back amongst the trees.

'Lie here.' He pushed her down and made her lie flat, with her face to the ground. He began piling dead leaves and fallen branches over her.

'Stay here! Do not try to run. Don't move or speak until we are gone.'

He flashed the torch briefly over the mound of dead branches to make certain she was covered, then he left her and hurried back to the graveside, unbuckling the flap of his pistol holster as he went. Two spaced pistol shots cracked out in the night, so loud and unexpectedly that she jumped and her heart raced wildly.

Then she heard Hammed shout, 'Come, you men. Let's get this thing finished.'

They trooped back into the grove, and she heard the sound of their spades and the thump of earth clods falling into the grave.

'I cannot see what I am doing, lieutenant,' a voice complained. 'Where is your torchlight?'

'You don't need a light to fill a hole,' Hammed snarled. 'Get on with your work. Tramp that loose soil down. I don't want anybody stumbling on this place.'

She lay quietly, trying to stop the wild tremors that shook her body. At last the sound of the shovels let up, and she heard Hammed's voice again.

'That will do. Make certain you leave nothing here. Back to the truck!'

Their footsteps and their voices died away. At a distance she heard the truck engine whirl and fire. The headlights shone through the trees as the truck backed and filled, turning in the direction from which they had come.

Long after the sound of the engine had died away completely, she continued to lie under the pile of dead branches. She was still shaking with the cold and weeping softly and silently with exhaustion and pain and relief. Then slowly she pushed the branches off herself and crawled to the trunk of the nearest tree. She used it to pull herself up to her feet, and then stood there, swaying weakly in the darkness.

It was only then that guilt overwhelmed her. 'I have betrayed Mek,' she thought sickeningly. 'I have told everything to his enemies. I must warn him. I must get back to him and warn him.'

She pushed herself away from the treetrunk and blundered back through the darkness towards the track.

The only means of ascertaining if they had solved Taita's codes correctly was to play out the moves he had listed. They went very carefully through the tunnels of the maze, stepping out the moves that he had noted and marking them on the walls in white chalk figures.

There were eighteen moves set out on the winter face of the stele. Using Royan's first interpretation of the symbols, they were able to advance through twelve of these. Then they found themselves at a dead end, confronted by a blank stone wall and unable to make the next move.

'Damnation!' Nicholas kicked the wall, and when this had no effect he hurled the chunk of white chalk at it. 'I wish I could get my hands on that old devil. Castration would be the least of his worries.'

'Sorry.' Royan scraped the hair back out of her eyes. 'I thought I had it right. It must be the figures in the second column. We will have to invert them.'

'We will have to start again,' Nicholas groaned.

'Right at the very beginning,' she agreed.

'How do we know when we have finally got it right?' he wanted to know.

'If by following the clues we arrive at one of the winning combinations, a bao equivalent of checkmate, on precisely the eighteenth move. There will be no logical move after that, and we can assume we have worked through it correctly.'

'And what will we find if we ever reach that position?'

'I will tell you when we get there.' She smiled at him sweetly. 'Cheer up, Nicky. It's only just starting to hurt.'

Royan inverted the values of the second and third numbers of Taita's notations, taking the first as the cup value and the second as the file value. This time they completed only five moves before they were stymied and could proceed no further.

'Perhaps our assumption about the third symbol being the change of level is incorrect?' Nicholas suggested. 'Let's start again and give that the second value.'

'Nicky, do you realize just how many possible combinations there are, given the three variables?' She was at last starting to waver. 'Taita has assumed an intimate knowledge of the game. We have only the sketchiest notions of how it was played. It's like a grand master trying to explain to a novice the intricacies of the King's Indian Defence.'

'In Russian!' Nicholas embroidered the simile. 'At this rate we are getting nowhere in a hurry. There must be some other way of approaching it. Let's go over the epigrams Taita stuck in between the notations again.'

'All right. I'll read and you listen.' She hunched over her notes. 'The trouble is that a subtle variation of the translation might change the sense. Taita loved puns, and a pun can rely on a single word for effect. One wrong twist or slant to a word and we have lost it.'

'Try anyway,' Nicholas encouraged her. 'Remember that even Taita had never played bao in three dimensions before. If he left a clue it would have to be at the very beginning of the stele. Concentrate on the first couple of notations and the epigrams that separate them.'

'We'll try it that way,' Royan agreed. 'The first notation is the bee followed by the numbers five and seven and the sistrum.'

Nicholas grinned. 'Okay, I have heard that so often already that I will never forget it. What follows?'

'The first quotation.' She ran her finger over the hieroglyphics. '"*What can be given a name can be known. What is nameless can only be felt. I sail with the tide behind me and the wind in my face. O, my beloved, the taste of you is sweet upon my lips.*"'

'Is that all?' he asked.

'Yes, then the next notation. The scorpion and the number two and three and the sistrum again.'

'Slowly! Slowly! First things first. What can we make out of the "*sailing*" and the "*beloved*"?'

So they riddled and wrestled with the text of the stele, until their eyes burned and they had lost track of day or night. They were eventually recalled to reality by Sapper's voice echoing up the staircase. Nicholas stood up from the desk and stretched before he looked at his watch.

'Eight o'clock. But I'm not sure if that is morning or evening.'

Then he started as Sapper came up the staircase, and saw that his bald head was shining with moisture and his shirt was soaked.

'What happened to you?' Nicholas demanded. 'Did you fall into the sink-hole?'

Sapper wiped his face with the palm of his hand. 'Didn't anybody tell you? It's pissing with rain outside.'

They both stared at him in horror.

'So soon?' Royan whispered. 'It wasn't supposed to start for weeks yet.'

Sapper shrugged. 'Somebody forgot to tell the weatherman.'

'Has it set in?' Nicholas asked. 'What's the state of the river? Has the level started to rise yet?'

'That's what I came to tell you. I am going up to the dam, taking the Buffaloes with me. I want to keep an eye on it. As soon as it gets unsafe I will send a runner down to you. When I do that, don't stop to argue. Get out of here fast. It will mean that I expect the dam to burst at any moment.'

'Don't take Hansith with you,' Nicholas ordered. 'I need him here.'

When Sapper had gone, taking most of the workers from the tunnel with him, Royan and Nicholas looked at each other seriously.

'We are running out of time fast, and Taita still has us in a tangle,' Nicholas said. 'One thing I must warn you. When the river starts to rise—'

She did not let him finish. 'The river!' she cried. 'Not the sea! I was mistaken in the translation. I read it as "*tide*". I assumed Taita was referring to the sea, but it should have been "*current*". The Egyptians made no distinction between the two words.'

They both rushed back to the desk and her notebooks. '"*The current behind me and the wind in my face*",' Nicholas changed the quotation.

'On the Nile,' Royan exulted, 'the prevailing wind is always from the north, and the current always from the south. Taita was facing north. The north castle.'

'We assumed the symbol for the north was the baboon,' he reminded her.

'No! I was wrong.' Her face was alight with the fires of inspiration. '"*O, my beloved, the taste of you is sweet upon my lips.*" Honey! The bee! I had the symbols for the north and south inverted.'

'What about east and west? What can we find there?' He turned back to the texts with fresh enthusiasm. '"*My sins are red as carnelians. They bind me like chains of bronze. They prick my heart with fire, and I turn my eyes towards the evening star.*"'

'I don't see—'

'"*Prick*" is the wrong translation,' he stuttered eagerly. 'It should be "*sting*". The scorpion looking towards the evening star. The evening star is always in the west. The scorpion is the western castle, not the eastern castle.'

'We had the board inverted.' She jumped up excitedly. 'Let's play it that way!'

'We still have not determined the levels,' he objected. 'Is the sistrum the upper level, or is it the three swords?'

'Now that we have made this breakthrough, that is the only variable. We are either right or wrong. We will play the sistrum first as the upper level, and if that doesn't work we can play it the other way round.'

It was so much easier now. The intricacies of the maze had become less forbidding with familiarity. There were the large white chalk signs in Nicholas's handwriting on each corner and at each fork and T-junction of the tunnels. They moved swiftly through the complex twists and turns, their excitement rising sharply as they followed each notation and found the way still clear before them.

'The eighteenth move.' Royan's voice trembled. 'Hold both thumbs. If it takes us into one of the open files that threaten the opponent's south castle, then that will be the check coup.' She drew a deep breath and read it aloud to him. 'The bird. The numbers three and five. With the lower level symbol of the three swords.'

They paced it out and passed the five junctions into the lowest level of the maze, reading their position from the chalk marks on the stone blocks of the walls at each fork.

'This is it!' Nicholas told her, and they stood together and looked about them.

'There is nothing outstanding about this spot.' Disappointment was bitter in Royan's tone. 'We have passed over it fifty times before. It is just like any of the other turns.'

'That is exactly what Taita would have wanted. Hell! He wouldn't have put up a signpost saying "X marks the spot", would he now?'

'So what do we do?' She looked at him, for once at a loss.

'Read the last epigram from the stele.'

She had her notebook in her hand. '"*From the black and holy earth of this very Egypt the harvest is abundant. I whip the flanks of my donkey, and the wooden spike of the plough breaks new ground. I plant the seed, and reap the grape and the ears of corn. In time I drink the wine and eat the loaf. I follow the rhythm of the seasons, and tend the earth.*"'

She looked up at him. 'The rhythm of the seasons? Is he referring us to the four faces of the stele? The earth?' she asked and looked down at the slabs beneath their feet. 'The promise of reward from the earth? Under our feet, perhaps?' she asked.

He stamped his foot on the slabs, but the sound was dull and solid. 'Only one way to find out.' He raised his voice and it echoed weirdly through the labyrinth. 'Hansith! Come down here!'

Sapper sat on the high seat of his yellow front-end loader in the rain and cheerfully cursed his gang of Buffaloes, secure in the knowledge that they understood not a word of his insults. The rain swept over them in intermittent gusts off the high mountains. It was not yet the solid, drenching downpour of the true wet season. However, the river was rising sullenly, turning dirty blue-grey with the mud and sediment that it was bringing down.

He knew that the flood had not yet begun in earnest. The thunder that growled ominously along the mountain peaks like a pride of hunting lions was only the prelude to the vast celestial onslaught which would soon follow. Although the river was lapping the top course of gabions of Sapper's dam, and was roaring through the bypass that he had cut into the side valley, he was still holding it at bay.

His Buffaloes were packing more baskets with aggregate, using up the last of the steel mesh from the stores in the quarry. As soon as each of these was filled and wired closed, Sapper picked it up in the front bucket of the tractor and drove it down the bank of the Dandera. He reinforced all the weak spots in the dam wall, and then he began raising it another course. Sapper was fully aware of the overturning effect that the river would exert once it began to pour over the top of the wall. Nothing would be able to withstand its power once this happened. It would carry away a rock-filled gabion as if it were the branch of a baobab tree. It needed only a single breach in the wall to bring the entire structure tumbling and rolling down. He had no illusions as to just how swiftly the river could do its fatal work.

He knew that he dared not wait for the first breach to develop in the wall before he warned Nicholas and Royan in the chasm downstream. The river could easily outrun any messenger he sent, and once the wall began to go it would already be too late. It would be a matter of fine judgement, and he slitted his eyes against another gust of slanting rain that blew into his face. His instinct was to call them out of the chasm now – there was already less than twelve inches of free-board at the top of the wall.

However, he knew that Nicholas would be furious if he was made to evacuate the workings prematurely, and in so doing aborted all their efforts. Sapper was fully aware of the extreme risks that Nicholas had taken and of the crippling expenditure he had made to reach this stage. Before they had left England, he had hinted to Sapper of the straitened circumstances in which he found himself. Although Sapper did not understand the intricacies or the responsibilities of being a 'Name' at Lloyd's, there had been so much publicity in the British press that he could not but realize that, if their venture here failed, the next stop for Nicholas would be the bankruptcy courts – and Nicholas was his friend.

The squall of rain blew over, and a bright hot sun burst through the low cloud banks. The flow of the river seemed undiminished, but at least the water level on the dam wall was no longer rising.

'I'll give it another hour,' he grunted, engaging the gears of the tractor and easing her down the bank to place another gabion in position.

N icholas worked shoulder to shoulder with Hansith's gang as they began to strip the paving slabs from the floor of the lowest level of the maze. The joints between the slabs were so tight that, even using crowbars, they had difficulty prising them apart. In order to save time, Nicholas made the hard choice of going

400

into a destructive search. He put four of the strongest men in the team to work with home-made sledgehammers, lumps of ironstone on wooden shafts, to break up the slabs so that they could be more readily levered out of the floor. He felt guilty about the damage they were causing to the site, but the work went ahead very much faster.

The high spirits and enthusiasm of the men were at last beginning to wane. They had worked too long in the oppressive confines of the maze, and every one of them was fully aware of the rising level of the river at the head of the gorge, and of the mortal threat behind those waters. Their expressions were surly and there was little laughter or banter. But more worrying for Nicholas was the fact that at the beginning of this shift Hansith had reported the first desertions. Sixteen of his men had failed to report for duty. They had quietly rolled their blankets during the night, picked up whatever items of value or utility they found lying around the camp, and crept away into the darkness.

Nicholas knew that it was no use sending anyone after them – they had too much of a start, and would be halfway up the escarpment already. This was Africa, and Nicholas was certain that now that the rot had started it would spread very quickly.

He joked and jollied them along, not allowing them to sense his true feelings. He worked shoulder to shoulder and sweated along with them in the excavation in an attempt to hold them. But he knew that, unless they made another discovery under these slabs to keep their interest and expectations alight, he might wake up tomorrow to find that even the monks and the faithful Hansith were gone.

He had started lifting the slabs in the angle of the corner of the maze, and they worked out from there in both directions down the arms of the tunnel. His heart sank as they broke up each paving slab with the hammers only to find beneath it the solid stratum of the country rock with no indication of any joint or opening.

'It doesn't look very hopeful,' he muttered to Royan as he took a short break to drink from one of the water flasks.

She too was looking unhappy as she poured water from the flask into his cupped hands, so that he could wash the sweat and grime from his face.

'I may have got the symbols for the levels wrong,' she suggested. 'It is just the kind of trick Taita would play, to work out combinations which would both give a logical solution.' She hesitated before she appealed to him for guidance. 'Do you think I should start working back the other combination—'

Her question was interrupted by a bellow from Hansith. 'In the name of the Blessed Virgin, *effendi*, come quickly!'

They spun around together. In her haste Royan dropped the flask, which shattered at her feet. She did not seem to notice that it had drenched her legs, but ran back to where Hansith was standing with the hammer poised for another stroke.

'What is it—' she broke off as they both saw that beneath the paving slabs Hansith had uncovered another layer of dressed stone sills.

These were laid neatly across the floor of the tunnel from wall to wall, recessed into the surrounding rock, with knife-edge joints between them. Their sides were smooth and plain, without engravings or markings upon them.

'What is it, Nicky?' Royan demanded.

'Either it's another layer of paving, or it's a cover over an opening in the floor,' he told her eagerly. 'We won't know until we lift one of them.'

The stone sills were too thick and heavy to be cracked with the primitive hammers, although Hansith tried his best. In the end they were forced to dig around the first of them and lever it free. It took five men to raise the end of it and lift it off its foundation.

'There is an opening under it.' Royan went down on her knees to peer into the space that it had left. 'Some kind of open shaft!'

Once the first sill was removed it was easier to get a purchase on the others that blocked the rectangular opening. When they had cleared them all away, Nicholas shone the lamp down into the dark shaft that was revealed. It stretched from wall to wall of the tunnel, and the head room was sufficient for even Nicholas to stand up to his full height on the steps that led down at a forty-five degree angle.

'Another stairway,' he exulted. 'Surely this must be it. Even Taita must have exhausted all the false leads by now.'

The workmen were crowding up behind them, their sullen mood evaporating at this fresh discovery and the certainty of additional bonuses in silver dollars that they had earned.

'Are we going down?' Royan asked. 'I know we should be careful and check it for traps, but we are running out of time, Nicky.'

'You are right, as always. The time has come when we have to press on regardless.'

'Caution thrown to the winds.' She took his hand, laughing. 'Let's go down together.'

They descended side by side, one cautious step at a time, with the lamp held head high and the shadows retreating before them.

'There is a chamber at the bottom,' Royan exclaimed.

'Looks like a store room – what are all those objects stacked along the walls? There must be hundreds of them. Are they coffins, sarcophaguses?' The dark shapes were almost human, standing shoulder to shoulder, rank after rank, around the walls of the square chamber.

'No, I think those are corn baskets on one side,' she said, recognizing them. 'Those on the other side look like wine amphorae. Probably some sort of offering to the dead.'

'If this is one of the funeral store rooms,' said Nicholas in a voice tight with excitement, 'then we are getting very close to the tomb now.'

'Yes!' she cried. 'Look – there is another doorway on the far side of this store room. Shine the light over there.'

The beam picked out the square opening facing them across this lower chamber. It was inviting, beckoning them almost seductively. They almost ran down the last few steps into the chamber lined with the reed baskets and pottery wine jars. But as they reached the level floor of the store room they ran into an invisible barrier that stopped both of them dead and sent them reeling backwards.

'God!' Nicholas clutched at his throat, his voice a strangled choke. 'Get back. Got to get back.'

Royan was sinking to her knees, also gasping and hunting for breath.

'Nicky!' she tried to scream, but her breath was trapped in her lungs. She felt that a steel noose had encircled her chest and, as it tightened, the breath was being forced out of her.

'Nicky! Help me!' She was strangling, like a fish thrown up on the bank. The strength drained from her limbs, and her vision began to break up and fade. She did not have the strength to stand.

He stooped over her and tried to lift her, but he was almost as weak. He felt his own legs buckling, no longer able to support even his own weight.

'Four minutes,' he thought desperately as he suffocated. 'That's all we have got. Four minutes to brain death and oblivion. We have to get air.'

From behind her, he slipped his arms under her armpits and locked his hands together over her breasts. Again he tried to lift her, but his strength was gone. He began to walk backwards towards the stairs down which they had run so lightly, and every pace required a huge effort. She was already unconscious, lying inert in the circle of his arms. Her limp legs trailed across the stone floor as he dragged her back.

The lowest step caught his heels and he almost toppled over backwards. With an effort he regained his balance and lugged her back up the steps, her feet sliding and bumping loosely over the treads. He wanted to shout to Hansith for help, but he did not have the air in his lungs to utter a sound.

'If you drop her now, she's dead,' he told himself, and he struggled up another five steps, his lungs hunting for precious air and finding none. His strength oozed out of him a drop at a time as his vision slid and wobbled and distorted.

'Let me breathe,' he pleaded. 'Please God, let me breathe.'

Miraculously, like a direct answer to his prayer, he felt the precious oxygen slide down his panting throat and swell his lungs. At once his strength began flooding back and he tightened his grip around Royan's chest and lifted her bodily. He staggered up the remaining steps with her body in his arms and sprawled out of the mouth of the shaft on to the slabs of the tunnel at Hansith's feet.

'What is is, *effendi*? What has happened to you and the lady?'

Nicholas had no breath to answer him. He laid Royan in the position for mouth-to-mouth resuscitation, and slapped her cheeks.

'Come on!' he pleaded with her. 'Speak! Talk to me!'

There was no response, so he knelt over her, covered her open mouth with his own and blew down her throat, until from the corner of his eye he saw her chest swelling and inflating.

He sat back for a count of three. 'Please, my darling, please breathe!' There was no colour in her yellow, corpse-like face.

He bent over her and covered her mouth again, and as he filled her lungs with his own breath he felt her stir under him.

'That's it, my darling,' he told her. 'Breathe! Breathe for me.'

At the next breath she pushed him away and sat up groggily, staring round at the circle of faces that hovered over her anxiously. She picked out Nicholas's pale face amongst the black faces of the men.

'Nicky! What happened?'

'I am not sure – but whatever it was, it almost got both of us. How are you feeling now?'

'It was as though an invisible hand had me by the throat, and was strangling me. I couldn't breathe, and then I passed out.'

'It must be some kind of gas filling the lower levels of the passage. You were only out for less than two minutes,' he reassured her. 'It takes four minutes of oxygen starvation to kill the brain.'

'I have a terrible headache.' She pressed her fingers to her temples. 'I heard your voice calling me back. You called me "my darling".' She dropped her eyes.

'Just a little slip of the tongue.' He lifted her to her feet and for a moment she swayed against him, her breasts soft and warm against his chest.

'Thank you once again, Nicky. I am so deeply in your debt already, I will never be able to repay you.'

'I am sure we will be able to work something out.'

She was suddenly aware of the men's eyes watching her and drew away from him. 'What kind of gas? And how did it get there? Was it another of Taita's tricks, do you think, Nicky?'

'One of the gases of decay, most probably,' was his opinion. 'Because it is trapped in the lower part of the passage, it must be a heavier-than-air type. I would guess that it is probably carbon dioxide, although it could be something like methane. I think methane is heavier than air, isn't it?'

'Did Taita do it deliberately?' The colour was returning to her cheeks, and she was recovering swiftly.

'I don't know, but those baskets and jars are suspicious. I will be able to answer that question when we have had a chance to examine their contents.' He touched her cheek tenderly. 'How are you feeling? How is your headache?'

'Better. What do we do now?'

'Clear the gas from the chamber,' he told her, 'and as soon as possible.'

He used a candle from his emergency pack to test for the gas level in the shaft. With it burning in his right hand he went back down the steps, holding it low to the floor, descending a step at a time. The candle flame burned brightly, dancing to the movement of air as he went down. Then, abruptly on the sixth step above the floor level of the chamber, the flame turned yellow and snuffed out.

He marked the level on the wall in white chalk, and called up to Royan at the head of the shaft, 'Well, at least it's not methane. I am still here. Must be carbon dioxide.'

'Pretty conclusive test,' she laughed. 'If it goes boom, it's methane.'

'Hansith, bring down the blower fan,' Nicholas shouted to the big monk.

Holding his breath as though he were snorkelling under water, Nicholas carried the fan down the lower steps and set it up on the floor of the chamber. He set the fan speed at 'High' and immediately retreated up the shaft, drawing a huge breath as soon as he was above the chalk mark on the wall.

'How long will it take to clear the gas?' Royan asked anxiously, looking at her wrist-watch.

'I will test with the candle every fifteen minutes.'

It was an hour before the gas had dispersed enough to enable him to reach the floor of the chamber again, and breathe the air down there. Then Nicholas ordered Hansith to bring down a bundle of firewood and build a fire in the centre of the stone floor, to heat and circulate the air more rapidly.

While he was doing this, Nicholas and Royan examined one of the baskets that stood against the wall.

'The crafty old ruffian!' Nicholas muttered half in exasperation and half in admiration. 'It looks like a mixture of manure and grass and dead leaves, the same as a compost heap.'

They crossed the chamber, turned one of the pottery jars on its side, and studied the powder that spilled out of it. Nicholas took up a handful and rubbed it between his fingers, then sniffed it warily.

'Crushed limestone!' he muttered. 'Although it has long ago dried out and lost any odour, Taita probably soaked it with some form of acid. Vinegar, perhaps, or even urine would have done the trick. As it broke down the limestone, it formed carbon dioxide.'

'So it was another deliberate trap,' Royan exclaimed.

'Even so many thousands of years ago, Taita must have understood the processes of decay. He knew what gases those mixtures would produce. Amongst all the other accomplishments he boasts of, he must also have been a nifty chemist.'

'Furthermore, he must have known that without a draught or any movement of air, these heavy inert gases would hang here in the bottom of the chamber indefinitely,' she agreed. 'I expect that this shaft is designed like a U-trap. I bet that the passage rises again—' she pointed at the mysterious doorway in the far wall, 'in fact I can see the first steps even from here.'

'We will soon find out if you are right,' he told her, 'because that's exactly where we are heading right now – up those steps.'

apper had placed cairns of stones at the water's edge to monitor the river level. He watched them the way a stockbroker watches his ticker tape.

It had been six hours since the last rain squall had passed. The clouds over the valley had burned away in the hot, bright sunlight, although they still hung densely over the northern horizon. Their great dun-coloured thunderheads reared to the heavens, menacing and ominous, forming their own mighty ranges that dwarfed the mountains beneath them. At any time the downpour might begin up there in the highlands. Once that happened, Sapper wondered how long it would take the flood waters to reach them here in the Abbay gorge.

He dismounted stiffly from the tractor, and went down the bank to inspect his stone markers. The water level had fallen almost a foot in the past hour. He forced himself not to let his optimism bubble over – after all, it had taken only fifteen minutes for the river to rise the same amount. The final outcome was inevitable. The rains would come. The river would spate. The dam would burst. He looked downstream at the dam wall, and shook his head with resignation.

He had done as much as possible to delay that moment. He had raised the level of the dam wall almost four feet, and packed in another buttress behind the wall to strengthen it. There was nothing further for him to do, and he could only wait.

Climbing up the bank, he leaned wearily against the yellow steel of his machine and looked across at his team of Buffaloes, strewn along the bank like casualties on a battlefield. They had worked for two days to hold back the waters, and now they were exhausted. He knew that he could not call on them for another effort; the next time the river attacked, it would overwhelm them.

He saw some of the men stir and sit up, and their faces turned upstream. He heard their voices faint on the wind. Something was exciting their interest. He climbed up on to the tractor and shaded his eyes. The unmistakable figure of Mek Nimmur was coming down the trail from the direction of the escarpment, stocky and powerful in his camo fatigues, his gait determined. He was accompanied by two of his company commanders.

Mek hailed Sapper from a distance. 'How is your dam holding?' he called in Arabic, which Sapper did not understand. 'Soon it will rain on the mountains. You won't be able to hold out here much longer.' But his gestures towards sky and river were immediately intelligible to Sapper.

Sapper jumped down from the machine to greet him, and they shook hands cordially. They had recognized in each other the qualities of strength and professionalism that they both admired.

Mek seized his company commander, who spoke English, by the arm, and the man fell into his by now familiar role of interpreter.

'It is not only the weather that troubles me,' Mek confided in a low voice, and the interpreter relayed the information to Sapper. 'I have reports that the government troops are moving into position to attack us. My intelligence is that they have a full battalion moving down this way from Debra Maryam, and another force below the monastery at St Frumentius, moving up the Abbay river.'

'Pincer movement, hey?' said Sapper.

Mek listened to the translation and nodded gravely. 'I am heavily outnumbered and I don't know how long I will be able to hold them when they attack. My men are guerrillas. It is not our role to fight set-piece battles. It is the war of the flea for us. Hit and run. I came to warn you to be ready to pull out at short notice.'

'Don't worry too much about me,' Sapper grunted. 'I am a sprinter. Hundred yards dash is my speciality. It's Nicholas and Royan you should be thinking of, them in that ruddy rabbit warren of theirs.'

'I am on my way to them now, but I wanted to arrange a fall-back position. If we get cut off from each other in the fighting, Nicholas has cached the boats at the monastery. That is where we will assemble.'

'Okay, Mek—' Sapper stopped speaking and all three of them looked up the trail, where there was a fresh disturbance amongst the men along the bank. 'What's going on?'

'One of my patrols coming in,' Mek narrowed his eyes. 'There must be some new development.' He stopped speaking as he realized that

Sapper could not understand him, and then his expression changed as he recognized the small, slim figure that was being carried on a rough litter by the men of his patrol.

Tessay saw him running towards her and sat up weakly on the litter. The men lowered her to the ground and Mek went down on his knees beside the litter and placed both his arms around her. They held each other in silence for a long moment. Then Mek gently cupped her face in his hands and examined her swollen and scarred features. Some of the burns had become infected, and her eyes were slits beneath the bloated lids.

'Who did this to you?' he asked softly.

She mumbled incoherently through her black-scabbed lips. 'They made me—'

'No! Don't try to talk.' He changed his mind as her lower lip cracked open and a droplet of fresh blood welled up and glistened like a ruby on her skin.

'I have to tell you,' she insisted in a broken whisper. 'They made me tell them everything. The numbers of your men. What you and Nicholas are doing here. Everything. I am sorry, Mek. I betrayed you.'

'Who was it? Who did this to you?'

'Nogo and the American, Helm,' she said, and although he embraced her as gently as a father with his infant in his arms, his eyes were terrible.

The lower chamber of the tunnel was cleared of gas at last. Hansith's fire burned bright and steady in the middle of the floor, the rising hot air wafting away the noxious vapours and dispersing them through the upper levels of the maze, where they mingled with the cleaner oxygen-rich air and lost their toxicity. By this time Royan had fully recovered from the physical effects of the gassing, but her confidence was shaken, and she allowed Nicholas to lead the way up the steps that rose from the far side of the chamber.

'It's the perfect gas trap,' Nicholas pointed out to her as they climbed cautiously. 'No doubt at all that Taita knew exactly what he was doing when he built this section of the tunnel.'

'Surely he must have expected any interloper of his period to have either succumbed to his hellish devices, lost his way in the maze, or given up and turned back by now,' she reasoned.

'Are you trying to convince me that this was Taita's last line of defence, and that he has no more tricks in store for us? Is that it?' Nicholas asked as he took another step upwards.

'No. Actually I was trying to convince myself, and not having much success. I just don't trust him one little bit any more. I have come to expect the worst from him. I expect the roof to collapse on me at any moment, or the floor to open and drop us into a fiery furnace or something worse.'

They had descended forty steps down into the chamber, and the staircase they were now climbing was a mirror image of that. It rose at the same angle and the tread of each step was the same depth and width. As their heads rose above the fortieth step, Nicholas played the beam of the lamp down the spacious, level arcade that opened before them, and they were dazzled by a riot of colour and pattern, bright and lovely as a field of desert blooms after rain. The paintings covered the walls and ceiling of the arcade, stunning in their profusion, wondrous in their execution.

'Taita!' Royan cried in a voice that quivered and broke. 'These are his paintings. There is no other artist like him, I could never mistake it. I would know his work anywhere.'

They stood on the top step and gazed around in wonder. When compared to these, the murals in the long gallery seemed pale and stilted, the tawdry sham that they really were. This was the work of a great master, a timeless genius, whose art could enchant and enrapture now just as readily as it had four thousand years ago.

They moved forward slowly, almost involuntarily, down the arcade. It was lined on each side with small chambers, like the stalls in an oriental bazaar. The entrance to each was guarded by tall columns that reached up to the roof. Each column was a carved statue of one member of the pantheon of gods. Between them they held the high-vaulted ceiling suspended.

As they drew level with the first two stalls, Nicholas stopped and squeezed her arm.

'The treasure chambers of Pharaoh,' he whispered.

The stalls were packed from floor to ceiling with wonderful and beautiful things.

'The furniture store.' Royan's voice was as reverential as his as she recognized the shapes of chairs and stools and beds and divans. She went to the nearest chamber and touched a royal throne. The arms were twining serpents of bronze and lapis lazuli. The legs were those of lions with claws of gold. The seat and back were chased with scenes of the hunt, and wings of gold surmounted the high back.

Stacked behind the throne was a great profusion of other furniture. They recognized a screened divan, its sides enclosed in an exquisite lacework of ebony and ivory. But there were dozens of other items besides, most of them broken down into their separate parts so that it was not possible to guess what they were. They gleamed with precious metals and coloured stones in such confusion and variety that it was too much to take in in a single glance. Both the alcoves on either side of the arcade were stuffed with these marvellous collections. Royan shook her head in wonder, and Nicholas led her on. The walls that separated the alcoves were decorated with panels illustrating the *Book of the Dead*, and the journey of Pharaoh through the pylons, the dangers and the trials, the demons and the monsters that awaited him along the way.

'These are the paintings that were missing from the mock tomb in the long gallery,' Royan told him. 'But just look upon the face of the king. You can see he was a real person. Those are perfect royal portraits.'

The mural beside them depicted the great god Osiris leading Pharaoh by the hand, protecting him from the monsters that crowded close on either hand, waiting their chance to devour him. It showed the face of the king as he must truly have been, a man with a kind and gentle, if rather weak, face.

'Look at the figures,' Nicholas agreed. 'They are not stiff wooden dolls always stepping forward with the right foot. These are real men and women. They are anatomically correct. The artist understood perspective and had studied the human body.'

They came to the next pair of alcoves, and paused to peer into them.

'Weapons,' said Nicholas. 'Just look at that chariot!'

The panels of the chariot were covered with a skin of gold leaf, so that it dazzled the eye. The harness and traces seemed only to await the horses that would draw it into battle, and the quivers strapped to the side panels behind each tall wheel bulged with arrows and javelins. The cartouche of Mamose was emblazoned on the side panels.

Piled beside this magnificent vehicle were war bows whose stocks were bound with wire of electrum and bronze and gold. There were arrays of daggers with ivory handles and swords with blades of glistening bronze. There were racks of spears and pikes. There were shields of bronze, the targets decorated with scenes of war and the name of the divine Mamose. There were helmets and breastplates made from the skin of the crocodile, and the uniforms and regalia of the famous regiments of Egypt dressed the life-sized wooden statues of the king that stood in rows against the walls of the alcoves.

They walked on down the aisle, between more paintings and murals depicting the life and the death of the king. They saw him playing with his daughters and dandling his infant son. They saw him fishing and hunting and hawking, in council with his ministers and his nomarches, dallying with his wives and concubines, and feasting with the priests of the temple.

'What a chronicle of life in ancient times,' Royan breathed with awe. 'There has never been a discovery remotely like this before.'

Each of the persons in the panels had obviously been drawn from

410

life. They were real breathing living men and women, every face and every expression different, captured with the keen eye, the humour and the great humanity of the artist.

'That must be Taita himself.' Royan pointed out the self-portrait of the eunuch in one of the central panels. 'I wonder if he took poetic licence, or was he truly so noble and beautiful?'

They paused to admire the face of Taita, their adversary, and looked into his searching, intelligent eyes. Such was the skill of the artist that he watched them as keenly as they studied him. A small, enigmatic smile played on Taita's lips. The painting had been varnished, so that it was perfectly preserved, as if it had been painted the day before. Taita's lips seemed moist and his eyes gleamed softly with life.

'His complexion is fair and his eyes are blue!' Royan exclaimed. 'Although that red hair is almost certainly dyed with henna.'

'It is weird to think that, although he lived so long ago, he almost succeeded in killing us,' Nicholas said softly.

'In what land was he born? He never tells us that in the scrolls. Was it Greece or Italy? Was he from one of the Germanic tribes, or was he of Viking stock? We will never know, for he himself probably did not know his own origins.'

'There he is again in the next panel.' Nicholas pointed down the arcade to where the unmistakable face of the eunuch appeared in the throng that knelt in homage before the throne on which sat Pharaoh and his queen. 'Like Hitchcock, he seems to like to appear in his own creations.'

They went on past the treasure stalls in which were stored plates and goblets and bowls of alabaster and bronze chased with silver and gold, polished bronze mirrors and rolls of precious silk and linen and woollen cloth that had long ago rotted to shaggy black amorphous heaps. On the walls that divided these from the next set of stalls they saw re-enacted the battle with the Hyksos in which Pharaoh had been struck down, the arrow shot by the Hyksos king lodged in his breast. Then in the next panel Taita, the surgeon, bent over him with the surgical instruments in his hands, removing the blood-smeared barb from deep in his flesh.

Now they came to alcoves in which were stacked hundreds of cedarwood chests. The boxes were painted with the royal cartouche of Mamose, and with scenes of the king at his toilet: lining his eyes with kohl, painting his face with white antimony and scarlet rouge, being shaved by his barbers and dressed by his valets.

'Some of those chests will contain the royal cosmetics,' Royan murmured, 'and some of them will be Pharaoh's wardrobes of clothing. There will be costumes in them for every occasion in his after-life. I long to be able to unpack and examine them.'

411

The next set of wall panels showed the marriage of the king to the young virgin, Taita's mistress. The face of Queen Lostris was rendered with loving detail. The artist gloated on her beauty and exaggerated it, his brush strokes caressing her naked breasts and lingering on all her virtues until they epitomized feminine perfection.

'How much Taita loved her,' Royan murmured, and there was envy in her voice. 'You can see it in every line he drew.'

Nicholas smiled softly and put his arms around her shoulders.

There were hundreds more wooden chests stacked in the next alcoves. Painted on the lids were miniatures of the king decked in all his jewellery: his fingers and toes were thick with rings and his chest was covered with pectoral medallions, while bangles of gold adorned his arms and bracelets his wrists. In one portrait he wore the double crown of the two kingdoms of Egypt united, the red crown and the white with the heads of the vulture and the cobra on his brow. In another he wore the blue war crown, and on a third the Nemes crown with gold and lapis wings that covered his ears.

'If each of those chests contains the treasures depicted on its lid—' Nicholas broke off, unable to continue the thought. The possibility of such riches was daunting, and the imagination balked at the magnitude of it.

'Do you remember what Taita wrote in the scrolls? "*I cannot believe that such a treasure was ever before accumulated in one place at one time*"?' Royan asked him. 'It seems that it is all still here, every single gem and grain of gold. The treasure of Mamose is intact.'

Beyond the treasury there was another alcove lined with shelves on which stood the *ushabti* figures: dolls made of green glazed porcelain or carved from cedarwood. They were an army of tiny figures, men and women from all the trades and professions. There were priests and scribes and lawyers and physicians, gardeners and farmers, bakers and brewers, handmaidens and dancing girls, seamstresses and laundrymaids, soldiers and barbers, and common labourers. Each of them carried the tools and accoutrements of his or her trade. They would accompany the king to the after-world and there would work for Pharaoh, and would go forward in his place if he were ever called upon to perform a service for the other gods.

At last Nicholas and Royan came to the end of this fabulous arcade, and found their way closed off by a series of tall, free-standing screens, tabernacles that had been once fine white linen mesh but were now decayed and rotted into ribbons and streamers, dirty and shabby as old cobwebs. And yet the stars and rosettes of shining gold that decorated these curtains were still hanging in the mesh like fish in a fisherman's net. Through this ethereal web of silken wisps and golden stars they could make out the shape of another gateway beyond.

'That must be the entrance to the actual tomb,' Royan whispered. 'There is only a thin veil between us and the king now.'

They hesitated at the threshold, gripped by a strange reluctance to take the final step.

As an old warrior, Mek Nimmur had seen and treated most of the injuries that a man might sustain on the battlefield. His little guerrilla group did not have a doctor, or even a medical orderly. Mek himself treated most of his casualties, and he always had a medical kit close at hand.

He had the men carry Tessay to one of the huts near the quarry, where, screened by the grass walls, he stripped her of her tattered clothing and treated her injuries. He cleaned her burns and abrasions with disinfectant, and covered the worst of them with clean field dressings. Then he rolled her gently on to her stomach and snapped the glass phial off the needle of the disposable syringe which was preloaded with a broad-spectrum antibiotic.

She winced at the sting of the needle, and he said, 'I am not a very good doctor.'

'I would have no other. Oh, Mek! I thought I would never see you again. I did not fear death as much as I feared that.'

He helped her dress in the spare clothing from his pack, a sweatshirt and fatigues that were many sizes too large for her. He rolled up the cuffs for her, and his touch was gentle. His hands were those of a lover, not a soldier.

'I must look so ugly,' she whispered through her swollen, black-scabbed lips.

'You are beautiful,' he denied it. 'To me you will always be beautiful.' He touched her cheek carefully, so as not to harm the raw burns that covered it.

At that moment they heard the gunfire. It was still faint with distance, borne down from the north on the rain winds.

Mek stood up immediately. 'It has begun. Nogo is attacking at last.'

'It's all my fault. I told him—'

'No,' he told her firmly. 'It is not your fault. You did what you had to do. If you had not, they would have hurt you even worse than this. They would have attacked us, even if you had told them nothing.'

He picked up his webbing belt and strapped it around his waist. From far off they heard the crumping detonation of exploding mortar shells.

'I have to go now,' he told her.

'I know. Do not worry about me.'

413

'I will always worry about you. These men will carry you down to the monastery. That is the assembly point. Wait for me there. I cannot hope to hold Nogo for long. He is too strong. I will come to you soon.'

'I love you,' she whispered. 'I will wait for you for ever.'

'You are my woman,' he told her in his deep, soft voice, and then he ducked through the doorway of the hut and was gone.

When Nicholas touched the frame of the screen, fragments of the mesh veil tore free with even that tiny movement and fell to the tiles of the floor. The golden rosettes trapped in their folds tinkled on the stones. Now there was an opening in the curtain large enough for them to step through. They found themselves before the inner doorway. It was guarded on one side by a massive statue of the great god Osiris with his hands crossed over his chest, clutching the crook and the flail. Opposite stood his wife Isis, with the lunar crown and horns on her head. Their blank eyes stared out into eternity, and their expressions were serene. Nicholas and Royan passed between these twelve-foot-high statues and found themselves at last in the veritable tomb of Mamose.

The roof was vaulted, and the quality of the murals that covered it and the walls was different – formal and classical. The colours were of a deeper, more sombre hue, and the patterns more intricate. The chamber was smaller than they had anticipated; just large enough to accommodate the huge granite sarcophagus of the divine Pharaoh Mamose.

The sarcophagus stood chest-high. Its side panels were engraved in bas-relief with scenes of Pharaoh and the other gods. The stone lid was in the shape of a full-length effigy of the supine figure of the king. They saw at once that it was still in its original position, and that the clay seals of the priests of Osiris which secured the lid were intact. The tomb had never been violated. The mummy had lain within it undisturbed through the millennia.

But this was not what amazed them. There were two extraneous items within the otherwise classically correct tomb. On the lid of the sarcophagus lay a magnificent war bow. Almost as long as Nicholas was tall, the entire length of its stock was bound with coils of shining electrum wire, that alloy of gold and silver whose formula has been lost in antiquity.

The other item that should never have been placed in a royal tomb stood at the foot of the sarcophagus. It was a small human figure, one of the *ushabti* dolls. A glance confirmed the superior quality of the carving of this effigy, and both of them recognized the features instantly. Only

414

minutes before, they had seen that face painted upon the walls of the arcade, outside the tomb.

The words of Taita, from the scrolls, seemed to reverberate within the confines of the tomb, and hang like fireflies in the air above the sarcophagus:

> *When I stood for the very last time beside the royal sarcophagus, I sent all the workmen away. I would be the very last to leave the tomb, and after me the entrance would be sealed.*
>
> *When I was alone I opened the bundle I carried. From it I took the long bow, Lanata. Tanus had named it after my mistress, for Lanata had been her baby name. I had made the bow for him. It was the last gift from the two of us. I placed it upon the sealed stone lid of his coffin.*
>
> *There was one other item in my bundle. It was the wooden* ushabti *figure that I had carved. I placed it at the foot of the sarcophagus. While I carved it, I had set up three copper mirrors so that I could study my own features from every angle and reproduce them faithfully. The doll was a miniature Taita.*
>
> *Upon the base I had inscribed the words—*

Royan knelt at the foot of the coffin and pick up the *ushabti* figure. Reverently she turned it in her hands and studied the hieroglyphics carved into the base of the figure.

Nicholas knelt beside her. 'Read it to me,' he said.

Softly she obeyed. '"*My name is Taita. I am a physician and a poet. I am an architect and a philosopher. I am your friend. I will answer for you.*"'

'So it's all true,' Nicholas whispered.

Royan replaced the *ushabti* exactly as she had found it and, still on her knees, turned her face to his.

'I have never known another moment like this,' she whispered. 'I want it never to end.'

'It will never end, my darling,' he answered her. 'You and I are only just beginning.'

Mek Nimmur watched them coming, skirting the bottom slope of the hill. It took the trained eye of a bush-fighter to pick them out as they moved through the thick scrub and thorn. As he evaluated them he felt a twinge of dismay. These were crack troops, seasoned during long years of war. He had once fought with them against the Mengistu tyranny, and he had probably trained many of those men down there. Now they were coming against him. Such was the cycle of war and violence in this racked continent, where the endless struggles were fuelled and nurtured by the age-old tribal enmities and the greed and corruption of the new-age politicians and their outmoded ideologies.

But this was not the moment for dialectics, he thought bitterly, and focused his mind on the tactics of the battlefield beneath him. Yes! These men were good. He could see it in the way they advanced, like wraiths through the scrub. For every one of them he picked out, he knew there were a dozen others that remained unseen.

'Company strength,' he thought, and glanced around at his own small force. Fourteen men amongst the rocks, they could only hope to hit their adversary hard while they still had the advantage of surprise, and then pull back before Nogo ranged his mortars in on the hilltop where they lay.

He looked up at the sky and wondered whether Nogo would call in an air strike. Thirty-five minutes' flying time for a stick of those Soviet-built Tupolevs from the air base at Addis, and he could almost smell the sweet stench of napalm on the humid wind, and see the rolling cloud of flame sweeping towards them. That was the only thing his men really feared. But there would be no air strike – not this time, he decided. Nogo and his paymaster, the German von Schiller, wanted the spoils from the tomb that Nicholas Quenton-Harper had discovered in the gorge. They did not want to share any of it with those political fat cats in Addis. They would not want to draw any government attention to themselves and this little private campaign of theirs in the Abbay gorge.

He looked back down the slope. The enemy was moving in nicely, swinging around the hillside to intersect the trail along the Dandera river. Soon they must send a patrol up here to secure their flank before they could sweep on. Yes, there they were. Eight, no, ten men detaching from the main advance, and moving cautiously up the slope beneath him.

'I will let them get in close,' he decided. 'I would like to get them all, but that is too much to hope for. I would settle for four or five of them, and it would be good to leave a few squealers in the scrub.' He grinned cruelly. 'Nothing like a man screaming with a belly wound to take the fire out of his comrades, and make them keep their heads down.'

He looked across the rock-strewn slope, and saw that his RPD light machine gun was perfectly sited to enfilade their advance up the slope. Salim, his machine gunner, was an artist with that weapon. Perhaps, after all, he could hope to put down more than five of them.

'We will see,' thought Mek, 'but I must time it right.'

He saw that there was a gap in the ridge of rock just below him.

'They will not want to expose themselves by crossing the open ridge,' he judged. 'They will tend to bunch up and sneak through the gap. That will be the moment.'

He looked back at the RPD. Salim was watching him, waiting for his signal. Mek looked back down the slope.

'Yes,' he thought. 'Their line is bunching. The big one on the left is already out of position. Those two inside him are angling across towards the gap.'

Nogo's men's camouflage blended perfectly with the scrub, and the barrels of their weapons were wrapped with rags and scraps of camouflage netting so that they threw no sunlight reflections. They were almost invisible in the bush; it was only their movements and the skin tones that betrayed them. They were so close now that Mek caught the occasional gleam of one of their eyeballs but he still could not pick out their machine gunner.

He must silence the gun with his first burst. 'Ah, yes,' he thought with relief. 'There he is. On the right flank. I nearly missed him.'

The man was short and thick-set, with heavy shoulders and long arms, simian, carrying the gun easily on his hip. It was a Soviet-made 7.62mm RPD. The wink of brass from the cartridges in the ammunition belts festooned over those great shoulders had given him away.

Mek eased himself down and inched around the base of the rock that covered him. He slipped the rate-of-fire selector on his AKM to rapid, and laid his cheek on the wooden butt. It was his personal weapon. A gunsmith in Addis had trued the action and lapped the barrel for him, as well as glass-bedding the barrel into the stock. All this had been done to improve the accuracy of this notoriously inaccurate assault rifle. It was still no sniper's weapon, but with these modifications he could expect to place all his shots within a two-inch circle at a hundred metres.

The man carrying the RPD up the slope was now only fifty metres below where he lay. Mek glanced to his right to make sure that the three others were moving into the gap where Salim could take them out with a single burst; then he settled the pip of his foresight in the centre of the RPD machine gunner's belly, using his belt buckle as an aiming mark, and fired a tap of three.

The AKM rode up viciously and the triple detonation stung his eardrums, but Mek saw his bullets strike, stitching a row up the man's torso. One hit low in the belly, the second in the diaphragm and the third at the base of his throat. He spun around, his arms flinging out and jerking, and then crashed over backwards, out of sight in the underbrush.

All around Mek his men were firing. He wondered how many of them Salim had taken with that first burst, but there was no longer anything to see. The enemy were all down in cover. A faint haze of gunsmoke blued the air as they returned fire, and the scrub trembled and shook to the recoil and the muzzle blast of their weapons.

Then, in the uproar of fire, in the whine and wail of ricochets off the rocks, one of them began to scream.

'I am hit. In Allah's name, help me.' His cries rang eerily across the hillside, and the enemy fire slackened perceptibly. Mek clipped a fresh magazine on to the AKM.

'Sing, little bird. Sing!' he muttered grimly.

It required the combined strength of Nicholas, Hansith and eight other men to lift the lid off the stone sarcophagus. Staggering under its weight, they laid it carefully against the wall of the tomb. Then Royan and Nicholas stood on the plinth of the sarcophagus to look down into the interior.

Fitted neatly into the stone receptacle was an enormous wooden coffin. Its lid too was in the form of the reclining Pharaoh. He was in the posture of death with his hands crossed at his breast, clutching the flail and the crook. The coffin was gilded and encrusted with semi-precious stones. The expression on the face of the king's effigy was serene.

They lifted the coffin out of the sarcophagus, and its weight was less than that of the stone lid. Carefully Nicholas split the golden seals and the layer of hard dried resin that held the lid of the coffin in place. Within it they found another coffin, fitted perfectly, and when they opened that yet another coffin was revealed. It was like a nest of Russian dolls, one within the other, becoming smaller with each revelation.

In the end there were seven coffins, each of them progressively more ornate and richly decorated than the previous one. The seventh coffin was only slightly larger than a man, and it was made of gold. The polished metal caught the light of the lamps like a thousand mirrors and threw bright arrows and darts into every recess of the tomb.

When at last they opened the golden inner coffin they found that it was filled with flowers. The blooms had dried and faded, so their colour was sepia. Their scent had long ago evaporated, so that only the musky aroma of great age wafted up from the coffin. The petals were so dry and papery that they crumbled at the first touch. Beneath the faded blooms was a layer of the finest linen; once it must have been snowy white, but now it was brown with age and the stain of the juices from the flowers. Through the soft folds they saw once again the gleam of gold.

Standing on either side of the coffin, Nicholas and Royan peeled back the linen mesh. It crackled softly and tore like tissue paper under their fingers, but as it came away they both involuntarily gasped with wonder as the death-mask of Pharaoh was revealed. It was only fractionally larger than the head of a man, but it was a perfect image in every detail. Pharaoh's features had been preserved for all eternity in this extraordinary work of art. They stared in silent wonder into the obsidian and rock crystal eyes of Pharaoh, and Pharaoh gazed back at them sadly, almost accusingly.

It was a long time before either of them could summon the courage and presumption to lift it away from the head of the mummy. But when they did so, they found further evidence that in antiquity the body of the king and that of his general, Tanus, had been changed. The mummy that lay before them was obviously too large for the coffin that contained it. It had been partially unwrapped, and cramped into the interior.

'A royal mummy would have had hundreds of charms and amulets placed beneath the wrappings,' Royan whispered. 'This is the plainly dressed corpse of a nobleman and not that of the king.'

Nicholas gently lifted the inner layer of bandage away from the dead head and a thick coil of braided hair was revealed.

'The portraits of Pharaoh Mamose on the walls of the arcade show that his head hair was dyed with henna,' Nicholas murmured. 'Look at this.'

The braid was the colour of the winter grasses of the African savannah, gold and silver.

'There can be no doubt now. This is the body of Tanus. The friend of Taita and the lover of the queen.'

'Yes,' Royan agreed, her eyes soft with tears. 'He is the true father of Lostris's son, who became in his time the Pharaoh Tamose and the forefather of a great line of kings. So this is the man whose blood runs through the history of ancient Egypt.'

'In his way he was as great as any Pharaoh,' Nicholas said quietly.

t was Royan who roused herself first. 'The river!' she cried, with a razor edge to her voice. 'We cannot let all this go again, when the river rises.'

'Neither can we hope to save all of it. There is too much. A great mass of treasure. Our time here has almost run out, so we must pick out the most beautiful and important pieces and pack them into the crates. Lord alone knows if we even have time for that.'

So they worked in a frenzy in the short time that was left to them. They could not even think about saving the statues and the murals, the furniture and the weapons, the banqueting utensils and the wardrobes of costumes. The great golden chariot must stand where it had stood for four thousand years.

They removed the golden death-mask from over Tanus's head, but they left his mummy in the innermost of the golden coffins. Then Nicholas sent for Mai Metemma. The old abbot came with twenty of his monks to receive the holy relic of the ancient saint that he had been promised as his reward. Reverentially, chanting deep and slow, they bore Tanus's coffin away to its new resting place in the *maqdas* of the monastery.

'At least the old hero will be treated with respect,' Royan said softly. Then she looked around the tomb. 'We cannot leave the site like this, with the coffins thrown about and the lids discarded,' Royan protested. 'It looks as though grave-robbers have been at work here.'

'Grave-robbers is exactly what we are.' Nicholas smiled at her.

'No, we are archaeologists,' she denied hotly, 'and we must try to act like it.'

So they replaced the six remaining coffins one within the other, laid them back in the great sarcophagus, and finally replaced the massive stone lid. Only then did Royan allow them to begin selecting and packing the treasures they would take with them.

The death-mask was without any doubt the premier item in the entire tomb. It fitted neatly into one of the crates, with the wooden *ushabti* of Taita laid alongside it, packed with Styrofoam until it was firmly secured. Royan scribbled on the lid in waterproof wax crayon: 'Mask & Taita Ushabti'.

Their final selection was, perforce, hurried and superficial. They could not rip open every one of the cedarwood chests that were piled high in the alcoves of the arcade. The painted and gilded chests themselves were priceless artefacts, and should be treated with respect. So they allowed themselves to be guided by the illustrations on the lid of each. They discovered immediately that these were indeed an accurate inventory and catalogue of the contents. In the chest which showed Pharaoh decked in the blue war crown, they found the actual crown laid on gilded leather pillows that had been moulded to fit it exactly and to protect it.

Even in the short time left to them they became almost surfeited by the magnificence of the items they uncovered as they selected and opened the cedarwood chests. Not only the blue crown, but the red and white crown of the kingdoms united was there, and the splendid Nemes crown, all three in such a miraculous state of preservation that they might have been lifted from Pharaoh's brow that morning.

From the very outset it had to be a prerequisite that any artefact must be small enough to fit into one of the ammunition crates. If it were too large, no matter what its value or historical significance, then it had to be rejected and left in the tomb. Fortunately, many of the cedarwood chests containing the royal jewellery fitted snugly into the metal crates, so that not only the contents but also the chests themselves could be saved. However, the larger items, the crowns and the huge jewelled gold pectoral medallions, had to be repacked.

As the ammunition crates were filled, they carried them down and stacked them on the landing outside the sealed doorway, ready to be carried out. Including the crates that contained the eight statuettes of the gods from the long gallery, they had packed and catalogued forty-eight crates when they heard Sapper's unmistakable accents floating up the staircase.

'Major, where the hell are you? You can't bugger about in here any longer. Come on, man! Get your hairy arse out of here. The river is in full spate, and the dam is going to burst at any minute.'

Sapper came bounding up the staircase, but even he stopped in wonder and awe as he looked for the first time upon the splendours of the funeral arcade of Pharaoh Mamose. It took some minutes for him to recover from the shock and to revert to his old prosaic self again.

'I mean it, major! It's a matter of minutes, not hours. That ruddy dam is going to go. Apart from that, Mek is fighting in the hills at the head of the chasm. You can hear the gunfire even at the bottom of the cliff in Taita's pool. You and Royan have to get out and fast, I kid you not!'

'Okay, Sapper. We are on our way. Get back to the chamber at the bottom of those stairs. You saw those ammunition crates down there?' Sapper nodded, and Nicholas went on quickly, 'Have the men lug those crates out of here. Get them down to the monastery. I want you to supervise that part of it. We will follow you down the trail with the rest of them.'

'Don't mess around, major. Your life isn't worth a pile of old junk like this. Get moving now.'

'Get on with it, Sapper. But don't let Royan hear you call it a pile of old junk. You could be in really serious trouble.'

Sapper shrugged. 'Don't say I didn't warn you.' He turned and started back down the staircase.

'You know where the boats are stashed,' Nicholas shouted after him. 'If you get there before me, get them inflated and the crates lashed down. We will be right behind you.'

The moment Sapper was gone, Nicholas raced back down the arcade to where Royan was still at work in the treasury.

'That's it!' he shouted at her. 'No more time. Let's get out.'

'Nicky, we can't leave this—'

'Out!' He grabbed her arm. 'We are getting out now. Unless you want to share Tanus's tomb with him on a permanent basis.'

'Can't I just—'

'No, you crazy woman! Now! The dam will go at any moment.'

She broke away from him, snatched up some handfuls of left-over jewellery from the open chest at her feet, and began stuffing them into her pockets.

'I can't leave these.'

He seized her around the waist and swung her over his shoulder. 'I told you I meant it,' he said grimly, and ran with her down the arcade.

'Nicky! Put me down.' She kicked with outrage, but he continued running down into the chamber at the foot of the staircase.

Hansith and his men were carrying the last few packed ammunition crates up the staircase on the far side of the chamber. They balanced the crates easily on their heads and went up the steps with alacrity.

Here Nicholas set Royan down on her own feet again. 'Will you promise to behave now? We aren't playing games. This is deadly serious – I mean deadly, if we get trapped down here.'

'I know.' She looked contrite. 'I just couldn't bear to leave the rest of it.'

'Enough of that. Let's go.' Nicholas grabbed her hand and dragged her after him. After the first few steps she shook her hand free and started to run in earnest, outstripping him and reaching the top of the staircase a few paces ahead of him.

Even under their burdens the porters were making good time. Caught up in the long hurrying column, Nicholas and Royan wound their way back through the maze, grateful for the signposts at each corner, and made it down the central staircase into the ruined long gallery without taking a wrong turning. Sapper was waiting for them at the ruins of the sealed doorway, and grunted with relief when he saw them amongst the porters.

'I thought I told you to go on ahead and get the boats ready,' Nicholas shouted at him.

'Couldn't trust you not to be bloody stupid.' Sapper looked miserable. 'Wanted to make sure you didn't hang about in there.'

'I am touched, Sapper.' Nicholas punched his shoulder, and then they ran down the approach tunnel and clattered over the bridge across the sink-hole.

'Where is Mek?' Nicholas panted at Sapper's back as he jogged in front of him. 'Have you seen Tessay?'

'Tessay is back. She had a nasty experience. She was in a terrible mess. Seems she got badly knocked about.'

'What has happened to her?' Nicholas was appalled. 'Where is she?'

'It looks like she fell into the hands of von Schiller's gorillas and they beat the hell out of her. Mek's men are taking her down to the monastery. She will wait for us at the boats.'

'Thank God for that,' Nicholas muttered, and then louder, 'What about Mek?'

'He is trying to hold off Nogo's attack. I have been hearing rifle fire and grenades and mortar shells all morning. He too is going to fall back and wait for us at the boats.'

They ran the last few yards down the tunnel ankle-deep in slush and water, and at last crawled over the wall of the coffer dam on to the rocky ledge around Taita's pool. Nicholas looked up to see Hansith's porters scrambling up the bamboo scaffolding ladder towards the top of the cliff, each of them hauling up one of the ammunition crates.

At that moment he caught a sound that he recognized instantly. He cocked his head to listen and then told Royan grimly, 'Gunfire! Mek is fighting it out, but it's pretty darned close.'

'My bag!' Royan started towards her thatched shelter at the foot of the cliff. 'I must get my kit.'

'You won't need your make-up or your pyjamas, and I've got your passport.' He seized her arm and turned her back towards the foot of the ladder. 'In fact the only thing you need now is plenty of space between you and Colonel Nogo. Come along, Royan!'

They swarmed up the bamboo scaffolding and when they reached the cliff top Royan was surprised to discover that, although the earth was wet underfoot from the recent rain squalls, the sun was high and hot. She had lost all sense of time in the cold, gloomy passages of the tomb, and now she held up her face to the sunlight and drank it in gratefully for a moment while Nicholas checked the porters and made certain that they were all out of the chasm.

Sapper set off at the head of the column along the trail through the thorn forest, with the file of porters strung out behind him. Nicholas and Royan waited until all the men were on the pathway before they themselves brought up the rear of the column. The sound of the fighting was frighteningly close now. It seemed to be almost at the brink of the chasm close behind them, less than half a mile away. The crackle of automatic fire gave a spring and a lift to the feet of the porters, and the entire party raced back through the forest to reach the main trail down to the monastery before they were cut off by Nogo's advance.

Before they reached the junction of the paths, they ran into a party of stretcher-bearers carrying a litter. They too were headed down towards the monastery. Nicholas thought the person they were carrying was one of the wounded guerrillas of Mek's force. But even when he caught up with them it took a moment for him to recognize Tessay's swollen and burned face.

'Tessay!' He stooped over her. 'Who did this to you?'

She looked up at him with the huge dark eyes of a wounded child, and told him in halting, broken words.

'Helm!' Nicholas blurted. 'I'd love to get my hands on that bastard.' At that moment Royan caught up with them, and she let out a small cry of horror as she saw Tessay's face. Then immediately she took charge of her.

Nicholas spoke quickly to one of the stretcher-bearers whom he recognized.

'Mezra, what is happening out there?'

'Nogo moved a force in from the east of the gorge. They outflanked us, and we are pulling out. This is not our kind of fighting.'

'I know,' Nicholas remarked grimly. 'Guerrillas must keep moving. Where is Mek Nimmur?'

'He is retreating down the eastern bank of the chasm.' As Mezra replied, they heard a renewed outburst of firing behind them. 'That is him!' Mezra nodded. 'Nogo is pushing him hard.'

'What are your orders?'

'To take Lady Sun to the boats and wait for Mek Nimmur there.'

'Good!' Nicholas told him. 'We will go with you.'

The Jet Ranger was flying low, hugging the contours of the land, never cresting the high ground. Helm knew that Mek Nimmur's *shufta* were armed with RPGs, rocket-launchers. In the hands of a trained man, these were deadly weapons against a slow-flying, unarmoured aircraft such as the Jet Ranger. The pilot's defence was to use the terrain as cover, weaving and twisting up the valleys so as to deny the rocketeers a clear shot.

Although the rain clouds were slumping down the escarpment into the Abbay gorge, the helicopter was keeping well below them. However, the sudden squalls of wind rocked the machine dangerously and splatterings of heavy raindrops rattled against the windshield. The pilot sat forward in the seat, leaning against his shoulder-straps as he concentrated on this dangerous low flying in these unpleasant conditions. Helm sat in the right-hand seat, beside the pilot. Von Schiller and Nahoot Guddabi were together in the rear passenger seat, both of them craning nervously to peer out of the side windows as the heavily wooded slopes of the valley streamed past, seemingly close enough to touch.

Every few minutes the radio crackled into life, and they could hear the terse transmissions of Nogo's men on the ground calling for mortar support or reporting objectives attained. The pilot translated the radio gabble for them, twisting round in his seat to tell von Schiller, 'There is a sharp fire-fight going on along the top of the chasm, but the *shufta* are on the run. Nogo is handling his force well. They have just dislodged a strong force from the hillside to the east of us,' he pointed out of the left-hand port, 'and they are hammering the *shufta* with mortars as they run.'

'Have they reached the spot in the chasm where Quenton-Harper was working?'

'It isn't clear. All a bit confused.' The pilot listened to the next burst of Arabic on the radio. 'I think that was Nogo himself speaking just then.'

'Call him up!' von Schiller ordered Helm, leaning over the back of his seat. 'Ask him if they have secured the tomb site yet.'

Helm reached across and lifted the microphone off its hook below the instrument panel. 'Rose Petal, this is Bismarck. Do you copy?'

There was a pause filled with static, and then Nogo's voice speaking English. 'Go ahead, Bismarck.'

'Have you secured the primary objective? Over.'

'Affirmative, Bismarck. All secured. All opposition suppressed. I am sending men down the ladder to clear the workings.'

Helm swivelled in his seat to look back at von Schiller. 'Nogo has men in the chasm already. We can go in and land.'

'Tell him not to let any of his men into the workings before I arrive,' von Schiller ordered sternly, but his expression was triumphant. 'I must be the first in there. Make him understand that.'

While Helm relayed his orders to Nogo, von Schiller tapped the pilot on the shoulder. 'How long to the objective?'

'About five minutes' flying time, sir.'

'Circle the site when you arrive. Don't land until we are sure Nogo has it under his control.'

The pilot lifted the collective and the sound of the rotors altered as they changed pitch. The helicopter slowed and then hovered in mid-air, while the pilot pointed down.

'What is it?' von Schiller followed his gesture. 'What do you see?'

'The dam,' Helm answered. 'Quenton-Harper's dam. He did a load of work down there.'

The wide body of trapped water gleamed grey and sullen under the rain clouds, tainted with the run-off from the highlands. The water diverted into the side canal boiled white and angrily down into the long valley.

'Deserted!' Helm commented. 'All Harper's men have pulled out.'

'What is that yellow object on the bank?' von Schiller wanted to know.

'That's the earth-moving machine. You remember? My informer told us about it.'

'Don't waste any more time,' von Schiller ordered. 'Nothing more to see here. Let's get on!'

Helm tapped the pilot's shoulder, and gestured downstream.

Sapper was waiting for them to catch up at the junction of the trail, where the diverted river was roaring down the valley in a torrent and had washed out a long section of the original track. The porters, strung out in a long line down the valley, each with an ammunition crate balanced on his head, were picking their way along the higher ground above the water.

Tessay's litter was near the rear of the column, with Royan and Nicholas trotting on each side of it and steadying it over the rough and uneven sections of the path.

'Where is Hansith?' Nicholas shouted at Sapper, shading his eyes to check the men ahead of him, and trying to pick out the big monk's distinctive form from amongst the others in the caravan.

'I thought he was with you,' Sapper shouted back. 'I haven't seen him since we left the chasm.'

Nicholas turned and stared back the way they had come, along the footpath through the thorn forest.

'Damn the man,' he grunted. 'We can't go back to look for him. He will have to make his own way down to the monastery.'

At that moment they heard the faint but familiar flutter of rotors in the hot, humid air below the lowering cloud masses.

'The Pegasus chopper! Sounds as though von Schiller is heading directly for Taita's pool. He must have known all along exactly where we were working,' said Nicholas bitterly. 'Not wasting any time. Like a vulture coming in to a fresh carcass.'

Royan was also looking up at the sound, trying to pick out the shape of the aircraft against the dark clouds. Her face was flushed from the run, the tendrils of sweat-damp hair dangled down her cheeks. 'If those swine are allowed to enter our tomb it will be a dreadful desecration of a sacred place,' she said angrily.

Suddenly Nicholas reached across the litter and took her arm. His expression was stern and determined. 'You are right. Go on down to the monastery with Tessay. I will follow you later.' Before she could protest or question him, he strode across to Sapper.

'I am putting the two women in your care, Sapper. Look after them.'

'Where are you going, Nicky?' Royan had come up behind him, and overheard his orders to Sapper. 'What are you going to do?'

'One little chore. Won't take me long.'

426

'You aren't going back there?' She was horrified. 'You will get yourself killed or worse. You saw what Helm did to Tessay—'

'Don't fuss yourself, my love,' he laughed, and before she realized what he intended he kissed her full on the lips. While she was still flustered and confused by this display in front of so many men, he pushed her gently away.

'Take care of Tessay. I will meet you at the boats.'

Before she could protest further, he turned and struck out up the valley at a long-legged lope which carried him over the rough terrain so swiftly that she had no further chance to prevent him.

'Nicky!' she screamed after him despairingly, but he pretended not to hear and kept going, following the diverted river upstream, back towards the dam.

The Jet Ranger followed the convoluted course of the river below the dam. At moments they could look directly down into the narrow gap between the high cliffs, into the shaded depths of the chasm, almost dry now, with only the occasional gleam of the shrunken and still pools.

'There they are!' Helm pointed dead ahead. There was a small cluster of men on the brink of the chasm.

'Make sure they aren't *shufta*!' There was fear in von Schiller's voice.

'No!' Helm reassured him loudly. 'I recognize Nogo, and that tall one beside him in the white *shamma* is the monk Hansith Sherif, our informer.' He shouted above the engine beat at the pilot, 'You can go in and land. There! Nogo is waving you in!'

The moment the skids of the helicopter touched the ground, both Nogo and Hansith ran forward. Between them they helped von Schiller down from the passenger cabin and hustled him clear of the spinning rotors.

'My men have secured the area,' Nogo assured him. 'We have driven the *shufta* down the valley towards the river. This man is Hansith Sherif, who has been working beside Harper in the tomb. He knows every inch of the tunnels.'

'Does he speak English?' Von Schiller looked up at the tall monk eagerly.

'A little bit,' Hansith answered for himself.

'Good! Good!' Von Schiller beamed at him. 'Show me the way. I will follow you. Come on, Guddabi, it's about time you did some work for the money I am paying you.'

Hansith led them quickly to the head of the scaffolding, where von

427

Schiller paused and looked down nervously into the gloomy depths of the chasm. The bamboo framework seemed flimsy and rickety, the drop deep and terrifying. Von Schiller was on the point of protesting when Nahoot Guddabi whimpered behind him.

'He does not expect us to climb down there, does he?'

His terror bolstered von Schiller immediately, and he turned on Nahoot with relish. 'It is the only access to the tomb. Follow the man down. I will be close behind you.'

When Nahoot still hesitated, Helm put a calloused hand in the small of his back and shoved him forward.

'Get on with it. You are wasting time.'

Reluctantly Nahoot started down the scaffolding after the monk, and von Schiller followed him. The framework of bamboo shook and swayed under their combined weight and the drop to the rocks below sucked at them, but at last they reached the ledge beside Taita's pool. There they stood in a small group, staring about them in awe and wonder.

'Where is the tunnel?' von Schiller demanded as soon as he had regained his breath, and Hansith beckoned to him to follow him to the wall of the small coffer dam.

Here von Schiller paused and looked around at Helm and Nogo. 'I want you to remain on guard here. I will enter the tomb with Guddabi and this monk. I will send for you when you are needed.'

'I would feel happier to be with you, to protect you, Herr von Schiller—' Helm began, but the old man frowned at him.

'Do as I tell you!' And with Hansith steadying him he climbed stiffly down the wall of the coffer dam into the mouth of the tunnel. Nahoot Guddabi followed him closely.

'The lights? Where does the power come from?' von Schiller wanted to know.

'There is a machine,' Hansith explained, and at that moment they heard the soft burble of the generator ahead of them. None of them spoke again as they moved down the entrance tunnel after Hansith, until they reached the bridge over the dark waters of the sink-hole.

'This is very rough construction,' Nahoot muttered, his uneasiness at last giving way to professional interest. 'It does not remind me of any other Egyptian tomb I have ever inspected. I think we may have been misled. It is probably some native Ethiopian workings.'

'You are making a premature judgement,' von Schiller admonished him. 'Wait until we have seen the rest of what this man has to show us.'

Von Schiller steadied himself with a hand on Hansith's shoulder as they crossed the bobbing pontoons of baobab wood, and he scrambled ashore on the far side with relief. They started up the rising section of the tunnel and passed the high-water mark.

428

As soon as the construction of the walls changed to packed and dressed stone, Nahoot remarked on it. 'Ah! I was disappointed at first. I thought we had been duped, but now one can see the Egyptian influence.'

They reached the landing outside the ruined gallery on which stood the Honda generator. By now both von Schiller and Nahoot were sweating with exertion and trembling with excitement.

'This looks more and more promising. It may very well be a royal tomb,' Nahoot exulted. Von Schiller pointed to the plaster seals stacked against the side wall where Nicholas and Royan had abandoned them. Nahoot fell to his knees beside them and examined them eagerly, his voice trembling as he cried out.

'The cartouche of Mamose, and the seal of the scribe Taita!' He looked up at von Schiller with shining eyes, 'There can be no doubts now. I have led you to the tomb as I promised you I would.'

For a moment von Schiller stared at him, speechless in the face of such bare-faced arrogance. Then he snorted with disgust and stooped to peer through the open doorway into the long gallery.

'This has been destroyed!' he cried in horror. 'The tomb has been annihilated.'

'No, no!' Hansith assured him. 'Come this way. There is another tunnel beyond.'

As they picked their way through the rubble and wreckage, Hansith told them in halting, broken English how the roof of the gallery had collapsed, and how he, Hansith, had found the true entrance under the ruins.

Nahoot stopped every few paces to examine and exclaim over the scraps of painted plaster that had survived the fall of the roof. 'These must have been magnificent. Classical work of the highest order—'

'There is more to show you. Much more,' Hansith promised them, and von Schiller snarled at Nahoot.

'Leave these damaged sections now. Time is running out on us. We must hurry on directly to the burial chamber.'

Hansith led them up the hidden staircase into the maze of the bao, and then through the twists and turns to the lowest level.

'How did Harper and the woman ever find their way through this?' von Schiller marvelled. 'It's a rabbit warren.'

'Another concealed staircase!' Nahoot was amazed, and stuttered with excitement as they descended into the gas trap where the ranks of amphorae had stood undisturbed for thousands of years, and then climbed the last flight of stairs to the beginning of the funeral arcade.

Now both of them were stunned by the splendour of the murals and the majesty of the great god images that guarded the length of the arcade. They stood side by side unable to move, frozen with awe as they gazed about them.

'I never expected anything like this,' von Schiller whispered. 'This exceeds anything that I ever hoped for.'

'The rooms on each side are filled with treasures.' Hansith pointed down the arcade. 'There are such things as you have never dreamed. Harper was able to take very little with him – a few small boxes. He has left piles of goods, stacks of chests.'

'Where is the coffin? Where is the body that was in the tomb?' von Schiller demanded.

'Harper has given the body, in its golden coffin, to the abbot. They have taken it away to the monastery.'

'Nogo will soon fetch it back for us. You need not worry about that, Herr von Schiller,' Nahoot assured him.

As though the spell that held them was shattered by this promise, they started forward together, slowly at first, and then both of them began to run. Von Schiller tottered into the nearest store room on his old, stiff legs, and giggled like a child on Christmas morning as he gazed upon the piled treasures. 'Incredible!'

He dragged down one of the cedarwood chests from the nearest stack, and ripped off the lid with trembling fingers. When he saw the contents he was struck speechless. He knelt over the chest and began to weep softly with emotion too overwhelming to express in words.

icholas was banking on the fact that Nogo's men would be driving along the cliff tops to reach Taita's pool, and that he would have a free run up the course of the diverted stream to the dam site. He took no precautions against running into them, other than to pause every few minutes to listen and peer ahead. He knew that he had little time left to him. He could not expect the rest of the party to wait for him at the boats and endanger themselves for this whimsy of his.

Twice he heard automatic gunfire in the distance, coming from the direction of the chasm, down towards the pool. However, the chance he took paid off, and he reached the dam site without running into any of Nogo's forces. He did not, however, push his luck too far. Before approaching the dam openly, he climbed the hillside above it and surveyed the area. It gave him time to recover from the hard run up the valley, and to check that Nogo had not left men to guard the dam, although he considered this unlikely.

He could see that the yellow front-loader tractor was still parked on the bank high above the wall where Sapper had left it. He could also see no sign of any human presence, no armed Ethiopian army guards. He grunted with relief and wiped the sweat out of his eyes with his shirtsleeve.

Even with his naked eye he could see that the water was lapping the top of the wall and squirting through the gaps and chinks between the gabions. Yet from where he stood the wall still seemed to be holding well, and it would need another foot rise in the level of the backed-up river to overturn it.

'Well done, Sapper,' he thought, grinning. 'You did a hell of a job.'

Nicholas studied the level of the river and the condition of the waters that were being held back by the wall. The flow down from the mountains was much stronger than when he had last been here. The river bed was brimming from bank to bank, and some of the trees and bushes at the edge were already partially submerged, bowing and nodding as the swift current tugged at them. The flood was a sullen grey colour, fast and hostile, swirling into the pond of the dam before finding the outlet into the side channel and tearing down it, growling like a wild animal released from its cage, brimming into spume and white water as it felt the sharp fall into the valley.

Next he looked towards the escarpment of the gorge. It was blotted out by banks of dark, menacing cloud that obscured the northern horizon. At that moment a squall of wind swept over him, cold with the threat of rain. He needed no further urging and started down the slope towards the dam, slipping and sliding in his haste. Before he reached the bottom, the squall of wind had turned to cold rain. It flung needles into his face and plastered his shirt to his body.

He reached the tractor and scrambled up into the driver's seat. There was a moment of panic when he thought that Sapper might have removed the key from its hiding-place under the seat. He scrabbled for it for a few seconds until his fingers closed over it, and then let out a sigh of relief.

'Sapper, for a moment there you were very close to death. I would have broken your neck with my own hands.'

He thrust the key into the ignition lock and turned it to the pre-heat position, waiting for the coil light on the dashboard to turn from red to green.

'Come on!' he muttered impatiently. Those few seconds of delay seemed like a lifetime. Then the green light flashed and he twisted the key to start.

The engine fired at the first turn and Nicholas hooted, 'Full marks, Sapper. All is forgiven.'

He gave the machine time to warm up to optimum operating temperature, slitting his eyes against the rain as he waited and looking around at the hills above him, fearful that the sound of the engine might

431

bring Nogo's gorillas swarming down on him. However, there was no sign of life on the rainswept heights.

He eased the tractor into her lowest gear and turned her down the bank. Below the dam wall the water that was finding its way through the gaps was less than hub-deep. The tractor bounced and ground its way through the boulder-strewn watercourse. Nicholas stopped the machine in the middle of the river bed while he studied the downstream face of the dam wall for its weakest section. Then he lined up below the centre of the wall, at the point where Sapper had shored up the raft of logs with rows of gabions.

'Sorry for all your hard work,' he apologized to Sapper, as he manoeuvred the steel scoop of the tractor to the right height and angle before attacking the wall. He worried the gabion he had selected out of its niche in the row, reversing and thrusting at it until he could get the scoop under it and drag it free. He pulled away and dropped the heavy wire mesh basket over the waterfall, then drove back and renewed the attack.

It was slow work. The pressure of the water had wedged in the gabions, keying them into the wall so it took almost ten minutes to free the second basket. As he dropped that one over the waterfall, he glanced for the first time at the fuel gauge on the dashboard of the tractor and his heart sank. It was registering empty. Sapper must have neglected to refuel it: either he had exhausted the fuel supply or he had not expected ever to use the machine again when he abandoned it.

Even as Nicholas thought about it the engine stuttered as it starved. He reversed it sharply, changing the angle of inclination so that the remaining fuel in the tank could slosh forward. The engine caught and cleared, running smoothly and strongly once again. Quickly he changed gear and ran back at the wall.

'No more time for finesse,' he told himself grimly. 'From here on in it's brute force and muscle.'

By removing two of the gabions he had exposed a corner of the log raft behind them. This was the vulnerable part of the wall. He worked the hydraulic controls and lifted the scoop to its highest travel. Then he lowered it carefully, an inch at a time, until it hooked over the end of the thickest log in the jam. He locked the hydraulics and thrust the tractor into reverse, gradually pouring on full power until the engine was roaring and blowing out a cloud of thick blue diesel smoke.

Nothing gave. The log was jammed solidly and the wall was held together by the keying of the gabions into each other and the enormous pressure of water behind them. Despairingly, Nicholas kept the throttle wide open. The lugged tyres spun and skidded on the boulders under them, throwing a tall shower of spray high into the air and churning out loose rock and gravel.

'Come on!' Nicholas pleaded with the machine. 'Come on! You can do it.'

The engine beat faltered again as she starved for fuel. She spluttered and coughed, and almost stalled.

'Please!' Nicholas begged her aloud. 'One more try.'

Almost as if it had heard him, the engine fired again, ran unevenly for a few moments, and then abruptly bellowed at full power again.

'That's it, my beauty,' Nicholas yelled, as it lurched and hammered against the wall.

With a sound like a cannon shot the log snapped and the top end of it flew out of the wall, leaving a long, deep hole through which the river poured triumphantly, a thick, solid column of dirty grey water.

'Thar she blows!' Nicholas shouted, jumping down from the driver's seat. He knew there was not enough time left for him to drive the tractor out of the river bed. He could move more quickly on his own feet.

The current seized his legs, trying to pull them out from under him. It was like one of those childhood nightmares when monsters were pursuing him and, despite his every effort, his legs would only move in slow motion. He glanced back over his shoulder, and at that instant he saw the central section of the dam wall burst, blowing outward in a violent eruption of furious waters. He struggled on another few paces towards the bank before the deep and turbulent tide picked him up. He was helpless in its grip. It swept him away, over the waterfall and down, down into the hungry maw of the chasm.

'These are the royal crook and sceptre of the Pharaoh,' cried von Schiller in a voice that was gusty and faint with emotion as he lifted them out of the cedarwood chest.

'And this is his false beard and his ceremonial pectoral emblem.' Nahoot knelt beside him on the floor of the tomb under the great statue of Osiris. All the ill feelings between them were forgotten in the wonder of the moment as they examined the fabulous treasures of Egypt.

'This is the greatest archaeological discovery of all time,' von Schiller whispered, his voice tremulous. He pulled his handkerchief from his pocket and dabbed at the perspiration of excitement that trickled down his cheeks.

'There is years of work here,' Nahoot told him seriously. 'This incredible collection will have to be catalogued and evaluated. It will be known for ever as the von Schiller hoard. Your name will be perpetuated for all time. It is like the Egyptian dream of immortality. You will never be forgotten. You will live for ever.'

A rapturous expression crossed von Schiller's features. He had not considered that possibility. Up until this moment he had not considered sharing this treasure with anybody, except in his particular way with Utte Kemper, but Nahoot's words had awakened in him the old impossible dream of eternity. Perhaps he might make arrangements for it to be made accessible to the public – but only after his own death, naturally.

Then he thrust the temptation aside. He would not debase this treasure by making it available to the common rabble. It had been assembled for the funeral of a pharaoh. Von Schiller saw himself as the modern equivalent of a pharaoh.

'No!' he told Nahoot violently. 'This is mine, all mine. When I die it will go with me, all of it. I have made the arrangements already, in my will. My sons know what to do. This will all be with me in my own grave. My royal grave.'

Nahoot stared at him aghast. He had not realized until that moment that the old man was mad, that his obsessions had driven him over the edge of sanity. But the Egyptian knew that there was no point in arguing with him now – later he would find a way to save this marvellous treasure from the oblivion of another tomb. So he bowed his head in mock acquiescence.

'You are right, Herr von Schiller. That is the only fitting manner to dispose of it. You deserve that form of burial. However, our main concern now must be to get all of it to safety. Helm has warned us about the danger of the river, of the dam bursting. We must call him and Nogo. Nogo's men must clear out the tomb. We can ferry the treasure in the helicopter up to the Pegasus camp, where I can pack it securely for the journey to Germany.'

'Yes. Yes.' Von Schiller scrambled to his feet, suddenly terrified at the prospect of being deprived of this wondrous hoard by the flooded river. 'Send the monk, what is his name, Hansith, send him to call Helm. He must come at once.'

Nahoot jumped up to his feet. 'Hansith!' he shouted. 'Where are you?'

The monk had been waiting at the entrance to the burial chamber, kneeling in prayer before the empty sarcophagus which had contained the body of the saint. He was torn now between religious conviction and greed. When he heard his name called he genuflected deeply, and then rose and hurried back to join von Schiller and Nahoot.

'You must go back to the pool where we left the others—' Nahoot started to relay the orders, but suddenly a strange, distracted expression crossed Hansith's darkly handsome features and he held up his hand for silence.

'What is it?' Nahoot demanded angrily. 'What is it that you can hear?'

Hansith shook his head. 'Be quiet! Listen! Can't you hear it?'

'There is nothing—' Nahoot began, but then broke off suddenly, and wild terror filled his dark eyes.

There was the softest sound, gentle as the sigh of a summer zephyr, lulling and low.

'What do you hear?' von Schiller demanded. His hearing had long ago deteriorated, and the sound was far beyond the range of his old ears.

'Water!' whispered Nahoot. 'Running water!'

'The river!' shouted Hansith. 'The tunnel is flooding!' He whirled round and went bounding down the funeral arcade with long, lithe strides.

'We will be trapped in here!' screamed Nahoot, and raced after him.

'Wait for me,' von Schiller yelled, and tried to follow. But he soon fell behind the two much younger men.

The monk, however, was far ahead of both of them as he took the flight of stairs up from the gas trap two at a time.

'Hansith! Come back! I order you,' Nahoot cried despairingly in his wake, but he caught only a flash of the monk's white robe as he darted into the first twist of the labyrinth.

'Guddabi, where are you?' von Schiller's voice quavered and echoed through the stone corridors. But Nahoot did not reply as he ran on in the direction which he thought the monk had taken, passing the first turn in the maze without even glancing at the chalk marks on the wall. He thought he heard Hansith's racing footsteps ahead of him, but by the time he had turned the third corner he knew he was lost.

He stopped with his heart racing savagely and the bitter gall of terror in the back of his throat.

'Hansith! Where are you?' he screamed wildly.

Von Schiller's voice came back to him, ringing weirdly down the passageways, 'Guddabi! Guddabi! Don't leave me here.'

'Shut up!' he screamed. 'Keep quiet, you old fool!'

Panting heavily, the blood pounding in his ears, he tried to listen for the sound of Hansith's feet. But he heard only the sound of the river. The gentle susurration seemed to emanate from the very walls around him.

'No! Don't leave me here,' he screamed, and began to run without direction, panic-stricken, through the maze.

ansith took each twist and turn unerringly, with the terror of dreadful death driving his feet. But at the head of the central staircase his ankle twisted under him and he fell heavily. He tumbled down the steeply inclined shaft, bumping and rolling the full length, gathering speed as he went until he reached the bottom and lay sprawled on the agate tiles of the long gallery.

He dragged himself to his feet, bruised and shaken by the fall, and tried to run on. But his leg gave way under him again, and he fell in a tangle. His ankle was badly sprained and would not carry his weight. Nevertheless he dragged himself up a second time and hobbled down the gallery, supporting himself with one hand on the shattered wall.

When he reached the doorway and crawled through it on to the landing beside the generator the sound of the water came up the tunnel. It was much louder now – a low, reverberating growl which almost blotted out the soft, discreet hum of the generator.

'Sweet loving Christ and the Virgin, save me!' he pleaded as he staggered and lurched down the tunnel, falling twice more before he reached the lower level.

On his knees he peered ahead, and in the glare of the electric lights strung along the roof of the tunnel he could make out the sink-hole below him. He did not at first recognize it, for it had all changed. The water level was no longer lower than the paved floor on which he sprawled. It was brimming, a great swirling maelstrom, and the water pouring into it was being sucked away through the hidden outlet almost as fast as it entered from the tunnel mouth on the far side. The pontoon bridge was tangled and half-submerged, bobbing and canting and rearing as it fought its retaining cables like an unbroken horse on a tether.

From Taita's pool a roaring river of water was boring down the far branch of the tunnel across the sink-hole. The tunnel was flooding rapidly, the water already reaching halfway up the walls, but he knew that it was the only escape route from the tomb. Every moment he delayed, the flood became stronger.

'I have to get out through there.' He pushed himself to his feet again.

He reached the first pontoon of the bridge, but it was careering about so madly that he dared not attempt to remain upright upon it. He dropped to his hands and knees, crawled out on to the flimsy structure and managed to drag himself forward from one pontoon to the next.

'Please God and St Michael help me. Don't let me die like this,' he prayed aloud. He reached the far side of the sink-hole and groped for a handhold on the roughly hewn walls of the tunnel.

He found a hold with his fingertips and pulled himself into the mouth of the tunnel, but now the full force of the water pouring down the shaft struck his lower body. He hung there for a moment, pinned by the raging waters, unable to move a pace forward. He knew that if his grip failed he would be swept back into the sink-hole and sucked down into those terrible black depths.

The electric bulbs strung along the roof of the tunnel ahead of him still burned brightly, so that he could see almost to the open basin of Taita's pool where the bamboo scaffolding would offer escape to the top of the chasm. It was only two hundred feet ahead of him. He gathered all his strength and pulled himself forward against the raging waters, reaching forward from one precarious handhold to the next. His fingernails tore and the flesh smeared from the tips of his fingers on the jagged rock, but he forced his way onwards.

At last he could see daylight ahead of him, filtering from Taita's pool. Only another forty feet to go, and he realized with a surge of relief and joy that he was going to make it out of the deadly trap of the shaft. Then he heard a fresh sound, a harsher, more brutal roar as the full flood of the burst dam poured down the waterfall into Taita's pool. It found the entrance to the tunnel and came down it in a solid wave, filling the passageway to the roof, ripping out the wiring of the lights and plunging Hansith into darkness.

It struck him with such force that it seemed to be not mere water but the solid rock of an avalanche, and he could not resist it. It tore him from his insecure perch and plucked him away, tossing him backwards, spinning him down the length of the shaft that he had gained with so much effort, and hurling him into the sink-hole beyond. He was swirled end over end by the crazed waters. In the darkness and wild confusion he did not know which direction was up and which down, but it made no difference for he could not swim against its power.

Then the sink-hole seized him full in its grip and sucked him swiftly and deeply down. The pressure of the water began to crush him. One of his eardrums burst, and as he opened his mouth to scream at the agony of it the water spurted down his throat and flooded his lungs. The last thing he ever felt was when he was flung against the side wall of the sink-hole, travelling as fast as the falling waters, and the bones of his right shoulder shattered. He could not scream again through his sodden lungs, but soon the pain faded into oblivion.

As his corpse was drawn swiftly through the subterranean shaft it became mangled and dismembered on the jagged rock sides, and was no longer recognizable as human by the time it was discharged through the butterfly fountain on the far side of the mountain. From there the torn fragments were washed down the diverted Dandera river to join, at last, the wider and more stately waters of the Blue Nile.

he waters pouring through the gap in the dam wall picked up the yellow front-loader and tumbled it over the waterfall into the chasm as though it were a child's toy. Nicholas had a glimpse of it in the air below him. Even as he fell himself, he realized that if he had stayed with the machine he would have been crushed beneath it. The huge machine struck the surface of the pool in a fountain of white spray and disappeared.

Nicholas followed it down, falling free, even managing to keep his head uppermost, feet foremost, as he swooped down the waterfall. The flood that carried him cushioned his fall, so that instead of being dashed against the exposed boulders at the bottom, he bounced and tumbled in the racing torrent. He came to the surface fifty yards downstream, tossed his wet hair out of his eyes and glanced around him quickly.

The tractor was gone, swallowed deep into the pool at the foot of the waterfall, but ahead of him was a small island of rock in the middle of the river. With a dozen overarm strokes he swam to it and clung to a rocky spur. From there he looked up at the sheer walls of the chasm and remembered the last time he had been trapped down here. The elation he had felt at the destruction of the dam and the flooding of Pharaoh's tomb evaporated.

He knew that he would not be able to climb those slick, water-smoothed cliffs that offered no handholds and which belled outwards in an overhang over his head. Instead he weighed the chances of working his way back upstream to the foot of the falls. From here it looked as though there was some sort of funnel or crevice up the east side of the chute which might offer a ladderway to the top, but it would be a hard and dangerous climb.

The volume of water coming over the falls was not as heavy as he had expected, considering the vast body of water that was being held back by the dam. He realized then that the greater part of the wall of gabions must still be in place and that this torrent was only the result of water escaping through the narrow gap he had torn in the centre of the wall. The remaining gabions must still be holding in place under their own weight. However, he realized that they could not hold much longer and that the river must soon plough them aside and burst through in full force. So he abandoned the idea of swimming back to the foot of the falls.

'Have to get out of its way,' he thought desperately, as he imagined being caught up in the terrible flood which would certainly come down at any moment. 'If I can reach the side somewhere, perhaps find a ledge, climb above the flood.' But he knew it was a forlorn hope. He had swum the length of the canyon once before without finding a handhold on the slick walls.

'Swim ahead of it?' he thought. 'A slim chance, but the only one I have.' He kicked off his boots, and gathered himself. He was about to push off from his temporary refuge, when he heard the rest of the dam wall high above him give way.

There was a rumbling roar, the crackle of logs snapping and breaking, the grating and grinding of heavy gabions being thrown around like empty rubbish cans, and then suddenly and terrifyingly a solid wave of grey water burst over the top of the falls, carrying with it a wall of trash and debris.

'Oh mother! Too late. Here comes the big one!'

He shoved off from his rock, turning downstream, and swam with all his strength, kicking and flailing his arms in a wild crawl stroke. He heard the roar of the approaching wave and glanced back over his shoulder. It was overhauling him swiftly, filling the chasm from wall to wall, fifteen feet high and curling at the top. He had a fleeting mental image from his youth, waiting to surf that notorious wave at Cape St Vincent, hanging on the line-up and seeing it humping up behind him, this great wall of water, so mountainous and so overwhelming.

'Ride it!' he told himself, judging the moment. 'Catch it like a slider.'

He clawed through the water, trying to get up speed to ride up the wall. He felt it seize him and lift him so violently that his guts swooped, and then he was on the crest of it. He arched his back and tucked his arms behind him in the classic body-surfer's position, hanging in the face of the wave, slightly head down, the front half of his body thrust clear of the water, steering with his legs. After the first few terrifying seconds he realized that he was riding her high and had some control; his panic abated and he was overcome by a sense of wild exhilaration.

'Twenty knots!' He estimated his speed by the giddy blur of the canyon walls passing him on either side. He steered away from the nearest wall, sliding across the face, taking up station in the centre of the wave. He was carried along by the wave and by the thrilling sensation of speed and danger.

The increased depth of water in the chasm covered the dangerous, knife-sharp rocks, enabling him to ride clear of them. It smoothed out the waterfalls and the chutes, so that instead of dropping down them and plummeting below the surface of the pool beneath he slid down them with a smooth rush, holding his position in the face of the wave with a few quick overarm strokes or a kick of the legs.

'Hell! This is fun!' He laughed aloud. 'People would pay money to do this. Beats the hell out of bungee jumping.'

Within the first mile the wave began to lose its shape and impetus as it spread out down the canyon. Soon it would no longer have the power to hold him up in the surfing position, and he glanced around him swiftly. Floating near by, keeping pace with him in the flotsam of debris from the dam, was one of the treetrunks that had formed part of the raft with which Sapper had plugged the gap in the wall.

He steered across to this ponderous piece of timber. It was thirty feet long and floated low in the flood, its back showing like that of a whale. Its branches had been roughly hacked away by the axemen, and the spikes that remained provided secure handholds. Nicholas pulled himself up on to the treetrunk, lying on his belly, facing downstream, with his legs still dangling in the water. Swiftly he recovered his breath and felt his full strength returning.

Although it had smoothed out and lost its wave formation, the flood was still tearing down the chasm at a tremendous pace. 'Still not much under ten knots,' he estimated. 'When this lot hits Taita's pool, I pity von Schiller and any of his uglies who are in the tomb. They are going to stay in there for the next four thousand years.' He threw back his head and laughed triumphantly. 'It worked! Damn me to hell, if it didn't work just the way I planned it.'

He stopped laughing abruptly as he felt the treetrunk veer across the river towards one of the canyon walls.

'Oh, oh! More trouble.'

He rolled to one side of the treetrunk and kicked out strongly. His ungainly vessel responded, swinging heavily across the current. It was sluggish steering, not enough to avoid contact with the rock wall entirely, but instead of striking full-on it was merely a glancing collision that pushed him back again into the main flow of the current.

He was gaining confidence and expertise every moment, 'I can ride her all the way down to the monastery!' he exclaimed delightedly. 'At this rate of knots I might even get to the boats before Sapper and Royan.'

Looking ahead, he recognized this stretch of the chasm that he was hurtling through.

'This is the bend above Taita's pool. Be there in another minute or two. I expect the scaffolding has been washed away by now.'

He pulled himself as high on the log as he could without upsetting its balance, and peered ahead, blinking the water out of his eyes. He saw the head of the falls above Taita's pool racing towards him, and he braced himself for the drop.

The long, smooth chute of racing water opened ahead of him, and the moment before he flew down it he had a glimpse into the basin of rock below it. He saw at once that his expectations had been premature. The bamboo scaffolding had not been entirely washed away, although it was badly damaged. The lowest section was gone, but the upper part hung drunkenly down the rock cliff, just touching the surface of the racing waters. It was swaying and swinging loosely as the current snatched at it, and incredulously he realized that there were at least two

440

men trapped on the flimsy structure, clinging desperately to the ladder-way of lurching, clattering poles. Both of them were trying to claw their way up it to the top of the cliff.

In that fraction of a second Nicholas saw a flash of steel-rimmed spectacles under a maroon beret, and realized that the man nearest the top of the cliff was Tuma Nogo. Then Nogo succeeded in reaching the top of the scaffolding and disappeared over the top of the cliff. That one glance was all Nicholas had time for before his log was plunged into the water-chute, gathering speed until it was tearing downwards at a steeply canted angle. The point dug in as it hit the surface of the pool at the bottom, and the log almost pole-vaulted end over end, but Nicholas clung on to his handholds, and gradually it righted itself.

For a few moments the log was stalled in the vortex below the falls, but almost at once the current grabbed it again and it gathered speed, bearing away down the length of Taita's pool as ponderously as a wooden man-o'-war.

Nicholas had a second of respite in which to look around the basin of Taita's pool. He saw at once that the entrance tunnel to the tomb was entirely submerged and, judging by the water level up the cliff wall, it was already fifty feet or more beneath the surface. He felt a leap of triumph. The tomb was once more protected from the depredations of any other grave-robber.

Then he looked up the battered remnants of the bamboo scaffolding skewed down the cliff, torn half away from the ancient niches in the rock, and he saw the other man still clinging to the wreckage. He was twenty feet above the water level, and seemed frozen there like a cat in the high branches of a windswept tree.

At that moment Nicholas realized that his log was swinging in the grip of the river, curling in towards the dangling scaffold. He was about to try to steer it clear, when the man on the framework high above him turned his head and looked down at him. Nicholas saw that he was a white man, his face a pale blob in the gloom of the canyon, and a moment later he recognized him with a stab of hatred through the chest.

'Helm!' he exclaimed. 'Jake Helm.'

He had an image of Tamre, the epileptic boy, crushed beneath the rockfall, and of Tessay's burned and battered face. His outrage and hatred surged. Instead of steering the log away from the scaffold, he reversed his thrust and swung in towards the cliff. There was a breathless interval when Nicholas thought he might miss, but at the last moment the leading end of the log swung sharply and the point of it crashed into the trailing end of the bamboo, hooking on to it.

The log's weight and momentum were irresistible. The bamboo poles crackled and snapped like dry kindling, and then the whole rickety structure tore loose from the wall and came crashing down over the log. Helm swung out overhead, then released his grip and dropped feet first into the water close alongside the log. He went deep below the surface. While he was under, Nicholas pulled himself up to sit astride the log and grabbed a length of bamboo pole that had broken off the scaffolding and was floating alongside his perch.

The log was trapped in a back eddy of the swollen river, and now it began to spin slowly in the slack water outside the main current. Nicholas was still riding high on the log. He hefted the bamboo, swinging it back and forth like a baseball bat, to get the feel of it. Then he cocked it over his shoulder and waited for Helm to show himself.

A second later the Texan's head broke out, streaming water. His eyes were screwed closed, and he let out a gasp of water and air and tried to suck in a breath. Nicholas aimed the pole at his head and swung with all his strength, but just at that moment Helm opened his eyes and saw the blow coming.

He was as quick as a water snake, rolling his head under the swinging club so that it merely touched the side of his cropped blond head and then glanced away. Nicholas was thrown off balance by his own swing, and before he could recover Helm had drawn a quick breath and ducked below the surface again.

Nicholas poised the club, ready to strike a second time, peering down into the murky water, muttering angrily at himself for having missed the first blow while he still had the advantage of surprise. He had no illusions about what he was in for, now that Helm had been warned.

The seconds drew out with no sign of his adversary reappearing, and Nicholas looked behind him anxiously, trying to anticipate where he would come up again. For a long minute nothing happened. He lowered the club nervously, and changed his grip so as to be ready to stab in any direction with the sharp broken tip.

Suddenly his left ankle was seized in a crushing grip below the water and, before he could grab a handhold to resist, Nicholas was jerked from his seat on the log and went over backwards into the river. As he plunged beneath the water he felt Helm's fingers clawing at his face. He grabbed one of the fingers and wrenched it back, feeling it snap in his grasp as he forced it back towards its own wrist. But Helm was galvanized by the agony of the dislocated joint, and one of his long muscular arms whipped around Nicholas's neck like the tentacles of an octopus.

The two of them came to the surface for a moment, both of them drew one quick, harsh breath, then Helm forced Nicholas's head backwards and water flooded into his open mouth. The lock on his neck tightened, and he felt the tension on his vertebrae. It was a killer grip. If Helm had only had a solid purchase he could have exerted the last ounce of pressure which would have snapped his spine. But Nicholas kept rolling back in the direction of the thrust, giving with it, and preventing Helm from bringing all his strength to bear. As he went over he saw Helm's face in front of his, magnified and distorted through the tainted grey water. He looked monstrous and evil.

As Helm rolled over the top of him Nicholas locked both hands around his waist to hold him firmly, then brought up his right knee between Helm's legs, hard into his crotch, and felt the bone of his kneecap make contact. The bunch of genitals was full and rubbery; Helm contorted and his lock on Nicholas's neck eased. Nicholas used the slack to reach down and grab a handful of Helm's damaged testicles and twist them savagely. He saw the man's face inches in front of his own twist into a rictus of pain and Helm pulled away from him, releasing his lock on Nicholas's throat and reaching down to grab his wrist with both hands.

Again they came to the surface close alongside the floating log, and Nicholas realized that the current had taken hold of them again and was carrying them away through the outlet of Taita's pool into the full stream of the river. Nicholas released his grip on Helm's balls and with his other hand aimed a punch at his face, but they were too close to each other and the blow lacked power. It glanced off Helm's cheek, and Nicholas tried to lock his extended arm around his neck, going for a headlock himself. Helm hunched his head down on his shoulders, slipping under the hold. Then suddenly he reached forward fast as a striking adder and sank his teeth into Nicholas's chin.

The surprise was complete, and the pain was excruciating as his teeth locked into the flesh. Nicholas shouted and clawed at Helm's face, going for his eyes, trying to drive his fingernails through the lids. But Helm squeezed his eyes tight closed and his teeth cut in ever deeper, so that Nicholas's blood welled up and oozed from the corners of Helm's mouth.

The log was still floating beside them, inches from the back of Helm's head. Nicholas seized his ears, one in each hand, and twisted him around in the water. He could see over the top of Helm's head, while Helm's vision was blocked. There was a nub of raw wood sticking out of the tree trunk where an axe had hacked away a side branch. The cut was at an angle, leaving a sharp spike. Through tears of agony Nicholas lined up the spike with the back of Helm's head. He could feel Helm's teeth almost meeting in the flesh of his face. They had cut through the lower lip so that blood was starting to fill Nicholas's mouth. Helm was worrying him like a pit-bull in the arena, wrenching his head from side to side. Soon he would come away with a bloody mouthful of Nicholas's flesh.

With all the strength of pain and desperation, Nicholas hurled himself forward, and, using his upper body and his grip on the sides of

443

Helm's head, drove him on to the sharp wooden spike. The point found the joint between the vertebrae of the spine and the base of Helm's skull, going in like a nail and partially severing the spinal cord. Helm's jaws sprang open as he went into spasm. Nicholas pulled away from him with a flap of loose flesh hanging from his chin, and blood streaming and spurting from the deep ragged wound.

Helm was impaled upon the spike, like a carcass on a butcher's hook. His limbs twitched and the muscles of his face convulsed, his eyelids shivered and jumped like those of an epileptic, and his eyeballs rolled back into his skull so that only the whites showed, flashing grotesquely in the gloom of the chasm.

Nicholas pulled himself up on to the log beside the Texan's body, and hung there panting and bleeding in gouts down his chin on to his chest. Slowly the log revolved under the eccentric weight distribution, and Helm began to slide off the spike. His skin tore with a sound like silk parting, and the vertebrae of his spine grated on wood. Then the corpse, at last quiescent, flopped face down into the water and began to sink.

Nicholas would not let him go so easily. 'Let's make sure of you, dear boy,' he grated through his swollen, bleeding mouth. He spat out a mouthful of blood and saliva as he stretched out and grabbed the back of Helm's collar, holding him face down in the water under the log. They picked up speed rapidly down the last stretch of the canyon, but Nicholas held on doggedly, drowning any last spark of life from Helm's carcass, until at last it was torn from his grip by the current and he watched it sink away into the grey, roiling waters.

'I'll give your love to Tessay,' Nicholas called after him as he disappeared. Then he gave all his concentration to balancing the log and staying aboard for the ride through the tumbling, racing current. At last he was spewed out through the pink rock portals into the bottom reach of the Dandera river. As he was swept beneath the rope suspension bridge he slid off the log and struck out for the western bank, very much aware of the terrible drop into the Nile that lay half a mile downstream.

Sitting on the bank, he tore a strip from the tail of his shirt. Then he bound up his wounded chin as best he could, strapping it around the back of his head. The blood soaked through the thin wet cotton, but he knotted it tighter and it began to staunch the flow.

He stood up unsteadily and pushed his way through the strip of thick riverine bush which bounded the river, until at last he struck the trail that led down to the monastery and hobbled down it on his bare feet. He only stopped once, and that was when he heard the sound of the helicopter taking off from the top of the cliff above the chasm far behind him.

He looked back. 'Sounds as though Tuma Nogo made it out of

444

there, more's the pity. I wonder what happened to von Schiller and the Egyptian,' he muttered grimly, fingering his injured face. 'At least none of them are going to get into the tomb, not unless they dam the river again.' Suddenly a thought occurred to him.

'My God, what if von Schiller was already in there when the river hit?' He began to chuckle, and then shook his head. 'Too much to hope for. Justice is never that neat.' He shook his head again, but the movement started his wound aching brutally. He clutched his bandaged jaw with one hand and started down the trail again, breaking into a trot as he reached the paved causeway that led down to the monastery.

Nahoot Guddabi ran full into von Schiller around a corner of the maze, and in a peculiar way the old man's presence, even though he was of no conceivable value in this crisis, steadied him and kept at bay the panic that threatened at any moment to boil over and overwhelm him. Without Hansith the maze was a weird and lonely place. Any human company was a blessing. For a moment the two of them clung together like children lost in the forest.

Von Schiller still carried part of the treasure that they had been examining when Hansith had panicked and run. He had Pharaoh's golden crook in one hand and the ceremonial flail in the other.

'Where is the monk?' he screamed at Guddabi. 'Why did you run off and leave me? We have to find the way out of these tunnels, you idiot. Don't you realize the danger?'

'How do you expect me to know the way—' Nahoot began furiously, and then broke off as he noticed the chalk notations on the wall behind von Schiller's shoulder, and for the first time realized their significance.

'That's it!' he exclaimed with relief. 'Harper or the Al Simma woman have marked it out for us. Come on!' He started down the tunnel, following the signposting. However, by the time they came out on the central staircase almost an hour had passed since Hansith had left them. As they hurried down the staircase into the long gallery the sound of the river rose to a pervading hiss, like the breathing of a sleeping dragon.

Nahoot broke into a run and von Schiller staggered along behind him, his aged legs weakening with fear.

'Wait!' he shouted after Nahoot, who ignored his plea and ducked out through the opening in the plaster-sealed doorway. On the landing the generator was still running smoothly, and Nahoot did not even glance at it as he hurried down the inclined shaft in the bright dazzle of the light bulbs along the roof.

He turned the corner still at a run, and stopped dead as he realized that the tunnel below him was flooded, right back up to the level of the ancient high-water mark on the masonry blocks of the walls. There was no sign of the sink-hole or the pontoon bridge. They were submerged under fifty feet or more of water.

The Dandera river, guardian of the tomb down all the ages, had resumed its duty. Dark and implacable, it sealed the entrance to the tomb as it had done these four thousand years past.

'Allah!' whispered Nahoot. 'Allah have mercy on us.'

Von Schiller came around the corner of the tunnel and stopped beside Nahoot. The two of them stared in horror at the flooded shaft. Then slowly von Schiller sagged against the side wall.

'We are trapped,' he whispered, and at those words Nahoot whimpered softly and sank to his knees. He began to pray in a high, nasal sing-song. The sound infuriated von Schiller.

'That will not help us. Stop it!' He swung the golden flail in his right hand across Nahoot's bowed back. Nahoot cried out at the pain and crawled away from von Schiller.

'We must find a way out of here.' Von Schiller's voice steadied. He was accustomed to command, and now he took charge.

'There must be another way out of here,' he decided. 'We will search. If there is an opening to the outside then we should feel a draught of air.' His voice became firmer and more confident. 'Yes! That's what we will do. Switch off that fan, and we will try to detect any movement of air.'

Nahoot responded eagerly to his tone and authority, and hurried back to switch off the electric fan.

'You have your cigarette lighter,' von Schiller told him. 'We will light tapers from these.' He pointed at the papers and photographs that Royan had left lying on the trestle table by the doorway. 'We will use the smoke to detect any draught.'

For the next two hours they moved through all levels of the tomb, holding aloft the burning tapers, watching the movement of the smoke. At no point could they detect even the faintest movement of air in the tunnels, and in the end they came back to the flooded shaft and stared despairingly at the pool of still black water that blocked it.

'That is the only way out,' von Schiller whispered.

'I wonder if the monk escaped that way,' said Nahoot as he slumped down the wall.

'There is no other way.'

They were silent for a while; it was difficult to judge the passage of time in the tomb. Now that the river had found its own level there was no movement of water in the shaft, and the faint and distant sound of the current running through the sink-hole seemed merely to enhance the silence. In it they could hear their own breathing.

Nahoot spoke at last. 'The fuel in the generator. It must be running low. I did not see any reserves—'

They thought about what would happen when the small fuel tank ran dry. They thought about the darkness to come.

Suddenly von Schiller screamed, 'You have to go out through the shaft to fetch help. I order you to do it.'

Nahoot stared at him in disbelief. 'It's over a hundred yards back through the tunnel to the outside, and the river is in flood.'

Von Schiller sprang to his feet and stood over Nahoot threateningly. 'The monk escaped that way. It's the only way. You must swim through the tunnel and reach Helm and Nogo. Helm will know what to do. He will make a plan to get me out of here.'

'You are mad.' Nahoot backed away from him, but von Schiller followed him.

'I order you to do it!'

'You crazy old man!' Nahoot tried to scramble to his feet, but von Schiller swung the heavy golden flail, a sudden unexpected blow in Nahoot's face that knocked him over backwards, splitting his lips and breaking off two of his front teeth.

'You are mad!' he wailed. 'You can't do this—' but von Schiller swung again and again, lacerating his face and shoulders, the heavy golden tails of the whip cutting through the thin cotton of his shirt.

'I will kill you,' von Schiller screamed, raining blows on him. 'If you don't obey me I will kill you.'

'Stop!' Nahoot whined. 'No, please, stop. I will do it, only stop.'

He crawled away from von Schiller, dragging himself along the floor of the tunnel until he sat waist-deep in the water.

'Give me time to prepare,' he pleaded.

'Go now!' Von Schiller menaced him, lifting the whip high. 'Very likely you will find air trapped in the tunnel. You will find your way through. Go!'

Nahoot scooped a double handful of water and dashed it into his own face, washing away the blood that poured from one of the deep cuts in his cheek.

'I have to take off my clothes, my shoes,' he whimpered, pleading for time, but von Schiller would not allow him to leave the water.

'Do it where you are standing,' he ordered, brandishing the heavy whip. In his other hand he held the heavy golden crook. Nahoot realized that a blow from that weapon could crack his skull.

Standing knee-deep at the water's edge, Nahoot hopped on one foot as he pulled off his shoes. Then, slowly and reluctantly, he stripped to his underpants. His shoulders were deeply scored by the lash of the flail, fresh blood welling up and slithering like scarlet serpents down his back.

He knew that he had to placate this crazy old madman. He would duck under the surface and swim a short way down the tunnel, hold on to the side wall down there for as long as his breath lasted, and then swim back again.

'Go!' von Schiller shouted at him. 'You are wasting time. Don't think that I will let you get out of this.'

Nahoot waded deeper into the shaft until the water covered his chest. He paused there for a few minutes as he drew a series of deep breaths. Then at last he held his breath and ducked below the surface. Von Schiller stood waiting at the edge of the pool, staring down into it but unable to see anything beneath the black and ominous surface. In the lamplight Nahoot's blood stained the surface.

A minute passed slowly, and then suddenly there was a heavy swirl beneath the waters, and a human arm rose through the dark surface, hand and fingers extended as though in supplication. Then slowly it sank out of sight again.

Von Schiller craned forward, 'Guddabi!' he called angrily. 'What are you playing at?'

There was another swirl below the water, and something flashed like a mirror in the depths.

'Guddabi!' von Schiller's voice rose petulantly.

Almost as if in response to the summons, Nahoot's head broke out through the surface. His skin was waxen yellow, drained of all blood, and his mouth gaped open in a dreadful, silent scream. The water around him boiled as though a shoal of great fish were feeding below. As von Schiller stared in incomprehension, a dark tide rose up around Nahoot's head and stained the surface a rose-petal red. For a moment von Schiller did not realize that it was Nahoot's blood.

Then he saw the long, sinuous shapes darting and twisting beneath the surface, surrounding Nahoot, feeding upon his flesh. Nahoot lifted his hand again and extended it towards von Schiller, pleadingly. The arm was half-devoured, mutilated by deep half-moon wounds where the flesh had been bitten away in chunks.

Von Schiller screamed in horror, backing away from the pool. Nahoot's eyes were huge and dark and accusing. He stared at von Schiller and a wild cawing sound that was not human issued from his straining throat.

Even as von Schiller watched, one of the giant tropical eels thrust its head through the surface and its teeth gleamed like broken glass as it gaped wide, and then locked its jaws on to Nahoot's throat. Nahoot made no effort to tear the creature away. He was too far gone. He stared at von Schiller all the while that the eel, twisting and rolling into a gleaming ball of slimy coils, still hung from his throat.

Slowly Nahoot's head sank below the surface again. For long minutes the pool was agitated by the movements in its depth and the occasional gleam of one of the serpentine fish. Then gradually the surface settled as still and serene as a sheet of black glass.

Von Schiller turned and ran, back up the incline shaft, past the landing on which the generator still puttered quietly, blindly trying to get as far away as he could from that dreadful pool. He did not know where he was going, but followed any passageway that opened in front of him. At the foot of the central stairway he ran into the corner of the wall and stunned himself, falling to the agate tiles and lying there blubbering as a large purple lump rose on his forehead.

After a while he dragged himself to his feet and lurched up the stairs. He was confused and disorientated, his mind starting to break up in delirium, driven over the edge of sanity by horror and fear. He fell again, and crawled along the tunnel on his hands and knees to the next corner of the maze. Only then was he able to regain his feet to stagger onwards.

The steep shaft leading down into Taita's gas trap opened under his feet without him seeing it. He fell down the steps, jarring and bruising his legs and chest. Then he was on his feet again, reeling across the store room past the ranks of amphorae, up the far staircase and into the painted arcade that led to the tomb of Pharaoh Mamose.

He had tottered down half the length of it, dishevelled and wild-eyed and demented, when suddenly the lights dimmed for a moment, fading to a yellow glow. Then they brightened again as the generator sucked the last drops of fuel from the bottom of the tank. Von Schiller stopped in the centre of the arcade and looked up at the lights with despair. He knew what was coming. For another few minutes the bulbs burned on, bright and cheerfully, and then again they dimmed and faded.

The darkness settled over him like the heavy velvet folds of a funeral pall. It was so intense and complete that it seemed to have a physical weight and texture. He could taste the darkness in his mouth as it seemed to force its way into his body and suffocate him.

He ran again, wildly and blindly, losing all sense of direction in the blackness. He crashed headlong into stone and fell again, stunned. He could feel the warm tickle of blood running down his face, and he could not breathe. He whimpered and gasped and slowly, lying on his side, he curled himself into a ball like a foetus in the womb.

He wondered how long it would take him to die, and his soul quailed as he knew that it might take days and even weeks. He moved slightly, cuddling in closer to the stone object with which he had collided. In the darkness he had no way of telling that it was the great sarcophagus of Mamose that sheltered him. Thus he lay in the darkness of the tomb, surrounded by the funeral treasures of an emperor, and waited for his own slow but inexorable death.

The monastery of St Frumentius was deserted. The monks had heard the gunfire and the sounds of battle echoing down the gorge, and had gathered up their treasures and fled.

Nicholas ran down the long, empty cloister, pausing to catch his breath at the head of the staircase that led down to the level of the Nile and the Epiphany shrine where he had stored the boats. Panting, he searched the gloom of the deep basin below him into which the sunlight seldom reached, but the moving clouds of silver spray from the twin waterfalls screened the depths. He had no way of telling if Sapper and Royan were down there waiting for him, or if they had run into trouble on the trail.

He adjusted the tattered and bloodstained bandage around his chin, and then started down. Then he heard her voice in the silver mist below him, calling his name, and she came pelting up the slippery, slime-covered stairs towards him.

'Nicholas! Oh, thank God! I thought you weren't coming.' She would have rushed into his embrace, but then she saw his bandaged and blood-smeared face, and she stopped and stared at him, appalled.

'Sweet Mary!' she whispered. 'What happened to you, Nicky?'

'A little tiff with Jake Helm. Just a scratch, but I am not much good at kissing right now,' he mumbled, trying to grin around the bandage. 'You will have to wait for later.'

He put one arm around her shoulders, almost swinging her off her feet, as he turned her to face down the stairs again.

'Where are the others?' He hurried her down.

'They are all here,' she told him. 'Sapper and Mek are pumping the boats and loading.'

'Tessay?'

'She's safe.'

They scrambled down the last flight of steps on to the jetty below the Epiphany shrine. The Nile had risen ten feet since Nicholas had last stood there. The river was full and angry, muddy and swift. He could barely make out the cliffs on the far bank through the drifting clouds of spray.

The five Avon boats were drawn up at the edge. Four of them were already fully inflated, and the last one was billowing and swelling as the air was released into it from the compressed air cylinder. Mek and

Sapper were packing the ammunition crates into the ready boats and strapping them down under green nylon cargo nets.

Sapper looked up at Nicholas and a comical expression of astonishment spread over his bluff features, 'What the blue bleeding blazes happened to your face?'

'Tell you about it one day,' Nicholas promised, and turned to embrace Mek.

'Thank you, old friend,' he said sincerely. 'Your men fought well, and you waited for me.' Nicholas glanced at the row of wounded guerrillas that lay against the foot of the cliff. 'How many casualties?'

'Three dead, and these six wounded. It could have been much worse if Nogo's men had pushed us harder.'

'Still, it's too many,' said Nicholas.

'Even one is too many,' Mek agreed gruffly.

'Where are the rest of your men?'

'On the run for the border. Kept just enough of them with me to handle the boats.' Mek stripped the filthy bandage from Nicholas's chin. Royan gasped when she saw the injury, but Mek grinned.

'Looks as though you were chewed by a shark.'

'That's right, I was,' Nicholas agreed.

Mek shrugged. 'It needs at least a dozen stitches.' He shouted for one of his men to bring his pack.

'Sorry, no anaesthetic,' he warned Nicholas as he forced him to sit on the transom of one of the boats and poured antiseptic straight from the bottle.

Nicholas let out a gasp of pain. 'Burns, doesn't it?' Mek agreed complacently. 'But just wait until I start sewing.'

'This kindness will be written down against your name in the golden book,' Nicholas told him, and with an evil leer Mek broke the seal on a suture pack.

As Mek worked on the wound, pulling the edges together and tugging the thread tight, he spoke quietly so that Nicholas alone could hear. 'Nogo has at least a full company of men guarding the river downstream. My scouts tell me that he has placed them to cover the trails on both banks.'

'He doesn't know that we have boats to run the river, does he?' Nicholas asked through gritted teeth.

'I think it is unlikely, but he knows a great deal about our movements. Perhaps he had an informer amongst your workmen.' Mek paused as he pricked the needle into Nicholas's flesh, and then went on, 'And Nogo still has the helicopter. He will spot us on the river as soon as this cloud breaks.'

'The river is our only escape route. Let's pray that the weather stays socked in, like this.'

By the time Mek had tied off the last knot and covered Nicholas's chin with a Steri-Strip plaster, Sapper had finished inflating and loading the last boat.

Four of Mek's men carried Tessay's litter to one of the boats. Mek helped her aboard and settled her on the deck, making sure that she had one of the safety straps close at hand. Then he left her and hurried to where his wounded men lay in order to help them into the boats too. Most of them could walk, but two had to be carried.

After that he came back to Nicholas. 'I see you have found your radio,' he said, as he glanced at the fibreglass case that Nicholas had slung over his shoulder on its carrying strap.

'Without it we would be in big trouble.' Nicholas patted the case affectionately.

'I will take command of that boat, with Tessay.'

'Good!' Nicholas agreed. 'Royan will go with me in the lead boat.'

'You had better let me lead,' Mek said.

'What do you know about river running?' Nicholas asked him. 'I am the only one of us who has ever shot this river before.'

'That was twenty years ago,' Mek pointed out.

'I am an even better man now than I was then,' Nicholas grinned. 'Don't argue, Mek. You come next, and Sapper in the one behind you. Are there any of your men who know the river to command the other two boats?'

'All my men know the river,' Mek told him, and shouted his orders. Each of them hurried to the Avon he had been allocated. Nicholas gave Royan a boost over the gunwale of their boat, and then helped his men launch her down the rocky bank. As soon as the hull floated free they scrambled aboard and each man grabbed a paddle.

As they bent to their paddles, Nicholas saw at once that every man of his crew was indeed a riverman, as Mek had boasted. They pulled strongly but smoothly, and the light inflatable craft shot out into the main stream of the Nile.

The Avons were designed to accommodate sixteen, and were lightly loaded. The ammunition cases that held the grave goods from the tomb were bulky but weighed little, and there were not more than a dozen people in any one boat. They all floated high and handled well.

'Bad water ahead,' Nicholas told Royan grimly. 'All the way to the Sudanese border.' He stood at the steering sweep in the stern, from where he had a good forward view. Royan crouched at his feet, clinging to one of the safety straps and trying to keep out of the way of the oarsmen.

They cut across the current that was scouring the great stone basin below the falls, and Nicholas lined up for the narrow heads through which the river was escaping to the west. He looked up at the sky and saw through the spray that the rain clouds were low and purple. They seemed to sag down upon the tops of the tall cliffs.

'Luck starting to run our way,' he told Royan. 'Even with the helicopter they won't be able to find us in this weather.'

He glanced at his Rolex and the spray was beading the glass. 'Couple of hours until nightfall. We should be able to put a few miles of river behind us before we are forced to stop for the night.'

He looked back over his stern and saw the rest of the little flotilla bobbing along behind him. Thé Avons were reflective yellow in colour and stood out brilliantly even in the mist and murk of the gorge. He lifted his clenched fist high in the signal to advance, and from the following boat Mek repeated the gesture and grinned at him through his beard.

The river grabbed them and they shot through its portals into the narrow, twisted gut of the Nile. The men at the oars stopped paddling, and let the river take them. All they could do now was to help Nicholas to steer her through any desperate moments, and they crouched ready along the gunwales.

The high water in the gorge had covered many of the reefs of rock, but their presence below the surface was clearly marked by the waters that humped up in standing waves or foamed white in the narrows between them. The flood reached up high on either bank, dashing against the cliffs of the sub-gorge. If an Avon overturned, or even if a crew member were thrown overboard, there would be no place on this river to heave-to and pick up survivors.

Nicholas stood high and craned ahead. He had to pick his route well in advance, and once committed he had to steer her through. It all depended on his ability to read the river and judge her moods. He was out of practice, and he had that tight, hard cannonball of fear in the pit of his belly as he put the long sweep over and steered for the first run of fast green water. They went swooping down it, Nicholas holding their bows into it with delicate touches of the sweep, and came out into the bottom of it with all the other boats following them down in sequence.

'Nothing to it!' Royan laughed up at him.

'Don't say it!' Nicholas pleaded with her. 'The bad angel is listening.' And he lined up for the head of the next set of rapids that raced towards them with terrifying speed.

Nicholas steered through the gap between two outcrops of rock and they shot the barrel, gaining speed down the chute. It was only when they were halfway down that he saw the tall standing wave below them over which the river leaped. He put the sweep across and tried to steer round it, but the river had them firmly in its grip.

Like a hunter taking a fence they shot up the front of the standing wave, and then with a sickening lurch plummeted down the far side into the deep trough. The Avon folded across the middle, the bows almost touching the stern as she tried to pull through the hole in the river surface.

The crew were tumbled over each other and Nicholas would have been catapulted overside if it had not been for his body line and his grip on the steering sweep. Royan flung herself flat on the deck and hung on to the safety strap with all her strength as the Avon's buoyancy exerted itself and the boat bounded high in the air, whipping back elastically into its original shape, then hovered a moment and almost capsized before it crashed back, right side up.

One of the crew had been hurled overboard and was floundering alongside, carried along at the same speed as the flying Avon, so his comrades were able to lean out and haul him back on board. The cargo of ammunition crates had tumbled and shifted, but the nets had prevented any of them from being lost over the side.

'What did you do that for?' Royan yelled at him. 'Just when I was beginning to trust you.'

'Just testing,' he yelled back. 'Wanted to see how tough you really are.'

'I admit it, I am a sissy,' she assured him. 'You really don't need to do it again.'

Looking back, Nicholas saw Mek's boat crash through the trough just as they had, but the following craft had enough warning to steer clear and slip through the sides of the run.

He looked ahead again, and his whole existence became the wild waters of the river. His universe was contained within the tall cliffs of the sub-gorge as he battled to bring the racing Avon through. He did not know whether it was spray or rain that stung his cheeks and his wounded chin, and that flew horizontally into his eyes and half-blinded him. At times it was a mixture of the two.

An hour later Nicholas misjudged the rapids again, and they went in sideways and almost capsized. Two of his crew were hurled overboard. Steering fine and leaning outboard they managed to pull one of them from the river, but the other man struck a rock before they could reach him. He went under and did not rise again. None of them spoke or mourned him, for they were all too busy staying alive themselves.

Once Royan shouted up at Nicholas through the rattling spray and the thunder of the river all around them, 'Helicopter! Can you hear it?'

Half-deafened, he looked up at the lowering grey belly of the clouds that hung at the level of the cliffs, and faintly made out the whistle and flutter of the rotors.

'Above the cloud!' he shouted back, wiping the rain and the spray from his eyes with the back of his hand. 'They will never spot us in this.'

The onset of the African night was sped upon them by the low cloud. In the gathering darkness another hazard leaped upon them with no warning at all. One instant they were running hard and clear down a smooth stretch of the river, and the next the waters opened ahead of them and they were hurled out into space. It seemed that they fell for ever, although it was a drop of not more than thirty feet, before they hit the bottom and found themselves floating in a tangle of men and boats in the pool below the falls. Here the river was stalled for a moment, revolving upon itself while it gathered its strength for the next mad charge down the gorge.

One of the Avons had capsized and was floating belly up – even its highly stable hull had not been able to weather the drop down the falls. The crews of the other boats gathered themselves and then paddled across to drag the survivors from the water and to salvage the oars and other floating equipment. It took the combined efforts of all of them to right the overturned Avon, and then it was almost completely dark by the time they had it back on even keel.

'Count the crates!' Nicholas ordered. 'How many have we lost?'

He could hardly credit his good fortune when Sapper shouted back, 'Eleven still on board. All present and correct.' The cargo nets were holding well. But all of them, men and women, were exhausted and soaked through and shivering with the cold. Any attempt to go on in darkness would be suicidal. Nicholas looked across at Mek in the nearest boat and shook his head.

'There is a bit of slack water in the angle of the cliff.' Mek pointed towards the tail of the pool. 'We might be able to find moorings for the night.'

There was a stunted but tough little tree growing out of the vertical fissure in the rock, and they used this as a bollard and made a line fast to it. Then they lashed all the Avons together in a line down the cliff and settled in for the night. There was no chance of hot food or drink, and they had to make do with some cold tinned rations eaten off the blade of a bayonet, and a few chunks of soggy *injera* bread.

Mek scrambled over from his own boat and huddled down close beside Nicholas with one arm over his shoulder and his lips close to his ear.

'I have made a roll call. Another man missing when we went over the falls. We won't find him now.'

'I am not doing too well,' Nicholas admitted. 'Perhaps you should lead tomorrow.'

'Not your fault.' Mek squeezed his shoulders. 'Nobody could have done better. It was this last waterfall—' he broke off and they listened to it thundering away in the darkness.

'How far have we come?' Nicholas asked. 'And how much further to go?'

'It's almost impossible to tell, but I guess we are halfway to the border. Should reach there some time tomorrow afternoon.'

They were silent for a while, and then Mek asked, 'What is the date today? I have lost count of the days.'

'So have I.' Nicholas tilted his wrist-watch so that he could read the luminous dial in the last of the light. 'Good God! It's the thirtieth already,' he said.

'Your pick-up aircraft is due at Roseires airstrip the day after tomorrow.'

'The first of April,' Nicholas agreed. 'Will we make it?'

'You answer that question for me.' Mek grinned in the night without humour. 'What chances of your fat friend being late?'

'Jannie is a pro. He is never late,' said Nicholas. Again a silence fell, and then Nicholas asked, 'When we reach Roseires, what do you want me to do with your share of the booty?' Nicholas kicked one of the ammunition crates. 'Do you want to take it with you?'

'After we see you off on the plane with your fat friend, we are going to be doing some hot-footed running from Nogo. I don't want to be carrying any extra luggage. You take my share with you. Sell it for me – I need the money to keep fighting here.'

'You trust me?'

'You are my friend.'

'Friends are the easiest to cheat – they never expect it,' Nicholas told him, and Mek punched his shoulder and chuckled.

'Get some sleep. We will have to do some hard paddling tomorrow.' Mek stood up in the Avon as she pitched and rolled gently to the push of the current. 'Sleep well, old friend,' he said, and climbed across to the boat alongside, where Tessay waited for him.

Nicholas braced his back against the soft pneumatic gunwale of the Avon and took Royan in his arms. She sat between his knees and leaned back against his chest, shivering in her sodden clothes.

After a while her shivering abated, and she murmured, 'You make a very good hot-water bottle.'

'That's one reason for keeping me around on a permanent basis,' he said, and stroked her wet hair. She did not answer him, but snuggled closer, and a short while afterwards her breathing slowed as she fell into an exhausted sleep.

Although he was cold and stiff and his shoulders ached and his palms were blistered from wrestling with the steering oar, he could not find sleep as readily as she had. Now that the prospect of reaching the airstrip at Roseires loomed closer, he was troubled by problems other than those of simply navigating the river and battling his way through Nogo's men. Those were enemies he could recognize and fight; but there was something more than that which he would soon have to face.

456

Royan stirred in his arms and muttered something he could not catch. She was dreaming and talking in her sleep.

He held her gently and she settled down again. He had started to drift off himself when she spoke again, this time quite clearly. 'I am sorry, Nicky. Don't hate me for it. I couldn't let you—' her words slurred and he could make no sense of the rest of it.

He was fully awake now, her words aggravating his doubts and misgivings. During the rest of that night he slept only intermittently, and his rest was troubled by dreams as distressing as hers must have been to her.

In the pre-dawn darkness he shook Royan gently. She moaned and came awake slowly and reluctantly.

They bolted down a few mouthfuls of the cold rations that remained from the previous night. Then, as dawn lit the gorge just enough for them to see the surface of the river and the obstacles ahead, they pushed off from their moorings and the yellow boats strung out down the current. The battle against the river began all over again.

The cloud cover was still low and unbroken, and the rain squalls swept over them at intervals. They kept going all that morning, and slowly the mood of the river began to ameliorate. The current was not so swift and treacherous, and the banks not so high and rugged.

It was mid-afternoon and the clouds were still closed in solidly overhead as they entered a stretch where the river threaded itself through a series of bluffs and headlands, and they came upon another set of rapids. Perhaps Nicholas was more expert in his technique by now, for they swept through them without mishap, and it seemed to him that each stretch of white water was progressively less severe than the last.

'I think we are through the worst of it now,' he told Royan as she sat on the deck below him. 'The gradient and the fall of the river are definitely more gentle now. I think it is flattening out as we approach the plains of the Sudan.'

'How much further to Roseires?' she asked.

'I don't know, but the border can't be too far ahead now.'

Nicholas and Mek were keeping the flotilla closed up in line astern, so that orders could be shouted across the gaps between them and all the boats kept under their command.

Nicholas steered for the deeper water on the outside of the next wide bend, and as he came through it he saw that the stretch of river ahead seemed open and altogether free of rapids or shoals. He relaxed and smiled at Royan.

'How about lunch at the Dorchester grill next Sunday? Best roast beef trolley in London.'

He thought he saw a shadow pass across her eyes before she smiled brightly and replied, 'Sounds good to me.'

'And afterwards we can go back home and curl up in front of the telly and watch *Match of the Day*, or play our own little match.'

'You are rude,' she laughed, 'but it does sound tempting.'

He was about to stoop over her, and kiss her for the pleasure of watching her blush again, when he saw the dance of tiny white fountains spurting up from the surface of the river ahead of their bows, coming swiftly towards them. Then, moments later, he heard the crackle of automatic fire, the distinctive sound of a Soviet RPD.

He threw himself down over the top of Royan, covering her with his own body, and heard Mek bellowing from the boat behind them.

'Return fire! Keep their heads down.'

His men threw down their paddles and seized their weapons. They blazed away towards the inner curve of the bank from where the attack was coming.

The attackers were completely concealed amongst the rocks and scrub, and there was no definite target to shoot at. However, in an ambush like this it was essential to lay down as heavy a covering fire as possible, to keep the attackers' heads down and to upset their aim.

A bullet tore through the nylon skin of the Avon close to Royan's head and went on to slam into one of the metal ammunition crates. The sides of their craft offered no protection at all from the heavy fusillade that lashed them. One of their crew was hit in the head. The bullet cut the top off his skull like the shell of a soft-boiled egg, and he was flung over the side. Royan screamed more with horror than with fear, while Nicholas snatched up the assault rifle that the dead man had dropped and emptied the magazine towards the bank, firing short taps of three and raking the scrub that concealed their attackers.

The Avon still raced downstream on the current, spiralling aimlessly as she lost direction without the steering oar. It took them less than a minute to be carried past the ambush and around the next bend of the river.

Nicholas dropped the empty rifle and shouted across at Mek, 'Are you all right?'

'One man hit here,' Mek yelled back. 'Not too bad.'

Each of the boats reported their casualties: a total of one dead and three wounded. None of the wounded was in a serious condition, and although three of the boats had been holed, the hulls were made up of watertight compartments and were all still floating high.

Mek steered his Avon alongside Nicholas's and called across. 'I was beginning to think we had given Nogo the slip.'

'We got off lightly that time,' Nicholas called back. 'We probably took them by surprise. They weren't expecting us to be on the water.'

'Well, no more surprises for him now. You can bet they are on the radio already. Nogo knows exactly where we are and where we are headed.' He looked up at the cloud. 'We can only hope the cloud stays thick and low.'

'How much further to the Sudanese border?'

'Not sure, but it can't be more than another couple of hours.'

'Is the crossing guarded?' Nicholas asked.

'No. Nothing there. Just empty bush on both sides.'

'Let's hope it stays empty,' Nicholas muttered.

Within thirty minutes of the fire-fight, they heard the helicopter again. It was flying above the clouds, and as they listened it passed overhead, but out of sight, and headed on downstream. Twenty minutes later they heard it again, coming back in the opposite direction, and shortly after that it flew downstream again, still above the cloud.

'What the hell is Nogo playing at?' Mek called across to Nicholas. 'Sounds as though he is patrolling the river, but he can't get under the cloud.'

'My guess is that he is ferrying men downstream to cut us off. Now he knows we are using boats, he also knows that we can only head in one direction. Nogo isn't one to worry about international borders. He may even have realized by now that we are heading for Roseires. It's the nearest unmanned airstrip along the river. He could be waiting for us when we try to land.'

Mek steered his Avon closer and passed a line across, tying the two boats together so that they could talk in normal tones.

'I don't like it, Nicholas. We are going to walk right into them again. What do you suggest?'

Nicholas pondered for a long minute. 'Don't you recognize this part of the river? Don't you know precisely where we are yet?'

Mek shook his head. 'I always keep well away from the river when we cross the border, but I will recognize the old sugar-mill at Roseires when we get there. It's about three miles upstream from the airstrip.'

'Deserted?' Nicholas asked.

'Yes. Abandoned ever since the war began twenty years ago.'

'With this cloud cover, it will be dark in an hour,' Nicholas said. 'The river is slower now and not so dangerous. We can take a chance and keep on going after dark. Perhaps Nogo won't expect that. We might be able to give him the slip in the dark.'

'Is that the best you can do?' Mek chuckled. 'As a plan it sounds to me a bit like closing your eyes and hoping for the best.'

'Well, if somebody could tell me where the hell we are, and what time Jannie will arrive tomorrow, I might be able to come up with something a bit more specific.' Nicholas grinned back at him. 'Until that happens, I am flying by the seat of my pants.'

All of them were tense with strung-out nerves as they paddled on into the premature dusk beneath the thick blanket of cloud and rain. Even in the gathering darkness the crew kept their weapons cocked and locked, trained on either bank of the river, ready to return fire instantly.

'We must have crossed the border an hour ago,' Mek called to Nicholas. 'The old sugar mill can't be far ahead.'

'In the dark, how will you find it?'

'There is the remains of an old stone jetty on the bank, from which the riverboats taking the sugar down to Khartoum used to load.'

Night came down upon them abruptly, and Nicholas felt a sense of relief as the river banks receded into the murk and the darkness hid them from hostile eyes ashore. As soon as it was fully dark they lashed the boats together to prevent them becoming separated and then let the river carry them on silently, keeping so close in to the right-hand bank that they ran aground more than once, and some of the men had to slip over the side and push them out into deeper water.

The stone piers of the jetty at Roseires sprang out at them unexpectedly, and Nicholas's leading Avon slammed into them before he could steer clear. However, the crew were ready and they jumped over the side into chest-deep water and dragged the boat to the bank. Immediately Mek leaped ashore and, with twenty of his men, spread out into the overgrown canefields along the bank to secure the area and prevent a surprise attack by Nogo's men.

There was confusion and more noise than Nicholas felt was safe as the rest of the flotilla beached, and they began to bring the wounded ashore and unload the cargo of ammunition cases. Nicholas piggybacked Royan to the bank and then waded back to fetch Tessay. She was much stronger by now. The enforced rest during the voyage downriver had given her a chance to recover, and she stood up unaided in the Avon and climbed on to Nicholas's shoulders to be brought ashore.

Once on dry ground he let her slide down on to her own feet and asked her quietly, 'How are you feeling?'

'I will be all right now, thank you, Nicholas.'

He supported her for a moment while she recovered her balance and said quickly, 'I did not have a chance to ask earlier. What about Royan's message that she asked you to telephone from Debra Maryam? Did you get it through for her?'

'Yes, of course,' Tessay replied guilelessly. 'I told Royan that I had given her message to Moussad at the Egyptian Embassy. Didn't she tell you?'

Nicholas winced as though he had taken a low punch, but he smiled and kept his tone casual. 'It must have slipped her mind. Not important, anyway. But thanks nevertheless, Tessay.'

At that moment Mek came striding out of the darkness and spoke in a harsh whisper. 'This sounds like a camel market. Nogo will hear us from five miles away.' Quickly he took command and started to organize the shore party.

Once the last of the ammunition crates were unloaded, they dragged the boats into the canefields and unscrewed the valves that deflated the pontoons. Then they piled cane trash over them. Still working in the dark, they distributed the cargo of ammunition crates amongst Mek's men. Sapper took a case under each arm. Nicholas slung the radio over one shoulder and his emergency pack over the other, and balanced on his head the case that contained Pharaoh's golden death-mask and the Taita *ushabti*.

Mek sent his scouts forward to sweep the route out to the airstrip and make certain that they did not run into an ambush. Then he took the point and the rest of them strung out in Indian file along the rough, overgrown track behind him. Before they had covered a mile the clouds suddenly opened overhead, and the crescent moon and the stars showed through and gave them enough light to make out the chimneystack of the ruined mill against the night sky.

But even with this moonlight their progress was slow and broken by long pauses, for the stretcher-bearers carrying the wounded had difficulty keeping up. By the time they reached the airstrip it was after three in the morning and the moon had set. They stacked the ammunition cases in the same grove of acacia trees at the end of the runway where they had cached the pallets of dam-building equipment and the yellow tractor on the inward journey.

Although they were all exhausted by this time, Mek set out his pickets around the camp. The two women tended the wounded, working by the light of a small screened fire as they used up the last of Mek's medical supplies.

Sapper used the one electric torch whose batteries still held a charge, and he gave Nicholas a discreet screened light while he set up the radio and strung the aerial. Nicholas's relief was intense when he opened the fibreglass case and found that, despite its dunking in the Nile, the rubber gasket that sealed the lid had kept the radio dry. When he switched on the power, the pilot light lit up. He tuned in to the short-wave frequency and picked up the early morning commercial transmission of Radio Nairobi.

Yvonne Chaka Chaka was singing; he liked her voice and her style. But he quickly switched off the set so as to conserve the battery, and settled back against the bole of the acacia tree to try and get a little rest

461

before daylight broke. However, sleep eluded him – his sense of betrayal and anger were too strong.

Tuma Nogo watched the sun push its great fiery head out of the surface of the Nile ahead of them. They were flying only feet above the water to keep under the Sudanese military radar transmissions. He knew there was a radar station at Khartoum that might be able to pick them up, even at this range. Relations with the Sudanese were strained, and he could expect a quick and savage response if they discovered that he had violated their border.

Nogo was a confused and worried man. Since the débâcle in the gorge of the Dandera river everything had run strongly against him. He had lost all his allies. Until they were gone he had not realized how heavily he had come to rely on both Helm and von Schiller. Now he was on his own and he had already made many mistakes.

But despite all this he was determined to pursue the fugitives, and to run them down no matter how far he had to intrude into Sudanese territory. Over the past weeks it had gradually dawned upon Nogo, mostly by eavesdropping on the conversations of von Schiller and the Egyptian, that Harper and Mek Nimmur were in possession of treasure of immense value. His imagination could barely grasp the enormity of it, but he had heard others speak of tens of millions of dollars. Even a million dollars was a sum so vast that his mind had difficulty assimilating it, but he had a vague inkling as to what it might mean in earthly terms, of the possessions and women and luxuries it could buy.

Equally slowly it had dawned upon him that, now that von Schiller and Helm were gone, this treasure could be his alone; there was no longer any other person to stand in his way, other than the fleeing *shufta* led by Mek Nimmur and the Englishman. And he had overwhelming force on his side and the helicopter at his command.

If only he could pin the fugitives down, Nogo was certain he could wipe them out. There must be no survivors, no one to carry tales to Addis. After Mek and the Englishman and all their followers were dead it would be a simple matter to spirit his booty out of the country in the helicopter. There was a man in Nairobi and another in Khartoum whom he had dealt with before; they had bought contraband ivory and hashish from him. They would know how to market the booty to best advantage, although they were both devious men. He had already decided that he would not trust it all to one person but would spread the risk, so that even if one of them betrayed and cheated him—

His mind raced off on another tack, and he savoured the thought of great riches and what they could buy for him. He would have fine clothes and motor cars, land and cattle and women – white women and black and brown, all the women he could use, a new one for every day of his life. He broke off his greedy daydreams. First he had to find where the runaways had vanished to.

He had not realized that Harper and Mek Nimmur had inflatable boats hidden somewhere near the monastery. Hansith had not informed him of that fact. He and Helm had expected them to try to escape on foot, and all the plans to head them off before they could reach the Sudanese border had been based on that assumption. On Helm's orders, he had even set up a reserve fuel dump near the border where they expected Mek Nimmur to cross, from which they could refuel the helicopter. Without those supplies of fuel he would long ago have been forced to give up the chase.

Nogo had placed his men to cover the trails leading along the river bank towards the west, and he had not even considered guarding the river itself. It was quite by chance that one of his patrols had been in a position to spot the flotilla of yellow boats as they came racing downstream. However, there had not been enough warning to enable them to set up an effective ambush, and they had been able to fire on the boats only briefly before they escaped. They had not inflicted serious damage on any of the boats – at least, not enough to stop them getting through.

Immediately the company commander had radioed his report of this contact with Mek Nimmur, Nogo had started ferrying men downstream to the Sudanese border to cut off the flotilla. Unfortunately, the Jet Ranger could carry no more than six fully armed men at a time, and transporting them had been a time-consuming business. He had only succeeded in bringing sixty of his men into position before night had fallen.

During the night he fretted that the flotilla was slipping past him, and with the dawn they were in the air again. Fortunately the cloud had broken up during the night. There was still some high cumulus overhead, but they were now able to fly low along the river and search for any sign of Mek Nimmur's flotilla.

They had first flown back along the river on the Ethiopian side of the border, as far as the point where Mek Nimmur and Harper had been fired upon. They had picked up no sign of the boats, so Nogo had forced the pilot to turn back, cross the border and search the Sudanese stretch of the Nile. But Nogo had only been able to persuade his pilot to penetrate sixty nautical miles along the Nile into the Sudan before the man had rebelled. Despite the Tokarev pistol that Nogo held to his head, he had banked the Jet Ranger into a 180-degree turn and headed back low along the river.

By now Nogo knew he had been defeated and outwitted. He brooded unhappily in the front seat of the helicopter beside the pilot, trying to fathom out what had happened to his quarry. He saw the tall smokestack of the abandoned sugar-mill at Roseires poking up into the early morning sky, and he glowered at it angrily. They had passed the mill only a short while before on their way downstream.

'Turn in towards the north bank,' he ordered the pilot, and the man hesitated and glanced at him before he obeyed.

They passed directly over the building, flying lower than the chimney. The factory was roofless and the windows were empty rectangles in the broken walls. The boilers and machinery had been removed twenty years previously, and Nogo could look into the empty shell. The pilot hovered the aircraft while Nogo peered down, but there was no place where anyone could hide, and Nogo shook his head.

'Nothing! We have lost them. Head back upstream.'

The pilot lifted the machine's nose and turned away towards the river, obeying the order with alacrity. As the aircraft banked steeply, Nogo was looking down directly into the overgrown canefields verging the river when a flash of bright yellow caught his eye.

'Wait!' he shouted into his mike. 'There is something there. Go back!'

The helicopter hovered over the field, and Nogo gestured urgently downwards. 'Down! Put us down.'

As soon as the skids touched the earth, the stick of six heavily armed troopers dived out of the rear cabin and raced out to take up defensive positions. Nogo clambered out of the front door and ran into the overgrown bed of tall cane. One look was all he needed. The yellow boats had been deflated and folded and hastily covered. The earth around them had been churned up by booted feet. The tracks led away inland. The men who had made them had been heavily laden, for they had trodden deeply into the soft, sandy earth.

Nogo ran back to the helicopter and thrust his head in through the open cabin door. 'Is there an airstrip near here?' he shouted at the pilot, who shook his head.

'There is nothing shown on the chart.'

'There must have been one. The sugar-mill would have had a strip.'

'If there was one, it must have been decommissioned years ago.'

'We will find it,' Nogo declared. 'Mek Nimmur's tracks will lead us to it.' He sobered immediately. 'But I will have to bring up more men. Judging by his spoor, Mek Nimmur has at least fifty of his *shufta* with him.'

He left his men at the sugar-mill and flew back to the border with an empty rear cabin to pick up the first load of reinforcements.

464

ig Dolly! Come in, Big Dolly. This is Pharaoh. Do you read?' Nicholas put out his first call an hour before sunrise.

'If I know the way Jannie's mind works, and I should, he would plan to make his approach flight in darkness and arrive here as soon as there is enough light to pick up the strip and land.'

'If the Fat Man comes,' Mek Nimmur qualified.

'He will come,' said Nicholas confidently. 'Jannie has never let me down yet.' He thumbed the microphone and called again: 'Big Dolly! Come in, Big Dolly.'

The static hummed softly, and Nicholas retuned the set carefully. He called again every fifteen minutes as they huddled around the set in the dark under the acacia trees.

Suddenly Royan started to her feet and exclaimed excitedly, 'There he is. I can hear Big Dolly's engines. Listen!'

Nicholas and Mek ran out into the open, and turned their faces upwards, looking into the north.

'That's not the Hercules,' Nicholas exclaimed suddenly. 'That's another machine.' He turned and faced southwards, towards the river. 'Anyway, it's coming from the wrong direction.'

'You are right,' Mek agreed. 'That's a single engine, and it's not a fixed wing. You can hear the rotors.'

'The Pegasus helicopter!' Nicholas exclaimed bitterly. 'They are on to us again.'

As they listened, the sound of the rotors faded. Nicholas looked relieved. 'They missed us. They can't have spotted the Avons.'

They trooped back under the cover of the acacias, and Nicholas called again on the radio, but there was no reply from Jannie.

Twenty minutes later they heard the sound of the Jet Ranger returning, and they monitored it anxiously.

'Gone again,' said Nicholas after a while, but then twenty minutes later they heard it yet again.

'Nogo is up to something out there,' Mek said uneasily.

'What do you think it is?' Nicholas was infected by his mood. When Mek worried, there was usually a damned good reason to worry.

'I don't know,' Mek admitted. 'Perhaps Nogo has spotted the Avons and is bringing up more men before he comes after us.' He went out into the open and listened intently, then came back to where Nicholas crouched over the radio.

'Keep calling,' he said. 'I am going out to the perimeter to make certain my men are ready to hold Nogo off if he comes.'

The helicopter moved up and down the Nile at short intervals during the next three hours, but the lack of any further developments lulled them, and Nicholas barely looked up from the radio each time they heard the distant beat of the rotors. Suddenly the radio crackled, and Nicholas started violently at the shock.

'Pharaoh! This is Big Dolly. Do you read?'

Nicholas's voice bubbled over with relief as he replied, 'This is Pharaoh. Speak sweet words to me, Big Dolly.'

'ETA your position one hour thirty minutes.' Jannie's accent was unmistakable.

'You will be very welcome!' Nicholas promised him fervently.

He hung up the microphone and beamed at the two women, 'Jannie is on his way, and he will—'

He broke off and his smile shrivelled to an expression of dismay. From the direction of the river came the unmistakable rattle of AK-47 rapid fire, followed a few seconds later by the crump of an exploding grenade.

'Oh, dammit to hell!' he groaned. 'I thought it was too good to last. Nogo has arrived.'

He picked up the mike again and spoke into it expressionlessly. 'Big Dolly! The uglies have arrived on the scene. It's going to have to be a hot extraction.'

'Hang on to your crown, Pharaoh!' Jannie's voice floated back. 'I am on my way.'

During the next half-hour the sounds of the fighting along the river intensified until the rattle of small-arms fire was almost continuous, and gradually it crept closer to the far end of the airstrip. It was clear that Mek's men, spread out thinly along the river end of the strip, were falling back before the thrust of Nogo's men. And every twenty minutes or so there was the sound of the returning helicopter, as it ferried another stick of men to increase the pressure on Mek's scanty defence.

Nicholas and Sapper were the only able-bodied men left in the acacia grove, for all the others had gone out to defend the perimeter. The two of them moved the ammunition crates to the edge of the trees, where they could be loaded in haste once the Hercules landed.

Nicholas sorted out the cargo, reading the contents of each crate from the notations on the lids in Royan's handwriting. The crate containing the death-mask and the Taita *ushabti* would be the first to go aboard, followed by the three crowns: the blue war crown, the Nemes crown and the red and white crown of the united kingdoms of upper and lower Egypt. The value of those three crates probably exceeded that of all the rest of the treasure combined.

Once the cargo had been taken care of, Nicholas went down the row of wounded men and spoke to each of them in turn. First, he thanked them for their help and sacrifice, and then offered to take them out on the Hercules to where they could receive proper medical attention. He promised each of them that, if they accepted the offer, he would see to it that once they had recovered from their wounds they could return to Ethiopia.

Seven of them – those who were less seriously wounded and were able to walk – refused to leave Mek Nimmur. Their loyalty was a touching demonstration of the high regard in which Mek was held by his men. The others reluctantly agreed to be evacuated, but only after Tessay had intervened and added her assurances to Nicholas's. Then he and Sapper carried them to the point at the edge of the grove where Jannie would halt Big Dolly for the pick-up.

'What about you?' Nicholas asked Tessay. 'Are you coming out with us? You are still in pretty bad shape.'

Tessay laughed. 'While I can still stand on my two feet, I will never leave Mek Nimmur.'

'I can't understand what you see in that old rogue,' Nicholas laughed with her. 'I have spoken to Mek. He wants me to take his share of the booty with me. He won't be able to carry any extra luggage at the moment.'

'Yes, I know. Mek and I discussed it. We need the money to continue the struggle here.'

She broke off and ducked involuntarily, as a stunning explosion cracked in their eardrums and a tall column of dust leaped into the air close to the edge of the grove. Shrapnel whistled over their heads and twigs and leaves rained down on them.

'Sweet Mary! What was that?' Tessay cried.

'Two-inch mortar,' said Nicholas. He had not moved, nor made any attempt to take cover. 'More bark than bite. Nogo must have brought it in with his last flight.'

'When will the Hercules get here?'

'I'll give Jannie a call, and ask him.'

As Nicholas sauntered over to the radio set Tessay whispered to Royan, 'Are you English always so cool?'

'Don't ask me – I'm mostly Egyptian, and I am terrified.' Royan smiled easily and put her arm around Tessay. 'I am going to miss you, Lady Sun.'

'Perhaps we will meet again in happier times.' Tessay turned her head and kissed her impulsively, and Royan hugged her hard.

'I hope so. I hope so with all my heart.'

Nicholas spoke into the microphone. 'Big Dolly, this is Pharaoh. What is your position now?'

'Pharaoh, we are twenty minutes out, and hurrying. Did you have baked beans for dinner or is that mortar fire I hear in the background?'

'With your wit you should have gone on the stage,' Nicholas told him. 'The uglies have control of the south end of the strip. Make your approach from the north. The wind is westerly at about five knots. So any way you come in, it will be cross-wind.'

'Roger, Pharaoh. How many passengers and cargo do you have for me?'

'Passengers are six cas-evac plus three. Cargo is fifty-two crates, about a quarter of a ton weight.'

'Hardly worth coming all this way for so little, Pharaoh.'

'Big Dolly. Be advised, there is another aircraft in the circuit. A Jet Ranger helicopter. Colour green and red. It is a hostile, but unarmed.'

'Roger, Pharaoh. I will call again on finals.'

Nicholas went back to where the two women were waiting with the wounded.

'Not long now,' he told them cheerfully. He had to raise his voice to make himself heard above the din of mortar bursts and rapid small-arms fire.

'Just enough time for a cup of tea,' he said. He pushed a few twigs into the embers of the previous night's fire, then rummaged in his small emergency pack for the last of his tea bags while Sapper placed the smoke-blackened billycan back on the burgeoning flames.

They only had one mug between them. 'Girls first,' said Nicholas, passing it to Royan. She took a swallow and scalded her lips.

'Good!' she sighed, and then cocked her head. 'This time it is definitely Big Dolly I can hear.'

Nicholas listened and then nodded. 'I think you are right.' He stood up and went to the radio. 'Big Dolly. You are audible.'

'Five minutes to landing, Pharaoh.'

From where he stood, Nicholas looked down the long strip. Mek's men were retreating, flitting like smoke through the thorn scrub and firing back in the direction of the river. Nogo was pushing them hard now.

'Hurry along, Jannie,' he murmured, and then adjusted his expression as he turned back to the two women. 'Plenty of time to finish your tea. Don't waste it.'

The rumble of Big Dolly's engines was louder than the sound of gunfire now. Then suddenly she was in sight, coming in so low that she seemed to brush the tops of the thorn trees. She was enormous. Her wingspan reached from one side of the narrow overgrown strip to the other. Jannie touched her down short, and she blew out a long rolling cloud of brown dust behind her as he put the engines into reverse thrust.

Big Dolly went barrelling past the clump of acacia, and Jannie waved to them from the high cockpit. The moment he had bled off enough speed, he stood on his footbrakes and rudder bar. Big Dolly spun around in her own length and came roaring back down the strip towards them, her loading ramp beginning to drop open even before she reached them.

Fred was waiting in the open hatchway, and he ran down to help Sapper and Nicholas with the wounded men on the litters. It took only a few minutes to carry them up the ramp, and then they started loading the ammunition crates. Even Royan gave a hand, staggering up the ramp with one of the lighter crates clutched to her chest.

A mortar shell exploded a hundred and fifty yards beyond the parked Hercules, and then half a minute later a second shell fell a hundred yards short.

'Ranging shots,' Nicholas grunted, picking up a crate under each arm and running up the ramp.

'They have us in their sights now,' Fred shouted. 'We have to get out of here. Leave the rest of the cargo. Let's go! Go!'

There were only four crates still lying under the spreading branches of the acacia, and both Nicholas and Sapper ignored the order and ran back down the ramp. They snatched up a crate under each arm and raced back. The ramp was starting to rise and Big Dolly's engines roared as she began to taxi out. They hurled the crates over the tailboard of the rising ramp and then jumped up to grab a handhold and pull themselves aboard. Nicholas was the first up and reached down to haul Sapper in.

When he looked back, Tessay was a small, lonely figure under the acacias.

'Give Mek my love and thanks,' he bellowed at her.

'You know how to contact us,' she screamed back.

'Goodbye, Tessay.' Royan's voice was lost in the blast of the great engines, and the dust blew back in a sheet over Tessay so that she was forced to cover her face and turn away. The ramp hissed closed on its hydraulic rams, and cut out their last glimpse of her.

Nicholas put an arm around Royan's shoulders and hustled her down the length of the cavernous cargo hold and into one of the jump seats at the entrance to the cockpit.

'Strap yourself in!' he ordered, and ran up the steps to the cockpit.

'Thought you had decided to stay behind,' Jannie greeted him mildly, without looking up from his controls. 'Hold tight! Here we go.'

Nicholas clung on to the back of the pilot's seat as Jannie and Fred between them pushed forward the bank of throttle levers to full power, and Big Dolly built up speed until she was careering down the strip.

Looking over Jannie's shoulder, Nicholas saw the vague shapes of men in camouflage battledress amongst the thorn scrub at the end of the runway. Some of them were firing at the huge aircraft as it raced towards them.

'Those popguns aren't going to hurt her much,' Jannie grunted. 'Big Dolly is a tough old lady.' And he lifted her into the air.

They flashed over the heads of the enemy troops on the ground, and Jannie set her nose high in the climb attitude.

'Welcome aboard, folks, thank you for flying Africair. Next stop Malta,' Jannie drawled, and then his voice rose sharply, 'Oh, oh! Where did this little piss-cat come from?'

Directly ahead of them the Jet Ranger rose out of the thick scrub on the banks of the Nile. The angle of the helicopter's climb meant that the approaching Hercules was hidden from the pilot's view, and he continued to rise directly into their path.

'Only five hundred feet and a hundred and ten knots on the clock,' Fred shouted a warning at his father from the right-hand seat. 'Too low to turn.'

The Jet Ranger was so close that Nicholas could clearly see Tuma Nogo in the front seat, his spectacles reflecting the sunlight like the eyes of a blind man, and his face freezing into a rictus of terror as he suddenly saw the great machine bearing down on them. At the last possible moment the pilot put his aircraft over in a wild dive to try to clear the nose of the approaching Hercules. It seemed impossible to avoid the collision, but he managed to bank the lighter, more manoeuvrable machine over until it rolled almost on to its back. It slipped under the belly of the Hercules, and the men in the cockpit of Jannie's plane barely felt the light kiss of the two fuselages.

However, the helicopter was flung over on to its nose by the impact, until it was pointing straight down at the earth only four hundred feet below. While Big Dolly flew on, climbing away steadily on an even keel, the pilot of the Jet Ranger struggled to control his crazily plummeting machine. Two hundred feet above the earth the turbulence thrown out astern by the massive T56-A-15 turbo-prop engines of the Hercules, each rated at 4900 horsepower, struck the helicopter with the force of an avalanche.

Like a dead leaf in an autumn gale she was swept away, spinning end over end, and when she struck the ground her own engines were still squealing at full power. On impact the fuselage crumpled like a sheet of aluminium cooking foil, and Nogo was dead even before the fuel tanks exploded and a fireball engulfed the Jet Ranger.

As soon as Jannie reached safe manoeuvring altitude he brought Big Dolly around on her northerly heading, and they could look back over the wing at the Roseires airstrip falling away behind them. The column of black smoke from the burning helicopter was tar-thick as it drifted away on the light westerly wind.

'You did say they were the uglies?' Jannie asked. 'So rather them than us, then?'

nce Jannie had settled Big Dolly on her northerly heading, and they were sailing low over the open deserted Sudanese plains, Nicholas went back into the main hold.

'Let's get the wounded settled down comfortably,' he suggested. Sapper and Royan unbuckled their safety belts and went back with him to attend to the men lying where their litters had been dumped during the haste of the getaway from Roseires.

After a while Nicholas left them to it and went forward to the small, well-stocked galley behind the flight deck. He opened some canned soup and sliced hunks of fresh bread from the loaves he found in the refrigerator. While the tea water boiled, he found his small emergency pack, and took from it the nylon wallet which contained his medicines and drugs. From one of the vials he shook five white tablets into the palm of his hand.

In the galley he crushed the tablets to powder, and when he poured tea into two of the mugs he stirred the powder in with it. Royan had enough English blood in her veins never to be able to refuse a mug of hot tea.

After they had served soup and buttered toast to the wounded men, Royan accepted her mug from Nicholas gratefully. While she and Sapper sipped their tea, Nicholas went back to the flight deck and leaned over the back of Jannie's seat.

'What is our flying time to the Egyptian border?' he asked.

'Four hours twenty minutes,' Jannie told him.

'Is there any way that we can avoid flying into Egyptian air space?' Nicholas wanted to know.

Jannie swivelled around in his seat and stared at him with astonishment. 'I suppose we could make a turn out to the west, through Gadaffiland. Of course, it would mean an extra seven hours' flying time, and we would probably run out of fuel and end up making a forced landing somewhere out there in the Sahara.' He lifted an eyebrow at Nicholas. 'Tell me, my boy, what inspired that stupid question?'

'It was just a rare thought,' Nicholas said.

'Let it be not merely rare, but extinct,' Jannie advised. 'I don't want to hear it asked again, ever.'

Nicholas slapped his shoulder. 'Put it out of your mind.'

When he went back into the main hold, Sapper and Royan were sitting on two of the fold-down bunks that were bolted to the main bulkhead. Royan's empty tea mug stood on the deck at her feet. Nicholas sat down beside her, and she reached up and touched the bloodstained dressing that covered his chin.

'You had better let me see to that.' Her fingers were deft and cool on his hot inflamed skin as she cleaned the stitches with an alcohol

471

swab and then placed a fresh plaster over them. Nicholas felt a strong twinge of guilt as he submitted to her ministrations.

However, it was Sapper who was the first to show the effects of the doped tea. He lay back gently and closed his eyes, then a soft snore vibrated his lips. Minutes later Royan sagged drowsily against Nicholas's shoulder. When she was fast asleep, he let her down gently and lifted her feet up on to the bunk. He spread a rug over her. She did not even stir, and he had a moment's doubt about the strength of the tablets.

Then he kissed her forehead softly. 'How could I ever hate you?' he asked her softly. 'Whatever you did.'

He went into the lavatory and locked the door. He had plenty of time. Sapper and Royan would not wake for hours yet, and Jannie and Fred were happily ensconced on the flight-deck, listening to Dolly Parton tapes on the audio system.

When at last he had finished, Nicholas glanced at his wrist-watch and realized that it had taken him almost two hours. He closed the toilet seat and washed his hands carefully. Then he took one last careful look around the tiny cabin and unlocked the door.

Sapper and Royan were still fast asleep on the fold-down bunks. He went forward to the flight-deck, and Fred pulled his earphones down around his neck and grinned at him.

'Nile water. It's poisonous. You have been locked in the loo for the last couple of hours. Surprised that there is anything left of you.'

Nicholas ignored the jibe and leaned over Jannie's seat back. 'Where are we?'

With a thick forefinger Jannie stabbed the chart that he was balancing on his protruding belly. 'Almost in the clear,' he said complacently. 'Egyptian border in one hour twelve minutes.'

Nicholas remained standing behind his seat until Jannie grunted and lifted the microphone. 'Time to go into my act.'

'Hallo, Abu Simbel Approach!' he said in a Gulf States accent. 'This is Zulu Whiskey Uniform Five Zero Zero.'

There was a long silence from the Egyptian controller. Jannie grunted. 'He probably has a bint in the tower with him. Got to give him time to get his pants back on.'

Abu Simbel Control answered on his fifth call. Jannie launched into his tried and tested routine, feigning ignorance in fluent colloquial Arabic.

After five minutes, Abu Simbel cleared him to continue on north-wards, with an instruction to 'call again abeam Aswan'.

They flew on serenely for another hour, but Nicholas's nerves were screwing up tighter every minute.

Suddenly, without the least warning, there was a silvery flash ahead of them as a fighter interceptor, coming from below them, pulled up steeply across their bows. Jannie shouted with surprise and anger as another two warplanes rocketed up from under them, so close that they were buffeted by the turbulence of their jet trails.

They all recognized the type. They were MiG21 'Fishbeds' sporting the Egyptian air force livery, and with air-to-air missiles hanging in menacing pods under their swept-back wings.

'Unidentified aircraft!' Jannie yelled into his mouthpiece. 'You are on collision course. State your call sign!'

They all craned their necks and stared up through the Perspex canopy over the flight-deck. High above them they could see the three MiG fighters in formation circling against the blue of the African sky.

'ZWU 500. This is Red Leader of the Egyptian people's air force. You will conform to my orders.'

Jannie looked back at Nicholas, his expression forlorn. 'Something has gone wrong here. How the hell did they tumble to us?'

'You'd better do what the man says, Dad,' Fred advised miserably, 'otherwise he is going to blow us all over the sky.'

Jannie shrugged helplessly, and then spoke into his microphone mournfully. 'Red Leader. This is ZWU 500. We will cooperate. Please state your intentions.'

'Your new heading is 053. Execute immediately!'

Jannie brought Big Dolly around into the east and then glanced at his chart.

'Aswan!' he said dolefully. 'The Gyppos are taking us to Aswan. What the hell, I might as well warn Aswan tower that we have wounded on board.'

Nicholas went back to Royan's bunk and shook her awake. She was groggy and unsteady on her feet from the effects of the drug as she staggered to the lavatory. However, when she emerged again ten minutes later her hair was combed and she seemed alert and recovered from the mild draught that she had drunk in her tea.

There was the Nile ahead of them once more, and the town of Aswan on both banks, nestling below the first cataract and the impounded waters of the High Dam. Kitchener's Island swam like a green fish in the middle of the stream.

As the voice of the military controller at the Aswan airfield gave Jannie his orders, Big Dolly settled with unruffled dignity and lined up for the straight-in approach to the tarmac runway. The MiG fighters which had shepherded them in from the desert were no longer visible, but their presence high above was betrayed by their terse radio transmissions as they handed over their captive to the ground control.

473

Big Dolly sailed in over the perimeter fence and touched down, and the voice of the controller ordered them, 'Turn first taxi-way right.'

Jannie obeyed, and as he turned off the main runway there was a small vehicle with a sign on its roof which read, in both English and Arabic, 'FOLLOW ME'.

The vehicle led them to a row of camouflaged concrete hangars in front of which a ground crew in khaki overalls signalled them with paddles into a parking stand. As soon as Jannie applied his brakes and brought Big Dolly to a halt, a file of four armoured half-tracks raced out and surrounded the huge aircraft, training their turret weapons upon her.

Obedient to the instructions radioed by control, Jannie shut down his engines and lowered the tail ramp of the aircraft. No one on the flight-deck had spoken since they had landed. They stood crowded together, looking unhappy, peering out of the cockpit windows.

Suddenly a white Cadillac with an escort of armed motorcyclists, followed by a military ambulance and a three-ton transport truck, drove through the gate of the perimeter fence and came directly to the foot of the cargo ramp of the Hercules. The chauffeur jumped out and opened the door, and his passenger stepped out into the late afternoon sunshine. He was clearly a person of authority, dignified and composed. He wore a light tropical suit and white shoes, a panama hat and dark glasses. As he came up the ramp to where the five of them waited, he was followed by two male secretaries.

He removed his dark glasses and tucked them into his breast pocket. As he recognized Royan he smiled and lifted his hat, 'Dr Al Simma – Royan! You did it. Congratulations!' He took her hand and shook it warmly, not relinquishing his grip as he looked directly at Nicholas.

'You must be Sir Nicholas Quenton-Harper. I have been looking forward to meeting you immensely. Won't you please introduce us, Royan?'

Royan could not meet Nicholas's accusing scrutiny as she said, 'May I present His Excellency, Atalan Abou Sin, Minister of Culture and Tourism in the Egyptian government.'

'You may indeed,' said Nicholas coldly. 'What an unexpected pleasure, Minister.'

'I would like to express the thanks of the President and the people of Egypt for returning to this country these precious relics of our ancient but glorious history.' He made a gesture that encompassed the stack of ammunition crates.

'Please, think nothing of it,' said Nicholas, but he never took his eyes off Royan. She kept her face turned half-away from him.

'On the contrary, we think the world of what you have done, Sir Nicholas.' Abou Sin's smile was charming and urbane. 'We are fully aware of the expense to which you have been put, and we would not want you to be out of pocket in this extraordinarily generous gesture of yours. Dr Al Simma tells me that the expedition to recover these treasures for us has cost you a quarter of a million sterling.' He took an envelope from his inside pocket, and proffered it to Nicholas.

'This is a banker's draft drawn on the Central Bank of Egypt. It is irrevocable, and payable anywhere in the world. It is for the sum of £250,000.'

'Very generous of you, Your Excellency.' Nicholas's voice was heavy with irony as he slipped the envelope into his top pocket. 'I presume this was Dr Al Simma's suggestion?'

'Of course,' beamed Abou Sin. 'Royan holds you in the very highest regard.'

'Does she, now?' Nicholas murmured, still staring at her expressionlessly.

'However, this other small token of our appreciation was the suggestion of the President himself.' The minister snapped his fingers and one of his secretaries stepped forward with a leather-covered medal case, which he opened before he presented it to Abou Sin.

On a bed of red velvet nestled a magnificent decoration, a star encrusted with seed pearls and tiny pavé diamonds. In the centre of the star was a golden lion rampant.

Abou Sin lifted the star from its case and advanced on Nicholas. 'The Order of the Great Lion of Egypt, First Class,' he announced, placing the scarlet ribbon over his head. The star hung resplendent on Nicholas's grubby shirt-front, heavily stained with sweat and dust and Nile mud.

Then the minister stood aside and made a gesture to the army colonel who was standing to attention at the foot of the ramp. Immediately there was an orderly rush of uniformed men up the ramp. The detachment of soldiers obviously had their orders. First they picked up the litters on which the wounded Ethiopians lay.

'I am glad that your pilot had the good sense to radio ahead that you had wounded men on board. Rest assured that they will receive the best care available,' Atalan Abou Sin promised as they were carried down to the waiting ambulance.

Then the soldiers returned and began carrying the ammunition cases down the ramp. They were loaded neatly into the three-tonner. Within ten minutes Big Dolly's hold was bare and empty. A tarpaulin cover was roped down securely over the back of the loaded truck. An escort of heavily armed motorcyclists fell into formation around it, and then, with sirens wailing, the little convoy roared away.

'Well, Sir Nicholas.' Abou Sin held out his hand courteously, and Nicholas took it with an air of resignation. 'I am sorry to have taken you out of your way like this. I know that you will be anxious to continue on your journey, so I will not detain you further. Is there anything I can do for you before you leave? Do you have sufficient fuel?'

Nicholas glanced at Jannie, and he shrugged. 'We have plenty of juice. Thank you, sir.'

Abou Sin turned back to Nicholas, 'We are planning to build a special annexe to the museum at Luxor to house these artefacts of Pharaoh Mamose that you have returned to Egypt. In due course you will be receiving a personal invitation from President Mubarak to attend, as an honoured guest, the opening of that museum. Dr Al Simma, whom I am sure you know has been appointed the new Director of the Department of Antiquities, will be in charge of the museum. I am sure she will be delighted to review the exhibits with you when you come back.'

He bowed to Sapper and the two pilots.

'Go with God,' he said, and went down the ramp. Royan began to follow him, but Nicholas called softly after her.

'Royan!' She froze, and then turned her head slowly and reluctantly to meet his eyes for the first time since they had landed.

'I didn't deserve that,' he said, and then with a stab of emotion he realized that she was weeping softly. Her lips quivered and the tears ran slowly down her cheeks.

'I am sorry, Nicky,' she whispered, 'but you must have known that I am not a thief. It belongs to Egypt, not to us.'

'So everything that I thought there was between us was a lie?' he demanded remorselessly.

'No!' she said. 'I—' and then she broke off without finishing what she was going to say. She ran down the ramp into the sunlight to where the chauffeur was holding the back door of the limousine open for her. She slipped on to the seat beside Abou Sin without looking back, and the Cadillac pulled away and drove through the gate.

'Let's get the hell out of here, before these Gyppos change their minds,' said Jannie.

'What a splendid idea,' said Nicholas bitterly.

Once they were airborne again, Aswan Control cleared them for a direct flight northwards to the Mediterranean coast. The four of them, Jannie and Fred, Sapper and Nicholas, stayed together on the flight-deck and watched the long green snake of the Nile crawl along their right wingtip.

They spoke very little during this long leg of the flight. Once Jannie said quietly, 'So I can kiss my fee goodbye, I suppose?'

'I didn't really come along for the money,' said Sapper, 'but it would have been nice to be paid. Baby needs new shoes.'

'Does anybody want a cup of tea?' Nicholas asked, as though he had not heard.

'That would be nice,' said Jannie. 'Not as nice as the sixty grand that you owe me, but nice anyway.'

They flew over the battlefield of El Alamein, and even from twenty thousand feet they could pick out the twin monuments to the Allied and German dead. Then the blue of the sea stretched ahead of them.

Nicholas waited until the Egyptian coast receded behind them and then he let out a long, soft sigh.

'O, ye of little faith,' he accused them. 'When did I ever let you down? Everybody gets paid in full.'

They all stared at him long and hard, and then Jannie voiced their doubts. 'How?' he asked.

'Give me a hand, Sapper,' Nicholas invited, and started down the staircase. Jannie could not control his curiosity and handed over the controls to Fred. He followed the two Englishmen down to the lavatory on the main deck.

Sapper and Jannie watched from the doorway as Nicholas took the Leatherman tool from his pocket and lifted the cover of the chemical toilet. Jannie grinned as Nicholas started to work on the screws, holding the hidden panel in place. Big Dolly was a smugglers' aircraft, and these little modifications were evidence of the pains that Jannie and Fred had taken to adapt her to that role. There were a number of these hidey-holes cunningly built into the engine housings and other parts of the fuselage.

When they had flown back from Libya, the Hannibal bronzes had reposed in the secret compartment behind this panel. The location of the panel in the back of the toilet made it highly unlikely that any follower of Islam would want to investigate such an unclean area.

'So that's what you were doing in here for so long,' Jannie laughed as Nicholas lifted out the panel. His grin faded as Nicholas reached into the space beyond and carefully drew out an extraordinary object. 'My God, what is that?'

'The blue war crown of ancient Egypt,' said Nicholas. He handed it to Sapper. 'Lay it on the bunk, but treat it carefully.'

He reached into the compartment again, 'And this is the Nemes crown.' He handed it to Jannie.

'And this is the red and white crown of the two kingdoms. And this is the death-mask of Pharaoh Mamose. Last but not least, this is the *ushabti* of the scribe Taita.'

The relics lay on the fold-down bunk, and they stood and stared at them reverently.

'I have helped you bring out stone friezes and little bronze statues,' said Jannie softly. 'But nothing like this before.'

'But,' Sapper shook his head, 'the ammunition crates the Gyppos offloaded at Aswan? What was in them?'

'Five one-gallon bottles of chemical for the toilet,' said Nicholas, 'plus half a dozen spare oxygen cylinders, just to make up weight.'

'You switched them.' Sapper beamed at him. 'But how the hell did you know that Royan was going to scupper us?'

'She was right when she said I must have known she was no thief. The whole lark was out of character for her. She is,' he searched for the correct description, 'much too upright and honest. Not at all like the present company.'

'Thanks for the compliment,' said Jannie drily, 'but she must have given you more reason than that to make you suspicious.'

'Yes, of course.' Nicholas turned to him. 'The first real inkling I had was when we came back from Ethiopia the first time, and she immediately pushed off to Cairo. I guessed she was up to something. But I was absolutely certain only when I learned that she had passed a message, through Tessay, to the Egyptian Embassy in Addis. It was clear then that she had alerted them to our return flight.'

'The perfidious little bitch,' Jannie guffawed.

'Careful there!' said Nicholas stiffly. 'She is a decent, honest and patriotic young woman, warm-hearted and—'

'Well, well!' Jannie winked at Sapper. 'Please excuse my slip.'

Only two of the great crowns of ancient Egypt were set out on the polished walnut conference table. Nicholas had placed them on the heads of two genuine Roman marble busts that he had borrowed from a dealer with whom he did regular business here in Zurich. He had drawn the blinds over the tenth-storey windows, and arranged the lighting to show the crowns to the best effect. The private conference room that he had hired for the occasion was in the Bank Leu building on Bahnhofstrasse.

While he waited alone for the arrival of his invited guest, he reviewed his preparations and could find no fault with them. He went to the full-length mirror on one wall and tightened the knot of his old Sandhurst tie. The stitches had been removed from his chin. Mek Nimmur had done a first-rate job, and the scar was neat and clean. His suit had been made by his tailor in Savile Row, so it was in a muted chalk stripe and had been worn enough to have acquired just the right degree of casual bagginess. The only shiny items of his dress were the hand-made shoes from Lobb of St James's Street.

The intercom buzzed softly and Nicholas lifted the handset.

'There is a Mr Walsh to see you, Sir Nicholas,' said the receptionist at the desk in the bank lobby downstairs.

'Please ask him to come up.'

Nicholas opened the door at the first ring and Walsh glowered at him from the threshold.

'I hope you are not wasting my time, Harper. I have flown all the way from Fort Worth.' It was only thirty hours since Nicholas had telephoned him at his ranch in Texas. Walsh must have jumped into his executive jet almost immediately to have got here so soon.

'Not Harper. Quenton-Harper,' said Nicholas.

'Okay then, Quenton-Harper. But cut the crap,' Walsh said angrily. 'What have you got for me?'

'I am also delighted to see you again, Mr Walsh.' Nicholas stood aside. 'Do come in.'

Walsh strode into the room. He was tall and round-shouldered, his jowls drooping and wrinkled and his nose beaky. With his hands clasped behind his back he looked like a buzzard on a fence pole. *Forbes* magazine listed his net worth at 1.7 billion dollars.

Two men followed him into the room, and Nicholas recognized both of them. The antiquarian world was very small and incestuous. One of them was the professor of ancient history at Dallas University. Walsh had endowed the chair. The other was one of the most respected and knowledgeable antiques dealers in the United States.

Walsh stopped so suddenly that they both ran into him from behind, but he did not seem to notice.

'Son of a gun!' he said softly, and his eyes lit with the flames of fanaticism. 'Are those fakes?'

'As fake as the Hannibal bronzes and the Hammurabi bas-relief you bought from me,' said Nicholas.

Walsh approached the exhibits as though they were the cathedral communion plate and he the archbishop.

'These must be fresh,' he whispered. 'Otherwise I would have known about them.'

'Fresh out of the ground,' Nicholas confirmed. 'You are the first one to have seen them.'

'Mamose!' Walsh read the cartouche on the *uraeus* of the Nemes crown. 'Then the rumours are true. You have opened a new tomb.'

'If you can call nearly four thousand years old new.'

Walsh and his advisers gathered around the table, pale and speechless with shock.

'Leave us, Harper,' said Walsh. 'I will call you when I am ready to talk to you again.'

'Sir Nicholas,' he prompted the American. Nicholas knew that he had the upper hand now.

'Please leave us, Sir Nicholas,' Walsh pleaded.

An hour later Nicholas sauntered back into the conference room. The three men were seated around the table as though they could not bear to be parted from the two great crowns. Walsh nodded at his minions and they stood up and obediently but reluctantly filed from the room.

As soon as the door closed, Walsh asked brusquely, 'How much?'

'Fifteen million US dollars,' Nicholas replied.

'That's seven and a half mill each.'

'No, that's fifteen mill each. Thirty million the two.'

Walsh reeled in his chair. 'Are you crazy, or something?'

'There are those who think so,' Nicholas smiled.

'Split the difference,' said Walsh. 'Twenty-two and a half.'

Nicholas shook his head. 'Not negotiable.'

'Be reasonable, Harper!'

'Reasonability has never been one of my vices. Sorry.'

Walsh stood up. 'I am sorry too. Perhaps next time, Harper.'

He clasped his hands behind his back and stalked to the door. As he opened it, Nicholas called after him.

'Mr Walsh!'

He turned back eagerly. 'Yes?'

'Next time you may call me Nicholas, and I shall call you Peter, as old friends.'

'Is that all you have to say?'

'Of course. What else is there?' Nicholas looked puzzled.

'Damn you,' said Walsh, and came back to the table. He dropped into his chair. 'Damn you to hell and back!'

He sighed and pursed his lips, and then asked, 'Okay. How do you want it?'

'Two irrevocable bank drafts. Each for fifteen million.'

Walsh picked up the intercom, and spoke into it. 'Please ask Monsieur Montfleuri, your chief accountant, to come up here,' he ordered dolefully.

Nicholas sat at his desk in his study at Quenton Park. He stared at the panelling that covered the wall facing him. Although the panelling had originally come from one of the Catholic abbeys dissolved by Henry VIII in 1536 and had been bought by his grandfather almost a hundred years ago, it was newly installed in this setting.

He reached under the top of his desk and pressed the hidden button of the electronic control. A section of the panelling slid smoothly and silently aside to reveal the armoured plate glass of the display cabinet built into the wall behind it. At the same time the spotlights in the ceiling lit automatically, and their beams fell on the contents of the cabinet. The spots had been placed so that there was no reflection from the glass window to distract the eye, and the beams brought out the full glory of the double crown and the golden death-mask of Mamose.

He poured whisky into a crystal glass, and while he sipped it he savoured the thrill of ownership. But after a while he knew there was something missing. He picked up the Taita *ushabti* from the desk in front of him, and spoke to it as though he were addressing the subject himself.

'You knew the real meaning of loneliness, didn't you?' he asked softly. 'You knew what it was like to love someone you could never have.'

He set down the statuette and picked up the telephone. He dialled an international number and it rang three times before a man answered in Arabic.

'This is the office of the Director of Antiquities. How may I help you?'

'Is Dr Al Simma available?' he asked in the same language.

'Please hold the line. I am putting you through!'

'Dr Al Simma.' Her voice sent an electric thrill down his spine.

'Royan,' he said, and he could sense her shock in the long silence that followed.

'You!' she whispered. 'I did not think I would ever hear from you again.'

'I just rang to congratulate you on your appointment.'

'You cheated me,' she said. 'You switched the contents of three of the crates.'

'As a wise man once said, friends are the easiest to cheat – they don't expect it. You, of all people, should know the truth of that, Royan.'

'You have sold them, of course. I have heard a rumour that Peter Walsh paid twenty million.'

'Thirty million,' Nicholas corrected her. 'But only for the blue and the Nemes. Even as I speak to you, the red and white crown and the death-mask repose before me.'

'So now you can pay off your Lloyd's insurance losses. You must be very relieved.'

'You won't believe this, but the Lloyd's syndicate on which I am a Name has come up with much better results than were forecast. I wasn't really broke after all.'

'As my mother would say, "Bully for you."'

'Half of it has already gone to Mek Nimmur and Tessay.'

'At least that is a good cause.' Her tone tingled with hostility. 'Is that all you called to tell me?'

'No. There's something else that might amuse you. Your favourite author, Wilbur Smith, has agreed to write the story of our discovery of the tomb. He is calling the book *The Seventh Scroll*. It should be published early next year. I will send you a signed copy.'

'I hope he gets his facts straight this time,' she said drily.

They were both silent for a while, before Royan broke it. 'I have a mountain of work in front of me. If there is nothing else on your mind—'

'As a matter of fact there is.'

'Yes?'

'I would like you to marry me.'

He heard her draw breath sharply, and then after a long pause she asked softly, 'Why would you want anything so unlikely?'

'Because I have come to realize how much I love you.'

She was silent again, and then she said in a small voice, 'All right.'

'What do you mean, "All right"?'

'I mean, all right, I will marry you.'

'Why would you agree to anything so unlikely?' he asked.

'Because I have come to realize, despite everything, how much I love you back.'

'There is an Air Egypt flight from Heathrow at 5.30 this afternoon. If I drive like fury, I may just make it. But it gets me into Cairo rather late.'

'I will be waiting at the airport, no matter how late.'

'I am on my way!' Nicholas hung up, and went to the door, but suddenly he turned back and picked up the the Taita *ushabti* from the desk.

'Come on, you old rogue.' He laughed triumphantly. 'You are going home, as a wedding gift.'

EPILOGUE

They strolled along the corniche in the mauve evening. Below them the Nile ran on eternally green and slow and inscrutable, disposing of the secrets of the ages. At the point on the river bank, below the ruins of the temple of Ramesses at Luxor, where once the great barge of Pharaoh Mamose had docked with Taita and his beloved mistress upon her prow, they paused for a while and leaned upon the coping of the stone retaining wall. They gazed out to the darkening hills across the river.

Time had long since obliterated the funerary temple and the great causeway of Mamose, and other kings had built their own monuments over the foundations. No man had ever discovered the tomb that he had never occupied, but it must have been situated close to the secret opening in the rock through which Duraid Al Simma had entered the tomb of Lostris and discovered there the scrolls of Taita in their alabaster jars.

All four of them were silent in the gathering dusk, the shared silence of firm friendship. They watched a cruise boat pass, coming upriver with the tourists clustered upon her decks, still agog after ten days of voyaging from Cairo on these enigmatic waters, pointing out to each other the great pylons and engraved walls of Ramesses' temple, their excited voices small and inconsequential in the hush of the desert evening.

Then Royan slipped her arm through Tessay's and the two women walked on ahead. They made a lovely pair, slim and young and honey-skinned, their laughter gay and sweet, their dark heads ruffling in the sultry puffs of Saharan air off the desert. Nicholas and Mek Nimmur followed them, each watching his own woman fondly as they bantered.

'So now you are one of the fatcats in Addis, you, the hard man, the bush fighter, you are now a politician. I can hardly believe it, Mek.'

'There is a time to fight and a time to make peace.' Mek was serious for a moment, but Nicholas mocked him lightly.

'I see that now that you are a politician you have to practise your clichés and your platitudes.' Nicholas punched his arm lightly. 'But how did you swing it, Mek? From dirty *shufta* bandit to Minister of Defence in one mighty bound.'

'The money from the sale of the blue crown helped a little. It gave me the clout I needed,' Mek admitted, 'but they knew they could never hold a democratic election without me as a candidate. In the end they were eager to have me on board.'

'The only quibble I have with the deal is that you handed all that lovely hard-won lolly over to them,' Nicholas mourned. 'Hell, Mek, fifteen million iron men don't come along every day.'

'I didn't hand it to them,' Mek corrected him. 'It was paid into the state coffers, where I can keep an eye on what eventually happens to it.'

'Still, fifteen mill is a lot of bread,' Nicholas sighed. 'Try as I might, I cannot approve of such extravagance, but I must admit that I do approve of your choice of running mate in your bid for the Presidency in the coming elections.'

They both looked at Tessay's slim back and bush of springing black curls as she strode along ahead of them on shapely brown legs under the white skirt.

'I may not approve of you as Minister of Defence, but I can see that she makes a very charming Minister of Culture and Tourism in the interim government.'

'She will make an even more impressive Vice-President when we win next August,' Mek predicted easily, and at that moment Royan looked back over her shoulder at them.

'We'll cross the road here,' she called. Nicholas had been so engrossed that he had not realized they had come up opposite to the new annexe to the Luxor Museum of Antiquities. The two women waited for them to catch up and then they separated and each of them took the arm of her own husband.

As they crossed the wide boulevard, threading their way between the slow clip-clopping horse-drawn gharries, Nicholas leaned down and brushed her cheek with his lips. 'You are really quite delectable, Lady Quenton-Harper.'

'You make me blush, Sir Nicky,' she giggled. 'You know that I am still not used to being called that.'

They reached the other side of the thoroughfare and paused before the entrance to the museum annexe. The sloping roof was supported by tall hypostyle columns, miniature copies of those at the temple of Karnak. The walls were made of massive blocks of yellow sandstone, and the lines of the building were clean and simple. It was very impressive.

Royan led them to the entrance doors of the museum, which was not yet open to the public. The President was flying up on Monday for the official opening, and Mek and Tessay were to be the official representatives of the Ethiopian government at the opening ceremony. The guards at the door saluted Royan respectfully and hurried to open the heavy brass-bound doors to let them pass.

The interior was hushed and cool, the air conditioning carefully regulated to preserve the ancient exhibits. The display cases were built into the sandstone walls, and the lighting was subtle and artful. It showed off the wondrous treasures of the Mamose funerary hoard to full advantage. The exhibits, arranged in ascending order of beauty and archaeological importance, sparkled and glowed in their nests of blue satin, the royal blue of the Pharaoh Mamose.

The four visitors were quiet and reverential as they passed, their voices soft and subdued as they asked questions of Royan. Wonder and amazement held them enthralled. They paused at the entrance of the final chamber, the one that housed the most extraordinary and valuable items in this glittering collection.

'To think that this is only a small part of what treasure still remains in Mamose's tomb, sealed by the waters of the Dandera river,' whispered Tessay. 'It's so exciting that I can hardly wait for the adventure to continue.'

'I forgot to tell you!' Mek exclaimed, and it was clear from his triumphant grin that he had not forgotten at all, but had been merely waiting for the appropriate moment to impart his news. 'The Smithsonian have confirmed their grant to redam the Dandera and reopen the tomb. It will be a joint venture between the Institution and the governments of our two countries, Egypt and Ethiopia.'

'That is wonderful news,' Royan exclaimed delightedly. 'The tomb itself will be one of the great archaeological sites of the world, and a huge source of tourist revenue for Ethiopia—'

'Not so fast,' Mek interrupted her. 'There is one condition that they stipulate.'

Royan looked crestfallen. 'What is their condition?'

'They insist that you, Royan, take on the job of director of the project.'

She clapped her hands with delight, and then put on a mock-serious expression. 'However, I have my own condition before I accept,' she said.

'And what is that?' Mek demanded.

'That I am able to appoint my own assistant on the dig.'

Mek let out a roar of laughter. 'We all know who that will be.' And he clapped Nicholas on the back. 'Just make sure that none of the artefacts cling to his sticky little fingers!' he warned.

Royan hugged Nicholas around the waist. 'He has completely reformed, I will now give you final proof of that.' Still clinging to her husband, she led them into the last chamber.

Mek and Tessay stopped in the entrance, silent with awe as they stared at the contents of the free-standing display case of armoured glass in the centre of the room. The red and white crown of the united kingdoms of upper and lower Egypt stood side by side with the glistening golden death-mask of Pharaoh Mamose in the brilliant light of the overhead spotlights.

At last Mek Nimmur recovered from the shock. Advancing slowly to the front panel of the display case, he stooped to read aloud the brass plate fixed to the front of it: '*"The permanent loan of Sir Nicholas and Lady Quenton-Harper."*'

He turned back to stare at Nicholas incredulously. 'And you were the one who picked on me for turning over the money from the sale of the blue crown!' he accused him. 'How could you bring yourself to give up your share of the loot, Nicholas?'

'It wasn't easy,' Nicholas admitted with a sigh, 'but I was faced with a delicate ultimatum from a certain party who is not standing a million miles away from us at this very moment.'

'Don't feel too sorry for the poor boy,' Royan laughed. 'He still has a big lump of Peter Walsh's money tucked away in Switzerland, the proceeds of the sale of the Nemes crown. I was unable to talk him into handing everything over.'

'Enough of these public disclosures of my domestic affairs,' said Nicholas firmly. 'The sun is long gone, and it's whisky time. I think I saw a bottle of Laphroaig behind the bar at the hotel. Let's go and find out if I was mistaken.'

He took Royan's arm and led her away, and the other two followed closely, laughing delightedly at his discomfort.

DOWN

WITH

BIG

BROTHER

DOWN WITH BIG BROTHER

The Fall of the Soviet Empire

MICHAEL DOBBS

Alfred A. Knopf New York 1997

THIS IS A BORZOI BOOK
PUBLISHED BY ALFRED A. KNOPF, INC.

http://www.randomhouse.com/

This publication was prepared in part under a grant from
the Kennan Institute for Advanced Russian Studies of the
Woodrow Wilson International Center for Scholars,
Washington, D.C. The statements and views expressed
herein are those of the author and are not necessarily those
of the Wilson Center.

Library of Congress Cataloging-in-Publication Data
Dobbs, Michael.
Down with Big Brother : the fall of the Soviet empire / by
Michael Dobbs. — 1st ed.
p.   cm.
Includes bibliographical references and index.
ISBN 0-679-43179-9 (hardcover : alk. paper)
1. Soviet Union—Politics and government—1953–1985.
2. Soviet Union—Politics and government—1985–1991.
I. Title.
DK274.D63   1997
947.084—dc20   96-21607   CIP

Manufactured in the United States of America

First Edition

FOR LISA

His eyes refocussed on the page. He discovered that while he sat helplessly musing he had also been writing, as though by automatic action. And it was no longer the same cramped awkward handwriting as before. His pen had slid voluptuously over the smooth paper, printing in large neat capitals—

DOWN WITH BIG BROTHER
DOWN WITH BIG BROTHER
DOWN WITH BIG BROTHER
DOWN WITH BIG BROTHER
DOWN WITH BIG BROTHER

over and over again, filling half a page.

George Orwell, *1984*

CONTENTS

ACKNOWLEDGMENTS

THIS BOOK IS THE OUTCOME of reporting tours in Yugoslavia, Poland, and the Soviet Union between 1977 and 1993. But my interest in the former Communist world goes back long before that. I was eight weeks old when I first went to Russia, courtesy of my parents, Joseph and Marie Dobbs, who had met at the British embassy in Moscow in 1948. I was to visit Russia, in one capacity or another, under all Russian leaders from Stalin to Yeltsin. When I went to work in Yugoslavia and Poland, I was also following in the footsteps of my peripatetic parents. I therefore have them primarily to thank for ushering me into the shadow of Big Brother and getting me to write about the experience.

While gathering material for this book, I have benefited from the stimulating conversation and hospitality of friends, colleagues, and sources in many different countries. I mention many of these sources in the endnotes, but I would particularly like to thank a few people who assisted directly in my research. In common with other *Washington Post* reporters in Moscow, I was fortunate to be able to draw on the advice and assistance of Masha Lipman, a talented Russian journalist who has gone on to become managing editor of the news magazine *Itogi*. Here in Washington, I would like to thank two research associates, Brian Sloyer and Marian Alves, who spent long

hours at the Library of Congress on my behalf. I am also indebted to Mark Kramer, of Harvard University, who supplied me with many interesting documents from Soviet and East European archives.

My agent, Rafe Sagalyn, and my editor at Knopf, Ashbel Green, played key roles in encouraging me to write this book and shepherding it to completion. Other people who made helpful comments on the manuscript were Jeff Frank, now with *The New Yorker*, my former Moscow colleague Fred Hiatt, and David Brown, a medical reporter for the *Post*. Responsibility for any remaining errors rests with me. I would also like to thank Don Oberdorfer, a former diplomatic reporter for the *Post* and author of *The Turn*, for making available the transcripts of two Princeton University conferences on the end of the Cold War. These proved very helpful.

The collapse of communism was one of the great news stories of the twentieth century. I will always be grateful to the editors of the *Washington Post,* particularly Jim Hoagland and Michael Getler, for assigning me to cover many of its most dramatic episodes, beginning with the Polish labor unrest of August 1980. My understanding of the story was greatly enriched by talks with present and former *Post* reporters, including Bradley Graham, Jackson Diehl, Robert Kaiser, Dusko Doder, Celestine Bohlen, Gary Lee, Fred Hiatt, Margaret Shapiro, David Hoffman, Lee Hockstader, Dan Southerland, Blaine Harden, Mary Battiata, John Pomfret, Christine Spolar, and especially David Remnick. Nobody could wish for better colleagues.

I am happy to acknowledge the support of the Kennan Institute for Advanced Russian Studies of the Woodrow Wilson International Center for Scholars in Washington, D.C. The Kennan Institute provided me with both a fellowship and a congenial place to work, when I returned to Washington from Moscow in August 1993.

Most of all, I am grateful to my family for sharing in my adventures and putting up with my frequent absences. My wife, Lisa, has been my most attentive reader and perceptive critic. My children, Alex, Olivia, and Joseph, are not quite sure what communism was all about, but they know that it took up a lot of their father's time, long after it had been pronounced dead and buried. One day, they will read this book and understand what those tanks were doing roaring past our front entrance on August 19, 1991.

PREFACE

THE HAULING DOWN OF THE RED FLAG from the Kremlin at 7:35 p.m. on December 25, 1991, marked the end of the Soviet era, as surely as the storming of the Winter Palace in St. Petersburg on November 7, 1917, marked its beginning. But who can say, for certain, when the collapse of communism began?

One possible starting point for the story might be April 26, 1986, when the explosion at the Chernobyl nuclear power station demonstrated the technological incompetence of the Soviet regime. Another is March 11, 1985, when the fifty-four-year-old Mikhail Gorbachev was elected general secretary of the Soviet Communist Party. There are good arguments to be made in favor of August 31, 1980, when a Communist government formally surrendered the right to represent its own working class to an independent trade union. Or you could go all the way back to the death of Josef Stalin on March 5, 1953. After Nikita Khrushchev started destroying the reputation of the "Greatest Genius of All Times and Peoples," belief in a Communist utopia gradually waned.

For me personally, the anti-Bolshevik revolution began on May 8, 1980. This was the day I got my first close-up look at the guardians of Stalin's legacy. My only previous view of these men had been from a distance,

through the prism of a propaganda machine that depicted them as the exalted representatives of an infallible party, chosen by history to implement the will of the masses. Viewed up close, I was reminded of Hannah Arendt's phrase about the leaders of the Third Reich: the "banality of evil." The aura of bureaucratic anonymity—the ultimate source of their authority—was shattered.

I was living in Belgrade at the time. Josip Broz Tito, the father of Communist Yugoslavia and the last surviving legendary figure from World War II, had just died. On the day of the funeral, the Yugoslav capital was awash with foreign dignitaries. With the exception of President Carter, who did not wish to be seen shaking hands with Leonid Brezhnev less than five months after the Soviet invasion of Afghanistan, anybody who was anybody was there. The Soviet bloc sent its top leaders. The mourners included a Communist demigod, Kim Il Sung of North Korea, and one of the great mass murderers of the twentieth century, Pol Pot of Cambodia.

Through a security lapse, I managed to gate-crash the VIP enclosure on the strength of a simple press pass. For the next half-hour I was able to chat and mingle with the assembled high priests of Marxism-Leninism. There, in one corner of the VIP pen, stood the builder of the Berlin Wall and the undertaker of the Prague Spring, exchanging pleasantries, two cogs in a vast machinery of state repression. A few feet away, the president of Bulgaria was fussing over his fellow dignitaries, like some overeager waiter, desperate to please. While standing in line to view Tito's coffin, I found myself gazing into the dull, evil-looking eyes of the self-styled "Genius of the Carpathians." Nicolae Ceaușescu of Romania had one of the most unpleasant faces I have ever seen: deep, black lines around a long, pointed nose; a high forehead; crinkly gray hair. As a general rule, the more grotesque the personality cult surrounding this or that "Great Leader," the more mediocre its beneficiary turned out to be.

Seated in the middle of the gathering, like a medieval emperor receiving the homage of his vassals, was Big Brother himself. Leonid Brezhnev seemed to have trouble focusing on events around him. His face was bloated. He clung to Andrei Gromyko, his indispensable foreign minister, like a child clings to his nanny. "Where's Andrei Andreyevich," he murmured, in apparent panic, when Gromyko disappeared for a few seconds. He was surrounded by sycophants. "I want to thank you for your work for peace," fawned the president of Bangladesh, almost groveling on the red carpet. Brezhnev lifted his vast eyebrows. "We try our hardest," he croaked. "We are ready for anything in the struggle for peace."

At midday, the city of 1.5 million people fell silent in tribute to the man who had ruled Yugoslavia since 1945. All that could be heard in the normally noisy city were the chimes of clocks and the chirping of birds. Then, equally suddenly, the silence was interrupted by the wailing of factory sirens and the horns of ships on the nearby Danube and Sava rivers. A military band struck up a slow funeral march. Eight generals appeared on the steps of the Yugoslav parliament building, carrying the numerous medals of their commander in chief. The coffin itself was escorted by Tito's political heirs, the eight members of the new collective presidency, representing the ethnically diverse components of the Yugoslav federation. Vain to the end, Tito had decided that no single individual could possibly take his place. Instead, he was to be succeeded by a committee, each of whose members had a veto over the actions of all the others. It was a recipe first for paralysis, later for civil war.

When the procession reached Tito's residence, on a hill overlooking the Sava, the band began playing the "Internationale," the anthem of the worldwide Communist movement. The coffin was lowered into the vault, to be sealed with a marble slab inscribed with gold lettering, JOSIP BROZ TITO 1892–1980. The nonentities of the collective presidency shuffled self-importantly past. They were followed by kings and princes, presidents and prime ministers, Communist Party secretaries and Third World dictators—pillars of a seemingly permanent world order that was about to crumble.

BEFORE 1980, reporting from the Communist world had been an introverted pursuit. Our sources of information were limited to Western diplomats, official propagandists, a handful of brave dissidents. To hold an honest conversation with an ordinary person was practically impossible. Factories were completely off-limits, unless you were accompanied by a government chaperone. Censorship was so tight that we usually never heard of protests until they were long over. Our job was to put together a coherent picture of an entire society on the basis of isolated scraps of information. It was like a gigantic jigsaw puzzle, with hundreds of missing pieces.

This sedentary way of life disappeared virtually overnight. Within a few months of running into Poland's Edward Gierek at Tito's funeral, I was filing dispatches on his overthrow. Soon, I found myself covering strikes, hunger marches, coups, wars, and the remaking of the map of Europe. As a reporter from the *Washington Post,* first in Eastern Europe and then in the Soviet Union, I had a grandstand view of the "decade that shook the

world." Indeed, in a minor way, my colleagues and I became part of the revolution. Our reports were beamed back into the Soviet bloc by Western radio stations, breaking the information monopoly of one-party regimes.

My travels around the disintegrating Communist world took me from the Berlin Wall to Tiananmen Square, from tropical Nicaragua to the windswept island of Sakhalin. I visited places I had never dreamed of visiting, from a freezing orphanage in Bucharest to the inner corridors of Kremlin power. I wandered around KGB headquarters in Moscow, inspected the sites of nuclear explosions, and walked through the ruins of once graceful towns like Tbilisi and Vukovar. I was fortunate enough to meet most of the principal actors in the fall of communism, from Andrei Sakharov to Mikhail Gorbachev. I was the first Western journalist to be admitted to the Lenin shipyard in Gdańsk during the great strike of August 1980 by a then unknown Lech Wałęsa. A decade later, when Boris Yeltsin jumped on the tank outside the Russian parliament to rally resistance to an abortive Communist coup, I was in the crowd of one hundred or so Muscovites standing right in front of him.

The unraveling of the Communist empire was a great human drama, as great a drama in its own way as the original Bolshevik revolution. It changed the lives of millions of people, including many who had never lived in a Communist country but who had been touched by the Cold War. Some were inspired to acts of greatness; others were driven to their deaths. In the space of a decade, playwrights and electricians were magically transformed into presidents, dissidents into prime ministers, Marxists into nationalists, and general secretaries into jailbirds. Strategic assumptions that had shaped the thinking of a generation of diplomats and politicians were turned upside down. A superpower disappeared, and twenty new nation-states joined the United Nations. The familiar and seemingly petrified Cold War world—the world of Checkpoint Charlie and Dr. Strangelove—vanished forever.

JUST AS COMMUNISM cast a long shadow over the twentieth century, the consequences of the failed experiment in utopia will be felt well into the next century. Many of the disaster scenarios that could threaten the future of humankind—nuclear blackmail, environmental catastrophe, a large-scale war, the rise of a Mafia state—originate in the former Communist world. Integrating the post-Communist societies into the modern world is perhaps the biggest challenge facing the international community today.

In order to deal with this challenge, we must first understand how it

arose. The convulsions that have swept Eastern Europe and the former Soviet Union reflect the disintegration of a totalitarian ideology. The explosion of primitive nationalism has its roots in attempts by the old nomenklatura to preserve its power and privileges. The halting nature of economic reform in Russia is due, in large measure, to the inefficient structure of the Soviet economy, with the military-industrial complex grabbing the lion's share of the nation's resources. The cutthroat capitalism and Mafia-like mentality of the new bourgeoisie can be traced back to the systemic corruption of the Communist regime.

It will take the passing of at least one generation, and possibly two or three, to exorcise the ghosts of totalitarian rule. The rivers and steppes of the vast Eurasian landmass will be poisoned for decades from the fallout of nuclear accidents caused by the arbitrary and irresponsible decisions of Communist leaders. The Berlin Wall was breached in a single day, but many years will go by before East Europeans are accepted as citizens of the new Europe. Tens of thousands of Romanian orphans—the product of Ceauşescu's bizarre social policies—will grow up physically and intellectually stunted. Ethnic wars between Serbs and Croats, Armenians and Azerbaijanis, Russians and Chechens, will provide the fuel for massacres and countermassacres for many generations.

Big Brother may be dead, but the specter of communism will continue to haunt us for decades to come.

I

REVOLT

OF THE PROLES

If there was hope, it lay in the proles.

George Orwell, *1984*

*The march of freedom and democracy will leave Marxism-
Leninism on the ash heap of history.*

Ronald Reagan

ZARECHE

December 26, 1979

THE BLACK ZIL LIMOUSINES raced over the ice-bound Moskva River, past the pompous wedding-cake structure of the Ukraine Hotel, and down the rectilinear expanse of Kutuzov Avenue. Bundled up in long winter coats as protection against fifteen degrees of frost, militiamen ordered motorists to the side of the road with frantic waves of their white nightsticks. Plain-clothes agents loitered along the sidewalk, scanning the crowd for signs of suspicious activity. Tightly drawn white curtains and tons of bulletproof armor shielded the occupants of the speeding Zils from the curious stares of pedestrians, picking their way through the gray-brown sludge of the dreary Moscow winter.[1]

As members of the Politburo of the Central Committee of the Soviet Communist Party, the men inside the curtained limousines belonged to the Kremlin's inner elite. Their expressionless faces stared down from hoardings all across the Soviet Union. Their turgid speeches filled bookstores from Kaliningrad to Khabarovsk. Their physical needs were satisfied by the Ninth Directorate of the KGB security police, which supplied them with everything from country houses and pornographic movies to tailor-made suits and topflight medical attention. Cosseted by a powerful propaganda machine and a ubiquitous security apparatus, they were insulated from the

kind of pressures Western politicians deal with every day: public opinion polls, protest demonstrations, a hostile press. They were the faceless representatives of an infallible party.

The lights were green all down Kutuzov Avenue, one of a dozen highways that radiate outward from the Kremlin. Designed by Stalin as a grand entrance into the Soviet capital, with luxury apartment buildings for senior party officials on either side, Kutuzov Avenue led direct to Minsk, Warsaw, and Berlin. It was along this route that both Napoleon and Hitler had invaded Russia, losing everything in a fateful gamble with the vastness of the Russian landscape and the harshness of the Russian winter. The Zils and their police escort vehicles hugged the crest of the road, traveling at eighty miles an hour in the lane permanently reserved for the "big pine cones," *shiski*, as Muscovites referred to their leaders. A few hundred yards after the Triumphal Arch, commemorating Napoleon's defeat at the hands of General Kutuzov in 1812, the motorcade reached the city limits.

During the seventies the Soviet capital had grown to engulf vast tracts of surrounding pine forest. The city had expanded in all directions except one: westward, along the meandering Moskva River. Here, hidden among gentle hills, billowing birch trees, and picture book villages, was the playground of the ruling class. In the elaborate reward-and-punishment system devised by Stalin for maintaining control over his labyrinthine bureaucracy, there was no greater prize than a country house in this bucolic setting. For the Soviet elite—government ministers to nuclear scientists to prima ballerinas to army generals—a dacha was not only a place of rest but a form of escape from the oppressive atmosphere of the capital, with its noxious pollution and paranoid sense of being under constant surveillance.

The line of Zils turned left off the highway, ignoring several No Entry signs, onto an immaculately maintained country road that disappeared into the snow-covered forest. The motorcade traveled along the bank of the ice-bound Setun River and entered a private estate, surrounded by a ten-foot-high green wooden fence. Some twenty minutes after leaving the center of Moscow, the Zils pulled up in front of a mock neoclassical palace. Decorated in the ornate bourgeois style favored by Soviet leaders, it looked like a cross between an office building and a museum. The complex boasted indoor and outdoor swimming pools, tennis courts, and a private movie theater.[2]

The inhabitants of the curtained limousines had come to inform the general secretary of the Central Committee of the Soviet Communist Party of the final plans for the invasion of Afghanistan.

IT WAS DIFFICULT to tell it now, as one looked at his puffy face, parchment-colored skin, and dull, lifeless eyes, but Leonid Ilyich Brezhnev had once been a vigorous and gregarious politician. He had received little formal education. In fact, he had scarcely read a book in his life. Outside politics, his main interests were hunting, driving fast cars, and watching ice hockey games on television. He showed little enthusiasm for paperwork and was a poor public speaker. But in the Bolshevik phrase, he was "good with cadres." He took care of his own. His intellectual limitations had been outweighed by a remarkable instinct for the uses of power and patronage and a talent for forming alliances with his fellow apparatchiks. His intuitive sense of whom to flatter, whom to manipulate, whom to bribe, and, when necessary, whom to trample underfoot had taken him to the highest rungs of the Soviet bureaucracy.

His Politburo colleagues had consistently underestimated him. One of the main reasons why they had elected him general secretary to replace the disgraced Nikita Khrushchev in 1964 was that they were sick of strong, charismatic leaders. They wanted a malleable stopgap, and Brezhnev—nicknamed "the ballerina" because of his ability to change positions in line with prevailing opinion—seemed to fit the bill. They were correct in thinking that the new leader would be more easygoing than Khrushchev and would put an end to the upheavals that had shaken the party apparatus. But they seriously misjudged his staying power. Brezhnev had outlasted, and outmaneuvered, them all.

As he entered the sixteenth year of his reign, Brezhnev was a mixture of Communist demigod and national buffoon. The personality cult surrounding the general secretary, or *gensek*, had reached ludicrous proportions. Not content with depicting the doddering seventy-three-year-old leader as a wise and far-seeing statesman, the official media also presented him as a brilliant military strategist, a distinguished man of letters, and an outstanding contemporary thinker. "From Ilyich to Ilyich," shouted the propaganda posters, a slogan intended to compare Brezhnev with Vladimir Ilyich Lenin, the founder of the Soviet state. He was the proud holder of Party Card No. 000002. (Card No. 000001 was reserved for the dead Lenin.)

The more infirm and senile Brezhnev became, the more honors and accolades he received. By the end of his life he had accumulated more awards than Lenin, Stalin, and Khrushchev combined. Soviet history books had been rewritten to transform his undistinguished wartime exploits into a de-

cisive contribution to the defeat of Nazi Germany. His boastful ghostwritten reminiscences about World War II, *Malaya Zemlya* (Little Land), had been acclaimed a literary masterpiece by Soviet critics and printed in millions of copies. They were read out on radio and television, serialized in magazines, and "studied" in schools and party meetings.

All this was the cause of great ridicule among ordinary Soviet citizens. In public they joined in the officially orchestrated adulation of the general secretary, adopting resolutions to support his political initiatives and holding ceremonies to celebrate his birthday. In the privacy of their own homes they joked about his poor Russian and his narcissistic habits. After the publication of his memoirs in 1978, the villagers of Zareche began referring to the walled-in Brezhnev compound as Malaya Zemlya.[3]

Although his sayings and doings filled the front pages of Soviet newspapers, Brezhnev usually worked for no more than one or two hours a day. By the late seventies he was barely able to look after himself, let alone the affairs of a mighty superpower. Politburo meetings had been reduced to fifteen or twenty minutes. The general secretary rarely visited his Moscow apartment or his Kremlin office. He spent weeks at a time cooped up in the Zareche dacha or his favorite hunting lodge at Zavidovo, at the confluence of the Volga and Moskva rivers. Family life had become a burden to him. His tearaway daughter, Galina, had scandalized Moscow by her luxurious lifestyle and affairs with shady circus performers. His son-in-law, Yuri Churbanov, had become a front man for the Uzbek cotton Mafia. Brezhnev would shut himself up for hours in his study with his personal bodyguard, an old wartime buddy named Aleksandr Ryabenko, playing checkers or dominoes.

Brezhnev's true state of health was one of the Kremlin's most closely guarded secrets. It was clear to anyone who observed his stumbling gait, slurred speech, and vacant expression that he was a chronic invalid. But the extent of his physical and mental ailments was known only to three or four senior Politburo members and a handful of doctors, bodyguards, and relatives. The truth was that the world's largest country had been without an effective ruler since at least 1974, when the general secretary suffered a series of mild strokes caused by the medical condition known as arteriosclerosis of the brain.[4]

As the arteries of Brezhnev's brain hardened and became clogged, he lost control over many of his physical functions. Doctors observed a shocking, apparently irreversible change in their patient's personality, caused by the devastation of the central nervous system. Once jocular and unassuming, he

had lost the ability to view his own actions with a critical eye. At times he experienced fits of deep depression and burst into tears for the most trivial reason. At others he would have delusions of grandeur, reading aloud the obsequious articles about himself in the state-controlled press. He insisted on driving fast cars long after he had slipped into his second childhood. There were several occasions when he nearly killed himself and his terrified security guards by steering his limousine too closely to a cliff on the winding mountainous roads of Crimea, where he had a summer residence.[5] His vanity was fed by a retinue of sycophants, always ready to assure him that he was a superb driver, in addition to being the beloved father of the Soviet people.

What would normally have been a serious but possibly treatable illness had been greatly complicated by an addiction to sleeping pills and prescription drugs. Brezhnev had long suffered from chronic insomnia. His aides and cronies slipped him powerful tranquilizers, which he often washed down with his favorite vodka, Zubrovka. During the mid-seventies he had formed a doting relationship with a KGB nurse, who supplied him with a steady stream of pills without the knowledge of his doctors. The depressants had the effect of further weakening his nervous system, making him listless and inert and contributing to his symptoms of dementia. This in turn further aggravated his insomnia. It was a vicious cycle. One crisis followed another.

In an attempt to save the general secretary from himself, his doctors and bodyguards frequently resorted to petty deceit. They diluted the Zubrovka with boiled water, causing Brezhnev to look suspiciously at his glass and complain, "There's something about this vodka that's not quite right." On other occasions they gave him blank sleeping pills. The problem with this trick was that Brezhnev was unable to distinguish the real pills from the fake ones. Desperate to get to sleep, he would swallow increasingly large numbers of pills. The bodyguards worried that he might end up killing himself.[6]

Enormous effort went into preparing his public appearances. Special escalators were invented to permit the *gensek* to climb the steps of the Lenin Mausoleum in Red Square and his personal airplane. Politburo speechwriters were instructed to avoid the use of certain long words that he had difficulty pronouncing. Teams of resuscitation specialists accompanied him wherever he went. Special medical facilities were installed wherever he stayed. Doctors were under strict orders to do everything in their power to make sure that Brezhnev fulfilled his ceremonial obligations. The head of the Kremlin medical service, Yevgeny Chazov, later complained that the at-

tempt to camouflage the leader's true state of health was not only "hypo-critical" but also "sadistic."[7]

When Brezhnev gave a speech, his doctors never knew whether he would make it back from the podium. In October 1979, Chazov had accompanied his patient to ceremonies marking the thirtieth anniversary of the foundation of the German Democratic Republic. The trip almost ended in disaster after Brezhnev suffered an attack of chronic fatigue, losing sensation in his legs. An hour before a special session of the East German parliament body-guards carried the general secretary out of his residence. When the time came for him to make his speech, he was unable to move from his chair. Chazov sat horrified in the corner of the hall as the Polish and East German leaders, Edward Gierek and Erich Honecker, gripped their Soviet comrade by the elbows and frog-marched him to the lectern. Miraculously Brezhnev managed to wheeze his way through his thirty-five-minute speech without alerting Western reporters to his true condition.[8]

When it was all over, the Soviet Foreign Ministry lodged a formal protest with Poland over Gierek's "unfriendly gesture" in assisting Brezhnev to the lectern of the East German parliament. According to the Soviet démarche, the gesture had created the erroneous impression that Comrade Brezhnev was "infirm." Chazov later wrote that "gratitude" would have been more in order. "I am not convinced that Brezhnev would have been able to get up from his chair at all without outside help."[9]

BORN IN 1906, Brezhnev had watched Russia transform itself from a weak, practically defenseless country into a mighty superpower, feared and respected throughout the world. Soon after coming to power in 1917, the Bolsheviks had been forced to surrender territories containing one-third of Russia's urban population to Germany under the Treaty of Brest-Litovsk. By 1945 not only had they reconquered all the land they had lost, they had gained control over a vast chunk of Central and Eastern Europe. Victory in World War II had brought a five-hundred-mile buffer zone around the western fringes of the Slavic heartland. For Brezhnev and his colleagues, the true western border of the Soviet Union was now represented by the Elbe River, where Russian and American soldiers had linked up following the victory over the Third Reich. It was an empire that exceeded the wildest dreams of the tsars.

The Soviet empire was shaped in the form of concentric circles, radiating outward from Mother Russia. The "inner empire" was made up of nations,

such as Ukrainians, Georgians, Balts, Uzbeks, Kazakhs, and Armenians, that had all been incorporated into the Soviet Union proper. The next circle consisted of the "People's Democracies" of Eastern Europe, such as Poland, East Germany, and Hungary. The "outer empire" included Third World countries, like Nicaragua, Angola, and Afghanistan, that had shaken themselves free from the shackles of imperialism but had not yet reached the stage of "real socialism." In the last decade alone Marxist-Leninist parties had seized power in more than a dozen such countries, causing analysts in both Moscow and Washington to conclude that the worldwide "correlation of forces" was moving inexorably in favor of socialism.

Strategically, too, the global balance of power seemed to be shifting in favor of Moscow. During the past two decades the Soviet Union had embarked on a huge military buildup. From a position of clear inferiority when Brezhnev came to power, it had become the geostrategic equal of the United States. In some areas, such as tanks and heavy land-based missiles, it enjoyed a significant advantage. Six thousand long-range nuclear warheads were on permanent standby, ready to obliterate Washington and Chicago, New York and Los Angeles, at the touch of a button. Hundreds more medium-range missiles were targeted on West European cities, such as London, Frankfurt, and Paris.

Brezhnev regarded it as his duty to defend this legacy and pass it on intact to his successors. He based his actions on the tsarist principle that territory gained must never be surrendered. Translated into the wooden terminology of scientific socialism, the tsarist insistence on never taking a step back was known as the "irreversibility of history." Once a country had progressed from one stage of history to another—from feudalism to capitalism or from capitalism to socialism—there was no turning back. To countenance the possibility of a regression from socialism to capitalism was to question the whole basis of Marxist dialectics.

In private Brezhnev could be brutally frank about Soviet foreign policy goals. When Alexander Dubček and the other Czechoslovak reformers were kidnapped and brought to Moscow in August 1968, following the Soviet invasion of their country, the Soviet leader gave them a harsh lesson in realpolitik. "The results of the Second World War," he told Dubček, "are inviolable, and we will defend them even at the cost of risking a new war."[10]

A decade after the crushing of the Czechoslovak experiment in "socialism with a human face," the Soviet regime appeared both unchanging and unchangeable. There was a similar immutable quality about international affairs. The world seemed permanently split into two, ideologically opposed

camps. Restrained by a balance of nuclear terror, neither side possessed the means to secure victory over the other.

In reality, the state of Soviet society and economy was more brittle than practically anyone imagined. With his vacant gaze and shuffling walk, Brezhnev was the public face of a vast multinational empire already sinking into irreversible decline. By the fall of 1979 the Soviet Union had become a sclerotic giant. Its bureaucratic arteries had shriveled and hardened. Years of ideological indoctrination, or, more simply, years of lies, had produced an atmosphere of total cynicism. Edicts were issued from the center and promptly forgotten; grandiose projects were announced and never completed; statistics had ceased to have any meaning. In the surrealistic atmosphere of the late Brezhnev era, the government allocated billions of rubles to building imaginary factories and nonexistent railway lines. Years later it was discovered that the leaders of the Central Asian republic of Uzbekistan had been routinely reporting a fictitious cotton crop to Moscow and distributing the receipts among themselves.

Even the military-industrial complex—the leadership's number one priority—was not immune from the ills afflicting the rest of the economy. The Soviet Union might be ahead of the United States in tanks and rockets and number of men under arms, but it was losing a much more important race. Soviet generals had begun to voice serious concern about the lack of "smart weapons" capable of matching the sophisticated weaponry under development in the West. Although some official U.S. studies claimed to show that the Soviet Union was "ahead" or "catching up" in key areas of military technology, such as cruise missiles or antisubmarine warfare, Soviet scientists knew very well that this was not an accurate picture.[11] The Soviet Union was in danger of missing out altogether on the technological revolution that was transforming Western societies.

Unable to summon up the energy for internal renewal, Soviet leaders sought legitimacy through external expansion. They had become hostages to their own ideology. The dogma of the irreversibility of history meant that no part of the empire—however useless, however costly—could ever be surrendered. In his quest for global influence, Brezhnev had forgotten one of the cardinal lessons of realpolitik, knowing when to stop. In the words of Stalin's foreign minister, Vyacheslav Molotov, "You have to understand that there are limits to everything. Otherwise, you can choke."[12]

THE CRISIS CONFRONTING the most powerful men in the Soviet Union had been building for months. In April 1978 a small group of radical intel-

lectuals and left-wing army officers had seized power in Afghanistan, a mountainous country of fifteen million people on the Soviet Union's southern border, and proclaimed a socialist regime. Kremlin leaders found out about the coup from a dispatch by Reuters news agency.[13] Nevertheless, they began referring to the Afghan leaders as "comrades." Giddy with success, the ideologists pointed to the Afghan "revolution" as another triumph over the forces of imperialism. "Today, there is no country in the world that isn't ready for socialism," declared one apparatchik enthusiastically.[14]

With its clanlike political structure, almost medieval way of life, and 90 percent illiteracy rate, Afghanistan seemed an unlikely candidate for a workers' paradise. Within eighteen months of the rising of the red flag over Kabul, the "revolution" was on the verge of falling apart. The mullahs had called for a "holy war" against the godless Communists. Most of the countryside—and some big towns—were already under the control of antigovernment guerrillas. The army was disintegrating. The man who had proclaimed himself the "Great Leader of the April Revolution," a dreamy Marxist theorist named Mohammad Taraki, had issued numerous appeals for Soviet assistance.

Brezhnev had given Taraki much of what he wanted—tanks, helicopters, military advisers—but had drawn the line at direct Soviet involvement in the Afghan civil war. In early September he had publicly hugged and embraced Taraki at a ceremony in the Kremlin. Soon afterward came news that the Afghan president had been overthrown in a palace coup and arrested on charges of terrorism. When Brezhnev returned to Moscow from East Berlin on October 9, he was greeted by even more distressing news. Taraki was dead. The *Kabul Times* reported laconically that he had been suffering "for some time" from a "serious illness." In fact, he was murdered on the orders of his successor, Hafizullah Amin. A member of the palace guard later described how he had helped tie the "Great Leader" to a bed with a towel and had then suffocated him with a pillow. The death throes had lasted for fifteen minutes.[15]

Soviet leaders had grave doubts about the loyalty of the man now described by the Afghan mass media as the "Brave Commander of the Revolution." According to Soviet intelligence reports, Amin was pursuing sectarian and repressive policies that could trigger a truly popular revolt. In addition, he was suspected of planning diplomatic overtures to Washington. Amin had studied in the United States, and there were rumors that he might have been recruited by the CIA. While there was no hard evidence to support the allegations, Kremlin leaders had paranoid visions of the "imperialists" establishing electronic listening posts along their southern bor-

ders, monitoring everything that moved in Soviet Central Asia.[16] By November the KGB residency in Kabul had concluded that the "revolution" could be saved only through Amin's forcible removal from power. That in turn would require a Soviet military intervention.[17]

THE MEN WHO GATHERED at Brezhnev's dacha that cold December day in 1979 all had been born before the Bolsheviks staged their coup d'état in Petrograd. Like the general secretary himself, they were the products of their times. Peasant boys from the vast Russian plain, they owed their careers and positions entirely to the Soviet Communist Party. Their formative years had been marked by war, famine, and revolution. They all had felt what one of them later described as the "merciless . . . relentless gaze" of a great tyrant, who possessed the power of life and death over 250 million people.[18] The seemingly arbitrary disappearance of millions of Soviet citizens—including some of their own relatives and friends—had cleared the way for their own upward progress through the Soviet bureaucracy. Now old men, they were finally experiencing the rewards of a lifetime of unquestioning political obedience.

Apart from Brezhnev himself, there were four men in the room: the head of the KGB, Yuri Andropov; the defense minister, Dmitri Ustinov; the foreign minister, Andrei Gromyko; and the general secretary's closest aide and confidant, Konstantin Chernenko.[19] Each of these men owed his place in the Politburo to Brezhnev, and each had a personal interest in perpetuating the rule of a chronic invalid. In return for symbolic tribute, Brezhnev allowed his barons to run their fiefdoms as they pleased and bathe in his reflected glory.

As head of the KGB, the Committee for State Security, Andropov had been the first Politburo member to learn about the deterioration in Brezhnev's health. The Kremlin doctors reported directly to him. For a long time he had refused to share the information with his colleagues because he feared it could provoke a vicious struggle for power. "For the sake of peace in the country and in the party, for the well-being of the people, we must keep silent. Indeed, we must try to hide these failures of Brezhnev," he told Chazov. "If a struggle for power begins in conditions of anarchy, at a time when there is no strong leadership, it will lead to the collapse of the economy and the entire system."[20]

There was another reason for Andropov's caution. A premature power struggle could damage his own chances of becoming general secretary. In

Chazov's view, Andropov was "terrified" of other strong figures in the leadership, such as Aleksei Kosygin and Nikolai Podgorny. As their power dwindled and his own position grew stronger, Andropov dropped his objections to informing the Politburo about Brezhnev's state of health.

A tall, ascetic-looking figure with steel-rimmed glasses and brushed-back silver hair, Andropov ran a worldwide network of spies, informers, and agents provocateurs. The successor to Lenin's Cheka and Stalin's NKVD, the KGB was an empire within an empire. Known as the "sword and shield" of the Soviet Communist Party, the KGB was responsible for everything from rooting out dissidents and electronic eavesdropping to foreign intelligence gathering and providing protection for the leadership.

For the leader of such a seemingly all-powerful organization, Andropov had a remarkably keen sense of the fragility of Soviet power. His younger associates talked about his "Hungarian complex."[21] As a rising apparatchik in his early forties he had been dispatched as ambassador to Budapest. There he had experienced the seminal event of his career, an armed uprising in 1956 against the Communist regime and its violent suppression by Soviet tanks. From the windows of his embassy he had seen Communists strung up from lampposts. He himself had come under fire, on his way out to the airport to greet a senior Soviet emissary. His wife, Tatyana, had suffered a breakdown, from which she never fully recovered.[22] Andropov was stunned by the speed with which the apparently well-entrenched Stalinist regime in Hungary was swept away. It took just a few weeks for the dissatisfaction of a handful of intellectuals and military cadets to build up into a mighty protest movement. The secret police was disbanded in a matter of hours. Supposedly loyal Communist Party members transformed themselves overnight into fanatical anti-Communists.

There was another lesson that Andropov drew from the Hungarian uprising. Military power, ruthlessly applied, can stop a counterrevolution in its tracks. Furthermore, a successful demonstration of overwhelming force would deter future rebellions. As Soviet ambassador to Budapest Andropov had played a key role in crushing the uprising, persuading a former Hungarian prime minister to sign a letter "inviting" Soviet troops into the country.[23] Nearly a quarter of a century later he proposed applying the Hungarian scenario to Afghanistan.

Andropov's closest ally in the Politburo was Marshal Ustinov. Like the KGB chief, Ustinov spoke in the name of a tremendously powerful institution. With more than 180 divisions, and five million men under arms, the armed forces were an awe-inspiring colossus. Without the Red Army there

would have been no Soviet Union. No sacrifice was too great for the institution that had won the civil war for the Bolsheviks, driven out the German invader, and transformed a backward country into a global superpower. The army was both a source of national pride and an instrument for holding together a vast multinational empire. Every year more than a million eighteen-year-old Uzbeks and Russians, Lithuanians and Georgians were thrown into an ethnic melting pot for two years' compulsory military service. The army had the task of transforming these raw recruits into both good soldiers and good Soviet citizens.

An engineer by profession, Ustinov personified the military-industrial complex. At the age of thirty-three he had been picked by Stalin for a crucial task, supplying the Red Army with the weapons it needed to defeat the Wehrmacht. As people's commissar for armaments Ustinov had supervised the evacuation of the defense industry from European Russia to Siberia. Within six months of Hitler's invasion of Russia in June 1941, more than fifteen hundred defense factories had been physically transplanted one thousand miles to the east. The plant and equipment filled some one and a half million railway wagons.[24] It was one of the most stupendous organizational feats of World War II and a vital precondition for the Soviet Union's eventual victory. After the war Ustinov oversaw the construction of delivery systems for the Soviet atomic bomb. In short, he brought the Red Army from the age of cavalry to the age of nuclear weapons.

By the time Ustinov became Soviet defense minister in 1976, Soviet factories were churning out an average of five fighter planes, eight tanks, eight artillery pieces, and one intercontinental ballistic missile every day.[25] In Politburo discussions Ustinov routinely demanded greater resources for the military—and usually won the argument. It was clear to everyone in the leadership that military spending was draining the Soviet Union's economic resources, but no one had the courage to call a halt. Negotiations with the imperialists could be conducted only from a position of strength. As Brezhnev liked to say, "The people will understand us. For peace, it is necessary to pay a price."[26]

The defense minister had the qualities of a strong-willed Russian muzhik, or peasant. He was big-hearted and gregarious. With the possible exception of Andropov, he was the hardest-working member of the Politburo, regularly putting in fifteen-hour days when he was well over seventy.[27] Like many of the older generation of Soviet leaders, however, he was a Stalinist at heart. He never forgave Khrushchev for defiling the memory of the tyrant with his secret speech to the Twentieth Communist Party Congress

in 1956. By condemning Stalin's crimes, Khrushchev had dragged Soviet history through the mud and undermined the faith of the people in Communist ideology. "No enemy brought us as many misfortunes as Khrushchev," Ustinov told the other members of the leadership. "It's no secret that the Westerners have never liked us. But Khrushchev gave them enough arguments and ammunition to keep them well supplied for many years."[28]

The third member of the national security troika was Gromyko. For many people in the West, Gromyko was the physical embodiment of Soviet foreign policy. His dour demeanor—he was known on the diplomatic circuit as Grim Grom—seemed to sum up the Kremlin's approach to international relations. A talented linguist, the foreign minister had been around for so long that he had practically become a one-man institution. He had run errands for Stalin at Potsdam and Yalta, while the fate of postwar Europe was being decided, and helped draft the founding charter of the United Nations in San Francisco. He had sat next to Khrushchev when he banged his shoe on his desk at the UN General Assembly. He had negotiated with Charles de Gaulle and Zhou Enlai, Henry Kissinger and Ho Chi Minh.

Western newspapers had christened Gromyko Mr. Nyet because of the series of twenty-six vetoes that he delivered in the UN Security Council between 1946 and 1948 as the first Soviet representative to the world body. In the Kremlin, however, he was known as Comrade Yes because of his servility to his superiors.[29] A professional diplomat, Gromyko had climbed to the top of the Soviet bureaucracy by dint of loyalty and long service. He had achieved his ambition by becoming a full member of the Politburo in 1973 and would do nothing to jeopardize his privileged position. While Brezhnev's illness had significantly increased his policy-making responsibilities, Gromyko was reluctant to cross swords with more powerful Politburo figures, such as Ustinov and Andropov. On crucial national security questions, the opinions of the minister of defense and the chairman of the KGB were usually decisive.[30]

The last visitor to Zareche that day, Konstantin Chernenko, had little to do with the formulation of foreign policy. He was there by courtesy of his relationship with Brezhnev, whom he had known for more than three decades. He was the Kremlin's chief paper shuffler, responsible for drafting Politburo minutes. He performed a series of indispensable chores for the general secretary, such as compiling laudatory press clippings, doling out cigarettes, and swapping old war stories. Chernenko was such a dullard that aides and bodyguards laughed at him behind his back.

Chernenko had a favorite catchphrase—"everything's fine, everything's fine"—which he repeated endlessly. Occasionally this got him in trouble with his patron. One day, as he sat in his office, Brezhnev complained that he had been unable to sleep at all the previous night. Chernenko, who also suffered from insomnia, was barely awake at the time. "*Vsyo khorosho,*" he murmured, scarcely aware of what was happening around him. "Everything's fine."

"What's fine about that?" roared Brezhnev. "I can't sleep, and you go on with your 'Everything's fine.' "

"Ohhh," sputtered Chernenko, by now wide-awake, "that's not fine."[31]

THE GENERAL STAFF had serious doubts about the proposed invasion. Afghanistan's rugged terrain and warrior traditions had created enormous problems for both tsarist Russia and the British Empire. The generals' concerns were shared by Foreign Ministry officials, who feared the international repercussions of a Soviet move into Afghanistan. But Ustinov and Andropov were convinced that a massive show of force would intimidate the opposition and restore order in the country. What they had in mind was a short, sharp operation, somewhat like the invasion of Czechoslovakia in 1968. Protected and encouraged by the Soviet army, "healthy forces" would regain control of the Afghan party from the usurper, Amin. The presence of Soviet troops in the capital, Kabul, and other garrison towns would permit the Afghan army to suppress the antigovernment insurgency. Under no circumstances would Soviet soldiers be allowed to take part in combat operations against the mujahedin. The actual fighting would be done by Afghans.[32]

When the chiefs of the General Staff expressed skepticism about this plan, Ustinov summoned the dissenters to his office. He had two marsnals and a general stand at attention in front of his desk, beneath the portrait of Lenin. "Are generals now making policy in the Soviet Union?" he demanded angrily. "Your task is to plan specific operations and to carry out your orders."[33] The implied accusation of Bonapartism—regarded as a mortal sin by Soviet Communists—was enough to bring the dissenters into line. The generals saluted smartly and got to work.

Once the foreign policy troika had taken a decision to use force in Afghanistan, the only man capable of blocking the invasion was the *gensek* himself. But Brezhnev was distressed by the gruesome fate that had befallen Taraki, just a few days after their public embrace, and regarded Amin's re-

fusal to accept Soviet advice as a personal affront. "What will they say in other countries?" he had asked his aides, in a characteristic fit of emotion. "Is it possible to believe the word of Brezhnev if all his assurances of support and protection remain mere words?"[34]

The decision to invade had been endorsed by the Politburo on the evening of December 12. One by one, the twelve senior members of the leadership had joined Brezhnev in scrawling their names across the Central Committee resolution NR 176/125, approving a series of "measures" to be taken in country "A."[35] The measures were so secret that they could not be committed to paper. To prevent a possible leak via the Politburo typist, Chernenko wrote out the resolution by hand.

There were two stages to the operation. With Amin's agreement, three divisions of Soviet troops would be dispatched to Afghanistan with the ostensible purpose of "saving the revolution." They would then proceed to the second stage, the forcible removal of Amin and the installation of a more compliant Afghan leader. Soviet military planners envisaged Operation Storm as a gesture of "fraternal assistance" and invasion rolled into one.[36]

While the inner Politburo met at Brezhnev's dacha on December 26, a fleet of four hundred Soviet transport planes was already pouring into Kabul's Bagram Airport. A plane landed every three or four minutes, discharge troops and armored vehicles, and fly away for more without turning off its engines.[37] The operation was supervised by Ustinov, Andropov, and Gromyko, who reported the results to Brezhnev.

Convinced it was his duty to preserve the empire that had been put together with so much blood, the general secretary gave the order for Operation Storm to proceed. The following day Chernenko dictated a memorandum recording that the general secretary "approved the plan of action for the immediate future, as outlined by the comrades."[38] Shortly afterward Brezhnev was heard to boast that "it will all be over in three to four weeks."[39]

Many years later, when a search was made of the archives for the political decision that led to the bloody events of December 27, these two notes drafted by Chernenko were all that could be found. By that time the men who had taken the fateful decision to invade Afghanistan were long dead, and the Soviet Union itself was no more.

KABUL

December 27, 1979

HAFIZULLAH AMIN WAS CONVINCED that the Red Army was coming to his rescue. His personal envoy had just returned from Moscow with news that the Soviet Union was at last ready to provide Afghanistan with "fraternal assistance." The Kremlin had accepted his explanation for the overthrow and murder of Taraki, the original "Great Leader" of the Afghan revolution. Soon Amin's hold on power would be secure.

There had been some difficult moments. Over the past few weeks Communists loyal to Taraki had begun a campaign to assassinate members of the new regime. At the beginning of December they had succeeded in lightly wounding Amin and killing his nephew. Anti-Communist rebels had advanced to within a few miles of the capital, cutting the main north-south highway. For security reasons Amin had moved out of the House of the People in downtown Kabul a week earlier. His new residence was a monstrous three-story fortress, the Dār-ol-Amān Palace, built by a former Afghan king. Located at the base of the Hindu Kush mountains, seven miles southwest of Kabul, the palace was defended by an Afghan infantry brigade. Tanks guarded the only approach road, a winding serpentine.

Amin had some doubts about the loyalty of his own troops but trusted his Soviet advisers completely. He knew the Soviet leaders were angry with

him for killing Taraki but reasoned that they would support the winning side. Confident that he was the victor in the Afghan fratricide, Amin gratefully accepted Soviet offers of "protection." He allowed a battalion of elite troops from Soviet Central Asia—the so-called Muslim battalion—to take up positions near his palace.[40] Soviet advisers had intimate knowledge of his security arrangements. Frightened that Afghan cooks might try to poison him, Amin had even gone to the length of employing two cooks from the Soviet republic of Uzbekistan.

On December 27 Amin entertained government ministers at lunch. He wanted to show them his new residence and boast about his Soviet connections. "The Soviet divisions are already on their way. Everything is going fine," he assured his guests, referring to the thousands of Soviet troops already pouring into Bagram Airport. "I am in constant contact with Comrade Gromyko. We are discussing how to inform the world about the decision to grant us Soviet assistance."[41]

At the end of the lunch everybody at the table fell violently ill. Amin, together with many of his guests, lost consciousness. Soviet and Afghan doctors were summoned. Although this was obviously a case of mass food poisoning, it did not occur to anyone to suspect the Soviet kitchen staff.

The doctors were greeted by a tableau of wretchedness. All over the palace—in the hallways, on the staircases, in waiting rooms—prominent Afghans were lying in unnatural poses. Some were still unconscious. Some were doubled up, clutching their stomachs. Some were screaming with pain. The Soviet military doctors, who were not informed about the plot to overthrow the Afghan leader, were ushered into an upstairs room where Amin was lying on a bed, dressed only in a pair of shorts. His pulse was weak. His jaw was hanging down, and his eyes were rolling. The doctors pumped his stomach, injected him with antidotes for food poisoning, and attached drips to his veins. Suddenly his eyelids began fluttering. The "Brave Commander" was pulling through.

As he regained consciousness, Amin began asking questions. "What's happening in my house?" he demanded. "Who did this? Is this an accident—or some kind of diversion?"[42] But it still did not occur to him to suspect his Soviet comrades. "Believe it or not, this is the work of the Taraki group," he told his wife, who had not attended the luncheon.[43]

THE CRUMBLING AVENUES and twisting alleyways of Kabul were practically deserted as Grigori Boyarinov embarked on the mission that would

mark the start of the Soviet Union's last great colonial adventure. The evening curfew came into force at 7:00 p.m., and only security personnel were allowed on the streets. The sprawling mud slums on the outskirts of the city seemed peaceful. Confined to their homes, many Afghan families were preparing to sit down for dinner. Radios and television sets were blaring out from countless courtyards. The aroma of shashlik—a pungent mixture of oil, wood fires, and sizzling meat—filled the crisp winter air.

A plan to poison the Afghan leader and take him into custody had already gone awry. Amin had only nibbled at his food and had been able to make a premature recovery. His aides had resisted Soviet offers to transfer him to the Soviet military hospital in Kabul. Alarmed by the mass food poisoning, the Afghan authorities had begun to strengthen the guard around the palace. The Soviet attack, originally planned for eleven that night, would now have to be brought forward.

Crouching in an armored personnel carrier a couple of miles from the Dār-ol-Amān Palace, Boyarinov waited for the signal to launch the attack. The fifty-seven-year-old colonel was easily the most experienced member of the sixty-member assault team. Indeed he could probably claim to be the Soviet Union's leading expert on partisan warfare. As a young lieutenant in World War II he had earned numerous medals for bravery by parachuting behind German lines and causing havoc in the enemy's rear. He had gone on to write a dissertation on the subject, and he had also run a school for KGB snipers. For the last eighteen years he had served as head of the guerrilla warfare department at the KGB staff college, training the young men who would soon be going into battle beside him. Earlier that year Boyarinov had spent three months in Afghanistan, advising the Afghan Army and analyzing the military situation.

If there was going to be action in Afghanistan, Boyarinov wanted to be part of it. This handsome, well-built man, known to everyone as Grisha, felt an obligation to his "boys" in the Alpha and Zenith squads of the KGB. At the same time, like many professional officers, he had some reservations about the whole Afghan business. Before returning to Afghanistan, he had tried to cheer up a KGB colleague who had failed to win a place in the assault team. "Don't worry, we will get our fill of Afghanistan. It sounds bitter, I know, but I am afraid that this is going to last a long time."[44] After his superiors outlined the operation to him, he commented dryly to a friend, "Let's hope that the people who prepared this attack know what they are doing."[45]

Shortly before 7:30 p.m. Soviet commandos blew up the Kabul post office with 115 pounds of plastic explosive. The bomb knocked out the

telecommunications system of the Afghan capital. Echoing off the mountains that ring Kabul, the explosion served as a signal to groups of Soviet commandos scattered in different parts of the city to move into action. Within minutes Soviet and Afghan troops were battling for control of key buildings in the capital: the Interior Ministry; the headquarters of the General Staff; the central prison. Red tracer bullets and puffs of artillery smoke flashed across the nighttime sky. The Muslim battalion began firing on the Dār-ol-Amān Palace, and a column of armored cars moved up the serpentine approach road.

The assault plan went wrong from the start. The shelling began too early, depriving the attackers of the advantage of surprise. The shells seemed to bounce off the thick walls of the palace as if they were made of rubber. A burned-out Afghan bus blocked the palace driveway, forcing the Soviet commandos to make a dash for it on foot. Under heavy fire from the upper floors of the palace, they blasted their way into the ground floor with portable grenade launchers. Within the first few minutes of fighting at the palace, half the Soviet assault force lay sprawled on the ground, either dead or injured.

A splinter from a grenade caught Dmitri Volkov in the throat after he had captured an Afghan tank on the approach road to the palace. Gennady Zudin was shot in the head as he squatted behind one of the Corinthian columns that adorned the front of the palace. Valery Yemishev, one of the first men into the palace, had his right hand blown off by an Afghan grenade. A friend took fifteen seconds out of the battle to reconnect the dangling hand with a rubber band. One of the Soviet doctors, Viktor Kusnechenkov, was killed in the crossfire.

Inside the palace there was total chaos. To disguise their identities, the Soviet commandos had put on ill-fitting Afghan army uniforms. Since both sides were also using Soviet weapons, it was difficult to tell them apart. In order to recognize each other, the Soviets screamed Russian swearwords as they raked the long corridors of the palace with machine-gun fire. They would kick a door down, throw in a grenade, and proceed to the next room. Shrieks and groans could be heard from all directions. When it was all over, Soviet cleanup squads carted away two truckloads of Afghan corpses.

As he ran into the palace, Boyarinov was hit by shrapnel. His face and hands were bleeding. His thirty-man team had been given the task of securing the ground floor, but most of them had disappeared. Rushing down a corridor, he spotted the shell-shocked and seriously wounded Sergei Kuvilin.

"We have to destroy the communications center," Boyarinov shouted.

"There are none of us left. I'm alone."

"Well, there're two of us now."[46]

Boyarinov threw a few grenades into the communications center and then raced up the staircase to Amin's private apartment, leaving Kuvilin to cover the ground floor. At that moment a burst of automatic fire from somewhere up the staircase blew off Boyarinov's face.

AS SOVIET ARTILLERY SHELLS SLAMMED into the presidential palace, Hafizullah Amin instructed the commander of the guard to find out where the fire was coming from. "The Soviets will come to our assistance," he added confidently.[47]

The commander returned in panic a few minutes later. The telephones were not working. He had managed to reach army GHQ in Kabul by wireless. It too was under fire. No Afghan units had moved from their bases. There were no reports of mutiny or unrest. That left only one possibility: The palace was under attack by the "friendly army."

"That's impossible, you're lying," screamed Amin, throwing an ashtray at the unfortunate aide. "It's our own mutinous troops."[48]

Like Czechoslovakia's Alexander Dubček before him, Amin could not believe that his Soviet allies had turned against him. For all his brutality, the Afghan leader had retained an innocent faith in the homeland of world socialism that went back to his days as a student at Kabul University. As a young Communist he had regaled his followers with tales about the valiant Red Army. For this army to attack him was not just betrayal. It was sacrilege.

As the sound of gunfire grew louder, Amin rushed out of his room. Two Soviet doctors cowered behind a bar in the corridor. They could see the Afghan leader dressed in white shorts, with drips still sticking out of his bandaged arms. One of the doctors pulled the needles out of Amin's arms and dragged him to the bar. All of a sudden they heard a child crying somewhere in the darkness. It was Amin's five-year-old son. Seeing his father, the boy hurled himself at him, grabbing his legs. Father and son slumped down together beside the wall.

Soviet soldiers discovered the two bodies in a pool of blood. Evidently, they were caught in the crossfire. As they lay dying, the tyrant hugged the boy's head close to his chest.[49] After the fighting died down, a member of a rival Afghan faction insisted on carrying out a formal death sentence on Amin "in the name of the Party and the people."[50] The fact that the dicta-

tor was already dead did not deter him from pumping several more bullets into the corpse.

WHILE THE SOVIET COMMANDOS were mounting their assault on the Dār-ol-Amān Palace, the man who was shortly to succeed Amin as president of Afghanistan was cowering in a bunker on the other side of Kabul. Vain, garrulous, and a chronic alcoholic, Babrak Karmal had been one of the original leaders of the Afghan "revolution." After quarreling with Taraki and Amin he was sent into exile as Afghanistan's ambassador to Czechoslovakia. The KGB had smuggled him back into Kabul on December 23, 1979, four days before the invasion.[51]

Karmal later boasted that he had directed a "popular uprising" against the tyrannical Amin. In fact he had virtually nothing to do with the fighting. The first meeting of the new Afghan Politburo took place at the Soviet military base at Bagram Airport under the watchful eyes of Karmal's KGB bodyguards. It was here that Karmal appointed himself general secretary of the Central Committee of the People's Democratic Party of Afghanistan. It was here that he listened to his own prerecorded radio address to the Afghan people broadcast from a transmitter in the Soviet border town of Termez, in which he denounced Amin as an "agent of American imperialism."

"The day of freedom and rebirth has arrived," declared the new Afghan leader. "The tyrannical torture machine of Amin and his supporters—the savage butchers, hangmen, usurpers, and murderers of tens of thousands of our compatriots—has been smashed."[52]

Late that night, after Amin was dead, Karmal climbed into a Soviet armored car. The armored car joined a Soviet convoy, guarded by three tanks, moving cautiously in the direction of the city. As dawn broke, the convoy drove into the center of Kabul. It was a clear, crisp morning. Armed men were everywhere. Tanks and armored vehicles roared down streets littered with burning vehicles and the debris of bombed-out buildings. Karmal and his bodyguards were deposited at the Interior Ministry building, now firmly in the hands of Soviet troops.

As Afghanistan's new president was arriving in Kabul, another convoy was moving in the opposite direction. At the Kabul airport coffins containing the remains of the twelve Soviet commandos killed during the assault on Dār-ol-Amān were loaded onto transport planes.[53] There were special honors for Boyarinov, who was given the posthumous award of Hero of the So-

viet Union. They were the first casualties of a war that was to last nearly ten years and take the lives of more than thirteen thousand Soviet servicemen, in addition to half a million Afghans.

As they watched the coffins of their dead comrades being stacked on transport planes at Bagram Airport that wintry morning, the survivors of the attack on Amin's palace were convinced that the war was over. In fact it was just beginning.

The long-term results of the invasion were almost the exact opposite of the goals of Politburo leaders. Instead of crushing the Afghan opposition, they gave it new life. Instead of striking a blow against the imperialists, they provoked an unlikely coalition of the United States, China, and Saudi Arabia. And instead of defending the prestige of world socialism, they encouraged a generation of Soviet citizens to question where the world's second superpower was heading.

When the coffins were eventually unloaded on Soviet soil, there were no salutes and no marching band. The Kremlin did not want anyone to know that Soviet citizens were being killed in combat operations in Afghanistan. The funerals took place in secret. A standard formula was adopted to explain the fatalities of a nonexistent war to the families of the victims. Boyarinov and the others had died "while fulfilling their internationalist duty."

PITSUNDA

December 28, 1979

A WOODED PENINSULA JUTTING OUT into the Black Sea, the Georgian resort of Pitsunda has been known for its natural beauty since ancient Greece. Centuries-old pine trees stretch down to the water's edge, providing shelter from the sudden winter storms and harsh summer sun. In the first century A.D. the Greeks established a fortified trading settlement on the narrow peninsula, with strong walls to scare away pirates. A thousand years later the rulers of Byzantium transformed the fortress into a kind of medieval health spa with magnificent baths.

After Georgia had been incorporated into the Soviet Union, Pitsunda became a holiday resort for the Communist nomenklatura. Nikita Khrushchev liked the place so much that he had a luxurious villa built by the seashore, surrounded by an ugly concrete wall. Recreation facilities included an Olympic-size swimming pool, a gymnasium, and tennis courts. Two other, slightly less grandiose villas were built on adjacent plots of land for more junior leaders.[54] It was at Pitsunda, in October 1964, that Khrushchev learned of the Kremlin coup that forced him out of office.

As they walked down the winding paths of Khrushchev's old dacha that wintry afternoon, the two youngest members of the Politburo recognized that the Soviet Union was headed in the wrong direction. Both Mikhail

Gorbachev and Eduard Shevardnadze were convinced Communists, completely loyal to the system that had sponsored and promoted them. What distinguished them from the older members of the Politburo was a still-youthful energy and optimism, an almost naive belief in socialism's further perfectibility. There was a word for their generation in Russian: *shestidesyatniki,* "men of the sixties." Their formative years had been marked by Khrushchev's thaw, the brief interlude between the terror of Stalinism and the stagnation of the Brezhnev period. The previous generation, as represented by Brezhnev, had been brought up in an atmosphere of all-pervasive fear. Conservative to the core, they were loath even to tinker with the system, for fear of bringing the whole structure crashing down. The *shestidesyatniki,* by contrast, were full of confidence in their own abilities and itching for the chance to put things right. They had little firsthand experience of war and terror.

The generational differences between Soviet leaders were summed up by a joke that became popular during Brezhnev's twilight years. Stalin, Khrushchev, and Brezhnev are seated in a compartment of a train that breaks down in the middle of Siberia. After hours of waiting, an argument breaks out between the passengers over how to get the train moving again. "Let's shoot one of the drivers," suggests Stalin. "Then the other drivers will know that we mean business." "No, that's inhumane. We must abide by socialist norms," says Khrushchev. "Let's offer the drivers higher wages." Unable to agree, the two older men ask Brezhnev to adjudicate. He ponders the question for a long time. "I know," he replies finally. "Why don't we just close the blinds and pretend the train is moving? No one will know the difference."

The Soviet Union had been practically immobile now for fifteen years. Although Gorbachev and Shevardnadze had no clear idea how to get the train moving again, they understood that the first priority was acknowledging that it had stalled. That meant raising the blinds, letting in some fresh air, and ending the pretense about the country's advancing from one socialist triumph to another.

As the Politburo member in charge of agriculture Gorbachev had an excellent vantage point for observing the ruinous effects of central planning. The world's largest country—a country that possessed more acres of bountiful farmland than Canada and the United States combined—was unable to feed itself. A net exporter of grain before the 1917 Bolshevik Revolution, Russia was now compelled to scrounge for grain every year from the capitalist West. Russian peasants, corralled into vast state-run farms during Stalin's collectivization campaign, had forgotten how to farm. Instead of

producing goods for a market, they fulfilled the orders of bureaucrats. Prices were established by administrative fiat and bore little relation to real costs. The distorted price structure gave rise to many absurdities. Since the price of bread was heavily subsidized by the state and was lower than the equivalent price of grain, it made perfect economic sense for farmers to use loaves of bread as animal fodder.

Predictably enough, Gorbachev's early attempts to boost agricultural production met with complete failure. In 1979 the grain harvest was a disastrous 179 million tons, 40 million tons below target. The shortfall would have to be met by imports. As usual, Soviet leaders blamed the weather. But Gorbachev knew perfectly well that the real problem was with the way Soviet agriculture—and, by extension, the entire Soviet economy—was organized. Labor discipline was so poor that hundreds of thousands of kolkhozniks failed to show up for work every day. One-third of the food harvest was lost because of inadequate storage facilities, an outdated transportation system, and general mechanical failures. Tractors and combine harvesters left factories in such poor condition that they invariably had to be repaired as soon as they arrived on the farm.[55]

In public Gorbachev maintained the pretense that all was well. But he talked frankly with Shevardnadze, whom he had known for more than two decades. The two men had much in common. As young men Gorbachev and Shevardnadze had climbed the greasy pole of Soviet politics together, making their early career in the Komsomol, the Communist youth league. Gorbachev became first secretary of the Communist Party in his home region of Stavropol in 1970. At the age of thirty-nine he had in effect become Kremlin plenipotentiary for a predominantly agricultural district roughly the size of Illinois. Two years later Shevardnadze was chosen as Communist Party chief in his native republic of Georgia, on the other side of the Caucasus mountain range.

The two party bosses took their winter vacations together at Pitsunda. During a long walk through the pine woods Shevardnadze described his attempts to increase agricultural production in Georgia by offering peasants financial incentives. The experiment had horrified doctrinaire Marxists, who feared the reemergence of the so-called kulak class, the prosperous, stubbornly independent peasantry destroyed by Stalin. Shevardnadze had taken Gorbachev to meet one of the new kulaks, who kept ten dairy cows at his farmstead. The question now was what to do with this ideological monstrosity.

"If you like, we can de-kulakize him," said Shevardnadze in his thick Georgian accent. "Then there won't be any farm, milk, or livestock."

The party's new agriculture secretary laughed. "We could de-kulakize him, of course, so that your theoreticians won't get angry. But how are we going to improve rural life without this kind of kulak?" he replied.[56]

On another occasion Shevardnadze blurted out that everything was "rotten" in the Soviet Union. "We cannot go on living like this. We must think what we can do to salvage the country," he told Gorbachev. [57]

Both Gorbachev and Shevardnadze were experienced apparatchiks, adept in the ways of Soviet politics. They knew how to camouflage their "experiments" behind innocuous-sounding names. In return for occasional flashes of personal honesty, they joined the rest of the Soviet leadership in ritualistic displays of public hypocrisy.

Gorbachev had honed his sycophantic skills on the important visitors who passed through Stavropol. With its warm weather and mountain spas, the Stavropol region was a favorite vacation destination for the "big pine cones" from Moscow. The local Communist Party chief was responsible for humoring the big shots and helping them unwind from the burdens of office. Party bosses from places like Stavropol were even occasionally referred to as resort secretaries. The opportunities for corruption were immense. The party secretary in the neighboring Krasnodar region, Sergei Medunov, was a notorious bribe taker with close links to the local mob. Gorbachev, by contrast, had a reputation for relative honesty. All the same, for his own political survival, he was obliged to ply his visitors with gifts and cater to their various whims.[58]

An amateur actor in his youth, Gorbachev was particularly good at feigning sincerity. When he praised Brezhnev or spoke about the glorious future awaiting the next generation of Soviet citizens, his deep brown eyes seemed to light up with enthusiasm and conviction. At Politburo meetings he always deferred to his elders. When his turn came to speak, he would invariably support the leader's position, however absurd or hard-line. When the entire country was called upon to critique Brezhnev's memoir positively, Gorbachev displayed the required enthusiasm. At an ideological conference in Stavropol he praised the decrepit general secretary for his "titanic daily work," "deep philosophical penetration," and "talent for leadership of the Leninist type." "Communists, and all the workers of Stavropol, are boundlessly grateful to Leonid Ilyich Brezhnev for this truly party-spirited literary work," Gorbachev declared. He ordered all local newspapers to serialize the turgid volume "in response to the innumerable requests of the workers of Stavropol."[59]

If Gorbachev was a talented flatterer, Shevardnadze was a virtuoso. In

the Georgian tradition, he groveled at the feet of the powerful. At the Twenty-fifth Communist Party Congress in 1976, he lauded Brezhnev's "high competence, breadth of vision, concreteness, humanity, uncompromising class position, loyalty, principled position, skill at penetrating the soul of his interlocutor, and ability to create an atmosphere of trust between people." He expressed his nation's undying loyalty to its big Russian brother in unctuous tones. "They call Georgia a sunny land. But for us, comrades, the real sun rises not in the East, but in the North, in Russia, the sun of Leninist ideas."[60]

While resting at Pitsunda the future general secretary and his future foreign minister heard an announcement that was to cast a long shadow over their efforts to chart a new course for the Communist superpower. On the morning of December 28 Radio Moscow began retransmitting the speech by Babrak Karmal proclaiming the dawn of a new "day of freedom." A few hours later the radio reported that the Afghan government had sent an urgent request to the Soviet Union for "immediate political, moral, and economic aid, including military aid." "The government of the Soviet Union has met the request of Afghanistan," the announcer added, without elaboration.[61]

As candidate, or nonvoting, members of the Politburo, neither Gorbachev nor Shevardnadze had been informed about the plans to invade Afghanistan. Both men later claimed that they were shocked by the decision, which they described as a "fatal error" and a "crime against humanity."[62] In June 1980, however, they joined other Central Committee members in unanimously endorsing a resolution claiming that the Red Army had foiled "imperialist" plans to turn Afghanistan into a "bridgehead for military aggression" against the Soviet Union. Shevardnadze went out of his way to praise Brezhnev once again for his far-sighted leadership, hailing the invasion as "a brave, uniquely loyal, uniquely courageous step . . . that has been received with approval by every Soviet citizen."[63]

By sending troops to Afghanistan, Kremlin leaders imagined that they had bought a few years' peace and quiet, just as they had with the invasion of Czechoslovakia in 1968. They could not have been more wrong. While Gorbachev and the other Central Committee members were raising their hands to approve the provision of "fraternal assistance" to Afghanistan, even more serious trouble was brewing at the opposite end of their empire: in Poland.

GDAŃSK

August 15, 1980

THE GATES OF THE LENIN SHIPYARD were locked shut when I arrived on the second day of the strike that was to foreshadow the downfall of communism. A portrait of John Paul II, the Polish pope, had been attached to the front of the gate, like a talisman protecting the strikers from the fury of the Communist regime. The white and red Polish flag hung limply from the top of the gate. STRAJK OKUPACIJNY, "Occupation Strike," proclaimed a nearby placard. Workers in grimy overalls clutched the gray metal railings with their fists, gazing out at a crowd of several hundred sympathizers and relatives. The gate was adorned with freshly cut red and white flowers.

Hundreds of strikes had taken place around Poland over the previous few weeks to protest a rise in meat prices, but they had always been settled behind closed doors. Strike leaders calculated that the presence of journalists, particularly foreign journalists, would only complicate their negotiations with the regime. Communist ideologists regarded factories, coal mines, and shipyards as proletarian fortresses, built to withstand the assaults of class enemies. In years of wandering around the Soviet bloc, I had never once been permitted to visit a factory without being chaperoned by government officials.

To my amazement, the shipyard gates suddenly opened a crack, and I was ushered into the forbidden world. Marxist ideologists would never be able to come up with a satisfactory explanation for the scene that now confronted me: workers rebelling against the "workers' state." Strikers were lounging around on the grass, sitting on torn-up pieces of asbestos. Heated discussions were going on everywhere, as if people had just been released from a lifetime vow of silence. Some workers had scrambled on top of the shipyard walls, to honks of support from passing motorists. An incongruous touch was provided by several dozen patients from the shipyard hospital, who were wandering around in striped pajamas and red dressing gowns. When the strikers found out that I represented a Western newspaper, they came up and hugged me excitedly. Cries of "*Amerika, Amerika*" rippled around the shipyard.

I was led to a large hall, decorated with a statue of Vladimir Lenin at one end and a model sailing ship at the other. Negotiations were already under way between the strike committee and the shipyard director, Klemens Gniech. The man sitting opposite Gniech caught my attention immediately. A shortish figure, about five feet seven, he was dressed in a crumpled dark suit and a checkered, open-neck shirt. Apart from his oversize mustache, the first things I noticed were his quick, darting eyes, impish smile, and cheeky, rasping voice. He had the air of a born rabble-rouser.

"That's our leader. His name is Lech Wałęsa," whispered my guide, Gregorz Obernicowicz. "He's the person who decided to let you in."

Wałęsa understood, almost instinctively, that the ability to command public attention was his most valuable asset. He also realized that he could use the Western media to circumvent the information blockade imposed by the Communist authorities. Since childhood he had secretly listened to the broadcasts of Radio Free Europe and the BBC. He knew that any reports filed by a Western journalist about the shipyard strike would immediately be broadcast back to Poland by Western radio stations—and heard by millions of Poles.

Speaking the truth openly was Wałęsa's trump card. It was what distinguished him from the despised apparatchiks and gave him his authority. When I asked him that first day why he had decided to allow a foreign journalist into the shipyard—when other strike leaders had kept us out—he replied: "We want to show people that they do not have to be afraid."

Later on the strike in the Lenin Shipyard became an international media event. Negotiations were conducted under the glare of television arc lights. During the first few days, however, the atmosphere was extraordinarily inti-

mate. I felt as if I had wandered behind the scenes of an elaborate theater production. For years the Communist authorities had forced Western journalists to watch the show from the balcony. We suspected that what we were seeing on the other side of the proscenium arch was false but could never be sure. The actors had become thoroughly accustomed to the lines written for them by the party ideologists. Yet here they were, rebelling against the director and rewriting the script. The make-believe world created by Communist propaganda had been shattered.

Watching the workers gain confidence in one another, I understood why the authorities attached so much importance to walls and fences. In order to preserve and consolidate their power, the Communists had taken the strategy of "divide and rule" to its logical extreme. The most obvious wall was the one that divided Communist countries from the outside world: the Iron Curtain. But equally important were the internal walls that divided workers from intellectuals, crane operators from welders, Poles from Jews. Some of these barriers were real. They took the form of censorship, restrictions on freedom of movement, and a ban on independent organizations of any kind. But many were psychological, the legacy of decades of arbitrary rule and a climate of ingrained fear. Freedom of association was a mortal threat to the totalitarian regime. As the self-appointed instrument of historical progress, the Communist Party controlled an atomized and defeated society.

When I think back to the shipyard strike, what sticks in my mind most of all was the extraordinary lightness of spirit. There were many tense moments, particularly at the beginning, but the predominant mood was one of infectious gaiety. The warm August sunshine helped create a holiday atmosphere. But mostly it was the smiles on people's faces, the sense of walls coming down, the sheer irreverence and improbability of it all. When the workers were discussing what material to use for a monument to commemorate the victims of Communist repression, someone pointed to the life-size Lenin on the podium. "We won't be needing him anymore. Let's use that," he suggested, to ironic cheers.

There was a quality of self-liberation about the conversations that took place at the shipyard in August 1980. After years of lies, people were at last looking one another in the eye and telling the truth. They were learning not to be afraid, as Wałęsa had hoped. In the process they helped liberate the rest of us from our own preconceptions. We discovered that people we had previously dismissed as representatives of Marx's lumpen proletariat were individuals with hopes, worries, and diverse points of view.

I also remember the sight of the crowd standing outside the shipyard gate, stretching back as far as the eye could see. It was crowds like this— good-humored, self-disciplined, incredibly patient—that had greeted the pope on his return to Poland the previous summer. There were people in the crowd from all walks of life: factory workers; office employees; students. As they waited for a glimpse of Wałęsa, they held impromptu discussions. I was reminded of John Reed's account of the Russian Revolution. "For months in Petrograd, and all over Russia, every street-corner was a public tribune. In railway trains, street-cars, always the spurting up of impromptu debate, everywhere," wrote Reed in *Ten Days That Shook the World.*

Over the next decade I was to witness such scenes many times over as Poles—followed by Balts, Czechs, Ukrainians, Germans, and finally Russians—unmade the revolution that Reed had chronicled.

LECH WAŁĘSA WAS a child of postwar Poland. He had taken part in the great social upheavals that spawned the Communist world's first free trade union movement: the massive migration from the impoverished countryside; the struggle of the Catholic Church against an atheistic regime; the strikes and demonstrations along the Baltic coast in 1970. His life could almost be a symbol of Poland's postwar history, with its cycles of soaring hopes and bitter disappointments.

When Wałęsa was born, in the tiny village of Popowo, in central Poland, the country was under German occupation. A few months after his birth, in September 1943, his father was hauled off to a Nazi concentration camp, where he died two years later. By the time Lech went to school, Poland was firmly within the Soviet camp, having been liberated from the east by the Red Army. The Soviets grabbed the eastern part of the country for themselves, compensating the Poles with a two-hundred-mile swath of formerly German territory. They installed a Communist-led government in Warsaw, making sure that all the key posts were held by Moscow-trained apparatchiks. Everything about the new regime—from the crash industrialization program and ubiquitous secret police to the Stalinist architecture and uplifting slogans promising a socialist utopia—was based on the Soviet model.

A long history of struggle against foreign occupation, including Russian occupation, had prepared the Poles to resist attempts to Sovietize the country. At school children were encouraged to become Communist pioneers and follow the footsteps of "Grandpa Lenin." At home they were brought

up on tales of the epic anti-Russian uprisings of the nineteenth century and the "Miracle on the Vistula" in August 1920, when Marshal Józef Piłsudski's legions routed the Red Army. In their factories, on weekdays, workers were exposed to an unending stream of Marxist propaganda at obligatory Communist Party meetings. In church, on Sundays, they attended to spiritual needs that were beyond the reach of the seemingly all-powerful state.

In 1966, at the age of twenty-three, Wałęsa moved from central Poland to Gdańsk, following in the footsteps of millions of young Poles. Gdańsk, formerly the free town of Danzig, had been part of the territories "reclaimed" by Poland following the defeat of Nazi Germany. During the first wave of migration, immediately after World War II, the largely German population was driven out. A second wave of migration followed in the fifties and sixties, as the result of the Communist government's program of breakneck industrialization. A predominantly agricultural country was transformed into a predominantly urban one in the space of two decades.

There was a political rationale behind this social revolution. Marxist ideologists believed that the most effective way of consolidating the power of the party—and shattering the reactionary influence of the church—was to create an urban working class. The church could continue to wield its influence in the countryside, but the party would dominate the cities.

If the party had provided the new proletariat with decent working and living conditions, the strategy might have made some sense. But the factories and coal mines of the workers' state were sweatshops, more reminiscent of Dickensian England than the promised socialist utopia. The Lenin Shipyard, Wałęsa later recalled, lacked the most elementary conveniences for workers. "When I arrived, our shipyard looked like a factory filled with men in filthy rags, unable to wash themselves or urinate in toilets. To get down to the ground floor where toilets were located took at least half an hour, so we just went anywhere. You can't imagine how humiliating these working conditions were."[64] In rainy weather workers returned home soaked to the skin because there was no place to change. Safety standards were abysmal. Shortly after Wałęsa joined the shipyard as an apprentice electrician, twenty-two workers were burned alive in an explosion on a ship they were rushing to complete.

Living conditions for workers were equally primitive. The younger workers stayed in hostels, three or four to a room, with a kitchen and shower at the end of each corridor. Fights broke out frequently, particularly on payday, when workers drowned their misery in vodka. The areas around the hostels were wastelands of broken glass and uncollected garbage.

What Gdańsk did possess in abundance was the spirit of freedom. A strategically important port of nearly half a million people, the city has always looked outward. From the fourteenth to the seventeenth century, it was one of the most important trading posts in the Baltic. The magnificent old town, with its baroque and Gothic churches and Renaissance guild hall, was built during a period when Gdańsk was the respected trading partner of cities like Bruges, London, and Hamburg. The huge granaries along the banks of the Vistula River are a reminder of the time when Poland was Europe's largest grain exporter. During the Communist period, as Poland became a net importer of food, the grain started moving in the opposite direction.

Proclaimed a Free City after World War I, under League of Nations control, Gdańsk was the spark that ignited World War II. Hitler was determined to get Danzig back and cut Poland's land corridor to the sea. The first shots of the war were fired a few miles away, at the coastal fort of Westerplatte, by the German battle cruiser *Schleswig-Holstein* on September 1, 1939. To die or not to die "for Danzig" became a burning moral issue for millions of young Europeans who could barely locate the city on a map.

The city's reputation as a flash point for political unrest was strengthened by the workers' rebellion of December 1970. The first confrontation with the security forces had taken place right outside the shipyard gate. The workers had intended to march to the town hall with the centuries-old demands of Polish insurrectionaries, bread and freedom. Singing the Communist anthem, the "Internationale," they were greeted by a burst of automatic rifle fire. Within seconds dozens of demonstrators lay sprawled on the ground. The casualty toll from that single incident was four dead and fifteen injured.[65]

A member of the original shipyard strike committee, Wałęsa remained obsessed with the idea of honoring the memory of his fallen comrades. He remembered how the survivors had draped the murdered workers' helmets in black crepe and attached them to the shipyard gate. They had daubed the blood of the victims onto bedsheets to form four red crosses, which they hung from a window of the shipyard hospital. "We then sang the national anthem, laying particular stress on the words: *'We'll recover with the sword what the alien forces have taken from us.'* Loudspeakers had been set up on the gate so that the government pawns could hear what we had to say, and we began the chant, *'Murderers, murderers.'* "[66]

The Communist authorities were equally determined to erase all traces of the tragedy. The corpses of the victims had been spirited away in the mid-

dle of the night, to be buried in unmarked graves. Their relatives were warned to keep quiet or face the possibility of dismissal from work or losing their place in the line for housing. The Communist apparatchiks and army generals who gave the order to shoot were never punished. Promises to erect a monument to the dead were never kept. It was even unclear exactly how many people had died as a result of the disturbances. The official figure was fifty-five, but many people in Gdańsk suspected that the real number was much higher.

Wałęsa used anniversaries of the December 1970 riots to denounce the Communist authorities. He organized unofficial rallies outside gate number two of the shipyard to demand that the authorities keep their promise to erect a memorial to the dead. The number of people attending these rallies grew from six in 1976 to one hundred in 1977 to five hundred in 1978. In December 1979 the shipyard management had attempted to sabotage the commemoration by sending workers home early, ostensibly as an "energy-saving measure." But some five thousand people turned up to listen to Wałęsa call for the establishment of a free trade union, independent of Communist Party control. At the end of his speech he urged everybody in the crowd to return to the same spot the following year, bearing a large stone.

"We'll build a mound with those stones, we'll cement them over, and that will be our monument. We'll erect it ourselves.!"[67]

THE SHIPYARD STRIKE WAS originally planned for August 13, 1980. But Wałęsa had to help his long-suffering wife, Danuta, at home that day—she had just given birth to their fifth child—so the revolution was postponed for twenty-four hours.

The instigators of the strike were three young shipyard workers: Jurek Borowczyk, Ludwik Pradzynski, and Bogdan Felski.[68] They all were in their early twenties, with no family commitments, few inhibitions, and practically nothing to lose. They shared the anger of the older workers over the humiliating living conditions and the arrogance of the one-party state but did not share their sense of caution. They had still been children in December 1970, when Polish security forces opened fire on workers outside the shipyard, and had not experienced political defeat. The consumer culture of the seventies, promoted by the party as a means of diverting the attention of young people away from politics, had put them in touch with Western fashions and Western ideas. While older workers were awed by the repressive power of

the Communist government, for these young men, the regime was an irrelevance.

Borowczyk and his friends felt reasonably confident they could persuade their workmates to join a protest action. Tens of thousands of Polish workers had already staged strikes over the government's attempts to raise meat prices at at the beginning of July. On each occasion, the workers had called off their protest after being promised large pay increases by the government. Such victories meant little at a time of high inflation. Within a few months the workers were as bad off as before. It was essential that the Gdańsk strike be organized properly.

In order to sustain their protest and ensure that the whole shipyard came out on strike, the young radicals knew that they needed someone experienced. Wałęsa was an ideal choice. He enjoyed considerable authority in the shipyard as one of the leaders of the failed 1970 uprising. He was also well known in Gdańsk as a prominent member of the underground Baltic free trade union movement. There were other opposition figures in the city, who were better read and had greater strategic vision. But Wałęsa had a special talent: making a nuisance of himself in public. He would seize any opportunity to denounce the Communist regime. He would hop on a tram or bus and immediately start distributing antigovernment leaflets. When he took a taxi, he would try to convert the driver to the cause of free trade unions. Exasperated by his behavior, the shipyard management had fired him for insolence in 1976. The authorities frequently locked him up in prison for forty-eight hours at a time. But all attempts to control the feisty little electrician were useless. Wałęsa would even argue with his jailers.

In early August the management of the Gdańsk shipyard handed the free trade union the perfect excuse for a strike. It fired an elderly crane operator named Anna Walentynowicz five months before she was due for retirement. The dismissal letter accused Walentynowicz of "severe violations" of labor discipline. Her real crime was her persistence in distributing *Coastal Worker*, the free trade-union newsletter. The union decided to retaliate.

If there was a guiding mind behind the initial organization of the strike, it was Bogdan Borusewicz, the thirty-year-old chief editor of *Coastal Worker*. A graduate of the Catholic University of Lublin, Borusewicz had a long history of conflict with the authorities. During the student unrest of 1968 he had been sentenced to three years in prison for handing out illegal leaflets in Gdańsk. He was in close contact with intellectual and dissident circles in Warsaw. It was Borusewicz who recruited the three young men from the shipyard—Borowczyk, Pradzynski, and Felski—to bring their fel-

low workers out on strike. Accustomed to the ways of conspiracy, he insisted on the need for strict secrecy. Even Wałęsa was given less than twenty-four hours' notice of the final date of the strike.[69]

On the morning of August 14 the three young workers fanned out across the sprawling shipyard. Each was armed with a dozen posters and five hundred or so leaflets, printed on the illegal presses of *Coastal Worker*. Borowczyk headed for his department, K-5, on the other side of a canal that runs through the middle of the shipyard. Rusting away in a corner of the department were piles of imported steel-welding equipment, costing millions of dollars, which nobody had learned how to put to use properly.[70]

The workers crowded around Borowczyk as he began distributing leaflets in the locker room. Signed by the editorial board of *Coastal Worker*, the leaflets called for the reinstatement of Anna Walentynowicz. "The authorities frequently resort to isolating those who show leadership potential," the leaflets declared. "If today we fail to make our opposition felt, there will be no one to contest the increase in working hours, the violations of security rules, or the compulsory overtime. The best way of defending our own interests is to defend one another."[71] In order to broaden the appeal of the strike, Borowczyk added a second demand, a thousand-zloty pay rise.

His colleagues were sympathetic but frightened. "Why doesn't a larger department begin the strike?" asked one worker. "We're not standing here any longer, let's go back to the hall," said another, glancing around nervously. Borowczyk knew that if the workers went back to the hall, under the gaze of the foreman and the Communist Party secretary, all would be lost. He had no idea if other departments had joined the strike, but he decided to take a risk.

"Let's go to K-three and K-four," he said, referring to two giant hull-making departments. "They've both stopped."[72]

A group of about thirty workers agreed to follow him. Beneath a makeshift banner announcing their two demands, they marched back across the drawbridge to the main section of the yard. Everywhere knots of curious workers formed to watch them pass, a lonely band of determined men dwarfed by the towering cranes and red propaganda posters hailing the glorious Communist future. "Come with us," they chanted. *Khodz z namy*. It was the same cry that had reverberated around the shipyard a decade before. In little groups of three and four, workers clambered down from the half-finished ships to join the swelling procession. Someone switched on the shipyard warning sirens, the agreed signal for the beginning of the strike.

Wearing their blue-gray overalls and yellow hard hats, the workers

skirted the back of the electricians' hall, W-4, where Wałęsa had worked four years previously. They headed for the K-3 department at the far end of the shipyard, near gate number three. A crowd of several hundred workers had gathered outside K-3, reading the posters hung up by Ludwik Pradzyn-ski. The effect of the two groups coming together was electric. "Hurrah, hurrah," they cheered. Suddenly they no longer felt alone.

By now they were several thousand strong. Growing more confident, they marched very slowly around the entire shipyard once again, attracting supporters as they went. They ended up at gate number two, where the tragedy of December 1970 had occurred. But this time, instead of surging out onto the streets, they halted. A minute's silence was declared in memory of the fallen. Then, their throats sore with emotion, they sang the national anthem, "*Jeszcze Polska nie zginęła, Póki my żyjemy*," "Poland has not per-ished yet / So long as we live."

LECH WAŁĘSA HEARD THE WAILING of the shipyard sirens at home in Stogi, a drab working-class suburb of crumbling prefabricated apartment blocks on the eastern outskirts of Gdańsk. He knew exactly what it meant. The shipyard named for the founder of the world's first socialist state was on strike.

Family problems had prevented him from getting away any sooner. His trade union activities had caused him to miss the birth of his daughter Ania a few days before. Police had knocked on the door of their two-room apart-ment with an arrest warrant just as his wife, Danuta, was about to go into labor. Detaining opposition activists for forty-eight-hour stints, without bringing formal charges, was a standard form of official harassment. By the time he was released, baby Ania had already been born. The trauma of the birth, in a crowded, unsanitary hospital, had left Danuta exhausted and barely able to stand. She insisted that Lech get the older kids dressed and take them to school before rushing off to change the world.

As he rode the tramway to the shipyard, dressed in his most respectable clothes, a shabby gray suit that looked as if it needed a good dry cleaning, Wałęsa wondered why he had not been arrested again. He could see a Pol-ish Fiat trailing the tram: the secret police were keeping a close eye on him. The authorities were expecting trouble in Gdańsk. A few days previously the party's top ideologist had boasted that the police knew the names and addresses of twelve thousand opposition activists in Poland. Rounding up potential troublemakers in a city like Gdańsk was a relatively simple affair.

A dark thought flashed across Wałęsa's mind: *Perhaps they actually want us to go on strike, so they can gun us all down once again.* [73]

By the time he arrived at the shipyard thirty-five minutes later, he had overcome his doubts. He thought of baby Ania and the life that awaited her in the People's Poland. There was no going back. It was up to ordinary Poles to assume responsibility for their own destiny, regardless of the Machiavellian calculations of Communist Party apparatchiks.

A crowd of people was milling around gate number two, the main entrance to the shipyard. Wałęsa could see that the guards were checking every pass. In order to get back into the yard, from which he had been banished four years previously, he climbed over a nearby brick wall.

A meeting was under way in the main square of the shipyard, just outside the red-brick hospital building. The shipyard director, Klemens Gniech, was attempting to persuade the workers to end the strike. He appeared to be having some success. There were boos and catcalls, but some people were drifting back to work. Wałęsa climbed up on the excavator. "Do you know who I am?" he asked angrily, tapping Gniech rudely on the shoulder. "I worked in this shipyard for ten years, and still feel myself to be a shipyard worker. I have the confidence of the workforce. It's been four years since I lost my job."[74]

The director was so astonished that he found it difficult to speak. The workers cheered one of their own. Sensing that he had got the upper hand, the quarrelsome electrician threw in several more demands for good measure. These included his own reinstatement and the construction of a monument to the fallen shipyard workers. He upped the demand for a pay raise to two thousand zlotys. The cheers grew even louder. Feeling the crowd behind him, Wałęsa announced an "occupation strike" and promised the workers that he would be the "last one" to leave the shipyard.

"I landed a straight left and put him down so quickly that he almost fell out of the ring," Wałęsa recalled later. "I shouted at him that the workers wouldn't go anywhere if they weren't sure that they had obtained what they wanted. So they felt strong, and I became their leader."[75]

WARSAW

August 15, 1980

EDWARD GIEREK WAS ON HOLIDAY in the Soviet Union when he heard about the strike at the Lenin Shipyard. Vacations by the Black Sea had become an annual ritual for the men who served as Moscow's proconsuls in Eastern Europe. Every August, at Brezhnev's invitation, the first secretaries of the ruling Communist parties assembled at a nineteenth-century palace on the southern tip of the Crimea. Luxuriating in tsarist splendor, they inhaled the sea air, gloated over the misfortunes afflicting the capitalist world, and issued self-congratulatory communiqués.

The trips to the Crimea gave Gierek an opportunity to demonstrate his good standing with Brezhnev. The obligatory television pictures of the two Communist Party chiefs embracing each other on the cheeks sent a message to political rivals back home. That was one reason why he had gone ahead with his vacation at a time when labor unrest was sweeping the country. His Politburo colleagues might grumble about his economic policies and engage in the endless game of bureaucratic intrigue behind his back. But there was little chance that they would make any serious move against him as long as he appeared to enjoy the confidence of the Kremlin.

It had not been a restful vacation. Shortly after his arrival in the Crimea, at the end of July, Gierek had had an unpleasant interview with Brezhnev.

The *gensek* was greatly alarmed by a strike in the eastern Polish city of Lublin that had paralyzed the main Moscow–Berlin railway line.[76] For four days the Soviet Union had been without rail communications with its front-line troops in East Germany. Such a state of affairs was intolerable, Brezhnev made clear. Gierek had tried to reassure the old man. For a few days the strike wave appeared to subside. Then came the shattering news from Gdańsk.

A special plane was dispatched from Warsaw to bring the first secretary back home. From the airport he drove to Communist Party headquarters. As he walked through the oak doors of the Politburo conference room, his colleagues rose respectfully from their seats.[77]

The Politburo had been in emergency sessions since the previous day, when the Lenin Shipyard had gone on strike. The party secretary responsible for national security, Stanisław Kania, reported that the strike had already paralyzed most of the Gdańsk region. A wave of panic buying had been observed along the Baltic coast. There were signs of trouble spreading to other parts of the country. A state of alert had been ordered in the armed forces, and army and police reserves dispatched to Gdańsk.

"And where are all the party members?" demanded Gierek, seated at the head of the oval conference table, in the place of honor, directly beneath an oil portrait of Lenin.[78]

The question was directed at Kania, a thick-jowled apparatchik with a square peasant's face. During Gierek's absence in the Crimea he had been left in charge in Warsaw. He had paid a series of visits to trouble spots around the country, including Gdańsk, and understood something that Gierek had not yet grasped: The party had lost its authority.

"The party members are not strong enough to oppose what is now going on," he replied. "There were no signals that a strike was about to start in the shipyard. They were taken unawares. There is now a real danger that the situation could get out of control."[79]

Other Politburo members supported Kania. During the two weeks Gierek had been away, not a single day had gone by without a strike. Deteriorating standards of living had left rank-and-file party members demoralized. "Antisocialist elements" were exploiting the legitimate discontent of the workers. Economic demands were being transformed into political demands, including the establishment of free trade unions. Despite rigid censorship and the resolutely upbeat tone of the official media, news about fresh outbreaks of labor unrest traveled fast. Foreign radio stations, particularly Radio Free Europe, were devoting blanket coverage to the crisis.

The news from Gdańsk was politically devastating for Gierek. A former coal miner with a reputation for caring about workers, he had come to power on the wave of labor unrest in December 1970 that had sealed the fate of his predecessor, the autocratic Władysław Gomułka. Several weeks after his appointment, Gierek had visited the Lenin Shipyard to appeal to the workers for their "help." "We will help you, Comrade Gierek," the workers had shouted back. "*Pomożemy, Towarysz Gierek.*" *Pomożemy* had become the slogan of the Gierek regime.[80]

The first secretary understood the cutthroat world of party politics better than anyone else in the room. He suspected that his enemies in the Politburo were exploiting the latest outbreak of strikes to move against him.[81] He asked himself the question that Communist Party bosses usually ask themselves in such circumstances: Who stood to gain from his overthrow?

The answer seemed obvious: the security apparatus. During a period of social upheaval the armed forces and the Interior Ministry became the guarantors of political stability in the country. There could be no major shakeup in either institution until the strikes were over. With their vast network of agents and informers around the country, the security chiefs were also best placed to manipulate the unrest to their own advantage.

Kania seemed harmless enough. He was known to be fond of alcohol and was frequently incapable of serious work after lunch. In Communist Party circles such a weakness was not generally considered an obstacle to high office: It made a man more pliable, more dependent on his Politburo colleagues. Recently, however, Kania had been displaying some worrying signs of independence. Furthermore, he had a powerful ally in the defense minister, General Wojciech Jaruzelski.[82]

Like many high-ranking Polish Communists, Gierek could not understand why the security chiefs had allowed the labor unrest to grow and grow without taking elementary countermeasures. Had they wanted to put a stop to the strikes, he reasoned, it would have been a simple enough matter to isolate the principal troublemakers and prevent information reaching Western correspondents in Warsaw. But Kania had said repeatedly that the situation was under control and that Gierek should go ahead with his Crimean holiday. Now that the strikes were spreading along the Baltic coast, the task of restoring order was more difficult.

Gierek's first instinct was to counterattack. Obviously, he told the Politburo, the strikers were inspired by "outside forces."

"This is not something we need to discuss today, but we do need to think about it," said Gierek, suggesting he might favor an armed crackdown. "It

is clear that this period of tension cannot go on indefinitely. It may take a more dangerous form—and that would compel us to use force."[83]

Within hours of Gierek's return to Warsaw, the machinery of repression had moved into high gear, and columns of riot troops were moving in the direction of Gdańsk. The Polish government placed three army regiments stationed in the Gdańsk region on a state of alert. Soviet naval ships appeared off the Baltic coast. Warsaw Pact troops in East Germany and the western Soviet Union were called up for what the Soviet news agency Tass euphemistically described as "routine maneuvers."[84] Telephone communications with Gdańsk were cut. A task force was established in the Ministry of Interior to prepare a plan to crush the rebellion and normalize "the country's social and political situation." The plan, code-named Summer '80, envisaged the storming of the Lenin Shipyard by helicopter, the arrest of Wałęsa and other strike leaders, and twenty-four-hour surveillance of "antisocialist forces."[85]

The immediate priority was to contain the revolt within the Lenin Shipyard.

WHILE GIEREK WAS DEMANDING a smothering of information about the unrest in Gdańsk, a balding man in a moth-eaten silk dressing gown was busy dispensing it as rapidly as possible. Jacek Kuroń lived in a three-room apartment on Adam Mickiewicz Street, a fifteen-minute tram ride from the Central Committee building. Over the last month he had slept no more than three or four hours a night. He spent his days and nights on the phone, relaying information from the strike committees springing up around Poland to Western news organizations in Warsaw.

Kuroń's address book contained the names and telephone numbers of hundreds of opposition activists in towns and villages all over Poland, from Arłamow to Zakopane. Western correspondents used to joke that it was the most subversive document in the Soviet empire. Its owner sat behind a large wooden desk, littered with half-drunk cups of coffee, discarded cigarette packages, old newspapers, hastily scribbled notes, and a battered orange phone. A human dynamo, he was seldom in repose. He would dial one number, listen for fifteen or twenty seconds, and bark out a few commands. Practically hoarse from a surfeit of talking, smoking, and drinking, he would pause only to dial a new number. He talked at machine-gun speed—as if expecting the telephone to be cut off at any moment. In the rare moments when he was not on the phone, Kuroń devoted his attention to the

never-ending stream of visitors who tramped through his apartment. After the last visitor had left, he would slump down on a couch in the corner of the room for a few hours' sleep.

For Poland's Communist leaders, this disheveled personage was Lucifer incarnate, an "enemy of the state" and a "hireling of world imperialism." For the country's rapidly growing dissident movement, he had an almost godlike status. He was organizer, ideologist, and den mother rolled into one.

A former "Red Scout" and lecturer at Warsaw University, Kuroń had received an orthodox Marxist education. He had been active in the Communist youth movement and had appeared destined for a brilliant Communist Party career. But he had fallen out with the authorities in the early sixties for writing a Trotskyist critique that accused the Communist bureaucracy of exploiting the working class as ruthlessly as capitalists did. Since 1965 Kuroń had spent more than six years in jail for "antistate activities." While he was in prison, his political views had evolved. He found inspiration in Polish history books, particularly works about the great nineteenth-century insurrections against Russian rule. He ceased to think in Marxist terms. Although he never became a believer, he came to respect the Catholic Church for its role in preserving Poland's national identity. He began to consider the problem of how civil society could develop in the shadow of a totalitarian regime.

Contrary to what the official news media said about him, Kuroń did not advocate an all-out confrontation with the state. Indeed, he was convinced that society had no chance of winning a violent showdown with a heavily armed opponent. This was the lesson of the workers' rebellion of 1970.

The only solution was to bypass the party altogether. Society would ignore the institutions of the Communist regime and create its own unofficial structures, rolling back the frontiers of totalitarianism. By behaving *as if* they were free, Poles eventually would become free. Underground newspapers would make a mockery of government censorship. A "flying university," meeting in private homes, would circumvent the state education system. A network of civic defense committees would result in de facto freedom of association. The structures of Communist power would be preserved as an ideological fig leaf for the Kremlin, but Poland would become a pluralist society in all but name.

"Don't burn down party committees; found your own" was Kuroń's motto.

The free trade unionists in Gdańsk formed part of Kuroń's extended opposition family. At the heart of the network was the Workers' Defense Com-

mittee, known by its Polish initials as KOR. Founded in 1976 by a group of Warsaw intellectuals to assist the victims of police brutality, KOR soon developed into a political pressure group. Its members issued statements drawing attention to human rights violations and criticizing the Communist Party's management of the economy. KOR became a kind of umbrella organization for other opposition groups, ranging from peasants' defense committees to underground publishers. When a new wave of labor unrest broke out in July 1980 over a government plan to raise the price of meat, Kuroń established a strike information center in his apartment.

Kuroń and his friends recognized that the Polish Communists were not going to give up any of their hard-won political power willingly. They believed, however, that the stark facts of economic decline would oblige the regime to come to an understanding with the opposition. By holding down the living standards of ordinary people, the Communist countries of Eastern Europe had achieved some remarkably high rates of economic growth in the fifties and sixties. But the era of high growth rates had now come to an end. In 1979, for the first time in postwar Poland, the economy had actually shrunk by some 2 percent. The sacrifices had been in vain. The boom had turned into a bust.

The most immediate crisis facing the regime was a crippling foreign debt. During the early seventies the Gierek government had borrowed billions of dollars to finance grandiose investment projects. Western banks and governments had fallen over themselves to provide credit; the Soviet bloc was generally considered a "good risk." Surely, it was argued, the Kremlin would never allow one of its satellites to default. Gierek boasted about building "a second Poland." The idea was to construct hundreds of modern factories, dramatically increase the production of consumer goods, and pay back the loan with increased exports to the West. But the plan had misfired. Few of the projects selected by the supposedly omniscient planners had been economically justified. Most were the result of the personal whims of Polish leaders, large bribes from Western companies, or sheer bureaucratic incompetence. By 1980 Poland owed its creditors some eighteen billion dollars. Virtually every dollar that Poland earned in foreign exchange from exports was earmarked for servicing the debt.

The unofficial opposition was ready to help the government find a way out of the crisis—for a price. Polish society had to be allowed to develop its own "self-governing" institutions. The Communist Party would have to provide guarantees that it would no longer resort to arbitrary violence and would not renege on concessions extracted in moments of weakness. Lead-

ers who had previously been accountable to no one but themselves would have to submit to some kind of social control. At the very least, that meant open discussion of the economic and social catastrophe facing the country.

After the government had cut telephone and telex links between Gdańsk and Warsaw, the boundlessly energetic Kuroń devised a human relay system to circumvent the information blockade. As soon as something happened at the shipyard, his acolytes in the free trade union movement would drive a hundred miles or so in the direction of Warsaw. When they found a functioning telephone, they would call Kuroń. The system was cumbersome, but it worked.

On Saturday, August 16, Kuroń's informants reported that the strike committee had agreed to a compromise pay offer and had called off the strike. A few hours later came news that the shipyard workers had decided to continue the strike—in solidarity with other workers in the Gdańsk region.

As Kuroń relayed the story, Wałęsa had been on the point of going home to his wife and children when he was confronted by angry delegates from other factories. "If you abandon us, we'll be lost," screamed the representatives of the striking bus and tram drivers. "Buses can't face tanks." Several hundred predominantly young workers surged around Wałęsa, chanting, "Solidarity, Solidarity." Wałęsa grabbed a microphone and began speaking to the crowd gathered in front of the shipyard gates.[86]

"I promised you that I would stay here to the end. Who wants to go on with the strike?"

Chants of "We do," "We do."

"Who wants to end the strike?"

Silence.

"The strike goes on!"

It was a crucial moment, as Kuroń was quick to appreciate. The Communist authorities were dealing no longer with an isolated outbreak of labor unrest, but with a vast protest movement that would grow until it enveloped all sections of Polish society. As a first step the workers in Gdańsk had established an interfactory strike committee to represent the interests of striking workers all over the country. Wałęsa had been elected chairman. The workers' principal demand, stabbing like a dagger to the heart of Communist ideology, was free trade unions.

WARSAW

August 29, 1980

E<small>DWARD</small> G<small>IEREK</small> <small>REMEMBERED</small> with bitterness how the whole country had breathed a sigh of relief when he came to power. Striking workers along the Baltic coast had hailed him as one of their own. Communist app020ratchiks had predicted that he would help restore the party's depleted authority. The Kremlin had showered him with compliments, describing him as an "outstanding Marxist-Leninist." Even the West had joined in the applause for a personable Communist leader who seemed to understand the value of détente and economic cooperation. Everyone was sick and tired of Gomułka, who had been brought to power during a previous wave of workers' unrest, in 1956.

The wheel of Polish history had turned full circle, Gierek reflected. Everybody was turning on him, just as everyone had turned on Gomułka in December 1970. In the space of a few days he had become the object of almost universal derision. At the Lenin Shipyard in Gdańsk the same workers who had shouted, "We will help you, Comrade Gierek," ten years before greeted his most recent television appearance with jeers and catcalls. His allies in the Politburo seemed embarrassed to be associated with him. The Soviets were making ominous noises about the "threat to socialism" in Poland and the "mistakes" committed by the Polish leadership. Western leaders

who had once beaten a path to his door were gloating over the extraordinary challenge to his power. Everywhere, people were saying that he was finished.

As usual, ordinary Poles expressed their sentiments about their political leaders in a joke. "Question: What is the difference between Gierek and Gomułka? Answer: None, only Gierek doesn't realize it yet."

At Politburo meetings the Kania-Jaruzelski tandem was already taking aim at his economic policies. Jaruzelski, whom Gierek had earlier regarded as an ally, claimed he had learned about Poland's huge foreign debt from a broadcast on Radio Free Europe. Kania, the party secretary in charge of national security, complained that the Politburo had been treated with "total contempt."[87] Other Politburo members, who had previously groveled before the first secretary, joined in the attack. In order to appease the critics, Gierek had been forced to sacrifice six of his closest associates. He was under enormous stress. He felt isolated and abandoned.[88]

The first secretary was still surrounded by the trappings of power: the bulletproof limousine, the deferential secretaries, the security guards. The plain black telephone on his desk was a direct line to Brezhnev. A companion white telephone, with push buttons, provided instant communications with Communist Party leaders in other Soviet bloc countries, from Czechoslovakia to Bulgaria. Just along the hallway was a special communications room dominated by a large wall map of Poland with forty-nine miniature lightbulbs, one for each vojvodship (province). Seated behind a microphone, Gierek could speak directly to any provincial governor in the country. Or he could flick a switch to light up all forty-nine lightbulbs, representing forty-nine local Communist Party bosses ready to carry out his orders. It was a perfect example of the command economy transmitting instructions downward.[89]

To Gierek's dismay, the bureaucratic machine was no longer responding to his orders. It was not so much that someone else had grabbed the levers of power as that the levers themselves had ceased to function. Senior leaders appeared on television—and no one paid any attention. Instructions were issued to rank-and-file party members and promptly forgotten. The map in room 115 flashed its lights, but the list of striking factories grew ever longer. Communist Party branches in the Lenin Shipyard and hundreds of other proletarian bastions around the country had withered away overnight. The party itself—a mighty organization with more than three million members—was doing nothing. Its leaders had become generals without an army.

At first Gierek took comfort in the thought that the strike leaders did not represent the workers. He was disabused of this notion by the government representative in Gdańsk, Mieczysław Jagielski, who insisted that the strike had the "total support" of society. "My feeling is that we are going to have to agree to the creation of free trade unions," Jagielski reported on August 26. "Today the workers are still asking our permission [to establish their own unions]. Tomorrow they may not bother to ask us."[90]

The following day, August 27, the Soviet ambassador came to see Gierek with a letter describing the Kremlin's growing concern over events in Poland. Soviet leaders were outraged by the presence of so many foreign journalists in the Lenin Shipyard. They wanted a much more vigorous propaganda campaign against the strikers, citing the way Lenin had dealt with the "anarchosyndicalist" opposition in 1921. Gierek understood this to be a reference to the purges of opposition leaders and the Red Army's brutal suppression of a rebellion at the Kronshtadt naval base, with the loss of several thousand lives. Shaken by the comparison, he told the ambassador that the deployment of the army on the streets might only make things worse.

"A soldier in a tank is only effective if he is willing to shoot. These soldiers are Poles, and we don't know if they would be willing to shoot at workers."[91]

Gierek postponed a decision on what to do. He seemed to be hoping for a miracle or at least more concrete guidance from Moscow on how to deal with a crisis that confounded all Marxist-Leninist theory. The situation had continued to deteriorate, and by Friday, August 29, half the country was out on strike. By official count, some seven hundred factories were being occupied by around seven hundred thousand workers. "Strike alerts" had been declared in many of the country's remaining factories. The protests were on the verge of becoming a general strike. The labor unrest had spread from the Baltic coast to the textile city of Łódż in central Poland and the coal-mining region of Silesia in the south. Practically every sector of Polish industry was affected.

The news that the coal miners had joined the strike was a terrible blow. Gierek regarded Silesia as a personal fiefdom, the one region of Poland that would never betray him. Silesia had been the springboard from which he had launched his political career. Its people were reserved and industrious, not given to dramatic political gestures. The local security forces kept a tight rein on dissidents. As the situation in the rest of the country grew progressively worse, Gierek considered making a last stand in Silesia.

"We will withdraw from Warsaw to the South and then we will reconquer

the country vojvodship by vojvodship," he told an associate, in the desperate tone of a man who knows that he has already lost.[92]

Over the past two weeks the first secretary had changed his mind several times about how to respond to the labor unrest. In his memoirs, written ten years after the event, he claimed he consistently opposed the use of force. His Politburo colleagues and Soviet interlocutor present a different picture of his actions and state of mind during those tension-filled days. According to these accounts, Gierek considered calling for Soviet military assistance at the beginning of the crisis. His Politburo colleagues opposed the idea, and nothing came of it. At other times Gierek insisted that the protests be defused peacefully. Many different emotions were churning inside him: the desire to hang on to his job; bitterness at the disloyalty of those around him; concern for his own reputation.

"There were many different Giereks," recalled Kania, the man closest to him during this period. "Not only the early Gierek, the man of the early seventies, who had social support, and the later Gierek, who had to leave the political scene. In every period there were several Giereks, and during the most difficult times there were several Giereks in the course of a single day."[93]

Now Gierek sat quietly as the debate swirled around him at the Politburo meeting. His tactic of choice—procrastination—was no longer feasible. There were essentially two alternatives: agree to the demand for free trade unions or suppress the unrest by force. The Interior Ministry task force had devised a plan to storm the Lenin Shipyard and take over the Baltic ports. That morning, the head of the task force, General Bogusław Stachura, had reported that his men were ready "to liquidate the counterrevolutionary nest in Gdańsk."[94] In the Politburo the spokesman for the hard-liners (or men of cement, as they were known in Polish) was a former trade union boss named Władysław Kruczek, an elderly holdover from the Stalinist era. He demanded the immediate declaration of a state of emergency.

"The regime must begin to defend itself. Even the most beautiful speeches are not producing any results."[95]

This was the signal for the Politburo members in charge of security to mount a counteroffensive. Although they had secretly begun drawing up plans for a crackdown, they thought it was too early to put them into effect.[96] Kania described the proposal for Wałęsa's arrest as "a daydream." Jaruzelski, the practical military officer, pointed out that the Polish constitution made no provision for a "state of emergency." If force was used, the government would have to declare a "state of war" (*stan wojenny*), but such

a step was "unrealistic" at a time when half the country was on strike. One should not give orders that could not be carried out. A similar point was made by the police minister, Stanisław Kowalczyk. The security forces lacked the manpower to crack down everywhere at once. His men could seize port facilities in Gdańsk, but there would certainly be bloodshed.

The Politburo was in a quandary. Gierek's frantic appeals to Moscow for guidance had produced no result. Brezhnev was officially said to be "unavailable." The Kremlin was not prepared to issue a dispensation to the Poles to embrace the heresy of free trade unions, which it saw as tantamount to the "legalization of the antisocialist opposition."[97] On the other hand, Soviet leaders were frightened by what might happen if the Polish leadership failed to reach some kind of agreement with the workers. So they did what Soviet bureaucrats usually did when they could not make up their minds: They stopped answering their phones. They also put their own forces in the region on "full combat alert" and called up one hundred thousand military reservists.[98]

The first secretary summed up the mood of the meeting by telling his Politburo colleagues that free trade unions were unacceptable, ideologically and politically. There was, however, no other acceptable short-term solution. "We are being threatened with a general strike. We have to choose the lesser evil and then find a way of extricating ourselves from it."

GDAŃSK

August 31, 1980

THE LAST DAY OF THE STRIKE at the Lenin Shipyard began, as usual, with a mass. A wooden platform had been erected in the middle of the shipyard to form a makeshift altar, complete with carpet and wooden crucifix. A few yards away, on the wall of an administration building, was a faded hammer and sickle flag. A priest in resplendent white vestments broke a ceremonial wafer in front of ten thousand kneeling workers and television cameras from all over the world. Other priests fanned out through the crowd to hear mumbled confessions.

When the time came to sign the agreement giving workers the right to form independent labor unions, Wałęsa produced a foot-long souvenir pen of the pope's pilgrimage to Poland the previous year. It was a typical Wałęsa gesture, a tongue-in-cheek way of sending a message to millions of his fellow Poles. He knew that state television planned to broadcast large parts of the signing ceremony, and he wanted to distinguish himself from the party functionaries with whom he had been negotiating. He would never permit himself to become one of them. He also wanted to recognize publicly his debt to the man who had inspired the nation to voice its opposition to totalitarian rule. The ploy was successful. That evening Polish television viewers were permitted their first glimpse of the strikers who had been defying

the Communist government for the past two weeks. When they saw a worker with an oversize mustache and a pen with a portrait of the pope on it sitting next to some bureaucrats in expensive-looking suits, they immediately knew which side they were on.

Unusually for him, Wałęsa read his speech declaring an end to the strike from a prepared text. He paid tribute to Jagielski, the government negotiator, and "a certain rather reasonable group" in the Politburo that had resisted the use of force. "We reached agreement as Poles with Poles. . . . Did we achieve all we wanted, fulfill all our longings and our dreams? . . . Not everything. But we all know we gained a lot. . . . We got all we could in the present situation. The rest will be achieved because we have what matters most: our independent, self-governing trade unions. That is our guarantee for the future."[99] He stressed the words "independent" and "self-governing" as if they were a magical mantra, before concluding, "I declare the strike over."

It was Jagielski's turn to address the delegates and the huge crowd gathered outside in the brilliant August sunshine. The deputy prime minister had spent a fretful forty-eight hours, shuttling between Gdańsk and Warsaw for meetings with his Politburo colleagues and the Soviet ambassador. The Kremlin had never responded to the doctrinal query about free trade unions. Polish leaders had taken the Soviet silence as a sign that it was up to them to do whatever was necessary to bring the strikes to an end.

"Esteemed audience," Jagielski began. "We tried to show the practical limits of what we could undertake and actually implement. I reiterate and confirm what has been said. We talked as Poles should talk to one another, as Pole with Pole."

As he echoed Wałęsa's thought, Jagielski was interrupted by a loud burst of applause. By common consent, he had acquitted himself well during the weeklong negotiations. He had represented a corrupt and unpopular regime with dignity.

After the government delegation had departed, members of the strike committee hoisted Wałęsa onto their shoulders and carried him to gate number two one last time. A refrain of *Sto lat, sto lat* (May he live a hundred years) echoed around the shipyard. As Wałęsa scrambled on top of a forklift truck and punched his fists in the air in celebration of victory, the huge crowd broke out into chants of "Le-szek, Le-szek." It looked like a scene from a movie: the sea of jubilant, exhausted faces; the white and red Polish flag fluttering in the breeze; the red banner reading "Workers of all Factories, Unite!" Indeed, it soon became a movie. The crowd at the ship-

yard gate included Andrzej Wajda, who had just come up with an idea for a new film, to be called *Man of Iron.*

As the cheering died down, Wałęsa told the crowd that he had been unable to achieve anything by himself. "We did this together. Everybody together, that is power. That is strength." He then reminded his listeners why he kept coming back to gate number two. "My actions are connected to December 1970. Perhaps someone will accuse me of being a dictator, but I say we must always meet here on December 16. Always, always. We must always remember those who were killed."[100]

The chants of "Le-szek, Le-szek" started up again, this time with even greater force. Workers in yellow hard hats flung open the shipyard gates, and the strikers streamed out into the sun-filled streets of Gdańsk. At that moment everything seemed possible. August had been a triumph of memory over forgetting. In fact, the storm clouds were just beginning to gather.

WASHINGTON

December 3, 1980

MONITORING THE POLISH DRAMA from his office in the White House, President Jimmy Carter's national security adviser was becoming increasingly pessimistic. Like most Polish-Americans, Zbigniew Brzezinski had been exhilarated by the rise of Solidarity and the resurgence of Polish national feeling, but he also found it difficult to believe that the Kremlin would ignore such a serious challenge to its authority. The Soviet Union had shown repeatedly—in East Germany in 1953, Hungary in 1956, and Czechoslovakia in 1968—that it was willing to use force to defend its East European empire. Polish history was full of brave, but ultimately doomed, insurrections against Russian rule.

Brzezinski knew very well that the United States could not prevent Soviet tanks from rolling into Poland without being prepared to risk a nuclear war. But it could raise the stakes. If Washington had reason to believe that the Soviet Union was preparing to invade Poland, it had a duty to say so. In August 1968 the United States had picked up clear evidence of massive Soviet troop movements around Czechoslovakia but had failed to act on the information. American passivity, Brzezinski believed, had unwittingly strengthened the hand of the hard-liners in the Soviet Politburo. Had the Johnson administration warned Brezhnev of the devastating impact that an

invasion of Czechoslovakia was likely to have on East-West relations, history might have turned out differently. Brzezinski, the author of the standard university textbook on the Soviet bloc, was determined that Carter would not repeat LBJ's mistake. His strategy was to make as much noise as possible in order to dissuade the Soviets from military intervention.[101]

By the beginning of December American spy satellites had picked up information that seemed to support Brzezinski's worst fears. Satellite photos showed that civilian traffic along East Germany's border with Poland had dwindled to a trickle, suggesting that the frontier had been sealed. On Poland's border with the Soviet Union, soldiers were unfolding hospital tents and stockpiling ammunition. In northern Czechoslovakia long columns of tanks and artillery pieces were moving up to the frontier. The roads were icy and treacherous, making this an unusual time of year to be holding such a huge exercise. Occasionally a tank slithered into a ditch or a telegraph pole. In Poland itself the two Soviet tank divisions stationed near the southwestern town of Legnica were on a state of high alert.

The information gleaned from the spy satellites was confirmed by an exceptionally well-placed Polish agent. Disillusioned with communism and disgusted by the December 1970 massacre of workers in Gdańsk, Colonel Ryszard Kukliński had been cooperating with the CIA for almost a decade. He was an intelligence agent's dream. A brilliant staff officer completely trusted by the defense minister, General Jaruzelski, he had access to the innermost secrets of the regime. He had already supplied Washington with sensational details about Soviet war plans and the degree to which the Polish army was subject to Kremlin control. In October 1980, just three months after the creation of Solidarity, he had been invited to join a secret working group set up at the Ministry of Defense to lay the groundwork for the introduction of martial law. He was now able to provide the CIA with up-to-the-minute details of the Soviet campaign to intimidate the Polish government.[102]

In early December Kukliński reported that the Kremlin had presented Jaruzelski with an ultimatum. A total of eighteen Warsaw Pact divisions—fifteen Soviet, two Czech, and one East German—would enter Poland at midnight on December 8. Polish troops had been ordered to cooperate fully. The operation had been depicted as a routine exercise, code-named *Soyuz* (Alliance) 80. In reality it was an invasion in disguise. Jaruzelski was so shocked that he shut himself up in his office, refusing to see even his closest associates. He was particularly distressed by the fact that German troops would be participating in the operation. If the ultimatum were carried out,

German and Soviet armies would jointly dismember Poland for the second time in half a century. The Polish General Staff was stunned and paralyzed.[103]

The threat of a new partition of Poland galvanized Brzezinski into action. Having left Poland at the age of ten, shortly before the Nazi invasion, he had severed most of his ties with his former homeland. But he felt part of a remarkable Polish diaspora that included Karol Wojtyła, Pope John Paul II; Secretary of State Edmund Muskie; Israeli Prime Minister Menachem Begin; and the winner of the 1980 Nobel Prize for literature, Czesław Miłosz. (Throughout the Solidarity crisis the diaspora acted as a high-powered international think tank on Polish affairs. At one particularly tense moment the pope and the national security adviser conferred by phone in their native language.)

Brzezinski, the son of a prewar Polish diplomat, also had a slight connection with Jaruzelski, the general who was to declare war on Solidarity twelve months later. Brzezinski's older stepbrother and Jaruzelski both had attended a Catholic boarding school in Warsaw, run on military lines by the Marian friars.[104] The two boys spent much of their time reciting mass, parading up and down in dark blue uniforms, and singing songs glorifying Poland's military dictator, Marshal Piłsudski. When war broke out, the boys were scattered in different directions. The Jaruzelskis were deported to the Soviet Union, and later returned to Poland as standard-bearers for communism. The Brzezinskis ended up in Canada and the United States.

Over the past few days Brzezinski had urged Poles to sink their differences in the face of the Soviet threat. He advised Solidarity emissaries to consolidate their gains rather than risk a showdown. He also encouraged government leaders to tell Moscow they were determined to keep Poland within the Warsaw Pact but would resist a Soviet invasion. Once again his strategy was guided by a desire to avoid the mistakes of the past. The Soviets had been able to act with impunity in Czechoslovakia in August 1968, Brzezinski reasoned, because they knew in advance that there would be no resistance from the Czech army.[105]

Concerned that time was running out, the national security adviser now persuaded Carter to get on the "hot line" to Brezhnev. A teletype link between the White House and the Kremlin, the hot line was technologically inferior to the telephone since it did not allow voice communication. (Facsimile machines were installed only in 1986.) But the very fact that an American president was using a device that traced its origins to the 1962 Cuban missile crisis—when communications difficulties had brought the world to a brink of a nuclear war—served to underline the gravity of the moment.

In a few moments a rickety teletype machine down the corridor from Brezhnev's office was spitting out the president's message. It began on a note of reassurance: "I WISH TO CONVEY TO YOU THE FIRM INTENTION OF THE UNITED STATES NOT TO EXPLOIT THE EVENTS IN POLAND, NOR TO THREATEN LEGITIMATE SOVIET SECURITY INTERESTS IN THAT REGION."

Then came the threat: "AT THE SAME TIME, I HAVE TO STATE OUR RELATIONSHIP WOULD BE MOST ADVERSELY AFFECTED IF FORCE WAS USED TO IMPOSE A SOLUTION UPON THE POLISH NATION." The five-sentence missive was signed, somewhat incongruously, "BEST WISHES, JIMMY CARTER."[106]

At 1621 Washington time—twenty-one minutes past midnight in Moscow—word arrived from the Kremlin confirming receipt of the message.

MOSCOW

December 5, 1980

As THEY FLEW TO MOSCOW in answer to a summons from the Soviet leadership, Stanisław Kania and Wojciech Jaruzelski felt a sense of impending doom. They knew that the armies of their Warsaw Pact allies were camped around Poland's borders, ready to enter the country at any moment. Live ammunition had been distributed; field hospitals had been set up to take care of the wounded; communication lines were in place. Their attempts to arrange a private meeting with Brezhnev had been rebuffed. The Polish leaders had been excluded from the first day of the emergency Soviet bloc summit at which the fate of their country would be decided.

Kania, who had succeeded Gierek as first secretary of the Polish Communist Party, thought of his son, Mirek, who was serving in the army.[107] Nobody knew how Polish soldiers would react in the event of a Soviet invasion. Even if they were confined to barracks, there was a strong possibility of spontaneous resistance, which would almost certainly result in terrible bloodshed. Jaruzelski recalled the many Polish rebellions against foreign rule that had ended in bloody failure. His grandfather and two of his great-uncles had been sentenced to twelve years' exile in Siberia for taking part in the 1863 insurrection against the tsars.[108]

Like Brzezinski, Kania and Jaruzelski thought constantly about how the

Soviets had crushed the 1968 Prague Spring. The Czechoslovak reformers, under Dubček, had forfeited Moscow's confidence by talking about "socialism with a human face" and tampering with the holy grail of Marxist-Leninist ideology. The Polish Communists had adopted a different strategy. They presented themselves as trustworthy defenders of Soviet-style socialism in Poland. When other Soviet bloc leaders attacked them, they meekly agreed with the criticism. They acknowledged that the "antisocialist" forces posed a serious threat. At the same time, they argued that they were in control of the situation and had both the means and the will to defeat the enemies of socialism. They even hinted that if events really did get out of control, they themselves would appeal for "fraternal assistance."[109]

The Soviet leaders had selected a villa on top of the Lenin Hills as the site of the inquisition. The view over the winding Moskva River and the gilded domes of the Novodevichy monastery had attracted rulers and would-be rulers of Russia for centuries. From this spot, in September 1812, Napoleon had gazed out over the burning rooftops of Moscow after conquering an entire continent. Confronted with the scorched-earth tactics of the Russian army, he concluded that he had no choice but to retreat back to Paris at the head of his rapidly dwindling *Grande Armée*. It was the turning point of one of history's great military campaigns. In the Soviet period the Politburo had built a complex of luxurious guesthouses on top of the hills, surrounded by high concrete walls pierced by heavy wrought-iron gates. It was here that the Polish leadership would be confronted with evidence of the counterrevolution.

The Poles were shown into a large conference room, equipped with translation booths. The curtains were closed. Facing them across a vast square table, beneath heavy chandeliers, were the leaders of the Soviet Union and five other Warsaw Pact countries, who had met in private the previous day. Two of these leaders, János Kádár of Hungary and Gustáv Husák of Czechoslovakia, had come to power as the direct result of Soviet invasions. A third, Erich Honecker, had risen through the ranks of the Communist youth movement as Soviet tanks suppressed a workers' uprising in Berlin in 1953.

It was Honecker who played the role of Grand Inquisitor. Frightened that the "Polish disease" could spread to East Germany, he had been particularly active in lobbying for Soviet military intervention and was ready to contribute between two and four divisions to ensure its success. Before traveling to Moscow, he had obtained "plenipotentiary powers" from his Politburo colleagues in the event of an invasion.[110]

"There is a danger to the constitutional order. The internal Polish solu-

tion is almost exhausted. We are ready to help in the struggle with the counterrevolution. The Gdańsk agreement was a mistake, a capitulation to enemy forces. There must be no further retreat."[111]

A physical fitness fanatic, who exercised daily in his private gym, Honecker had plenty of experience defending "the gains of socialism." As East Germany's security chief he had supervised the construction of the Berlin Wall in August 1961. Dubbed the "Anti-Fascist Protection Wall" by the Communists, the one-hundred-mile-long network of concrete, barbed wire, and machine-gun posts was designed to prevent East Germans from fleeing to the West. Its lightning construction—one of Europe's largest cities was sliced into two halves overnight—was a source of great satisfaction to Honecker. He later recalled that "nothing essential" had been forgotten in an operation that had made the world "take notice" of the German Democratic Republic.[112]

Nicolae Ceaușescu, the maverick Romanian dictator feted in Western capitals for refusing to join the invasion of Czechoslovakia, joined in the attack. In an attempt to win popularity at home and dupe the West into granting him trading concessions, the self-styled "Genius of the Carpathians" claimed to be pursuing a policy of "national independence." In reality his regime was a virtual carbon copy of Stalin's. As the supreme leader (*conducător*) of Romania, Ceaușescu owed his power to an omniscient security service, a slavishly loyal party, and a personality cult of absurdist dimensions. He was astute enough to understand that all this could be undermined if the "Polish disease" were allowed to spread.

"Any concession is tantamount to capitulation by the Party," the *conducător* whined. "In addition to political methods, other steps must be taken that will strengthen the state authorities and smash the counterrevolution. There must be an element of force."

Now it was Kádár's turn. Installed in power by the Red Army following the 1956 uprising, the Hungarian leader had the reputation of being the most sophisticated and flexible of East European leaders. He had softened his "butcher of Budapest" image by promoting a consumer ideology known as goulash communism and experimenting with market mechanisms in the economy. But he remained brutally realistic about the limits of Soviet tolerance and the character of his Kremlin patrons. "Do you really not know the kind of people you're dealing with?" he had asked Dubček, in frustration, three days before Russian tanks rolled into Czechoslovakia.[113] His own carefully calibrated strategy could be jeopardized by the kind of revolutionary change now sweeping through Poland.

His voice breaking with emotion, Kádár told his Soviet bloc colleagues that what was happening in Poland was "a Polish affair" but had implications for "the entire socialist community." "We think that the Polish comrades will sort this out. But we must show solidarity with them and offer them our help."

"The military assistance rendered by other socialist countries to Czechoslovakia in 1968 turned out to be absolutely necessary," piped up Husák, who had been responsible for "normalizing" Czechoslovakia in the wake of the Soviet invasion. "In Poland the leadership is good, but it lacks courage and decisiveness."

Husák's eyes welled with tears. He was himself a victim of Stalinist repression and had served an eight-year prison sentence on trumped-up charges of "bourgeois nationalism." But this had not prevented him from purging the Czechoslovak party of almost one-third of its members after ousting Dubček. The stifling political atmosphere had made him a hated figure among Czechoslovak intellectuals, many of whom had been forced to take menial jobs, but Husák did not care. Intensely ambitious, he understood that the path to success in a Communist country was to carry out Moscow's wishes, without question.

After allowing everyone to have his say, the Kremlin leaders dragged their Polish counterparts off for a further round of browbeating, this time one-on-one. Jaruzelski tried to convince Ustinov that the Polish army—unlike the Czechoslovak army in 1968—was loyal and disciplined. The Soviet defense minister brushed him aside. Puffing himself up in his marshal's uniform and banging his fist on the table, he repeated over and over again: "It is necessary to act with determination, and in an offensive manner."[114]

The decisive encounter took place between the two party leaders. Kania tried to explain to Brezhnev that Soviet military intervention was likely to provoke a popular uprising, in addition to dealing a catastrophic blow to détente. He recalled how young Poles had attacked German tanks with Molotov cocktails during the Warsaw uprising at the end of World War II. No nation in Europe was willing to risk so much for its independence, he told Brezhnev. Finally, Kania promised the general secretary that the Polish Communist Party would not permit any change to the "constitutional order."

After Kania had finished, the decrepit Brezhnev uttered the enigmatic words that seemed to summarize the Kremlin's entire approach to the crisis. "Okay, we will not go in."

There was a pause as he struggled for breath.

"But if there are complications, we will go in. We will go in."
Another long pause.
"But without you, we won't go in."[115]

A few hours later the high command of the Warsaw Pact withdrew the order for eighteen divisions of highly trained combat troops to move into Poland at midnight on December 8 for the *Soyuz* 80 "maneuver."[116] The first stage of the crisis was over. The second was about to begin.

WHILE THE POLISH LEADERS FLEW home to Warsaw, the Soviet, East German, and Czechoslovak troops that had been expecting to crush the "counterrevolution" in Poland began to demobilize. As the days went by and the threat of a Soviet invasion failed to materialize, there were sighs of relief in Western capitals. Superpower relations, already seriously damaged by the invasion of Afghanistan, would not be thrown back into the ice age. But a tantalizing question remained: What had caused the old men in the Kremlin to pull back from the brink?

In their memoirs both Kania and Brzezinski claim some of the credit for persuading Brezhnev to back down. The arguments of Polish leaders, and the public and private warnings issued by the White House, must have had some impact on Soviet calculations. But Politburo records released in Moscow after the collapse of communism provide another explanation for Soviet restraint. The Soviet leaders had no intention of invading Poland, except possibly as a last resort, in the event of massive civil disorders. The Kremlin strategy all along was to pressure the Polish leadership to do its dirty work. Large-scale military maneuvers around the country's borders—which would certainly be observed by American spy satellites—was one particularly effective method of raising the psychological stakes. Repeated American warnings of a Soviet invasion of Poland may have inadvertently served Moscow's purposes by increasing the pressure on Warsaw to take drastic action against Solidarity.

Kremlin documents show that Soviet leaders began actively considering the martial law option as early as October, a full fourteen months before Jaruzelski eventually took the plunge. They knew about the contingency plans for a state of emergency and wanted the Polish leadership to put them into effect. Brezhnev contrasted the passivity of the Polish leadership with the repressive policies adopted by Tito's successors in Yugoslavia, who used the pretext of some minor labor unrest to arrest three hundred Albanian dissidents.

"Wałęsa travels from one end of the country to another and is treated in high esteem," Brezhnev grumbled. "Perhaps they really should introduce martial law."

Other Politburo members agreed. "If martial law is not introduced, then the situation is going to become more and more complicated," declared Ustinov. "There are rumblings in the [Polish] army."[117]

The ostentatious manner with which Soviet generals shared their invasion plans with their Polish colleagues also smacked of political intimidation. The Soviets even allowed a visiting Polish delegation to make copies of a map showing precisely where the eighteen Warsaw Pact divisions would be deployed. Polish staff officers accompanied Soviet advance troops on reconnaissance missions into Poland.[118] Looking back at the events of December 1980 twelve years later, Jaruzelski acknowledged that Soviet leaders had stage-managed the summit "to scare us out of our wits."[119] The deputy chief of staff of the Warsaw Pact, General Anatoly Gribkov, conceded that the Kremlin had sought to "put pressure on the Polish leadership and society in every possible way."[120]

The exercises produced their intended effect. After returning from Moscow, Jaruzelski ordered that preparations for martial law be accelerated. Lists were drawn up of four thousand leading Solidarity activists who would be interned as soon as a state of emergency was declared.[121]

By early 1981 the Kremlin strategy had become clear. "We must subject the Polish leadership to constant pressure," Ustinov told the Politburo on January 29. "We are planning maneuvers in Poland in March. I think we should extend these maneuvers so as to create the impression that our forces are ready [to intervene]."[122] Three months later a secret Kremlin document described the fear of a Soviet invasion of Poland as "a factor that restrains the counterrevolution" that should be "exploited to the maximum possible extent."[123]

The pressure on the Polish leadership reached a peak in early April, a few days after yet another well-advertised invasion scare. Soviet military planes began flying over Poland without requesting permission.[124] The Soviets then sent a military aircraft to take Kania and Jaruzelski to a secret meeting with Ustinov and Andropov. Remembering the fate that had befallen hundreds of thousands of their countrymen, the Polish leaders wondered if they would ever return.[125] The session took place in a railway carriage in a forest on the Soviet side of the border. For a full six hours Ustinov and Andropov accused the Poles of turning a blind eye to "counterrevolution" and failing to respond to "anti-Soviet attacks." The harangue continued until 3:00 a.m.

Kania and Jaruzelski sidestepped Soviet demands for the immediate introduction of martial law but promised "to restore order with our own forces." Andropov reported to the Soviet Politburo that the Polish comrades seemed "extremely tense," "nervous," and psychologically "worn out."[126]

While the Soviets continued to threaten military intervention, they had good reasons to avoid such a step. One reason was economic. As a senior Soviet official explained to Honecker, who was itching to teach the Poles a lesson, the Soviet economy was reeling from a series of three disastrous harvests. Oil production, which fueled both the military machine and the civilian economy, was nearly 10 percent below projected targets in 1980. In order to make up the shortfall, planners were counting on a sharp increase in exports of natural gas. But this was possible only with large-scale technical and financial assistance from Western countries.[127] If the West responded to an invasion of Poland with a trade embargo, the results could be catastrophic.[128]

The military-strategic considerations were even more compelling. Nearly a hundred thousand Soviet troops were already committed to Afghanistan. What had been planned as a swift and relatively painless operation was turning into a classic military quagmire, with no end in sight. Andropov, who had helped mastermind the invasion, now realized Soviet troops were ill prepared to fight an unconventional war. To some of his associates, he appeared to be having second thoughts about the whole operation.[129] An invasion of Poland would stretch the Kremlin's resources to the limit.

"In practice, we already have three fronts," said Ustinov, explaining the Soviet view of the world to Jaruzelski, as the two defense ministers inspected troops participating in a joint military exercise. Shouting to make himself heard above the roar of helicopter engines, the Soviet marshal ticked off the "fronts" one by one: Afghanistan; China, which was cooperating with the United States; and finally Poland, where Solidarity was acting as an imperialist "Trojan horse." The implication was that one of the fronts had to be liquidated.[130]

Mikhail Suslov, the Politburo ideologist and head of the commission on Poland, put the matter even more succinctly. He told his associates that the Soviet Union simply could not afford "a second Afghanistan."[131]

Like generals fighting the last war, both Polish and Western leaders were obsessed with the "Czech variant." The world had changed since 1968, and there were many differences between Czechoslovakia and Poland. Even if

the Kremlin had not been bogged down in Afghanistan, an invasion of Poland represented a much greater military challenge than the relatively peaceful Czechoslovak operation. There were more than twice as many Poles as there were Czechs and Slovaks, and the Poles had a history of resisting foreign armies. Furthermore, the Soviets never gave up on the Polish leadership, as they had with Dubček. Jaruzelski, in particular, was highly regarded in Moscow.[132]

At the secret meeting in the railway carriage in the Belorussian forest, Ustinov was disturbed by the depressed state of mind of Jaruzelski and Kania and their penchant for procrastination. But he brusquely brushed aside Jaruzelski's plea that he be allowed to resign because of exhaustion. "We need this pair," he told his Politburo colleagues a few days later.[133]

Soviet leaders treated their Polish counterparts as subordinates, bound by the discipline of the international Communist movement. When Brezhnev called Kania or Jaruzelski on the phone, he used the familiar *ty* form of address, as if he were speaking to a lowly apparatchik in Omsk or Tomsk. Polish leaders, by contrast, always took care to use the polite *vy* form in talking to Brezhnev. Kania and Jaruzelski replied to the Soviet leader's slurred monologues as if they were the distillation of human wisdom, meekly thanking him for his continued "trust" and "support." The Soviet treatment of Polish leaders was sometimes gratuitously insulting. The commander of the Warsaw Pact, Marshal Viktor Kulikov, even threw Kania out of his residence late one night, allegedly for being drunk.[134]

Soviet leaders had one enormous advantage in the high-stakes political poker game that took place around Poland in 1980 and 1981. They could see the other side's hand. The Poles and the Americans knew that the Soviets were in a position to invade, but they could only guess at the Kremlin's real intentions. The Soviets, by contrast, had access to detailed firsthand information of virtually everything that happened in the Polish Politburo. Their spies were everywhere: in factories, government offices, military barracks. The KGB resident in Poland knew everything going on in the Polish Security Ministry. The Polish army was integrated into the Soviet chain of command, with Soviet "advisers" and "inspectors" at every level.[135] Soviet leaders paid careful attention to Kania's drinking habits and Jaruzelski's fits of depression.

In the end this intimate knowledge of the strengths and weaknesses of their Polish "partners" allowed the Soviets to turn a losing hand into a winning one.

WARSAW

December 12, 1981

SLIM, STIFF, AND ALMOST PAINFULLY SHY Wojciech Jaruzelski was an enigma to his countrymen. They knew from his speeches that he was an orthodox Marxist who had absorbed the political lexicon of Poland's conquerors. They knew he was trusted by Moscow; otherwise he would not have become the youngest general in the Polish army at the age of thirty-three. But they were also impressed by his aristocratic bearing and perfect diction. There were rumors that his family belonged to the class of feudal landowners known as the *szlachta,* the privileged gentry that had been the backbone of the pre-Communist Polish republic. It was said that Jaruzelski and his family had suffered greatly at the hands of the Soviets. The real thoughts of this aristocratic general, whose accomplishments included fencing and horse riding, seemed forever concealed behind a pair of thick dark glasses.

In the forest lands northeast of Warsaw, in the tiny village of Trzeciny, where the young Wojciech had grown up, the sense of confusion was even greater. The villagers remembered his father, Władysław, who had cut a dashing figure with his saber when he went off to fight the Bolsheviks in the Polish-Soviet War of 1920. They remembered his mother, Wanda, a quiet, determined lady who had brought her children up to be good Catholics and good Poles, reading them stories about brave Polish heroes struggling

against Russian rule. Finally they remembered Wojciech himself, a timid, frail child who appeared in church without fail every Sunday, before being packed off to a strict Warsaw boarding school at the age of ten. The villagers found it difficult to believe that this was the same Wojciech who later became head of a Communist government and first secretary of the Polish Communist Party. Something must have happened to him. The story spread that the Soviets had kidnapped the real Wojciech and cunningly sent a Communist double back to Poland in his place.[136]

But it *was* the real Wojciech. Jaruzelski fitted the classic Marxist-Leninist profile of a "class enemy." His family could trace its heraldic crest, a blindfolded crow, back to the thirteenth century. His paternal grandfather had been sent in chains to Siberia after taking part in the great antitsarist insurrection of 1863. Because of his defiance, the family had lost most of its property. Despite his noble status, Władysław Jaruzelski was reduced to working as an administrator on the family's former estates. After the Red Army had occupied eastern Poland in September 1939, the Jaruzelski family fled to Lithuania, where they had relatives. A few days before Hitler attacked the Soviet Union, in June 1941, Jaruzelski senior was arrested as a "socially dangerous element." By the time he was released from a labor camp in January 1942, following a deal between Stalin and General Władysław Sikorski, the head of the Polish government-in-exile, this strong two-hundred-pound man had become an emaciated skeleton, weighing no more than a hundred pounds. He died of dysentery and malnutrition six months later.[137]

The rest of the family experienced almost equal hardship. At the time of his father's arrest Jaruzelski was deported to Siberia, along with his mother and sister. The trip, in an overcrowded goods train, took a month. He spent almost two years in Siberia as a virtual slave laborer, chopping down trees and hauling huge bags of flour around a warehouse. He suffered from excruciating back pains, which flared up again during periods of tension, such as in 1981. The secret police urged Jaruzelski to apply for Soviet identity papers, on the ground that eastern Poland had been incorporated into the Soviet Union. When he refused, he was thrown into prison with common criminals, who stole his belongings and beat him up. After three weeks of this treatment he accepted the NKVD offer. Shortly afterward he applied to join the Polish army that was being formed on Soviet soil under the leadership of a Communist officer, Zygmunt Berling. Joining this army, he explained later, represented a chance of "returning to Poland with a weapon in my hand."[138]

Jaruzelski had little sympathy for either Russia or for communism

when—as his party biography delicately put it—he "found himself" in the Soviet Union at the age of sixteen. At school he had belonged to a particularly zealous Catholic youth organization, known as the Soldiers of Mary. By his own account, he shared the anti-Soviet convictions of the *szlachta* class. His first impression of the Red Army had been of a horde of conquering barbarians. "What struck me first was how many of them there were," he wrote later. "I had the impression that there were thousands upon thousands of them, with their long gray overcoats and great piles of rifles. I had the sense of a force that was terrible, strange, hostile."[139] Yet, after returning to Poland from the Soviet Union, Jaruzelski became the devoted soldier of an alien ideology. In 1947, at the age of twenty-four, he experienced what he later described as a spiritual "rebirth." He applied to join the Polish Communist Party and was swiftly accepted.[140]

According to Jaruzelski, this stunning conversion took place in stages. In the Siberian taiga he discovered that ordinary Russians were not the Satans he had previously imagined them to be. He began to draw a distinction between the Russian people and their oppressive political system. He came to admire their incredible feats of endurance, the way they threw themselves into battle crying, "For Stalin, for the motherland." Communism could be cruel and terrible, but it had some redeeming features. The Communist aspiration for a fairer, more just society was not too far removed from the social values that Wanda Jaruzelski had sought to instill in her children, minus the traditional anti-Russian outlook of the *szlachta* class. The Communist Party seemed to offer a more realistic program of postwar reconstruction, and the rapid absorption of formerly German territories, than the bourgeois parties. It was not just soldiers like Jaruzelski who rallied around the party at the end of the war, but also intellectuals like Czesław Miłosz and Leszek Kolakowski.

Another explanation for Jaruzelski's ideological rebirth might begin with the personality of a superachiever. Ever since childhood he had striven hard to earn the approval of his superiors. At the Catholic boarding school in Warsaw he was considered an outstanding pupil. He soaked up the conservative opinions of his Marian teachers, chanting songs praising Poland's military dictator, Marshal Piłsudski, and avidly following the military campaign of Spain's General Franco. He was an enthusiastic Boy Scout, modeling himself on the hero scouts who had helped defend Poland against the "Red invader." Later in life he was equally zealous in seeking to impress the commanders of the Warsaw Pact and the members of the Soviet Politburo. After Solidarity came to power in 1989, he cultivated contacts with former dissidents like Adam Michnik, whom he had once thrown into prison.

In all these exploits there was an element of the odd man out, struggling for social acceptance. At school he was always the puniest child in the class. In Communist politics he was the offspring of the petty nobility who, by his own account, could never quite rid himself of an inferiority complex toward the "working class."[141] In retirement he was Poland's last Communist leader, fighting to salvage his historical reputation.

As he climbed up the bureaucratic ladder, Jaruzelski shut his eyes to many unpleasant facts. He had the soldier's habit of carrying out orders without asking questions. As defense minister in 1968 he had little compunction about ordering Polish troops to join the Soviet-led invasion of Czechoslovakia. It never occurred to him to doubt Soviet propaganda claims about stockpiles of German weapons and a Western plan to subvert Czechoslovakia.

Sometimes his lack of curiosity bordered on the abnormal. When he was elected Communist Party leader in October 1981, in succession to Kania, he was handed a key to the safe containing the innermost secrets and scandals of the Polish regime. Despite the notoriety of this safe, he never bothered to look through its contents. "I don't know how to explain this lack of curiosity," he later confessed. "It's probably very personal."[142]

Jaruzelski's five years in the Soviet Union had taught him a brutal lesson in realpolitik. The monthlong train trip to Siberia—a journey twice the width of the continental United States—had given him a sense of the vastness of Poland's eastern neighbor. He had gained an insight into the power of the Soviet system and the might of its armed forces. Breaking with Poland's romantic tradition, Jaruzelski prided himself on his realism. From his own experience he knew that resistance to such a huge empire was futile. It was his duty to save Poland from the horrors of yet another Russian invasion. As he remarked privately to a colleague, "Our historical mission is to prevent a Soviet intervention."[143]

Whatever the explanation for Jaruzelski's conversion to communism, the Soviets had every confidence in him. Shortly after his election as first secretary, he received a congratulatory telephone call from Brezhnev, who urged him to carry out his plan to crush the "counterrevolution." "There is nobody else in the PZPR [the Polish Communist Party] who enjoys as much authority as you," said the Soviet leader, reading haltingly from a prepared text.[144]

The Kremlin's trust in Jaruzelski seems strange in view of his class origins and long-standing Soviet suspicions of "Bonapartism," the meddling of the military in political affairs. The fact that Jaruzelski had endured Stalinist repression without kicking up a fuss made a favorable impression on

Soviet leaders. They also gave him credit for his wartime service, his work in building up the Polish army under Communist leadership, and his excellent Russian.[145]

Jaruzelski's official biography makes clear that he played a part in the bloody settling of accounts with the anti-Communist Home Army in the years immediately after World War II. He was a protégé of the Soviet generals who supervised the Polish Defense Ministry. According to one account, he was the only Polish general to vote against the dismissal, in 1956, of the Russian-born defense minister Marshal Konstantin Rokossowsky and his recall to the Soviet Union.[146] Jaruzelski was subsequently put in charge of political education in the armed forces, an extremely sensitive post reserved for someone who could get along with the Russians. When he was appointed defense minister in 1968 in succession to the nationalistically inclined Marian Spychalski, the Soviets were delighted.[147]

In his memoirs Jaruzelski describes himself as a "fanatical believer" in the doctrine of communism. "It went without saying that we had to defend our church and its dogmas."[148]

Soviet leaders occasionally complained that Jaruzelski lacked "courage" and "decisiveness." But they had no doubts at all about his "moral-political reliability."[149] They had studied his personal dossier thoroughly, and they knew their man.

STEP BY STEP JARUZELSKI had accumulated all the leading positions in the Polish People's Republic. He was commander in chief of the armed forces, prime minister, and first secretary of the Communist Party. All that remained was for the onetime "Soldier of Mary" to declare himself military dictator. But he could not make up his mind.

After his appointment as prime minister Jaruzelski had moved into the office of Poland's last military dictator, Marshal Piłsudski, on Ujazdowskie Avenue.[150] It was here that Piłsudski had organized his program of "national purification" following the coup d'état of 1926. The ghost of his right-wing predecessor seemed to haunt Jaruzelski as he struggled to find a solution to Poland's problems. As the crisis deepened, he frequently spent entire nights in the second-floor corner office, sleeping on a camp bed. Crushed by a sense of terrifying responsibility, he lay awake for hours. On several occasions he opened the drawer to his desk, where his service revolver lay. He gazed at the gun for minutes at a time, before closing the drawer again.[151]

Pressures were growing from all sides. There were rumors—yet again— of Soviet troops massing on the borders. Jaruzelski had no illusions about

what would happen to him in the event of an invasion. He remembered how Brezhnev had ordered Dubček's arrest a few days after kissing him warmly on both cheeks. The image of the Czechoslovak Communist leaders being brought to Moscow under arrest had obsessed him from the outset of the crisis.[152] The invasion of Czechoslovakia would be a picnic compared with the bloody catastrophe that would result if Soviet troops entered Poland.

The economy was another source of worry. Production had fallen by 12 percent in 1981, on top of the 4 percent drop in 1980 and 2 percent in 1979. The output of coal, Poland's principal hard-currency export, had plummeted as a result of the introduction of a forty-hour week for miners. The foreign exchange reserves were practically zero. Poland was almost entirely dependent on Moscow for supplies of raw materials. A few weeks earlier the Kremlin had threatened to slash gasoline exports to Poland by two-thirds. Deliveries of natural gas, phosphorus, iron ore, and cotton would be reduced by 50 percent. Without these supplies Polish industry would grind to a halt.[153]

Jaruzelski knew Western countries would react harshly to a crackdown on Solidarity. But he also had reason to believe that the newly formed Reagan administration would breathe a quiet sigh of relief over an "internal solution" to the Polish crisis. He knew that Washington was exceptionally well informed about the behind-the-scenes drama in Poland. His trusted aide Colonel Kukliński had defected to the West in early November with a complete blueprint of plans for martial law. Polish leaders feared that the Reagan administration would alert Solidarity to the coming danger, but nothing happened. Jaruzelski interpreted Washington's silence as tacit approval of his plans. He reasoned that the United States regarded martial law as a preferable alternative to a Soviet invasion, which would have devastating consequences for East-West relations.[154]

There is another explanation for the Reagan administration's failure to act on Kukliński's information: old-fashioned interagency rivalry. The handful of senior CIA officials who knew about Kukliński's existence were determined not to share their knowledge with anyone else in the U.S. government—even after their source had escaped from Poland. They themselves treated his warnings about martial law with skepticism, trusting the instinct of Solidarity leaders who believed that Jaruzelski would not dare send the Polish army against civilians.[155]

WHAT JARUZELSKI LATER DESCRIBED as "the most difficult day of my life" began, as usual, with his top military aides.[156] At 9:00 a.m. he sum-

moned the men charged with implementing the state of war (*stan wojenny*) to his office. The task of rounding up thousands of Solidarity activists and smashing any protest action fell to the interior minister, Czesław Kiszczak, a politically astute general who had previously served as head of military intelligence. Florian Siwicki, the armed forces chief of staff, would be responsible for the military aspects of the operation, including coordination with Soviet forces. Another longtime Jaruzelski protégé, Michał Janiszewski, was responsible for drafting martial law regulations and overseeing the state bureaucracy. Together these four generals formed the inner core of the new Military Council for National Salvation.

The generals fully expected Solidarity to unleash its ultimate weapon, a general strike. Workers would occupy their factories, just as they had done in August 1980. This time, however, the authorities were well prepared. There would be no need to order Polish soldiers to fire on Polish workers, something Jaruzelski had vowed never to do. In great secrecy the regime had assembled a force of thirty thousand professionally trained riot police, known by the Polish acronym ZOMO. Dressed to look like a swarm of Darth Vadars, with Plexiglas shields, gas masks, and water cannon, the ZOMO had the job of methodically breaking one strike after another. Poland's 320,000-strong armed forces would perform a backup role, providing security for government installations and intimidating the population with a massive show of military might. Moving thousands of tanks out of their barracks served the additional purpose of showing Soviet leaders that Jaruzelski was not in need of "fraternal assistance."[157]

Browbeaten by the Kremlin and pushed into a corner by Solidarity, the Polish high command was convinced that martial law represented the only way out of the crisis. In five days' time the opposition was planning to hold a huge protest demonstration in Warsaw. In another few days tens of thousands of soldiers would complete their military service, to be replaced by untrained conscripts, tainted by the Solidarity experience. The time to act was now, at the weekend, while the factories were empty.[158]

Jaruzelski had already succeeded in linking Operation X to promises of a Soviet economic bailout. At his insistence the Kremlin had sent its top planner, Nikolai Baibakov, to Warsaw a few days before to discuss a two-billion-dollar Polish wish list. As a result of these talks, a tacit understanding had been reached. If the Polish government took tough action to crush Solidarity, Moscow would help the country out of its economic mess.[159] Before issuing the final go-ahead for martial law, the general wanted to clarify Soviet military intentions toward Poland.

As was often the case in Communist Party politics, relations between Moscow and Warsaw were characterized by an extraordinary degree of intrigue and deceit. As Jaruzelski later remarked, he was dealing with people who were perfectly capable of showering you with kisses one day and sending troops to overthrow you the next.[160] He knew the Soviets maintained good relations with Polish hard-liners who were prepared to issue an "invitation" that could be used to justify military intervention. It was in Jaruzelski's interest to create the impression that there were certain circumstances under which he might himself appeal for Soviet assistance. That way he would retain the final word on whether or not to issue such an invitation.

This is the most plausible explanation for references in Soviet documents to a Polish request for military assistance, in the event that Operation X failed to restore order in the country. In addition to demonstrating his loyalty to Moscow, Jaruzelski wanted to sound out Soviet intentions. In his own words, he was constantly "probing" the other side.[161] Kremlin leaders suspected something of the kind. "Jaruzelski is displaying a certain cunning," said Suslov, chairman of the Politburo commission on Poland. "He is creating an alibi for himself with these requests. . . . Later he will be able to say, 'I turned to the Soviet Union for help and didn't receive the help I was asking for.' "[162]

In the presence of his three colleagues, Jaruzelski placed a call to Brezhnev on the morning of December 12. The general secretary was indisposed, so he was put through to Suslov, who was himself seriously ill. Exactly what was said during this telephone conversation has remained controversial. Soviet officials say that he asked for a pledge of Soviet help, if Operation X went wrong. Jaruzelski claims that he wanted an assurance that the Soviet Union would treat the introduction of martial law as an "internal" Polish affair.

"And what if things get complicated?" asked Jaruzelski, alluding to Brezhnev's enigmatic warning to Kania the previous year.

"Well, you have always said that you can handle this with your own forces," Suslov replied.[163]

A couple of hours later Ustinov phoned. The marshal wanted to stiffen Jaruzelski's backbone before the coming battle. As usual, the Soviet defense minister spoke in the hectoring tone used by a commanding officer to address a subordinate. He peppered his end of the conversation with words like *nastupat'* (attack) and *reshitel'no* (decisively).[164] Jaruzelski had heard these words frequently over the last sixteen months.

After listening to Moscow, Jaruzelski turned his attention to the situa-

tion in Gdańsk. Over the past ten days relations with Solidarity had deteriorated to an all-time low. The immediate cause of the crisis was the government's use of riot police to break up a strike by firefighter cadets. Solidarity leaders had responded to the storming of the firefighters' college—a dress rehearsal for a much more serious crackdown—by calling for antigovernment street demonstrations. They had returned to the movement's birthplace, the Lenin Shipyard in Gdańsk, to consider proposals for a referendum on free elections and the formation of a provisional government. In Jaruzelski's mind, the proposals were tantamount to the dismantling of Communist power in Poland.

The Solidarity National Commission was riddled with secret police informers, who sent reports back to Warsaw about the uncompromising mood of the meeting. By 2:00 p.m. Jaruzelski had heard enough. He instructed his aides to proceed with Operation X.[165]

GDAŃSK

December 12–13, 1981

IT SHOULD HAVE BEEN a moment of triumph. Lech Wałęsa was back in the Lenin Shipyard, sitting on the podium of the same conference hall where he had negotiated the Gdańsk agreement with Poland's Communist authorities. The conference hall was bathed in television arc lights. In the space of five hundred days Wałęsa had been transformed from an unsung dissident in a corner of the Soviet empire to an international media celebrity. He had traveled to Japan and France, received the acclaim of the International Labor Organization in Geneva, held talks with Pope John Paul in the Vatican. His exploits were followed with close attention in the Kremlin and the White House; his pithy turns of phrase were dissected by journalists from all over the world. He had been nominated for the Nobel Peace Prize and chosen as "Man of the Year" by *Time* magazine.

Usually Wałęsa enjoyed the media attention. He played up to the paparazzi, who followed him around Poland. He allowed himself to be photographed taking a bath, praying in church, scolding his children, thrusting his fists into the air in a gesture of victory.

On this occasion he was uncharacteristically somber and passive. He seemed oblivious of the dramatic debate whirling around him on how to respond to the latest government "provocations." Sitting slightly to one side,

he leafed through a pile of newspapers, making paper airplanes and fiddling with his new Czech pipe. His face looked swollen and white. He took no part in the voting as his colleagues passed a series of hard-line resolutions. Kuroń, the organizational brains behind Poland's political opposition, called for the formation of a coalition government. One of the radicals began to bait the Solidarity leader, insisting that he should at least take the floor.

"Leszek, you sit there like a maharaja, saying nothing. Speak to us."

"You're all talking so much rubbish here that we'd better check to see if someone has added anything to your food," Wałęsa snapped back.[166]

The endless arguments, with both the government and his own Solidarity colleagues, had worn Wałęsa down. He sensed that an approaching cataclysm would severely test the strength of the first free trade union in the Communist world. At his last meeting with Jaruzelski, in early November, the general had seemed unyielding. The balance of power within the regime appeared to be shifting in favor of the advocates of force. Several of Wałęsa's own advisers had warned him that the government was preparing for a showdown.

Bronisław Geremek, a medieval historian who had been advising Wałęsa since August 1980, voiced the fears of the intellectuals at the meeting of Solidarity's national commission. "We cannot win an all-out confrontation with the government," he told Solidarity leaders. "We're not prepared for one, but they are. Remember, it's they who will choose the time and place for such a confrontation, not we."

His words were received in silence.

Outside the conference hall, life was continuing normally. Thick snow lay on the ground. At the shipyard's number two gate, made famous in news pictures all over the world, a brisk trade was going on in Solidarity mementos. There were Solidarity wall calendars for 1982, posters, emblems of the pre-Communist eagle with the crown on the head, and dozens of lapel badges, including the cheeky new slogan, "I Love the Soviet Union." A banner had been strung across the shipyard entrance, calling for the establishment of a people's tribunal to punish "the murderers and thieves of the Polish people."

By early evening disquieting news began to arrive at the shipyard. A Solidarity representative in the town of Olsztyn, a hundred miles southeast of Gdańsk, phoned to say that ZOMO units had left their barracks in full battle gear. Telex messages reported army movements to the south and west of the city. Phone calls were made to the local militia chief, who told Solidar-

ity leaders "not to worry." A large-scale police operation was under way to crack down on crime in the Gdańsk region.

Just before midnight, an aide handed Wałęsa a piece of paper with the news: "All communications by telephone and telex have been cut."

The Solidarity leader rose to his feet. His face, lit up by the television lights, appeared even more swollen than before. He had what he later described as a "subconscious premonition" of what was about to happen but decided that resistance was pointless.[167]

"Ladies and gentlemen, we have no communications with the outside world. Perhaps they will be restored tomorrow, perhaps not. In connection with this, I wish you good night."

He stood up, threw his hands up in the air, as if to say, "There's nothing more I can do," and strode out of the room.

BY THE TIME WAŁĘSA REACHED his apartment on the outskirts of Gdańsk, ZOMO squads were knocking on the doors of known Solidarity supporters all over Poland. If there was no response, they simply smashed the door down. Those detained in Operation X included some of the best-known people in the country: writers, actors, historians, film producers, and academicians, in addition to straightforward union activists. In an attempt to make the roundup seem a little more evenhanded, a handful of former Communist leaders, including Gierek, were also detained. Some of the would-be internees were already dead, an indication that the lists had been drawn up many months previously.

At 2:00 a.m. ZOMO in pale blue battle dress surrounded the Monopol Hotel in Gdańsk, where members of the Solidarity National Commission were staying. All exits were blocked. The police went from room to room, handcuffing Solidarity officials and leading them out into waiting police trucks. Members of the antiterrorist squad in tightly fitting nylon jackets guarded the roof. The twenty-seven-year-old leader of the Warsaw branch of Solidarity, Zbigniew Bujak, observed the scene from across the street. He could not believe his eyes. His first thought was that the government had gone crazy. The whole of Poland would go on strike.[168]

The doorbell rang in Wałęsa's apartment building in Zaspa at around 3:00 a.m.[169] The Solidarity leader had gone to bed. His wife, Danuta, looked through the peephole to see the local Communist Party chief, Tadeusz Fiszbach, in the company of the provincial governor and half a dozen policemen with crowbars. A reputed liberal, Fiszbach had been woken a short

time before and ordered to put Wałęsa on a plane to Warsaw for "talks with Jaruzelski." He seemed upset. At first Wałęsa refused to go. After the governor told him that the ZOMO were ready to take him to Warsaw by force, he packed a few clothes and left. (Wałęsa never did meet with Jaruzelski. After a few weeks in a government villa outside Warsaw, he was taken to a hunting lodge near the Soviet border that had once been the playground of Poland's "red bourgeoisie.")

At 6:00 a.m. Jaruzelski appeared on television in full general's uniform, flanked by the Polish flag. "Our country has found itself at the edge of an abyss," he declared. "Poland's future is at stake: the future for which my generation fought."

In a voice laden with emotion, Jaruzelski accused Solidarity leaders of everything from "acts of terrorism" to economic sabotage. If the present situation were allowed to continue, he declared, the result would be "famine," "chaos," and "civil war." Socialism was the only path possible for Poland. With heavy heart, he announced that a state of war had been imposed on the entire country. A Military Council of National Salvation had been formed to bring the country back from the brink of disaster. Military tribunals were being established to punish anyone acting against the "interests of the state."

Jaruzelski ended his speech with the first line of the national anthem: "Poland has not perished as long as we live." As he spoke, the chords of the patriotic mazurka sung by exiled Polish legionnaires following the eighteenth-century partition of their country welled up in the background.

From Jaruzelski's point of view, the first few days of martial law went astonishingly well. A few Solidarity leaders—Bujak was the most important—managed to go into hiding, but most were arrested. As expected, workers at many large factories attempted to stage occupation strikes. All were broken up with brutal efficiency by the ZOMO, usually under the cover of the nighttime curfew. The Lenin Shipyard, regarded by the entire country as Solidarity's inner fortress, held out for less than a week. The organizers of the strike had trouble persuading the frightened workers to guard the perimeter of the shipyard, including gate number two. After establishing a psychological advantage, the ZOMO smashed the shipyard wall at several different points and rounded up the protesters.

The most serious casualties occurred at the Wujek coal mine in Silesia, where Solidarity supporters armed themselves with axes, chains, and iron rods. The miners had vowed to defend themselves after hearing of beatings and mass arrests elsewhere in Silesia. Fierce hand-to-hand combat broke

out after ZOMO units attacked the mine with tanks and helicopters, three days after the imposition of martial law. Encircled by the enraged miners in a narrow courtyard, the riot police opened fire. Nine protesters were killed. The wall where the miners died became a makeshift shrine. The victims' helmets lay on the top of the wall for months afterward, along with mounds of fresh flowers and messages of support for the banned trade union.[170]

With his massive blow against Solidarity, Jaruzelski succeeded in reversing the movement's principal accomplishment: overcoming the fear that had divided Pole from Pole. As was the case before August 1980, the Communist regime now controlled an atomized and defeated society. The psychological walls that Solidarity had succeeded in smashing went up again practically overnight. Ordinary people began to mistrust one another once more. Anyone could be a police informer. The desperate economic situation also helped the general. The priority for most families in the exceptionally cold winter of 1981 was not politics, but keeping warm and finding enough to eat.

It was enough to look at the faces of people in the streets the day after martial law was declared to see that Jaruzelski had won his gamble. The exuberance and sense of pride that had been the hallmark of the Solidarity period disappeared overnight. The people themselves were different. Millions of rank-and-file Solidarity supporters retreated to the safety of their apartments. Their place on the streets was taken by hundreds of thousands of people connected in some way with the Communist regime. They immediately began ripping down Solidarity posters, guarding public buildings, and issuing permits of one kind or another. Their cynical, dissolute faces wore expressions of immense relief. Such people had been around all along; they had just lain low, waiting for better times.

IN THE SHORT TERM Jaruzelski won his "war" with the Polish people. Operation X was a model of its kind, one that will be studied by would-be military dictators for a long time to come. The coup showed that it is possible to turn back the information revolution. The most sophisticated communications technology in the world is no protection against a totalitarian regime. A sufficiently determined dictator can lock up the photocopy machines, unplug the automatic telephone exchanges, and hunt down the typewriters and computers.

The cost of doing all this, however, was immense. In order to reimpose Communist Party control over Poland, Jaruzelski had to take the country

back into the Middle Ages. He turned an industrialized country in the heart of Europe into a land cut off from the outside world, a country without telephones and telex machines. He locked up ten thousand of the best and the brightest. He imposed a stifling censorship on the mass media, closing down hundreds of newspapers and obliging television news readers to wear military uniforms. The martial law decrees covered everything from the introduction of compulsory labor and political loyalty tests for millions of state employees to bans on recreational sailing and sales of gasoline. A dusk-to-dawn curfew was introduced. Poland's borders with the outside world were sealed. In order to prevent information from flowing freely around the country, travel without a permit was banned. Even savings accounts were frozen to prevent money from reaching Solidarity activists who had managed to avoid arrest.

There was no way a country burdened by such regulations could compete in the modern world. The restrictions were relaxed gradually, but Jaruzelski found that he had to rely on the support of Communist Party reactionaries to stay in power. That meant abandoning all hope of economic reform and condemning Poland to another decade of stagnation.

That was not all. For the Communist Party to be rescued by its own army was a humiliating admission of failure. During the period immediately after World War II, Polish Communists had felt a kind of revolutionary élan. Their success in rebuilding a war-ravaged country and incorporating the "western territories" acquired from Germany had won them popular support. By December 1981 it was clear that communism could maintain itself in Poland only with the aid of machine guns and internment camps. In order to save the system, Jaruzelski had to wage war against the working class. He replaced trade union leaders with military commissars and ordered tanks to smash their way into factories.

Paradoxically martial law may have been a blessing in disguise for Solidarity. After sixteen months of bruising struggles with the government, the movement was displaying the symptoms of a split personality. Some Solidarity leaders wanted the union to champion the cause of national independence; others wanted to put the emphasis on social matters. Some Solidarity activists saw themselves as spokesmen for workers in the huge industrial plants that were threatened by the free market; others regarded economic reform as a first step toward the junking of communism. Had history been allowed to take its normal course, these divisions would have led to an open split. The military crackdown had the effect of uniting the warring factions and preserving the Solidarity myth intact.

Packed off to internment camps by Jaruzelski, Solidarity leaders

regarded themselves as the modern-day equivalents of the Polish officers murdered by the Soviets at Katyn in World War II or the antitsarist insurrectionaries of 1830 and 1863. Like their forefathers, they felt they were suffering for a just cause, Poland's national independence. They were determined to live up to Piłsudski's motto: "To be conquered and not to surrender—that is victory." The battery of Polish national feeling, which had run down in the sixties and seventies, was once again fully charged.

In the end martial law was a Pyrrhic victory for Jaruzelski. Even in the darkest days of December 1981, when the nation was completely demoralized, it was clear that the wheel of Polish history would turn again. The people had been conquered, but they had not surrendered. There were limits to the restoration of the old order. Poles had changed as a result of the Solidarity experience, and Communist ideology had lost its power to motivate. The system of central planning had proved hopelessly inefficient and would have to be dismantled if Poland were to have any chance of escaping from the seemingly never-ending cycle of economic crises and political explosions. Jaruzelski and his advisers understood the need for sweeping changes, but were afraid to relax political controls because it would undermine the very basis of Communist Party power. The dilemma was irresolvable.

The crackdown in Poland was also a Pyrrhic victory for the Soviets. Once again, as in 1956 and 1968, they managed to stuff the genie of freedom back into the bottle. Eastern Europe had been made safe for "socialist democracy." Soviet tanks would continue to have the run of the vast strategic plain between Russia and Germany. On the other hand, Soviet leaders now bore the burden of helping Poland survive an economic blockade imposed by Western countries. They could not afford to be saddled with another international basket case, at a time of growing economic problems at home. Brezhnev complained to his Politburo colleagues that "we are stretched to the limit in our capacity to help the Poles, and they are making still more requests." He suggested that economic assistance be confined to prestige projects, "which should not impose great strains on our economy."[171]

Soviet economic planners had great difficulty persuading Brezhnev to make hard economic choices. Surrounded by sycophants and completely dependent on his doctors and bodyguards, the general secretary had lost touch with political reality. His political program consisted of trying to please everybody and accepting artificial tributes as his rightful due. Trapped in grandiose illusions, he imagined himself both infallible and irreplaceable.[172]

But he too was mortal.

MOSCOW

November 10, 1982

ON NOVEMBER 7 LEONID BREZHNEV presided over the annual Revolution Day parade in Red Square, an obligatory annual ritual for Soviet leaders. He stood for several hours on top of the Lenin Mausoleum in bitterly cold weather, waving feebly as T-72 battle tanks and nuclear missiles trundled across the ancient cobblestones. Immediately after the parade he was driven to his hunting lodge at Zavidovo for the holiday. On November 9 he returned to his dacha at Zareche. His personal barber got blind drunk and was unable to give him his regular afternoon shave, but Brezhnev was too sick to care very much.

"What a useless fellow," he murmured indulgently. "He's smashed again."[173]

As the general secretary fell into his dotage, he had become increasingly estranged from his unruly family and dependent on the KGB guards who looked after his every physical need. They were like wet nurses to him. They helped the seventy-five-year-old leader out of bed in the morning, changed his clothes, fed him his meals, played dominoes with him, put up with his moods, and worried about his health. It was like dealing with a small child.

On the evening of November 9 Brezhnev retired to bed early. He usually stayed up to watch the 9:00 p.m. television news program *Vremya*, but he was tired by the hundred-mile drive from Zavidovo. He complained that his

throat was hurting him. The following morning his bodyguards waited for his wife, Viktoria Petrovna, to emerge from his bedroom before going in to wake him up. It was a few minutes before nine o'clock. Brezhnev was lying on his side, apparently asleep.

"Leonid Ilyich, it's time to get up," said Vladimir Medvedev, the head of the night shift, as he gently shook the *gensek*.

There was no reaction. Medvedev began shaking Brezhnev more vigorously, but his eyes did not open. His body seemed cold. The bodyguards did what they were trained to do in such a situation: They pumped the old man's heart and gave him mouth-to-mouth resuscitation. They also called the chief Kremlin doctor, Yevgeny Chazov, who arrived on the scene twelve minutes later. Soon afterward an emergency medical team rushed into the room and started full-scale resuscitation procedures. It was clear to Chazov that all this frenetic activity was just for show. Brezhnev had been dead for several hours.[174]

The first Politburo member on the scene was the former KGB chief Yuri Andropov, the heir apparent. He gave an involuntary gasp as he looked at the lifeless corpse of the man who had led the Soviet Union for the past eighteen years. He stared intently at the dead leader's puffed-up face, which had turned a pale blue. Suddenly the reverie was over. Andropov said his good-byes and left.

THE SOVIET PEOPLE HEARD the news twenty-six hours later. The man chosen to make the death announcement on behalf of the grieving Politburo was Igor Kirillov, senior news reader for central television, who had served as the voice and face of Big Brother for almost two decades. A master of intonation and inflection, Kirillov had a knack for conveying Kremlin propaganda to the masses. His voice would drip with treacly pride as he announced the fulfillment of five-year plans. He read Politburo communiqués as if they were self-evident truths with which no honest person could possibly argue. Turning to news from capitalist countries—unemployment and crime were favorite topics—Kirillov switched instantly to moral indignation. For Brezhnev's death, he adopted a tone of voice that was both somber and reassuring.

"Dear comrades," Kirillov announced, pausing for effect. "The Communist Party of the Soviet Union and the whole Soviet people [pause] have suffered a grave loss [pause]. Leonid Ilyich Brezhnev [reverential inflection, long pause], loyal perpetuator of the great cause of Lenin [pause], ardent patriot [pause], outstanding revolutionary and fighter for peace and com-

munism [pause], an outstanding politician and statesman of our time [pause], has departed this life [long, mournful pause]."

But wait, comrades. All is not lost. "The people have learned from experience that whatever the turn of events and whatever the trials [pause], our party remains capable of carrying out its historic mission. [Voice assumes growing confidence.] The home and foreign policies of the CPSU elaborated under the leadership of Leonid Ilyich Brezhnev [reverential pause] will continue to be applied consistently and purposefully [final note of triumph before funeral music surges in the background]."

Years later, after the collapse of communism, Kirillov explained that he had been trained in the famous Stanislavsky school of acting, the Method.[175] In order to seem sincere, the actor must completely live the part. If he can convince himself that he is hopelessly in love, he can convince others. Like anyone else his age—he was born in 1932, at the height of Stalin's great terror—Kirillov knew about the gulag and the man-made famine that killed millions of people, but he put them out of his mind. He convinced himself that the party was right. Eventually, as the personality cult surrounding Brezhnev reached absurdist proportions, even Kirillov began to have doubts. But he still behaved *as if* he believed. He was the epitome of the system of doublethink that held a nation of 287 million people in its grasp.

KIRILLOV'S SIMULATION of ideological conviction was an apt analogy for the Brezhnev era. By and large, ordinary Soviets had ceased to believe in socialist ideology, but they continued to go through the motions. The whole country was engaged in a mass deceit. In the privacy of their kitchens people laughed at their doddering leader. In public they kept straight faces.

The Brezhnev period was later dismissed by Soviet historians as the "era of stagnation." It would be wrong to conclude, however, that nothing of significance happened in the Soviet Union during those years. The process of ideological disillusionment that took place under Brezhnev was an essential prelude to the Gorbachev revolution. During his eighteen years in power the regime gave up the battle to control the minds of its citizens, concentrating instead on their outward behavior. An all-embracing religion capable of mobilizing millions of people was transformed into an ideology for cynics. By the time Brezhnev died, the Soviet Union had lost its sense of mission. Even the general secretary no longer believed in the future socialist utopia.

"All that stuff about Communism is a tall tale for popular consumption," he told his brother, Yakov. "After all, we can't leave the people with no faith. The church was taken away, the tsar was shot, and something had to be substituted. So let the people build Communism."[176]

Compared with the scenes that had accompanied Stalin's death nearly thirty years earlier, Brezhnev's funeral was a restrained and unemotional affair. Stalin was terrifying and awe-inspiring even in death. In March 1953 Politburo members had quaked before him as he lay on his deathbed in his dacha. When they heard that the "Great Leader of All Times and All Peoples" had passed away, millions of people all over the country broke down and wept. The crowds were so great for the lying in state that more than five hundred people were trampled to death on the streets of Moscow. When Brezhnev died, Soviet citizens merely shrugged their shoulders. The elaborate funeral rites in Red Square—the coffin borne aloft by the surviving members of the Politburo, the wailing of factory sirens and firing of guns, Chopin's "Funeral March"—were practically identical. But there was no sense of real grief.

Curiously enough, the ideological crisis came at a time when ordinary Soviets were living better than ever before. The improvement in living standards fell far short of the regime's own promises. Standards of health remained dismal, meat and butter were rarities, and wages were low. Even so, Brezhnev's rule represented a respite from the terror and grinding poverty of the Stalinist period. Older people later looked back to the era of stagnation as a golden age, when bread cost sixteen kopecks a loaf, there was no unemployment, and every Soviet citizen was guaranteed five square meters of free housing. Russian families were beginning to acquire consumer luxuries like refrigerators and color television sets and could even dream of a tinny Soviet-made automobile.

Had Brezhnev's successors been able to sustain this gradual increase in living standards, there might have been no perestroika and no Second Russian Revolution. But this proved impossible at a time when the Soviet Union was waging war in Afghanistan, pouring money into the arms race with the United States, and propping up a string of Third World clients. By the early eighties it was clear to the thinking section of the Soviet elite that such profligacy could not continue forever. In order to meet the ever-growing cost of empire, Russia had been forced to ransack its treasure trove of natural resources. In other words, the country was living off its own future.

When the planners attempted to point this out to the decrepit *gensek,* he

would wave them away impatiently. It was an article of faith with Brezhnev that Russia's natural wealth was "inexhaustible."

"To hell with you and your figures," he once told Baibakov, the head of the state planning commission. "Let's go hunting."[177]

A FEW MONTHS AFTER Brezhnev's death, in April 1983, a group of a hundred or so Soviet economists and sociologists met in the Siberian city of Novosibirsk to discuss the eternal Russian questions: Who is guilty? What is to be done? Emboldened by Andropov's calls to get the world's second superpower moving again, the participants in the seminar tried to analyze the causes of the country's declining economic performance. They rejected the standard explanations—such as bad weather conditions, lack of skilled manpower, and low labor discipline—in favor of a much broader indictment of central planning. In the opinion of these scientists, the economy was trapped in a Stalinist rut of low productivity, shoddy output, and extravagant use of natural resources. The obsession with fulfilling targets established by supposedly omniscient planners was stifling individual initiative. The command-and-administer system, under which any economic decision of any significance was taken at the center, may have functioned reasonably well when the country's industrial infrastructure was still being formed. But it was incapable of meeting the challenges of the modern economy.

To avoid problems with the censors, the organizers of the Novosibirsk conference took care to wrap their conclusions up in Marxist-Leninist jargon. They limited circulation of their findings to fifty-eight numbered copies. Each was stamped "Confidential—for official use only." Despite these precautions, a copy of the report made its way to the West, where it caused an overnight sensation.[178] The so-called Novosibirsk report provided an insight into a growing behind-the-scenes debate in the Soviet Union on how to meet the challenges posed by the technological revolution that was sweeping the rest of the industrialized world. Behind the monolithic and seemingly stagnant facade something was stirring.

Under Stalin the Soviet Union had adopted a simplistic formula for economic growth. Increases in output were believed to be directly proportional to greater inputs of the "factors of production": manpower, raw materials, and land. If necessary, force would be used to achieve the desired result. In the 1930s, at the height of Stalin's industrialization campaign, thirty million peasants were forcibly uprooted from the countryside to provide slave labor for socialist industry. Another fifteen to thirty million Soviet citizens fell

victim to terror or famine. The Bolshevik leaders were convinced that the goal of building a socialist utopia justified any sacrifice. Their hubris was breathtaking. "There are no fortresses Bolsheviks cannot storm," one of Stalin's collaborators boasted. "Our task is not to study the economy, but to change it. We are not bound by any law."[179]

The extensive economic model was retained by Stalin's successors, with only slight modifications. Both Khrushchev and Brezhnev had a weakness for huge projects that would exploit the country's untapped resources. Khrushchev developed the virgin lands of northern Kazakhstan in a vain attempt to solve the food crisis. Brezhnev ordered a railway line to be built across the frozen tundra of northern Siberia to reach the copper reserves of Udokan and the gold mines of Yakutia. By the early eighties the Soviet Union led the world in such basic economic indices as the production of iron, coal, timber, and cement. It boasted the world's biggest hydroelectric dam, largest steel factory, heaviest tractors, most powerful rockets. At the same time, industry was unable to produce a decent razor blade or meet the demand for toilet paper.

What the Novosibirsk reformers proposed was a switch from extensive to intensive growth. Quality, not quantity, would become the new buzzword. Western studies had shown that a Soviet factory consumed two to three times as much energy as a Western plant to produce an inferior product. The technological gap between the Soviet Union and the West was growing all the time. By 1982, the year of Brezhnev's death, the Soviet Union trailed the United States in the number of computers per head by a factor of 1:400 and in the number of industrial robots by 1:15.[180]

Compared with later critiques of the Soviet economy, the Novosibirsk report was fairly tame. By contemporary standards, however, it was revolutionary. It challenged the official Leninist dogma that the Soviet Union was already a "classless society" and predicted that economic reform would trigger a political struggle between different interest groups. It also called for a total "restructuring" of the system of economic management to encourage individual initiative.

Nobody realized it yet, but a new political slogan had just been launched, a slogan that would transform the Communist world: perestroika.

NOWA HUTA

June 22, 1983

WHILE THE LEADERS of world communism were bidding farewell to Brezhnev, a little drama was being played out on the periphery of the Soviet empire that captured the scale of the ideological challenge confronting his successors. The workers of Nowa Huta, a city of two hundred thousand people in southern Poland, had taken a passionate dislike to a statue to Vladimir Ilyich Lenin adorning their central square. They had marched on it, scrawled anti-Communist graffiti on it, and attempted to pull it down with picks and ropes. On one occasion they had even set the father of the international proletariat on fire, drenching his billowing overcoat in gasoline and blowing off one of his hands.

Determined to protect Vladimir Ilyich from his ungrateful offspring, the Communist authorities erected a corrugated iron fence around the charred two-story-high monument. Thousands of ZOMO riot police moved into Nowa Huta. Armed policemen patrolled the square day and night. At moments of tension a dozen police vehicles threw a defensive circle of steel around the statue. Water cannon were stationed nearby to repel a surprise attack.

For a nation still reeling from the psychological shock of martial law, there was a delicious irony to these events. Nowa Huta—Polish for "new

steelworks"—had been planned as a model socialist community. Poland's rulers had wanted a socioeconomic laboratory where they could turn God-fearing Polish peasants into the new proletarian man described by Marx and Lenin. They saw the town as a political counterweight to the nearby city of Kraków, Poland's ancient capital, which they regarded as a bastion of conservative reaction. The construction of Nowa Huta in the early 1950s was accompanied by a propaganda barrage about the incredible feats of "heroes of socialist labor," which served as inspiration for Andrzej Wajda's film *Man of Marble*. To celebrate its completion, the giant Nowa Huta steelworks received the hallowed name of Lenin.

There were hundreds of similar "model" towns all over the Soviet empire, from Karl-Marx-Stadt in East Germany to Komsomolsk-on-Amur in the Soviet Far East. They were uniform in their soul-destroying drabness, gridlike layouts, and pompous style of municipal architecture. Lenin Avenue always led to Lenin Square, dominated by a huge statue of Lenin, right arm thrust up in classic taxicab-hailing pose. The biggest building in each square was always the headquarters of the local Communist Party, and the party secretary always had his offices on the second floor. Faded propaganda banners—with slogans like "Glory to the Communist Party" and "We Promise to Fulfill the Goals of the Five-Year Plan"—adorned the pot-holed streets. The stores had names like Food Products No. 8, Bakery No.12, and Hairdresser. The gray apartment buildings had a makeshift, slapped-together quality about them, as if nobody cared whether the walls were straight or the balconies fell into the street. There was even a distinctly socialist smell. The blend of odors varied slightly from country to country, but the basic ingredients were always the same: low-octane gasoline, body odor, unwashed frying pans, cheap perfume, brown coal, cabbage, dried urine, and musty newsprint.

Many of these towns were company towns, built around a single state-owned factory, such as a steelworks or a coal mine or a big defense plant, visible for miles around. The factory dominated the lives of the townspeople, just as it dominated the landscape. It provided them with jobs and poisoned the air they breathed and the water they drank. It organized day care centers and summer camps for their children and exposed them to an unending stream of Communist propaganda. It distributed housing and acted as an extension of the police state: If you misbehaved, you would be crossed off the ten-year waiting list for an apartment.

Nowa Huta differed from other model socialist towns in one very important respect. At the corner of Karl Marx Avenue and Great Proletarian

Avenue stood a soaring concrete structure that had not been part of the original plan. Topped by a huge steel cross, the Church of Our Lady, Queen of Poland was known to everyone in town as the Ark. The struggle to prove the planners wrong had infused the entire community with a sense of defiance.

The first cross had appeared on this site in 1957, in the wake of the popular upheavals that swept Gomułka to power. Over the next decade the cross was repeatedly torn down by police and stubbornly put up again by the local inhabitants. Finally, in 1967, seventeen years after the building of Nowa Huta, the archbishop of Kraków had dug a spade into the earth to break the ground for the town's first church. It took another decade of bureaucratic obstruction and arbitrary shortages of building materials to complete the Ark. Much of the work, including carrying two million stones from mountain streams, was done by local inhabitants with their bare hands. Consecrating the completed church in 1977, the archbishop had declared: "Nowa Huta was built as a city without God, but the will of God and the people who worked here prevailed. Let this be a lesson."[181]

The archbishop had gone on to become Pope John Paul II, the first non-Italian pope in 455 years. On his first pilgrimage back to his homeland, in 1979, Karol Wojtyła had been refused permission to visit the Ark. So he had said mass across the cornfields, in Kraków, against the backdrop of the dark, satanic steel mill. Now he was returning to Poland once again, and this time he would be visiting Nowa Huta. Frustrated in their attempts to pull down the local Lenin monument, the inhabitants of the "city without God" were determined to show the world where their loyalties really lay.

THE POPE'S FIRST VISIT had provided the spiritual boost that had paved the way for the rise of Solidarity. By turning out to greet their countryman, and becoming part of the millions-strong crowd that followed his every move, Poles acquired a sense of solidarity with one another. Never again would they feel alone and isolated, as they had during the dark days of totalitarianism. If anyone was isolated, it was Poland's Communist rulers.

During the 1979 pilgrimage John Paul had spoken in a voice that was simple and direct, quite unlike the voice of the Communist regime. He talked of the thirty-five-year Communist experience as a transitory phenomenon, insignificant in comparison with Poland's thousand-year devotion to the Roman Catholic Church. It was a message that came across clearly on the first day of the visit, in Warsaw's Victory Square, when the pope attacked the state for attempting to create an atheistic society. "Christ

cannot be kept out of the history of man in any part of the globe," he had thundered. The crowd greeted his words with a ten-minute burst of applause, ending with rhythmic chants of "We want God, we want God."[182]

From that moment onward, Karol Wojtyła became the uncrowned king of Poland.

During his weeklong tour of Poland the pope had elaborated on one of his favorite themes, the spiritual unity of Europe. He saw his beloved Kraków as part of a European-wide civilization, in which political boundaries were more or less irrelevant. In Wojtyła's Europe, the Europe of 966, when Poland was first converted to Christianity, there was no Iron Curtain and no Berlin Wall. Priests, scholars, and ideas traveled freely from one town to another. The pope was convinced that his election was God's way of reminding Western Europe that Poles, Czechs, Slovaks, Croats, Serbs, Bulgars, and even Russians were also part of a much broader Christian civilization.

Born in 1920, the year Poland defeated Soviet Russia in the "Miracle on the Vistula," Karol Wojtyła had firsthand experience of family tragedy, backbreaking labor, and political oppression. He had scarcely known his mother, a schoolteacher, who died when he was only six, while giving birth to a stillborn girl. His father, who had served in the Austro-Hungarian army, was killed in the opening year of World War II. "At the age of twenty," Wojtyła later recalled, "I had already lost all the people I loved and even the ones I might have loved, such as my big sister who had died, I was told, six years before my birth."[183] Psychologists have speculated that the future pope sought compensation for the maternal love he never received in the Marian cult of the Black Madonna.

As a theological student in Kraków Wojtyła experienced the terror of German occupation. A particularly brutal Nazi gauleiter, Hans Frank, installed himself in the royal Wawel Castle with orders from Hitler to treat the Poles as a slave race. "The standard of living in Poland must be kept low," Hitler instructed. "The priests will preach what we want them to preach. Their task is to keep the Poles quiet, stupid, and dull-witted."[184] Wojtyła saw Kraków Jews being taken to the death camp at Auschwitz, just a few miles down the road. Polish intellectuals were disposed of in a similar fashion. The Germans put Wojtyła to work, first in a stone quarry and later carrying buckets of lime in a water purification plant. On the night of August 6, 1944, the Gestapo arrested all Polish males between the age of fifteen and fifty in retaliation for the Warsaw uprising. Had they found Wojtyła, they would probably have killed him. Fortunately for the young theologian, he was given shelter by the archbishop of Kraków, Prince Adam Sapieha.

Wojtyła lived in the residence on Franciscan Street, off and on, for nearly

fifteen years, as both student and archbishop. When he returned in June 1983, as pope, it was as if he were coming home. He greeted the nuns by name and sang and joked with the thousands of young people who waited to greet him in the street outside. "Holy Father, we trust you," they chanted. "Save Poland."

On the last full day of his visit the pope said mass on the Błonie, the vast meadow in front of Wawel Castle. Banners reading "Solidarity Lives" and "There Is No Freedom Without Solidarity" fluttered above the crowd of two million people. Alluding to Jaruzelski's imposition of martial law, the pope urged his listeners never to give up. The nation had been "called to victory," he declared.

As he said these words, two million people raised their hands silently in the air in the V for victory sign. An underground Solidarity leader, Eugeniusz Szumiejko, who had managed to escape the police roundup, was standing at the back of the huge throng, on top of an embankment. All of a sudden he saw a sea of black heads submerged in a wave of white fists.[185] It was an awe-inspiring sight, proof that Jaruzelski had been unable to crush the spirit that had given birth to Solidarity. At the end of the mass a large chunk of the crowd set off on foot for Nowa Huta, beneath their Solidarity banners, to see the pope consecrate a new church.

"*Khodz z namy*," they chanted, the battle cry of 1970 and 1980. "Come with us. There will be no beatings today."

When they reached the site of the new church, they joined a congregation of a quarter of a million people. The entire population of the "city without God" had turned out to greet the pope. Here was proof that history could not be reversed by tanks, internment camps, and corrugated iron fences, that martial law too would pass, and that Nowa Huta's two-story monument to the founder of world communism would one day come down.

THE KREMLIN GREETED THE NEWS of Pope John Paul's triumphant return to his homeland with ill-concealed fury. The Soviet mass media accused Polish priests of inciting parishioners to acts of "political hooliganism" and inspiring "counterrevolutionary disturbances." Soviet leaders urged their Polish counterparts to crack down hard on the "reactionary" wing of the Catholic Church.

"The Polish Communist Party isn't putting much effort into the struggle with the church," Gromyko, the Soviet foreign minister, complained to his Politburo colleagues. "Things have reached the point when thousands

upon thousands of people are crawling on their knees before the Roman pope." [186]

Jaruzelski resisted Moscow's advice to crack down on the church. He tried to explain that he needed the church as an "ally" in his campaign to ensure peace and quiet in Poland and regain respectability at home and abroad. The Kremlin potentates remained hostile. Their suspicions were voiced by the youngest member of the Politburo, who presented himself as an ardent believer in the monotheistic faith of communism. "Jaruzelski is trying to paint the situation in rosy colors," he told his colleagues. "We must clarify his real intentions. We must find out whether he wants to introduce a pluralistic system of government in Poland." [187]

Such were the views of Mikhail Sergeyevich Gorbachev a year before he became general secretary of the Communist Party of the Soviet Union.

II

REVOLT

OF THE MACHINES

In Poland, in August 1980, it was human beings who went on strike. In the Soviet Union, we are witnessing a strike of inanimate objects.

Adam Michnik

All that is human must retrograde if it does not advance.

Edward Gibbon, *Decline and Fall of the Roman Empire*

SAKHALIN ISLAND

September 1, 1983

AFTER RONALD REAGAN'S ELECTION as fortieth president of the United States, the Pentagon began publishing annual reports on the Soviet military threat. Packed with color illustrations of missiles that could hit New York and Los Angeles, charts depicting the growing Warsaw Pact advantage in tanks and men under arms, and grainy photographs of nuclear submarines, the glossy brochures portrayed a world in which the balance of power was shifting inexorably in favor of the Communist superpower. With each edition of *Soviet Military Power*, an ever greater proportion of the earth's surface was daubed in red. Sinister red arrows reached out across the world's major sea-lanes, showing the Kremlin straining to achieve the goal of a thousand-ship navy. Much of Asia, Africa, and Latin America was covered with blotches and symbols denoting the presence of Soviet, Cuban, or East German military advisers. No part of the globe, not even the United States, seemed entirely safe from the encroaching Red menace.

Thanks to satellite technology, American military planners were able to observe a Soviet arms buildup that was unprecedented for peacetime. If anything, they underestimated the extent of the buildup, failing to detect many of the nuclear warheads that were rolling off Soviet production lines. There was something missing, however, from this bird's-eye view: an understanding of ground-level reality.

99

Viewed up close, the Soviet military machine was neither as awesome nor as efficient as it appeared from the sky. The military-industrial complex suffered from the same weaknesses as the rest of the Soviet economy: incompetence, waste, technological backwardness, bureaucracy. Despite devoting an ever-increasing proportion of their country's economic resources to the military, Soviet leaders still felt insecure.

Several years later, when the Cold War was already winding down, Soviet military chiefs presented their American counterparts with a map that reflected their view of the world. In sharp contrast with American maps, the Soviet map depicted a vast country encircled by enemies. To the east there were the Chinese, waiting for a chance to expand into the underpopulated vastness of Siberia. To the south, the Muslims, with whom Russia had waged war for five hundred years. To the west, the ideologically irreconcilable forces of imperialism. And all around, the rival superpower, with its military bases, electronic listening posts, subversive radio "voices," and all-conquering consumer culture.

To defend themselves against these multiple threats, Kremlin leaders propagated the doctrine of a "sacred" border. The frontiers of the Soviet state had been consecrated with the blood of millions of soldiers and could never be altered. It was the patriotic duty of every citizen to defend these borders to the end. Half a million soldiers were assigned to patrol the frontier. Soviet air defenses alone consisted of some twenty-five hundred interceptor aircraft, five thousand early warning radar systems, and ten thousand surface-to-air-missiles, deployed along a five-thousand-mile arc from Kamchatka to Kaliningrad.[1]

The orders were clear: "Use weapons and combat equipment" to destroy any intruder. When the test finally came, the border guards almost fluffed it.

GENNADY OSIPOVICH CLIMBED into the cockpit of his Su-15 interceptor jet an hour before dawn on September 1, 1983. He was given the coordinates of an unidentified "military" target approaching the island of Sakhalin from the direction of Kamchatka, a volcanic peninsula that juts down from the eastern tip of Russia. His mission was to destroy the target if and when it crossed back into Soviet airspace. At 5:42 a.m., Sakhalin time, he received the order to take off.

By the time Osipovich was finally airborne, the "intruder" plane had been wandering across Soviet territory for almost an hour. Four fighter planes had been scrambled over Kamchatka to bring it down, but they had lost touch with their target as it headed out over the Sea of Okhotsk. It later

turned out that eight out of the eleven tracking stations on Kamchatka and Sakhalin were not functioning properly.[2]

A veteran pilot with ten years' experience in the Far East, Osipovich knew that the boastful talk about the Soviet Union's impenetrable borders was a myth. In fact, there were gaping holes in the system. The Americans seemed to delight in testing the mettle of Soviet pilots. U.S. fighter aircraft would head directly for the border, only to veer away at the last moment. American RC-135 intelligence-gathering planes were constantly buzzing around. The war of nerves was taking its toll. Six months previously a squadron of planes from the U.S. Pacific fleet had brazenly violated Soviet airspace over the Kurile Islands, an archipelago seized from Japan at the end of World War II. A high-level commission had berated the Soviet pilots for their lack of vigilance.[3]

Personal initiative was not a quality that was prized in the Air Defense Force (PVO). The Soviet top guns who flew high-performance combat planes sometimes dismissed their PVO colleagues as "robots" controlled from the ground. Osipovich's Sukhoi-15 was a typical PVO plane, a cumbersome gas guzzler, fast-climbing but difficult to maneuver. One Soviet defector described it as little more than "a high-altitude missile platform."[4] The range of PVO planes was limited. After a Soviet fighter pilot flew a state-of-the-art MiG-25 to Japan, orders were issued to ensure that PVO planes never had enough fuel to reach a foreign airfield. That meant a maximum flying time of forty to fifty minutes, barely enough to complete a mission.[5]

After roughly ten minutes' flight Osipovich caught sight of the intruder through a thin layer of cloud. At first it looked like a flying dot, two to three centimeters across. The flashing navigation lights were clearly visible against the nighttime sky. When he got closer, to a distance of around three miles, he could observe the silhouette of a strange, humpbacked plane. It was large, unlike anything he had ever seen before.

At 6:15, Osipovich's headphones crackled with an order to "prepare to fire." Ground control on Sakhalin addressed him by the call sign 805 and asked if his missile systems were "locked on" to the target.

"I am locked on," replied the pilot, watching a row of lights on his control panel beginning to flash. The interceptor was equipped with two R-98 air-to-air missiles. Upon release, one of the missiles was programmed to home in on a source of infrared radiation, such as aircraft exhaust. The other missile was guided to its target by radar. Attempting to get a little closer to the intruder, Osipovich turned on his afterburner. The radio crackled an order that he could not make out.

"Say again."

The voice of ground control rose to a shout. "Eight-zero-five, the target has violated the state border, destroy the target!"[6]

But there was to be a last-minute reprieve for KAL 007. Down on the ground, frantic messages were flying between air force bases on Sakhalin, a thousand-mile-long slither of starkly beautiful mountains rising from a plain that bristled with military installations. The duty officer for Osipovich's squadron was startled by the extraordinarily "stupid" behavior of the intruder. Suicide missions were not the American style. He told a colleague from a neighboring fighter division that it all seemed "very suspicious." "I don't think the enemy is so stupid. Can it be one of ours?" Next, he called a control post at Makarov, on the eastern tip of the island, to check on the progress of the intruder.

"It hasn't bombed us yet," came the cheerful reply.[7]

At the command control center in Khabarovsk, four hundred miles to the west, there were similar doubts about the identity of the "target." The duty officer thought the intruder plane could be a passenger aircraft. "All necessary steps must be taken to identify it," he insisted. His superior, General Kamenski, was also troubled. "Maybe it is some civilian aircraft, or God knows what," he told the commander of air defenses on Sakhalin, General Kornukov.

"What civilian?" exploded Kornukov, who had been dragged out of bed forty-five minutes earlier and informed that an American RC-135 was heading straight toward his island. He knew the penalties for letting such a plane escape. "It has flown over Kamchatka. It came from the ocean, without identification. I am giving the order to attack."[8]

Seconds later even Kornukov began having some doubts. Straining to make sense out of the nocturnal drama, he countermanded his earlier order to shoot down the intruder. "Are there navigation lights or not?" he suddenly barked out. In the next minute he repeated the question five more times. The absence of navigation lights would be proof of the plane's hostile intent. The question was relayed to Osipovich.

"The air navigation light is on; the flashing light is on," he radioed back.

"Flash the interceptor's lights as a warning signal," ordered Kornukov. "Order him to approach the target, rock wings at it, and force it to land." To still the hubbub that was coming in over his headset, he gave another order to the commander of Osipovich's squadron: "Stop that horsing around at the command post. Only you, I, and the controller are to talk. No one else."[9]

Positioned behind and slightly below the intruder plane, Osipovich fired four bursts of armor-piercing shells, 243 rounds in all. In response, the target appeared to reduce speed, forcing Osipovich's Su-15 to shoot ahead. Both planes had now crossed the island from east to west—a twelve-minute flight—and were heading out into the Sea of Japan. In the thick moon haze of the predawn sky, it seemed to Osipovich that the target was taking evasive action. He knew that if he slowed down, he would stall. So he dived two thousand feet and banked around for a second run at the intruder. His thoughts were consumed by the flashing lights of his instrument panel.[10]

THE 240 PASSENGERS on board Korean Airlines flight 007 from Anchorage to Seoul were oblivious of the drama just outside their portholes. Some had covered themselves in blankets and had drowsed off. Others were waiting for the cabin crew to come around with breakfast as the plane flew over Japan on its approach to South Korea. Most of the window shades were down, for the in-flight movie. Up on the flight deck the crew were suppressing yawns and engaged in desultory conversation about vacations and customs procedures. The talk turned to the location of the airport currency exchange.

"What kind of money do you wish to exchange?" asked one crew member. "Dollar to Korean money is all right."

"Yes."

"That is in the domestic building."

"It could be open nine o'clock in the morning. It could be ten o'clock."[11]

It did not occur to Captain Chun Byung-in and his colleagues that they had flown in and out of Soviet airspace for more than two hours and were being tracked by Soviet interceptors. Shortly after leaving Anchorage, they had programmed the well-trodden route to Seoul into the Boeing's computer. At this moment they believed themselves to be more than two hundred miles to the east, in international airspace, off the coast of Japan. But a tragic error had occurred. Instead of following the recognized route, the plane had followed a constant magnetic heading that had brought it right over Soviet territory. The onboard inertial navigation system had failed to engage, either because the pilots had switched it on too late or because someone had flipped the switch to the wrong position. There had been many opportunities to catch the error, but the flight was long and tedious, and nobody noticed that the plane was drifting off its assigned route.[12]

At the moment when Osipovich was attempting to attract his attention

with a burst of cannon fire, Captain Chun was talking to air traffic control in Tokyo. He received permission to climb two thousand feet to an altitude of thirty-seven thousand feet, a routine fuel-saving maneuver at this point in the flight. Osipovich interpreted the climb as an attempt to escape.

BY NOW THE INTRUDER PLANE was heading out of Soviet airspace, and the generals down on the ground were beginning to panic. If it got away, they would be accused of dereliction of duty and could face dismissal. There was no time left to identify the target positively. Osipovich was running out of fuel. He had no more than ten to fifteen minutes' flying time remaining. In theory he could have tried to communicate with the intruder aircraft on the internationally recognized 121.5 megahertz emergency frequency. But that would have meant retuning his radio and losing contact with his ground controllers. There was no time for that either.[13]

At 6:21, just as dawn was breaking over the island of Sakhalin and KAL 007 was flying out of Soviet airspace, Kornukov made his final decision. The air crackled with commands.

"Fire missiles, fire on target six-zero–six-five, destroy target six-zero–six-five."

"Get Osipovich to fire, and soon!"

"Carry out the task, destroy!"

"Bring one-six-three in behind Osipovich to guarantee destruction!"

"Eight-zero-five, approach target and destroy target!"

As he spun around behind the Boeing, Osipovich had only one thought in his mind: to down the enemy plane. He had even dreamed of such a moment. This would be the culmination of his career as a Soviet interceptor pilot. He stubbed his index finger to release the heat-seeking missile. Two seconds later he fired the radar-guided missile.

"Launch executed," he radioed back.

It took the missiles roughly thirty seconds to cover the five miles between the two planes. Then Osipovich saw a burst of yellow flame from the tail section. The navigation lights went out immediately. At first the plane seemed to climb. But as he peeled off to the right, he could see the intruder plane plummeting toward the sea.

"The target is destroyed," he announced excitedly.[14]

THE KREMLIN

September 2, 1983

THE DESTRUCTION of Korean Airlines flight 007 was a spectacular example of what the historian Barbara Tuchman has described as the "March of Folly," action that flies in the face of national self-interest. By shooting 269 innocent people out of the sky, the Soviets seemed to confirm the "evil empire" tag that had been stuck on them by President Reagan.

Soviet leaders compounded the public relations disaster of shooting down a civilian aircraft by refusing—for almost a week—to acknowledge what they had done. The first statement by the official Tass news agency about the incident failed to mention any shots. It claimed that an unidentified aircraft, flying "without navigation lights," had violated Soviet airspace. Soviet interceptors had attempted to guide the plane to the "nearest airfield," but the intruder had ignored all the "signals and warnings" and "continued its flight in the direction of the Sea of Japan." These claims were a gift to conservatives in the United States, who had no illusions about Moscow's willingness "to lie and to cheat," in Reagan's phrase. Soviet responsibility for the shootdown was easily demonstrated. The Americans simply played a tape of the exchanges between Sakhalin ground control and the interceptor pilot to a hushed session of the UN Security Council.

No single individual was to blame for this self-inflicted disaster. It re-

flected the collective woodenheadedness of a system that had sidetracked Russia into decades of self-imposed isolation, a system that suppressed dissenting opinions and was unable to deal flexibly with new challenges, a system that prized ideology over common sense. It was the same wooden-headedness that had caused Kremlin leaders to murder millions of their own citizens in the name of progress, to devastate their country's natural environment for short-term economic gain, to persecute its most outstanding writers and scientists, and to stumble into an unpopular, unwinnable war in Afghanistan despite numerous warnings about the risks of such an enterprise. The system was so powerful, and so well entrenched, that it seemed to paralyze virtually all who lived in its shadow.

LESS THAN TEN MONTHS had passed since Brezhnev's death, but they had taken their toll on Yuri Andropov. Worn down by rapidly failing health and awesome responsibilities, the new Soviet leader looked like a skeleton. Even longtime associates had difficulty recognizing him. He spent much of his time in a hospital room, cluttered with medical equipment and Kremlin telephones, sitting in an ancient dentist's chair with a high headrest that allowed him to shift his position at the press of a button. In the summer of 1983 his kidneys had given out entirely, and he had to be hooked up to a dialysis machine twice a week.[15] For the Soviet people the general secretary had become a kind of ghostly presence that could be felt and sensed but was never seen. If he needed to communicate with the nation, he did so in written form, through a statement "from the Soviet leadership," or a Tass communiqué, or perhaps an interview in *Pravda*.

The Andropov era had begun on a hopeful note. After the drift and stagnation of the Brezhnev years, most Soviet citizens welcomed any sign of change, however modest. They were impressed by the new leader's attempts to shake the bureaucracy out of its torpor. An anticorruption drive targeted at former Brezhnev cronies helped bolster the image of the former KGB chief as a stern but just ruler who would get the country moving again. At last Russia had a real *khozyayin*, master, who would punish idlers and restore a sense of order and discipline. Desperate for vigorous leadership, many Russians reacted positively to such token gestures as a series of police raids on Moscow bathhouses in the middle of the day to crack down on absenteeism.

Among the Communist Party elite, the wizened man in the dentist's chair was regarded as the best of his generation. Fifteen years at the head of

the world's largest spy agency had given Andropov a unique insight into the true condition of the Soviet Union and the extent to which it lagged behind its capitalist rivals. Compared with Brezhnev, he was decisive and energetic. He understood the need for change and seemed open to new ideas. But there was a hard side to the dying Soviet leader that went back to his days as a rising apparatchik under Stalin. Unlike younger members of the Politburo, who had never experienced war or revolution, Andropov knew that Soviet power rested on the ability of a ruthless minority to impose its will on the majority. Reform was necessary, but it had to be tightly controlled.

In Andropov's view, the secret of ruling a country as vast as Russia was never to show weakness. This applied to both domestic policy and foreign affairs. The enemies of socialism were lying in wait, ready to pounce the moment the dictatorship of the proletariat displayed signs of indecision or disunity. Events should not be allowed to reach the point where the only solution was overwhelming military force. That meant keeping a watchful eye on dissent and nipping protests in the bud, *before* they grew into a major challenge to the regime. In Politburo discussions before he became general secretary, Andropov was always calling for firm measures against would-be dissenters and wayward intellectuals. He liked to quote the Leninist dictum that "A revolution is worth something only if it knows how to defend itself."[16]

"It is very easy to destroy a social order, particularly one in which there are many hidden reasons for dissatisfaction, where nationalism is just under the surface," Andropov told his associates. "Dissidents are enemies of our social system, although they conceal their aims beneath demagogic slogans."[17]

For all his sophistication and willingness to experiment, Andropov remained a prisoner of the system. A revolutionary mind-set prevented him from challenging its basic features: the overwhelming weight of the military-industrial complex; central planning; the dominance of politics over economics. Like many Soviet leaders, he had become a victim of his own absolute power.

Andropov was a great admirer of Eisenstein's epic film *Ivan the Terrible,* a thinly disguised apologia for autocratic rule that had been made to order for Stalin. He was particularly impressed by a scene early on in the movie, when the new tsar is attempting to impose his will on the rebellious boyars. The boyars grumble that neither Europe nor Rome will recognize the young ruler, to which a Jesuit priest retorts, "He who is strong will be recognized by everybody." Andropov would cite these words approvingly when arguing

the need for a tough stance vis-à-vis the American "imperialists." "Both we and the Americans live according to this principle," he told his associates. "Neither of us wants to appear weak."[18]

Like Stalin and Ivan the Terrible before him, Andropov lived in a world dominated by scheming domestic enemies and hostile foreign powers. The only way to survive in such a world, and ensure the well-being of his people, was through ruthlessness, cunning, and a large dose of paranoia.

Military strength was the foundation stone of the Russian state. The obsession with security frequently undermined the Kremlin's other foreign policy goals, which required a "peacemaker" image. Even as general secretary Andropov was reluctant to go against the wishes of the military-industrial complex. When the Korean airliner affair erupted, the Foreign Ministry urged him to assume responsibility for the shootdown, while accusing the United States of organizing a deliberate intrusion into Soviet airspace. But the defense minister, Ustinov, was categorically opposed to admitting that the Soviet Union had destroyed a civilian airliner.

"Don't worry," he told Andropov in a conference call to his hospital room. "Everything will be all right. Nobody will be able to prove anything."[19]

EVER SINCE THE DAYS OF STALIN, Politburo meetings had followed a well-established ritual. They were less a forum for open debate than a weekly loyalty ceremony for members of the party's inner elite. The course of the proceedings was usually predetermined by the general secretary and a handful of powerful vassals, each of whom enjoyed a great deal of autonomy in running his particular fiefdom. There was always a strict pecking order around the Politburo table. Junior members were expected to give the floor to their elders and then chime in respectfully in support of the established party line. By voicing ritualistic support for a particular decision, they automatically assumed responsibility for it. The process was then repeated over and over again, all the way down the party hierarchy, until it became binding on all eighteen million Soviet Communists. Under the rules of "democratic centralism," once the Politburo had taken a formal decision, no dissent was permitted.

In its language and rituals the Politburo resembled a group of Mafia dons who have clawed their way to the top of a gigantic protection racket. The Communist Party was at root a conspiracy. The original purpose of the conspiracy—the building of an earthly utopia—had long since been forgot-

ten. Ideology had given way to cynicism, but the gang mentality had remained. In order to preserve their power and privileges, the party bosses understood that they had to stick together.

Contrary to the cherished notion of some Kremlinologists, the Politburo was not divided into hawks and doves. Under both Brezhnev and Andropov, all Politburo members were hawks by definition. (The only way for a dove to survive when surrounded by hawks is to become a hawk itself.) It was part of the ritual that everyone prove his credentials by sounding at least as hawkish as the previous speaker. Disagreements were expressed in nuances and subtle differences of emphasis, rather than open argument. The biological law of Kremlin politics was survival of the blandest. That meant having an intuitive feel for the emerging consensus—as spelled out by the *gensek* or one of his top vassals—and climbing on board. All Soviet politicians, with the partial exception of the *gensek*, were required to wear a mask.

In Andropov's absence, the Politburo debate on the Korean airliner affair was opened by Konstantin Chernenko, the wheezing asthmatic who used to light Brezhnev's cigarettes. Thanks to his late patron, he was now the party's chief ideologist. He reacted to the destruction of a civilian airliner—and the deaths of 269 people—as a bureaucrat whose orderly world has been disturbed by an unwelcome intrusion.

"One thing is clear," he sputtered, "we cannot allow foreign planes to overfly our territory freely. No self-respecting state can allow that."[20]

Next to speak was Defense Minister Ustinov, who was determined to defend the honor of the military establishment. His report to the Politburo included several blatant lies, designed to relieve his subordinates of all responsibility. His assertion that the Boeing 747 was flying "without warning lights" flatly contradicted the testimony of the interceptor pilot. He insisted that "repeated instructions" had been given to the intruder to land at a Soviet airfield and that warning shots had been fired "with tracer shells, as stipulated in international rules."

"My opinion is that in this situation we must show firmness and remain cool," the defense minister barked. "We should not flinch. If we flinch, it gives all kinds of people the opportunity to overfly our territory."

The only Politburo member who might have had the authority to stand up to Ustinov was Andrei Gromyko, who would be required to bear the brunt of international outrage over the shooting down of a civilian airliner. But the seventy-four-year-old foreign minister was exceptionally cautious. This survivor of Stalin's purges had managed to climb to the top by always

backing the winning side. Every gene in his body told him not to get into an argument with someone as forceful as Ustinov. If he judged that the timing was right, "Grim Grom" could be an effective advocate for arms control negotiations with the United States in internal Politburo discussions. Faced with a choice between antagonizing the military and abandoning policy positions favored by the Foreign Ministry, he almost always chose the latter. He did not want his ministry to acquire a dovish reputation.[21]

Gromyko told the Politburo that the Soviet military had acted "correctly" in shooting down the Korean plane. At the same time, he believed that the Soviet Union should anticipate the likely thrust of "imperialist propaganda" and acknowledge that "shots were fired." "We should say so frankly, so as not to allow our adversary to accuse us of being deceitful. Our main argument should be that the plane was flying over Soviet territory and had penetrated an exceptionally long way into our territory."

Now it was Mikhail Gorbachev's turn to speak. The youngest member of the Politburo was in a delicate position. Everyone knew he was a favorite of Andropov, who had encouraged him to broaden his range of interests beyond agriculture. His elders needed his youthful energy and competence, but they also felt threatened by him. Here was a man who could push them all aside. In order to retain their confidence and have a shot at the top job, Gorbachev had to tread a very fine line. He had to prove that he could be an enthusiastic and creative spokesman for the party without threatening the vested interests of any section of the Soviet bureaucracy.

Gorbachev resorted to the standard stratagem of Kremlin politics: When in doubt, attack the "forces of imperialism." He told his colleagues that the Americans must have been aware of the unauthorized incursion into Soviet territory. The length of time that the Korean plane had been in Soviet airspace, some two hours, showed that this was a well-planned "provocation."

"It's no use keeping quiet now; we must go on to the offensive," he concluded, striking a hawkish note.

That evening, in keeping with Andropov's declared intention of introducing greater "openness" into political life, the Soviet people were informed that the Politburo had met. A communiqué read out on the main television news bulletin said that the subjects under discussion included "improving the production of color television sets" and measures "to increase labor productivity."[22] There was no mention of the KAL tragedy. It took another five days for the Soviet authorities to acknowledge that they had indeed shot down a civilian airliner. On September 10 the Kremlin

moved over to the offensive, just as Gorbachev had proposed, broadcasting a television interview with the man who had blasted the Korean airliner out of the sky.

GENNADY OSIPOVICH WAS SHOCKED and bewildered. He tried hard to conceal his feelings, but his mental anguish was apparent to anyone who met him. His normally firm handshake was cold and lifeless. His expression seemed hopelessly distracted. He behaved like someone suffering from an attack of nausea or perhaps a merciless tongue-lashing from a superior. Wrapped up in his own world, he seemed to tune out of a conversation and gaze off into the distance.

"Perhaps there was no one on the plane," he would say to no one in particular. Or, "Who can tell me exactly how many seats there are on this Boeing?"23

The pilot's world had turned upside down several times in the space of a few days. When he brought his Su-15 back to Sokol Air Base, he was greeted like a hero. The entire regiment turned out to welcome the man who had shot down an "intruder." There were hugs, kisses, and celebratory shots of vodka. The younger pilots looked at him with envy, but Osipovich felt a twinge of anxiety. He phoned Kornukov, the general who had given the order to "destroy the target," to find out what had really happened. Perhaps the plane had been "one of ours"?

"No," the general had replied in his gruff tone. "It was a foreigner. So make a hole in your shoulder boards for a new star."24

Then the rumors started. Western radio stations reported that the Soviet Union had shot down a passenger airplane, with 269 people on board. Government commissions arrived from Moscow. There were endless questions and investigations. The higher-ups, trained in the art of playing it safe, began to look strangely at Osipovich.

"Why are they treating me as if I am insane?" the pilot complained to a journalist for the army newspaper *Red Star*, who had flown in to interview him. "For days I have not even been able to go to the bathroom by myself. They keep me locked up."25

The journalists had been fully briefed before leaving Moscow. Their task was to get the interceptor pilot to confirm the official propaganda line about downing a "spy plane." That meant mouthing the same lies that the Soviet Union had been telling the rest of the world. The entire script had already been written in Moscow. All Osipovich was required to do was to memorize

his lines and repeat them in front of the camera. He did as instructed, but the result seemed hopelessly artificial and wooden. The television correspondent was dissatisfied

The pilot asked for a break. Someone produced a bottle of vodka, which he downed in a succession of quick shots. He felt more relaxed now. When he reappeared in front of the television cameras, the words of outrage and indignation seemed to come spontaneously. He spoke about the threat of a nuclear war, describing how he had been scheduled to give a talk on "peace" to a school in Sakhalin on the very day that the United States organized its provocation. The television reporter, Aleksandr Tikhomirov, asked if he was certain that the intruder had been an "enemy plane."

"Yes, this is what I thought," replied Osipovich, slouching in an easy chair. "After it crossed our border, it only made me more certain. This enemy aircraft which had broken into our territory was now flying over my home. It passed almost over our base. People at this time are peacefully sleeping, and he's up there on a spying mission."[26]

THE KOREAN AIRLINER TRAGEDY was a cathartic experience for both superpowers. It brought them closer to nuclear Armageddon than at any time since the 1962 Cuban missile crisis, but it also laid the psychological foundation for a new era in East-West relations. Like punch-drunk fighters clutched in a deadly embrace, the leaders of Russia and America staggered to the edge of a cliff, looked over the edge, and then took a step back.

Hearing the rhetorical missiles hurtling back and forth between Moscow and Washington, one could be forgiven for concluding that the world was on the edge of an abyss. The Reagan administration accused the Kremlin of "a crime against humanity" and the deliberate "massacre" of 269 innocent civilians. The Soviets responded by depicting Reagan as a "madman," comparable to Adolf Hitler, who wanted to dominate the world. At the same time, however, there was a reassuring predictability about these barbs. It was as if each side knew that it possessed the means to inflict unacceptable devastation on its rival and was therefore compelled to find other ways of giving vent to its hostility. The balance of terror was matched by a balance of rhetoric.

The rhetorical confrontation between Moscow and Washington came against the background of a trial of strength over the deployment of American missiles in Western Europe. If the Kremlin could convince Western public opinion that Reagan was pushing the world to the brink of a nuclear

confrontation, the battle was almost won. The Reagan administration, by contrast, wanted to portray itself as tough but reasonable. The Korean airliner affair represented a major public relations defeat for Andropov, from which he never really recovered. The deployment of American Pershing and Cruise missiles—the Western response to the earlier deployment of Soviet SS-20 missiles targeted on Western Europe—went ahead on schedule.

The Soviets lost the struggle for Western public opinion. But there was another, equally significant battle taking place—the battle for Reagan's own mind—and here, ironically, Andropov had more success. The war psychosis in Moscow helped convince the president that it would be unwise to push the Soviets too far. A cornered enemy could react in an irrational way. Reagan was surprised to learn in late 1983 that "many people at the top of the Soviet hierarchy were genuinely afraid of America and Americans . . . as potential aggressors who might hurl nuclear weapons at them in a first strike."[27] He felt an obligation to dispel such ideas.

Reagan's own horror of nuclear war was strengthened by watching a preview of the ABC television movie *The Day After*, which depicted the destruction of Lawrence, Kansas, in a nuclear exchange with the Soviet Union. Some administration officials were concerned that the movie could play into the hands of Soviet propagandists, but the commander in chief had a different reaction. "It's powerfully done, all $7 million worth. It's very effective and left me greatly depressed," he noted in his diary. "We have to do all we can to have a deterrent and to see there is never a nuclear war."[28]

There would be no dramatic changes in superpower relations as long as Kremlin politics revolved around a hospital bed. The dying Andropov had indicated, in a note to the Politburo, that he wanted the young and energetic Gorbachev to be his successor. But his wishes were thwarted by a geriatric cabal that could not stomach the thought of a new generation's taking over the leadership. When Andropov died in February 1984, the crown passed to the seventy-year-old Chernenko, himself mortally ill. Gorbachev's hopes of becoming general secretary were dashed by the seventy-eight-year-old prime minister Nikolai Tikhonov. "Mikhail is still very young," Tikhonov was overheard telling his associates. "It's unclear how he would behave in such a position. Kostya is the one we need."[29]

The biological imperative could not be ignored forever, however. The age of the dinosaurs was nearly over.

THE KREMLIN

March 10, 1985

NIGHT HAD ALREADY FALLEN as the black Zils sped between St. Basil's Cathedral and the executioner's stand on the southern fringe of Red Square. As the limousines approached the fortified walls of the Kremlin, the traffic lights on the facade of the 205-foot-high Spassky Gate switched automatically from red to green. Dressed in knee-length boots and long winter overcoats, the guards snapped to attention, saluting their rulers. It seemed an unusual time for Politburo members to be gathering in the Kremlin—nearly 10:00 p.m. on a Sunday—but the guards had been trained never to question the habits of their secretive leaders.

Inside the Kremlin the Zils turned right in front of the Ivan the Great bell tower, completed by Boris Godunov in 1600, past the glittering cathedrals where the tsars had been crowned and buried for more than three hundred years. Then another right, past another set of guards and a pair of wrought-iron gates, halting outside a mustard-colored palace alongside the Kremlin wall. Shaped in the form of a triangle, this three-story building formed a kind of inner citadel, a kremlin within the Kremlin. In tsarist times it had housed the Senate and the Palace of Justice. After Lenin moved the capital back to Moscow from Petrograd in March 1918, the Senate building became the headquarters of the new regime. A red flag fluttered

from its round copper roof, held aloft by a mechanical gust of air. Viewed from Red Square on the other side of the wall, the flag crowned a symbolic tableau of Soviet power, centered on Lenin's tomb and flanked by the glittering red stars on top of the Spassky and Nikolai gates.

Nearly seven decades of Soviet history had been concentrated in this building. It was here that Lenin had ordered the murder of the tsar and his family, here that Stalin had organized the purges of his political opponents and run the military campaign against the Nazi invader, here that the monster Beria had been arrested by his frightened Politburo colleagues. Even the granite steps over which Stalin's heirs now entered the building bore their own legend. To be summoned "to the steps," in the language of the party nomenklatura, meant to be granted an audience with Stalin himself.[30] As they mounted the steps, the dictator's intimidated subordinates often had no idea what to expect. An angry glance could be a prelude to promotion. A smile could mean death. It all depended on a tyrant's whim.

But times had changed, and on this occasion Soviet leaders had all been expecting a summons "to the steps." Konstantin Chernenko, the lackluster bureaucrat who succeeded Andropov as *gensek*, had been battling lung disease and pneumonia for weeks. At 7:20 that evening he had finally died, at the age of seventy-three. For the third time in just over three years it was necessary to choose a new tsar.

The Politburo members took the elevator to the third floor of the Senate building, where the general secretary had his office. Stepping out of the elevator, they found themselves in a long, high-ceilinged corridor, with an immaculate red runner down the middle and doors on either side. Which door they entered depended on their seniority. Voting members traditionally gathered in a walnut-paneled room, next to the *gensek*'s office. Candidate, or nonvoting, members met with Central Committee secretaries in a more modest room, nicknamed the *predbannik*, Russian for the dressing room of a bathhouse. When the appointed time came, the two groups met together in the Politburo Room, shaking hands like two rival football teams before the big match. The purpose of this unwritten Kremlin tradition was to allow the *gensek* to consult with the most senior Soviet leaders before the start of the meeting. Key decisions were often taken in the Walnut Room, without any note takers present, and ratified in the Politburo Room.[31]

As he waited to greet his fellow Politburo members that Sunday evening, Mikhail Gorbachev was still a few steps away from supreme power. He had been chairing sessions in Chernenko's absence, but he knew that some members of the old guard were counting on one of their own, Viktor Grishin, to

block his rise to the top. As the Moscow Communist Party boss the seventy-one-year-old Grishin had gained a reputation for both inefficiency and corruption. A few weeks earlier he had attempted to project himself as Chernenko's heir apparent by helping the dying leader cast his vote on nationwide television. Prime Minister Tikhonov was also maneuvering behind the scenes to block Gorbachev's candidature. But rank-and-file members of the Central Committee were solidly for Gorbachev. After thirteen months of Chernenko both the party and the country wanted a change.

The key figure in the succession was Andrei Gromyko, the veteran foreign minister, who had served every Soviet leader since Stalin. Now that Ustinov was dead, there was no one in the Politburo who could match Gromyko's prestige and authority. He had been around for as long as anyone could remember, having joined the Communist Party in 1931, the year of Gorbachev's birth. He had had his differences with Gorbachev in the past and was irritated by the rave notices that Gorbachev had received in the Western press, following a triumphant tour of Britain in December 1984. At the same time, he had made a realistic assessment of the balance of political forces. His own son, Anatoly, was a strong Gorbachev supporter. By anointing Gorbachev, he would cement his own position as the Soviet Union's elder statesman.

By prior arrangement, Gorbachev and Gromyko had agreed to meet in the Walnut Room a few minutes before the arrival of everyone else. The younger man used the occasion to solicit Gromyko's support openly.

"We have to unite our forces. This is a critical moment," said Gorbachev.

"It seems to me that everything is clear."

"I am counting on the fact that you and I will cooperate."[32]

Confident that he had Gromyko's backing, Gorbachev then approached Grishin to offer him a consolation prize, chairmanship of the Funeral Commission. The Moscow Communist Party boss was an astute enough politician to understand that the apparently courteous offer concealed a trap. If he accepted the prestigious, but purely honorific, position of head of the Funeral Commission, he ran the risk of appearing to make another unseemly grab for power, without gaining anything concrete in return. Cautiously he replied that the post had traditionally gone to the person who had been standing in for the general secretary. He urged Gorbachev to take the job, hoping perhaps that he would encounter opposition from older Politburo members.[33]

"There's no need to hurry," said Gorbachev, calculating that his own support would build, as the wishes of regional party secretaries became known. "Let's think about this carefully overnight."

Entering the Politburo Room, Gorbachev moved his chair a little to one side of the place traditionally occupied by the general secretary. Proprieties had to be observed. The mood in the room was still "The king is dead," rather than "Long live the king." The Politburo attended to a number of seemingly minor details, such as listening to a medical report on Chernenko, preparing the obituary, picking a date for the funeral, and summoning members of the policy-making Central Committee to Moscow. Then Gromyko spoke. He was adamant that Gorbachev be appointed chairman of the Funeral Commission. This was his way of signaling that he supported the younger man's candidature for *gensek*. While there were a few murmurs about unnecessary speed, no one opposed the proposal.[34]

In addition to Gromyko, Gorbachev had another very influential supporter. While working in the Central Committee apparatus in Moscow, he had forged an alliance with Yegor Ligachev, the secretary in charge of cadres. A Siberian with an authoritarian manner and appetite for hard work, Ligachev had been chosen by Andropov to purge the party of incompetent officials. Like Gorbachev, Ligachev was disgusted with the drift of the Brezhnev years. Over the past three years he had been traveling round the Soviet Union, replacing longtime Brezhnev cronies with younger men. He kept his finger on the pulse of the network of party officials who controlled the nation on a day-to-day basis. These regional chieftains, who held some 40 percent of the seats on the Central Committee, had played a key role in getting rid of Khrushchev in 1964. If there was a deadlock in the Politburo, as there would be if Grishin pushed his own candidature, their word would be decisive. Ligachev had counted heads. They were practically unanimous for Gorbachev.

Two members of the old guard who might have come out in support of Grishin were absent from the crucial Politburo meeting. The party boss of Kazakhstan, a Brezhnev holdover named Dinmukahamed Kunayev, arrived in Moscow only on the following day. The Ukrainian Communist Party chief, Vladimir Shcherbitsky, was stranded in San Francisco on an official visit. His flight home was mysteriously delayed until after the leadership question was settled. The delay may have been entirely coincidental, but Kremlin conspiracy theorists automatically suspected a plot by the pro-Gorbachev forces.[35]

At around 3:00 a.m., after settling organizational matters with Ligachev, Gorbachev went home to his dacha in the Moscow countryside, one of the many perks of a Politburo member. His wife, Raisa, was waiting up for him. However late he returned from work, it was their invariable custom to take an evening walk together. This was partly Gorbachev's way of unwinding

after a long day in the office. But it was also a way of talking things over with his closest confidante in a place where they could be sure that there were no microphones.

As they strolled through the snow-covered garden, Gorbachev blurted out that there was a good chance that he would be elected *gensek* the following day. Despite some doubts, he thought he should take the job. He had worked hard as the Politburo member in charge of agriculture but had not been able to achieve "anything substantial." Championing reform in the present political climate was like beating one's head against a brick wall. The Soviet people were "full of hope," and he had no right to disappoint them.

"We can't go on living like this. There has to be change," added the fifty-four-year-old peasant boy from the rolling plains of southern Russia.[36]

While Gorbachev was talking with Raisa, his allies were busy summoning the three hundred members of the Central Committee to Moscow from every part of the Soviet empire. They gathered, the following afternoon, in their marble-paved conference hall, on the opposite side of Red Square from the Kremlin. For perhaps the first time since the overthrow of Khrushchev in 1964, there was a sense of real political tension in the air. The Politburo had just met for a second time, and nobody knew what had been decided. It was clear to everybody that the Soviet Union stood at a crossroads. In private conversations in the lobby, younger party officials discussed what they would do if the Politburo blocked the general desire for change. Some threatened to organize a collective protest if Gorbachev was not the official candidate for *gensek*.

A door on the left of the stage opened, and the Politburo members filed into the room, in order of seniority. As they took their places on the podium, beneath a thirty-foot mosaic of Lenin in red and orange, the hubbub of conversation died away. As second secretary Gorbachev called for a moment of silence in honor of the departed leader. Then Gromyko walked to the rostrum. The tension mounted. Could the veteran foreign minister be making his own bid for the leadership? There was a heart-stopping preamble as Gromyko paid the ritualized tribute to Chernenko. Then the words that everybody had been waiting for:

"The Politburo has unanimously agreed to recommend," he rasped, staring stone-faced at the hall, as if he were delivering another *nyet* to the UN Security Council, "Mikhail Sergeyevich Gorbachev—"[37]

A roar of applause burst from the hall. Suddenly everyone was on his feet, clapping and smiling. Everybody in the room, even the tough old party

bosses who had wanted desperately to stop his nomination, was a Gorbachev supporter now. The tension of the last twenty-four hours had burst. The new general secretary, the youngest Soviet leader since Lenin, sat alone on the podium, head bowed, as if embarrassed by the adulation. He made a gesture to stop the cheering, but it went on and on.

The world's first socialist state had a new tsar.

OVER THE NEXT SIX YEARS, as the assumptions of the postwar world were turned upside down, Western analysts were to marvel over how a man like Mikhail Gorbachev had emerged from the obscurity of the Russian provinces. After a succession of geriatric *genseks*, the sight of a Soviet leader who could talk without notes and walk unassisted was itself cause for wonder. The fact that the new leader was willing to challenge ideas and habits sanctified by more than sixty years of Communist tradition seemed nothing short of miraculous. How had the Soviet system, the most durable totalitarian regime of the twentieth century, produced such a man?

The truth was that Gorbachev did not emerge out of nowhere. He represented a generation of political activists who grew up in the shadow of a great tyrant and lived all their lives in a socialist state. It was a generation whose Communist faith had been severely tested but never entirely undermined, a generation that had become accustomed to endless political and moral compromises, a generation waiting patiently for the chance to correct its predecessor's mistakes. The new general secretary of the Communist Party of the Soviet Union shared the dreams and nightmares of the *shestidesyatniki* generation, its strengths and failings, its beliefs and illusions.

Mikhail Sergeyevich Gorbachev was born on March 2, 1931, in the village of Privolnoye in the fertile steppes that stretch northward from the Caucasus Mountains. In Russian the word *privolnoye* has two connotations: wide, open spaces and freedom. There was a sense of both in the northern Caucasus. The area was populated in the seventeenth and eighteenth centuries by Cossack peasants fleeing serfdom in Russia and Ukraine. In return for their freedom, the Cossacks helped defend the southern border of the Russian empire from the Muslim tribes of the Caucasus. There was enough land for everybody. Misha's maternal great-grandparents had moved here from Ukraine; his paternal great-grandparents were from the Voronezh region of central Russia.

The Ukrainian side of the family, the Gopkolos, appear to have supplied

Gorbachev with his charisma and romantic spirit. He inherited the dark brown eyes of his Ukrainian grandmother, Vasilisa, and the talkativeness and occasional stubbornness of his mother. It was Vasilisa who decided to have him baptized, at the height of Stalin's persecution of the Orthodox Church. He remembered the Ukrainian folk songs that he learned from his mother and grandmother and as general secretary would occasionally sing them to his guests in his soft baritone.[38] The Russian side of the family had given him a sense of moderation and a willingness to compromise. His facial characteristics, particularly his smile, resemble those of his father, Sergei.[39]

The year of Gorbachev's birth coincided with Stalin's murderous collectivization campaign. Determined to catapult backward Russia into the ranks of the industrialized countries, the dictator decreed that peasants pool their land and machinery in giant state-run kolkhozes, or collective farms. In order to drive independent farmers out of business and increase the supply of food and labor to the cities, he used the technique of compulsory procurement quotas. Anyone who showed even token resistance to the new order was dubbed a "class enemy" and relentlessly persecuted.

The consequences of forced collectivization were particularly dramatic in the northern Caucasus, the Russian breadbasket, and Ukraine. Robert Conquest, the chronicler of the "harvest of sorrow," estimates that roughly one million people died in the northern Caucasus alone as the result of the famine of the early thirties.[40] Hundreds of thousands of rich peasants, or kulaks, were deported. Sometimes entire families were wiped out. The mortality rate among children under the age of two was particularly high. For a village boy, the chances of surviving this man-made disaster were little better than one in two. In his memoirs Gorbachev recalls the large number of empty, half-destroyed houses in his village, whose occupants had died of hunger.[41]

Nearly every family in the land was touched by the terror, and the Gorbachevs were no exception. In 1934, when Misha was only three, his paternal grandfather, Andrei, was denounced by a neighbor for hiding grain and "sabotaging" the spring sowing plan. A stubborn individualist, Andrei Gorbachev had refused to join the collective farms that were being established in the Stavropol region during these years. After a typically farcical trial he was sent off to Siberia to cut timber. Deprived of their principal means of support, the family swiftly became destitute. Within months three out of Andrei's six children had died of starvation.

The fact that Gorbachev managed to survive at all was probably due to

his Ukrainian grandfather, Panteley Yefimovich Gopkolo, who played a key role in the early collectivization campaign. As the first chairman of the local collective farm Grandfather Gopkolo was one of the most powerful men in the village. One of his jobs was to extract grain from the other peasants, including, presumably, Andrei Gorbachev. But then, in 1937, at the peak of the purges, Panteley Gopkolo was arrested in the middle of the night and accused of belonging to "an underground right-Trotskyist counterrevolutionary organization." The transformation of persecutors into persecuted was a reflection of the general paranoia of the times. Gorbachev recalls that his own home became a "plague house," which nobody dared visit for fear of being associated with an "enemy of the people." "Even the neighbors' kids refused to have anything to do with me," he recalled in his memoirs. "This is something that remained with me for the rest of my life."[42]

In a typically Soviet twist of fate, Grandfather Gopkolo was released and rehabilitated shortly before the outbreak of war. He served for a further seventeen years as chairman of the Red October collective farm, insisting, "Stalin has no idea what the NKVD [secret police] is doing."

Political repression was so widespread in the thirties that it was impractical for the party to limit recruitment to workers and peasants with completely clean family records. Many of Gorbachev's colleagues had similar skeletons in their personal files. That in itself was not an obstacle to high office, provided they kept quiet about it. To have raised such a matter in public would have raised doubts about one's "political reliability." So for almost six decades Gorbachev never talked about the sufferings of his family. He did not ask to see KGB files on his grandfathers until after the abortive hard-line coup of August 1991. As he later explained, he was unable to break through the "spiritual barrier" of loyalty to the Communist Party.[43]

It is a measure of the psychological legacy of Stalinism that Gorbachev, like many others, was unable to rid himself of the illusion that a noble purpose had been served by all this suffering. The sacrifices of those close to him became a reason not for rejecting the Soviet system but for continuing to believe in it. "Am I supposed to turn my back on my grandfather, who was committed to the Socialist idea?" Gorbachev asked rhetorically in November 1990. "Can I go against my father, who defended Kursk, forded the Dnieper River knee-deep in blood, and was wounded in Czechoslovakia? When cleansing myself of Stalinism and all other filth, should I renounce my grandfather and father and all they did?"[44]

For the older generation of Soviet officials, the salient fact of Gorbachev's biography was that he was the first general secretary too young to

participate in what Russians call the Great Patriotic War. It is hard to over-estimate the central place of the war in Soviet life—it took the lives of twenty million Soviet citizens—and the impact it had on the way of think-ing of successive leaders. For men like Brezhnev and Andropov, the mem-ory of how the Germans had reached the gates of Moscow and Leningrad in a four-month blitzkrieg in 1941 held ever-present lessons. It explained their obsession with security, their paranoid fears of foreign encirclement, their deeply ingrained conservatism. Experience had taught them that it was fatal ever to relax their guard. For them, the victory over the Nazi invader was the ultimate proof of the superiority of the Communist system. With-out Stalin's forced industrialization, the Soviet Union would never have been able to produce the tanks and guns that eventually enabled the Red Army to triumph over the most formidable military machine the world had ever known. Without the purges and show trials, the country would have been racked by internal division.

When the Germans invaded, Gorbachev was only ten. The Nazi occu-pation of the Stavropol region lasted too short a time—just five months—to make much impression on him. Marshal Sergei Akhromeyev, who survived the nine-hundred-day siege of Leningrad and went on to become military adviser to the future *gensek*, had a typical older man's reaction to this lack of wartime experience. Gorbachev, he wrote in his memoirs, repre-sented a generation that had never been forced "to fight against Fascist tanks armed only with rifles and Molotov cocktails, to watch powerlessly as German warplanes swooped down on your comrades and yourself, to with-draw hundreds of kilometers [as the invader] burned our cities and villages, killed peaceful civilians, and destroyed our national wealth."[45] What Gor-bachev had witnessed was the horrific aftermath of war: the hunger and cold; the uncertainty about the fate of one's relatives; the backbreaking labor of reconstruction. The old soldier speculated that those experiences may have contributed to the "pacifist" inclinations of his boss.

Gorbachev's formative years coincided not with the war but with the death of Stalin in March 1953 and the Khrushchev thaw. At the time he was an impressionable young law student at Moscow State University. He had arrived in the capital in 1950, with little more than the clothes on his back. The collective farm chairman's grandson was exactly the kind of per-son that the party wanted to recruit for the most prestigious educational institution in the country. He had the right "class" background. At high school near Privolnoye, he had completed his graduating thesis on the sub-ject "Stalin Is Our Battle Glory, Stalin Is the Flight of Our Youth."[46] He

was an active member of the Communist youth organization, the Komsomol, and had even won a state decoration, the Order of the Red Banner of Labor, for his work as a combine operator. It was at the university that he met his future wife, Raisa Titorenko, a stylish young philosophy student from Siberia.

While Gorbachev's political opinions were entirely orthodox, he did display a certain intellectual independence. Precocious and self-confident, he would argue with his teachers, both in high school and at the university. He joined in the freewheeling debates in the student dormitory. Comments that he made to his Czech roommate, Zdenek Mlynář, show that he was well aware of the gulf between Communist ideology and Soviet reality. On one occasion the two students were watching a propaganda film, entitled *The Cossacks of Kuban*, that glorifies the collective farms of the northern Caucasus. When the film showed peasant tables groaning with food and drink, it was too much for Gorbachev, who told Mlynář how little the *kolkhozniki* really had to eat. On another occasion, after a lecture on "kolkhoz law," Gorbachev made clear to his Czech friend that the most important law for the *kolkhozniki* was brute force.[47]

A few months after Stalin's death, Gorbachev returned to the Stavropol region to help out with the harvest and train in the local prosecutor's office. After the heady atmosphere of Moscow State University, he was struck by the "passivity and conservatism" of provincial life. "I am so depressed by the situation here," he wrote his future wife. "Especially the manner of life of the local bosses. The acceptance of convention, subordination, with everything predetermined, the open impudence of officials, and the arrogance. When you look at one of the local bosses, you see nothing outstanding apart from his belly. But what aplomb, what self-assurance, and the condescending, patronizing tone!"[48]

Khrushchev's denunciation of Stalin's crimes came as a huge shock to Gorbachev, who had been brought up to revere "the Father of the Peoples." But it also enabled him to bring his political ideals into line with the reality he saw around him. Now, once again, he had something to believe in. If the Communist Party could succeed in ridding itself of the "Stalinist filth," it would lead the country to the promised utopia.

Gorbachev was a delegate to the Twenty-second Communist Party Congress in 1961 that voted to remove Stalin's body from the mausoleum in Red Square, where it had lain alongside Lenin's. Held in the new Palace of Congresses in the Kremlin, the congress was infused with a spirit of optimism that reflected the mood of the times. Khrushchev had just defeated a Sta-

linist clique in the Politburo, led by former Foreign Minister Molotov. The Russians had beaten the Americans into space; one of the delegates to the congress was Yuri Gagarin. Russia was still a poor and backward society, but it was making rapid strides in all areas. Economic growth rates were high. Internationally, colonial empires were falling apart. Imperialism was in obvious retreat. The faithful gathered in the Kremlin had no difficulty believing Khrushchev when he assured them the Soviet Union would overtake the United States in per capita production by 1970 and achieve full communism by 1980.

The hopes of the *shestidesyatniki* generation received a shattering blow in August 1968, when Soviet troops invaded Czechoslovakia to crush Dubček's experiment in "socialism with a human face." The invasion set the cause of reform back by a generation not only in Eastern Europe but also in the Soviet Union, where there was an abrupt shift back to neo-Stalinist policies. Gorbachev visited Czechoslovakia a year after the invasion, as a member of a Soviet Communist Party delegation that also included Ligachev. It was an uncomfortable, disquieting experience for him. "When we went into factories, nobody wanted to talk to us," he later recalled. "The workers did not reply to our greetings, they demonstratively turned away. It was an unpleasant sensation."[49]

Gorbachev kept his feelings under tight control. It was at this point that his political career took off, thanks in large measure to his friendship with Dmitri Kulakov, a former Stavropol Communist Party chief, who was the Politburo member for agriculture.[50] Other powerful patrons were Yuri Andropov and Mikhail Suslov.

THE SHESTIDESYATNIKI INHERITED from Khrushchev a conviction that the Communist Party could be cleansed of its impurities and lead the masses to a better life. It was this belief that sustained them during the long years of stagnation, when the world's largest country seemed to be drifting aimlessly. When Gorbachev told Raisa on the eve of his election as *gensek* that "there has to be change," the last thing he had in mind was the kind of revolutionary change that actually took place. In a speech to Communist Party activists less than three months previously, he had spoken of the need for a technological revolution that would allow the Soviet Union "to enter the new millennium as a great and flourishing state."[51] He wanted to strengthen the Communist system, not to bury it. It was to take him almost eight years to acknowledge publicly that this hope had rested on an "illusion."

"We were like Khrushchev. We wanted to improve the system, to give it more oxygen, a second breath," Gorbachev recalled in 1993, two years after the failed Communist coup. "When I felt that the post of *gensek* would be offered to me, I racked my brains about what to do. I knew what was wrong with the country. We couldn't just go on as before. There was already a big budget deficit; national income was falling; our machinery was obsolete; our technology was outdated; there were no goods in the shops; oil production was declining. And what did we have to export? Only oil and vodka. I saw all this very clearly. We understood that there had to be reforms, that more freedom should be given to producers, to the regions. We knew that it was necessary to free society of many restrictions. We thought we could do all this within the framework of the existing system."[52]

The goal that Gorbachev set himself was without precedent in Russian history. Other Russian rulers—Ivan the Terrible, Peter the Great, and Stalin, to name but a few—had attempted to jolt Russia out of its backwardness and catch up with the West. But all had relied on the coercive power of a centralized state to mobilize the masses. The whip and the executioner's block were the instruments of choice for Russian reformers. Gorbachev and his allies understood that the repressive tradition was a large part of the problem; a technological revolution could not be carried out by an alienated, apathetic workforce. Russia's new leader wanted to realize the "immense potential of socialism" by releasing the energies of individual human beings.

Gorbachev knew that his revolution would have to start from above. In contrast with a country like Poland, with its long history of struggle against totalitarian rule, Soviet society lacked an independent voice. But the latest successor to Lenin and Stalin realized very quickly that the revolution would have to be continued from below. Otherwise it would be smothered by the army of bureaucrats, just as Khrushchev's thaw had been smothered.

THE KREMLIN

March 14, 1985

IN ORDER TO IMPRESS their foreign guests with the majesty and might of holy Russia, the tsars ordered a temple of military glory to be built in the heart of the Kremlin. Constructed from the finest marble and parquet, the two-hundred-foot-long room was known as St. George's Hall, after the highest military decoration that imperial Russia could bestow. The white and gold walls bore lists of Russian military conquests, from Poland to Alaska, the coats of arms of provinces that had been absorbed into the empire, and the names of the commanders who had defeated Napoleon.

The Communists had continued the tsarist tradition of marking great occasions with splendid banquets in St. George's Hall. It was here that Stalin feted the victory over Nazi Germany in 1945 and here that Khrushchev welcomed Gagarin on his return home from man's first journey into space. It was here too that Kremlin receptions were held following the funerals of general secretaries and world leaders formed their first impressions of the new masters of a country that stretched across eleven time zones and possessed more than thirty-five thousand nuclear missiles.

The initial assessment of most of the foreign guests was that Gorbachev would make a formidable opponent. The new *gensek* appeared in the hall flanked by his seventy-nine-year-old prime minister and his seventy-five-

year-old foreign minister. In addition to being younger and more energetic than these men, he had a much more engaging personal style. He mingled easily with the guests and had a Western politician's way of looking his interlocutor sincerely in the eye. But he seemed to be cut from essentially the same ideological cloth as the men by his side. Most of the foreigners who met with him that day concluded that Gorbachev's emergence as Soviet leader amounted to little more than a face-lift for a totalitarian state.

The sense of Western unease was expressed by the West German chancellor Helmut Kohl, whose country would benefit most dramatically from the policies of the new Soviet leader. He later compared Gorbachev's public relations skills with those of the Nazi propaganda chief, Joseph Goebbels. East European politicians were equally skeptical. They were unimpressed when Gorbachev told them that the Kremlin would respect the "sovereignty" and "independence" of the socialist camp. "Brezhnev used to use very similar words. It didn't mean very much at the time," recalled Wojciech Jaruzelski, after the empire had collapsed.[53] Gorbachev told the Polish leader that any "attempt to undermine the socialist order" in Eastern Europe would be completely unacceptable. There could be no relegalization of Solidarity.

The American delegation, led by George Bush, was ushered into a nearby room for an eighty-five-minute private audience with Gorbachev. The vice president was weary of Kremlin funerals: "You die, we fly" had become the unofficial motto of the Bush entourage. This was the third time in forty months that he had watched the Byzantine farewells in Red Square. After his return to Washington he described Gorbachev as an "impressive idea salesman" but made it clear that he expected little change in basic Kremlin policies. The shift was one of style, rather than substance. Five weeks later the American ambassador to Moscow, Arthur Hartman, flew to Washington to deliver an initial progress report on Gorbachev to Ronald Reagan. "Hartman confirms what I believe," the president noted in his diary, "that Gorbachev will be as tough as any of their leaders. If he wasn't a confirmed ideologue, he would never have been chosen by the Politburo."[54]

Perhaps the most perceptive comment about the new Soviet leader came from Margaret Thatcher. Gorbachev had visited London three months earlier and had impressed the British prime minister with his agile mind and willingness to talk about any subject under the sun. "We can do business with Mr. Gorbachev," she had declared then. They shared some similar traits, notably a supreme self-confidence and a restless desire for change.

Unlike many Western leaders, Thatcher realized that Gorbachev was sincere in his desire to reform the Communist system, but she doubted he would be successful. "Gorbachev thinks that there are problems with the way the system works," she told George Shultz, the American secretary of state. "He thinks he can make changes to make it work better. He doesn't understand that the system is the problem."[55]

NIZHNEVARTOVSK

September 4, 1985

THE SCALE OF THE TASK confronting Gorbachev soon became evident. Within months of his election the Soviet Union received another economic jolt: For the first time in many years oil production had begun to decline. The fall received little attention in the West, where people were more interested in the personality of the new leader, but it was destined to shape the whole course of Gorbachev's reform effort. His ambitious industrial modernization schemes depended on large-scale investment. If the oil boom turned into a bust, none of this would be possible. His perestroika reform movement, at least as originally conceived, was doomed to fail.

The discovery of vast oil reserves in western Siberia in the late sixties had given the economy and the regime a new lease on life. The oil came on stream at a particularly fortunate time for Brezhnev and his colleagues. The Stalinist command-and-administer system had ceased to work effectively but could not be jettisoned without undermining the foundations of the Communist state. Scared by the Prague Spring, Soviet leaders were opposed to anything that smacked of free market economics. Thanks to the windfall gains from oil exports, economic reform could be postponed almost indefinitely. Equally fortunately the boom coincided with a severe energy crisis in the West, caused by the explosion of oil prices in the wake of the 1973 Arab-Israeli War. Soviet propagandists seized on pictures of angry motorists be-

sieging gas stations in America and Western Europe as evidence of the terminal bankruptcy of capitalism. Seen through their eyes, the energy crisis was a purely capitalist phenomenon that could not happen in a "planned" economy.

The oil bonanza had allowed the Kremlin to finance grain imports, service its rising foreign debt, and bankroll its Third World allies. Soviet petrodollars had covered the costs of the war in Afghanistan, the stationing of Cuban troops in Angola and Ethiopia, and the salaries of more than 150,000 technical advisers in seventy-six countries. In the decade that followed the first oil shock, the Soviet Union earned some three hundred billion dollars from oil exports to the West.[56] Huge as this figure may seem, it represented only a small slice of the pie. Roughly 75 percent of Soviet oil production was reserved for domestic consumption. A further 10 to 15 percent was earmarked for client states. From Warsaw to Havana, from Hanoi to Managua, corrupt and inefficient Communist regimes were kept afloat by plentiful supplies of cheap Siberian energy. On the domestic market, oil cost even less: a few cents a gallon. As long as the oil kept flowing, factory managers had little incentive to change their ways.

"The oil money was a kind of drug," said Stanislav Shatalin, a Soviet economist who later became an adviser to Gorbachev. "Like any drug, it created the illusion of strength, while destroying the body even more and making the disease even more fatal."[57]

In retrospect, the energy crisis was a blessing in disguise for the West. By forcing factories to cut costs and introduce new energy-saving techniques, it had the effect of speeding up the technological revolution already under way in many Western countries. The Soviet Union, by contrast, wandered further into an economic fantasy land, where the laws of supply and demand were replaced by bureaucratic decree. Soviet managers became accustomed to apparently limitless supplies of cheap raw materials. By the mid-eighties the average factory was consuming two or three times as many raw materials as an American plant to make a vastly inferior product. When the energy crisis finally caught up with the Communist world, the impact was devastating.

The first sign of the approaching calamity came at the end of the seventies, when planners warned Brezhnev that the Soviet Union was living beyond its means. In October 1981 the Kremlin finally decided to cut oil deliveries to Eastern Europe by 10 percent, provoking protests from its clients. The East German leader Erich Honecker was particularly vehement, arguing that he would not be able to explain the sudden rise in energy costs to his "working class."[58] Anxious to keep everyone happy, the indeci-

sive Brezhnev scaled back the proposed cutbacks. The savings turned out to be marginal.

By the time Gorbachev came to power, the signs of crisis were so obvious that they could no longer be ignored. Addressing a Politburo session a month after his election, the new *gensek* ticked off examples of the Soviet Union's economic backwardness one by one. He concentrated on the dismal state of agriculture, the field in which he had most experience. In the food industry, he told his colleagues, manual labor still accounted for nearly two-thirds of total output. Labor productivity was 60 percent below Western levels. Every year a third of the harvest was lost because of waste and inefficiency. More than three hundred Soviet towns were without water supplies and sewers. Half the streets in urban areas were unpaved.[59]

"If we don't break this trend, then by the end of the century we will be transformed into a Third World country," Gorbachev told his colleagues, a candid assessment censored from the official transcript released to the Soviet press.[60]

The scale of the new leader's ambitions had made the problem of resource allocation even more acute. In his first few months in office Gorbachev ripped through the country like a tornado, exposing structural defects in Soviet society that went back many decades. There was so much that needed fixing. The goal was clear: to get the nation moving again by replacing plant and equipment and increasing the productivity level of ordinary workers. What was unclear was where the money to pay for such a gigantic modernization program was going to come from.

It was a classic guns-versus-butter dilemma. One option was to cut military spending. But that was impossible at a time when relations with the United States were still contentious. Shortly after his election the defense chiefs persuaded Gorbachev to *increase* the military budget. A secret Politburo resolution pledged that defense spending would rise by an annual rate of 4.5 percent a year throughout the 1986–90 plan period, outpacing the planned growth in national income.[61] A second option was to cut consumption. But that was unacceptable in view of the popular expectations released by Gorbachev's election. If people were to be persuaded to work harder, they needed more incentives, not fewer.

In the middle of this debate, news from western Siberia caused Gorbachev to revise both his travel plans and his economic calculations. The oil boom of the Brezhnev years was running dry. Unless urgent measures were taken, the Kremlin would lose its most reliable source of hard currency.

As HIS TUPOLEV 134 AIRCRAFT skirted the fringe of the Arctic Circle, thirty-five thousand feet above the world's largest oil field, Gorbachev had a bird's-eye view of the economic foundations of Soviet power. The pristine taiga—wave after wave of undulating forest—gave way to a nightmarish industrial wasteland. It looked as if someone had taken a knife to a vast green canvas and slashed wildly from side to side. A great tangle of roads, pipelines, and oil derricks stretched for hundreds of miles on either side of the Ob River. Every so often the slashes coalesced into an ugly blotch of unpaved streets, apartment blocks slapped together from concrete slabs, and factories belching fire and smoke into a perpetually gloomy sky.

For generations of Russians, Siberia was not only a place but also an idea. Traditionally the name had conjured up two conflicting images in the Russian mind: the idea of freedom and the idea of tyranny. The vast unexplored spaces made Siberia the Russian equivalent of the American West, a land of promise and opportunity that attracted pioneers who wanted to escape the ubiquitous bureaucracy. But Siberia was also a place of banishment for the political opponents of tsars and general secretaries, associated in many people's minds with the repression of millions of people and uniquely harsh climatic conditions.

During the Communist period Siberia became synonymous with yet another idea, the notion that the Soviet Union was a land of "limitless" resources. Exploiting these resources, the Bolsheviks believed, was purely a matter of political will. The ends always justified the means. If the leadership decided that a project was of overriding national importance, the human and environmental costs became irrelevant. Any sacrifice was justified in the name of the ultimate goal, the construction of a Communist society. In pursuit of this utopia, Stalin launched an heroic onslaught against nature and turned Siberia into a vast prison camp. He mobilized millions of slave laborers to build canals and railways across its frozen wastes, scour its mountains for uranium, and construct munitions factories around its shores.

The Siberian treasure trove sustained Soviet-style communism long after it had reached the point of natural exhaustion. It was to Siberia that the Brezhnev generation of leaders looked for salvation from the economic crises affecting the rest of their empire. When the centralized economy experienced serious bottlenecks in the early seventies, the Politburo ordered construction of a two-thousand-mile railway line, known as the BAM, to tap the fabulous mineral wealth of northern Siberia. When the cotton-growing regions of Central Asia began to run dry because of overexploita-

tion, the planners had a simple solution: Divert Siberian rivers from north to south. When the Kremlin's superpower burden started to become intolerable in the late seventies, Siberian oilmen were instructed to redouble their efforts. Siberia fulfilled the function of a raw materials appendage to the Communist empire, a colonial outpost that could be mercilessly exploited. For Brezhnev and his colleagues, any attempt to question the myth of Siberia's "inexhaustible" wealth was ideologically unacceptable.

From an economic point of view, Siberia made Soviet-style communism possible. It was also where its death throes would be most visible. Eventually even nature rebelled against its rapacious masters.

The city to which Gorbachev was now headed, Nizhnevartovsk, was a typical example of the Stalinist approach to economic development. A quarter of a century earlier all that had stood on this desolate spot were several hundred wooden huts belonging to the native Khant population. The nomadic Khants lived off the reindeer in the surrounding forests and the abundance of fish in the Ob River. Geologists had identified a nearby swamp—known to the natives as Samotlor (Dead Lake)—as a probable oil deposit. In early 1965 several drilling teams set out to explore the site. The working conditions were appalling. There were no roads, and temperatures were forty to fifty degrees below zero. It took the drilling teams more than a month to hack their way through the marshes. But when they sank their drills into the frozen earth, they found more oil than they had even dreamed about. The oil began to come on stream in significant amounts at the beginning of the seventies.

Over the course of the next decade the Samotlor field produced more oil than Kuwait. Every fourth barrel of Soviet oil—the equivalent of the country's entire export surplus—came from this remote corner of western Siberia. The pioneers who discovered the field were showered with medals. Desperate for anything that could be turned into hard currency, Soviet leaders repeatedly raised production targets. In order to keep pace with the demands from Moscow, the oilmen began cutting corners. In their haste to get the oil out of the ground, they skimped on infrastructure and paid no attention to the surrounding environment. They used crude extraction techniques that caused the fields to become waterlogged and lose their natural pressure. They left valuable timber to rot in the swamp, rather than take the trouble of processing it. Instead of building pipelines to remove the excess natural gas, they simply torched it. Every day enough gas was burned off from the oil fields around Nizhnevartovsk to heat several European cities.[62]

With sensible conservation techniques, the Samotlor field could have

continued to produce large amounts of oil for many decades. But the oil was extracted in such a slipshod fashion that the natural life of the field was unnecessarily shortened. By the time Gorbachev came to power, production had already entered a sharp decline.

Scarcely any of the oil wealth trickled down to the people of Nizhnevartovsk. Home to more than three hundred thousand people, the city had a transient, makeshift quality about it, as if the flimsy apartment blocks and potholed streets would be abandoned to the taiga as soon as the oil wells dried up. An entire quarter of the city consisted of nothing but metal wagons designed as temporary accommodation for oil workers. Frequently three or four families were forced to share a single outdoor toilet, despite sub-zero temperatures for more than half the year. For serious shopping, residents were obliged to fly to Moscow, three hours away by plane. Recreational and cultural facilities were practically nonexistent.

As Gorbachev stepped out of the bulletproof Zil that had been specially flown in from Moscow, the crowd surged forward. The Kremlin security men had trouble preventing the grimy oil workers from sweeping the general secretary and his fashionably coutured wife, Raisa, off their feet. Wherever they went, the couple was greeted by a wall of cheering, inquisitive people. The local party bureaucrats, anxious to avoid an embarrassing scene, hovered uneasily in the background. The expressions on their faces suggested an unctuous desire to humor the new leader, combined with alarm over his unpredictable ways.

It was an encounter between two different worlds: the apparatchiks in their homburgs and heavy overcoats and the unshaved, unwashed masses in their threadbare anoraks and woolen ski caps. And there, bobbing up and down in the middle of this tableau vivant, was the smiling face of the Soviet Union's new leader, arm outstretched to the people, like a modern-day *tsarbatushka* (little father).

The sight of a Communist Party leader rubbing shoulders with ordinary people seemed miraculous to the inhabitants of Nizhnevartovsk, as it did to the rest of the country when it was broadcast on television that evening. The propaganda machine had done its best to drain of any individuality the men who waved feebly from the top of Lenin's tomb on national feast days. Like the hierarchs of the Russian Orthodox Church, Communist leaders derived their authority from participation in endless rituals, rather than their ability to impress the masses with their brilliance. The aura of mystery and

anonymity that surrounded these men was one of the principal sources of the durability of the regime.

In order to achieve his goal of pushing the world's second superpower into the twenty-first century, Gorbachev knew he had to extricate himself from the grasp of the conservative party apparatus, which had no interest in challenging the status quo. If he allowed himself to become a prisoner of the bureaucracy, change would be glacial. The solution was to forge a direct link with the long-suffering Russian people, the *narod*, over the heads of the apparatchiks. This would provide him with the independent power base he needed to push through his program of reform.

"Let us put them [the bureaucrats] under control. You from one end, and us from the other," he told an appreciative audience at one of his stops. "Without the support of the workers, no policy is worth anything. If it is not supported by the working people, it is no policy, it is some farfetched thing."[63]

By the time he arrived in Nizhnevartovsk, Gorbachev had already discovered a magical tool for awakening the slumbering masses. He was the first general secretary to understand the power of television. As a rising apparatchik he had seen how television had helped destroy public confidence in leaders like Brezhnev and Chernenko by broadcasting their obvious infirmities to an increasingly disillusioned nation. Now he proposed using the same medium to project himself as a dynamic new leader tackling the problems of ordinary people. The state-run television network gave him a captive audience. Every evening, at precisely nine, across the eleven time zones of the Soviet Union, 150 million people tuned in to the news show *Vremya*, broadcast on all main channels. The lead story during those early days was almost always Mikhail Gorbachev, hectoring local officials, diving into crowds, explaining his policies to attentive workers. He combined the roles of newsmaker and news editor. *Vremya* producers often received a telephone call from Gorbachev or one of his close aides with detailed instructions on what to include in the show and what to delete.[64]

Television cameras accompanied Gorbachev practically everywhere he went in western Siberia. Here he embraced the notion of the "human factor" as the decisive element in the revolution that he was attempting to unleash. Like many visitors to Siberia, he was struck by the contrast between the riches that were pouring out of the ground and the squalor in which people were forced to live. As he toured supermarkets, drilling rigs, and gas compressor stations, he was besieged by complaints about shoddy housing, poor food supplies, air pollution, outdated equipment, and the lack of con-

sumer goods. The ends had clearly *not* justified the means. The Stalinist system of economic management had created a monster that fed on itself, producing little benefit either for the country or for its inhabitants.

The new *gensek* was shaken to learn that for all the billions of rubles that it had contributed to the central treasury, Nizhnevartovsk did not possess a single public movie house. Movies were screened occasionally at a Communist Party youth club, but tickets were hard to acquire. All this troubled Gorbachev as he flew to the regional capital, Tyumen, for a meeting with local party officials. The next morning he got up early to revise the text of the speech that his aides had prepared for him.[65] He agreed with the planners that urgent measures had to be taken to reverse the decline in oil production. But there was another message he wanted to convey: The entire economy had to be reoriented toward the individual.

"It is embarrassing for us to talk about the millions of tons of oil and cubic meters of gas when a drilling foreman says to us that the greatest incentive in Nizhnevartovsk is to be given a ticket to see a film," he told party workers, gathered in front of him like dim-witted schoolchildren. "Why, at the end of the day, do we need to extract millions of tons of oil and gas? Not so that we can simply talk and brag about such quantities, but so that people's lives can be improved, so that the economy becomes stronger, so that our defenses can be strengthened, so that the people's living conditions can be improved. That is why all this is necessary."[66]

During those early barnstorming trips around the country Gorbachev frequently discarded the speeches that had been prepared for him in advance. He modeled his speaking style on the early Bolsheviks, who could keep audiences spellbound through the sheer force of their oratory. Speaking extemporaneously provided a contrast with his immediate predecessors, who were barely able to read from prepared texts. On the other hand, it caused him to ramble, the occupational disease of an all-powerful leader who is rarely contradicted. The points he was trying to make could easily get lost in an avalanche of words. Sometimes he got carried away with his own rhetoric, forgetting the point that he intended to make.

While the new tsar had a very clear sense about what was wrong with the Russian economy, he had a much hazier idea of how to put it right. Stripped of their revolutionary rhetoric and good intentions, his early policies often boiled down to more of the same. He still proclaimed an undying faith in the socialist system of centralized distribution. His attitude to Lenin remained deeply reverential. On the subject of market economics, Western visitors found that he was practically illiterate. Given these ideological limitations

and the ingrained habits of Soviet bureaucrats, it was not surprising that the party bosses in western Siberia responded to the new leader's criticisms and exhortations in the traditional way. They drilled hundreds more wells and increased the pressure on work crews to meet plan targets. Little attention was paid to the maintenance and repair of existing wells or the rational, long-term development of oil fields. Only token efforts were made to improve the living conditions of oil workers. *Uskorenie* (acceleration) became the slogan of the day.

Over the next two years oil production did increase slightly. But the frenetic drilling of new wells had the effect of making matters even more chaotic, exacerbating the problem of waterlogged fields. By 1988 Soviet production was in steep and irreversible decline. Even more alarming, at least in the short term, was a decision by Saudi Arabia in the summer of 1985 to increase its oil production dramatically. Shortly after Gorbachev's visit to Siberia, world oil prices crashed. By the first quarter of 1986 the Soviet Union would be able to fetch no more than ten to twelve dollars a barrel for its oil, compared with a peak of nearly forty dollars in 1980. During Gorbachev's first two years in office the country's hard currency export earnings fell by almost a third.

Perestroika was doomed before it had even begun.

GORBACHEV'S TRIP TO Western Siberia turned out to be important for another reason: It marked the high point of his ill-conceived antialcohol campaign, which did more to alienate the Russian people than any other single action. With hindsight, it was probably the most spectacular blunder committed by the new leadership during the early stage of perestroika.

Drink had been the scourge of Russian life for many centuries. "The greatest pleasure of the people is drunkenness, in other words forgetfulness," noted the marquis de Custine during his visit to Russia in 1839.[67] The Brezhnev regime tacitly encouraged vodka sales, which provided a valuable source of tax revenue and helped ensure the political acquiescence of the population. Consumption of hard liquor had almost quadrupled during the Brezhnev period. By the time Gorbachev came to power, alcoholism had reached epidemic proportions. Official studies showed that 70 percent of all crimes were related to alcohol. Drink was blamed for widespread absenteeism at work, a sharp increase in the divorce rate, and a dramatic drop in male life expectancy.

The driving forces behind the antialcohol campaign were two Politburo

members who had played an important role in helping Gorbachev become general secretary, Yegor Ligachev and Mikhail Solomentsev. Ligachev was a puritan, disgusted with the moral decay that he saw all around him. He had already tried to enforce a ban on alcohol in his hometown of Tomsk. Solomentsev was a reformed alcoholic who waged war on drink with the enthusiasm of the convert. Together they persuaded the Politburo to adopt draconian restrictions on the production and sale of alcohol. Tens of thousands of liquor stores across the country were closed down; centuries-old vineyards in the Caucasus were plowed up; alcoholic beverages were banned from official receptions. The sale of alcohol was prohibited altogether before 2:00 p.m. The few liquor stores that were permitted to remain open were constantly besieged by long lines of frustrated customers.

The effect of this campaign was to drive one of Russia's largest and most profitable businesses underground. Sugar became a "deficit item" overnight, as the production of illegally brewed moonshine shot up. Unable to buy vodka from government stores, people switched to any available substitute. Thousands of desperate alcoholics died from imbibing noxious substances, such as eau de cologne, glue, window-cleaning liquid, and shoe polish. The government surrendered its jealously guarded monopoly over alcohol sales to criminal gangs. The loss of tax revenue from alcohol sales left a hole in the state budget that was never repaired. From 1985 onward there was a growing imbalance between the money income of the population and the supply of goods and services. Since the government continued to fix prices by administrative fiat, the result was widespread shortages. By the time the antialcohol campaign was quietly abandoned in 1988, the authorities had lost control over the monetary system.

Although Gorbachev was not the principal instigator of the antialcohol drive, he supported it wholeheartedly. In the public mind it was viewed as *his* campaign. Jokes soon circulated at the new leader's expense. Russians started referring to him as *mineralny sekretar* (mineral water secretary), instead of *generalny sekretar* (general secretary). He was undaunted by the criticism. At Politburo meetings he made clear that he regarded the struggle against alcohol as part of the struggle for communism. What was at stake, he told his colleagues, was the "genetic future" of the nation. When the deputy head of the state planning agency, Gosplan, objected that the move toward prohibition would deprive the state of up to 12 percent of its revenues, Gorbachev cut him short. "Vodka is not going to bring us to communism," he snarled.[68]

Gorbachev's determination to impose sobriety on his countrymen, even

against their will, revealed an authoritarian streak in his personality that contrasted with his talk of democracy and openness. "Bear in mind, this is not for a day or two, or even for a year. It is forever," Gorbachev told the oil workers of Nizhnevartovsk, wagging his index finger at them, like an angry patriarch.[69] The workers applauded sullenly, without any intention of changing their ways.

GENEVA

November 19, 1985

THE DAY AFTER HIS APPOINTMENT as general secretary, Gorbachev had written a private memorandum to himself, outlining his political priorities. Improving relations with the United States, the leading imperialist country, was at the top of the list.[70] The time had come to put the memorandum into effect. He would have a face-to-face meeting with Ronald Reagan, a man Kremlin propagandists had compared with Hitler in his obsessive quest for world domination.

Close to one hundred photographers from all over the world were on hand to record the first handshake between a Soviet general secretary and an American president in more than five years. The practice of regular summit meetings had been suspended as a result of the Soviet invasion of Afghanistan in 1979 and the political turmoil in Moscow. Reagan, who was already in the second term of his presidency, had geared himself up for a summit with first Andropov and then Chernenko. But, as he later complained, the Soviet leaders "kept dying on me."[71] Now, in Gorbachev, he had finally found a young and vigorous leader with whom he could talk.

Reagan had a visceral dislike of Communists that went back to his days as a trade union activist in Hollywood after the Second World War and his suspicion that the Reds were attempting to take over the American movie industry. At his first presidential news conference he had spoken of Soviet

leaders as if they were soulless automatons, willing to "commit any crime, to lie, and to cheat" in order to promote the goal of worldwide revolution.[72] Yet as he pumped Gorbachev's hand in the courtyard of the Villa Fleur d'Eau on Lake Geneva, he found "something likable" about him. "There was warmth in his face and his style, not the coldness bordering on hatred I'd seen in most senior Soviet officials I'd met until then," he recalled later.[73]

A small army of White House advance men had spent weeks discussing how Reagan could break the ice with Gorbachev. They had crawled over the grounds of the nineteenth-century château, with measuring tapes and tele-photo lenses, looking for the best camera angles. It was important to estab-lish the right atmosphere, an amalgam of intimacy, parity, informality, and security. Finally they settled on a cozy boathouse down by the lake, a hun-dred yards from the main house, with a picturesque fireplace. It was an image maker's dream. After strolling down to the lake, the two most pow-erful men in the world would sit down opposite each other in overstuffed chairs, by a blazing fire, and address the great issues of war and peace. This would be the "Fireside Summit." If that evoked memories of the reassuring fireside chats of Franklin Delano Roosevelt—one of Reagan's great he-roes—so much the better.[74]

The summit began on an inauspicious note, with arguments over ideol-ogy and human rights. "At the beginning it was more like a dispute between the number one Communist and the number one capitalist than a working dialogue between the world's two most powerful leaders," Gorbachev re-called later.[75] To ease the tension, Reagan suggested a walk in the fresh air. The younger man accepted with alacrity. By the time they got to the sum-mer house, a fire was already blazing in the hearth, attended by a bureau-crat with top-level security clearance.

As Gorbachev settled into his armchair, the president consulted his script, typed on a deck of four-by-six index cards, which he occasionally shuffled. He had given some thought to how to address his Soviet guest. In the end, he settled for "Mr. General Secretary," having been persuaded that the use of "Mikhail" on the first occasion might be misconstrued. Having got the formalities out of the way, he staked out some common ground. Here we are, he said, the two of us, sitting opposite each other in this room You, like me, were born in an obscure hamlet, in the middle of a huge coun-try. From these poor and humble beginnings, we have risen to become the leaders of America and Russia.

"We're probably the only people in the world who could start World War III. And we're also the only two people, perhaps, in the world that could prevent World War III."[76]

At first glance, it would be hard to think of any two men more different than the seventy-four-year-old president and the fifty-four-year-old *gensek*. One had made a career out on anticommunism; the other dreamed of giving communism a new lease on life. One was bored by the details of public policy and would happily abandon his briefing books for another viewing of *The Sound of Music*; the other was a workaholic who devoured position papers and intelligence assessments, underlining interesting passages with an iridescent marker. One held fast to certain immutable principles; the other was a compromiser born and bred. One was an amiable character, who liked telling jokes; the other didn't much care for jokes and could be a bit of a bully.

Yet for all these differences Reagan was correct when he suggested to Gorbachev that they had a great deal in common. At the most basic level they both were superb actors, with the power of communicating ideas and feelings to large numbers of people. Reagan had been trained in the great movie studios of Hollywood. A natural television performer, he knew how to control his gestures and his voice to evoke a sense of empathy from his audience. At times he even seemed to model himself after characters in his own movies. Gorbachev, by contrast, had received his thespian initiation on the stage of High School No. 1 in Krasnogvardeyskoye. He was so convincing as the romantic lead in nineteenth-century Russian comedies that he once considered taking up acting as a career.[77] He learned the art of attracting the attention of a live audience through deliberately exaggerated gestures, dramatic finger pointing, and a flamboyant stage presence.

There was a visionary, almost prophetic quality about both Reagan and Gorbachev. They were optimists, convinced they could make the world a better place. Unlike many politicians, they allowed themselves to dream, and their dreams and illusions became part of the geopolitical calculations of great powers. Reagan's optimism was the unclouded optimism of a man who had lived the American dream and wanted others to share in his good fortune. At times it bordered on nostalgia. By proposing a space shield that would protect America from incoming nuclear missiles, the president hoped to re-create the security and well-being of his youth. Gorbachev's optimism derived from his experience as a young man growing up during the heady years of the political thaw that had followed the death of Stalin. The general secretary was convinced that if socialism could only be cured of its Stalinist deformities and abuses, everything was still possible.

The two leaders also shared a horror of nuclear war. The dawning of the nuclear age had linked the destinies of America and Russia, creating a symbiotic relationship based on mutual insecurity. The vast open spaces that

had allowed Russia to repel invasions by Napoleon and Hitler meant nothing when the Kremlin could be destroyed by a nuclear missile fired from an American submarine with scarcely any warning. The ocean that had protected America from foreign aggression for two centuries could be crossed by a Soviet warhead in less than thirty minutes. For the first time since the Revolutionary War against the British, there was a direct threat to the American heartland.

PRIOR TO THE GENEVA SUMMIT Reagan had met very few Russian politicians. He had had a brief encounter with Brezhnev in California in 1973 and a more substantive meeting with Gromyko in the White House in September 1984. It was easy to demonize such men. They seemed to take pride in acting as the faceless representatives of a totalitarian ideology. As Gromyko remarked on one occasion, "My personality doesn't interest me." Their stolid appearance and stonewall negotiating technique confirmed Reagan's view of East-West relations as a titanic struggle between good and evil.

Although he had battled with Hollywood leftists in the late forties and early fifties, the president's knowledge of communism and Communists was largely theoretical. Much of it derived from a book of spurious Lenin quotations, *The Ten Commandments of Nikolai Lenin*, given to him by a friend out in California.[78] He kept the book in a drawer of his desk in the Oval Office and frequently referred to it when he wanted to make a point about Soviet perfidy. A favorite quotation, which he tried out on many foreign and congressional leaders, was: "We will not have to take the last bastion of capitalism, the United States. It will fall into our outstretched hand like overripe fruit."[79] Soviet experts in the administration went to some trouble to show that this and many other quotations in the book were false.

Reagan never abandoned his belief that communism was intrinsically evil. But he did change his tactics for dealing with Soviet leaders, to the dismay of some of his conservative supporters. He stopped referring to the Soviet Union as an "evil empire" driven by a fanatical desire for world domination. In early 1984, in a calculated opening to Moscow, he was already musing what would happen if "Ivan and Anya" found themselves sharing a shelter from the rain with "Jim and Sally." He concluded that the "common interest" of ordinary people in creating a "world without fear" was a phenomenon that transcended "all borders."[80]

The struggle for Reagan's soul was symbolized by a rift in the administration. On one side were the pragmatists, led by Secretary of State George Shultz, who were impressed by Gorbachev and wanted to take advantage of

the new political climate in the Soviet Union. On the other were the ideologues, represented by Defense Secretary Caspar Weinberger, who regarded the changes in Moscow as largely cosmetic and were deeply skeptical about the benefits of arms control negotiations. In his heart Reagan sided with the ideologues. But his political instincts and his confidence in the negotiating skills that he had developed in Hollywood told him that the time had come for a serious dialogue.

Nancy Reagan played an important role in persuading her husband to adopt a mellower, more conciliatory tone toward the Kremlin during the run-up to the 1984 presidential election. She was disturbed by public opinion polls suggesting that the president's harsh Cold War rhetoric could cost him votes. "Ronnie, you have to present a more peaceful image," she told her husband during a trip on Air Force One, in earshot of National Security Adviser Robert McFarlane.[81]

The first lady was strengthened in her conviction that Gorbachev would make a worthy negotiating partner for the president by her astrologer friend Joan Quigley, who had studied the personal horoscopes of the two leaders. The astrologer explained to Nancy Reagan that "Ronnie's Mercury," the "planet of ideas and the mind," was very close to "Gorbie's Venus," the "planet of love." This showed that Gorbachev would "love and embrace the ideas that the American president would bring him." The celestial chemistry between the two leaders had "breathtaking possibilities," but it was essential that Reagan jettison the "evil empire attitude" before traveling to Geneva. The precise departure time of Air Force One for Geneva—8:35 a.m. on November 16, 1985—was chosen by Quigley in order to put Gorbachev's planet "in the ascendant" on her chart, so that he "would be drawn to Ronnie."[82]

In order to reach the point at which he could have a real conversation with Gorbachev, Reagan needed more than just an astrologer. He also had to have a kindred spirit to exorcise his ideological demons, to help him see the Russians as three-dimensional human beings rather than two-dimensional villains. The key figure here was Suzanne Massie, the voluble author of several popular books about Russian history, who had a gift for talking on Reagan's wavelength. During the course of eighteen unpublicized meetings with the president, she fed him a mixture of street-corner anecdotes, salty jokes, and ancient folk wisdom about Russia that sparked his interest in a vast and contradictory land. Many of Reagan's favorite Russian aphorisms—including the endlessly repeated *Doverai, no proverai* (Trust, but verify)—came from Massie.

Massie's own twenty-year love affair with Russia had been ignited by a family tragedy. Her son, Bobby, was a hemophiliac. In the course of dealing with his illness, she and her husband, Robert Massie, became fascinated by the life of the most famous hemophiliac of all, the tsarevich Aleksis, and the curative powers of the mad monk Rasputin. (The research eventually blossomed into a best-selling book, *Nicholas and Alexandra*, by Robert Massie.) When she traveled to Leningrad for the first time in 1967, she felt an immediate kinship with the Russian people. "It was like finding a huge family that belonged to me, but that I had never known existed," she later wrote.[83] She was banned from visiting the Soviet Union for ten years after a search at the Moscow airport turned up an address book filled with Russian names and phone numbers. By the time she got back, in September 1983, in the middle of the KAL crisis, she was alarmed to discover that communication between the two superpowers had virtually broken down. Convinced that someone had to correct the demonic views that each side held about the other, she badgered the White House for a meeting with Reagan.

"Do Soviet leaders really believe in their ideology?" was Reagan's first question when they finally got together.

"I can't answer that," Massie replied. "All I can tell you is what Russians say about their leaders. They call them the Big Bottoms. They think the only thing their leaders are interested in is their chairs, their positions. Ideology is unimportant."[84]

Talking to the president, Massie found, was rather like talking to her curmudgeonly great-uncle. He had certain *idées fixes* about Russia that he had picked up from friends in California who knew very little about the place. But he had a sense of humor about himself, was eager to learn more about the country he had already labeled the "focus of evil in the modern world," and had no problems with his ego. For a man with the reputation of being the "great communicator," he was enigmatic. It was difficult to read what was going on in his mind. He seemed to relax when the bureaucrats left the room. During their one-on-one sessions Massie tried to give the president a sense of the variety and diversity of Russia. She told him what it was like to live in a communal apartment, what people talked about while standing in line, what Russians were like as people. She also sought to bolster his confidence in negotiating with Gorbachev, who was already being built up in the American press as some kind of superman.

"You are stronger than he is in every way," she told the president before he left for Geneva. "You have a lot of experience; you are older and wiser; you are secure in the hearts of your countrymen." Russians, she added, were

basically "ungovernable." "If you were president of that country, you really would be in trouble."

RONALD REAGAN TOOK the biblical prophecy of Armageddon seriously. When he read references in the Book of Revelations to a star that would fall from heaven, poisoning everything in its path, he thought of the effects of nuclear war. Far from guaranteeing the peace, nuclear weapons were inherently immoral, in Reagan's view, because they would bring about the end of human civilization. "For the first time ever, everything is in place for the battle of Armageddon and the second coming of Christ," he had declared in 1971.[85] If this was the case, it was obviously the responsibility of the statesman to protect his people from the promised Day of Judgment.

During the 1980 presidential election campaign, Reagan had an experience that strengthened his view that something had to be done to protect the American people from the threat of nuclear annihilation. He was touring the headquarters of the North American Aerospace Defense Command (NORAD), which has the task of detecting incoming nuclear warheads. An underground city hidden deep in the Cheyenne Mountain, in Colorado, the NORAD command post could serve as the setting for a James Bond movie. Banks of radar detectors and computers keep track of everything from flocks of birds migrating south for the winter to a Soviet intercontinental ballistic missile lifting off from the deserts of Kazakhstan. Sophisticated communications devices ensure that the information can be flashed instantaneously to the president, wherever in the world he might be. Watching the flickering consoles and giant screens pinpointing hundreds of Soviet missile sites, Reagan asked the NORAD commander what could be done if the Soviets were to fire a missile at an American city.

"Nothing," the general replied, in the eerie stillness of his mountain fortress. "We would pick it up right after it was launched, but by the time the officials of the city could be alerted that a nuclear bomb would hit them, there would be only ten or fifteen minutes left. That's all we can do. We can't stop it."

The answer stunned Reagan. He found it difficult to believe, much less accept, that the United States had no defense against Soviet missiles. As he flew back home to Los Angeles, he confided his astonishment to an aide. "We have spent all that money and have all that equipment, and there is nothing we can do to prevent a nuclear missile from hitting us."[86]

Reagan's shock at American vulnerability to a nuclear attack blossomed into the launching of a top-priority program to intercept and destroy in-

coming Soviet missiles. In a televised address from the Oval Office on March 23, 1983—just two weeks after the "evil empire" speech—he outlined his vision of how to avoid a nuclear Armageddon. He appealed to scientists who had spent half a century developing nuclear weapons "to give us the means of rendering these nuclear weapons impotent and obsolete."[87] The doctrine of mutually assured destruction—MAD for short—would be superseded by a new Fortress America doctrine. This time, however, America would be protected not by the ocean but by an invisible, space-based shield. The official name for the program was the Strategic Defense Initiative (SDI), a phrase designed to emphasize its peaceful intent. But the technologies involved—lasers, particle beams, and kinetic energy weapons—seemed so fantastic that journalists were soon referring to Reagan's plan as "Star Wars," after the blockbuster science-fiction film.

The president's announcement was greeted with dismay in Moscow. Kremlin leaders viewed it as a further escalation of the arms race, designed to deprive the Soviet Union of its hard-won military parity. They could not accept American assurances that SDI was purely defensive. Their reasoning was simple. If the United States succeeded in deploying an antimissile system that protected American cities from incoming warheads, it would enjoy a huge strategic advantage. Such a development would allow Washington to launch a first strike against the Soviet Union with impunity or, at the very least, engage in nuclear blackmail. The alternative—being dragged into another exhausting high-tech race with the rival superpower—was equally alarming to Soviet leaders.

It did not take Gorbachev long to realize that the Soviet Union could not afford to match the American investment in "Star Wars." At the Geneva summit he offered Reagan a sweeping trade-off. The Kremlin would agree to a 50 percent reduction in the nuclear arsenals of the two superpowers, including its own SS-18 missiles, in return for a pledge from Washington to respect a 1972 treaty banning ballistic missile defenses. If the United States refused to compromise, the Soviet Union would be forced to take "countermeasures." Rather than compete directly with SDI by building its own nuclear shield, it would attempt to overwhelm the American defenses with bigger and better offensive missiles.

"Everything is coming to a halt if we can't find a way to prevent the arms race in space," the Soviet leader warned.[88]

"I'm talking about a shield, not a spear," replied Reagan, departing from his prepared notes. "Even if everybody reduces [offensive missiles] by 50 percent, it's still too many weapons. SDI gets around that."

"It's emotional . . . one man's dream," Gorbachev shot back, exasper-

ated by Reagan's stubbornness. "I want to reduce the number of weapons, but SDI is threatening a new arms race."

FOR ALL HIS SHORTCOMINGS—the seemingly eccentric ideas and notorious inattention to detail—Ronald Reagan possessed an incredible political sense. His adversaries repeatedly underestimated him. His aides were amazed by his ability to glide through life, with seemingly minimal effort, achieving goals that were beyond the reach, or even the imagination, of workaday politicians. Even for those close to him, this was a paradox that was difficult to explain. "He knows so little," marveled the detail-obsessed McFarlane shortly after his resignation as national security adviser in 1984, "yet he accomplishes so much."[89]

Part of the reason for Reagan's success in dealing with the Soviets was his abiding faith in the strengths of the American system of government. Shortly after he became president, a French intellectual named Jean-François Revel wrote a book entitled *How Democracies Perish* that became a bible for many American conservatives. It begins with an alarming prediction: "Democracy may, after all, turn out to be a historical accident, a brief parenthesis that is closing before our eyes." The central thesis of the book is that it is futile to expect that economic crises would cause the mellowing or disintegration of Communist states. According to Revel, it is far more likely that the opposite would happen. In order to cover up their internal failures, Soviet leaders would become more aggressive, more militaristic. Totalitarian societies were, by their very nature, cohesive and well regimented. There was a growing danger that they would overwhelm the fragile Western democracies.

Reagan did not share the view that the Russians were ten feet tall. His political sixth sense told him that democracy was a much stronger form of government than totalitarianism, precisely because of its pluralistic nature. He believed instinctively that communism's death knell was already sounding, a conviction that he expressed in his speeches. "In an ironic sense, Karl Marx was right," he told the British Parliament in June 1982. "We are witnessing today a great revolutionary crisis, a crisis where the demands of the economic order are conflicting directly with those of the political order. But the crisis is happening not in the free, non-Marxist West, but in the home of Marxism-Leninism, the Soviet Union."[90] Reagan's prediction that the "march of freedom and democracy" would leave communism on the "ashheap of history" seemed like a vain hope at the time—certainly to thinkers like Revel—but it proved astonishingly accurate.

In his dealings with Gorbachev, Reagan displayed a flexibility and tactical finesse that belied his reputation as a Cold War warrior. His ingrained optimism, and his confidence in himself, led him to go further down the road to disarmament than many conservatives thought wise. "I bet the hard-liners in both our countries are bleeding when we shake hands," he joked to the Soviet leader at the end of three days of discussions in Geneva.[91] It was almost as if there were two very different Reagans: the confrontational Cold War ideologue and the pragmatic Hollywood negotiator.

One Reagan spoke as if treaties with Communist states were not worth the paper they were written on. The other concluded one of the most sweeping arms control agreements in history with the rival superpower. One Reagan denounced the Soviet Union as an "evil empire." The other traveled to the heart of that empire and joined his Soviet counterpart in burying the Cold War. One Reagan spoke as if the only language that the Communists understood were force. The other was a dreamer who thought he could convince a Communist leader of the superiority of the capitalist system by flying with him in a helicopter over the villas and swimming pools of Southern California.

There was an objective need for both Reagans in the collapse of communism. Had the president failed to respond vigorously to the Soviet arms buildup or the invasion of Afghanistan, the Kremlin would have had less incentive to change its ways. On the other hand, if he had heeded the advice of his right-wing friends and spurned the olive branch offered by Gorbachev, a historic opportunity to negotiate a peaceful end to the Cold War might have been lost.

"If Reagan had stuck to his hard-line policies in 1985 and 1986, Gorbachev would also have been forced to take a much tougher position," said Anatoly Dobrynin, the veteran Soviet ambassador in Washington. "Otherwise he would have been accused by the rest of the Politburo of giving everything away to a fellow who does not want to negotiate. We would have been forced to tighten our belts and spend even more on defense. Remember the party still had everything under control at that time, and this was a realistic option."[92]

Reagan's dream of constructing a nuclear shield around the United States bedeviled his future dealings with Gorbachev. But the president's initiative also had the effect of altering the political dynamics between Moscow and Washington by exposing Soviet economic weakness. In a perverse kind of way it may have helped pave the way for the dramatic breakthrough in superpower relations.

The launching of "Star Wars" provoked a contradictory reaction in the

Soviet Union. Supported by some sections of the military, politically well-connected weapons developers immediately began an intense lobbying effort to be given the resources to counter the American program. A decision was taken to significantly increase defense spending during the 1986–90 plan period. At the same time, the prospect of a new high-technology arms race had a sobering impact on Kremlin policy makers.

"The Russians really believed that Reagan would do what he said he was going to do. The perception was the reality. They believed. This may have been Reagan's greatest achievement. He conveyed political will," said Suzanne Massie, who helped Reagan prepare for his meetings with Gorbachev.[93] "The SDI program had a long-lasting impact on us," acknowledged Aleksandr Bessmertnykh, a leading American expert in the Foreign Ministry. "We realized that we were approaching a very dangerous situation in the strategic counterbalance we had been living in."[94]

GENEVA MARKED A CRUCIAL STEP on Gorbachev's long journey from a collective farm in an obscure corner of the Soviet Union to the center of the world stage. Like Reagan, he was a complex, contradictory personality. He was a man with a soaring vision for his country, yet at times he could be infuriatingly obtuse. He earned the reputation in the West of being a decisive man of action, but there were long periods when he seemed gripped by indecision. He could work himself up into an emotional frenzy and then behave as if nothing had happened. He could be incredibly charming and almost heartlessly cold.

Some of these contradictions were explored in a psychological portrait of the Soviet leader that the Central Intelligence Agency prepared for Reagan on the eve of the Geneva summit. Among several passages carefully underlined by the president with his blue biro were the following: "Gorbachev has a greater measure of self-confidence, even arrogance, than recent Soviet leaders about his ability to revitalize the Soviet system, deal effectively with foreign leaders, and restore credibility to Soviet diplomacy. . . . Behind the smile and approachability, Gorbachev—like Khrushchev before him—has a tough, hard-nosed side. . . . Although Gorbachev's background and approach are unusual, he remains a product of the Soviet system."[95]

Shortly after the Geneva summit Gorbachev entered what one of his top aides later described as his Lenin phase.[96] He would pore over the writings of the founder of the Soviet state, searching for some clue to the country's future direction. At times he even picked up a volume of Lenin's collected

works from his desk and read a passage out loud, remarking on its relevance to contemporary problems. This interest in Lenin's writings was unusual for Soviet leaders. Politburo members quoted Lenin all the time but rarely went to the bother of actually reading him. But Gorbachev evidently regarded himself as the modern-day equivalent of the great revolutionary leader.

The keeper of the Leninist flame was also the ultimate Soviet yuppie. Everything about Gorbachev—from his fastidious clothes sense to his obsessive work habits—made him a symbol of upward mobility in an ostensibly classless society. As he moved upward—from the Privolnoye kolkhoz to a Moscow university dorm to a meteoric career in the Communist Party—he displayed a natural facility for making and discarding allies and collaborators. He had very few lifetime friends. His wife, Raisa, a beautiful and ambitious woman who had seemed a cut above him when he courted her at the university, was the ideal partner for him on this journey. His opinions and ideals remained his own, but the way he looked at the world was heavily influenced by those around him.

Joining the club of world leaders was the ultimate step up for the peasant boy from Stavropol. He began to look at the problems of his own country and its relationship with the rest of the world from a different perspective. The opinions of Reagan and Kohl and Thatcher began to matter to him almost as much as those of his Politburo associates. Some of his aides later complained that the *gensek* allowed the praise of Western leaders, and the "Gorbiemania" of the crowds, to go to his head. Always keen to improve himself, he had Dale Carnegie's best-seller *How to Win Friends and Influence People* translated into Russian. He successfully adopted its precepts: the firm handshake; the sincere smile; the technique of remembering little details about his interlocutors.[97]

A man of insatiable curiosity, Gorbachev soaked up facts and impressions of life in the West. As his plane flew over a city like Paris or London, he would look down at the tidy streets and neat little houses, making mental comparisons with the languorous squalor of street life in the Soviet Union. No detail was too small for his attention.

Gorbachev's goal in going to Geneva was to create the right international climate for his domestic programs. To accomplish perestroika (restructuring), he needed a *peredyshka* (respite or breathing space) from the East-West competition. A few months after the Geneva meeting, he outlined his new foreign policy strategy in a candid speech to a specially convened conference of Soviet ambassadors. The United States, he declared, was attempting to "exhaust" the Soviet Union economically by dragging it

into a ruinous arms race. The central task of Soviet diplomacy was to "create the best possible conditions" for social and economic development at home. The most basic requirement was peace with the West, "without which everything else is pointless." But it also involved abandoning outmoded ways of thinking. Pragmatism, not ideology, would become the watchword for Soviet foreign policy. Rather than dig themselves into entrenched positions, Soviet diplomats would be required to display political imagination and tactical flexibility. Gorbachev did not want his representatives to be nicknamed Mr. Nyet by their Western colleagues.[98]

The reference to "Mr. Nyet" was aimed at Gromyko, the diplomat who had embodied Soviet foreign policy for almost four decades. In one of his first acts as Soviet leader, Gorbachev had pushed the seventy-five-year-old foreign minister upstairs to the largely ceremonial position of chairman of the Supreme Soviet, the country's de facto head of state. He had entrusted the task of representing the Soviet Union abroad to his old friend Eduard Shevardnadze, the man who had originally come up with the expression "We cannot go on living like this." Shevardnadze knew very little about foreign affairs, having spent most of his political career in his native republic of Georgia. Far from disqualifying him from the job of foreign minister, his ignorance of the way things were done in the past may actually have been an asset, in Gorbachev's eyes. He needed a new face to embody his policies toward the rest of the world.

Gorbachev's talk about "new thinking" angered the Kremlin old guard. "What kind of new thinking?" spluttered the octogenarian Boris Ponomarev, who had been in charge of the party's foreign policy department for a quarter of a century. "We already have the right thinking. Let the Americans change their thinking!"[99]

WHEN GORBACHEV LOOKED into Reagan's eyes in Geneva, he still saw the face of world imperialism. He resented the president's attitude of moral superiority and eagerness to subject him to long lectures on human rights. "I felt that my interlocutor was so weighed down by stereotyped thinking that it was really difficult for him to reason soberly," he complained.[100] He had little time for small talk and was put off by Reagan's penchant for telling anecdotes and jokes and his lack of knowledge of detailed arms control issues. After their first meeting he made a comment to his chief foreign policy aide that suggested he did not believe that Reagan was up to the job. "He would make a very pleasant next-door neighbor, but a president . . ."[101]

At the same time, Gorbachev understood that Reagan was politically strong and had the overwhelming support of his own people. He concluded that Reagan was a person with whom it was possible "to do business," the very phrase that Mrs. Thatcher had used about Gorbachev himself two years before.[102]

Soviet fears of a nuclear first strike by the United States faded after the Geneva meeting. Gorbachev accepted Reagan's assurances that he was not a warmonger intent on the physical destruction of the rival superpower. He achieved his primary goal going into the summit, a joint statement proclaiming that "a nuclear war cannot be won—and must never be fought."[103] The Soviet leader took such rhetoric seriously. When military aides came to him a few weeks later with a routine contingency plan for the outbreak of nuclear war, he brusquely pushed them away. "Up until now, we assumed in our planning that a war [with the United States] is possible. But now, while I am general secretary, don't even put such plans, such programs on my desk."[104]

The antinuclear sentiments of both leaders were soon strengthened by a man-made nuclear catastrophe that seemed to fit right in with the biblical prophecy of Armageddon that had impressed Reagan so much: "A great star fell from the sky, flaming like a torch; and it fell on a third of the rivers and springs. The name of the star was Wormwood; and a third of the water turned to wormwood, and men in great numbers died of the water because it was poisoned" [Revelation 8:10]. The Ukrainian word for "wormwood" is *chernobyl*.

CHERNOBYL

April 26, 1986

SUMMER HAD COME EARLY to the picture book villages around the Chernobyl nuclear plant in northern Ukraine. It was that magical time of year when, with scarcely any warning, the rivers unfreeze, the snows melt, and the countryside turns a deep shade of green. Spring had been compressed into a few fleeting days, giving local residents barely enough time to unseal their windows, pack away their heavy winter coats, and plant a new crop of vegetables. The scent of pine trees and apple blossoms filled the air. Day and night fishermen lined the banks of the cooling pond of the power plant, casting their nets for the young fish that teemed in the warm wastes.

Carved out of the primeval forest, Chernobyl was known as a good place to raise a family. Recreational facilities were excellent. The dormitory town of Pripyat, where most Chernobyl employees had their apartments, was cleaner and better planned than most Soviet industrial communities. The glittering white power plant was a pleasant contrast with the pollution-spewing industrial dinosaurs that enveloped many urban areas in clouds of black smoke. Dominating the surrounding woodlands, the power plant seemed almost as benign as the meandering Pripyat River. Its four reactors emitted no odor, and scarcely any noise, other than a barely discernible hum. Nobody worried about environmental hazards. For years the Soviet government had assured everybody that nuclear power was perfectly safe.

As he paced up and down the control room of Reactor No. 4, Chernobyl's deputy chief engineer felt tired and irritable. Anatoly Dyatlov had been on duty for more than twelve hours. His subordinates had messed up a routine experiment to see if the reactor could operate under electricity generated by its own turbines, allowing the power in the reactor to fall to unacceptably low levels. There had been some discussion about terminating the experiment prematurely, but Dyatlov ordered it to continue. Soon the ordeal would be over, and he would be able to go back to bed.

The first explosion came in the form of a heavy thud, at 1:23 a.m. It was followed by a series of tremors, like an earthquake, and a mighty whoosh of steam. Then another deafening bang from somewhere deep inside the building shook the plaster off the ceiling and extinguished the overhead lights. It sounded to Dyatlov as if a huge gas tank had exploded. Others thought that the building was under attack by terrorists or even that war with the United States had finally broken out. The dozen or so engineers in the control room strained to read their instruments by the light of the emergency circuits.

"Everybody to the reserve switchboard," shouted Dyatlov.[105]

Seconds later he countermanded his order. Darting from one control panel to another, he realized that what had happened was not a minor accident but something much more terrible. Computer readouts showed that the turbine pressure was zero. In other words, steam from the reactor was no longer turning the turbines that generated electricity. Pressure in the water channels was also zero, meaning that cool water was no longer being pumped through the reactor. Most alarming of all, the instruments showed that the power in the reactor was increasing wildly when it should have been decreasing.

"I thought my eyes were coming out of my head. There was no way to explain it," Dyatlov recalled later.

In Chernobyl types of reactors, nuclear fission is controlled by lowering dozens of neutron-absorbing graphite rods into the reactor core. Normally the rods are lowered mechanically, but in an emergency they can also be lowered by gravity. To Dyatlov's horror, neither procedure seemed to work. For some reason, the rods had jammed in their sockets, about a third of the way down. The reactor was out of control.

The foreman in charge of the reactor rushed into the room. Pale and panic-stricken, Valery Perevozchenko was probably the first person to appreciate the scale of the catastrophe because he had seen it begin. He had been standing on a galley above the reactor lid, a huge metal circle made up of 1,661 pressurized steel tubes, each containing 770 pounds of nuclear fuel. The engineers referred to the lid colloquially as the *pyatachok* (five-kopeck

piece). Without warning, the *pyatachok* seemed to come alive. Viewed from above, it looked as if 1,661 steel cans were popping open simultaneously, in response to some inexplicable force beneath.[106] Seconds after Perevozchenko ran out of the hall, a terrifying blast ripped off the *pyatachok,* leaving a gaping hole in the roof of the reactor hall.

No one believed the foreman when he announced that the reactor had exploded. According to the textbooks, this was technically impossible. Dyatlov was still thinking of ways to control the nuclear reaction. He turned to two trainees, who had been observing the experiment, and ordered them to attempt to pull the graphite control rods down by hand. Protective clothing was nowhere to be found, so the trainees rushed off without respirators or masks. After they left, Dyatlov realized that he had probably sent two young men to their deaths for no useful purpose. If the control rods would not come down mechanically or by gravity, there was no way to bring them down manually. He ran after them, but it was too late.[107] They had already disappeared into the smoke-filled inferno. By the time they returned, half an hour later, both had received lethal doses of radiation.

The fishermen along the banks of the reactor pool also had a grandstand view of the explosion. They saw a pillar of flame and red-hot chunks of nuclear fuel shoot up into the dark sky, accompanied by a thunderclap that sounded like a sonic boom. Without knowing what was happening, the fishermen had just witnessed a radioactive release equivalent to ten of the atom bombs that had been dropped on Hiroshima. They continued to watch, entranced, as teams of firefighters battled the blaze from the half-destroyed roof of the turbine hall. The temperature was so high that the roof seemed to melt under the firemen's feet. Radioactive debris littered the entire area, emitting a sinister glow. As soon as one fire was put out, others started.

As dawn approached, the fishermen could see that the men up on the roof were sluggish and disoriented. Soon they began to feel nauseated. Their skin turned black, and they felt a burning sensation inside their chests. They were suffering from "nuclear tan."[108]

Unable to do anything in the control room, Dyatlov decided to survey the damage. In the turbine hall he was greeted by a scene of unimaginable devastation. Flames were leaping up through huge holes in the ceiling. Water was spurting in different directions, spilling over the machinery. There was a constant clicking sound from short circuits. Great chunks of roofing had fallen onto the floor, puncturing oil tubes that immediately exploded into flames. The air was thick with radioactive dust, which created a burning feeling in the chest and lungs and a tightening of the skin.

On one of his sorties out of the control room the engineer came across a worker from the reactor hall, Anatoly Kurguz, who had been singed by radioactive steam. The whole of his body was covered in blisters, and he was in terrible pain. Dyatlov could see the blisters hanging down from his face, like pieces of dead flesh. He ordered Kurguz to report to the medical unit in the administrative building. It turned out that the first-aid station was closed, one of many signs of the hubris of Chernobyl managers. Neither Dyatlov nor anyone else had any idea how much radioactivity had been released by the explosion. Their Geiger counters were capable of measuring only relatively modest levels of radiation and were already flickering off the scale. More powerful instruments had been locked away in safes, on the assumption that they would never be needed.

When Dyatlov inspected the damaged reactor, he discovered that two entire walls of the building were missing. By this time he was feeling nauseated, having exposed his body to destructive beta and gamma rays. He grabbed some computer printouts and took them to the administrative building, where the plant director, Viktor Bryukhanov, was on the phone to Moscow. The director was insisting that the reactor was intact and the fire under control. Dyatlov was too sick to argue with his boss. He felt as if there were nothing left of his insides. He mumbled something about a fault in the shutdown mechanism and left the room. He spent the rest of the night throwing up, alongside his companions from the control room.

A turbine engineer by profession, Bryukhanov knew little about nuclear power. His real skill lay in knowing how to please the bosses, while making sure that his subordinates received their annual bonuses for "fulfilling the plan." Ever since his appointment as the first director of the Chernobyl plant in 1970, at the remarkably young age of thirty-five, he had been under constant pressure to meet plan targets. He had pushed ahead with the construction of new reactors, ignoring warnings about sloppy building practices and violations of safety procedures. Four years earlier a small explosion had occurred in the core of Reactor No. 1, releasing some radioactivity into the air. Bryukhanov's main concern then had been to hush up the incident and repair the damaged reactor as quickly as possible. The following year he had succeeded in commissioning the fourth unit three months ahead of schedule, an achievement that earned him the title Hero of Socialist Labor.

Anxious to salvage his reputation as an efficient manager, Bryukhanov reported that Reactor No. 4 was still functioning and radiation levels at the plant were "within normal limits." He based this claim on the fact that the

Geiger counters were incapable of registering more than one thousand microroentgens per second, a relatively modest amount. When a civil defense worker finally unearthed a much more powerful instrument and took measurements showing catastrophic levels of radiation, the director refused to believe him.

"There's something wrong with your instrument. Fields that high are impossible," he snapped. "Get that thing out of here, or toss it in the garbage."[109]

NUCLEAR ACCIDENTS CAN OCCUR anywhere, but Chernobyl was a uniquely Soviet catastrophe. It was the almost inevitable consequence of the rapacious attitude toward nature that was an inherent part of the Soviet system of economic development. In the revolutionary mind-set, nature was subordinate to man. "We cannot wait for favors from nature," Soviet propagandists liked to proclaim. "Our task is to take them from her." In the end nature was bound to take its revenge, one way or another.

"The Russian soil was able to support the Communists for fifty years. It can't put up with them much longer," said Adam Michnik, one of the intellectual forces behind the Polish Solidarity movement, referring to Chernobyl and a host of other man-made disasters. "In Poland, in August 1980, it was human beings who went on strike. In the Soviet Union we are witnessing a strike of inanimate objects."[110]

In the immediate aftermath of Chernobyl, the government blamed the disaster on Bryukhanov, Dyatlov, and their subordinates. It was true that they had ignored safety rules and made serious errors of judgment. The investigation showed that the operators had switched off the emergency cooling system to Reactor No. 4 so that it would not interfere with the turbine experiment. They had failed to observe proper shutdown procedures. At a secret trial in July 1987 both Dyatlov and Bryukhanov were sentenced to ten years' imprisonment for "violations of discipline." Four other operators received prison sentences ranging from two to ten years. The prosecution described the defendants as "nuclear hooligans."

By producing a few scapegoats, the court neatly absolved everybody else of responsibility. The verdict deflected attention away from a series of major design flaws in the Chernobyl type of reactor, such as the lack of a containment structure to prevent leaks of radioactivity. It turned out that such reactors were chronically unstable at low levels of power, but no one had bothered to inform the operators about this defect. The operators were also unaware that under certain circumstances, the emergency shutdown mech-

anism could trigger a fatal surge of power. This is precisely what happened at Chernobyl. To have admitted all this at the time would have raised questions about the whole future of the nuclear power industry. It was much easier to blame "operator error."

The real villain of Chernobyl was not the operators or even the designers of the flawed reactor, but the Soviet system itself. It was a system that valued conformity over individual responsibility, concerned with today rather than tomorrow, a system that treated both man and nature as "factors of production" that could be mercilessly exploited. Eventually something had to break.

The violation of safety procedures was the norm, rather than the exception, in Soviet factories. So too was the obsession with secrecy that deprived the operators of the Chernobyl plant of basic information about the design of the reactor and previous nuclear accidents. But perhaps the gravest shortcoming of the system was the way it suppressed the notion of individual responsibility. The physical bravery displayed by many of the six hundred thousand "liquidators" who took part in the Chernobyl cleanup efforts— beginning with the operators themselves and the firemen who fought the blaze on the roof of the turbine hall—was remarkable. Equally remarkable was the moral cowardice that caused otherwise decent individuals to go along with senseless and reprehensible decisions, including a fatal delay in the evacuation of hundreds of thousands of people from heavily contaminated areas. When the Ukrainian Communist Party chief insisted that May Day parades go ahead in Kiev despite the fact that radioactive winds were blowing in the direction of the capital, hardly anyone stood up to protest.

This moral failing was eventually recognized by one of the leaders of the Soviet nuclear industry, academician Valery Legasov, who committed suicide on the second anniversary of the disaster. Shortly before his death he gave an interview in which he complained that technology had been permitted to outpace morality. He explained that the previous generation of Soviet scientists—men like Sakharov, Kurchatov, and Kapitsa—had stood "on the shoulders of Tolstoy and Dostoevsky." They had been educated in the spirit of beautiful literature, great art, and a "correct moral sense." But somewhere along the line the connection with Russia's prerevolutionary traditions had been broken. "Soviet man" was technically developed but morally stunted.

"We will not cope with anything if we do not renew our moral attitude to work," Legasov concluded.[111]

The Soviet system made a catastrophe like Chernobyl unavoidable. It then compounded the tragedy by an insistence on secrecy so absurd that it

was ultimately self-defeating. The attempted cover-up was all the more grotesque because it came when the rest of the world was in the throes of an information revolution that rapidly revealed the magnitude of the disaster.

ONE OF THE FIRST DECISIONS taken by Bryukhanov in the early-morning hours of Saturday, April 26, was to order nonessential telephone lines around Chernobyl to be cut.[112] It was an apparatchik's instinctive reaction to a major disaster. To the Communist bureaucratic mind, there is nothing more frightening than loss of control. Panic could be avoided by keeping the population in the dark.

During those first few hours after the explosion, thousands of people living in the immediate vicinity of the power plant received potentially fatal doses of radiation. Unaware of the danger, people took advantage of the warm weather to tend their gardens, visit friends, and play outside with their children. Local officials later boasted that sixteen couples were married in Pripyat that day, proving how "normal" everything was less than two miles away from the burning reactor.

Years later the people of Pripyat would have reason to curse the lack of information. Thousands died because of mysterious illnesses. The health of tens of thousands of others was permanently ruined. Leukemia rates soared. "If we had known what had happened, of course we would have remained indoors and taken precautions. God knows how much radiation we might have been spared," said Nadezhda Spachenko, a Chernobyl engineer, whose children soon began to suffer chronic headaches, nosebleeds, swollen thyroid glands, and general fatigue.[113]

In the best Soviet tradition, the investigation of the Chernobyl disaster was entrusted to the very people who were largely responsible for the tragedy. The first government commission arrived on the scene eighteen hours after the explosion. It was headed by Deputy Prime Minister Boris Shcherbina and included the designers of the failed reactor. Shcherbina was a leader of the old school, a little Napoleon who could instill terror in his subordinates with a harsh remark or withering glance. He had served as minister of oil and gas, a job that involved relentless cracking of the whip to ensure the fulfillment of planned targets. Promoted to the post of deputy prime minister in charge of the entire energy sector, he had attempted to apply similar methods to the building of nuclear power stations, a policy that had resulted in a sharp fall in safety standards. His handling of the emergency was summed up by a phrase that he used soon after his arrival in Pripyat: "Panic is worse than radiation."[114]

The evacuation of Pripyat finally got under way at 1:30 p.m. on April 27, thirty-six hours after the disaster. Believing they would be allowed to return in a few days, after the emergency was over, the residents left most of their belongings behind. Within a couple of hours a city of forty-eight thousand people had been turned into a ghost town. Pets had to be left behind because their hair was dangerously radioactive. For a few days packs of sick and hungry dogs roamed the streets, turning increasingly ferocious as it became clear that their masters would never return. Eventually they were rounded up and shot. In later years Pripyat became an eerie testimonial to the early Gorbachev era, with faded propaganda banners hailing the forthcoming May Day holiday.

It was not until the radioactive cloud reached Sweden on April 28, two and a half days after the explosion, that the rest of the world found out that a major nuclear disaster had occurred. An emergency Politburo session was convened in Moscow to consider how to respond to inquiries from Western governments and media organizations. After some debate, the Politburo decided to provide as little information as possible. That evening, a television announcer read a terse four-line communiqué from the Soviet government: "An accident has taken place at the Chernobyl power station, and one of the reactors was damaged. Measures are being taken to eliminate the consequences of the accident. Those affected by it are being given assistance. A government commission has been set up." Censors instructed Soviet editors to refrain from publishing anything about Chernobyl other than the official government communiqué.

Deprived of information, Soviets living in the immediate vicinity of Chernobyl exposed themselves to further danger, at a time when people thousands of miles away, in Western Europe, were drinking powdered milk and scrubbing vegetables. On Tuesday, April 29, U.S. intelligence analysts were stunned to see satellite pictures of an open-air soccer game taking place less than a mile from the smoldering reactor. A barge was sailing peacefully down the Pripyat River as if nothing had happened.[115] The second stage of the evacuation, affecting eighty-five thousand people living within an eighteen-mile radius of the power plant, did not begin until May 5, more than a week after the explosion. Apart from a few privileged officials, scarcely anyone in the zone received potassium iodide pills that might have afforded some protection against fast-decaying radioisotopes, such as iodine 131.

By insisting on secrecy, the government commission exposed many more people than necessary to high doses of radiation. Hundreds of thousands of "liquidators"—mainly young people of child-bearing age—were ordered to

take part in the cleanup effort. Many evacuees ended up in places that were only a little less dangerous than those they had left. Shcherbina ignored expert advice and ordered a new city, Slavutich, to be built on contaminated ground, to house Chernobyl workers and their families. In order to reduce the numbers of people requiring medical treatment, the government secretly approved a tenfold increase in "safe" radiation levels two weeks after the accident. For three years meat and milk from the contaminated region were mixed with clean meat and milk from other regions and sold all over the country.[116]

Chernobyl was a symbol of the failure of the command-and-administer system. But in an ironic way, it was also an instrument of retribution against the system and its hitherto untouchable representatives. Most of the senior officials involved in the Chernobyl cleanup understood very little about radiation or nuclear physics. Through a combination of ignorance and bravado, they took needless risks. One deputy minister received a fatal dose of radiation in a top Moscow clinic after being assigned a bed previously used by a Chernobyl firefighter.[117] A later investigation showed that the nursing staff had failed to change the bed linen, so patients were contaminating one another.

Shcherbina himself died under mysterious circumstances in August 1990, at the age of seventy, after what the Soviet press described as "a serious illness." He had exposed himself to needless risks by eating contaminated food and flying over the reactor without protective clothing, but it was unclear whether his death was caused by radiation. In 1988 he had issued a secret decree forbidding doctors from citing radiation as a cause of death or illness.[118]

THE KREMLIN

July 3, 1986

THE SOVIET UNION's most eminent nuclear scientists sat at little desks in front of Mikhail Gorbachev, like disobedient schoolchildren summoned to explain themselves before the headmaster. A portrait of Lenin gazed down severely from the walls of the Kremlin conference hall. Politburo members and ministers shifted uneasily in their chairs, uncertain who would be the next target of the general secretary's wrath.

Under Brezhnev, Politburo meetings had been pro forma affairs, often lasting little more than twenty or thirty minutes. By long-established ritual, they took place every Thursday, on the third floor of the government building in the Kremlin, beginning on the stroke of 11:00 a.m. Many crucial decisions, such as the invasion of Afghanistan, were made by a handful of Brezhnev cronies and not even discussed by the full Politburo. After Gorbachev came to power, there was a complete change of routine. Politburo meetings turned into marathon brainstorming sessions that frequently lasted for eight or ten hours. The new *gensek* liked to include as many people as possible in the decision-making process. At times of crisis seventy or eighty people might crowd into the gloomy Politburo conference hall, to be subjected to long harangues by Gorbachev.[119]

"For thirty years, you told us that everything was perfectly safe," the Soviet leader fumed, addressing the nuclear barons. "You assumed we would

look up to you as gods. That's the reason why all this happened, why it ended in disaster. There was nobody controlling the ministries and scientific centers. And for the moment, I can see no signs that you have drawn the necessary conclusions. In fact, it seems that you are attempting to cover everything up."[120]

Rage and frustration had been building up inside Gorbachev for weeks. Apart from the immense destruction and suffering that it had caused, Chernobyl had been a public relations catastrophe. It could not have occurred at a worse time. Naturally the West had seized on the catastrophe, and the initial cover-up, as evidence that nothing had really changed in the Soviet Union. His own reputation as a dynamic new leader was in tatters. Western commentators had made much of the fact that it had taken eighteen days for him to go on Soviet television with a personal account of the disaster. They had described his eighteen-minute speech as "defensive" and "uninformative."

Gorbachev was angry with the Western media and the Reagan administration for criticizing his performance and questioning his commitment to reform. He was depressed by the stories of bureaucratic heartlessness and incompetence that had come to his attention. Most of all, he was furious about the difficulty of obtaining fast and accurate information from his own subordinates. He believed that the leadership had been misled about the reliability of the Chernobyl type of reactor, radioactivity levels in the disaster zone, and much more. He accused the nuclear chieftains of using a cult of secrecy to safeguard their vested interests, refusing to share information even with the Central Committee and the government. Free from outside control, they had created a mini-empire riddled with "the spirit of servility, sycophancy, persecution of dissidents, window-dressing, personal connections, and clans."

"We're going to put an end to all this," Gorbachev pledged. "We have suffered great losses, and not only economic ones. There have been human victims, and there will be more. We have been damaged politically. All our work has been compromised. Our science and technology have been discredited as a result of what has happened. . . . From now on, what we do is going to be visible to our entire people and the whole world. We need full information."

As the expanded Politburo meeting wore on, horrifying facts began to emerge about safety standards in the Soviet nuclear power industry. At Chernobyl alone there had been an average of twenty accidents a year. Most were attributable to design defects. "We were heading toward a major dis-

aster," acknowledged Prime Minister Nikolai Ryzkhov. "If it hadn't happened now, it could have taken place at any moment."[121]

The *gensek* was in no mood for excuses. When a deputy minister insisted that the reactor was structurally sound except for one small detail—the lack of a containment structure—he gave vent to his anger. "You astonish me. Everybody is saying that the reactor has shortcomings and is dangerous, but you are still defending the honor of the uniform." The apparatchik was fired two weeks later, along with several other ministers and deputy ministers.

In public Gorbachev continued to defend the system that made such disasters possible. He placated the Politburo old guard by attacking the West for an "unrestrained anti-Soviet campaign" and insisted that the Soviet Union would continue with its ambitious nuclear power program. In private, however, he was radicalized by the traumatic experience of Chernobyl. In conversations with aides, he complained more and more frequently that perestroika was proceeding too slowly and would have to be accelerated. He still saw the Communist Party as the spearhead of his revolution, but there would clearly have to be a vast shakeup in its ranks before it could become an effective instrument of change. The party, like the nuclear industry, could no longer be answerable only to itself. It would have to submit to some form of outside control.[122]

His weapon in this battle was glasnost (openness). First and foremost, Gorbachev wanted more information for himself and the Politburo. But he also saw the need for more information for the general public, which would be his ally in his struggle to reform the party. In the weeks since Chernobyl, he had been bombarded by complaints from newspaper editors about the lack of glasnost.[123] Designed to prevent panic, the ban on information had had precisely the opposite effect, in the view of the editors. Rumors spread by word of mouth. In Kiev, a city of 2.5 million people, ninety miles south of Chernobyl, panic-stricken residents had camped out at railway stations for days on end, storming departing trains. Everybody knew that Communist Party officials responsible for censoring the news media were evacuating their own families from the capital.

In response to these protests and the outcry in the West, the flow of information about Chernobyl gradually increased. Gorbachev also used the crisis as a pretext to appoint new editors to magazines and journals, such as *Ogonyok*, *Moscow News*, and *Novy Mir*, which quickly became standard-bearers for glasnost.

FOR THOSE WHO DEALT with Chernobyl, the disaster was a turning point in their lives and professional careers. For Marshal Akhromeyev, who sent tens of thousands of conscripts to clean the mess up, it was an event comparable to Hitler's invasion of the Soviet Union in June 1941. Legasov, the nuclear scientist who committed suicide, compared Chernobyl with such epoch-making catastrophes as the destruction of Pompeii. For Prime Minister Ryzkhov, struggling to cope with collapsing oil prices and falling alcohol revenues, the disaster represented another blow to the nation's finances. For Grigori Medvedev, a nuclear engineer who wrote the first detailed account in Russian of the disaster, Chernobyl marked "the final, spectacular collapse of a declining era."[124]

The effect on Gorbachev was summed up by his foreign policy aide Anatoly Chernyayev. Chernobyl, he writes in his memoirs, was a "time bomb" that exploded on Gorbachev's watch but had been ticking away for decades beneath the foundations of Soviet society.[125] There would be many more such explosions. Gorbachev was fated to pay for the mistakes of his predecessors.

JALALABAD

September 25, 1986

WHAT RUDYARD KIPLING CALLED the Great Game had been played out
in the inhospitable mountains around the Khyber Pass for more than two
centuries. The object, according to the nineteenth-century British strategists
who drew up the rules, was nothing less than "the domination of the
world."[126] Successive British viceroys of India had nightmares of Russian
troops pouring through the pass and achieving the age-old tsarist dream of
a warm-water port on the shores of the Indian Ocean. To prevent this
geopolitical nightmare from taking place, it was essential to control the
northern approaches to the pass.

In the updated twentieth-century version of "the Game," everything was
reversed. The Kremlin gerontocrats were plagued by visions of an "imperialist" threat to their Central Asian republics, the soft underbelly of the Soviet empire. In order to forestall this threat, they had invaded Afghanistan
only to encounter unexpectedly strong opposition from the descendants of
the same tribesmen who had spent years fighting the British. Determined to
make things difficult for the Russians, the "imperialists" secretly supplied
the tribesmen with weapons and provided training bases on the southern
side of the Khyber Pass. The Soviets responded by attempting to seal the
border with Pakistan.

Like the British before them, the Soviets established a strong garrison in Jalalabad, halfway between the Afghan capital, Kabul, and the Pakistani border town of Peshawar. A brigade of two thousand elite *spetsnaz* (special assignment) troops was camped out around the airport. By intercepting rebel communications with mobile eavesdropping equipment, they were able to locate mujahedin caravans crossing over into Pakistan. Once a caravan had been pinpointed, a squadron of Mi-24 helicopter gunships would be dispatched to strafe the area with rockets and machine-gun fire. Paratroopers would arrive aboard Mi-8 transport helicopters, protected by the Mi-24s. After several hours of bombardment, a column of tanks, armored cars, and mortars would move in to finish the job.

Operation Curtain, as it was dubbed by the Soviets, was launched in April 1984. Inevitably there were setbacks as well as successes. Supported by the local population, the mujahedin possessed a superb intelligence network and were often able to turn the tables on their Soviet tormentors. But the results were sufficiently impressive to persuade Gorbachev to authorize an escalation in the war in the spring of 1985, shortly after he came to power.[127] For the first time in six years the Soviets seemed to have a chance of winning "the Game"—provided, of course, that the "imperialists" did not succeed in turning one of their pawns into a queen.

IN SEPTEMBER 1986 a small band of mujahedin led by a Commander Ghaffar left a guerrilla training camp in Pakistan and crossed the Khyber Pass. They crawled undetected to within a mile of the Jalalabad airport. From a well-hidden position, on a small hill overlooking the airfield, Ghaffar's men could observe Soviet soldiers moving around inside the perimeter fence. Soviet tanks and armored personnel carriers stood at each end of the runway. The mujahedin had split into three teams of three men each, deployed in a rough triangular formation, within shouting distance of one another. They had been waiting, crouched behind the bushes, for more than three hours now. Each team was equipped with one of the most sophisticated pieces of electronic gadgetry yet devised by the U.S. Army, the Stinger missile, a portable air defense system capable of downing an enemy aircraft from a distance of three miles.

In midafternoon, as the shadows were lengthening over the mountains, Ghaffar's patience was finally rewarded. No fewer than eight Mi-24 helicopter gunships—the most hated weapon in the Soviet arsenal—were approaching for a landing. The commander gave a shout. The three marksmen hoisted the launchers onto their shoulders and trained the sights onto the

approaching Mi-24s, with their telltale glass-covered noses and rocket pods hanging down beneath the fuselage. With a flick of his left thumb, each marksman punched a button that instructed the missile's electronic brain to sense the infrared heat being emitted from the helicopter engines. There was a series of loud pinging sounds, the signal that the missiles had locked on to their targets. Ghaffar shouted, "Fire," and the marksmen pulled the triggers. Ecstatic chants of *Allah o Akbar* (God is great) rose into the air as the missiles whooshed into the sky at a speed of more than twelve hundred miles per hour.

Seconds later two of the helicopters burst into flames and plummeted to the ground. There was a wild scramble as the firing parties reloaded. Two more missiles were fired, downing another helicopter. The first five Stinger missiles ever fired in combat had resulted in three kills and two misses, a 60 percent success rate. The mujahedin were jubilant. An Afghan cameraman attempting to record the scene for the benefit of the spymasters in Peshawar was so excited that his film consisted mainly of blurred shots of sky, stony ground, and black smoke pouring from the wreckage.[128]

There was jubilation too in the White House and the Pentagon when news of the ambush reached Washington. The Stinger missile had become a well-publicized symbol of U.S. clandestine support for the Afghan rebels in their struggle against the Soviet invader. The "most overt covert operation in history," somebody called it. Together with the decision to supply satellite intelligence and other high-tech American weaponry to the mujahedin, it helped change the course of the Afghan War.

From now on it would be much more difficult for the Soviets to conduct the kind of low strafing of rebel positions that had proved so effective in 1985 and early 1986. The scope of *spetsnaz* hunt-and-destroy missions was much reduced. Soviet pilots would change their operating procedures, flying at high altitude, beyond the range of the mujahedin. When they came in to land, they adopted a curious corkscrew technique, descending in a tight spiral and firing flares every few seconds to confuse the homing devices of the Stingers. The Soviet Defense Ministry was so taken aback by the new weaponry that it promised the title "Hero of the Soviet Union" to the first soldier to capture a Stinger from the mujahedin. The first batch of intact Stingers was delivered to Moscow in the fall of 1986.[129]

By invading Afghanistan in December 1979, Brezhnev and his colleagues handed the West a diplomatic victory that had hitherto proved way beyond the reach, or even the imagination, of the smartest policy makers in

Washington, London, or Paris. The spectacle of Soviet aggression against a Muslim Third World country—one of the founding members of the non-aligned movement—brought the most unlikely political bedfellows together. In the space of a few months a remarkable anti-Soviet coalition had taken shape. It spanned the entire ideological spectrum: American capitalists and Chinese Communists, conservative Saudi princes and Iranian Islamic fundamentalists, Pakistani generals and European peaceniks. The only people left in Moscow's camp were diehard Kremlin clients.

The Politburo was aware that there would be near-universal condemnation of its action. A few days after the invasion a prominent Moscow think tank warned Soviet leaders that they were up against "the united resources of the U.S., other NATO countries, China, Australia, the Islamic states, and an army of Afghan insurgents."[130] Such warnings fell on deaf ears. Soviet leaders were convinced that the international hue and cry would soon die down, just as it had after the invasion of Czechoslovakia in 1968.

In addition to howls of outrage, the invasion of Afghanistan caused an immediate toughening in Western policies toward Moscow. The American president, Jimmy Carter, reacted to Brezhnev's adventure with the fury of a jilted suitor. He believed he had done his best to improve relations with the rival superpower, but his good intentions had been mistaken for weakness. He had been duped and betrayed by his would-be Soviet partners. He commented bitterly that he had learned more about the real nature of the Soviet Union in a few days than in the previous three years of his presidency. Describing the invasion as "the greatest threat to peace since the Second World War," he authorized a series of actions designed to punish the Soviets and bolster American defenses.[131] Publicly announced sanctions included a ban on high-technology exports to the Soviet Union, an embargo on grain sales, a delay in ratifying the SALT-2 arms treaty, and a boycott of the 1980 Summer Olympics in Moscow. Privately Carter also approved covert arms supplies to the Afghan resistance and military consultations with China.[132]

The Reagan administration expanded these measures into an anti-Soviet crusade, led by a former World War II spymaster named William Casey. A Wall Street millionaire, Casey had been appointed director of the Central Intelligence Agency as a reward for managing Reagan's presidential campaign. His Jesuit upbringing had taught him to view international politics as an eternal struggle of good against evil. He saw himself as the foreign policy conscience of the administration. His wartime experiences—he had organized an intelligence network behind German lines—had made him a firm believer in the value of covert action. Convinced that clandestine oper-

ations had contributed significantly to the defeat of Nazi Germany, he wanted to apply similar methods to the Soviet Union. "It is important . . . to understand how clandestine intelligence, covert action, and organized resistance saved blood and treasure in defeating Hitler," he writes in his wartime memoirs, published posthumously. "These capabilities may be more important than missiles and satellites in meeting crises yet to come, and point to the potential for dissident action against the control centers and lines of communication of a totalitarian power."[133]

In Casey's view, intelligence could not be neutral. Intelligence without action was pointless. The war had to be taken into the enemy camp. He needed to find a place, he told associates, "to start rolling back the Communist empire."[134] In March 1985, Casey got what he wanted—a presidential directive to push the Soviet army out of Afghanistan. Prior to 1985, the American strategy had been simply to bleed the Soviets. The new objective was to help mujahedin win the war. From mid-1985 onwards, the CIA began pouring weapons into Afghanistan, via the guerrilla training camps in Pakistan.[135]

A shambling bear of a man, with the look of an absentminded professor, Casey inspired strong opinions. To his detractors, he was an irresponsible ideologue, so blinded by his hatred for the Soviets that he was unable to view the world objectively. Secretary of State George Shultz complained repeatedly that the CIA was feeding him false information about the Soviet Union, vastly overrating its military and economic capabilities. He blamed Casey for a series of intelligence disasters beginning with the Iran-contra affair.[136] To his admirers, Casey was the unsung hero of the final phase of the Cold War, the backstage mastermind who devised a strategy for bringing a Communist superpower to its knees. His methods for rolling back communism may have been crude, but they were effective. By the time he resigned as CIA director in January 1987, the "evil empire" was in clear retreat.

Whatever one thought of Casey, one had to be impressed by his energy and single-mindedness. Sick with cancer and in his early seventies, he was still crisscrossing the globe in his specially equipped black C-141 Starlifter aircraft to tend to his cherished anti-Soviet coalition. In order to save time and avoid unnecessary stopovers, the plane often was refueled in midair by a KC-10 tanker. The CIA director traveled at night to avoid attention, and checked into hotels under assumed names such as Smith and Black, in cloak-and-dagger tradition. A typical trip included stops in Tokyo, Beijing, Islamabad, Riyadh, Jerusalem, Ankara, and Rome. He discussed strategy with the Chinese, finances with the Saudis, and logistics with the Paks. Pak-

istani intelligence officials were soon referring to him as "the wanderer" or "the cyclone."[137]

On one such trip, in October 1984, Casey was taken by helicopter to visit the secret mujahedin training camps in Pakistan near the Afghan border. After watching the rebels learning how to make bombs with CIA-supplied explosives, he startled his Pakistani hosts by suggesting ways in which the war could be extended to the Soviet Union itself. Stage one of the plan involved the smuggling of subversive literature across the Afghan-Soviet border, to be followed by weapons to encourage local uprisings. A few months later the CIA shipped ten thousand Uzbek-language versions of the Koran to Pakistan for distribution in Soviet Central Asia.[138]

Back in Washington, meanwhile, a bureaucratic war was under way within the administration over the supply of Stingers to the mujahedin. The Joint Chiefs of Staff did not want to hand their wonder weapon over to a bunch of illiterate Afghans. The CIA bureaucracy was concerned that the Stinger could be easily traced back to the United States, a violation of the most basic principle of covert warfare, plausible deniability. The main advocates of the deployment of the Stinger were conservative members of Congress and a few well-placed bureaucrats, such as Morton Abramowitz, chief of intelligence at the State Department, who feared that the Soviets might overwhelm the Afghan resistance. In interagency discussions Abramowitz argued that it was important to bring home to the new Soviet leadership the costs of remaining in Afghanistan. As long as Gorbachev could blame the war on his predecessors, he could be persuaded to get out. The United States should not allow "Brezhnev's war" to become "Gorbachev's war."[139]

The president authorized the transfer of four hundred Stingers to the mujahedin in February 1986, but more than six months elapsed before they showed up in Afghanistan. As was often the case in Washington, the presidential decision triggered more bureaucratic infighting over how it would be implemented. The army succeeded in delaying deployment for weeks by insisting that the entire stockpile of Stingers was needed by U.S. troops in Germany. It then demanded that security in mujahedin training camps in Pakistan be upgraded to American standards.[140] By the time these objections were sorted out, a series of press leaks had alerted the Soviets that the missiles were on their way.

In an attempt to second-guess the internal Kremlin debate about Afghanistan, U.S. policy makers staged mock Politburo sessions in the Pentagon basement.[141] Officials took turns playing Soviet leaders, arguing

among themselves about how to respond to the latest challenge to their authority. The hawks argued in favor of a further escalation of the war and armed incursions into Pakistan to destroy the guerrilla training camps. The doves insisted that one Afghanistan was enough, and it was time to pull Soviet troops out. Intelligence reports from a well-placed agent in Moscow, suggesting that the Soviet military was extremely nervous about Gorbachev, supplied a touch of authenticity to these mock debates.[142]

In fact, nobody in Washington really knew what was happening behind the Kremlin's thick brick walls.

THE KREMLIN

November 13, 1986

THE GENERAL SECRETARY WAS in a combative mood. At his second meeting with Reagan, in Reykjavik, he and the president had come close to bargaining away their entire nuclear arsenals. Had it not been for Reagan's obsession with "Star Wars," which torpedoed the agreement at the last moment, they would have changed the course of world history. Gorbachev had returned home frustrated and disappointed by the setback, but with a grudging respect for the "human qualities" of his American partner. It seemed to him that Reagan was genuinely interested in promoting peace.[143] He was more determined than ever to tackle the vast range of issues that were impeding progress in superpower relations.

At the top of Gorbachev's agenda was Afghanistan.

"We have been waging war in Afghanistan for six years now. If we don't change our approach, we'll be there for another twenty or thirty years," Gorbachev told his Politburo colleagues, gathered in the Kremlin for their regular Thursday meeting. "We must end this process in the swiftest possible time."[144]

Like a chessplayer moving his pieces into position before an offensive, Gorbachev had prepared carefully for this moment. He had been raising the subject of Afghanistan at Politburo sessions within a few months after his

appointment as *gensek*, suggesting that the time had come "to leave."[145] He came to the meetings armed with letters from ordinary Soviet citizens and war veterans and read them out loud to his colleagues. "We cannot explain to the soldiers what is going on," a political officer had written. "Why do we have to kill civilians, destroy villages, burn down settlements? What are we fighting for?"[146]

After "educating" his Politburo colleagues, Gorbachev had got to work on the Afghan leadership. In May 1986 he summoned Babrak Karmal to Moscow and told him bluntly that the time had come to quit.[147] He then sent emissaries to Kabul to persuade the new Afghan leader, Mohammad Najibullah, to embrace a policy of "national reconciliation." The issue now was not whether Soviet troops should be pulled out of Afghanistan but how and when and what kind of country they would leave behind.

Out of the half dozen men who had made the decision to invade Afghanistan, the only one still alive and still in power was Andrei Gromyko, now Soviet president. Gorbachev was amused by the speed with which the former foreign minister had "restructured" himself during the first two years of perestroika.[148] Perhaps that explained his astonishing longevity. By the fall of 1986 the chief apologist for the invasion had become a leading advocate of withdrawal.

Sidestepping the question of his own responsibility, Gromyko acknowledged that the gamble had failed. The Soviet leadership had "underestimated" the difficulties that it would encounter. The social conditions in Afghanistan—a backward, almost medieval state—had not been ripe for socialism. There was little domestic support for the "revolution." The Afghan army was plagued by desertion. The United States was doing its best to trap the Soviet Union in a long, drawn-out war.

"We must seek a political solution," Gromyko concluded. "Our people will breathe a sigh of relief if we undertake steps in this direction."

Gorbachev knew he could count on the other key figures in the room. His prime minister, Nikolai Ryzhkov, had been complaining for months that the war was placing an unbearable strain on the Soviet Union's finances. The cost of the war had doubled over the past two years. The Kremlin was spending as much on the upkeep of 100,000 troops temporarily deployed in Afghanistan as on 380,000 troops permanently stationed in East Germany, along the front line with NATO. Annual expenditures on Afghanistan were roughly comparable to the cleanup effort after Chernobyl.[149]

Afghanistan was far from being the only economic basket case propped

up by Kremlin largess. As glasnost took hold in the Soviet Union, the issue of "fraternal assistance" became increasingly controversial. Every year Moscow sent shiploads of Zhiguli cars to Nicaragua, prefabricated barracks to Guinea-Bissau, radio stations to Angola, and factories to Cuba. Even the normally lucrative international arms trade turned out to be unprofitable for the Soviet Union. Revolutionary governments in Africa, the Middle East, or Latin America practically never paid hard cash for the mountains of weapons that they received from Moscow. Accustomed to viewing the world through ideological glasses, Soviet leaders chalked their losses up to "socialist solidarity." Eventually, however, even they understood they were being conned.

"I learned to my cost what the weapons trade with 'friends' was all about," Ryzkhov said later. "An ever-growing debt. Endless negotiations, in which requests for rescheduling payments were interspersed with threats not to pay at all. Constant appeals to our 'sense of friendship.' "[150]

Gorbachev had already lined up military backing for his attempts to end the war. The key figure here was Marshal Akhromeyev, who had helped draw up the invasion plans. The armed forces chief of staff was a complex personality, at once diehard Communist and ardent patriot. Like his patron Dmitri Ustinov, the marshal revered Stalin for his wartime leadership. A few weeks after Gorbachev's election Akhromeyev had proposed turning the Soviet Union into an "armed camp," ready at all times to defend itself against the imperialists. On certain matters, however, he was a progressive. He was opposed to the Soviet Union's frittering away its resources on Third World countries like Ethiopia.[151] He had helped facilitate arms negotiations with the United States. American negotiators were extremely impressed with him, crediting him with several important breakthroughs. As far as they were concerned, he was a "first-class military man": direct, authoritative, and very loyal.[152]

The commanders on the ground had told Akhromeyev that the Fortieth Army would have to be doubled in size in order to fulfill the Politburo's order to seal the border with Afghanistan. That would mean redeploying elite combat troops from the NATO front line or the militarily sensitive Chinese border. Even then there would be no guarantee of success. The Soviet Union could not support three fronts at once.[153]

A soldier-intellectual, Akhromeyev understood that the conditions of combat in Afghanistan were vastly different from those of the Great Patriotic War. When the Russian soldier was fighting to defend his own homeland, he could perform incredible feats. In Afghanistan he felt himself to be an intruder, obliged to wage war against the local population on behalf of

an unpopular government. The chief of staff believed that the army had acquitted itself well in Afghanistan, under extremely adverse circumstances. The mujahedin were no match for Soviet units in set-piece battles. But the ability to seize territory had little practical significance in a land where the enemy could melt back into the mountains and wait for the Soviets to leave. The Soviet army had been given an impossible mission.

"The military fulfills the tasks that are assigned to it, but the results are zero. Military gains are not being consolidated by political gains," the marshal complained, attempting to shift the blame back to the civilians. "We control Kabul and the provincial centers, but we cannot establish political authority on the territory that we seize. We have lost the struggle for the Afghan people. Only a minority of the population supports the government."

The Politburo session ended in general agreement. The Kremlin would promote a political settlement between the Communist government in Kabul and the mujahedin. Soviet troops would be withdrawn in stages, over the next two years. The dream of building socialism in a backward, feudal society was officially abandoned. The goal now was to ensure "a neutral state" on the Soviet Union's southern border. For the first time in nearly seventy years the Politburo was acknowledging that defections from the Soviet bloc were possible. Revolutions could, after all, be reversed.

The empire had begun to crack.

ENDING THE WAR in Afghanistan had been high on the list of political priorities that Gorbachev had drawn up for himself on his first day in office. Accomplishing this goal was not so simple, however. Unlike many struggles over domestic policy, the Afghanistan debate did not divide the Politburo into conservatives and reformers. The real battle over the modalities of Soviet withdrawal took place in Gorbachev's own mind.

"Afghanistan did not fit naturally into the ideological struggle for perestroika. There was consensus on this issue. Everyone in the Politburo, including conservatives like Ligachev, was in favor of withdrawal," said Gorbachev's foreign policy adviser, Anatoly Chernyayev.[154]

Gorbachev talked about the war as "a past sin," grumbling to his colleagues, "Soon they will be sticking this label onto us."[155] At the same time, according to Chernyayev, he still saw the conflict through the prism of East-West confrontation. He was susceptible to pressure from radical Third World leaders, such as Mengistu Haile Mariam of Ethiopia, who argued that the Kremlin would lose all credibility if it abandoned one of its allies.

American support for the mujahedin helped convince Soviet leaders that they were fighting an unwinnable war. "The situation now is worse than it was six months ago," said Gromyko in November 1986, two months after the first Soviet helicopters were shot down by Stingers. Akhromeyev complained that, even with fifty thousand soldiers deployed along the border with Pakistan, it was proving impossible to close off all the supply routes used by the Afghan resistance.

Once the decision to leave had been made, however, the U.S. covert action program may have had the paradoxical effect of delaying withdrawal. This, at least, is the view of former Gorbachev aides, who argue that it was extremely difficult for Moscow to leave a country that had been turned into a superpower battlefield. "American arms supplies only dragged out the war," insisted Aleksandr Yakovlev, the ideological brains behind perestroika. "Gorbachev, Shevardnadze, and myself were deeply convinced that we did not need Afghanistan and had no business being there. We would have lost the war anyway. We should have learned from the British that Afghanistan is a country that cannot be conquered. But the struggle between the two political systems sometimes drove us and the Americans to do stupid things. We all lost touch with reality."[156]

Over the next few months the war continued to escalate. By early 1987 there were 120,000 Soviet troops in Afghanistan, up from 75,000 at the beginning of the war.[157] Both the cost of the war and the number of casualties continued to rise. It took the Soviets another twenty-seven months to extricate themselves from the Afghan quagmire.

The decision to leave Afghanistan paved the way for the release from internal exile of the human rights campaigner Andrei Sakharov. The father of the Soviet hydrogen bomb had been banished to the closed city of Gorky in January 1980 for daring to criticize the invasion of Afghanistan in public. It was now obvious that he had been right all along, although this was too much for the Politburo to acknowledge. When Gorbachev phoned Sakharov to tell him that he was free to return to Moscow, he offered no apology and no explanation.

"Go back to your patriotic work!" the *gensek* ordered.[158]

Emboldened by Sakharov's release and the about-face on Afghanistan, Gorbachev's more radical aides urged him to turn his attention to military reform. Articles began appearing in the Soviet press on hitherto taboo themes, such as nepotism and corruption in the military. The general secretary had been waiting for a chance to assert his control over the Soviet Union's bloated armed forces. A few months later he was presented with an opportunity that was almost literally heaven-sent.

MOSCOW

May 28, 1987

IT WAS BORDER GUARDS' DAY, one of those typical Soviet holidays when the regime congratulated the "defenders of the socialist motherland" and reminded the population of the ever-present "imperialist threat." As usual, there were fireworks over the Moskva River and laudatory articles in *Pravda* hailing the vigilance of some unsung KGB officer stationed in a remote frontier post. Unusually for Moscow, there were also brawls in Gorky Park, as groups of vodka-drenched border guards intimidated passersby and sang lewd songs. It was an early sign that public discipline was breaking down in conditions of glasnost.

While the border guards were whooping it up in Gorky Park, the commanders of Soviet air defense were trying to figure out the significance of a mysterious blip on their radar screens. The blip had first made its appearance in the early afternoon, in the Leningrad region, and was assigned the number 8255. It seemed to be traveling south toward Moscow, at an altitude of around eighteen hundred feet. After the inevitable bureaucratic delay—duty officers feared that they would be penalized for raising a false alarm—a MiG-23 interceptor jet was sent up to investigate. The pilot reported spotting "a light sports plane flying just below the clouds."

The high command was skeptical. There were no private sports planes in Russia. After the KAL affair would any sane pilot intrude into Soviet air-

space without filing a flight plan? More MiGs were sent up to investigate, but they lost sight of the "target" in the low clouds. There was more confusion as another unidentified blip—a weather front or a hot-air balloon—merged with 8255 and then separated again. Soviet pilots spent the next two hours chasing a phantom. As the blip approached Moscow, the generals racked their brains over the identity of the mystery target in a telephone conference.

"I'm afraid it was birds, small birds," said Major General Gvozdenko, one of the commanders of the national air defense system.[159]

"No," objected Major General Reznichenko, in charge of Moscow's air defenses that day. "The pilots saw it."

"They didn't see anything. Those pilots are always seeing things."

"But the pilot is very insistent. A plane appeared from somewhere."

Frustrated by such stubbornness, Gvozdenko changed his approach. "Do you realize," he told his colleague, "if we say it's a plane, the higher-ups are going to badger everybody? They're going to say, 'If you saw a plane, then look for it.'"

Reznichenko's superior, Lieutenant General Brazhnikov, joined the conversation. "It's a weather formation, or birds. That's the most likely."

"It would be nice if it really were a weather formation," said Reznichenko, allowing himself to dream for a moment. "But what if it's a plane? And it comes down because it runs out of fuel. Then [the higher-ups] will really start yelling at us, 'What did you do, and why did you do it this way and not that way?'"

"So it comes down," argued Gvozdenko, still thinking about ways to cover himself. "We tracked it consistently. We sent fighters up."

As the senior general present Brazhnikov realized that it was time to make a decision. "Okay, we have to make a report. What is it to be: birds, a weather formation, or a target?"

The general in charge of the radar system, Aleksandr Gukov, was in a quandary. "I can't make a decision," he told Brazhnikov. "I doubt it is a weather formation. It's moving too fast."

A few minutes later Gukov came back on the line. A good soldier, he knew how to please his superiors. "Our conclusion is that it is a weather formation," he reported.

"But, Aleksandr Ivanovich, you're so contradictory," said Brazhnikov, exasperated. "Two minutes ago you said it couldn't be a weather formation."

"You made a decision. It's up to us to work these things out."

Brazhnikov decided he preferred the birds explanation. "Try to remember what the north and Siberia are like at this time of year," he told Gukov. "Do geese fly for a long time?"

"Yes, they do. The Leningraders decided it was birds."

"Well, there you are, and you were saying a weather formation. Why should weather formations stand out against such a cloudy background? It seems very doubtful."

"We should go along with the decision of the Leningraders and show solidarity," said the radar commander, amid chortles from his fellow generals. "There's just one thing that confuses me. Birds fly north in the spring. But this is coming *from* the north."

"I still think we will conclude that it was geese," said Brazhnikov firmly, bringing the debate to a close. "So, Aleksandr Ivanovich, it will be birds."

"Yes, sir, understood, let it be birds."

Seventy minutes later a single-engine Cessna 172 sports plane flew low over the Kremlin, buzzing the Lenin Mausoleum. After circling Red Square a couple of times, the Cessna landed on an expanse of cobblestone between the domes of St. Basil's Cathedral and the Kremlin's Spassky Gate. A bespectacled young pilot, dressed in a red flying suit, got out. Mathias Rust, a nineteen-year-old bank clerk trainee from Hamburg, told the crowd that he wanted to talk to Gorbachev about "world peace."

NEWS THAT A WEST GERMAN teenager had managed to penetrate Soviet air defenses and fly 450 miles unchallenged across Soviet territory to the inner sanctum of Soviet power provoked one of Gorbachev's most spectacular temper tantrums. He was out of the country at the time, attending a Warsaw Pact meeting in Berlin. "It's a national shame. This is as bad as Chernobyl," he exploded when Marshal Akhromeyev reached him by phone late that night.[160]

In accordance with long-established tradition, the entire Politburo was at the airport to welcome the general secretary back home from Berlin. There were the usual smiles and comradely bear hugs, but Gorbachev's eyes flashed with anger as he greeted his colleagues. According to his chief of staff, Gorbachev suspected that the generals had permitted Rust's plane to reach Red Square in a deliberate attempt to cause him political embarrassment. After this incident he would never trust the military again.[161]

"They have disgraced the country, humiliated our people," he told an aide, referring to the military leadership. "Well, so what, let everybody see

where power lies in this country. It lies with the political leadership, the Politburo. We will put an end to all this hysterical chatter about the military being in opposition to Gorbachev, about their wanting to replace him."[162]

At an emergency Politburo meeting the following day Gorbachev lambasted "the complete helplessness of the Defense Ministry" and accused senior generals of being "apprehensive" of perestroika. Turning to the defense minister, Marshal Sergei Sokolov, he said, "Under the present circumstances, if I were you, I would resign at once."[163] Sokolov stood at attention and resigned on the spot. More than 150 lower-ranking officers were dismissed or disciplined for "negligence."

To add insult to injury, Gorbachev selected a relatively unknown general, Dmitri Yazov, as his new minister of defense, passing over dozens of more senior officers. The military hierarchy deeply resented being singled out for such degrading treatment and the accompanying barrage of criticism in the Soviet media but could do nothing. As Akhromeyev acknowledged in his memoirs, its guilt was "undeniable."

The Rust incident was widely interpreted as a sign of Gorbachev's political dominance. However, it turned out to be one of the last occasions that the general secretary was able to impose his will on a united Politburo. Opposition to his policies was growing within the leadership, from both left and right. The battle for perestroika had just begun.

MOSCOW

October 21, 1987

AS A REVOLUTIONARY ELITE, committed to building a utopian society by force, the Communists understood that they would always be a minority. In order to impose their views on the majority and stay in power, they had to stick together. If cracks were allowed to appear in the Communist monolith, the party would lose its aura of historical infallibility. The entire system would rapidly fall apart. That was why there was no greater crime in the Bolshevik lexicon than "factionalism." The traitor within was more dangerous than the enemy without.

The "unshakable unity" of the Communist movement was of course a myth. The East European Communist parties, particularly the Polish party, were riven by internal struggles. The Soviet party accommodated hard-line Stalinists, social democrats, and careerists without any ideology at all. The doctrine of democratic centralism permitted party members to express their opinions freely—at least in theory—provided they abided by the decisions of "higher authorities." What was banned was organized opposition to the "party line," as promulgated by the leadership. This included the creation of factions within the party or—an even bigger heresy—any attempt to influence the internal debate by appealing to public opinion. The men who waved to the crowds from the top of the Lenin Mausoleum were

expected to speak with a single voice and abide by a single code of behavior.

The iron conventions of Communist Party politics were to be shattered by a Siberian named Boris Yeltsin. Constructed like a human bulldozer with very poor brakes, he was accustomed to pushing aside any obstacle that lay in his path. Six feet four inches tall, with a pugnacious face and a mane of white hair, he had an almost animal sense of power and territory. Hardworking, stubborn, independent, self-confident to a fault, he was what the Russians call a *nastoiashchii nachalnik* (a real boss). His leadership abilities propelled him upward, from running a construction site in the Ural Mountains to regional party secretary to the Politburo in Moscow.

"For more than thirty years now, I have been a boss," he writes in his memoirs. "That's exactly what people of my social class in Russia are called. Not a bureaucrat, not an official, not a director, but a boss. I can't stand the word—there's something about it that smacks of the chain gang. But what can you do? Perhaps being first was always a part of my nature, but I just didn't realize it in my early years."[164]

In addition to being a natural leader, Yeltsin was a born rebel. As a child he was always getting into scrapes. His boxer's nose, which is broken in the middle, was the result of a childhood fight with older boys, when he was whacked across the face with the shaft of a cart. A few years later, during the war, he stole a hand grenade from the ammunition store. It exploded while he was attempting to dismantle it, blowing off two fingers of his left hand.

The young Boris had an ingrained disdain for authority figures. He was expelled from school at the age of twelve after publicly accusing the head teacher of abusing the children "mentally and psychologically."[165] It was a drama that repeated itself over and over again, as he made his way from a remote Siberian village to the corridors of Kremlin power. He got into arguments with university professors, construction foremen, plant directors, party secretaries. The plot and cast of supporting characters changed, but the climactic scene always remained the same: a furious denunciation of a powerful—and, in Yeltsin's eyes, unworthy—superior.

It was this combination of leader and rebel that made Yeltsin such a formidable opponent. If he could not climb to the top of the Communist Olympus, he would destroy the party from within. With his intimate knowledge of nomenklatura politics and his skill at exposing the party's internal divisions, he was more dangerous than any dissident.

"It was as if there were two people inside Yeltsin," recalled his loyal aide

Lev Sukhanov. "The first Yeltsin was a party leader, accustomed to power and privilege, and devastated when it was all taken away. The second Yeltsin was a rebel, who rejected the rules of the game imposed by the system. These two Yeltsins fought each other."[166]

The man who was to become the first freely elected leader in Russia's thousand-year history was born on February 1, 1931, in the squalid village of Butko, on the eastern side of the Ural Mountains, which divide Europe from Asia. The Yeltsin family owned a windmill, a threshing machine, five horses, and four cows. This was enough to qualify as kulaks, or rich peasants, by the standards of Stalin's collectivization campaign. Boris's mother, religiously devout, like most Russian peasants, made sure that he was christened soon after birth. In this and some other respects Yeltsin's childhood resembles that of Mikhail Gorbachev, his almost exact contemporary and future political nemesis. The main difference is that Yeltsin was a product of the great Russian heartland, while Gorbachev was born on the southern fringes of the country, where there was no tradition of serfdom.

Like the Gorbachevs, the Yeltsin family suffered as a result of the murderous collectivization drive. When Boris was three years old, his father and uncle were accused of being kulaks and "wreckers" and given three-year terms in a labor camp. This blemish on the family record was something the Yeltsins, like the Gorbachevs, blanked out of their lives. Although Yeltsin had vivid memories of his father's being dragged away in the middle of the night, he never mentioned the incident publicly until long after the collapse of communism.[167]

In 1955, the year Gorbachev graduated from the law school of Moscow State University, Yeltsin completed his studies in the construction faculty of the Urals Polytechnic in Sverdlovsk, formerly Ekaterinburg. A bastion of the military-industrial complex, Sverdlovsk was even more tightly sealed off from the outside world than other Soviet cities. The city was entirely off-limits to foreigners until 1991. For an ambitious young man like Yeltsin, there was no alternative to "Soviet reality." He devoted his energy to making the system work.

Yeltsin's former associates in the city describe him as a tough and unforgiving taskmaster. Appointed regional party secretary in 1976, the former builder ran the city like a giant construction site, setting firm deadlines and personally inspecting the work of his subordinates. If a project was not completed on time, he made sure that someone was punished. In one celebrated incident he announced he would travel along a projected 220-mile highway from Sverdlovsk to the northern town of Serov in exactly a year. Officials

from every village and town along the route were told to accompany him. Those who failed to complete their allotted sections on time were warned that they would be thrown off the bus and made to walk.

In his autobiography, *Against the Grain*, Yeltsin recalls the "intoxicating sense of power" enjoyed by regional party bosses who ran their fiefdoms like little tsars. "Whether I was chairing a meeting, running my office, or delivering a report, everything that one did was expressed in terms of pressure, threats, and coercion. At the time, these methods did produce some results, especially if the boss in question was sufficiently strong-willed."[168]

Yeltsin's ability to get things done earned him considerable popularity in Sverdlovsk. It also impressed his superiors in Moscow, notably the party secretary in charge of cadres, the conservative Yegor Ligachev. At Ligachev's recommendation Yeltsin was transferred to the Soviet capital in April 1985, a month and a half after Gorbachev became general secretary. By the end of the year Yeltsin had been promoted to the key post of secretary of the Moscow party committee.

As Moscow party chief Yeltsin quickly displayed a talent for popular, crowd-pleasing gestures. He fired dozens of bureaucrats, encouraged people to air their grievances, and began to reorganize the notoriously corrupt retail trade. To demonstrate his concern for ordinary Muscovites, he rode the crowded, ramshackle buses that brought workers in from their dreary suburbs and toured the half-empty grocery stores where housewives scavenged for food. A television crew often accompanied him on these occasions, provoking complaints from Politburo colleagues that he was seeking "cheap popularity." Yeltsin's real crime was that he was breaking the unwritten code of conduct for Soviet leaders. By ostentatiously giving up his Zil limousine, even for a few hours, he was undermining the system of nomenklatura privileges. A Soviet leader's authority derived from his position in the bureaucracy, rather than his standing with the people. By daring to distinguish himself from his fellow apparatchiks, Yeltsin was destroying the party's monolithic facade.

In seeking to establish his own direct link with the *narod*, Yeltsin was following a trail blazed by Gorbachev. What he failed, or refused, to understand was that they were playing by different sets of rules. As the supreme leader of the state a general secretary was permitted to have his own unique personality. His underlings were expected to remain faceless members of the collective. Besides, there was a hesitant, conditional quality about Gorbachev's relationship with the masses. For Gorbachev, glasnost was a means to an end, a way of bringing pressure on the party from outside. The party

remained the ultimate source of his power. Yeltsin, by contrast, was coming dangerously close to rejecting party discipline altogether.

In the early stage of perestroika, Yeltsin and Gorbachev had been natural allies. When his reform plans ran into a brick wall, Gorbachev used the human battering ram from Siberia to clear a way forward. It was important that the Politburo have a radical wing, to balance the naturally conservative majority. That way the general secretary could present himself as a man of compromise. As Yeltsin notes in his memoirs, "If Gorbachev didn't have a Yeltsin, he would have to invent one. . . . In this real-life production, the parts have been well cast, as in a well-directed play. There is the conservative Ligachev, who plays the villain; there is Yeltsin, the bully-boy, the madcap radical; and the wise, omniscient hero is Gorbachev himself. That, evidently, is how he sees it."[169]

The Moscow experience had radicalized Yeltsin. He understood that the old command-and-administer methods would no longer work. He was frustrated that he was no longer his own master, as he had been in Sverdlovsk. Instead of helping him, his Politburo colleagues seemed intent on undermining his authority. He was particularly upset with his old patron Ligachev, who had come to personify the party machine. As the second-ranking figure in the leadership Ligachev chaired meetings of the all-powerful Secretariat, which supervised the work of lower party bodies. Yeltsin complained that the Secretariat was constantly interfering in Moscow's affairs. For his part, Ligachev dismissed Yeltsin as a demagogue, who talked a lot and did very little.

The stage was set for one of the most dramatic showdowns of the Gorbachev era.

A SENSE OF EXCITEMENT surged through the wood-paneled conference hall as Gorbachev strode to the podium at precisely 10:00 a.m. There was a single item on the agenda of the Central Committee: the speech on Soviet history that the general secretary intended to deliver to mark the seventieth anniversary of the Bolshevik Revolution on November 7. In a democracy the subject matter would have sounded arcane. In a crumbling dictatorship, such as the Soviet Union, it was electrifying, because it went to the heart of the way the country had been ruled and the kind of society it aspired to become. In a totalitarian state, writes George Orwell in his novel *1984*, "He who controls the present controls the past. He who controls the past controls the future."

The conference hall—the same room where Gorbachev had been elected general secretary two and a half years earlier—was packed. Sitting in front of the *gensek* were the cream of the Soviet nomenklatura: party secretaries; generals; ministers; leading cultural figures; industrialists. A thick autumn fog had closed the city's airports, and several dozen Central Committee members from distant parts of the country had been unable to reach Moscow in time for the plenum. Their places were taken by the commanders of military districts and regional party bosses. Like a pope delivering an encyclical, the general secretary was promulgating a new party line. When the conclave was over, the cardinals of the Communist Church would go forth and spread the Word.

The message that Gorbachev wanted to convey on this occasion was that the party had erred and strayed from the one true faith. Stalin was bad, but Lenin was good. Salvation lay at hand if the party could cleanse itself of the Stalinist "filth" and return to its Leninist roots. Communism not only could but must be reformed.

After the obligatory preamble, hailing the "colossal, grandiose achievements" of the revolution, Gorbachev set about demolishing the reputation of the man who had led the Soviet state for twenty-nine of its seventy years. He poured scorn on the notion that Stalin was somehow unaware of the mass repressions committed by his underlings. Stalin's personal involvement, he told Central Committee members, was fully documented and "unforgivable." To illustrate his point, he gave some specific figures. Only one member of the 1924 Politburo—Stalin himself—survived the great purges. Other victims of the terror included 60 percent of the delegates to the 1934 congress, 70 percent of the Central Committee that they elected, "thousands of Red commanders who constituted the flower of the army on the eve of Hitler's aggression," and "many thousands of honest party and nonparty people."[170] (This was a grotesque underestimate. The total number of Stalin's victims, including those who died as a result of artificially induced famines and the forced resettlement of entire nations, which Gorbachev did not mention, is generally believed to lie in the range of thirty to forty million.)

By the standards of the time, it was a bold speech. Getting the Politburo to agree to the paragraph about Stalin's "crimes" had been a major breakthrough, requiring weeks of argument. As usual, however, it took the general secretary far too long to make his point. As he droned on—for an hour, for two hours, for four hours—his attacks on the enemies of perestroika got lost in a general ideological fog. Perhaps this was his intention. In order to

destroy the totalitarian monster, he had to proceed by stealth. If his Communist party followers had understood where he was leading them, they would certainly have rebelled a great deal sooner than they eventually did. A master of Kremlin intrigue, Gorbachev had perfected the art of camouflaging a major policy shift behind a rhetorical smoke screen. He would casually throw out the seed of a new idea and then sit back and watch it grow, adjusting his moral judgments to the political needs of the moment.

As far as Yeltsin was concerned, Gorbachev's talent for vacillation and compromise was also his greatest failing. He was sick of the Byzantine maneuverings, the interminable ideological discussions, the constant sabotage of the apparatchiks. The fawning atmosphere surrounding the general secretary was another source of irritation. Yeltsin never forgot the fact that just a few years previously Gorbachev was running a relatively unimportant agricultural region, whereas he, Yeltsin, had been responsible for one of the most important industrial fiefdoms in the country.[171] While he admired Gorbachev's courage for launching perestroika, at a time when he could have sat still and enjoyed the perquisites of power, Yeltsin was disillusioned by the lack of concrete results.

Yeltsin had come to the Central Committee plenum with a scrap of paper listing his grievances. He knew that the action he was about to take was politically suicidal, at least in traditional Communist Party terms. At the back of his mind there may have been a vague sense that the ground rules of Soviet politics were changing and he could carve out a new role for himself. Popular dissatisfaction with growing economic difficulties—hardships that many people associated with perestroika—was becoming a factor that the leadership could no longer ignore. But his main motivation was almost certainly psychological. It was the same inner voice that had urged him to get up at his school graduation ceremony, at the age of eleven, and denounce the teacher for being a sadist. The voice told him to screw his courage to the sticking point, say what was on his mind, and damn the consequences.[172] When Gorbachev finished speaking, he raised his hand.

Ligachev was in the chair. At first he did not see his political enemy, even though he was sitting in the front row with other candidate members of the Politburo. The second secretary was about to bring the plenum to its customary close, a unanimous endorsement of everything the general secretary had said, when Gorbachev interrupted him.

"Comrade Yeltsin has some kind of statement to make."

Yeltsin's speech was disjointed. A smoother politician would have focused his attacks on one or two vulnerable targets. But Yeltsin scattered

his criticism in all directions, taking on the entire political establishment. He began by denouncing Ligachev and the powerful Central Committee Secretariat for "an intolerable style of work" that relied on "bullying reprimands" and constant "dressings down." He then moved on to the failures of perestroika. The people were disillusioned by two or three years of empty promises, and their faith had "begun to ebb." The party's authority was falling. He concluded with a direct assault on Gorbachev's style of leadership. He claimed to detect the beginnings of a new "personality cult" in the excessive adulation of certain Politburo members toward the general secretary. If left unchecked, such a tendency could become very dangerous. He was implying, in effect, that the father of glasnost could become another Stalin. Gorbachev's face flushed with rage at this observation.[173]

There was a long pause as the burly Siberian collected his thoughts and summoned up his courage to say one last thing: "I am clearly out of place as a member of the Politburo. For various reasons. There is the question of my experience, and other factors too, including the lack of support from some quarters, particularly Comrade Ligachev. That has led me to ask you to release me from the duties of a candidate member of the Politburo."[174]

"Having said all that, I sat down," Yeltsin recalled later. "My heart was pounding, and seemed ready to burst out of my ribcage. I knew what would happen next. I would be slaughtered, in an organized, methodical manner, and the job would be done almost with pleasure and enjoyment."[175]

Events developed exactly as Yeltsin had foreseen. Gorbachev was furious that the ritual display of unity on a festive occasion had been shattered. While on holiday, he had received a letter from Yeltsin outlining his grievances and threatening to resign. But he thought he had persuaded his protégé to postpone the showdown until after the anniversary celebrations.[176] His own political maneuvering room had been drastically reduced. He now had no alternative but to sit back and watch the conservatives tear the most radical member of the Politburo to bits.

First to speak was Ligachev, the darling of the apparatchiks, who accused Yeltsin of "the purest form of slander." By daring to suggest that the public was losing confidence in perestroika, Yeltsin had "raised doubts about our entire policy." Other speakers accused the Moscow party boss of being a "quitter," a "wrecker of party unity," a "demagogue," a "coward," a "nihilist." In all, twenty-five members of the Central Committee took the floor in the debate. Only one had a remotely kind word to say for Yeltsin. That was Georgi Arbatov, the Kremlin's resident Americanologist, who praised the heretic for his "courage," while joining the others in deploring the rift in party unity.

Numerous foreign dignitaries had been invited for the seventieth anniversary celebrations, and the show had to go on. Yeltsin appeared on the top of the Lenin Mausoleum with the rest of the leadership for the big military parade on November 7. But he was already feeling the burden of social ostracism. As soon as the celebrations were over, he was thrown to the wolves.

Yeltsin was taken to the hospital on November 9. According to his own account, he was suffering from nervous tension, severe chest pains, and excruciating headaches. Gorbachev later accused him of staging a fake suicide by slashing himself across the rib cage with a pair of office scissors. "I was already aware of Yeltsin's propensity for invention," the Soviet leader wrote later.[177]

Three days later Gorbachev summoned Yeltsin to a plenary session of the Moscow party committee. In his memoirs Yeltsin describes how he was pumped full of drugs and hauled before his accusers. "I could not understand such cruelty," he wrote later. "My head was spinning, my legs were crumpling under me, I could hardly speak because my tongue wouldn't obey. . . . Scarcely able to shuffle my feet, I was almost like a robot."[178]

The Moscow plenum resembled a Stalinist show trial. Ligachev with a smile of triumph on his face sat up on the podium beside Gorbachev. There was little pretense of giving Yeltsin a fair hearing. Instead his erstwhile colleagues and subordinates lined up to denounce him in the harshest possible way. Few of them knew what Yeltsin had actually said at the Central Committee meeting—the proceedings were not published until two years later—but they attacked him anyway. Working for Boris Nikolayevich was "torture," said one district secretary. Another accused him of being the only person in Russia who did not "love Moscow or Muscovites." A third official criticized his "cruelty." A fourth complained that his regular personnel changes had become a "bad joke." After his tormentors had had their say, Yeltsin did what the accused nearly always did on such occasions. He meekly confessed his "guilt" before the party and before "Mikhail Sergeyevich Gorbachev, whose prestige in our organization, in our country, and in the whole world is so high."[179]

When it was all over, Yeltsin collapsed across the table. As he was leaving the room, Gorbachev saw him out of the corner of his eye and turned back. He grabbed Yeltsin by the elbow and led him back to his old office. They sat there, talking for a while, before an ambulance came to collect Yeltsin and take him back to the hospital. A few days later Yeltsin got a

phone call from Gorbachev, offering him a job as deputy head of the state building conglomerate, Gosstroi. It was a ministerial-level position, but outside the charmed circle of Politburo members and Communist Party secretaries. Yeltsin accepted immediately.

"I will never allow you back into big-time politics," the general secretary added.[180]

Rarely have more fateful words ever been spoken by a Russian leader.

MOSCOW

March 14, 1988

THE OFFICIAL BLACK CARS deposited the men responsible for molding Soviet public opinion outside an imposing portico on Staraya Ploshchad (Old Square) emblazoned with the words "Central Committee of the Communist Party of the Soviet Union." Uniformed KGB guards snapped to attention as the editors in chief entered the building, flashing the little red booklets that identified them as members of the nomenklatura. The visitors checked their coats into the ground floor cloakroom and then took the elevator to the fifth floor, where the party's ideology secretary had his office.

If the Kremlin was the symbolic heart of the Soviet Union, the place where the Politburo held its regular Thursday meetings and foreign leaders were received, Old Square was the political nerve center. For decades the virtually unchecked authority of the totalitarian state had been concentrated in a labyrinth of buildings between the Lubyanka Prison and the Kremlin. Everything of significance that happened in the Soviet Union—from the approval of five-year plans to the appointment of a factory director in faraway Siberia—was grist to its bureaucratic machinery. Central Committee departments issued binding instructions to ministers and newspaper editors, army officers and Russian Orthodox bishops, factory managers and ambassadors. A special communications system, nicknamed the

vertushka, linked the Central Committee with every important decision maker in the country.

Occupying a city block, the Central Committee was a luxuriously appointed bureaucratic machine. No expense was spared to ensure that everything was in perfect running order, in stark contrast with the rest of Moscow, with its crumbling facades and potholed streets. Every office was repainted once a year. A special furniture factory produced the desks, cupboards, lecterns, and long conference tables that adorned the offices of the apparatchiks. An entire section of the Ministry of Health—the Ninth Directorate—looked after the health of Soviet leaders. The Central Committee's own farm supplied ecologically uncontaminated food for the staff restaurants, thus ensuring that the "servants of the people" did not have to eat the same poisoned food products as the people they served. When a senior official needed a new suit or a pair of shoes, he was outfitted by a special Central Committee tailor or shoemaker. Lower-level employees had access to a special section of the Gum department store on Red Square.

In the Communist utopia created by the apparatchiks for their own benefit, every rung on the bureaucratic ladder had its own special privileges and rewards. Dachas, medals, clothing allowances, and even cemetery lots all were distributed according to a Byzantine table of ranks. Instructors had the right to a new fur hat once every two years, while secretaries and drivers were limited to one every three years. A visitor could tell where power lay in the Central Committee by following the carpet runner in the hallway. It glided past the offices of ordinary apparatchiks but made right-angle detours into the suites of the top leaders. Another telltale sign was the portraits of the Communist deities. When a bureaucrat reached the rank of deputy head of department, he was automatically allocated a portrait of Marx instead of the standard portrait of Lenin. Heads of department had large portraits of both Marx and Lenin on their walls. Then there was the question of how tea was served. A lower-ranking official was served tea on a plain tray. Once he reached the rank of chief of sector, the tray suddenly sprouted a napkin. In apparatchik-speak, the promotion was referred to as "receiving the napkin."

The fifth floor of the old Central Committee building, where the editors in chief alighted from the elevator, was the inner sanctum of the Communist cathedral. The carpet runners were thicker here than on other floors of the building, the brass lamps in the corridors had a special sheen that came from daily polishing, and the walnut-paneled offices were large enough to accommodate entire committees. Voices were kept to a respectful hush. This

was the only place in the building where an official was permitted to sit directly beneath the portrait of Lenin. (Elsewhere the portrait was placed a little to one side.) It was as if the founder of the Soviet state were speaking to future generations through the occupants of these offices. Everything was done to bolster the impression that they were his spiritual heirs.

Apart from the chief ideologist, only two other people had offices on the fifth floor: the secretary in charge of the Soviet economy and the *gensek* himself. The ideology secretary's office was in a front corner of the building, with a fine view of KGB headquarters and the towering statue of Feliks Dzerzhinsky, the founder of the Soviet secret police. For more than a quarter of a century the "gray cardinal" of Kremlin politics, Mikhail Suslov, had held court in this office, defending the purity of Marxist-Leninist dogma. Suslov, a stern figure of unbending rectitude, with the manner of a dried-up professor, had struck fear into an entire generation of Soviet and foreign Communists with his withering denunciations of anyone who dared think differently. Suslov was to ideology what Gromyko was to foreign policy: Comrade Nyet. As far as he was concerned, all change was bad, almost by definition. When Suslov finally died, in 1982, Office No. 2 was inhabited in turn by Yuri Andropov, Konstantin Chernenko, and Mikhail Gorbachev. The latest occupant of the office was Yegor Ligachev.

Together with many senior apparatchiks, Ligachev had unpleasant memories of Office No. 2. He himself had been the target of some of Suslov's tirades.[181] In many ways, however, the former party secretary from Tomsk was a worthy successor to the "gray cardinal." He was energetic, incorruptible, and ideologically blinkered. His entire adult life had been spent in the service of the party. Like Gorbachev and Yeltsin, Ligachev had direct experience of the Stalinist terror. His father-in-law, a Red Army general, had been arrested in 1936 on the absurd charge of being an "Anglo-Japanese-German spy" and executed at the end of a ten-minute trial. As a Communist youth leader in 1949 Ligachev himself had come under suspicion of "Trotskyism" and had been lucky to escape arrest.[182] But his faith in socialism had never wavered. His subordinates were sick of hearing him talk about his seventeen years in Siberia—that "severe but wonderful land"—as the happiest and most satisfying period of his life. Ligachev was a short, gruff man, with the face of a pugilist, who had an imperious manner and a voice that brimmed with moral certainty. When he opened his mouth, it was as if he were speaking for the entire Central Committee.

In the early days of perestroika, Ligachev and Gorbachev had seen eye to eye. Dismayed by the stagnation of the Brezhnev era, they shared a com-

mon determination to breathe new life into socialism. Ligachev was happy to serve as Gorbachev's hatchet man, purging the party of incompetent and corrupt officials and whipping its regional organizations into line. If glasnost meant diagnosing the defects of the planned economy and putting them right, he was all for it. As time went on, however, he became increasingly alarmed over the direction that glasnost was taking and the party's inability to control events. He later said that he began having serious doubts about the political course being followed by Gorbachev from late 1987 onward. "At some point this man became something else. He underwent a political rebirth. As our economic difficulties mounted, he began to look for solutions that led to the destruction of everything we believed in."[183]

Ligachev had a puritan's distaste for such undesirable social phenomena as pornography and rock concerts. But what really enraged him was what he saw as the increasingly revisionist and negative attitude toward Soviet history. In his view, giving editors the green light to denounce Stalin's "crimes" had opened the floodgates to a general "blackening" of everything the party had accomplished since 1917.

As ideology secretary Ligachev had done his best to prevent glasnost from getting out of hand. He had hit the roof in September 1987, when the weekly *Moscow News* dared publish an obituary of the émigré Russian writer Viktor Nekrasov, a nonperson as far as Kremlin propagandists were concerned. But Ligachev was finding his job increasingly difficult. Holding back the rising tide of anti-Sovietism was like trying to plug a leaking dike. He ran frantically from one gap in the Soviet Union's ideological defense system to another, yelling at newspaper editors and giving speeches bemoaning the loss of traditional Communist values, but the waters kept on rising. The ideological dam had been breached in dozens of places. Unless dramatic action was taken, there was a serious danger that it would be swept away altogether.

Ligachev's problem was that the traditional methods—a discreet telephone call here, a party reprimand there—no longer worked as effectively as they had. Once-servile mass media organs, such as *Moscow News* and *Ogonyok*, had managed to slip out of his grasp. New television programs, such as *Vzglyad* (Glance), aimed at the youth audience, were constantly testing the ideological limits, running items about Afghan war veterans or the spread of AIDS or hard-currency prostitutes. In the Baltic states censorship regulations were getting particularly lax. At the beginning of March a Russian-language journal in Latvia had begun publishing Orwell's *Animal Farm*, the classic denunciation of totalitarianism.

The party's monopoly over the dissemination of information was also being undermined by the technological revolution. Up until very recently every photocopier in the country had been kept under lock and key. Such tight control was no longer feasible if the Soviet Union wanted to compete in the modern world. Preventing the politically unreliable from getting their hands on the latest generation of information technology–such as VCRs, computers, laser printers, satellite dishes, and fax machines—was equally daunting.

The time had come to mount a general counteroffensive. Like a commander in chief briefing his generals, the ideology secretary intended to outline his plan of attack at his meeting with the editors in chief.

LIGACHEV'S PROBLEMS WERE COMPOUNDED by the fact that two floors below, another Politburo member was intent on taking Soviet society in an altogether different direction. An owlish figure with bushy eyebrows and a fondness for three-piece suits, Aleksandr Yakovlev was the most erudite member of the leadership, and also the most radical. By temperament and political conviction, he and Ligachev were polar opposites. Ligachev was overbearing and insensitive to others. Yakovlev was introspective and easily offended. Ligachev wanted to maintain a tight grip over what Soviet citizens should be permitted to read and say. Yakovlev favored shining the torch of glasnost on previously taboo subjects, including the holy of holies, Lenin himself. If Ligachev was the hero of the apparatchiks, Yakovlev was the darling of the intellectuals.

At sixty-four, Yakovlev was nearing the end of an epic intellectual journey. It had taken him from a tiny village on the banks of the Volga River, in the historic heart of Russia, to the heart of Soviet power; from a once-ardent faith in the "shining" socialist future to a conviction that Soviet-style communism was doomed. Back in 1985 he had believed, along with Gorbachev, that the system could be reformed. The desperate rearguard action put up by his fellow apparatchiks during the first two years of perestroika had destroyed his remaining illusions. By his own account, the turning point came in January 1987, when he and Gorbachev had come up with a proposal for competitive elections to party posts. The intention had been to introduce a degree of democracy within the party and unleash the latent energy of the Soviet elite, but the result had been a storm of protests from the nomenklatura.

"That is when it became clear to me that the system could not be re-

formed. It had to be broken," said Yakovlev in 1993. "At first I thought that we could achieve what we wanted to achieve by eliminating the stupidities associated with the Brezhnev version of socialism and allowing people to display some initiative. But it turned out that the system would not permit this. The system is based on fear and the lack of individual responsibility. Any attempt by an individual to use his initiative was bound to shake the system to its foundations."[184]

Yakovlev's ideological conversion had been long and tortuous, and it involved the painful rethinking of many deeply held beliefs. The descendant of Yaroslavl serfs, he was impressed by the way in which a backward, rural country managed to transform itself into a modern industrial state, vanquishing illiteracy in the process. His father, Nikolai, had fought with the Reds in the civil war and, like Gorbachev's grandfather, became the first chairman of the local collective farm. Unlike Gorbachev, however, Yakovlev had little direct experience of the terror. Nikolai Yakovlev managed to avoid arrest through the simple stratagem of leaving the village for several days at a time when the secret police were rounding up "enemies of the people." Like everybody else in the Soviet Union, the NKVD had a plan to fulfill. After grabbing the required quota of "enemies" from the Yaroslavl region, it moved on. When he learned that the coast was clear, Yakovlev's father returned home.[185]

At the age of seventeen Yakovlev went idealistically to war, shouting, "For Stalin! For the motherland!" with his friends as they charged German lines. As a lieutenant in the marines he saw a lot of gruesome action. Neither side bothered with prisoners. Many of his friends were killed. He would have been killed himself had it not been for the tradition in the Soviet Marines of never leaving a wounded soldier on the battlefield. When he was riddled by Nazi machine-gun fire in a swamp outside Leningrad, his friends dragged him to safety. Four of them sacrificed their lives in the process, but Yakovlev was saved. He returned home a permanent cripple. Of his school year, only three students out of every one hundred survived the war.

Yakovlev's first faint doubts about Stalin occurred after the war, when he saw how the regime treated Soviet prisoners coming home from Germany. Instead of being greeted as heroes and helped to begin a new life, the POWs were packed off to prison camps again—Soviet camps this time—for fear that they might be ideologically contaminated. "There was no way I could accept this. It was a terrible shame," said Yakovlev later. His doubts were strengthened in 1956, when he sat in the balcony of a Kremlin meeting hall as Nikita Khrushchev denounced Stalin's crimes in his celebrated "secret speech." The accounts of purges, deportations, and mass atrocities "turned

me inside out," Yakovlev recollected. "No one looked at anyone else. There was only silence as Khrushchev revealed fact after fact, each one worse than the last."[186]

Fate decreed that Yakovlev would witness another epoch-making event, the Soviet invasion of Czechoslovakia in 1968. By that time he had risen to become acting head of the propaganda department of the Central Committee. He arrived in Prague a day after the Red Army acted to crush Dubček's experiment in socialism with a human face as the ideological watchdog for a group of Soviet journalists. It quickly became clear to Yakovlev that the official explanation for the invasion—a "Jewish-American conspiracy" to overthrow socialism in Czechoslovakia—was a lie. During his five-day visit he saw Czechoslovak citizens burn the Soviet flag and attack Soviet tanks with Molotov cocktails. He heard them chanting, "Fascists, fascists," at the army that had supposedly come to provide "fraternal assistance." He saw Dubček—reviled by Yakovlev's fellow propagandists as a traitor to communism—being greeted as a national hero on his return from captivity in Moscow. "My visit to Czechoslovakia left a lasting impression on me," he told me. "It was a sign that the system was doomed."[187]

Like many of his colleagues, Yakovlev took care to conceal his personal views. Without an ability to lead a double life, he would not have survived in the bureaucracy, much less prospered. He claims that he gave Brezhnev an accurate account of the "real state of affairs" in Czechoslovakia. But his report must have been couched in extremely diplomatic terms since he was given a state award for his work in Prague and remained in his propaganda job for several more years. It was only after the collapse of communism and his retirement from high office that he talked about his Czechoslovak experiences in public.

The other great intellectual influence on Yakovlev was foreign travel. He was the only Politburo member with detailed personal knowledge of life in Western countries. As a rising apparatchik he had spent a year at Columbia University in 1958, in the first Soviet-American student exchange. Although he was impressed by American hospitality and technological achievements, he reacted negatively to moralizing lectures from his hosts about the inherent superiority of capitalism. Decades later he still smoldered at the memory of the Manhattan store clerk who asked him to remove his hat to check if it really was true that Communists had horns. He vented his resentment in a series of stridently anti-American tracts, with such titles as *The Ideology of the American Empire, The U.S.A.—from Great to Sick*, and *On the Edge of an Abyss*.

After getting into a literary brawl with Russian nationalists in 1972,

Yakovlev was sent into gilded exile as ambassador in Canada. He remained there for ten years, observing the workings of a Western democracy from up close and the tragicomic goings-on of the late Brezhnev era from afar. The Canadian experience gave Yakovlev the ability to view the problems of his own country with a degree of intellectual detachment. It also provided a relaxed setting for a remarkable series of conversations with Gorbachev in May 1983, during which the two men explored many of the ideas that ultimately led to perestroika. Gorbachev, then the youngest member of the Politburo with responsibility for agricultural affairs, was making his international debut with a ten-day visit to Canada. Yakovlev had the job of showing him around.

Yakovlev had met Gorbachev on several occasions in the early seventies but did not know him well. However, they had a very close friend in common, a man called Mark Mikhailov, who was from Stavropol, Gorbachev's hometown, and had worked for Yakovlev in the Central Committee. Thanks to this mutual friend, they knew that they could be frank with each other. The informal nature of Gorbachev's trip also helped. Hopping around Canada in an old prop-driven Convair plane, they discovered that they had remarkably similar views. At one stop their Canadian host failed to show up, and they had a long two-hour walk through the cornfields until they were caught in the rain. "I took advantage of the circumstances and told him what I really thought. He did the same," said Yakovlev.[188] Far from KGB eavesdroppers and their doddering Kremlin colleagues, they talked about the "stupidities" of Soviet foreign policy and the need for a radical change of direction at home.

Gorbachev brought Yakovlev back from his Canadian exile and helped him become director of a prestigious Moscow think tank, the Institute for World Economy and International Relations. After he became general secretary, he promoted Yakovlev to the Politburo and made him his closest confidant. Yakovlev was Gorbachev's ideas man, the intellectual powerhouse behind perestroika.

Although Yakovlev and Ligachev were political opposites, in one respect they were very similar. They both were skilled apparatchiks, accustomed to wielding power behind the scenes. On the basis of long experience, they had an intuitive feel for the backstage intrigues of the Central Committee bureaucracy. Although Yakovlev had a following among Moscow intellectuals, he lacked the populist instincts of a man like Yeltsin. Yakovlev believed that the real fight was in the Politburo, not on the streets, and that Yeltsin was harming the cause through his emotional, erratic behavior.

The supreme operating rule of big-time Kremlin politics was the principle of plausible deniability. Instructions were given verbally, often by telephone, in such a way that they could not be traced back to their source. Sometimes they consisted of little more than a wink and a nod. Like Ligachev, Yakovlev exerted his influence through a network of well-placed allies. He acted as the political patron of the self-proclaimed "kamikazes of glasnost," the radical newspaper editors who were constantly probing the ideological limits. They took responsibility for what appeared in their newspapers, but it was understood that he would protect them in a crisis.

A typical example of Yakovlev's methods came in October 1986 with the release of the anti-Stalinist film *Repentance*, one of the major breakthroughs of glasnost. A Felliniesque allegory set in Stalin's native Georgia, *Repentance* dealt with some of the most explosive issues of Soviet history as well as contemporary politics. Yakovlev knew that it would be difficult to get such a work approved by Politburo conservatives. In order to skirt around this obstacle, he reached a confidential understanding with the director of the film, Tengiz Abuladze. *Repentance* would not be officially released. Instead it would be shown by private invitation to select audiences. The number of screenings grew and grew until virtually the whole country had seen the film. *Repentance* became a nationwide sensation.

Once censorship was relaxed, Soviet journalists and filmmakers needed little encouragement from above to expose the dark secrets of the past. Nevertheless, conservatives like Ligachev soon began to view Yakovlev as the evil puppeteer, pulling the strings of his glasnost puppets. They blamed him for all their setbacks. In his memoirs Ligachev denounces Yakovlev as the éminence grise who distorted the true course of perestroika through his manipulation of the media. Doing battle with such a man was like fighting shadows. "We had no idea what a powerful and dangerous weapon the media could be in [conditions of] *glasnost* and pluralism. Aleksandr Yakovlev, who had spent many years in the West, naturally had a much better understanding of this than other members of the Politburo. From the very beginning he established a personal control over the right radical press."[189]

If socialism was to be saved, Ligachev knew that he had to fight back.

LIKE YAKOVLEV, LIGACHEV HAD his network of like-minded editors, who regarded him as their political patron. In March 1987 one of these editors, Valentin Chikin, launched a journalistic broadside against glasnost in

his newspaper, *Sovietskaya Rossiya*. It came in the form of a full-page article, headlined I CANNOT BETRAY MY PRINCIPLES, signed by an obscure Leningrad chemistry teacher named Nina Andreyeva. The headline was borrowed from a recent Gorbachev speech, but the article itself was the antithesis of practically everything the general secretary stood for. Andreyeva defended Stalin, called for a "class struggle both at home and abroad," and denounced the informal political groups that were springing up around the country. It was, Gorbachev said later, a direct assault "against perestroika."[190]

Exactly who was behind Andreyeva's tract later became a matter of great controversy. The radicals immediately suspected that Chikin was acting with Ligachev's protection and encouragement. The two men were certainly in close contact during this period. Ligachev repeatedly denied that he had anything to do with the article *before* publication, and the case against him has never been proved. Given the way such matters were handled, it is unlikely that a "smoking gun" will ever be found. In a sense it is irrelevant because the real issue with the Nina Andreyeva article was what happened *after* publication.

Had "I Cannot Betray My Principles" been the musings of a lone chemistry teacher, no one would have raised an eyebrow. By 1988 glasnost was well advanced, and opinions similar to Andreyeva's appeared in the press every day. What attracted attention, however, was their exceptionally prominent display in a leading party newspaper. The three-column photo spread of the author, wearing a Bolshevik-style leather jacket, surrounded by adoring students, was a signal to readers that her views had official approval. For the conservatives it was a call to arms.

The attempt to turn "I Cannot Betray My Principles" into the new party line began the day after publication, on the fifth floor of the Central Committee. Ligachev had deliberately avoided inviting the editors of the two most radical periodicals, *Ogonyok* and *Moscow News*, to the meeting, which took place in the Politburo conference room, around the corner from his office. After a few remarks about propaganda support for the spring sowing campaign and the development of livestock breeding, the ideology secretary turned to the subject that was uppermost in his mind.

"Have you read the article by Nina Andreyeva?" he asked the editors.

"Yes, we've read it," replied Ivan Laptev, the editor in chief of *Izvestia*. The official organ of the Soviet Parliament, *Izvestia* had become a strong supporter of glasnost, which Laptev feared could be endangered if Ligachev got his way.

"It's an excellent article, a wonderful example of party political writing. I would ask you, comrade editors, to be guided by the ideas of this article in your work," enthused Ligachev in his stentorian voice. He then turned to the head of the Tass news agency, regarded by thousands of provincial newspapers as the official voice of the Kremlin.

"Tass should distribute this article at once."[191]

His instructions were immediately carried out. Dozens of provincial newspapers republished the article. Party organizations across the country held special meetings to study it. Telegrams from "honest workers," supporting Andreyeva's views, flooded into the Central Committee. One morning the Communist Party newspaper *Pravda* even printed Ligachev's name ahead of his Politburo colleagues, elevating him to almost equal status with Gorbachev.[192] The liberal intelligentsia was in despair. Without a signal from the top, no one dared respond to Andreyeva and *Sovietskaya Rossiya*. People remembered the Brezhnev period of stagnation, when Khrushchev's thaw had turned back into a freeze, with little warning. The fate of perestroika seemed to lie in the balance.

Ligachev had timed his counteroffensive well. When he met the editors, Gorbachev had just left Moscow on an official visit to Yugoslavia. Yakovlev had flown off to Outer Mongolia, eight time zones away. It took three weeks for them to formulate a response.

THE KREMLIN

March 23, 1988

THE POLITBURO DEBATE over the Nina Andreyeva affair erupted unexpectedly. Gorbachev finally got around to reading the article on his return from Yugoslavia, on Saturday, March 19. He spent the weekend pondering its significance. The general secretary was uncertain how to react. On the one hand, he had no desire for a showdown with Ligachev, the party's deputy leader. On the other, if this was a deliberate assault on perestroika, as his radical advisers insisted, there would have to be some kind of reply.

The Politburo was not due to meet until the following Thursday, for its regular weekly meeting. On Wednesday, however, fate intervened. Several thousand collective farmers from all over the Soviet Union had descended on the Kremlin for their first congress in more than twenty years. As was customary on such occasions, Gorbachev opened the meeting with a two-hour speech. Behind him, on the stage of the Palace of Congresses, a vast, plushly decorated auditorium built to house big propaganda events by day and performances of *Swan Lake* by night, were most of his Politburo colleagues. When the *gensek* finally got through exhorting the kolkhozniks to be more efficient and display more initiative, the Politburo members filed backstage to the Presidium Room for tea and sandwiches. Without warning the chitchat turned to Nina Andreyeva.

"Yes," said Vitaly Vorotnikov, the prime minister of the Russian Federation, emphatically. "There was an article the other day in *Sovietskaya Rossiya*. A real, politically correct article. It was a model for our ideological work."[193]

Ligachev jumped into the conversation, with more lavish praise of Andreyeva. "It's good that the press is finally showing these . . ." He left the end of the sentence unspoken, realizing he was in polite company. "Otherwise everything would go to pieces."

The Politburo patriarch, Andrei Gromyko, supported Ligachev. "I think it was a good article. It will put everything back in its proper place." His fellow septuagenarian Mikhail Solomentsev, who had helped Ligachev organize the failed antialcohol campaign, added his two kopecks' worth in favor of Nina Andreyeva.

Gorbachev suddenly realized that he could not let the conversation continue in this fashion. Four full Politburo members, out of a total of thirteen, had just endorsed a political platform that was fundamentally different from his own. Unless he took a clear stand, he could quickly find himself in a minority, supported only by the two hard-core liberals Yakovlev and Shevardnadze. He would then be forced to embrace the views expressed in "I Cannot Betray My Principles" or resign.

"If you consider this article to be a model, then we have to clarify a few things. I have a different view."

"Well, well," shot back Vorotnikov, an Andropov protégé and early supporter of Gorbachev, increasingly dismayed by the radical direction that perestroika had taken.

"What do you mean 'well, well'?"

There was an awkward silence as Gorbachev and Vorotnikov glared at each other, and the other Politburo members glanced uneasily around the room.

"This smells of a schism," said Gorbachev fiercely, using the Russian word *raskol*, a Bolshevik term of abuse. "The article was directed against perestroika. I have never objected if someone expresses his personal opinion. Whatever views you want—in the press, in letters. But I've been told that there have been attempts to turn this article into a party directive. In some party organizations they are already adopting it as a resolution, like in the old days. The press has been forbidden to utter a word against it."

At this point Gorbachev decided to gamble everything on the strongest card in his hand, his immense political prestige, both at home and abroad. His Politburo critics may have tapped into a groundswell of Communist

Party dissatisfaction with the way perestroika was going, but they were disorganized and leaderless. Ligachev was a divisive, controversial figure. The rules of party discipline, plus ingrained habits of obedience, made it difficult for the conservatives to mount an open challenge to the general secretary. Their aim, at this stage, was not to replace the leader but to make him their spokesman. Gorbachev understood the contradiction in their position and exploited it brilliantly.

"I am not going to fight for my chair. But as long as I am here, as long as I occupy this position, I shall insist on the idea of perestroika," he declared, hinting that he was prepared to resign. "No, this is not going to succeed. We will discuss this matter in the Politburo."

THE POLITBURO MEETING LASTED for two days, an unprecedented length of time, even by glasnost standards. It began in the Kremlin on Thursday and continued all day Friday on the fifth floor of Old Square, in the same conference hall where Ligachev had heaped praise on the Andreyeva article, less than a fortnight previously. Much of the debate was taken up by the general secretary's long monologues. A mixture of waffling visionary and determined politician, Gorbachev had a unique ability to envelop an audience in billowing clouds of rhetoric, exhausting and disorienting everybody with his tortuous logic. The confusion of a good argument seemed to clarify his thinking and serve as a platform for action. He liked to quote Lenin: "The most important thing in any endeavor is to get involved in the fight, and in that way learn what to do next."[194] He could talk himself out of almost any crisis.

On this occasion the role of attack dog was played by Yakovlev, who took the Andreyeva article apart line by line. "This is an antiperestroika manifesto," he declared bluntly. He was supported by the prime minister, Nikolai Ryzhkov, who made an impassioned defense of perestroika and suggested that Ligachev be relieved of his position as ideology secretary. Ever the unctuous Georgian, Foreign Minister Shevardnadze described what was happening in the Soviet Union as the "major event of the twentieth century." "The issue here is nothing less than the salvation of socialism," he enthused. "A primitive approach could compromise our magnificent enterprise."[195]

Now that the debate had been framed in terms of perestroika—for or against—the outcome was clear. No one wanted to be labeled a "splitter" or "destroyer of party unity." The remaining Politburo members all hastened

to endorse the party line, as laid down by Gorbachev and Yakovlev. The conservatives soothed their consciences by grumbling about the "irresponsible" media. "Of course we are all for glasnost," remarked Gromyko, eager to make up for his lapse earlier in the week. "But it is intolerable that the Soviet people are presented in the press as a people of slaves, a people of lackeys. The thesis developed by *Sovietskaya Rossiya* was a reaction to this slander."

As the debate swirled around the question of who had issued the order to discuss Andreyeva's article at party meetings, Ligachev maintained a sullen silence. He later said that he found the atmosphere at the Politburo session "oppressive." It reminded him of a "witch-hunt." Yakovlev was clearly intent on making him take political responsibility for the affair and ousting him from the leadership. He was ready to defend himself, if necessary.[196]

Gorbachev decided not to press the point. He had won an important victory. He had got the Politburo to agree to issue an authoritative reply to Andreyeva in the pages of *Pravda*, to be drafted by Yakovlev. By now it was clear that he had the support of the Politburo's wobbly-kneed majority, who were willing to go along with practically anything their leader said. Wishing to avoid an open break with the conservatives, the general secretary helped Ligachev cover his traces. Like his opponents, he had an ingrained fear of *raskol*. He thought that little would be gained in having a Politburo composed of like-minded people if it was unable to push its decisions through the generally reactionary *apparat*, the vast bureaucratic machine that actually ran Russia.[197]

Pravda published its counterblast to "I Cannot Betray My Principles" on April 5, ending three weeks of national uncertainty about the future of perestroika. The unsigned editorial insisted that there were no "taboo subjects" and "no going back" to the policies of the past. A few weeks later Ligachev was relieved of his ideological portfolio and given the thankless job of rescuing Soviet agriculture from its chronic state of crisis.

THE NINA ANDREYEVA AFFAIR was a turning point for both the Soviet Union and Gorbachev. The floodgates of glasnost were opened once and for all. The trickle of revelations about the country's Stalinist past now became a veritable deluge. There was something new every day: the television premiere of Mikhail Bulgakov's "anti-Soviet" masterpiece *The Heart of a Dog*; the publication, by an Estonian newspaper, of the secret protocols

of the Molotov-Ribbentrop pact, demonstrating the collusion between the Soviet Union and Nazi Germany; a theater production of *Hope Against Hope*, Nadezhda Mandelshtam's epic description of the gulag; the decision by a Moscow court to release Vladimir Nabokov's erotic novel *Lolita*. The rewriting of Soviet history became so extensive that Soviet secondary schools were obliged to cancel all history exams, pending the release of new textbooks.

The rebirth of history triggered a sense of political exhilaration that transcended class barriers. The homeland of world socialism became a gigantic "debating society," in Gorbachev's phrase.[198] Highbrow intellectuals, frightened that they might miss something, spent hours glued to their television sets. Brawny workers thumbed through fat literary journals in search of a long-banned work by Akhmatova or Solzhenitsyn. Former prison camp inmates cast aside decades of caution and told their stories in public for the first time. Archivists for government agencies devoted their spare time to drawing up lists of the "repressed." A group called Memorial succeeded in gathering tens of thousands of signatures in several weeks to support demands for a center to commemorate Stalin's victims. Suddenly everybody seemed to have an opinion and was not afraid to voice it.

Gorbachev sensed this national mood and responded to it. By now he saw himself as a man of destiny, chosen by history to accomplish something very special. To a far greater extent than any of his colleagues, he had staked his reputation on the success of perestroika. He was the tsar-liberator, the farsighted ruler who had given the serfs their freedom. At Politburo meetings he occasionally compared himself to the great Lenin, who had launched a revolution through the sheer force of his political will. There was no going back now.

"You have certain goals in which you believe, and you are sure that you are right," he told his fellow Politburo members. "If this is the case, you have to go on, right to the end. Otherwise what kind of man are you, and why do you occupy this position? You have the country, the whole world, behind you. If you panic at the slightest setback, like some weak fellow, if you cry 'Help' and behave like an opportunist who is concerned only with saving his own skin, then all is lost."[199]

The Andreyeva affair made Gorbachev realize that he could no longer entrust his revolution solely to the party. He was taken aback by the strength of bureaucratic resistance to his ideas. "Now I realize the kind of people I've been working with," he told his chief of staff.[200] "You can forget about perestroika with people like that." He complained that many of his

Politburo colleagues lacked the political imagination to grasp the significance of what was happening in the Soviet Union. "It's as if there's a ceiling, right here," he said, waving a hand above his head.[201] The political
system would have to be opened up to outside forces.

At the end of the two-day Politburo meeting on the Andreyeva case,
when everybody was too exhausted to pay much attention, Gorbachev exploded one of his rhetorical bombs. "The people" were demanding changes
in the electoral system. Serious consideration would have to be given to how
to implement the Leninist slogan "All power to the Soviets," the representative organs that had, up until now, provided a constitutional fig leaf for
Communist dictatorship. The entire relationship between the party and the
Soviets would have to be "rethought."

Stripped of the ideological trappings, what the general secretary was
proposing was an end to seven decades of one-party rule.

LABOR CAMP PERM-35

July 8, 1988

MART NIKLUS FELT like the man in the proverbial time machine. An un-repentant Estonian nationalist, he had been dispatched to a "strict regime" labor camp in the Urals in 1980, at a time when the Brezhnev regime was preoccupied with the crises in Poland and Afghanistan. His contact with the outside world had been minimal. He spent his days sewing cords onto elec-tric irons. When he reached the required daily norm of 522 finished electric irons, he was allowed to take a forty-five-minute walk in a thirty-foot-long cage. If he protested, he was thrown into an unheated isolation cell, ten feet long, three feet wide, and six feet high. The nerve roots in his back had be-come chronically inflamed from sitting in the same position, day after day. Now he was going home.

Like many Estonians, Niklus was a man with a long memory. He re-membered how the Red Army had marched into his hometown of Tartu in June 1940, when he was a nine-year-old boy. He remembered how his coun-try had been incorporated into the Soviet Union against its will and how the cream of the Estonian nation had been deported to Siberia. He remembered the postwar purges and the campaign of terror against private farmers. Un-like most of his countrymen, however, he did not keep quiet about what he had seen. At Tartu University he organized groups of students to listen to

Western radio stations. He made copies of the text of the secret protocols of the Molotov-Ribbentrop pact—unearthed by Western historians in the former Nazi archives—and distributed them as widely as he could. He tried to stage street demonstrations on Estonia's prewar independence day. The authorities considered him a "dangerous recidivist." They sentenced him to long prison terms for "anti-Soviet agitation," only to see him resume his seditious activities as soon as he was released. By 1988 the former zoologist had spent nearly twenty of his fifty-seven years in Soviet penal institutions.

Since his most recent incarceration three general secretaries had died in office, and nothing had changed at Perm-35. The new general secretary had come into office, angrily denying that the Soviet Union had a human rights problem.[202] Vague rumors had reached the camp—the last remaining outpost in the once-sprawling "Gulag Archipelago"—of new political slogans, like glasnost and perestroika. But no one seemed to know what they meant. Initially Niklus was skeptical that they meant anything at all. As recently as 1986 a fellow political prisoner, Anatoly Marchenko, had died of the treatment he received at Perm-35. When Niklus asked a prison guard when they could expect to see some "restructuring" in the gulag, he was told: "We don't know. We only follow the rules; we have received no instructions."[203]

Niklus began to suspect that something might be changing when several nearby labor camps were closed. The population of Perm-35 began to decline. By mid-1988 there were only several dozen political prisoners left in the camp that had once housed such eminent anti-Soviet "hooligans" as Natan Shcharansky, Vladimir Bukovsky, and Yuri Orlov. On June 15 Niklus received a visit from two officials of the Estonian KGB. They brought him a food parcel from home, gave him some chocolates—an unimaginable luxury in Perm-35—and asked, very politely, if he would like to write a letter to his mother. He was permitted to receive Estonian newspapers, and soon he was reading about a demonstration in Tartu demanding his release. On June 30, still sitting in prison, he read an interview with a senior official announcing that he had already been freed and was on his way home. His reaction was to begin an immediate hunger strike.

It took another week for the release order to make its way down through the prison bureaucracy. On July 8 Niklus was escorted out of the barbed-wire enclosure, and taken to the Perm railway station. He sent a telegram to his mother, hoping that someone would show up at Tartu railway station to help him with his luggage. Then, still dressed in the striped black clothes reserved for specially dangerous prisoners, he boarded a train to a country of newspaper fable, the land of perestroika.

The "dangerous recidivist" was unprepared for the welcome he received in Tartu. Thousands of well-wishers showed up at the train station, offering him flowers and waving the long-banned flag of the prewar Estonian republic. There were banners with slogans like "We want perestroika without the KGB" and "We want to leave the Soviet Union." "It was the most fantastic moment of my life," Niklus recalled later. "They didn't simply carry my bags; they carried me, on their shoulders. Everyone wanted to touch me." He was paraded around the town, like a returning sports hero, and made a little speech about Estonian independence. Within two hours he heard his halting, emotional words being broadcast over the same state radio that had once denounced him as an "enemy of the Soviet people." That evening there was a mass meeting in Tartu's medieval town square to celebrate his return.

There were many times, during those first few weeks of freedom, when the former political prisoner could scarcely believe what was happening around him. Ordinary people now voiced opinions that had earned Niklus long terms in the gulag. A few weeks after his release, Estonia's Communist-run television station broadcast a program to mark the forty-ninth anniversary of the Molotov-Ribbentrop pact. There was a graphic picture of sinister black arrows, marked with swastikas, devouring most of Poland. Then large red arrows coming from the direction of the Soviet Union swallowed up the rest of Poland, plus the Baltic states. There were shots of the Soviet and German foreign ministers, Vyacheslav Molotov and Joachim von Ribbentrop, congratulating each other in Berlin. The camera then panned to a rally, addressed by Yuri Afanasiev, a prominent Russian historian. Afanasiev not only admitted the existence of the secret protocols—a fact still denied by Soviet leaders—but described them as a "historical injustice that we have no right to keep silent about."[204]

Events in Estonia, and the other Baltic states, now moved with breathtaking speed. That summer hundreds of thousands of Estonians—out of a population of 1.5 million—took part in patriotic song festivals. The mass outpouring of national sentiment was dubbed "The Singing Revolution." By October Estonian nationalists and reform-minded Communists had formed a mass political movement, or popular front, ostensibly to "support perestroika." Niklus was chosen as one of the founding delegates to the Congress, taking his place alongside doctors and factory managers. Within weeks similar mass movements had been launched in the neighboring republics of Latvia and Lithuania. It soon became clear that the real goal of these "pro-Gorbachev" movements was the restoration of Baltic indepen-

dence. Once-reactionary Communist Party officials scrambled to lead the revolution or get left hopelessly behind. By November the hitherto pliant Estonian Parliament had declared what amounted to home rule and legalized private property.

THE HARD-LINERS IN MOSCOW could scarcely contain their anger. The head of the KGB reported to the Politburo that "nationalistic forces" were consolidating their positions in the Baltic states, and the situation was getting out of hand. At Gorbachev's suggestion, the Politburo voted to send Aleksandr Yakovlev on a fact-finding trip to Lithuania, to see what could be done to rein in the pro-independence groups. To the conservatives' dismay, Yakovlev delivered a remarkably sanguine report, depicting events in the Baltic republics as totally in keeping with perestroika. People were drawing attention to social and economic grievances that had festered for decades and taking power into their own hands, he insisted. There was no cause for alarm.[205]

The behind-the-scenes political crisis came to a head in late November in the Walnut Room of the Kremlin, the place where the inner leadership gathered prior to Politburo sessions. Ligachev and his allies complained that the country was falling apart. Estonia had taken the first step to real independence. Ethnic disturbances had broken out in the Caucasus, between Armenians and Azerbaijanis. Crowds had set alight several Soviet tanks in the Azerbaijani capital, Baku, and two Russian soldiers had been killed. Demonstrators had carried portraits of the ayatollah Khomeini through the streets.

"Where are we going?" asked Vorotnikov, the Politburo member who had praised Nina Andreyeva's article.

"I said back in March that it is time to show our power, to restore order, to show these bums. How much can we tolerate?" said Ligachev. "Everything is falling apart. Discipline has broken down. The state is beginning to collapse."[206]

At first Gorbachev listened to Ligachev's ranting with a slightly ironic expression on his face. According to his foreign policy adviser, Anatoly Chernyayev, his political intuition told him that the Baltic states would probably break away. He did not want this to happen, but he felt powerless to prevent it. Unlike the conservatives, he would not allow himself to abandon perestroika, which he regarded as his life's work. He concluded that the best form of defense was attack.

"Why are you trying to frighten me all the time, Yegor? You keep on asking what this perestroika of ours has brought us? Where are we going? What's happening with us? This does not scare me."

Gorbachev felt politically stronger now than he had in March, during the Nina Andreyeva affair. Two of Ligachev's allies, Gromyko and Solomentsev, had retired from the Politburo. Ligachev himself had been shunted aside. For the first time since his election as general secretary, in March 1985, Gorbachev threatened to resign.

"If you consider that we have chosen the wrong path, that I am doing something wrong, then let's go next door." He nodded in the direction of the Politburo Room, on the other side of the tall walnut doors. "I will resign. On the spot! And I won't express a word of resentment. Choose who you want, and let him run things as best he can."

Gorbachev got his way once again. But there was a price to be paid for his stubbornness. Politburo unanimity—the method by which the Communist Party had imposed its will on a recalcitrant nation for more than seventy years—was a thing of the past. By now the split in the leadership had become impossible to hide.

NEW YORK

December 7, 1988

THE PEASANT BOY from Stavropol had come a long a way. Rarely in the thirty-three-year history of the United Nations had a visiting dignitary been accorded such a reception by the General Assembly. At the end of his address, presidents, foreign ministers, and ambassadors from 158 countries gave him a standing ovation. Mikhail Gorbachev sat in a thronelike white chair, as the applause of the world community echoed in his ears. For once the Soviet showman seemed nervous, as if overwhelmed by all the attention. He took a handkerchief out of his pocket to wipe his mouth. Then, a little stiffly, he rose to his feet to acknowledge the applause.

During the course of his one-hour speech Gorbachev effectively abandoned seven decades of Bolshevik ideology. He renounced the Marxist-Leninist idea of a never-ending "class struggle," substituting instead the "primacy of universal human values," including individual rights that had long been denied by Moscow. He declared an end to the "Cold War" that had consumed the energies of two superpowers for as long as most Americans and Russians could remember. He insisted that the Soviet Union could no longer remain a "closed society," isolated from the world economy. And he paved the way for the political liberation of Eastern Europe by pledging to respect the "freedom of choice" of other peoples and renouncing the use

of force in international relations. As a token of the Kremlin's new intentions, he announced a unilateral reduction in the size of the armed forces by half a million men.[207]

Normally jaded New Yorkers greeted the general secretary like a latter-day Messiah. The welcome exceeded all expectations. Gorbachev's aides had warned him that New York was a cynical city, indifferent to the comings and goings of even the most distinguished foreign visitors, except when they tied up traffic.[208] The forty-five-car Soviet motorcade was greeted by cheers and smiling faces wherever it appeared.

There were chants of "Gorbie, Gorbie" and handmade placards hailing "the peacemaker." His name was in lights on Broadway. WELCOME, COMRADE GENERAL SECRETARY GORBACHEV, announced the electronic signboard in Times Square, flashing the Communist hammer and sickles like an advertisement for a soft drink. On Wall Street dealers tore themselves away from their computer screens to applaud the leader of world communism. In the media frenzy surrounding the visit, anyone touched, or spoken to, by Gorbachev shared in his reflected glory. "He was standing right here," marveled elevator operator Gary Benaccio, still shaking his head as he told CBS how he had escorted the Soviet leader 107 stories to the top of the World Trade Center. "He looked like a regular tourist."

The popular adulation had a double-edged effect. The cheering crowds left an indelible impression on everyone in the Soviet delegation, most notably the general secretary himself. Gorbachev had seduced the West, but the West had seduced him in its turn. The triumphant reception strengthened his conviction that perestroika was right and necessary, not just for the Soviet Union but for all humanity. He was no longer just another Soviet leader with a thick neck; he was a man who could change the world.

Foreign trips offered Gorbachev a respite from his growing domestic problems. On this occasion, however, the respite was short-lived. As the Soviet leader's Zil sped away from the United Nations, he received a telephone call from Moscow over the scrambled Kremlin communications network. On the other end of the line was a very agitated Ryzkhov. There had just been a terrible earthquake in Armenia. Entire cities had been destroyed. There were thousands of victims. Gorbachev listened to the prime minister in grim silence as the crowds in the streets continued to chant his name. That evening a gloomy and dejected general secretary told his aides that he was cutting short his foreign tour and returning home.[209]

YEREVAN

December 11, 1988

THERE COULD HARDLY HAVE BEEN a greater contrast between the bright lights of Manhattan and the wrenching misery of Armenia. "In my entire life, I've never seen one-thousandth of the suffering I've seen here," said Gorbachev, after picking his way through the rubble of Leninakan and Spitak.[210] The grief-stricken survivors greeted him with indifference, even hostility. They wanted to know why high-rise apartment blocks had collapsed so easily, why scientists had been unable to predict the devastating tremors, why the rest of the country was slow in sending help.

Had the Armenian earthquake occurred in a Western country, it would have caused enormous damage and significant loss of life. But what would have been a manageable natural disaster in the West became an overwhelming man-made catastrophe in the Soviet Union. Shoddy construction practices and corruption among local officials caused the casualty toll to rise to the tens of thousands. Nearly half a million people were left without housing. Few buildings in the affected area had been constructed to withstand powerful tremors, despite the fact that earthquakes are commonplace in the Caucasus region. A subsequent investigation showed that steel rods that should have been used to reinforce concrete structures had been stolen and sold on the black market, leaving multistory apartment blocks as flimsy as matchboxes.

In the aftermath of the earthquake Soviet civil defense organizations proved hopelessly overstretched and ill equipped. Although they had the means to blow up the world and intimidate their neighbors in Europe and Asia, Soviet leaders were unable to organize an efficient relief effort in their own country. Troops were rushed to the area but were unable to provide assistance to the population because they lacked suitable equipment for removing the piles of rubble. In conditions of glasnost, it was impossible to conceal the inefficiency of the transportation system, the lack of decent medical care, the appalling housing conditions. Like Chernobyl, the Armenian earthquake became a metaphor for a sociopolitical system that was militarily powerful but economically crippled, technologically advanced but socially backward.

The abrupt transition from international triumph to domestic tragedy highlighted the challenge facing Gorbachev. Persuading Reagan and the American people to take a more benign view of the "evil empire" was easy compared with the awesome task of getting the Soviet Union back on its feet. The man who had been acclaimed as a miracle worker on the international stage seemed to have little to offer his own people except lectures and exhortations. In the West Gorbachev was applauded as the leader who had put an end to the Cold War and slashed the Soviet armed forces. At home his countrymen were beginning to refer to him as a *boltun* (chatterbox), a man of fine phrases devoid of practical meaning.

Nowhere had political support for Gorbachev plummeted so far, so fast as in Armenia, a small Christian nation that had traditionally looked to Russia for protection from the Turks. A year earlier the Armenians had looked up to Gorbachev as a hero. Thanks to glasnost, they had been permitted to give vent to a long-standing national grievance: Stalin's decision to make the mountainous region of Karabakh part of Turkic Azerbaijan, against the wishes of its predominantly Armenian population. A series of huge demonstrations had taken place in the streets of Yerevan to demand self-determination for Karabakh. At first Gorbachev had seemed sympathetic to the Armenians. After watching a KGB tape of the rallies in February 1988, he told his Politburo colleagues that there was "nothing anti-Soviet" about the protests.[211] He was impressed that many of the demonstrators even carried his own portrait as they marched.

By December, however, Gorbachev's views had radically changed. The upsurge of national feeling in Armenia had provoked a counterreaction in Azerbaijan. There had been anti-Armenian riots in Sumgait, an Azerbaijani town with a large Armenian minority. Hundreds of thousands of Ar-

menians and Azerbaijanis had been forced to flee from their homes. It was the first sign of a new, and ominous, political trend that would accompany the collapse of communism: ethnic cleansing.

The general secretary displayed his mounting political frustration at the end of his visit to Armenia. He used an interview with Soviet television about the earthquake to lash out at Armenian nationalists as "adventurists" and "political gamblers," who were exploiting the misery of their people for their own ends. Shortly afterward he ordered the arrest of the leadership of the Karabakh committee, which had organized the rallies in Yerevan.

Something profound had happened in the Soviet Union in the two and a half years since Chernobyl. It was no longer just the "inanimate objects" that were revolting against Communist rule, in Adam Michnik's phrase. In the Caucasus and the Baltic states the revolt had been joined by "animate objects." Soon the wave of popular discontent would spread to the politically somnolent Slavic heartland of the Soviet Union. The "revolution from above" had become a "revolution from below."

Gorbachev was no longer in control of his own revolution.

III

REVOLT

OF THE NATIONS

Where the Russian flag has once been hoisted, it cannot be lowered.

Nicholas I, 1850

Comrades, we have every right to say that we have solved the nationality question in this country.

Mikhail Gorbachev, November 1987

TERMEZ

February 15, 1989

MIKHAIL GORBACHEV REMEMBERED the pictures of American helicopters lifting off from the rooftop of the U.S. Embassy in Saigon, with marines pushing away Vietnamese citizens as they tried desperately to clamber aboard. It would be a "shame," he told his aides, if Soviet troops were to "run away" from Afghanistan as the Americans had done in Vietnam.[1] He wanted the Red Army's withdrawal from Afghanistan to be orderly and dignified, in keeping with the Soviet Union's superpower status.

In accordance with Gorbachev's wishes, everything possible was done to create the illusion that the Red Army had "fulfilled its internationalist duty." As column after column of tanks and armored cars swept across the "Friendship Bridge" spanning the muddy Amu Darya River—the ancient Oxus—a military band struck up a patriotic march. Regimental standards fluttered proudly in the breeze. Battle-hardened veterans, their faces bronzed in the Afghan sun, were showered with kisses and carnations by relieved relatives. Everyone seemed to be wearing a medal of some kind. "The Order of the Motherland Has Been Fulfilled," proclaimed a red banner strung up across a makeshift parade ground.

The patriotic slogans and parade ground hurrahs could not, however, conceal the bitterness felt by many of the returning troops over a futile nine-

year war. As they crossed back into Soviet territory, commanders spoke contemptuously about the politicians who had sent them to Afghanistan and the Communist regime they had attempted to defend.

"It's like the Middle Ages there," said a *spetsnaz* colonel, gesturing in the direction of the country he had just left. "The Afghan people were simply not prepared for a socialist revolution."

"It was a tragedy," acknowledged another veteran. "We helped a government that did not have the support of the Afghan people."[2]

Although the Geneva accords provided for the complete withdrawal of Soviet troops by February 15, 1989, there had been considerable skepticism in Western capitals about whether Gorbachev would keep his promise. From the time of Peter the Great Russian history had been one of almost continuous expansion, interrupted by the occasional foreign invasion and domestic cataclysm. Over the course of several centuries Russian rulers had succeeded in establishing their dominance over much of the Eurasian landmass, an area inhabited by more than a hundred ethnic groups. To hang on to these vast territories, Russia had to convince its many enemies that retreat was out of the question. If it started abandoning colonial outposts, however obscure and however costly to defend, its credibility as a great power would be called into question.

The Russian territorial doctrine was succinctly expressed by Tsar Nicholas I in 1850, after one of his naval officers had seized some territory belonging to China along the Amur River. The officer had acted on his own initiative, without orders from St. Petersburg, and some of the tsar's advisers were in favor of surrendering the territory, which had little strategic value. But Nicholas saw things differently. "Where the Russian flag has once been hoisted, it cannot be lowered," he declared. The tsar's stubbornness and inflexibility produced the desired impression on foreign rulers. "The Russian policy of aggression is slow and steady, but firm and unchangeable," noted the emir of Afghanistan some thirty years later. "If once they make up their minds to do a thing, there is no stopping them, and no changing their policy."[3]

The Bolsheviks followed a similar territorial doctrine to the tsars, although they dressed it up in Marxist-Leninist language. Two years after the invasion, in 1982, *Pravda* described the Afghan Revolution as "irreversible because it is a people's revolution, and because it enjoys the support and solidarity of the Soviet Union."[4] Soviet leaders had an additional reason for wanting to retain what amounted to the world's last great colonial empire. Together with victory over Nazi Germany in the Great Patriotic War, the

existence of a steadily expanding network of client states was the major accomplishment of the Soviet regime. Here was concrete proof that communism was on the move, ideological justification for decades of economic hardship and political repression. Soviet citizens might live in penury and squalor, but history was on their side. Sooner or later communism would triumph throughout the world.

It was this doctrine—the doctrine of the irreversibility of history—that was being undermined by the withdrawal from Afghanistan. If the forces of socialism were defeated in Afghanistan, the Kremlin would find it difficult to hold on to places like Nicaragua, Ethiopia, and Poland.

IT TOOK LIEUTENANT GENERAL BORIS GROMOV, the last Soviet commander in Afghanistan, a week to make the three-hundred-mile drive along the mountainous Salang Highway from Kabul to Termez. This was the same route that the Soviets had used to invade the country nine years earlier. An outpost founded by Alexander the Great and sacked by Genghis Khan, Termez had been incorporated into the tsarist empire in the late nineteenth century, during the great thrust to the south. The springboard for the Russian conquest of Afghanistan had become the main reentry point for Soviet troops returning home.

The long convoys of Soviet military vehicles proceeded cautiously, knowing they could be ambushed by the guerrilla fighters who now controlled more than four-fifths of Afghanistan. To protect the highway from sudden attack, Soviet special forces had systematically destroyed hundreds of Afghan villages perched in the towering mountains on either side of the road. Everywhere they looked, the retreating troops could see the detritus of a war that had cost the lives of fifteen thousand of their own comrades and more than a million Afghans. They drove past roofless mud-brick houses, bullet-splattered walls, and fields of forlorn tree stumps that had once been luxuriant orchards. Rusting carcasses of bombed-out tanks and the twisted wreckage of army trucks littered the sides of the highway.

A month before his departure from Kabul, Gromov had received a message from the Afghan guerrilla commander who controlled the heights around the Salang Highway, Ahmad Shah Massoud. "We have put up with war and your presence in our country for nearly ten years now," the missive read. "God willing, we will put up with you for a few more days. But if you begin military action against us, we will give you a worthy response." Despite Massoud's offer of a cease-fire, skirmishes had broken out between the

mujahedin and the departing Soviet troops. In retaliation, Gromov had launched Operation Typhoon. In its last military action in Afghanistan, the Red Army carried out more than a thousand helicopter attacks against suspected mujahedin positions in the Salang area and blasted their supply bases with long-range missiles.[5]

The rest of the withdrawal proceeded smoothly enough. The weather proved more troublesome for the Soviets than the mujahedin, who refrained from harassing their enemies on their way out. Several soldiers were killed in avalanches that had blocked the eleven-thousand-foot-high Salang Pass for days at a time. The Fortieth Army reached the border without further losses.

Gromov spent his last night in Afghanistan in the town of Khairaton, on the southern side of the "Friendship Bridge." Like his men, he was immensely relieved to be going home. He had spent nearly six years in Afghanistan, on three separate tours of duty, and had little illusion about the ability of Najibullah's Afghan regime to survive without Soviet assistance. For nearly a decade the Afghan Communists had manipulated the Soviets into waging war on their behalf. In theory the Soviet "internationalist" fighters had been defending the "cause of socialism." In practice, Gromov realized, they had been defending an unpopular government from its domestic opponents. They had failed to win the hearts and minds of the Afghan people. The leaders the Soviets had helped install and keep in power were inept, corrupt, and entirely dependent on foreign assistance.[6]

Gromov had had a difficult time explaining to his men what they were doing in Afghanistan. The standard formula—"fulfilling their internationalist duty"—was no longer adequate. Until Gorbachev came to power, the Soviet Union had refused to acknowledge it was fighting a war in Afghanistan. Instead of being hailed as heroes on their return home Afghan war veterans were treated like pariahs. The motherland seemed ashamed of them and was reluctant to acknowledge their sacrifices. It soon became clear to Gromov that he and his men were in an unwinnable war. In this situation it was his duty to reduce Soviet combat losses to a minimum. This was the goal he had set for himself following his appointment as commander of the Soviet "limited contingent" in Afghanistan in 1987.[7]

As he made a final tour of inspection of the Soviet military barracks at Khairaton, Gromov was sickened by the sight of warehouses overflowing with hundreds of thousands of tons of food and building materials. It was not just human lives that had been squandered in Afghanistan. The war had disrupted the Soviet economy, absorbing resources and contributing to

widespread shortages of ordinary household items. In a few hours' time these huge stockpiles of sugar, flour, cement, and roof tile would be handed over to the Afghan army. Gromov knew from bitter experience what would happen next. A few weeks before, Afghan soldiers had ransacked the Soviet military barracks in the southern city of Jalalabad, carrying away everything from television sets and air conditioners to beds and doorframes. Many of the stolen items quickly ended up on the black market.[8]

Gromov had promised himself that he would be the last Soviet soldier to leave Afghanistan. He told journalists he would walk alone across the "Friendship Bridge," once he knew all his men were safely on Soviet territory. As he crossed the border, he would turn back in the direction of Afghanistan and "say what needed to be said." When word of his intention reached Moscow, it caused some alarm at the Defense Ministry, which did not appreciate flamboyant gestures by independently minded combat generals.

"Why are you leaving last, and not first, as a commander should?" growled the defense minister, Dmitri Yazov, when he finally reached Gromov over a secure Kremlin telephone line in Khairaton.

"This was my own decision as the commander of the army," the forty-six-year-old general replied. "I consider that five and a half years' service in Afghanistan gives me the right to make a small breach of army tradition."[9]

Yazov grunted but said nothing.

FOR GROMOV, THE WAR WAS ENDING as it began, in a shameful silence. He resented the fact that neither Gorbachev nor any other Soviet leader could be bothered to come to Termez to welcome the troops home. Even the defense minister and his deputies had chosen to avoid the ceremonies, which were being presided over by low-level officials from the republic of Uzbekistan. In effect his troops had been left to organize their own homecoming. Moscow had rejected his repeated pleas to follow tradition and award the Fortieth Army a collective medal for its service in Afghanistan. It was as if the Politburo wanted to wash its hands of the whole Afghanistan adventure, Gromov thought, and put the blame on the soldiers who had carried out the orders of their political superiors.

He lay awake most of the night, thinking about what he had seen and done since he first arrived in Afghanistan in January 1980, a month after the invasion. A sense of emptiness and betrayal overwhelmed him. Despite winning every set-piece battle they had fought with the mujahedin, his troops

had lost the war because they lacked the necessary political support from the Afghan people. In Gromov's view, the Soviet Union had suffered a political rather than a military defeat. But it was a defeat nonetheless. The consequences of such a shattering setback were impossible to predict. The future—for both the country and the army—was clouded with uncertainty.

Gromov also thought about the price his own family had paid while he was waging war. During his second tour of duty in Afghanistan his wife had been killed in an air crash. His two sons, Maksim and Andrei, had grown up without a father or a mother. He had been away from home long enough.

He finally got to sleep around 4:00 a.m. An hour later he was awakened by the noise of engines being revved up and soldiers joking about the end of the war. He dressed carefully, asking an adjutant to inspect his uniform from all sides, to ensure that he would be picture-perfect as he crossed the "Friendship Bridge." He ordered guards to be withdrawn from the last remaining Soviet outposts around Khairaton. Outside on the parade ground five hundred soldiers of the 201st Reconnaissance Division were lined up next to their armored personnel carriers, waiting for the command to move off. Gromov gave the troops a pep talk, telling them they would go down in history as the last battalion of Soviet troops to leave Afghanistan. As they paraded past his reviewing stand, he noticed that many of the men had tears in their eyes.

A few minutes later Gromov climbed into his own APC to drive the final mile into Soviet territory. The "Friendship Bridge" was deserted. In the distance, on the Soviet side of the wrought-iron bridge, he could see a crowd of journalists and well-wishers, including fourteen-year-old Maksim. He jumped down from the vehicle and proceeded on foot. At the center of the bridge, on the state boundary line, he turned back in the direction of the country he had just left and said "what needed to be said."

Speaking in a soft voice, so that no one could hear him, the last commander of the Fortieth Army roundly cursed the leaders who had dispatched a million Soviet boys to defend the "cause of socialism" in a backward, mountainous land, with a long tradition of fighting foreign invaders. And he asked for forgiveness from the mothers of the fifteen thousand soldiers who had never returned from Afghanistan.[10]

MOSCOW

March 26, 1989

ACCORDING TO STANDARD MARXIST-LENINIST THEORY, a metropolis is meant to exploit its colonies for its own benefit, using them as a source of cheap raw materials and a dumping ground for shoddy industrial goods. In the Soviet case, precisely the opposite had happened. Russia exported oil at heavily discounted prices to places like Estonia, Poland, and Cuba. Sometimes it received overpriced consumer items in return for this oil; at other times, nothing at all. Third World trouble spots like Afghanistan, Ethiopia, and Nicaragua were a constant drain on the Soviet treasury. Under communism it was impossible to draw a line between exploiting and exploited nations. The rapacious system of central planning exploited everyone, Russians most of all.

Geopolitical setbacks overseas and economic devastation at home caused Russians to turn away from foreign adventure and examine their own problems. Thanks to glasnost, they were able to compare their standard of living with that of other people. They were dismayed to find that they were at the bottom of the pile. Vast territories and unprecedented military might had brought ordinary Russians nothing but pain and further economic suffering. The social compact of the Brezhnev era—pride in the Soviet Union's superpower status combined with a low but gradually increasing standard of living—was disintegrating.

The revolt of ordinary Russians was the essential precondition for the successful rebellions in Eastern Europe. The subject nations wanted their freedom. Russians wanted an end to their economic misery. Eventually these two elements gelled into a grand political bargain that was to transform the Communist world.

Mikhail Gorbachev was the first Soviet leader to show any real concern for the opinions of his countrymen. In the spring of 1988, in the wake of the Nina Andreyeva affair, he had made a strategic decision. He would make use of public opinion in his battle against the nomenklatura. Frustrated by the opposition of Communist Party bureaucrats to his reforms, he came up with a device for circumventing them altogether. Citing the Bolshevik slogan "All Power to the Soviets," he proposed creating a powerful legislature. The old Supreme Soviet, a rubber-stamp body packed with party hacks and a few token milkmaids, would be replaced by a real parliament.

The announcement that the Soviet Union would hold its first-ever contested election on March 26, 1989, provoked a wave of political excitement. Soon the entire country was caught up in a gigantic debate, which unfolded in television studios, city squares, meeting halls, classrooms, army barracks, and the columns of newspapers. The hubbub of voices was both bewildering and exhilarating. Fear melted away like the packed ice on Russian rivers after the long winter, cracking open with a mighty cacophony of sound. Suddenly everybody seemed to have an opinion. Walls were plastered with political slogans; housewives standing in line for groceries vented their spleen at the government; anti-Communist tracts were distributed on street corners.

As the elections approached, the apparatchiks began to panic. Voting procedures had been designed to give official candidates a built-in advantage, but in many cases this was not sufficient to ensure their election. The prospect of hundreds of Communist Goliaths being slain by populist Davids made for a riveting spectacle. This was a struggle for personal—as much as political—survival. In the Soviet Union political connections were the key to a privileged lifestyle: a larger apartment; improved food rations; opportunities for foreign travel; access to a government dacha; better medical services; a car perhaps. Losing one's place in the nomenklatura was devastating, psychologically, professionally, and even economically.

In many people's eyes, the struggle for democracy in the Soviet Union was symbolized by high-profile opposition candidates, like Boris Yeltsin and Andrei Sakharov. Both men overcame enormous bureaucratic resistance to get their names on the ballot. Yeltsin, the turncoat Politburo member, had decided to run for a city-wide seat in Moscow, representing six

million voters. Frantic attempts by the Communist authorities to discredit him only increased his popularity among ordinary Muscovites. Sakharov was nominated to fill one of the deputy slots reserved for the prestigious Academy of Sciences, a body that had joined in the Kremlin's campaign to revile him for his human rights activities and opposition to the war in Afghanistan. The bureaucrats who ran the academy had initially attempted to block his candidacy but were forced to climb down following a series of angry protest meetings by rank-and-file scientists.

By Western standards, the election campaign was extraordinarily low-tech. There were no slickly made television advertisements, no image makers or spin doctors, no fund-raising drives, no campaign staffs. There weren't even many political posters in evidence, just the occasional scruffy sheet of typewritten paper tacked to a wall, describing the "program" of one or another of the candidates. The most important platform for propagating a candidate's ideas was the political meeting.

The Communist Party dug deep into its bag of dirty tricks in order to rig the election in its favor. Party officials packed nomination meetings with their own activists, preventing opposition candidates from getting their names on the ballot. Many apparatchiks ran unopposed in rural districts, where people were still afraid to express their opinions.

When the election returns came in, the apparatchiks received a hugh shock. In most places where there was a clear choice, the party-approved candidate was defeated. The list of the vanquished read like a who's who of Soviet public life: Politburo members, generals, cosmonauts, government ministers, and the mayors or party bosses of Moscow, Leningrad, Kiev, Minsk, and many other big cities. In Moscow Yeltsin crushed his official Communist rival by a stunning margin of thirteen to one. In the Baltic states popular front movements that were already beginning to toy with the words "national sovereignty" and "independence" crushed Communist Party candidates. In Ukraine, which had previously been regarded as a bastion of reaction, five regional Communist Party bosses were defeated by national-ist candidates.

The election results surprised and delighted Moscow intellectuals, who had previously regarded the Soviet people as a dark, inchoate mass unre ceptive to democratic ideas. "After this, my country will never be the same again," enthused the poet Andrei Voznesensky, a spokesman for the *shesti-desyatniki* generation. "We intellectuals always saw ourselves as the symbol of democracy, but we thought the people weren't ready for it. The joyful thing about all this is that in many ways we have been proved wrong."[11]

Despite the powerful showing of the reformers, the conservatives were

still assured a built-in majority in the new legislature. One-third of the 2,250 seats in the Congress of People's Deputies had been reserved for Communist-dominated "social organizations," including the party itself. Communist Party candidates also did well in the countryside and traditionally conservative areas of the country, such as Central Asia and Belarus.

The apparatchiks had suffered a serious reverse, but they were hardly out of the game. Within days of their setback at the polls, they were galvanized into action by nationalist disturbances in the turbulent Transcaucasian republic of Georgia, birthplace of Josef Stalin. The counterattack would not be long in coming.

TBILISI

April 9, 1989

HIS LEFT HAND RESTING ON A SILVER STAFF, the patriarch of the Georgian Orthodox Church waited patiently for silence. The broad tree-lined avenue in front of him was packed with people. Illuminated by hundreds of flickering candles, their predominantly young faces bore expressions of expectancy and determination. One of the most ancient peoples of the Caucasus, inhabiting the mythical land of the Golden Fleece, Georgians were imbued with a sense of unique national identity. His Holiness Ilya II knew that it would be difficult to persuade his compatriots to back down now. But he felt a duty to try.

"In the name of God the Father, God the Son, and God the Holy Spirit. God is with us."[12]

A hush descended over the crowd as Georgia's eighty-two-year-old patriarch pronounced his blessing. It was 3:15 a.m., and some ten thousand people were now crammed into the plaza in front of the Georgian parliament, on Rustaveli Avenue, Tbilisi's principal thoroughfare. Some of the demonstrators held placards with slogans, handwritten in Georgian and in English, like "We Demand an Independent Georgia," "Down with Soviet Power," and "Russian Occupiers, Go Home." Others waved the banned black, red, and white flag of the pre-Communist Georgian republic, which

had enjoyed a brief independence between 1918 and 1921, before its conquest by the Red Army. The color black was intended to symbolize the Georgian nation's tormented past, red its bloodstained present, and white its glorious future.

On his way to the parliament building from his residence in the old town, the patriarch had seen Soviet troops and armored cars massing in Lenin Square, a few hundred yards away. Georgian officials had told him that the army planned to use force to disperse the demonstrators. He spoke slowly, with long pauses, hoping that reason would prevail over emotion.

"All of Georgia appreciates you. The nation understands what you are doing. It knows how important it is. But we cannot ignore the real danger that is facing us, right now. That is why I came to bless you and ask you to leave."

Now in its fifth day, the protest outside the parliament building had begun as a hunger strike by several hundred students to denounce attempts by the Abhazian minority to secede from Georgia. As they listened to speeches by opposition activists, the protesters became increasingly radical and nationalistic. There had been demands for the formation of a provisional government to kick out the Communists and restore Georgian independence. Frightened of losing control, the authorities had called in the army. The previous day a column of tanks and armored cars had driven through the streets of the capital, while helicopters flew overhead. Far from intimidating the people of Tbilisi, this military display had only fueled their ardor. As rumors spread of an imminent crackdown, the size of the crowd grew steadily. The unarmed protesters blocked the approaches to the building with barricades, made out of city buses with deflated tires and abandoned concrete trucks.

Flanking the patriarch, on the stone steps of the floodlit parliament building, were the most prominent leaders of the opposition. Alongside them, squatting in makeshift plastic tents that had been pitched on a little stretch of grass next to the steps and facing their supporters in the square, were the original hunger strikers. A few minutes earlier the demonstrators had been dancing and singing Georgian folk songs. As they listened to Ilya, pleading with them to disperse, their mood became somber and defiant.

The patriarch tried again. "It is possible that there are only a few minutes left. We have a chance to go to the cathedral and pray there."

"We're not going," one of the demonstrators shouted.

"We won't take a step back," others cried. "We have taken an oath not to leave."

Suddenly the whole crowd began to chant: "Long live Georgia," "Long live Georgian independence."

The patriarch knew what was about to happen but felt powerless to do anything more. "Do you want to die?" he murmured to one of the protesters, standing beside him. As he left the plaza, the passionate voice of one of the nationalist firebrands, twenty-eight-year-old Irakli Tsereteli, boomed over the loudspeakers.

"Tonight we will be reborn. We will remain on the path of democracy, the path of independence, the path of God. God is with us."

"Amen," the crowd roared back.

"God is with us."

"Amen."

"We have taken an oath never to retreat. The best sons of Georgia will keep that oath, against the will of our enemies."

"We have sworn."

WHILE THE PATRIARCH WAS ADDRESSING the demonstrators outside the Georgian parliament, the man who would determine their fate was pacing up and down Lenin Square. At fifty-three, Colonel General Igor Rodionov was one of the most experienced commanders in the Soviet army. He had served in Afghanistan, where he had annoyed his superiors by refusing to open fire on unarmed civilians. As commander in chief of the Transcaucasian military district, he had spent much of the past year in endless negotiations with warring factions in Armenia and Azerbaijan. He had also been involved in relief operations in Armenia following the earthquake of December 1988. He was a fanatical believer in order and discipline, and his life revolved around the army. He regarded the region's squabbling politicians with contempt.

Outsiders who met Rodionov were impressed by his intelligent, well-educated veneer. But they were also struck by another side to his character, a total, almost blinkered loyalty to the Communist Party. Here was a man who had grown up entirely within the system. Like many of his colleagues in the military, he was dismayed by the massive political upheavals taking place in the Soviet Union. The anti-Soviet and anti-Russian slogans pasted up all over Tbilisi slogans like "Down with Russian Imperialism"—offended him deeply. He regarded the protesters who had taken over the plaza as revolutionary subversives, attempting to overthrow the constitutional order. As far as the general was concerned, this was not a peaceful demonstration. It was an "anti-Soviet orgy."[13]

At first Rodionov had been reluctant to involve the army in the Georgian crisis. Ensuring public order was a matter for the police, not the military. But as the demands of the demonstrators grew steadily more outrageous, he changed his mind. The republic's leaders were no longer able to control events. The local security forces were already stretched to the limit by the upheavals in the Black Sea region of Abhazia. Rodionov concluded that only the army had the means, and the political will, to restore order. The Defense Ministry in Moscow had dispatched two thousand troops to Tbilisi to assist him.

Precisely who gave orders for force to be used against the demonstrators outside the parliament building later became a subject of intense political controversy. Soviet leaders, from Gorbachev downward, denied any knowledge of the affair. But in those predawn moments in Lenin Square, the chain of command seemed perfectly clear. Despite his strong political views, Rodionov was not the kind of officer who would launch a military operation by himself without the authorization of his superiors.

A subsequent investigation showed that the general had received written instructions from the Soviet Defense Ministry to take the parliament building "under control." How this was to be done was left vague, but "the center" was kept fully informed of the military preparations. A deputy defense minister and several senior Central Committee officials were in Tbilisi, monitoring the crisis. The decision to apply force was endorsed by local party leaders, who later claimed that they were in constant communication with the center, through KGB channels. Several minor operational details, including a last-minute decision not to use water cannon against the demonstrators, were also "agreed" with Moscow.[14]

At 3:30 a.m. Rodionov in Lenin Square received a telephone call from Dzumber Patiashvili, the first secretary of the Georgian Communist Party, who was at home. The two men spoke over a radiotelephone. Under the influence of his Russian deputy, Patiashvili had earlier firmly supported the use of force against the demonstrators. He was convinced that there was no other way of preserving Communist Party power in Georgia. But now he was beginning to panic. His subordinates had told him about the demonstrators' refusal to heed the patriarch. There were too many people in front of the parliament building.

Perhaps, he suggested to Rodionov, the operation should be postponed for a little while?

The general said it was too late. Emotions were at a fever pitch. If the army backed down now and failed to restore order, anything could happen. He promised Patiashvili that there would be "no complications."[15]

Rodionov returned to his commanders in a determined mood. The short, pugnacious man was convinced of the righteousness of his cause. His troops were lined up beneath the outstretched arms of the gigantic Lenin statue in the middle of the square, as if receiving the blessing of the father of Soviet communism. The armored cars were revving their engines.

"Let's begin," the general announced. It was exactly 4:00 a.m.[16]

" EVERYONE DOWN ON THEIR KNEES," shouted Tsereteli as the troops began their slow march up Rustaveli Avenue, in the direction of the parliament building. "They won't beat you if you are on your knees."[17]

A chant of "Our Father, which art in heaven, hallowed be thy name" echoed from the loudspeakers around the plaza. "Thy kingdom come. Thy will be done in earth, as it is in heaven."

"Give us this day our daily bread," shouted the hunger strikers, sitting on the grass alongside the broad steps leading up to the parliament building, itself set back some fifty yards from the avenue.

Ten thousand voices–young, defiant, seemingly ready for any sacrifice— joined in the prayer. "Forgive us our trespasses as we forgive those that trespass against us."

The demonstrators could see the headlights of four armored personnel carriers moving toward them through the darkness, occupying the width of the avenue. Behind the APCs they could see a line of Interior Ministry troops, thwacking their plastic shields with heavy rubber truncheons. Behind those troops came several companies of paratroopers, who had been given the task of guarding the parliament building once the plaza in front of it was cleared. Except for the sharpened metal spades that were part of their regular equipment, the paratroopers were unarmed.

Cries of "Georgia, Georgia" filled the air, as the *spetsnaz* troops moved forward behind the APCs, herding people in front of them. By 4:10 a.m. the troops had formed a human barricade of shields and armor across the middle of Rustaveli Avenue, splitting the crowd in two. Riot police swarmed down side streets next to the parliament building, trapping everybody sitting in the vicinity of the fourteen stone steps and the adjacent patch of lawn. By barricading the side streets with trucks, the demonstrators had sealed off their own means of escape.

The patch of lawn next to the parliament building was filled with frantic people, crammed into an increasingly tight space. As the troops pushed inward from both sides, the hunger strikers struggled to their feet, kicking and screaming. Several dozen riot police were equipped with aerosol cans of a

toxic nerve gas, known familiarly as cherry gas, or *cheryomukha*, which they sprayed at the demonstrators. Others lashed out with rubber truncheons. At one point the police line seemed to be breaking. Rodionov ordered paratroopers into the breach. In order to gain some breathing space, they struck out with the only weapon at their disposal, their metal entrenching tools. In the general crush of human bodies, the weakest were trampled underfoot and were soon struggling for breath.

"They're killing people in there. Help them," shouted the demonstrators outside the police barricade. "Fuck the bastards."

Determined to rescue the hunger strikers, the demonstrators found a large wooden pole, which they attempted to ram through the line of shields and rubber truncheons. Occasionally a bloody figure ran through a chink in the line, assisted by Georgian militiamen, many of whom were beaten by Soviet soldiers as they helped the demonstrators form an escape route. Soon the entire avenue became a battleground. Tear gas canisters exploded overhead as young men, wearing kerchiefs, attacked the armored cars with sticks and stones. Ambulance sirens wailed. Curses filled the air.

"This is for Stalin," yelled a Russian soldier, beating a demonstrator with his truncheon.

"Fuck the bastards, they're all drunk," shouted a Georgian, smelling the alcohol-soaked breath of one of the riot police.

When it was all over, sixteen bodies were collected from the patch of lawn next to the parliament building and the nearby steps. The faces of the victims were bloated and swollen, symptoms of asphyxiation.[18] Ambulance teams noticed a smell of rotten fruit on the breaths of some of the victims, suggesting that nerve gas had been fired at them from close range. Most of the victims were women, ranging in age from sixteen to seventy, the least able to defend themselves in the crush.

After the violence outside the parliament building, the troops chased the crowds down Rustaveli Avenue, toward Republic Square, firing tear gas as they went. By sunrise another three demonstrators had been fatally injured in other parts of the city. Some 250 people were taken to the hospital. Many were suffering from a combination of "crowd crush" and toxic gas poisoning. Others displayed deep welts from the long rubber nightsticks of the *spetsnaz*. Several dozen had stab wounds, apparently caused by the little spades wielded by paratroopers.

THE MEN WHO ORDERED the violent dispersal of the Tbilisi rally wanted to prevent the disintegration of the Soviet empire. But as frequently hap-

pened during the final crisis of communism, the outcome of their action was the precise opposite of their intention. Instead of dampening the nationalistic spirit of the Georgian people, they gave it a tremendous boost. Instead of establishing a precedent for the use of force to suppress unauthorized gatherings, they provoked a furious debate over the role of the army in domestic political conflicts. Instead of saving communism in Georgia, they only hastened its end.

A few years before, such incidents would have been hushed up. In conditions of glasnost, this was impossible. The spectacle of soldiers beating and killing defenseless civilians, just as the country was starting its transition to democracy, shocked people throughout the Soviet Union. In Georgia itself the events of April 9 soon became the stuff of popular legend, much of it distorted.

No one exploited the myth of "Bloody Sunday" in Tbilisi more effectively than Zviad Gamsakhurdia. The fifty-year-old son of the republic's best-loved writer, Gamsakhurdia identified himself with Georgian national aspirations. His father, Konstantine, specialized in historical epics, describing the long struggle of the Georgian nation against the other peoples of the Caucasus. His novels were set against a background of snowcapped peaks and rugged mountains and peopled by beautiful Georgian maidens, noble princes, and heroic warlords, after one of whom he named his son. It was easy for Zviad, listening to these stories, to imagine that he had been given the mission of uniting Georgia against its many enemies.

The older Gamsakhurdia's writings had found favor with the most eminent Georgian of all. Born Joseph Djugashvili, Stalin had listened to similar tales of Georgian bravery and banditry from his mother. Although he was a scourge of Georgian nationalism, Stalin had a sentimental attachment to Georgian folklore. He permitted Konstantine Gamsakhurdia several eccentricities that would have got other writers into serious trouble. Older residents of Tbilisi still remember how the writer liked to parade around the town dressed in medieval Georgian costume like a prince. As long as he stuck to historical themes and avoided politically delicate subjects, such as the war between Russia and Georgia, nobody bothered him. He was on good terms with the local Communist leaders, including Eduard Shevardnadze. In return for his services to Georgian literature, the Gamsakhurdia family was rewarded with a magnificent villa overlooking the capital, protected by a high iron gate.

When Georgian nationalism began to stir again in the aftermath of Stalin's death, Zviad Gamsakhurdia was right in the middle of the ferment. He had had his first run-in with the authorities in 1957, at the age of eigh-

teen, when he was convicted of "anti-Soviet agitation" for distributing sub-versive pamphlets. Two years later he was in trouble again, this time for get-ting into a fight with a policeman. On both occasions, however, he received relatively light suspended sentences. His father's fame helped him stay out of jail. Like his father, Zviad Gamsakhurdia had an ambiguous relationship with the Communist regime, a mixture of defiance and accommodation. He was sent to prison in 1978 for founding a Georgian human rights group and giving interviews to foreign correspondents. The following year, however, he was released after a television interview in which he publicly recanted his "mistakes." Rival dissidents accused him of collaborating with the KGB.

By 1989 the Georgian dissident movement had splintered into dozens of factions and subfactions, as opposition leaders vied for influence. In the struggle to shape public opinion, Gamsakhurdia junior coined the slogan "Georgia for the Georgians." Although Georgians accounted for only two-thirds of the republic's 5.5 million people, he believed they deserved an ex-clusive voice in its political affairs. In his view, minority groups, such as Abkhazians, Ossetians, and Armenians, were all second-class citizens.

"Georgia is a unitary independent state, and therefore there can be no concessions to the separatists in Abkhazia and southern Ossetia," he told the meeting outside the parliament building. "The representatives of all other nations are merely guests on Georgian land, who can be shown the door at any time by their hosts."[19]

In many ways, Gamsakhurdia's brand of xenophobic nationalism was as authoritarian and myopic as the Communist ideology it sought to replace. He convinced his followers that independence would lead automatically to prosperity, as the Kremlin would no longer have the opportunity to "ex-ploit" Georgia economically. In his patriotic zeal he ignored the fact that Georgia relied on other Soviet republics for practically all its oil and gas, 94 percent of its grain, 93 percent of its steel, and 82 percent of its timber. His assumption that ethnic minorities would meekly accept the will of the Geor-gian majority turned out to be another fatal miscalculation, which laid the basis for a prolonged civil war.

In the emotional aftermath of the Tbilisi "massacre," reason and com-mon sense were in short supply. Revolted by the shedding of innocent blood, Georgians rallied around the leaders who denounced the Soviet "im-perialists" the loudest. At this point the Communist authorities made a se-ries of blunders that played right into the hands of the nationalists. They arrested Gamsakhurdia and other opposition leaders, endowing them with the halos of martyrs. Then, for almost two weeks, the army denied using

toxic gas against the demonstrators. Panic swept the city as hundreds of people were admitted to local hospitals with symptoms of poisoning. Anti-Soviet sentiment reached a fever pitch. By the time Gamsakhurdia was released from prison several weeks later, the role of one of his father's heroes seemed ready-made for him. A year and a half after "Bloody Sunday," he was to win the first free election in Georgian history, by a two-to-one margin.

For ordinary Soviets, the Tbilisi tragedy became a chilling reminder of just how easily democratic reforms could be reversed. It was a lesson driven home a few weeks later, by an even greater tragedy on the other side of the Communist world.

BEIJING

May 17, 1989

"WE SALUTE THE AMBASSADOR OF DEMOCRACY," read the placards in Tiananmen Square, the symbolic heart of the world's most populous nation. "In the Soviet Union, They Have Gorbachev. What Do We Have?"

When Mikhail Gorbachev decided to put an end to three decades of enmity between the Soviet Union and China, he could scarcely have imagined the turmoil he would unleash. During the course of his three-day stay in Beijing, authority on the streets of the Chinese capital had passed from the "People's government" to the people themselves. The ostensible purpose of the visit was overshadowed by the biggest display of popular defiance in the history of Communist China. On the eve of Gorbachev's arrival, several thousand students began a hunger strike in Tiananmen Square to publicize their demand for democratic reforms. By the day he left, the protest had spread to dozens of provincial cities. In Beijing alone more than a million people poured into the streets to express support for the students and call for the removal of unpopular Chinese leaders, beginning with Deng Xiaoping.

The demonstrators represented every conceivable walk of life. There were schoolchildren and steelworkers, bankers and bellhops, diplomats and doctors, artists and artisans. There were contingents from the training school of the Public Security Bureau, the Chinese secret police, and the Peo-

ple's Liberation Army. Even Beijing's notorious criminal gangs, the *liu-mang*, took part in the festivities, declaring a moratorium on petty crime for the duration of the protest and acting as the self-appointed guardians of public order.

The protesters arrived in the center of the city on bicycles and pickups, in trucks and buses, by taxi and on foot. As they marched down the Avenue of Heavenly Peace, past the luxury hotels that were the sign of China's explosive economic growth, and the entrance to the Forbidden City, where Deng and other Chinese leaders had their residences, to Tiananmen Square, the normally drab city became the backdrop for an astonishing political carnival. A host of sounds filled the air: the sirens of ambulances evacuating weakened hunger strikers from the square, the applause of bystanders, the drumbeats of marching bands, firecrackers, bicycle bells, and chants of "Down with corruption" and "We want democracy." There were cries of "Deng Xiaoping, go and play bridge," a reference to the favorite pastime of the ailing eighty-four-year-old leader. One group of protesters climbed to the roof of the History Museum, overlooking the hundred-acre square, and erected large banners reading "We Are the Soul of China" and "Perseverance Is Victory."

It was a Communist regime's worst nightmare, a popular uprising embracing all sections of society. The masses were symbolically reoccupying the square where Mao Zedong, standing on top of Tiananmen Gate, had proclaimed the People's Republic on October 1, 1949. A secular shrine bordered by the Forbidden City and the Great Hall of the People, Tiananmen Square had played a fateful role in Chinese history. It had been the setting for nationalist riots and fanatical Red Guard rallies, military parades and student protests, solemn state funerals and dissident demonstrations. But it had never witnessed scenes like this.

Watching the sea of humanity pour into the square, I was reminded of the early days of the Solidarity movement. The size of this demonstration was several times larger than anything I had seen in Poland, even during the pope's visit, but the exuberance and infectious gaiety of the crowds were very similar. After decades of passively submitting to totalitarian rule, the people were rebelling against their masters. The artificial barriers between different social classes and different age-groups were being swept away, allowing a pulverized and atomized society to discover its own strength. What had long been banned was suddenly permitted. As in Poland in August 1980, there was a sense of sheer improbability about what was happening that left people rubbing their eyes in disbelief.

The protests forced extensive changes in Gorbachev's schedule, begin-

ning with the arrival ceremony, which was moved from Tiananmen Square to the airport. The switch was made so abruptly that protocol officials were unable to roll out the usual red carpet. On his second day in Beijing, Gorbachev had to be smuggled into the Great Hall of the People through an obscure service entrance in the rear because the rest of the building was under siege by students. Planned excursions to the Forbidden City and the Imperial Palace were canceled. On the final day of the visit hundreds of journalists battled their way into the Great Hall for a promised end-of-summit press conference, only to learn that Gorbachev was stranded at his official residence, six miles away. There was only one solution. Since the Soviet leader was unable to reach his own press conference, the conference would have to go to him. The resulting obstacle chase, through streets filled with banner-waving demonstrators, was one of the zanier highlights of my journalistic career.

All semblance of organization and protocol had irretrievably broken down. We poured out of the Great Hall, followed closely by a small army of Soviet and Chinese officials, interpreters, and technicians. A motley fleet of bicycles, rickshaws, and minivans was commandeered for the mad dash across town. Cheered on by a carload of Gorbachev's security men, a dozen of us piled onto the back of a passing pickup. "Follow us," the KGB men shouted as they careered down an avenue filled with chanting protesters. Entering the spirit of the occasion, one of the security men held up a photo of Gorbachev and began flashing victory signs at the delighted demonstrators. Miraculously a path opened up through the million-strong multitude. Gripping the back of the pickup, we made a triumphant entrance to the government guesthouse where Gorbachev was staying. Soldiers in white gloves treated us as if we had arrived in a chauffeur-driven limousine, saluting smartly and waving our truck down a long driveway lined with artificial lakes and ornamental pagodas. Our friendly KGB escorts never made it to the news conference. Their decrepit Soviet Lada overheated in a gigantic traffic jam. They were last seen gazing disconsolately under the hood as steam billowed from the radiator.

While many Chinese students regarded Gorbachev as a symbol of democracy, he was careful not to say anything that would embarrass his official hosts. He used the press conference to express the hope that the crisis would be resolved through "dialogue" and "negotiation." But he also seemed to chide the protesters for wanting to move too far, too fast. "We, too, have hotheads who want to renovate socialism overnight," he told Chinese officials at one point. "But it doesn't happen like that in real life. Only in fairy tales."[20]

GORBACHEV HAD GOOD REASON not to gloat over the misfortunes of the Chinese Communists, for he had numerous troubles of his own. After four years in power, the length of an American presidential term, his political authority was rapidly eroding. He could no longer evade responsibility for the economic cataclysm hanging over the Soviet Union by denouncing the misguided policies of his predecessors. He himself was also to blame.

His political position seemed secure enough. Shortly before leaving for Beijing, Gorbachev had succeeded in purging the Central Committee of one-quarter of its members, replacing representatives of the old guard with his own supporters. In other respects, however, his policies were beginning to unravel. Perestroika contained within it the seeds of its own destruction.

By introducing elements of democracy into a totalitarian state, Gorbachev had released destructive centrifugal forces that were threatening to tear the Soviet Union apart. The upheavals in Georgia were a symptom of long-smoldering nationalist grievances that were spreading around the fringes of the old Russian empire and threatening to spill over into the traditional Slavic heartland. The relaxation of central controls had also had a devastating impact on the economy. The old rules had ceased to apply, but no new rules had been devised to take their place. The Soviet Union had entered a kind of economic twilight zone, where nobody could be sure of anything. The once-rigid five-year plan had been reduced to a catalog of empty promises. The ruble had plummeted in value because of a succession of catastrophic budget deficits. Since prices were still controlled by the state, the result was long lines and rationing by scarcity. Unable to rely on the promises of the planners and mistrusting their own currency, consumers and producers had retreated to a primitive barter system.

Gorbachev was paying the price for allowing political reform to outpace economic reform. The Chinese leaders, by contrast, had made dramatic strides toward a market economy but continued to deny freedom to their citizens. Both variants of reform were inherently unstable. The students who surged onto the streets of Beijing during Gorbachev's visit were a perfect illustration of the disparity between economic progress and political stagnation. It was no longer possible to seal the Middle Kingdom from the outside world. Thanks to Deng's modernization campaign and "open-door policy," tens of thousands of Chinese students had studied at universities in the United States and Europe. Millions more had been affected by the information revolution that had swept across Chinese campuses. The more the

students learned about the rest of the world, the more critical they became of the defects in their own society and the abuse of power by the Communist elite. Li Chaojie, a philosophy student at Beijing University, was speaking for many of his fellow protesters when he told me: "In China, power means money, the ability to do whatever you want. Corruption is everywhere. That is why we need democracy: in order to make those in power responsible for their actions."[21]

By the time Gorbachev arrived in Beijing, it was clear not only that communism had failed but that reform communism had also failed. China and the Soviet Union had taken opposite paths to reform, and both were in deep crisis. The Chinese reforms ignored the yearning for freedom; the Soviet reforms ignored the yearning for a better life.

In some respects, the course of the two reform efforts was preordained. Gorbachev was haunted by the memory of the 1964 Kremlin coup against Nikita Khrushchev, the last reformer to hold the office of general secretary. When the nomenklatura judged that Khrushchev had gone too far, they simply got rid of him, and nobody made the slightest protest. In order to prevent the same thing from happening to him, Gorbachev attempted to create new political institutions to counterbalance the power of the party. By unleashing the forces of glasnost, he ensured that the public would know what was going on and have the ability to react. "I often said to my colleagues when we began perestroika: 'If we do not think up something new, we will meet the same fate as Khrushchev,'" Gorbachev later acknowledged. "That was when we started on the first free elections."[22]

For the Chinese Communists, the Gorbachev tactic of arousing public opinion against the nomenklatura was frighteningly reminiscent of their Cultural Revolution. Chairman Mao had used a similar strategy in the mid-sixties, when he saw his dream of a socialist utopia begin to fade. The excesses of the Red Guards had left thousands of senior Chinese Communists, Deng included, with an abiding horror of spontaneous mass movements that could not be strictly controlled by the party. The fact that Gorbachev intended perestroika to be a peaceful revolution mattered little to Deng, who feared a general descent into chaos and anarchy. The memory of how he had been forced to make a humiliating self-criticism, stripped of all his leadership positions, separated from his family, and shipped off to the countryside was the most searing experience of his life, more terrible even than the Long March. His eldest son, a student at Beijing University, had been paralyzed from the waist down after leaping out of a fourth-floor window in an attempted suicide, while being persecuted by Red Guards.[23]

Now that he was back in power, the quality that Deng prized above all else was stability.

As long as Gorbachev was in Beijing, the students were assured a measure of protection. Indeed, knowing that the government would hesitate to use violence against them while the world was watching, they had timed their protest to coincide with his visit. But the sense of security provided by the presence of thousands of foreign journalists and live television coverage of events in Tiananmen Square was illusory. It took the Chinese authorities less than thirty-six hours after Gorbachev's departure to begin to reassert their control.

At 12:55 a.m., on Saturday, May 20, the loudspeakers in the square suddenly came to life with a hysterical tirade from Li Peng, the hard-line prime minister. Drowsy students emerged from their tents and buses to hear the man they considered their archenemy announce that martial law was being imposed on Beijing. His voice rising to a shriek, Li said that the leadership had decided to take "decisive and firm measures to put an end to the turmoil" and protect the socialist system in China. Troops had been authorized to use force to clear the square of hunger strikers and their supporters.

The speech was greeted by a deafening chorus of boos and chants of "Down with Li Peng," "Long live democracy," and "Victory belongs to us." By the time the prime minister finished speaking, tens of thousands of demonstrators were defiantly singing the "Internationale" and flashing victory signs. They scrawled their response to martial law on a banner plastered across the Monument to People's Heroes, just opposite the mausoleum housing Chairman Mao's embalmed remains: "We Came Here on Our Feet; We Will Leave Only on Our Backs."

The government followed up on its declaration of martial law by pulling the plug on live television coverage of the drama in Tiananmen Square. "Your task is over," a Foreign Ministry official told CNN. "You came here to report on Gorbachev. Gorbachev is gone." But when troops were sent to reoccupy the square, their path was blocked by makeshift barricades and human ramparts erected by tens of thousands of ordinary Beijing citizens.

Over the next few days the mood of the students switched repeatedly between fear, exhilaration, paranoia, exhaustion, elation, and back to fear again. Gangs of motorcyclists roared from one end of the city to the other to gather information on behalf of the hunger strikers. Many of the reports contradicted each other. The army was advancing. No, it was retreating.

The reformers were winning, and Li Peng was about to resign. No, it was the hard-liners who were winning, and Zhao Ziyang, the liberal Communist Party chief sympathetic to the students, who was under house arrest.

Lost in all of this was the position of the diminutive eighty-four-year-old Communist who had rebounded from disgrace several times to become de facto emperor of China. It was Deng Xiaoping, the great survivor of Chinese politics, who would have the last word.

BEIJING

June 3–4, 1989

AS RUMORS FLEW AROUND THE CITY that the People's Liberation Army was advancing on Tiananmen Square, thousands of Chinese students huddled around the base of the Monument to People's Heroes. A rickety white foam-and-plaster "Goddess of Democracy" rose high above their heads, facing the huge portrait of Chairman Mao at the entrance to the Forbidden City. Raising their right hands, the students swore a solemn oath: "For the sake of our country's democratization, for the sake of our country's real prosperity, for the sake of preventing our country from being usurped by a small band of conspirators ... I will devote my young life to protect Tiananmen and the Republic. I may be decapitated, my blood may flow, but the people's square will not be lost. We are willing to lose our young lives to fight to the very last person."[24]

Several miles away, in a special nuclear-safe command center in the Fragrant Hills district of the city's western suburbs, China's octogenarian leaders awaited news of the military operation against their own people.[25] Deng Xiaoping later insisted that China's future would have been "too terrible to imagine" had he not taken "firm action."[26] How could twenty-year-old students presume to know better than a veteran revolutionary, a man who had accompanied Mao on the Long March and survived the turmoil of the Cultural Revolution?

249

Over the past three weeks Deng had been humiliated in front of Gorbachev and the whole world. Not only had the students refused to allow him to revel in his greatest diplomatic triumph—the first Sino-Soviet summit in more than three decades—but they had publicly demanded his resignation. In an unsubtle pun on his given name, Xiaoping, which sounds like the Mandarin for "little bottle," they had smashed bottles on the pavements outside the Great Hall of the People. A decade earlier students had paraded through the streets of Beijing carrying glass bottles to express their support for Deng in his struggle against the ultraradical Gang of Four.

The issue now was very simple. Who had the greater political legitimacy: the students or the Communist Party leadership? The answer to that question was equally obvious. He who controlled Tiananmen Square, the symbolic heart of China, had traditionally claimed the right to represent "the people." It all boiled down to a question of power.

Shortly after the students swore to uphold democracy, a long column of tanks and armored cars started to move on the square from the west. Before going into battle, the troops had stood in front of their commanders and taken an oath of their own, to uphold law and order and prevent a recurrence of political "turmoil" in China. They were under orders to "recover the square" at any cost. This time they would not permit themselves to be deflected by unarmed protesters blocking their path as had happened just two weeks previously.

The first serious clashes occurred at a traffic circle at Gongzhufen, about ten blocks west of the square. As the motorized column forced its way through a barricade of buses and overturned taxis, demonstrators began pelting the troops with bricks and stones. The troops opened fire, first over the heads of the crowds but then directly at them. Enraged civilians grabbed hold of a couple of soldiers and tore them to pieces. A few blocks later the cycle of violence repeated itself, this time with greater fury. The Avenue of Heavenly Peace became a hellish battleground: flaming barricades; soldiers shooting indiscriminately from their AK-47s; panic-stricken civilians screaming abuse; army vehicles set alight with Molotov cocktails; bodies sprawled everywhere; the continuous wail of ambulance sirens. Eyewitnesses reported that the troops lost all sense of proportion, raking nearby apartment buildings with gunfire and slashing the dead with their bayonets.

By 2:30 a.m. the troops had sealed off the square from three sides, leaving a small gap in the southeast corner, through which the students would be permitted to flee. A well-known rock star from Taiwan, Hou Dejian, negotiated with the army for a peaceful withdrawal. "The students sang the

Internationale, their hands tightly clasped together," recalled Chai Linh, who had been elected commander of Tiananmen Square by her fellow students. "We were crying."27 As the students made their retreat, chanting, "The People's Army should not shoot at the people," they were savagely beaten by riot police with long nightsticks. The troops moved in behind them, sweeping aside the tent city that had been home to the hunger strikers for the past month and knocking down the "Goddess of Democracy." Later the army claimed that there were no killings within the narrow confines of the square. Nevertheless, it was clear to everybody that several thousand deaths had occurred within the immediate vicinity. Observing the carnage from the seventh floor of the Beijing Hotel, on the northeast corner of the square, the veteran American journalist Harrison Salisbury was reminded of Chairman Mao's dictum: "All power comes from the barrel of a gun."28

Determined not to allow its prize to slip from its grasp, the People's Liberation Army established machine-gun posts around the square, and mowed down anybody who got too close. Later that morning Radio Beijing boasted that Tiananmen had been cleansed of "trash" and "returned to the people." As far as China's Communist rulers were concerned, they and "the people" were one.

MOSCOW

May 25–June 9, 1989

THE MARQUIS DE CUSTINE VISITED RUSSIA in 1839. Although he spent less than three months in St. Petersburg and Moscow, the French aristocrat wrote a travelogue that some have hailed as the best book ever written about Russia by a foreigner. A habitué of the literary salons of Paris, anxious to establish a reputation as an outstanding writer, the marquis was snobbish, opinionated, and frequently condescending. Unlike his more celebrated contemporary Alexis de Tocqueville, who had toured America a few years earlier, Custine had little sympathy for the country that provided him with his material. But his observations about Russian despotism—a brutally repressive political system that had created what Custine described as a "nation of mutes"—contained insights that have stood the test of time.

Nations are mute only for a time—sooner or later the day of discussion arises; religion, policy, all speak and all explain themselves in the end. Thus, as soon as speech is restored to this silenced people, one will hear so much dispute that an astonished world will think it has returned to the confusion of Babel. . . . In a nation governed like this one, passions boil a long time before breaking out; while the danger approaches from hour to hour, the evil is prolonged, and the crisis de-

layed. Even our grandchildren may not see the explosion; but we can say to-day that explosion is inevitable, while we cannot predict the time.[29]

One and a half centuries later, when Mikhail Gorbachev granted the Soviet Union its first real parliament, the Congress of People's Deputies, many of these prophecies were realized. In Custine's phrase, the "day of discussion" had arrived.

It came in the form of a torrent of words that brought a country of 280 million people to a virtual standstill. For thirteen days Russians and Ukrainians, Balts and Uzbeks, Armenians and Azeris took part in a festival of free speech, the likes of which they had never seen before. Industrial production sank from Kaliningrad to Kamchatka as coal miners, factory managers, and government bureaucrats tuned in to the Kremlin soap opera. The debates were televised live, so there was no question of government censorship and no way of predicting what would happen next. At the beginning of the opening session a bearded actor from Latvia hijacked the proceedings by striding to the podium to call for a "minute's silence in memory of those who died in Tbilisi." Gorbachev and other Politburo members seemed taken aback by this unscripted intervention but were nonetheless forced to their feet.

Over the course of the next two weeks the deputies competed with one another to shatter long-standing political taboos. Everything was a matter for public discussion: from the war in Afghanistan to the spread of AIDS to the privileges of the Communist elite to the nature of the one-party system itself.

Every day brought a fresh sensation, the toppling of some hitherto sacrosanct Communist icon or a dramatic clash between reformers and conservatives. A truck driver from Kharkov accused Gorbachev of falling victim to flattery and allowing his wife, Raisa, to gain too much influence. He sarcastically compared the Soviet leader with the "great Napoleon," who, under the influence of assorted sycophants, including his consort, Josephine, had transformed France from a republic into an empire.[30] An Olympic weight-lifting champion launched an all-out attack on the KGB, which he said bore responsibility for "the destruction or persecution of millions of people." He called on the security organs to vacate Lubyanka Prison, where people who were "the pride and flower of our nations" were tortured and hurt.[31]

Not to be outdone, a historian, Yuri Karyakin, demanded that Lenin's

body be removed from its mausoleum by the Kremlin wall, the pantheon of Communist heroes. "Tanks roll across Red Square and the body vibrates. Scientists and artists touch up his face. This is a nightmare. It's all done for the sake of appearances. There is nothing there."[32] His words produced a stunned silence in the normally noisy hall.

One of the most riveting exchanges occurred when General Rodionov was called upon to explain his actions in Tbilisi on the night of April 9. Jeered by the radicals and cheered by the conservatives, the general depicted himself as the victim of a Stalinist witch-hunt by the mass media. He described the demonstration in front of the parliament building as a "provocation" and poured scorn on Georgian leaders for attempting to blame the military for what had happened. Minutes later the deputies were treated to an emotional speech from Patiashvili, who had resigned as Georgian first secretary immediately after the tragedy. Choking back tears, Patiashvili accused Rodionov of lying to him about the "degree of cruelty" that would be used against the population and concealing the use of entrenching tools and toxic gas.[33]

Mixed in with the rhetorical fireworks and occasional blasphemy were grim facts about life in the Soviet Union that had long been concealed from ordinary people. Revelations about environmental catastrophes, abysmal standards of public health, and economic lunacy poured out of the congress. An eminent biologist reported that 20 percent of the population lived in ecological disaster zones, where every third person could be expected to develop cancer. In some parts of the country infant mortality exceeded African levels. One-fifth of all the sausages in the Soviet Union and 42 percent of dairy products for children contained poisonous chemicals.[34] An agricultural specialist complained that the Soviet Union produced ten times as many combines and five times as many tractors as the United States but only half the amount of wheat. Distinguished scientists were obliged to do their calculations on abacuses because of the shortage of computers and even electronic calculators.[35]

For sheer political theater, the first session of the Congress of People's Deputies offered a breathtaking spectacle. First, there was the setting itself, a modernistic, glass-fronted hall in the heart of the Kremlin, overlooking the golden onion domes of the fifteenth-century Cathedral of the Assumption. Then there was the plot: Democracy comes to the one-party state. Finally there was the extraordinary cast of characters: Communist Party leaders and former political prisoners, Red Army generals and black-robed Orthodox priests, poets and nuclear scientists. Most of the Soviet elite took part in the work of the congress.

The action in the lobbies was as interesting as the speeches from the podium. After yelling at one another across an opera-size stage dominated by a huge statue of Lenin, the deputies would stream out into the marble-tiled lobbies to be confronted by cameras and microphones. For a press corps whose knowledge of Soviet leaders had traditionally been restricted to what little they chose to reveal in *Pravda*, it was a dream come true. In the space of a few hours a moderately energetic reporter could pick up quotes from the head of the KGB, Andrei Sakharov, Boris Yeltsin, a couple of cosmonauts, half a dozen Politburo members, and a representative sampling of Soviet intellectuals. Occasionally Gorbachev himself made an appearance in the halls, provoking a mass stampede. Television cameramen would shove legislators aside in a mad dash to get within shouting distance of the general secretary, bashing one another with their metal stepladders and long boom mikes.

Such were the birth pangs of Soviet democracy. What we reporters were not only witnessing but actively helping to accelerate with our undignified behavior was the demythologizing of Kremlin power. Communist demigods were being transformed into ordinary mortals before our eyes. Soviet politics, which had previously been restricted to a tiny elite, was now taking place in full view of the entire world. There was no more mystery.

It was a key moment in the downfall of communism and the eventual disintegration of the Soviet Union. The Communist Party's monolithic facade was the primary source of its political strength. Once Soviet politicians began speaking with many voices, allowing their own power bases to take precedence over party discipline, the cement that had been holding together a vast multinational country rapidly became unstuck.

OF THE OUTSIZE PERSONALITIES who dominated the First Congress of People's Deputies, two men stood out: Mikhail Gorbachev and Andrei Sakharov. They were the antipodes around whom the debate swirled. This was a clash of characters, rather than political opinions. Deep down inside, they shared a similar vision for their country. They wanted Russia to abandon its centuries-old messianic complex—the tsars had referred to Moscow as the Third Rome—and become part of the mainstream of world civilization. The question was how to achieve this grandiose goal, a problem that had preoccupied Russian reformers from Peter the Great onward.

Gorbachev was the supreme tactician. He proceeded by stealth, taking one step backward and two steps sideways for every one and a half steps forward. He was ready to make an alliance with anyone, in order to secure a

temporary political advantage. He was adept at hiding his true intentions beneath a fog of Communist rhetoric; he redefined the word "socialism" until it was deprived of any practical meaning. He was the master conjurer and illusionist. At times he was so clever that he even outsmarted himself. His intricate sleights of hand left him dizzy and disoriented, unsure about the direction in which he was moving or whether to support or condemn the revolution that he himself had unleashed. The physical strain of keeping the show on the road was so overwhelming that it was easy to lose sight of broader political objectives. After presiding over several hours of raucous parliamentary debate at the congress, he would retire to the Presidium Room in utter exhaustion.[36]

Sakharov, by contrast, was the ultimate man of principle. He was an antipolitician, who rejected the "art of the possible" in favor of a policy of speaking the truth at all times. He was impervious to the things that motivate most politicians: power, popularity, and the prospect of high office. He was unmoved by the opinion of his fellow parliamentarians or even his constituents. Hardened by decades of official persecution and the ostracism of many of his fellow scientists, he lived his life in accordance with a set of humanitarian values that he had worked out for himself. He had no interest in compromise, coalition building, or finding a common language with his political opponents. He did, and said, what he thought was right. His health had suffered as a result of the lack of proper medical attention during his six-year exile in the city of Gorky and several long hunger strikes. He was a poor orator, speaking haltingly and frequently becoming flustered. He lacked Gorbachev's debating skills or Yeltsin's talent for exciting crowds. But there was a clarity to Sakharov's thinking—the ability to go to the heart of a problem—that is the hallmark of a great scientist. As the debate raged around him, he would appear to drift off into his own self-contained world. But his mind continued to whir. All of a sudden he would snap out of his reverie and march to the rostrum, to make the essential point that had eluded everyone else.

Since Gorbachev had telephoned Sakharov in Gorky in December 1986 to inform him of his release from internal exile, there had been little personal contact between the two men. Their dealings with each other at the congress mirrored the stormy relationship between the father of perestroika and the pro-democracy forces he had let loose. At first Gorbachev treated Sakharov respectfully, protecting him from what one radical deputy called the "aggressive-obedient majority" and ensuring that he had ample time at the podium. The general secretary recognized the moral authority of the

Nobel Peace Prize laureate and wanted to tap into it. He viewed Sakharov as a one-man "loyal opposition," who could act as a political counterweight to the reactionaries and serve as a moderating influence on the radicals. As the congress wore on, however, Gorbachev became increasingly irritated with Sakharov and his constant moralizing.

There was a behind-the-scenes skirmish between the two men on June 1, halfway through the congress. Sakharov was concerned about the growing gap between words and deeds that was undermining public support for perestroika. Deciding that the time had come for a "frank talk," he asked to see the general secretary at the end of the evening session. They sat down together on the edge of the vast stage, underneath the towering statue of Lenin. As was his custom, Sakharov went immediately to the heart of the matter, telling Gorbachev that public confidence in his leadership had dropped "almost to zero." People were tired of listening to empty promises. The time had come to stop playing politics and decide, once and for all, whose side he was on.

"The country, and you personally, are at a crossroads. Either accelerate the process of change to the maximum, or try to retain the command-and-administer system in all of its aspects. In the first case, you will have to rely on the Left, and you'll be able to count on the support of many brave and energetic people. In the second case, you know yourself whose support you'll have, but they'll never forgive you for backing perestroika."[37]

A week of boisterous debate had exhausted Gorbachev. "His usual smile for me—half kindly, half condescending—never once appeared on his face," Sakharov later recalled. Gorbachev understood that the Soviet Union was facing a deepening crisis, but the kind of decisive action that Sakharov was demanding went against all his political instincts. For Gorbachev, politics was a constant compromise, a never-ending process of tacking one way and then another.

"I stand firmly for the ideas of perestroika," he replied. "But I'm against running around like a chicken with its head cut off. We've seen many 'big leaps,' and the results have always been tragedy and backtracking. I know everything that's being said about me. But I'm convinced the people will understand my policies."

For Sakharov, the only way out of the crisis was to push the revolution begun by Gorbachev to its logical conclusion. That meant stripping the apparatchiks of their power and vesting supreme authority in a democratically elected parliament. He wanted the congress to adopt a Decree on Power, abolishing the one-party state, severely restricting the authority of the

KGB, and paving the way for direct presidential elections. He pointed out that Gorbachev had never received a popular mandate and had never even faced a contested election. (A block of 100 seats in the 2,250-seat congress had been reserved for Communist Party nominees, led by the general secretary.)

"I'm very concerned that the only political result of the congress will be your achievement of unlimited personal power," Sakharov told Gorbachev. "Besides, you're vulnerable to pressure, to blackmail by people who control the channels of information. Even now, they're saying you took bribes in Stavropol, 160,000 rubles has been mentioned. A provocation? Then they'll find something else. Only election by the people can protect you from attack."

"I'm absolutely clean. And I'll never submit to blackmail. Not from the right, not from the left!"

At this point Gorbachev would almost certainly have won a popular election. Virtually everyone, including his opponents, conceded that he was irreplaceable. But he could not break ranks with his Politburo colleagues, most of whom were horrified by the thought of running for office, so he resisted Sakharov's suggestion. When his closest political ally, Aleksandr Yakovlev, advised him to give up the post of general secretary in order to become president, he replied that the party was a "monster" that must not be permitted to escape from his grasp.[38]

Gorbachev could never decide whether he was leader of the party, or leader of the country, or, as Sakharov put it, "the leader of the nomenklatura or the leader of perestroika." The contradiction remained unresolved until the very end, fatally undermining his authority. In the eyes of the apparat, he was a destroyer. In the eyes of the people, he was first and foremost a Communist.

THE FOLLOWING DAY the "aggressive-obedient majority" went on the offensive. Like Sakharov, the apparatchiks wanted to know whose side Gorbachev was on. Their instrument for getting the general secretary to reveal his hand was an emotional speech by a legless Afghan war veteran, attacking Sakharov for lack of patriotism.

Sergei Chervonopisky evoked an immediate wave of sympathy from the hall as he hobbled painfully to the rostrum on his crutches. He began by denouncing the shameful treatment of the former "fighting internationalists" and the primitive state of the Soviet prosthetics industry, which remained

"at the level of the Stone Age." He depicted the Tbilisi tragedy as an anti-military "provocation" and accused the liberal media of carrying out an "unprecedented persecution" of the Soviet army. He then read out an open letter from a group of paratroopers denouncing Sakharov for his "irresponsible, provocative" statements about the war in Afghanistan.[39] The Nobel laureate had claimed in a newspaper interview that Soviet helicopters had opened fire on Soviet soldiers to prevent them from deserting to the enemy.

Inspired by thunderous applause from the conservatives, Chervonopisky now turned his sights on Gorbachev. Noting that more than 80 percent of the deputies were Communists, he said the time had come to pin their colors to the mast. He accused the general secretary of failing to even mention the word "communism" in his report to the congress.

"I am a convinced opponent of sloganeering and window dressing, but today I will proclaim three words for which I believe we all, without exception, must fight."

Here the speaker paused dramatically. Expressing ideology in the form of a sacred trilogy had an almost mystical appeal for Russian conservatives. Everyone in the hall was familiar with the reactionary tsarist slogan—"Orthodoxy, Autocracy, Nationalism"—and they wondered what new rallying cry the disabled war veteran could have in mind. Chervonopisky pronounced his triple formula slowly and deliberately: "State, Motherland, Communism."

The three words brought most in the hall to their feet, for the loudest ovation of the congress. Politburo members, seated discreetly to one side of the hall, joined in with enthusiasm. At first Gorbachev remained seated, applauding politely. But as the cheering turned to a rhythmic clapping, he too rose. Remaining seated required an almost physical effort of willpower. "I felt some powerful force propelling me up out of my seat, compelling me to join the standing ovation," the radical deputy Anatoly Sobchak recalled later. Determined not to succumb to the "mass hysteria," he grabbed the armrests of his chair. "I remembered that feeling from my army service, marching to a military band. But that was only a parade. Here it was more like a battle."[40]

Attempting to defend himself, Sakharov went to the rostrum to say that he had the greatest respect for the ordinary Soviet soldier. His bony head cocked slightly to one side, his words almost whistling through the gaps in his teeth, he ignored the growing uproar as best he could. "The war in Afghanistan was a criminal one, a criminal adventure. . . ." (Here he raised

his voice above the shrieks of derision that poured down on him from all sides.) "A criminal adventure undertaken by unknown persons. We do not know who bears responsibility for this enormous crime against the motherland. This crime cost the lives of almost a million Afghans, a war of destruction was waged against an entire people."

The conservatives were shouting so loudly now that Sakharov could hardly be heard. Few deputies were listening to what he had to say anyway. He seemed a beaten, dejected figure, as isolated as he had ever been. Still he pressed ahead. "I came out against sending Soviet troops into Afghanistan, and for this I was exiled to Gorky." Noise in the hall, shouts of "Apologize," "Shame on you." "Precisely this was the main reason, I am proud of this. . . ." The words were almost drowned out by jeers and whistles. "I am proud of this exile to Gorky, as a decoration that I received. . . . I do not apologize to the entire Soviet army, as I have not insulted it. I was insulting neither the Soviet army nor the Soviet soldier." Noise in the hall. "I was accusing those who gave this criminal order to send Soviet troops into Afghanistan." General pandemonium, jeers, chants of "Away with Sakharov," scattered applause.

After Sakharov had finished, the "aggressive-obedient majority" set about him with a vengeance. One by one deputies who had remained silent during the invasion of Afghanistan climbed to the rostrum to accuse Sakharov of slander and dishonor. It was as if they were justifying their own subservience by venomously attacking the one man in the Soviet Union who had had the courage to speak out. The verbal lynching was reminiscent of the way Yeltsin had been treated after daring to criticize Gorbachev and Ligachev at the Politburo meeting eighteen months earlier. Nobody came to Sakharov's aid; the radicals were stunned into silence. Although Gorbachev seemed embarrassed by what was happening, covering his face with his hands, he did nothing to stop the attacks.

The onslaught reached a climax with a vituperative speech by a teacher from Uzbekistan. Her voice choked with tears, Tursun Kazakova said Sakharov had canceled out all his previous services to the nation "by this one action." "You have insulted the entire army, the entire people, all our fallen who have given up their lives," she screamed. "I have nothing but contempt. You should be ashamed!"

This hysterical performance brought those in the hall to their feet for yet another standing ovation. This time, however, Gorbachev remained in his seat.

As long as the Soviet Union remained a semifree country, with a semi-

democratic parliament, Sakharov continued to obey the dictates of his own conscience. He trusted the good sense of the millions of ordinary Soviet citizens who were following the proceedings on television. He was right about that. As a result of the congress, Sakharov achieved an almost heroic stature. Letters and telegrams of support poured into his apartment on the Moscow ring road and the Academy of Sciences, which had attempted to block his nomination.

A few weeks after the congress the country's most popular newspaper, *Argumenty i Fakty*, ran a poll among its twenty million readers to nominate the "best deputy." Sakharov topped the list, Yeltsin was second, and Gorbachev was a distant seventeenth. The general secretary was so annoyed by this result that he attempted to fire the editor, who refused to resign. Whether Gorbachev liked it or not, glasnost had come of age.

TWO DAYS AFTER THE COMMUNIST WORLD had been shaken by the earthquakes in China and Poland, Mikhail Gorbachev sought inspiration at the shrine of Vladimir Ilyich Lenin. When the congress broke for lunch, deputies were invited to join the Soviet leadership in making a ritual pilgrimage to the mausoleum, in Red Square, where Lenin's body had lain in state for six decades. In the company of the international press corps, Gorbachev led the Politburo on the half mile hike through the Kremlin grounds.

Surrounded by a moving wall of bodyguards and television cameras, his wife, Raisa, by his side, Gorbachev was his usual ebullient self as he headed for the Kremlin's ancient Spassky Gate. He seemed to relish all the attention. For all its rowdiness and unpredictability, the first Congress of People's Deputies had represented an unquestioned political triumph for the father of glasnost. He had dominated the proceedings from the very beginning, alternately charming and cajoling the deputies, making up the rules as he went along, doing everything he could to steer the unruly congress in the direction he wanted. For someone who had risen through the ranks of a totalitarian state and had no experience of democratic debate, it was an amazing performance. Gorbachev took to parliamentary democracy instinctively. He knew how to twist arms, make deals, bend rules, win votes, exploit the media. He could outtalk, outmaneuver, and outargue everyone else in the room. Thanks to his ability to think fast on his feet, he was usually two or three steps ahead of his political opponents. He was also incredibly persistent. He understood that nothing is ever final in politics and that

the political struggle continues even when it appears to be over. He was the great improviser, the Houdini of Soviet politics, the statesman with nine lives.

The rest of the Politburo fell in line behind Gorbachev as he strode past the palaces and cathedrals of the Kremlin, waving cheerfully at astonished tourists. The contrast between the charismatic Soviet leader and these bureaucratic drones was stunning. They walked clustered together in a grim silence, fending off attempts by reporters to ask questions about events in China and Poland. It was enough to look at their somber, melancholy faces to guess what was running through their minds. Gorbachev may have come into his element, but their world was falling apart. The powers and privileges that they had worked all their lives to achieve were being stripped away from them, as rival centers of authority appeared in the country. During the past few days they had been forced to observe the debates in the congress from the wing of the vast hall, rather than the traditional place of honor on the presidium. It was a bewildering, humiliating experience.

For several months now, as Gorbachev acquired the status of an international superstar, other Soviet leaders had felt themselves increasingly left out in the cold. "We felt some kind of zone, or curtain, separating him from other members of the Politburo," Vitaly Vorotnikov wrote in his memoirs. "We believed in Gorbachev for a very, very long time. We pinned our hopes on him, and were unable to imagine what kind of paths he would lead us down. Alas, we realized what was happening far too late. [By that time], the pseudodemocratic train had gained such speed that it had become impossible to stop." Half in admiration, half in disgust, Vorotnikov cited Gorbachev's unique ability to create a rhetorical mist "so that each of the opposite sides began to think that the *gensek* supported its position."[41]

The congress may not have been democratic enough for Sakharov and his supporters. For oligarchs like Vorotnikov, it was far too democratic. They were losing their ability to control events. During the breaks they gathered backstage, in the old Presidium Room, to grumble about the antics of the radicals and express alarm about the direction in which the country was headed. Gorbachev's chief of staff later wrote that he had never seen Politburo members look so alarmed. "Most of them realized that a door had just been opened, and a motley crowd had burst through it. They were frightened by the kind of sentiments the crowd was voicing in front of the entire nation."[42]

It was a decisive moment. Everyone understood that the genie of freedom had escaped from the bottle and that only massive repression would

succeed in stuffing it back in. The bloodshed in Tiananmen Square and the revolution by ballot box that was under way in Poland had crystallized the options facing Gorbachev. In the phrase of one of his Communist Party aides, he now stood at "a political and moral crossroads."[43] His revolution from above had become a revolution from below. He could permit the revolution to continue, in the knowledge that reformers like himself would ultimately be swept away, or he could use force to stop the revolution in its tracks. That would mean abandoning the hope of radical economic reform for another generation and risking an all-out confrontation with the West.

LED BY GORBACHEV, the Politburo members passed through the fortified Spassky Gate, with its four-sided clock and crenellated green spire, topped by a red star, onto the cobblestoned vastness of Red Square. Still fending off reporters' questions, they marched into the boxlike red marble mausoleum in the center of the square. The KGB honor guards snapped to attention as Lenin's modern-day heirs disappeared inside the black marble doors and descended into a dimly lit basement, where the temperature was kept at fifty-nine degrees Fahrenheit.

The body of the dead Bolshevik lay on a bed, beneath a bulletproof glass shield that had withstood several physical assaults, including a visitor who blew himself up with homemade explosives in 1973. Only Lenin's waxlike hands and head—which housed a brain purportedly 25 percent larger than that of the average human—were visible above the blanket. Hidden wires connected the body to an underground control room, where teams of scientists monitored its condition twenty-four hours a day. (The Russian press later claimed that most of the corpse was moldy, following a bungled restoration job during World War II, when it was evacuated to Siberia to prevent it from falling into the hands of the advancing Nazis.) The subterranean complex also included a secret workout room, where KGB officers were encouraged to get into shape, after a hard day guarding Vladimir Ilyich's physical remains.

The Soviet leaders filed past the body in an atmosphere of hushed reverence. As they emerged into the sunlight, they ran into the mob of journalists and cameramen, yelling questions about the events in Beijing. Gorbachev hemmed and hawed, saying that he was watching developments in China with "concern" but that every government was responsible for its own actions.

"At the press conference in China, I said we are in favor of a dialogue be-

tween the state and Party organs, working people, and students. The answer to these questions can only be decided through dialogue. This is also my position now."[44]

The equivocal position adopted by Gorbachev provoked much grumbling from the radicals. Anxious to forestall similar tragedies at home, they demanded a forthright condemnation of Beijing and a clear definition of the circumstances in which it was permissible to use force to break up demonstrations. Yeltsin described the actions of the Chinese army as "a crime against humanity." Sakharov called for the withdrawal of the Soviet ambassador from Beijing. The *gensek*, however, refused to make things any clearer. He was determined to preserve his freedom of maneuver.

It was Gorbachev's fate to operate in the shadowy world between politics and morality, where right and wrong are always relative and everything depends on the final result. In the cutthroat world of Kremlin politics, morality was a luxury that a statesman could ill afford. The primary goal was political survival. Had Gorbachev taken the kind of absolutist moral position favored by Sakharov, he would almost certainly have been stabbed in the back by his own colleagues.

At the same time, he did remain true to certain basic principles. Although he dabbled with violence himself and closed his eyes to its use by other Soviet leaders, he never permitted a forcible reversal of the political processes that he had set in motion. In 1989 he still had the power to stop the Second Russian Revolution in its tracks, before it accelerated out of control and the Soviet empire disintegrated. But he deliberately failed to use this power because he feared it would only lead to massive bloodshed and smother all hope of reform for another generation. He rejected the Tiananmen option. He permitted the revolution to proceed, behind a fog of rhetoric that confused supporters and opponents alike. The creation of this verbal smoke screen was arguably his greatest achievement.

Gorbachev's resolve and political skill were soon to be put to the test by a series of dramatic events in Eastern Europe.

WARSAW

June 4, 1989

WHILE THE CHINESE PEOPLE'S ARMY was suppressing the last vestiges of popular resistance around Tiananmen Square, another Communist regime on the other side of the world was submitting its record to the judgment of the electorate. For the first time in more than forty years, the citizens of Poland had been granted the right to express their opinions through the ballot box. They were using their newfound freedom to deliver a massive rebuff to their self-appointed rulers.

The stark choice confronting Communist leaders, in the face of mounting popular discontent, was summed up by two evocative sounds. There was the rat-tat-tat of machine guns in China, as security forces splattered unarmed protesters with bullets. And there was the scrrratch-scrratch-scratch of voters' pens in Poland crossing out the names of Communist parliamentary candidates. It was the choice between suppression of the people and submission to the people, dictatorship and democracy, violence and nonviolence. It had its clearest expression on June 4, 1989.

The Polish Communists had already tried mass repression, and it had failed to resolve any of Poland's underlying problems. Store shelves were no fuller than in December 1981, when Jaruzelski imposed martial law. Workers had not become more productive. Factories still churned out substan-

dard goods that were practically impossible to sell on world markets; even the Soviets had complained about the quality. The foreign debt crisis was graver than ever. The environment had suffered further devastation, and standards of public health had continued to decline. The psychological shock of martial law was rapidly wearing off. After a period of stunned resignation, strikes and other forms of protest were again becoming commonplace. The government was preparing a package of sweeping austerity measures, including large-scale layoffs and big price increases. Sooner or later another social explosion seemed inevitable.

In theory Jaruzelski still had the possibility of resorting to martial law once again, an option favored by Communist Party hard-liners. This time around, however, martial law would probably have to be accompanied by mass bloodshed. Repression on such a scale went against his own character and the trend of events in the Soviet Union under Gorbachev. Using force against the population would also kill off any prospect of radical economic reform.

It was here that the comparison with China broke down. In China the transition to free markets was already well under way when Deng Xiaoping sent tanks to crush the student protests. The chaos and confusion of the Cultural Revolution, coming on top of the disastrous Great Leap Forward, had produced a backlash within the Communist Party in favor of economic pragmatism. In Poland, by contrast, the reformers lacked a reliable political base, either inside or outside the ruling party. If Jaruzelski chose the path of violence, he would be forced to rely on the most reactionary wing of the Communist Party, which saw free enterprise as a mortal threat. Without popular support, there could be no reform and no chance of escaping the seemingly endless cycle of repression and revolt.

The alternative to repression was dialogue with the opposition. Jaruzelski decided to give Solidarity the chance of participating in discussions about Poland's future in return for helping keep the peace. In order to carry out this U-turn, he had to quell a revolt from his own ranks. At a session of the policy-making Central Committee he and his key supporters silenced the critics by threatening to resign en masse.

The precise shape of the proposed Round Table and the placement of the guests became the subject of protracted negotiations. The finest carpenters in the land were commissioned to construct a huge doughnut-shaped table, with accommodation for up to sixty people. This magnificent piece of furniture was nearly twenty-eight feet in diameter, providing a safety margin of three feet over and above the world's longest-recorded spitting distance.[45] It

was periodically assembled, disassembled, uncovered, covered, brought to Warsaw and returned to the manufacturer as both sides maneuvered for political advantage. Subtables and sub-subtables were added. Finally, on February 6, 1989, jailers and jailed sat down together around the now-mythical table, their view of one another partially obscured by floral decoration. Two months later they announced that they had reached agreement on the relegalization of Solidarity and the first semifree elections in the history of People's Poland.

In keeping with Jaruzelski's determination to introduce democracy in carefully regulated doses, everything was done to ensure that the Communists won these trial elections. Senior members of the Jaruzelski government were permitted to run unopposed on a "National List." An official candidate would be considered "elected" as long as a majority of voters did not go to the trouble of putting a cross through his name. Of the seats in the Sejm, the lower chamber of the parliament, 65 percent would be reserved for the Communists and their allies. Solidarity, meanwhile, would be restricted to contesting the remaining 35 percent of "open" seats in the lower chamber and all one hundred seats in the less powerful Senate.

On election day polling places were decorated in bright red and white bunting, the Polish national colors. The Communist candidates concealed their political loyalties as best they could, hiding behind the anonymity of the National List. But there was no doubt about the identity of the Solidarity representatives. Their photographs had all been taken individually with Wałęsa at the Lenin Shipyard in Gdańsk and turned into campaign posters, which were plastered up all over Poland. Shortly before the election Solidarity had designed a final campaign poster that summarized what was at stake after forty-four years of uninterrupted Communist rule. It was a photo of the actor Gary Cooper in full cowboy regalia. "High Noon, June 4," the slogan declared.

Everybody expected the Solidarity candidates to do well, but the results were stunning. In the first round of the election Solidarity won 160 out of the 161 seats in the Sejm that it was allowed to contest, and 92 seats in the Senate. Only 2 members of the National List managed to secure the 50 percent of the votes needed for election. After four decades of enforced unanimity and sham elections, the temptation to "throw the bums out" was simply too great for ordinary voters to resist. In fact they took what one voter described as an "almost sensual pleasure" in putting crosses through the names of well-known Communists—from the prime minister down. "I crossed out all of them," said a voter in Warsaw, "because every one of them

is compromised. They promised us things so many times in the past, and every time they failed."[46]

This was not the result Solidarity had wanted. As he voted in Gdańsk, Wałęsa had told reporters that "too big a percentage of our people getting through would be disturbing, and might force a fight on us." He himself voted for all the names on the National List, with the exception of Interior Minister Czesław Kiszczak, his onetime jailer. Solidarity leaders knew that Jaruzelski still had the support of the army and the police. After winning their lopsided victory, they had to guard against seeming too triumphant. "We knew we had won, but we couldn't express our happiness too openly because we also knew that they had all the guns," recalled Bronisław Geremek, the leader of the Solidarity parliamentary group.[47]

When party leaders got together to discuss the results of the election, their mood was bleak and defeatist. "The election results are terrible," conceded Jaruzelski. Like a commander struggling to keep his troops together in retreat, the general parceled out commands and assignments. He ordered a new round of discussions, with everybody from the Roman Catholic Church to the "allies," apparatchik-speak for the Kremlin. Outwardly he seemed calm and in control, but aides who knew him well could see that he was going through another bout of intense mental anguish.[48] He wanted so much to go down in Polish history as the father of democracy, but he had been unable to shake off his popular image as the general in dark glasses who had imposed martial law. His reward for choosing the path of dialogue and reconciliation, rather than the path of violence and oppression, was massive rejection by the voters.

Like Gorbachev before him, Jaruzelski made the mistake of thinking he could control the pace and scope of change. He thought he could persuade Solidarity to share responsibility for painful economic reforms without giving the movement real power. He believed that the transition to democracy would be gradual. But events had assumed a momentum of their own. By agreeing to talks with Wałęsa, he had triggered a political process that was to lead inexorably to his own downfall.

At the official inquest into the party's electoral defeat on June 5, different explanations were suggested for the debacle. Some accused Solidarity of being too aggressive; some blamed the influence of the Catholic Church; some criticized the party for elementary political mistakes. But it was the minister for economic reform, Władysław Baka, one of the defeated candidates on the National List, who put the matter most cogently. "The people simply didn't want us anymore," he told his comrades.[49]

That evening the official Communist Party spokesman went on television to concede the obvious: "The elections had the character of a referendum, and Solidarity won a clear majority." The following day, June 6, the outgoing Communist prime minister, Mieczysław Rakowski, invited his inner circle to breakfast. Everybody was tired, and there was a *fin de régime* atmosphere about the meeting. The scale of the disaster was summed up by the acerbic government spokesman Jerzy Urban, who just a few months ago had been describing Wałęsa as a "private citizen" and Solidarity as a "nonexistent organization."

"This is not just a lost election, gentlemen. It's the end of an age."[50]

FOROS

August 22, 1989

THE CRIMEA HAD BEEN a favorite vacation spot for Russian rulers ever since Catherine the Great captured it from the Turks in the late eighteenth century. A subtropical paradise of palm trees and vineyards, the mountainous peninsula jutting into the Black Sea was considered the jewel in the imperial crown. Tsars and general secretaries came here every year to take restorative cures, breathe the balmy sea air, and escape the cares of state. When power changed hands, a new palace invariably appeared along the winding coastal road, each more magnificent than the last.

Soon after he became Soviet leader, Gorbachev decided that he too deserved a grandiose summer residence. The site he chose was on the southernmost tip of the Crimea, midway between the historic towns of Sevastopol and Yalta, in a particularly dramatic and isolated spot. A two-thousand-foot-high ridge rose behind the rocky beach, creating a sun-drenched semicircular bowl, sandwiched between the mountains and the sea.

Construction of the residence began in 1987 and was accorded top priority. Thousands of soldiers labored around the clock to complete the private resort, which included tennis courts, outdoor and indoor swimming pools, a helicopter landing pad, a cinema, and secret communications facil-

ities. Hundreds of tons of topsoil were trucked in to create a shady land-scape, along with an instant orchard of peach trees. A hotel was built for bodyguards and service staff. The Gorbachev family residence itself was a tasteless architectural mishmash, consisting of two concrete boxes, with sloping red-tiled roofs, joined by a covered bridge. A sixty-foot glass esca-lator provided access to the beach. From the outside the compound looked like a cross between a luxury hotel and an inhospitable prison camp, sur-rounded by watchtowers and several high metal fences.

From the start there was an air of ill omen about Foros. The *gensek's* bodyguards took an immediate dislike to the place, which they nicknamed the "frying pan" because it was so hot. In the fall landslides would dislodge rocks from the surrounding mountains, cutting off the approach roads. Work on the residence was as slipshod as it was rushed. Shortly after the first family moved in, in the summer of 1988, an oak beam fell on the head of Gorbachev's grown-up daughter, Irina. She had to spend a week in the surgery ward of the local hospital, and there was some concern she would suffer permanent brain damage. After that incident the bodyguards began jumping up and down on the beds and chairs, to test the solidity of the fur-niture.[51]

By the time of Gorbachev's second vacation in Foros in August 1989, it was not just the villa that was crumbling about him. The entire Soviet em-pire, assembled so arduously by his predecessors, was in the process of falling apart. The Soviet withdrawal from Afghanistan had been a harbin-ger of things to come.

THE ROT HAD GONE furthest in Poland, traditionally the most trouble-some of the East European satellites, with the Communist Party's deva-stating electoral defeat. To make matters worse, the party had been deserted by long-subservient political allies and could no longer command a parlia-mentary majority. A leading Communist reformer, General Kiszczak, had tried, and failed, to form a government. In order to break the impasse, Soli-darity had proposed a compromise: "Your President, Our Prime Minis-ter."[52] Jaruzelski would be permitted to stay on as a largely ceremonial head of state but would be obliged to accept a Solidarity-led government.

Communist power was unraveling elsewhere in Eastern Europe as well. In Hungary a liberal Communist regime was physically dismantling the Iron Curtain erected by Stalin at the end of World War II to seal his empire from the West. On May 2 Hungarian soldiers had begun tearing down the

barbed-wire fences and watchtowers along the border with Austria. When President Bush visited Budapest in July, his Hungarian hosts presented him with a symbolic piece of the Iron Curtain in a glass display case. News that gaping holes had appeared in the once-impenetrable border spread quickly. Within weeks thousands of East Germans, chafing against draconian travel restrictions in their own country, were attempting to use Hungary as a transit point to the West.

To a certain extent, Gorbachev was prepared for these developments. During his meetings with East European leaders he had repeatedly warned of the danger of "lagging behind" events. He and his advisers understood that the era of Soviet domination of Eastern Europe was coming to an end, even if they did not expect the end to come so suddenly. In a speech to the European Parliament in Strasbourg, in July, he had called for the Cold War to be "consigned to oblivion" and had acknowledged explicitly, for the first time, that socialist revolutions were reversible: "The social and political orders of certain countries changed in the past, and may change again in the future. However, this is exclusively a matter for the peoples themselves to decide; it is their choice. Any interference in internal affairs, or any attempts to limit the sovereignty of states—including friends and allies, or anyone else—are impermissible."[53] In effect Gorbachev was abandoning the so-called Brezhnev doctrine of limited sovereignty. According to this doctrine, the security and well-being of the socialist community were indivisible. If socialism was endangered anywhere in the Soviet bloc, it was the duty of all other socialist countries to provide "fraternal assistance." There could be no defections from the socialist camp.

Burying the Brezhnev doctrine was facilitated by the fact that Soviet ideologists had always denied its existence. The term was an invention of Western Sovietologists, summarizing the arguments used by Moscow to justify the invasion of Czechoslovakia. In theory the Soviet Union remained committed to the principles of equality, independence, and noninterference in international affairs. Gorbachev's contribution was to give real content to what had hitherto been an empty slogan. When the Czechoslovak leader Gustáv Husák asked him for advice about personnel changes in the Communist Party, an area of vital concern to Brezhnev, Gorbachev refused to get involved. "It's clearer to you what you should do than to us in Moscow," he replied airily.[54] His spokesman began talking about the "Sinatra doctrine": Let everyone be able to say, "I do it my way."[55]

"There never was any formal decision to refrain from the use of force in Eastern Europe," said Aleksandr Yakovlev, who helped Gorbachev devise

his foreign policy strategy. "We simply stopped being hypocritical. For years we had told the entire world that these countries were free and independent, even though this was obviously not the case. There was no need to take a formal decision. We just had to implement what was already official policy."[56]

Traditionally, Soviet foreign policy had been a prerogative of the general secretary. Although Ligachev and other conservatives repeatedly bemoaned the loss of Soviet influence in Eastern Europe at Politburo meetings, they were reluctant to challenge Gorbachev in an area that was clearly his responsibility. By his own account, Ligachev was more concerned about propping up socialism in East Germany than in Poland. He regarded the formation of a Solidarity-led government as Poland's "internal affair."[57]

By the time the conservatives realized what was happening, it was too late. The dominoes had begun to fall.

GORBACHEV LIKED FOROS because it enabled him to escape the hothouse world of Kremlin politics. Dressed in shorts, a sports cap, and hiking boots, he spent two hours a day strolling through the mountains above the dacha with Raisa. Bodyguards trailed behind, with rucksacks loaded up with mineral water, two-way radios, and Kalashnikov sub-machine guns. Sometimes the Gorbachev family took an excursion by boat, down the indented Crimean coastline, as far as the white tsarist palace at Livadia, where Stalin, Roosevelt, and Churchill had decided the fate of Europe in the dying days of World War II.

Outside visitors were rarely invited to Foros. The general secretary had no desire to socialize with his Politburo colleagues; there had always been a terrible sense of isolation and loneliness at the summit of Kremlin power. Gorbachev was surrounded by sycophantic courtiers, but he had very few personal friends. One outsider to penetrate the Gorbachev family circle was his foreign policy aide, Anatoly Chernyayev. The former diplomat regarded himself as the representative of Russia's liberal intelligentsia in the Gorbachev court. He served as a debating foil for the general secretary and helped him with his speeches and theoretical works about perestroika. His meticulous, handwritten diary reflects Gorbachev's concerns that summer, and the sense of a political and economic order that was falling apart:

> Socialism is disappearing in Eastern Europe. Western Communist parties are collapsing everywhere where they have been unable to identify themselves with a national idea. . . . But the main thing is the

disintegration of myths and unnatural forms of life in our own society. The planned economy is falling apart, the "image" of socialism is
disappearing. Ideology, as such, no longer exists. The empire is falling
apart. The party has lost its leading, dominating role, and repressive
force, and is breaking up. The power [of the centralized state] has
been shattered, and nothing has yet filled the vacuum. Signs of chaos
are accumulating. . . .[58]

For Gorbachev, the upheavals in Eastern Europe were a sideshow to the
main event, the revolution in the Soviet Union itself. Everywhere he looked,
there were threats and challenges. Scarcely a day went by without a new crisis: an upsurge of ethnic violence in Uzbekistan; nationalist protests in the
Baltic states; strikes by hundreds of thousands of coal miners in Ukraine
and Siberia. His own ability to influence events and manipulate the public
debate was rapidly declining, a process he found deeply frustrating. In private conversations with Chernyayev, he railed at the press for "stirring
things up" and at the Balts for their selfish preoccupation with national independence, which threatened to torpedo the entire experiment in controlled reform. He was also troubled by the growing militancy of ethnic
Russians, who had hitherto formed the backbone of the Soviet state.

"If Russia rises up, then it will really begin," he commented bitterly. "It
will be the end of empire."

The dwindling personal authority of the father of perestroika was only
part of a much larger crisis of power throughout the Soviet bloc. Moscow
could no longer issue commands and expect them to be obeyed from Vilnius
to Vladivostok, much less in Berlin and Budapest. Local authorities, and
even individual citizens, were deciding for themselves which instructions
they would implement. Students were evading the draft, factory managers
were ignoring the plan, and newspaper editors were throwing Central Committee instructions into the garbage.

The crisis of power was particularly evident in the economic field. The
centralized system of distribution had virtually broken down under the
strain of the deepening economic crisis. Shortages of almost everything,
from television sets to toilet paper, were causing local authorities to look for
ways to protect their own consumers. A "shopping-bag war" had broken
out in early 1989, when Czechoslovakia and East Germany banned the export of children's clothing and certain food items to neighboring socialist
states. The Soviet Union countered with a similar prohibition on the export
of refrigerators, washing machines, and caviar. Regions, cities, and even vil-

lages had joined the rush toward protectionism. In the middle of August Moscow city authorities announced that shoppers would have to produce residence permits in order to purchase a wide range of "deficit" items. The planned economy, with its rigidly formulated quotas and deadlines, had effectively given way to a rudimentary system of barter. In the absence of a free market, it was everyone for himself.

When the American secretary of state, James A. Baker III, visited Moscow in May, he urged Gorbachev to take the first step toward the creation of a market by abolishing state controls over prices. The Soviet leader had been resisting similar advice from his own economists because he feared a popular backlash over rising prices. Baker, a former treasury secretary, urged Gorbachev to act quickly while he still enjoyed a "credit of trust." "If we did this, people really would lose confidence in us," Gorbachev replied. "We are already twenty years late with price reform. It's impossible to turn things around in two or three years."[59]

What Baker failed to understand—and Gorbachev could not acknowledge—was that the "credit of trust" in perestroika had already expired.

ALTHOUGH GORBACHEV WAS PREOCCUPIED with domestic affairs, he could not help paying some attention to events in Poland during his Foros vacation. Negotiations were under way for the formation of a Solidarity-led government under the premiership of Tadeusz Mazowiecki, a veteran Catholic editor and former political prisoner. The Communists had been promised two ministerial portfolios—defense and internal affairs—but wanted more. Everybody understood that a major turning point in the postwar history of Eastern Europe had been reached. For the first time ever a ruling Communist Party was on the threshold of surrendering effective political power.

Communist leaders elsewhere in Eastern Europe were dismayed by the prospect of a Solidarity-led government in Poland, but most of them understood that they were powerless to prevent it. The exception was the maverick Romanian dictator, Nicolae Ceauşescu. A Stalinist diehard who headed the most repressive regime in Eastern Europe, Ceauşescu had managed to win plaudits from Western statesmen by occasionally distancing himself from Moscow. In August 1968 he had been the sole Soviet bloc leader to condemn the invasion of Czechoslovakia, on the ground that it violated the principle of national sovereignty. The threat to Communist rule in Poland caused a 180-degree turn in Ceauşescu's foreign policy. From

being the champion of national independence he had now became the staunchest advocate of the defunct Brezhnev doctrine.

At midnight on August 19 the Polish ambassador in Bucharest was hauled out of bed and presented with an urgent diplomatic note from the Romanian government, setting forth Ceaușescu's views on the crisis. Denouncing Solidarity as the hireling of "international imperialism," the note called on the Polish army to facilitate the formation of a "government of national salvation," led by the Communists. It said that the remaining Warsaw Pact countries had both the right and the obligation to take joint action to defend the "cause of socialism" in Poland.[60] Precisely what kind of action Ceaușescu had in mind was not specified, but the note implied that he favored some kind of decisive military intervention.

Poland rejected the Romanian demand, as did other Warsaw Pact members. Three days later, on August 22, Gorbachev endorsed the formation of a Solidarity-led government in Poland, in a forty-minute telephone conversation with Mieczysław Rakowski, the new leader of the Polish Communist Party. Gorbachev had taken a personal dislike to the megalomaniac Romanian *conducător* and his domineering wife, Elena. The grotesque personality cult surrounding the couple reminded him of the worst days of Stalin. At Warsaw Pact meetings Ceaușescu had been gratuitously offensive, pouring scorn on perestroika and presenting Romania as the model for other Communist countries to follow. The debate became so heated during one session that the bodyguards outside the room were sent away, so that they would not hear two general secretaries yelling at each other. Relations between the two wives were equally bad-tempered.[61]

"Ceaușescu fears for his own skin," Gorbachev told Rakowski, dismissing the Romanian call for a Warsaw Pact intervention in Poland.[62]

Although he had no intention of stopping the formation of a Solidarity-led government, Gorbachev was troubled by the stunning electoral defeat suffered by Communist reformers in Poland. He felt a political kinship with Jaruzelski, the first East European leader to embrace the ideas of perestroika, and apply them in his own country. As their reward for leading the rest of the Soviet bloc in the transition to democracy, the Polish reformers had been unceremoniously booted out of office. There were worrying portents here for the Soviet Union and for Gorbachev himself. He told Rakowski that the only solution was the construction of a new political party, purged of conservatives.

"You must build a new party. You won't be able to accomplish anything with the old lot. Not even crap," he told Rakowski, apologizing for his use of the Russian vernacular.

The Soviet leader insisted that Moscow would stick by the Polish reformers and continued to support the "line of agreement" pursued by Jaruzelski. Soviet "support" for Poland would remain unchanged, provided the Polish "opposition" behaved in a reasonable and responsible way. If the opposition attempted to overthrow the existing "constitutional order," then the Kremlin would be obliged to review its policy toward Poland. "You can tell that to the opposition." Gorbachev did not say precisely what he had in mind, but the implication was that the Soviet Union would cut back supplies of subsidized oil and raw materials.

Without the threat of military force to back it up, it was inevitable that this latest line in the sand would soon be swept away. Events were now moving faster than anyone, including Gorbachev, could possibly anticipate. The next few months were to witness the crumbling of Moscow's East European empire and the shattering of a geopolitical arrangement that had been in place for more than four decades.

THE PACE OF CHANGE began to accelerate a few hours after Gorbachev got off the phone with Rakowski. Unbeknownst to either man, the foreign minister of Hungary made a decision, in the privacy of his Budapest home, that led inexorably to the fall of the Berlin Wall less than three months later.

Gyula Horn was grappling with the kind of excruciating moral and political dilemma familiar to many Communist reformers that summer. Over the past few months Hungary had been transformed into a holding pen for tens of thousands of East German refugees. Very few were political dissidents. For the most part they were young people, fed up with the austerity of life under communism and the never-ending snooping of the secret police. They had given up on their dogmatic Communist leaders, who seemed allergic to the very idea of reform, and were voting with their feet. From Hungary they wanted nothing more than safe passage to the bright lights of capitalism in West Germany. "There is no future for us in the East" was a common refrain. The foreign minister had to decide whether to let them go or keep them penned up in the Communist East.

On the one hand, Hungary had binding treaty obligations to East Germany. Under a bilateral agreement, signed in 1968, the Hungarian government had undertaken not to permit East German citizens to travel to the West via Hungary. If Budapest violated this treaty, Horn feared that Communist hard-liners in Berlin, Prague, and Bucharest would find a way of getting even. On the other hand, he knew that his government would appear hypocritical, and hopelessly behind the times, if it failed to live up to its new

humanistic principles. A few months earlier Hungary had signed international agreements pledging to promote freedom of travel between states and to protect the rights of refugees. The way the Hungarian government handled the issue of East German refugees was a crucial test of the sincerity of its commitment to democracy and human rights.

After a sleepless night, pacing up and down his sitting room, the fifty-seven-year-old foreign minister made up his mind. He decided to abrogate the treaty with East Berlin and let the refugees go. Hungarian leaders had earlier taken the precaution of informally testing the waters with Moscow. The Soviets appeared to have no objection.

"There was no other way," Horn recalled later. "We had to look for the humanist solution, no matter what sort of conflict might arise. It was quite obvious to me that this would be the first step in a landslide-like series of events."[63]

BERLIN

November 9, 1989

THERE WAS NO MORE enduring symbol of the Cold War than the Berlin Wall. For more than a generation the wall exemplified the confrontation between communism and capitalism, East and West, dictatorship and democracy. Its images became ingrained in the popular imagination: Soviet and American tanks barrel to barrel at Checkpoint Charlie; John Kennedy declaring, "*Ich bin ein Berliner*," at the Brandenburg Gate; the spy swaps on the Glienicke Bridge; a series of dramatic escapes; Ronald Reagan shouting, "Mr. Gorbachev, tear down this wall!"

The wall was the quintessential dividing line, not merely between two parts of a single city but between two rival ideologies and two contrasting ways of life. This was not just *a* wall. It was *the* wall. On one side of the wall were the bright lights of the Ku'damm, with its luxurious department stores and garish sex shows. On the other side were the ubiquitous hallmarks of socialism: dimly lit streets, crumbling apartment blocks, and ugly statues to worthy proletarians. One side of the wall was a monotonous white; the other, a riot of cheeky, multicolored graffiti. On one side of the wall people drove Mercedes and BMWs. On the other they drove the Trabant, a car variously described as "a sardine-can on wheels" and a "plastic tank." On one side of the wall was a society that permitted its citizens to travel freely; on the other side, a society that needed a wall to prevent them from fleeing.

The East German authorities had erected the wall in the course of a single day—on August 13, 1961—in order to stem the flood of refugees to the West. Before the wall was built, half a million people crossed the city every day, and hundreds never returned. Since the end of World War II some three million East Germans had left their homeland, one of the largest mass migrations in European history. Most of the refugees were professionals, such as doctors and engineers, who believed that there was no future for them under communism. Fifty percent were under the age of twenty-five. The German Democratic Republic was threatened with demographic extinction.

At first the wall consisted of rolls of barbed wire, demarcating the Soviet and Western sectors of Berlin. Streets were arbitrarily cut into two. In some places the line went through the middle of a house. Friends, neighbors, even members of the same family ended up in different worlds. Thousands of East German soldiers ensured that the Western sector of the city was sealed tight as swiftly as possible. Tanks and armored cars were deployed beneath the Brandenburg Gate. Subway stops were barricaded; houses were boarded up; bridges were destroyed. Frightened of unleashing a nuclear confrontation with the Soviet Union, Western leaders were forced to sit back and watch.

"We're going to close Berlin," Nikita Khrushchev had boasted to his generals. "We'll just put up serpentine barbed wire, and the West will stand there like dumb sheep. And while they're standing there, we'll finish a wall."[64]

Events turned out precisely as Khrushchev predicted. By the end of the year the barbed wire had been replaced by a concrete wall, twelve feet high, encircling the Western enclave of Berlin. Over the next quarter century the East German authorities worked on perfecting what was officially described as the "anti-Fascist defense barrier," until every conceivable hole was plugged. In its completed form the wall was 104 miles long, including 66 miles of reinforced concrete slabs. Built of the hardest concrete, to withstand ramming, each slab was six inches thick and weighed two and a half tons. The slabs were cemented together and topped with asbestos piping. Extra protection was provided by 302 observation towers, 65 miles of trenches, 259 dog runs, and 20 massive concrete bunkers.[65] Next to the wall was a death strip of constantly raked sand, at least a hundred yards wide, equipped with hundreds of mines and automatic firing devices.

Despite these precautions, thousands still managed to escape the "socialist paradise" in all manner of brave and ingenious ways. They flew over

the wall in hot-air balloons and homemade flying machines, burrowed under it in tunnels, and rammed it with steel-plated trucks. In order to attain their freedom, one group of refugees dressed themselves up as Soviet army officers and walked through the border unchallenged. Others crawled through stinking sewers and slid down homemade chair lifts. One family sailed across the Baltic in a homemade submarine. The escapees included several hundred East German border guards. Later human rights organizations compiled a list of 825 people who had lost their lives trying to flee to the West.[66]

For many people, in both East and West Germany, the wall seemed a permanent feature of their lives. It was so solidly built that it was difficult to imagine its ever coming down. Erich Honecker, the man who had supervised its construction, boasted in early 1989 that the wall would still be around in "fifty or one hundred years' time."[67] The West German chancellor, Helmut Kohl, did not believe that the fall of the wall was imminent. On a visit to Poland on November 8, 1989, he reacted with incredulity when Lech Wałęsa predicted that the wall would be down in a matter of "weeks."

"You are a young man," Kohl scoffed. "This is something that is going to take many years."[68]

Twenty-four hours later the chancellor was obliged to interrupt his trip to Warsaw and return home because of extraordinary developments from Berlin.

IT HAD BEEN a generally soporific news conference, dedicated to the political and economic reforms under way in East Germany. The regime's propaganda chief, Günter Schabowski, was exhausted. The last few weeks had seen a whirlwind of political changes, including the overthrow of Honecker and the collective resignation of the Politburo. The refugee crisis had reached a climax. Almost a million East German citizens had applied to emigrate. Tens of thousands were leaving every day without waiting for permission, via the circuitous routes that had opened up in Hungary and Czechoslovakia. Pro-democracy demonstrations were getting larger by the day. The previous weekend, on November 4, an estimated half million people had paraded through the streets of Berlin to demand free elections and free travel. Schabowski himself had attempted to speak at this rally and had been roundly jeered.

"Wir sind das Volk," the demonstrators had chanted. "We are the people."

The East German people were reclaiming their sovereignty, just as their Polish neighbors had done in August 1980 and June 1989. Never again would they permit their self-appointed representatives to speak in their name; never again would they participate in the pretense that they had surrendered power voluntarily to a Soviet-sponsored "people's democracy" on German soil. Like other East German reformers, Schabowski sensed that the days of the "dictatorship of the proletariat" were numbered. But he had no idea of the historical upheaval that he was about to unleash.

The propaganda chief peered at the throng of journalists above his half-moon glasses and announced that he would take one more question. Someone at the back of the room wanted to know about the new travel regulations under consideration by the East German leadership. Schabowski shuffled through his papers to find a government statement that the new party leader, Egon Krenz, had shoved into his hand moments before the press conference with the comment "This will do us a power of good."[69] It was couched in the usual bureaucratese, a deliberately woolly style of language that permitted the authorities to make grand-sounding concessions that could be retracted as soon as officials started examining the fine print.

From now on, Schabowski announced, East German citizens could "apply for" private trips abroad "without preconditions." Furthermore, the authorities would issue visas for "permanent departures"—i.e., emigration—without delay. Such departures could be made through all border crossings, including the checkpoints leading into West Berlin. The spokesman did not notice a sentence on the other side of the paper embargoing the news until 8:00 a.m. the following day.

There was nothing specifically in the communiqué about the Berlin Wall, and the procedure for approving tourist trips to the West was still unclear. What the apparatchiks had in mind was an orderly line that could still be controlled. The spectacle of tens of thousands of East German refugees camping out in West German embassies in Czechoslovakia and Hungary had been deeply embarrassing to them. If this pressure could be relieved, senior Politburo members believed, then the German Democratic Republic could still be saved.

Schabowski felt a twinge of panic as he read out the reference to "West Berlin." As the Politburo member responsible for Berlin he knew that any decision concerning the city's status had to be agreed with the four "occupying powers"—the Soviet Union, the United States, Britain, and France. "I hope the Soviets know about this," he thought. "This thing affects the four-power status."[70]

Among the reporters who attended the news conference, both German and foreign, there was confusion over what the government announcement really meant.[71] On the face of it, the propaganda chief seemed to be saying that travel through the wall was now permissible for East German citizens. On the other hand, anyone with experience of Communist bureaucrats knew that their words did not always mean what they appeared to mean. Everything depended on implementation.

By the time Schabowski finished speaking, it was already 7:00 p.m. The East German television news show *Aktuelle Kamera* went on the air half an hour later. Reporters had no time to clarify matters, so they decided to broadcast the statement verbatim without explanation.

What happened next was extraordinary, something that went against the habits of subservience carefully nurtured by the Communist authorities. Instead of waiting for official clarification, thousands of East Berliners simply took matters into their own hands and headed for the Western sector of the city. It was as if they really did believe that they, not the Communist government, were the true representatives of "the people." When they reached the six crossing points leading to West Berlin, they were given the usual runaround. The border guards claimed to know nothing about the new regulations. "It's all nonsense, go home," said some. "We have no instructions," said others.

As the crowds built up behind them, and Western television news crews arrived to film the scene, people began to argue with the border guards about the meaning of Schabowski's statement. "Open the gate! Open the gate!" they chanted. "The wall must fall." The vast majority of those clamoring to get out had no intention of leaving East Germany permanently. They merely wanted to taste life on the other side of the wall. "Let us go and see the Ku'damm and we'll come right back," they shouted. "We'll come back."

By this stage the border guards were beginning to panic. They had been trained as an elite force, ready to protect the frontiers of the socialist state with their lives. Up until a few days ago these hard-faced young men had orders to shoot would-be escapees on sight. In the past their word had been law. They possessed overwhelming force and the will to use it. Ordinary citizens had no choice but to obey their arbitrary commands. But now, even though they retained their weapons, the guards found themselves besieged and outnumbered by crowds of angry citizens, who refused to take no for an answer. At around 9:00 p.m. commanders on duty at the border posts began flooding their superiors in the Stasi, the German secret police, with anxious telephone calls. They were told to "hang on" for clarification.

At the Bornholmer Strasse crossing point, in the northern suburbs of the city, the pressure of the crowd was becoming uncontrollable. There were chants of "Open up, open up." Shortly before 11:00 p.m. the dam finally broke when the crowd pushed back the red and white frontier post. Soon the border guards were enveloped in a sea of humanity. "It made me wonder why we had been standing in that place for the past twenty years," Captain Helmut Stoss told reporters later.[72] When Security Ministry officials finally found out what was happening, they reluctantly issued orders to let the people pass.

At Checkpoint Charlie, the gateway to the American sector of the city, the crowds had to wait until midnight before the border was opened. A great roar went up from the Western side of the wall as the first East Berliners pushed through the eerie, real-life set of countless espionage movies, flashing victory signs and waving their blue identity cards in the air. People poured out of a nearby bar to greet the new arrivals with bottles of champagne and gifts of West German money.

"I just can't believe it!" exclaimed thirty-four-year-old Angelika Wache as she emerged blinking into a hundred flashguns.

"I don't feel like I'm in prison anymore," shouted another young man. Torsten Ryl, twenty-four, told reporters that he had come over to see what the West was like and intended to return. "Finally, we can really visit other states, instead of just seeing them on television or hearing about them." To the cheers of the crowd, a West Berliner handed him a twenty deutsche mark bill and told him to "go have a beer."[73]

In the meantime, dozens of youths from West Berlin had clambered on top of the wall at the Brandenburg Gate and had begun to taunt the police on the other side. The old Prussian memorial to victories past, a six-column arch topped by the Goddess of Victory in a chariot pulled by four horses, was regarded by many Germans as the symbol of German unity, a reminder of the country they had lost following their defeat in World War II. A few hours previously it was unthinkable even to approach the wall at this point because it was so heavily guarded. But now people began to dance on it, in full view of astonished television viewers around the world. At around 1:00 a.m. the *Wessis* (Westerners) were joined by *Ossis* (Easterners), at which point the East German police turned a water cannon on the revelers, a gesture that was greeted by derisory hoots and whistles from the crowd. One young man nonchalantly opened up an umbrella to protect himself from the shower of water.

"*So ein tag, so wunderschön,*" sang the crowds on both sides of the wall. "What a day, what a wonderful day."

The next few days were a riotous street party as East Berliners poured into the forbidden city. Within forty-eight hours of the opening of the wall, nearly two million East Germans had crossed over into the West. Westerners showered them with flowers and chocolate and thumped the roofs of their decrepit Trabant cars in welcome. The sight of two-stroke "Trabis" choking the streets of West Berlin became a token of the new era, along with Mstislav Rostropovich playing his beloved cello by Checkpoint Charlie. In a flood of warm feeling toward their Eastern neighbors, some Westerners even began referring to the poisonous fumes emitted by the Trabis as the "perfume of freedom." Soon the people of Berlin and Leipzig switched from chanting, "We are the people" ("*Wir sind das Volk*") to chanting, "We are *one* people" ("*Wir sind ein Volk*").

Later the generosity and hospitality of *Wessis* wore off, along with the novelty of having their poor relations coming to visit. Familiarity bred suspicion, even contempt. The euphoria felt by *Ossis* at their sudden liberation was replaced by bitterness and anger toward their Communist rulers for having cheated them for so long. But for a few glorious days a city that had experienced so much sorrow and tragedy became the scene of unadulterated joy.

"For twenty-eight years, since the construction of the Wall on August 13, 1961, we have longed and hoped for this day," the mayor of West Berlin, Walter Momper, told a rally in front of City Hall. "We Germans are now the happiest people in the world."[74]

AT THE SOVIET EMBASSY on Unter der Linden, the elegant tree-lined avenue bisecting the Brandenburg Gate, diplomats had watched, spellbound and uncomprehending, as crowds of East Berliners took the wall by storm. For nearly four and a half decades the embassy had served as a kind of viceregal palace, the channel through which the Kremlin controlled its prize possession. Few decisions of any consequence in the German Democratic Republic were made without the Soviet ambassador's being consulted or at least informed. But now momentous events were taking place on its own doorstep, and the Soviet Embassy knew less about what was going on than West German television.

Some eight hours after the wall had first been breached, the embassy received a panicky telephone call from Moscow. It was the desk officer for the socialist countries section of the Soviet Foreign Ministry. "What is happening at the wall?" he demanded. "Every news agency in the world is going crazy."[75]

A political officer at the embassy briefly recounted the events of the past few hours, beginning with Schabowski's extraordinary press conference.

"Has all this been agreed with us?" the desk officer asked incredulously.

The East German government had informed the embassy about its plan to allow would-be refugees to travel directly to West Germany without going through Czechoslovakia or Hungary. The ambassador, Vyacheslav Kochemasov, had in turn informed the Soviet Foreign Ministry, which had raised no objection to the plan. But the embassy knew nothing at all about the decision to permit ordinary East Germans to come and go as they pleased through the wall. It was inconceivable that the GDR authorities would fail to consult Moscow on such a delicate matter, particularly one that affected the four-power status of Berlin. Perhaps, the diplomat suggested delicately, this information had been conveyed through back channels, without the embassy's being informed. It was also possible that Krenz had chosen to get in touch with Gorbachev directly, over the *vertushka*.

Inquiries were made, and it soon turned out that the inconceivable had in fact occurred. Nobody in Moscow knew anything. Half an hour later Ambassador Kochemasov received a telephone call from the East German Foreign Ministry.

"Last night's decision was forced upon us," a senior East German official explained apologetically. "Any delay could have had very dangerous consequences. There was no time for consultations."

It took many months for Soviet and East German officials to piece together exactly what had happened that night and to explain the failure in communications. The original draft of the new travel regulations, the draft that had been shown to Soviet diplomats, had not addressed the issue of tourist visits at all. It had dealt exclusively with the problem of "permanent exits." This had seemed anomalous to a team of four mid-level East German interior ministry officials and Stasi lawyers, who were charged with preparing the final draft. "We were supposed to come up with regulations for the citizen who wanted to leave the country forever, but we weren't supposed to let out the citizen who just wanted to visit his aunt?" one of the Interior Ministry officials recalled later. "That would have been schizophrenic."[76] To make good this omission, on the morning of November 9, the officials inserted a vaguely worded paragraph opening the way for "private trips," without going into detail about the accompanying formalities.

The new draft was submitted to the Politburo during its lunch break. The leaders had more pressing matters on their minds, such as their own political survival, and paid little attention to the wording. They approved the

draft, while sipping their coffee. At around 5:00 p.m. the resolution was presented to the policy-making Central Committee. Hardly any of the 213 members understood the text. There was only one question. "Has this been agreed with the Soviet comrades?" someone asked. "Yes," replied Krenz, distracted by the excitement of the last few days.[77]

NEWS THAT THE BERLIN WALL had fallen came as a shock to Gorbachev, but he quickly adjusted to the new reality. For months he had been lecturing the ultraconservative East German leadership on the need for flexibility. "In politics life severely punishes those who fall behind," he had told Honecker in October 1989, during ceremonies to mark the fortieth anniversary of the foundation of the German Democratic Republic.[78] The visit to Berlin gave Gorbachev a firsthand insight into the depth of Honecker's political isolation. Standing on the podium for an anniversary parade, he could hear young East Berliners chanting, "Gorbie, help us." Many of the demonstrators were members of the Communist youth organization.

Polish prime minister Mieczysław Rakowski was standing just behind Gorbachev. Since he spoke good German and Russian, he could act as the Soviet leader's interpreter. "Do you understand what they are screaming?" he whispered into Gorbachev's ear.

"Yes, I understand it."

"This is the end."[79]

On his return home Gorbachev told his Politburo colleagues that Honecker's days in power were numbered. [80] Sure enough, the old Stalinist was forced to resign less than two weeks later, a victim of his stubborn refusal to countenance any kind of serious change.

Soviet diplomats in East Berlin frequently complained that it was very difficult to get the Kremlin leadership to focus on the growing crisis in East Germany. By late 1989 Gorbachev was almost totally preoccupied with the deteriorating situation at home. At first he had not even wanted to attend the jubilee celebrations, as he did not believe there was anything he could do to influence the course of events. It was only as the result of very active lobbying by Kochemasov that he agreed to participate.[81]

Gorbachev's attitude to Germany was heavily influenced by the fact that he belonged to the postwar generation of Kremlin politicians. He was the first Soviet leader since Stalin not to be filled with atavistic horror by the thought of a reunited Germany outside the Soviet orbit. Indeed a divided Germany struck Gorbachev as unnatural and unsustainable over the long

term. Deep down he regarded the reunification of Germany as "inevitable," even though he did not expect it to occur within the immediately foreseeable future.[82] History itself would decide such questions, he liked to say. A week before the wall came down, he told East German leaders that reunification was "not a problem of current politics."[83]

In reacting to events in East Germany, Gorbachev remained faithful to his precept that every Communist Party was responsible for events in its own country, a position that he had first enunciated at a meeting of East European leaders in 1986. During a visit to Moscow in June Honecker had complained that he was coming under increasing pressure from "government circles" in West Germany to make political concessions. "This pressure needs to be adequately countered," he told Gorbachev in an indirect appeal for Soviet assistance. The Soviet leader expressed solicitude and said he had warned Kohl against "exploiting" the popular discontent in East Germany. But he made clear that the Soviet Union did not intend to get directly involved.[84]

As Honecker's political authority began to unravel, Gorbachev adopted the stance of a detached bystander. His main concern was to keep the half million Soviet troops stationed in East Germany out of the crisis. In conversations with colleagues and aides, the general secretary insisted that the revolution be permitted to take its natural course without interference from outside.[85] To make sure that his instructions were carried out, he sent Yakovlev to Berlin and other East European capitals with a very simple message. "I had to make the point over and over again. We are not going to interfere," Yakovlev said later. "Please, we told them, make your own calculations, but make sure you understand that our troops will not be used, even though they are there. They will remain in their barracks and will not go anywhere, under any circumstances."[86]

During what later became known as the October Revolution in Leipzig, Soviet officials urged Honecker and Krenz not to use force against hundreds of thousands of young people who were defying a ban on demonstrations. There was concern in Moscow about the possibility of an anti-Soviet "provocation." In order to prevent this from happening, Soviet troops were confined to barracks, and all military maneuvers canceled, for the duration of the demonstrations.[87] Similar instructions were issued in the hours immediately after the fall of the Berlin Wall.[88]

Twenty-four hours after the wall had been breached, Ambassador Kochemasov received official instructions from Moscow, belatedly endorsing what had happened. He conveyed an oral message from Gorbachev to

Krenz, accepting the East German explanation for the failure in communication and adding, "Everything was done completely correctly. Act in a similar way in the future—energetically and confidently."[89]

The wall was no more. Nearly four and a half decades of Soviet domination over Eastern Europe had come to an end.

PRAGUE

November 24, 1989

AS THE HERO of the Prague Spring stepped out onto the balcony high above Wenceslas Square, three hundred thousand people burst out into a deafening roar of "DUBČEK, DUBČEK." An elderly, slightly stooping figure, with white hair and a gentle smile, Alexander Dubček waited for the chanting to subside. Then he uttered the slogan that had inspired millions of his countrymen in 1968 and caused a panic-stricken Soviet Politburo to send tanks rumbling into Czechoslovakia.

"Long live socialism with a human face!"[90]

More chants of "Freedom, freedom!" and "Long live Dubček." The long, narrow square echoed with the sound of people jangling key chains, their way of telling Dubček's Stalinist successors that the time had come to quit.

For more than two decades Czechoslovakia's hard-line Stalinist regime had done its best to turn Dubček into a nonperson. When the state-controlled news media deigned to mention him at all, it was only to ridicule him. After being forced to resign as first secretary of the Czechoslovak Communist Party in April 1969, he had been given a series of low-level jobs, each one more degrading than the last. For most of his countrymen, Dubček's weary face evoked a bygone age. On his way over to Wenceslas Square, people had stared at him in amazement as if they had seen a ghost.

Yet here he was, basking in the applause of hundreds of thousands of people. Around the country virtually the entire population of Czechoslovakia was watching the scene on live television. Dubček's return to Wenceslas Square and the fact that it was witnessed by so many people represented "the triumph of remembering over forgetting," in the phrase of the exiled Czech writer Milan Kundera.

Wenceslas Square, in the heart of Prague, had been the focal point of popular resistance to the Soviet invasion of Czechoslovakia in August 1968. For a long time the stone facade of the National Museum at the top of the square had borne the pockmarks of machine-gun fire, following a shoot-out between a Czech sniper and Soviet soldiers. Here Soviet troops had shot dead an eleven-year-old boy as he tried to ram a Czechoslovak flag down the barrel of a Red Army tank. Here, on January 16, 1969, a Czech student named Jan Palach had burned himself to death in a protest against the abandonment of the ideals of the Prague Spring. In retrospect, Palach's death marked the last spasm of the democracy movement. Palach too had become a nonperson.

After Dubček's ouster from office, power had passed to a group of neo-Stalinists led by the Slovak leader Gustáv Husák. "Normalization" became the slogan of the day. Within a few years half a million Dubček supporters had been expelled from the Communist Party. Those who refused to recant were forced to take menial jobs as street sweepers, boiler men, and night watchmen. Tight censorship of the news media was reimposed. Independent political groups and trade unions were shut down. Czechoslovakia closed its borders with the outside world once more.

The country remained a reactionary backwater long after Gorbachev had unleashed his glasnost campaign in the Soviet Union. For Husák and his colleagues, glasnost represented a mortal political threat. Their power derived directly from the Soviet invasion. They knew very well that a public discussion of the invasion would fatally undermine their own legitimacy. During meetings with Soviet leaders in 1989 they repeatedly rejected attempts to reopen the question. Anything associated with the Prague Spring, including use of the very word "reform," was taboo. Like Honecker in East Germany, the Czech leaders resisted pressure from Moscow for the adoption of more liberal policies, believing it would trigger a political avalanche that would sweep them from office.

"They lived under the shadow of the 1968 syndrome," Gorbachev wrote later. "They would become hysterical at the slightest hint in the Soviet press about the possibility of an official reevaluation of 1968."[91]

The implementation of "normalization" was so thorough and so perva-

sive that it effectively ended political debate in Czechoslovakia. For years organized resistance to the regime had been confined to a handful of restless intellectuals, the most prominent of whom was Václav Havel, the country's leading playwright. Most people were too scared to side openly with the dissidents. The memory of the invasion and the massive political repression that followed discouraged them from expressing their true opinions. As Havel himself said in 1988, "our fellow countrymen sympathize with us, but they do not support us."[92]

As anti-Communist rebellions swept through the rest of Eastern Europe, the hard-line Czechoslovak leadership found itself politically and ideologically isolated. After the fall of the Berlin Wall it was clear to everybody that Czechoslovakia was next in line. All that was needed was some spark to galvanize the dormant and apathetic masses into action and help them overcome their fear of the regime. That spark occurred on Friday, November 17, after the government had used force to break up a peaceful student demonstration demanding political freedom. Hundreds of demonstrators were taken to the hospital, and there were rumors (which later turned out to be false) that a student had been beaten to death.

Over the next week the protests grew until they came to envelop the whole country. Havel and his dissident friends launched a mass movement, known as Civic Forum, to investigate police brutality and demand the resignations of those responsible. Civic Forum's targets included Husák, who had been kicked upstairs to become president, and his successor as the Communist Party leader, Miloš Jakeš. Day by day more and more people packed into Wenceslas Square to support Civic Forum's demands.

As fear melted away, the people of Prague took a perverse delight in flaunting forbidden symbols, as if to make clear to the regime that the attempt to wipe out the country's collective memory had failed utterly. By November 24 the streets of the city were plastered with portraits of Palach and Dubček. There were also numerous pictures of Tomáš Masaryk, the social democrat who had presided over the birth of an independent Czechoslovak state in 1919, and his son, Jan, who had served as foreign minister after World War II and been hounded to his death by the Communists. As symbols of the country's liberal, pre-Communist traditions, the two Masaryks had been consigned to the political void along with Palach, Dubček, and Havel. Another nonperson who reemerged into public life on November 24 was Marta Kubisova, an actress banned from the stage for twenty-one years for performing anti-Communist songs. The crowd roared its approval as she stepped onto the balcony of the newspaper *Free Word* to

sing a haunting song about a seventeenth-century Bohemian hero who fought for the liberation of his people.

Then it was Dubček's turn. There were delirious cheers when he demanded the ouster of all Communist Party leaders tied to the Soviet invasion. "Twenty years ago we tried to reform socialism, to make it better," Dubček told the crowd. "In those days the army and the police stood with the people, and I am sure it will be the same again today."

"*Dubček na hrad, Dubček na hrad,*" chanted the crowd. "Dubček to the castle." In other words, Dubček for president. (Hradčany Castle was the official residence of the head of state, Gustáv Husák.)

Dubček was followed out onto the balcony by Havel. They stood for a moment together under the television arc lights, holding each other's arms and acknowledging the cheers of the crowd. They were an odd couple, the former Communist Party leader in a gray suit alongside the dissident in his scruffy jeans and open-neck shirt. To the crowd down below, it seemed like the most natural union in the world. "Dubček-Havel," they chanted. The revolutions of 1968 and 1989 had finally come together.

HAVEL AND DUBČEK HAD REACHED Wenceslas Square by very different routes. By personality and background, they were almost polar opposites. They represented two distinct political traditions, but in the end they arrived at the same point.

Dubček was the son of a Slovak carpenter, who had emigrated briefly to the United States, only to return home thoroughly disillusioned with capitalism. One of the founders of the Czechoslovak Communist Party, Dubček's father took his family to live in the Soviet Union for thirteen years, at the height of Stalin's terror. During World War II both Dubček and his brother, Julius, fought with the Slovak partisans against the Nazis; Julius was killed during one of these battles. Such impeccable Communist credentials gave Dubček a head start as he began his climb up the party's bureaucratic ladder at the end of the war.[93]

Havel, by contrast, was the son of a rich Czech businessman. His uncle owned Czechoslovakia's biggest film studios. After the Communists staged their coup d'état in 1948, the Havel family assets were seized by the state. Havel himself was prevented from entering the university because of his class origins. Instead he became a stagehand at a theater and eventually a playwright. He took a special delight in satirizing the absurdities of communism.

The two political traditions came together briefly in 1968, when Dubček set out to prove that communism need not be synonymous with dictatorship. The Action Program drawn up by the reformers in the Czech leadership was to find an echo many years later in the ideas of perestroika. It promised a return to the rule of law as well as respect for freedom of assembly and freedom of the press. The grotesque personality cult that had traditionally surrounded Communist Party leaders was dismantled. Many years later a Czech dissident recalled how impressed he had been when a newspaper published a picture of Dubček diving into a swimming pool. "We had never seen a picture of a Communist Party first secretary in bathing trunks before," said Peter Uhl, editor of an underground human rights journal.[94] Havel described the Prague Spring as "an unbelievable dream." It was the first time in his life he had really felt free.

Although Dubček rebelled against the Stalinist variant of communism, he remained loyal to both socialism and the Soviet Union. The climactic moment in his political career came in the early-morning hours of August 21, 1968, when he learned that Soviet troops had landed in Prague. His first reaction was incredulity: How could the Soviet leaders do such a thing "*to me*"?[95] As he later acknowledged in his autobiography, he had totally misjudged the character of the people he was dealing with. "I did not believe the Soviet leaders would launch a military attack on us. . . . It took the drastic, practical experience of the coming days and months for me to understand that I was in fact dealing with gangsters."[96]

Shortly afterward Soviet paratroopers burst through the doors of Dubček's office and announced they were taking the Czechoslovak leadership "into custody." Dubček and his fellow Politburo members were flown to Moscow under armed guard. During the subsequent "negotiations" with Brezhnev, Dubček maintained a dignified silence, refusing to recant the humanistic ideals of the Prague Spring. At the same time, he chose to avoid a public confrontation with Brezhnev or the hard-liners in the Czechoslovak leadership, such as Husák. His position was close to that of the character in Havel's play *The Memorandum*, who hopes he can "salvage this and that" if only he can sidestep an "open conflict" with his ruthless deputy. The attempt to save what could be saved ended in total failure and Dubček's expulsion from the Communist Party.

During the deadening years of normalization Dubček was kept under de facto house arrest. Police surveillance was relaxed after Gorbachev visited Prague in April 1987 and signaled his support for some of the ideas of the Prague Spring. Even then Dubček preferred to keep his head down. When

I called on him at his home in Bratislava in August 1988, on the twentieth anniversary of the invasion, he chatted amicably about his three grandchildren and his hopes of visiting Italy. But he refused to respond to a harsh attack that had just been published in the Communist Party newspaper *Rude Pravo*, accusing him of "personal responsibility" for the invasion because of his failure to rein in "the extremists." "It's not that I am afraid, simply that the time is not right," he explained.[97]

There could scarcely have been a greater contrast with Havel, who believed that the only way of dealing with a lawless regime was to confront it head-on. Like the founders of Solidarity in Poland, Havel was determined to follow his conscience whatever the consequences. He talked about "living in truth." By behaving as a free citizen in an unfree nation, he would show his countrymen that it was possible to challenge the seemingly all-powerful regime. Over time, he believed, more and more people would join the ranks of the opposition, as the absurdities of the Communist system became apparent.

The first cracks in the Communist monolith appeared in 1977, when Havel and a handful of other dissidents published a document drawing attention to human rights violations in Czechoslovakia. The idea behind Charter '77, according to Havel, was to provide society with a voice, "to straighten up as a human being once more after being humiliated, gagged, lied to, and manipulated." The fact that the charter initially attracted only a few hundred signatories was unimportant. What mattered was that civil society, which had previously been given up for dead, was once again showing signs of life. The charter became the inspiration for Civic Forum.

These activities earned Havel the hatred of the regime and the status of public enemy number one. His plays were performed in New York, London, eventually even Warsaw and Moscow—but not in Prague. He had spent more than five years in prison and had been arrested countless times, most recently in January 1989, for commemorating the twentieth anniversary of Palach's self-immolation. When not in prison, he was the subject of almost constant police harassment and surveillance.

Havel's defiance had its roots in an intellectual tradition stretching back more than three centuries. In 1620 the Habsburg armies crushed the forces of the Czech nobility at the Battle of the White Mountain. Twenty-seven ringleaders of an attempted uprising were publicly executed in Prague's Old Town Square. For the next three hundred years, until Czechoslovakia won recognition as an independent state after World War I, Prague was a provincial outpost. Czechs were excluded from the political life of the empire, and

the official language, in Prague as in Vienna, was German. The role of preserving and defending the Czech language and national consciousness fell
to the writers.

I visited Havel in his farmhouse in the rolling hills of northern Bohemia
in August 1988. At that time the oppressive Husák regime was still well in
control, if a little rattled by events in the Soviet Union. Prospects for a nationwide uprising seemed slim, but Havel was remarkably buoyant and optimistic. "This situation cannot go on forever," he told me. "Something has
to change here. Nobody knows when and how that change will come, but it
will come. There is too great a distance between the official ideology and the
state of mind of society."[98]

WHILE HAVEL AND DUBČEK WERE SPEAKING to the delirious crowds in
Wenceslas Square, the panic-stricken Czech leaders were holding a crisis
session of the party's policy-making Central Committee. Long-festering
splits within the leadership had burst out into the open. Husák's successor
as first secretary, Miloš Jakeš, was in favor of using force to break up the
demonstrations. But his Politburo colleagues lacked the stomach for decisive measures.

As the protest demonstrations grew in strength, the Prague police became increasingly demoralized. Jakeš prepared a last-ditch plan to shore up
his crumbling authority. He would order the People's Militia, a twenty-five-
thousand-strong force answerable only to the party leadership, into Prague
factories to counter the influence of students who were trying to drum up
support for a general strike. He also hoped to use the militia to reestablish
his control over state television, which had begun to broadcast coverage of
the demonstrations. The Politburo approved the plan on the evening of
Tuesday, November 21.

The results fell way short of the decisive show of force that would have
been required to restore the status quo. It was too little too late. When the
People's Militia squads appeared at the factories, they were booed and
jeered, in some cases even attacked. The interior minister, who was responsible for the police, refused to go along with the plan. Other Politburo members, including the Prague party boss, looked for ways of distancing
themselves from the discredited Jakeš. The demoralized and leaderless militia went home.

At the Central Committee meeting on November 24, one member after
another got up to denounce the leadership for the use of violence against

the demonstrators. Prime Minister Ladislav Adamec, the leading reformer on the Politburo, denounced the use of "extraordinary measures," saying it would only "further aggravate" the situation.[99] Eventually even Jakeš joined in the ritualistic breast-beating and self-criticism. "We have underestimated completely the processes taking place in Poland, Hungary, and especially recently in the German Democratic Republic," he told his colleagues. "Our restructuring has been accompanied by many wonderful words, without the necessary deeds."[100]

Like other disgraced Communist leaders, Jakeš was devastated by the way in which once-trusted subordinates turned on him as soon as the going got rough. "Beforehand, they had been raising their hands to vote yes," he told an interviewer later. "Suddenly, everything was wrong. I could do nothing right."[101]

THE FINAL ACT of the day's drama took place in the Magic Lantern Theater, a hundred yards from the bottom of Wenceslas Square. The Magic Lantern served as the headquarters of the democracy movement, performing a similar function to that of the Lenin Shipyard in Gdańsk during the heyday of Solidarity. It was here that Civic Forum leaders plotted strategy, student activists drew up manifestos, and Havel held his daily press conferences.

On the evening of November 24 Havel was joined on the Magic Lantern stage by Dubček. Journalists wanted to know how Dubček's ideas had changed during the twenty years since he had dropped out of public life. Not at all, was the answer. "I believe in the reformability of socialism," Dubček replied. "We must look truth in the eyes and depart from everything that is wrong." As Dubček spoke, Havel wore a pained expression. "Socialism is a word that has lost its meaning in our country," he told journalists. "I identify socialism with men like Mr. Jakeš."[102]

As the two men were discussing their differing views of socialism, someone rushed onstage to deliver a whispered message. Television had just announced that Jakeš and the entire Politburo had resigned. The theater erupted in applause. Havel and Dubček jumped to their feet to embrace each other and flash the V for victory sign. A supporter emerged from the wings of the theater carrying a bottle of champagne and some glasses. Havel proposed a toast: "Long live a free Czechoslovakia." Dubček downed the champagne in one long gulp.

Outside in Wenceslas Square crowds of people, amazed by the latest turn

of events, gathered in front of store windows to watch the television news. Then they began lighting firecrackers and sparklers. Taxi drivers leaned on their horns. Four soldiers in uniform ran laughing through the square, waving a red, white, and blue Czechoslovak flag. A single trumpeter led a crowd of revelers to the statue of St. Wenceslas, ringed by hundreds of flickering votive candles. The first snowflakes of winter had begun to fall.

It was spring again in Prague.

BUCHAREST

December 21, 1989

THE DICTATOR STOOD on his balcony, gazing out across a sea of demonstrators bearing his portrait and red banners extolling his wise and brilliant leadership. His high-pitched voice had become one continuous shriek, denouncing "foreign imperialists" and "fascist hooligans" for disturbing the workers' paradise. When he paused for breath, the crowd responded with rhythmic chants of "Ceauşescu-Romania" and "Hoorah, hoorah." The dictator modestly raised his hand to silence the deafening roars of approval. Then he resumed his ranting, slicing the air with the palm of his hands as he screamed into the microphone.

Demonstrations of popular support for the *conducător*, supreme leader, of the Romanian people always followed the same ritual. Party organizers were instructed to dispatch fixed quotas of "ordinary Romanians" to the site of the rally. The demonstrators were issued banners and told what slogans to chant. The front rows of the rally were filled with members of the secret police, the Securitate, who led the chanting and provided a physical barrier between the *conducător* and his "supporters." The volume level was routinely boosted by prerecorded applause, relayed through strategically placed banks of loudspeakers.

During his twenty-four years in power Nicolae Ceauşescu had come to

depend on the adulation of those around him. Dozens of museums had been built in his honor, to cater for his insatiable thirst for *omagiu* (homage). Romanian newspapers compared him with Napoleon and Alexander the Great. A court painter depicted him carrying an orb and scepter, ascending through the clouds with his wife, Elena, accompanied by cherubic young Communist pioneers and white doves, symbolizing his quest for peace. His favorite poet referred to him as a "lay god," with a voice of "planetary resonance" that echoed to the corners of the earth.[103] Impressed by Ceaușescu's occasional disagreements with Moscow, Western leaders had joined in the chorus of applause. Richard Nixon hailed his "profound understanding of the world's major problems." The queen of England invited him to Buckingham Palace and made him a Knight Grand Cross of the Order of the Bath, the highest award she could bestow on a foreign leader.

For twenty-four years the applause had never faltered. But on this day something went terribly wrong.

It started with a low murmuring at the back, where the ordinary people stood. As the *conducător* ranted on, the murmurs turned to boos and whistles. There were shouts of "Freedom," "Democracy," and, ominously, the same chant that had sealed the fate of East Germany's Communist leaders: "*We* are the people." Gradually the cries of protest swelled, so that they could no longer be drowned out by the Securitate cheerleaders and the tape-recorded applause of the loudspeakers.

As they watched the live broadcast from Palace Square in Bucharest, millions of Romanians could hear the growing rumble of discontent. They saw a puzzled look spread across Ceaușescu's deeply lined face, to be replaced by annoyance and finally by outright fear. They saw him raise his right hand in an ineffectual attempt to silence the hecklers. They saw him open and close his mouth, as nothing came out. For the first time ever their leader seemed at a loss for words. His eyes darted back and forth, searching the crowd. A bodyguard rushed forward to pull the president away from the balcony. Television viewers could hear Elena's frantic comments to her husband: "Promise them something, talk to them." Martial music swelled up in the background. Then the television screens went blank.

In an attempt to win over the crowd, Ceaușescu promised across-the-board wage and pension hikes. They responded with boos and hisses. The illusion of his omniscient power had been shattered once and for all. Both the people in the square and millions of television viewers at home had sensed his vulnerability.

Even before the wave of anti-Communist revolution swept Eastern Eu-

rope, Ceauşescu was a man obsessed with personal security. Fearing assassination plots, he refused to eat anything that had not been professionally tasted. When he appeared in public, he was always surrounded by the Securitate. He had a personal hygiene fetish and would douse his hands in alcohol before and after meeting foreign dignitaries. Mistrusting outsiders, he appointed his relatives to key posts in the governments. "Socialism in one family" became a Romanian joke. Elena was considered the number two person in the regime; son Nicu was heir apparent; brother-in-law Ilie Verdeţ rose to the post of prime minister; another brother-in-law, Manea Mănescu, was deputy prime minister. Other relatives held key positions in the army, the Ministry of Trade, and the Ministry of Internal Affairs. Few people outside the charmed circle of relatives were permitted to remain in sensitive posts for more than a few years.

Convinced of his own infallibility and irreplaceability, Ceauşescu was prepared to do almost anything to remain in power. As his political position grew more precarious, he began lobbying other Communist leaders for urgent action to save the cause of socialism in Eastern Europe. In private conversations with his aides Gorbachev referred to Ceauşescu as the "Romanian führer" and made clear that he would be happy to see him deposed. During one visit to Bucharest the Soviet leader had accused Ceauşescu of terrorizing Romanians and isolating them from the rest of Europe.[104]

By early December it was clear that the *conducător* was in serious trouble. The flash point came in the western Romanian city of Timişoara, where thousands of demonstrators took to the streets to defend a Lutheran priest threatened with deportation for his human rights activities. On Ceauşescu's orders, soldiers fired into the crowds, killing dozens of people. "We'll fight to the last," he had told his security chiefs, only hours beforehand. "Fidel Castro is right. You do not shut your enemy up by talking to him like a priest, but by burning him."[105]

The events in Timişoara provoked a wave of national revulsion against the Ceauşescu regime. As news of the killings spread by word of mouth— the state-run media were prohibited from reporting antigovernment demonstrations—casualty figures became grossly inflated. The rumors of thousands of dead jolted Romanians from their long torpor. The rally in Palace Square represented a last, desperate gamble by Ceauşescu to prove he still had public opinion behind him. The live television pictures of the crowd jeering and booing the tyrant served as a signal to ordinary Romanians to take to the streets.

That afternoon and evening there were riots on the streets of Bucharest.

Crowds massed in the center of the city, outside Communist Party build-ings, chanting, "Timişoara, Timişoara." Periodically the protesters were dispersed by water cannon and bursts of gunfire from Securitate sharp-shooters. The next morning the crowds were back, tearing down portraits of Nicolae and Elena and besieging the Central Committee building in Palace Square, where the couple was holed up. The streets were full of tanks and armored cars, but their occupants showed little enthusiasm for using force against the demonstrators. In University Square, around 11:00 a.m., sol-diers allowed demonstrators to scramble on board their armored vehicles. Soon a new chant went up: "The army is with us, the army is with us."[106]

As the demonstrators broke into the Central Committee building, a white helicopter took off from the roof, with the Ceauşescus aboard. It flew first to Snagov, a town spa forty miles northeast of Bucharest and the site of one of many presidential residences scattered around Romania. Inside the palace Ceauşescu attempted to get in touch with Communist Party secre-taries around Romania by phone and rally their support. Minutes later the helicopter flew off again. The dictator wanted to go to the oil-producing city of Piteşti, which he had heard was quiet, but the helicopter pilot had differ-ent ideas. Claiming that the French-built craft had been spotted by radar and could be shot down at any moment, he deposited the Ceauşescus by the side of a country road.

For the next few hours the deposed first couple wandered around the Ro-manian countryside in a series of hijacked cars. Abandoned by their body-guards, they were finally arrested by the army in the town of Tîrgovişte, just south of the Carpathian Mountains. Ceauşescu was unable to accept the fact that he was being held prisoner by his own army. He alternated between bouts of deep depression and rantings about "betrayal." "How could you arrest me?" he berated his captors. "I am your commander-in-chief."[107] He complained that his fate was "decided in Malta," a reference to a Gor-bachev-Bush summit three weeks earlier. When his captors offered him reg-ular army food, he pushed it away, describing it as "inedible crap." At night he and Elena huddled together in the same bed, two old people hugging each other and bickering at the same time.

Over the next three days the Ceauşescus could hear gunfire around the army barracks where they were being held. In Tîrgovişte, as in other Ro-manian towns, Securitate sharpshooters were conducting a furious last-ditch stand. Their strategy was to create an atmosphere of total confusion and panic by taking potshots at civilians and attempting to storm key gov-ernment buildings. The sound of shooting encouraged Ceauşescu to believe

that a civil war was raging in Romania and it was only a matter of time before he was rescued.

In fact Ceaușescu's supporters were fighting a losing battle. A new transitional government, known as the National Liberation Front, was gradually imposing its authority. By Christmas Eve the new rulers had had enough. In order to deprive the Securitate of a rallying point, they decided to rid Romania of the Ceaușescus once and for all.

The "trial" took place on the afternoon of Christmas Day in a small schoolroom that had been transformed into an improvised courtroom. The proceedings lasted for fifty-five minutes and were as grotesque a parody of the "rule of law" as anything that had occurred under Ceaușescu himself. No attempt was made to prove the charges, which included "murder of more than sixty thousand people," "subversion of the national economy," and "depositing more than one billion dollars in foreign banks." The military judge acted as one of the prosecutors. After failing to persuade the Ceaușescus to plead diminished responsibility through insanity, the court-appointed defense counsel conceded at the end of the trial that his clients were guilty as charged.

Still dressed in the same dark overcoat that he had worn in Bucharest, the fallen *conducător* stubbornly refused to acknowledge the court's authority or answer its questions. Over and over again he insisted that only his own rubber-stamp parliament, the Grand National Assembly, had the right to put him on trial. When Elena screamed at the court, he patted her on the hand, as if to say that it was not worth arguing with such insignificant people. From time to time he gazed impatiently at his watch, rolling his eyes at the ceiling at the impudence of those who presumed to judge him.

"I am president of the country and supreme commander of the army. I do not recognize you," he snarled. "I do not answer the questions of a gang which carried out a coup."[108]

After the court delivered the preordained verdict—capital punishment—Ceaușescu maintained a sullen dignity. According to the official account, as he was led away, he hummed the opening bars of the "Internationale." Elena was more shrill, screaming at the soldiers who took her away that she had been "like a mother" to them. "We want to die together," she insisted at one point. When one of the soldiers bumped into her, she turned on him furiously. "Go fuck your mother," she yelled.

The soldiers led the Ceaușescus out into an adjoining courtyard and placed them against a whitewashed wall. A firing squad was waiting. The four executioners opened up with automatic rifles, firing more than thirty

rounds apiece. The bodies of the "beloved father and mother" of the Romanian people crumpled to the ground.

MANY OF THE OFFICIAL charges against the Ceauşescus turned out to be wildly exaggerated. The new National Salvation government later acknowledged the total number of those killed during the "revolution" was more like one thousand than forty thousand.[109] No hard evidence was ever found to support allegations that the dictator had stashed away millions of dollars in Swiss banks. On the other hand, the economic, social, and psychological devastation wrought on Romania by Ceauşescu during his twenty-four-year rule was incalculable. It will probably take the country many generations to recover from the effects of his megalomania. Hailed by Communist propagandists as the path to national grandeur, Ceauşescu's policies had turned Romania into the most impoverished and backward country in Eastern Europe, with the possible exception of Albania. The so-called Golden Era was an age of unrelenting economic hardship and brutal political repression.

Hardly any of Ceauşescu's grandiose schemes ever came to fruition, but the cost of attempting to implement them was enormous. Determined to boost the population of Romania from twenty-two million to thirty million by the year 2000, the tyrant virtually outlawed abortion and contraception. The result was a surge in the number of unwanted children, a jump in the infant mortality rate, and the deaths of thousands of women who attempted illegal abortions every year. Intent on creating a modern industrialized state, he poured money into prestige projects, such as a vastly expanded oil-refining industry, which worked at only 10 percent of capacity. The country's once-prosperous agricultural sector was ruined. To build a capital city that would be worthy of him, Ceauşescu tore up some of the oldest sections of Bucharest to make way for a vast and hideous "People's Palace," with more than a thousand rooms, decorated with five-ton chandeliers and acres of white marble. At the same time, he ordered hundreds of villages razed to the ground in the name of "systematization" and "civilization." To pay for his visionary ideas, he deprived ordinary Romanians of heat, food, and electricity.

Reporting from Romania in the aftermath of Ceauşescu's overthrow was like reporting from a country just liberated after a devastating war. The difference was that Romanians were being freed not from a foreign occupier but from their own domestic tyrant. It was as if a huge weight had been lifted from the national psyche. People seemed dazed by their experiences.

There was a kind of stunned relief among Romanians that they had survived the experiment in "scientific socialism." Wherever one went—factories, schools, hospitals, orphanages—people shouted out stories that they had scarcely dared whisper to trusted intimates a few days before. The story that caught the world's attention, because it best summed up the biological and psychological degradation of the nation, was the plight of Romania's orphaned and abandoned children.[110]

ORPHANAGE-SCHOOL No. 6 on the outskirts of Bucharest, home to 226 shivering, undernourished children, was typical of hundreds of other Dickensian establishments scattered around Romania. Although the children suffered from a wide variety of ailments, including AIDS, rickets, and tuberculosis, the most common sickness was frostbite. In winter the temperature in the orphanage, a three-story concrete barracks, frequently fell below freezing because of severe energy cuts ordered by Ceauşescu. Children wore knitted caps and mittens to keep warm, even while indoors. They received lukewarm baths on Wednesdays and Saturdays. They lived in rooms of ten beds each, off long, gloomy corridors that were permanently dark because of a shortage of lightbulbs. The curriculum was dominated by lessons in blind adulation for the dictator who tormented them. "The people, Ceauşescu, Romania, the party," they would chant whenever a visitor came into the room, lit only by a forty-watt lightbulb, the maximum permitted. The children were taught politically uplifting songs that mocked the cold and dark reality of their surroundings.

> *How beautiful, how beautiful is my life,*
> *I can become what I want.*
> *I am a patriotic hawk of the fatherland.*
> *Today the country is taking care of my childhood.*
> *How beautiful, how beautiful is my life.*
> *For my country, one day,*
> *I will sacrifice everything.*

When news of Ceauşescu's overthrow reached the orphanage, staff and children went from room to room, tearing down his portraits. Some girls even gouged his eyes out. Within a week the orphanage director was telling the children lurid tales about how the dictator had turned former orphans into Securitate killers. Everybody recalled how the orphanage had previously been housed in much more lavish accommodations in the center of

Bucharest that had been demolished to make way for one of Ceauşescu's pet projects. "You saw what Ceauşescu did," shouted Titza Batezatu. "He killed children; he shot children. He only pretended to love you, but in fact he shot you."

"Ceauşescu was a criminal," said Rodica Bruiso, a look of hatred crossing her twelve-year-old face.

"That's right," piped up eighteen-year-old Mikhaila Baiban. "He had dozens of palaces built for himself, while the people starved."

The scene in the orphanage was the direct result of the bizarre social policies pursued by the "Genius of the Carpathians." In 1966, a year after Ceauşescu came to power, Romania adopted legislation providing for prison terms of up to five years for illegal abortions. An abortion was permitted only if a woman had already had five children. In 1986 the law was tightened further to ban abortions for any woman under the age of forty-five unless her life was endangered. There were severe penalties for doctors carrying out illegal abortions. These draconian restrictions were combined with a failure to create suitable living conditions for raising large families. Many women who were unable to face the prospect of having more children, and were too poor to bribe doctors for illegal abortions, attempted to self-abort. Others had the children only to abandon them later.

Under Ceauşescu the Bucharest Municipal Hospital dealt with an average of three thousand failed abortions every year, including two hundred women who required major surgery. Many other women were too frightened to report to the hospital. The head of the hospital's gynecological section estimated that well over a thousand women died in Bucharest every year as a result of bungled abortions. Gangrene of the uterus and permanent sterility were frequent complications.

Unlike many Western leaders, ordinary Romanians were not taken in by Ceauşescu. Not far from Orphanage-School No. 6 was a former children's playground that had been hastily converted into a "cemetery of heroes." Hundreds of candles flickered in memory of demonstrators killed by Securitate snipers or crushed by tanks during the final death throes of the Ceauşescu regime. Adorning the grave of fourteen-year-old Marian Mulescu, shot by security police beneath the dictator's balcony in Palace Square, was a placard recording his last conversation with his mother as he lay dying in the hospital.

"Why did you go down to the square, my son?"

"I went there for freedom."

KATYN

April 14, 1990

AFTER DECADES OF LIES the time had come to tell the truth about the thousands of Polish officers massacred in the forest of Katyn by the Soviet secret police. By a quirk of history, this task had been assigned to Wojciech Jaruzelski, Poland's last Communist ruler and president of the first post-Communist republic. The man who had devoted the better part of his life to keeping Poland part of the Soviet bloc was eager to prove he could be an equally devoted servant of the new order.

Dressed in the uniform of a four-star general, Jaruzelski stepped forward to lay a wreath on the grave of the murdered officers. As he straightened himself up, a volley of rifle shots disturbed the quietness of the birch grove. A military chaplain led the crowd in prayers. Hundreds of tiny flags, bearing inscriptions such as "To my beloved husband, murdered in Katyn" and "To our father, killed on the orders of Stalin and Beria," fluttered in the breeze.

"They fought for a free Poland, and they were slaughtered as innocents," Jaruzelski wrote in the remembrance book. "Far from their homes and their native land, they remained faithful to Poland and their soldiers' honor until the last moment. To the Polish officer, and the victim of Stalinist crimes, is due eternal honor."

A few months earlier such a ceremony would have been impossible. Even though there was overwhelming evidence implicating the Soviet secret police in the murder of the Polish officers, Kremlin propagandists had always insisted that the Nazis were responsible. Like his Communist predecessors, Jaruzelski had accepted the Russian version of events, prohibiting the Polish press from any discussion of Katyn. It was only after Communist rule had begun to unravel in Poland that he shifted his position. After the Solidarity election victory in June 1989 Jaruzelski urged Gorbachev to acknowledge Soviet responsibility for the tragedy on the ground that it was impeding the development of normal relations between the Soviet Union and Poland.

The Polish obsession with Katyn was part of a frenzied reexamination of history all over the former Soviet empire. The Balts wanted to know the truth about the Molotov-Ribbentrop pact, which had permitted Stalin to crush their independence at the outset of World War II. Czechs and Slovaks insisted on being told the names of the Politburo traitors who had requested "fraternal assistance" from the Soviet Union in 1968 to suppress the Prague Spring. Hungarians demanded political rehabilitation for the leaders of the 1956 Budapest uprising against the Communist dictatorship. East Germans combed through Stasi records to discover which of their friends and neighbors had been spying on them.

Exactly half a century earlier, in April 1940, the spot where Jaruzelski now stood had been a killing field. The NKVD, Stalin's secret police, brought the Polish officers here in prison vans known as Black Ravens. The officers were frisked for valuables and forced to kneel alongside a line of deep pits. It was easy to see why the NKVD had chosen the clearing in the forest as a suitable execution site. It was a quiet and secluded place where they could work undisturbed. It was also convenient, right next to a summer vacation home for NKVD employees and only a thirty-minute drive from the main Moscow–Minsk railway line.

The NKVD executioners were trained to kill with brutal efficiency. Soviet pistols tended to overheat with heavy use, so they used a German-made pistol, the Walther 7.65 mm, considered more reliable. They took aim at the nape of the victim's skull, so that the bullet passed neatly through his brain, emerging between the nose and the hairline. Perfected in the early days of the revolution, this method caused instant death with minimal consumption of bullets. An assistant usually stood by to reload the eight-shot semiautomatic pistol. The bodies were neatly stacked in layers of twelve. There could be anywhere between two hundred and three thousand bodies per pit.

When the pit was full, it was filled in with heavy sand and landscaped with birch trees.[111]

The Germans stumbled on what had happened at Katyn after invading the Soviet Union in June 1941. Acting on a tip from a local peasant, they dug up the skeletons of 4,143 Polish officers. The mass graves also contained personal effects such as letters, snapshots, bracelets, and leather cavalry boots. The discovery was a propaganda windfall for the Nazis, who used it to drive a wedge between the Poles and the Soviets. It was also an embarrassment for the Western Allies, who needed to keep on good terms with Stalin in order to win the war.

From the historians' point of view, the most important find were twenty-two diaries, which make it possible to reconstruct what happened to the officers in the seven months between their arrests and brutal executions. After their capture by the Red Army, the officers were interned in a Russian Orthodox monastery at Kozielsk, 150 miles south of Moscow. All attempts to "reeducate" them or persuade them to remain in the Soviet Union failed. Proud of their national traditions, they defied the Soviet military authorities by holding prayer meetings in their barracks and singing the Polish national anthem. Their proud demeanor, unquenchable optimism, and beautifully cut leather boots astonished their Soviet jailers. Despite all the evidence to the contrary, they persisted in believing that their homeland would soon be liberated.

Toward the end of March 1940 the prisoners picked up rumors that the camp was about to be closed. The Soviet Union had never declared war on Poland. The officers hoped to be sent to a neutral country and eventually rejoin the exiled Polish army. The NKVD encouraged such rumors, hinting that they were going "to the West" or "to home." On April 3 the first group of three hundred or so prisoners left Kozielsk to the exuberant cheers of their countrymen. They were fed a good meal before leaving the camp, leading to speculation that the Soviets wanted to fatten them up prior to releasing them. After a twenty-four-hour ride in windowless wagons, they were pushed off the train at a place called Gniezdovo.

"At [the Gniezdovo] station, we were loaded into prison cars under strict guard," noted Lieutenant Wacław Kruk in a diary entry dated April 8. "Optimistic as I was before, I'm now coming to the conclusion that this journey does not bode well."[112]

One of the Polish officers, Major Adam Skolski, managed to keep writing his diary until a few moments before he died. "From dawn, the day started in a peculiar way. Departure in lorries fitted with cells; terrible.

Taken somewhere into a forest, something like a country house. Very thorough search of our belongings. They took my watch, which showed time as 6:30 (Polish time) 8:30 (Soviet time); asked about a wedding ring. Ruble, belt, and pocket knife taken away."[113]

FOR GORBACHEV, glasnost had never been an end in itself. It was a means to an end, a way of bringing outside pressure to bear on the apparatchiks who actually made decisions. Historical truth was a powerful political weapon to be used sparingly, in accordance with changing circumstances, and at the most opportune time. This was one area where he enjoyed an advantage over his bureaucratic rivals. As general secretary he was the custodian of the regime's most terrible secrets.

The secrets were stuffed in large envelopes, tied with string, and sealed with wax. There were around two thousand of these envelopes, all neatly filed away in cupboards in the Kremlin apartment once occupied by Stalin, down the corridor from the general secretary's office. This was the celebrated *osobaya papka* (special file), containing documents so secret that they were circulated and preserved in one copy only. Anybody who checked the documents out was obliged to sign for them. Many of the envelopes in the *osobaya papka* could be opened only by the general secretary himself or with his personal authorization.[114]

The contents of the *osobaya papka* were politically and ideologically devastating. Here, in black and white, were documents that laid bare the cynicism and opportunism of Soviet leaders, from Lenin onward. There were orders, signed by Lenin, for the murder of priests and "class enemies" and for a policy of "Red Terror" against the enemies of the revolution. There were documents proving that Stalin was responsible for the deaths of millions of his countrymen, and not just "thousands," as Gorbachev himself maintained as late as November 1987. There was the official Russian-language text of the secret Molotov-Ribbentrop pact between the Soviet Union and Nazi Germany, providing for the dismemberment of Poland and the Baltic states, a document that Moscow had long denounced as a forgery. There were the squalid details of Kremlin power struggles, including the murder of the secret police chief Lavrenti Beria and the plot against Khrushchev. There were documents outlining preparations for the invasions of Hungary and Czechoslovakia. And there were two large envelopes devoted to Katyn.

An item in Envelope No. 1 revealed the shameful truth: The Polish offi-

cers had been killed on Stalin's direct orders. It was a typewritten memorandum from Beria to the dictator, recommending the "supreme penalty—shooting" for Polish officers and Poles suspected of belonging to "various counter-revolutionary organizations." Stalin had scrawled his approval across the top of the document, and other Politburo members had also affixed their signatures. Another handwritten report, submitted to Nikita Khrushchev by the head of the KGB, gave a precise figure for the number of Poles executed at Katyn and two other sites: 21,857. It recommended destroying the personnel records of the murdered Poles on the ground that they no longer had any "operational" or "historical" value and were potentially embarrassing.[115]

Gorbachev had the opportunity to discover the truth about Katyn from the moment he became general secretary. However, he showed little interest in the matter until it became a subject of hot political controversy. In the spring of 1987 he set up a joint Soviet-Polish commission to investigate so-called blank spots in relations between the two countries. Official historians from both sides were instructed to comb the archives to produce an agreed-upon version of history. Despite numerous meetings, the commission failed to make much progress largely because the Soviet representatives were not authorized to question the official line. Polish historians concluded that the purpose of the blank spots campaign was to obfuscate rather than to clarify, postponing the moment when Moscow would finally admit responsibility for Katyn.

Two years later, in the spring of 1989, pressure began to mount from the Polish side for a resolution of the Katyn affair. With contested elections approaching, and in the wake of the Round Table agreement with Solidarity, Jaruzelski was anxious to demonstrate his national credentials. For the Polish Communist Party to continue to deny Soviet guilt—in the face of overwhelming evidence—would be politically suicidal. In March 1989 a Polish spokesman announced that everything pointed to the conclusion that "the crime was committed by the Stalinist NKVD."[116]

The Polish about-face put Gorbachev in a difficult spot since he had earlier insisted that there was no conclusive evidence of Soviet guilt. Far from being dead and buried, the Katyn mystery had now become a live political issue. In a memorandum dated March 22, 1989, the top Soviet officials dealing with Poland warned Gorbachev that the Katyn affair could explode in his face and urged him not to procrastinate any further. "In this case, time is not our ally," the memorandum concluded. "It might be preferable to explain what really happened, and who specifically is responsible for what

happened, and close the issue there. The costs of this course of action would be lower, in the final analysis, than the damage caused by our inaction."[117]

Preoccupied with his own domestic problems, Gorbachev effectively shelved this recommendation. But according to his former chief of staff Valery Boldin, he did order his own search of the *osobaya papka*. Boldin later recalled:

> He called me in and asked me to show him everything we had on the Katyn affair. Two envelopes were found. I ordered them from the archives, and I brought them to him unopened, exactly the way I received them from the archives. He opened both envelopes himself, read what was inside, and sealed them back with Scotch tape. He did not give the material to me to read. He told me, "This is indeed the material concerning Katyn. It needs to be kept so that it is quite safe." I put the material in a new envelope and sealed it properly. . . . All the documents that were kept in the archives on this subject were handed over to him.[118]

In accordance with the rules of the *osobaya papka*, archivists duly noted that the documents were signed out to Boldin on April 18, 1989, and returned in a new envelope. It was the first time that any Kremlin official had examined the file in more than eight years.

Gorbachev insists he was never shown the documents relating to Katyn or equally damning evidence on the Molotov-Ribbentrop secret protocols.[119] He has challenged the veracity of his former chief of staff, pointing out that Boldin played a leading role in the August 1991 coup. He has also posed the rhetorical question, Why should the father of glasnost, the man who did more than any other Soviet leader to publicize the ghastly atrocities of the Stalin era, have any reason to lie about Katyn?[120]

Boldin's reliability as a historical witness is certainly open to question. On this occasion, however, he seems more credible than Gorbachev. In April 1989 he was still the perfect apparatchik, faithfully carrying out his master's wishes. He had no reason to conceal documents from his own boss. On the contrary, he wanted to impress the general secretary with his loyalty and zeal. The idea that he would have kept such explosive material to himself is so improbable that few Russian officials outside Gorbachev's immediate entourage believe it. Even Yakovlev, the Politburo member directly responsible for historical matters, has accused the former Soviet leader of lying: "There was a huge fuss about this. Gorbachev kept telling me: 'Find

the documents, keep looking.' And he told Jaruzelski: 'Press harder on Yakovlev, let him look for these documents.' It put me in such a difficult position. During my talks with Jaruzelski, I felt like a fish in a hot frying pan. . . . I later discovered that he [Gorbachev] had hid the facts about Katyn all along."[121]

There is a plausible answer to Gorbachev's rhetorical question about why he should have concealed the most damning documents about Katyn when he allowed so much else to come to light, and it goes to the heart of his political identity and character. The father of glasnost was a master obfuscater and manipulator. He was in favor of openness, but on his terms. He believed in doling out the truth in small, politically calculated doses. He could have totally destroyed the legitimacy of the Communist system with a series of spectacular revelations, but he had no interest in doing so. He was a reformer, not a revolutionary. In the case of the Katyn archives, he wanted to prevent a wave of anti-Sovietism in Poland. He did not want to antagonize the conservative wing of his own Politburo, at a time when he needed its support to create a powerful presidency. A host of such considerations are likely to have run through his mind as he stuffed the incriminating documents back into the envelope.

In short, the time was not yet ripe.

Later on, when the time was ripe, he had his own historical reputation to consider. The way Boldin tells it, Gorbachev became trapped in his own Byzantine political manipulations. His attempt to control the flood of revelations from the archives had led him to conceal valuable documents from both his own colleagues and the international community. Having lied once, he was obliged to lie again, for reasons of consistency.

When Gorbachev revised his position about Soviet responsibility for Katyn in April 1990, he did so for primarily pragmatic reasons. Independent research in both Poland and the Soviet Union had exploded the long-standing claim of German guilt and Soviet innocence. Jaruzelski was coming to Moscow and wanted to go down in history as the man who had persuaded the Soviets to "tell the truth" about Katyn. From Moscow's point of view, it was better to concede Soviet guilt to Jaruzelski than to his anti-Communist rivals. According to a secret Kremlin memorandum, it was necessary to find a way "to seal the political problem and at the same time avoid an explosion of emotion." The challenge facing Soviet leaders was to come up with a version of history that would set the record reasonably straight, at the "lowest [political] cost."[122]

When Gorbachev received Jaruzelski in the Kremlin, he told the Polish

leader that the available evidence indicated that the Katyn massacre had been carried out on the orders of "Beria and his henchmen."[123] This formula had the effect of shifting responsibility for the massacre away from the Soviet state toward an individual who was later executed for his crimes. The contents of the *osobaya papka* were still considered too shocking to be made public.

If this is a correct interpretation of Gorbachev's handling of the Katyn affair, he made one fatal miscalculation. He assumed that the secrets of the *osobaya papka* would remain under lock and key virtually indefinitely. He underestimated the political challenge he faced from Boris Yeltsin, who had been nursing a festering sense of grievance about his ouster from the leadership two and a half years previously.

Over the next eighteen months the rivalry between Gorbachev and Yeltsin gradually came to dominate the Soviet political scene. Theirs was to be a fight to the death, involving every conceivable weapon in the Kremlin arsenal, including the *osobaya papka*.

MOSCOW

May 29, 1990

BORIS YELTSIN DESCRIBED the brutal essence of Kremlin politics when he observed that leaders "have never voluntarily parted with power in Russia." In the second volume of his memoirs, *The Struggle for Russia*, he tried to explain this "medieval principle" to a predominantly Western audience: "It's as if leaders were told: you have been given power, so hang on to it. Don't let it go for anything. Whoever is on top must step on those below. . . . That is the vertical structure of society. Russia is one and indivisible. Everyone strives upward, to the very top. Higher and higher still. Once you have scrambled to the top, the altitude is so dizzying, you cannot back down."[124]

Russian leaders had every incentive to hang on to power. In the West the shock of losing high office is cushioned by new opportunities; there is a revolving door between public and private life. In the Soviet Union losing power was tantamount to losing everything. Under Stalin, ousted Politburo members were lucky to stay alive. Stalin's successors were more humane. Instead of shooting their defeated rivals, they humiliated them, sending them off to run power stations in Siberia and embassies in Latin America. It was not physical destruction, but it was political destruction, and it was accompanied by the loss of many of the privileges enjoyed by members of the Kremlin circle.

When Yeltsin was expelled from the Politburo in February 1988, he was obliged to give up many privileges, including his Zil limousine and country dacha. The psychological trauma of losing power was even greater. His telephone fell silent; people whom he had regarded as friends and colleagues disappeared from his life; his information network dried up overnight. His former comrades in the Kremlin nomenklatura treated him as a political outcast. He lay awake at night, suffering from appalling headaches, obsessively reviewing every step that he had taken and every word that he had said. There were times when he felt like "crawling up the wall" and could hardly restrain himself from "crying out loud."

"Politically, I was a corpse," he later wrote. "All that was left where my heart had been was a burnt-out cinder. Everything around me was burnt out, everything within me was burnt out."[125]

Traditionally once a person was tossed out of the charmed inner circle of Soviet power, there was no way back. The victors made sure of that. Yeltsin, however, had the wit to realize that the rules of Kremlin politics were changing rapidly because of Gorbachev's glasnost campaign. For the first time in seven decades, public opinion was becoming a real factor in Soviet decision making. Gorbachev made use of public opinion in his fight with the bureaucracy. Yeltsin, however, was the first Soviet politician to understand that power could come from the people rather than from the party.

The role of people's tribune suited the Siberian. Although he had been a *nachalnik* (boss) for most of his life, he knew what it was like to be an underdog. Born dirt poor, he had suffered abuse as a child. More recently he had been disgraced by Gorbachev and the party leadership and had many scores to settle. His immense physical strength and sportsman's training made him a natural fighter. He had a lot of stamina. He knew almost instinctively how to appeal to a crowd. Like Poland's Wałęsa, he was able to sense what his listeners were thinking and shape his message to what they wanted to hear. Through a skillful mixture of good humor, common sense, and outright demagoguery, he tapped into the anger of the masses and used it as a weapon against his political opponents.

It was Gorbachev who had inadvertently supplied Yeltsin with the vehicle for his political resurrection, with his decision to create a partially free parliament, the Congress of People's Deputies. After Sakharov's death in December 1989 Yeltsin became the leader of the "democratic opposition" to Gorbachev.

The Soviet Union's deepening economic crisis played straight into Yeltsin's hands. By the summer of 1990 most Russians had lost interest in

Gorbachev's foreign policy triumphs and the dramatic improvement in relations with the United States. Soviet television viewers reacted to pictures of Germans and Americans chanting, "Gorbie, Gorbie," with snorts of contempt. Reductions in nuclear arsenals were welcome, but what most interested ordinary Russians were everyday concerns like a good pair of shoes and the length of the line outside the local bread store.

In developing his own political style and identity, Yeltsin did everything to distinguish himself from his former patron. Gorbachev rode around in a long motorcade of Zils; Yeltsin flaunted his dilapidated Moskvich, the Soviet equivalent of the despised East German Trabi. Gorbachev once confided that he shared state secrets with his wife, Raisa; Yeltsin took the view that wives had no business poking their noses into politics.[126] Gorbachev had a penchant for long-winded speeches that could go on for two or three hours at a time; when Yeltsin spoke, he was always succinct and concrete. As his popularity declined, Gorbachev seemed to retreat back into his Kremlin fortress and shy away from direct contact with ordinary Russians; Yeltsin made a point of getting out into the Russian heartland and listening to what ordinary people were saying.

But the differences went deeper than style and personality, to the most crucial question of all: Was communism finished? Despite a willingness to redefine the word "socialism," so that it lost much of its meaning, Gorbachev was unwilling to abandon Communist ideology altogether. He prattled on about the irrevocable "socialist choice" that Russia had allegedly made in November 1917. Lenin remained an unassailable authority for him. Yeltsin, on the other hand, was undergoing an ideological conversion that was both painful and public. Spurred on by his conflict with the Communist Party establishment, he had reexamined his most basic political beliefs, and he had come to the conclusion that he was no longer a Communist.

A turning point in Yeltsin's intellectual development occurred during his first visit to the United States in September 1989, more specifically his first visit to an American supermarket, in Houston, Texas. The sight of aisle after aisle of shelves neatly stacked with every conceivable type of foodstuff and household item, each in a dozen varieties, both amazed and depressed him. For Yeltsin, like many other first-time Russian visitors to America, this was infinitely more impressive than tourist attractions like the Statue of Liberty and the Lincoln Memorial. It was impressive precisely because of its ordinariness. A cornucopia of consumer goods beyond the imagination of most Soviets was within the reach of ordinary citizens without standing in line for hours. And it was all so attractively displayed. For someone brought

up in the drab conditions of communism, even a member of the relatively privileged elite, a visit to a Western supermarket involved a full-scale assault on the senses.

"What we saw in that supermarket was no less amazing than America itself," recalled Lev Sukhanov, who accompanied Yeltsin on his trip to the United States and shared his sense of shock and dismay at the gap in living standards between the two superpowers. "I think it is quite likely that the last prop of Yeltsin's Bolshevik consciousness finally collapsed after Houston. His decision to leave the party and join the struggle for supreme power in Russia may have ripened irrevocably at that moment of mental confusion."[127]

Sukhanov devotes an entire chapter of his book *Tri Goda s Yetsinym* (Three Years with Yeltsin) to describing the wonders of the Houston supermarket. He records Yeltsin's amazement at being told that the store stocked thirty thousand separate items. (The average Soviet store stocked fewer than a hundred, and many of these were usually "unavailable.") Every aisle was an eye-opener for the visitors from Moscow. Scarcely had they recovered from the shock of the cheese section, where they saw "red cheese, brown cheese, and lemon-orange cheese," than they were "literally shaken" by the quality of produce in the vegetable section. They were particularly struck by the radishes, which were as large as good-size potatoes back home and seemed to sparkle beneath the brilliant light of the store. Reluctantly they had to move on from the vegetables to the pastry section.

"You could spend hours in the pastry section," exclaimed Sukhanov. "As a spectacle this probably surpassed Hollywood. At the counter there was a customer waiting for a huge cake, made in the form of a hockey stadium. The players were made of chocolate. It was a real work of art, but the main thing was that it was available for purchase, completely available."[128]

On the plane, traveling from Houston to Miami, Yeltsin seemed lost in his thoughts for a long time. He clutched his head in his hands. Eventually he broke his silence. "They had to fool the people," he told Sukhanov. "It is now clear why they made it so difficult for the average Soviet citizen to go abroad. They were afraid that people's eyes would open."[129]

The former party apparatchik understood the yearning of the *narod*— the long-suffering Russian people—for a normal life, its anger at being deceived and humiliated. He, too, had been humiliated. He, too, had been deceived. He would help the *narod* secure its revenge against the party establishment. The *narod*'s revenge would also be his.

Dominated by a monumental marble statue of Lenin, set between Corinthian columns, the long conference hall of the Grand Kremlin Palace had witnessed some of the most dramatic events of the Soviet era. Here Stalin had reached the apotheosis of his political power, at the Seventeenth Party Congress in 1934, when he was officially described as "the greatest man of all ages and nations."[130] Here, too, the Gorbachev generation of Communists had listened, heads bowed, to Khrushchev's impassioned denunciation of Stalin's crimes, in his "secret speech" to the Twentieth Congress in 1956. Under Brezhnev the hall had been reserved for meetings of the Supreme Soviet. Every year newspapers around the world had carried the ritual photograph of doddering Politburo members raising their right hands in unanimous approval of party policy.

After serving as a totalitarian echo chamber for more than five decades, the great Kremlin hall had finally been turned into a real debating chamber. A large electronic scoreboard, placed to one side of Lenin, kept track of the innumerable votes. There were long lines of people waiting to speak at the microphones scattered around the hall. Outside, in the lobby, journalists rushed frantically about, nabbing deputies as they came out of the hall. Tables were piled high with draft resolutions, political pamphlets, official transcripts. On one side of the lobby there was a line of display boards, filled with telegrams from voters. The texts varied, but the message was always the same: The people's candidate for chairman of the new Russian parliament was Boris Nikolayevich Yeltsin.

Egged on by Gorbachev, who accused Yeltsin of turning his back on "socialism," the Communists did everything they could to prevent the renegade from gaining the highest political post in Russia. But their efforts to smear him backfired. The Communist candidate was so unappealing—both politically and physically—that he had trouble gaining the votes of all his fellow Communists. Independent deputies resented the Soviet president's open interference in the election process. The longer they took to make up their minds, the more telegrams supporting Yeltsin poured into the Kremlin. After two inconclusive rounds of voting, Yeltsin was finally elected speaker on the third ballot, by a margin of just four votes.

Minutes after his triumph Russia's new leader walked out of the Kremlin to thank the *narod*. They had been waiting patiently for hours, standing beneath St. Basil's Cathedral and listening to radio transmissions of the debate. When they caught sight of their hero's silver gray pompadour, they rushed toward him with a roar, chanting, "Victory, victory."

"My struggle is the people's struggle," Yeltsin boomed, addressing his supporters from a grassy mound beneath the red-ocher Kremlin wall. "This

is an important step in the victory of democracy. Now we need to continue the fight for the independence and sovereignty of Russia, for the revival of its national, economic, and spiritual image, so that Russia will live as it did before."[131] Acknowledging the cheers of the crowd with his fist, he crammed himself into the front seat of his Moskvich and was driven away.

In addition to a huge political constituency, Yeltsin now had a political stage vast enough to vie with that occupied by Mikhail Gorbachev. Russia was by far the largest, and most important, of the Soviet Union's fifteen republics. Stretching from the Baltic to the Pacific, Russia occupied 76 percent of the Soviet landmass, an area nearly twice the size of the entire United States. Its 142 million population equaled that of all the other republics combined. The republic accounted for 90 percent of Soviet oil production, 76 percent of natural gas output, and 89 percent of foreign trade earnings. It was no exaggeration to say that the Russian colossus held the key to Gorbachev's success or failure.

Not only was Russia vast, but it was also ideally suited to the theme that Yeltsin had made his own, the yearning of ordinary people for a decent standard of living. Other nations had independence movements to distract them from their economic misery. Russia had nowhere else to go; it was the heart of the empire. The empire, however, had brought Russia nothing but headaches. The economic devastation left behind by seven decades of communism had caused many Russians to question the national tradition of constant territorial expansion, a tradition embraced by tsars and general secretaries alike. For the first time in many centuries Russians were ready to shed their traditional great power aspirations if this would lead to an improvement in their own living standards. It was a conscious turning inward, away from empire.

The buzzword in this debate was "sovereignty." One of the first steps taken by the new Russian parliament under Yeltsin's leadership was the adoption of a "declaration of sovereignty," asserting the primacy of Russian laws over Soviet laws. The parliament also asserted a right of ownership and control over all natural resources on the territory of the Russian Republic. After a one-year transition period Russia would insist that the other Soviet republics begin paying world prices for oil, gas, and other raw materials.[132] As Gorbachev was quick to appreciate, such a step threatened to destroy one of the last bonds holding the empire together. If Russia took control of its vast natural resources, his bargaining power would be much reduced not only with the Baltic states but also with Slavic republics such as Ukraine. The whole basis of Soviet power, and his personal authority as president of

the Soviet Union, would be undermined. The prediction that he had made at Foros the previous summer—"if Russia rises up . . . it will be the end of empire"—was in the process of coming true.

Yeltsin, by contrast, had discovered the perfect political weapon to use against his former Communist comrades. By leading the struggle for "sovereignty," he would wrest power away from Gorbachev and the hated "center." But the fight was sure to be fierce, and he needed allies. In order to make the necessary alliances, he was prepared to share his weapon with others. Not only republics but provinces, towns, and even villages had the right to be sovereign, he assured his supporters. "Take as much sovereignty as you can swallow," he told provincial leaders shortly after his election. In Yeltsin's conception, the entire structure of political power in Russia would be rebuilt from the bottom up, on a contractual basis. The possibility that the sovereignty weapon might one day be used against him appears to have never occurred to Yeltsin. If it did, he put it out of his mind. That was tomorrow, and this was today.

After almost three years in the political wilderness, he was back at the center of power, and it felt exhilarating. The new speaker took possession of an enormous office in the White House, a massive building on the Moskva River, where the Russian government had its headquarters. He visited the White House in the company of Sukhanov, who had helped him recover from despair at the Soviet Building Ministry, Gosstroi. The sight of the luxurious office, with its soft modern sheen, gave Sukhanov a "pleasant tingle," he later recalled.

"Look, Boris Nikolayevich, what an office we have seized!" Sukhanov exclaimed.

"We haven't just seized an office," Yeltsin replied. "We have seized the whole of Russia."[133]

MOSCOW

December 20, 1990

As IT TURNED OUT, Yeltsin was wrong. He and the "democrats" had not "seized" the whole of Russia. Not yet, anyway. What they had "seized" was a luxurious office in the center of Moscow, as Sukhanov had been astute enough to observe. For the time being, their power did not extend very far beyond the Moscow Ring Road. Mother Russia—vast, lethargic, bankrupt, disillusioned—continued to elude them.

The popularly elected Russian Congress of People's Deputies had proclaimed its authority over the whole of Russia. It passed resolutions, issued edicts, and adopted laws. The blizzard of paper, however, had little visible impact on real life. The "power ministries"—the military, the KGB, the police—remained under tight Communist Party control. Months after giving up its constitutionally guaranteed monopoly of power, the party continued to exercise its influence through a ubiquitous old-comrade network. The titles on office doors were changed to emphasize the shift of power from the party to elected bodies, but the occupants of the offices usually remained the same.

The bureaucrats used the centralized distribution system to remind Yeltsin who was boss. When the new speaker demanded an official residence outside Moscow, he was allocated a room in a seedy vacation home for low-

level clerks. After much complaining, he was eventually permitted to move in with a deputy minister of agriculture. The Ninth Directorate of the KGB, which was responsible for ensuring the safety of Soviet leaders, did its best to prevent Russia's new rulers from gaining access to government cars and government communications systems. Weapons were a particularly sensitive issue. Fearing a crackdown by the hard-liners, Yeltsin attempted to build up a Russian security service that would be independent of the KGB. Since the Russian government did not control any munitions factories of its own, it had to scavenge whatever weapons it could. By the time a coup eventually did take place, in August 1991, the White House arsenal consisted of sixty assault rifles, a hundred pistols, two bulletproof jackets, and five walkie-talkies.[134]

Just because the Communist Party apparatus was successful in denying real power to Yeltsin did not mean that nothing had changed. The impotence and incompetence of the nomenklatura became increasingly apparent, as Russia sank further into an economic morass. The bureaucrats controlled everything, but there was little they could do with their power, other than hang on to it. The system of centralized distribution had ceased to function effectively, but the apparatchiks were loath to get rid of it, for fear of undermining their own authority. The result was political paralysis. Rival legislatures competed with one another to churn out laws and edicts that nobody respected. Unable to halt the disintegration of the economy, provincial governments attempted to protect their own citizens by resorting to total rationing and erecting customs barriers. The mood was everyone for himself.

There was a brief surge of optimism in early September, when Gorbachev and Yeltsin both embraced a plan to introduce a Western-style mixed economy over a period of five hundred days. The five-hundred-day plan, as it was known, envisaged the denationalization of 80 percent of the Soviet economy, the abolition of central planning, and the liberalization of foreign trade activity. Prices would be freed; the ruble would be made convertible; collective farms would be disbanded; private property would be recognized. What is more, all this would happen relatively painlessly. What Soviet economists called the monetary overhang—the phenomenon of too much money chasing too few goods—would be eliminated by the proceeds of a bankruptcy sale of state assets.

The five-hundred-day plan turned out to be another utopian dream. There was no such thing as a painless transition from central planning to a free market. The economists who drew up the plan underestimated the op-

position they would encounter from the people who actually ran the economy: factory directors; collective farm chairmen; representatives of the military-industrial complex. These people coalesced into a powerful lobbying group. Scarcely a week went by without the convening of a conference to denounce the "ruinous" plans of the radicals and demand a return to well-tried "administrative methods." The political pressure on Gorbachev became intense. Prime Minister Ryzkhov warned of political and economic disintegration. The kolkhoz chairmen threatened to withhold food from the cities if the five-hundred-day plan was implemented. Military deputies in the Soviet parliament went so far as to call for the president's removal from office, unless he acted decisively to prevent "the collapse of the country."[135]

In the end Gorbachev simply "got frightened," in the words of his leading economics adviser.[136] His own popularity had dropped to an all-time low of 21 percent. In the Soviet parliament the "democrats" were an insignificant force. The five-hundred-day plan contained many interesting ideas, but they existed only on paper. The harsh Russian winter was approaching. Gorbachev could not afford to antagonize the factory managers and bureaucrats, who were actually running the country, or the generals and secret police chiefs, who constituted his final line of defense against Yeltsin. It was here that real power lay. He decided to bow to political reality and beat a tactical retreat.

During the fall of 1990 the radicals watched in dismay as Gorbachev appeared to move steadily to the right. In early December he dismissed his progressive interior minister, Vadim Bakatin, who had incurred the wrath of the conservatives by failing to crack down on Baltic separatism. A few days later he issued a decree ordering all state enterprises to abide by the instructions of the central planners. In a speech to the Soviet parliament he called for "resolute measures" to keep the country together. But the biggest shock was yet to come.

EDUARD SHEVARDNADZE WAS particularly alarmed by the growing influence of the conservatives. The foreign minister considered himself a political soul mate of Gorbachev and one of the intellectual fathers of perestroika and "new thinking." He recalled his talk with Gorbachev on the beach at Pitsunda in the early eighties. In his emotional Georgian way Shevardnadze had blurted out that everything was "rotten" in the Soviet Union, and it was impossible "to go on living like this." In a sense, everything had begun with that conversation.

It was difficult for Shevardnadze to keep track of his old friend's constant zigzags, but one thing seemed clear: Gorbachev was drifting away from him. The president had chosen to surround himself with representatives of the traditional power structures—the Communist Party, the military, the KGB. As the conservative attacks mounted, the foreign minister thought he was being made to shoulder the blame for the Kremlin's international setbacks, while the president basked in the praise. One incident in particular rankled with him. On October 15, the day Gorbachev was awarded the Nobel Peace Prize, a rancorous "Who lost Germany?" debate erupted in the Soviet parliament. Shevardnadze later complained that he had been left to fend off the attacks of the reactionaries for permitting a reunited Germany to become a member of NATO. "The only thing I needed, wanted, and expected from the President was that he take a clear position: that he rebuff the right-wingers, and openly defend our common policy. I waited in vain."[137]

After a sleepless night Shevardnadze made his decision. He wrote out his resignation statement, by hand, in the early-morning hours of December 20, 1990. He informed his daughter in Tbilisi and his two closest aides at the Foreign Ministry. They expressed their support for the action he was about to take. Then he left for the Kremlin.[138]

A stunned silence fell on the Congress of People's Deputies as Shevardnadze embarked on what he described as "the shortest and most difficult speech of my life." Thumping the air with his right fist, his Georgian accent thicker than ever, he berated the "comrade democrats" for scattering "into the bushes" while the fate of perestroika was being decided. Then came the disjointed words that made headlines around the world: "Dictatorship is coming; I state this with complete responsibility. No one knows what kind of dictatorship this will be and who will come—what kind of dictator—and what the regime will be like. I want to make the following statement: I am resigning. . . . I cannot reconcile myself to the events taking place in our country, and to the trials awaiting our people. I nevertheless believe that the dictatorship will not succeed, that the future belongs to democracy and freedom."[139]

As Shevardnadze delivered his bombshell, Gorbachev listened impassively from his seat on the podium a few feet away. He later acknowledged he was "hurt" by his friend's failure to inform him in advance, but his face betrayed no emotion at the time.[140] When the speech was over, he clutched his forehead and looked down at his papers.

The team that had launched the Soviet Union on its great experiment

back in 1985 had gone its separate ways. Yegor Ligachev had joined the hard-line opposition after accusing Gorbachev of presiding over the dismantling of socialism. Aleksandr Yakovlev, the ideological brains behind glasnost, had effectively retired from active politics. Prime Minister Nikolai Ryzkhov had become a victim of the government's rock-bottom popularity. Now it was Shevardnadze's turn to quit. Gorbachev had never been so alone.

The filmmaker Ales Adamovich summed up the Soviet leader's predicament in a speech to the congress. "By losing such allies as Shevardnadze, you are losing your own strength, your prestige," he told Gorbachev. "If this process goes on, the president will soon be surrounded by colonels and generals. They will surround the president, making him a hostage. Gorbachev is the only leader in Soviet history who has not stained his hands with blood, and we would like to remember him for that. But a moment will come when they will instigate a bloodbath, and later they will wipe their bloodstained hands against your suit, and you will be to blame for everything."[141]

It did not take long for Adamovich's prediction to come true.

IV

REVOLT

OF THE PARTY

The most dangerous moment for a corrupt regime is when it attempts to reform itself.

Alexis de Tocqueville

A revolution is only worth something if it knows how to defend itself.

Vladimir Lenin

MOSCOW

December 22, 1990

EDUARD SHEVARDNADZE HAD BASED his warning about an "approaching dictatorship" on his acute political intuition. He had watched the conservatives mobilize their forces to oppose the five-hundred-day plan, and he feared Gorbachev might be wilting under the pressure. He regarded the Tbilisi massacre of April 1989 as a dress rehearsal for a much broader armed crackdown. There had been an intensive parliamentary investigation into the Tbilisi events, but no one had ever been punished. The foreign minister began to suspect that there were "hidden forces . . . lurking behind the president's back" who were ready to resort to "criminal actions." The fact that Gorbachev was willing to shield these people was deeply disturbing to him. One day he could bear it no longer and decided to confront his old friend with his suspicions.

He reached the president over the *vertushka* as he was being driven to the Kremlin from his country dacha. The twenty-five-minute drive was always a good opportunity to catch Gorbachev alone, before he got submerged in daily business.

"Acts of violence are the end of perestroika, and of your reputation . . ."

"What are you thinking?" Gorbachev exploded. "How can it even occur to you that I would allow something like that to happen?"[1]

329

Shevardnadze's suspicions were well founded, even though he had no concrete evidence to back them up. By the time he delivered his bombshell to the congress, the machinery of repression was already in motion. Plans for a nationwide crackdown were already being hatched in the Lubyanka Prison, headquarters of the Committee for State Security. Surveillance of opposition activists had been intensified. KGB agents were following Yeltsin around the clock and had even bugged his favorite sauna with a re-mote-control radio. In an effort to gather incriminating information, wire-taps were ordered against hundreds of people, from the prime minister of Russia and the mayor of Moscow to Yeltsin's tennis coach and Raisa Gorbachev's hairdresser. Eventually the net was widened to include many of Gorbachev's own advisers, such as Shevardnadze, Yakovlev, and the author of the five-hundred-day plan, the economist Stanislav Shatalin.[2] Transcripts of these intercepted conversations were later discovered in the safe of Valery Boldin, Gorbachev's chief of staff.

In the fall of 1990 the KGB chairman, Vladimir Kryuchkov, began bombarding Gorbachev with letters, outlining alleged plots by the "demo-crats" to seize power.[3] He urged the president to agree to the imposition of a nationwide state of emergency. At a Politburo session in late November he called for the establishment of direct presidential rule across the entire So-viet Union and the suspension of parliamentary institutions.[4] Gorbachev opposed the plan but did agree to the drafting of emergency legislation and to KGB preparations for a crackdown.

On December 8 Kryuchkov summoned two key aides to his fourth-floor office in the Lubyanka, one floor up from the office previously occupied by Andropov. Citing a request from Gorbachev, he instructed them to prepare a memorandum on measures to "stabilize" the situation in the country, along with the draft declaration on a state of emergency that could be sub-mitted to the Supreme Soviet.[5] Three days later the KGB chairman went on television to claim that "destructive elements," funded and supported from abroad, were attempting to "shatter our society and government and de-stroy Soviet rule." Such paranoid talk had not been heard in public from a Kremlin leader since the onset of perestroika.

If there were any doubts about Kryuchkov's conviction that a strong-arm solution was necessary, they were dispelled at the winter session of the Congress of People's Deputies. On December 22, two days after Shevard-nadze had warned of "dictatorship," the KGB chairman appeared before the congress to demand "decisive measures" to put an end to ethnic vio-lence. The thrust of his speech was that Soviet leaders had to be ready to

spill a little blood in order to save the country from an even worse fate. "Esteemed comrade deputies! Is not blood already being shed? Do we not learn almost every day, when we switch on our television sets and open our newspapers, of new human fatalities, of the deaths of innocent people, including women and children? I do not wish to frighten anyone, but the Committee for State Security is convinced that if the situation in our country continues to develop along the present lines, we will not be able to escape sociopolitical shocks that are even more serious and more grave."

Aware that Communist Party power could not be restored through legal, democratic methods, Kryuchkov was setting out the argument for using force. His speech ran counter to Gorbachev's repeated insistence that all problems be resolved through "exclusively political means" but was fully consistent with traditional Communist dogma. Before 1985 Soviet leaders had no compunction about using violence in order to defend "the revolution." "Bloodshed is inevitable," Defense Minister Ustinov had argued during a Politburo debate about the Polish crisis in April 1981. "If we fear it, then we will give up position after position. All the gains of socialism could be put at risk."[6]

As Lenin liked to say, "A revolution is only worth something if it knows how to defend itself."

Since the early days of the revolution Soviet power had rested on the Communist Party, the Red Army, and the security organs. Of these three pillars, only the "organs" had remained relatively unscathed after five tumultuous years of perestroika.

The party had been forced to give up its monopoly of political power, guaranteed under Article VI of the Soviet Constitution. Dispirited by the revelations of Stalinist atrocities, rank-and-file Communists were deserting the party. The once-monolithic ruling elite had lost its cohesiveness, following the defection of reformers like Yeltsin. The army too was a shadow of its former self. Its morale had been shaken by the debacle of Afghanistan, massive draft evasion, and a series of ethnic wars around the periphery of the Soviet Union. Decimated by budget cuts, it was now an army in retreat, more concerned with finding housing for officers thrown out of Poland and East Germany than fending off military threats from outside.

By contrast, the KGB had managed to survive, more or less intact, as the "shield and sword" of the Soviet state. The "organs" had made token gestures to glasnost, such as appointing a press officer and providing infor-

mation about the fate of the victims of Stalin's terror. The infamous Fifth Directorate, charged by Andropov with crushing the dissident movement, had been renamed the Directorate for the Protection of the Constitution. The public relations campaign to show a kinder, gentler face of the secret police reached its apogee earlier in 1990 with the appointment of a "Miss KGB." Little had changed, however, in the way the committee went about its business. Its responsibilities ranged from watching over Soviet borders to guarding the Politburo, from hunting down economic "saboteurs" to chasing foreign spies, from handling government communications to spreading disinformation. The KGB continued to keep tabs on suspected dissidents and use illegal wiretaps. It was later revealed that its vast network of informers included the prime minister of Lithuania and the patriarch of the Russian Orthodox Church.

The budget and manpower of the KGB remained at preperestroika levels. To this day nobody knows precisely how many people worked for the "organs." According to Kryuchkov's successor, Vadim Bakatin, the KGB had 480,000 full-time employees in September 1991, a figure challenged by some independent experts as being too low.[7] The KGB payroll included some 12,000 foreign intelligence workers, 90,000 agents in provincial cities, 220,000 border guards, and several divisions of *spetsnaz* troops. These "special assignment" troops included the Alpha Group that had stormed the presidential palace in Kabul in December 1979. During the fall of 1990 Kryuchkov persuaded Gorbachev to transfer to the KGB several regular army units, including the Vitebsk Paratroopers Division, and two motorized rifle divisions.[8]

Like his predecessors, Kryuchkov placed great importance on the revolutionary traditions of the KGB, inherited from Lenin's Cheka and Stalin's NKVD. A four-story monument to the founder of the Cheka, Feliks Dzerzhinsky, stood outside the Lubyanka. The spirit of "Iron Feliks" seemed to permeate the entire organization. KGB officers referred to themselves proudly as Chekists, graduated from the Dzerzhinsky Academy, and venerated the memory of the father of the Red Terror. Although some junior officers were infected by the democratic spirit of perestroika, ideological vigilance remained the order of the day at the senior levels of the KGB. When Bakatin was given the task of dismantling the KGB in the wake of the failed coup of August 1991, he was amazed by the low quality of the committee's analytical work and the general lack of professionalism. The obsession with ideology was even apparent in the nuclear bomb shelter that had been prepared for the commander in chief, where the only books on the shelves were the complete works of Lenin.

"It would have been funny if it hadn't been so pathetic," Bakatin commented. "The Communist core of the KGB had decided that this was what the head of state really needed at such a critical moment."[9]

The dangers of relying on such a powerful organization with such a blinkered view of the world were apparent to many of Gorbachev's liberal advisers. But he brushed their fears aside. He had every confidence in the loyalty of the KGB.[10] He frequently boasted about how well informed he was about everything that was happening in the Soviet Union. Far from considering the KGB a potential threat to perestroika, he regarded it as an essential ally. At a time of general political upheaval the "organs" were a pillar of political stability, a counterweight to the forces arrayed behind Yeltsin. Like other Kremlin leaders, particularly those who had spent most of their careers in the provinces, Gorbachev had great respect for the supposed omniscience of the KGB. The thick red dossiers, with their "eyes only" reports for the general secretary, were part of the mystique of Kremlin power.

Gorbachev knew that Kryuchkov and the representatives of the "power structures" were trying to push him into declaring a state of emergency. He struck a kind of Faustian bargain with "the organs." He would use them to defeat Yeltsin and then shake himself free. As he later explained, he was trying to "outmaneuver" both the conservatives and the democrats.

"A politician has to have a sense of tactics. I was being criticized from both sides. It was necessary for me to steer between one extreme and the other. I was playing for time."[11]

Gorbachev should have known that bargaining with the KGB was a little like bargaining with the devil.

VLADIMIR ALEKSANDROVICH KRYUCHKOV had the kind of bland, featureless face that merges into the crowd. Western correspondents had difficulty identifying him at the first Congress of People's Deputies in May 1989, seven months after his appointment as head of the KGB. Few of the legislators knew who he was, and there was little in his official portrait to distinguish him from the other faceless apparatchiks. He seemed the perfect subordinate: soft-spoken, self-disciplined, eager to please.

He had made his career in the shadow of Yuri Andropov. Their association went back to the Hungarian crisis of 1956, when Kryuchkov served in the Soviet embassy in Budapest under Andropov. The uprising and its subsequent suppression by the Red Army were an ordeal by fire for both the ambassador and his thirty-two-year-old press attaché. Together they had

the task of convincing the rebels that Soviet troops were withdrawing permanently from Hungary at a time when Khrushchev was planning to send them back into Budapest in overwhelming force. The experience provided Kryuchkov with a powerful lesson in the uses of misinformation and military might to stop a counterrevolution in its tracks. When Andropov was transferred back to Moscow, to be put in charge of a Central Committee department dealing with socialist countries, he took Kryuchkov along as his aide.

When Andropov was appointed head of the KGB in 1967, he asked his assistant to accompany him. A party apparatchik inexperienced in intelligence work, Kryuchkov aroused some resentment among KGB professionals. Many were openly contemptuous, regarding him as an obsequious bureaucrat who owed his position entirely to Andropov's patronage. "He was a meticulous paper shuffler, a master at working the Soviet bureaucracy," recalled Oleg Kalugin, a career KGB general who had many arguments with Kryuchkov. "Kryuchkov catered completely to Andropov's wishes, and unfortunately the KGB chairman had worked with Kryuchkov so long that he couldn't see his assistant's myriad shortcomings. In reality, Kryuchkov knew little of the outside world, and even less about intelligence. He had a serious intellectual inferiority complex and was extremely jealous of his colleagues' successes. He was the kind of man who gloated when you stumbled and then, if the opportunity arose, would push you even further down. He was, in short, a real bastard."[12]

In order to retain the confidence of his masters, Kryuchkov had to display utter loyalty and devotion to the cause. Like other KGB officers, he was required to submit a detailed personal biography, drawing attention to any conceivable character flaw or compromising family connection. He acknowledged that his sister was an alcoholic who had been convicted of theft. He took care to inform his superiors that he had broken off all ties with both her and with a politically unreliable older brother, who had conveniently disappeared from his life at the end of the war by moving to the Soviet Far East.[13]

Andropov appointed Kryuchkov head of the foreign intelligence arm of the KGB, the First Chief Directorate, in 1974. He served in this position for the next fourteen years, impressing his subordinates with a seemingly limitless capacity for work and a total absence of humor. A physical fitness fanatic, he had the habit of squeezing tennis balls to strengthen his grip while conducting meetings. He rose every day at 5:45 a.m., in order to allow time for a full regimen of outdoor exercises, regardless of the weather and when

he had gone to bed. This routine continued after he became chairman of the KGB in October 1988. He would summon officials to his Moscow dacha and make them wait while he finished his early-morning run around the estate. A Zil would then take the party to the Lubyanka.[14]

The fact that Kryuchkov had served Andropov for many years boosted his standing with Gorbachev. The general secretary believed that the new KGB chief would continue Andropov's crusade against corruption and Brezhnevite "stagnation."[15] He had every condidence in Kryuchkov's loyalty, seeing him as a consummate acolyte, who had spent his entire life fulfilling the wishes of his superiors. It was difficult to imagine such a creature leading a coup against his commander in chief. When he was eventually presented with evidence of Kryuchkov's betrayal, he initially refused to believe it.[16]

Treason was probably the last thing on Kryuchkov's mind in December 1990. His aim was not to lead a coup himself but gradually to maneuver Gorbachev into cracking down on the "antisocialist" opposition. The country was on the verge of disintegration, but the "course of events" could still be reversed through decisive action. Soviet history was full of examples of Communist Party leaders reasserting their authority when all seemed lost. There were textbook scenarios for what he had in mind in the KGB archives, in files marked "Kronshtadt, 1921," "East Berlin, 1953," "Budapest, 1956," "Prague, 1968," "Kabul, 1979," and "Warsaw, 1981." The party and the KGB had decades of experience in the art of seizing and retaining power. It was what they did best.

The KGB chief was convinced that political chaos and economic disruption had left many Soviet citizens yearning for a "strong hand." If the authorities displayed sufficient determination and tactical skill, they might be able to restore order without excessive violence and bloodshed. But first of all, it was necessary to organize a trial run.

VILNIUS

January 13, 1991

THE CONVOY OF FOUR T-72 TANKS and sixteen armored cars roared up the winding path to the television tower, on the top of a hill, overlooking the Lithuanian capital. As the tanks approached, swinging their gun turrets menacingly and firing deafening blanks, several thousand demonstrators rushed toward the eleven-hundred-foot tower. From the tops of the armored cars, Soviet soldiers trained powerful spotlights on the crowd. An amplified voice boomed out of the darkness. "Brother Lithuanians! In the name of the National Salvation Committee, I announce that all power in the republic is now in our hands. This is the power of simple working people: workers, peasants, and servicemen. The power of people like you."[17]

There were jeers and whistles from the demonstrators, who had linked arms, forming a human barricade, ten to twelve people deep, around the television tower. Chants of "*Lietuva, Lietuva*" (Lithuania, Lithuania) and "*Laisve, laisve*" (Freedom, freedom) filled the cool nighttime air.

"True, some of you have come under the influence of deceits, lies, demagoguery, and intimidation," the male voice went on. "These are the weapons the authorities have used up to now, playing games in the Lithuanian parliament and government. They expressed the interests of rich people, fraudulent people, corrupt elements. This is not our course."

By now it was clear where the voice was coming from, a loudspeaker mounted on top of one of the armored cars. The speaker did not identify himself, but Lithuanian investigators later said it belonged to Juozas Jermalavičius, chief ideologist of the pro-Moscow wing of the local Communist Party.[18] Installed in power by Soviet tanks, Jermalavičius and his comrades had suffered a humiliating defeat in the first free elections in Lithuania in half a century. When the Lithuanian parliament declared independence on March 11, 1990, by a majority of 124 to 0, the pro-Moscow deputies walked out. Ten months later they announced the formation of a "National Salvation Committee," with the task of restoring "Soviet power" in Lithuania. The members of the committee refused to reveal their identity, saying they feared for their lives.

"I ask you not to resist," the voice continued, first in Lithuanian and then in Russian, as the tanks pushed aside a few small trucks and cars that had been blocking the path to the television tower. "I ask you to go home. Your parents, your mothers and fathers, your brothers and sisters, your grandfathers and grandmothers are waiting for you. Go home. Confrontation is senseless."

The Lithuanian defenders stood their ground, shouting defiance at the approaching tanks. They had been expecting such a confrontation for several days now. Over the past week the Kremlin had stepped up its campaign of intimidation, dispatching thousands of paratroopers to the Baltic states to hunt down draft dodgers. Events seemed to be following a planned scenario. First, Gorbachev had dispatched an angry letter to the Lithuanian leaders demanding their allegiance to the Soviet Constitution. Then Soviet troops began seizing public buildings, gradually restricting the authority of the democratically elected Lithuanian government. They also took the precaution of disarming an elite Lithuanian antiriot squad, the only force capable of opposing them. Air and rail traffic, in and out of Vilnius, was halted. Finally, at midnight on January 12, a delegation of "workers" had attempted to deliver a petition to the Lithuanian government, demanding that it surrender power to the National Salvation Committee. The "workers," many of whom reeked of alcohol, had been hustled away for questioning by nervous pro-independence activists.

At the time the incident seemed inconsequential. But the leaders of the shadowy National Salvation Committee needed a pretext, however flimsy, for appealing to the commander of the Soviet military garrison in Vilnius for "assistance." This was it. Shortly after 1:00 a.m. armored columns appeared on the streets of Vilnius, prompting Lithuanian leaders to broadcast

a frantic appeal to the population to defend strategic buildings like the television tower.

Rolandas Jankauskas was at a Vilnius discotheque when he heard the appeal. He had just turned twenty-two. He had left the Soviet navy two months previously, after completing his compulsory military service. Singing and laughing, Jankauskas and his friends poured out of the disco to see where the tanks were headed. At roughly the same time a twenty-three-year-old seamstress, Loreta Asanaviciute, ran into an old friend while walking home after a party. The friend asked her to go with her to the television tower, on Cosmonaut Avenue, where large crowds were beginning to gather. Impulsive and full of life, Asanaviciute immediately agreed.[19]

Jankauskas and Asanaviciute were among the first Lithuanian victims of the attack on the television tower. He fell to the ground as the troops began advancing toward the tower, throwing stun grenades and firing shots into the air. Seconds later he was crushed under the wheels of an armored personnel carrier. Asanaviciute was one of several Lithuanians hit by a tank clearing a path for the advancing troops. The right side of her body bore the marks of caterpillar tracks.

After failing to disperse the demonstrators by firing over their heads, the Soviet attackers aimed their AK-47 assault rifles directly into the crowd. Seven of the eleven Lithuanian civilians killed during the assault on the tower were hit by bullets. Sporadic shooting continued in the vicinity of the tower for a further ninety minutes. That night, out of more than four hundred injured, a total of fifty-three people were taken to hospitals in Vilnius with bullet wounds. At Hospital No. 1, in the center of the city, there were horrific scenes of carnage: charred faces; crushed legs; ripped-out intestines. "Some of the things I have seen tonight made my hair stand on end," said Dalia Steibilene, the doctor on duty when the fighting broke out. "We knew that this kind of violence was happening in the Caucasus, but nobody thought that anything like this would happen in peaceful Lithuania."[20]

Soviet officials later claimed that members of the crowd had opened fire on the Soviet army. But they failed to produce any evidence to support their assertion, and none of the foreign journalists at the scene saw any firearms in the hands of the defenders.

Spearheading the assault force was a group of thirty or so men in black helmets, their eyes shielded by bulletproof visors, who smashed their way through the plate glass windows at the base of the television tower. They seemed more organized and disciplined than the rest of the attacking force. They talked to one another constantly, via radio sets attached to the backs

of their helmets. Once inside the tower, they moved methodically from floor to floor, pushing aside the barricades erected by the Lithuanian defenders and dismantling the booby traps. Their presence in Vilnius was meant to be a closely guarded secret. Within a matter of days it was to become a matter of nationwide controversy, and a serious embarrassment to their masters in Moscow.

MORE THAN A DECADE HAD PASSED since Yevgeny Chudesnov had taken part in the operation to overthrow Amin. He still remembered the fragrant aroma of shashlik, rising from hundreds of bonfires, as he drove through the deserted streets of Kabul that cold winter night. A veteran of the Alpha Group, he had become almost immune to the rattle of gunfire and the deafening sound of explosions.

If the KGB was the sword and shield of the Soviet state, the Alpha Group was the sword and shield of the KGB. Modeled on the British SAS and the American Delta squad, the two hundred or so members of the Alpha Group were superbly trained and equipped. These Soviet Rambos had extensive experience in freeing hostages, disarming terrorists, and storming buildings. Since the takeover of Amin's palace in December 1979, they had carried out hundreds of delicate missions in different parts of the Soviet Union, achieving almost mythic status in the eyes of Kremlin leaders. The head of the Alpha Group reported directly to the chairman of the KGB. The force was the last line of defense for a Soviet Union threatened with disintegration.

Chudesnov and sixty-four of his colleagues had arrived in Vilnius after nightfall on January 11, on a special flight from Moscow.[21] The following day they received their orders. They were instructed to seize control of three facilities: the TV tower, the radio transmission center, and the Vilnius television station. A Soviet army paratroop regiment would provide the necessary support. Chudesnov was put in charge of the subgroup that was to capture the television station.

There were large crowds of people standing around the television station, just as there had been at the TV tower. After catching his first glimpse of these crowds, Chudesnov had a fleeting hope that the operation would be called off at the last moment.[22] The armored convoy drove past the television station, but then it turned back, and he and his men were ordered into battle. They jumped out of their armored cars and dived into the human barricade, throwing stun grenades. One of the stun grenades hit a twenty-

eight-year-old Lithuanian defender in the chest, killing him on the spot.[23] As the Alpha Group entered the building, a female announcer was broadcasting an emotional message to millions of Lithuanians.

"We address all those who can hear us," she said, looking straight at the camera. "It is possible that the army can break us with force and close our mouths, but no one will make us renounce our freedom and independence."

Seconds later Lithuanian television went off the air.

Chudesnov was running along the corridor of the television center when he heard a voice behind him. It was a young lieutenant, Viktor Shatskikh, a recruit to the Alpha Group. "Yevgeny Nikolayevich, I feel a pain in my back," he murmured. When Chudesnov examined the wound, he saw that a bullet had penetrated a hinge in the lieutenant's body armor, ripping open his right lung. He died shortly afterward. It was never established whether he had been shot by a Lithuanian sniper's bullet, as the Soviet military later claimed, or friendly fire.

This was a disaster. If anyone found out that the Alpha Group had taken part in the storming of the television center, the official cover story would be blown apart. It would no longer be possible for Kremlin leaders to deny knowledge of the events in Lithuania. There would be a chain of evidence linking the National Salvation Committee to Kryuchkov and possibly to Gorbachev.

All night the generals in charge of the operation had been broadcasting messages to one another, full of strange talk about "big boxes," "cucumbers," and "tomatoes." Decoded, these were cryptic references to tanks, bullets, and explosives. After Shatskikh's death, a note of panic crept into the radio traffic.

"A two-hundred-kilo load has appeared. Over."

"What do you mean, a two-hundred? Over."

"The people who came with you in helmets, they say they have a two-hundred. Do you understand me? Over. "

The conversation continued for some minutes. "The people in helmets" was code for the Alpha Group. "A two-hundred-kilo load" was Afghan veterans' slang for a coffin with a corpse in it.

"This is Granite-Eighty-two. Listen to me, and tell this to everybody else. About those striped ones in helmets, the ones who worked up in front. They weren't there. Okay? You don't know anything about them. Over."

"Understood. Over."[24]

The KGB did its best to disown Shatskikh and cover up its role in the attempted coup in Lithuania. Stories in the Soviet press described the dead

officer as a "paratrooper." When the "two-hundred-kilo load" was transported back to Moscow, there was no KGB representative at the airport to take delivery. Kryuchkov and other KGB leaders failed to show up for the funeral. This know-nothing stance shocked other members of the Alpha Group.[25] They had risked their lives for leaders who were unwilling to take responsibility for their actions and insisted on hiding their true identities behind an anonymous National Salvation Committee. By the time the "organs" finally got around to acknowledging that a KGB officer had been killed in Vilnius, the damage had been done. Cracks of dissent had appeared in the KGB's avenging "sword."

A PEDANTIC MUSIC PROFESSOR with a little goatee, Vytautas Landsbergis seemed an unlikely spokesman for a nation attempting to break away from the Soviet empire. His speeches were dry, even dull. He had never been a prominent dissident. Prior to his emergence as the head of the Lithuanian independence movement, Sajudis, he was best known as the world's leading authority on Mikolajus Čiurlonis, a turn-of-the-century Lithuanian composer and painter. One of his first actions after being elected chairman of the Lithuanian Parliament was to have a piano moved into his office. He held up a parliamentary debate on independence with a long discourse on whether Lithuanians should sing the national anthem in the key of F sharp, as was traditional, prior to the Soviet occupation. Landsbergis was determined to convince his fellow legislators that it was impossible to sing that high.[26]

After the assault on the television facilities Landsbergis appealed to the population to defend the parliament building. By dawn a crowd of seven to eight thousand unarmed civilians had gathered around the yellow stone building in the center of Vilnius. Inside, several hundred volunteers were busy transforming the symbol of the country's independence into a sandbagged bunker. Their weapons consisted of a few dozen hunting rifles, Molotov cocktails, and fire hoses.

As an emergency session got under way in the parliamentary chamber, gas masks were distributed to the deputies. A Catholic priest blessed everyone present. Landsbergis was wearing under his jacket a bulletproof vest that made him look even more rotund and professorial than usual. He had spent the last few hours frantically trying to reach Gorbachev, only to be told that the Soviet leader was "unavailable." His fury at Gorbachev was almost matched by his anger with President Bush for his inactivity in the face

of Soviet aggression. He complained that Bush was completely preoccupied with the crisis in Kuwait, and preparations for Desert Storm.

"The Americans have sold us out," he fumed, waving his hands. "Bush should ring Gorbachev on the hot line and tell him that, whatever the situation in the gulf, murder in Lithuania is also murder. If Gorbachev doesn't stop this, nobody will defend Gorbachev from his own murderers. He will be a zero for the West and a zero for his colonels."[27]

What Landsbergis lacked in charisma, he made up for in stubbornness. In the ten months since the Lithuanian declaration of independence, Soviet leaders had done everything in their power to persuade the little nation of 3.7 million people to back down. They had sent columns of tanks and armored cars past the parliament building. They had shut down the gas pipelines. They had banned travel by foreign citizens to and from Lithuania, erecting a kind of cordon sanitaire around the country. The political and economic pressure failed to make much impression on the diminutive music professor. He shut himself up in his spacious presidential office, played his beloved Čiurlonis on the piano, and refused to budge.

Such intransigence infuriated Gorbachev, a compromiser born and bred. The Soviet leader could not understand why his adversary failed to play by the normal rules of the political game and was so obsessed with the outward symbols of Lithuanian independence. But it seemed entirely logical to Landsbergis, who had devoted his life to studying the symbolist movement inspired by Čiurlonis. "Everyday difficulties do not exist for him. He thinks you can do without such things as gasoline," explained his wife, Gražyna. "He is guided by a single motivating idea—the freedom of Lithuania."[28]

The Lithuanian leader was a product of the inbred world of Catholic intellectuals who managed to preserve the nation's identity in the face of terrible adversity. His maternal grandfather, Juonas Jablonskis, had been a fierce defender of the Lithuanian language. His paternal grandfather, Gabrielus Landsbergis, had helped lead the struggle against tsarist rule in the late nineteenth century and had been deported to Siberia for his activities. The ideas of such men were passed down to future generations, even as the Baltic states were crushed by the Stalinist and Nazi military machines. The Soviet occupation of Lithuania in June 1940 left a vivid impression on eight-year-old Vytautas. "Look, the Mongols have arrived," he whispered to his older brother as the Soviet troops, who included a large proportion of Central Asians, took over the country.[29]

During the dreary years of Soviet occupation Landsbergis devoted his energy to defending Lithuanian culture from "Sovietization." His interest

in Čiurlonis, who played an important part in the resurgence of Lithuanian culture, was a form of intellectual dissent. "For many years cultural activity meant political activity," he later recalled. "By protecting our culture, we also protected our national identity. Otherwise we would have been Russified—first in language and later in thinking."[30]

SYMBOLS WERE JUST ABOUT ALL Lithuanians had to hang on to that grim winter, as the Soviet army strengthened its grip on their country. The bloodshed at the television tower united Lithuanians as never before. The more the Kremlin propaganda machine sought to justify the assault, the more they flaunted their long-banned national symbols: the yellow, green, and red flag; the white knight on horseback; the schematic outline of a medieval castle.

The ultimate symbol of Lithuania's defiance of Moscow and its passionate desire for independence was now the parliament building itself. Ordinary people, who had never shown much interest in politics, mounted an around-the-clock vigil outside the bunkerlike building. Fearing a tank attack, workers erected a twelve-foot-high concrete wall on three sides of the virtually undefended building and dug a fifteen-foot ditch. The wall soon became a display case for anti-Soviet graffiti. "Gorbie, hell is waiting for you," read one slogan in English, next to a crude drawing of Gorbachev, with horns growing out of his head. "The Red Army is Red Fascism," proclaimed another.

A nearby strand of barbed wire served as a collection point for the symbols of Soviet occupation: passports, conscription papers, Communist Party cards. Day and night Lithuanians threw piles of Soviet propaganda booklets on the bonfires in front of the parliament building. Even if their cause was doomed, the defenders of independence had the satisfaction of keeping warm by the embers of the complete works of Lenin and multivolume histories of the Soviet Communist Party. Many people brought their children along with them, so that they could describe Soviet tyranny to *their* children and grandchildren.

Bundled up against the cold, a three-year-old girl named Zhivele Kaslauskas listened to her parents discuss Lithuania's chances of gaining full independence, before taking her home to bed. "It may take years, but in the end I am sure we will win," said her father, Alvidas. "This empire cannot last. One day Russians themselves will rise up against it."[31]

Inside the legislature the atmosphere was tense and claustrophobic.

Lithuanian democracy was less than a year old, and already it was being forced to defend itself from armed attack. The deputies were scared. "If the military attacks, we're going to become human torches. Look at all this wood and fabric," whispered one terrified legislator as rumors spread of an imminent assault.[32] The spectacle of the freely elected representatives being issued gas masks and hunkering down behind concrete barricades was both shocking and ominous.

Soon such a sight would become commonplace, from Tallinn to Tbilisi, from Moscow to Sarajevo. Big Brother refused to go quietly, without a fight.

MOSCOW

January 14, 1991

THE BLOODSHED IN VILNIUS CAUSED a wave of revulsion and apprehension throughout the Soviet Union. There had been a lot of speculation about "a move to the right" by Gorbachev, but it was difficult to tell exactly what was going on behind the Kremlin walls. Finally, everything seemed clear. The reformer was turning his back on his own reforms. The sick joke about *pere-stroika* (restructuring) giving way to *pere-strelka* (a shoot-out) was in the process of being realized.

The time had come for a final parting of the ways between Gorbachev and the radical intellectuals, who had been his most enthusiastic supporters during the early stages of perestroika. As news of the massacre outside the television tower spread, they poured onto the streets of Moscow and other cities, carrying banners with slogans like "Gorbachev Is the Saddam Hussein of the Baltics!" and "Give Back the Nobel Peace Prize." Yuri Afanasiev spoke for many Moscow intellectuals when he blamed the killings on a "dictatorship of reactionary circles" made up of the military, the KGB, and the Communist Party. "And at the head of that party dictatorship stands the initiator of perestroika, Mikhail Sergeyevich Gorbachev," he added bitterly.[33] There was an upsurge in resignations from the Communist Party, beginning with the entire staff of *Moscow News*, one of the flagships of glasnost.

When the Soviet parliament debated the events in Lithuania the follow-ing day, Gorbachev was unrepentant. He insisted he had known nothing about the violence until it was over, "when they woke me up." But he refused to criticize the army's decision to provide military assistance to the self-appointed National Salvation Committee, whose members did not even have the courage to identify themselves. Indeed he put the blame for what had happened on Landsbergis and other Lithuanian leaders, accusing them of "violating" the Soviet Constitution.

"I don't see how we will make progress with such people in charge," he told the deputies. "Lithuania has treated us like a foreign country."[34]

There were only two possible explanations for the line that Gorbachev was taking, and both were equally disturbing. Either the commander in chief was in control of his own security forces, or he wasn't. In the first case he was the accomplice of hard-liners, who were attempting to mount a coup against a democratically elected parliament. In the second case he had be-come their puppet. By refusing to discipline his subordinates, he had effec-tively condoned a flagrantly illegal act. His failure to condemn the violence was an implicit invitation to the would-be putschists to try again.

Documents unearthed following the failed coup of August 1991 demol-ish the cover story about the commander of the Vilnius military garrison's responding to an "appeal" from the National Salvation Committee. The de-cision to use force was made not in Vilnius but in Moscow, where Soviet mil-itary leaders had been preparing for such a confrontation over many months. A few semiliterate handwritten jottings discovered in the diary of Defense Minister Dmitri Yazov and dated March 22, 1990—less than two weeks after Lithuania had declared its independence—provided an insight into what was being planned:

- Issue a warning. Not recognize their laws! Bring pressure to bear.
- If necessary, act resolutely!
- What are we to draw on? The old government cannot be resusci-tated.
- To draw on the committee and set up committees everywhere!
- To be ready to take the TV center?![35]

A subsequent diary entry, for April 9, 1990, shows that Soviet leaders were considering the imposition of direct presidential rule on Lithuania at that time. But Gorbachev opposed the use of force, partly for fear of of-fending international public opinion. "We cannot take the strap to Lithua-

nia's 'behind,'" Yazov quoted him as saying. "The issue of Lithuania far transcends the framework of the Union! Is the Lithuanian issue becoming a world–international issue?"

It turned out that the puppeteers in Moscow had planned everything in advance, including a "general strike" by ethnic Russians and an attempt to storm the parliament building:

- General strike! A telegram will be sent for them to abolish their resolutions, restore the constitution.
- About 200 armed men, in the Hall and the Supreme Council.
- An appeal will be made.
- The publishing house belongs to the CPSU (Soviet Communist Party)—capture it!

On the Saturday that the KGB dispatched the Alpha Group to capture the television center, Kryuchkov drove to the Kremlin for a secret meeting with his fellow plotters. According to Kremlin records, the session began at 7:15 p.m. and broke up at 2:10 a.m., shortly after the shooting had begun in Vilnius.[36]

What is most intriguing about this meeting, which took place in the office of Gorbachev's chief of staff, Valery Boldin, was the list of participants. In addition to Kryuchkov and Boldin, it included Valentin Pavlov, who was about to become Soviet prime minister, Oleg Baklanov, the head of the military-industrial complex, and Oleg Shenin, a Communist Party secretary in charge of organizational matters. These men were to become the key figures in the State Committee for the State of Emergency, which seized power from Gorbachev eight months later.

THE REMAINING LIBERALS in Gorbachev's entourage were sickened by the use of military force in Lithuania and the president's refusal to condemn it. They recalled Shevardnadze's warnings of "an approaching dictatorship." Now each of them faced a crisis of conscience. They could do the honorable thing and resign, leaving Gorbachev in the clutches of the hard-liners. Or they could stick with him in the hope that he would have a change of heart.

The president's economics adviser, Nikolai Petrakov, chose to resign, after signing a collective protest letter to the *Moscow News* accusing a "regime in its death throes" of launching an "open war" on the republics.[37] The foreign policy adviser, Anatoly Chernyayev, dashed off a long memo to

Gorbachev, describing his sense of "torment" and "shame," but never submitted it.[38] Several other staffers, including the presidential press spokesman, Vitaly Ignatenko, were talked out of resigning by Yakovlev, who insisted that this was not the time to abandon the president. Meeting in Yakovlev's office on Monday afternoon, the dissenters decided on a different course of action: They would persuade Gorbachev to fly to Vilnius and "bow before the dead."

Yakovlev went to see Gorbachev, who agreed with the plan. He instructed his staff to draft a speech that he could deliver to the Lithuanian parliament. By Tuesday, however, the president had once again changed his mind. "Some comrades are against the idea," he told his aides, evidently referring to Kryuchkov. "They say it is impossible to guarantee the security of the president."[39]

Although Gorbachev refused to apologize for the use of force in Lithuania, he did put a brake on the machinery of repression. If everything had gone the way the hard-liners planned, presidential rule would have been declared in all three Baltic republics, and parliamentary activity suspended. The bloodshed in Vilnius, combined with the spectacle of tens of thousands of unarmed civilians taking to the streets to defend their parliaments and the outrage of the Russian intelligentsia, caused Gorbachev to reconsider his position. He would not permit his hard-line associates to push events to their logical conclusion.

The men who had gathered in Boldin's office in the Kremlin drew their own conclusions from Gorbachev's hesitation and prevarication. There was no point in restoring "socialist order" on the periphery of the empire if the center could not be relied upon. The script was fine, but it was necessary to make a few alterations. Next time they would begin at the center and proceed from there to the republics.

MOSCOW

April 5, 1991

As WINTER GAVE WAY to spring, the shock of the attempted coup in Lithuania began to fade. Ordinary Soviet citizens had other, more pressing matters on their minds, including the problem of finding enough to eat. The economy was in free fall. Shortages were spreading from one sector of industry and agriculture to another, creating a devastating ripple effect. In the past Soviet leaders might have been able to make up for the fall in production by increasing imports of grain and industrial goods. But the country's foreign exchange reserves were practically exhausted. In the words of a government report, the world's first socialist state was "on the verge of bankruptcy."[40]

The real mystery about the Soviet Union's command economy is not that it collapsed when it did but that it managed to survive for so long. Economic power was concentrated in the hands of a small group of bureaucrats at the top of the pyramid. Even if these apparatchiks had been totally omniscient and supremely intelligent, it would still have been physically impossible for them to match the collective wisdom of the millions of individuals who form a Western-style "marketplace." The Stalinist system of central planning could cope with grandiose tasks, like building nuclear bombs and producing thousands of tanks, because it was good at mobilizing resources to achieve a specific goal. The more complex the economy became, the more

349

inefficient the system proved to be. The command economy lacked the myriad self-correcting mechanisms of a market economy. When a capitalist entrepreneur makes a wrong decision, he is quickly put right by millions of consumers; a similar error by a Soviet bureaucrat could go undetected for years, with horrendous consequences.

In the end there was only one self-correcting mechanism that mattered in a totalitarian state as powerful and self-sufficient as the Soviet Union: the country's ability to support such a profligate and hopelessly inefficient system. Because Russia was a land of fabulous natural wealth, it took some time before this mechanism kicked into operation. As long as Kremlin leaders could export enough oil and natural gas to ensure Soviet citizens a basic standard of living and bankroll military adventures in the Third World, they had little incentive even to think about reform. It was no coincidence that Mikhail Gorbachev came to power just as the petrodollars were beginning to run out.

Even with a committed reformer occupying the post of general secretary, the system proved very resistant to change. Prior to 1991 there were hidden reserves that could be tapped to extend the life of the command economy by a few more months. When oil exports started to decline, there were still plentiful deposits of natural gas. When the gas industry began experiencing difficulties, the planners switched their attention to timber and precious metals. When all else failed, the Kremlin could always borrow money on international markets. The Soviet Union's credit rating remained relatively high until 1990.

By 1991 it was no longer possible to disguise the gravity of the economic crisis. Oil exports had slumped by 50 percent since 1989 because of a decline in domestic production. After climbing slowly during the seventies and early eighties, the Soviet Union's hard-currency debt had more than doubled under Gorbachev to $68 billion.[41] Western bankers were reluctant to lend Moscow any more money, without firm guarantees of repayment. In a sign of financial desperation, Kremlin leaders now began authorizing massive sales of gold bullion to shore up the collapsing balance of payments. When the figures were published later that year, Western bankers were shocked to discover that the Soviet Union's gold reserves had shrunk to 240 million metric tons, worth about $3 billion, a fraction of earlier estimates.[42]

The myth of Soviet financial respectability had been shattered for good.

JUST BECAUSE THE ECONOMY WAS a shambles and ordinary Soviets had extraordinary difficulty making ends meet did not mean that it was impos-

sible for enterprising, well-connected individuals to make a lot of money. In fact, the opposite was true. The greater the economic chaos and confusion, the greater the opportunities for personal enrichment. In a country that was increasingly out of touch with economic reality, someone with a firm grasp of the laws of supply and demand could become a millionaire overnight.

The simplest way of making a fortune was to find a way of purchasing goods and raw materials at artificially low Soviet prices and turn around and sell the same goods for much higher free market prices. The profit margin was often staggering. This was the trail blazed by the country's first millionaire, Artyom Tarasov, one subsequently followed by the vast majority of successful Soviet businessmen. Tarasov, an engineer working for the Moscow City Council, devised a method for turning Soviet junk into American dollars. He scoured Russia for scrap metal, which he purchased with rubles at dirt-cheap prices. He exported the metal to Western countries and used the proceeds to purchase personal computers, which he was able to re-sell in Russia for a huge profit. Business soared.

By the end of 1990 Tarasov had moved on to the even more lucrative oil trade. He persuaded the newly appointed Russian government to grant his company, Istok, a license for the export of several million barrels of Russian oil. He was able to purchase the oil for the ruble equivalent to eighty-five cents a barrel and sell it abroad for around twenty dollars a barrel in hard currency. These transactions yielded millions of dollars in profits. Under the terms of Tarasov's agreement with the Russian authorities, Istok was permitted to keep the funds in a French bank account. There was one, very important caveat, however. The entire hard-currency proceeds of the sale would be used to purchase consumer goods that had already been promised to Russian farmers, under an incentive scheme known as Harvest '90.[43]

At the beginning of April 1991 came news that Tarasov and his principal business partner had fled the country. The money earmarked for Harvest '90 had vanished from the French bank account. The Russian farmers had lost out once again. According to Russian investigators, the only benefit the farmers ever derived from an import-export deal designed to offer them new hope was several thousand pairs of defective rubber boots. The state prosecutor's office accused Tarasov of "misappropriation" and "breach of trust," but failed to bring formal charges because of the statute of limitations.[44] Tarasov maintained his innocence all along and refused to cooperate with the investigation, saying that it was inspired by his political enemies.

Hundreds of similar get-rich schemes were implemented in the early

months of 1991. A subsequent parliamentary investigation showed that only a small proportion of the several billion dollars earned by semiprivate companies like Istok during 1990–91 ever returned to Russia.[45] These were halcyon days for the emerging class of nomenklatura capitalists.

Behind every successful entrepreneur stood a bureaucrat with the power to grant or withhold a license of some kind and a foreign partner willing to ignore how the license was obtained. In many cases these relationships outlasted the collapse of communism. The key to understanding how *biznes* is conducted in the new Russia frequently lies in knowing who was pals with whom in the old Communist Party and KGB. "What we have in Russia is a pseudomarket, not a real market," explained Aleksandr Rudenko, a prominent businessman in St. Petersburg, who made his fortune during this early period. "The state has a monopoly over the export of basic goods. The economic conditions have been created in which people who are well connected can steal like crazy. You get three or four officials to sign a piece of paper authorizing you to do something, and you have it made."[46]

By refusing to follow Western advice and liberalize prices, Gorbachev fostered the development of the privileged new class. In a market economy entrepreneurs make their profits from tiny percentages. The more imperfect the market, the bigger the potential profit from buying and selling. In the dying days of the Soviet Union the profit margins were so huge that few people who were in a position to manipulate the market to their advantage were able to resist the opportunity. The absurdities of the "planned economy" were screaming to be exploited.

Some of the scams were perfectly legal, if morally questionable. In November 1989 the government slashed the tourist rate of the ruble by 90 percent but left the official rate unchanged. Foreigners living in the Soviet Union were allowed to purchase foreign airline tickets in devalued tourist rubles, even though the price was still calculated at the official ruble rate. As a result, a round-trip business class fare to Paris or London cost less than a hundred dollars, one-tenth of the previous price. For a few glorious months members of the Western community thought nothing of flying to Stockholm to catch the latest Hollywood movie or taking a weekend trip to Rome to visit a new trattoria. Dream vacations in Africa, Australia, and Latin America suddenly became affordable. Since few people bothered to fly economy class anymore, Western airlines flying in and out of Moscow upgraded most of their seats to first class and business class. Everyone was happy. The only obvious loser was the Soviet Foreign Trade Bank, which collected devalued rubles from the foreigners and paid out real dollars to

the airlines. It was hardly surprising that the bank went bankrupt shortly after the loophole was finally closed, almost a year later.

For years one of the few real constraints against private enrichment at the expense of the state was the fear of getting caught. Thanks to Gorbachev, however, even that inhibition had now vanished. The bureaucrats who controlled the Soviet economy scrambled to profit from their positions. It took surprisingly little time for once-doctrinaire Marxists to transform themselves into born-again capitalists. Red Army generals in East Germany stopped worrying about the threat from NATO and began selling fuel and military supplies on the black market. KGB officials, trained to root out any manifestation of free enterprise, founded commodity exchanges. Officials at Gosplan, the state planning agency, used their intimate knowledge of how the Soviet economy actually worked to launch their own trading companies.

Nowhere was the enthusiasm for "nomenklatura capitalism" more apparent than in the Central Committee of the Soviet Communist Party. By the spring of 1991 the inner sanctum of Marxism-Leninism had become a den of money changers.

FOR MOST OF ITS EXISTENCE the Soviet Communist Party never had to concern itself with the problem of raising funds. When the party needed money—whether to build dachas for deserving apparatchiks, to pay for the limousines used by Politburo members, or to finance Western Communist parties—it simply issued an instruction to the state bank. In a one-party state there was no distinction between the party and the state. The Politburo's orders were the law of the land.

The symbiotic relationship between party and state was shaken in February 1990, when the Congress of People's Deputies voted to abolish Article VI of the Soviet Constitution. When it lost its constitutionally guaranteed monopoly of political power, the Communist Party also lost the right to plunder the state treasury as it saw fit. Even though the party was still an immensely wealthy organization—its property holdings alone were worth billions—its financial managers were extremely worried. The new Russian parliament, headed by Yeltsin, was threatening to levy taxes on a long list of party assets, including its vast media empire, and hundreds of rest homes, hospitals, and vacation resorts.

Determined to protect its economic privileges, the party began to search for ways of hiding its wealth from prying eyes. In a secret memorandum,

dated August 23, 1990, Deputy General Secretary Vladimir Ivashko proposed channeling some of the assets to commercial firms controlled by trusted Communist Party members.[47] Assistance would be given to the front organizations to engage in foreign trade activity, in order to generate an "independent source" of hard currency for the party's international operations. Communist members of the Soviet and Russian parliaments would ensure that the appropriate legal framework was created to defend the party's commercial interests. Secrecy was essential, of course. Only a very small group of leaders would know the identity of the "friendly firms" or their true relationship with the party.

Ivashko's plan was hardly original. A similar scheme—to channel funds to pro-Moscow organizations around the world—had been in operation for several decades. "Friendly firms" controlled by foreign Communist parties were granted special trading privileges in the Soviet Union, enabling them to purchase raw materials at deeply discounted prices. A typical example of such an operation was the delivery of free or subsidized newsprint to left-wing publishing houses in Italy and Greece. Some of the newsprint was resold at market prices, in order to provide income for political activities. An alternative method of subsidizing "friendly firms" was to purchase goods from them at inflated prices. After the failed coup of August 1991 Russian prosecutors drew up a list of around one hundred foreign companies that received Soviet subsidies of one kind or another.[48]

In order to put Ivashko's ideas into effect, the Central Committee recruited a KGB colonel, well versed in the art of clandestinely channeling funds to "friendly firms." Leonid Veselovsky had previously served as a KGB field officer in Portugal, where he was responsible for contacts with the local Communist Party. Soon after his appointment he wrote a memorandum for his new bosses describing a mechanism for shifting party funds to the West by starting joint stock companies in countries "with a mild taxation system," such as Switzerland. According to his plan, details of which were later leaked to the Russian press, the companies would be headed by trusted party agents.[49]

The extent to which the Communist Party succeeded in laundering its assets later became a subject of great political controversy. After the failed coup Russian prosecutors claimed to have traced billions of rubles of party funds that had been "loaned" to Russian companies and joint ventures. The list of alleged recipients of Communist largess included some of the best-known Russian banks and holding companies. Hardly any of this money was ever recovered, leading prosecutors to complain that their investigation

was blocked for political reasons. Veselovsky himself insisted that most of his ideas for shifting party assets overseas never got beyond the planning stage.[50]

What is clear, however, is that many apparatchiks chose precisely this moment to launch their own careers as private businessmen. Veselovsky himself was a prime example of this phenomenon. In early 1991, while still working for the Central Committee, he hooked up with a flamboyant Canadian millionaire named Boris Birshtein. A Soviet émigré who had once run a textile factory in Lithuania, Birshtein understood the importance of establishing a mutually beneficial relationship with well-placed bureaucrats. That, after all, was the way *biznes* had always been conducted in Russia. Personal connections were the key to business success. "You just need to get in the saunas, and that's where you really do business," he boasted to a Western reporter.[51]

Unlike most foreign businessmen, Birshtein deliberately flaunted his wealth. With his fleet of private jets, sable-lined coat, and diamond-studded brooch, he was almost a caricature of the Russian idea of the successful capitalist. When he came to Moscow, he hired the biggest limousine possible and traveled from office to office in a motorcade worthy of a head of state. The Moscow Police Department, which had itself benefited from Birshtein's generosity, was happy to provide the tycoon with an impressive escort.

By his own account, Veselovsky helped Birshtein rent a luxurious party-owned mansion on the Lenin Hills that had previously been reserved for such visiting foreign dignitaries as Fidel Castro and Henry Kissinger. The two men hit it off immediately. Veselovsky provided Birshtein with introductions to party bureaucrats, whose assistance was essential for the conclusion of lucrative foreign trade deals. Birshtein permitted Veselovsky to escape from the stifling world of party apparatchiks into the world of private jets and diamond brooches. After the negotiations for the mansion had been concluded successfully, Birshtein offered his new friend a one-year contract as a "consultant."

"He was influential and intelligent. He had a Ph.D. in economics," Birshtein recalled later. "We started to think about different businesses. He said, 'I'm sick of the party. It's all bullshit. I want to leave.' It was then that I offered to hire him."[52]

The relationship between Birshtein and Veselovsky proved beneficial for both men. The Canadian millionaire helped the former KGB colonel move to Switzerland, giving him the use of a lakeside villa in Zurich and a silver Mercedes. In the meantime, Birshtein's own fortunes began improving

sharply. Prior to 1991 his private Toronto-based company, Seabeco, had been struggling with creditors and disgruntled former employees. In 1991 business suddenly took off. The Seabeco Group spawned dozens of off-shoots, including a number of highly profitable joint ventures with Russian trading companies. The business grew and grew until, one day, Birshtein overreached himself. At the peak of his influence, in September 1993, he was caught up in a sensational bribery scandal involving the Russian security minister and declared persona non grata.[53]

EXCEPT FOR THE FACT that it attracted a lot of attention, because of the mystery surrounding Communist Party finances, there was nothing unusual about Veselovsky's transformation from apparatchik to businessman. There was a *fin de régime* atmosphere in Moscow in the spring of 1991, and bureaucrats were lining up to jump ship before it was too late. Many of Veselovsky's colleagues in the Central Committee apparatus found jobs in the emerging private sector at this time, as "experts" or "consultants." Veselovsky himself later said that from April 1991 onward practically all the senior officials in the administration department of the Central Committee were involved in commercial activity of one kind or another.[54]

This was a crucial turning point. In the past Communist ideology had provided the ultimate justification for the power and privileges of the Soviet elite. But many members of the elite were now discovering that they could maintain their privileged positions in society even without the ideology. If they were clever enough and agile enough they could trade their positions in the old Communist regime for equally comfortable positions in the nascent capitalist order. In many cases they were trading up. Why drive a Volga when you could be driving a Mercedes? It was no longer necessary to pretend that they were the vanguard of the proletariat, chosen by history to build a socialist utopia.

Not all members of the elite arrived at this conclusion at precisely the same time, of course. Some apparatchiks lacked the wits to succeed as entrepreneurs; some were scared by the thought of changing careers in midstream; some believed that the Communist Party was the only organization capable of holding the Soviet Union together. Mixed in with the thousands of careerists and cynics—people who worried only about their "bottoms," to use the popular expression—were a few true believers. What mattered, however, was that the party was no longer a monolith. And once it ceased to be a monolith, it was no longer invincible.

The collapse of communism unleashed a ruthless struggle for the vast economic resources that had previously been controlled by the state. The nomenklatura capitalists grabbed whatever they could, while the going was good. In many cases assets were sold off for practically nothing; this was "grab-it-ization" rather than privatization. The wild scramble for property that got under way in the Soviet Union at the beginning of 1991 represented the relatively benign form of this struggle for power and wealth. But the potential for violence was always just beneath the surface, as events in Yugoslavia soon demonstrated.

BOROVO SELO

May 2, 1991

THE FALL OF THE BERLIN WALL produced a wave of self-congratulation in Western capitals. When communism collapsed in Eastern Europe, many people in the West assumed that the new order would be represented by politicians like Václav Havel and Lech Wałęsa, who had spent most of their lives struggling against totalitarian dictatorship. The slaying of the Communist dragon appeared to represent the final victory of the liberal, free market values dear to Western democracies. Adam Smith and Thomas Jefferson had triumphed over Karl Marx and Vladimir Lenin.

The sense of victory was short-lived. Just because communism was in its death throes did not mean that democracy had triumphed. Communism was more than just an ideology; it was a guide to political action, a tested method of achieving, and retaining, supreme power. Like a malevolent virus, communism possessed a unique ability to adapt to changing circumstances. A skillful Communist leader knew how to exploit the divisions in society, how to rouse the have-nots against the haves, how to employ populist demagoguery to rout his political opponents. If circumstances required, such a leader might even be prepared to switch ideologies, in the interests of retaining supreme power. This was a struggle in which the ends always justified the means.

Nowhere did Communist leaders have greater success in shedding their ideological skins than in Yugoslavia. The role of political trailblazer came naturally to the Yugoslav Communists. Apart from Russia, Yugoslavia was the only country in Eastern Europe where the Communists had come to power through their own efforts, rather than with foreign assistance. Under their leader Josip Broz Tito, the Yugoslav Communists had conducted a successful guerrilla campaign against the Nazi occupation of their country in World War II. They had consolidated their power after 1948 by refusing to submit to Stalin. This act of defiance made Yugoslavia a favorite of the West and a candidate for billions of dollars of economic assistance. But the liberal, easygoing facade presented by Yugoslav Communists was deceptive. When their power and privileges came under threat, they put up a more ruthless fight than any of their more orthodox, Soviet-sponsored comrades, with infinitely more tragic results.

The key figure in the Yugoslav Communist Party was Slobodan Milošević of Serbia. A master of bureaucratic intrigue, Milošević had moved to fill the political vacuum created by Tito's death in 1980. He was the first Communist leader anywhere in Eastern Europe to understand the power of nationalism. By giving voice to long-repressed ethnic grievances, he succeeded in becoming the undisputed leader of Serbia, the largest and most powerful of Yugoslavia's six republics. It was a virtuoso performance. In the space of a few months a stolid, rather colorless Communist Party functionary re-created himself as the father of the Serb nation. Far from coming to an end with the collapse of the old Communist order, history was just getting started again, after a hiatus of almost half a century. Milošević had the sense to realize this and to exploit the rebirth of history for his own purposes.

Milošević, a shy, almost reclusive figure, seemed an unlikely nationalist firebrand. He kept his emotions so tightly under control that it was difficult to guess what he was feeling or thinking. He rarely smiled. When he was angry, his jaw might sometimes jut out a little, but his bland, fleshy face remained as expressionless as ever. His personal life has been marked by dogged hard work, family tragedy, and a striking absence of close friends. Both of his parents had committed suicide when he was young. At school he seemed uninterested in the favorite pastimes of his classmates, such as chasing girls and playing basketball. With the exception of his wife, Mirjana Marković, a hard-boiled Marxist ideologist, whom he married just out of high school, he had few confidants.

Milošević made his early career in the labyrinthine economic bureau-

cracy of the Communist state, running an energy company and serving as president of the leading Serbian bank. Up until the mid-1980s his speeches were full of standard denunciations of nationalism. When he spoke in public, he used the wooden language favored by Communist bureaucrats, which was difficult for ordinary people to decipher. He seemed an almost perfect product of the apparatchik class: There are practically no photographs of him in anything other than the apparatchik's uniform of dark suit and white shirt. He rose through the ranks of the party apparatus by displaying total loyalty to his superiors and never stepping out of line.

One of the distinguishing features of the international Communist movement was an ingrained suspicion of any leader who attempted to develop a popular power base outside the party. The party's strength lay in its unity. Only a very few exceptionally confident Communist leaders had dared to violate the taboo against involving the masses in internal party disputes. In China Mao had launched the Cultural Revolution in an attempt to outflank the hidebound party apparatchiks. In the Soviet Union Gorbachev had used glasnost to drum up popular support and put his conservative Politburo rivals on the defensive. Milošević employed essentially the same tactic. Before his death Tito had decreed that he would be succeeded by a collective leadership, made up of the representatives of Yugoslavia's many different ethnic groups. In Milošević's view, this arrangement had become a recipe for political paralysis. By stoking up the passions of the Serbian masses, he would become the single most powerful politician in the country and inherit Tito's mantle.

The key moment in Milošević's transformation from Communist to nationalist came in April 1987, when he visited the province of Kosovo, in southern Serbia. The very fact that he was willing to make such a trip was a sign that he was looking for ways of distinguishing himself from his fellow bureaucrats. Modern-day Kosovo is a dirt-poor Third World kind of a place, 90 percent of whose inhabitants are Albanian. In the thirteenth and fourteenth centuries, however, Kosovo was the core of a powerful Serbian state. When Serbs think of Kosovo, they automatically think of the most fateful episode in their history. In 1389 a battle took place that ended Serbia's existence as an independent nation-state for nearly five hundred years. Dressed in heavy chain mail, the Serbian knights were decimated by the lightly clad, and much more mobile, Turkish cavalry. Although the Serbian prince, Lazar, was killed on the battlefield, he left behind a legend of heroism and chivalry that sustained his countrymen for generations to come. In Serbian mythology, military defeat was transformed into moral victory and immortalized in an epic poem promising Serbs revenge against "the Turks":

> *Whoever is a Serb and of Serbian birth,*
> *And who does not come to Kosovo Polje*
> *to do battle against the Turks,*
> *Let him have neither a male*
> *nor a female offspring,*
> *Let him have no crop.* [55]

Milošević went to Kosovo to attend a Communist Party conference investigating complaints by local Serbs of harassment and persecution by the Albanian majority. The meeting took place on the very site of Prince Lazar's defeat, in the village of Kosovo Polje, better known in English as the Field of Blackbirds, on the outskirts of the Kosovo capital, Priština. During the meeting thousands of Serbs and Montenegrins tried to force their way into the hall, to voice their grievances. The Serbs began pelting the police with stones.[56] The police blocked their path, beating them back with truncheons. At this point Milošević emerged from the hall to speak to the angry throng. He was confronted by a wizened old Serb with a white mustache and a splendid crop of white hair, who complained that the police had been beating him. After listening to the old man, Milošević uttered the words that were to give birth to a new legend and change the course of Yugoslav history: "Nobody has the right to beat you."[57]

This single sentence earned Milošević an instant place in Serbian mythology, alongside Prince Lazar. He stayed in the building until dawn, listening to Serbs pour out their grievances against the Albanian-dominated provincial government of Kosovo. Overnight he was transformed from an anonymous Communist bureaucrat to a people's tribune. When he appeared in public, he was greeted by chants of "Slobo, Slobo." He had hit upon the magic formula that would propel him to supreme power. He had the ability not only to identify with the masses and voice their grievances but also to manipulate their emotions for his own ends. A Serbian political rival compared the new Milošević with the character in the Charlie Chaplin film *The Great Dictator,* "when they wave the flags and he realizes his power."[58]

In the hands of a political master like Milošević, nationalism was a potent weapon. Had he accused his political opponents of betraying socialism, the country would have laughed. By labeling them traitors to the nation, he united the whole of Serbia behind him. He adopted the nationalist battle cry, *"Samo Sloga Srbina Spašava"* (Only Unity Will Save the Serbs). In the Serbian Cyrillic script, *S* is written as *C*. The four back-to-back *C*s became the symbol of the Serbian nationalist movement. The new ideology enabled

Milošević to preserve the one-party state in all but name. There would be very little economic reform and only token democratization. The key institutions of Communist power—propaganda, big companies, banks— remained firmly under the control of Milošević and his allies.

In September 1987 the hero of Kosovo Polje ousted his longtime patron and mentor, Ivan Stambolić, as leader of the Serbian Communist Party. It was an act of spectacular political ingratitude that sent a warning to politicians all over Yugoslavia. Next, Milošević took his "antibureaucratic revolution" on the road. Thanks to his control over the media, primarily television, he was able to mobilize huge crowds to intimidate his political opponents and force them out of office. Within a short time, pro-Milošević leaders had come to power in the Serbian provinces of Kosovo and Vojvodina, as well as the Serb-inhabited republic of Montenegro. The series of mass rallies reached an emotional climax on June 28, 1989, the six hundredth anniversary of the Battle of Kosovo Polje. For twelve months a coffin said to contain the mummified remains of Prince Lazar had been making a triumphal tour of Serbian villages, being greeted at every stop by crowds of wailing mourners. On the great day itself more than a million Serbs crowded onto the Field of Blackbirds to hail Milošević as the reincarnation of the fallen prince.

At a time when Communist leaders all over Eastern Europe were being chased out of office, Milošević was climbing to new heights of power by exploiting nationalist grievances. Nationalism stood him in good stead in March 1991, when his regime faced its most serious crisis. Tens of thousands of opposition demonstrators took to the streets of Belgrade to protest against the official manipulation of the mass media. As they attempted to take over the television station, dubbed the Bastille by Milošević's opponents, one of the protesters was killed by a police bullet. There were hundreds of arrests. The government declared a state of emergency and attempted to crush the uprising with tanks. The huge show of force further inflamed the demonstrators, who set up a street "parliament" in the center of Belgrade that attracted hundreds of thousands of people.

The police brutality severely dented Milošević's halo. The leader who had risen to power on the populist slogan "Nobody has the right to beat you" was "beating" his own people. In order to defuse the protests, he was obliged to make a tactical retreat, dismissing some of the most obnoxious members of his entourage, including the television chief. He then served notice that Serbia was preparing for war. Nationalism became a way of diverting attention from the economic and political crisis threatening the country.

Milošević outlined his strategy for carving a Greater Serbia out of the disintegrating Yugoslav federation at a secret briefing for regional party chiefs on March 16. He told them they had a sacred duty to defend the three million Serbs who lived outside Serbia proper, mainly in Croatia and Bosnia-Herzegovina. If the rights and freedoms of Serbs in other Yugoslav republics were threatened, the country's internal borders would have to be redrawn, if necessary by force. This was no time for pro-democracy demonstrations or whining about the unprecedented decline in living standards. Serbia was surrounded by enemies, and national unity was essential. The course of future events would be decided by the strong, not the weak.

"We consider that it is the legitimate right and interest of the Serb people to live in a single state. This is the beginning and end of our policy," he announced, to thunderous applause. "If we must fight, then, by God, we will fight. I only hope no one will be so crazy as to fight against us. We may not know how to work well or to do business well, but at least we know how to fight well."[59]

MILOŠEVIĆ WAS RIGHT to criticize the political paralysis that had gripped Yugoslavia in the years since Tito's death. The country was drifting from one crisis to another. Bold action was needed to resolve the economic mess left behind by decades of Communist rule, but this proved impossible under the rules of consensus laid down by Tito. By the mid-1980s Yugoslavia had become virtually ungovernable. The federal government was extremely weak, and unable to impose its authority on the country. It seemed impossible for the republics to reach agreement on an austerity package to slash the budget deficit and allow loss-making factories to go bankrupt.

At first many American diplomats in Belgrade were favorably impressed by Milošević. They hoped the Serbian leader would use his newfound authority to break the political logjam and push through the necessary democratic reforms. It gradually became clear that Milošević had no intention of destroying the monopoly system that provided him with his own power base. Instead of supporting the federal government's hesitant attempts to introduce market reforms, he worked behind the scenes to sabotage them. Instead of damping down nationalism, he used his control over the media to stoke the flames.

The nationalist explosion in Serbia soon led to a counternationalism in Croatia, Yugoslavia's second largest republic. In April 1990 Croats went to the polls and elected a leader who was almost a mirror image of Milošević. Like his Serb counterpart, Franjo Tuđman was a former Communist. He

had fought with Tito's partisans during the Second World War and gone on to become one of the youngest generals in the Yugoslav People's Army. His conversion to nationalism had come earlier than that of Milošević—he was one of the leading figures in an outpouring of Croatian national sentiment in the early 1970s known as the Euphoria—but his political philosophy was remarkably similar. Like Milošević, he was suspicious of genuine political pluralism. He regarded himself as the symbol of Croatia's centuries-old desire for independent statehood and believed that the whole nation should rally around him.

The two leaders were alike even in their denunciations of each other. Zagreb television became a bizarre parody of Belgrade television. Tuđman was always the lead story on Croatian television news, just as Milošević's sayings and doings dominated Serbian newscasts. The hate-filled language used by the two television stations was practically interchangeable; only the targets were different. Zagreb attacked the "terrorist, hegemonistic" policies of Serbia, while Belgrade attacked the "terrorist, hegemonistic" policies of Croatia. Both sides used long-forgotten World War II epithets against the other. Croatian commentators referred to Serbian leaders as "chetniks," the name used by Serbian royalists who fought against Tito's partisans. Serbian commentators referred to Croatian leaders as "ustashi," after the brutal Croatian fascists who established a pro-Nazi puppet regime in Zagreb during the war.

There was, however, one important difference between the leaders of Serbia and Croatia. For Milošević, nationalism was a means to an end, preserving his own power. For Tuđman, restoring Croatian independence was the supreme goal. Whereas Milošević was cold and calculating, Tuđman was emotional and narrow-minded. He had much less political experience than his Serbian rival and made numerous errors of judgment. One of the most serious was his insensitivity to the traumas of the 600,000-strong Serb minority in Croatia.

During the war hundreds of thousands of Serbs had been massacred by the ustashi. Tuđman did little to allay Serb concerns about the place they would occupy in an independent Croatian state. The Croatian parliament adopted national symbols that were offensive to many Serbs, including the red and white checkerboard that had been used by the ustashi regime. (Tuđman argued that it was a perfectly respectable Croatian emblem that long predated the ustashi.) After winning the 1990 elections, his Croatian Democratic Union (HDZ) began a systematic purge of Serbs from the police force, the education system, and even industry. Croats argued that such

a step was only fair, since the Serbs had been overrepresented in Croatia under the Communists. While it was certainly true that the Serb minority in Croatia had enjoyed special privileges in the past—this was part of Tito's delicate ethnic balancing act—mass dismissals were a provocative act under the circumstances. Tuđman played into the hands of the Serbian propagandists.

Given the hard-line attitudes on each side and the ghastly memories of the older generation of Serbs, conflict was almost inevitable. The two nationalisms fed on each other, but they also competed. There was little room for compromise, particularly in the border regions of Croatia, where many Serbs lived. The first signs of trouble came in August 1990, in Krajina, a stony plateau just inland from the Dalmatian coast, where Serbs had been living since the sixteenth century. The Krajina Serbs declared their "autonomy" from the rest of Croatia and appealed to the Serb-dominated Yugoslav army for assistance. That army provided the population with weapons and political support, preventing the Tuđman government from establishing its authority in the region.

For the next nine months the country waited for the spark that would ignite a full-scale war. It came at the other end of Croatia, on the border with Serbia proper, in an obscure little village called Borovo Selo.

THE BOROVO SHOE AND TIRE FACTORY LIES in a bend in the Danube River on the fertile Slavonian plain, a few miles across the cornfields from the town of Vukovar. Founded in 1931 by a Czech entrepreneur named Jan Bata, the factory soon achieved a reputation for high-quality products. During the years before World War II it was a model of modern production techniques, progressive management, and ethnic harmony. The workforce was predominantly Croat and German, together with some Serbs, whose ancestors had been brought to Slavonia to serve as frontiersmen in the Austro-Hungarian army.

The Communist victory caused a social and political upheaval at the Borovo factory. The former owners were expropriated, and the factory was taken over by the state. All the Germans were expelled. Croat managers were arrested, on suspicion of cooperating with the ustashi regime. In order to provide the factory with manpower and reward their own supporters, the victorious Communists began a major resettlement program. The place of the departing Germans was taken by Serbs and Croats from impoverished mountain regions near the Adriatic coast. There was immediate friction

between the newcomers—hardened mountain people who had borne the brunt of the fighting during the war—and the native inhabitants. The mountain Serbs described the Slavonian Serbs as Schwabs, Germans. The local Serbs, many of whom were prosperous landowners, regarded the Krajina Serbs as lazy and uncouth. There were similar differences between the Slavonian Croats and the Croats from Herzegovina. These divisions later became very significant.

Ethnic hatreds had faded into the background during the postwar years. The Titoist slogan of "Brotherhood and Unity" had an effect, particularly when reinforced by the threat of long prison terms against anyone suspected of stirring up ethnic hatred. People stopped thinking of themselves as Serb or Croat. Mixed marriages were commonplace. By 1981, the year after Tito's death, 22 percent of the local population was describing itself to census takers as Yugoslav, a catchall adjective for "South Slav."

"There was little to distinguish Serbs from Croats," recalled Nikola Radaković, a Serb director of the shoe factory. "We were born in the same hospital, went to the same schools, chased the same girls, and sang the same songs. We spoke the same language and wore the same kind of clothes. In fact, we were the same."[60]

The Borovo factory became a showcase for the Yugoslav system of "workers' self-management," which Tito invented to distinguish his brand of socialism from the Soviet variety. Delegations of admiring foreign visitors toured the factory and met the "worker-directors" who had been "elected" from the shop floor. In theory, it sounded as if Yugoslavia had the best of both worlds. Factories belonged to the workers, but there was meant to be free competition between different collectively owned enterprises. In fact, self-management was largely a fig leaf for continued Communist Party control. All appointments to senior management positions had to be cleared by the party. Most factory directors were Serbs, generally considered more "politically reliable" than Croats.

At first the system worked reasonably well. In return for their political passivity, the "worker-owners" were never fired. Loss-making departments were not closed down. The sixties and seventies were boom years for Yugoslavia—Western governments rewarded Tito's defiance of Moscow with generous credits—but it was a false prosperity. By normal accounting standards, the Borovo factory was losing money. Factory managers later acknowledged that they spent much of their time juggling the books, in an ultimately futile attempt to conceal the losses. In order to meet the monthly payroll, they were obliged to take out huge bank loans, which were never

paid back. The factory had long since ceased to invest in plant and equipment. As a result, two investment cycles were missed, and much of the shoe-making machinery was antiquated.

The logical answer to the factory's problems would have been to dismiss half the workforce and raise the productivity of the other half by purchasing new machinery. When an attempt was finally made to follow such a strategy in 1988, the workers promptly went on strike. They camped outside the federal parliament building in Belgrade for weeks until the government caved in to their demands and granted the factory temporary relief from its debts. The government funded such loans by printing billions of new dinars, a course of action that led inexorably to hyperinflation. By the late eighties the Borovo factory had become a gigantic industrial dinosaur, employing more than twenty thousand workers. It was a symbol of everything wrong with the socialist economy: a bloated workforce; obsolescent technology; low productivity. It was also an ethnic time bomb, waiting to explode.

"The political crisis in Yugoslavia was the direct result of economic collapse," said Josip Kovač, a Croat who worked in the factory's financial department. "When two people are fighting for the same job, all their differences come to the surface: nationality; religion; political affiliation. If everyone had work, we would not have seen such political turmoil."[61]

At first there was little overt support in the Vukovar region for the nationalist parties. During the municipal elections of 1990 a majority of Croats and Serbs had voted for the nonsectarian Social Democratic Party. But the tradition of ethnic harmony broke down in the face of the growing economic crisis and the propaganda war between Belgrade and Zagreb. In early 1991 the Tudman government began a concerted drive to replace "disloyal" Serbs with "loyal" Croats at all levels. In Vukovar Serbs were tossed out of the police force after they refused to wear the checkerboard emblem of the new Croatian state. As soon as it became clear that the Borovo factory was irretrievably bankrupt, several departments were forced to close. The Serbs suffered the brunt of the mass dismissals. Unemployed Croats could always find jobs in the police force, which was looking for recruits to fill the places vacated by the Serbs.

As important as the ethnic divisions between Serb and Croat were the differences between the plains people and the mountain people. The harvests were so abundant in this part of the world that anyone with land was assured a good income. In the farming villages of Slavonia there were many households with Mercedes cars and private swimming pools. Such people had no reason to fight for an even higher standard of living. They got on

well with their Serb and Croat neighbors. By contrast, the landless immigrants felt the full force of the economic recession and had little attachment to the status quo. The bankrupt shoe factory became a natural recruiting ground for the rival militias and police forces that sprang up around Vukovar. The dispossessed on both sides became the officers in the coming war.

Pitting the poor against the rich was a standard Communist technique, and the Communists-turned-nationalists used it to perfection. Nationalist politicians like Milošević formed a de facto alliance with the desperate and the disgruntled. There is evidence that the Serbian secret police helped organize the paramilitary forces that spread havoc and terror, first in Croatia and later in Bosnia.[62] In return for doing most of the fighting, the militia groups were promised the spoils of war.

The first barricades went up in early April around the Serb-inhabited settlement of Borovo Selo. This dreary industrial suburb a couple of miles down the road from the shoe factory was home to many unemployed Serb workers. Their plight had attracted the interest of Serb nationalists in Belgrade, including the leader of an extreme-right chetnik party, Vojislav Šešelj. The chetniks had done their best to stir up anti-Croat sentiment among the former Borovo workers and made sure that they had plenty of weapons to "defend" themselves from a Croat attack.

There were wild men on the Croat side too. In mid-April a group of HDZ members led by Gojko Šušak, the founder of a Canadian pizza company and adviser to Tuđman, decided to teach the Serbs a lesson. They forced the local police chief, Josip Reihl-Kir, a moderate who had worked tirelessly to reduce ethnic tensions, to take them to Borovo Selo. Approaching the village through the cornfields, they fired three shoulder-launched missiles at Serb positions. The missiles did not do much damage, but they were seized upon by the Belgrade propaganda machine as proof that Croatia was bent on war. Šušak, who rose to become defense minister in the Croatian government, later boasted that he had fired the first shell against the Serbian "aggressors" in eastern Slavonia.[63]

THE ETHNIC TINDERBOX WAS IGNITED on Thursday, May 2. The Serbs of Borovo Selo had been celebrating May Day, a traditional Yugoslav feast day, and the village was adorned with the Yugoslav blue, white, and red tricolor emblazoned with the Red Star. Across the cornfields, in the predominantly Croat settlement of Borovo Naselje, people had hung out the Croatian checkerboard.

Shortly after midnight two Croatian police cars drove into town, from the direction of Borovo Naselje. The policemen began to haul down the Yugoslav flag from a post and immediately found themselves surrounded by angry Serbs. Shots were fired; each side later accused the other of firing first. Two of the Croatian patrolmen were detained by Serb vigilantes, and the others fled. In response the Croat authorities dispatched a group of twenty armed policemen to Borovo Selo to investigate the fate of the patrolmen.

As the Croatian police vehicles entered the village, they were ambushed by Serb militants. During the resulting battle twelve of the Croatian policemen and three Serb irregulars were killed. That afternoon Yugoslav People's Army units arrived in Borovo Selo, with the declared aim of keeping the warring ethnic communities apart. A few days later the Croatian authorities released photographs purporting to show the mutilated corpses of three of the police. One had an arm chopped off, another had been slashed across the face, while the third had the skin ripped off his back. Such atrocities had been commonplace in World War II and were a gruesome reminder of what could happen again if war were allowed to break out between the rival ethnic communities.

The Croatian police chief, Josip Kir, had favored a policy of negotiating with the rebel Serbs. But he was no longer able to control his own side. Šušak and the other hard-liners had taken over. Convinced that his own life was in danger, Kir begged his superiors to transfer him back to Zagreb. The day before he was due to leave, he was murdered by one of his own subordinates in what his wife described as a politically motivated killing.[64]

Once it had been set in motion, the downward spiral toward uncontrollable violence proved impossible to stop. Croat activists set up barricades on the outskirts of Borovo Naselje, next to the shoe factory. Soon former workmates who had happily shared their lunch breaks together were shooting at one another across the cornfields. Within a few weeks the sniper fire had been replaced by artillery barrages and tank salvos. Croatian national guardsmen moved into Borovo Naselje, while the Yugoslav army formed a defensive ring around Borovo Selo, less than half a mile away. Serbs living in predominantly Croat communities were forced out of their houses at gunpoint; the houses were then blown up from the inside. The same thing happened to Croat families that found themselves on the wrong side of the ethnic dividing line. Each side accused the other of planning a massacre.

The toughest fighters on both sides were almost invariably the poor immigrants whose families had arrived from the mountains on the "trains without a timetable" in Tito's social revolution after World War II. Up until

recently many of these people had been stuck in demeaning jobs at the Borovo shoe factory. The Croat commander of Borovo Naselje, Blago Zadro, was a typical example. He was a Herzegovinian, from the Dalmatian hinterland. Before the war he had a job mixing chemicals and rubber, a particularly unpleasant task. After his department had been closed down, he spent three months in the reorganized Croatian police force. He also had a high position in the local branch of the HDZ.[65]

The Serb commander of Borovo Selo, Vitomir Devetek, had a similar background. He too came from the mountains, and he too had been working in a dead-end job at the factory, producing bulletproof vests. Along with dozens of other Serbs, he had been dismissed in March after refusing to sign a loyalty oath to the republic of Croatia. His forces included thirty-five Serbs fired from the Vukovar Police Department.

"The Croatian people must understand. They will never have the independent state they imagine in their sick heads," Devetek told an American reporter in early July as he patrolled the front line. "Sooner or later, we will attack Borovo Naselje and liberate it. Then we will liberate Vukovar."[66]

MOSCOW

August 17, 1991

VLADIMIR KRYUCHKOV was convinced that the world's first Communist state was headed for political disintegration and economic catastrophe. He had used every trick in the KGB disinformation manual to persuade Gorbachev to impose a nationwide state of emergency. He had accused Lithuanian independence activists of launching an armed uprising and firing on Soviet troops. He had planted stories about a conspiracy by Western bankers to wage "financial war" against the Soviet Union by flooding the country with cheap rubles. He had talked about CIA plots to recruit Soviet leaders as "agents of influence" and destroy the rival superpower. He had even informed Gorbachev about a bizarre scheme by opposition activists to storm the Kremlin with "hooks" and "ladders."[67]

At first it seemed that all this disinformation might be producing the desired effect. The president had gone along with some of the KGB chief's schemes to curb the democratic opposition and restore order in the country. At the crucial moment, however, he had called a halt to the machinery of repression. Over the past few months Gorbachev had drifted away from the hard-liners and formed an alliance with republican leaders who were intent on grabbing as much power as possible from the center.

Time was running out for Kryuchkov. Leaders from all over the country

were due to come to Moscow on August 20 to sign a new Union Treaty, bringing to an end seven decades of centralized rule. The USSR—the Union of Soviet Socialist Republics—would cease to exist. Its place would be taken by a much looser confederation, to be known as the Union of Sovereign States.

The decision to omit any mention of "socialism" from the constitution of the new state was alarming enough. Even more troubling were indications that there would not be a place for "principled Communists" in the new order. The KGB had recorded a conversation between Gorbachev and the two most influential republican leaders, Boris Yeltsin of Russia and Nursultan Nazarbayev of Kazakhstan, at the end of July. After a grueling round of negotiations on the new Union Treaty at the president's dacha at Novo-Ogaryevo, the three leaders had turned their attention to possible personnel changes. At Yeltsin's insistence, part of the conversation had been held on the balcony, to avoid eavesdroppers. But the microphones had nevertheless picked up their remarks, and the transcript made devastating reading.

Yeltsin had argued forcefully that nobody would believe in the new Union Treaty unless Gorbachev replaced the most "odious" members of his entourage. At the top of his list was Kryuchkov, who had the attempted coup in Lithuania "on his conscience." Nazarbayev supported the demand for a purge and mentioned the name of Boris Pugo, the hard-line interior minister. Yeltsin later recalled that Gorbachev seemed tense but agreed that both security chiefs would be removed. The three leaders also decided to replace the prime minister, Valentin Pavlov, who had allied himself with the conservatives.[68]

Kryuchkov now knew that in all likelihood he would not remain head of the KGB very much longer. If he was going to act, he would have to do so soon. On August 6, the day Gorbachev left for his annual vacation in the Crimea, Kryuchkov instructed his aides to prepare the necessary documents for a state of emergency.

The groundwork for a coup had already been laid. Over the course of many weeks Kryuchkov had put out feelers to other members of the leadership. He knew that many of them thought the same way he did. Pavlov had already tried, and failed, to persuade the Supreme Soviet to grant him emergency economic powers. The defense minister, Dmitri Yazov, was constantly complaining about the humiliation of the army and the decline in the Soviet Union's military readiness. The party secretary in charge of the military-industrial complex, Oleg Baklanov, was convinced that Gorbachev was running the Soviet defense industry into the ground. The secretary in

charge of personnel matters, Oleg Shenin, was angry that the party was losing its influence. The president's chief of staff, Valery Boldin, was another malcontent, even though he took care to hide his disdain for Gorbachev behind a veil of sycophancy. These men met together regularly to bemoan the fate of a once-great superpower.

On Saturday, August 17, Kryuchkov invited his fellow conspirators to a KGB facility, near the Moscow Ring Road. The complex included a sauna, a swimming pool, a video room. It was a secure and pleasant place to meet, and the KGB chief often entertained here. On this occasion, however, he led his guests onto the veranda. Even he was cautious about being overheard. He served vodka to Yazov, Shenin, and Pavlov. The others preferred whiskey. Plates of bacon lard, a traditional Russian delicacy, were served as an appetizer.

"I am ready to resign right now," said Pavlov, who understood that his days as prime minister were numbered. "The situation is catastrophic. The country is on the threshold of hunger. Nobody wants to carry out orders anymore. The only hope is a state of emergency."[69]

"I deliver regular reports to Gorbachev about the extremely difficult situation, but he scarcely reacts," complained the KGB chief. "He interrupts the conversation, changes the subject. He doesn't believe my information."

At Kryuchkov's suggestion, the participants in the meeting decided to form a Committee for the State of Emergency, to be known by its Russian initials, GKChP. They would send a delegation to the Crimea to make a last attempt to persuade Gorbachev to declare his own state of emergency. If he refused, he would be interned in his dacha. Vice President Gennady Yanayev would announce that the president was "ill," and he would assume power. Yanayev was not yet part of the plot, but the conspirators thought they could talk him into joining. He was weak and malleable.

There was a discussion about who would go to Foros to break the news to the president. It was agreed that Kryuchkov and Yazov should remain in Moscow, to make the necessary preparations. Boldin, who had worked with Gorbachev for the past fifteen years, would be made part of the delegation, in order to underline the seriousness of the revolt.

"*Et tu, Brutus?*" joked Yazov, who owed his own promotion to defense minister in 1987 to Gorbachev. Everybody laughed.

FOROS

August 18, 1991

IT WAS A SLOW SUNDAY AFTERNOON. For the past eight hours Lieutenant Colonel Vladimir Kirillov had been cooped up inside a locked room. He spent most of his time watching television. Outside his window the sea sparkled invitingly beneath the hot Crimean sun.

Suddenly the television set flickered and died. An emergency light began flashing on the electronic console in front of Kirillov. Almost instinctively the colonel started to check the telephones on his desk. The two-way intercom with the commander in chief was out of order. So was the direct line to the Defense Ministry in Moscow. Even the internal phone system within the presidential compound at Foros was down. With the exception of a nuclear strike by the rival superpower, Kirillov's worst nightmare had just been realized. The man in charge of the Soviet nuclear codes had no way of communicating with his superiors. The clock on the wall showed the time as 1632.

A few feet away from Kirillov lay a black briefcase containing the Soviet nuclear codes. This was the modern-day orb and scepter that distinguished the leader of a nuclear superpower from ordinary mortals. From the outside it looked like an ordinary attaché case. This is precisely what it was. The designers of the nuclear command and control system had leafed through some Western mail-order catalogs, picked out a Samsonite briefcase with a

lightweight aluminum frame, and adapted it to their needs. The electronic equipment inside the briefcase would allow Gorbachev to launch thousands of nuclear missiles at the touch of a button, in the event of a surprise attack on the Soviet Union.[70]

Kirillov and his colleagues were required to carry the commander in chief's *chemodanchik* (little suitcase) wherever he went. They followed him to the Kremlin in the morning and back to his dacha at night. They accompanied him on trips to foreign countries, waiting patiently in a reception room as he conferred with world leaders. When he went on vacation, they tagged along too.

The nuclear command post at Foros was located in a two-story guesthouse, fifty yards away from Gorbachev's personal residence. At any one time there were always three people on duty: two "officer-operators" and a communications specialist. The work was organized into three twenty-four-hour shifts. When they were not on duty, the nuclear aides lived in a military rest home, several miles away from the presidential compound.

Only one telephone out of an entire bank of communications devices in the command post was still working. This was a radiotelephone to the government communications center at Mukhalatka, a few miles down the road. When the operator answered, Kirillov asked to be put through to Moscow immediately.

"We have no communications with anybody," the operator replied. "There's been an accident."[71]

The nuclear aides were beginning to panic when there was a loud knocking at the door. The chief of Soviet ground forces, General Valentin Varennikov, was standing in the corridor with half a dozen other officers, most of whom Kirillov did not know.

"How are your communications?" barked the general.

"There aren't any," replied the colonel.

"That's how it should be," said Varennikov, evidently pleased. He told Kirillov that the interruption in communications would last approximately twenty-four hours, adding, "The president knows all about it." With that he and the others disappeared in the direction of Gorbachev's residence. When the colonel tried to find out more, he was told by one of the people who had come with Varennikov to "mind your own business."

"A GROUP OF COMRADES is here to see you, Mikhail Sergeyevich."

Gorbachev looked up from his papers to see the ingratiating face of the head of his personal guard, Vladimir Medvedev. He was seated behind

the desk of the study in his Crimean residence, with a magnificent view of the Black Sea. His annual vacation was practically over. He felt rested and in generally good health, although his back was giving him some problems. He had suffered an attack of lumbago the previous day, while walking in the hills around Foros. That morning his personal physician had given him some injections to relieve the pain. "Do whatever you want," the president had joked. "Remove the nerve, a vertebra, even the leg, but I must be in Moscow on August 19."[72] When Medvedev entered the room, Gorbachev had been working on the speech he planned to deliver at the signing ceremony for the new Union Treaty, which he saw as his last chance of holding the country together.

"What comrades?" he asked sharply. "I am not expecting anyone."[73]

The president was angry. He rarely invited Kremlin officials to visit him while he was on vacation. When he was at Foros, he preferred to be alone with his immediate family: Raisa, their daughter, Irina, her husband, Anatoly, and their two children. For outsiders to show up uninvited at his private retreat was a gross breach of protocol. It was also a serious violation of the elaborate security arrangements that surrounded a Soviet leader. Gorbachev wanted to know why his bodyguards had permitted the visitors to enter the compound.

"They came with Plekhanov," Medvedev replied nervously.

This, at least, explained how the "comrades" had managed to get past the guards. Lieutenant General Yuri Plekhanov was head of the Ninth Directorate of the KGB, the division responsible for the protection of Soviet leaders. The president's bodyguards ultimately reported to him. It was Plekhanov who had devised the seemingly impenetrable security system around the residence, which consisted of three circles of guards, a total of five hundred superbly armed men. There were the president's personal bodyguards, headed by Medvedev. There were KGB soldiers, who were responsible for defending the internal perimeter of the compound and manning five high watchtowers. Finally there were border troops, who patrolled the outside of the compound. Every year Plekhanov spent a few days at Foros, to ensure that the system was functioning properly.

"Okay, let them wait a little," Gorbachev told Medvedev. He planned to ask Kryuchkov what was going on. The fact that a group of Soviet leaders would come to visit him in Foros on the eve of his departure for Moscow struck him as strange. But he had confidence in the KGB chief, who seemed the model of the loyal subordinate. While he was at Foros, he spoke to him almost every day by phone.

The president picked up the *vertushka*, but it was dead. He picked up a second phone, a third, and a fourth, with the same frustrating result. Finally he removed the cover from a special red phone reserved for the commander in chief. This was the hot line to the defense minister and the chief of the General Staff, for use in the event of a nuclear attack on the Soviet Union. No one else was permitted to touch this phone, even to dust it. It too had gone dead. Gorbachev now had no doubt that an attempt was under way to overthrow him. He looked at his watch. It was 4:50 p.m.

He rushed outside onto the veranda, where his wife was resting after a day by the beach. During the past six years he had shared all his hopes and worries with her. Now he told her that he detected "a plot." It was the only plausible explanation for the unprecedented communications blackout, combined with the sudden arrival of uninvited visitors. Even the television set had been disconnected. They had to prepare themselves for a period of enforced isolation, perhaps even arrest.

"If they think that they will get me to change my policies, they will not succeed. I will not give in to any blackmail or threats," said Gorbachev after a moment's silence. "This will be difficult for all of us, for the whole family. We have to be ready for anything."[74]

"You have to make this decision yourself, but I will be with you, whatever happens."

Raisa fetched Irina and Anatoly. They understood that anything could happen. As Raisa said later, "We all knew our history, its terrible pages." They remembered how the last Kremlin reformer, Nikita Khrushchev, had been stripped of all his posts and exiled to a Moscow dacha from one day to the next. Russian history was replete with leaders who had been executed, tortured, and thrown into prison. One by one, the members of Gorbachev's family said they supported his decision not to give in to blackmail.

His mind made up, Gorbachev returned to his study, where the "comrades" were already waiting for him. Half an hour had gone by, and they were getting nervous. There were five of them altogether: Baklanov, Shenin, Boldin, Varennikov, and Plekhanov. All were in suits. Gorbachev, who was dressed in shorts and a sweater, immediately began throwing questions at them.

"Who sent you?"

"The committee."

"What committee?"

"The committee set up to deal with the emergency situation in the country."

"Who set it up? I didn't create it, and the Supreme Soviet didn't create it. Who created it?"[75]

Gorbachev's office was small, and there were not enough chairs for everybody. The visitors were nervous, unsure of themselves. They had not been expecting such a hostile reception from the president, a compromiser to his fingertips. They thought they would haggle with him and reach "a mutually agreed solution."[76] But this time the president seemed in no mood to compromise. He glared at Plekhanov and ordered him rudely out of the room. As far as he was concerned, Plekhanov was a flunky, and flunkies had no business meddling in politics.

The visitors told Gorbachev the names of some of the members of the Emergency Committee. The list included the vice president, the prime minister, the defense minister, the interior minister, the KGB chief. He jotted down the names on a notebook with a blue felt pen. These were people he knew and trusted, people whom he himself had promoted to the top positions in the state and government.

The only member of the committee who had come to Foros was Baklanov, and he did most of the talking. He told Gorbachev that he had two alternatives. He could either sign a decree implementing a state of emergency or temporarily transfer his power to Vice President Yanayev. When Gorbachev said that republican leaders were due to sign the new Union Treaty on August 20, Baklanov interrupted him: "There won't be any signing ceremony."

"Yeltsin has already been arrested," Baklanov added. A few seconds later he corrected himself: "He will be arrested."[77]

"You and the people who sent you are irresponsible. You will destroy yourselves, but that's your business. To hell with you. But you will also destroy the country and everything we have already done. Tell that to the committee that sent you."

Gorbachev was working himself up for one of his long monologues, his preferred style of political discourse. He browbeat the conspirators, just as he browbeat the parliament and Central Committee, telling them repeatedly to "go to hell." The Soviet Union faced many crises, he told them, but a state of emergency was no way to resolve them. The country's problems could be solved only by democratic means. Anyone who thought otherwise was an "adventurer" and a "criminal." Nothing would come of their plans.

"Only people bent on committing suicide could now propose introducing a state of emergency in the country. I will not have anything to do with it."

"Mikhail Sergeyevich," pleaded Boldin, hitherto the most sycophantic of the president's aides, who was standing by the window, "you don't understand what the situation in the country is."

"Shut up, you prick," Gorbachev shot back. "How dare you give me lectures about the situation in the country."[78]

Varennikov, barely able to contain himself, was sitting across the table from Gorbachev. The former commander of the Soviet military operation in Afghanistan had a voice that carried naturally to the most distant corner of a parade ground. He was used to giving orders, not receiving them. He bellowed at his commander in chief as if he were a junior officer who had just disgraced the regiment.

"Resign!"[79]

Varennikov launched into a tirade of his own, complaining about the way in which the Soviet armed forces had been "humiliated," particularly over the withdrawal from East Germany. Why, he wanted to know, were separatist, nationalist forces being allowed to run riot? Why was the president ignoring the constitution he had sworn to uphold?

Gorbachev brushed aside the general's demand for his resignation and, for good measure, pretended that he had forgotten Varennikov's name and patronymic.

"Valentin Ivanovich, is it? Well, just listen, Valentin Ivanovich. The people are not a battalion of soldiers to whom you can issue the command 'right turn' or 'left turn, march,' and they will do just as you tell them. It won't be like that."[80]

After hurling some more Russian swearwords at his former subordinates, Gorbachev told them they were "criminals" who would be held responsible for their actions. As the conspirators left the room, he shook them by the hand.

Raisa was sitting in the hall with her daughter and son-in-law. She was frightened that the conspirators would arrest her husband on the spot. She was particularly shocked to see Boldin among the group that had confronted her husband since she regarded him as a friend of the family. He stopped a short distance from her but did not say anything. Shenin and Baklanov said hello.

"Why have you come here?" she asked Baklanov.

"Force of circumstances," he replied, adding, "We are your friends."

He held out his hand to say good-bye, but Raisa refused to take it.[81]

MOSCOW

August 18, 1991

GORBACHEV'S COLLEAGUES HAD GATHERED in the prime minister's office, on the second floor of the government building in the Kremlin. They were seated around a long conference table, covered with green baize. Bottles of mineral water, half-drunk cups of tea and coffee, plates full of biscuits and sandwiches, and top secret documents were scattered around the table. Cigarette smoke hung in the air.

The participants in the meeting had arranged themselves on either side of the table, in order of seniority. The most senior officials were farthest from the door. Whenever someone came into the room, there would be a shuffling of places, in order to preserve the Kremlin pecking order. But the seat at the head of the table—the place reserved for the chairman of the meeting—was always left vacant. It was as if none of the men around the table were willing to assume individual responsibility for the events that were taking place. All sought refuge behind the anonymity of the collective. In the absence of Gorbachev, they were effectively leaderless.

Vice President Yanayev arrived late and reeking of alcohol. The conspirators were hoping he would agree to declare himself acting president, but he had yet to give his consent. He had spent the afternoon in the company of an old drinking buddy at a government rest home outside Moscow. His somewhat disheveled appearance provoked a sarcastic comment from

Prime Minister Pavlov, who had also been drinking heavily that afternoon, having attended a homecoming party for his son.

"Here we are, discussing important matters, and the vice president is wandering about somewhere," Pavlov remarked jocularly as Yanayev entered the room.[82]

The vice president sat down in his usual place, to the immediate left of the empty chair. The place opposite was reserved for the speaker of the Soviet parliament, Anatoly Lukyanov, who had also been summoned to the Kremlin at short notice. The wily Lukyanov was insisting that his name be removed from the list of members of the GKChP. As the representative of the legislative authority he could not take part in the work of the executive.

The meeting had been convened by Kryuchkov, on the pretext that the president was "ill" and urgent measures were necessary to stabilize the situation in the country. Now that he had isolated the president, the KGB chief had the delicate task of broadening the plot to include other members of the leadership. Gorbachev's "illness" was a convenient fiction that enabled everyone at the meeting to hide behind a cloak of legality.

Yanayev allowed the debate to swirl around him. He was unsure what position to take, and his alcoholic stupor made it even more difficult for him to think straight. He had talked to Gorbachev a few hours previously by phone—the president had told him he was flying back to Moscow on the nineteenth—so he knew perfectly well that he was not seriously ill. He shared his colleagues' dismay at the state of the country and believed that a "strong hand" was the only solution. On the other hand, he had never had any pretensions to being a leader, far less a dictator.

Like most Russians, Yanayev had been surprised by his election as vice president eight months earlier. The press had dismissed him as a colorless bureaucrat who had managed to reach the top by never sticking his neck out. After writing a doctoral thesis on Trotskyism and anarchism, he had spent most of his career in the Communist youth organization, the Komsomol. He had also worked for the official trade union organization, which was known as a refuge for mediocrities. Yanayev's lackluster biography and weak personality had caused a revolt in the Congress of People's Deputies when Gorbachev proposed him for the post of vice president. Even his jokes fell flat. Questioned by deputies about the state of his health, he replied, "I perform my husbandly duties satisfactorily." (According to Russian prosecutors, Yanayev was a notorious womanizer.) It took two ballots to get him elected, but Gorbachev seemed satisfied with his choice. The president did not want a strong number two, who might one day challenge him.

Shortly after 10:00 p.m. the delegation that had visited Gorbachev in

Foros burst into the room. They too had been drinking, on the plane home. Shenin and Baklanov gave their accounts of the meeting with the president, complaining that he had refused to go along with their perfectly reasonable suggestions for a state of emergency. Yanayev attempted to find out precisely what was wrong with Gorbachev but had no success.

"What's the matter with you? We're not doctors," said one of the group. "We were just told, 'He's sick.' "[83]

Realizing that the others wanted him to declare himself acting president, Yanayev began to squirm. He protested that Lukyanov, who had known Gorbachev since the university, would be a better choice. The Supreme Soviet speaker was adamantly opposed to this idea. He had come to the meeting armed with a copy of the constitution, which he had helped draft. The constitution was clear, he told Yanayev. If the president is incapacitated, for whatever reasons, the vice president must take over.

"According to the constitution, you become acting president, not me. My job is to convene the Supreme Soviet."[84]

At this point, Kryuchkov shoved a piece of paper across the table to Yanayev. It contained a single typewritten sentence:

> In connection with the inability of Gorbachev, Mikhail Sergeyevich, to fulfill his duties as President of the USSR, due to his state of health, I assume the responsibilities of President of the USSR from August 19, 1991, on the basis of article 127^7 of the Constitution of the USSR.
> USSR Vice President
> G. I. Yanayev

"Don't you understand?" said Kryuchkov, one of the few people in the room still sober. "Unless we save the harvest, there will be hunger. In a few months the people will come out onto the street. There will be civil war."[85]

"Perhaps we shouldn't say that he is ill," mused Yanayev, smoking one cigarette after another. "They might not understand us properly. There will be all sorts of speculation, talk. People will immediately want to know when he is going to get better."

"If we don't link this with Gorbachev's illness, what other basis do we have for assuming his responsibilities? Now is not the time to investigate whether or not he is ill. We have to save the country."[86]

There was silence around the table as everyone waited for the vice president to make up his mind.

"I won't sign this decree," he said finally. "I do not consider myself morally or professionally ready to assume these responsibilities."[87]

Everybody around the table attempted to calm Yanayev down. They told him that the GKChP would take care of everything. His duties would be limited to signing a few decrees. When Gorbachev's state of health improved, he would naturally resume his old duties.

"Sign, Gennady Ivanovich," said Kryuchkov softly.

Yanayev took out his pen and signed the document in a shaky hand.

MOSCOW

August 19, 1991

SHORTLY AFTER SIX THE NEXT MORNING, Yeltsin's youngest daughter, Tanya, flew into his bedroom, yelling, "Papa, get up! There's been a coup!"

"That's illegal," said Yeltsin, still half asleep. Just six weeks previously he had been sworn in as the first popularly elected president of Russia in a millennium, and his own children were already making jokes about a coup.

Tanya told her father what she had just heard on television. Gorbachev had been replaced for "reasons of health." A committee with a strange-sounding acronym had been appointed to run the country, in order to impose a state of emergency. Its members included Kryuchkov, Yazov, Yanayev. By now Yeltsin was wide-awake. His first reaction to the coup was the same as that of millions of other Soviet citizens when they heard the news that Monday morning either by switching on the television or from telephone calls from their friends.

"Are you kidding me?"[88]

Still in his nightclothes, Yeltsin dragged himself to the television set. A stern middle-aged matron was reading from a pile of decrees.

"The holding of meetings, street processions, demonstrations, and also strikes is forbidden. In the case of necessity, a curfew and military patrols will be introduced. Important government and economic installations will

be placed under guard. Decisive measures will be taken to stop the spreading of subversive rumors, actions that threaten the disruption of law and order and the creation of interethnic tension, and disobedience to the authorities responsible for implementing the state of emergency. Control will be established over the mass media. . . ."

Like most senior officials, Yeltsin had spent the weekend at his dacha in the bucolic Moscow countryside. After long negotiations with the central authorities, the Russian government had finally been allocated a complex of a dozen state dachas in the village of Arkhangelskoye, on the Moskva River, a twenty-five-minute drive from the center of the city. All of Yeltsin's key aides, including Russian Parliament Speaker Ruslan Khasbulatov and Russian Prime Minister Ivan Silayev, had weekend homes in the same compound. They began assembling at Yeltsin's dacha as soon as they heard the news.

The immediate priority was to establish how much support the coup leaders enjoyed across the country. None of the republican leaders seemed very eager to take the Russian president's call. He had just returned from an official visit to Kazakhstan and thought he had a good relationship with the Kazakh leader, Nazarbayev. The day before, they had toasted their success in persuading Gorbachev to accept a new Union Treaty. This morning, however, Nazarbayev was extremely cautious in committing himself, one way or the other.

"It is obvious that this is a coup. Gorbachev has been stripped of power by force. How do you intend to react?" Yeltsin said down the phone line to Alma-Ata.[89]

Nazarbayev replied that he did not yet have enough information to make any kind of public statement. A similar wait-and-see position was adopted by the leaders of Ukraine and Belarus when Yeltsin finally managed to get through to them.

At least the *vertushka* was still functioning. Yeltsin used it to call Yanayev but was told that the "acting president" was "resting" after working all night. He then placed a call to Gorbachev in Foros. A few minutes later the government telephone operator called back to say the call could not be put through.

The most significant call that Yeltsin made from Arkhangelskoye that morning was to the paratroop commander, General Pavel Grachev. The two men had first met just a few weeks before, during the Russian presidential election campaign. Displaying the sixth sense that was his political hallmark, Yeltsin understood that he might one day need the support of the mil-

itary. After a campaign stop in the provincial town of Tula, he had made a point of attending a paratroop training exercise nearby. Grachev had been his host. After watching paratroopers float down from the sky, the two men repaired to a hut by a lake, where they downed numerous bottles of vodka. Yeltsin went for a nude swim in the lake. As the banquet ended, officers and politicians repeatedly assured each other of their "eternal love and friendship."[90]

In his alcoholic haze, the future president of Russia had posed a crucial question to the Afghan war hero. "If our lawfully elected government in Russia were ever threatened—a terrorist act, a coup, efforts to arrest the leaders—could the military be replied upon? Could you be relied upon?"

"Yes, we could," Grachev had replied.[91]

Unbeknownst to Yeltsin, Grachev had played a key role in drafting the plans for a state of emergency. On Kryuchkov's invitation, he had joined a working group of senior KGB and Defense Ministry officials that began preparing for a crackdown as soon as Gorbachev left for Foros. The documents drawn up by Grachev and his colleagues formed the basis of the decrees issued by the GKChP that had been read over television that morning. When Yeltsin reached him on the phone, the general was supervising the deployment of tens of thousands of troops into the capital, including the Tula Division. Defense Minister Yazov had put him in charge of the military side of the coup.

The Russian president asked Grachev if he remembered the conversation they had had in Tula a few weeks previously. After a long pause Grachev replied nervously that he was duty-bound to obey the orders of his superiors. But then he added, "Wait a minute, Boris Nikolayevich, I'll send you a security detachment."[92]

Yeltsin thanked Grachev, and they said good-bye. There was something about the general's tone of voice that was encouraging. For a military officer, who knew that someone might be listening in to the telephone conversation, he had seemed sympathetic.

"Grachev's on our side," Yeltsin told his wife, Naina, as he put down the phone.

While Yeltsin was on the phone, the other Russian leaders had begun drafting an appeal to the citizens of Russia. They understood there was little point negotiating with the members of the GKChP. Their best hope was to take a firm stand on the issue of constitutional legality. There could be no compromise with the people who had overthrown the democratically elected president of the Soviet Union.

Since there was no typewriter available, Khasbulatov began writing out

the appeal by hand. "We are confronted with a right-wing, reactionary, anticonstitutional coup," the speaker wrote as the others leaned over his shoulder, making suggestions. "We urge the citizens of Russia to give a worthy answer to the putschists and demand that they return the country to normal constitutional development." When they signed their appeal, Yeltsin, Silayev, and Khasbulatov had no way of knowing if it would ever reach the outside world.

In fact distributing the appeal turned out to be an amazingly simple operation. Unlike Jaruzelski, in December 1981, Kryuchkov and his colleagues had failed to lay the proper groundwork for their coup. There was no mass roundup of the political opposition. Soviet borders with the outside world remained open. Independent radio stations were still on the air. The telephones were working. The party apparatchiks who had set up the GKChP seemed to assume that once they got rid of Gorbachev, the rest of Soviet society would fall meekly into line. They were operating according to the rules of the last Kremlin coup—against Nikita Khrushchev, in October 1964—when Moscow's control over information had been total.

The information revolution had caught up with Russia by 1991, and there were dozens of ways to get the news out. The president's daughters began by faxing it to a group of Yeltsin supporters in the nearby town of Zelenograd. Son-in-law Lyosha then sent a copy to the aerospace design office where he worked. Someone else called the White House, the headquarters of the Russian government. Within an hour Yeltsin's call for popular resistance had been photocopied, faxed, broadcast, and E-mailed all over the world. It was an impressive achievement in a land where all copy machines had been kept under lock and key up until 1989.

Yeltsin had been so preoccupied with organizing resistance to the coup that he did not have time to change out of his slippers and tennis shorts. When he decided to drive to the White House, his family helped him get dressed in his working clothes. It was then that he uttered what later became one of the catchphrases of the coup: "Can one of you women find some socks for the president of Russia?"[93]

Before leaving Arkhangelskoye, Yeltsin put on a bulletproof vest offered to him by one of his security guards. The sight of the vest, peeking out of his smart brown suit, made his family understand the risks he was running. His wife and daughters suddenly felt afraid. By now several dozen Russian security men, with assault rifles, had taken up positions around the dacha.

"What are you protecting with that bulletproof vest?" Naina wanted to know. "Your head is still unprotected. And your head is the main thing."

As the president climbed into his Zil limousine, his wife began to worry

about the tanks already reported to be heading in the direction of Moscow. Yeltsin did his best to sound confident.

"We have a little Russian flag on our car. They won't stop us."[94]

The presidential Zil hurtled along the winding country road that led from Arkhangelskoye to Moscow, followed by a cortege of Russian government vehicles. They were heading due east, and the morning sun was shining directly in their faces, making it difficult to see the road ahead. As they turned onto the Minsk highway, they overtook hundreds of tanks, armored cars, and troop trucks, crawling toward the center of town. The line of military vehicles seemed endless. The troops had been woken up at 4:30 that morning and ordered to head toward Moscow in full combat gear. Similar columns were advancing from the north and the south.

Dozens of journalists, both Soviet and Western, were already assembled at the White House. If there was going to be significant resistance to the men who had seized power from Gorbachev, this vast edifice on the left bank of the Moskva River would almost certainly be the rallying point. Designed by a committee of Soviet architects, in the worst traditions of post-Stalinist modernism, the nineteen-story building was an unlikely symbol for Russia's fledgling democracy. It was possible to get utterly lost wandering around its corridors. It was the kind of building where if you wanted to reach the cafeteria on the top floor, you first had to take an elevator to the eighth floor, go down a corridor, descend two flights of stairs, and then take another elevator. As it turned out, the maze of corridors and underground tunnels provided the defenders of the White House with the basis of an effective security system.

In his first appearance before the press Yeltsin seemed pale and shaken. He seemed overwhelmed by the magnitude of his task. None of the other republics was in a hurry to come to Russia's aid, and the sight of the firepower being brought into the city by his enemies was fresh in his mind. The situation looked hopeless. "At least fifty tanks are on their way to this building," he told journalists, after a whispered consultation with an aide. "Anybody who wants to save himself can do so."[95]

When he returned to his office, on the fifth floor of the White House, Yeltsin could see a column of tanks lined up along the embankment. A group of Muscovites had surrounded the tanks and were arguing with the crews. Nobody seemed afraid, even though radio and television were spewing out the dire warnings of the GKChP against anyone who dared resist the state of emergency. "All at once, I felt a jolt inside," he recalled later in his memoirs. "I had to be out there right away, standing with those people."[96]

A roar went up from the crowd when they spotted the towering figure of the Russian president striding purposefully down the ceremonial steps in the front of the White House. They broke into chants of "Yeltsin, Yeltsin" and "Down with the Communist Party." Surrounded by aides and security guards, Yeltsin approached Tank No. 110 of the Taman Division and posed for pictures. Television cameras whirred as he shook the hand of the tank commander. The crew seemed dazed, utterly bewildered by what was happening.

"Apparently they are not going to shoot the president of Russia just yet," Yeltsin quipped to the crowd.[97]

Friendly hands helped Yeltsin up onto the tank. A dozen security guards and Russian deputies climbed up after him. Someone held up the white, blue, and red tricolor that had been the Russian flag prior to the 1917 Bolshevik Revolution. The president stood by the gun turret and straightened himself up tall, raising his right hand for silence. He twisted his face into a defiant scowl and began to read from the "Appeal to the Citizens of Russia" that he and his colleagues had written earlier that morning.

"The use of force is absolutely unacceptable," Yeltsin boomed. "We are absolutely sure that our compatriots will not permit the tyranny and lawlessness of the putschists, who have lost all sense of shame and honor, to be confirmed. We appeal to military personnel to display their high sense of civic courage and refuse to participate in the reactionary coup."

As he stood on top of the tank, surrounded by cheering supporters, Yeltsin felt both a surge of energy and an intense sense of relief. It was like the time he had stood up in school and accused his headmistress of sadism. Everything was clear now. An intensely complicated political struggle had just been reduced to a case of us against them. *They*—the authority figures—had the guns. But *he*, Yeltsin, had a burning sense of moral conviction and political legitimacy. He also had the people on his side.

FOROS

August 19, 1991

OVERNIGHT GORBACHEV'S PRIVATE PLAYGROUND in the Crimea had been transformed into a luxurious—and very isolated—jailhouse. The president had become a prisoner of the security forces assigned to protect him. There was no way for the Gorbachev family to escape from Foros, just as there was no way for outsiders to penetrate the security fences that surrounded the compound. Fire engines had been parked across the helicopter landing pad to forestall any rescue attempt. Border guards blocked all the approach roads to Camp Dawn, the KGB code name for the dacha. The previous night Gorbachev's personal secretary had counted the lights of sixteen naval ships surrounding the bay.[98]

On the grounds of the dacha itself, a standoff had developed between two rival groups of security guards. The presidential bodyguards—with the exception of General Medvedev—had remained loyal to Gorbachev. No attempt had been made to disarm them, and they were permitted to continue protecting the president. The task of guarding the perimeter of the compound had been taken over by a fresh contingent of KGB men, who had arrived from Moscow with the conspirators. They took over control of the gates, impounded all the vehicles, and decided who would enter and leave. They also possessed the only means of communication with the outside world.

One of the first people to attempt to enter Camp Dawn after the coup was the president's senior nuclear aide, Colonel Viktor Vasilyev.[99] He had the job of taking over responsibility for the *chemodanchik* from Kirillov and escorting Gorbachev back to Moscow. Together with his two assistants, he reported to the entrance gate of Foros around eight on the morning of August 19. None of the trio had any idea what had happened in the country. There was no television and no telephone in the military rest home where they were billeted.

After examining their passes, the guard asked the nuclear aides to wait, while he phoned his superiors. A few minutes later a KGB colonel appeared and told them the passes were no longer valid. When they asked why, he suggested they listen to the radio, which was broadcasting GKChP decrees over and over again.

It took many hours for the Defense Ministry to decide what to do with Gorbachev's nuclear briefcase. They were in no particular hurry. The *chemodanchik* had ceased to be operational from the moment that communications were interrupted with Foros, at 4:32 p.m. the previous day. (The defense minister and chief of the General Staff possessed identical pieces of equipment, which they could have used in the event of a nuclear attack on the Soviet Union.) The significance of the *chemodanchik* was now symbolic, rather than practical. Without it, Gorbachev was no longer the commander in chief. This happened, without any ceremony, at 2:00 p.m. on August 19, when a jeep arrived for the nuclear aides. They flew back to Moscow that evening, aboard the presidential plane, taking the *chemodanchik* with them.

THE CONSPIRATORS HAD CUT OFF the television and radio cable to the presidential compound. Gorbachev, however, still had a little Sony transistor radio that he used to listen to the news while shaving. He spent the night fiddling with the dial, desperate for any news about the plans of the GKChP. There was nothing until shortly after six that morning, when Radio Moscow began broadcasting the announcement that Yanayev had taken over as "acting president."

Apart from his bodyguards and private secretary, the only aide that Gorbachev had taken with him to Foros was his foreign policy adviser, Anatoly Chernyayev, who had been helping him write an article outlining several scenarios for the future development of the country. These included the imposition of a state of emergency, a course Gorbachev raised only to reject. When the conspirators arrived, Chernyayev was staying in the guesthouse

behind the presidential mansion and was unable to leave the compound. He was to remain by Gorbachev's side throughout the coup.

On Monday morning Chernyayev found the president lying in bed, writing notes to himself. His back was still giving him problems, and any movement was painful for him. Together, they tried to analyze the coup's chances of success. Gorbachev was contemptuous of the putschists. He did not believe they would be able to put the economy back on its feet or restore order. In the long term they were doomed. In the short term, however, he feared that they might come out on top.

"This could end very badly," he said gloomily. "In this situation, I trust Yeltsin. He will not give in to them, he will not make any concessions. There could be bloodshed."[100]

Raisa Gorbachev put herself in charge of security. Shattered by the betrayal of Boldin and Plekhanov, she was now hypervigilant. The GKChP announcement that Gorbachev was incapable of performing his duties because of ill health terrified her. The plotters' next step, she reasoned, would be to turn her husband into a real invalid, in order to support their previous statements. Fearing a possible poisoning attempt, she kept the family from eating any food not already stocked on the premises. Her daughter, Irina, collected all the fruit in the house and hid it in a cupboard, to ensure that the children would have something to eat.[101] Convinced the entire house was bugged, Raisa insisted that confidential conversations be held out in the open.

After lunch the entire Gorbachev family plus Chernyayev took the enclosed glass escalator down to the rocky beach. While the children swam in the sea, Gorbachev and Chernyayev sat in a little changing hut, planning the president's next move. Gorbachev decided to bombard the leaders of the GKChP with constant demands, as a means of psychological pressure. Chernyayev jotted down his first orders, which he later handed to Plekhanov's deputy, the GKChP representative at Foros:

1. I demand the immediate restoration of government communications.
2. I demand the immediate dispatch of the presidential plane, so that I can return to work.

By Monday afternoon the security guards who remained loyal to Gorbachev had rigged up a makeshift television aerial. The television set was working again, in time for the GKChP press conference that evening. Like

everybody else in the country, Gorbachev was more struck by the way the coup leaders looked than by what they had to say. It was a pathetic sight. The advocates of a "firm hand" seemed terribly nervous and unsure of themselves. Yanayev was unable to keep his hands from shaking, as he promised to restore law and order in the country.

Equally revealing was the journalists' lack of respect toward the would-be saviors of the nation. After six years of glasnost, they clearly had no intention of surrendering their hard-won freedoms. "Do you realize that you have carried out a state coup?" asked a twenty-four-year-old reporter for *Nezavisimaya Gazeta*, Moscow's latest independent newspaper. "Which comparison do you find more appropriate: 1917 or 1964?" The Bolshevik coup or the removal of Khrushchev? Other reporters wanted to know if Yanayev would be seeking the advice of Chilean General Pinochet and why the Soviet people had not been told exactly what was wrong with Gorbachev.

After watching the pitiful performance of the coup leaders, Gorbachev decided to make his own appeal to the Soviet and international public. After midnight he sat down to record his message, in front of the family video camera. "Everything that has been said concerning the state of my health is false. On the basis of this lie, an anti-constitutional coup d'état has been carried out. The legitimate president of the country has been barred from carrying out his duties. . . . I am under arrest and nobody is allowed to leave the territory of the dacha. I am surrounded by troops from both the sea and the land. I don't know whether I shall succeed in getting this out, but I shall try to do everything to see that this tape reaches freedom."[102]

Gorbachev read the appeal four times in succession. His daughter, Irina, and his son-in-law, Anatoly, cut the tape into four sections. They wrapped each section separately in a tiny paper envelope and sealed it with Scotch tape. Then they began to rack their brains over how to smuggle his message out of Camp Dawn.

MOSCOW

August 20, 1991

MARSHAL DMITRI YAZOV HAD SCARCELY SLEPT in the two nights since he had ordered his troops to occupy the streets of their own capital. He was depressed and irritable. He had joined the plot against his commander in chief after becoming convinced that Gorbachev was leading the Soviet Union to disaster and destroying its armed forces. But the more he saw of his fellow conspirators, the more he wondered whether he had made the right choice. Half of them were drunkards; the other half were incompetent.[103]

The attempt to reestablish Soviet power was not going well. Moscow was buzzing with rumors that half a dozen tanks of the Taman Division had defected to the Yeltsin camp. They had been assigned to take up positions at the Kutuzov Bridge, a couple of hundred yards from the White House. After talks with Russian leaders, Major Sergei Yevdokimov had agreed to move his tanks, deploying them in a defensive position around the parliament building, with their gun turrets facing outward. There were other signs of dissent as well. A paratroop training academy in Ryazan had declared its support for Yeltsin, as had garrisons on the island of Sakhalin and the Kamchatka peninsula, eight time zones to the east. Morale among the five thousand troops now occupying the center of Moscow was reported to be poor.

"What have we got ourselves into?" muttered Yazov at a meeting of his

senior commanders, at six o'clock Tuesday morning, as he reviewed the situation in the army.

Opposition to the GKChP even extended to the defense minister's own family. His wife, Emma, had reacted to the coup with shock and dismay. Although she was recovering from a serious automobile accident, she had ordered a car to take her to the Defense Ministry, on Arbat Square, half a mile from the Kremlin. Weeping and sobbing, she had hobbled into Yazov's office in a plaster cast.

"Dima, this means civil war. You have to stop this nightmare. Call Gorbachev."[104]

Hurt by his wife's tears, Yazov explained gently that there was no way of communicating with the president. "Emma, please understand, I am alone."

As they were talking, the television in the corner of the office began broadcasting the press conference by Yanayev and the other members of the GKChP. Emma wanted to know why he was not with them. By way of reply, he waved his hand dismissively in the direction of his colleagues.

"Dima, look at who you have got involved with. You always laughed at these people. Phone Gorbachev."

The defense minister felt torn between his loyalty to the president and his loyalty to the Soviet Union, or at least his vision of it. Bluff and straightforward, he had tried to steer clear of palace intrigues. This was one reason why Gorbachev had confidence in him, despite his limited intellectual horizons and lack of a formal education. At sixty-seven he was an officer of the old school whose entire life had revolved around his military service and Communist Party membership. He had joined the army as a teenager, during World War II, and had twice been wounded at the front. Soon he would be celebrating his fifty-year jubilee with the Soviet armed forces.

Yazov could not bring himself to betray his fellow conspirators so soon after betraying Gorbachev. He ordered the military preparations for the takeover of the Russian parliament to continue.

AT THE WHITE HOUSE Yeltsin also had hardly slept the previous night. His situation looked desperate. The building was virtually undefended. Workers had practically ignored his call for an immediate general strike against the GKChP. Although there had been protest rallies here and there, most of the population seemed indifferent to what was going on in Moscow.

But the Russian president had one great advantage: He was a fighter who thrived on adversity. As both an athlete and a politician he was at his best

when he was twenty points down and struggling to remain in the game. The ability to perform almost superhuman feats, interspersed with periods of prolonged idleness, is a common Russian trait, which Yeltsin possessed to an almost exaggerated degree. His burst of political activity during the coup was in marked contrast with the strange passivity of the plotters, who virtually dropped out of sight after their disastrous press conference.

When he climbed onto the tank outside the White House, Yeltsin became the symbol of democratic opposition to the new regime. By the second day of the coup he had issued a series of presidential decrees that laid the legal and constitutional basis for defying the authority of the GKChP. In quick succession he summoned the Russian parliament into extraordinary session, issued warrants for the arrest of the coup leaders, suspended the activity of the Russian Communist Party, and named himself commander in chief of all Soviet troops on the territory of Russia. The soldiers patrolling the streets of Moscow were now faced with a choice of whom to obey: Yazov or Yeltsin.

AT NOON ON TUESDAY, AUGUST 20, Soviet security chiefs gathered in the office of the deputy defense minister, Vladislav Achalov, to discuss an attack on the White House. Most of the uniformed participants at the meeting were well acquainted with one another since they had all served in Afghanistan. The Interior Ministry forces were represented by Boris Gromov, the last commander of the Soviet Fortieth Army. Sitting next to him was the paratroop commander, Pavel Grachev. The commander of the Alpha Group, Viktor Karpukhin, was wearing his combat fatigues. Also present was Valentin Varennikov, the loudmouthed commander of Soviet land forces, who had demanded Gorbachev's resignation in Foros two days earlier.

A KGB general, Genii Ageev, opened the meeting by outlining Operation Thunder. It hinged on careful coordination among the army, the KGB, and the Interior Ministry. Grachev's paratroopers would be responsible for establishing a security perimeter with a radius of a thousand yards around the White House. They would prevent demonstrators from entering the entire area between the Moskva River and the American Embassy. Gromov's forces would then drive a wedge through the crowds of Yeltsin supporters who already surrounded the parliament. KGB troops, led by the Alpha Group, would move in behind the Interior Ministry forces and storm the building, firing grenade launchers as they went. A squadron of military helicopters would land on the building from the roof.

Once inside the White House, the Alpha Group would arrest the Russian leadership, shooting any resisters. Special ten-man units of KGB troops would comb the building for Yeltsin supporters. These units would include photographers, who had the task of taking pictures of White House defenders using firearms. The photographs would allow the GKChP to claim that the other side shot first.

Both Grachev and Gromov had grave doubts about the operation, but they kept their thoughts to themselves. Instead they raised practical objections, pointing out that they would have to bring more troops into Moscow in order to implement the plan worked out by the KGB. Grachev insisted that the participants in the meeting hear a report from his subordinate, General Aleksandr Lebed, who had just completed a reconnaissance mission around the White House.

"Big crowds are gathering," Lebed told the security chiefs. "They are erecting barricades. It will be impossible to complete this operation without significant casualties. There are many armed men inside the White House."[105]

"General, it is your duty to be an optimist," exploded Varennikov, who had been demanding Yeltsin's arrest ever since the start of the coup. "You are bringing pessimism and uncertainty into this room."

Like many other senior officers, Lebed felt confused and bewildered. For the past forty-eight hours, he had been caught up in an incomprehensible nightmare. On Monday, he had been instructed by Grachev to report to the White House and help organize the "defense and protection" of the building. Against whom was unclear: he did not hear about the formation of the GKChP until late Monday afternoon. He had negotiated with Yeltsin aides to station tanks around the building, with their gun barrels facing outwards. "In spite of all my efforts, I could not figure out what was going on," he later recalled, describing his position as "humiliating." On Tuesday morning, equally mysteriously, Grachev had instructed him to remove his tanks from the White House. "Again, I understood nothing." It seemed to Lebed that he was taking part in some "idiotic game" straight out of the theater of the absurd. Later, he would be hailed as a hero for his role in defending the White House. But, as he wrote in his memoirs, "I was following orders when I led my troops into Moscow, and I was following orders when I led them out again."[106]

DURING THE AFTERNOON rumors of Operation Thunder began to filter down to the troops who had taken up positions around the center of

Moscow. In most units the news of an imminent attack on the Russian parliament was greeted with alarm. In the day and a half since their deployment in the capital, the troops had been involved in endless debates with Muscovites about the legality of the state of emergency and the whereabouts of Gorbachev. The prospect of opening fire on their fellow Russians filled them with dread. The operation was set for 3:00 a.m. on Wednesday.

The debates were particularly lively in Manezh Square, alongside the Kremlin wall, which had been occupied the previous day by KGB *spetsnaz* units from the Moscow area. In recent months they had been training to support the Alpha Group in unspecified "antiterrorist operations." They were well motivated and combat-ready. But even they were beginning to have doubts about their latest assignment.

The operation had begun badly. Driving into central Moscow, they had been delayed by a traffic accident, involving two armored personnel carriers and a passenger car. A soldier was taken to the hospital with a concussion. By the time the armored column reached the Manezh, the entrances to the square were blocked with trolley-buses. The *spetsnaz* had pushed the trolley-buses out of the way with the help of special engineering equipment, only to be confronted with crowds of unarmed civilians. None of the soldiers in the Manezh had any training in crowd control. Clearing the square of demonstrators, without resorting to force, had occupied the rest of the day.

That night the troops had attempted to get some rest in the holds of their armored cars. But they were constantly interrupted by visits from delegations of people's deputies, representing both the Russian parliament and the Moscow City Council. The deputies distributed packages of Yeltsin decrees, appealing to the troops to ignore the orders of the GKChP and heed the authority of the Russian parliament. The *spetsnaz* officers were impressed by the red badges worn by the deputies in their lapels, a sign of their official status. Discussing the situation among themselves, they gradually reached the conclusion that Gorbachev's overthrow had been unconstitutional. The officers' uneasiness encouraged the deputies to push harder.

"Let's all go to the Kremlin right now, and settle all this with Yanayev," suggested Boris Nemtsov, a legislator from the Volga River city of Nizhni Novgorod, only half in jest.[107]

"No, boys, that's your business," replied a *spetsnaz* colonel. "But you do whatever you want. We won't stop you."

In the early evening the *spetsnaz* troops received an order to withdraw from the Manezh and return to their barracks at Teplyi Stan in southwest Moscow. They were told that they would be taking part in a "special oper-

ation" later that night. Every soldier was required to equip himself with a bulletproof vest and two clips of live ammunition. The entire division was placed on battle alert. The officers were convinced that they would soon be ordered to attack the White House. For the first time in their military careers they began to argue about whether to fulfill an order.

"I won't give an order to shoot," one company commander told his men. "Act according to your conscience."[108]

"If I am ordered to shoot, I will obey the order," said a lieutenant.

After some debate the officers reached a decision. They would halt at the first barricade, switch off their radios, and refuse to take any further part in the storming of the parliament building.

As the *spetsnaz* column pulled out of the Manezh, one of the APCs was flying the Russian tricolor rather than the red Soviet flag. Given the circumstances, it was an extraordinary act of defiance. Plainclothes KGB men accompanying the column launched an immediate inquiry and established that the flag had been raised on the orders of a platoon commander, Captain Oleg Nevzorov. They told him to take it down, adding, "We'll deal with you later."

ALL DAY LARGE CROWDS HAD BEEN GATHERING in front of the White House. Grachev used the network of Afghan war veterans to send word to Russian leaders that a decision to storm the building had been made. The best chance of avoiding such a catastrophe, he told them, would be to appeal to Muscovites to defend the building. The attacking forces would certainly be very reluctant to shoot unarmed civilians.[109]

The defenders of the White House spent the afternoon erecting barricades from pieces of scrap metal and ripped-up cobblestones. A local transportation company provided dozens of heavy vehicles, which were used to block all the approach roads to the parliament building and the bridges across the river. Soon the area around the White House resembled the scene in Tiananmen Square in 1989, shortly before the military assault. Tens of thousands of people stood in a series of circles around the building, arms linked, ready to sacrifice their lives in the event of a military assault. Many people carried pocket transistor radios, most of which were tuned to the independent Ekho Moskvy (Echo of Moscow) station, which was providing regular updates about troop movements.

A large section of the crowd was composed of young people, many of whom had shown little previous interest in politics. It had taken a coup to jolt them out of their apathy and make them realize that they had a stake in

the political future of the country. Members of the new entrepreneurial class were also well represented at the barricades. Brokers on the Moscow commodity exchange had demonstrated their support for Yeltsin by marching to the White House carrying a three-hundred-foot-long Russian tricolor.

As the brilliant sunshine of the first two days of the coup turned to a steady drizzle, the mood of the White House defenders grew steadily more bleak. Everything seemed to indicate that the final preparations for the assault were under way. At first the attack was expected in the early evening. All women were ordered to leave the building. The twenty ground-floor entrances were secured with barricades. Shortly after 6:00 p.m. deputies who had gathered in Yeltsin's office in the fifth floor began issuing panicky statements over Echo Moskvy, suggesting that Russian democracy was doomed.

"I appeal to you, my brother officers," said Aleksandr Rutskoi, the Russian vice president and a former Afghan war hero. "Think of the orders that you are being given. The interests you are defending are not those of the state, but those of the junta. Nobody will forgive you."[110]

At the peak of the tension deputies still inside the White House noticed a sudden surge of activity outside. The focal point was an elderly man with a shock of white hair attempting to force his way through the concentric lines of defenders. There was a great deal of shouting and pushing and shoving going on. Some people were urging that the man be let into the building, while others were insisting that he be kept out.

"I must see Yeltsin," the old man kept yelling above the hubbub, a look of total determination on his face.

The intruder's identity eventually became clear. It was the world-renowned musician Mstislav Rostropovich, who had been stripped of his Soviet citizenship by the Brezhnev regime in 1978 because of his friendship with Aleksandr Solzhenitsyn. Rostropovich had played his cello by the Berlin Wall in November 1989 and was determined to defend the cause of freedom in his native Russia. He had heard about the coup in Paris and had taken the first available Air France flight to Moscow. He had bluffed his way past the border guards, telling them he had come to participate in a conference of Russian compatriots that was being held in the Soviet capital. They had granted him a visa on the spot. From the airport he had taken a taxi directly to the White House. Russian deputies later joked that he was the only person to succeed in storming the building during the coup.[111]

The sight of Rostropovich pushing his way past the barricades at such a critical moment did not please all the defenders of the White House.

Nemtsov, the deputy from Nizhni Novgorod, feared that a nervous defender might be tempted to open fire. Yeltsin, however, immediately understood the symbolic value of having such a celebrated figure by his side. He permitted the sixty-four-year-old cellist to stand guard for a time outside his fifth-floor office with a borrowed AK-47 assault rifle.[112] The irrepressible Rostropovich was soon swapping Lenin jokes with his fellow defenders and insisting that everyone address him as Slava.

THE KEY ROLE IN STORMING the White House had been assigned to the Alpha Group, the crack KGB antiterrorist squad that had already performed so many sensitive operations for the Kremlin. Several dozen Alpha members had been deployed in the woods outside Yeltsin's dacha in Arkhangelskoye early on Monday morning. It would have been easy for them to have ambushed the Russian president as he drove into Moscow, but the order to move never came. Confident that he was master of the situation, Kryuchkov preferred to wait until his opponent made a false move. It was a fatal mistake. By Tuesday afternoon the price of arresting Yeltsin had risen many times.

The Alpha commander, Viktor Karpukhin, assembled his principal subordinates at 5:30 p.m., following his return from the Defense Ministry. He outlined the plan for Operation Thunder.

"Who gave this order?" asked Mikhail Golovatov, the deputy Alpha commander.

"The order is from the government."

"Is it a written order?"

"The order is from the government," Karpukhin repeated testily.[113]

Golovatov and the subcommanders understood the mood of the rank and file much better than did Karpukhin, a much-decorated Hero of the Soviet Union, who was always rushing off for talks with "the bosses." They knew that ordinary Alpha members were fed up with being used as pawns in the never-ending Kremlin chess game. The seizure of the television facilities in Vilnius eight months earlier had been the last straw. The politicians who had ordered the Alpha Group into action against a crowd of unarmed civilians had refused to assume any responsibility for the resulting bloodshed. They had even tried to disown the young Alpha lieutenant who was killed during the operation.

When one of the subcommanders described the plan to storm the White House as "senseless," Karpukhin lost his temper. He called the youthful de-

fenders of the building "suckers" who would crumble before a determined attack. He ordered his subordinates to prepare for the assault by conducting a reconnaissance of the area around the parliament building.

The reconnaissance mission only confirmed their worst fears. There were some fifty thousand people gathered around the White House, including several thousand armed defenders. Operation Thunder was feasible enough on the technical level—the Alpha subcommanders estimated that they could storm the building in fifteen to thirty minutes—but the losses, on both sides, would be enormous. It was likely that half the members of the SWAT team would be wiped out during the assault.

Golovatov, who had led the attack on the Lithuanian television facilities, conducted an informal opinion poll among his men. One by one they expressed their objections to the operation.

"We will not go to the White House to kill people," one of the men insisted.

"And we will not lead you there," replied Golovatov.[114]

INSIDE THE WHITE HOUSE the nerveracking tension was more than some of the defenders could bear. Around 8:00 p.m. Yeltsin received a call over the office intercom from the Russian prime minister, Ivan Silayev, who had conducted some of the negotiations with the GKChP. He said he had allowed his staff to leave the building and intended to go home himself. He sounded depressed and defeated.

"I want to say good-bye, Boris Nikolayevich. Tonight, everything will be over with us. This is reliable information. Let them come and get us at home. Good-bye."[115]

Soon after the prime minister's desertion Yeltsin broadcast an appeal over Echo Moskvy for as many people as possible to come to the White House: "Citizens of Russia! At this fateful hour, support those to whom you entrusted the fate of the country during the elections. The people of Russia must pool their efforts to defeat the forces of reaction. You must oppose the tanks and armored personnel carriers with the united determination not to permit dictatorship. Unity and solidarity—these are the keys to our victory ... The days of the conspirators are numbered. Law and constitutional order will triumph. Despite everything, Russia will be free!"[116]

Even though the 11:00 p.m. curfew announced by the GKChP was fast approaching, thousands of Muscovites responded to the Russian president's appeal. Earlier in the evening Dmitri Komar, who had served in Afghanistan, had told his friends that he had seen "enough fighting" for a

lifetime. After listening to Yeltsin, however, he decided to head for the barricades. The twenty-three-year-old former paratrooper asked a friend to tell his parents that he would not be home that night.

"It is my duty to be there. Tell Mama that I am spending the night with my classmates. She mustn't worry."[117]

Ilya Krichevsky, a twenty-eight-year-old architect and amateur poet, had also spent the evening listening to the reports on Ekho Moskvy. Shortly after 10:00 p.m. the phone rang. It was an old army friend, suggesting they check out the protests around the White House. They agreed to meet by the nearby Barrikadnaya metro station, so named because it had been the scene of a popular insurrection against the tsarist regime in 1905. Ilya pulled on his brown parka and the black and red cowboy boots that were the envy of all his friends. His father stopped him as he was heading for the door and asked him where he was going.

"For a stroll."

"What do you want to do that for? You just heard there is a curfew."

"I won't go far."[118]

THE PHONES WERE ALSO RINGING all evening in the offices of the so-called power ministers, the men who ran the Soviet security apparatus. The commanders of Operation Thunder were all waiting for each other to make the first move. No one wanted to be responsible for a bloodbath around the White House, but neither were they willing openly to defy the GKChP. Each, in his own way, was playing a double game.

In the late evening Grachev received a phone call from the head of the air force, Yevgeny Shaposhnikov. The air force commander had a reputation for "democratic" sympathies, and Grachev trusted him. He complained that the "riffraff" in the Kremlin wanted to use him as a scapegoat. As Shaposhnikov later remembered the conversation, the paratroop commander said he would resign or shoot himself rather than order an attack on the White House. They discussed several options, including sending paratroopers to arrest the GKChP or even bombing the Kremlin.

"No, that will lead to complete confusion, and endanger lives," said Grachev. "Let's just sit by our phones, and try to avert any stupidities."[119]

After their telephone conversation both Grachev and Shaposhnikov sent word to Yeltsin, via intermediaries, that they would not permit their men to be used in an assault on the White House.

THE FIRST SHOTS WERE FIRED shortly after midnight, half a mile from the White House, on the Garden Ring Road. A column of a dozen armored cars from the Taman Division had driven past the American Embassy and was headed toward the Foreign Ministry, skirting the area around the Russian parliament. As they approached the underpass beneath Kalinin Avenue, the soldiers in the lead APC could see a barricade in front of them. It was made of Moscow city buses, scrap metal, and concrete blocks.

As the armored column entered the tunnel, stones, bottles, and paving stones rained down from above. Hundreds of White House defenders were gathered on the ramp, leading from the Garden Ring to Kalinin Avenue. They had little doubt that the long-awaited assault on the parliament building was getting under way. Chants of "Russia, Russia" filled the air, interspersed with cries of "Fascists," "Bastards," and "Get out of here."

Inside the cabin of the lead APCs the crews were beginning to panic. The way ahead was blocked, and it was impossible to turn around. They decided to batter their way through the barricade. After rocking backward and forward and repeatedly slamming the buses, two of the APCs managed to break free, crushing the leg of a White House defender. The enraged demonstrators jumped onto the APCs that remained boxed up in the tunnel and threw tarpaulins over the visors so that the drivers could no longer see where they were going. Soldiers who stuck their heads above their hatch were forced to surrender. Others fired their weapons into the air, in an attempt to scare away their tormentors.

Four hours after responding to Yeltsin's radio appeal, Dmitri Komar found himself in the center of the action. As a teenager he had dreamed of becoming a fighter pilot. His experiences in Afghanistan—which he refused to talk about, even to his family—had turned him off a military career. But now, as the sound of gunfire echoed through the streets of Moscow, he was once again in his element.

Emboldened by the methylated spirits that he had been gulping back in the course of the evening, Komar climbed on top of APC No. 536. The rear hatch had come loose as a result of repeated collisions with the barricade, and Komar began to climb down into the cabin. The gunner thought he was attempting to take control of the APC and ordered him to get out. Komar refused. The gunner fired his automatic rifle. The shots missed Komar but caused him to lose his balance. He toppled off the vehicle and smashed his head open on the road beneath.[120]

"Fascists, murderers," screamed the crowd as it became clear that one of the White House defenders had been mortally wounded. After dragging Komar's body to the side of the road, the demonstrators surrounded the

APC and began trying to climb on it. From the rampway above, people began hurling firebombs onto the vehicle. Soon smoke filled the tiny cabin, making it difficult for the crew to breathe.

Afraid he was about to be lynched, the gunner of APC No. 536 fired a volley of shots into the air from his AK-47 assault rifle. The shots ricocheted off the half-opened hatch and hit half a dozen demonstrators. One of the demonstrators, Vladimir Usov, was hit in the head with a bullet and subsequently crushed by thirty tons of heavy armor.

Ilya Krichevsky, the amateur poet with the black and red cowboy boots, also found himself in the thick of the fighting that night. The former tank gunner had hoped to talk the troops out of joining the expected assault on the White House. After witnessing the deaths of Komar and Usov, he began throwing stones at APC No. 536. As he ran toward the vehicle, his fist thrust into the air in front of him, he was hit in the forehead by a bullet. He died instantly.

WHEN THE SHOOTING BEGAN, Yeltsin's bodyguards began to implement a secret plan to allow the Russian president to escape from the White House. They hustled him down into the basement garage and bundled him into his bulletproof Zil. The garage exited onto a side street, less than five hundred yards from the new American Embassy compound. Russian officials had already secured the agreement of American diplomats to grant the president refuge if his life was in danger.

Yeltsin sat in the limousine for several minutes, as the sound of street fighting raged aboveground. He later said that he categorically refused to leave the White House, once he understood what was happening.[121] He and his aides spent much of the rest of the night in an underground bomb shelter, behind a hermetically sealed steel door. Whether this would have saved his life in the event of an attack on the building is unclear. Russian prosecutors later learned that the KGB possessed blueprints of the labyrinth of tunnels and bunkers beneath the White House and were guarding all the exits.

ON THE OTHER SIDE of the barricades, some units had already begun to implement the initial stages of Operation Thunder. Shortly after midnight the KGB *spetsnaz* left their barracks in Teplyi Stan in full battle formation. They headed down Lenin Avenue and along the Mozhaisk Highway, on a route that led directly to the White House.

The security chiefs who had attended the noon meeting at the Defense Ministry were busy consulting with one another over the *vertushka*. Resorting to standard Soviet army tactics of prevarication and confusion, Grachev had held off sending his paratroopers to the White House, where they were meant to clear the way for the Alpha Group. When the fighting erupted outside the U.S. Embassy, Grachev called Gromov, to find out what the Interior Ministry troops were doing.

"They are standing still. And they are not going anywhere," replied the last commander of Soviet troops in Afghanistan.[122]

Grachev then received a call from Karpukhin. The Alpha commander said he was waiting, with his men, underneath a bridge on the other side of the river from the White House. (This information later turned out to be false. The Alpha Group remained in its barracks that night.) After feeling Grachev out, Karpukhin announced that his men would not be participating in the operation.

"Thank you," replied Grachev. "My men are no longer in Moscow. I am not taking another step."

AT KGB HEADQUARTERS Kryuchkov had been waiting all night for reports on the attack on the White House. Around two o'clock he received shattering news from Defense Minister Yazov. The army had decided not to participate in the operation. After hearing his subordinates describe the scene around the White House, Yazov had ordered a halt to all troop movements.

The KGB chairman asked the security chiefs to see him in his office on the fifth floor of the Lubyanka. Yazov refused to attend and sent his deputy Achalov. When Achalov entered the room, he was greeted by shouts of rage from the GKChP members, gathered around the table.

"So you chickened out?" asked Baklanov, who had led the delegation to Foros.

Quarrels broke out over who was responsible for the fiasco. KGB officials accused the military of cowardice and incompetence; Baklanov attacked Kryuchkov for failing to cut communication lines to the White House; the generals blamed the civilians. Eventually Kryuchkov bowed to military reality and told his fellow conspirators, in his soft voice, "Well, it looks as though we'll have to call the operation off."[123]

The coup had effectively collapsed.

FOROS

August 21, 1991

THERE WAS NOW ONLY ONE HOPE LEFT for the conspirators: to plead forgiveness from Gorbachev. The fact that they considered it at all was a measure of their desperation. They had locked the president up for four days, cut off his communications, and taken away his nuclear codes. But they also knew about his rivalry with Yeltsin and his penchant for endless political maneuvering. They had taken advantage of these characteristics in the past. If they could persuade Gorbachev that they had been motivated by patriotic concerns, such as a desire to save the union, there was a chance he might agree to a compromise.

In the presidential compound at Foros, Gorbachev and his family listened all day to the radio. They heard about the shooting incidents near the White House, the continued defiance of the Russian parliament, and the withdrawal of troops from the capital. It was clear that the coup was crumbling. Senior state and Communist Party officials, who had kept silent during the early stages of the coup, were going on Moscow radio to denounce the GKChP and express allegiance to the country's lawful president.

Although most of the news was encouraging, there was also cause for concern. Raisa Gorbachev was particularly alarmed when she heard, over the BBC, that Kryuchkov had agreed to allow a delegation of parliamen-

tarians to fly to Foros to confirm that the president was incapable of carrying out his duties. After three nights without sleep she concluded that the conspirators were planning to turn her husband into a real invalid, in order to justify their earlier lies.[124] In her panic she began looking for places for him to hide. She was so frightened that she suffered a mild stroke. For a few hours she was unable to talk or move her arm.

Shortly before five in the afternoon a long line of Zils and Volgas swept through the gates of Camp Dawn. The putschists—Kryuchkov, Yazov, Baklanov, Lukyanov—had flown to the Crimea in the presidential airplane. They had nearly two hours' head start on another plane carrying Russian leaders, led by Vice President Aleksandr Rutskoi and Prime Minister Silayev. They were determined to get to Gorbachev first, so that they could present him with their version of events.

As the limousines drew up to the presidential mansion, bodyguards who had remained loyal to Gorbachev leaped out of the bushes and aimed their automatic rifles at the visitors.

"Halt!"[125]

The bodyguards directed the putschists to the guesthouse, where Chernyayev had his quarters. A presidential adviser, Chernyayev ranked well below most of the visitors, who occupied high state offices. When they saw him, however, they immediately began scraping and bowing. Defeat and humiliation were etched across their faces. He looked at them stone-faced and walked away in disgust. Later Gorbachev's personal secretary, Olga Lanina, caught a glimpse of Yazov smoking and crying. She could hear the defense minister muttering to himself, "I'm a damned old fool."[126]

Gorbachev had a bodyguard tell the putschists he would not meet with any of them until his communications were restored. They replied that this would take some time.

"Tell them I am not in a hurry to go anywhere," said Gorbachev.[127]

The communications were restored at 6:38 p.m., as suddenly as they had been interrupted seventy-four hours earlier. From his second-floor study Gorbachev phoned the most important republican leaders, starting with Yeltsin. In subsequent calls he began to reassert his control over the country and his prerogatives as commander in chief. He deprived the putschists of their access to the *vertushka*, placed the Kremlin guard under his personal command, ordered the minister of aviation to allow Rutskoi's plane to land at the nearby military airfield. He then called President Bush, who was on holiday in Kennebunkport, Maine, to let him know that the coup had failed and thank him for his public expressions of support.

The Russian delegation arrived at the compound around 8:00 p.m., soon

after Gorbachev got off the phone with Bush. They were immediately shown into the presidential mansion. It was a jubilant Slavic reunion. Rutskoi and Silyayev rushed to embrace the president. There were hugs and kisses and tears all around. Everybody wanted to talk at once and relive the drama of the past three days. In the emotion of the moment both Gorbachev and the Russians forgot that they had been mortal political enemies just a few weeks before.

The Russians were flatly opposed to any meeting between Gorbachev and the "traitors," who were still in the guesthouse. The president said he would talk only to Lukyanov, his old college friend, and Vladimir Ivashko, the deputy secretary-general of the Communist Party. Both men claimed that they had had nothing to do with the GKChP and had resisted the coup, as best they could. Gorbachev listened to their explanations impatiently. "Don't hang noodles on my ears," he told the parliamentary speaker, a Russian idiom for "You don't fool me."

"Listen, Anatoly, we've known each other for forty years. You should have thrown yourself in front of the guns. You delayed convening the Supreme Soviet for almost a week. What do you mean, you did this, you did that? If you were on the side of legality and the president, you should have summoned the Supreme Soviet the very next day. That's what Yeltsin did."[128]

Overriding the objections of Raisa, who was still under the shock of the imprisonment, Rutskoi insisted that everybody return to Moscow that night. The victory over the GKChP was still tenuous and needed to be consolidated. A former Afghan war hero, he supervised all the security arrangements himself. The Gorbachev family would fly in the Russian plane, together with the Russian delegation. Kryuchkov was separated from his security guards and given a seat in the back of the plane. Yazov and the other conspirators were put in the presidential jumbo.

As the plane headed back to Moscow, everybody finally began to relax. There were toasts to the president's good health and the victory over dictatorship. "We are flying into a new era," Gorbachev announced.[129]

In the aft section of the plane Kryuchkov sat deep in thought, clutching his briefcase and staring out the porthole into the night. A Rutskoi aide and former KGB employee, General Aleksandr Sterligov, sat beside him. The KGB chief made little effort to converse although at one point he sighed that he would probably have "to resign" as a result of the events of the past few days. After landing in Moscow, he made a move to leave the plane with the presidential party.

"Wait a little bit," said Sterligov.

A few minutes later Kryuchkov again rose from his seat.

"Wait a little bit more."

There was an uncomfortable pause. "I think I understand what is happening," Kryuchkov said slowly.

"You have understood correctly."

The chairman of the KGB was charged with high treason and taken to Lefortovo Prison.[130]

MOSCOW

August 23, 1991

ALTHOUGH GORBACHEV INSISTED that he was "a different person returning to a different country," he initially failed to understand the extent of the changes that had occurred in the Soviet Union during his three-day captivity in Foros. Instead of going straight to the White House from the airport to salute the defenders of democracy, he went home to bed. At a press conference the following day he continued to insist that the Communist Party was a "progressive force" despite the treachery of its leaders. He said he personally would remain faithful to the "socialist choice."[131]

The extent to which Gorbachev had misjudged the mood of the country became clear that night when tens of thousands of anti-Communist demonstrators marched on KGB headquarters in Lubyanka Square. Chanting, "Freedom, freedom," and, "Down with the KGB," they attempted to tear down the statue of Feliks Dzerzhinsky, the founder of the secret police. In order to forestall a riot, the Moscow city authorities sent cranes to pluck "Iron Feliks" from his pedestal in the center of the square. Behind the crenellated curtains of the Lubyanka, sharpshooters stood guard, ready to resist the storming of the building, as senior KGB officials shredded documents.

By the following morning popular rage had shifted to police headquarters on Petrovka Street and the Central Committee building on Old Square.

The victorious Yeltsin camp was afraid that the street revolution was getting out of hand. Something had to be done to channel the emotions of the mob in an orderly direction and bring the revolution to an end.

At the urging of Moscow city officials, Yeltsin's chief of staff, Gennady Burbulis, dashed off a memorandum calling on Gorbachev to halt the "intensive destruction of documents" under way in the Central Committee. "An order from the general secretary is needed to temporarily suspend the activity of the C.C. building," Burbulis wrote. He then took the note to Gorbachev for approval.

"I agree," scrawled the last general secretary of the Soviet Communist Party across the top right-hand corner. "M. Gorbachev. 23 VIII 91."[132]

There was no time to type the note out properly. At police headquarters on Petrovka Street, people were already climbing the iron fence around the building. It was important to divert this crowd to Old Square, two miles across town.

"The mayor needs your help," Moscow city officials shouted into a megaphone. "Everyone to the Central Committee." A radical air force major took the microphone and urged the demonstrators to continue with the business in hand. But the opportunity to settle accounts with the hated Communist Party had the desired effect. A large section of the crowd began drifting away.[133]

Over on Old Square, meanwhile, the representatives of the Moscow City Council were wondering how to deliver Gorbachev's instruction to "suspend" the work of the Central Committee. First, they tried the ceremonial front entrance flanked by two marble columns that was traditionally reserved for members of the inner Politburo. The stone-faced KGB guards refused them admittance. Then they walked around to the back. After some heated discussion they were eventually shown up to the second-floor office of Nikolai Kruchina, the chief administrator of the Central Committee.

Kruchina rose from his desk as his uninvited visitors came through the soundproofed double doors that separated his spacious office from the anteroom for secretaries. A bearded man with a thin, youthful face shoved a crumpled piece of paper into his hand.

"You must order the immediate evacuation of the building," said the man, who introduced himself as Vassily Shakhnovsky, chief of staff to the mayor of Moscow. "Otherwise our supporters will come in and throw you out."[134]

Kruchina read the piece of paper. When he saw the signature "Gorbachev" scrawled across the top, it was as if his neat, well-ordered world had suddenly exploded.

"It cannot be done. You can't just close the entire Central Committee down like this," he said flatly, glancing at the clock on his wall, which was approaching 3:00 p.m.

"Look outside your window. There is a huge crowd out there. They will tear everyone inside here to pieces, unless you go quietly."

Kruchina went to the window that overlooked Old Square. He parted the white silk drapes and peeked out. A human chain, made up of thousands of people with linked arms, had been formed around the building. Behind them stood more people. Some waved their fists in the air; others held up placards with slogans like "Long Live Democracy," "Put the Putschists on Trial," and "Chase the Apparatchiks Out of the Central Committee." Chants of "Down with the party" filtered through the double-glazed windows. Here and there people were tearing up party membership cards.

There was a scattering of police officers in the crowd, but they seemed to be taking the side of the demonstrators. A loudspeaker had been hooked up on top of a police car and was relaying a live broadcast from the Russian parliament building. Loud cheers went up from the crowd when a legislator got up to demand the disbanding of the Communist Party as a "criminal organization."

Kruchina began to reconsider his position. With the exception of the KGB guards, he had no security forces to call on. In two hours the building would in any case start to empty for the weekend. The note signed by Gorbachev spoke only of a "temporary" suspension of Central Committee activities, not its permanent closure. If the apparatchiks refused to leave the building, they might be attacked by a vengeful crowd. He decided to allow Shakhnovsky and his colleague Yevgeny Sevastyanov to use the emergency public address system.

A secretary was summoned to lead the men from the mayor's office to another part of the labyrinthine complex, where the public address system was located. There they went through the same arguments they had already been through with Kruchina. "What do you mean, you want us to leave the building? Is there a bomb in here or something?" said Konstantin Mishin, the deputy business manager, in an attempt at a joke. The Gorbachev note shocked the former Komsomol leader. His political instinct told him to order the women Central Committee workers to leave and the male comrades to stand and fight. But here was an instruction from the man who was still the general secretary of a party run on the principle of democratic centralism: Decisions made at the top are binding on everyone lower down.

"Once the leadership had made a decision, we had to comply," Mishin said later. "In the past discipline had always been one of the principal

sources of our strength as a party. But at that moment it turned into a fatal weakness."[135]

Mishin showed the visitors how to operate the public address system. Sevastyanov, the mayor's chief of security, sat down in front of the electronic console.

"A representative of the mayor of Moscow is addressing you," he announced, speaking into the microphone. "By agreement with the president, in connection with recent events, a decision has been made to seal this building. You have one hour in which to leave. You may take your personal belongings with you, but everything else is to be left behind."

The message was repeated twice. Sevastyanov and Shakhnovsky could hear the announcement echoing around the vast complex. As they came out of the room housing the public address system, they heard the patter of feet in the corridors. The apparatchiks were already leaving the building. "Like rats leaving a sinking ship," thought Shakhnovsky, torn between disgust and jubilation.

IN MANY DEPARTMENTS frantic attempts were under way to prevent secret documents from falling into the hands of the Yeltsin camp. Valentin Falin, the secretary in charge of the International Department, gave orders for the sign on his door to be changed to read "V. I. Falin, People's Deputy of the USSR." He calculated that the democrats would think twice before violating parliamentary immunity. He told his aide Anatoly Smirnov to destroy lists of left-wing parties in the West that had received financial aid from the Kremlin. When the order to evacuate the building came over the intercom, officials in the department began to panic. Piles of documents were dumped in the shredding machine, along with large paper clips. Unable to digest the metallic paper clips, the machine ground to a halt.[136]

Around the corner at the staff canteen on Ipatyev Lane, an oppressive silence had settled over the potted plants and neatly laid tables. The guards were checking the red admittance cards for one of the best restaurants in Moscow. Waitresses in rusty-colored aprons were flitting between the tables, collecting written orders from the customers. A few apparatchiks were slurping down their last bowls of subsidized borsch. Suddenly a maître d' came rushing in. "It's all over. They're sealing the building off." The silence was broken by a lone, sullen voice: "What are you so happy about? You used to feed us; now you will feed the Americans."[137]

As the bureaucrats fretted over their fate, several dozen Moscow police-

men had entered the building to reinforce Shakhnovsky and Sevastyanov. Sevastyanov ordered them to guard the entrances. Periodically he and Shakhnovsky appeared at one of the windows on the ground floor to tell the impatient crowd what was going on.

"The activity of the Central Committee has been suspended," said Shakhnovsky, holding up the scrap of paper signed by Gorbachev to loud applause. Muscovites stared at the general secretary's signature, as if it were some magical token.

"Friends, the next act of our life will be to take the stars off the Kremlin," announced Sevastyanov. "But remember, there are provocateurs here, extremist forces. Do not give any pretext to those who would like to sow disorder here."[138]

The crowd, meanwhile, was enjoying the public humiliation of Gorbachev, relayed live by radio and television from the White House, on the other side of Moscow. This was Yeltsin's revenge for his own disgrace almost four years previously at the hands of Gorbachev and the party elite. Now it was Gorbachev who was down and Yeltsin who was extracting his pound of flesh.

The occasion itself was humiliating enough. Betrayed by his aides, the Soviet president had been saved from political and perhaps physical annihilation by Yeltsin and the Russian parliament. Now he was trying to explain to them why he had placed so much trust in leaders who were prepared to lock him up in his own dacha. The deputies jeered and booed. Gorbachev waved his right forefinger in the air, trying in vain to get them to end his torment. Then Yeltsin approached the lectern. Towering over the president, he ordered him to read the minutes of a cabinet meeting that revealed the depths of his aides' betrayal.

"Go on, read it now," Yeltsin insisted, jabbing his powerful right forefinger at Gorbachev.

Amazed at the effrontery of his former protégé, Gorbachev looked at Yeltsin for a second with hatred in his eyes. Then, realizing that he was trapped, he smiled weakly. Yeltsin turned away, unable to conceal the look of triumph on his face, shaking his head in disbelief at the turn history had taken.

A few minutes later Yeltsin invited the chamber to join him in "a little bit of relaxation," a decree suspending the activities of the Russian Communist Party. A protesting Gorbachev urged the deputies to remain "democrats to the end." He was drowned out by loud applause and stamping of feet. "The decree has been signed," the Russian president announced with a

sneer. The demonstrators ringing the Central Committee building on Old Square roared their approval.

FOR SEVEN DECADES after the 1917 Revolution the Communist Party had deliberately cultivated a sense of mystery as a key to maintaining its own power. Separated from the people they ruled by a wall of ritual, party leaders acquired an aura of omniscience and aloofness. Scarcely anything was known about their private lives or personal political views. No ordinary mortal was allowed to know how these bureaucratic supermen acquired their fine clothes, what kinds of books and films they enjoyed, or how they made a seemingly miraculous appearance on top of Lenin's tomb in Red Square on public holidays. Everything was hidden behind the veiled curtains of the Central Committee building and the limousines that swept through the silent city. As the mysteries were gradually explained, the party's grip over society was automatically undermined. Now the final curtain was ripped away, to reveal a group of frightened and rather unremarkable people, more intent on saving themselves than the regime they served.

As the apparatchiks left the Central Committee building, they passed through two lines of democrats chanting, "Shame, shame." A piercing whistling filled the air as grim-faced bureaucrats in gray suits and white shirts emerged in single file. Occasionally a Yeltsin activist would order an apparatchik to open his briefcase, to make sure that he was not smuggling any papers out of the building.

Yuri Prokofiev, the Moscow Communist Party chief, was grabbed by an angry mob when he emerged from a door next to the Central Committee cafeteria. For a few seconds it seemed as if he might be lynched. He was rescued from the crowd by several policemen and shoved into a passing taxi to a deafening chorus of jeers.

In the early seventies a network of secret tunnels had been constructed underneath Moscow for use in just such an emergency. An underground shuttle train connected the Central Committee building on Old Square, KGB headquarters, and the Kremlin; another metro line led to KGB safe houses and nuclear command posts deep in the Moscow countryside. The victorious Russian leaders were determined not to allow Communist Party officials to make use of these facilities. As soon as they had received reinforcements, Shakhnovsky and Sevastyanov posted guards at the entrances to the tunnels to prevent anyone from escaping.

An exception was made for several members of Gorbachev's personal

staff who were working in their offices inside the building at the time it was taken over. The president's foreign policy adviser, Chernyayev, refused to follow the disgraced apparatchiks out into the street. It was a question of personal dignity. Chernyayev had remained at Gorbachev's side during his imprisonment in Foros. He believed that he should be spared the whistles of a vengeful crowd. Yeltsin's men eventually relented. Chernyayev was escorted to the Kremlin via the underground tunnel.[139]

By 9:00 p.m. there was practically no one left in the massive building on Old Square. The KGB guards had been sent away. After being carried along by the tide of tumultuous events, Vassily Shakhnovsky found himself virtually alone in the silent building, which was protected by a few dozen Moscow militiamen.

The past four and a half days had been like a blur for Shakhnovsky, who had left the Communist Party at the same time as Yeltsin. He had scarcely had time to sleep, let alone think, as he rushed from one crisis to another. Now, unexpectedly, he found himself wandering around a darkened and deserted inner citadel of the worldwide Communist movement. Accompanied by the building's newly appointed commandant, Aleksandr Sokolov, he decided to tour his new domain. He checked the entrances. He looked into the storerooms, glancing over a large batch of recently imported video equipment. He poked his head into the cavernous office of the party's general secretary on the fifth floor and the Politburo conference room just down the corridor.

Then, suddenly, it hit him. Turning to Sokolov, he announced in awestruck tones: "Aleksandr Ilyich, we have just closed down the Central Committee of the Communist Party of the Soviet Union."

MOSCOW

August 24, 1991

WHILE THE VICTORS WERE CELEBRATING their triumph, the vanquished were agonizing over their defeat. On the day the Communist Party was banned, Gorbachev's military adviser, Marshal Akhromeyev, sat in his Kremlin office, pondering the collapse of the coup. Eventually he took out a pen and began to write.

First, he wrote a note to the speaker of the Soviet parliament, submitting his resignation as a people's deputy. Then he prepared an eight-hundred-word farewell address to his fellow deputies. He acknowledged supporting the putsch against his commander in chief, an action he described as a "conscious breach of my military oath." He had known nothing about the plot in advance. But he had been convinced for at least a year that the Soviet motherland was hurtling toward "destruction." He had therefore felt morally obliged to assist anyone who acted to prevent such a tragedy, even though he doubted the coup attempt would succeed. It had been impossible to stand on the sidelines at a time when the multinational state was disintegrating and the armed forces were on the verge of breakup.

"These three ideas—the state, the [Soviet] people, the armed forces—have given meaning to my life and the lives of millions of other people. It follows that my life is now losing its meaning," he wrote.[140]

The sixty-eight-year-old marshal had heard about the coup attempt

while on holiday at Sochi, on the Black Sea coast. He had immediately made arrangements to return to Moscow to offer his services to the GKChP. He had helped draw up plans for the storming of the White House and the arrest of the defiant Russian leadership, spending the night on the couch in his Kremlin office. When it became clear that the putsch was falling apart, he wrote in his diary: "Let history take note: They protested against the ruin of a great state. And let history judge who was right and who was guilty."

After writing several letters to old army friends, Akhromeyev went home to his government dacha. His wife, Tamara, was still in Sochi. But his daughters, Natasha and Tatyana, were at home, together with their children. Their father seemed nervous and preoccupied but self-controlled. For the first time since the coup he appeared eager to have a heart-to-heart conversation with them.

The family had dinner and then sat together on the veranda, eating a huge watermelon and listening to the breeze rustling through the tall fir trees. Natasha and Tatyana steered clear of the subject of Gorbachev, believing it would only upset their father. Instead they encouraged him to reminisce about his wartime exploits. He talked again about the epic siege of Leningrad, in which he had almost starved to death, shriveling to just eighty-five pounds, and the defeat of Hitler's armies at Stalingrad, which he had also witnessed.

Natasha finally asked her father about the coup. "You always said that a coup was impossible. And now it's happened, and the minister of defense even took part in it. How do you explain that?"

Akhromeyev thought a little before replying, "Even now it's impossible for me to explain it."[141]

The following morning at nine Akhromeyev left for the Kremlin in his official Volga. He seemed cheerful, promising to take his granddaughter for a walk in the garden that evening. Half an hour later Natasha called to say she would pick her mother up at the airport that afternoon.

Akhromeyev made a first, bungled attempt to kill himself a few minutes after Natasha's phone call. He tied a noose to the window frame, but the rope broke after he put his weight on it. He wrote a note at 9:45 a.m. describing what had happened. Later that morning he was seen wandering around the Kremlin corridors, apparently on his way to the canteen. At midday he called his driver at the car pool, saying he needed a car by 1:00 p.m. The driver waited and waited, but the marshal never showed up.

Shortly before 10:00 p.m. the Kremlin duty officer making his rounds of the main government building saw the door of room 19A slightly ajar. It

seemed very late for someone to be working. He pushed the door open and saw Akhromeyev's thin, wizened body slumped over a radiator beneath a window. Around the neck of the corpse was a white nylon cord, the other end of which was attached to the metal handle of the window. A wooden chair lay off to one side. The corpse was dressed in the uniform of a marshal of the Soviet Union.[142]

The investigators found half a dozen notes on Akhromeyev's desk. One envelope contained a fifty-ruble bill and a note to his aide, asking him to settle a bill at the Kremlin canteen for food and drink consumed during the coup. Another note asked his colleagues in the army to help his family with the funeral arrangements. There was a private letter for his wife. And there was a note that was apparently meant to serve as his political epitaph:

> I cannot live when my motherland is dying and everything that I ever believed in is being destroyed. My age and my previous life give me the right to leave this life. I fought to the end.
>   Sergei Akhromeyev. August 24, 1991[143]

Nikolai Kruchina returned to his office in the Central Committee on the evening of Sunday, August 25, for a meeting with the building's new administrators. He seemed calm enough as he talked about the transfer of Communist Party property to the Russian government and the social needs of a thousand or so unemployed bureaucrats. As the meeting broke up, a little after 9:00 p.m., Shakhnovsky happened to say: "And, of course, we will need to have a special discussion about the party's finances."[144]

The business manager's face went pale. "Okay, okay, let's talk about it tomorrow," he said, abruptly ending the conversation. He collected some belongings from an anteroom and departed. Shakhnovsky was left with the impression of an honest, hardworking bureaucrat who had some reason to feel ashamed. Perhaps it had something to do with the use of party money to establish covert commercial structures, he thought.

Kruchina was driven to his home on Pletnev Lane in the city center, one of several luxury apartment blocks reserved for top party officials. At around 10:30 p.m. he said good night to his wife and retired to his study, saying that he had "a little work" to do. He scribbled a couple of letters and put his affairs in order.

"My conscience is clear," he told his family, in one of the notes. "I am not a criminal. I am a coward." He underlined the word "coward."[145]

As dawn broke over Moscow, suffusing the city of gold-domed churches, crumbling tenements, and pompous "wedding cake" skyscrapers in a red

glow, he went out onto the fifth-floor balcony, climbed over the railing, and hurled himself to his death.

NEARLY SEVENTY-FOUR YEARS after seizing power in an armed insurrection, the Soviet Communist Party had ceased to exist. At the time of its demise it had fifteen million members. Not a single one of them put up any resistance. All it had taken to shut down the building that had served as the headquarters of a worldwide revolutionary movement were a dozen militiamen and several pounds of stamped paper. When the end came, the Communists were too exhausted and too dispirited to fight back.

Terminal exhaustion had set in after a period of "threescore years and ten," the biblical life span of the human organism. The Communists had exhausted the land they had ruled for nearly three-quarters of a century, a land as bountiful in many ways as North America. They had exhausted their capacity to expand the frontiers of socialism. They had exhausted their own people with unfulfilled promises of an unattainable utopia. In short, they had exhausted their own great idea, an idea that had moved millions by its grandeur and simplicity, the idea of building paradise upon this earth.

The durability of communism and the speed with which it collapsed were two sides of the same coin. There came a point at which the strengths of the system—massive repression, rigid centralization, an all-embracing ideology, the obsession with military power—turned into fatal weaknesses. By ruthlessly suppressing all manifestations of nationalism and political dissent, the Bolsheviks created the conditions for the simultaneous collapse of communism and the Soviet state. When the end came, nobody was prepared to help them.

History will identify many claimants to the title of vanquisher of communism. Pope John Paul II exposed the moral failings and political isolation of Communist leaders; Andrei Sakharov emphasized the universality of human rights at a time when most of his compatriots kept silent; Lech Wałęsa led a workers' rebellion against the workers' state; the Afghan mujahedin proved that the Red Army was not invincible; Ronald Reagan challenged Soviet leaders to an armaments race they could not possibly win; Boris Yeltsin shattered the monolithic unity of the Soviet Communist Party; Mikhail Gorbachev allowed millions of Soviet citizens to confront their tragic past.

All these contributions were significant, but none of them was decisive. Communism was not defeated by any one individual or even a combination of individuals. In the last resort communism defeated itself.

EPILOGUE

The Union of Soviet Socialist Republics is ceasing its existence.

Presidents of Russia, Ukraine, and Belarus,
December 1991

The people feel no mercy: You do good and no one thanks you.

Alexander Pushkin, *Boris Godunov*

SARAJEVO

September 22, 1991

BY THE TESTIMONY of those who knew them, Sergei Akhromeyev and Nikolai Kruchina took their own lives because they were unable to conceive
of a place for themselves in the new post-Communist order. The collapse of
the party each had served loyally for more than four decades represented the
collapse of all their beliefs. There were other such personal tragedies during
the twilight days of communism—both in the Soviet Union and in Eastern
Europe—but they were the exceptions rather than the rule. For the most
part the apparatchik class was remarkably successful in adapting to the
changing times.

The archetype of the Communist-turned-nationalist was the Serbian
president Slobodan Milošević. By the fall of 1991 he was well on the way to
achieving the goal of a Greater Serbia that he had outlined back in March,
shortly after the student riots that almost toppled him from power. Serb
separatists supported by Milošević had seized control of roughly 20 percent
of the neighboring republic of Croatia. The Yugoslav People's Army
(JNA), the largest military force in the Balkans, was rapidly turning into an
exclusively Serbian army. The Croatian town of Vukovar, on the Danube,
was under siege by a combined force of the JNA and Serbian militia. It was
at this point that Milošević turned his attention to the republic of Bosnia-

Herzegovina, where 1.5 million Serbs lived alongside 2 million Muslims and 800,000 Croats.

A patchwork quilt of different ethnic groups and religious traditions, straddling the centuries-old divide between Rome and Byzantium, Austro-Hungary and Turkey, Bosnia was Yugoslavia in miniature. It was also the proverbial Balkan tinderbox, waiting for the match that would ignite a much larger explosion. Everybody remembered how a few shots fired by a young Serb student in Sarajevo in June 1914 had ignited World War I. Three-quarters of a century later Bosnia no longer held the strategic importance it once did for the great powers. But it seemed destined to play a decisive role in the outcome of the Yugoslav civil war and the larger question of whether a "new world order" could be constructed on the rubble of communism.

Bosnia had managed to keep out of the fighting between Serbia and Croatia by acting as the honest broker in the conflict. For this political balancing act to work, the Bosnian Muslims had to be able to play the Croats off against the Serbs. If Croatia succeeded in breaking away from the Yugoslav federation, the precarious ethnic balance in Bosnia would be fatally disturbed. The republic would be faced with a terrible choice. It could declare its own independence, risking an armed revolt by Serb nationalists. Or it could remain inside a shrunken Serb-dominated Yugoslavia, a course of action that would be bitterly opposed by Croats and Muslims. For a glimpse of what life would be like in such a state, they had only to look across the border. At the same time as it was complaining about the mistreatment of Serbs by Croatia, the Milošević regime was denying elementary civic rights to the Albanian and Muslim minorities in Kosovo and Sandžak.

As Bosnia teetered on the edge, Milošević took a series of steps designed to ensure that he would be in a position to dictate the future course of events, whatever the Bosnian leadership decided. First, he established a political network in the republic, based on the nationalist Serbian Social Democratic Party (SDS), which had been the main instrument for provoking the rebellion in Serb-inhabited regions of Croatia. Next, he used his JNA connections to make sure that his Bosnian clients would enjoy an overwhelming advantage in weapons and ammunition over their future opponents. The Milošević government pursued a consistent, well-thought-out strategy of arming the Bosnian Serbs for the coming war from late 1990 onward. The code name for this strategy was RAM.

The existence of the RAM plan was first revealed by the federal prime

minister, Ante Marković, during a showdown with Milošević's supporters in September 1991.[1] At the time little was known about RAM, except for its name. But the pieces in the jigsaw puzzle gradually fell into place, as large consignments of weapons turned up at SDS branches and Serb-controlled police stations all over Bosnia. In some cases the weapons were handed over directly by the four JNA army corps stationed in Bosnia, whose commanders were all Serb. In other cases they were sent from Serbia. It later turned out that the Bosnian interior minister, a Muslim businessman named Alija Delimustafić, was partly aware of what was going on. He turned a blind eye to shipments of arms from Belgrade to Croatian Serbs, in return for drop-offs of flak jackets for his police force. Some of the weapons earmarked for the Croatian Serbs were retained by the Bosnian Serbs.[2]

In September 1991 the Serb campaign of political and military infiltration of Bosnia moved into the open. Copying the strategy of the Croatian Serbs, the Bosnian Serbs formally declared the "autonomy" of four Serb-inhabited regions, covering roughly 60 percent of the territory of Bosnia-Herzegovina. At the same time, Serbia's ally Montenegro dispatched a force of several thousand reservists to occupy strategic positions in the hills above Mostar, the capital of Herzegovina. The Muslims and Croats responded to this mini-invasion by mobilizing their own reservists, a move denounced by SDS leaders as a prelude to "civil war."[3] The JNA then mobilized its twenty thousand troops in Bosnia-Herzegovina, against the wishes of the republic's collective presidency.

There is compelling evidence that most of these developments were orchestrated from Belgrade. The SDS leader, Radovan Karadžić, was regarded as Milošević's loyal ally and client at this point. Two months previously, Milošević had urged the JNA to take up positions along the Neretva River, in support of the Serbian population in Herzegovina. The purpose of this exercise was to provide military security for "all those territories where Serbs lived" until the final breakup of Yugoslavia. In September, army leaders had finally set about implementing his plan.[4]

THE DAY AFTER the Montenegrin reservists were deployed around Mostar, I took a flight from Belgrade to Sarajevo. I was researching a series of articles about the metamorphosis of communism into nationalism: Yugoslavia seemed like a textbook study of the dangers facing the Soviet Union following the collapse of central authority. Although Western governments were doing their best to ignore the growing tensions in Bosnia, it was

already clear to anyone who followed developments in Yugoslavia that this would be the next great flash point.

The Muslim-led Bosnian government was desperate for international attention. Making as much noise as possible was its only real political weapon, given the fact that Serb nationalists already enjoyed an overwhelming advantage in firepower. Within hours of arriving in Sarajevo, I was invited to observe the work of a government commission investigating the events in Herzegovina. Soon I found myself in the back of a black Mercedes, driving through the gorges of the wild Neretva Valley, in search of the Montenegrin reservists. Sitting next to me was the head of the commission, Rusmir Mahmutcehajić, a deputy prime minister. As we drove past the scene of epic World War II battles between Tito's Communist partisans and the Germans, he gave me his interpretation of the latest developments in the republic.

"This is the final stage in Milošević's plan to create a Greater Serbia. It will be very difficult for us to avoid a war. There will be resistance—political, social, and even terrorist—from Bosnia. Milošević is like Hitler. The world must understand what will happen if he is not stopped. There will be genocide. He is a crazy man. How can we believe his assurances to us when the Albanians of Kosovo do not have any rights? He thinks we will be easy prey, but he is wrong."[5]

Following behind us was a long line of BMWs, Opels, and Mercedes, the cars of choice for senior government officials. The composition of the commission was a case study in Bosnian coalition politics. Led by Mahmutcehajić, a Muslim, it included a Serb and a Croat. The Serb representative was a deputy police minister, nominated for the post by Karadžić's SDS Party. Other than keeping an eye on everyone else, he appeared to have little interest in the work of the commission. His face wore a look of supercilious amusement. When I asked him what the commission was likely to achieve, he shrugged his shoulders and replied, "Nothing." Each member of the commission was accompanied by his own personal bodyguards, who eyed one another suspiciously. The Muslim and Croatian bodyguards were decked out in shiny suits and dark glasses; the Serbs, in Rambo-style combat fatigues. All were heavily armed.

In between listening to news bulletins from the front, Mahmutcehajić speculated on Milošević's reasons for sending the Montenegrin reservists into Herzegovina. Version one: to carve out a Serb-dominated region on the eastern bank of the Neretva. Version two: to occupy the mountainous hinterland above the medieval Adriatic city of Dubrovnik, cutting it off from

the rest of Croatia. Version three: to destabilize the sociopolitical situation in Bosnia-Herzegovina, in advance of any move by the Muslim-led government to declare independence. In view of subsequent events, all these explanations appear perfectly plausible.

As we drove on, we saw more armed men, representing a bewildering array of factions and paramilitary forces. Some saluted as we drove past. Others scowled. Finally the government motorcade pulled into a mixed Muslim and Croatian village. A crowd quickly gathered around us. "This is not a Yugoslav army; it is a Serbian army," shouted one villager. "They are behaving like beasts; they are drunkards," screamed another. "They were firing at us all night," yelled a third. "Give us weapons. Nobody is safe any longer," shouted a fourth.

"Weapons, weapons," the villagers chanted together, looking as tough and as rugged as the mountains that rose around them.

As we toured more villages on the eastern bank of the Neretva, the cause of the commotion became clearer. A long line of trucks and tourist buses had arrived from Montenegro, disgorging some three thousand disheveled reservists. Part of this ragtag army was billeted at the Mostar military airfield, but others were camped out in the open. When they were not lobbing shells into Croatian and Muslim villages, the reservists spent most of their time scouring local bars for women and shooting their guns into the air. The arrival of the reservists had seriously strained intercommunal relations in the area. Muslims and Croats viewed the newcomers as a direct threat. Serbs saw them as a potential ally in a future battle, even though they were careful not to show their satisfaction in public.

After crisscrossing the Herzegovinian countryside, we eventually came across several dozen Montenegrins lounging outside Slobo's bar in the tiny village of Potkosa. The tables were littered with empty beer bottles. The government ministers got out of their limousines. There was a clatter of safety catches being released and cartridge clips being jammed into position as the two armed groups faced each other across the remote mountain road.

"Hi, guys. Can I speak to whoever is in charge?" said the deputy prime minister, trying to be friendly.

There was no reply. The Montenegrins played with their automatic rifles. The deputy prime minister retreated.

The sun was dipping behind the starkly beautiful mountains when the motorcade moved off. Suddenly we heard the sound of shouting. Our police escort had practically run into a barricade blocking the road, half a mile up

the hill from Slobo's bar. Excited-looking soldiers waving M-76 automatic sniper rifles and Kalashnikovs appeared out of the woods on one side of the road. A row of ruined houses on the other side blocked any escape route. Each of the twenty or so cars in the motorcade was covered by an armed soldier.

"Turn your engines off. Don't move," shouted the soldiers, aiming their weapons directly at us.

Our driver reached instinctively for his German-made pistol. But he quickly understood that the situation was hopeless. We had driven into an ambush. One shot, and there would have been a bloodbath. During the moments that followed, we were left to ponder the true balance of power in Bosnia-Herzegovina. The ministers who were trapped in their Mercedes and BMWs could lay claim to the legitimacy of the ballot box, but it was the other side that possessed the guns. Furthermore, the government was itself bitterly divided over the future of the republic. The Serb members of the government commission shared the views and goals of the people who were threatening us with their guns. There was little doubt which side was better placed to win an eventual confrontation.

After about ten minutes the deputy prime minister was allowed to leave his car and approach the command post on foot. After another ten minutes of tense negotiations a JNA officer appeared and ordered us to return to Sarajevo. The gunmen disappeared back into the woods, as silently as they had emerged.

BACK IN SARAJEVO, the politicians were quarreling over the significance of the Montenegrin incursion and the prospects for avoiding all-out war. The Muslim politicians were desperate for foreign intervention. They were bombarding both the European Community and the United Nations with appeals for peacekeepers to be sent to Bosnia *before* rather than *after* real fighting broke out. Preoccupied with the disintegration of the Soviet Union and the war between Croatia and Serbia, no Western capital showed any sign of listening to these appeals.

The clandestine arming of the Serb population had presented the Muslim-led government with a terrible dilemma. Militarily it would have been prudent for it to arm its own supporters, just as the Zagreb government had done prior to the outbreak of war in Croatia. Politically, however, such a step would have provoked a final rupture with the SDS and the collapse of the multiparty coalition. Rightly or wrongly, the Bosnian president, Alija

Izetbegović, believed that the best chance for preserving peace lay in being as conciliatory as possible toward the Serb minority. For this reason, he chose the opposite path to that followed by Franjo Tuđman of Croatia. In Bosnia, unlike in Croatia, Serbs could not legitimately complain of discrimination. Attempts by Belgrade television to portray Izetbegović as a Muslim fundamentalist bent on creating an Islamic state in the heart of Europe would have been laughable had they not been so sinister.

A short man with a sad, rumpled face and a kindly smile, Izetbegović struck a tragic figure in the fall of 1991. In his doubts and well-meaning equivocations, he was more like Hamlet than the ayatollah Khomeini. He still believed that the best chance of preserving Bosnia-Herzegovina as a multiethnic community lay in preserving Yugoslavia as a federal state. As proof of his sincerity, he had gone along with JNA demands for the disbanding of territorial defense units established by Tito, on the ground that they could become the basis of rival ethnic armies. But the army had double-crossed him. Instead of remaining neutral in the conflict, it had distributed arms to Serb rebels. In what was supposed to be a training exercise, the JNA was even preparing for the coming war by digging artillery positions in the mountains above Sarajevo.[6]

As the leader of an ethnically based party, Izetbegović must bear his share of responsibility for the fratricide that tore Bosnia apart. At the time, however, his main failing appeared to be an excessive optimism and naiveté. After the European Community recognized the breakaway republics of Croatia and Slovenia in December 1991, he believed he had no choice but to take Bosnia out of a Yugoslavia that would be dominated by Milošević. But he failed to provide his own people with the means of defending themselves against the inevitable Serb onslaught. He deluded himself into thinking that war in Bosnia-Herzegovina was unlikely for the simple reason that it was too ghastly to contemplate.

"The result of a war here would be terrible," he told me in the presidency building in Sarajevo. "There would be neither victors nor vanquished. It would be a catastrophe. Every second person in the republic has a weapon, either legally or illegally. It would mean a general war in Yugoslavia. Everybody has an interest in Bosnia, and everybody would be drawn into such a war. The war would spread to Serbia, through Sandžak and Kosovo. A war in Bosnia-Herzegovina would lead to war in Europe."[7]

The headquarters of Karadžić's SDS Party was only a few hundred yards away from the president's office, but it was like entering a different world. Unlike Izetbegović, Karadžić knew exactly what he wanted and had

a clear strategy for achieving it. He made no secret of his belief that Serbs were entitled to two-thirds of Bosnia-Herzegovina—even though they accounted for only one-third of the population—and were prepared to go to war to attain their territorial goals. There could scarcely have been a greater contrast between the soft-spoken Muslim intellectual and the ranting Serb nationalist, who had previously worked as a psychiatrist for the Sarajevo football team.

The day I went to see Karadžić, Sarajevo was buzzing with reports of a fax that he had allegedly sent to SDS offices around Bosnia. A copy of the "instructions" was published by the Sarajevo newspaper *Oslobođenje*, along with an SDS statement that it was a "dirty fabrication." "In the event of resistance to the legitimate and humane demands of the Serbian people, you must be merciless," Karadžić had supposedly told his followers. "An eye for an eye, and a tooth for a tooth."[8]

Although Karadžić denied issuing such instructions, he used similar language in my presence. He interrupted our conversation several times to take telephone calls from regional SDS chiefs and discuss plans for full-scale mobilization. "The destiny of Serbia is at stake," he screamed down the phone. "This is our historic hour. We must act now."

Turning his attention to me, he laid out his own idiosyncratic version of Bosnian history. "The Muslims are trying to dominate Bosnia. They want to create an Islamic state here, but we Serbs are not going to let them. You cannot force Christians to live in a Muslim state. Look at what happened in Lebanon. The Bosnian Muslims are really Serbs who were forced to convert to Islam, when the Turks were here. They have a very high birthrate. They are waiting until they make up fifty percent of the population, and then they will proclaim their Islamic state. I don't understand why America is supporting this anti-Serb coalition."

I asked him if he would agree to some kind of loose confederation between Bosnia and Serbia, an idea then under discussion. He shook his pompadour of scruffy gray hair in a vigorous no.

"We will never agree to this. A confederation is not a stable type of state. Attempts to create a confederation can only end by war or by disintegration. Probably both. They cannot take our territory."

The kind of state Karadžić had in mind became clear when he produced a map purporting to show that many Bosnian towns with majority Muslim populations were really "Serb." This was at the height of the so-called war of the maps, when every ethnic group was making absurd territorial claims. In retrospect, however, Karadžić's map was a remarkably farsighted docu-

ment. This was more or less what Bosnia was to look like in a year's time, after hundreds of thousands of Muslims had been chased from their homes by "ethnic cleansing."

LEAVING KARADŽIĆ'S HEADQUARTERS ON that golden fall afternoon, I felt a stab of nostalgia for a city and a way of life that seemed threatened with extinction. Sarajevo, built along a narrow river valley, surrounded by high mountains, was a seductive blend of East and West, old and new. The slender minarets of dozens of mosques dotted the hillsides, next to squat Orthodox churches and solid Austro-Hungarian buildings like the post office and Bosnian presidency. The cobblestoned old town, the Baš-Čaršija, was a blaze of oriental bustle and color. Farther along the Miljačka Valley were the modern skyscrapers of the Communist era, which would have been eyesores in many other places but added to the city's eclectic charm. Full of coffeehouses and nightclubs, Sarajevo was a tolerant, hedonistic city, echoing with gaiety and laughter.

It was in Sarajevo that I had first felt the distant rumbling of the political earthquake that was to sweep away the old order. It was May 4, 1980, a Sunday. I entered the city at dusk, having just driven up from Dubrovnik, through the Neretva Valley. The traffic seemed unusually chaotic, cars rushing in all directions, ignoring the most elementary traffic regulations. When I checked into the Europa Hotel in the Baš-Čaršija, the receptionist was crying. He told me that Tito had died less than an hour before. Like many people in Sarajevo, he was terrified by the thought of what would happen to his country now that the man who had held it together for thirty-five years was gone. The television in the corner of the reception was showing old newsreel footage of Tito threatening to deliver a decisive rebuff to any invader. "In the same way we fought the Germans in the war, we were ready to fight in 1948, we are ready to fight now, and we will be ready to fight in the future too, when I am gone," the old marshal was declaring.

Bosnia had remained at peace for more than a decade after Tito's death, but its luck was now running out. The threat was coming not from without—as Tito had suggested—but from within. The legitimate government was attempting to deal with a fifth column, right in its midst, and was too weak to defend itself effectively. The Serbian nationalists in Sarajevo and Belgrade had resorted to a proven technique of aggression. As I walked away from my meeting with Karadžić, I was reminded of the situation in Czechoslovakia, prior to the Nazi takeover in 1938. By whipping up the na-

tionalist sentiment of the German population in the Sudetenland, the Nazis were able to occupy the entire country with very little resistance. The rest of the world stood by and did nothing.

It did not take a great deal of imagination to predict the fate that awaited Sarajevo in the event of war. It already had a name, Vukovar.

VUKOVAR

November 19, 1991

WHEN THE YUGOSLAV ARMY and Serb militiamen finally entered Vukovar after shelling it mercilessly for eighty-seven days, they discovered a nightmarish wasteland of death and destruction. Bullet-riddled bodies littered the rubble-strewn streets; stray dogs wandered amid the burning apartment buildings; burned-out cars and tanks lined roads strewn with land mines; survivors emerged blinking into the sunlight from their cellars and basements, crying in horror at the scene of devastation around them. Not a single wall, door, or roof seemed to have escaped the downpour of artillery shells, bombs, and bullets. Even the trees had been chopped to pieces.

Before the war began, Vukovar was a charming town on the Danube River, known for its baroque churches and large shoe factory. Now it resembled a picture of Dresden after the Allied bombing campaign. Europe had not witnessed destruction like this since the Second World War. The Serb victors spoke of "liberating" Vukovar from the Croatian "fascists," but there was precious little left to "liberate." If there was ever a case of destroying a city in order to save it, this was it.

For Croats, Vukovar had become a symbol of their determination to resist Serbian aggression. It was their Stalingrad. For weeks Radio Vukovar

had been broadcasting messages from its weak UHF transmitter: "Vuko-var is still fighting. Vukovar has not fallen." The town was defended by some fifteen hundred poorly armed policemen and volunteers. Yet for almost three months, they held out against an attacking force of some twenty thousand men, supported by tanks, artillery, and aircraft. When the JNA sent a column of tanks into the suburb of Borovo Naselje in mid-September, it was decimated by Croat militiamen, using shoulder-held grenade launchers. Unable to capture Vukovar in a ground assault, the JNA changed tactics and pulverized the town from the air with rockets, mortars, and bombs. Forced to take refuge in the basements, the townspeople drank rainwater and ate stale crusts of bread in order to survive. Many died for lack of medical care.

Atrocities were committed on both sides. Rival commanders thought nothing of executing civilians for suspected treachery or merely because of their ethnic origin. In addition to the thousands of people who lost their lives as a result of the shelling, hundreds simply disappeared. Fighting was particularly fierce around the Borovo shoe factory, on the northern ap-proaches to the town.

When the JNA and Serb militia groups closed in on Vukovar in early November, the Croat defenders fought for every house and every cellar, until they ran out of ammunition. Several hundred defenders managed to escape across the cornfields. Several hundred others surrendered to the army and were reasonably well treated. Croat fighters who were captured by Serb irregulars were often executed on the spot, sometimes in full view of the foreign journalists who had been permitted to witness the final "libera-tion" of the city.[9]

By the time their ordeal was finally over, both Serb and Croat survivors were too shell-shocked to display much relief. "My life has no meaning any-more," said Marina Rodić, a Croat woman, who lost her husband and her son during the fighting. "Nobody won in Vukovar, we all lost," said Milan Bosnić, a Serb who spent sixty-three days in a cellar.[10]

The most controversial incidents occurred at the hospital, which had taken dozens of direct hits during the course of the fighting. The basement was full of injured soldiers and civilians. On November 19 the facility was cordoned off by JNA troops and Serb paramilitaries. The United Nations peace envoy, Cyrus Vance, attempted to gain access but was rebuffed by a JNA officer, Major Veselin Slavančinin, commander of the artillery units that had flattened much of the city.[11] The major claimed that the hospital was mined, and he could not guarantee the safety of international ob-

servers. But both sides agreed that the 420 Croat patients in the hospital would be evacuated to Croatian-held territory.

The following day the Serb soldiers separated two hundred lightly wounded male patients from the other patients. "They ordered anybody who was able to walk to board the buses which were waiting at the back door of the hospital," recalled Viktor Đurisić, a severely injured Borovo factory worker. "We never saw these people again."[12]

According to eyewitness testimony compiled by United Nations experts, the prisoners were taken to a large building used as a garage for farm equipment in the nearby village of Ovčara. Here they were beaten so severely that at least two men were killed. Serb soldiers then divided them into groups of about twenty men. "One by one, each group was loaded onto a truck and driven away. At intervals of about fifteen to twenty minutes, the truck returned empty and another group was loaded onto it."[13]

Following information provided by a Croat who managed to escape from the truck, UN investigators located a mass grave at the head of a wooded ravine, five minutes down the road from Ovčara. There were hundreds of bullet holes in nearby trees and piles of spent Kalashnikov cartridges on the ground. Roman Catholic crosses and rosary beads found on several exhumed bodies indicated that the corpses were Croat rather than Serb. After examining the site, the experts concluded that the executioners had stood "on the northwest side of the grave [and shot] diagonally toward the southeast and into the trees." The forensic evidence of a massacre was buttressed by eyewitness testimony. "Since five in the afternoon to one in the morning, we were killing them in Ovčara," a Serb paramilitary was reported to have boasted, while swigging back plum brandy over breakfast. "They were begging, crying, and pleading that they had not been shooting our people."[14]

Over the next few years many more such atrocities were committed, both in Croatia and in Bosnia. Half a century after the civilized world had learned about the horrors of Auschwitz and Buchenwald and vowed, "Never again," concentration camps and torture centers were once again established on European soil. Words like "genocide" and "ethnic cleansing" once again entered the vocabulary. By the time a peace agreement was finally reached in late 1995, an estimated quarter of a million people had been killed in the former Yugoslavia, and nearly three million driven from their homes.

The destruction and killing of Vukovar were repeated, in seemingly endless variations, in Dubrovnik, Tbilisi, Sarajevo, Srebrenica, Dushanbe,

Grozny, and dozens of smaller towns and villages across the former Communist world. Vukovar was only the beginning.

WESTERN LEADERS HAD the opportunity—some would say the historical obligation—to step in before the fighting got out of hand. Yugoslavia was, in part, an American creation. President Woodrow Wilson had taken the lead in creating a kingdom of Serbs, Croats, and Slovenes at the Paris Peace Conference in 1919, from the rubble of the Ottoman and Austro-Hungarian empires. After World War II the country had been a key element in the East-West balancing act. The United States extended informal security guarantees to Yugoslavia to forestall a Soviet invasion after Tito had broken away from Moscow in 1948. U.S. officials visiting Belgrade never missed the opportunity to voice support for the country's "independence, nonalignment, and territorial integrity."

It had been clear for some time that Yugoslavia was headed for a violent breakup. In October 1990 the Central Intelligence Agency issued a confidential report predicting that the country would fall apart within eighteen months. The CIA believed there was a "high probability" that the policies of nationalist brinkmanship pursued by Milošević and Tuđman would plunge the country into civil war.[15]

Instead of acting on these warnings, the Bush administration treated the crisis as a primarily European matter. For most of 1991 President Bush and Secretary of State James A. Baker III had been preoccupied by the Gulf War and the disintegration of the Soviet Union. Accustomed to the geostrategic certainties of the Cold War, they linked the U.S. national interest in Europe almost exclusively to the containment of communism. The Western failure in Yugoslavia was a failure, above all, of political imagination. The collapse of Communist regimes in Eastern Europe had produced a state of false euphoria in Western capitals. There was boastful talk about a "new world order" and "the end of history." Seduced by their own rhetoric, American policy makers failed to see that nationalism was replacing communism as the principal threat facing the Western democracies and that Yugoslavia would be the first real battleground of the post-Communist era.

Far from coming to an end, history was just getting started again, after a forced hiatus of many decades. The Yugoslav crisis was emblematic of the kind of challenge that would soon become characteristic of the new epoch. Other Miloševićs and Tuđmans were springing up all over the former Communist world. The Cold War was giving way to a new kind of ideological struggle. On one side were those who believed in the American ideal of a

pluralistic democracy, based on free markets, free institutions, and free speech. On the other were those who had a political and economic interest in erecting barriers to the free exchange of people, goods, and ideas. By whipping up ethnic hatreds that had lain dormant for decades, the Communists-turned-nationalists were able to perpetuate their own power.

Like communism, nationalism had a natural ability to reproduce itself, until checked by a superior force or brought down by its internal contradictions. It thrived in conditions of economic chaos, offering ready-made scapegoats and ostensibly painless solutions to deep-seated problems. By the end of 1991 the virus of nationalism had spread to large parts of Eastern Europe, casting a shadow over the democratic achievements of the previous two years. The visitor had the impression of traveling back in a time machine to 1945 or 1917. Flags, national symbols, political parties, even street names had been revived—all as they had been before the Communists came to power. It was as if the region had suddenly woken up from a long political hibernation.

In some countries the virus of nationalism assumed a relatively benign form. One such case was Czechoslovakia, where Czechs and Slovaks were able to work out a reasonably amicable divorce. In many other places, however, it was a recipe for fratricidal war. By the fall of 1991 the seeds of future disaster had already been sown in the former Soviet republics of Georgia, Tajikistan, Azerbaijan, and Moldova. In the Caucasus a retired Soviet air force general named Dzokhar Dudayev was busy forming his own sixty-thousand-strong army. Within weeks he was to declare himself president of Chechnya, a country that few Westerners even knew existed.

There was a limit, of course, to what Western governments could do to contain the nationalist genie. America had never shown any interest in the Caucasus. Yugoslavia, however, was another matter. The country straddled a centuries-old geopolitical fault line between Byzantium and Rome, Islam and Christianity, East and West. The United States had already been dragged into two world wars sparked off by conflicts in Eastern Europe. During the Cold War successive American presidents had made clear that they would react vigorously to Soviet aggression in Yugoslavia. If the West was prepared to stand up to the newly resurgent forces of nationalism, then surely this was the place.

The first and best opportunity for drawing the line occurred during the winter of 1990 to 1991, when it became clear that Yugoslavia was hurtling toward disintegration. Senior Bush administration officials later expressed regret that they failed to intervene decisively at this point.[16] One possible course of action would have been for the United States to have convened a

pan-European congress to devise and impose a set of ground rules for Yugoslavia's breakup, including guarantees for the protection of ethnic minorities. Without strong American leadership, the Europeans were unable to reach a common approach. The Germans had political, historical, and economic ties to Croatia and Slovenia, which were part of the old Austro-Hungarian Empire. Britain and France, by contrast, had historical ties to Serbia. The divisions between Western governments sent a series of confusing signals to Yugoslav leaders.

The next opportunity for decisive action came in the fall of 1991, when the JNA was laying siege to the towns of Vukovar and Dubrovnik. Dubrovnik, in particular, could have been easily defended by NATO ships patrolling the Adriatic. An architectural jewel on Croatia's Dalmatian coast, it had a six-hundred-year history of resisting foreign invaders. In October 1991 Serb gunners in the mountains above Dubrovnik began raining shells and wire-guided rockets down on the walled city. The NATO supreme commander, General John Galvin, later told Congress that his warships would have had little difficulty taking out the Serb artillery. "We could have sent the U.S. Sixth Fleet . . . into the Adriatic, and with very little military action, we could have shown the determination of Western nations that this did not get out of hand," he testified.[17]

Another opportunity to prevent the war from spreading occurred several weeks later, when Bosnian leaders begged Western governments to send a few hundred peacekeepers to prevent the war between Serbia and Croatia from engulfing their republic. Although U.S. officials listened sympathetically to the pleas of Bosnian President Alija Izetbegović, they did nothing. The United States was not prepared to act unilaterally. The United Nations took the view that Bosnia was still at peace and therefore not in need of peacekeepers. United Nations envoy Cyrus Vance believed it would be "premature" to send peacekeepers to Bosnia.[18] Instead the United Nations imposed an arms embargo against all six former Yugoslav republics, a course of action that directly benefited the Serbs, already armed to the teeth.

During 1991 the Bush administration made only one serious effort to prevent the coming catastrophe in Yugoslavia, and it ended in disaster. On June 21 Baker made a one-day visit to Belgrade to urge the squabbling Yugoslav politicians to resolve their differences peacefully. He used the occasion to warn Yugoslav leaders of the "dangers of disintegration" and announce that Washington would not recognize any republic that attempted to secede from the federation. Within five days of his departure both Croatia and Slovenia had declared independence. Although Baker spoke out against the use of force by the federal government, Milošević interpreted his

endorsement of a united Yugoslavia as a green light for sending in the army to crush the secessionist movements. He issued secret orders to the Yugoslav army to defend Serb-occupied territories in both Croatia and Bosnia.[19]

The failed attempt at diplomacy left Baker deeply discouraged. He returned to Washington convinced that the United States "did not have a dog in that fight," as he later put it. After listening to the leaders of Serbia, Croatia, and Bosnia, he complained that it was difficult to get past the fifteenth century. His assessment was shared by the president, who, like many people in Washington, had trouble sorting out the bewildering complexity of Balkan politics. Bush would listen to his foreign policy experts with a distracted expression on his face and then remark, "Tell me again what this is all about."[20]

The lack of interest on the part of Bush and Baker meant that Yugoslavia was a low priority for the administration. Responsibility for handling the crisis was shifted to Deputy Secretary of State Lawrence Eagleburger and National Security Adviser Brent Scowcroft, who had the reputation of being "Balkan experts," having served in the U.S. Embassy in Belgrade. Supported by the Pentagon, both men concluded that American interests were best served by keeping out of what was essentially a European crisis. "The Europeans kept on telling us that this was a problem on their own doorstep, and they would like to take the lead," Scowcroft said later. "We were happy to let them do so."[21]

The State Department did its best to distance itself from the crisis. In October, the Yugoslav ambassador to Washington had a long talk with Eagleburger about the "new mood of isolationism" in America. Reporting back to Belgrade, he quoted Eagleburger as saying that the end of the Cold War had greatly reduced Yugoslavia's strategic importance. The United States no longer felt any need to engage itself vigorously in places like Yugoslavia as a counterweight to Soviet expansionism.[22]

Yugoslav leaders observed the disarray in Western capitals and drew the appropriate conclusions. It was clear that the West, led by the United States, lacked the stomach to get involved in a Balkan imbroglio. In the spring of 1991 Milošević had sent the Yugoslav defense minister on a secret mission to Moscow to find out whether the Soviet Union would help Yugoslavia resist a Western military intervention. The Russians replied that the question did not arise. According to their intelligence sources, the West had absolutely no intention of intervening in Yugoslavia whatever the circumstances.[23]

The Serbian leaders knew that they could act with virtual impunity.

BYELOVEZHSKY FOREST

December 8, 1991

THE SNOW WAS FALLING lightly when the leaders of Russia, Ukraine, and Belarus reached Brezhnev's old hunting lodge in the Belorussian forest. It was a perfect winter day: The air was cold and crisp. The president of Belarus, Stanislav Shushkevich, sought to play the genial host by suggesting a walk through the pine trees or even a spot of hunting, but no one took up his offer. The other leaders were much too nervous and excited to think of recreation. They had gathered at this out-of-the-way hunting lodge to bury the Soviet Union.

Close to the Polish border, the Byelovezhsky nature reserve was a perfect spot for a secret assignation. The nearest city of any size, Brest-Litovsk, was fifty miles away. The hunting lodge was guarded by special troops, who had sealed off all the approach roads. The press corps had been left behind in Minsk, the capital of Belarus. Gorbachev was spending the weekend at his dacha outside Moscow, fretting that the leaders of the three Slavic republics had left him out of their discussions. Neither he nor anybody else in Moscow had any inkling of the events taking place deep in the forest.

By the time the republican leaders gathered in Byelovezhsky Forest, the power of the central government had diminished dramatically. Scarcely a day went by without news of some fresh snub to Gorbachev. In early No-

vember the Soviet president flew to Madrid to meet his friend George Bush; he returned home to discover that no fewer than seventy federal ministries had been abolished by the republics. Without consulting Gorbachev, the Russian government under Boris Yeltsin had decided to stop paying taxes to the central treasury and take control of oil and gas deposits on Russian territory. By late November some commentators were already comparing Gorbachev's power with that of the queen of England.

But the most serious blows to Gorbachev's authority were still to come. On December 1 presidential elections were held in Ukraine, the Soviet Union's second most populous and powerful republic after Russia, together with a referendum on independence. Ukrainians voted in favor of independence by a margin of nearly nine to one. They chose a former Communist ideologist, Leonid Kravchuk, as Ukraine's first president. Eager to establish his nationalist credentials, he announced that he saw no future for the Soviet Union. "Gorbachev's ability to interfere after the referendum will be reduced to zero," he told reporters as he cast his ballot. "You can't oppose a movement of millions of people."[24]

When they met in the Kremlin several days later, Yeltsin told Gorbachev that he could not imagine a new union without fifty-three million Ukrainians. "If things don't work out, we will have to think of other variants," he added enigmatically.[25] Gorbachev interpreted this to mean that Yeltsin would put pressure on Kravchuk to reach a compromise. The Siberian, however, had a different solution in mind.

Yeltsin and his advisers had been thinking about doing away with the Soviet Union for some months. The defeat of the August coup had completely altered the balance of power between Russia and the center. Gorbachev could do nothing without Yeltsin's consent. Even so, Yeltsin knew that he would not be complete master of his own house as long as the Soviet president was around. He was contemptuous of Gorbachev's endless political maneuverings which, he believed, had brought the country to the brink of civil war. And he could never forget the political humiliation that he had suffered in 1987, when Gorbachev had hauled him out of a hospital bed to face his vengeful Communist Party accusers. He had suffered debilitating bouts of depression, insomnia, and a nervous breakdown because of Gorbachev. The time had come to even the score.

It took twenty-four hours to draw up the Soviet Union's death sentence and prepare the birth certificate for the new Commonwealth of Independent States. Aides to the three leaders stayed up all night, working on the text of a joint statement. The extreme secrecy and haste surrounding the

meeting greatly complicated this task. There were no photocopy machines in the hunting lodge. When officials wanted to make copies of the documents, dissolving the Soviet Union, they had to feed them through a pair of linked fax machines. Only two typists were on hand to prepare the documents in three languages.[26]

By the afternoon of December 8 everything was ready. One by one, Yeltsin, Kravchuk, and Shushkevich signed a joint communiqué declaring that "the Union of Soviet Socialist Republics is ceasing its existence as a subject of international law and a geopolitical reality." They also laid claim to the nuclear warheads stationed on their territories.

All that remained now was to inform the rest of the world. The sequence of telephone calls made by the Byelovezhsky conspirators was indicative of their priorities. At the top of their list was Nursultan Nazarbayev, the president of Kazakhstan, the only non-Slavic republic to possess nuclear weapons. At that moment Nazarbayev was in the air, en route to Moscow. Yeltsin attempted to contact the plane, hoping to persuade Nazarbayev to fly to Belarus directly. But Soviet air traffic control refused to put the call through, and Nazarbayev remained out of contact until his plane landed at the Moscow airport. Angry that his Slavic colleagues had failed to consult with him earlier, he refused for several days to sign the communiqué dissolving the Soviet Union.

Next on the list was President Bush. If the Byelovezhsky agreements went into effect, twelve new countries would emerge from the rubble of the Soviet Union. (The three Baltic states had succeeded in establishing their independence immediately after the coup.) Swift international recognition was essential to the success of this operation. Otherwise, bickering and territorial disputes might break out among the former Soviet republics, raising the prospect of a replay of the Yugoslav tragedy on a much larger stage.

The simplest way of reaching the American president would have been via the Soviet government communications network, the *vertushka*, which was still under Gorbachev's control. Suspicious of his rival, Yeltsin decided to place the call through a regular telephone operator. A few minutes later, the operator called back in a panic: She could not make herself understood by the White House switchboard. The Russian foreign minister, Andrei Kozyrev, a fluent English speaker, got on the phone. He had to explain patiently to the White House operator exactly who Boris Yeltsin was and why it was so important that he be permitted to speak to the president.[27]

Calls were also put through to the Soviet and Russian defense ministers, to tell them what had happened. It was only after all these calls that the con-

spirators got around to informing Gorbachev about the disappearance of his country and, by logical extension, his job. This time the call was made by the president of Belarus, the junior member of the troika. The other two leaders listened in to the conversation on extensions. They knew only too well what Gorbachev's reaction was likely to be.

By the time Shushkevich finally reached him, the Soviet president was fuming. He had spent the last few hours frantically calling his aides and trying to find out what was going on in the Byelovezhsky Forest. Nobody seemed to know anything. He felt almost as impotent as he had back in August, when his communications were taken away from him altogether. He told reporters later that he was "stunned" that Yeltsin did not have the decency to call him personally.

"Why is it you who called me?" Gorbachev demanded after Shushkevich filled him in on the agreement. "You mean you have already decided everything?"

When the soft-spoken Shushkevich confessed that not only had the agreement been signed but that Bush had already been informed, Gorbachev exploded. "This is a disgrace. You've been speaking with the president of the United States, and you failed to speak with the president of your *own* country? This is shameful."[28]

MOSCOW

December 25, 1991

WHEN YELTSIN RETURNED to Moscow, he hesitated about going to the Kremlin to inform the Soviet president officially that he had lost both his job and his country. There were rumors that the Alpha Group had been placed on alert and was preparing to arrest "the Byelovezhsky troika" for the attempted overthrow of the state. Speaking by phone to Gorbachev, Yeltsin suggested that he might be taken prisoner if he ventured into the massive red-brick fortress.

"What's the matter with you?" asked Gorbachev incredulously, still employing the familiar *ty* form of address used for subordinates. "Have you gone out of your mind?"[29]

Yeltsin need not have worried. Gorbachev was furious at the leaders of the three Slavic republics, but he had no intention of using force to remain in power. The failure to conclude a new Union Treaty represented the collapse of everything he had been trying to achieve for the last nine months. He regarded the dissolution of the Soviet Union as a political and economic disaster that could only lead to more pain and turmoil. In the end, however, it was up to ordinary Soviet citizens to accept or reject the Byelovezhsky agreements.

"I will respect the choice made by the representative organs of the people," he told an interviewer. "Let the people themselves decide."[30]

Gorbachev had begun perestroika by attempting to involve ordinary people in decisions previously made by a closed circle of Kremlin leaders. After unleashing the unpredictable force of public opinion, he had gradually lost control over his own revolution. It had taken him places he had never intended to go, and now it threatened to devour him completely. But the successor to Lenin, Stalin, Khrushchev, and Brezhnev remained true to the political choice that he had made when he launched perestroika. Unlike his predecessors, he would not resort to force to impose his will.

Over the next two weeks Gorbachev did everything he could to mobilize public opinion against the dissolution of the once-mighty Soviet super-power. He issued appeals, made statements, gave interviews. He tried to persuade the parliaments of individual Soviet republics to reject the decisions that had been taken in their name. He met with military leaders, newspaper editors, Nobel laureates. None of this activity had the slightest effect. Exhausted by the endless political debates and their own rapidly deteriorating living standards, the *narod* had lost interest in what the tsar had to say.

THERE WAS STILL SOME UNFINISHED BUSINESS to take care of before Gorbachev could lay down his burden. On December 23 he finally had a nine-hour meeting in the Kremlin with Yeltsin, his political nemesis. The two leaders discussed the transfer of the nuclear *chemodanchik* and a suitable presidential pension. (It was decided that Gorbachev would receive the ruble equivalent of forty dollars a month, plus a limousine and half a dozen bodyguards.) Gorbachev then summoned his aide Yakovlev to witness the formal handing over of the Kremlin secrets to Yeltsin.

Together, the three men ripped open the buff manila envelopes containing the evidence of Stalin's most terrible crimes. They examined the map of Europe drawn up by Molotov and Ribbentrop in August 1939, carving up Poland and the Baltic states between the Nazis and the Communists. They pored over Stalin's instructions to the NKVD to exterminate the cream of the Polish officer corps, interned at Katyn. Yakovlev, in particular, was shocked by the contents of the presidential archive, the *osobaya papka*. As the head of an official commission investigating the Stalinist era he had been looking for these documents for years, but Gorbachev had always assured him that they could not be found.

"How can this be?" he asked Gorbachev.[31]

The president claimed that he had only just found out about the damning documents from the archivists, who had gone through the *osobaya papka* prior to the transfer of power to Yeltsin. Yakovlev looked at his old

friend in amazement and disbelief. Yeltsin squirreled the incident away in his unforgiving memory. It would come in handy later, when he needed ammunition to use against the father of glasnost.

Gorbachev knew that he could expect little sympathy from Yeltsin. But he was taken aback by the abrupt change in the attitude of once-fawning bureaucrats and security personnel. As it became clear that he was on the way out, they seemed to go out of their way to slight him. Russian security guards instructed Raisa to clear the family's personal effects out of the presidential dacha. By the end of his rule Gorbachev's writ did not even extend to the sixty-nine acres of the Kremlin. It was all part of the time-honored Russian tradition of kicking a fallen leader.

Shortly after 5:00 p.m. on December 25 Gorbachev put through a call to President Bush, who was spending Christmas at Camp David. He struck a statesmanlike tone for his final telephone conversation with the leader of the rival superpower. He assured the president that there was no need to worry about the security of the Soviet nuclear arsenals and asked him to do what he could to support the new Confederation of Independent States, particularly Russia. Bush told Gorbachev that what they had achieved together "will go down in history."[32]

Gorbachev spent his last hour in power in his office on the third floor of the Kremlin, next door to the Politburo conference hall. His aides guessed that the president did not want to be left alone with the nuclear button and his resignation statement. So they kept him company, reminiscing about his years as a regional Communist Party boss in Stavropol. A few minutes before 7:00 p.m. he walked into an anteroom where a television studio had been set up. There were close to a dozen people in the room, including executives from Soviet television and CNN, which was broadcasting the speech to 153 countries around the world.

There was a brief discussion between his aides over whether he should sign the decree giving up his duties as commander in chief before or after the resignation statement. Gorbachev interrupted the argument to ask his press secretary for a pen. He tried it out on a blank sheet of paper. "I need something softer," he complained. A CNN representative took out his pen and handed it to Gorbachev, who signed the piece of paper on the spot.

At precisely 7:00 p.m., he began to address the 280 million citizens of the Soviet Union. Reading from a prepared text in a pale green binder, he tried to explain to the *narod* one last time why he had launched perestroika in the first place. He told them the Soviet Union had been lagging behind Western countries despite the abundance of land, oil, and natural resources. He said

he was proud of his role in ending the Cold War and helping Soviet citizens regain their freedom. Toward the end of his ten-minute speech he put particular emphasis on a few sentences he had written himself and inserted into the text at the last moment:[33] "It is vitally important to preserve the democratic achievements of the last few years. They have been paid for through the suffering of our entire history, our tragic experience. They must not be given up, under any circumstances or under any pretext. Otherwise all our hopes for a better future will be dashed."

Less than half an hour after Gorbachev finished speaking, at 7:35 p.m., the red Soviet flag was hauled down from the Kremlin for the last time. Moments later the white, red, and blue tricolor of Yeltsin's Russia rose in its place. There was some scattered applause, and a few whistles, from the handful of tourists gathered in Red Square. A light snow was falling.

Seventy-four years after the storming of the Winter Palace in St. Petersburg, the Soviet Union had ceased to exist.

OF ALL THE OUTSTANDING LEADERS of the twentieth century—Lenin, Mao, Stalin, Hitler, Roosevelt, Churchill—the last general secretary of the Soviet Communist Party was surely the most contradictory. His name will be associated with epoch-making developments that were the very opposite of his original intention. He was the Communist who dismantled communism, the reformer who was overtaken by his own reforms, the emperor who allowed the world's last great multinational empire to break apart. He wanted to lead the Soviet Union into the information age but was destined to preside over its downfall. He launched a revolution and ended up becoming one of its victims.

Gorbachev's most important contribution lay not so much in what he *did*, as in what he *permitted* to happen, almost in spite of himself. If Ronald Reagan was the Great Communicator, Gorbachev was the Great Facilitator. In contrast with the early Bolsheviks, who set out to create utopia by force, Gorbachev permitted history to resume its natural course. He sought not to change the course of history but to swim in its tide. Even after it had become clear where his revolution was leading, he did not draw back from the consequences of his own actions.

Gorbachev's mistakes, like his political vision, were mistakes on the grand scale. He clung to the illusion that the Communist Party was capable of reforming itself long after it had been hopelessly discredited. An enthusiastic proponent of elections for other people, he never submitted his own

record to the judgment of the voters. A decisive moment occurred in 1989, when he rejected the idea of a direct election and allowed himself to be nominated for a bloc of uncontested seats in the new Soviet parliament. Up until that point he could probably have won a popular mandate— the economy had not yet started to unravel, and his prestige was still high— but he chose to show solidarity with his Politburo colleagues. His loyalty to the party cost him dearly during the final showdown with Yeltsin, when he found himself without a reliable political weapon. He renounced the use of the machine gun but failed to secure the legitimacy of the ballot box. He was never able to answer satisfactorily Andrei Sakharov's question at the first Congress of People's Deputies: "Whose side are you on, Mikhail Sergeyevich?"

The other major failure was his handling of the economy. Gorbachev did more to hasten the end of the "evil empire" through his muddled economic policies than anything Reagan could possibly have devised. The deficit in the state budget had risen from just over 3 percent when Gorbachev came to power to a staggering 30 to 50 percent by the time he stepped down. Things started going wrong almost from the moment he arrived in office. The disastrous antialcohol campaign of 1986–87 eliminated the single most effective source of government revenue. In order to plug the deficit, government presses worked overtime, churning out increasingly worthless paper rubles. Gorbachev compounded his mistake by refusing to liberalize prices, a course of action that led to chronic shortages of both consumer goods and industrial components. This was the beginning of one of the most catastrophic economic slides ever experienced by an industrialized society.

These were monumental errors, but they served a historical purpose. The transition from communism to capitalism was never going to be smooth. The totalitarian order established by Lenin and Stalin was so formidable and so deeply rooted in the Soviet psyche that it could not be demolished head-on. To remain in power and continue his reforms, Gorbachev had to proceed by stealth. This master of Kremlin intrigue bobbed and weaved among the rival factions, hiding his true intentions beneath a fog of Communist rhetoric. Duplicity and obfuscation were his required talents; political survival was the supreme imperative. Had he been clearer about his goals, it is likely that his Politburo colleagues would have attempted to get rid of him much earlier. By the time they finally understood what was happening, it was too late. The party had been destroyed from within.

The Soviet Communist Party was prepared to fight to remain in power as long as this was a serious option. The repressive power of the totalitar-

ian state meant that domestic rebellions could be ruthlessly crushed. From the moment such a state possessed nuclear weapons, it became invulnerable to foreign invasion. The only way out, therefore, was death by economic exhaustion.

The irony is that the last general secretary had to fail in order to succeed in the larger historical mission of vanquishing communism. Gorbachev came to power promising to reverse several decades of Soviet economic decline and revitalize the Marxist-Leninist idea. Had he succeeded, the system would have received a new or at least a temporary lease on life. There would have been less pressure for significant political reform. The deepening economic crisis made the transition to democracy possible but also fraught with danger because it left many people yearning for the security of the authoritarian past.

In the long run the collapse of Soviet communism was inevitable, for the simple reason that it was too top-heavy a structure to bear its own weight. But there was nothing inevitable about the timing of the collapse or the manner in which it occurred. History will record that it was Gorbachev who set in motion the chain of events that led to the disintegration of the world's first socialist state. Through a strange amalgam of genius and incompetence, idealism and egotism, naiveté and cunning, the onetime peasant boy from Privolnoye dealt a fatal blow to the most durable dictatorship humankind has ever known.

By seeking to reinvigorate the Communist system, Gorbachev succeeded in destroying it.

GLOSSARY

NOTES ON SOURCES

NOTES

BIBLIOGRAPHY

INDEX

GLOSSARY

OF FOREIGN TERMS

KOR Workers' Defense Committee (human rights group)

MKS Interfactory Strike Committee

PZPR Polish United Workers' Party (Communist Party)

Solidarity Solidarity trade union

stan wojenny martial law (literally warlike state)

szlachta petty nobility

vojvodship province

ZOMO riot police

Alpha Group elite KGB antiterrorist squad

apparat bureaucratic machine

apparatchik bureaucrat

Central Committee policy-making body of CPSU

chemodanchik little suitcase (nuclear codes)

CPSU Communist Party of the Soviet Union

dacha country house

gensek general secretary of CPSU

GKChP Committee for the State of Emergency (formed during August 1991 coup attempt)

glasnost openness

Gosplan State Planning Agency

Gosstroi State Construction Agency

KGB Committee for State Security (secret police), successor to Lenin's Cheka and Stalin's NKVD

455

kolkhoz   collective farm

kolkhoznik   collective farm worker

kremlin   a fortified place

kulak   landed farmer (prior to collectivization)

Lubyanka   headquarters of KGB

muzhik   peasant

narod   people, the masses

nomenklatura   roster of officials nominated by Communist Party

osobaya papka   special file, top secret Communist Party documents

perestroika   restructuring

plenum   full Central Committee meeting

Politburo   executive leadership of CPSU Central Committee (composed of full and alternate members)

PVO   Antiaircraft defense

shestidesyatniki   men of the sixties, the generation that matured under Khrushchev

spetsnaz   KGB "special assignment" troops

stagnation   term applied to Brezhnev era

Staraya Ploshchad   old square headquarters of Communist Party

terror   term applied to Stalin's rule

thaw   term applied to period of political liberalization under Khrushchev

vertushka   Soviet government communications system

Volga   car used by mid-level officials

Vremya   television news

White House   headquarters of Russian government

Zhiguli   popular compact car

Zil   limousine used by senior party officials

SERBO-CROAT

chetnik   Serbian nationalist (World War II term)

HDZ   Croatian Democratic Union (governing party in Croatia)

JNA   Yugoslav People's Army

SDS   Serbian Social Democratic Party of Bosnia (led by Radovan Karadžić)

ustashi   Croatian nationalist (World War II term)

OTHER

conducător   supreme leader (Romanian)

mujahedin   Islamic guerrilla fighter

Securitate   Romanian secret police

Stasi   East German secret police

Trabi   popular East German car

NOTES ON SOURCES

THE COLLAPSE of communism opened up a treasure trove of previously untapped sources. In writing this book, I have drawn on interviews with direct participants, memoirs of Soviet and East European leaders, declassified archival materials, contemporary newspapers, and my own reporting notes. Unless otherwise stated, all interviews are with me. I have tried to provide a named citation for all direct quotations. During the course of my research I gathered transcripts of numerous meetings of the Soviet Politburo, which are marked in the notes with the Russian abbreviation TsKhSD. The translations are my own. Because access to the Soviet archives is still restricted, I have deposited copies of these materials with the National Security Archive in Washington, D.C.

Also helpful in reconstructing events were three documentary television programs prepared by the British Broadcasting Corporation by Brian Lapping Associates, *The Second Russian Revolution*, the *Fall of the Berlin Wall*, and *Yugoslavia: Death of a Nation*. I am grateful to Norma Percy and Brian Lapping for permission to quote from the original transcripts of *The Second Russian Revolution*, which are deposited at the library of the London School of Economics. Publishing details of all books cited in the notes are provided in the bibliography. I have used the following abbreviations in the notes:

BBC British Broadcasting Corporation transcript service

CDSP Current Digest of the Soviet Press

CNN Cable News Network

FBIS Foreign Broadcast Information Service

ICAO International Civil Aviation Organization

LAT Los Angeles Times

MN Moscow News

NSC National Security Council

NYT New York Times

RFE/RL Radio Free Europe/ Radio Liberty

TsK KPSS Central Committee of Soviet Communist Party

TsKhSD Center for Storage of Contemporary Documentation

UN United Nations

WP Washington Post

NOTES

I: REVOLT OF THE PROLES

1. Weather report, *NYT,* December 27, 1979, p. B8.

2. Sergo Mikoyan, son of the former Soviet leader Anastas Mikoyan, provided me with the details of Brezhnev's dacha. See also the memoirs of his doctor, Yevgeny Chazov, *Zdorov'ye i Vlast',* pp. 86–87.

3. Roy Medvedev, "The Advantages of Mediocrity," *Moskovskie Novosti* (Moscow), September 11, 1988, pp. 8–9, translated in *CDSP,* vol. XL, no. 36, p. 5.

4. For a detailed discussion of Brezhnev health problems, see Chazov, pp. 115–44, and former bodyguard Mikhail Dokuchayev, "Devyatka," *Novoye Vremya* (Moscow), no. 32 (1993), pp. 36–40.

5. Chazov, p. 128.

6. Vladimir Medvedev, *Chelovek Za Spinoi,* pp. 148–49.

7. Chazov, p. 134.

8. Ibid., pp. 149–51. For Western reports of the incident, see *NYT,* October 7, 1979, p. A1, and Reuters dispatches from Berlin on October 6, 1979.

9. Chazov, p. 150. See also Edward Gierek, *Przerwana Dekada,* pp. 93–94.

10. Zdenek Mlynář, *Nightfrost in Prague,* p. 156.

11. See, for example, Defense Department estimates for 1980 reproduced in David Holloway, *The Soviet Union and the Arms Race,* pp. 134–40. The U.S. Defense Department publication *Soviet Military Power* (1981, p. 71) also claimed that the Soviets had "dramatically reduced" the U.S. lead in "virtually every important basic technology" during the 1970s.

12. Vyacheslav Molotov, *Molotov Remembers: Conversations with Felix Chuev,* p. 8.

13. Deputy Soviet Foreign Minister Georgi Kornienko, *Novaya i Noveishaya Istoria* (Moscow), no. 3 (May–June 1993), p. 107.

14. Ibid., p. 108.

15. Statement of Captain Abdul Hadud, reported in Colonel A. Lyakhovski and Lieutenant Colonel V. Zabrodin, "Secrets of the Afghan War," *Armiya* (Moscow), no. 6 (March 1992), pp. 60–61.

16. For Soviet suspicions of Amin, see report by the Politburo Commission on Afghanistan, quoted in Aleksandr Lyakhovski, *Tragediya i Doblest' Afgana,* pp.

102–3. See also Kornienko, p. 110, Georgi Arbatov, *The System* p. 119, and Anatoly Dobrynin, *In Confidence*, p. 436.

17. For KGB view, see memoirs of Col. Aleksandr Morozov, former KGB deputy station chief in Afghanistan, published in *New Times* (Moscow), no. 38–41 (1991).

18. Andrei Gromyko, *Memoirs*, p. 99.

19. Memorandum signed by Konstantin Chernenko, December 27, 1979, TsKhSD. Copy in author's possession.

20. Chazov, p. 133.

21. Arbatov, p. 266.

22. Larisa Vasilieva, *Kremlin Wives*, p. 219.

23. *NYT*, April 3, 1994. For details of Andropov activity in Budapest, see also *Izvestia,* July 24, 1992, and Arnold Beichman and Mikhail S. Bernstam, *Andropov*, pp. 145–60.

24. Alexander Werth, *Russia at War*, pp. 213–17.

25. *Soviet Military Power* (1981), p. 12.

26. Chazov, p. 90.

27. Ibid., p. 205.

28. Transcript of Politburo session, July 12, 1984, TsKhSD.

29. Arbatov, p. 198.

30. For Gromyko's reasons for supporting invasion of Afghanistan, see reminiscences of former Foreign Minister Aleksandr Bessmertnykh and Gorbachev foreign policy aide Anatoly Chernyayev at Princeton University conference on the Cold War, vol. III, February 26, 1993.

31. Vladimir Medvedev, p. 130.

32. *Voenno-Istoricheskii Zhurnal* (Moscow), no. 11 (1993), pp. 30, 35.

33. Chernyayev, Princeton conference, vol. III, pp. 22–23. See also Dobrynin, p. 439.

34. Chazov, p. 152.

35. A copy of the handwritten resolution, obtained from TsKhSD, was published in the *Washington Post,* p. A1, on November 15, 1992. The only full Politburo member not to countersign the resolution was Andrei Kosygin, who was gravely ill at the time and resigned from his post as Soviet prime minister shortly afterward. According to Kornienko, p. 110, the decision to invade was taken jointly by Brezhnev, Suslov, Andropov, Ustinov, and Gromyko.

36. *Voyenno-Istoricheskii Zhurnal* (Moscow), no. 11 (1993), pp. 32–34.

37. Henry S. Bradsher, *Afghanistan and the Soviet Union*, p. 179.

38. Chernenko memorandum, December 27, 1979, TsKhSD. See also Dobrynin, p. 439.

39. Dobrynin, p. 440.

40. *Armiya,* no. 6 (March 1992), p. 66.

41. *Armiya,* nos. 7 and 8 (April 1992), p. 54. In reconstructing the events of December 27, I have also drawn on Mikhail Boltunov, *Alpha—Sverkhsekretnii Otryad KGB.* For an Afghan perspective, I turned to Raja Anwar, *The Tragedy of Afghanistan*, which confirms many of the details of the Soviet accounts.

42. *Armiya,* nos. 7 and 8, p. 55.

43. Anwar, p. 189.

44. Boltunov, p. 37.

45. Ibid., p. 44.

46. Ibid., p. 72.

47. *Armiya,* nos. 7 and 8, p. 57.

48. Ibid.

49. Ibid., pp. 55–56. See also Lyakhovski, pp. 144–51.

50. Ibid., p. 56.

51. Boltunov, pp. 86–89. For Karmal's character and alcoholism, see also Leonid Shebarshin, *Ruka Moskvi*, pp. 206–09.

52. Foreign Broadcast Information Service (FBIS-SOV-79-251), December 28, 1979, pp. D1–2.

53. Casualty figures for the storming of Amin's palace remain contradictory.

These come from *Armiya* nos. 7 and 8, p. 56, the semiofficial Soviet account of the incident.

54. The description of Khrushchev's old dacha comes from Sergo Mikoyan, who spent family vacations here in the fifties and sixties. Conversation with author, March 1994.

55. For a discussion of Soviet agricultural problems during this period, see Valery Boldin, *Ten Years That Shook the World*, p. 35. Also Zhores A. Medvedev, *Gorbachev*, pp. 103–12.

56. Eduard Shevardnadze, *The Future Belongs to Freedom*, pp. 23–26.

57. At a press conference on October 15, 1992, Gorbachev said this conversation had taken place in December 1979. In his memoirs (p. 37), Shevardnadze also places the conversation in Pitsunda but says it took place in the winter of 1984, shortly before Gorbachev became Soviet leader.

58. Boldin, p. 36.

59. *Stavropolskaya Pravda*, May 6, 1978. Quoted in Zhores Medvedev, p. 216.

60. XXV Congress of the CPSU. Official stenographic record. Politizdat, 1976. Vol. I, p. 186.

61. FBIS-SOV-79-251, p. D3.

62. Shevardnadze, p. 26. Interview, March 1994.

63. CPSU Central Committee resolution, June 23, 1980, TsKhSD. Lyakhovski, p. 113.

64. Lech Wałęsa, *A Way of Hope,* p. 44.

65. Roman Laba, *The Roots of Solidarity*, pp. 15–56.

66. Wałęsa, *A Way of Hope,* p. 70.

67. Neal Ascherson, *The Book of Lech Wałęsa*, p. 55. See also Jean-Yves Potel, *Gdansk: La Mémoire ouvrière 1970–1980*, pp. 156–59.

68. Wałęsa, *A Way of Hope,* p. 117. For Borowczyk's account of the strike, see Stan Persky and Henry Flam, *The Soli-*

darity Sourcebook, pp. 73–78. *Solidarity*, no. 11, August 30 1980 (the shipyard strike bulletin), interviewed the strike insti-gators. *The Polish August* (editor Oliver MacDonald) contains a full English translation of all the strike bulletins.

69. Persky and Flam, p. 74.

70. Interview with strike committee member Gregorz Obernikowicz, August 14, 1980.

71. Wałęsa, *A Way of Hope*, pp. 117–18.

72. Solidarity strike bulletin, no. 11.

73. Wałęsa, *A Way of Hope*, pp. 116–17.

74. There are several different versions of this speech. This one is from an exhaustive Polish account of the strike by Andrzej Drzycimski and Tadeusz Skutnik, *Gdańsk Sierpień '80,* p. 437. See also interview with Orianna Fallaci, March 1981, reprinted in Persky and Flam, p. 102.

75. Persky and Flam, p. 102.

76. Gierek, p. 169.

77. After the collapse of communism, the building was transformed into the Warsaw Stock Exchange.

78. Politburo transcript for August 15, 1980, in Zbigniew Włodek, ed., *Tajne Dokumenty Biura Politycznego: PZPR a Solidarność 1980–1981*, pp. 28–34.

79. Ibid., p. 29.

80. Gierek speech to Gdańsk shipyard workers on January 25, 1971. See article by Mieczysław Rakowski, *Polityka,* no. 12 (March 21, 1981).

81. Gierek, p. 160.

82. For Gierek's suspicions of his Politburo colleagues, see Gierek, pp. 155–60. In their memoirs, both Kania and Jaruzelski deny that they were part of a plot to unseat the first secretary.

83. Włodek, p. 33.

84. *August 1980: The Strikes in Poland*, p. 11.

85. Files of the Summer '80 task force, which remained in existence until early

1982, were published in *Życie Warszawy*, May 12, 1994, *Ekstra*, pp. 1–3. See also Jerzy Jachowicz, "Tajemnice Wojny z Narodem," *Gazeta Wyborcza* (November 7, 1990), p. 1, and Włodek, p. 24.

86. Interview with Kuroń, August 17, 1980.

87. Politburo meeting, August 23, Włodek, pp. 54–57.

88. Gierek, p. 165.

89. Interview with Czesław Szalanski, Gierek's personal electrician, July 1993.

90. Politburo meeting, August 26, Włodek, pp. 70–72.

91. Gierek's report to the Politburo on his meeting with Ambassador Aristov, August 28, Włodek, p. 78. In his memoirs (p. 168) Gierek claims that Brezhnev called him on the direct Kremlin line, offering to "lend a hand" if he "grabbed the contras by the muzzle." There is no other documentary evidence to support Gierek's version of the telephone conversation with Brezhnev, and both Kania and Jaruzelski are skeptical that it ever took place. Gierek maintains that both men were present when the Soviet leader called and listened to the conversation, but Kania and Jaruzelski deny this. Since Gierek has proved to be a less than reliable witness on several other points, his memoirs should be treated with caution.

92. Stanisław Kania, *Zatrzymać Konfrontację*, p. 32.

93. Ibid., p. 32. Kania's account of Gierek's actions during this period is supported by Jaruzelski and former KGB resident Vitaly Pavlov. In an interview in June 1993, Pavlov said that he had learned from confidential sources that Gierek wanted to raise the question of Soviet military assistance at the Politburo, but Kania was opposed.

94. *Życie Warszawy*, May 12, 1994, p. 1. See also Kania, p. 33.

95. Politburo meeting, August 29, Włodek, pp. 84–90. At the time there were widely reported rumors that a much more formidable figure, Central Committee secretary Stefan Olszowski, was also in favor of the use of force. See, for example, Timothy Garton Ash, *We the People: The Revolution of 89*, p. 62, or Neal Ascherson, *The Polish August*, p. 162. Olszowski may have used Kruczek as a stalking horse, but the Politburo record shows that he himself adopted a more moderate wait-and-see position, insisting only on "consultations" with the Kremlin and a vigorous propaganda campaign against the strikers.

96. Interview with Colonel Ryszard Kukliński, *Kultura* (Paris, April 1987), translated in *Orbis*, no. 32 (Philadelphia, Winter 1988), p. 14. According to Kukliński, a party-state leadership staff was established on August 24, 1980, and immediately began drawing up preparations for martial law.

97. The Soviet Politburo set up a commission under Suslov to follow events in Poland on August 25. Portions of the Suslov commission archives were declassified in August 1993, in connection with President Yeltsin's visit to Poland, and published in booklet form. See *Dokumenty Teczka Susłowa*, pp. 12–25.

98. Politburo memorandum, August 28, 1980, quoted by Mark Kramer, "New Evidence on the Polish Crisis," Cold War International History Project Bulletin, no. 5 (1995), p. 120.

99. A. Kemp-Welch, ed., *The Birth of Solidarity*, p. 140.

100. The scene at the gate is recorded in the films *Man of Iron* and *Workers '80*.

101. Zbigniew Brzezinski, *Power and Principle*, p. 465.

102. Interview with Kukliński in *WP*, September 27, 1992, p. A1. See also portrait of Kukliński by Ben Weiser in *WP* magazine, December 13, 1992.

103. Kukliński interview in *Kultura*, pp. 3–57, partially translated into English in *Orbis* 32 (1988), pp. 7–31. The *Orbis* issue

(pp. 32–48) also contains extracts from Brzezinski's White House diaries, covering the Polish crisis of December 1980. For Jaruzelski's account of these events, see Wojciech Jaruzelski, *Les Chaînes et le Refuge,* pp. 237–39.

104. Brzezinski interview, April 1994. See also Jaruzelski, *Les Chaînes et le Refuge,* pp. 24–29.

105. Brzezinski, *Orbis,* p. 36.

106. Ibid., p. 37.

107. Kania, p. 84.

108. Jaruzelski, *Les Chaînes et le Refuge,* pp. 16, 242.

109. Ibid., p. 239. At a press conference in Warsaw on December 4, a Communist Party spokesman, Jozef Kłasa, said Polish Communists had the "right and duty" to seek help from other socialist states in the event of a "real threat to socialism" but would not make such a request "lightly." *WP,* December 5, 1980, p. A20.

110. Deutschland Archiv, no. 3, March 1993, p. 336. See also *Moskovskie Novosti,* no. 48 (November 28, 1993), p. 12.

111. Kania, p. 88.

112. Honecker obituary, *LAT,* April 29, 1994.

113. Mlynář, p. 157.

114. Jaruzelski, *Les Chaînes et le Refuge,* p. 240.

115. Kania, p. 91. Vitaly Svietlov, a Soviet Communist Party official who served as interpreter, remembers the conversation slightly differently. He quotes Brezhnev as saying, "Okay, there will be no maneuvers. But if we see that they are overthrowing you, we will go in." Interview, *Gazeta Wyborcza,* no. 291 (December 11, 1992), p. 14.

116. Kania, pp. 92–93.

117. Politburo minutes, October 29, 1980, TsKhSD.

118. Jaruzelski, *Les Chaînes et le Refuge,* p. 237. See also article by General Anatoly Gribkov, deputy chief of staff of the Warsaw Pact, in *Voyenno-Istoricheskii*

Zhurnal (Moscow), no. 9 (September 1992), p. 55.

119. Jaruzelski, *Les Chaînes et le Refuge,* p. 241. Jaruzelski maintains that Brezhnev canceled the invasion plans because of opposition from Kádár and Ceauşescu but provides no evidence to support this conclusion.

120. Gribkov, p. 54.

121. Kukliński, *Kultura* (Paris, April 1987), pp. 25–26.

122. Politburo session, January 22, 1981, TsKhSD.

123. Report of Suslov commission on Poland, April 16, 1981, TsKhSD. Published in booklet form in *Dokumenty Teczka Susłowa,* p. 40.

124. Kukliński, *Orbis* (Winter 1988), p. 22.

125. Jaruzelski, *Les Chaînes et le Refuge,* p. 256.

126. Politburo session, April 9, 1981, TsKhSD. For the Polish leaders' version of this meeting, see Jaruzelski, *Les Chaînes et le Refuge,* pp. 253–57, and Kania, pp. 120–23.

127. Dispatch from Moscow, *WP,* December 3, 1980, p. A21.

128. Information from East German archives. *Moskovskie Novosti,* no. 48 (November 28, 1993), p. 12.

129. Arbatov, p. 272.

130. Jaruzelski interview, August 1993. Jaruzelski points to this conversation with Ustinov as a veiled threat of Soviet military intervention.

131. Gorbachev interview, *Trybuna* (Warsaw, November 9, 1992), p. 2.

132. See, for example, Suslov's comments at Politburo session, October 29, 1980, TsKhSD, or the Suslov commission report of April 16, 1981, published in *Dokumenty Teczka Susłowa,* p. 38.

133. Politburo meeting, April 9, 1991, TsKhSD.

134. Kukliński, *Orbis,* p. 23.

135. Interview with KGB resident Pavlov, July 1993. Pavlov denied that the KGB recruited Polish citizens directly, but see Wojciech Jaruzelski, *Stan Wojenny Dlaczego*, pp. 346–49, and Kukliński, *Orbis* pp. 28–30.

136. Jaruzelski learned about this legend when he received a visit from one of his former neighbors after becoming president of Poland in 1989. Interview with author, August 1993.

137. Jaruzelski interview. See also Jaruzelski, *Les Chaînes et le Refuge*, pp. 41–66.

138. Jaruzelski interview.

139. Jaruzelski, *Les Chaînes et le Refuge*, p. 50.

140. Ibid., p. 116.

141. Ibid., p. 38.

142. Ibid., p. 279.

143. Miecyzsław Rakowski, *Jak To Się Stało*, p. 25.

144. *Dokumenty Teczka Susłowa*, p. 52.

145. Svietlov interview, *Gazeta Wyborcza*.

146. Jan Nowak, *Wojna W Eterze*, p. 255.

147. Janusz Rolicki, *Edward Gierek Replika*, p. 84.

148. Jaruzelski, *Les Chaînes et le Refuge*, p. 146.

149. See, for example, Soviet Politburo discussion, October 29, 1980, in which Gromyko describes Jaruzelski as a "reliable person" but expresses concern about his statement that "Polish soldiers will not fire on Polish workers." TsKhSD.

150. Czeslaw Kiszczak, *Generał Kiszczak mówi...*, p. 129.

151. Jaruzelski, *Les Chaînes et le Refuge*, p. 291.

152. Rakowski, p. 25.

153. Jaruzelski, *Les Chaînes et le Refuge*, p. 272.

154. Interview with Polish government spokesman Jerzy Urban, "CIA had agent on Polish General Staff," *WP*, June 4,

1986. See also Jaruzelski, *Stan Wojenny Dlaczego*, pp. 356–58.

155. Interview with former NSC staffer Richard Pipes, June 2, 1994. According to Pipes, the CIA held information provided by Kukliński so tightly that it never entered the bureaucratic "machine." Even Secretary of State Alexander Haig was unaware of Kukliński's existence. Pipes later learned that the CIA considered Kukliński's warnings "extremely implausible." The CIA has never provided a full explanation for its handling of the Kukliński affair.

156. Jaruzelski, *Stan Wojenny Dlaczego*, p. 404.

157. Jaruzelski interview, August 1993.

158. Kiszczak, pp. 129–30.

159. *Dokumenty Teczka Susłowa*, p. 78. Jaruzelski, *Stan Wojenny Dlaczego*, pp. 390–91.

160. Jaruzelski interview, August 1993.

161. Ibid.

162. Politburo session, December 10, 1981, TsKhSD, translated in Cold War International History Project Bulletin, no. 5 (1995), p. 137.

163. Jaruzelski interview, *Gazeta Wyborcza*, December 14, 1992, p. 13. No official transcript of this conversation has yet been published. The former KGB resident in Warsaw, Pavlov, claims that Suslov declined a request by Jaruzelski for military assistance in the event of difficulties in enforcing martial law. He quotes Suslov as saying, "We will help you materially, financially, and politically, but not with armed force." Interview with *Gazeta Wyborcza*, February 20, 1993, p. 15.

164. *Gazeta Wyborcza*, December 14, 1992, p. 13.

165. Jaruzelski testimony to Sejm commission, March 9–10, 1993. *Sąd Nad Autorami Stanu Wojennego*, p. 235.

166. I have relied on the account of my *WP* assistant, Marek Olbrich, who was

present for this final Solidarity session in Gdańsk.

167. Interview, *WP*, November 16, 1982, pp. A1–A14.

168. Bujak interview, Maciej Łopiński et al., *Konspira*, p. 5.

169. Wałęsa, *A Way of Hope*, pp. 207–10.

170. Dobbs, *WP*, January 17, 1982, p. A1; March 14, 1982, p. A1.

171. CPSU Politburo debate, January 14, 1982, translated in Cold War International History Project Bulletin, no. 5 (1995), p. 138.

172. Chazov, p. 148.

173. Vladimir Medvedev, p. 176.

174. Chazov, pp. 168–69.

175. Interview, December 1992.

176. Luba Brezhneva, *The World I Left Behind*, p. 162.

177. *MN*, no. 21, 1992, p. 16.

178. A copy of the report was leaked to *Washington Post* Moscow correspondent Dusko Doder (*WP*, August 3, 1983, p. A1). The full text of the Novosibirsk report was published in Tatiana Zaslavskaya, *A Voice of Reform*, pp. 158– 83. Zaslavskaya described the background to the report in an interview with the author in August 1987.

179. Quoted in Henry Rowen and Charles Wolf (eds.), *The Future of the Soviet Empire*, p. 26.

180. Brzezinski, p. 36.

181. *LAT*, November 7, 1981, pp. 1, 8.

182. Peter Hebblethwaite and Ludwig Kaufmann, *John Paul II*, p. 108.

183. David Willey, *God's Politician*, p. 30.

184. Hebblethwaite and Kaufmann, p. 34.

185. Interview with Szumiejko, *Konspira*, p. 208.

186. Politburo session, April 26, 1984, TsKhSD.

187. Ibid.

11: REVOLT OF THE MACHINES

1. *Soviet Military Power* (1981), p. 64.

2. *Report of the Completion of the Fact-finding Investigation Regarding the Shooting Down of Korean Airlines Flight 007* (International Civil Aviation Organization, 1993), p. 49. Christopher Andrew and Oleg Gordievsky, *KGB—The Inside Story*, p. 497.

3. Osipovich interview in *Izvestia*, January 24, 1991, translated in FBIS-SOV-91-025, p. 8. See also Seymour M. Hersh, *"The Target Is Destroyed,"* pp. 17–19.

4. Alexander Zuyev, *Fulcrum*, pp. 124–26.

5. Osipovich, op. cit.

6. ICAO annex, pp. 65–66.

7. Ibid., pp. 146, 149.

8. Ibid., p. 103.

9. Ibid., pp. 127–29.

10. Osipovich, p. 11.

11. ICAO annex, pp. 9–10.

12. ICAO report, pp. 56–59.

13. Osipovich, p. 13.

14. ICAO annex, p. 72.

15. Chazov, p. 181. Arbatov, p. 286.

16. See, for example, speech marking fiftieth anniversary celebrations of KGB, December 20, 1967, reprinted in Martin Ebon, *The Andropov File*, pp. 166–76.

17. Chazov, p. 175.

18. Ibid., p. 90.

19. S. F. Akhromeyev and G. M. Kornienko, *Glazami Marshala i Diplomata*, p. 49.

20. Politburo session, September 2, 1983, TsKhSD, published in *Rossiyskie Vesti*, August 25, 1992, pp. 1–4, translated in FBIS-SOV-92-167, p. 7.

21. Akhromeyev and Kornienko, pp. 45–46.

22. *Rossiyskie Vesti*, loc cit.

23. *Izvestia*, May 23, 1991, p. 6, translated in FBIS-SOV-91-104, p. 5.

24. Interview with Osipovich, *Izvestia*,

January 25, 1991, p. 7, translated in FBIS-SOV-91-025, p. 12.

25. *Izvestia*, May 23, 1991.

26. *NYT*, September 11, 1983, p. A16.

27. Ronald Reagan, *An American Life*, p. 588.

28. Ibid., pp. 585–86.

29. Gorbachev, *Zhizn' i Reformi*, vol. 1, p. 249.

30. Yegor Ligachev, *Inside Gorbachev's Kremlin*, p. 70.

31. Nikolai Ryzhkov, *Perestroika— Istoria Predatel'stv*, p. 78.

32. Gorbachev, *Zhizn' i Reformi*, vol. 1, p. 264.

33. Grishin testimony for the BBC television series *The Second Russian Revolution*. See also Anatoly S. Chernyayev, *Shest' Let s Gorbachevym,* pp. 30–31, and Boldin, p. 59.

34. Roxburgh, *The Second Russian Revolution,* pp. 5–6. See also Ryzhkov, pp. 78–79. Ligachev (pp. 68–70) gives a slightly different version of events, but his testimony is colored by a wish to emphasize his own role in Gorbachev's election.

35. See, for example, comments by Georgi Arbatov in *The Second Russian Revolution.*

36. Gorbachev address to former classmates, June 16, 1990, recorded by BBC for *The Second Russian Revolution.* Gorbachev also referred to this incident in a talk to American intellectuals in Washington in June 1990. (FBIS-SOV-90-107, p. 15.) See also Raisa Gorbachev, *I Hope*, pp. 4–5, and Gorbachev, *Zhizn' i Reformi*, vol. 1, p. 265.

37. Boldin, pp. 62–63. See also Chernyayev, pp. 29–30.

38. *MN*, no. 7, February 11, 1993, p. 15.

39. Raisa Gorbachev, p. 110. See also Gail Sheehy, *Gorbachev*, p. 40.

40. Robert Conquest, *The Harvest of Sorrow*, p. 303.

41. Gorbachev, *Zhizn' i Reformi*, vol. 1, p. 42.

42. Ibid., p. 38.

43. Ibid., p. 39.

44. Speech on Central TV, November 29, 1990.

45. Akhromeyev and Kornienko, pp. 61–62.

46. Gorbachev, *Zhizn' i Reformi*, vol. 1, p. 66.

47. Zdeněk Mlynář, "Il Mio Compagno di Studi Mikhail Gorbachev," *L'Unità* (Rome, April 9, 1985), p. 9.

48. Raisa Gorbachev, p. 66.

49. Gorbachev, *Zhizn' i Reformi*, vol. 1, p. 157.

50. Ibid., p. 106.

51. Robert G. Kaiser, *Why Gorbachev Happened*, p. 76.

52. Interview, August 1993.

53. Interview, September 1993.

54. Reagan, *An American Life*, pp. 614–15.

55. George Shultz, *Turmoil and Triumph*, p. 568.

56. Edward Jay Epstein, "Petropower and Soviet Expansion," *Commentary*, (July 1986), p. 26.

57. Dobbs, "Oil's Skid Fuels Gorbachev's Reforms," *WP*, May 28, 1990, pp. A1, 18.

58. Soviet Politburo transcript, October 29, 1981, TsKhSD.

59. Chernyayev, p. 40.

60. Interview with Abel Aganbegyan, BBC/Lapping.

61. *Izvestia*, June 8, 1990. According to former Prime Minister Ryzkhov, the decision was taken because of the "prevailing international situation and our military doctrine."

62. See Gorbachev, *Zhizn' i Reformi*, vol. 1, p. 285.

63. BBC, September 6, 1985, SU/8049/ C/1.

64. Testimony of *Vremya* producer Eduard Sagalayev. See David Remnick, *Lenin's Tomb,* pp. 146–47. See also Boldin, pp. 110–11.

65. Boldin, p. 100.

66. BBC, September 9, 1985, SU/8051/C/1.

67. Marquis de Custine, *Empire of the Czar,* p. 437.

68. Chernyayev, p. 39.

69. BBC, September 6, 1985, SU/8049/C/1.

70. Interview with Gorbachev foreign policy adviser Chernyayev, July 1993. See also Gorbachev, *Zhizn' i Reformi,* vol. 1, p. 276.

71. Ronald Reagan, *Speaking My Mind,* p. 247.

72. Presidential press conference, January 29, 1981.

73. Reagan, *An American Life,* p. 635.

74. Donald T. Regan, *For the Record,* pp. 308–09.

75. Gorbachev, *Zhizn' i Reformi,* vol. 2, p. 14.

76. Lou Cannon, *President Reagan: The Role of a Lifetime.* p. 280. See also Reagan, *An American Life,* pp. 636–37.

77. Testimony of school friend Yuliya Karagodina, see Remnick, pp. 155–56.

78. Interviews with NSC adviser Robert McFarlane, December 1993, and former State Department official Tom Simons. Jack Matlock, the former NSC specialist on the Soviet Union, also referred to the spurious Lenin book during the Princeton conference, February 26, 1993, Session IV.

79. Interview with college radio stations, September 9, 1985.

80. Televised address to the American people, January 16, 1984. The "evil empire" speech was delivered to the National Association of Evangelicals in Orlando, Florida, on March 8, 1983.

81. McFarlane interview, December 1993.

82. Joan Quigley, *What Does Joan Say?,* pp. 126–30.

83. Robert and Suzanne Massie, *Journey,* p. 190.

84. Massie interview, March 1994.

85. Daniel Schorr, "Reagan Recants; His Path from Armageddon to Détente," *LAT,* January 3, 1988. See also Cannon, pp. 289–91.

86. Martin Anderson, *Revolution,* pp. 82–83.

87. Televised address, March 23, 1983.

88. This exchange occurred at the Soviet Embassy on November 20. See Don Oberdorfer, *The Turn: From the Cold War to a New Era,* pp. 147–50.

89. Shultz testimony, Princeton conference, Session IV.

90. Address to the British Parliament, June 8, 1982.

91. Kaiser, p. 119.

92. Interview, July 1994.

93. Interview, March 1994.

94. Princeton conference, Session II.

95. NSC memorandum, November 12, 1985, provided to author by Robert McFarlane.

96. Boldin, pp. 95–96.

97. Dusko Doder and Louise Branson, *Gorbachev—Heretic in the Kremlin,* pp. 16–17.

98. *Vestnik* (Soviet Foreign Ministry publication), no. 1 (August 1987). Quoted by Oberdorfer, p. 162.

99. Chernyayev, p. 61.

100. Ibid., p. 70.

101. A. M. Aleksandrov-Agentov, *Ot Kollontaia do Gorbacheva,* p. 289.

102. Gorbachev, *Zhizn' i Reformi,* vol. 2, p. 14.

103. Dobrynin, p. 586.

104. Chernyayev, Princeton conference, Session II.

105. Dyatlov interview, April 1992. The most detailed English-language accounts of the disaster are Grigori Medvedev, *The Truth About Chernobyl* and Piers Paul Read, *Ablaze*.

106. Grigori Medvedev, pp. 73–76.

107. Dyatlov interview.

108. Grigori Medvedev, p. 87.

109. Grigori Medvedev, p. 114.

110. Interview with author, see *WP*, August 21, 1988, p. A10.

111. Yuri Shcherbak, *Chernobyl, a Documentary Story*, pp. 152–54.

112. Interview with Shcherbak, *The Second Russian Revolution*, Part II, BBC-TV, March 1991.

113. Interview, April 1991.

114. Grigori Medvedev, p. 167.

115. Nigel Hawkes, *The Worst Accident in the World*, p. 122.

116. "Lies about Chernobyl," *Izvestia*, April 24, 1992.

117. Grigori Medvedev, p. 204.

118. "Chernobyl, Symbol of Soviet Failure," *WP*, April 26, 1991.

119. For atmosphere at Politburo meetings, see, for example, Boldin, pp. 162–65.

120. Chernyayev, pp. 87–88.

121. Secret Politburo documents on Chernobyl, *Izvestia*, April 17, 1993, pp. 1 and 5.

122. Chernyayev, pp. 89–90.

123. See, for example, memorandum to Gorbachev from *Pravda* science editor Vladimir Gubarev of May 16, 1986, published in *Rodina* (Moscow), no. 1 (1992).

124. Grigori Medvedev, p. ix.

125. Chernyayev, p. 88.

126. For a classic definition of the Great Game, see George N. Curzon, *Russia in Central Asia*.

127. For Soviet *spetsnaz* tactics, see B. V. Gromov, *Ogranichenni Kontingent*, pp. 198–205, and "Taini Afghanskoi

Voini," *Armiya* (Moscow), no. 10 (May 1992), pp. 50–51.

128. Muhamad Yousaf, *The Bear Trap*, pp. 174–77.

129. Lyachowski, p. 379.

130. Confidential memorandum to Brezh-nev from Institute of World Economy director Oleg Bogomolov. *WP*, April 26, 1988.

131. Bradsher, pp. 189–99.

132. Brzezinski interview with author, April 1994.

133. William Casey, *The Secret War Against Hitler*, p. xiv.

134. Joseph E. Persico, *Casey*, p. 7.

135. Natonal Security Decision Directive 166. See Robert Gates, *From the Shadows*, pp. 348–49.

136. See Shultz, pp. 691, 844, 866.

137. Yousaf, pp. 78–79.

138. Ibid., pp. 189–95. *WP*, July 19, 1992, p. A1.

139. Abramowitz interview with author, January 1994.

140. Interview with Michael Pillsbury, former Defense Department official, January 1994.

141. Ibid.

142. The agent was probably Dmitri F. Polyakov, a general in the Soviet Air Defense Command. He was executed after Aldrich Ames identified him to the KGB in 1986.

143. Chernyayev, p. 115.

144. Official Politburo minutes, November 13, 1986, TsKhSD; Chernyayev, p. 130.

145. Dobrynin, p. 442.

146. Chernyayev interview, July 1993.

147. Dobrynin, p. 443.

148. Chernyayev interview, July 1993.

149. For Soviet estimate of costs of Afghan War, see Ryzhov, pp. 232–33, Chernyayev, p. 193, and Akhromeyev and Kornienko, p. 167.

150. Ryzkhov, p. 231.

151. Chernyayev, pp. 14, 25, 192.

152. See, for example, comments by Paul Nitze, Princeton conference, Session III.

153. Gromov, p. 219, Akhromeyev and Kornienko, p. 167.

154. Interview, July 1993.

155. Chernyayev, p. 120.

156. Interview, June 1993.

157. Gromov, p. 254.

158. The conversation took place on December 16, 1986. Andrei Sakharov, *Memoirs*, p. 615.

159. *Pravda*, May 28, 1992, p. 3.

160. Akhromeyev and Kornienko, p. 76.

161. Boldin, p. 167.

162. Chernyayev, p. 159.

163. Dobrynin, p. 625.

164. Boris Yeltsin, *The Struggle for Russia*, p. 179.

165. Boris Yeltsin, *Against the Grain*, pp. 18–22.

166. Lev Sukhanov, *Tri Goda s Yeltsinym*, p. 143.

167. Yeltsin, *Struggle for Russia*, p. 98.

168. Yeltsin, *Against the Grain*, p. 67.

169. Ibid., p. 156.

170. *Izvestia,* no. 2, 1989, TsKh KPSS, pp. 214–15.

171. Yeltsin, *Against the Grain*, p. 76.

172. Ibid., p. 144.

173. Boldin, p. 235.

174. *Izvestia,* TsKh KPSS, p. 241.

175. Yeltsin, *Against the Grain*, p. 147.

176. Chernyayev, p. 135.

177. Gorbachev, *Zhizn' i Reformi*, vol. 1, p. 374.

178. Yeltsin, *Against the Grain,* pp. 153–54. Gorbachev maintains that Yeltsin's condition was stable.

179. *Moskovskaya Pravda*, November 13, 1987.

180. Boris Yeltsin, *Ispoved' na Zadannuyu Temu*, p. 178. This crucial quote was inexplicably dropped from the English version, *Against the Grain*. Gorbachev says this conversation took place before the Moscow party plenum.

181. Ligachev, pp. 83 and 264.

182. Ibid., pp. 256–60.

183. Interview, April 1993.

184. Interview, June 1993.

185. Interview with *Komsomolskaya Pravda*, June 5, 1990. For additional details on Yakovlev's family background, see profile by Bill Keller, *NYT Magazine,* February 19, 1989.

186. Speech marking hundredth anniversary of Khrushchev's birth, *Moscow Times,* April 16, 1994.

187. Interview, June 1993.

188. Ibid.

189. Ligachev, p. 105.

190. Chernyayev, p. 204.

191. BBC, *The Second Russian Revolution,* Part II; BBC/Lapping interviews with Laptev, Starkov, and Belyayev. See also Roxburgh, pp. 83–87. For Ligachev's self-serving account of the incident, see pp. 298–307.

192. *Pravda*, March 19, 1988.

193. Chernyayev, pp. 204–05.

194. Dobrynin, p. 737.

195. This account is reconstructed from Chernyayev and the Politburo transcript of the March 25 debate, published in Mikhail Gorbachev, *Avant-Mémoires*, pp. 211–30. See also Vitaly Vorotnikov, *A Bylo Eto Tak,* pp. 198–203.

196. Ligachev, pp. 304–08.

197. Chernyayev, pp. 208–12.

198. Interview with *WP*, May 18, 1988.

199. Gorbachev, *Avant-Mémoires*, p. 215.

200. Boldin, p. 169.

201. Chernyayev, p. 204. See also Vorotnikov, p. 234.

202. See, for example, Gorbachev press conference in Paris, October 6, 1985.

203. Interview with Niklus, October 1988.

204. Dobbs, "Gorbachev Plan Wins Support in Estonia," *WP,* October 17, 1988, p. A1.

205. Ligachev, pp. 137–40. Interview with Yakovlev, June 1993.

206. Chernyayev, p. 250.

207. FBIS-SOV-99-236, December 8, 1988, pp. 11–19.

208. Chernyayev, p. 267.

209. Ryzkhov, p. 179; Chernyayev, p. 267.

210. *WP,* December 12, 1988, p. A1.

211. Politburo meeting, February 29, 1988, TsKhSD.

III: REVOLT OF THE NATIONS

1. Chernyayev interview, July 1991.

2. Interviews with author, Termez, February 6, 1989.

3. Abdur Rahman, quoted in *Afghanistan, the Great Game,* p. 3.

4. Quoted in *WP,* February 13, 1989, p. A1.

5. Gromov, pp. 327–28.

6. Ibid., p. 311.

7. Ibid., p. 258.

8. Ibid., pp. 312, 342.

9. Ibid., p. 341.

10. Ibid., p. 347.

11. Dobbs, "Soviet Voters' Revolt Carries Hidden Dangers for Gorbachev," *WP,* March 29, 1989, p. A18.

12. Videotape of demonstration by Georgian filmmaker Eldar Shengalaya.

13. Rodionov address to Congress, May 30, 1989 (FBIS-SOV-89-125-S), p. 8. For an outsider's impressions of Rodionov, see Anatoly Sobchak, *Tbiliskii Izlom,* pp. 79–80, 108–10.

14. Sobchak, pp. 134, 70–71. Defense Ministry instructions to Rodionov are reprinted on p. 211.

15. For Rodionov's version of the conversation, see Ibid., p. 130. For Patiashvili's, see FBIS-SOV-89-125-S, p. 13.

16. Sobchak, p. 132.

17. This account is reconstructed from videotape of the demonstration and Sobchak, pp. 138–44.

18. In addition to Sobchak commission investigation, the report prepared by Physicians for Human Rights, "Bloody Sunday—Trauma in Tbilisi," February 1990, was very helpful.

19. KGB transcript, Sobchak, p. 66.

20. *WP,* May 18, 1989, p. A38.

21. See Dobbs, "Gorbachev, Deng to Meet on Rough Roads to Reform," *WP,* May 14, 1989, p. A1.

22. "Tale of Two Reformers," *Moscow Times,* April 16, 1994, p. 8.

23. Patrick Tyler, "Deng's Daughter Opens a Long-Shut Door," *NYT,* January 13, 1995, p. A1.

24. Orville Schell, *Mandate of Heaven,* p. 137.

25. Harrison Salisbury, *Tiananmen Diary,* p. 161.

26. *NYT,* January 13, 1995, p. A1.

27. Testimony quoted in Yi Mu and Mark Thompson, *Crisis at Tiananmen,* p. 268.

28. Salisbury, p. 56.

29. Custine, p. 346 ff. This translation taken from *Journey for Our Time,* George Prior, 1980, pp. 154–56.

30. Speech by Leonid Sukhov, FBIS-SOV-89-112-S, p. 25.

31. Speech by Yuri Vlasov, FBIS-SOV-89-127-S, p. 34.

32. Speech by Yuri Karyakin, FBIS-SOV-89-142-S, p. 10.

33. FBIS-SOV-89-125-S, pp. 5–14.

34. Speech by Alexei Yablokov, FBIS-SOV-89-159-S, pp. 23–27.

35. Speech by Yuri Chernichenko, FBIS-SOV-89-134-S, pp. 18–20.

36. Boldin, p. 224.

37. Andrei Sakharov, *Moscow and Beyond, 1986–1989*, pp. 131–32.

38. Yakovlev interview, July 1993.

39. FBIS-SOV-89-142-S, p. 3. See also Anatoly Sobchak, *For a New Russia*, pp. 31–33, and Sakharov, *Moscow and Beyond*, pp. 133–35.

40. Sobchak, *For a New Russia,* p. 32.

41. Vorotnikov, pp. 239, 260–61.

42. Boldin, pp. 226–28.

43. Interview with Andrei Grachev, December 1989.

44. *WP*, June 7, 1989, p. A17.

45. Wałęsa, *The Struggle and the Triumph*, pp. 167 and 174.

46. *WP*, June 5, 1989, p. A1; "The Curtain Rises," *LAT*, December 17, 1989, p. Q6.

47. Interview, July 1993.

48. Rakowski, p. 227.

49. Ibid., p. 228. See also official transcript of meeting, published in *Kultura* (Paris), no. 3 (1993), pp. 41–51.

50. "The Curtain Rises," *LAT*, p. Q6.

51. Yan Kasimov, "Holiday-making in Crimea," *MN*, no. 34, 1992, p. 10.

52. Title of editorial by Adam Michnik, *Gazeta Wyborcza*, July 4, 1989.

53. *WP*, July 7, 1989, p. A19.

54. Gorbachev, *Zhizn' i Reformi*, vol. 2, p. 355.

55. *WP*, October 27, 1989, p. A22.

56. Interview, August 1993.

57. Interview, April 1993.

58. Chernyayev, pp. 294–95.

59. Ibid., p. 295.

60. Rakowski, p. 254.

61. Interview with Georgi Shakhnazarov, Gorbachev adviser, July 1993.

62. Rakowski, pp. 244–45.

63. Blaine Harden, "Refugees Force a Fateful Choice," *WP*, January 14, 1990, p. A35.

64. Peter Wyden, *Wall*, p. 23.

65. Information from Checkpoint Charlie Museum.

66. Reuters dispatch from Berlin, August 18, 1995.

67. Wyden, p. 681.

68. Interview with Wałęsa adviser Bronisław Geremek, who was present at the conversation, July 1993.

69. BBC/Lapping, *Fall of the Wall*, Part II.

70. Reconstruction of events leading to fall of the wall by *Der Spiegel*, October 8, 1990. See also Elizabeth Pond, *Beyond the Wall*, pp. 1–3, 130–34.

71. Peter Ross Range, *When Walls Come Tumbling Down.*

72. BBC/Lapping, *Fall of the Wall.*

73. *Time* magazine, European edition (November 20, 1989), p. 15.

74. November 10, 1989. Complete text reprinted in Harold James and Marla Stone, eds., *When the Wall Came Down*, pp. 46–49.

75. Eyewitness account of former Soviet diplomat Igor Maksimichev, *Nezavisimaya Gazeta*, November 10–11, 1993.

76. *Der Spiegel* 41 (1990), pp. 104–09.

77. *Nezavisimaya Gazeta*, November 10, 1993.

78. Gorbachev, *Zhizn' i Reformi*, vol. 2, p. 412.

79. *Der Spiegel* 40 (1995), pp. 66–81.

80. Boldin, p. 143.

81. Kochemasov interview, *MN*, November 29, 1992, p. 12.

82. Chernyayev, p. 304.

83. East German Communist Party archives. Quoted in Hannes Adomeit, *Post-Soviet Affairs* (July–September 1994), p. 215.

84. Kochemasov, *op. cit.*

85. BBC/Lapping interview with presidential adviser Yuri Osipyan.

86. BBC/Lapping interview.

87. Kochemasov, *op cit.* See also Yakovlev.

88. *Nezavisimaya Gazeta*, November 10, 1993.

89. Ibid.

90. "Dubček Returns; Prague Spring Reformer Cheered in Wenceslas Square," *WP*, November 25, 1989, p. A1.

91. Gorbachev, *Zhizn' i Reformi*, vol. 2, p. 353.

92. Interview, August 1988.

93. See Alexander Dubček, *Hope Dies Last*, pp. 8–73 passim.

94. Interview, August 1988. See Dobbs, "The Czech's Long Dissent; Playwright Vaclav Havel, 20 years after the Soviet Invasion," *WP*, August 22, 1988, p. C1.

95. Mlynář, *Nightfrost in Prague*, p. 146.

96. Dubček, p. 178.

97. Dobbs, "The Autumn of Alexander Dubček," *WP*, August 17, 1988, p. A12.

98. Dobbs, "The Czech's Long Dissent."

99. "Police Riot Sticks Spawn a Revolution," *WP*, January 14, 1990, p. A39.

100. *WP*, November 25, 1989, p. A1.

101. David Pryce-Jones, *The Strange Death of the Soviet Empire*, p. 335.

102. "A Brutal Mistake Sparks a Revolution," *LAT*, December 17, 1989, p. Q12.

103. Dobbs, "Romania's Cult of the Personality," *Guardian* (London, June 20, 1980).

104. Chernyayev, p. 81; Gorbachev, *Zhizn' i Reformi*, vol. 2, p. 397.

105. Transcript of Political Executive Committee meeting, published in *România Libera*, January 10, 1990.

106. Eyewitness testimony to author, December 1989.

107. Edward Behr, *Kiss the Hand You Cannot Bite*, p. 17.

108. Transcript of trial, quoted in John Sweeney, *The Life and Evil Times of Nicolae Ceauşescu,* p. 225.

109. Ibid., p. 217.

110. Author's contemporaneous notes. See Dobbs, "Dictator's Dream Took Harsh Toll," *WP*, January 5, 1990, p. A1.

111. Interview with former NKVD executioner Vladimir Tokaryev, *Observer* (London, October 6, 1991), p. 1.

112. 82nd Congress. *The Katyn Forest Massacre,* p. 1661.

113. Ibid., p. 1660.

114. Interview with Dmitri Volkogonov, January 1995. See also *Komsomolskaya Pravda*, October 15, 1992, p. 3.

115. Yeltsin provided Poland with copies of Katyn documents in October 1992. For facsimiles and English translation, see Wojciech Materski et al., *Katyn: Documents of Genocide.*

116. "The Katyn Documents: Politics and History," RFE/RL research, vol. 2, no. 4 (January 22, 1993), p. 27.

117. Joint memorandum from Shevardnadze, Falin, and Kryuchkov, in author's possession. See also Materski and RFE/RL, "The Katyn Documents," pp. 28–29.

118. Interview, January 1993. See Dobbs, "Gorbachev's Veracity Challenged," *WP*, January 22, 1993, p. A23.

119. In interview, Boldin said he showed Gorbachev original copies of the secret Soviet-German protocols in July 1987. Gorbachev continued to insist that the originals could not be found.

120. Statement to author, January 1993.

121. Interview, June 1993.

122. Falin memorandum, February 22, 1990, quoted in RFE/RL, "The Katyn Documents," p. 29.

123. Official Tass statement, April 15, 1990.

124. Yeltsin, *Struggle for Russia*, p. 291.

125. Yeltsin, *Against the Grain*, pp. 157–58.

126. Ibid., p. 164.

127. Sukhanov, pp. 145 and 150.

128. Ibid., p. 146.

129. Ibid., p. 153.

130. Mikhail Heller and Aleksandr Nekrich, *Utopia in Power*, p. 251.

131. Author's contemporary notes. "Yeltsin wins presidency of Russia," *WP*, May 30, 1990, p. A1.

132. Dobbs, "Yeltsin Presses for Sovereign Russia," *WP*, May 31, 1990, p. A1.

133. Yeltsin, *Struggle for Russia*, p. 18. For a slightly different account of the conversation, see Sukhanov, p. 269.

134. Yeltsin, *Struggle for Russia*, pp. 20–21.

135. Viktor Alksnis interview with *Sovietskaya Rossiya*, reported in "Conservative calls on Gorbachev to get tough," *WP*, November 22, 1990, p. A62.

136. Petrakov interview, February 1991.

137. Shevardnadze, p. 212.

138. Ibid., p. 197.

139. Ibid., pp. 223–26.

140. "Shevardnazde quits as foreign minister," *WP*, December 21, 1990, p. A1.

141. Quoted in Kaiser, pp. 388–89.

IV: REVOLT OF THE PARTY

1. Shevardnadze, p. 215.

2. Yevgenia Albats, *The State Within a State*, pp. 279–80.

3. Radio interview with coup investigator, FBIS-SOV-92-024, p. 61.

4. Vadim Bakatin, "Neizbezhnaya Otstavka," *Znamya* (Moscow), no. 12 (1991), pp. 216–19.

5. Albats, p. 277.

6. Politburo debate, April 2, 1981, TsKhSD.

7. Vadim Bakatin, *Izbavleniye ot KGB*, p. 46.

8. Albats, p. 24.

9. Bakatin, *Izbavleniye ot KGB*, p. 44.

10. Ibid., p. 50.

11. Interview, August 1993.

12. Oleg Kalugin, *The First Directorate*, pp. 243–44.

13. V. Stepankov and E. Lisov, *Kremlyovskii Zagovor*, pp. 53–54.

14. Interview with Kryuchkov's wife, *Moskovskaya Pravda*, August 22, 1992 (FBIS USR-92-119), p. 10. See also Andrew and Gordievsky, p. 446, and Leonid Shebarshin, *Iz Zhizni Nachalnika Razvedki*, pp. 7–9.

15. Gorbachev interview with Yuri Shchekochikhin, *Literaturnaya Gazeta*, December 4, 1991 (FBIS-SOV-91-233), p. 26.

16. Chernyayev, p. 484.

17. The author was a witness to these events. See "Soviet troops seize Lithuania's TV station" and "Lithuania under Soviet military curfew," *WP*, January 13, 1991, p. A1, and *WP*, January 14, p. A1, p. A13.

18. Interview with Lithuanian Procurator General Paulaskas, *Izvestia*, January 14, 1992 (FBIS-USR-92-013), p. 28.

19. Interviews with victims' relatives, January 1991. See also official statement by Lithuanian Deputy Procurator General Norkunas, February 18, 1991.

20. Interview, January 13, 1991.

21. Stepankov and Lisov, pp. 272–79.

22. Boltunov, p. 188.

23. Norkunas statement.

24. Radio conversation intercepted by Lithuanian authorities. See *Literaturnaya Gazeta* (Moscow, July 10, 1991), p. 3.

25. *Komsomolskaya Pravda*, August 28, 1991, p. 4. (FBIS-SOV-91-171), p. 35.

26. Remnick, p. 238.

27. Interview, January 13, 1991, 7:00 a.m.

28. Interview, May 1990. See Landsbergis profile, "Unlikely revolutionary leader

Lithuanian drive," *WP*, May 7, 1990, p. A13.

29. Interview, May 1990.

30. Ibid.

31. *WP*, January 17, 1991, p. A18.

32. *WP*, January 14, 1991, p. A16.

33. Remnick, p. 389.

34. *WP*, January 15, 1991, p. A1.

35. *Literaturnaya Gazeta* (July 15, 1992), p. 12. (FBIS-USR-92-097), p. 117.

36. Stepankov and Lisov, p. 271.

37. *MN*, no. 3 (1991), p. 1.

38. Chernyayev, p. 411.

39. *New Times*, no. 12 (1992), p. 12. In interview in August 1993, Gorbachev said he never had any intention of following the "advice" of Yakovlev and Ignatenko, adding that his presence was needed in Moscow.

40. Vneshekombank report. Quoted in Stepankov and Lisov, p. 304.

41. "Republics assume Kremlin debt," *WP*, October 30, 1991, p. A31.

42. *Moskovskie Novosti*, no. 46 (November 17, 1991), p. 9. "Much of Soviet gold is sold," *WP*, September 28, 1991, p. A1.

43. Copies of export licenses, provided by Istok, are in author's possession. The Russian press ran numerous articles on the Harvest '90 scandal, notably *Izvestia*, October 21–26, 1992, and *Trud*, December 30, 1992.

44. Resolution to dismiss charges in Istok case, Russian ministry of Internal Affairs, July 4, 1994, in author's possession. Tarasov subsequently returned to Russia as a People's deputy with parliamentary immunity from prosecution. See also statement by Russian prosecutor-general Nikolai Marakov to Supreme Soviet, June 24, 1993.

45. Makarov statement.

46. Interview, September 1992. See Dobbs and Coll, "Ex-Communists are

scrambling for Quick Cash," *WP*, February 1, 1993, p. A1.

47. Stepankov and Lisov, pp. 302–03.

48. Interview with Soviet prosecutor Sergei Aristov, March 1993.

49. *Komsomolskaya Pravda*, January 22, 1992.

50. Interview, January 1993.

51. Stephen Handelman, *Comrade Criminal*, p. 372.

52. Interview, September 1993.

53. Yeltsin, *Struggle for Russia*, pp. 224–34.

54. Veselovsky memorandum, September 24, 1991, leaked to *Komsomolskaya Pravda*.

55. Quoted in Robert D. Kaplan, *Balkan Ghosts*, p. 39.

56. BBC/Lapping, *Death of Yugoslavia*, Program 1.

57. BBC videotape of meeting.

58. Former Mayor of Belgrade Bogdan Bogdanović, quoted by Stephen Engelberg, *NYT Magazine*, September 1, 1991.

59. Slavoljub Đjukić, *Između Slave i Anateme,* p. 187.

60. Interview, Vukovar, July 1993. This section is based on a reporting trip to Yugoslavia and Croatia for a series about the legacy of communism. See Dobbs, "Yugoslavia Maps a Road to Ruin," *WP*, September 5, 1993, p. A1.

61. Interview, Zagreb, July 1993.

62. See, for example, Roger Cohen, "In the Balkans, Doing Well by Waging War," *NYT* "Week in Review," March 26, 1995, p. 4.

63. Laura Silber and Allen Little, *Yugoslavia: Death of a Nation*, pp. 140 and 146.

64. BBC/Lapping. *Death of Yugoslavia*, Program 3.

65. Interview with former Borovo managing director Vladimir Husar, Zagreb, July 1993.

66. Mary Battiata, "In Croatia, Time

Heals No Ethnic Wounds," *WP*, July 13, 1991, p. A1.

67. Yakovlev interview, August 22, 1991.

68. Yeltsin, *Struggle for Russia*, p. 39; interview with Gorbachev, BBC *Second Russian Revolution*, final program.

69. Stepankov and Lisov, p. 85.

70. Interview with inventor, *Komsomolskaya Pravda*, January 28, 1992, p. 2. (FBIS-SOV-92-019, p. 7.)

71. Stepankov and Lisov, p. 138; "During the Soviet coup, who held nuclear control?" *WP*, August 23, 1992, p. A1.

72. "Physician Tells of Pre-Coup Events at Foros," *Izvestia*, September 24, 1991 (FBIS-SOV-91-185).

73. Stepankov and Lisov, p. 9; Gorbachev press conference, Moscow, August 22, 1991.

74. Gorbachev press conference; interview with Raisa Gorbachev, *Trud*, September 3, 1991; Gorbachev, *Zhizn' i Reformi*, vol. 2, p. 558.

75. Mikhail Gorbachev, *The August Coup*, p. 19.

76. Boldin, p. 26.

77. Stepankov and Lisov, p. 13.

78. Chernyaev diary, *Izvestia*, September 30, 1991.

79. Gorbachev, *August Coup*, p. 21. Stepankov and Lisov, p. 14.

80. Gorbachev, *August Coup*, p. 23.

81. Stepankov and Lisov, p. 15; extracts from prosecutor's report, *Novaya Yezhednevnaya Gazeta*, August 6, 1993, p. 3; TV interview with Raisa Gorbachev, FBIS-SOV-91-194, p. 32.

82. Stepankov and Lisov, p. 89.

83. Prosecutor's report, *Novaya Yezhednevnaya Gazeta*, July 30, 1993, p. 3.

84. Ibid.

85. Stepankov and Lisov, p. 90.

86. Prosecutor's report.

87. Stepankov and Lisov, p. 90.

88. Yeltsin, *Struggle for Russia*, p. 54.

89. Khasbulatov memoirs, *Rossiiskaya Gazeta*, August 19, 1992, pp. 1–3.

90. Aleksandr Lebed, *Za Derzhavu Obidno*, p. 381.

91. Yeltsin, *Struggle for Russia*, p. 58. Author was present at the maneuvers.

92. Ibid., p. 58.

93. *Komsomolskaya Pravda*, August 19, 1992, p. 1.

94. Yeltsin, *Struggle for Russia*, pp. 42 and 61.

95. Yeltsin press conference, attended by author.

96. Yeltsin, *Struggle for Russia*, p. 68.

97. In presence of author.

98. Chernyaev diary, *Izvestia*, September 30, 1991.

99. Stepankov and Lisov, pp. 139–43.

100. Chernyaev, p. 485; Chernyaev diary.

101. Gorbachev, *Zhizn' i Reformi*, vol. 2, p. 566.

102. Gorbachev, *August Coup*, pp. 91–92.

103. Yazov testimony, *Izvestia*, October 10, 1991, p. 7.

104. Stepankov and Lisov, pp. 132–33.

105. Ibid., p. 161.

106. Lebed, pp. 383–411.

107. Sergei Grigoriev, *Istina Momenta*, p. 190.

108. Ibid., pp. 21–26.

109. Stepankov and Lisov, p. 175.

110. *WP*, August 21, 1991, p. 24.

111. Grigoriev, pp. 49–50, 200.

112. Yeltsin, *Struggle for Russia*, p. 86.

113. Stepankov and Lisov, pp. 171–73.

114. Interview with *Literaturnaya Gazeta*, *CDSP*, vol. XLIII, no. 37 (August 28, 1991), p. 20.

115. Khasbulatov memoirs *Rossiiskaya Gazeta*, August 19, 1992.

116. Grigoriev, p. 33.

117. Yu. Kazarin and B. Yakovlev, eds., *Smert' Zagovora*, p. 110.

118. *Moscow* magazine (November–December 1991).

119. Victoria Bonnell, ed., *Russia at the Barricades*, p. 205.

120. Interview with the prosecutor general, quoted in *Krasnoye ili Beloye?*, pp. 124–29. See also Kazarin and Yakovlev, pp. 94–97.

121. Yeltsin, *Struggle for Russia*, pp. 92–93.

122. Grachev interview, *Izvestia*, September 4, 1991. See also Grachev and Gromov testimony to prosecutors, *MN*, no. 29 (1994), p. 8; Stepankov and Lisov, pp. 174–76.

123. Stepankov and Lisov, pp. 183–84.

124. Interview with Raisa Gorbachev, quoted in *Krasnoye ili Beloye?*, pp. 141–42.

125. Chernyayev diary.

126. Quoted in Stuart H. Loory et al., *Seven Days That Shook the World*, p. 148.

127. Gorbachev press conference, August 22, 1991.

128. Chernyayev interview, July 1993.

129. Chernyayev diary.

130. N. Gulbinskii and M. Shakina, *Afganistan, Kreml', Lefortovo*, p. 135.

131. Gorbachev press conference, August 22, 1991.

132. Copy of document in author's possession.

133. CNN video film.

134. Shakhnovsky interview, May 1992.

135. Mishin interview, May 1992.

136. Smirnov testimony to Russian Constitutional Court, July 29, 1992.

137. *MN* (September 1, 1991).

138. CNN video.

139. Interview with CC official, August 1991.

140. *Den'* (January 19, 1992), p. 1.

141. Interview with Akhromeyev family, June 1992.

142. Stepankov and Lisov, p. 239.

143. *Sovietskaya Rossiya*, September 28, 1991, p. 6.

144. Interview, June 1992.

145. Stepankov and Lisov, p. 236.

EPILOGUE

1. *Vreme* (Belgrade, September 23, 1991), p. 7.

2. Interview with *Vreme* military correspondent Miloš Vasić, August 1994.

3. Interview with SDS leader Radovan Karadžić, September 1991.

4. Borisav Jović, *Posledni Dani SFRJ*, pp. 349, 386.

5. Author's notes. See Dobbs, "Bosnian Republic Resembles Tinderbox Waiting to Explode," *WP*, September 24, 1991, p. A1.

6. John Kifner, "With Little, Bosnians Sharpen Fighting Skills," *NYT*, December 5, 1993. See also Tom Gjelten, *Sarajevo Daily*, pp. 75–76, and captured JNA documents published by State Commission for War Crimes in Bosnia-Herzegovina, Bulletins no. 3 and 4, March–April 1993.

7. Interview, September 23, 1991.

8. *Oslobođenje*, Sarajevo, September 23, 1991, p. 3.

9. Chuck Sudetic, *NYT*, November 21, 1991, p. A1.

10. Dusan Stojanovic, AP dispatch, November 19, 1991.

11. Blaine Harden, "Serbs Blamed for Mass Croatian Grave," *WP*, January 26, 1993.

12. Interview, Vinkovci, July 1993.

13. UN Security Council Document, S/25274, February 10, 1993, p. 29.

14. Harden.

15. Don Oberdorfer, "Despite Accurate

Warning, U.S. Failed to Act on Balkans," *WP*, July 2, 1993, p. A1.

16. Interviews with former Secretary of State Lawrence Eagleburger and former National Security Adviser Brent Scowcroft, December 1995.

17. Testimony to House Armed Services Committee, May 25, 1993, H201-11.

18. Interview with former U.S. ambassador to Belgrade Warren Zimmermann, March 1995.

19. Jović, p. 349.

20. Interview with Scowcroft. See also Dobbs, "Bosnia Crystallizes U.S. Post–Cold War Role," *WP*, December 3, 1995, p. A1.

21. Interview, December 1995.

22. Jović, pp. 395–96.

23. Ibid., p. 295.

24. "Ukraine seen going independent," *WP*, December 2, 1991, p. A1.

25. Andrei Grachev, *Kremlyovskaya Khronika*, p. 339.

26. Yeltsin, *Struggle for Russia*, p. 112. See also Fred Hiatt and Margaret Shapiro, "Snubs Helped Seal Old Union's Fate," *WP*, December 14, 1991, p. A1.

27. *WP* interview with Kozyrev, December 1991, see Hiatt and Shapiro, ibid.

28. Kozyrev interview. See also Grachev, p. 343.

29. Grachev, p. 344.

30. Ibid., p. 352.

31. Yakovlev interview, July 1993.

32. "Gorbachev: The Final Hours," ABC *Primetime Live*, December 26, 1991; Grachev, p. 390.

33. Grachev, p. 389.

BIBLIOGRAPHY

Akhromeyev, S. F., and G. M. Kornienko. *Glazami Marshala i Diplomata*. Mezhdunarodnie Otnosheniya, 1992.

Aksyutin, Yuri V., ed. *L. I. Brezhnev: Materiali k Biographii*. Politicheskaya Literatura, 1991.

Albats, Yevgenia. *The State Within a State*. Farrar, Straus, and Giroux, 1994.

Aleksandrov-Agentov, A. M. *Ot Kollontaia do Gorbacheva*. Mezhdunarodnie Otnosheniya, 1994.

Anderson, Martin. *Revolution*. Harcourt, Brace, Jovanovich, 1988.

Andrew, Christopher, and Oleg Gordievsky. *KGB—The Inside Story*. Hodder and Stoughton, 1990.

Anwar, Raja. *The Tragedy of Afghanistan*. Verso, 1988.

Arbatov, Georgi. *The System*. Times Books, 1992.

Ascherson, Neal. *The Polish August*. Penguin, London, 1981.

———, et al. *The Book of Lech Wałęsa*. Penguin, 1982.

August 1980: The Strikes in Poland. Radio Free Europe Research, 1980.

Bakatin, Vadim. *Izbavleniye ot KGB*. Novosti, 1992.

Baker, James A., III. *The Politics of Diplomacy*. Putnam, 1995.

Behr, Edward. *Kiss the Hand You Cannot Bite*. Villard Books, 1991.

Beichman, Arnold, and Mikhail S. Bernstam. *Andropov*. Stein and Day, 1983.

Beschloss, Michael R., and Strobe Talbott. *At the Highest Levels*. Little, Brown, 1993.

Boldin, Valery. *Ten Years That Shook the World*. Basic Books, 1994.

Boltunov, Mikhail. *Alpha—Sverkhsekretnii Otryad KGB*. KEDR, 1992.

Bonnell, Victoria, et al., eds. *Russia at the Barricades*. M. E. Sharpe, 1994.

Bradsher, Henry S. *Afghanistan and the Soviet Union*. Duke University Press, 1985.

Brezhneva, Luba. *The World I Left Behind*. Random House, 1995.

Brzezinski, Zbigniew. *The Grand Failure*. Charles Scribner, 1989.

———. *Power and Principle*. Farrar, Straus, and Giroux, 1983.

Cannon, Lou. *President Reagan: The Role of a Lifetime*. Simon and Schuster, 1991.

Carrère d'Encausse, Hélène. *Decline of an Empire*. Newsweek Books, 1979.

Casey, William. *The Secret War Against Hitler*. Regnery Gateway, 1988.

Chazov, Yevgeny. *Zdorov'ye i Vlast'*. Novosti, 1992.

Chernyayev, Anatoly S. *Shest' Let s Gorbachevym*. Progress, 1993.

Conquest, Robert. *The Harvest of Sorrow*. Oxford University Press, 1986.

Curzon, George N. *Russia in Central Asia*. 1889.

Custine, Marquis de. *Empire of the Czar*. Anchor Books, 1990.

Dobbs, Michael, et al. *Poland, Solidarity, Walesa*. McGraw-Hill, 1981.

Dobrokhotov, L. N., ed. *Gorbachev-Yeltsin: 1500 Dnei Politicheskogo Protivostoyaniya*. Terra, 1992.

Dobrynin, Anatoly. *In Confidence*. Times Books, 1995.

Doder, Dusko, and Louise Branson. *Gorbachev—Heretic in the Kremlin*. Viking, 1990.

Dokumenty Teczka Suslowa. Interpress, 1993.

Drzycimski, Andrzej, and Tadeusz Skutnik. *Gdańsk Sierpień '80*. AIDA, 1990.

Dubček, Alexander. *Hope Dies Last*. Kodansha International, 1993.

Đukić, Slavoljub. *Između Slave I Anateme*. Filip Visnjić, 1994.

Ebon, Martin. *The Andropov File*. McGraw-Hill, 1983.

Feschbach, Murray, and Alfred Friendly, Jr. *Ecocide in the USSR*. Basic Books, 1992.

Garton Ash, Timothy. *We the People: The Revolution of 89*. Granta Books, 1990.

Gates, Robert M. *From the Shadows*. Simon and Schuster, 1996.

Gierek, Edward. *Przerwana Dekada*. FAKT publishing house, 1990.

Gjelten, Tom. *Sarajevo Daily*. HarperCollins, 1995.

Glenny, Misha. *The Fall of Yugoslavia*. Penguin, 1992.

Gorbachev, Mikhail. *The August Coup*. HarperCollins, 1991.

———. *Avant-Mémoires*. Odile Jacob, 1993.

———. *Zhizn' i Reformi*. Novosti, 1995. 2 vols.

Gorbachev, Raisa. *I Hope*. HarperCollins, 1991.

Grachev, Andrei. *Kremlevskaya Khronika*. Eksmo, 1994.

Grigoriev, Sergei. *Istina Momenta*. Respublika, 1992.

Gromov, B.V. *Ogranichennii Kontingent*. Progress, 1994.

Gromyko, Andrei. *Memoirs*. Doubleday, 1989.

Gulbinskii, N., and M. Shakina. *Afganistan, Kreml', Lefortovo*. Lada-M, 1994.

Gwertzman, Bernard, and Michael T. Kaufman, eds. *The Decline and Fall of the Soviet Empire*. Times Books, 1992.

Handelman, Stephen. *Comrade Criminal: Russia's New Mafia*. Yale University Press, 1995.

Hawkes, Nigel, et al. *The Worst Accident in the World*. Pan Books, 1986.

Hebblethwaite, Peter, and Ludwig Kaufmann. *John Paul II*. McGraw-Hill, 1979.

Heller, Mikhail, and Aleksandr Nekrich. *Utopia in Power*. Summit Books, 1986.

Hersh, Seymour M. *"The Target Is Destroyed."* Random House, 1986.

Holloway, David. *The Soviet Union and the Arms Race*. Yale University Press, 1983.

Hopkirk, Peter. *The Great Game*. Oxford University Press, 1991.

James, Harold, and Marla Stone, eds. *When the Wall Came Down*. Routledge, 1992.

Jaruzelski, Wojciech. *Les Chaînes et le Refuge*. Jean-Claude Lattès, 1992.

———. *Stan Wojenny Dlaczego*. BGW, 1992.

Jović, Borisav. *Posledni Dani SFRJ*. Politika, 1995.

Kaiser, Robert G. *Why Gorbachev Happened*. Simon and Schuster, 1991.

Kalugin, Oleg. *The First Directorate*. St. Martin's Press, 1994.

Kania, Stanisław. *Zatrzymać Konfrontację*. BGW, 1991.

Kaplan, Robert D. *Balkan Ghosts*. St. Martin's Press, 1993.

Kazarin, U., and B. Yakovlev, eds. *Smert' Dogovora*. Novosti, 1992.

Katyn Forest Massacre. 82nd U.S. Congress, 1951–1952.

Kemp-Welch, A. ed. *The Birth of Solidarity*. Macmillan Press, 1983.

Kennedy, Paul. *The Rise and Fall of the Great Powers*. Random House, 1987.

Khrushchev, Nikita. *Khrushchev Remembers*. Little, Brown, 1970.

Kiszczak, Czesław. *Generał Kiszczak Mówi . . .* BGW, 1991.

Klass, Rosanne, ed. *Afghanistan—The Great Game Revisited*. Freedom House, 1987.

Krasnoye ili Beloye? Terra, 1992.

Kto yest' Kto. Novoye Vremya, 1993.

Laba, Roman. *The Roots of Solidarity*. Princeton University Press, 1991.

Lebed, Aleksandr. *Za Derzhavu Obidno*. Moskovskaya Pravda, 1995.

Ligachev, Yegor. *Inside Gorbachev's Kremlin*. Pantheon Books, 1993.

Loory, Stuart H., et al. *Seven Days That Shook the World*. Turner, 1991.

Lyakhovski, Aleksandr. *Tragediya i Doblest' Afgana*. GPI Iskona, 1995.

Łopiński, Maciej, et al. *Konspira*. University of California Press, 1990.

MacDonald, Oliver, ed. *The Polish August*. Left Bank Books, 1981.

Maksimichev, Igor'. *Poslednii God GDR*. Mezhdunarodnie Otnosheniya, 1993.

Malcolm, Noel. *Bosnia—a Short History*. New York University Press, 1994.

Massie, Robert and Suzanne. *Journey*. Knopf, 1975.

Materski, Wojciech, et al. *Katyn: Documents of Genocide*. Polish Academy of Sciences, 1993.

Matlock, Jack F., Jr. *Autopsy of an Empire*. Random House, 1995.

McFarlane, Robert C. *Special Trust*. Cadell & Davies, 1994.

Medvedev, Grigori. *The Truth About Chernobyl*. Basic Books, 1991.

Medvedev, Roy. *Lichnost i Epokha: Politicheskii Portret Brezhneva*. Novosti, 1991.

———, and Giulietto Chiesa. *Time of Change.* Pantheon Books, 1989.

Medvedev, Vadim. *Raspad.* Mezhdunarodnie Otnosheniya, 1994.

Medvedev, Vladimir. *Chelovek Za Spinoi.* Russlit, 1994.

Medvedev, Zhores A. *Gorbachev.* Norton, 1986.

Mlynář, Zdeněk. *Nightfrost in Prague.* C. Hurst and Co.,1980. American edition: Karz publishers.

Molotov, Vyacheslav. *Molotov Remembers: Conversations with Felix Chuev.* Ivan R. Dee, 1991.

Morrison, John. *Boris Yeltsin: From Bolshevik to Democrat.* Dutton, 1991.

Narodnie Deputati SSSR. Izdanie Verkhovnogo Soveta SSSR, 1990.

Nowak, Jan. *Wojna w Eterze.* Odnowa, 1956.

Oberdorfer, Don. *The Turn: From the Cold War to a New Era.* Poseidon Press, 1991.

Pavlov, Valentin. *Gorbachev-putch: Avgust iznutri.* Delevoi Mir, 1993.

Persico, Joseph E. *Casey.* Viking, 1990.

Persky, Stan, and Henry Flam. *The Solidarity Sourcebook.* New Star Books, 1982.

Pipes, Richard. *The Russian Revolution.* Knopf, 1990.

Pond, Elizabeth. *Beyond the Wall.* Brookings Institution, 1993.

Potel, Jean-Yves. *Gdansk: La Mémoire ouvrière 1970–1980.* Maspero, 1982.

Pryce-Jones, David. *The Strange Death of the Soviet Empire.* Henry Holt, 1995.

Quigley, Joan. *What Does Joan Say?* Birch Lane Press, 1990.

Rakowski, Mieczysław. *Jak To Się Stało.* BGW, 1991.

Read, Piers Paul. *Ablaze.* Random House, 1993.

Reagan, Ronald. *An American Life.* Simon and Schuster, 1990.

———. *Speaking My Mind.* Simon and Schuster, 1989.

Reed, John. *Ten Days That Shook the World.* Penguin, 1991.

Regan, Donald T. *For the Record.* St. Martin's Press, 1989.

Remnick, David. *Lenin's Tomb.* Random House, 1993.

Rolicki, Janusz. *Edward Gierek Replika.* BGW, 1990.

Rowen, Henry S., and Charles Wolf, Jr. eds. *The Future of the Soviet Empire.* St. Martin's Press, 1987.

Roxburgh, Angus. *The Second Russian Revolution.* BBC Books, 1991.

Ryzkhov, Nikolai. *Perestroika—Istoria Predatel'stv.* Novosti, 1992.

Sakharov, Andrei. *Memoirs.* Knopf, 1990.

———. *Moscow and Beyond, 1986–1989.* Knopf, 1991.

Salisbury, Harrison. *The New Emperors.* Avon Books, 1993.

———. *Tiananmen Diary.* Little, Brown, 1989.

Schell, Orville. *Mandate of Heaven.* Simon and Schuster, 1994.

Schweizer, Peter. *Victory.* Atlantic Monthly Press, 1994.

Sejm commission, March 9–10, 1993. *Sąd nad autorami Stanu Wojennego.* BGW, 1993.

Shane, Scott. *Dismantling Utopia: How Information Ended the Soviet Union.* Ivan R. Dee, 1994.

Shawcross, William. *Dubcek.* Simon and Schuster/Touchstone, 1990.

Shcherbak, Yuri. *Chernobyl, a Documentary Story.* Macmillan, 1989.

Shebarshin, Leonid. *Iz Zhizni Nachalnika Razvedki.* Mezhdunarodnie Otnosheniya, 1994.

———. *Ruka Moskvi,* Tsentr-100, 1992.

Sheehy, Gail. *Gorbachev.* Mandarin, 1991. American edition: *The Man Who Changed the World: The Lives of Mikhail S. Gorbachev.* HarperCollins, 1990.

Shevardnadze, Eduard. *The Future Belongs to Freedom.* Free Press, 1991.

Shultz, George P. *Turmoil and Triumph.* Macmillan, 1993.

Silber, Laura, and Allan Little. *Yugoslavia: Death of a Nation.* TV Books, 1996.

Sobchak, Anatoly. *For a New Russia.* Free Press, 1992.

———. *Tbiliskii Izlom.* Sretenie, 1993.

Steele, Jonathan. *Eternal Russia.* Harvard University Press, 1994.

Stepankov, Valentin, and Yevgeny Lisov. *Kremlyovskii Zagovor.* Ogonyok, 1992.

Stokes, Gale. *The Walls Came Tumbling Down.* Oxford University Press, 1993.

Sukhanov, Lev. *Tri Goda s Yeltsinym.* Vaga, 1992.

Sweeney, John. *The Life and Evil Times of Nicolae Ceauşescu.* Hutchinson, 1991.

Thompson, Mark. *A Paper House: The Ending of Yugoslavia.* Vintage, 1992.

U.S. Defense Department. *Soviet Military Power.* 1981.

Vasilieva, Larisa. *Kremlin Wives.* Arcade, 1993.

Vorotnikov, Vitaly. *A Bylo Eto Tak.* Soviet Veteranor, 1995.

Wałęsa, Lech. *The Struggle and the Triumph.* Arcade, 1992.

———. *A Way of Hope.* Henry Holt, 1987.

Werth, Alexander. *Russia at War.* Dutton, 1964.

Willey, David. *God's Politician.* Faber and Faber, 1992.

Włodek, Zbigniew, ed. *Tajne Dokumenty Biura Politycznego PZPR a Solidarność 1980–1981.* Aneks, 1992.

Wyden, Peter. *Wall.* Simon and Schuster, 1989.

Yakovlev, Aleksandr N. *Predislovia; Obval; Posleslovie.* Novosti, 1992.

Yeltsin, Boris. *Against the Grain.* Jonathan Cape, 1990. Original Russian version: *Ispoved' na Zadannuyu Temu.* Sredne-Uralskoye Publishing House, 1990.

———. *The Struggle for Russia.* Times Books, 1994.

Yi, Mu and Mark Thompson. *Crisis at Tiananmen.* China Books, 1989.

Yousaf, Muhamad. *The Bear Trap.* Leo Cooper, 1992.

Zaslavskaya, Tatiana. *A Voice of Reform.* M. E. Sharpe, 1989.

Zimmerman, Warren. *Origins of a Catastrophe.* Times Books, 1996.

Zuyev, Alexander. *Fulcrum.* Warner Books, 1992.

INDEX

A NOTE ABOUT THE AUTHOR

MICHAEL DOBBS WAS BORN in Belfast, Northern Ireland. He has spent much of his journalistic career reporting from Communist countries: from 1977 to 1980 as a special correspondent based in Yugoslavia for the *Washington Post*, the London *Guardian*, and the BBC; and from 1981 to 1995 as the *Washington Post*'s bureau chief in Warsaw and Moscow (with an intervening stint in Paris). He is currently a diplomatic reporter for the *Post*.

In addition to having received the Overseas Press Club award for interpretation of foreign news in 1990 and a National Press Club award for best diplomatic reporting in 1995, Dobbs has held fellowships at the Russian Research Center at Harvard University and at the Woodrow Wilson Center in Washington, D.C. He lives in Bethesda, Maryland, with his wife and three children.

A NOTE ON THE TYPE

THE TEXT OF THIS BOOK was set in a typeface called Times New Roman, designed by Stanley Morison (1889–1967) for *The Times* (London), and introduced by that newspaper in 1932. Among typographers and designers of the twentieth century, Stanley Morison was a strong forming influence, as typographical adviser to the Monotype Corporation of London, as a director of two distinguished English publishing houses, and as a writer of sensibility, erudition, and keen practical sense. In 1930 Morison wrote: "Type design moves at the pace of the most conservative reader. The good type-designer therefore realizes that, for a new fount to be successful, it has to be so good that only very few recognize its novelty. If readers do not notice the consummate reticence and rare discipline of a new type, it is probably a good letter." It is now generally recognized that in the creation of Times Roman, Morison successfully met the qualifications of his theoretical doctrine. In addition to being arguably the most widely used roman type in the world today, Times New Roman enjoys an undisputed popularity in its Cyrillic version.

Display type is Figural, a work of the foremost Czech type designer Oldřîch Menhart (1897–1962).

Composed by Crane Typesetting Service,
Charlotte Harbor, Florida

Printed and bound by Berryville Graphics,
Berryville, Virginia

Designed by Misha Beletsky